## About the Author

COUNT LEV NIKOLAYEVICH TOLSTOY, commonly known the world over as Leo Tolstoy, was born in 1828 in Tula, near Moscow. His parents, who both died when he was young, belonged to the Russian nobility, and throughout his life Tolstoy remained conscious of his aristocratic heritage. His novels *War and Peace* and *Anna Karenina* have become classics of world literature, and he is revered as one of the greatest writers of the nineteenth century. He died in 1910 at the age of eighty-two.

## About the Translator

ANDREW BROMFIELD was born in Yorkshire and lives near London, having spent several long periods living in Moscow, where he cofounded and edited the literary journal *Glas*. He is best known for his English translations of the work of Victor Pelevin and Boris Akunin.

# WAR AND
# PEACE

LEO TOLSTOY
*Photograph, Moscow, 1868*

# WAR AND PEACE

## ORIGINAL VERSION

LEO TOLSTOY

*Translated by Andrew Bromfield*
*Introduction by Nikolai Tolstoy*

**ecco**
*An Imprint of HarperCollinsPublishers*

# ecco

*An Imprint of* HarperCollins*Publishers*

First published in Great Britain in 2007 by HarperCollins Publishers.
The first U.S. edition was published in 2007 by Ecco, an imprint of
HarperCollins Publishers.

HarperCollins books may be purchased for educational, business, or
sales promotional use. For information please write: Special Markets
Department, HarperCollins Publishers, 10 East 53rd Street, New York,
NY 10022.

FIRST HARPER PERENNIAL edition published 2008.

Library of Congress Cataloging-in-Publication Data is available upon
request.

ISBN 978-0-06-079888-8

10   11   12   ID/RRD   10   9   8   7   6   5   4   3

# CONTENTS

# INTRODUCTION

Ben Jonson is said to have criticized Shakespeare when told that 'hee never blotted out line', and Sir Walter Scott was similarly an author who wrote with extraordinary rapidity and accuracy. Leo Tolstoy, in contrast, regularly rewrote and restructured much of his work, on occasion spending years immersed in elaborate correction. It is not surprising, therefore, that *War and Peace*, the longest major Russian novel ever written, occupied the greater part of the decade 1863 to 1873. He had been mulling over the potential of an historical novel some years before that, but his earliest drafts for the book dating from 1863 show that it was then that he decided to write a work whose setting would be the dramatic events associated with Russia's wars against Napoleon. Two years later he published the first section in the literary journal *Russkii Vestnik* under the title *1805*, and the second entitled *War* appeared a year later in 1866.

Although Tolstoy's prime concern lay with exploration of human character, he was fascinated by the grand drama of historical events. He had experienced war in the Balkans, the Caucasus, and the Crimea, and from a cheerfully unreflecting Russian patriot he became increasingly concerned to discover the underlying rationale of a phenomenon which perversely legitimated lying, spying, murder, cruelty, and rapine on a grand scale – vices which civil society is at pains to suppress. Conventional historians of the day recounted events in terms of grand strategy carried out by commanders executing complex manoeuvres, which proved successful or unsuccessful according to their talents and those of their adversaries. Tolstoy – who had known at first hand the smoke, din, fire, terror, and heady intoxication of battle – saw in contrast only the interplay of confusion, chance, and a multitude of disparate factors far beyond the capacity of individuals to control or even understand.

All this is well known: what is less so is the extent to which Tolstoy pursued painstaking researches as an historical novelist. His best biographer, the Englishman Aylmer Maude, suggested that *War and Peace* was not an historical novel in the true sense, since the age in which his story is set remained within the memory of his parents' generation. But this is to do Tolstoy an injustice. His notes and correspondence illustrate the remarkable extent to which he sought to reconstruct the past, whether pacing the battlefield at Borodino or investigating recondite details ranging from the extent to which men still wore hair powder in 1805 to the fact that the copse in which Pierre Bezukhov and Dolokhov fought their duel was pine rather than birch.

One of Tolstoy's major problems was that of establishing the precise nature of his genre. As he explained to Katkov, the editor of *Russkii Vestnik*, in January 1865: 'the work is not a novel and is not a story, and cannot have the sort of plot whose interest ends with the dénouement. I am writing this in order to ask you not to call my work a novel in the table of contents, or perhaps in the advertisement either. This is very important to me, and I particularly request it of you'.

Those sections which appeared in 1865 and 1866 were but the introduction to a much larger work, which by the end of 1866 he believed he had completed. Over the previous six months he had written 726 pages of manuscript, which he felt brought the work to a satisfactory conclusion. His pleasure in writing was intense, and as he explained later he 'generally enjoyed good spirits', and on days when his work had gone well, he would gleefully announce that he had left 'a bit of my life in the inkstand'.

It is this version which comprises the present work, which was first made available to the Russian general reader seven years ago, and is here presented for the first time in English. The title Tolstoy proposed was *All's Well That Ends Well*, from which it may be correctly inferred that it had a happy ending. There can be no doubt that he intended this version to be published, for which he engaged as illustrator a talented artist named Nikolai Sergeievich Bashilov. Tolstoy and Bashilov enjoyed a close and constructive collaboration. Thus when the author explained that he had based the character of Natasha in large part on his sister-in-law Tatiana, the artist's task was the easier since he was her uncle. Sadly, Bashilov's increasing illness made it ever harder for him to meet insistent deadlines imposed by the author and publisher, and at the end of 1870 he died while undergoing a health cure in the Tyrol. Consequently the early editions of the novel remain unillustrated, and it was not until 1893 that an able successor to Bashilov was found in the form of Leonid Pasternak, father of the novelist Boris.

*War and Peace* 'as we know it' was published in six volumes in 1868–69. By that time Tolstoy had extensively revised *All's Well That Ends Well*, radically altering its conclusion and carrying the story forward in part as a reminder that life does not come to a gratifying halt with marriage. Two years later he wrote disparagingly: 'I've stopped writing, and will never again write verbose nonsense like *War and Peace*. I'm guilty, but I swear I'll never do it again'. However he had not reached the end of his creative activity, and in 1873 set about further extensive restructuring. 'I've started to prepare a second edition of War and Peace and to strike out what is superfluous – some things need to be struck out altogether, others to be removed and printed separately', he wrote to a literary friend in March. 'And if you can remember, remind me of what is bad. I'm afraid to touch it, because there is so much that is bad in my eyes that I would want to write it again after refurbishing it'.

Even this was not the end of the story, for when his wife came to issue a fresh collected edition of his works in 1886 it was the 1868–69 version that she chose. Whether this was Tolstoy's choice remains unknown, but he can scarcely have disapproved. This illustrates the extent to which he envisaged his creation as a living entity subject to continual modification, and confirms the desirability of making public the first version he completed. Whether the final 'canonical' edition represents an improvement must be left to readers to judge, and the present publication at last provides means of effecting the comparison.

Those who have never read War and Peace will be able to enjoy experiencing Tolstoy's first heady production of that wonderful work, and those who have will undergo the stimulating experience of being able to compare it with its predecessor. Apart from the truncated conclusion, attentive readers will note many differences of detail and emphasis. My own interest was particularly aroused by subtle variations in the treatment of Dolokhov, the bold and on occasion cruel lover of Pierre's faithless wife Hélène. Based on Tolstoy's cousin, the noted duellist and adventurer Feodor Ivanovich Tolstoy, whose larger-than-life personality clearly fascinated the novelist, he erupts as another fictional counterpart into the marvellous short story 'Two Hussars', where in the space of twenty-four hours he turns upside down the sleepy life of a provincial town. The writer was fortunate in possessing a family and friends pre-eminently adaptable to the most exotic of fictive requirements.

As he wrote to his cousin Alexandra, a lady in waiting to the Empress, during the writing of All's Well That Ends Well: 'you possess that Tolstoyan wildness that's common to us all. Not for nothing did Feodor Ivanovich have himself tattooed'. His words might have as aptly been applied to the larger-than-life author himself.

*Nikolai Tolstoy*, 2007

# A NOTE ON THE TRANSLATION

Like most literary classics, *War and Peace* has generated a long and distinguished tradition of English translations. But while most are based on the 'classical' 1500-page text, the present translation is based on an earlier, shorter text that is now being translated into English for the first time.

This shorter Russian text was brought out in 2000 by the Moscow publisher Igor Zakharov as 'the first complete edition of the great novel *War and Peace*'. His edition, however, was in fact derived from an earlier edition which, although unknown to the world at large, had long been familiar to literary specialists as the first draft, recovered by the Tolstoy scholar Evelina E. Zaidenshnur. This text, together with a 60-page commentary, had been published as a scholarly monograph in 1983, in vol. 94 of the Academy of Sciences journal *Literaturnoe Nasledstvo* (Literary Heritage), although much of the material had appeared earlier still in the 90-volume Jubilee edition of Tolstoy's Collected Works.

Evelina Zaidenshnur's reconstruction was an extraordinary achievement, the fruit of fifty years' painstaking paleographical detective work in the massive archive held by the Tolstoy Museum in Moscow. This work had culminated in the first, full working version whose last page contains the word: '*Konets*' or 'The End'. Known to have reached completion in December 1866, this draft had soon been dispersed in the process of rewriting that began shortly after. Zaidenshnur's text was a mosaic of manuscripts retrieved from across the archive and reassembled through the careful matching of Tolstoy's original handwriting, ink and paper and close examination of his numerous notebooks, diaries and letters for clues and references to the work in progress.

Zaidenshnur's edition offers us a coherent narrative which, despite its occasional roughness and sketchiness and obvious differences, is often as polished and fine as the later, canonical version. Inevitably, however, in the long process of deciphering several thousands of pages of impenetrable scrawl, crisscrossed with cancellations, messily overwritten and with scribbled additions ballooning into the margins, there were errors and oversights in transcription. Words were misread, sentences misplaced.

Nevertheless, as befitted a scholarly enterprise, the text included multiple variants in brackets (cancelled words as well as alternative readings) and the entire project was described in meticulous depth. It was this essentially academic text, shorn of its scholarly apparatus and its variants, somewhat rewritten and with none of its original French, that was reissued in 2000 by Zakharov as 'the first' *War and Peace*, and promoted as 'half the usual length, less war and more peace, no philosophical digressions', and so on. Although the English translation that follows is based largely on that edition, frequent reference has also been made to Zaidenshnur's edition as well as the later 'classical' text.

Claiming this as the 'original' *War and Peace*, might, as one reviewer remarked, 'cause purists to wince'. This version is not, however, intended as substitute for the canonical version so much as its complement, rather as a brilliant sketch, or series of sketches, stands in relation to the final canvas of a great masterpiece. Complete if unpolished, this version still offers authentic delights, especially to those readers new to Tolstoy (and for whom there await all the greater pleasures of the longer text). Many familiar scenes – the Rostovs' banquet, the hunt, the dancing, for example – are already here, although they will later be placed in settings of altogether grander, more universal proportions. Devotees and scholars (above all those unable to read the original Russian) will value this version meanwhile for the rare insights it offers into the 'creative laboratory' of a consummate artist. Close comparison will point to the scattered phrases in the one that blossom into major themes and characters (such as Platon Karataev) in the other. Or reveal how elements in the early draft are cast aside, redeployed, or amplified in the ruthless process of reshaping, refining and rearranging that duly occurs on the large scale and the small. Sympathies switch from one figure to another; attributes migrate; names are reassigned; a single character splits into two, while several meld into one; new faces enter, others depart. And while the storyline takes significant new turns, so the weave of its telling grows increasingly intricate. The creation of *War and Peace*, as R.F. Christian and K. Feuer have shown, was dynamic in process – there was no exact plan, it evolved in the writing: Tolstoy's unfolding philosophy would shape his narrative as much as the narrative would shape his philosophy. After several false starts (which would all leave their traces), new ideas would be tried out continually as each draft was refashioned. The difference in treatment is most apparent in the endings, where the hastily outlined 'happy' ending of this first full version gives way to closing scenes that subtly recapitulate the grand themes which resonate throughout the mature work – life and death, peace and war, and so on – and suggest continuity rather than conclusion. This early draft, then, catches the work at a crucial stage in its development, just when Tolstoy was poised to expand his core text into what would finally emerge as the *War and Peace* that we know.

In accordance with the convention of the day Tolstoy, even before his draft was complete, had already submitted the opening parts for publication, and three instalments, under the overall title *1805*, appeared in 1865 and 1866 in the journal *Russkii Vestnik* (Russian Herald). However, conceiving his work as a single entity, Tolstoy abandoned serial publication. The end of his first full draft was reached in December 1866, but dissatisfied with its scope, Tolstoy withdrew to his estate at Yasnaya Polyana, took a break over the new year holidays and then embarked on three further years of intense research and rewriting, during which he would gradually transform what was now more or less a family chronicle (and which he considered calling *All's Well That Ends Well*) into the monumental epic that would be entitled *War and Peace*. Over the next few years Tolstoy travelled to battle sites, devoured memoirs and histories, and talked with old soldiers who could still recall the events of their youth. His finished text, amplified and elaborated, would be almost twice its original length.

Although the full-length version was initially published in six volumes between 1868 and 1869, it would undergo yet further extensive revision before appearing in 1873 as the single, four-volume set that Tolstoy had originally envisaged. This second edition of 1873 is regarded by some as the most authoritative. However, Tolstoy continued to make changes in subsequent editions, adjusting details of style, translating the many passages of French into Russian, rearranging the text and removing the more intrusive of his philosophical digressions to a separate section at the end. The divisions into volumes, parts and chapters differed with each edition. Moreover, by the 1880s, Tolstoy had lost interest in the publication of his own work and handed his copyrights to his wife, Sofia, and she failed to ensure that earlier amendments were incorporated into later editions. Thus among the six editions that came out between 1868 and 1886, no two are alike, and a consensus has never been reached as to which of them is best or definitive.

Further complications dog the question of an 'authorised' version. Tolstoy's wife had copied the entire work out seven times in the course of its composition, but along the way had acted as editor, making her own changes, and censoring and suppressing whatever could be deemed offensive or dangerous. Others had a hand in this too, but – odd as it may seem today – this was done with Tolstoy's agreement.

His attitude should be placed in context. In Russia, because political and philosophical ideas were denied open public debate, they found expression in literature and poetry, and while this resulted in a uniquely rich body of work freighted with powerful allusions, the poets and writers themselves were turned into potential subversives with state censors routinely scrutinising their every word. Hence we find Tolstoy telling his editor P.I. Bartenev on 6 December 1867: 'I give you *carte blanche* to cross out everything that strikes you as dangerous. You know better than I what is possible and what is not.' And again on 8 December 1867: '. . . I am beginning to fear that censorship or the printers could give us nasty trouble. I place my only hope about these two matters in you.'

Tolstoy's very earliest attempts, during the 1850s, at what would become *War and Peace* were clearly engaged with the politics of his own day. His initial central figure was an ageing Decembrist revolutionary (an older Pierre Bezukhov) returning to Russia from exile after serving his sentence for participating in the unsuccessful uprising of December 1825 (from which came the name 'Decembrist'). To portray him in depth, however, Tolstoy saw that he needed to understand his hero's youth. This had been shaped by the year 1812, when Russia had rejoiced at the disaster of Napoleon's failed invasion. Yet that year could not be separated from 1807 and 1805, when it had been Russia's turn to be shamed by Napoleon, this time in direct military defeat. Thus Tolstoy's focus had kept pushing ever further back from his own time to that of his grandfather, and in the end his narrative would deal with those early years alone. What came to concern him were not historic events in themselves so much as the continuity, the cyclicity, of ideas: although centred on Russia's confrontation with Napoleon, the book's main sweep of action is framed by the unseen French revolution which has taken place before the story opens and the Decembrist uprising which will take place after it ends. Both are signalled in the ardent aspirations of the young: first in Pierre who has returned from post-revolutionary Paris, then in Andrei's young son, who eagerly eavesdrops on political talk that heralds the forthcoming change. Tolstoy's contemporaries (as well as the censors) could easily catch these implications and read this apparent work of history as a comment on their own times. In his great transformation, Tolstoy's point of departure had become his point of arrival.

The more he researched the intricacies of the past, the more Tolstoy came to distrust accepted histories with their false view of great men and great events. As his perspective lengthened, so it widened from the life of a single individual to encompass the interwoven fates of whole families and the destinies of nations. The scope likewise broadened beyond his own social class of princes and emperors to include all Russian society down to the peasants and common soldiers, whom he would duly regard as the bedrock of wisdom and patriotism. With his mass of personal evidence and detailed reminiscence, Tolstoy blended fact with fiction until the two could barely be told apart: mythic figures from history were brought to life as convincingly as his imaginary inventions, all invested alike with well documented words and actions and animated by incisive psychological insight. Tolstoy taught lessons in reading as well as in life: what looks significant here will be insignificant there, what seemed trivial before seems important after. In the teeming tumult of life, in the unstoppable onrush of events no one can ever know or determine his or her place or fate.

These philosophical reflections were shaped into essays and discursive digressions that were initially incorporated into the flow of the narrative (but were later amended or removed). Yet *War and Peace* is more than just story and lecture: the texture itself embodies the philosophy that it expounds. Keen to free himself from novelistic constraints, Tolstoy turned his creation into what Henry James would disparage as a 'loose baggy monster', a vast web of the 'accidental and the arbitrary'. But apparent inconsistencies turn out to be continuous threads that form and reform in a stream of flux and inconsequence: the lives of central figures are revealed at significant moments in sharply observed episodes; bystanders are briefly caught by the limelight, then vanish for ever in the flow of the text. Even the central characters flourish and fade as we turn the pages. The reader thus turns spectator, immersed, watching, puzzling, remembering, the process of reading akin to living itself. What strikes us as strange – some unexplained personage here, some name mentioned there – may be part of the overall design, the text consciously rendered as random and unfathomable as human existence.

It is hard, however, to distinguish intentionality from inadvertence in an early draft such as this. While the anomalies in Zaidenshnur's edition are usually ascribed to the misreading of manuscript, some of them might not be outright mistakes but rather the tentative signs of Tolstoy's developing ideas. Although the more obvious anomalies have been corrected, some still remain in the Zakharov edition. Should these be conveyed into English, or seamlessly resolved, and if so, how? The loyalties of a translation are always torn between the future reader and the past source. The present translation treads a fine line between the two, sometimes offering close recreations, warts (so to speak) and all, but at other times making minor adjustments, which often means bringing the text anachronistically into line with the canonical version. The following illustrates a minor adjustment. In a sentence that occurs in both early drafts, but is cut from the canonical version, Pierre, at the English Club, drinks something called 'Alito Margo'. This non-existent potion was clearly a misreading of Tolstoy's Russian scrawl for 'Château

Margaux', a French wine that was probably unknown to scholars in the Soviet period, but has been rendered thus in the English.

In occasional places, to bridge puzzling jumps that occur in the source texts, words have been added in square brackets for the sake of continuity.

Those familiar with the canonical *War and Peace* may wonder about the general absence of French from this edition, that language having constituted some 2.5 per cent of Tolstoy's original text. Accurately depicting the period in which the book is set, Tolstoy shows the Russian upper classes complacently writing and conversing in French, but this conceals an irony, for he also shows not only how the speaking of French alienated the aristocracy from their own native people, but also how it compromised their declared allegiance when Russia was at war with France.

Whereas Zaidenshnur (1983) faithfully reproduces all the French from Tolstoy's original manuscripts, the Zakharov version (2000) translates every word into Russian. This is less contentious than it might seem, for Tolstoy himself, when criticised for featuring so much French in his first edition of 1868–9, translated it all into Russian for the second edition of 1873. He also employed various compensatory techniques, telling the reader, for example, that someone was speaking in French when the words themselves were Russian. Posthumous editions would in due course restore the French to the main text and relegate Tolstoy's Russian translations to footnotes. Soviet editions with the French were called 'classical', while cheaper 'popular' editions remained all-Russian.

But questions of readability aside, the loss of French deprives the text of a crucial subtlety, for Tolstoy constantly uses language as a gauge of sincerity and realism: French signals artificiality and remoteness, Russian signals integrity and groundedness, and folk idiom true earthy wisdom.

English translations have seldom reproduced all, if any, of the French. The present version restores it in 'gestural' form only (*eh bien! O dieu!*), to give a flavour of its original presence and remind the reader of its impact.

Names in Tolstoy present special problems. In the original manuscripts the names of chief protagonists are French throughout – André, Nicolas, Pierre and so on – although affectionate forms are always Russianised. The present translation uses the Russian forms Andrei and Nikolai, for example, but retains the French Hélène and Pierre, partly because of their uniqueness in the wider literary tradition. Transliteration of foreign words aims for readerly access rather than scholarly precision.

Place names follow Tolstoy's idiosyncratic usage and most of his odd, unexplained names of people and apparently inconsistent dates or ages have been left. At that period, Russians used the Julian calendar, which was twelve days behind the Gregorian calendar then in general use elsewhere in Europe. But historical accuracy was of little concern to Tolstoy, and he wrote: 'An historian and an artist describing an historic epoch have two quite different tasks before them.' And given the deliberately distorted, impressionistic quality of certain passages, such details as the age assigned to a character seem to be not so much chronologically precise as approximations in development and mentality.

Tolstoy's spelling is erratic but has generally been regularised. However, the alternate spellings of Bonaparte/Buonaparte follow the original draft exactly, for they subtly register the Russians' changing view of the French leader's repeated self-inventions, tracing the rise of this 'upstart' from low-born Corsican soldier (Buonaparte) to French general (Bonaparte) to Emperor (Napoleon). Russians would have perceived an audible difference between the derisively drawled vowel-sounds of Italian 'Bu-o-na-par-te', and the contemptuous snort of the French 'Bonaparte'.

Finally we come to the slightly vexed question of Tolstoy's style. Tolstoy was an experimental writer who rejected the nineteenth century novel with its conventions and pretensions, above all to authorial invisibility. He wished to convey widely differing experiential effects, many of them rooted in the visual: his writing is often craggy and rough, yet it achieves a piercing clarity that is as merciless as it is miraculous. This relentless percipience is relieved by softer moments of impressionism, such as his famous false-naive technique of *'ostranenie'* or 'defamiliarisation' (numbingly tragic on the battlefield, wryly comic in the theatre). Similarly impressionistic are the long, winding sentences with their many clauses that hasten along in the recreation of swiftly passing time. Sometimes the slipping syntax that results from this haste has been corrected in English, but sometimes it has been left, true to the original. Such slippage could well be part of Tolstoy's deliberate deformations. His generally hurtling manner has a brusqueness and vigour that purposely fly in the face of literary forebears (especially the gentilities of Turgenev, with whom he quarrelled). His use of the same unvarying adjective throughout a single passage, in grand disregard for fine style, creates an unrepentant hammering effect in Russian but raises problems in English, which abhors repetition of this kind. Whilst the present translation introduces small variations in the name of stylistic euphony, it occasionally mimics that repetition to enable readers to feel the force and strangeness of the original. Time and again Tolstoy insisted that this work was neither a novel nor a poem nor a history, and he would have loathed the idea of its being recast in translation as the very thing, a neat and tidy story, that he so strenuously sought to avoid.

Tolstoy's presence in the text is felt everywhere, but especially in his use of the parenthetical aside, whereby the authorial voice suddenly and unashamedly disrupts the story to offer a comment or explanation, revealing a contempt for the very artifice of fiction with which it is beguiling us. In the Russian, this change of voice mid-dialogue carries no warning punctuation, but in the translation it is isolated by the usual marks. In this, as in so many other respects, Tolstoy's virtuoso brilliance prefigures the modernists of the twentieth century: Vladimir Nabokov, for example, writing in English almost a hundred years later, would perfect the art of parenthesis with his famous: '(picnic, lightning)', but well before that Joseph Conrad and Virginia Woolf were just two among the many whose admiration had taken the sincerest form it could, that of imitation. The present translation has tried to convey some of the special qualities that make this early version of *War and Peace*, written with the energy of an artist who was still feeling his way to greatness, so deserving of our close attention.

*Jenefer Coates*
Editor

*Andrew Bromfield*
Translator

Approximate equivalents of old Russian measurements:

*arshin* = 28 inches           or   71 cm

*desyatina* = 3.6 acres        or   1.45 hectares

*pood* = 36 lbs                or   16 kilograms

*sazhen* = 7 feet or 2.3 yards or   2.1 metres

*vershok* = 1.75 inches        or   4.5 cm

*verst* = 2/3 or .66 mile      or   1 kilometre

# LIST OF ILLUSTRATIONS

# WAR AND
# PEACE

# PART ONE

TOLSTOY
*Photograph 1862*
*Autograph on mounting:*
"1862. I took this myself. Count L. N. Tolstoy.
Photograph at Yasnaya Polyana."

# I

"*Eh bien, mon prince*, so Genoa and Lucca are now merely estates, the private estates of the Buonaparte family. *Non*, I warn you, if you don't say this means war, if you still defend all these vile acts, all these atrocities by an Antichrist (for I really do believe he is the Antichrist), then I no longer know you, you are no longer *mon ami*, you are no longer, as you put it, my devoted slave. But, anyway, how do you do, how are you? I see I am frightening you, do come and sit down and tell me what's going on."

These were the words with which, in July 1805, the renowned Anna Pavlovna Scherer, lady-in-waiting and confidante of the Empress Maria Fedorovna, greeted the influential and high-ranking Prince Vasily, who was the first to arrive at her *soirée*. Anna Pavlovna had been coughing for several days, and had what she called the *grippe* (*grippe* then being a new word, used only by the few), and therefore had not attended at court nor even left the house. All of the notes she had sent out in the morning with a scarlet-liveried servant had contained the same message, without variation:

> *If, Count (or Prince), you have nothing better to do, and the prospect of an evening in the company of a poor invalid is not too alarming, then I should be delighted to see you at home between seven and ten o'clock.*
> *Annette Scherer.*

"*Dieu*, what a fierce attack!" replied the prince with a faint smile, not in the least perturbed by this reception as he entered, wearing his embroidered court dress-coat, with knee-breeches, low shoes and starry decorations, and a serene expression on his cunning face.

He spoke that refined French in which our grandfathers not only spoke, but also thought, and with the gently modulated, patronising intonation that was natural to a man of consequence who had grown old in society and at court. He went up to Anna Pavlovna and kissed her hand, presenting to her the bald, perfumed top of his head, which gleamed white even between the grey hairs, then he calmly seated himself on the divan.

5

"First of all, tell me how you are feeling, *ma chère amie*? Do set your friend's mind at rest," he said, without changing his tone of voice, in which, beneath the decorum and sympathy, there was a hint of indifference and even mockery.

"How can you expect me to feel well, when one is suffering so, morally speaking? How can anyone with feeling stay calm in times like these?" said Anna Pavlovna. "You are here for the whole evening, I hope?"

"But what about the festivities at the English ambassador's? Today is Wednesday. I really do have to show my face," said the prince. "My daughter will be calling to take me there."

"I thought today's celebrations had been cancelled. I do declare all these fêtes and fireworks are becoming an utter bore."

"Had they but known you wished it, they would have cancelled the celebrations," said the prince by force of habit, like a wound-up clock, voicing things that he did not even wish to be believed.

"Don't tease me. *Eh bien*, what has been decided following this dispatch from Novosiltsev? You know everything."

"What can I say?" the prince said in a cold, bored voice. "What has been decided? It has been decided that Buonaparte has burnt his boats, and we are apparently prepared to burn ours too."

Whether Prince Vasily's words were wise or foolish, animated or indifferent, he uttered them in a tone that suggested he was repeating them for the thousandth time, like an actor speaking a part in an old play, as though the words were not the product of his reason, not spoken from the mind or heart, but by rote, with his lips alone.

By contrast, Anna Pavlovna Scherer, despite her forty years, was full of an impulsive vivacity which long practice had scarcely taught her to curb within the limits of courtly decorum and discretion. At every moment she seemed on the point of uttering something improper, yet although she came within a hair's breadth, no impropriety ever burst forth. She was not good-looking, but the rapturous enthusiasm of which she herself was aware in her glance and in the vivacity of her smile, which expressed her infatuation with ideal causes, evidently furnished her with that quality which was called interesting. From Prince Vasily's words and his expression it was clear that the circles in which they both moved had long ago adopted the unanimous opinion that Anna Pavlovna was a sweet, good-hearted enthusiast and patriot who dabbled in matters that were not entirely her concern and often took things to extremes, but was lovable for the sincerity and ardour of her feelings. Being an enthusiast had become her position in society, and sometimes, even when she did not really wish it, she played the enthusiast simply in order not to disappoint the expectations of those who knew her. The

PRINCE VASILY
*Drawing by M. S. Bashilov, 1866*

restrained smile that played constantly on Anna Pavlovna's face, although it did not become her faded features, was an expression, as it is in spoilt children, of a constant awareness of her own charming defect, of which she neither wished, nor was able, nor felt it necessary, to rid herself.

The contents of the dispatch from Novosiltsev, who had set out to Paris for peace negotiations, were as follows.

On arriving in Berlin, Novosiltsev had learned that Bonaparte had issued a decree annexing the Genoese Republic to the French Empire, while at the same time he was declaring his desire for reconciliation with

England through the mediation of Russia. Novosiltsev, having halted in Berlin on the surmise that such coercive action on the part of Bonaparte might well alter the Emperor's intentions, had requested His Majesty's decision on whether he should move on to Paris or return home. The reply to Novosiltsev had already been drawn up and was due to be forwarded the following day. The seizure of Genoa was the long-sought pretext for a declaration of war, to which the opinion of court society was even more readily inclined than the military. The reply stated: "We do not wish to conduct negotiations with a man who, while declaring his desire to make peace, continues with his encroachments."

All this was the very latest news of the day. The prince evidently knew all these details from reliable sources and related them to the lady-in-waiting in jocular fashion.

"Well, and where have these negotiations led us?" Anna Pavlovna asked, continuing with the conversation, as before, in French. "And what is the point of all these negotiations? It is not negotiations, but death for the death of the martyr that the scoundrel needs," she said, flaring her nostrils and swinging round on the divan, then smiling.

"How very bloodthirsty you are, *ma chère*! Not everything in politics is done as it is in the drawing room. There are precautionary measures to be taken," Prince Vasily said with his melancholy smile which, though unnatural, had made itself so much at home on the prince's old face after thirty years of constant repetition that its unnaturalness seemed quite normal. "Are there any letters from your family?" he added, evidently considering this lady-in-waiting unworthy of serious political conversation and attempting to lead her on to a different subject.

"But where have all these precautionary measures led us?" Anna Pavlovna persisted, refusing to give way.

"If nothing else, to discovering the opinion of that Austria of which you are so fond," said Prince Vasily, clearly teasing Anna Pavlovna and not wishing to allow the tone of the conversation to move beyond the facetious.

But Anna Pavlovna had become heated.

"Oh, don't you talk to me about Austria! Perhaps I don't understand anything, but Austria does not want war and never has wanted it. She is betraying us. Russia alone must be the saviour of Europe. Our benefactor is aware of his high calling and he will be faithful to it. That is the one thing in which I believe. Our kind and wonderful sovereign is destined for the very greatest of roles in this world, and he is so virtuous and good, that God will not abandon him, and he will fulfil his calling to crush the hydra of revolution, which is more horrible than ever in the person of this assassin and villain. We alone must redeem the blood of the martyr. In whom can we place our hope, I ask you? England, with her commercial spirit, will not and cannot understand the lofty soul of Emperor Alexander. She has refused to evacuate Malta. She wishes to see, she seeks an ulterior motive in our actions. What did they say to Novosiltsev? Nothing. They did not understand, they cannot understand the selflessness of our Emperor, who wants nothing for himself but wishes everything possible for the good of the world. And what have they promised? Nothing. And even what they have promised will never be done! Prussia has already declared that Buonaparte is invincible and all of Europe is powerless against him . . . And I don't believe a single word that Hardenberg or Haugwitz say . . . This vaunted Prussian neutrality is no more than a trap. I believe only in God and the exalted destiny of our dear Emperor. He will save Europe!" She stopped abruptly, with a mocking smile at her own vehemence.

"I think," the prince said with a smile, "that if you had been sent instead of our dear Wintzengerode, you would have taken the Prussian king's assent by storm. You are so eloquent. Are you going to give me tea?"

"In a moment. *A propos*," she said, composing herself once again, "I have a most interesting person coming today, the Vicomte de Mortemart, he is related to the Montmorencys through the Rohans, one of the best families of France. He is one of the good émigrés, the real ones. He behaved very well and has lost everything. He was with the Duc d'Enghien, with the hapless holy martyr while he was visiting Etenheim. They say he is quite a darling. Your charming son Hippolyte has promised to bring him here. All our ladies are quite beside themselves over him," she added with a smile of disdain, as though she were sorry for the poor ladies who could think of nothing better to do than fall in love with the Vicomte de Mortemart.

"Apart from yourself, naturally," said the prince in his gently mocking tone. "I have seen him in society, this vicomte," he added, evidently little interested by the prospect of seeing Mortemart. "Tell me," he said in a deliberately careless fashion, as if he had just remembered something, even though his enquiry was in fact the main purpose of his visit, "is it true that the Dowager Empress desires the appointment of Baron Funke as First Secretary in Vienna? It would appear that this baron is something of a nonentity."

Prince Vasily wished to have his own son appointed to this position, which others were attempting to obtain for the baron through the Empress Maria Fedorovna.

Anna Pavlovna hooded her eyes almost completely in order to indicate that neither she, nor anyone else, could judge what was desirable or pleasing to the Empress.

"Baron Funke has been recommended to the Dowager Empress by her sister," was all that she said, in a tone that was particularly aloof and melancholy. The moment Anna Pavlovna mentioned the Empress's name, her face suddenly presented an expression of profound and sincere devotion and respect, combined with the sadness that she felt every time she mentioned her exalted patroness in conversation. She said Her Highness had been pleased to show great regard for Baron Funke, and once again her gaze was veiled with melancholy.

The prince lapsed into indifferent silence. Anna Pavlovna, with her characteristic courtly and feminine adroitness and prompt tact, felt a desire at once to tweak the prince's nose for having ventured to speak in such a way about a person recommended to the Empress, and at the same time to console him.

"By the way, *à propos* your family," she said, "did you know that your daughter is the delight of all society? They think her quite as lovely as the day. The Empress very often asks after her: 'Where is my Belle Hélène?'"

The prince bowed in token of his respect and gratitude.

"I often think," Anna Pavlovna continued after a moment's silence, moving closer to the prince and smiling at him affectionately, as though indicating in this way that the conversation on politics and society was at an end, and the heart-to-heart talk was about to begin, "I often think how unfairly happiness is sometimes distributed in life. What have you done fate to have given you two such marvellous children – excluding Anatole, your youngest, him I do not like," she interjected categorically, raising her eyebrows. "Such charming children. And really, you appreciate them far less than anyone else, and therefore you do not deserve them."

And she smiled her rapturous smile.

"*Que voulez-vous?* Lavater would have said I lack the bump of paternity," said the prince listlessly.

"Stop your joking. I wanted to have a serious talk with you. You know, I am displeased with your younger son. I don't know him at all, but he appears to have set himself out to earn a scandalous reputation. Just between ourselves" (her face assumed a melancholy expression) "he was spoken of at Her Majesty's, and people feel sorry for you . . ."

The prince did not reply, but she gazed meaningfully at him in silence as she waited for a reply. Prince Vasily frowned.

"What would you have me do?" he said at last. "You know I have done everything that a father can for their education, and both of them have turned out fools. Hippolyte at least is a docile fool, but Anatole is a rowdy one. That is the only difference," he said, smiling more unnaturally and animatedly than usual, and in so doing revealing with unusual distinctness something coarse and disagreeable in the folds that formed around his mouth, making Anna Pavlovna think it could not be very pleasant to be the son or daughter of such a father.

"And why do men like you have children? If you were not a father, there would be nothing I could reproach you with," said Anna Pavlovna, raising her eyes thoughtfully.

"I am your devoted slave, and I can confess this only to you. My children are the bane of my existence. They are my cross. That is how I explain things to myself. What would you have me do? . . ." He fell silent, as a gesture of submission to a cruel fate. "Ah yes, if only one could choose to have them or not at will . . . I am certain that in our time such an invention will be made."

Anna Pavlovna did not much like the idea of such an invention.

"You have never thought of marrying off your prodigal son Anatole. They do say that old maids have a mania for marrying people off. I am not yet aware of this weakness in myself, but I do have one little person who is very unhappy with her father, a kinswoman of ours, the Princess Bolkonskaya."

Prince Vasily did not reply, although with the quickness of wit and memory natural to people of high society he indicated with a movement of his head that he had taken note of this information.

"Indeed, d'you know that this Anatole costs me forty thousand a year," he said, evidently incapable of curbing his gloomy train of thought. He was silent for a moment.

"What will happen in five years' time, if things carry on like this? Such are the rewards of being a father. Is she rich, your princess?"

"Her father is very rich and mean. He lives in the country. You know, the famous Prince Bolkonsky, retired from service under the deceased Emperor and nicknamed the King of Prussia. He's a very intelligent man, but an eccentric and a difficult character. The poor girl is so unhappy. She has a brother, he's the one who recently married Lise Meinen, and is now Kutuzov's adjutant, he lives here and will be coming this evening. She is the only daughter."

"Listen, *ma chère* Annette," said the prince, suddenly catching hold of the other person's hand and for some reason tugging it downwards. "Arrange this business for me and I shall be your most devoted slave for ever. She comes from a good family and is rich. That is all I require."

And with those free and familiar, graceful movements that were so characteristic of him, he raised the lady-in-waiting's hand and kissed it, and having kissed it he waved the hand through the air as he sprawled back in his armchair, gazing away to the side.

*"Attendez,"* said Anna Pavlovna, pondering. "I will have a word today with Lise, young Bolkonsky's wife. And maybe it will all be settled. I shall begin to study my trade as an old maid with your family."

## II
---

Anna Pavlovna's drawing room began filling up little by little. The highest nobility of St. Petersburg arrived, people who differed greatly in age and character, but were alike in terms of the society in which they all lived: the diplomat Count Z. arrived, covered in stars and decorations from all the foreign courts, then came the Princess L., a fading beauty, the wife of an envoy; a decrepit general entered, clattering his sabre and wheezing; then Prince Vasily's daughter, the beautiful Hélène, entered, having called to collect her father in order to go on with him to the ambassador's festivities. She was wearing a ball gown and her *insigne* as a lady-in-waiting. The young little Princess Bolkonskaya, known as the most enchanting woman in St. Petersburg, also arrived; she had married the previous winter and now no longer appeared at great society events on account of being pregnant, but she still went out to small *soirées*.

"You have not yet met . . ." or "I don't think you know my aunt . . ." said Anna Pavlovna to each of her guests as they arrived, leading them across with great seriousness to a little old woman with tall bows on her cap who had come gliding out of the next room as soon as the guests had begun to arrive; she introduced each by name, slowly shifting her gaze from guest to aunt, before moving aside. All of the guests performed the ritual of greeting this aunt who was known to no one, in whom no one was interested and whom no one wanted to meet. Anna Pavlovna followed their greetings with sad, solemn concern, tacitly giving approval. In speaking to each of them the aunt used the same expressions, whether they concerned the guest's health, her own health or the health of Her Majesty, which today, thank God, was improved. Concealing their haste out of a sense of decorum, all who approached the old woman left with a feeling of relief at an onerous duty fulfilled, never to approach her again for the entire evening. Of the ten or so gentlemen and ladies already present, some were gathered by the tea table, some were in the nook behind the trellis, and some by the window: all of them made conversation and moved freely about from one group to another.

The young Princess Bolkonskaya arrived with her needlework in a velvet bag embroidered in gold. Her pretty little upper lip with its faint hint of a dark moustache was too short to cover her teeth, but it opened all the more sweetly for that and occasionally stretched down more sweetly still to touch her lower lip. As is always the case with thoroughly attractive women, her fault – the shortness of her upper lip and her half-open mouth – seemed to be her special, very own beauty. Everyone was gladdened by the sight of this pretty mother-to-be so full of health and vitality, who bore her condition so lightly. Just looking at her, being with her and talking for a while made old men as well as bored, sullen young men feel as though they themselves were growing like her. Anyone who spoke with her and saw the radiant smile that accompanied her every word and the brilliant white teeth that were constantly visible, thought he was especially charming that day. Every one of them thought so. Waddling with short, quick steps, the little princess moved round the table with her needlework bag hanging from her arm and, adjusting her dress, sat herself down happily on the divan beside the silver samovar, as though whatever she did was amusing to herself and to everyone around her.

"I've brought along my work," she said, opening the top of her reticule and addressing everybody at once.

"Now, Annette, don't you play any nasty tricks on me," she said, addressing the hostess. "You wrote that you were only having a little *soirée*, and see how poorly dressed I am." And she spread out her arms to show off her elegant grey gown trimmed with lace and girdled with a broad ribbon under the bosom.

"Don't you worry, Lise, you will always be the loveliest of all," replied Anna Pavlovna.

"You know, my husband is abandoning me, he's going off to get himself killed," she continued in the same tone, addressing the general. "Tell me, whatever is the point of this loathsome war?" she asked, turning to Prince Vasily and, without waiting for a reply, turned to Prince Vasily's daughter, the beautiful Hélène: "You know, Hélène, you are becoming too lovely, just too lovely."

"What a delightful creature this little princess is!" Prince Vasily said quietly to Anna Pavlovna.

"Your charming son Hippolyte is madly in love with her."

"The fool has taste."

Shortly after the little princess entered, a stout young man with short-cropped hair came in, wearing spectacles, light-coloured knee-breeches after the fashion of the time, a high ruffle and brown tailcoat. Despite the fashionable cut of his clothes, this fat young man was clumsy and awkward, in the way that healthy peasant lads are clumsy and awkward. But he was unembarrassed and resolute in his movements. He halted

THE LITTLE PRINCESS
*Drawing by M. S. Bashilov, 1866*

for a moment in the centre of the drawing room and, failing to locate the hostess, bowed to everyone except her, despite the signs she was making to him. Taking the old aunt for Anna Pavlovna herself, he sat down beside her and began speaking, but finally realising from the aunt's astonished face that this was not the right thing to do, he stood up and said:

"I beg your pardon, mademoiselle, I thought you weren't you."

Even the impassive aunt blushed at these senseless words and waved with a despairing expression to her niece, beckoning for help. Anna Pavlovna left the other guest with whom she was occupied and came across.

"It's so very good of you, Monsieur Pierre, to come to visit a poor invalid," she said to him, smiling and exchanging glances with her aunt.

Pierre then did something even worse. He sat down beside Anna Pavlovna with the expression of a man who intended to stay for some time and immediately started talking about Rousseau, of whom they had spoken at their last meeting but one. Anna Pavlovna had no time for this. She was busy listening, watching, arranging and rearranging her guests.

"I cannot understand why," said the young man, peering significantly at his interlocutress over the top of his spectacles, "everyone so dislikes *The Confessions*, when the *Nouvelle Héloïse* is far more inferior."

The fat young man expressed his meaning awkwardly, challenging Anna Pavlovna to an argument and completely failing to notice that the

14

PIERRE BEZUKHOV
*Drawing by M. S. Bashilov, 1866*

lady-in-waiting had absolutely no interest whatever in which work was good or bad, especially now, when she had so many other things to think of and remember.

"'May the last trumpet sound when it will, I shall appear with this book in my hand,'" he said, smiling as he quoted the first page of *The Confessions*. "No, *madame*, if you read the book, you will love the man."

"Yes, of course," replied Anna Pavlovna, in spite of holding entirely the opposite opinion, and she surveyed her guests, wishing to get to her feet. But Pierre continued:

"It's not just a book, it's an entire work. *The Confessions* is a total confession. Is that not so?"

"But I have no desire to be his confessor, Monsieur Pierre, his sins are too vile," she said, rising to her feet with a smile. "Come along, I shall introduce you to my cousin."

And having rid herself of this young man who did not know how to behave, she returned to her concerns as mistress of the house and continued listening and watching, ready to offer assistance whenever conversation flagged, like the foreman of a spinning mill who, with his workers all at their places, keeps pacing about, watching that the spindles all keep turning. And just as the foreman of the spinning mill, on noticing that a spindle has stopped or is squeaking strangely or loudly, hurries across and adjusts it or sets it moving as it should, so Anna Pavlovna approached a circle that had fallen quiet or was talking too much and, with a single word or slight rearrangement, set her regular, decorous conversational engine in motion once again.

## III

Anna Pavlovna's *soirée* was in full swing. On various sides the spindles were humming away smoothly and steadily. Apart from the aunt, beside whom there sat only a single elderly lady with a thin, tearful face, somewhat out of place in this brilliant company, and the fat Monsieur Pierre who, following his tactless conversations with the aunt and Anna Pavlovna, had remained silent for the entire evening and, evidently being acquainted with hardly anyone there, merely gazed around with lively interest at those who were walking about and talking more loudly than others, the remaining company had divided into three circles. At the centre of one was the beautiful Princess Hélène, Prince Vasily's daughter, in the second it was Anna Pavlovna herself, in the third it was the little Princess Bolkonskaya – pretty, rosy-cheeked and very pregnant for her young age.

Prince Vasily's son Hippolyte – "your charming son Hippolyte" as Anna Pavlovna invariably called him – made his entrance, as did the expected vicomte, over whom, according to Anna Pavlovna, "all our ladies" were quite beside themselves. Hippolyte came in peering through a lorgnette, and without lowering this lorgnette, drawled loudly but indistinctly, "the Vicomte de Mortemart" and immediately, paying no attention to his father, seated himself beside the little princess and, inclining his head so close that very little space remained between his face and hers, he began to tell her something obscure and private, laughing.

The vicomte was an attractive-looking young man, with mild features and manners who evidently considered himself a celebrity but, being well brought up, modestly permitted the company in which he found himself to take advantage of his person. Anna Pavlovna was obviously offering him to her guests as a treat. Just as a good maître d'hôtel presents as a supreme delicacy that piece of beef which no one would wish to eat if they had seen it in the filthy kitchen, so this evening Anna Pavlovna served up the vicomte to her guests as something supremely refined, although the gentlemen who were staying at the same hotel and played billiards with him every day saw him as little more than a master of cannon shots, and did not feel in the least bit fortunate to have met the vicomte and spoken with him.

Talk immediately turned to the murder of the Duc d'Enghien. The vicomte said the duke had been killed by his own magnanimity and that there were particular reasons for Bonaparte's animosity.

"Ah! Do tell us about that, vicomte," said Anna Pavlovna.

The vicomte bowed slightly as a token of acquiescence and smiled courteously. Anna Pavlovna walked round the vicomte and invited everyone to listen to his story.

"The vicomte was personally acquainted with the duke," Anna Pavlovna whispered to one person.

"The vicomte is a marvellous raconteur," she declared to another.

"So obviously a man of good society," she said to a third, and thus the vicomte was served up to the company in a tasteful manner in the best possible light, like roast beef on a hot dish garnished with fresh green herbs.

The vicomte, about to begin his story, gave a delicate smile.

"Move over here, *chère* Hélène," said Anna Pavlovna to the beautiful princess, who was sitting a little distance away, at the centre of a different circle.

Princess Hélène was smiling. She stood up, wearing that same constant smile of a perfectly beautiful woman with which she had entered the drawing room. With a slight rustle of her white ball gown trimmed with its plush and fur, and a gleam of white shoulders, glossy hair and diamonds, she stepped between the men who had made way for her and, looking at none of them, but smiling at all as though obligingly granting each one the right to admire the beauty of her figure and well-formed shoulders and her bosom and her back that were greatly exposed in the fashion of the day, and seeming to bring with her all the splendour of a ball, she went over to Anna Pavlovna. Hélène was so lovely that not only was there not a shade of coquetry to be seen in her, but she seemed, on the contrary, to be ashamed of the all-too-overwhelming power of her undeniable beauty. It was as though she wished to diminish her beauty and could not. "What a beautiful woman!" said all who saw her.

As though overcome by something quite extraordinary, the vicomte shrugged his shoulders and lowered his eyes as she seated herself before him and illuminated him with that same unvarying smile.

"*Madame*, truly I fear for my abilities before such an audience," he said, bowing his head and smiling.

The princess, finding it needless to respond, rested the elbow of her shapely, exposed arm on the table. She waited, smiling. Throughout the whole story she sat up straight, glancing occasionally either at her beautiful, well-fleshed arm, the shape of which had changed in pressing against the table, or at her even more beautiful bosom, on which she adjusted her diamond necklace; several times she rearranged the folds of her gown and every time that she was impressed by something in the story, she glanced round at Anna Pavlovna and immediately assumed the very same expression that the lady-in-waiting's face wore, then settled once again into her radiant smile. Following Hélène, the little princess had also come over from the tea table.

"*Attendez-moi*, I'll get my needlework," she said. "Now, what ever are you thinking of?" she asked, addressing Prince Hippolyte. "Fetch me my *ridicule*."

The little princess, smiling and chatting on all sides, promptly made everyone shuffle about as she took her place, and then cheerfully sat rearranging herself.

"Now I'm all right," she said and, requesting them to begin, she took up her work. Prince Hippolyte, after bringing her work-bag, had gone round behind her and, drawing up an armchair, sat close beside her.

The charming Hippolyte was striking for his uncommon resemblance to his beautiful sister, but even more for the fact that, despite the resemblance, he was amazingly ugly. The features of his face were precisely the same as those of his sister, but in her case everything was constantly illuminated by a buoyant, self-sufficient, youthfully vital smile and an exceptional, classical beauty of body, while in the brother's case, on the contrary, the same face was clouded by idiocy and invariably expressed a self-opinionated peevishness, while the body was puny and weak. The eyes, nose and mouth – all seemed to be clenched into a single indeterminate, dull grimace, and the hands and legs always assumed unnatural positions.

"It isn't a ghost story, is it?" he asked, having seated himself beside the princess and hastily set his lorgnette to his eyes, as though he could not speak without this instrument.

"Most decidedly not, my dear fellow," said the astonished storyteller, with a shrug of his shoulders.

"The thing is, I absolutely detest ghost stories," he said in a tone that made it clear that he uttered words first and only realised what they meant afterwards.

Because he spoke with such self-confidence, no one could tell whether what he had said was very clever or very stupid. He was dressed in a dark-green frock coat and knee-breeches in the flesh-pink shade that

HIPPOLYTE KURAGIN
*Drawing by M. S. Bashilov, 1866*

he called *cuisse de nymphe éffrayée*, with stockings and shoes. He had seated himself as far back as possible in the armchair, facing the raconteur, and placed one hand, with one plain and one engraved signet ring, upon the table in front of him in such an outstretched pose that it clearly cost him a great deal of effort to maintain it at that distance, and yet he held it there throughout the story. In the palm of his other hand he clasped his lorgnette, teasing up with that same hand the curly "titus" coiffure that lent his elongated face an even odder expression and, as though he had just remembered something, he began looking first at his hand with the rings, extended in display, then at the vicomte's feet, and then he twisted himself entirely around with a rapid, lurching movement, the way he did everything, and stared long and hard at the Princess Bolkonskaya.

"When I had the good fortune to see the late lamented Duc d'Enghien for the last time," the vicomte began in a tone of mournful elegance, surveying his listeners, "he spoke in the most flattering terms of the beauty and genius of the great Mademoiselle Georges. Who does not know this brilliant and charming woman? I expressed my surprise as to how the duke could have come to know her, not having been in Paris in recent years. The duke smiled and told me that Paris is not as far from Mannheim as it might seem. I was horrified and informed his highness of my terror at the thought of his visiting Paris. 'Sir,' I said, 'God only knows whether even here we are not surrounded by turncoats and traitors and whether your presence in Paris, no matter how secret it may be, is not known to Buonaparte!' But the duke only smiled at my words with the chivalry and courage which constitute the distinguishing trait of his line."

"The house of Condé is a branch of laurel grafted on to the tree of the Bourbons, as Pitt recently said," Prince Vasily pronounced in a monotone, as though he were dictating to some invisible clerk.

"Monsieur Pitt put it very well," his son Hippolyte added laconically, twisting abruptly on his armchair, his trunk in one direction and his legs in the other, after hastily snatching up his lorgnette and directing his sights at his parent.

"In short," continued the vicomte, addressing himself primarily to the beautiful Princess Hélène, who kept her gaze fixed on him, "I had to leave Etenheim and only later learned that the duke, in the impetuosity of his valour, had travelled to Paris and paid Mademoiselle Georges the honour not only of admiring her, but also of visiting her."

"But he had an attachment of the heart for the Princess Charlotte de Rohan Rochefort," Anna Pavlovna interrupted passionately. "They said that he was secretly married to her," she added, evidently frightened by the imminent content of this tale, which seemed to her too free in the presence of a young girl.

"One attachment is no hindrance to another," the vicomte continued, smiling subtly and failing to perceive Anna Pavlovna's apprehension. "But the point is that prior to her intimacy with the duke, Mademoiselle Georges had enjoyed intimate relations with another person."

He paused.

"That person was called Buonaparte," he announced, glancing round at his listeners with a smile. Anna Pavlovna, in her turn, glanced around uneasily, seeing the tale becoming ever more dangerous.

"And so," the vicomte continued, "the new sultan from the *Thousand and One Nights* did not scorn to spend frequent evenings at the home of the most beautiful, most agreeable woman in France. And Mademoiselle Georges" – he paused, with an expressive shrug of his shoulders – "was obliged to make a virtue of necessity. The fortunate Buonaparte would usually arrive in the evening, without appointing the days in advance."

"Ah! I see what is coming, and it fills me with horror," said the pretty little Princess Bolkonskaya with a shudder of her lissom, shapely shoulders.

The elderly lady, who had been sitting beside the aunt the whole evening, came to join the raconteur's circle and shook her head with an emphatic, sad smile.

"It is terrible, is it not?" she said, although she had obviously not even heard the beginning of the story. No one paid any attention to the inappropriateness of her remark, nor indeed to her.

Prince Hippolyte promptly declared in a loud voice:

"Georges in the role of Clytemnestra, how marvellous!"

Anna Pavlovna remained silent and anxious, still not having finally made up her mind whether the tale that the vicomte was telling was proper or improper. On the one hand, it involved evening visits to actresses, on the other hand, if the Vicomte de Mortemart himself, a relative of the Montmorencys through the Rohans, the finest representative of the St. Germain district, was going to make unseemly talk in the drawing room, then who, after all, knew what was proper or improper?

"One evening," the vicomte continued, surveying his listeners and becoming more animated, "this Clytemnestra, having enchanted the entire theatre with her astonishing interpretation of Racine, returned home and thought she would rest to recover from her fatigue and excitement. She was not expecting the sultan."

Anna Pavlovna shuddered at the word "sultan". Princess Hélène lowered her eyes and stopped smiling.

"Then suddenly the maidservant announced that the former Vicomte Rocroi wished to see the great actress. Rocroi was the name that the duke used for himself. He was received," the vicomte added, and after pausing for a few seconds in order to make it clear that he was not telling all that he knew, he continued: "The table gleamed with crystal, enamel, silver and porcelain. Two places were set, the time flew by imperceptibly, and the delight . . ."

Unexpectedly at this point in the narrative Prince Hippolyte emitted a peculiar, loud sound, which some took for a cough, others for snuffling, mumbling or laughing, and he began hastily fumbling after the lorgnette which he had dropped. The narrator stopped in astonishment. The alarmed Anna Pavlovna interrupted the description of the delights which the vicomte was depicting with such relish.

"Do not keep us in suspense, vicomte," she said.

The vicomte smiled.

"Delight reduced hours to minutes, when suddenly there came a ring at the door and the startled maid, trembling, came running in to announce that a terrible Bonapartist Mameluke was ringing and that his appalling master was already standing at the entrance . . ."

"*Charmant, délicieux,*" whispered the little Princess Bolkonskaya, jabbing her needle into her embroidery as if to indicate that the fascination and charm of the story had prevented her from continuing her work.

The vicomte acknowledged this mute praise with a grateful smile and was about to continue when a new person entered the drawing room and effected the very pause that was required.

# IV

This new person was the young Prince Andrei Bolkonsky, husband of the little princess. It was clear, not so much from the way the young prince had arrived late and was yet received in the most polite fashion by the hostess, as from the way that he made his entrance, that he was one of those young people who are so pampered by society that they have come to despise it. The young prince, a slightly short but slim man, was extremely handsome, with dark hair and a brownish complexion and a somewhat languorous air; he was dressed with exceptional elegance and had tiny hands and feet. Everything about his appearance, from his bored and weary gaze to his measured saunter, made the sharpest possible contrast to his lively little wife. He was evidently not only acquainted with everyone present in the drawing room, but so sick of them all that he found it utterly tedious even to look at or listen to them, since he knew in advance exactly how everything would go. Of all the people there that he found so very boring, he seemed to find none more so than his own pretty wife. He turned away from her lovely face with a faint, sour grimace that spoiled his handsome features, as if he were thinking: "You were the last thing this company required to make it utterly loathsome to me."

He kissed Anna Pavlovna's hand with an expression that suggested he would have given God only knew what to be spared this onerous duty and, squinting his eyes till they were almost closed, he surveyed the assembled company.

"You have a large gathering," he said in a high, thin voice, nodding to one person while proffering his hand to another, holding it out to be shaken.

"You intend to go to the war, prince?" said Anna Pavlovna.

"General Kutuzóv," he said, stressing the final syllable, *zóff*, like a Frenchman, and removing a glove from a perfectly white, tiny hand with

22

which he rubbed his eye, "General-in-Chief Kutuzóv has asked me to be his adjutant."

"But what about Lise, your wife?"

"She will go to the country."

"And are you not ashamed to deprive us of your delightful wife?"

The young adjutant puffed out his lips to make a derisive sound of the kind that only the French make, but said nothing.

"*André*," said his wife, addressing her husband in the same flirtatious tone in which she addressed strangers, "do come here and sit down and listen to the story the vicomte is telling us about Mademoiselle Georges and Buonaparte."

Andrei narrowed his eyes and sat down as far away as possible, as though he had not heard his wife.

"Pray continue, vicomte," said Anna Pavlovna. "The vicomte was telling us how the Duc d'Enghien visited Mademoiselle Georges," she added, addressing the new arrival, so that he could follow the continuation of the story.

"The purported rivalry between Buonaparte and the duke over Mademoiselle Georges," said Prince Andrei in a tone suggesting it was absurd for anyone not to know about that, and he slumped against the armrest of his chair. At this point the young man in spectacles named Monsieur Pierre, who had not taken his delighted, affectionate gaze off Prince Andrei from the moment he entered the drawing room, approached him and grasped him by the arm. Prince Andrei was so incurious that, without even glancing round, he twisted his face into a grimace that expressed annoyance with whoever was touching his epaulette, but on seeing Pierre's smiling face, Prince Andrei also broke into a smile, and suddenly his entire face was transformed by the kind and intelligent expression that suffused it.

"What's this? You here, my dear Horse Guard?" the prince asked with delight, but also with a slightly patronising and supercilious inflection.

"I knew that *you* would be," replied Pierre. "I'll come to you for supper," he added quietly, in order not to disturb the vicomte, who was continuing with his story. "May I?"

"No, you may not," said Prince Andrei, laughing and turning away, but letting Pierre know with a gentle squeeze of his hand that he need not have asked.

The vicomte was telling them that Mademoiselle Georges had implored the duke to hide, that the duke had said he had never hidden from anyone, and that Mademoiselle Georges had said to him, "Your highness, your sword belongs to the King and to France" and that the duke had after all hidden himself under the laundry in the next room, and that when Napoleon had become unwell, the duke had emerged from under the laundry and seen Buonaparte there before him.

"Charming, quite exquisite!" said a voice among the listeners.

Even Anna Pavlovna, having observed that the most difficult part of the tale had been negotiated successfully, calmed down and was quite able to enjoy the story. The vicomte warmed to his task and, rolling his r's powerfully, declaimed with the animation of an actor . . .

"The enemy of his house, the usurper of the throne, the man who stood at the head of his nation, was here, before him, prostrate and motionless on the ground and perhaps at his last gasp. As the great Corneille said: 'Malicious glee surged in his breast and outraged majesty alone helped him repel it.'"

The vicomte stopped and, as he prepared to proceed with his story with still greater verve, he smiled, as though reassuring the ladies, who were already over-excited. Quite without warning during this pause, the beautiful Princess Hélène looked at her watch, exchanged glances with her father, and the two of them suddenly stood up, their movements disturbing the circle and interrupting the story.

"We shall be late, papa," she said simply, all the while beaming her smile at everyone.

"Do forgive me, my dear vicomte," said Prince Vasily to the Frenchman, affectionately tugging him down by the sleeve to prevent him rising from his seat. "These wretched festivities of the ambassador's deprive me of my pleasure and interrupt you."

"So awfully sorry to forsake your exquisite *soirée*," he said to Anna Pavlovna.

His daughter, Princess Hélène, began making her way between the chairs, gently restraining the folds of her gown, with the smile on her lovely face beaming ever more radiantly.

# V

Anna Pavlovna requested the vicomte to wait while she showed Prince Vasily and his daughter out through the next room. The elderly lady who had previously been sitting with the aunt and had then so foolishly expressed her interest in the vicomte's story, hastily rose to her feet and followed Prince Vasily to the entrance hall.

The former pretence of interest had completely vanished from her face. That kind, tearful face now expressed only anxiety and fear.

"What can you tell me, prince, about my Boris?" she said, as she caught up with him in the hallway (she pronounced the name Boris with a distinctive stress on the "o"). "I cannot stay here in St. Petersburg any longer. Tell me, what news can I bring my poor boy?"

Although Prince Vasily listened to the elderly lady unwillingly, almost impolitely, and even showed his impatience, she smiled at him affectionately and imploringly, and to prevent him leaving took him by the arm.

"What trouble would it be for you to have a word with His Majesty, and he would be directly transferred to the Guards," she pleaded.

"Believe me, I will do all that I can, princess," replied Prince Vasily, "but it is difficult for me to ask His Majesty; I would advise you to appeal to Razumovsky through Prince Golitsyn, that would be wiser."

The elderly lady bore the name of Drubetskaya, one of the finest family names in Russia, but she was poor and, having long since withdrawn from society, she had forfeited her former connections. She had come here now solely to obtain an appointment to the Guards for her only son. It was only in order to see Prince Vasily that she had had herself invited to Anna Pavlovna's *soirée*, and it was only for that reason that she had sat listening to the vicomte's story. She was alarmed at Prince Vasily's words; her once-beautiful face expressed, for a moment, something close to disdain. She smiled again and clutched Prince Vasily's arm more tightly.

"Listen, prince," she said, "I have never once petitioned you for anything and I never will, and I have never once reminded you of my father's friendship towards you. But now I entreat you in God's name, do this for my son and I shall regard you as my benefactor," she added hastily. "No, do not be angry, but promise me. I have asked Golitsyn and he refused. Be the same good fellow you always were," she said, trying to smile, despite the tears in her eyes.

"Papa, we shall be late," said Princess Hélène, turning her beautiful head on her classical shoulders as she waited by the door.

Influence in society is capital which, if it is not to diminish, must be protected. Prince Vasily knew this and, realising that if he began asking for everyone who begged him, he would soon be unable to ask for anyone at all, he rarely made use of his influence. In Princess Drubetskaya's case, however, her renewed appeal prompted something akin to a pang of conscience. She had reminded him of the truth: that he had been obliged to her father for the first steps in his own career. In addition, he could see from her manner that she was one of those women, especially mothers, who, once they have taken an idea into their heads, will never relent until their wishes have been granted, otherwise they are prepared to carry on badgering every day and every minute and even create scenes. It was this final consideration that swayed him.

"My dear Anna Mikhailovna," he said with the customary familiarity and boredom in his voice, "for me it is almost impossible to do what you wish, but in order to prove to you that I love you and honour the memory of the late count, your father, I shall do the impossible. Your son shall be transferred to the Guards, here is my hand on it. Are you content?"

And he shook her hand, tugging it downwards.

"My dear man, you are my benefactor! I expected nothing less from you," the mother lied and demeaned herself, "I knew how kind you are."

He was about to leave.

"Wait, just one more word. Since he will move to the Guards . . ." she said and stopped short. "You are on good terms with Mikhail Ilarionovich Kutuzov, recommend Boris to him as an adjutant. Then my mind would be at rest, and then . . ."

Anna Mikhailovna begged, like a gypsy, for her son: the more she was given, the more she wanted. Prince Vasily smiled.

"That I do not promise. You have no idea how Kutuzov has been besieged since he was appointed commander-in-chief. He told me himself that all the ladies of Moscow have conspired to give him their children as adjutants."

"No, promise me, I shan't let you go, my dear man, my benefactor . . ."

"Papa," the beauty repeated in the same tone as before, "we shall be late."

"Well, *au revoir*. You see?"

"Then tomorrow you will put it to His Majesty."

"Without fail, but concerning Kutuzov I do not promise."

"No, promise me, promise, Vasily," Anna Mikhkailovna said as he left, with the smile of a young coquette which once must have been natural to her, but now was quite out of place on her kind, careworn face. She had clearly forgotten her age and sought out of habit to employ all the ancient feminine wiles. But as soon as he went out her face once again assumed the cold, artifical expression it had worn previously. She returned to the circle in which the vicomte was continuing with his story and once again pretended to be listening, waiting until it was time to leave, since her business was already done.

# VI

The end of the vicomte's story went as follows:

"The Duc d'Enghien took out of his pocket a vial of rock crystal mounted in gold which contained the elixir of life given to his father by the Comte St. Germain. This elixir, as is well known, possessed the property of bringing the dead, or the almost dead, back to life, but it was not to be given to anyone but members of the house of Condé. Outsiders who tasted the elixir were cured in the same way as the Condés, but they became implacable enemies of the ducal house. A proof of this can be seen in the fact that the duke's father, wishing to restore his dying horse, gave it these drops. The horse revived, but several times afterwards it attempted to kill its rider and once during a battle it carried him into the republicans' camp. The duke's father killed his beloved horse. In spite of this, the young and chivalrous Duc d'Enghien poured several drops into the mouth of his enemy Buonaparte, and the ogre revived."

" 'Who are you?' asked Buonaparte.

" 'A relative of the maid,' replied the duke.

" 'Lies!' cried Buonaparte.

" 'General, I am unarmed,' replied the duke.

" 'Your name?'

" 'I have saved your life,' replied the duke.

"The duke left, but the elixir took effect. Buonaparte began to feel hatred for the duke and from that day on he swore to destroy the unfortunate and magnanimous youth. Having learned who his rival was from a handkerchief dropped by the duke, which was embroidered with the crest of the house of Condé, Buonaparte ordered his minions to contrive a conspiracy between Pichegru and Georges as a pretext, then had the heroic martyr seized in the dukedom of Baden and killed.

"The angel and the demon. And that was how the most terrible crime in history was committed."

With this the vicomte concluded his story and swung round on his chair in an excess of agitation. Everyone was silent.

"The murder of the duke was more than a crime, vicomte," said Prince Andrei, smiling gently, as though he were making fun of the vicomte, "it was a mistake."

The vicomte raised his eyebrows and spread his arms wide. His gesture could have signified many things.

"But what do you make of the latest farce, of the coronation in Milan?" asked Anna Pavlovna. "In this new farce, the peoples of Genoa and Lucca declare their wishes to Mr. Buonaparte and Mr. Buonaparte sits on a throne and grants the people's wishes. Oh, it is exquisite! Why, it's enough to drive one insane. Just imagine, the entire world has lost its wits."

Prince Andrei turned away from Anna Pavlovna, as if to imply that the talk was leading nowhere.

"God has given me the crown. Woe betide him who touches it,"

Prince Andrei declared proudly, as though they were his own words (they were in fact those of Bonaparte when the crown was set upon his head). "They say he looked awfully fine as he pronounced those words," he added.

Anna Pavlovna glanced sharply at Prince Andrei.

"I hope," she continued, "that that was the drop which will finally make the glass run over. The sovereigns can no longer tolerate this man who is such a threat to everything."

"The sovereigns? I do not speak of Russia," said the vicomte with courteous despair, "but the sovereigns! What did they do for Louis XVI, for the Queen, for Elizabeth? Nothing!" he continued, growing animated. "And believe me, they are now being punished for their betrayal of the Bourbon cause. The sovereigns? They send their ambassadors to greet this usurper of the throne."

And with a contemptuous sigh he again shifted his position. At these words Prince Hippolyte, who had been looking at the vicomte through his lorgnette the whole time, suddenly turned his entire body towards the little Princess Bolkonskaya and, after asking her for a needle, began to show her, by drawing with the point on the table, the Condé coat of arms. He expounded it to her with an expression as intent as if the princess had asked him to do it.

"The Condé coat of arms consists of a shield with a staff gules engrailed with a staff azure," he prattled. The princess listened, smiling.

"If Buonaparte remains on the throne of France for another year," said the vicomte, continuing the chief conversation with the air of a man who is listening to no one, but merely pursuing his own train of thought on a matter which he knows better than everyone else, "then things will be carried too far by all the intrigues, violence, exiles and executions. Society, I mean good society, French society, will be exterminated for ever, and then what?"

He shrugged his shoulders and spread his hands.

"The Emperor Alexander," said Anna Pavlovna with the melancholy that always accompanied her talk of the imperial family, "has declared that he will allow the French themselves to choose their own form of government. And I think there can be no doubt that, once it is liberated from the usurper, the entire nation will throw itself into the arms of the legitimate King," said Anna Pavlovna, striving to be as gracious as possible with the émigré and royalist.

"Oh, if only that happy moment could come!" said the vicomte, inclining his head in gratitude for this mark of attention.

"And what do you think, Monsieur Pierre?" Anna Pavlovna sweetly asked the fat young man whose awkward silence was irksome to her as a polite hostess. "What do you think? You have recently come from Paris."

While waiting for a reply, Anna Pavlovna smiled at the vicomte and the others, as if to say: "I must be polite even with him; you see, I still speak to him, even though I know he has nothing to say."

# VII

"The entire nation will die for its Emperor, for the greatest man in the world!" the young man said suddenly in a loud and vehement voice, without any preamble whatsoever, resembling a young peasant lad fearful of being interrupted and deprived of the opportunity to express himself in full. He glanced round at Prince Andrei. Prince Andrei smiled.

"The greatest genius of our age," Pierre continued.

"What? That is your opinion? You are joking!" screeched Anna Pavlovna, her fright prompted less by the words that the young man uttered than by the animation, so spontaneous and entirely improper, that was expressed in the full, fleshy features of his face, and still more by the sound of his voice, which was too loud and, above all, too natural. He made no gestures and spoke in short bursts, occasionally adjusting his spectacles and glancing around, but it was clear from his whole appearance that no one could stop him now and he would express his entire view, regardless of the proprieties. The young man was like a wild, unbroken horse who, until saddled and stirrupped, is quiet and even timid and in no way different from other horses, but who, as soon as the harness is put on him, suddenly begins for no clear reason to pull in his head, and rear and buck in the most ludicrous manner possible, without knowing why himself. The young man had evidently sensed the bridle and begun his ludicrous bucking.

"Nobody in France even thinks about the Bourbons nowadays," he continued hastily, so that no one would interrupt him, and constantly glancing round at Prince Andrei, as though he was the only one from whom he expected encouragement. "Do not forget that it is only three months since I returned from France."

He spoke in excellent French.

"Monsieur le vicomte is absolutely right to suppose that in a year it will be too late for the Bourbons. It is already too late. There are no more royalists. Some have abandoned their fatherland, others have become Bonapartists. The whole of St. Germain pays homage to the Emperor."

"There are exceptions," the vicomte said superciliously.

The worldly, experienced Anna Pavlovna looked anxiously by turns at the vicomte and the improper young man and could not forgive herself for imprudently inviting this youth without first getting to know him.

The improper youth was the illegitimate son of a rich and renowned grandee. Anna Pavlovna had invited him out of respect for his father, bearing in mind also that Monsieur Pierre had just returned from abroad, where he had been educated.

"If only I had known that he was so badly brought up and a bonapartist," she thought, looking at his big, close-cropped head and his large, fleshy features. "So this is the upbringing they give young men nowadays. You can tell a man of good society straight away," she said to herself, admiring the vicomte's composure.

"Almost the entire nobility," Pierre continued, "has gone over to Bonaparte."

"So say the Bonapartists," said the vicomte. "It is hard these days to discover the opinion of the French public."

"As Bonaparte said," Prince Andrei began, and involuntarily everyone turned in the direction of his voice, which was low and indolent, but always audible because of its self-assurance, waiting to hear exactly what Bonaparte had said.

"'I showed them the path to glory, but they did not want it,'" Prince Andrei continued after a brief silence, again repeating the words of Napoleon. "'I opened up my ante-chambers and the crowds rushed in.' I do not know how justified he was in saying that, but it was clever, viciously clever," he concluded with an acid smile and turned away.

"He did have the right to speak out like that against the royalist aristocracy; it no longer exists in France," Pierre put in, "or if it does, then it carries no weight. And the people? The people adore the great man, and the people have chosen him. The people are without prejudice; they have seen the greatest genius and hero in the world."

"He might be a hero to some," said the vicomte, not replying to the young man and not even looking at him, but addressing Anna Pavlovna and Prince Andrei, "but after the murder of the duke there is one more martyr in heaven and one less hero on earth."

Anna Pavlovna and the others had no time to appreciate the vicomte's words before the unbroken horse continued his novel and amusing bucking.

"The execution of the Duc d'Enghien," Pierre continued, "was a state necessity, and I see precisely greatness of soul in the fact that Napoleon was not afraid to take upon himself alone the responsibility for that act."

"You approve of murder!" Anna Pavlovna exclaimed in a ghastly whisper.

"Monsieur Pierre, how can you see greatness of soul in murder?" said the little princess, smiling and drawing her work closer to her.

"Ah! Oh!" said various voices.

"Magnificent," Prince Hippolyte suddenly said in English, and began slapping his open hand against his knee. The vicomte merely shrugged.

"Is the murder of the duke a good deed or a bad one?" he said, surprising everyone with his high-toned presence of mind. "One or the other . . ."

Pierre sensed that this dilemma had been posed for him so that if he replied in the negative, they would force him to repudiate his admiration for his hero, but if he replied in the positive, that the deed was a good one, then God alone knew what might happen to him. He replied in the positive, unafraid of what would happen.

"This deed is a great one, like everything that this great man does," he said audaciously, paying no attention to the horror expressed on all of their faces except the face of Prince Andrei, or to the contemptuous shrugs; he carried on talking on his own, even though his hostess clearly did not wish it. Everyone exchanged glances of amazement as they listened to him, except Prince Andrei. Prince Andrei listened with sympathy and a quiet smile.

"Surely he knew," continued Pierre, "what a furious storm the death of the duke would stir up against him? He knew that for this one head he would be obliged once again to wage war against the whole of Europe, that he would fight, and would be victorious again, because . . ."

"Are you Russian?" asked Anna Pavlovna.

"I am. But he will be victorious, because he is a great man. The death of the duke was necessary. He is a genius and the difference between a genius and ordinary people is that he does not act for himself, but for humanity. The royalists wished to inflame once again the internal war and revolution that he had suppressed. He needed domestic peace, and with the execution of the duke he set an example that made the Bourbons stop their intrigues."

"But, *mon cher* Monsieur Pierre," said Anna Pavlovna, attempting to overcome him by meekness, "how can you call the means to the restoration of the legitimate throne intrigues?"

"Only the will of the people is legitimate," he replied, "and they drove out the Bourbons and handed power to the great Napoleon."

And he looked triumphantly over the top of his spectacles at his listeners.

"Ah! The *Social Contract*," the vicomte said in a quiet voice, evidently reassured at having recognised the source from which his opponent's views were derived.

"Well, after this . . . !" exclaimed Anna Pavlovna.

But even after this Pierre continued speaking just as uncivilly.

"No," he said, growing more and more animated, "the Bourbons and the royalists fled from the revolution, they could not understand it. But this man rose above it, and suppressed its abuses while retaining all that is good – the equality of citizens and freedom of speech and of the press, and only because of *this* did he acquire power."

"Indeed, but if, having taken power, he had returned it to the rightful king," said the vicomte ironically, "then I should call him a great man."

"He could not have done that. The people gave him power only so that he could rid them of the Bourbons, and because the people saw in him a great man. The revolution itself was a great thing," continued Monsieur Pierre, demonstrating with this audacious and challenging introductory phrase his great youth and desire to express everything as quickly as possible.

"Revolution and regicide are a great thing! After this . . ."

"I am not talking of regicide. When Napoleon appeared, the revolution had already run its course, and the nation put itself into his hands of its own accord. But he understood the ideas of the revolution and became its representative."

"Yes, the ideas of plunder, murder and regicide," the ironic voice interrupted once again.

"Those were the extremes, of course, but that is not what is most important, what is important are the rights of man, emancipation from prejudices, the equality of citizens; and Napoleon retained all of these ideas in full force."

"Liberty and equality," the vicomte said derisively, as though he had decided finally to demonstrate seriously to this youth the full stupidity of his words. "All high-sounding words which have been compromised long ago. Who does not love liberty and equality? Our Saviour preached liberty and equality. But after the revolution were people any happier? On the contrary. We wanted liberty, but Buonaparte is destroying it."

Prince Andrei looked with a merry smile by turns at Monsieur Pierre, at the vicomte and at his hostess, and evidently found this unexpected and indecorous episode amusing. During the first minute of Pierre's outburst Anna Pavlovna had been horrified, for all her experience of the world, but when she saw that, despite the sacrilegious sentiments expressed by Pierre, the vicomte did not lose his temper, and when she became convinced that it was no longer possible to suppress what was being said, she gathered her strength and joined forces with the vicomte to assail the orator.

"But, my dear Monsieur Pierre," said Anna Pavlovna, "how do you explain a great man who was capable of executing a duke or, in the final analysis, simply a man, without a trial and without any proven guilt?"

"I would like to ask," said the vicomte, "how Monsieur Pierre explains the Eighteenth Brumaire. Surely this is deceit? It is cheap swindling, in no way resembling the conduct of a great man."

"And the prisoners whom he killed in Africa?" the little princess interjected at the same point. "That is awful." And she shrugged her little shoulders.

"He is a scoundrel, no matter what you say," said Prince Hippolyte.

Monsieur Pierre did not know whom to answer, he glanced round at them all and smiled, and the smile exposed his uneven black teeth. His smile was not the same as other people's, which merge into the absence of a smile. On the contrary, when his smile came, his serious, even rather sullen face instantly disappeared and a different one replaced it; childish, kind, even a little stupid, and seeming to beg forgiveness.

The vicomte, who was seeing him for the first time, realised that this Jacobin was by no means as terrible as the things that he said. Everyone fell silent.

"Well, do you want him to answer everyone at once?" Prince Andrei's voice rang out. "Besides, in the actions of a statesman one should distinguish between the actions of the individual and those of the general or the emperor. So it seems to me."

"Yes, yes, of course," put in Pierre, delighted at the support that had been offered him. "As a man, he is great on the Bridge at Arcole, in the hospital in Jaffa, where he offers his hand to victims of the plague, but . . ."

Prince Andrei, evidently wishing to mitigate the awkwardness caused by Pierre's oration, half-rose to his feet, preparing to leave and signalling to his wife.

"It is difficult," he said, "to judge people of our own time, posterity will judge them."

Suddenly Prince Hippolyte stood up, halting everybody by gesturing with his hands and requesting them to be seated, and began speaking:

"Today I was told a quite charming Moscow anecdote, I simply must regale you with it. I beg your pardon, vicomte, I shall tell it in Russian, otherwise the whole point of the story will be lost."

And Prince Hippolyte began speaking in Russian with the same accent with which French people who have spent a year in Russia speak. Everyone paused, so keenly and insistently did Prince Hippolyte demand their attention for his story.

"There is à Moscou a certain lady. And she be very mean. She needed have two footmen behind a carriage. And very tall. That was to her taste. And she had chambermaid who was tall also. She said . . ."

At this point Prince Hippolyte began pondering, evidently struggling to figure something out.

"She said . . . yes, she said, 'Girl, put livery on and go with me to carriage to make visits.'"

Then Prince Hippolyte snorted and began to chortle far sooner than his listeners, which was something of a disadvantage to the narrator. However, many of them, including the elderly lady and Anna Pavlovna, did smile.

"She set off. Suddenly strong wind appeared. Girl lose her hat and long hair tumble down all loose . . ."

Then he could hold out no longer and burst into fitful laughter, and through this laughter he said:

"And so the whole world find out . . ."

That was how the anecdote ended. Although it was not clear why he told it or why it absolutely had to be told in Russian, Anna Pavlovna and the others were nonetheless grateful for Prince Hippolyte's courtesy, which had put such an agreeable end to Monsieur Pierre's disagreeable and discourteous outburst. Following the anecdote the conversation broke up into petty gossip about the next ball and the last, a play, and when and where people would see each other again.

# VIII

Having thanked Anna Pavlovna for her charming *soirée*, the guests began taking their leave.

Pierre was ungainly. Fat and broad, with huge hands that seemed to have been made for swinging one-*pood* weights, he had no idea, as they say, of how to enter a salon and even less idea of how to leave it, that is, of how to make his farewells and say something particularly agreeable before his exit. In addition, he was absent-minded. As he stood up, instead of taking his own hat he grabbed hold of a three-cornered hat with a general's panache and held it, tugging at the plume, until the general finally requested him with some animosity, or so it seemed to Pierre, to hand it back. But all of his absent-mindedness and his inability to enter a salon and converse appropriately within it were redeemed by an expression so good-natured and open that, despite all his short-comings, even those whom he had placed in an embarrassing position could not help finding him likeable. Anna Pavlovna turned towards him and, expressing her forgiveness of his outburst with Christian meekness, nodded to him and said:

"I hope to see you again, but I also hope you will change your opinions, my dear Monsieur Pierre."

To these words he made no response, but merely bowed and once again displayed to everybody his smile that said nothing, except perhaps this: "Opinions are all very well, but see what a fine, good-natured fellow I am." And everybody, even Anna Pavlovna, could not help but feel it.

"You know, my dear fellow, your way of thinking tends to raise the roof," said Prince Andrei, buckling on his sabre.

"I don't mean it to," said Pierre, lowering his head, peering over his spectacles and coming to a standstill. "How is it possible to see nothing in either the revolution or Napoleon except the personal interests of the Bourbons? We ourselves do not appreciate how much we are indebted precisely to the revolution . . ."

Prince Andrei did not wait to hear the end of this discourse. He went out into the entrance hall and, presenting his shoulders to the servant, who threw on his cloak, he lent an indifferent ear to the idle chatter of his wife and Prince Hippolyte, who had also come out into the hallway. Prince Hippolyte was standing beside the delightful pregnant princess and staring hard at her through his lorgnette.

"Go in, Annette, you'll catch cold," said the little princess, taking her leave of Anna Pavlovna. "It's settled," she added quietly.

Anna Pavlovna had already managed to talk over with Lise the putative marriage of Anatole and Lise's sister-in-law and to request the princess to influence her husband.

"I am relying on you, *chère amie*," said Anna Pavlovna, also quietly, "you will write to her and let me know how her father views the matter. *Au revoir*." And she left the entrance hall.

Prince Hippolyte moved still closer to the little princess and, leaning his face down to hers, began saying something to her in a half-whisper.

Two servants, one the princess's and the other his, stood waiting for them to finish talking, holding a shawl and a redingote and listening to their French speech, which they could not understand, but with expressions that suggested they did understand and did not wish to show it. The princess as always smiled as she spoke and laughed as she listened.

"I am very glad I did not go to the ambassador's," said Prince Hippolyte, "so boring . . . An excellent *soirée*. Was it not, excellent?"

"They say the ball will be very fine," replied the princess, twitching her lip with the faint moustache. "All the beautiful society ladies will be there."

"Not all, because you will not be there, not all," said Prince Hippolyte, laughing gleefully and, seizing the shawl from the manservant, even shoving him back, he began arranging it on the princess. Either out of clumsiness or on purpose, no one could have told which, he did not lower his arms for a long time after putting the shawl in place, and appeared to embrace the young woman.

She moved away from him gracefully, still smiling, turned round and looked at her husband. Prince Andrei's eyes were closed, he looked tired and sleepy.

"Are you ready?" he asked his wife, running his eye over her. Prince Hippolyte hastily donned his redingote, which in the new style hung below his heels, and ran out, tripping over it, onto the porch after the princess, whom a servant was helping into a carriage.

"Princess, *au revoir*," he shouted, tripping over his tongue in the same way as over his feet.

Gathering her skirts, the princess prepared to take her seat in the darkness of the carriage; her husband began adjusting his sabre; Prince Hippolyte, on the pretext of being helpful, kept getting in everyone's way.

"Permit me, sir," said Prince Andrei in Russian to Prince Hippolyte, who was preventing him from passing.

This "permit me, sir" had a ring of such cold contempt that Prince Hippolyte hastily stepped aside and began apologising and swaying agitatedly from one foot to the other, as though in pain from some fresh wound, still raw and smarting.

"I'm expecting you, Pierre," said Prince Andrei's voice.

The postillion set off with the carriage wheels rumbling. Prince Hippolyte laughed fitfully as he stood on the porch, waiting for the vicomte, whom he had promised to drive home . . .

"*Eh bien, mon cher*, your little princess is very nice, very nice," said the vicomte after he and Hippolyte had got into their carriage. "*Mais très bien.*" He kissed the tips of his fingers. "And perfectly French." Hippolyte snorted and began laughing.

"And you know, you are quite *terrible*, with your innocent ways," the vicomte continued. "I pity the poor husband, this poor little officer posturing as some ruling prince."

Hippolyte snorted again and said through his laughter:

"And you said that Russian ladies were not as good as French. You just need to know how to go about it."

## IX

Reaching the house first, Pierre, as if he lived there, went through into Prince Andrei's study and immediately, as was his habit, lay on the

PIERRE BEZUKHOV
*Drawing by M. S. Bashilov, 1866*

divan, taking down the first book he came across on the shelf (it was Caesar's *Commentaries*) and, leaning on his elbows, set about reading it from the middle with as much interest as if he had been immersed in it for some two hours. As soon as Prince Andrei arrived he went straight through to his dressing room, emerging into the study five minutes later.

"What did you do to Madame Scherer? She'll now fall quite seriously ill," he said to Pierre in Russian with a protective, cheerful and amicable smile as he came in, now dressed in a heavy velvet smoking jacket, rubbing his small white hands, which he had evidently just washed once again.

Pierre swung his whole body round, making the divan creak, and turned his eager face to Prince Andrei, who was shaking his head.

Pierre nodded guiltily.

"I didn't wake up until three. Would you believe that we drank eleven bottles between the five of us?" (Pierre always addressed Prince Andrei formally, while the prince spoke to him in a more informal manner. This was a habit they had acquired as children, and it had never changed.) "Such splendid fellows. That Englishman's a marvel!"

"That's one pleasure I have never understood," said Prince Andrei.

"What are you saying? You are a quite different kind of person, remarkable in every way," Pierre said sincerely.

"At our dear Anatoly Kuragin's place again?"

37

"Yes."

"I can't think why you associate with that trash!"

"But he really is a fine chap."

"He's trash!" Prince Andrei said curtly and frowned. "Hippolyte is a very bright boy, though, isn't he?" he added.

Pierre laughed, setting his entire body shaking so that the divan began creaking again. "In *Moscou* there is a certain lady," he mimicked through his laughter.

"But you know, he really is a good chap," the prince interceded for Hippolyte. "Well then, have you finally decided on anything? Are you going to be a Horse Guard or a diplomat?"

Pierre sat up on the divan, drawing his legs under him.

"Can you imagine, I still don't know? I don't like either choice!"

"But you have to decide on something, don't you? Your father's waiting."

At the age of ten Pierre had been sent abroad with his tutor, an abbot, and had stayed there until he was twenty. When he returned to Moscow, his father had dismissed the abbot and told the young man: "Now go to St. Petersburg, take a look around, get to know people and think about which path to choose. I agree to anything. Here is a letter for you to Prince Vasily, and here is money. Write to me about everything, I will help you with everything." Pierre had been trying to choose a career for three months now, and he had still got nowhere. This was the choice which Prince Andrei had mentioned to him. Pierre rubbed his forehead.

"I understand military service, but explain this to me," he said. "Why are you – you understand everything – why are you going to this war, against whom, after all? Against Napoleon and France. If it were a war for liberty, I would understand, I would be the first to join the army, but to help England and Austria against the greatest man in the world . . . I do not understand how you can go."

"You must see, *mon cher*," Prince Andrei began, perhaps unwittingly wishing to conceal his own vagueness of thought from himself, suddenly beginning to speak in French and changing his former sincere tone for a formal and cold one, "one can take an entirely different point of view on this question."

And, as though everything he mentioned were his own personal business or that of his intimate acquaintances, he proceeded to expound to Pierre the view then current in the highest circles of St. Petersburg society of the political mission of Russia in Europe at that time.

Since the revolution Europe had been plagued by wars. The cause of the wars, apart from Napoleon's ambition, stemmed from an imbalance of power in Europe. One great power was needed to take the matter in hand with strict impartiality and, through alliances, to define new state boundaries and establish a new balance of power in Europe together with a new people's law, by virtue of which war would become impossible and all misunderstandings between states would be settled by mediation. Russia had taken this selfless role upon herself in the forthcoming war. Russia would seek only to return France to its boundaries of 1796, allowing the French themselves to choose their own form of government, and also to restore the independence of Italy, the Cisalpine kingdom, the new state of the two Belgiums and the new German Alliance, and even to restore Poland.

Pierre listened attentively, several times respectfully restraining his impulse to contradict his friend.

"Do you see that this time we are not being as foolish as we seem?" Prince Andrei concluded.

"Yes, yes, but why won't they propose this plan to Napoleon himself?" Pierre exclaimed. "He would be the first to accept it, if this plan were sincere: he would understand and love any great idea."

Prince Andrei paused and rubbed his forehead with his small hand.

"And apart from that, I am going..." He stopped. "I am going because the life that I lead here, this life – does not suit me!"

"Why not?" Pierre asked in amazement.

"Because, my dearest friend," said Prince Andrei, standing up with a smile, "for the vicomte and Hippolyte to wander from one drawing room to the next and mull over nonsense and tell fairytales about Mademoiselle Georges or about some 'girl' is all well and good, but that role will not do for me. I cannot stand it any longer," he added.

Pierre's glance expressed his agreement.

"But here's another thing. Why is Kutuzov important? And what does it mean to be an adjutant?" asked Pierre with that rare naïvety possessed by some young people who are not afraid of exposing their ignorance with a question.

"You're the only person who could possibly not know that," Prince Andrei replied, smiling and shaking his head. "Kutuzov is Suvorov's right hand, the best Russian general."

"But how can you be an adjutant? Doesn't that mean they can order you about?"

"Of course, an adjutant's influence is absolutely insignificant," Prince Andrei replied, "but I have to make a start. Besides, it is what my father wanted. I shall ask Kutuzov to give me a unit. And then we shall see..."

"It will be strange, it's bound to be, for you to fight against Napoleon," said Pierre, as though assuming that as soon as Prince Andrei reached the war he would have to engage, if not in single-handed combat, then at least in very close action against Napoleon himself.

Prince Andrei smiled pensively at his own thoughts, twisting the wedding ring on his third finger with a graceful, effeminate gesture.

# X

A woman's dress rustled in the next room. As if he had just woken up, Prince Andrei shook himself and his face assumed the expression it had worn in Anna Pavlovna's drawing room. Pierre lowered his feet from the divan. The princess came in. She was wearing a different dress, more homely but just as elegant and fresh. Prince Andrei stood up and courteously moved up an armchair for her by the fireplace, but there was such intense boredom on his face as he did so, the princess would surely have taken offence, had she been able to see it.

"Why, I often wonder," she began, as always in French, as she hastily seated herself in the armchair, "why did Annette never marry? How foolish you all are, gentlemen, for not marrying her. Forgive my saying so, but you understand nothing at all about women."

Pierre and Prince Andrei involuntarily exchanged glances and said nothing. But neither their glance nor their silence embarrassed the princess in the least. She carried on prattling in the same way as before.

"What a wrangler you are, Monsieur Pierre," she said to the young man. "What a wrangler you are, Monsieur Pierre," she repeated, fussily settling herself into the large armchair.

Folding her little hands over the mound of her waist, she stopped talking, evidently intent on listening. Her face assumed that distinctive, serious expression in which the eyes seem to be gazing inwards – an expression that only pregnant women have.

"I keep arguing with your husband as well; I cannot understand why he wants to go to war," said Pierre, addressing the princess without a trace of the inhibition so usual in relations between a young man and a young woman.

The princess started. Apparently Pierre's words had touched a sore spot.

"Ah, that is just what I say!" she said with her society smile. "I do not understand, I absolutely do not understand, why men cannot live without war. Why is it that we women do not want anything, do not need anything? Why you, you can be the judge. I keep telling him: here he is my uncle's adjutant, a most brilliant position. Everybody knows him so well and appreciates him so. The other day at the Apraksins' I heard one lady ask: 'Is that the famous Prince Andrei?' On my word of honour."

She laughed.

"He is asked everywhere. He could quite easily be an aide-de-camp . . . Do you know that only two days ago His Majesty spoke to him most graciously? Annette and I were saying how very easy it would be to arrange. What do you think?"

Pierre looked at Prince Andrei and, noticing that his friend did not like this conversation, made no reply.

"When are you leaving?" he asked.

"Oh, don't talk of our leaving, don't even mention it! I don't wish to hear of it," said the princess in the same skittish, capricious manner in which she had spoken with Hippolyte in the drawing room, and which was so obviously unsuited to a family circle of which Pierre was ostensibly a member.

"Today, when I thought about having to break off all these dear, precious connections . . . And then, you know, Andrei."

She blinked significantly at her husband.

"I'm afraid, I'm so afraid!" she whispered, quivering all the way down her back.

Her husband looked at her as though he were surprised to have noticed that there was someone else apart from Pierre and himself in the room; however, he enquired of the princess with cold civility:

"What are you afraid of, Lise? I can't understand it," he said.

"See what egoists all men are! All, all of them egoists! Out of nothing but his own whimsy, God only knows why, he is abandoning me, shutting me away alone in the country."

"With my father and sister, do not forget," Prince Andrei said quietly.

"All the same alone, without *my* friends . . . And he does not want me to be afraid." Her tone was peevish now, her short little lip was raised, lending her face an expression that was not joyful, but feral, squirrel-like. She stopped speaking, as if she found it improper to talk of her future delivery in front of Pierre, while this was in fact the very essence of the matter.

"Even so, I do not understand what you are afraid of," Prince Andrei enunciated slowly, keeping his eyes fixed on his wife.

The princess blushed and fluttered her hands in despair.

"No, Andrei, it's just as I said: you have changed so much, so very much."

"Your doctor says you should go to bed earlier," said Prince Andrei. "You ought to go to bed."

The princess said nothing, and suddenly her short lip with the faint moustache began trembling. Prince Andrei stood up and, with a shrug of his shoulders, began pacing around the room.

Pierre gazed through his spectacles in naïve surprise, first at one, then at the other and began fidgeting on the spot, as if he kept wanting to get up and then changing his mind.

"What does it matter to me that Monsieur Pierre is here," the little princess said suddenly, and her pretty face suddenly dissolved into a tearful, unlovely grimace. "I have wanted to ask you for a long time, Andrei: What has made you change so much towards me. What have I done to you? You are going to the army, you have no pity for me. Why?"

"Lise!" was all that Prince Andrei said, but the word expressed both supplication and threat and also, above all, the assurance that she would regret what she had said; but she continued hastily:

"You treat me like a sick woman or a child. I see everything. You were not like this six months ago, were you?"

"Lise, will you please stop this," said Prince Andrei even more emphatically.

Pierre, who had become more and more agitated in the course of this conversation, stood up and walked across to the princess. He seemed unable to bear the sight of her tears and was ready to start crying himself.

"Calm down, princess. It only seems like that to you, because, I assure you, I myself have experienced . . . the reason . . . because . . . No, I beg your pardon, this is no place for an outsider . . . Please, calm down . . . Goodbye . . . Please excuse me . . ."

He bowed, preparing to leave. Prince Andrei took his arm and stopped him.

"No, wait, Pierre. The princess is so kind, she would not wish to deprive me of the pleasure of spending the evening with you."

"Yes, he thinks only of himself," said the princess, making no effort to restrain her angry tears.

"Lise," Prince Andrei said coldly, raising his tone of voice to a level that indicated his patience had been exhausted.

Suddenly the angry, squirrel-like expression on the princess's beautiful little face was replaced by an expression of fearful appeal that aroused compassion; she cast her husband a sullen glance out of her lovely eyes, and her face assumed the timid expression of a dog rapidly but feebly wagging its lowered tail in a confession of guilt.

"*Mon Dieu, mon Dieu!*" said the princess and, gathering up the folds of her dress in one hand, she went up to her husband and kissed him on his brown forehead.

"*Bon soir*, Lise," said Prince Andrei, rising and kissing her hand courteously, as though it were a stranger's.

# XI

The friends were silent. Neither said a word. Pierre kept glancing at Prince Andrei; Prince Andrei rubbed his forehead with his small hand.

"Let's go and have supper," he said with a sigh, getting up and moving towards the door.

They entered a dining room newly decorated in an elegant and rich style. Everything, from the napkins to the silver, porcelain and crystal, bore the special imprint of that newness and elegance which distinguish the household of a young married couple. In the middle of supper Prince Andrei leaned his elbows on the table and, like a man who has held something in his heart for a long time and suddenly decides to speak out, he began talking with an air of nervous irritation that Pierre had never seen in his friend before.

"Never, never marry, my friend, that is my advice to you, do not marry until you can tell yourself that you have done everything that you could, and until you have stopped loving the woman that you have chosen, until you can see her clearly, or you will commit a grievous and fatal error. Marry as an old man no longer good for anything ... Or everything that is fine and exalted in you will be destroyed. It will all be frittered away on trifles. Yes, yes, yes! Do not look at me with such amazement. If you expect anything of yourself in the future, then you will feel at every step that for you everything is over, all doors are closed, except to the drawing room, where you will stand on the same level as the household flunkey and the idiot ... I tell you!"

He gestured emphatically with his hand.

Pierre removed his spectacles, which changed the expression of his face, making his kindness even more obvious, and looked at his friend in surprise.

"My wife," continued Prince Andrei, "is a lovely woman. She is one of those rare women with whom one need not be concerned for one's honour; but, my God, what would I not give now not to be married! You are the only person I have told about this, because I am so fond of you."

As he said this Prince Andrei resembled even less than before the gentleman who had sprawled in Anna Pavlovna's armchair, narrowing his eyes as he pronounced French phrases through clenched teeth. Every muscle in his lean, brownish face was quivering in nervous animation; his eyes, in which the fire of life had earlier seemed extinguished, now glowed brightly, glinting and glittering. It was clear that the more listless he seemed at ordinary times, the more intensely energetic he was at such moments of almost morbid agitation.

"You don't understand why I say that," he went on. "It's an entire life story. You talk about Bonaparte and his career," he said, although Pierre had not even mentioned Bonaparte. "You talk about Bonaparte, but Bonaparte graduated from a course at the artillery college and went out into the world when there was war and the road to glory was open to everyone."

Pierre looked at his friend, clearly prepared in advance to agree with whatever he might say.

"Bonaparte went out into the world and immediately found the place he was meant to occupy. And who were his friends? Who was Josephine Beauharnais? My five years of life since I left the Corps de Pages have been nothing but drawing rooms, balls, illicit affairs, idleness. Now I am setting out to war, to the greatest war that there has ever been, and I know nothing and am good for nothing. I am amiable and sharp-tongued, and I am listened to at Anna Pavlovna's, but I have forgotten what I used to know. I have only just begun to read, but it is all a jumble. And there can be no soldier without knowledge of military history, mathematics and fortifications. And this stupid society, without which my wife cannot live, and these women . . . I have known success in high society. The most exquisite of women have flung themselves at me. But if you could only know what all these exquisite women are like, and women in general! My father is right. He says that nature is not all-wise, because she was unable to devise a means for the propagation of human-kind without woman. Egotism, vanity, stupidity, pettiness in all things – that is all women for you when they show themselves as they are. Look at them in society and there seems to be something to them, but there is nothing, nothing, nothing! No, do not marry, my dear friend, do not marry," Prince Andrei concluded, and he shook his head as emphatically as if everything he had said were a truth that no one could possibly doubt.

"I think it is funny," said Pierre, "that *you* regard *yourself, yourself* as unqualified, and your life as a spoiled life. You have everything, every-thing ahead of you. And you . . ."

He did not say what it was Andrei did, but his tone alone revealed how highly he thought of his friend and how much he expected from him in the future.

In the very best, the most friendly and direct of relationships, flattery or compliments are necessary, as grease is needed to make wheels turn.

"I'm a failure," said Prince Andrei, but from the proud way in which he raised his handsome head so high and the bright gleam in his eyes, it was clear how little he believed in what he had said. "But why bother talking about me? Let's talk about you," he said, pausing for a moment and smiling at his own consoling thoughts. That smile was instantly reflected on Pierre's face.

"Why bother talking about me?" said Pierre, extending his mouth into a carefree, jolly smile. "What am I? I am an illegitimate son."

And suddenly, for the first time in the whole evening, he blushed a deep crimson. It had obviously cost him a great effort to say that. "With no name and no fortune. But what of it, it is really . . ."

But he did not say what it really was.

"I am free for the time being, and I like it. I simply do not know what I ought to start doing. I wanted to ask your serious advice."

Prince Andrei looked at him with kindly eyes. But even so his friendly and affectionate glance expressed an awareness of his own superiority.

"You are dear to me, especially because, in the whole of our high society, you are the only person who is alive. You're fortunate. Choose whatever you like, it doesn't matter. You will always fit in anywhere, but just one thing: stop going to see these Kuragins, leading that kind of life. It doesn't suit you at all: all this bingeing and playing the hussar, and all the rest of it."

"Do you know what," said Pierre, as if a happy thought had just occurred to him, "seriously, I've been thinking that for a long time. Living like that I cannot make decisions, or think anything through. My head hurts, I have no money. He invited me today, I shan't go."

"Give me your word, your word of honour, that you won't go!"

"Word of honour."

"Make sure, now."

"Of course."

# XII

---

It was after one in the morning when Pierre left his friend's house. It was a bright St. Petersburg June night. Pierre got into a cabby's carriage with the intention of going home. But the closer he came, the more strongly he felt the impossibility of getting to sleep on this night that was more like an evening or a morning. He could see for a long way in the empty streets. He pictured Prince Andrei's animated, handsome face and heard his words – not about his relations with his wife (that did not interest Pierre) – but his words about the war and the future life that might await his friend. Pierre loved and admired his friend so unconditionally that he could not accept that, the moment Prince Andrei desired it, everyone would not acknowledge him as a remarkable and great man, whose nature was to command, not to obey. Pierre simply could not imagine that anyone at all, even Kutuzov, for instance, would have the courage to issue commands to a man so evidently born to take the leading role in everything as he conceived Prince Andrei to be. He imagined his friend before the assembled troops, on a white steed, with a terse, forceful speech on his lips; he imagined his courage, his successes, his heroism and everything that most young men imagine for themselves. Pierre recalled that he had promised to repay a small gambling debt today to Anatoly, at whose house the usual company of gamblers had been due to gather that evening.

"Go to Kuragin's," he said to the driver, thinking only of where he could spend the remainder of the night, and completely forgetting the promise he had given Prince Andrei not to visit Kuragin.

On arriving at the porch of the large house in which Anatole Kuragin lived beside the Cavalry Guards barracks, he recalled his promise, but immediately, as happens with those people who are described as lacking in character, he wanted desperately to go in and take another glance at that dissolute life with which he was so familiar and so bored, and the thought came to him of itself that the promise he had given did not mean anything and, moreover, he had also promised Anatoly, before Prince Andrei, that he would bring the money he owed: finally, he thought that all these words of honour were mere conventions, without any definite meaning, especially if you realised that tomorrow perhaps he would die or something so unusual would happen to him that nothing would be honourable or dishonourable any longer.

He walked up to the well-lit porch, on up the stairs and went in through an open door. There was nobody in the sumptuous entrance hall, but there were empty bottles lying about, a heap of bent playing-cards in the corner, cloaks and galoshes; there was a smell of wine; he could hear talking and shouting in the distance.

Evidently the gambling and supper were already over, but the guests had not yet departed. Pierre took off his cloak and went into the first room, in the centre of which there stood a life-size statue of a racehorse. Here he could hear the racket from the next room more clearly, the familiar sound of six or eight men laughing and shouting. He went into the next room, where the remains of supper were still on the table. About eight young men, all without frock coats and mostly in military riding breeches, were crowding around an open window and all shouting incomprehensibly in Russian and French.

"I bet a hundred with Chaplin!" shouted one.

"Make sure you don't support him!" shouted another.

"I'm for Dolokhov!" shouted a third. "Part our hands, Kuragin!"

"All in one breath, or you've lost!" shouted a fourth.

"Yakov, let's have the bottle, Yakov!" shouted the master of the house, a tall, statuesquely handsome fellow standing in the middle of the crowd. "Stop, gentlemen. Here he is, Pierre!"

"Ah! Pyotr! Petrusha! Peter the Great!"

"Peter the Stout!" everybody began shouting from every side, crowding round him.

Every one of the red or blotchy young faces expressed delight at the sight of Pierre, who removed his spectacles and wiped them as he looked at all this crowd.

"I don't understand a thing. What's going on?" he asked with a good-humoured smile.

"Stop, he's not drunk. Give me a bottle," said Anatole, and taking a glass from the table, he went up to Pierre.

"First of all, drink."

Pierre began drinking glass after glass without speaking, peering out from under his brows at the drunken guests, who had crowded round the window again, discussing something that he did not understand. He drank one glass at a gulp; Anatole poured him another with a meaningful expression. Pierre drank it resignedly, but more slowly than the first. Anatole poured a third. Pierre drank that one too, although he paused twice in order to catch his breath. Anatole stood beside him, gazing by turns with his beautiful, big eyes at the glass, the bottle and Pierre. Anatole was a handsome fellow: tall and full-bodied, white-skinned and ruddy-cheeked; he had such a high chest that his head was inclined backwards, which gave him a haughty air. He had a lovely fresh mouth, thick light-brown hair, slanting black eyes and a general appearance of strength, health and the good nature of vivacious youth. But his beautiful eyes with the wonderful, regular black brows seemed to have been made less for looking than for being looked at. They seemed incapable of changing their expression. It was only clear that he was drunk from his red face, and even more so from his unnaturally out-thrust chest and the wide stare of his eyes. Even though he was drunk and the upper half of his mighty body was clad in nothing but a shirt open at the chest, from the faint aroma of perfume and soap which surrounded him, mingling with the smell of the wine he had drunk, from his hairstyle, painstakingly pomaded in place that morning, from the elegant cleanness of his plump hands and superbly fine linen, from that distinctive whiteness and delicate smoothness of his skin, the aristocrat was apparent even

47

in his present condition, by virtue of the habit, acquired in childhood, of painstaking and lavish care for his own person.

"Come on, drink it all! Eh!" he said seriously, handing Pierre the last glass.

"No, I don't want to," said Pierre, faltering halfway through the glass. "Well, what's going on?" he added with the expression of a man who has fulfilled his initial obligation and believes that he now has the right to join in the common pursuit.

"Drink it all, eh?" Anatole repeated, opening his eyes wider, lifting the unfinished glass in his white hand, his arm bared to the elbow. He had the look of a man doing something important, because at that moment he was focusing all his energy on holding the glass straight and saying exactly what he wanted to say.

"I told you, I don't want to," replied Pierre, putting on his spectacles and walking away.

"What are you shouting about?" he asked the crowd that had gathered round the window. Anatole stood and thought for a moment, handed the glass to a servant and, smiling with his lovely mouth, also went over to the window.

On Fridays Anatole Kuragin received everyone at his home, they played cards and ate supper there, then spent most of the night out. On that day the session of faro had developed into a protracted game for high stakes. Anatole had lost a little, and since he had no passion for gambling, but played out of habit, he had soon dropped out. One rich man, a life-hussar, had lost a lot, and one Semyonovsky Regiment officer, Dolokhov, had won from everyone. After the game they had sat down to supper very late. An extremely serious Englishman, who described himself as a traveller, had said that he had been given to believe that Russians drank far more heavily than he discovered they actually did. He had said that in Russia they drank nothing but champagne, but if they would drink rum, then he proposed a wager that he would drink more than anyone else present. Dolokhov, the officer who had won more than everyone else that evening, had said it wasn't worth making a wager simply on a bottle of rum, and he had offered to drink the whole bottle without taking it from his lips, and also while sitting on the second-floor window-ledge with his legs dangling outside. The Englishman had proposed the wager. Anatole had accepted the wager for Dolokhov, that is, that Dolokhov would drink the full bottle of rum sitting on the ledge. Pierre came in just when the servants were starting to remove the frame that prevented anyone from sitting on the outside window-ledge. The second-storey window was high enough for someone falling from it to be killed. Drunken and amicable faces on all sides kept telling Pierre what was going on, as if it were particularly important for Pierre to know the state of affairs. Dolokhov was an officer in a Guards infantry regiment, of medium height, sinewy and solidly built, with a broad, full chest, extremely curly hair and light-blue eyes. He was about twenty-five. Like all infantry officers, he wore no moustache, and his mouth, the most striking feature of his face, was fully visible. It was an extremely agreeable mouth, despite the fact that it almost never smiled. The lines of this mouth were curved with remarkable subtlety. At its centre the upper lip pressed down vigorously on the firm lower one; sharp folds in the corners constantly formed something like two smiles, one on each side, and all of this, together with a direct, somewhat insolent, but ardent and intelligent gaze, produced such an extraordinary impression it made people wonder about the owner of such a beautiful and strange face. Women liked Dolokhov, and he was fully convinced there was no such thing as a woman whose character was entirely above reproach.

Dolokhov was a young man of good family, but not rich, although he lived extravagantly and gambled constantly. He almost always won; but no one, not even in his absence, dared to attribute his constant success to anything other than good luck, a clear mind and indomitable will-power. In their hearts, everyone who gambled with him assumed he was a card-sharp, although they did not dare to say so. Now, when he had proposed his strange wager, the drunken company took an especi-ally keen interest in what he intended to do, precisely because those who knew him knew that he would do what he had said. Pierre also knew it and that was the only reason why he greeted Dolokhov without attempting to raise any objection to his intentions.

The rest of the company consisted of three officers, the Englishman, who had been seen in St. Petersburg in the most diverse circles, and a certain Moscow gambler, a fat married man who was much older than everyone else, and yet was on familiar terms with all these young people.

The bottle of rum had been brought; the frame that prevented anyone sitting on the sloping ledge of the window was being broken out by two servants in gaiters and kaftans, who were clearly working in haste, feeling intimidated by the shouted advice from the gentlemen surrounding them.

With his chest thrust out, his expression unchanging, neither walking round the others nor asking them to make way, Anatole forced his strong body through the crowd at the window, went up to the frame, wrapped both his white hands in a frock coat that was lying on a divan, and struck at the panes of glass, breaking them out.

"Now now, your excellency," said a servant, "you're only getting in the way and you'll cut your hands."

"Get out of it, you fool, eh?" said Anatole. He took hold of the crossbeam of the frame and began pulling. Several other hands also joined in; they pulled, and the frame sprang out of the window with a crack, so that those pulling it almost fell over.

"Out with it all, or they'll think I'm holding on," said Dolokhov.

"Listen," Anatole said to Pierre. "You understand? The Englishman's boasting . . . eh? . . . National pride? . . . Eh? . . . All right? . . ."

"All right," said Pierre, gazing with a sinking heart at Dolokhov as, grasping the bottle of rum in his hands, he approached the window, through which could be seen the light of the sky, where dawn and dusk were merging. Rolling up the sleeves of his shirt purposefully after sticking the bottle of rum in his pocket, Dolokhov leapt smartly up to the window.

"Listen!" he shouted, standing on the sill and addressing the room.

Everybody stopped talking.

"I wager" (he spoke in French so that the Englishman would understand him, but he did not speak that language too well) "I wager fifty imperials . . . Want to make it a hundred?" he added, addressing the Englishman.

"No, fifty," said the Englishman.

"All right, fifty imperials, that I will drink this whole bottle of rum without lifting it from my lips, and that I'll drink it sitting outside the window, on this spot here" (he leaned out and pointed to the jutting slope of the wall outside the window) "and without holding on . . . Right?"

"Very good," said the Englishman.

Anatole turned towards the Englishman and, grabbing him by the button of his tailcoat and looking down on him from above (the Englishman was short), he began explaining in English what was already clear to everyone.

"Stop!" cried Dolokhov, banging the bottle against the side of the window to draw attention to himself. "Stop, Kuragin, listen. If anyone else does the same, then I pay a hundred imperials. Understand?"

The Englishman nodded, without making it at all clear whether he intended to accept this new wager. Anatole kept hold of the Englishman and even though the latter tried to convey by nodding that he had understood everything, Anatole translated Dolokhov's words into English for him. A young, skinny boy, a life-hussar who had lost that evening, climbed up into the window, stuck his head out and looked down.

"Oooh . . ." he exclaimed, looking out and down through the window to the stone of the pavement.

"Attention!" yelled Dolokhov and jerked the officer out of the window. He jumped awkwardly back down into the room, tripping over his tangled spurs.

Setting the bottle on the window-ledge so it would be easy to pick up, Dolokhov climbed cautiously and carefully out of the window. Lowering his legs and wedging himself against the sides of the window with both hands, he shifted his position, settled himself, lowered his hands, moved a little to the right, then to the left and took hold of the bottle. Anatole brought two candles and set them on the windowsill, although it was already quite light. Dolokhov's back in the white shirt and his curly head were lit up from both sides. Everybody was crowding round the window. The Englishman was standing at the front. Pierre was smiling without speaking. The old Muscovite, his face frightened and angry, suddenly pushed forward, trying to grab Dolokhov by the shirt.

"Gentlemen, this is stupidity, he'll fall and be killed," he said. Anatole stopped him.

"Don't touch him, you'll startle him, he'll be killed. Eh? . . . What then? . . . Eh?"

Dolokhov looked round, adjusting his position and once again wedging himself with his hands. His face was neither pale nor red, but cold and angry.

"If anyone tries to meddle again," he said, uttering each word separately through thin, compressed lips, "I'll chuck him down there right now. It's slippery enough to slide right off, but he interferes with his stupid nonsense . . . Right!"

After saying "Right!" he turned back again, lowered his hands, picked up the bottle and raised it to his mouth, tilting his head back and throwing his free hand upwards for balance. One of the servants, who had begun clearing up the broken glass, stopped in a bent-over position with his eyes fixed on the window and Dolokhov's back. Anatole stood up straight, his eyes wide open. The Englishman pursed his lips and watched from the side. The old Muscovite fled into the corner of the room and lay down on a divan with his face to the wall. Some stood still with their mouths open, some with their hands raised. Pierre covered his face, where a faint, forgotten smile still lingered, although it now expressed horror and fear. Nobody said a word. Pierre took his hands away from his eyes; Dolokhov was sitting in the same position, but his head was tilted right back so that the curly hair at the back touched the collar of his shirt and the hand holding the bottle was rising higher and higher, shuddering with the effort. The bottle was clearly emptying and at the same time rising higher, as his head tilted back. "What is taking so long?" thought Pierre. It seemed to him that more than half an hour

DOLOKHOV'S WAGER WITH THE ENGLISHMAN
*Drawing by M. S. Bashilov, 1866*

had gone by. Suddenly Dolokhov leaned backwards bodily and his hand began shaking nervously: this shuddering was enough to shift his whole body sitting on the steep slope. He changed position and his hands and head began to shake even more strongly from the effort. One hand was raised to grab hold of the windowsill, but then lowered again. Pierre closed his eyes and told himself that he would not open them again. Suddenly he sensed everything around him beginning to stir. He peeped: Dolokhov was standing on the windowsill, his face pale and elated.

"Empty!"

He tossed the bottle to the Englishman, who deftly caught it. Then Dolokhov jumped down from the window. He smelled strongly of rum.

"Eh? How's that? Eh?" Anatole asked everybody. "What a splendid trick!"

"To hell with the lot of you!" said the old Muscovite. The Englishman had taken out his purse and was counting out the money. Dolokhov was scowling in silence. Pierre, in a bewildered state, walked around the room, smiling and breathing heavily.

"Gentlemen, who wishes to wager with me? I'll do the same," he suddenly blurted out. "And I don't even need a wager, so there. Tell them to give me a bottle. I'll do it . . . tell them."

"What are you saying? Have you lost your mind? Who's going to let you? You get dizzy on the stairs," voices said on every side.

"It was mean of us to leave Dolokhov to sacrifice his life alone. I'll drink it, let me have a bottle of rum!" shouted Pierre, hammering on the table with a determined, drunken gesture, and he started clambering up to the window. They grabbed him by the arms and led him off to the next room. But Dolokhov was unable to walk; they carried him over to a divan and doused his head with cold water.

Someone wanted to go home, someone suggested not going home but on to somewhere else, all of them together: Pierre insisted on this more than anyone. They put on their cloaks and set off. The Englishman went home and Dolokhov fell into a half-dead, insensible sleep on Anatole's divan.

# XIII

Prince Vasily kept the promise that he had made to the elderly woman at Anna Pavlovna's *soirée* who had petitioned him about her only son Boris. His Majesty was informed of him and, unlike other young men, he was transferred to the Semyonovsky Guards regiment as an ensign. But Boris was not appointed an adjutant or attached to Kutuzov, for all Anna Mikhailovna's soliciting and scheming. Shortly after Anna Pavlovna's *soirée*, Anna Mikhailovna went back to Moscow, straight to her rich relatives the Rostovs, with whom she stayed in Moscow and in whose house her adored little Borenka had been educated since he was a child and had lived for years. Now, though he had only just been taken into the army, he had immediately been made a Guards ensign. The Guards had already left St. Petersburg on the 10th of August and her son, who had remained in Moscow to be fitted for his uniform, was due to catch them up on the road to Radzivilov.

It was the name-day of two members of the Rostov family – the mother and her youngest daughter, both called Natalya. All morning, teams of horses had been constantly driving up and away, bringing well-wishers to Countess Rostova's large house on Povarskaya Street, which was known to the whole of Moscow. The countess and her elder daughter sat in the drawing room with the guests, who endlessly came and went. The countess was a woman with a thin, oriental-looking face, about forty-five years old, clearly exhausted by her children, of whom she had had twelve. A slowness in her movements and speech, due to her frailty, lent her a grave air that inspired respect. As part of the household, Princess Anna Mikhailovna Drubetskaya sat beside her, helping with the business of receiving the guests and engaging them in conversation. The young people were in the back rooms, feeling no need to participate in the receiving of visits. The count was greeting and seeing off the guests and inviting them to dinner.

"I am very, very grateful, *ma chère* or *mon cher*" (he said *ma chère* or *mon cher* to everyone without exception, making not the slightest distinction between people of higher or lower standing than himself), "for myself and for my dear name-day girls. Be sure to come for dinner, now. I cordially invite you on behalf of the whole family, *ma chère*."

He spoke these words to everyone without exception or variation, with an identical expression on his plump, jolly, clean-shaven face, and with an identically firm handshake and repeated short bows. After seeing off one guest, the count went back to another who was still in the drawing room: drawing up an armchair and with the air of a man who likes and knows how to enjoy life, rakishly planting his feet wide apart and setting his hands on his knees, he swayed impressively, ventured conjectures concerning the weather and consulted people about his health, sometimes in Russian, sometimes in very bad but self-assured French, then once again, with the air of a man who is tired but resolute in the fulfilment of his duty, went to see the guest off, arranging the sparse grey hairs on his bald patch, and once again invited the guest to dinner. Sometimes on his way back from the hallway he went via the conservatory and the footmen's room to look into the large marble hall, where they were laying the table for eighty places and, looking at the footmen carrying the silver and porcelain, extending the tables and spreading out the damask tablecloths, he called over Dmitri Vasilievich, the nobleman's son who managed all his affairs and said:

"Right, Mitenka, now you make sure everything is all right. Good, good," he said, surveying with satisfaction the huge extended table. "And don't forget the order of the wines; the whole thing is in the serving. See to it . . ." And he walked away, sighing complacently, back to the drawing room.

"Marya Lvovna Karagina and her daughter!" the countess's huge footman announced in a deep bass as he stepped through the doors of the drawing room.

The countess thought for a moment and took a sniff from a gold snuffbox decorated with a portrait of her husband.

"These visits have quite worn me out," she said. "Well then, she shall be the last I receive. She is very prim and proper. Show her in," she said to her servant in a sad voice, as if she were saying: "Very well then, finish me off."

A tall, plump lady with a proud face and her pretty little daughter entered the drawing room in a rustling of dresses.

"Dear countess, how long it has been . . . she has had to stay in bed, the poor child . . . at the ball at the Razumovskys . . . and Countess Apraksina . . . I was so glad."

The sound of lively women's voices interrupting each other mingled with the sound of dresses rustling and chairs being drawn up. There began one of those conversations which are initiated precisely in order that, at the first pause, one may rise, rustle one's dress, and say: "I am so delighted! Mama and Countess Apraksina wish you good health . . ." – and, rustling one's dress yet again, proceed to the hallway, put on one's fur coat or cloak and depart.

The conversation turned to the most important news in town at the time, the illness of a famous, rich and handsome man of Empress Catherine's day, the old Count Bezukhov, and his illegitimate son Pierre, who had behaved so improperly at Anna Pavlovna Scherer's *soirée*.

"I feel awfully sorry for the poor count," said the guest, "his health was bad enough already, and now comes this distress from his son. It will be the death of him!"

"What's that?" asked the countess, as though she did not know what her guest was talking about, despite having already heard the reason for Count Bezukhov's distress at least fifteen times.

"That's modern-day education for you! While he was abroad," the guest continued, "this young man was left to his own devices and now they're saying in St. Petersburg that he has done such terrible things, he has been banished here with a police escort."

"Well, I never!" said the countess.

"He chose his friends badly," Princess Anna Mikhailovna interjected. "They say that he and Prince Vasily's son, and a certain Dolokhov, got up to God only knows what. And they have both suffered for it. Dolokhov has been reduced to the ranks and Bezukhov's son has been banished to Moscow. As for Anatole Kuragin – his father hushed things up somehow. He managed to stay in the Horse Guards regiment."

"But what can they have done?" asked the countess.

"They are absolute bandits, especially Dolokhov," said the guest. "He is the son of Marya Ivanovna Dolokhova, such a respectable lady, but what of it? Can you imagine, the three of them got hold of a bear from somewhere and took it off with them in a carriage to see some actresses? The police came running to calm them down, and they caught the local policeman, tied him back to back with the bear and threw the bear into the Moika river; the bear was swimming along with the policeman on top of it."

"A fine figure of a policeman, *ma chère*," the count exclaimed, splitting his sides laughing, with an air of approval which suggested that, in spite of his age, he would not have minded taking part in such fun and games.

"Oh, how terrible! What is there to laugh at, count?"

But the ladies laughed too, despite themselves.

"They barely managed to rescue the unfortunate man," the guest continued. "And that is the clever way in which the son of Count Kirill Vladimirovich Bezukhov amuses himself!" she added. "And they said he was so well brought-up and intelligent. This is what all that foreign upbringing has led to. I hope no one here will receive him, despite his wealth. They wanted to introduce him to me. I positively refused: I have daughters."

"But this is a quite excellent prank, *ma chère*. Good for them!" said the count, making no attempt to restrain his laughter.

The guest looked at him in prim annoyance.

"Ah, *ma chère* Marya Lvovna," he said in his badly pronounced poor French, "youth must sow its wild oats. Really and truly!" he added. "Your husband and I were no saints either. We had our little peccadilloes too."

He winked at her; the guest did not reply.

"Why do you say that this young man is so rich?" asked the countess, leaning away from the girls, who immediately pretended not to be listening. "Surely he only has illegitimate children. And I think . . . Pierre is also illegitimate."

The guest gestured vaguely.

"He has twenty illegitimate children, I believe."

Princess Anna Mikhailovna intervened in the conversation, clearly wishing to demonstrate her connections and her knowledge of all the affairs of high society.

"That is the point," she said significantly, and also in a half-whisper. "Count Kirill Vladimirovich's reputation is well known . . . He has lost count of his children, but this Pierre was his favourite."

"What a fine man he was," said the countess, "only last year! I never laid eyes on a more handsome man."

"He is greatly changed now," said Princess Anna Mikhailovna. "What I wanted to say," she continued, "is that on his wife's side, the direct heir to the entire estate is Prince Vasily, but Pierre was greatly loved by his father, who provided for his education and wrote to His Majesty . . . So no one knows, if he dies (and he is in such a bad way that it is expected any minute, and Lorrain has come from St. Petersburg), who will get this immense fortune, Pierre or Prince Vasily. Forty thousand souls and millions upon millions. I know this so well, because Prince Vasily told me himself. And Kirill Vladimirovich is a third cousin of mine on my mother's side, and he was Borya's godfather," she added, as though she attached no importance whatever to that circumstance.

"Prince Vasily arrived in Moscow yesterday. He is going for some audit, I am told," said the guest.

"Yes, but between you and me," said the princess, "that is a mere pretext: he has actually come to see Count Kirill Vladimirovich after hearing that he is in such a bad way."

"Nonetheless, *ma chère*, it was an excellent prank," said the count and then, noticing that the senior guest was not listening to him, he turned to the young ladies. "That policeman cut a fine figure, I imagine."

And demonstrating the policeman waving his arms, he began laughing again with that resonant bass laughter that shook his entire plump body, the way people laugh who always eat and, especially, drink well.

# XIV

Silence fell. The countess looked at her guest with a polite smile, but without disguising the fact that she would now be not in the least offended if her guest were to get up and leave. The guest's daughter was already adjusting her dress and glancing enquiringly at her mother, when suddenly from the next room there was the sound of several male and female feet running towards the door, the clatter of a stool dragged and overturned, and a thirteen-year-old girl with the skirt of her short muslin frock oddly tucked up came bursting into the room and stopped in the middle. She seemed to have misjudged her speed and galloped so far in by accident. That very same moment four figures appeared in the doorway: two young men – one a student with a crimson collar, the other a Guards officer – a fifteen-year-old girl and a fat, ruddy-cheeked boy in a child's smock.

The count leapt up and, swaying on his feet, spread his arms wide around the girl who had run in.

"Ah, there she is!" he cried, laughing. "The name-day girl! *Ma chère* name-day girl!"

"My dear, there is a time for everything," the countess said to her daughter, obviously merely in order to say something, because it was clear at a glance that her daughter was not the least bit afraid of her. "You're always spoiling her," she added, speaking to her husband.

"Hello, my dear, happy name-day to you," said the guest. "What a charming child!" she added, addressing her flattery to the mother.

The black-eyed, large-mouthed and plain but lively little girl, with her childish, exposed little shoulders heaving and contracting in their bodice after the fast run, with her tangle of black curls swept backwards, thin little bare arms and fast little legs in little lacy pantaloons and little open shoes, was at that sweet age when the little girl is no longer a child, but the child is not yet a young woman. Twisting away from her father, quick and graceful and evidently unused to the drawing room, she ran across to her mother and, paying no attention to her rebuke, hid her flushed little face in the lacework of her mother's mantilla and burst into laughter.

"Mama! We wanted to marry Boris . . . Ha, ha! . . . To the doll . . . Ha, ha! Yes . . . Ah . . . Mimi . . ." she said through her laughter. "And . . . Ah . . . He ran away."

She pulled a large doll out from under her skirt and showed it to them: a black, broken-off nose, a cracked cardboard head and kidskin bottom, legs and arms that dangled loosely at the elbows and knees, but still with a fresh, elegant, carmine smile and thick-black, arching brows.

The countess had been acquainted for four years with this Mimi, Natasha's inseparable friend, a gift from her godfather.

"You see?" And Natasha could not say any more (everything seemed funny to her). She fell down onto her mother and broke into such loud, resounding laughter that everybody, even the prim and proper guest, began laughing in spite of themselves. This laughter could even be heard in the footman's room. The countess's menservants exchanged smiling glances with the visiting liveried footman, who had been sitting glumly on his chair all the while.

"Now, off with you, you and your monster!" said the little girl's mother, pushing her daughter away in feigned anger. "This is my youngest, a spoilt little girl, as you can see," she said to the guest.

Tearing her little face away for a moment from her mother's lacy shawl and glancing up at her, Natasha said quietly through her tears of laughter:

"I feel so embarrassed, mama!" And quick as could be, as if she were afraid of being caught, she hid her face again.

The guest, obliged to admire the family scene, felt it necessary to take some kind of part in it.

"Tell me, my dear," she said, addressing Natasha, "who is this Mimi to you? Your daughter, I suppose?"

Natasha did not like this guest and the tone in which she condescended to make conversation with a child.

"No, *madame*, she's not my daughter, she's a doll," she said, smiling boldly, got up off her mother and sat down beside her eldest sister, demonstrating in this way that she could behave like a big girl.

Meanwhile the entire young generation (Boris the officer, Anna

Mikhailovna's son; Nikolai the student, the count's eldest son; Sonya, the count's fifteen-year-old niece; and little Petrushka, the youngest son) had all distributed themselves round the drawing room as if they had suddenly been dropped into cold water and were clearly struggling to restrain within the limits of decorum the excitement and merriment that were still glowing in every feature of their faces. It was plain to see that out there, in the back rooms from which they had come running in so impetuously, their conversations had been more fun than the talk here of town scandals, the weather and Countess Apraksina.

The two young men, student and officer, were childhood friends, both the same age and both handsome, although they were quite unalike. Boris, a tall, fair-haired youth, had a long face with fine, regular features. A calm and thoughtful mind was expressed in his pleasant grey eyes, but in the corners of his still hairless lips there lurked a constantly mocking and slightly cunning smile, which instead of spoiling his expression, seemed in fact to add spice to his fresh, handsome face that was so obviously still untouched by either vice or grief. Nikolai was not very tall, with a broad chest and a very subtle, fine figure. His open face, with soft, wavy, light-brown hair surrounding a prominent, broad forehead, and the ecstatic gaze of his half-closed, prominent brown eyes, always expressed the impression of the moment. Little black hairs had already appeared on his upper lip, and impetuosity and enthusiasm were expressed in his every feature. Both young men bowed and took seats in the drawing room. Boris did this fluently and easily; Nikolai, on the contrary, with almost childish resentment. Nikolai glanced by turns at the guests and the door, evidently with no desire to conceal the fact that he was bored, and hardly even answered the questions put to him by the guests. Boris, on the contrary, immediately found the right tone and informed them with mock gravity that he had known this Mimi doll as a young girl when her nose was still perfect, that she had aged a lot in the five years he had known her, what with her head splitting open right across the skull. Then he enquired after the lady's health. Everything he said was simple and decorous, neither too witty nor too foolish, but the smile playing about his lips indicated that even as he spoke he did not ascribe the slightest importance to his own words and was speaking purely out of a sense of decorum.

"Mama, what is he speaking like a grown-up for? I don't want him to," said Natasha, going up to her mother and pointing at Boris like a capricious child. Boris smiled at her.

"You just want to play dolls with him all the time," replied Princess Anna Mikhailovna, patting Natasha's bare shoulder, which shrank away nervously and withdrew into its bodice at the touch of her hand.

"I'm bored," whispered Natasha. "Mama, nanny is asking if she can go visiting, can she? Can she?" she repeated, raising her voice, with that characteristic capacity of women for quick-wittedness in innocent deception. "She can, mama!" she shouted, barely able to restrain her laughter and, glancing at Boris, she curtseyed to the guests and walked as far as the door, but once outside it started running as fast as her little legs could carry her. Boris became pensive.

"I thought you wanted to go too, *maman*. Do you need the carriage?" he said, blushing as he addressed his mother.

"Yes, off you go now and tell them to get it ready," she said, smiling. Boris went out quietly through the door and set off after Natasha; the fat boy in the smock ran behind him angrily, as if he were annoyed by some interruption to his studies.

# XV

Of the young people, aside from the countess's elder daughter, who was four years older than her sister and already behaved like a grown-up, and the young lady visitor, the only ones left in the drawing room were Nikolai and Sonya the niece, who sat there, with that rather artificial, festive smile that many adults believe they should wear when present at other people's conversations, repeatedly casting tender glances at her cousin. Sonya was a slim, petite brunette with a gentle gaze shaded by long eyelashes, a thick black plait wound twice around her head and sallow skin on her face and especially on her bare, lean but graceful and sinewy arms and neck. With the smoothness of her movements, the gentle flexibility of her little limbs and her rather cunning and reticent manner she involuntarily reminded people of a beautiful but still imma-ture kitten that would become a delightful cat. She evidently thought it proper to indicate her interest in the general conversation with her festive smile but, against her will, her eyes gazed out from under their long lashes at her cousin, who was leaving for the army, with such passionate girlish adoration, that her smile could not possibly have deceived anyone for even a moment, and it was clear that the little cat had only sat down in order to spring up even more energetically and start playing with her cousin just as soon as they got out of this drawing room.

"Yes, *ma chère*," said the old count, addressing the guest and pointing to his Nikolai. "His friend Boris there has been appointed an officer, and out of friendship he does not want to be left behind, so he's abandoning university and this old man and he's going to join the army. And there

SONYA
*Drawing by M. S. Bashilov, 1866*

was a place all ready for him in the archive and everything. How's that for friendship!" the count queried.

"But after all, they do say that war has been declared," said the guest.

"They've been saying that for a long time," the count said, still speaking vaguely. "They'll say it again a few times, and then again, and leave it at that. How's that for friendship, then!" he repeated. "He's joining the hussars."

Not knowing what to say, the guest shook her head.

"It's not out of friendship at all," responded Nikolai, flaring up and speaking as if he were defending himself against a shameful slander. "It's not at all out of friendship, it's just that I feel a calling for military service."

He glanced round at the young lady guest: the young lady was looking at him with a smile, approving the young man's action.

"We have Schubert, the colonel of the Pavlograd Hussars Regiment, dining with us today. He's been on leave here and is going to take him back with him. What can one do?" said the count, shrugging and speaking jocularly about a matter that evidently pained him a great deal.

For some reason Nikolai suddenly became angry.

"But I told you, papa, that if you don't wish to let me go, I shall stay. I know I'm no good for anything but military service. I'm not a diplomat, I don't know how to conceal what I feel," he said, gesticulating too enthusiastically for his words and glancing all the time with the coquettishness of handsome youth at Sonya and the young lady guest.

The little cat, devouring him with her eyes, seemed ready at any second to launch into her game and demonstrate her full feline nature. The young lady continued to approve him with her smile.

"Perhaps something might just come of me," he added, "but I am no good for anything here . . ."

"Well, well, all right!" said the old count. "He's always getting worked up. Bonaparte has turned everyone's heads: everyone thinks about how he rose from a corporal to an emperor. Well, then, if it pleases God . . ." he added, not noticing the guest's mocking smile.

"Well, off you go, off you go, Nikolai, I can see you're keen to be off," said the countess.

"Not at all," her son replied, but nonetheless a moment later he got up, bowed and left the room.

Sonya carried on sitting a little longer, smiling more and more falsely all the while, then got up, still with the same smile, and went out.

"How very transparent all these young people's secrets are!" said Countess Anna Mikhailovna, pointing to Sonya and laughing. The guest laughed.

"Yes," said the countess, after the ray of sunshine that this young generation had brought into the drawing room had disappeared, and as if she were answering a question that no one had asked her, but which was constantly on her mind. "So much suffering, so much worry," she continued, "all borne so that we can rejoice in them now. But even now, truly, there is more fear than joy. You're always afraid, always afraid! It's the very age that holds so much danger for girls and for boys."

"Everything depends on upbringing," said the guest.

"Yes, you are right," the countess continued. "So far, thank God, I have been my children's friend and I have their complete trust," she said, repeating the error of many parents who believe their children keep no secrets from them. "I know I shall always be my daughters' first confidante and if Nikolenka, with his fiery character, should get up to mischief (boys will be boys), then it would be nothing like those Petersburg gentlemen."

"Yes, they are splendid, splendid children," agreed the count, who always resolved matters that he found complicated by finding everything splendid. "Just imagine! Decided to join the hussars! What about that, *ma chère*!"

"What a sweet creature your youngest is," said the guest, glancing round reproachfully at her own daughter, as though impressing on her with this glance that that was how she ought to be in order to be liked, not the stiff doll that she was. "Full of fun!"

"Yes, full of fun," said the count. "She takes after me! And what a voice, real talent! She may be my own daughter, but it's no more than the truth when I say she'll be a singer, another Salomini. We've engaged an Italian to teach her."

"Is it not rather early? They do say it's bad for the voice to train it at this age."

"Oh no, not at all too early!" said the count.

"And what about our mothers getting married at twelve and thirteen?" added Countess Anna Mikhailovna.

"She's already in love with Boris, how do you like that?" said the countess, smiling gently, glancing at Boris's mother and, clearly replying to the thought that was always on her mind, she went on: "Well now, you see, if I were strict with her, if I forbade her . . . God knows what they would do in secret" (the countess meant that they would have kissed), "but as it is I know every word she says. She'll come running to me this evening and tell me everything herself. Perhaps I do spoil her, but I really think that is best. I was strict with my elder daughter."

"Yes, I was raised quite differently," said the elder daughter, the beautiful Countess Vera, with a smile. But a smile did not adorn Vera's face in the way it usually does: on the contrary, her face became unnatural and therefore unpleasant. The elder daughter Vera was good-looking, she was clever, she was well brought up. She had a pleasant voice. What she had said was just and apt but, strange to say, everyone, even the guest and the countess, glanced round at her as though they wondered why she had said it and felt uneasy.

"People always try to be clever with their oldest children, they want to make something exceptional of them," said the guest.

"No point in pretending, *ma chère*! The little countess tried to be clever with Vera," said the count. "But what of it? She still turned out splendid."

And then, noticing with the intuition that is more perceptive than the intellect that Vera was feeling embarrassed, he went over to her and stroked her shoulder with his hand.

"Excuse me, I have a few things to see to. Do stay a bit longer," he added, bowing and preparing to go out.

The guests stood up and left, promising to come to dinner.

"What a way to behave! Ugh, I thought they would never leave!" said the countess after she had seen the guests out.

# XVI

When Natasha came out of the drawing room and started running, she only got as far as the conservatory. There she stopped, listening to the talk in the drawing room and waiting for Boris to come out. She was already beginning to feel impatient and stamped her foot, preparing to burst into tears because he was not coming immediately. When she heard the young man's footsteps, not quiet, but rapid and discreet, the thirteen-year-old girl quickly dashed in among the tubs of plants and hid.

"Boris Nikolaevich!" she said in a deep bass, trying to frighten him, and then immediately started laughing. Catching sight of her, Boris shook his head and smiled.

"Boris, come here please," she said with a look of significant cunning. He went over to her, making his way between the tubs.

"Boris! Kiss Mimi," she said, smiling mischievously and holding out her doll.

"Why shouldn't I kiss her?" he said, moving closer and keeping his eyes on Natasha.

"No, say: 'I don't want to.'"

She moved away from him.

"Well, I can say I don't want to as well, if you like. Where's the fun in kissing a doll?"

"You don't want to? Right, then come here," she said and moved away deeper into the plants and threw the doll onto a tub of flowers. "Closer, closer!" she whispered. She caught hold of the officer by his cuffs and her blushing face was filled with fearful solemnity.

"But do you want to kiss me?" she whispered barely audibly, peering at him warily, smiling and almost crying in her excitement.

Boris blushed.

"You're so funny!" he said, leaning down towards her and blushing even more, but not trying to do anything and biding his time. The faint hint of mockery was still playing on his lips, on the point of disappearing.

She suddenly jumped up onto a tub so that she was taller than him, put both arms round him so that her slim, bare hands bent around his neck and, flinging her hair back with a toss of her head, kissed him full on the lips.

"Ah, what have I done!" she cried, then slipped, laughing, between the tubs to the other side of the plants, and her frisky little footsteps squeaked rapidly in the direction of the nursery. Boris ran after and stopped her.

"Natasha," he said, "can I tell you something really special?"

She nodded.

"I love you," he said slowly. "You're not a child. Natasha, do what I'm going to ask you."

"What *are* you going to ask me?"

"Please, let's not do what we just did for another four years."

Natasha stopped and thought for a moment.

"Thirteen, fourteen, fifteen, sixteen," she said, counting on her slim little fingers. "All right! Is it settled, then?" And a serious smile of joy illuminated her vivacious though not beautiful face.

"Yes!" said Boris.

"For ever?" the girl said. "Until death itself?"

And, taking him by the arm, she calmly walked with him into the nursery. Boris's handsome, refined face turned red and the expression of mockery disappeared entirely from his lips. He thrust out his chest and sighed in happiness and contentment. His eyes seemed to be gazing far into the future, four years ahead, to the happy year of 1809. The young people gathered once again in the nursery, where they loved to sit most of all.

"No, you shan't leave!" shouted Nikolai, who did and said everything passionately and impetuously, grabbing Boris by the sleeve of his uniform jacket with one hand and pulling his arm away from his sister with the other. "You have to get married."

"You have to! You have to!" both the girls cried.

"I'll be the sexton, Nikolaenka," shouted Petrushka. "Please, let me be the sexton: 'Oh Lord have mercy!'"

Although it might seem incomprehensible how much fun young men and girls could find in the wedding of the doll and Boris, one look at the exultation and joy expressed on all their faces when the doll, adorned with Seville orange blossom and wearing a white dress, was set on its kidskin bottom on a little post and Boris, who was ready to agree to anything, was led up to her, and little Petrusha, having donned a skirt, pretended he was the sexton – one look at all this was enough to share in this joy, even without understanding it.

During the dressing of the bride, for decency's sake Nikolai and Boris were banished from the room. Nikolai walked to and fro, sighing to himself and shrugging his shoulders.

NATASHA ROSTOV AND BORIS DRUBETSKOY
*Drawing by M. S. Bashilov, 1866*

"What's the matter?" asked Boris.

Nikolai glanced at his friend and gestured despairingly with his hand.

"Ah, you don't know what just happened to me!" he said, clutching his head in his hands.

"What?" asked Boris, in a calm, humorous tone.

"Well, I'm going away, and she . . . No, I can't say it!"

"But what is it?" Boris asked again. "Something with Sonya?"

"Yes. Do you know what?"

"What?"

"Agh, it's incredible! What do you think? Do I have to tell my father after this?"

"But what?"

"You know, I don't even know myself how it happened, I kissed Sonya today: I have acted vilely. But what am I to do? I am madly in love. But was it bad of me? I know it was bad . . . What do you say?"

Boris smiled.

"What are you saying? Did you really?" he asked in sly, mocking amazement. "Kissed her straight on the lips? When?"

"Why, just now. You wouldn't have done that? Eh? You wouldn't have. Have I acted badly?"

"Well, I don't know. It all depends on what your intentions are."

"Well! But of course. That's right. I told her. As soon as they make me an officer, I shall marry her."

"That's amazing," declared Boris. "How very decisive you are!"

Nikolai laughed, reassured.

"I'm amazed that you have never been in love and no one has ever fallen in love with you."

"That's my character," said Boris, blushing.

"Oh, yes, you're so very cunning! It's true what Vera says," Nikolai said and suddenly began tickling his friend.

"And you're so very awful. It is true, what Vera says." And Boris, who disliked being tickled, pushed his friend's hands away. "You're bound to do something extraordinary."

Both of them, laughing, went back to the girls to conclude the rite of marriage.

# XVII

The countess felt so tired after the visits that she gave orders not to receive anyone else, and the doorman was given strict instructions to invite everyone who might still arrive with congratulations to dine. Besides that, she wanted to have a confidential talk with her childhood friend Anna Mikhailovna, whom she had not seen properly since her arrival from St. Petersburg. Anna Mikhailovna, with her careworn and agreeable face, moved closer to the countess's armchair.

"I shall be entirely candid with you," said Anna Mikhailovna. "There are so few of us old friends left. That is why I value your friendship so."

The princess looked at Vera and stopped. The countess squeezed her friend's hand.

"Vera," said the countess, addressing her elder, and obviously less loved daughter. "How can you be so completely tactless? Surely you can tell you are not needed here? Go to your sisters or . . ."

The beautiful Vera smiled, apparently not feeling in the least insulted, and went to her room. But as she passed by the nursery she noticed two couples in there, seated symmetrically at the two windows. Sonya was sitting close beside Nikolai, who, with his face flushed, was reading her the first poem that he had ever composed. Boris and Natasha were sitting by the other window without speaking. Boris was holding her hand and he let go of it when Vera appeared. Natasha picked up the little box of gloves standing beside her and began sorting through them. Vera smiled. Nikolai and Sonya looked at her, got up and left the room.

"Natasha," said Vera to her younger sister, who was intently sorting through the scented gloves. "Why do Nikolai and Sonya run away from me? What secrets do they have?"

"Why, what business is it of yours, Vera?" Natasha asked protectively in her squeaky voice, continuing with her work. She was evidently feeling even more kind and affectionate towards everyone because of her own happiness.

"It's very stupid of them," said Vera in a tone that Natasha thought sounded offensive.

"Everyone has their own secrets. We don't bother you and Berg," she said, growing heated.

"How stupid! You'll see, I'm going to tell mama how you carry on with Boris. It's not right."

"Natalya Ilinishna treats me perfectly well. I can't complain," he said sarcastically.

Natasha did not laugh and looked up at him.

"Don't, Boris, you're such a diplomat" (the word *diplomat* was very popular with the children, in the special meaning which they gave to this word), "it's really boring," she said. "Why is she pestering me?"

She turned to Vera.

"You'll never understand," she said, "because you've never loved anyone, you have no heart, you're nothing but Madame de Genlis" (this nickname, which was regarded as very insulting, had been given to Vera by Nikolai) "and your greatest pleasure is to cause trouble for others. You can flirt with Berg as much as you like."

She blurted this out hurriedly and flounced out of the nursery.

The beautiful Vera, who had such an irritating, disagreeable effect on everyone, smiled again with the same smile that meant nothing and, apparently unaffected by what had been said to her, went up to the mirror and adjusted her scarf and hair. As she gazed at her own beautiful face, she visibly turned colder and calmer than ever.

# XVIII

In the drawing room the conversation was continuing.

"Ah, my dear," said the countess, "in my life too not everything is roses. Do you think I cannot see that with the way we live, our fortune will not last long? And it's all the club, and his generous nature. When we are in the country, what rest do we get there? Theatres, hunts and God knows what else. But there I am talking about myself! Now, how did you arrange everything? I am constantly amazed at you, Annette, at your age, the way you gallop off in a carriage on your own, to Moscow, to St. Petersburg, to all the ministers and all the important people, and you know how to deal with them all, I am amazed! Well, how did everything go? I don't know how to do anything of that sort."

"Ah my darling," replied Princess Anna Mikhailovna. "God grant that you may never know how hard it is to be left a widow with no support and with a son whom you love to distraction. One can learn to do everything," she continued with a certain pride. "My lawsuit taught me that. If I need to see one of these bigwigs, I write a note: 'Princess so-and-so wishes to see so-and-so', and I go myself in a cab, two or three times if necessary, even four, until I get what I want. I don't give a jot what people think of me."

"Well, how did you ask for Borenka?" asked the countess. "After all, your son is a Guards officer, but Nikolai is going as a cadet. I have no one to intercede for me. Whom did you petition?"

"Prince Vasily. He was very kind. Now he has agreed to everything, and informed His Majesty," Princess Anna Mikhailovna said ecstatically, completely forgetting all the humiliation that she had gone through to achieve her goal.

"And has he grown old, Prince Vasily?" the countess asked. "I haven't seen him since our dramatics at the Rumyantsevs'. I think he has forgotten all about me. He used to run around after me," the countess recalled with a smile.

"He is the same as ever," replied Anna Mikhailovna. "The prince is courteous, positively brimming over with compliments. His high position has not turned his head at all. 'I regret that I can do so little for you, my dear princess,' he said to me, 'ask what you will.' Yes, he is a splendid man and an excellent relative. But you know, Nathalie, how I love my son. I don't know what I would not do for his happiness.

And my circumstances are so bad," Anna Mikhailovna continued sadly, lowering her voice, "so very bad that I am now in a quite appalling situation. My miserable lawsuit is consuming everything I have and never makes progress. Can you believe that I do not have, literally do not have, ten kopecks to spare, and I have no idea where to get the money for Boris's uniform." She took out a handkerchief and began to cry. "I need five hundred roubles, and I have one twenty-five-rouble note. I am in such a state. My only hope now is Count Kirill Vladimirovich Bezukhov. If he will not support his godchild – after all, he is Boris's godfather – and provide him with something to live on, then all my efforts will have been wasted, I shall have no money to fit him out."

The countess shed a few tears and pondered something without speaking.

"I often think, perhaps it is a sin," said the princess, "but I often think: there is Count Kirill Vladimirovich Bezukhov living alone . . . it's an immense fortune . . . and what is he living for? Life is a burden to him, and Borya is only about to start living."

"He is bound to leave something to Boris," said the countess.

"God knows. These rich men and grandees are such egotists. But nonetheless I shall go to him now, and take Boris, and tell him to his face what is the matter. Let people think what they will of me, I really do not care, when my son's destiny depends on it." The princess got to her feet. "It is now two o'clock. And you are dining at four. I shall have enough time to go there and back." And with the bearing and manners of a practical St. Petersburg lady who knows how to make good use of her time, Anna Mikhailovna sent for her son and went out into the front hall with him.

"Goodbye, my darling," she said to the countess, who saw her to the door. "Wish me success," she added, whispering so that her son would not hear.

"You are going to Count Kirill Vladimirovich, *ma chère*," the count said from the dining room as he emerged into the hallway. "If he is feeling better, invite Pierre to dine with us. He has been here before, he danced with the children. You absolutely must invite him. Well, we shall see how Taras excels himself today. They say Count Orlov never had such a dinner as we shall have today."

# XIX

"My dear Boris," Princess Anna Mikhailovna said to her son as Countess Rostova's carriage, in which they were sitting, drove along the straw-covered street and into the wide, sand-strewn courtyard of the unfamiliar colonnaded house belonging to Count Kirill Vladimirovich Bezukhov. "My dear Boris," said his mother, freeing her hand from under her old coat and laying it on her son's arm in a gesture of timid affection, "please, set aside your pride. Count Kirill Vladimirovich is after all your godfather, and your future fate depends on him. Remember that, be nice, as you know how to be."

"If only I knew that anything would come of it, apart from humiliation," her son replied coldly. "But I promised and I am doing it for you. Only this is the last time, mama. Remember that."

Even though the carriage was standing at the entrance, the doorman scrutinised the mother and son who, without giving their names, had walked straight up between the two rows of niched statues and into the glazed vestibule, and he asked, casting a significant glance at the countess's shabby coat, whom they wished to see, the princesses or the count, and, on learning that it was the count, he informed them that his excellency was feeling worse today and his excellency was not receiving anyone.

"We can leave," the son said in French, evidently delighted at this news.

"My friend!" the mother said in an imploring tone of voice, touching her son's arm again, as though this touch could calm or excite him.

Boris, fearful of creating a scene in front of the doorman, said nothing, with the expression of a man who has decided to drain his bitter cup to the last drop. Without unbuttoning his greatcoat, he looked enquiringly at his mother.

"My dear fellow," said Anna Mikhailovna in a soft voice, addressing the doorman, "I know that Count Kirill Vladimirovich is very ill . . . that is why I have come . . . I am a relative . . . I will not disturb him, my dear fellow . . . And I would only need to see Prince Vasily Sergeevich, he is staying here, after all. Announce us, please."

The doorman tugged morosely on a cord leading upstairs and turned away.

"Princess Drubetskaya to see Prince Vasily Sergeevich," he called to the footman in knee-breeches, shoes and tails, who had come running down and was peering out from under the overhang of the stairs.

The mother straightened the folds of her dyed silk dress and, with a

PRINCESS ANNA MIKHAILOVNA DRUBETSKAYA AND HER SON BORIS
*Drawing by M. S. Bashilov, 1866*

glance at herself in the tall Venetian pier glass set into the wall, strode briskly up the stair-carpet in her down-at-heel shoes. "My dear, you promised me," she said again to her son, trying to rouse him with the touch of her hand. Lowering his eyes, the son walked on gloomily.

They entered a hall from which one of the doors led into the chambers allotted to Prince Vasily.

As the mother and son, walking out into the centre of the room, were contemplating asking the way from an old footman who had jumped to his feet at their arrival, the bronze handle of one of the doors turned and Prince Vasily emerged, dressed simply in a velvet smoking jacket with only a single star, accompanied by a handsome, dark-haired man. This man was the famous St. Petersburg physician Lorrain.

"So it is definite," the prince was saying.

"Prince, *errare est humanum*, but . . ." the doctor replied, burring his r's and pronouncing the Latin words with a French accent.

"Very well, very well . . ."

Noticing Anna Mikhailovna and her son, Prince Vasily dismissed the doctor with a bow and approached them without speaking, but with an interrogatory air. The son was astonished to see the profound grief that was suddenly expressed in Princess Anna Mikhailovna's eyes.

"Indeed, what distressing circumstances we are obliged to meet in, prince . . . Well, how is our dear invalid?" she said, disregarding the cold, insulting gaze directed at her and addressing the prince as her best friend, with whom she could share her woe. Prince Vasily looked in baffled enquiry, first at her, then at Boris. Boris bowed politely. Prince Vasily, making no response to the bow, turned back to Anna Mikhailovna and answered her question with a movement of the head and lips which signified the very worst prospect for the invalid.

"Surely not!" exclaimed Anna Mikhailovna. "Oh, that is terrible! The very idea is appalling . . . This is my son," she added, indicating Boris. "He wished to thank you himself."

Boris bowed politely once again.

"Believe me, prince, a mother's heart will never forget what you have done for us."

"I am glad to have been able to do something to please you, my dear Anna Mikhailovna," said Prince Vasily, adjusting his jabot, expressing far greater self-importance with his gesture and tone of voice to his satisfied suppliant here in Moscow than he had managed in St. Petersburg, at Anna Scherer's *soirée*.

"Try to serve well and be worthy," he added, addressing Boris with severity. "I am so glad . . . Are you here on leave?" he enunciated in his impassive tone of voice.

"I am awaiting orders, your excellency, to take up my new posting," Boris replied, betraying neither annoyance at the prince's sharp tone nor a desire to engage in conversation, but speaking so calmly and coldly that the prince regarded him more closely.

"Do you live with your mother?"

"I live in the house of Countess Rostova," said Boris and added, again coldly, "your excellency."

He evidently said "your excellency" not so much in order to flatter the other man as to restrain him from familiarity.

"That is the Ilya Rostov who married Natalya Z.," put in Anna Mikhailovna.

"I know, I know," said Prince Vasily in his monotonous voice, with a typical Petersburgian's contempt for everything Muscovite.

"I never could understand how Natalya could bring herself to marry that ill-bred bear of a man. A perfectly stupid and ridiculous individual. And a gambler into the bargain, so they say," he said, thereby demonstrating that for all his contempt for Count Rostov and his like, and for all his important affairs of state, he was not above listening to the rumours of the town.

"But a very kind man, prince," Anna Mikhailovna remarked, smiling with feeling, as though she were also aware that Count Rostov deserved such a low opinion, but was asking the prince to pity the poor old man.

"What do the doctors say?" the princess asked after a brief pause, once again with an expression of great sadness on her tearful face.

"There is not much hope," said the prince.

"And I so much wanted to thank my uncle once more for all his kindnesses to me and Borya. He is his godson," she added in a tone which suggested that this news ought to delight the prince highly.

Prince Vasily began thinking and frowned. Anna Mikhailovna realised that he was afraid of discovering in her a rival for Count Bezukhov's inheritance. She hastened to reassure him.

"If it were not for my genuine love and devotion to my uncle," she said, pronouncing the word with an especially casual confidence, "I know his character, noble and straightforward, but he has only the princesses here ... They are still young." She inclined her head and added in a whisper: "Has he fulfilled his final duty, prince? How precious those final minutes are! After all, things cannot get any worse, he must be made ready, if he is in such a bad way. We women, prince," she said, smiling sweetly, "always know how to say these things. I must see him, no matter how painful it is for me, I am already accustomed to suffering."

The prince had evidently understood what she was saying, and he had also understood, as he had at Anna Scherer's *soirée*, that Anna Mikhailovna was not easily to be put off.

"I fear that meeting might be too hard on him, dear Anna Mikhailovna," he said. "Let us wait until the evening, the doctors have predicted a crisis."

"But one must not wait, prince, at moments like this. Think, it concerns the salvation of his soul. Aah! The duty of a Christian is a terrible thing." A door from the inner rooms opened and one of the princesses, the count's nieces, emerged, with a beautiful, but cheerless, cold face and a long waist quite astonishingly out of proportion with her legs.

Prince Vasily turned to her.

"How is he?"

"Still the same. But now there's all this noise," said the princess, examining Anna Mikhailovna like a stranger.

"Ah, my dear, I did not recognise you," Anna Mihailovna said with a glad smile, springing nimbly across to the count's niece. "I have come to help you care for your uncle. I can well imagine how much you have suffered," she added sympathetically, rolling her eyes upwards.

The princess did not even smile, but excused herself and went away. Anna Mikhailovna took off her gloves and, consolidating the gains she had made, settled down in an armchair, inviting Prince Vasily to sit beside her.

"Boris," she said to her son with a smile. "I am going in to see the count . . . my uncle, and meanwhile you, my friend, go to see Pierre, and don't forget to pass on the invitation from the Rostovs. They want him to come for dinner. He should not go though, I think," she said, turning to the count.

"On the contrary," said the prince, suddenly quite clearly out of sorts. "I should be glad if you would relieve me of that young fellow. He simply hangs about here. The count has not asked for him once."

He shrugged. A footman led the young man down one staircase and up another to Pyotr Vladimirovich's rooms.

## XX

Boris, thanks to his placid and reserved character, was never at a loss in difficult situations. But now this placidity and reserve were intensified still further by the cloud of happiness that had enveloped him since morning and through which he seemed to see people's faces, so that observation of his mother's behaviour and her character became less upsetting. He found the position of petitioner, in which his mother had placed him, painful, but he himself felt in no way to blame.

Pierre had still not managed to choose a career for himself in St. Petersburg and had indeed been banished to Moscow for disorderly conduct. The story that had been recounted at Count Rostov's house was correct: his presence had made Pierre a party to the tying of the policeman to the bear. He had arrived several days earlier and put up, as always, at his father's house. Although he had assumed that his story was already known in Moscow and that the ladies surrounding his father, who were always hostile towards him, would use the opportunity to irritate the count, nonetheless on the day of his arrival he had gone to his father's apartments. On entering the drawing room, the princesses' usual haunt, he had greeted the ladies sitting there with their embroidery frames and a book, from which one of them was reading aloud. There were three of them. The eldest, a tidy, strict spinster with a long waist, the one who had come out to Anna Mikhailovna, was reading: the younger two, both rosy-cheeked and pretty, only distinguishable from each other by the fact that one had a mole above her lip which made her much prettier, were working at their embroidery frames. Pierre was received like a corpse or a carrier of plague. The eldest princess interrupted her reading and looked at him in silence with fearful eyes: the younger one with the mole, a cheerful and giggly individual, leaned over her embroidery frame to conceal the smile occasioned, no doubt, by the scene that was to come, which she foresaw would be amusing. She tugged at a strand of wool and bent her head close as though examining the stitchwork, scarcely able to restrain her laughter.

"Hello, cousin," said Pierre. "Do you not recognise me?"

"I recognise you only too well, too well."

"How is the count's health? May I see him?" Pierre asked awkwardly, as always, but without embarrassment.

"The count is suffering both physically and morally, and you seem to have taken pains to inflict as much moral suffering on him as possible."

"May I see the count?" Pierre repeated.

"Hmm! If you wish to kill him, to finish him completely, you may see him. Olga, go and see if the broth is ready for uncle, it will soon be time," she added, thereby indicating to Pierre that they were busy and fully occupied with comforting his father, whereas he was obviously occupied only with causing him distress.

Olga went out. Pierre stood for a moment, looked at the sisters, bowed and said:

"Then I shall go to my room. When it is possible, you will let me know."

He went out and heard the quiet laughter of the sister with the mole ringing behind him.

The following day Prince Vasily had arrived and installed himself in the count's house. He summoned Pierre and told him, "My dear boy, if you behave here in the same way as in St. Petersburg, you will come to

76

a very bad end: I have nothing more to say to you. The count is very, very ill, you should not see him at all."

Since then no one had bothered Pierre, who, wherever he happened to be, was content with his own thoughts and walked around his room, occasionally halting in the corners, making threatening gestures at the wall, as if he were running an invisible enemy through with a sword, and peering severely over the top of his spectacles, and then recommencing his stroll, repeating inaudible words to himself, shrugging his shoulders and throwing his hands up in the air.

"England is done for!" he said, frowning and pointing at someone. "Pitt, as a traitor to the nation and the people's law, is condemned to . . ." He had not yet finished pronouncing sentence on Pitt, imagining at that moment that he was Napoleon himself and having already completed, together with his beloved hero, the dangerous crossing via the Pas de Calais and conquered London, when he saw a young, well-proportioned, handsome officer entering his room. He halted. Pierre, who had seen Boris only rarely, had left him as a fourteen-year-old boy and did not remember him at all, but in spite of that, in his typical brisk and genial manner he took him by the hand and smiled amicably, displaying his bad teeth.

"Do you remember me?" asked Boris. "*Maman* and I came to see the count, but it seems he is not quite well."

"Yes, it seems he is unwell. Everyone is bothering him," replied Pierre, completely failing to notice that by saying this he appeared to be reproaching Boris and his mother.

He was trying to recall who this young man was, but Boris thought he had caught some hint in Pierre's words.

He flushed and looked at Pierre boldly and sardonically, as much as to say: "I have nothing to be ashamed of." Pierre could think of nothing to say.

"Count Rostov has invited you to come for dinner today," Boris continued after a silence that was rather long and awkward for Pierre.

"Ah! Count Rostov!" Pierre said cheerfully. "So you are his son, Ilya. Can you imagine, for a moment I didn't recognise you. Do you remember how we went to the Sparrow Hills with Madame Jacquot?"

"You are mistaken," Boris said unhurriedly, with a bold and rather sardonic smile. "I am Boris, Princess Anna Mikhailovna Drubetskaya's son. It is Rostov senior who is called Ilya, and his son is Nikolai. And I have never known any Madame Jacquot."

Pierre began waving his hands and his head about as though he had been attacked by a mosquito or bees.

"Ah, this is terrible! I have confused everything. I have so many relatives in Moscow! You are Boris . . . yes. Right then, you and I have agreed on that. Well, what do you think of the Boulogne expedition? The English will really be in trouble if Napoleon crosses the Channel. I think an expedition is very likely. As long as Villeneuve does not blunder."

Boris knew nothing about any Boulogne expedition, he did not read the newspapers and this was the first time he had heard of Villeneuve.

"Here in Moscow we are more concerned with dinners and gossip than politics," he said in his calm, sardonic tone. "I know nothing about all this and have no thoughts on it. Moscow is concerned with gossip above all else," he continued. "And what they are talking about now is you and the count."

Pierre smiled his kind smile, as though afraid that his interlocutor might say something that he would regret. But Boris spoke distinctly, clearly and coolly, looking straight into Pierre's eyes.

"Moscow has nothing better to do than gossip," he continued. "Everybody is concerned with whom the count will leave his fortune to, although he might perhaps outlive us all, which I wish with all my heart."

"Yes, it is very difficult," Pierre interjected. "Very difficult." Pierre was still afraid that this boy-officer might inadvertently become involved in a conversation that would be embarrassing for him.

"But it must seem to you," said Boris, blushing, but without changing his voice or pose, "it must surely seem that everybody is only concerned to get something from the rich man."

That is how it is, thought Pierre.

"But what I wish to tell you, in order to avoid any misunderstandings, is that you would be greatly mistaken if you were to count myself and my mother among those people. We are very poor, but I, at least, speaking for myself, precisely because your father is rich, do not consider myself his relative and will never ask for anything or accept anything from him," he concluded, growing more and more heated.

It took Pierre a long time to understand, but when he did, he leapt up off the divan, seized hold of Boris by the hand with his characteristic speed and clumsiness and, blushing far more than Boris, began speaking with a mixed feeling of shame and hurt.

"But listen . . . That's very strange! How could I . . . And who could ever think . . . I know quite well . . ."

But Boris again interrupted him.

"I am glad I have made everything clear. Perhaps you find it disagreeable, forgive me," he said, soothing Pierre instead of being soothed by him, "but I hope I have not offended you. I make it a rule to say everything directly. What shall I tell them? Will you come to the Rostovs for dinner?"

And Boris, evidently because he had relieved himself of his onerous duty, extricating himself from one awkward situation and placing the other man in another, became cheerful and relaxed.

"Now, listen," said Pierre, calming down. "You are an amazing person. What you said just now is fine, very fine. Of course, you do not know me, we have not seen each other for so long . . . we were still children . . . You imagine me as . . . but I understand, I understand you very well. I could not have done that, I would not have had the courage, but it is all fine. I am very glad to have met you again. Strange," he added with a smile, after pausing briefly, "what you imagined me to be like!" He laughed. "Well, what of it! You and I shall get to know each other better. Please." He shook Boris's hand.

"You know, I have never been at the count's house before. He has never invited me. I feel sorry for him, as a man . . . But what can be done?" said Boris, smiling with cheerful good-nature. "And do you think Napoleon will manage to ferry his army across?" he asked.

Pierre realised that Boris wanted to change the subject and, feeling the same way, began to expound the advantages and disadvantages of the Boulogne undertaking.

A manservant came to summon Boris to his mother, the princess. The princess was leaving. Pierre promised to come to dinner and then, in order to become closer friends with Boris, he shook his hand firmly, gazing affectionately into his eyes through his spectacles . . . When Boris left, Pierre continued to walk round the room for a long while, no longer running through an invisible enemy with a sword, but instead smiling at the recollection of this likeable, intelligent and resolute young man.

As happens in early youth, and especially when one is lonely, Pierre felt an irrational affection for this young man and resolved to become friends with him.

Prince Vasily was seeing off the princess. The princess was holding a handkerchief and her face was wet with tears.

"It is terrible! Terrible!" she said. "But no matter what it might cost me, I shall perform my duty. I shall come to spend the night. He cannot be left like this. Every minute is precious. I do not understand why the princesses are delaying. Perhaps God will help me find the means to prepare him! Goodbye, prince, may God give you strength . . ."

"Goodbye, my dear," replied Prince Vasily, turning away from her.

"Ah, he is in a terrible state," the mother said to her son as they were getting back into the carriage. "He hardly recognises anybody. Perhaps it will be for the best."

"I do not understand, dear mama, what is his attitude to Pierre?" her son asked.

"The will will reveal all, my friend, our fate depends on it too . . ."

"But what makes you think he will leave us anything at all?"

"Ah, my friend! He is so rich and we are so poor!"

"That is still not sufficient reason, dear mama."

"Oh, my God! My God! How pitiful he is!" exclaimed his mother.

# XXI

When Anna Mikhailovna and her son left to go to Count Kirill Vladimirovich Bezukhov's house, the countess sat alone for a long time, applying her handkerchief to her eyes. Eventually she rang.

"What is the matter, my dear," she said angrily to the girl who had kept her waiting for several minutes. "Do you not wish to serve here? Then I'll find another place for you."

The countess was feeling grief-stricken at her friend's humiliating poverty and was therefore in a bad humour, which always expressed itself in her calling the servant girl "my dear" and addressing her formally.

"Sorry, ma'am," said the maid.

"Ask the count to come to me."

The count waddled up to his wife with a rather guilty air, as always.

"Well now, my little countess. What a fine Madeira and woodcock sauté there will be! I have tried it; I was right to give a thousand roubles for Taras. He's well worth it!"

He sat down beside his wife, propping his arms rakishly on his knees . . . and ruffling up his grey hair. "What is your pleasure, little countess?"

"Now then, my friend, what's that stain you have there?" she said, pointing at his waistcoat. "It is the sauté, I suppose," she added, smiling. "Look, count, I need some money."

Her face grew sad.

"Ah, my little countess!" said the count and he began busily taking out his wallet.

"I need a lot, count, I need five hundred roubles." And taking out her batiste lawn handkerchief, she rubbed her husband's waistcoat with it.

"Straight away, straight away. Hey, is anyone there?" he shouted in the kind of voice only used by people who are certain that those they are calling will come dashing headlong at their summons. "Send Mitenka to me!"

Mitenka, a nobleman's son who had been raised in the count's house,

80

and who now managed all his affairs, entered the room with silent steps.

"Now then, my dear chap," the count said to the deferential young man, "will you bring me . . ." he thought for a moment. "Yes, 700 roubles, yes. And be sure not to bring torn and dirty notes like last time, but good ones, for the countess."

"Yes, Mitenka, please, nice clean ones," said the countess, sighing sadly.

"Your excellency, when do you wish me to bring it?" said Mitenka. "If you please, may I know what . . . Then, please, do not bother yourself," he added, noticing that the count had already begun breathing rapidly and heavily, which was always a sign of the onset of rage. "I almost forgot . . . Do you wish me to bring it this very minute?"

"Yes, yes, do, bring it now. Give it to the countess."

"Pure gold, that Mitenka of mine," the count added, smiling, when the young man left the room. "Nothing's ever impossible. I can't stand that sort of thing. With him, everything's possible."

"Ah, money, count, money, how much grief it causes in the world!" said the countess. "But I do need this money very badly."

"You, my little countess, are a notorious spendthrift," said the count and, after kissing his wife's hand, he went back to his study.

When Anna Mikhailovna came back from Count Bezukhov's house, the money, all in brand new notes, was already lying on the low table under the countess's handkerchief, and Anna Mikhailovna noticed that the countess seemed agitated about something and looked sad.

"Well then, my friend?" asked the countess.

"Ah, what a terrible state he is in! He is unrecognisable, he is so bad, so bad: I spent a moment with him and didn't even say two words . . ."

"Annette, for God's sake, do not refuse me," the countess said suddenly, blushing, which looked very strange with her ageing, thin, solemn face, as she took the money out from under the handkerchief.

Anna Mikhailovna instantly realised what the matter was and eagerly leaned over in order to hug the countess at the proper moment.

"This is for Boris from me to have his uniform made . . ."

Anna Mikhailovna embraced her eagerly and wept. The countess wept too. They wept because they were friends, and because they were kind-hearted, and because they, who had been friends from their youth, were concerned with such a base item as money, and because their youth was past and gone . . . But for both, their tears were gratifying.

# XXII

Countess Rostova and her daughter and an already large number of guests were sitting in the drawing room. The count showed the male guests through into the study, offering them his own connoisseur's collection of Turkish pipes. From time to time he came out and asked if *she* had arrived yet. They were expecting Marya Dmitrievna Akhrosimova, known in society by the nickname of the fearsome dragon, a lady renowned not for her wealth or her distinctions, but for her straightforward thinking and frank simplicity of manner. Marya Dmitrievna was known to the royal family, she was known to the whole of Moscow and the whole of St. Petersburg, and both cities, while marvelling at her, chuckled in secret over her rudeness and told jokes about her: nonetheless everyone without exception respected and feared her.

In the smoke-filled study the conversation was about the war, which had been declared in a manifesto, and about the levy. No one had yet read the manifesto, but everyone knew it had been published. The count sat on the ottoman between two other men who were smoking and talking. The count himself did not smoke or talk but, inclining his head first to one side and then to the other, he watched the smokers with evident enjoyment and listened to the conversation of his two neighbours, whom he had pitted against each other.

One of the speakers was a civilian, with a wrinkled, bilious, clean-shaven, thin face, a man already approaching old age, although he was dressed like a most fashionable young man: he was sitting with his legs up on the ottoman, with the air of being quite at home and, having thrust the amber mouthpiece deep into his mouth from one side, was fitfully drawing in the smoke and screwing up his eyes. He was a well-known Moscow wit, the old bachelor Shinshin, a cousin of the countess, who was referred to in the salons of Moscow as an affected fop. He seemed to be speaking with condescension towards his conversation partner. The other, a fresh, pink Guards officer, irreproachably washed, buttoned and combed, was holding the amber mouthpiece in the centre of his mouth and drawing the smoke in lightly with his pink lips, releasing it in rings from his shapely mouth, which seemed expressly made for the blowing of smoke rings. He was the lieutenant Berg, an officer of the Semyonovsky Regiment, with whom Boris was to travel to the regiment and about whom Natasha had been teasing Vera, the eldest of the young countesses, calling Berg her fiancé. Berg moved on from conversation about the war to his own affairs, unfolding his future plans for service in the army, and was evidently very proud to be conversing with such a celebrity as Shinshin. The count sat between them and listened carefully. The pastime that the count found most agreeable, apart from playing boston, which he greatly loved, was playing the role of listener, especially when he managed to pit two lively and loquacious conversation partners against each other. Although Berg was clearly not a loquacious partner, the count observed on Shinshin's lips a mocking smile that seemed to say: "Watch how I sort out this little officer." And the count, without the slightest animus against Berg, was amusing himself by discovering the wit in Shinshin's every word.

"Well, come on, old man, my highly esteemed Alphonse Karlovich," Shinshin said, laughing and combining, in the manner which was the distinguishing feature of his speech, the most trivial Russian expressions with refined French phrases. "Aren't you counting on having an income from the treasury, and don't you want the regiment to pay you a little something too?"

"Oh no, Pyotr Nikolaevich, I simply wish to demonstrate that there are far fewer advantages to being in the cavalry than in the infantry. Now, just imagine my situation, Pyotr Nikolaevich."

Berg always spoke very precisely, calmly and politely. His conversation always concerned only himself, and he always remained calmly silent while the talk was of something that had no direct connection with him. He could remain silent like this for hours at a time, without feeling the slightest embarrassment himself or provoking it in anyone else. But as soon as the conversation concerned him personally, he would begin speaking at length and with obvious enjoyment.

"Just imagine my situation, Pyotr Nikolaevich, if I were in the cavalry, I would receive no more than two hundred roubles every four months, even at the rank of lieutenant, but now I receive two hundred and thirty," he said with a gleeful, self-satisfied, egotistical smile, regarding Shinshin and the count as if it were obvious to him that his success would always be the main goal of everyone else's desires.

"What's more, Pyotr Nikolaevich, having transferred to the Guards, I'll be more easily noticed," Berg continued, "and there are openings in the Guards infantry far more often. And then, imagine for yourself how well I can get by on two hundred and thirty roubles."

He paused and then continued triumphantly:

"I can put money away and send some to my father as well," he said and blew out a smoke ring.

"The accounts are balanced. As the proverb says, a German can thresh grain on the head of an axe," said Shinshin, moving the amber mouth-piece to the other side of his mouth and winking at the count.

The count burst out laughing. The other guests, seeing Shinshin making conversation, came over to listen. Berg, failing to notice either mockery or indifference, related at length and in precise detail how, by moving to the Guards, he had already gained one rank's advantage over his corps comrades, and how in wartime the company commander might well be killed so that he, as the remaining senior officer, could very easily become company commander, and how everybody in the regiment loved him, and how pleased his papa was with him. The listeners all waited with the count, hoping for something funny, but nothing funny came. Berg was clearly relishing telling them all this, and had not the slightest suspicion that other people might have their own reasons for listening. But everything he told them was so nice and proper, the naïvety of his young egotism was so transparent, that he quite disarmed his listeners and even Shinshin stopped laughing at him. He thought Berg not worth talking to.

"Well, old man, whether you are in the infantry or the cavalry, you will always get ahead anywhere, that I prophesy. I predict a brilliant career for you," he said, patting Berg's shoulder and lowering his legs from the ottoman. Berg smiled in delight. The count, followed by the guests, went out into the drawing room.

## XXIII

It was that moment before a formal dinner when the guests, all assembled in their finery and anticipating the summons to the *hors d'oeuvres*, refrain from starting long conversations yet feel they ought to keep moving about and not remain silent, lest they show impatience to take their seats at the table. The hosts keep glancing at the door and occasionally exchange glances with each other. The guests try to guess from these glances for whom or for what they are still waiting: an important relative who is late or the food which, according to the infor-mation from the kitchen, is not yet ready. In the servants' room the servants have not yet been able to start discussing the ladies and gentle-men, because they keep having to get up for new arrivals.

In the kitchen meanwhile the cooks are growing fierce and ill-tempered, moving in their white hats and aprons between the stove, the spit and the oven and shouting at the kitchen boys, who at such moments become especially timid. The coachmen at the entrance draw up in lines and, having settled down comfortably on their coachboxes, chat among themselves or drop into the coachmen's room to smoke a pipe.

Pierre arrived and sat awkwardly in the middle of the drawing room, on the first armchair he came across, blocking everybody's way. The countess tried to induce him to speak, but he gazed naïvely around through his spectacles, as though searching for someone, replying in monosyllables to all the countess's questions. He was in people's way, and he was the only one who was unaware of it. A large number of the guests, knowing about the incident with the bear, looked at this big, fat, meek man with curiosity, wondering how such an unassuming duffer could possibly have played such a trick on a policeman.

"Did you arrive recently?" the countess asked him.

"*Oui, madame*," he replied, looking around the room.

"Have you not seen my husband?"

"*Non, madame*," he said, smiling quite inappropriately.

"I believe you were in Paris recently? How very interesting."

"It was very interesting," he replied, debating with himself where that Boris, to whom he had taken such a liking, could have got to.

The countess exchanged glances with Princess Anna Mikhailovna. Anna Mikhailovna realised that she was being asked to entertain this young man and, seating herself beside him, began to talk about his father, but he answered her as he had the countess, in words of a single syllable. The guests were all occupied with each other. The sound of dresses rustling could be heard on every side. "The Razumovskys . . . It was quite exquisite . . . You are most kind . . . Countess Apraksina . . . Apraksina . . ."

The countess rose and went out to the entrance hall.

"Marya Dmitrievna?" her voice said in the hall.

"The very same," replied a gruff woman's voice, and then into the room came Marya Dmitrievna, who had arrived with her daughter.

All the young and even the older ladies, apart from the most elderly, stood up. Marya Dmitrievna halted in the doorway, and from the height of her corpulent frame, holding high her beautiful fifty-year-old head with its grey ringlets, she ran her eye over the guests. Marya Dmitrievna always spoke in Russian.

"Dear name-day girl and children," she said in her loud, rich voice that subdued all other sounds. "I would have paid you a visit this morning, but I don't like roaming about in the mornings. I suppose, you old sinner," she said to the count, who was kissing her hand, "you are probably bored in Moscow? Nowhere to run the dogs? But what's to be done, old man, when these little chicks grow up . . ." She indicated her daughter, who was quite unlike her mother, a rather attractive young lady who appeared as tender and sweet as her mother appeared coarse. "Like it or not, you have to look for suitors for them. There are yours, now, and all of them of age." She pointed to Natasha and Sonya, who had come into the drawing room.

When Marya Dmitrievna arrived, everyone had gathered in the drawing room, anticipating the exodus to the dinner table. Boris came in as well, and Pierre immediately attached himself to him.

"Well now, my Cossack." (Marya Dmitrievna always called Natasha a Cossack.) "What a winner this girl's become!" she said, stroking Natasha, who had approached her hand fearlessly and happily. "I know she's a little scallywag, and she ought to be whipped, but I adore her."

From out of her vast reticule (Marya Dmitrievna's reticule was known to everyone for the abundance and variety of its contents) she extracted a pair of sapphire drop earrings and, after handing them to the glowing, ruddy-cheeked name-day girl, instantly turned away from her and, catching sight of Pierre, said to him:

"Hey, hey, my dear fellow! Here, come over here." She spoke with a deliberately quiet, modulated voice, the way people speak to a dog that they want to scold. "Here, my dear fellow . . ."

Pierre, somewhat alarmed, went over, gazing at her through his spectacles naïvely and merrily, like a schoolboy, as though he fully intended to enjoy the forthcoming amusement as much as everyone else.

"Come here, come here, dear fellow! I was the only one to tell your father the truth when he got into a predicament and it's God's own will that I should tell you too."

She paused. Nobody said a word, waiting for what would happen next and sensing this was only the preamble.

"A fine boy, what can I say! What a fine boy! His father's on his deathbed, but he's having fun, mounting a policeman on a bear. For shame, my good fellow, for shame! You'd do better to go off to the war."

She turned away and proffered her hand to the count, who could barely restrain his laughter. Pierre simply winked at Boris.

"Well then, to table, I think it's probably time," said Marya Dmitrievna. The count and Marya Dmitrievna went in first, followed by the countess, who was escorted by the colonel of the hussars, an important man, for he would be taking Nikolai to his regiment; then came Anna Mikhailovna and Shinshin. Berg lent his arm to Vera. Marya Dmitrievna's daughter Julie, who constantly smiled and rolled her eyes and had not let Nikolai get away from her side since the moment she had arrived, went to the table with him. They were followed by other couples, extending right across the hall, and behind all of them the single figures of children, tutors and governesses. Footmen began bustling about, chairs clattered, music struck up in the gallery and the guests took their places. The sounds of the house musicians gave way to the sounds of knives and forks, the voices of the guests, the quiet footsteps of the venerable, grey-haired footmen. The countess sat at the head of one end of the table with the ladies, Marya Dmitrievna on her right, and Anna Mikhailovna on her left. At the other end sat the count with the gentlemen, the colonel of hussars on his left and Shinshin on his right. Along one side of the long table sat the more senior young: Vera beside Berg, Pierre beside Boris; and along the other side sat the children with their tutors and governesses. The count peered past the crystal, the bottles and bowls of fruit at his wife, although in fact all he could see was her tall cap with its light-blue ribbons, while he assiduously poured wine for his neighbours, without forgetting himself. The countess also, while not forgetting the obligations of a hostess, cast meaningful glances past the pineapples at her husband, the redness of whose bald head and face contrasted, it seemed to her, more sharply than usual with his grey hair. At the ladies' end there was a continuous, even babbling; at the male end the voices sounded louder and louder, especially that of the colonel of hussars, who ate and drank so much, growing redder and redder as he went, that the count kept holding him up as an example to the other guests. Berg was quietly telling the disagreeably smiling Vera about the advantages of wartime from the financial point of view; Boris was naming the guests at the table for his new friend Pierre and exchanging glances with Natasha, who was sitting facing him. Pierre, who had involuntarily absorbed the contempt of St. Petersburg for Muscovites, confirmed with his own observations all that he had heard about the manners of Moscow society. It was all true: the prim conventionality (dishes were served to guests according to rank and age), the narrowness of interests (no one was concerned with politics) and the warm hospitality, to which he nonetheless did full justice. Of the two soups, he chose the turtle to start with, then ate the pie, then the woodcock sauté that the count had liked so much; he did not miss a single dish, or a single wine, which the butler thrust out mysteriously from behind his neighbour's shoulder in a napkin-swathed bottle, intoning quietly: "Dry Madeira, Hungarian, Rheinwein" and so on. He held up whichever crystal wineglass with the count's monogram first came to hand from the set of four that stood before every place-setting and he drank with pleasure, looking at the guests with an expression that grew increasingly agreeable. Natasha, sitting opposite him, looked at Boris the way thirteen-year-old girls look at a boy whom they have kissed for the first time that morning and with whom they are in love, smiling now and again.

Pierre continually glanced at her and was met by the gaze and the smile intended for Boris.

"Strange," he whispered to Boris, "she is not good-looking, the younger Rostov girl, this little black-haired one here, but what a lovely face! Don't you think so?"

"The elder girl is better-looking," replied Boris, smiling almost imperceptibly.

"No, but just fancy that! All the features are irregular, but how wonderfully lovely she is."

And Pierre kept looking at her. Boris expressed surprise at Pierre's having such strange taste. Nikolai was sitting far away from Sonya beside Julie Akhrosimova, replying to her affectionate and ecstatic utterances, while constantly glancing at his cousin to reassure her and make her feel that wherever he might be, at the other end of the table or the other end of the world, his thoughts would always belong to her alone. Sonya smiled ostentatiously, but she was clearly already tormented by jealousy, turning pale and red by turns and straining with all her might to hear what Nikolai and Julie were saying to each other. Natasha, to her chagrin, was sitting with the children, between her little brother and a fat governess. The governess looked around uneasily, constantly whispering something to her charge and immediately glancing at the guests in anticipation of approval. The German tutor was trying to remember all the various kinds of dishes, desserts and wines in order to describe it all in detail in a letter to his family at home in Germany, and was highly offended that the butler with the bottle wrapped in a napkin carried it past without serving him. The German frowned and tried to pretend that he had not wished to be given this wine, but he was offended, because no one would understand that he wanted the wine not to quench his thirst, not out of greed, but out of genuine intellectual curiosity . . .

## XXIV

Natasha was clearly unable to sit still. She pinched her brother and winked at the governess, at which fat Petrusha almost burst his sides laughing, and suddenly she leaned her entire body across the table towards Boris, horrifying the governess as she did so by spilling the kvass from her glass all over the pristine tablecloth and, ignoring the rebuke that followed, demanding all his attention for herself. Boris craned towards her and Pierre also listened to hear what this little black-haired creature would say. Despite her irregular features, to his strange fantasy she seemed far more attractive to him than anyone else he had seen at this table.

"Boris, what's for dessert?" asked Natasha, raising her eyebrows with an emphatic air.

"I really don't know."

"Yes, very lovely!" Pierre whispered with a smile, as though someone were arguing with him about this.

Natasha at once noticed the impression she had made on Pierre and smiled at him happily, even giving him a brief nod and tossing her curls as she looked at him. He could make what he would of that. Pierre had still not spoken a word to Natasha, but with this single mutual smile they had already said that they liked each other.

At the men's end of the table, meanwhile, the conversation was growing ever more animated. The colonel told everyone that the manifesto declaring war had already been published in St. Petersburg and a copy which he himself had seen had been delivered by courier that day to the commander-in-chief.

"And what the devil do we want to fight Napoleon for?" said Shinshin. "He's already beaten the stuffing out of Austria. I'm afraid it might be our turn now."

The colonel was a thickset, tall, sanguine German, evidently a veteran and a patriot. He took offence at Shinshin's words.

"Because, my tear sir," he said, speaking correct Russian, but pronouncing it in a typically German fashion. "The Emperor knows what he's toing. He has said in the manifesto that he cannot remain intifferent to the tanger that is threatening Russia and the security of its empire, its tignity and the sacred nature of its alliances," he went on, for some reason giving special emphasis to the word "alliances", as though that were the very essence of the matter and, with the infallible official memory that was so characteristic of him, he repeated the opening words of the manifesto: ". . . 'and the desire, which constitutes the sole and imperative goal of the sovereign, to establish peace in Europe on firm foundations has prompted the tecision to move part of his army abroad at once and make fresh efforts for the achievement of this purpose.' That is the reason why, my tear sir," he concluded, downing a glass of Lafitte with didactic emphasis and glancing round at the count for encouragement.

"Do you know the saying: 'Erema, Erema, better stay home and whittle a spindle that's your own'?" asked Shinshin, sprawling back in his chair with a wry grimace. "It happens to fit us remarkably well. If even Suvorov has been smashed to smithereens, and where are our Suvorovs now? I ask you," said the wit, constantly skipping from Russian to French and grimacing affectedly.

"We must fight to the last trop of blood," said the colonel, thumping the table in a gesture that was not entirely good form, "and tie for our Emperor, and then everything will be all right. And tiscuss as lit-tell," he said, drawing out the word "little" especially, "as lit-tell as possible," he concluded, again addressing the count. "That is how we old hussars see things, and that's all. And what is your opinion, young man and young hussar?" he added, turning to Nikolai who, having heard them talking about the war, had abandoned his female conversation-partner and was staring wide-eyed at the colonel, all ears for what he had to say.

"I agree with you entirely," replied Nikolai, blushing furiously, fidgeting with his plate and shifting his wineglasses about with a resolute and desperate air, as if he were exposed to great danger at that very moment. "I am convinced that Russians must die or conquer," he said, then felt, as did the others after the word had been uttered, that it was too exalted and grandiloquent for the present occasion and therefore embarrassing, but the fine, impressionable youthfulness of his open-hearted face made his outburst moving to the others rather than comic.

"That is glorious, what you said, glorious," said Julie, sighing and lowering her eyelids in the depth of her feeling. Sonya began to tremble all over and blushed up to her ears, behind her ears and down to her neck and shoulders as Nikolai was speaking. Pierre listened carefully to what the colonel said and nodded his head approvingly, although, by his own reasoning, he believed that patriotism was stupidity. Yet involuntarily he sympathised with every sincerely spoken word.

"That is splendid. Very good, very good," he said.

"A genuine hussar, young man," cried the colonel, thumping the table again.

"What are you making so much noise about?" Marya Dmitrievna's rich voice suddenly asked across the table. "Why are you banging on the table?" she said to the hussar, as always saying out loud what others were only thinking. "Who are you getting so angry with? Perhaps you think you have the French in front of you?"

"I am speaking the truth," said the hussar, smiling.

"It is all about the war," the count shouted across the table. "My son is going, Marya Dmitrievna, my son is going."

"And I have four sons in the army, but I'm not grieving. Everything is God's will, you can die lying on the stove in your own hut, and God can spare you in battle," said Marya Dmitrievna's rich voice, audible without the slightest effort from the other end of the table.

"That's right."

The conversation became more focused once again, the ladies' at their end of the table, the men's at theirs.

"I bet you won't ask," said Natasha's little brother, "I bet you won't ask!"

"I will," replied Natasha.

Her face suddenly became flushed, expressing a desperate and gay determination, the determination that an ensign has when he throws himself into the assault. Half rising to her feet, with eyes sparkling and her smile barely contained, she addressed her mother:

"Mama!" her full-throated voice rang the entire length of the table.

"What is it?" the countess asked in fright but, seeing from her daughter's face that it was a piece of mischief, she waved her hand at her strictly, making a threatening and forbidding movement with her head.

The conversation fell silent.

"Mama! What will it be for dessert?" the little voice rang out even more decisively, without breaking, naïvely but with an awareness of its own naïvety.

The countess tried to frown, but an involuntary smile of love for her favourite child had already sprung to her lips. Marya Dmitrievna wagged a thick finger.

"Cossack!" she said menacingly.

Most of the guests looked at the heads of the table, not knowing how they should take this prank.

"I'll teach you!" said the countess.

"Mama, what will it be for dessert?" Natasha cried, boldly and with capricious merriment now, confident in advance that her prank would be well received. Sonya and fat Petya hid laughing faces.

"See, I did ask," Natasha whispered to her little brother without taking her eyes off her mother and without altering the naïve expression on her face.

"Ices! Only they won't give you any," said Marya Dmitrievna. Natasha saw that she had nothing to be afraid of, and so this time she wasn't even afraid of Marya Dmitrievna.

"Marya Dmitrievna, what kind of ices? I don't like ice cream."

"Carrot ices."

"No, what kind? Marya Dmitrievna, what kind?" she almost shouted. "I want to know."

Marya Dmitrievna and the countess laughed, and then all the guests laughed too. They all laughed, not at Marya Dmitrievna's answer, but at the inconceivable boldness and smartness of this little girl who knew how to talk to Marya Dmitrievna like that and dared to do it.

"Your sister is charming," said Julie.

Natasha only desisted when she was told there would be pineapple ices. Before the ices they served champagne. The music started up again,

91

the count kissed his little countess and as they rose, the guests congratulated the countess and clinked glasses across the table with the count,
the children and each other. Julie clinked glasses with Nikolai, letting
him know with her glances that this clinking had another important
meaning. Footmen began bustling about again, chairs clattered, and in
the same order as before, but now with redder faces, the guests returned
to the drawing room and to the count's study.

# XXV

The card tables had all been set up, parties sat down to play boston,
and the count's guests settled themselves throughout the two drawing
rooms, the sitting room and the library. Marya Dmitrievna scolded Shinshin, with whom she was playing.

"You're so good at criticising everybody else, but you couldn't even
guess that with the queen of hearts you should lead a heart."

The count, fanning out his cards, struggled to abstain from his customary after-dinner sleep and laughed at everything. The young people,
encouraged by the countess, gathered around the clavichord and harp.
At everybody's request Julie first played a little piece with variations on
the harp and then, together with the other girls began asking Natasha
and Nikolai, known for their musicality, to sing something. Natasha, to
whom they appealed more than anyone else, neither agreed nor refused.

"Wait, I'll try," she said, moving to the other side of the clavichord
and, trying out her voice, she quietly sang several pure full-throated
notes that were surprisingly moving. Everyone fell silent as the sounds
faded away in the lofty, high-ceilinged room.

"I can, I can do it," she said, happily tossing back her curls, which
were tumbling over her eyes.

Pierre, very red in the face after dinner, went over to her. He wanted
to look at her from closer up and see how she would talk to him.

"And why might you not be able to?" he asked as simply as if they
had known each other for a hundred years.

"There are some days when the voice just isn't any good," she said
and moved over towards the clavichord.

"And today?"

"It's excellent," she said, addressing him with as much enthusiasm
as if she were praising somebody else's voice. Pierre, pleased to have
seen how she spoke, went over to Boris, whom he liked almost as much
today as Natasha.

"What a lovely child, that little black-haired girl," he said. "Even though she isn't good-looking."

After the boredom of isolation in his father's big house, Pierre found himself in that happy, young man's state of loving everyone and seeing nothing but good in everyone. At dinner he had still unwittingly despised the Moscow public from the elevated height of St. Petersburg. But now he already felt that only here in Moscow did people know how to live and he even thought how good it would be to visit this house every day, and listen to this little black-haired girl sing and talk, and look at her.

"Nikolai," said Natasha, going up to the clavichord, "what shall we sing?"

"Perhaps 'The Spring'," replied Nikolai. He was clearly beginning to find it impossible to put up with the importunate Julie, who thought he ought to be overjoyed at her attentions.

"Well come on, come on, Boris, come over here," Natasha called. "And where's Sonya?" She glanced around and, seeing that her friend was not in the room, ran to get her.

"The Spring", as it was known at the Rostovs, was an old four-part song which they had been taught by their music teacher, Dimmler. This "Spring" was usually sung by Natasha, Sonya, Nikolai and Boris, who, although he did not have any special talent or voice, had a good ear and with his characteristic exactitude and imperturbability could learn a part and hold his own. While Natasha was gone, they started asking Nikolai to sing something. He refused in a manner that was almost uncivil and morose. Julie Akhrosimova, smiling, went up to him:

"Why so gloomy, all of a sudden?" she asked. "Though I do understand. For music, and for singing especially, you have to be in the mood. It's the same for me. There are certain moments . . ."

Nikolai frowned and walked towards the clavichord. Before he sat down he noticed that Sonya was not in the room and he almost wanted to leave.

"Nikolai, don't make me beg you, it's absurd," said the countess.

"I'm not trying to make you beg, *maman*," Nikolai replied and he opened the clavichord, banging the lid with an abrupt movement, and sat down.

He thought for a moment and began a little song by Kavelin:

> *Why say that fateful word, "adieu",*
> *When you are parting from your love,*
> *As if life has abandoned you,*
> *And happiness is gone for ever?*

*Say rather, "till we meet again",*
*Say, "till our joy returns anew".*
*Dismiss time with this sweet refrain,*
*To your own love remaining true.*

His voice was neither good nor bad, and he sang indolently, as though fulfilling a tedious obligation, but despite that, the entire room fell silent, the young ladies swayed their heads and sighed, and Pierre concealed his teeth behind a gentle, faint smile that looked especially funny on his fat, full-blooded face, remaining like that until the end of the song.

Julie closed her eyes and sighed so loudly that the entire room could hear her.

Nikolai sang with the sense of measure that he so badly lacked in life and which in art cannot be acquired by any study. He sang with a lightness and freedom which demonstrated that he was not labouring, but singing just as he spoke. Only when he began to sing did he express himself not like the child he seemed to be in life, but like a man in whom passions were already stirring.

# XXVI

Meanwhile Natasha, running first into Sonya's room and not finding her there, ran through into the nursery, but she was not there either. Natasha realised Sonya was on the chest in the corridor. The chest in the corridor was the "vale of sorrows" for the younger female generation in the Rostov house. And there indeed was Sonya lying on the trunk, face down on nanny's grubby striped eiderdown, with her gossamer-fine pink frock all crumpled beneath her, sobbing into her hands so violently that her bare, brown little shoulders were shuddering. Natasha's face, festive and animated all day long and now even more brightly radiant in preparation for singing, which always made her excited, suddenly darkened. Her eyes grew still, then her sturdy neck, well formed for singing, began to quiver, the corners of her lips turned down and in an instant her eyes were wet with tears.

"Sonya! What is it? What's wrong? Oh-oh-oh!" And Natasha, opening her large mouth and making herself utterly ugly, began bawling like a child without knowing the reason why, just because Sonya was crying. Sonya wanted to lift her head up, she wanted to answer, but she could not and only hid herself away all the more. Still crying, Natasha sat down on the blue eiderdown and hugged her friend. Gathering all her strength, Sonya sat up and began wiping away the tears and telling her what was wrong.

"Nikolai is leaving in a week, his . . . papers . . . have been issued . . . he told me himself . . . But I still wouldn't have cried . . ." (she showed Natasha the piece of paper that she was holding in her hand: it was the poem written by Nikolai), "I still wouldn't have cried, but you can't . . . nobody can understand . . . what a fine soul he has . . ."

And she began crying again because his soul was so fine. Sonya felt that no one apart from her could understand the sublime loveliness, nobility and tenderness – all the finest virtues of this soul. And she really did see all these peerless virtues, firstly because Nikolai, without knowing it himself, showed her only his very best side, and secondly because she wished with all the strength of her heart to see only the beautiful things in him.

"You are lucky . . . I don't envy you . . . I love you, and Boris too," she said, recovering a little strength, "he is kind. For you there are no obstacles. But Nikolai is my cousin . . . we need to . . . the Metropolitan himself . . . even then it's impossible . . . And then, if mama" (Sonya thought of the countess as her mother and called her mama) ". . . she'll say that I'm ruining Nikolai's career, that I'm heartless and I'm ungrateful, but truly . . . so God help me" (she crossed herself) ". . . I love her so much, and all of you, only Vera . . . But why? What have I done to her? I'm so grateful to you all that I would sacrifice everything, but I don't have a thing . . ."

Sonya could not carry on and again she hid her face in her hands and the eiderdown. Natasha began trying to comfort her, but it was clear from her face that she understood the full significance of her friend's grief.

"Sonya!" she said suddenly, as if she had guessed the genuine cause of her cousin's distress. "Tell me, Vera said something to you after dinner, didn't she?"

"Yes, Nikolai wrote out this poem himself, and I copied out some others: she found them on my table and said she would show them to mama, and she said that I was ungrateful, that mama would never allow him to marry me. And he's going to marry Julie. You see the way she looks at him. Natasha? What did I do?"

And she started crying again, more bitterly than before. Natasha raised her up, embraced her and, smiling through her own tears, began reassuring her.

"Sonya, don't believe her, my darling, don't believe her. Remember how the two of us and Nikolai spoke about things in the divan room, remember, after supper? We decided how everything would be. I don't remember exactly, but remember how everything was so good and everything was possible. Uncle Shinshin's brother is married to his cousin, and we're only second cousins. And Boris says it's perfectly possible. You know, I told him everything. And he's so clever and so good," said Natasha, feeling, just as Sonya did about Nikolai, and for the same reasons, that no one in the world apart from her could know all the treasures that were contained in Boris ... "Sonya, don't you cry, my darling, my sweet Sonya." And she kissed her, laughing. "Vera's mean. Forget her. Everything is going to be all right, and she won't tell mama, Nikolai will tell her himself."

She kissed the top of Sonya's head. Sonya sat up, and the little kitten became lively again, her eyes began to sparkle and it seemed as if any moment she would wave her tail, jump down on her soft paws and start playing with a ball of wool just as she ought to.

"Do you think so? Really? Honest to God?" she said, rapidly straightening her dress and putting her hair in order.

"Really, honest to God!" replied Natasha, tidying a vigorous lock of stray hair back into her friend's plait, and they both laughed.

"Now, let's go and sing 'The Spring'."

"Yes, let's."

Sonya, having brushed off the fluff and tucked the poem into her bosom up by her neck and prominent collar bones, her face flushed, ran with Natasha on light, happy feet along the corridor to the drawing room. Nikolai was finishing the final couplet of his song. He saw Sonya, his eyes lit up, a smile appeared on his mouth that was open to sing, his voice became stronger and more expressive, and he sang the final couplet even better than the ones before.

> How sweet, bath'd in the moon's bright ray,

– he sang, looking at Sonya, and they understood how much all this meant – the words and the smile and the song although, strictly speaking, it all meant nothing.

> In fancy's happy mood, to say:
> This world still holds one, dear to see,
> Whose thought and dreams are all of thee!
> And her fair fingers still do stray
> Across that gentle harp and play,
> Sighing sweet passion's harmony,
> With urgent pleas that summon thee.
> One day – when bliss will be on hand ...
> Oh woe! Lest first my life should end.

He sang only for Sonya, but everyone felt a happy, warm feeling in their hearts when he finished and stood up from the keyboard with his eyes moist.

"Charming! Enchanting!" said voices on every side.

"This romance," said Julie with a sigh as she went up to him, "is bliss. I understand everything now."

During the singing Marya Dmitrievna had got up from the table and stood in the doorway to listen.

"Bravo, Nikolai," she said. "You move the heart. Come here, give me a kiss."

# XXVII

Natasha whispered to Nikolai that Vera had just upset Sonya by stealing the poems and saying all sorts of nasty things to her. Nikolai blushed and immediately strode determinedly across to Vera and began whispering to her that if she dared to do anything unpleasant to Sonya, then he would be her enemy for life. Vera tried to make excuses and apologised and observed, also in a whisper, that it was not proper to talk about it now, indicating the guests who, noticing some sort of unpleasantness between brother and sister, had moved away.

"I don't care, I'll say it in front of everyone," Nikolai said almost loudly, "that you have a wicked heart and you take pleasure in hurting people."

Having said his piece and still trembling in agitation, Nikolai walked over to the far corner of the room, to Boris and Pierre. He sat down beside them with the resolute and gloomy air of a man who is now capable of anything and whom it is best not to bother with questions. Pierre, however, as distracted as ever, failed to notice Nikolai's state of mind and, feeling in a state of great contentment, intensified still further by the pleasurable sensations of the music, which always affected him deeply despite his being incapable of singing a single note in tune, he said to Nikolai:

"How splendidly you sang!"

Nikolai did not answer.

"What rank will you have in your regiment?" Pierre asked, simply in order to ask him something else.

Nikolai, forgetting that Pierre was in no way to blame for the unpleasantness Vera had caused him or for Julie's irritating attentions, glared at him angrily.

"They suggested I petition for an appointment as a gentleman of the bedchamber, but I refused, because I wish my position in the army to be due to nothing but my own merits ... and not to perching on the heads of people more worthy than myself. I am joining as a cadet," he added, very pleased that he had so soon been able to demonstrate his nobility to his new acquaintance and to use the military expression, "perch on someone's head", that he had only just overheard from the colonel.

"Yes, I am always arguing with him," said Boris. "I don't see anything unfair in joining straightaway as a major. If you don't merit that rank, they will reject you, and if you do merit it, you can be useful all the sooner."

"Yes, well, you are a diplomat," said Nikolai. "I believe it's an abuse of one's position and I do not wish to start with abuse."

"You are absolutely right, absolutely," said Pierre. "What's that, the musicians? Will there be dancing?" he asked timidly, hearing the sounds of instruments tuning up. "I have never been able to learn a single dance properly."

"Yes, I think mama ordered it," replied Nikolai, glancing cheerfully round the room and mentally seeking his own lady among the others. But just then he spotted a group that had gathered around Berg and the good mood that he had recovered was once again replaced by morose bitterness.

"Ah, do read it, Mr. Berg, you read so well, I'm sure it must be very poetic," Julie was saying to Berg, who was holding a piece of paper. Nikolai saw that it was one of his own poems which Vera, out of sheer spite, had shown to the whole company. The poem was as follows:

### The Hussar's Farewell

*Oh, do not grieve me as we part,*
*Do not torment your dear hussar,*
*But be his sword-arm's joyful heart,*
*Bright inspiration for his war.*

*I need my courage for the battle,*
*So stay these tears, so bitter-sweet,*
*I long to earn a victor's laurels,*
*So I may cast them at thy feet.*

When he had written the poem and given it to the object of his passion, Nikolai had thought it was beautiful, but now he suddenly felt it was exceptionally bad and, even worse, laughable. Seeing Berg with his poem in his hand, Nikolai halted and then, with his nostrils flared, his face scarlet, his lips pursed, he strode rapidly and resolutely towards the group, waving his arms. Boris, spotting his intentions in time, blocked his way and grabbed him by the arm.

"Listen, that would be stupid."

"Let go, I'll teach him a lesson," said Nikolai, forcing his way forwards.

"He's not to blame, let me go over there."

Boris went up to Berg.

"That poem was not written for the whole world," he said, holding out his hand. "If you please!"

"Ah, so it is not for everybody! Vera Pavlovna gave it to me."

"It's so lovely, there is something very melodic about it," said Julie Akhrosimova.

"'The Hussar's Farewell'," said Berg, and had the misfortune to smile. By now Nikolai was standing in front of him, holding his face close and glaring at the unfortunate Berg with wild eyes that seemed to pierce right through him.

"You find something funny? What do you find funny?"

"No, I didn't know it was you who . . ."

"What's it to you whether it was me or not? Reading other people's letters is a base act."

"I beg your pardon," said Berg, blushing in alarm.

"Nikolai," said Boris. "Monsieur Berg was not reading other people's letters . . . You're about to do something stupid. Listen," he said, putting the poem in his pocket, "come over here, I want to have a word with you."

Berg immediately moved away to join the ladies and Boris and Nikolai went out to the sitting room. Sonya ran out after them.

Half an hour later all the young people were dancing the écossaise and Nikolai, having talked with Sonya in the sitting room, was once again the same merry and agile dancer as always, and now felt astonished at his own irascibility and annoyed at his indecent outburst.

Everybody was feeling very jolly, even Pierre, who confused the figures as he danced the écossaise under Boris's supervision, and Natasha, who for some reason split her sides with laughter every time she glanced at him, which pleased him greatly.

"How funny he is, and how splendid," she said first to Boris, and then to Pierre himself, straight to his face, looking naïvely up into his eyes.

In the middle of the third écossaise, chairs began moving in the sitting room, where the count and Marya Dmitrievna were playing cards, and most of the honoured guests and the old folks, stretching themselves after sitting so long and putting their wallets and purses back into their pockets, came out through the doors into the hall. At the front came Marya Dmitrievna and the count, both with cheerful faces. The count offered his curved arm to Marya Dmitrievna in a gesture of facetious politeness, almost balletically. He drew himself erect and his face was illuminated by an extraordinary smile of rakish cunning, and as soon as they had finished dancing the final figure of the écossaise, he clapped his hands to the musicians and shouted up into the gallery, to the first violin.

"Semyon! Do you know the Daniel Cooper?"

This was the count's favourite dance, danced by him in his youth (strictly speaking, the Daniel Cooper was one figure of the anglaise).

"Look at papa," cried Natasha so loudly that everyone could hear, bending her curly head down to her knees and setting the entire hall ringing with her peals of laughter. And indeed, everyone who was there in the hall gazed with a smile of joy at the jolly little old man beside his stately lady, Marya Dmitrievna, who was taller than he, as he curved his arms and shook them in time, straightened his shoulders, turned out his feet, tapping them lightly and, with the smile spreading further and further across his round face, prepared his audience for what was to come. As soon as the jolly, challenging strains of the Daniel Cooper began to ring out like a merry vagabond song, all the doors of the hall were suddenly crammed full, by male faces on one side and, on the other, by the smiling female faces of all the servants who had come out to look at their master making merry.

"Our old father! What an eagle he is!" said a nanny from one door. The count danced well and he knew it, but his lady did not know how to dance at all and had no wish to dance well. Her massive body was held rigidly upright with her powerful arms lowered (she had handed her reticule to the countess) and only her severe but beautiful face danced. Everything that was expressed in the whole of the count's rotund figure Mariya Dmitrievna expressed only in the ever brighter and wider smile on her face and her twitching nose. But while the count, working himself up more and more, captivated his audience with the sudden surprise of his nimble arabesques and the light capering of his soft legs, Marya Dmitrievna, by taking the very slightest pains in moving her shoulders or curving her arms, in turning and stamping her feet, produced no less an impression for her efforts, which were appreciated by everyone in view of her corpulence and customary severity. The dance grew more and more lively. The other dancers were unable to attract the

100

DANCING THE DANIEL COOPER
*Drawing by M. S. Bashilov, 1866*

slightest attention to themselves, and gave up trying. All eyes were riveted on the count and Marya Dmitrievna. Natasha tugged at the sleeves and dresses of everyone around her, who in any case already had their eyes

101

fixed on the dancers, and demanded that they watch her dear papa. In the pauses in the dance the count struggled to catch his breath, waving his hand to the musicians and shouting for them to play faster. Quicker and quicker, ever more jauntily, the count twirled this way and that, hurtling around Marya Dmitrievna, now on his tiptoes, now on his heels and finally, having swung his lady back to her place, he took the final bow, drawing his supple leg back behind him, lowering his perspiring head with its smiling face and stretching out his curved right arm in a broad sweep amid thunderous applause and laughter, especially from Natasha. Both dancers stopped, struggling to catch their breath and wiping their faces with fine lawn handkerchiefs.

"That's how they used to dance in our time, *ma chère*," said the count.

"Hurrah for Daniel Cooper!" puffed Marya Dmitrievna, breathing out long and hard.

# XXVIII

While at the Rostovs' house they were dancing the sixth anglaise to weary musicians playing out of tune and the weary footmen and chefs were preparing supper, discussing among themselves how the masters were able to keep on eating – they had only just finished their tea and now it was supper time again – at this very hour, Count Bezukhov suffered his sixth stroke, and with the doctors declaring there was no hope of recovery, the sick man was given mute confession and communion, and preparations began to be made for extreme unction, filling the house with the bustle and anxious anticipation usual at such moments. Outside the house, beyond the gates, concealing themselves from the carriages that were arriving, a throng of undertakers waited in anticipation of a rich commission for the count's funeral. The commander-in-chief of Moscow, who had repeatedly sent his adjutants to enquire after the count's condition, came himself that evening to take his leave of one of the representatives of the age of Catherine the Great. The count was said to be seeking someone with his eyes, asking for them. A mounted servant was sent for both Pierre and Anna Mikhailovna.

The magnificent reception room was full. Everyone rose respectfully when the commander-in-chief, who had spent about half an hour alone with the sick man, emerged, barely responding to their bows and trying to walk as quickly as possible past the glances trained on him by the doctors, clergymen and relatives. Prince Vasily, grown thinner and paler over the last few days, walked beside him, and everyone watched the commander-in-chief shake his hand and repeat something quietly to him several times.

Having seen the commander-in-chief out, Prince Vasily sat down on his own on a chair in the hall and crossed one leg high over the other, leaning his elbow on his knee and covering his eyes with his hand. Everyone could see he was suffering and no one approached. After sitting in this way for some time he stood up and, walking with unusual haste, glancing around with eyes that seemed either angry or frightened, went down the long corridor to the rear of the house to see the eldest princess.

The people in the dimly lit room talked between themselves in a faltering whisper, falling silent and glancing round with eyes full of questioning anticipation at the door leading to the dying man's chambers every time it gave out a faint creak as someone came out or went in.

"Man's span," said an old man, a clergyman, to a lady who had sat beside him and was listening to him naïvely. "Even as thy span is fixed, thou shalt not exceed it."

"I wonder, isn't it too late to administer extreme unction?" asked the woman, adding an ecclesiastical title, as if she had no opinion of her own on this account.

"It is a great mystery, *madame*," replied the clergyman, running his hands over his bald patch, over which several strands of greying hair had been carefully combed.

"Who's that? Was that the commander-in-chief himself?" someone asked at the other end of the room. "How young he looks . . ."

"And he's over sixty! Did they say the count can't recognise anyone? They wanted to administer extreme unction."

"I knew of one man who had extreme unction seven times."

The second princess simply came out of the sick man's room with tearful eyes and sat beside Lorrain, the famous young French doctor, who was sitting in a graceful pose next to a portrait of Catherine the Great, leaning his elbows on the table.

"Excellent," said the doctor, replying to a question about the weather today, "excellent weather, but then, my princess, Moscow is so like the countryside."

"Yes indeed, is it not?" said the princess, sighing. "Well, can he have something to drink?"

Lorrain pondered the question.

"Has he taken his medicine?"

"Yes."

The doctor glanced at his Bréquet watch.

"Take a glass of boiled water and add a pinch" (with his slim fingers he showed her what a pinch meant) "of cream of tartar."

"It has nefer happent," said a German doctor to an adjutant, "that anyvone has surfifed a third stroke."

"And how full of life he was!" said the adjutant. "And who will all this wealth go to?" he added in a whisper.

"Takers will be found," the German replied, smiling.

Everyone glanced round at the door again as it creaked and the second princess, who had prepared the drink indicated by Lorrain, carried it in to the sick man. The German doctor approached Lorrain.

"Can he hold on until tomorrow morning?" the German asked, speaking in badly pronounced French.

Lorrain, pursing his lips, wagged his finger severely in front of his nose in a gesture of denial.

"Tonight and no later," he said quietly with a decorous smile of self-satisfaction at his own ability to understand and convey the patient's condition clearly, and walked away.

Meanwhile Prince Vasily opened the door into the eldest princess's room. The room was in semi-darkness, there were only two icon lamps burning in front of the icons and there was a pleasant smell of incense and flowers. The entire room was crammed with little chiffoniers, closets and tables. The white coverlets of a high feather bed could be seen behind a screen. A little dog began barking.

"Ah, it is you, cousin."

She stood up and arranged her hair, which was always, even now, so uncommonly smooth that it seemed to have been made in a single piece with her head and covered with lacquer.

"What is it, has something happened?" she asked. "I am so frightened already."

"Nothing, everything is still the same, I only came to finish talking business with you, Katish," said the prince, seating himself wearily in the armchair from which she had just risen. "My, how you have warmed it," he said, "come, sit here, let us talk."

"I thought something might have happened," said the princess, and with her unvarying calm, strict, stony decorum she sat facing the prince, preparing to listen.

"Well then, my dear?" said Prince Vasily, taking the princess's hand and by force of habit pulling it downwards.

It was obvious that this "well then" concerned many things that they both understood without naming them.

The princess, with her stiff, straight waist that was absurdly long for her legs, looked directly and fearlessly at the prince with her prominent grey eyes.

She shook her head and looked at an icon with a sigh. Her gesture could have been taken either as an expression of grief-stricken devotion or an expression of weariness and hope to rest soon. Prince Vasily took the gesture as an expression of weariness.

"Do you think," he said, "it is any easier for me? I am as exhausted as a post horse, but even so I have to talk to you, Katish, and very seriously too."

Prince Vasily stopped speaking and his cheeks began twitching nervously, first on one side, then on the other, lending his face an unpleasant expression such as never appeared on Prince Vasily's face when he was in society drawing rooms. His eyes were also not the same as usual: they either glared with facetious insolence or gazed around in fright.

The princess, holding the little dog on her knees with her dry, thin hands, looked attentively into Prince Vasily's eyes, but it was clear that she would not break the silence with a question, even if she had to remain silent until morning. The princess had one of those faces on which the expression remains the same, regardless of how the expression changes on another person's face.

"Well, you see, my dear princess and cousin, Ekaterina Semyonovna," Prince Vasily continued, evidently resuming what he had been saying with a certain inward struggle, "at moments such as this, one has to think of everything. We have to think about the future, about you . . . I love all of you like my own children, you know that."

The princess gazed at him as drearily and rigidly as ever.

"Finally, I have to think about my family too," Prince Vasily continued, angrily pushing the little table away from him and not looking at her, "you know, Katish, that you three Mamontov sisters, together with my wife, we are the count's only direct heirs. I know how painful it is for you to talk and think of such things. And it is no easier for me, my friend, I am over fifty and I have to be prepared for anything. Do you know that I have sent for Pierre and that the count pointed directly at his portrait and demanded that he be brought to him?"

Prince Vasily looked enquiringly at the princess, but could not tell whether she understood what he had just said or was simply looking at him.

"I never cease praying to God for one thing," she replied, "that He will have mercy on him and allow his noble soul to depart in peace from . . ."

"Yes, yes, quite so," Prince Vasily interrupted impatiently, wiping his bald patch and angrily moving back towards himself the little table that he had pushed away, "but ultimately . . . ultimately the point is, you know yourself that last winter the count wrote a will in which he left the entire estate, bypassing the direct heirs and us, to Pierre."

"It doesn't matter how many wills he wrote!" the princess said calmly. "He could not leave anything to Pierre. Pierre is illegitimate."

"My dear," Prince Vasily said abruptly, hugging the little table close to him, becoming more animated and starting to speak more rapidly, "but what if a letter was written to His Majesty and the count had asked to adopt Pierre? You realise that in reward for the count's services his request would be granted . . ."

The princess smiled as people smile when they think they know some matter better than those with whom they are speaking.

"I shall tell you more," Prince Vasily continued, seizing hold of her hand, "the letter was written, although not sent, and His Majesty knew of it. It is only a question of whether it has been destroyed or not. If not, then as soon as it is all over" – Prince Vasily sighed, in this way making it clear what he meant by "all over" – "and they open the count's documents, the will and the letter will be sent to His Majesty and his request will probably be granted. Pierre, as the legitimate son, will receive everything."

"And our part?" the princess asked, smiling ironically, as though anything at all but that could happen.

"But, my dear Katish, it is as clear as day. He is then the sole legitimate heir to everything, and you will not receive even that much. You must know, my dear, whether the will and the letter were written and whether they have been destroyed. And if for some reason they have been forgotten, then you must know where they are, and find them, because . . ."

"This is just too much!" the princess interrupted him, smiling sardonically without changing the expression of her eyes. "I am a woman, you think that we are all stupid, but I know this much, that an illegitimate son cannot inherit . . . *Un bâtard*," she added, hoping that this translation would finally demonstrate to the prince that his argument was groundless.

"But after all, why can you not understand, Katish! You are so intelligent: why can you not understand that if the count has written His Majesty a letter in which he requests him to declare his son legitimate, in that case Pierre will no longer be Pierre, but Count Bezukhov, and then under the will he will receive everything? And if the will and the letter have not been destroyed then, apart from the consolation of having been virtuous and everything that follows from that, you will be left with nothing. That is certain."

"I know that the will was written, but I also know that it is invalid, and you seem to take me for a complete fool," the princess said with the expression that women assume when they believe that they have said something witty and insulting.

"My dear princess, Ekaterina Semyonovna," Prince Vasily began impatiently, "I did not come here in order to swap insults with you, but in order to speak with a dear, good, kind, truly dear friend about your own interests. I tell you for the tenth time that if the letter to the sovereign and the will in favour of Pierre are among the count's papers, then you, my dearest, and your sisters too, are not the heirs. If you do not believe me, then believe people who know these things: I have just been speaking with Dmitri Onufrievich," (he was the family lawyer), "and he said the same."

Something clearly suddenly changed in the princess's thoughts: her thin lips turned pale (her eyes remained the same) and as she began to speak her voice burst out in loud tones that she herself had evidently not expected.

"That would be good," she said. "I never wanted and I do not want a thing." She threw her little dog off her knees and adjusted the pleats of her dress. "That is his gratitude, that is his thanks to the people who have sacrificed everything for him," she said. "Excellent! Very good! I do not want a thing, prince."

"Yes, but you are not alone, you have sisters," Prince Vasily replied. But the princess would not listen to him.

"Yes, I had known this for a long time, but I had forgotten that apart from meanness, deceit and intrigues, apart from ingratitude, the blackest ingratitude, I could expect nothing in this house . . ."

"Do you or do you not know where this will is?" asked Prince Vasily, his cheeks twitching even more violently than before.

"Yes, I was stupid, I still believed in people, and loved them, and sacrificed myself. But the only ones who prosper are those who are base and vile. I know who is behind these intrigues."

The princess was about to stand, but the prince held her back by the arm. The princess had the air of someone suddenly disillusioned with the whole of humankind: she glared angrily at the prince.

"There is still time, my friend. Remember, Katish, that this was all done suddenly, in a moment of anger and sickness, and then forgotten. It is our duty, my dear, to correct his mistake, to make his final minutes easier and not allow him to commit this injustice, not allow him to die with the thought that he has rendered miserable those people . . ."

"Those people who have sacrificed everything for him," the princess interjected, attempting to stand once again, but the prince prevented her, "which he has never appreciated, No, cousin," she added with a sigh, "I shall remember that in this world one must not expect any reward, that in this world there is neither honour nor justice. In this world one must be cunning and wicked."

"Now, listen, calm yourself; I know your noble heart."

"No, my heart is wicked."

"I know your heart," the prince repeated, "I value your friendship, and I should wish you to hold the same opinion of me. Calm yourself and let us talk plainly while there is still time – perhaps a day, perhaps an hour: tell me everything that you know about the will, most importantly of all, where it is, you must know. We will take it now and show it to the count. He must have forgotten about it and will wish to destroy it. You understand that my only wish is to carry out his wishes religiously; that is the only reason why I came here. I am only here in order to help him and you."

"I understand everything now. I know who is behind these intrigues. I know," said the princess.

"That is not the point, my dearest."

"It is your protégée, your dear Princess Drubetskaya, Anna Mikhailovna, whom I would not wish to have as a maidservant, that loathsome, repulsive woman."

"Let us not waste time."

"Oh, do not speak to me! Last winter she wormed her way in here and said such vile things, such abominable things about all of us, especially about Sophia, I cannot even repeat them – that the count became ill and would not see us for two weeks. That was the time, I know, when he wrote that repulsive, loathsome document, but I thought that the paper meant nothing."

"That is the whole point – why did you not say anything to me earlier?"

"In the mosaic document case that he keeps under his pillow! Now I know," the princess said, not answering him. "Yes, if I have a sin to answer for, it is my hate for that horrible woman," the princess almost shouted, completely changed now. "And why does she come worming her way in here? But I shall speak my mind to her, I shall. The time will come."

"For God's sake, in your righteous wrath do not forget," said Prince Vasily, smiling faintly, "that thousand-eyed envy is following our every move. We must act, but . . ."

## XXIX

While these conversations were taking place in the reception room and the princess's quarters, the carriage with Pierre (who had been sent for) and Anna Mikhailovna (who had deemed it necessary to travel with him), was driving into Count Bezukhov's courtyard. As the wheels of the carriage began crunching gently across the straw spread under the windows, Anna Mikhailovna realised, on addressing her travelling companion with words of consolation, that he was asleep in the corner of the carriage and she woke him up. Once awake, Pierre followed Anna Mikhailovna out of the carriage and only then thought about the meeting with his dying father that awaited him. He noticed that they had driven up to the rear entrance, not the main one. Just as he stepped down from the footboard, two men in tradesmen's clothes darted hastily away from the entrance into the shadow of the wall. Halting for a moment, Pierre made out several other similar figures in the shadow of the house on both sides. But neither Anna Mikhailovna, nor the servant, nor the coachman, who could not have failed to see these people, took any notice of them. "Perhaps that is how things should be," Pierre thought to himself and followed Anna Mikhailovna inside. Anna Mikhailovna walked hurriedly up the dimly lit, narrow stone staircase, calling to Pierre, who was falling behind, to hurry. Not understanding why he had to go to the count, and even less why he had to go by the back staircase, he nevertheless decided that, judging from Anna Mikhailovna's certainty and haste, it was definitely necessary. Halfway up the stairs they were almost knocked over by some men with buckets who came running down towards them, clattering their boots. These people pressed themselves back against the wall to let Pierre and Anna Mikhailovna past, and showed not the slightest surprise at the sight of them.

"Is this the way to the princesses' apartments?" Anna Mikhailovna asked one of them.

"Yes, it is," the servant replied in a loud, bold voice, as if now everything were permitted, "the door's on the left, ma'am."

"Perhaps the count did not send for me," said Pierre as he reached the landing, "I should go to my room."

Anna Mikhailovna halted and waited for Pierre to draw level with her.

"Ah, my friend," she said touching his arm with the very same gesture that she had used with her son that morning. "Remember that he is your father ... perhaps in the final agony." She sighed. "I loved you immediately, like a son. Trust in me, Pierre. I shall not forget your interests."

Pierre did not understand anything: once again he had the feeling, even more strongly, that this was how everything ought to be, and he meekly followed after Anna Mikhailovna, who was already opening the door.

The door led into the lobby of the back entrance. The eldest princess's old manservant was sitting in the corner, knitting a stocking. Pierre had never been in this wing of the house, he had not even suspected the existence of these apartments. Anna Mikhailovna enquired after the princesses' health from a girl who was overtaking them with a carafe on a tray, calling her "my dear" and "darling", and dragged Pierre further on along the stone corridor. The first door to the left from the corridor led into the princesses' living quarters. In her haste (just as everything in that house was being done in haste at that moment) the maid with the carafe had not closed the door and, as they walked past, Pierre and Anna Mikhailovna automatically glanced into the room where the eldest princess and Prince Vasily were sitting close to each other, talking. Seeing them walking by, Prince Vasily made an impatient gesture and drew himself back, while the princess leapt to her feet and slammed the door with all her might in a furious gesture, locking it.

This gesture was so unlike the princess's constant composure and the fear expressed on Prince Vasily's face was so uncharacteristic of his normal pompous gravity that Pierre halted and looked enquiringly at his guide through his spectacles. Anna Mikhailovna did not express any surprise, she only smiled gently and sighed, as if indicating that she had been expecting all of this.

"Be a man, my friend, I shall look out for your interests," she said in response to his glance and set off even more quickly along the corridor.

Pierre did not understand what was going on, and even less what it meant to look out for someone's interests, but he did understand that all of this was as it ought to be. The corridor brought them out into the dimly lit hall adjoining the count's reception room. It was one of those cold and sumptuous rooms that Pierre knew from the formal wing. But even in the middle of this room there was a bath standing empty and water had been spilled on the carpet. A servant and a junior deacon with a censer tiptoed out towards them, paying no attention to them. They entered the reception room that Pierre knew so well, with its two Italian windows, its doors to the winter garden, the large bust and the full-length portrait of Catherine the Great. The same people, in almost the same places as before, were still sitting in the reception room, whispering to each other. Everyone fell silent and glanced round at Anna Mikhailovna as she entered, with her careworn, pale face, and at Pierre, big and fat, who was following her with his head meekly lowered.

Anna Mikhailovna's face expressed the realisation that the decisive moment had arrived, and she entered the room with the bearing of a practical St. Petersburg lady, without letting Pierre away from her, even more boldly than in the morning. She evidently felt that leading after her the person whom the dying man wished to see guaranteed that she would be admitted. Casting a swift glance over everyone present in the room and noticing the count's confessor, she glided smoothly across to him and, without exactly stooping but suddenly becoming shorter, she respectfully accepted the blessing of first one clergyman, then another.

"Thank God I am in time," she said to one clergyman, "we relatives were all so afraid. This young man is the count's son," she added more quietly. "A terrible moment!"

After uttering these words, she walked up to the doctor.

"My dear doctor," she said to him, "this young man is the count's son . . . is there any hope?"

Without speaking, the doctor raised his eyes and his shoulders in a rapid movement. Anna Mikhailovna raised her eyes and shoulders in exactly the same movement, almost closing her eyes, sighed and moved away from the doctor to Pierre. She addressed Pierre in a tone of especial deference and gentle sorrow:

"Trust in His mercy," she said to him and, having indicated a small divan for him to sit on and wait, she herself moved soundlessly towards the door at which everyone kept looking and, after a barely audible sound, this door closed behind her.

Pierre, having decided to obey his guide in all things, walked towards the divan that she had pointed out to him. As soon as Anna Mikkhailovna left the room, he noticed that the glances of everyone there were directed at him with something more than curiosity and sympathy. He noticed that everyone was whispering to each other, pointing him out with their eyes, seemingly in fear or even servility. They were showing him a respect that they had never shown him before: a lady he did not know, who had been speaking with the clergymen, got up from her seat and offered it to him; an adjutant picked up a glove that Pierre dropped and handed it to him. The doctors respectfully fell silent as he walked past them and moved aside to allow him space. Pierre at first tried to sit in a different place, in order not to inconvenience the lady, he wanted to pick up the glove himself and walk round the doctors, who were not standing in his way at all; but he suddenly sensed that it would be improper, he sensed that on this night he was an individual who was obliged to perform some terrible, universally expected ritual and that therefore he must accept services from everybody. He accepted the glove from the adjutant without a word, and sat in the lady's place, setting his large hands on his knees, symmetrically positioned in the naïve pose of an Egyptian statue, having decided to himself that all this was exactly as it ought to be and that this evening, in order not to become confused

or do anything stupid, he ought not to act according to his own understanding, but submit himself entirely to the will of those who were
leading him.

Less than two minutes went by before Prince Vasily majestically
entered the room in his kaftan with three starry orders, holding his head
high. He seemed to have grown thinner since the morning; his eyes were
larger than usual when he glanced round the room and saw Pierre. He
went up to him, took his hand (which he had never done before) and
tugged it downwards, as though he wished to test how firmly it was
attached.

"Bear up, bear up, my friend. He has asked to see you. That is
good . . ." and he was about to leave. But Pierre felt it necessary to ask:

"How is . . ." He stopped short, not knowing whether it was proper
to call the dying man the count, but ashamed to call him father.

"He has suffered another stroke, half an hour ago. Bear up, my
friend . . ."

Pierre was in such a confused state of mind that at the word "stroke"
he imagined a blow from some object. He looked at Prince Vasily,
perplexed. Only afterwards did he realise that a stroke was the name of
the illness. Prince Vasily said a few words to Lorrain as he walked by
and went in through the door on tiptoe. He did not know how to walk
on tiptoe and his entire body bobbed up and down awkwardly. The
eldest princess followed him, then the clergymen and junior deacons
went through and a servant also went in at the door. There was the
sound of things being moved behind the door and finally Anna
Mikhailovna came running out with the same pale face set firm in the
performance of her duty and, touching Pierre's arm, said:

"God's mercy is inexhaustible. The rite of extreme unction is about
to begin. Let us go."

Pierre went in through the door, walking across the soft carpet, and
noticed that the adjutant and the lady he did not know and some other
servant all followed him in, as if there were no longer any need to ask
permission to enter this room.

## XXX

Pierre knew this large room, divided by columns and an arch, its floor
completely covered with Persian carpets, very well. The section of the
room beyond the columns, where on one side there was a tall mahogany
bedstead standing under silk curtains, and on the other an immense

icon case with holy images, was brightly and beautifully illuminated, in the same way as churches are lit during the evening service. Standing under the illuminated *rizas* of the icon frame was a long Voltairian couch, and lying on the couch, which was padded at the top with snow-white, uncreased, pillows that had evidently only just been changed, covered up to the waist by a bright green quilt, lay the familiar majestic figure of Pierre's father, Count Bezukhov, with that grey mane of hair reminiscent of a lion above the broad forehead, and those large, characteristically noble, wrinkles on the handsome reddish-yellow face. He was lying directly under the icons; both of his large, chubby hands had been freed from under the quilt and were lying on top of it. A wax candle had been set between the thumb and index finger of his right hand, which was lying palm-down, and an old servant, leaning forward out of his armchair, was holding it in place. The clergymen were standing over the couch in their magnificent, glittering robes, with their long, loose hair flowing down over them, holding lighted candles and slowly and solemnly intoning the service. A little way behind them stood the two younger princesses, one clutching her handkerchief and the other pressing hers to her eyes, and in front of them the eldest, Katish, with a spiteful and determined expression, not taking her eyes off the icons for a moment, as though she were telling everyone that she could not answer for herself if she looked away. Anna Mikhailovna, her face expressing meek sorrow and universal forgiveness, and the unknown lady were standing by the door. Prince Vasily was standing at the other side of the door, close to the couch, behind a carved velvet-upholstered chair, the back of which he had turned towards himself, resting his left hand with a candle on it, and was crossing himself with his right hand, each time raising his eyes upwards as he touched his fingers to his forehead. His face expressed serene piety and devotion to the will of God. "If you do not understand these feelings, then so much the worse for you," his face seemed to say.

Behind him stood the adjutant, the doctors and the male servants; as if they were in church, the men and the women had separated. Everyone there was silent, crossing themselves, and all that could be heard were the words of the service, the rich, restrained, bass singing and, in the moments of silence, the shifting of feet and sighs. Anna Mikhailovna, with that air of importance which indicated she knew what she was doing, walked across the entire room to Pierre and handed him a candle. He lit the candle and, distracted by observing the people around him, began crossing himself with the same hand that was holding it.

One of the younger princesses, Sophia, the rosy-cheeked, giggly one with the mole, was watching him. She smiled, hid her face in her

THE DEATH OF COUNT BEZUKHOV
*Drawing by M. S. Bashilov, 1866*

handkerchief and did not uncover it for a long time, but glancing at Pierre, she started laughing again. She clearly did not feel able to look at him without laughing, but was unable to stop herself looking at him, and to avoid temptation she quietly moved behind a column. In the middle of the service the voices of the clergymen suddenly fell silent and they said something to each other in a whisper; the old servant holding the count's hand stood up and turned to face the ladies. Anna Mikhailovna stepped forward and, leaning over the sick man from behind the back of the couch, beckoned Lorrain to her with her finger. The French doctor, who was standing without a lighted candle and leaning back against a column in the respectful pose of a foreigner demonstrating that, despite the difference in faiths, he understands the great importance of the rite that is being performed and even approves of it, walked over to the patient with the inaudible steps of a man in the full prime of his strength, picked up the free hand from the green quilt with his slim white fingers and, turning away, began taking the pulse and thinking. They gave the sick man something to drink and fussed around him a little, then went back to their places once again and the service continued. During this break Pierre noticed that Prince Vasily came out from behind his chair and, with that same expression which indicated that he knew what he was doing, and if other people did not understand him, then that was so much the worse for them, did not walk across to the sick man but passed by him, joining the eldest princess, and together they moved into the back of the bedroom, towards the tall bedstead under the silk curtains. From the bed the prince and the princess both went out through the back door: but just before the end of the service they returned, one after the other, to their places. Pierre paid no more attention to this circumstance than to any other, having decided once and for all in his own mind that everything that took place in front of his eyes that evening necessarily had to be as it was.

The sounds of church chanting ceased and the voice of one of the clergyman respectfully congratulated the sick man on having taken the sacrament. The sick man lay there as lifeless and motionless as ever. Everyone around him began to stir, there was a sound of footsteps and whispering, among which Anna Mikhailovna's whisper stood out most sharply of all.

Pierre listened as she said:

"He must be moved to the bed, it will be quite impossible here . . ."

The doctors, princesses and servants crowded round the sick man so tightly that Pierre could no longer see that reddish-yellow head with the grey mane which, despite the fact that he also looked at other faces, had never been out of his sight for a moment throughout the service. Pierre guessed from the cautious movements of the people who had surrounded the couch that they were lifting up the dying man and moving him.

"Grip my hand, you'll drop him like that," he heard one of the servants whisper in alarm. "From underneath . . . once more," voices said, and the heavy breathing and foot-shuffling became more urgent, as though the weight they were carrying was more than they could manage.

The bearers, whose number included Anna Mikhailovna, drew level with the young man, and for a moment he could see behind the people's backs and heads the high, bloated, open chest and fat shoulders of the sick man, raised upwards by the people who were holding him under the arms, and the grey, curly lion's mane. The head with the unusually broad brow and cheekbones, the beautiful, sensuous mouth and the majestically cool gaze had not been disfigured by the nearness of death. It was the same as Pierre had known it three months ago, when the count had sent him to St. Petersburg. But this head swayed helplessly to the uneven gait of the bearers and the cool, detached gaze did not know what to settle on.

Several moments passed in commotion beside the tall bedstead: the people who had been carrying the sick man dispersed; Anna Mikhailovna touched Pierre's arm and said: "Come." She and Pierre approached the bed on which the sick man had been placed in a ceremonial pose that was evidently related to the sacrament that had just been celebrated. He was lying with his head propped up high on a pillow. His arms were laid out symmetrically on the green silk quilt, palms down. When Pierre approached, the count looked at him, but looked at him with that gaze, the meaning and import of which no man can understand. That gaze either said absolutely nothing at all, except that as long as one has eyes, one must look somewhere, or it said too much. Pierre halted, not knowing what he should do, and glanced enquiringly at his guide, Anna Mikhailovna. With a rapid gesture of her eyes, Anna Mikhailovna indicated the sick man's hand, blowing a kiss to it with her lips. Pierre, painstakingly craning his neck forward to avoid catching the quilt, did as she advised and pressed his lips to the broad-boned, fleshy hand. The hand did not even twitch, nor did a single one of the count's muscles. Pierre again glanced enquiringly at Anna Mikhailovna, asking what he ought to do now. With her eyes Anna Mihailovna indicated to him the armchair standing by the bed. Pierre obediently began sitting down on the chair, continuing to ask with his eyes whether he was doing as he ought. Anna Mikhailovna nodded approvingly. Pierre again assumed the symmetrical pose of an Egyptian statue, clearly regretting that his awkward and fat body occupied such a large amount of space and exerting all his inner strength to appear as small as possible. He looked at the count. The count looked at the spot where Pierre's face had been when he was standing. Through her expression Anna Mikhailovna demonstrated her awareness of the touching gravity of this final moment of meeting between father and son. This continued for two minutes, which seemed like an hour to Pierre. Suddenly a trembling began in the large muscles and wrinkles of the count's face. The trembling intensified, the handsome mouth twisted (it was only at this point that Pierre realised how close his father was to death) and a vague, hoarse sound issued from the distorted mouth. Anna Mikhailovna looked hard into the sick man's eyes and, trying to guess what it was he wanted, pointed first to Pierre, then to the drink, then pronounced Prince Vasily's name in a whisper, then pointed to the quilt. The sick man's eyes and face expressed impatience. He made an effort to glance at the servant who was standing fixedly at the head of the bed.

"His excellency wants to turn on his other side," the servant whispered and stepped up in order to turn the count's heavy body to face the wall.

Pierre stood up in order to assist the servant.

While they were turning the count over, one of his arms fell back helplessly, and he made a vain effort to pull it across. Whether or not the count noticed the glance of horror with which Pierre watched that helpless arm, or whether some other fleeting thought passed through his dying mind at that moment, he looked at the insubordinate arm, at the expression of horror on Pierre's face, then again at the arm, and a weak smile of suffering, quite unsuited to his features, flickered across his face, seeming to express mockery at his own helplessness. At the sight of that smile, Pierre unexpectedly felt a trembling in his chest and a tingling in his nose, and tears clouded his vision. They turned the sick man onto his side, facing the wall. He sighed.

"He has fallen asleep," said Anna Mikhailovna, noticing one of the princesses coming to take their place. "Let us go."

Pierre left the room.

# XXXI

There was no longer anyone in the reception room apart from Prince Vasily and the eldest princess, who were sitting under the portrait of Catherine the Great and talking animatedly about something. As soon as they saw Pierre and his guide, they fell silent. The princess hid something, or so it seemed to Pierre, and whispered:

"I hate the sight of that woman."

"Katish has ordered tea to be served in the small drawing room," Prince Vasily said to Anna Mikhailovna, "why don't you go and take some refreshment, my poor Anna Mikhailovna, or your strength will give out."

He said nothing to Pierre, merely squeezed his arm with feeling just below the shoulder. Pierre and Anna Mikhailovna went through into the small drawing room.

"Nothing is so restorative after a sleepless night as a cup of this excellent Russian tea," Lorrain said with an expression of restrained vivacity, sipping from a fine handleless Chinese cup as he stood in the small round drawing room in front of the table laid with a tea set and a cold supper. Everyone who was present in Count Bezukhov's house that night had gathered round the table in order to restore their strength. Pierre remembered this little drawing room very well, with its mirrors and little tables. During balls at the count's house Pierre, who did not know how to dance, had loved to sit in this small hall of mirrors and observe the ladies in their ball gowns, with diamonds and pearls adorning bare shoulders, passing through this room, examining themselves in the brightly illuminated mirrors that repeated their reflections several times over. Now that same room was barely lit by two candles in the middle of the night and a set of tea things and supper dishes stood untidily on a single little table, and a diverse collection of dull people were sitting there, talking to each other in whispers, demonstrating with their every movement and every word that no one was forgetting what was happening just then and what was yet to take place in the bedroom. Pierre did not eat, although he felt hungry. He glanced round enquiringly at his guide and saw her tiptoeing back out into the reception room, where Prince Vasily and the eldest princess had remained. Pierre assumed that this too was as it ought to be and, after waiting for a moment, he followed her. Anna Mikhailovna was standing beside the princess and they were both talking at the same time in excited whispers:

"Be so good, my dear princess, as to permit me to know what is necessary and what is not," said the younger woman, evidently still in the same state of excitement in which she had slammed the door of her room.

"But my dear princess," Anna Mikhailovna said mildly and earnestly, blocking the way from the bedroom and not allowing the eldest princess to pass, "will it not be too distressing for poor uncle at such a moment, when he is in need of rest? A discussion of worldly matters at such a moment, when his soul has already been prepared . . ."

Prince Vasily was sitting in an armchair in his familiar pose, with one leg crossed high over the other. His cheeks were twitching violently and had sunk so that they appeared fatter at the bottom, but he had the air of a man little interested in the two ladies' conversation.

"Listen, my dear Anna Mikhailovna, leave Katish to do as she knows best. You know how the count loves her."

"I do not even know what is in this document," said Katish, turning towards Prince Vasily and indicating the mosaic document case that she was holding. "I only know that the genuine will is in his bureau, and this forgotten piece of paper . . ." She tried to walk round Anna Mikhailovna, but with a little hop Anna Mikhailovna barred her way once again.

"I know, my dear, kind princess," said Anna Mikhailovna, grabbing hold of the document case with one hand so tightly that it was clear that she would not let it go easily. "My dear princess, I beg you, I implore you, have pity on him. I implore you."

The eldest princess said nothing. The only thing to be heard were the sounds of the struggle for the document case. It was evident that if she were to speak, it would be to say something unflattering to Anna Mikhailovna. Anna Mikhailovna was clinging on tight, but despite that, her voice remained as sweet and syrupy as ever.

"Pierre, come over here, my friend. I think he has a place in a family council, does he not, prince?"

"Why do you say nothing, cousin?" the eldest princess suddenly screeched so loudly that they heard it in the drawing room and took fright at the sound of her voice. "Why do you say nothing, when anyone who wishes to can take it upon themselves to interfere and make scenes at the door of a dying man's room? Schemer!" she whispered venomously and tugged on the document case with all her strength, but Anna Mikhailovna took a few steps forward in order not to be separated from the case and renewed her grip.

"Oh!" said Prince Vasily in reproachful amazement. He stood up. "This is absurd. Come now, let go, I tell you."

The eldest princess let go.

"And you."

Anna Mikhailovna did not obey him.

"Let go, I tell you. I take everything on myself. I shall go and ask him. I . . . enough of this from you."

"But prince, after such a great sacrament, allow him a moment's peace. You, Pierre, tell us your opinion," she said to the young man, who had come right up close to them and was staring in astonishment at the princess's embittered face that had lost all decorum, and at Prince Vasily's twitching cheeks.

"Remember that you will answer for all the consequences," Prince Vasily said severely. "You do not know what you are doing."

"Loathsome woman," screeched the eldest princess, unexpectedly throwing herself at Anna Mikhailovna and snatching away the document case. Prince Vasily lowered his head and spread his arms in despair.

At that moment the terrible door at which Pierre had been looking for so long and which had always opened so quietly, was noisily thrown wide open, banging against the wall, and the middle princess ran out fluttering her arms in the air.

"What are you doing?" she said in a desperate voice. "He is dying, and you leave me alone!"

The eldest princess dropped the document case. Anna Mikhailovna quickly bent down, snatched up the object of contention and ran into the bedroom. The eldest princess and Prince Vasily came to their senses and followed her. The first to emerge a few minutes later was the eldest princess, her face pale and cold and her lower lip bitten. At the sight of Pierre, her face assumed an expression of irrepressible spite. "Yes, now you can rejoice," she said, "this what you were waiting for." Bursting into sobs, she hid her face in her handkerchief and ran out of the room.

119

THE STRUGGLE FOR THE DOCUMENT CASE
*Drawing by M. S. Bashilov, 1866*

The eldest princess was followed out of the bedroom by Prince Vasily. He staggered as far as the divan on which Pierre was sitting and fell onto it, covering his eyes with his hand. Pierre noticed that he was pale and his lower jaw was jerking and shuddering feverishly.

"Ah, my friend," he said, taking Pierre by the elbow, and there was a sincerity and infirmity in his voice that Pierre had never noticed in it before. "We sin so much, we deceive so much, and all for what? I am over fifty, my friend . . . for me . . . Everything will end in death, everything. Death is terrible." He burst into tears.

Anna Mikhailovna was the last to emerge. She walked across to Pierre with slow, quiet steps.

"Pierre!" she said.

Pierre looked at her enquiringly. She kissed the young man on the forehead, wetting his face with her tears. She paused before speaking.

"He has passed away . . ."

Pierre looked at her through his spectacles.

"Come with me, I will walk with you. Try to cry; nothing brings more relief than tears."

She led him into the dark drawing room, and Pierre was glad that no one there could see his face. Anna Mikhailovna left him there, and when she returned he was sound asleep with his head lying on his hand.

The next morning Anna Mikhailovna said to Pierre:

"Yes, my friend, it is a great loss for all of us, and especially for you. But God will support you, you are young and now, I hope, the owner of immense wealth. The will has not yet been opened. I know you well enough to be sure that it will not turn your head, but it imposes obligations on you, and you must be a man."

Pierre said nothing.

"Afterwards perhaps I shall tell you that if I had not been there, God only knows what might have happened. You know that two days ago my uncle promised me not to forget Boris, but he had no time. I hope, my friend, that you will carry out your father's wish."

Pierre did not understand anything and, blushing shyly, which was something that he rarely did, he stared at Anna Mikhailovna without speaking. After her talk with Pierre, Anna Mikhailovna drove back to the Rostovs' house and went to bed. On waking in the morning, she told the Rostovs and all her acquaintances the details of Count Bezukhov's death. She said that the count had died as she herself would wish to die, that his end was not merely touching but edifying, that she could not recall it without tears, and that she did not know who had behaved best during those terrible and solemn moments, the father, who had remembered everything and everyone in his final moments and spoken such touching words to his son, or Pierre, who had been a pitiful sight, he was so crushed, and how, despite that, he had tried to conceal his sorrow in order not to distress his dying father.

"It is hard, but it is salutary; the soul is exalted when one sees such people as the old count and his worthy son," she said. She also spoke, in disapproving terms, of the actions of the princess and Prince Vasily, but only in a whisper and as a great secret.

# XXXII

At Bleak Hills, the estate of Prince Nikolai Andreevich Bolkonsky, they were expecting the arrival of the young Prince Andrei and his princess any day, but this anticipation did not disrupt the strict order which life followed in the home of the old prince. Ever since he had been exiled to the country under Tsar Paul, General-in-Chief Nikolai Andreevich Bolkonsky, known in society as the King of Prussia, had never left Bleak Hills, living there with his daughter, Princess Marya, and her companion Mademoiselle Bourienne. Even during the present reign, although he had been granted permission to enter the two capitals, he had continued to live in the country without leaving it once, saying that if anybody needed him, then that person would have to travel the one hundred and fifty *versts* to Bleak Hills, but he had no need of anyone or anything. There were, he would say, only two sources of human vice: idleness and superstition; and only two virtues: activity and intelligence. He conducted his daughter's education himself and, in order to develop in her both of the principal virtues, until the age of twenty he gave her lessons in algebra and arranged her entire life in a pattern of ceaseless study. He himself was constantly occupied either with writing his memoirs, or calculations from higher mathematics, or turning snuffboxes on a lathe, or working in the garden and supervising the construction projects which went on unceasingly on his estate, or reading his favourite authors. Since the primary condition of effective activity is order, in his life order was also carried to the ultimate degree of precision. His appearances at table were all made under the same unvarying conditions, not just at the same hour, but the same minute. With the people who surrounded him, from his daughter to the servants, the prince was brusque and unvaryingly demanding and therefore, not being cruel, he inspired fear and respect such as not even the most cruel of men could have easily commanded. Despite the fact that he was retired and now had no influence in affairs of state, every high official in the province where the prince's estate lay regarded it as his duty to report to him and, just like the architect, the gardener and Princess Marya, waited for the appointed hour of the prince's appearance in the high-ceilinged waiting room. Everyone in that waiting room experienced the same feeling of respect and even fear at that moment when the enormous, tall door of the study opened and the old man's short figure appeared in that powdered wig, with those small, dry hands and grey, beetling brows which sometimes, when he scowled, veiled the bright gleam in his intelligent and youthful-looking eyes.

On the morning of the day of the young couple's arrival, Princess Marya, following her custom, entered the footman's room at the usual time for the morning salutation, crossing herself fearfully and inwardly reciting a prayer. Every day she went in and every day she prayed for this daily meeting to pass successfully.

The powdered old manservant sitting in the footman's room rose quietly to his feet and declared in a whisper: "If you please!"

From behind the door she could hear the regular sounds of a lathe. The princess timidly tugged at the door, which always opened easily and smoothly, and stopped in the doorway. The prince was working at the lathe and, after glancing round, he continued with what he was doing.

The huge study was filled with things that were obviously in constant use. The large desk with books and maps lying on it, the tall glazed bookcases of the library with keys in their doors, the marble table for writing in a standing position, with an open notebook lying on it, the turner's lathe with the tools laid out and wood shavings scattered around it – everything evinced constant, varied and ordered activity. The movements of the small foot shod in a Tatar boot sewn with silver thread and the firm pressure of the lean, sinewy hand betrayed in the prince the strength of fresh old age, still stubborn and capable of great endurance. After making a few more turns, he removed his foot from the pedal of the lathe, wiped off his chisel, dropped it into a leather pocket attached to the lathe, went over to the desk and called his daughter to him. He never blessed his children and, after presenting her with his stubbly cheek, still unshaven that day, he merely said, looking her over severely and yet at the same time with attentive affection: "Are you well? Well then, sit down!" (As always, he spoke curtly and abruptly, opening the geometry notebook written in his own hand and moving his armchair up with his foot.)

"For tomorrow!" he said, rapidly locating the right page and marking from one paragraph to another with his tough nail. The princess bent down over the notebook on the table. "Wait, there's a letter for you," the old man said suddenly, taking an envelope written in a woman's hand out of a pocket fixed above the desk and tossing it onto the desk.

Blotches of red covered the princess's face at the sight of the letter. She hastily took it and bent over it.

"From Héloise?" the prince asked, his cold smile revealing teeth that were still sound, but gapped and yellowed.

"Yes, from Julie Akhrosimova," said the princess, with a timid glance and a timid smile.

"I shall let two more letters through, but I shall read the third one," the prince said strictly, "I fear you are writing a lot of drivel. I shall read the third one."

"Read this one if you wish, father," replied the princess, blushing even more intensely and offering him the letter.

"The third one I said, the third one," the prince shouted curtly, pushing the letter away. Leaning his elbows on the desk, he pulled across the notebook with the geometry diagrams.

"Well now, my lady," the old man began, bending down close to his daughter and placing one hand on the back of the chair in which the princess was sitting, so that the princess felt herself enveloped on all sides by her father's long-familiar acrid scent of tobacco and old age.

"Well now, my lady, these triangles are congruent: be so good as to show me the angle *abc* . . ."

The princess glanced in fright at her father's gleaming eyes, so close to her: red blotches flooded across her face and it was clear that she did not understand anything and was so afraid that her fear would prevent her from understanding all of her father's subsequent explanations, no matter how clear they might be. Whether the teacher was at fault or the pupil, every day the same scene was repeated: everything blurred in front of the princess's eyes, she could not see anything, she could not hear anything, she could only feel her strict father's dry, stern face beside her, feel his breath and his smell and only think about getting out of the study as quickly as possible and mastering the problem in the calm freedom of her own room. The old man lost his temper: he scraped the chair on which he was sitting away from the desk and then back towards it again, trying to control himself and not fly into a passion, yet almost every time he did fly into a passion, upbraiding her and sometimes flinging the notebook away.

The princess gave the wrong answer.

"Well, what a fool you are!" cried the prince pushing the notebook aside and turning away sharply: but he immediately rose to his feet, strode up and down, touched the princess's hair with his hands and sat down again. He moved his chair up closer to the desk and continued his exposition in a forcibly restrained voice.

"This will not do from you, princess," he said as the princess, having picked up the notebook with the set lessons and closed it, was preparing to leave. "Mathematics is a great matter, my lady. And I do not want you to be like our stupid young ladies, I do not want that. You will enjoy it when you get used to it." He patted her on the cheek. "You'll forget all about this foolishness." She was about to go out, but he stopped her with a gesture and took a new book with uncut pages off the tall table.

124

THE MATHS LESSON
*Wood engraving by K. I. Rikhai after the drawing by M. S. Bashilov, 1866*

"And here we have a certain *Key to the Sacrament* which your Héloise sends you. Religious. But I don't interfere in anybody's faith. I've looked it through. Take it. Right, off you go, off you go!"

He patted her on the cheek and locked the door behind her himself.

## XXXIII

Princess Marya went back to her room with the sad, frightened expression which rarely left her and made her unlovely, unhealthy face even less lovely, and sat down at her writing desk, adorned with miniature portraits and cluttered with notebooks and books. The princess was as disorganised as her father was organised. She put the geometry note-book down and impatiently unsealed the letter. Though she was not yet reading, but merely weighing, as it were, the pleasure to come, as she turned over the small pages of the letter her face was transformed; she became visibly calmer, she sat in her favourite armchair in the corner of the room, beside an immense pier glass, and began reading. The letter was from the princess's closest friend since her childhood: this friend was that same Julie Akhrosimova who had been at the name-day celebra-tions at the Rostovs' house. Marya Dmitrievna Akhrosimova's estate bordered on Prince Bolkonsky's and she spent two months of the sum-mer in the country. The prince respected Marya Dmitrievna, although he made fun of her. Marya Dmitrievna addressed nobody but the prince with formal politeness, and she held him up as an example to all modern-day people.

Julie wrote as follows:

> *Chère et excellente amie. What a fearful and terrible thing separation is! However much I try to tell myself that half of my existence and my happiness lies in you, that despite the distance that separates us, the bonds that unite our hearts are indissoluble, my heart revolts against fate and, for all the pleasures and distractions by which I am surrounded, I cannot suppress a certain secret sadness that I have felt in the depths of my heart since the time of our separation. Why are we not together, like last summer, in our large study, on the blue divan, on the divan of 'confessions'? Why can I not, as I did three months ago, draw new moral strength from your glance, so gentle, calm and astute, which I loved so much and which I see before me as I write to you?*

Having read to this point, Princess Marya sighed and glanced round into the pier glass that stood on her right. The mirror reflected her unlovely, weak body and thin face. The eyes, always sad, now regarded themselves in the mirror with especial hopelessness. "She is flattering me," the princess thought, then turned away and continued reading. Julie, how-ever, was not flattering her friend: the princess's eyes, large, deep and radiant (sometimes it seemed as if beams of warm light radiated from them), really were so fine that very often, despite the plainness of all the rest of her face, these eyes became more alluring than beauty itself. But the princess had never seen the fine expression of her eyes, the expression that they assumed in those moments when she was not thinking about herself. Her face, like everybody else's, assumed an artificial, unnatural, foolish expression whenever it looked at itself in the mirror. She con-tinued reading:

*The whole of Moscow is talking of nothing but the war. One of my two brothers is already abroad, the other is with the Guards, who are on the march to the border. Our dear sovereign is leaving St. Petersburg, and it is assumed that he intends to expose his own precious life to the fortunes of war. God grant that the ogre of Corsica who is subverting the order of Europe may be overthrown by the angel whom the Almighty in His mercy has set over us as our ruler. In addition to my brothers, this war has also deprived me of one of the connections that lie closest to my heart. I speak of the young Nikolai Rostov, who in his enthusiasm was unable to endure inaction and left the university in order to join the army. I confess to you, dear Marya, that despite his extreme youth, his departure for the army was a great sorrow for me. This young man, about whom I spoke to you last summer, has in him so much of the nobility and genuine youthful valour that one encounters so rarely in our times among the old men of twenty. In particular, he has such an open and feeling heart. He is so pure and full of poetry that my relations with him, for all their fleeting nature, have been one of the sweetest consolations of my own poor heart, which has already suffered so much. I will tell you some time about our parting and all that was said at that parting. It is all still too fresh . . . Ah! my dear friend, you are fortunate not to know these scalding delights, these scalding sorrows. You are fortunate because the latter are ordinarily stronger than the former. I know very well that Count Nikolai is too young to become anything other than a friend to me. But this sweet friendship, these relations that are so poetic and so pure, have been my heart's necessity. But enough of that.*

*The main news with which the whole of Moscow is occupied is the death of old Count Bezukhov and his legacy. Can you believe that the three princesses received some mere trifle, Prince Vasily received nothing at all and Pierre is the heir to everything and, in addition, has actually been declared a legitimate son and therefore Count Bezukhov and the owner of the largest fortune in Russia! They say that Prince Vasily played a quite disgusting role in this whole business and that he departed for St. Petersburg in a state of great confusion. I confess to you that I have a very poor understanding of all these affairs to do with last wills and testaments; I only know that since the young man whom we all knew by the simple name of Pierre became the Count Bezukhov and the owner of one of the finest fortunes in Russia, I have been amusing myself by observing the change in the tone of the* mamans *who have marriageable daughters and of the young ladies themselves with regard to this gentleman who, let it be said in parentheses, has always seemed to me quite insignificant. Only my* maman *continues to criticise him with her usual harshness. Since everyone has been amusing themselves for two years now by seeking out fiancés for me, whom for the most part I do not even know, Moscow's matrimonial gossip now makes me the Countess Bezukhova. But you understand that I do not desire that in the least. On the subject of marriages, do you know that recently the universal aunty, Anna Mikhailovna, confided to me in the very strictest secrecy a scheme to arrange your marriage? And to none other than Prince Vasily's son Anatole, whom they wish to settle by marrying him to a wealthy noble spinster, and the parents' choice has fallen on you. I do not know how you will regard this matter, but I considered it my duty to forewarn you. They say that he is very good-looking and a great hothead. That is all I was able to learn about him.*

*But enough idle chatter. I am finishing my second page, and* maman *has sent for me in order to go to dinner at the Apraksins'.*

*Read the mystical book that I am sending you. It is immensely popular here. Although there are some things in it which are hard for the feeble human intellect to comprehend, it is an excellent book, reading it calms and exalts the soul. Goodbye. My compliments to your father and my greetings to Mademoiselle Bourienne. I embrace you with all my heart.*

*Julie*

*P.S. Send me news of your brother and his delightful wife.*

The princess thought for a moment, smiling pensively, so that her face, lit up by her radiant eyes, was totally transformed, then suddenly, getting up and walking with ungainly steps across to the desk, she took out a sheet of paper and her hand began moving across it rapidly. This is what she wrote in reply:

*Chère et excellente amie. Your letter of the 13th brought me great joy. You still love me, my poetic Julie. The separation, concerning which you speak so very badly, has clearly not had its usual effect on you. You complain of separation, but what then should I say, if I but dared – I, who am deprived of all those who are dear to me? Ah, if we did not have religion to console us, life would indeed be dismal. Why do you attribute such a strict view to me when you speak of your weakness for a young man? In that regard I am strict only with myself. I know myself sufficiently well to understand completely that, without making myself ridiculous, I cannot experience those feelings of love which seem so sweet to you. I understand these feelings in others and although, never having experienced them, I cannot approve, neither do I condemn them. It only seems to me that Christian love, love for one's neighbour, love for one's*

128

enemies, is more worthy, sweeter and finer than those feelings which can be inspired by the beautiful eyes of a young man in a poetic and loving young girl such as you.

News of the death of Count Bezukhov reached us before your letter and my father was very affected by it. He said he was the penultimate representative of a great age, and that now it was his turn, but he would do everything in his power to ensure that his turn came as late as possible. May God preserve us from that misfortune.

I cannot share your opinion of Pierre, whom I knew as a child. It seemed to me that he always had a beautiful heart, and that is the quality which I value most highly in people. As for his inheritance and the role that was played in it by Prince Vasily, it is all very sad for both of them. Ah, my dear friend, the words of our dear Saviour that it is easier for a camel to pass through the eye of a needle than for a rich man to enter into the Kingdom of Heaven – those words are terribly just. I pity Prince Vasily, and Pierre even more. That such a young man should be burdened with such a huge fortune – the number of temptations that he will have to endure! If I were asked what I desire above all else in the world, then I desire to be poorer than the poorest of beggars. I thank you a thousand times, my dear friend, for the book you have sent me, and which is creating such a stir in Moscow. However, since you tell me that among the many good things it contains there are some that the feeble human intellect cannot fathom, it seems to me superfluous to engage in incomprehensible reading, which for that very reason could not be of any benefit. I have never been able to understand the passion that certain individuals have for confusing their own thoughts by their attachment to mystical books which merely provoke doubts in their minds, and inflame their imaginations, lending them an exaggerated character entirely contrary to Christian simplicity. Let us rather read the Apostles and the Gospel. Let us not attempt to fathom the mystical content of these books, for how can we, pitiful sinners, know the terrible and sacred mysteries of Providence while we are still prisoners of the fleshly integument that erects an impenetrable veil between us and the Eternal? Let us rather limit ourselves to the study of the great laws which our Heavenly Saviour left to us for our guidance here on earth, let us try to follow them and try to realise that the less we allow our intellect to roam at will, the more pleasing we shall be to God, who rejects all knowledge that does not come from Him, and that the less we delve into that which He has preferred to conceal from us, the sooner He will grant us this revelation through his own divine reason.

My father has said nothing to me about a bridegroom, he has said only that he has received a letter and is expecting a visit from Prince

*Vasily; as far as marriage plans involving myself are concerned, I must tell you, my dear, inestimable friend, that in my opinion marriage is a divine institution to which one should submit. No matter how hard it might be for me, if it should please the Almighty to impose on me the obligations of a wife and a mother, I shall endeavour to fulfil them as faithfully as I can, with no concern for the study of my own feelings regarding the one whom He shall give me for a husband.*

*I have received a letter from my brother which notifies me of his arrival in Bleak Hills, together with his wife. This joy will be short-lived, since he is leaving us in order to take part in this war, into which we have been drawn, God only knows how or why. The echoes of war are not only heard where you are, at the centre of affairs and society, they are heard and make themselves painfully felt here too, among the agrarian labours and peace and quiet that townspeople usually imagine in the country. My father talks of nothing but campaigns and marches, of which I understand nothing, and two days ago, as I was taking my usual stroll along the village street, I saw a heart-rending scene. It was a party of recruits, enlisted from among our peasants, being sent to the army. If you could have seen the state of the mothers, wives and children of those who were leaving, and heard the sobbing and wailing on both sides. Well might one think that humanity has forgotten the laws of its Heavenly Saviour, who taught us love and forgiveness, and that it believes the greatest virtue lies in the art of killing others.*

*Goodbye, my dear, kind friend. May our Heavenly Saviour and his most Holy Mother preserve and keep you under their holy and mighty protection.*

*Marya.*

"Ah, you send your letter, princess, I have already sent mine. I wrote to my poor mother," the ever-smiling Mademoiselle Bourienne said in her rapid and pleasant voice, burring her r's and introducing an entirely different, frivolously cheerful and complacent world into the aura of bleak, introspective melancholy surrounding Princess Marya.

"I must warn you, princess," she added, lowering her voice, "that the prince has quarrelled with Mikhail Ivanovich." Burring her r's with especial vigour and listening to herself with pleasure, she said, "He is very much out of sorts, so gloomy. I warn you, you know . . ."

"Oh, no, no," replied Princess Marya. "I asked you never to tell me what mood my father is in. I do not permit myself to judge him, and I would not wish others to judge him either."

The princess glanced at the clock and, noticing that she had already missed five minutes of the time that she should have been using to play the clavichord, she set off with a frightened air to the sitting room. Between twelve and two o'clock, in accordance with the established daily routine, the prince rested and the princess played the clavichord.

# XXXIV

The grey-haired valet was dozing in his chair, listening to the count snoring in the huge study. From behind closed doors at the far side of the house, came the sounds of difficult passages, repeated for the twentieth time, in a sonata by Dussek.

At this moment a carriage and a *britzka* drove up to the porch and Prince Andrei got out of the carriage, helping his little wife out politely but coldly, as always, and letting her go ahead of him. Grey-haired Tikhon, wearing a wig, stuck his head out of the door of the footman's room, announced in a whisper that the prince was resting and hastily closed the door. Tikhon knew that neither the arrival of the son of the house nor any other unusual events could be allowed to disrupt the daily routine. Prince Andrei clearly knew this quite as well as Tikhon; he looked at his watch, as if to check whether his father's habits had changed since the last time he had seen him and, having ascertained that they had not, he addressed his wife.

"He will get up in twenty minutes. Let us go through to Princess Marya," he said.

The little princess had changed in the time that had elapsed. The bulge of her waist had become significantly larger, she bent further backwards now and had become extremely fat, but her eyes were still bright and her short, smiling lip with the faint moustache lifted just as merrily and endearingly when she spoke.

"But this is a palace!" she said to her husband, looking around with the expression worn by people offering praise to the host at a ball.

"Let's go, come on, come on."

Looking around, she smiled at Tikhon and her husband and the footman showing them the way.

"Is that Marie playing? Quiet, let us take her by surprise."

Prince Andrei followed her with a courteous, sad expression.

"You have grown old, Tikhon," he said as he walked past the old man, who kissed his hand, which he wiped with a fine lawn handkerchief.

Just before the room from which they could hear the sound of the clavichord, a pretty blonde Frenchwoman skipped out of a side door. Mademoiselle Bourienne seemed quite beside herself with delight.

"Ah, what a joy for the princess," she said to them. "At last, I must let her know."

"No, no, please . . . You are Mademoiselle Bourienne; I am already acquainted with you from the friendship that my sister-in-law feels for you," said the little princess, kissing the Frenchwoman. "She is not expecting us."

They approached the door of the divan room, from behind which they could hear the same passage being repeated over and over again. Prince Andrei stopped and frowned, as though in anticipation of something unpleasant.

Princess Lise went in. The passage broke off in the middle, there was a cry, Princess Marya's heavy footsteps and the sounds of kissing and muffled voices. When Prince Andrei went in, his wife and his sister, who had only seen each other once for a short time during Prince Andrei's wedding, were clasped tightly in each other's arms, still pressing their lips to the same spots which they had found in that first moment. Mademoiselle Bourienne was standing beside them, pressing her hands to her heart and smiling devoutly, obviously equally prepared either to burst into tears or burst out laughing. Prince Andrei shrugged and frowned, in the way that lovers of music frown when they hear a false note. The two women released each other and then once again, as though afraid of missing their chance, they grabbed each other by the hands, began kissing each other's hands and pulling their own away, and then again began kissing each other on the face and then, to Prince Andrei's absolute astonishment, they both burst into tears and started hugging and kissing each other again. Mademoiselle Bourienne burst into tears too. Prince Andrei obviously felt awkward and embarrassed, but to the two women it seemed quite natural that they should be crying, they seemed never to have imagined that this meeting could have taken place in any other way.

"Ah, my dear! Ah, Marie." Both women suddenly started talking at once and burst into laughter. "I had a dream . . ." – "So you were not expecting us? Ah, Marie, you have grown so thin . . ." – "And you have put on so much weight . . ."

"I recognised the princess immediately," interjected Mademoiselle Bourienne.

"And I never even suspected," exclaimed Princess Marya. "Ah, Andrei, I didn't even see you there."

Prince Andrei and his sister kissed, hand in hand, and he told her that she was the same old cry-baby that she always used to be. Through her tears, Princess Marya turned on her brother the warm, loving, gentle gaze of her large, radiant eyes, so lovely at that moment that his sister, always so plain, seemed beautiful to him. But that very instant she turned back to her sister-in-law and began squeezing her hand without speaking. Princess Lise spoke incessantly. Every now and then her short upper lip with the light moustache flew down for an instant, touched the right spot on the rosy-pink lower lip and then once again her smile was revealed in a bright gleam of teeth and eyes. She related an incident that had happened to them on Mtsensk Mountain, which could have proved dangerous in her condition, and then immediately announced that she had left all her dresses behind in St. Petersburg and God only knew what she would wear here, and that Andrei had changed completely, and that Kitty Odyntsova had married an old man, and that there was a perfectly serious suitor for Princess Marya, but they would talk about that later. Princess Marya was still staring silently at her brother's wife and her lovely eyes were filled with both love and sadness, as if she pitied this young woman but could not express to her the reason for her pity. She was clearly caught up in her own train of thought now, independently of what her sister-in-law was saying. In the middle of Lise's account of the latest festivities in St. Petersburg, Princess Marya turned to her brother.

"And are you definitely going to the war, Andrei?" she said with a sigh. Lise sighed too.

"Tomorrow, in fact," Marya's brother replied.

"He is abandoning me here, and God only knows why, when he could have had a promotion . . ." Princess Marya did not hear her out and, still following the thread of her own thought, she indicated her sister-in-law's belly with an affectionate glance and asked: "Will it be soon now?"

The little princess's face changed. She sighed.

"Two months," she said.

"And you are not afraid?" asked Princess Marya, kissing her again. Prince Andrei winced at this question. Lise's lip moved down. She moved her face close to her sister-in-law's and suddenly burst into tears again.

"She needs to rest," said Prince Andrei. "Don't you, Lise? Take her to your room, and I shall go to father. How is he, still the same?"

"The same, the very same, I do not know how you will find him," the princess replied happily.

"The same routine, and the walks along the avenues? The lathe?" asked Prince Andrei with a barely perceptible smile, indicating that, much as he loved and respected his father, he understood his weaknesses.

"The same routine, and the lathe, and still mathematics and my geometry lessons," Princess Marya replied happily, as though her lessons in geometry were one of the most joyful memories of her life.

# XXXV

When the twenty minutes remaining until the time for the old prince to rise had elapsed, Tikhon came to announce the young prince to his father. The old man made an exception to his regular habits in honour of his son's arrival: he ordered him to be admitted while he was dressing for dinner. The prince dressed in the old style, in a kaftan with powdered hair. As Prince Andrei entered his father's apartments – not with the peevish expression and manners that he affected in society drawing rooms, but with the animated face that he wore when he was talking with Pierre – the old man was sitting in his dressing room on a broad armchair upholstered in morocco leather, wearing a dressing gown and presenting his head to Tikhon's hands.

"Ah! The soldier! So you want to conquer Bonaparte?"

That was how the old man greeted his son. He shook his powdered head, as far as the plait being woven by Tikhon's hands would allow it.

"Make sure you set about him well, or he'll soon be listing us among his subjects. Greetings." And he proffered his cheek.

The old man was in a good mood following his nap before dinner. (He said that sleep after dinner was silver, but sleep before dinner was golden.) He peered happily at his son from under his thick, beetling brows. Prince Andrei approached his father and kissed him on the spot he indicated. He did not respond to his father's favourite topic of conversation – poking fun at modern military men, and especially at Bonaparte.

"Yes, I have come to see you, father, and with a pregnant wife," said Prince Andrei, following the movement of every feature of his father's face with eager eyes full of respect. "How is your health?"

"The only people who are unwell, brother, are fools and profligates, and you know me, busy from morning till night, abstemious, so I am well."

"Thank God," said his son, smiling.

"God has nothing to do with it. Well now, tell me," he continued, returning to his favourite hobby-horse, "how the Germans and Bonaparte have taught you to fight according to this new science of yours that they call strategy."

Prince Andrei smiled.

"Allow me to gather my wits, father," he said with a smile which showed that his father's weaknesses did not prevent him from respecting and loving him. "I've not even settled in yet."

134

"Lies, lies," cried the old man, shaking his pigtail to see whether it was firmly plaited and grabbing his son by the arm. "The house is all ready for your wife. Princess Marya will show her around and chatter away nineteen to the dozen. That is their womanish business. I am glad she is here. Sit down, talk to me. Mikhelson's army I can understand. Tolstoy's too . . . a simultaneous expedition . . . But what is the southern army going to do? Prussia, neutrality . . . that I know. But what of Austria?" He talked on in this way, rising from his armchair and walking around the room with Tikhon chasing after him and handing him articles of clothing. "And what about Switzerland? How will they cross Pomerania?"

Prince Andrei, seeing the urgency of his father's demands, began expounding the plan of operations for the proposed campaign, unwillingly at first, but then growing ever more animated and from force of habit unwittingly switching over from Russian to French in the middle of his narrative. He told his father how an army of ninety thousand was to threaten Prussia in order to draw her out of neutrality and involve her in the war, how a part of these forces was to combine with the Swedish forces at Strahlsund, how two hundred and twenty thousand Austrians in combination with a hundred thousand Russians were to operate in Italy and on the Rhine, how fifty thousand Russians and fifty thousand English would land in Naples, and how in the end an army of five hundred thousand was to attack the French from all sides. The old prince showed not the slightest interest in this account, as if he were not listening, continuing to dress himself as he walked, but he interrupted it unexpectedly three times. Once he halted it by shouting:

"White, the white one!"

This meant that Tikhon had not handed him the waistcoat he wanted. The second time he halted it by asking: "Will she have the child soon?" And on being told in reply that it would be soon, he shook his head reproachfully and said: "Not good! Carry on, carry on."

The third time, as Prince Andrei was concluding his description, the old man began singing in an old man's voice, out of tune: "*Malbrook s'en va-t-en guerre. Dieu sait quand reviendra.*" His son only smiled.

"I don't say this is a plan of which I approve," said the son, "I have only told you what is the case. Napoleon has already drawn up his own plan, no worse than this one."

"Well, you have not told me anything new." And he muttered rapidly and pensively to himself: "God knows when he'll come back."

"Go to the dining room."

Prince Andrei went out. Father and son had not spoken at all about their own affairs.

At the appointed hour the prince, powdered, fresh and shaved, entered the dining room, where his daughter-in-law, Princess Marya, Mademoiselle Bourienne and the prince's architect were waiting for him. By a strange whim of the prince, the architect was allowed at the table, although according to his station this insignificant individual could not possibly have expected any such honour. The prince, who in his life firmly maintained the distinctions between the various estates and rarely allowed even important provincial officials to join him at table, had suddenly decided to use the architect Mikhail Ivanovich, who was blowing his nose into a checked handkerchief in the corner, to demonstrate that all people are equal, and repeatedly impressed on his daughter that Mikhail Ivanovich was in no way inferior to either of them. At table, when he expounded his sometimes strange ideas, it was to the tongue-tied Mikhail Ivanovich that he appealed most often.

In the dining room, as immense and high-ceilinged as all the rooms in the house, the prince's entrance was awaited by the members of the household and the footmen standing behind each chair: the butler, with a napkin over his arm, surveyed the table setting and winked at the menservants, his agitated gaze constantly flitting from the wall clock to the door through which the prince was due to appear. Prince Andrei looked at the huge gold frame, which was new to him, containing a chart of the genealogical tree of the princes Bolkonsky, which was hung opposite an equally huge frame with a badly painted depiction (evidently by the hand of a household artist) of a crowned prince, who was supposed to have been a descendant of Riurik and the founder of the Bolkonsky line. Prince Andrei looked at this genealogical tree, shaking his head and laughing, in the manner in which people gaze at a portrait that is funny because it is such a good likeness.

"How clearly I recognise him in all of this," he said to Princess Marya, who had come over to him.

Princess Marya looked at her brother in surprise. She did not understand what he was smiling at. Everything that their father did inspired in her a respect that was not subject to discussion.

"Everyone has his own Achilles' heel," Prince Andrei continued. "With his immense intelligence, to give way to such triviality!"

To Princess Marya the audacity of her brother's judgement was incomprehensible and she was preparing to protest, when the anticipated footfalls were heard from the study; the prince entered briskly, as he always did, elated and in disarray as though deliberately representing in his hastiness the antithesis of the strict order of the house. At that very moment the large clock struck two and another clock responded in a thin voice from the drawing room; the prince halted and, from beneath the dense, beetling brows, his animated, glittering, stern eyes surveyed them all and came to rest on the young Princess Lise. At that moment the young princess experienced the same feeling that is experienced by courtiers at the entrance of the Tsar, the feeling of fear and respect which this old man inspired in everyone close to him. He stroked the princess's hair and then patted the back of her head with a movement that was clumsy, but to which she felt herself obliged to submit.

"I am glad, very glad," he said and, glancing keenly into her eyes once again, he walked quickly away and sat in his place.

"Sit down! Sit down! Mikhail Ivanovich, sit down!"

He indicated the place beside himself to his daughter-in-law and a footman moved the chair out for her. In her pregnant condition the space was cramped.

"Oho!" said the old man, surveying her rounded waist. "You were in a hurry, that's not good."

He gave a dry, cold, disagreeable laugh, the way he always laughed, with his mouth alone and not his eyes.

"You need to walk, walk as much as possible, as much as possible," he said.

The little princess did not hear, or did not want to hear, what he said. She said nothing and seemed embarrassed. The prince asked her about her father, and the princess began speaking and smiled. He asked her about acquaintances that they had in common, the princess brightened up even more and began to tell him about them, conveying greetings to the prince and relating the town gossip. As soon as the conversation touched on things that had happened, the princess became visibly more at ease.

"Princess Apraksina, the poor thing, lost her husband and cried her eyes out," she said, growing more and more animated.

As she became ever more animated, the prince regarded her ever more severely, and suddenly, as though he had now studied her sufficiently and formed a clear impression of her, he turned away and addressed Mikhail Ivanovich.

# XXXVI

"Well now, Mikhail Ivanovich, our Buonaparte is having a hard time of it. From what Prince Andrei" (he always referred to his son in this way in the third person) "has told me, huge forces are gathering against him! Yet you and I have always considered him an insignificant individual."

Mikhail Ivanovich, who quite definitely did not know when *you and I* had said any such thing about Bonaparte, but realised that he was necessary for the preamble to this favourite topic of discussion, glanced in surprise at the young prince, wondering to himself what would come of this.

"I have a great tactician here!" the prince said to his son, indicating the architect, and the conversation moved on to Bonaparte and the modern-day generals and statesmen. The old prince seemed convinced, not only that all the current public figures were mere boys with no grasp of the essentials of either warfare or statecraft, and that Bonaparte was an insignificant little Frenchman, who was only successful because there were no Potemkins and Suvorovs to oppose him; he was even convinced there were not really any political troubles in Europe, nor any war either, but that there was a comic puppet play of some kind being acted out by modern-day people pretending that they were doing something serious. Prince Andrei cheerfully endured his father's jibes at the new men, challenging his father to discussion and listening to him with evident pleasure.

"Everything from the old times may seem so fine," he said, "but did not that same Suvorov fall into a trap set for him by Moreau and was he not unable to get out of it?"

"Who told you that? Who told you?" cried the prince. "Suvorov!" And he swept aside his plate, which Tikhon deftly caught. "Suvorov! . . . Two of them, Friedrich and Suvorov . . . Moreau! Moreau would have been a prisoner if Suvorov had had a free hand, but he had the Hofs-kriegswurstschnappsrat sitting on his hands. You go and you'll recognise those Hofskriegswurstrats soon enough. Suvorov couldn't best them, so how will Mikhailo Kutuzov cope? No, my friend," he continued, "you and your generals can't manage against Bonaparte, you have to get in a Frenchman, you set a thief to catch a thief. They've sent the German Pahlen to New York, to America, to get the Frenchman Moreau," he said, alluding to the invitation that had been sent that year to Moreau to enter service with the Russians. "Wonderful! Tell me, were the Potemkins, Suvorovs and Orlovs all Germans, then? I tell you, brother, either all of you up there have lost your minds or I'm so old that I've lost mine. May God be with you, but we shall see. Bonaparte's a great general for them now! Hm!

"Mikhail Ivanych!" the old prince cried to the architect, who was setting about his *entrée* in the hope they had forgotten about him. "Didn't I tell you that Bonaparte was a great tactician? He says so too."

"But of course, your excellency," replied the architect.

The prince laughed his cold laugh once again.

138

"Bonaparte was born under a lucky star. He has excellent soldiers. That's all."

And the prince began analysing all the mistakes which, in his opinion, Bonaparte had made in all his wars, and even in affairs of state. His son did not object, but it was clear that, no matter what arguments might be presented to him, he was as little capable of changing his opinion as the old prince. Prince Andrei listened, suppressing his objections and marvelling, despite himself, at how this old man who had spent all these years alone out in the countryside could know all the military and political affairs of Europe in recent years in such great detail, and discuss them with such subtlety.

"Do you think I am an old man and do not understand the present state of affairs?" said the prince in conclusion. "I have it all right here. I don't sleep for nights at a time. Well, where is this great general of yours, where has he shown his mastery?"

"That would be a long story," his son replied.

"Off you go to your Buonoparte! Mademoiselle Bourienne, here is one more admirer of your lackey-emperor," he shouted in excellent French.

"You know, prince, that I am not a Bonapartist."

"'God knows when he'll be back . . .'," the prince sang out of tune, and laughed on an even falser note as he got up from the table.

Throughout the argument and the rest of dinner the little princess said nothing, but from time to time she glanced in fright, now at Princess Marya, now at her father-in-law. When they got up from the table, she took her sister-in-law by the hand and drew her into the next room.

"What a clever man your father is," she said. "Perhaps that is why I am afraid of him."

"Ah, but he is so kind!" said Princess Marya.

# XXXVII

Prince Andrei was leaving in the evening of the next day. The old prince, not deviating from his routine, had gone to his own quarters after dinner. The little princess was with her sister-in-law. Prince Andrei, wearing a travelling frock coat without epaulettes, had packed with his valet in the rooms allocated to him. Having personally inspected the carriage and the packing of the trunks, he ordered them to be loaded. The only things left in the room were those that Prince Andrei always carried with him: a travelling casket, a large silver wine-case, two Turkish pistols and a sabre, a present from his father that had been brought from the Ochakov campaign. Prince Andrei's travelling accessories were all in excellent order: everything was new and clean, packed in cloth covers and carefully tied with string.

At moments of departure and change in their lives, people who are capable of reflecting on their actions are usually plunged into a serious state of mind. At such moments the past is usually reviewed and plans for the future are made. Prince Andrei's expression was very pensive and tender. With his hands set behind his back, swinging round each time in a natural gesture untypical of him, he was striding quickly back and forth from corner to corner across the room, gazing straight ahead and shaking his head thoughtfully. Was he afraid of going to war, or sad at leaving his wife? Perhaps both? However, clearly not wishing to be seen in such a state, he halted when he heard footsteps in the passage, hastily unclasped his hands and stood by the table, as if he were tying on the lid of his casket, and assumed his perennial calm and impenetrable expression. They were the heavy footsteps of Princess Marya.

"They told me you had ordered the luggage to be loaded," she said, panting (she had evidently been running), "and I wanted so much to have another talk with you alone. God only knows for how long we are parting yet again. You are not angry with me for coming? You have changed so greatly, Andriusha," she added, as though in explanation of her question.

She smiled as she pronounced the word "Andriusha". She clearly found it strange to think that this stern, handsome man was the same little boy Andriusha, the curly-headed, mischievous companion of her childhood.

"But where is Lise?" he asked.

"She was so tired, she fell asleep on the sofa in my room. Andrei! What a treasure your wife is," she said, sitting on the divan facing her brother. "She is a perfect child, such a darling, cheerful child. I have quite fallen in love with her."

Prince Andrei said nothing, but the princess noticed the ironic and disdainful expression that appeared on his face.

"But one must be tolerant of little weaknesses; who does not have them, Andrei? Do not forget that she was educated and grew up in high society. And then her present situation now is far from rosy. One must always put oneself in the other person's place. To understand all is to forgive all. How do you think the poor thing feels, after the life to which she is accustomed, parting with her husband and being left alone in the country, and in her condition? It is very hard."

Prince Andrei smiled, looking at his sister, as we smile when listening to people whom we think we can see through.

"You live in the country and you do not find this life so terrible," he said.

"I am a different case. What is the point of talking about me? I do not want any other life, I cannot want it, because I do not know any other life. But Andrei, think what it means for a young society woman to be buried in the country for the best years of her life, alone, because dear papa is always occupied and I . . . you know me . . . how meagre my interests are for a woman accustomed to the best society. Madame Bourienne is the only . . ."

"I greatly dislike her, your Bourienne," said Prince Andrei.

"Oh no, she is very good and kind and, above all, to be pitied. She has no one, no one at all. To tell the truth, not only do I not need her, she is an inconvenience. You know I have always been solitary, and now more so than ever. I like to be alone . . . Father likes her very much. She and Mikhail Ivanich are the two people with whom he is always kind and gentle, because he has been a benefactor to them both. As Sterne says: 'We don't love people so much for the good they have done us, as for the good we have done them.' Father found her as an orphan in the street, and she is very good-natured. Father loves the way she reads, and she reads aloud to him in the evenings. She reads beautifully."

"But tell me truly, Marya, I think you must sometimes find father's character hard to bear?"

"I? I? What should I wish for?" she said, evidently speaking from the heart.

"He has always been brusque, and now he is becoming rather difficult, I think," said Prince Andrei, clearly in order to bewilder or test his sister by speaking of their father so lightly.

"You have so many good points, Andrei, but you have a certain pride of intellect," said the princess, as always following the train of her own thoughts rather than the course of the conversation, "and that is a great sin. How can we possibly judge our father? And even if it were possible, then what feeling, apart from profound respect, can a man such as our father inspire? I am so content and happy with him. My only wish would be for you all to be as happy as I am."

Her brother shook his head mistrustfully.

"The one thing that I do find hard – I will tell you truly, Andrei – is father's way of thinking where religion is concerned. I don't understand how a man of such immense intelligence can fail to see what is as clear as day and can go so far astray! This is my only unhappiness. But even here I have recently seen some improvement. Lately his jibes have been less barbed, and he has received one particular monk and spent a long time talking with him."

"Well, I fear that you and the monk are wasting your efforts, Masha," Prince Andrei said mockingly but affectionately.

"Ah, *mon ami*! I only pray to God and hope that he will hear me. Andrei!" she said timidly after a moment of silence. "I have something very important to ask you."

"What, my dear?"

"No, promise you won't refuse. It will give you no trouble at all and is in no way unworthy of you. You will simply console me. Promise, Andriusha," she said, thrusting her hand into her reticule and grasping something inside without withdrawing it, as though this something that she held was the object of her request and could not be revealed until she had received his promise to fulfil her request. She looked at her brother with a timid, imploring expression.

"Even if it were a lot of trouble . . ." Prince Andrei replied, as if he could guess what it was all about.

"You think what you like. I know you're just the same as father. Think what you like, but do this for me. Do it, please! Father's father, our grandfather, wore it in all the wars." She still did not take the thing she was holding out of her reticule. "Well, do you promise me?"

"Of course, but what is the problem?"

"Andrei, I shall bless you with the icon, and you must promise me that you will never take it off. Do you promise?"

"So long as it doesn't weigh two *poods* and won't sprain my neck. Anything to please you," said Prince Andrei but, instantly noticing the sorrowful expression that his sister's face had assumed at his jest, he repented. "I shall be very glad, truly, very glad, my dear friend," he added.

"Against your will He will save you and spare you and turn you to Him, because in Him alone lie both truth and peace," she said in a voice trembling with feeling, solemnly holding up in front of her brother with both hands a little old oval icon of the Saviour with a dark face, set in a silver *riza* and hung on a finely worked little silver chain. She crossed herself, kissed the little icon and held it out to Andrei.

"Please, for me . . ."

Bright rays of kindly light shone from her timidly glowing eyes. Those radiant eyes illuminated her always sickly, thin face and made it beautiful. Andrei wanted to take the icon, but she stopped him. Andrei understood: he crossed himself and kissed the icon. At one and the same time his expression was tender (he was touched), loving, affectionate and mocking.

"Thank you, my dear." She kissed his clear, brown forehead and sat down on the divan again. Neither of them spoke for a moment.

"I was telling you, Andrei, be kind and generous, as you always used to be. Don't judge Lise harshly," she began. "She is so loving, so kind and her position now is very difficult."

"I do not believe, Masha, that I've ever told you I had reason to reproach my wife for anything or that I felt dissatisfied with her. Why are you saying this to me?"

Princess Marya blushed in patches and fell silent, as though she felt guilty.

"I have said nothing," he went on, "but *something has been said* to you. And that makes me sad."

The red blotches grew even more intense on Princess Marya's forehead, neck and cheeks. She wanted to say something, but could not utter the words. Her brother guessed. After dinner the little princess had wept, saying she had a premonition that the birth would be disastrous, that she was afraid, and she had complained of her wretched fate, her father-in-law and her husband. When the tears stopped, she had fallen asleep. Prince Andrei felt sorry for his sister.

"Know one thing, Masha, there is nothing with which I can reproach *my wife*, I never have reproached her and never will; and there is nothing with which I can reproach myself concerning her, and it will always be so, no matter what my circumstances might be. But if you wish to know the truth . . . Do you wish to know if I am happy? No. Is she happy? No. Why is this? I do not know . . ."

So saying, he got to his feet, walked over to his sister, bent down and kissed her on the forehead. The lustrous glow of her beautiful eyes was unusually pensive and kind; however, he was not looking at his sister, but over her head into the darkness of the open door.

"Let us go to her, we must say goodbye. Or you go on without me, wake her up, and I will come in a moment. Petrushka!" he shouted to his valet. "Come here, take these things away. This goes on the seat, this on the right side."

Princess Marya stood up and went towards the door. She stopped.

"If you had faith, you would turn to God in prayer for Him to grant you the love that you do not feel, and your prayer would be heard."

"Yes, is that so?" said Prince Andrei. "Go, Masha, I will come in a moment."

On the way to his sister's room, in the gallery connecting one wing with the other, Prince Andrei encountered the sweetly smiling Mademoiselle Bourienne, crossing his path for the third time that day in remote passageways, with her rapturous and naïve smile.

"Ah, I thought you were in your room," she said, for some reason blushing and lowering her pretty eyes. Prince Andrei glared hard at her. "I love this gallery, it's so mysterious here."

An expression of bitter fury suddenly erupted on Prince Andrei's face, as if she and her kind were to blame for some misfortune in his life. Remaining silent and avoiding her eyes, he stared at her forehead and hair, but with such disdain that the Frenchwoman blushed and walked away without a word.

As he drew close to his sister's room, the Princess Lise was already awake, and through the open door he could hear her merry little voice, hurrying out the words one after another. She was speaking as if she wanted to make up for lost time after long restraint.

"Yes, just imagine, the old Countess Zubova with false curls and with false teeth, as if she were defiantly mocking the years . . . Ha-ha-ha."

Prince Andrei had already heard this precise phrase about the Countess Zubova and the same laugh from his wife in the company of strangers about five times. He quietly entered the room. The little princess, rotund and rosy, with her needlework in her hands, was sitting in an armchair, prattling incessantly, picking over her St. Petersburg reminiscences and running through her phrases. Prince Andrei went up to her, stroked her hair and asked if she was rested now after the journey. She made some reply and then continued with the same conversation.

The coach and team of six horses were standing at the entrance. Outside it was a warm autumn night. The coachman could not see the shafts of the carriage. On the porch people were bustling about with lanterns. The large windows of the huge, beautiful house were ablaze with lights. The domestics were jostling in the lobby, wishing to say goodbye to the young prince; all the members of the household were standing in the hall: Mikhail Ivanovich, Mademoiselle Bourienne, Princess Marya and Princess Lise. Prince Andrei had been called to the study by his father, who wanted to take his leave of him face to face. Everybody was waiting for them to come out.

When Prince Andrei entered the study, the old prince was sitting writing at the desk in his old man's spectacles and the white dressing gown in which he never received anyone. He glanced round.

"Are you going?" And he started writing again.

"I've come to take my leave."

"Kiss me here." He pointed to his cheek. "Thank you, thank you."

"What are you thanking me for?"

"For not putting things off, not clinging to a woman's skirt. Duty above everything. Thank you, thank you!" And he carried on writing so that splashes of ink flew from his creaking pen. "If there is something you need to say, say it. I can do these two things at the same time," he added.

"About my wife . . . I already feel guilty for leaving a pregnant woman on your hands . . ."

"Don't tell lies. Say what you want to say."

"When the time comes for my wife to give birth, during the final days of November, send to Moscow for the *accoucheur* . . . Let him be here."

The old prince stopped what he was doing and fixed his son with a strict eye, as if he did not understand.

"I know that no one can help, if nature will not," said Prince Andrei, clearly embarrassed. "I agree that out of a million cases, only one turns out badly, but it is our fantasy, hers and mine. They have said things to her, she has seen it in a dream, and she is afraid."

"Hm . . . hm . . ." the old prince mused to himself, carrying on writing. "I will do it." He dashed off his signature, suddenly turned quickly towards his son and laughed. "A bad business, eh?"

"What is bad, father?"

"The wife!" said the old prince with curt emphasis.

"I do not understand," said Prince Andrei.

"But there is nothing to be done, my friend," said the prince, "they are all like that, you can't get unmarried again. Don't worry, I won't tell anyone, but you know it yourself."

He took hold of his son's hand with his own bony little hand, shook it, glanced straight into his son's face with his quick, lively eyes that seemed to see right through people, and laughed his cold laugh again.

The son sighed, confessing with this sigh that his father had understood him. The old man continued folding and sealing letters, grabbing up and throwing down the sealing wax, seal and paper with his customary rapidity.

"It can't be helped. She's a beauty! I will do everything. Don't you worry," he rattled out during the process of sealing.

Andrei said nothing; he was glad to know that his father had understood him. The old man stood up and held out a letter to his son.

"Listen," he said, "do not concern yourself about your wife: everything that can possibly be done, will be done. Now listen: give this letter to Mikhail Illarionovich. I have written that he should place you somewhere really useful and not keep you as an adjutant for long. A loathsome position. You tell him that I remember him and love him. And write to say how he receives you. If he is good, serve him. The son of Nikolai Andreich Bolkonsky will never serve under anyone out of charity. Well, now come here."

He spoke so rapidly that he did not finish half his words, but his son was used to understanding him. He led his son over to the bureau, lowered the lid, pulled out a drawer and took out a notebook filled with his own large, tall, narrow handwriting.

"I am certain to die before you. So that you know, here are my memoirs, send them to the Emperor after my death. Now, here is a bank note and a letter. It is a prize for the person who will write a history of Suvorov's wars. Send it to the Academy. Here are my remarks, when I am gone read them for yourself, you'll find them useful."

Andrei did not tell his father that he was sure to live a long time yet. He realised that he should not say that.

"I will do everything you say, father," he said.

"Well, and now goodbye." He gave his son his hand to kiss and embraced him. "Remember one thing, Prince Andrei – if they kill you, it will hurt this old man badly . . ." He paused unexpectedly, then suddenly continued in a shrill voice: "But if I learn that you have not conducted yourself like the son of Nikolai Bolkonsky, I shall be ashamed."

"You did not need to tell me that, father," said the son, smiling.

The old man paused.

"And I also wanted to ask you," continued Prince Andrei, "if I should be killed and if I should have a son, keep him by your side, as I was telling you yesterday, let him grow up with you, please."

"Not let your wife have him?" the old man said and laughed joyfully. They stood facing each other without speaking. The old man's quick, lively eyes gazed directly into his son's. Something twitched in the lower part of the old prince's face.

"Farewell, on your way," he said suddenly said. "On your way!" he shouted in a loud, angry voice, opening the door of the study.

"What is it, what?" the little princess and Princess Marya asked, catching sight of Prince Andrei and, for just a moment, the figure of the old man in a white dressing gown, glancing out of the doorway, wearing his old man's glasses and no wig, shouting in an angry voice.

Prince Andrei heaved a deep sigh and gave no answer.

"Well," he said, turning to his wife, and this "well" sounded like a cold sneer, as if he were saying: now try getting up to your tricks.

"Already, Andrei?" said the little princess, freezing like ice and looking at her husband in terror. He put his arms round her. She shrieked and fell on his shoulder in a faint.

He carefully drew away the shoulder on which she had slumped and glanced into her face, then seated her gently in an armchair.

"Goodbye, Marya," he said quietly to his sister, then they kissed each other, holding hands, and he strode rapidly out of the room.

Princess Lise lay in the armchair and Mademoiselle Bourienne massaged her temples. Princess Marya, with her tearful, beautiful eyes, supported her sister-in-law and continued to gaze at the door through which Prince Andrei had left, making the sign of the cross after him.

From the study, like gunshots, came the rapidly repeated, angry sounds of the old man blowing his nose. As soon as Prince Andrei had left, the door of the study opened swiftly and the old man emerged, a severe figure in a white dressing gown.

"Has he gone? That's good, then," he said and, casting a furious glance at the insensible little princess, he shook his head reproachfully and slammed the door shut again.

# PART TWO

# I

---

In October 1805, Russian forces were occupying the villages and towns of the Archduchy of Austria, with the fresh regiments that kept arriving from Russia and burdening still further the local population on whom they were quartered, setting up camp around the Braunau fortress. Kutuzov had made his own headquarters in Braunau.

On the 8th of October, one of the infantry regiments newly arrived at Braunau was stationed half a mile from the town, anticipating a review by the commander-in-chief. Despite the non-Russian countryside and surroundings – fruit orchards, stone walls, tiled roofs, mountains visible in the distance – the regiment adopted exactly the same attitude towards the non-Russian people who gazed at the soldiers full of curiosity, as might any Russian regiment who were preparing themselves for an inspection anywhere in the middle of Russia. The soldiers, in heavy uniforms with high-hoisted knapsacks and rolled-up greatcoats around their shoulders, and the officers, in light uniforms with long, slim swords that knocked against their legs, felt as much at home here as in any district of Russia, as they surveyed the familiar ranks all around them, and the familiar strings of carts behind the ranks, and the more familiar, even too-familiar, figures of their superiors ahead of the ranks and, up further ahead, the tethering-posts of the Uhlan Regiment and the artillery batteries that had travelled with them throughout the campaign.

The evening before, during the final day's march, an order had come through that the commander-in-chief would inspect the regiment in marching formation. However, the wording of the order had seemed unclear to the regimental commander and the question had arisen as to whether it meant in marching dress or not – but a council of battalion commanders had finally decided, on the grounds that it was always better to bow too low than not to bow low enough, to present the regiment in parade dress, which meant that the soldiers, after a day's march of thirty *versts*, had not been allowed a wink of sleep, but had spent the whole night mending and cleaning, while the adjutants and company commanders had been numbering off and transferring men to the reserve, so that by morning, instead of the straggling, dirty crowd it had been the day before on the final leg of the march, the regiment presented a well-ordered body of three thousand men, every one of whom knew his place and his job and every one of whom had every button and strap in place, all brilliantly clean. Not only was the exterior in good order, but if the commander-in-chief had chosen to peep under the uniforms, then on every man he would have seen an equally clean shirt and in every knapsack he would have found the complete regulation number of items, "lock, stock and barrel", as the soldiers say. There was only one circumstance concerning which no one could feel assured. That was the footgear. More than half of the soldiers had boots that were badly battered and split, and no matter how much they tried to patch up these defects, they were an insult to military eyes accustomed to good order. However, this shortcoming was not due to any fault of the regimental commander since, despite repeated requests, he had not been allocated any supplies from the relevant Austrian department, and the regiment had covered three thousand *versts* on foot.

The regimental commander was an ageing, ruddy-faced general with greying eyebrows and whiskers, stout, thickset, and deeper from front to back than across his shoulders. He was wearing a brand-new uniform that still bore the creases from being folded, with thick gold epaulettes which, rather than hanging down, seemed to raise his corpulent shoulders higher. The regimental commander had the air of a man who is happily performing one of life's most solemn duties. He strode to and fro in front of the line and as he strode, he swaggered with every step, arching his back slightly. It was clear that the regimental commander was admiring his regiment, that he was happy with it and that all his mental powers were occupied with nothing other than the regiment. And yet despite this, his swaggering gait seemed to suggest that, in addition to military interests, no small place was occupied in his heart by the interests of social life and the fair sex.

"Well, Mikolai Mitrich, dear fellow," he said with feigned careless-ness, addressing a battalion commander (the battalion commander leaned forward, smiling; it was clear that they were happy). "Well, Miko-lai Mitrich, dear fellow, we had a pretty tough time of it all right last night" (he winked). "But things seem all right" (he looked over the regiment). "I don't think the regiment looks too bad. Eh?" He was evidently speaking ironically.

The battalion commander understood his jolly irony and laughed.

"It wouldn't be dismissed from a parade ground, even the Empress Meadow, what?" said the regimental commander, laughing.

At this point, two horsemen hove into sight on the road from the town, which had been posted with signalmen. These were an adjutant and, riding behind him, a Cossack. The regimental commander looked hard at the adjutant and turned away, concealing beneath his demeanour of indifference the alarm that this sight had provoked. He only glanced round again when the adjutant was just three steps away, and with that subtle air of simultaneous civility and familiarity which field commanders use to address younger and more junior officers attached to their commanders-in-chief, he prepared to listen to what the adjutant had to say.

The adjutant had been sent from the general staff to confirm to the regimental commander what had not been clearly expressed in the previous day's order, that is to say, that the commander-in-chief wished to see the regiment in precisely the same condition in which it had marched, in greatcoats, guns covered and without any preparations.

The previous day a member of the Hofkriegsrat in Vienna had arrived to see Kutuzov with proposals and demands to proceed as soon as possible to unification with the army of the Archduke Ferdinand and Mack, and Kutuzov, who did not consider this unification advantageous, was intending to present to the Austrian general, among other arguments in support of his opinion, the lamentable condition in which troops were arriving from Russia. This was the commander-in-chief's purpose in wishing to meet the regiment: the worse the condition of the regiment, the more pleased its commander-in-chief would be. Although the adjutant did not actually know all these details, he conveyed to the regimental commander the commander-in-chief's absolute insistence that the men should be in greatcoats with guns covered, otherwise the commander-in-chief would be displeased. After listening to these words, the regimental commander lowered his head, twitched his shoulders and, without speaking, spread his arms wide in a sanguine gesture.

"A fine mess we've made of it now," he said, without raising his head. "I told you so, Mikolai Mitrich, in marching order means in greatcoats," he told the battalion commander reproachfully. "Oh, my God!" he added, but there was not a trace of irritation in his words and his gesture, only zeal to serve his commander and the fear of failing to please him. He stepped forward resolutely. "Company commanders!" he shouted in a voice accustomed to command. "Sergeant-majors! How soon will *his excellency* be here?" he asked the adjutant with an expression of polite respect that was evidently intended for the individual of whom he was speaking.

"In an hour, I think."

"Will we have time to change them?"

"I don't know, general . . ."

The regimental commander, approaching the ranks himself, gave

153

instructions to change back into greatcoats. The company commanders went dashing to their companies, the sergeant-majors began bustling about (the greatcoats were not in perfect order), and all at once the previously orderly and silent squares of men heaved and sprawled and began buzzing with talk. On all sides soldiers began running off or running back, hoisting up knapsacks with a jerk of the shoulder and tugging the straps over their heads, unrolling greatcoats and raising their arms high to thrust them into the sleeves.

Half an hour later they were all back in their previous formation, except now the squares had changed from black to grey. The regimental commander walked out in front of the regiment, again with his swaggering gait, and looked it over from a distance.

"What's this now? What's this?" he shouted, halting and grabbing at his sword-knot with his hand twisted inwards. "Number three company commander to the general!" "Commander to the general! Number three company to the general," murmured voices in the ranks and an adjutant ran off to look for the tardy officer. When the sounds of the zealous voices, now crying "the general to number three company" reached their intended destination, the officer required appeared from behind the company, and although he was an elderly man and no longer accustomed to running, he set off at a trot towards the general, tripping clumsily over the toes of his boots. The captain's face expressed the anxiety of a schoolboy who has been told to recite a lesson that he has not properly learned. Blotches appeared on a nose already red, evidently from over-indulgence, and the shape of his mouth kept shifting. The regimental commander looked the captain over from head to toe as he approached, wheezing and checking his stride as he drew closer.

"You'll be dressing the men in sarafans soon! What's that?" shouted the regimental commander, thrusting out his lower jaw and pointing at a soldier in the ranks of the third company in a greatcoat the colour of high-quality factory cloth that was different from the other greatcoats. "Where were you? When the commander-in-chief is expected, you leave your post? Eh? I'll teach you to dress men up for an inspection in fancy kaftans! Eh?"

Keeping his eyes fixed on his superior, the company commander pressed his two fingers harder and harder against the peak of his cap, as though he now saw his only salvation in this pressing. The battalion commanders and adjutants stood somewhat further back, not knowing which way to look.

"Well, why don't you say anything? Who's that you've got dressed up like a Hungarian?" the regimental commander joked sternly.

"Your excellency . . ."

154

"What's that, 'your excellency'? Your excellency, your excellency! But what's wrong, your excellency, nobody knows."

"Your excellency, that's Dolokhov, the demoted . . ." the captain said quietly, with an expression which seemed to suggest that in a case of demotion, an exception could be made.

"What, has he been demoted to field-marshal, or to private? If he's a private, he must be dressed the same as everyone else, in regulation uniform."

"Your excellency, you yourself gave him permission on the march."

"Permission? I gave permission? You're always the same, you young people," said the regimental commander, cooling down a little. "I gave permission. Say anything to you and you go and . . . What?" he said, growing irritated again. "Be so good as to dress the men properly."

And, after glancing round at the adjutant, the regimental commander set off towards the regiment, with that swaggering gait that still somehow expressed a certain partiality for the fair sex. It was clear that he was enjoying his own irritation and as he passed along the line of the regiment, he sought further pretexts for his wrath. After upbraiding one officer for a poorly polished badge and another for the unevenness of his line, he approached the third company.

"What way is that to stand? Where's your leg? Where is it?" the regimental commander yelled with a note of suffering in his voice, when he was still five men away from the soldier dressed in the bluish greatcoat.

This soldier, who differed from all the others in the fresh complexion of his face and especially of his neck, slowly straightened out his bent leg and looked the general straight in the face with his bright and insolent gaze.

"Why the blue greatcoat? Off with it! Sergeant-major! Change his coat . . . the rott . . ." He was not able to finish what he was saying.

"General, I am obliged to carry out orders, but not obliged to endure . . ." the soldier said with passionate haste.

"No talking in the ranks! No talking, no talking!"

". . . not obliged to endure insults," Dolokhov said in a loud, resonant voice with an expression of unnatural solemnity that struck everyone who heard him unpleasantly. The eyes of the general and the soldier met. The general fell silent, and he angrily tugged at his tight scarf.

"Be so good as to change your dress, if you please," he said, walking away.

# II

---

"He's coming!" a signalman shouted at just that moment.

The regimental commander, flushing, ran up to his horse, took hold of the stirrup with trembling hands, threw his body across, righted himself, drew his sword and, with a cheerfully resolute face, his mouth opened to one side, prepared to shout. The regiment fluttered like a bird settling its feathers and froze.

"Atten-tion!" shouted the regimental commander in a heart-stopping voice that was happy for himself, strict towards the regiment and welcoming to his approaching superior.

With its springs rattling gently, the tall, light-blue Viennese carriage harnessed in tandem raced at a brisk trot along the broad unsurfaced road lined with trees, and galloping behind the carriage came the retinue and an escort of Croats. Sitting beside Kutuzov was an Austrian general in a white uniform that looked strange among the black Russian ones. The carriage halted at the regiment. Kutuzov and the Austrian general were talking quietly and Kutuzov smiled gently as stepped down heavily, lowering his foot from the footboard. It was exactly as if those three thousand men holding their breath as they gazed at the two of them and the regimental commander did not even exist.

A shout of command rang out and again the regiment shuddered as it jangled and presented arms. The commander-in-chief's weak voice rang out in the deathly silence. The regiment bellowed: "Good Health to You, Your Ex-ex-ex-ency!" And then everything froze again. At first Kutuzov stood still on one spot while the regiment moved, then Kutuzov began walking along the ranks, with the white general beside him and accompanied by the retinue.

From the way in which the regimental commander saluted the commander-in-chief, boring into him with his eyes, standing to attention and drawing himself up, the way he leaned forward as he followed the generals along the ranks, scarcely restraining his quivering swagger, the way he jumped at the commander-in-chief's every word and movement, it was clear that he took even greater pleasure in carrying out the duties of a subordinate than the duties of a superior. Thanks to the strict discipline and diligence of the regimental commander, the regiment was in capital condition in comparison with others that were arriving in Braunau at that time. There were only two hundred and seventeen stragglers and sick. In reply to the chief-of-staff's question concerning the

KUTUZOV
*Engraving by Cardelli*

needs of the regiment the regimental commander, leaning forward, made bold to report in a whisper and with a deep sigh that their footwear had suffered very, very badly.

"Well, it's the same song everywhere," the chief-of-staff said nonchalantly, smiling at the general's naïvety and thereby indicating that what seemed to the regimental commander to be a peculiar misfortune was the common lot of all the forces who were arriving and it had been foreseen. "You'll set that to rights here, if you're quartered here a while."

Kutuzov walked along the ranks, halting from time to time and saying a few warm words to officers whom he knew from the Turkish War, and sometimes even to soldiers. Glancing at their shoes, he shook his head sadly several times and pointed them out to the Austrian general with an expression as if he were not reproaching anyone for this, but could not help seeing how bad it was. Each time this happened, the regimental commander ran forwards, afraid of missing what the commander-in-chief was saying about the regiment. Walking behind Kutuzov at a distance from which every softly spoken word could be heard, came the twenty or so members of his retinue. The gentlemen of the retinue clearly did not feel the same superhuman fear and respect for Kutuzov as the regimental commander was exhibiting. They were talking among themselves and sometimes laughing. Walking closest of all behind the commander-in-chief was a handsome adjutant. It was Prince Bolkonsky. Walking alongside him was a tall cavalry staff officer, extremely fat, with a kind, smiling, handsome face and moist eyes. This massive officer could hardly restrain the laughter provoked by the dark-haired officer of the hussars walking alongside him. This cornet officer of the hussars was staring, with a straight face and fixed expression in his eyes, at the regimental commander's back and mimicking his every movement with a serious expression. Every time the regimental commander quivered and leaned forward, the officer of hussars quivered and leaned forward in precisely the same way. The fat adjutant laughed and nudged the others to get them to watch the amusing fellow.

"*Mais voyez donc*, do look," said the fat officer, nudging Prince Andrei. Kutuzov walked slowly and listlessly past the thousands of eyes that were rolling out of their sockets as they tried to follow the commander. On drawing level with the third company, he suddenly halted. The retinue, not having anticipated this halt, involuntarily advanced closer to him.

"Ah, Timokhin!" said the commander-in-chief, recognising the captain with the red nose who had been rebuked for the blue greatcoat.

It had seemed quite impossible to stand more rigidly to attention than Timokhin had stood when the regimental commander was rebuking him. But when the commander-in-chief addressed him, he drew himself up so very far that had the commander-in-chief looked at him a moment longer, the captain would have been quite incapable of sustaining his pose, and so Kutuzov, clearly understanding his situation and wishing the captain, on the contrary, nothing but good, hastily turned away. A barely perceptible smile ran across Kutuzov's plump face.

"A comrade from back at Izmail," he said. "A brave officer. Are you pleased with him?" Kutuzov asked the regimental commander.

And the regimental commander, reflected yet again in the hussar cornet's movements as if in an invisible mirror, quivered, stepped forward and replied:

"Very pleased, your excellency."

"He had a weakness," said Kutuzov, smiling and moving away from him. "He drank."

The regimental commander took fright, wondering whether he was to blame in this matter and made no reply. Kutuzov began telling the Austrian general something, speaking in French. At that moment the cornet of the hussars noticed the face of the captain with the red nose and tightly tucked-in belly, and mimicked his face and pose so precisely that the fat officer was unable to restrain his laughter. Kutuzov swung round. The cornet was clearly able to control his face just as he wanted; in the moment it took for Kutuzov to turn round, the cornet had already managed to assume first a grimace and then the most serious, respectful and innocent expression. But there was something ingratiating and ignoble in his bird-like face and twitching figure with its high-raised shoulders and long, thin legs. Prince Andrei turned away from him with a frown.

The third company was the last, and Kutuzov began thinking, clearly trying to recall something. Prince Andrei stepped out of the retinue and, speaking in French, said quietly:

"You instructed me to remind you about the demoted man Dolokhov in this regiment."

"Where is Dolokhov here?" asked Kutuzov.

Dolokhov, now kitted out in a grey soldier's greatcoat, did not wait to be called out. A handsome, trim figure of a soldier with blond hair and clear blue eyes stepped out from the ranks. He measured out his stride with a perfection that made his skill strikingly obvious and left an unpleasant impression precisely because of its excessive precision. He walked up to the commander-in-chief and presented arms.

"A complaint?" asked Kutuzov, frowning slightly. Dolokhov did not reply. He was playing on his position, without feeling the slightest embarrassment, and noted with evident delight that the regimental commander shuddered and blanched at the word "complaint".

"This is Dolokhov," said Prince Andrei.

"Ah!" said Kutuzov. "I hope that this lesson will reform you, be a good soldier now. The Emperor is merciful. And I shall not forget you if you deserve it."

The wide-open, light-blue eyes gazed at the commander-in-chief as insolently as at the regimental commander, as if tearing asunder with their expression the veil of convention that set the commander-in-chief and the soldier so far apart.

"I have one request to make, your excellency," he said in his resonant, firm, unhurried voice, with its dry, ecstatically bombastic tone. "I request you to give me a chance to make amends and prove my devotion to His Majesty the Emperor and to Russia."

Dolokhov uttered this theatrical speech with animation (he flushed brightly as he said it). But Kutuzov turned away. The same smile that altered only the eyes flitted across his face as when he had turned away from Captain Timokhin. This time too he turned away and frowned, as if wishing in this way to state that everything that Dolokhov had said to him, and everything that he could have said, had already been known to him for a long, long time, that he was tired of all this, and that all this was not at all what was needed. He turned away and set off towards the carriage.

# III

The regiment broke up into companies and set out for its appointed quarters not far from Braunau, where it hoped to obtain shoes and clothes and to rest after its days of hard marching.

"Don't hold it against me, Prokhor Ignatych," said the regimental commander, overtaking the third company as it moved towards its quarters and approaching its captain, Timokhin, who was walking at the front. Having dealt successfully with the review the regimental commander's face expressed irrepressible joy. "Service to the Tsar . . . I have to . . . sometimes you give someone in the ranks a dressing down . . ." (he seized Timokhin's hand with joyful agitation). "I'll be the first to apologise, you know me . . . well . . . I hope . . . Most grateful." And he held his hand out again to the company commander.

"For goodness' sake, general, how would I dare," the captain replied, his nose reddening. He smiled, revealing with his smile the lack of two front teeth, smashed out with a musket butt at Izmail . . .

"Yes, inform Mr Dolokhov that I shall not forget him, he needn't worry. But tell me, please, I have been wanting to ask what . . . how is he behaving himself? And all that . . ."

"In the line of service he's very correct, your excellency . . . as for his character . . ." said Timokhin.

"What, what about his character?" asked the regimental commander.

THE MILITARY REVIEW: KUTUZOV AND DOLOKHOV
*Drawing by M. S. Bashilov, 1867*

"There are days on end, your excellency," said the captain, "when he comes over all bright and clever and good-natured. Then all the soldiers love him, your excellency. But some days he's a wild beast. In Poland he nearly killed a yid, by your leave . . ."

"Well yes, well yes," said the regimental commander, "still, one must have pity on a young man in misfortune. Important connections, after all . . . connections . . . So just you mind . . ."

"Yes, your excellency," said Timokhin, making it clear with his smile that he understood his superior's wishes.

"Well yes, yes."

The regimental commander sought out Dolokhov in the ranks and reined in his horse.

"Till the first action, then epaulettes," he said, addressing Dolokhov. Dolokhov glanced round but did not say anything and did not alter the expression of his sneering, smiling mouth.

"Well, that's all right, then," the regimental commander continued. "A glass of vodka each for the men from me," he added loudly, so that the soldiers would hear. "I thank you all. God be praised!" And he rode round the company and approached the next one.

"Now he really is a good man, someone you can serve under," Timokhin said to a subaltern walking beside him.

"Heart's the word all right . . ." (the regimental commander was nicknamed the king of hearts). "Didn't he say anything about extra pay?" asked the subaltern.

"No."

"That's bad."

The regimental commander's happy mood had infected Timokhin. After talking with the subaltern, he went up to Dolokhov.

"Well, old man," he said to Dolokhov, "after you talking to the commander-in-chief, our general's turned sweet on you as well."

"Our general's a swine," said Dolokhov.

"It won't do to go saying things like that."

"Why not, if it's true?"

"But it won't do, and by saying that you're offending me."

"I don't wish to offend you, because you're a good man, but he . . ."

"Come, come, that won't do."

"All right, I won't."

The commander's happy mood after the review was transmitted to the soldiers as well. The company marched along merrily. On all sides there were soldiers' voices talking to each other.

"How come they said Kutuzov was half-blind, with one eye."

"Well he is! As one-eyed as they come."

"Nah . . . brother, he's sharper-eyed than you are, boots and leg wrappings and all, he looked everything over."

"The way he looked at my feet, brother . . . Well! I thought . . ."

"And that other one with him was an Austrian, looked like he'd been daubed with whitewash. White as flour. Scours it up, I reckon, like a weapon."

"What about it, Fedeshou, did he say as when the counter-attack will start, you were standing closer? Everyone was saying Boonaparte himself is stationed at Braunovo."

"Boonaparte stationed! They're talking nonsense, the fools! Don't know a thing. The Prussian's up in arms now! And the Austrian, you know, he's putting him down. Soon as he makes peace, then the war with Boonaparte will start up. And he says Boonaparte's stationed at Braunovo! Shows you what kind of fool he is. Don't go believing everything you hear."

"Look, those damn billeting officers! There's the fifth company already turning into a village, they'll have their gruel cooked and ready before we even get to where we're going."

"Give us a rusk, you devil."

"Did you give me that baccy, yesterday? So there, brother. Well, never mind, have it anyway."

"They could at least call a halt, or we'll cover another five *versts* without a bite."

"Wasn't it really grand the way the Germans gave us carriages at Olmütz! Riding along real grand, like."

"But the folks round here, my friend, are a desperate lot altogether. Back there they was like the Poles, all under the Russian crown, but now, brother, there's nothing but Germans everywhere."

"Singers to the front!" the captain's voice shouted.

About twenty men ran out in front of the company from various lines. The choirmaster drummer turned to face the singers and with a wave of his hand launched into a long, drawn-out soldier's song that began: "Barely dawn, the sun was just rising . . ." and ended with the words: "And so, brothers, there'll be glory for us and Father Kamensky . . ." This song had been composed in Turkey, and now it was being sung in Austria, the only change being that they replaced "Father Kamensky" with "Father Kutuzov".

After rattling off these final words in smart soldier fashion and waving his hands as if he were throwing something down on the ground, the drummer, a lean and handsome soldier of forty or so, looked the singer-soldiers over sternly and screwed his eyes shut briefly. Then, after making certain that all eyes were fixed on him, he seemed to lift some invisible, precious object above his head cautiously with both hands, hold it there for a few seconds and suddenly fling it down recklessly.

"*Ah, you bowers, bowers mine . . .*" – "*Ah, new bowers mine,*" twenty voices sang, joining in, and the spoon-player, despite the weight of his equipment, bounded forward and started walking backwards in front of the company, working his shoulders and menacing someone here and there with his spoons. The soldiers walked with a broad stride, swinging their arms in time to the song, falling into step despite themselves. From behind the company there came the sound of wheels, the crunch of springs and the clatter of horses' hooves. Kutuzov and his retinue were returning to the town. The commander-in-chief gave a sign for the men to continue marching freely, and his face and the faces of all his retinue expressed pleasure at the sound of the song, at the sight of the dancing soldier and the soldiers of the company marching along merrily and briskly. In the second row, on the right flank, the side on which the carriage was overtaking the company, they could not help but notice a handsome blue-eyed, broad, thickset soldier who was marching along especially briskly and gracefully in time to the song and who glanced merrily at the faces of the men riding past with an expression that seemed to say he pitied everyone who was not marching with the company just then. The cornet of hussars with the high shoulders fell back from the carriage and rode up to Dolokhov.

The cornet of the hussars, Zherkov, had at one time belonged to the wild social circle led by Dolokhov. Zherkov had met Dolokhov abroad as a private, but at the time had not deemed it necessary to recognise him. Now he addressed him with the joyful greeting of an old friend.

"My dearest friend, how are you?" he said to the sounds of the song, matching his horse's stride to the stride of the company.

"Greetings, brother," Dolokhov replied coldly, "as you can see."

The brisk song lent a special significance to the tone of rakishly familiar merriment with which Zherkov spoke, and to the deliberate coldness of Dolokhov's replies.

"Well, how are you getting on with your people, with the commander?" asked Zherkov.

"All right, they're fine people. How did you worm your way on to the staff?"

"I was attached. I'm on duty."

They said nothing for a moment. *She loosed the brave falcon from out her right sleeve*," said the song, making them feel spry and cheerful despite themselves. Their conversation would probably have been rather different, had they not been speaking against the sound of singing.

"Is it true then, they've beaten the Austrians?" asked Dolokhov.

"God only knows, they say so."

"I'm glad," Dolokhov replied curtly and clearly, as the song required.

"Why not come to see us some evening, you can have a game of faro," said Zherkov.

"Have you come into big money, then?"

"Come."

"I can't. I swore an oath. I don't drink and I don't play until they promote me."

"Well then, that's until the first action . . ."

"We'll see that when the time comes . . ." They were silent again.

"Do call in if you need anything, everyone at headquarters will help," said Zherkov.

Dolokhov laughed.

"No need to worry about me. If I want something, I won't bother to ask, I'll take it." And Dolokhov glared spitefully into Zherkov's face.

"All right, I was only . . ."

"Well, and I was only."

"Goodbye."

"Good health."

> And way up high, and far away,
> To mine own native parts . . .

Zherkov spurred on his horse, which grew frisky and shuffled its feet three times, deciding which one to start with before it galloped off, overtaking the company and catching up with the carriage, all in time to the song.

# IV

On returning from the review, Kutuzov went through into his study with the Austrian general and, calling to an adjutant, ordered him to bring several documents relating to the condition of the troops that were arriving and the letters received so far from the Archduke Ferdinand. Prince Andrei Bolkonsky entered the commander-in-chief's study with the required papers. Kutuzov and the Austrian member of the Hofkriegsrat were sitting in front of a plan laid out on the desk.

"Ah . . ." said Kutuzov, glancing round at Bolkonsky and seeming with this sound to invite the adjutant to wait, then he continued with the conversation he had begun in French.

"I say only one thing, general," Kutuzov said with a pleasing elegance of expression and intonation that obliged one to listen closely to every single unhurriedly spoken word. It was clear that even Kutuzov listened to himself with pleasure. "I say only one thing, general, that if the business depended on my personal wishes, then the will of His Majesty the Emperor Franz would have been carried out long since. I would have joined with the archduke long ago. And believe me, on my honour, that for me personally to hand over the supreme command of the army to a general more knowledgeable and skilled than I am, of which Austria has such an abundance, and lay down this entire onerous responsibility, for me personally it would be a real joy. But circumstances are sometimes stronger than we are, general." And Kutuzov smiled with an expression which suggested that he was saying: "You have every right not to believe me, and it is actually all the same to me whether you believe me or not, but you have no excuse for telling me so. And that is the entire point."

The Austrian general appeared dissatisfied, but he could not help replying to Kutuzov in the same tone of voice.

"On the contrary," he said in a peevish and angry tone that contradicted the flattering meaning of the words he was speaking, "on the contrary, your excellency's contribution to the common cause is highly valued by His Majesty, but we believe that the present delay is depriving the glorious Russian troops and their commanders-in-chief of the laurels which they are accustomed to reap in battles" – concluding with a phrase that he had obviously prepared.

Kutuzov bowed, without altering his smile.

"I am convinced of it, and, on the basis of the last letter with which His Highness the Archduke Ferdinand has favoured me, I believe that the Austrian forces, under the command of such a skilled aide as General Mack, have already won a decisive victory and are no longer in need of our assistance," said Kutuzov.

The general shuddered and frowned. Although there had been no positive news of the Austrians' defeat, there were too many circumstances that confirmed the general unfavourable rumours, and therefore Kutuzov's assumption of an Austrian victory sounded very much like a jibe. But Kutuzov smiled meekly, still with the same expression, which said that he had the right to assume this. Indeed, the latest letter that he had received from Mack's army had informed him of a victory and the highly advantageous strategic position of the army.

"Let me have that letter," said Kutuzov, addressing Prince Andrei. "There, if you would kindly look," and with a mocking smile on the corners of his lips, Kutuzov read the Austrian general the following passage in German from Archduke Ferdinand's letter:

"We have fully consolidated forces, about seventy thousand men, so that we can attack and smash the enemy if he should cross the Lech. Since we already control the Ulm, we can, if the enemy should not cross the Lech, retain the advantage of commanding both banks of the Danube, then at any moment, cross the Danube, assault his line of communication, recross the Danube lower down and, if the enemy should think of turning his entire force against our faithful allies, prevent him from realising that intention. We shall accordingly await in good spirits the time when the Imperial Russian Army shall be fully prepared and then together we shall easily find a way to prepare for the enemy the fate which he deserves."

Kutuzov sighed heavily as he finished this sentence and gave the member of the Hofkriegsrat an attentive and affectionate look.

"But you are aware, your excellency, of the wise rule that enjoins us to assume the worst," said the Austrian general, evidently wishing to have done with the jokes and get on with business. He glanced round with displeasure at the adjutant.

"I beg your pardon, general," Kutuzov interrupted him and also turned to face Prince Andrei. "Listen, my dear fellow, you get all our scouts' reports from Kozlovsky. Here are two letters from Count Nostitz, here is a letter from His Highness Archduke Ferdinand, and there is this too," he said, handing him several papers. "And out of all this you compose a memorandum in immaculate French, a note to present clearly all the news that we have had about the operations of the Austrian army. Right, that's it, and present it to his excellency."

Prince Andrei inclined his head politely as a sign that, from the very first words, he had understood not only what was said, but also what Kutuzov would have liked to say to him. He gathered up the papers and, taking his leave with a bow, he walked quietly across the carpet and went out into the reception room.

Despite the fact that it was less than three months since Prince Andrei had left Russia, he had changed greatly in that time. In the expression of his face, his movements and his gait there was almost no trace of the former dissembling and weary lassitude. He had the air of a man who did not have time to think about the impression he was producing on others, and was occupied with something agreeable and interesting. His face expressed greater contentment with himself and the people around him; his smile and his glance were more cheerful and attractive.

Kutuzov, whom he had overtaken in Poland, had received him very warmly, promising not to forget him, and had singled him out from the other adjutants, taking him with him to Vienna and giving him the more serious assignments. On Kutuzov's staff, among his comrades and colleagues, and in the army in general, Prince Andrei had two entirely opposite reputations, just as he had had in St. Petersburg society. Some, the minority, recognised that Prince Andrei was different in some way from themselves and from everyone else and, expecting great things from him, they heeded, admired and imitated him. And with these people

Prince Andrei was simple and agreeable. Others, the majority, did not like Prince Andrei, and thought him a puffed-up, cold and disagreeable individual. But with these people the prince knew how to comport himself in such a way that they respected and even feared him. He was closest of all to two people: one of them was a St. Petersburg friend, the good-hearted, fat Prince Nesvitsky. Prince Nesvitsky, immensely rich, carefree and jolly, fed the entire headquarters staff and bought their drink, always laughing at anything that was even remotely funny, and incapable of understanding or believing in the possibility of acting basely or of hating anyone. The other was a man with no title, Captain Kozlovsky from the infantry regiment, who had had no education to prepare him for society and even spoke French badly, but who was carving out a career by hard work, zeal and intelligence, and for this campaign had been recommended and taken on for special assignments for the commander-in-chief. Bolkonsky had befriended him willingly, if patronisingly.

On emerging from Kutuzov's study into the reception room, Prince Andrei took his papers across to Kozlovsky, the man on duty, who was sitting by the window with a book on fortification. Several military men in full uniform with timid expressions on their faces were waiting patiently at the other side of the room.

"Well, what is it, prince?" asked Kozlovsky.

"I have been ordered to draw up a memorandum about why we are not advancing."

"And why is that?"

Prince Andrei shrugged.

"I think you were right," he said.

"And is there no news from Mack?" asked Kozlovsky.

"No."

"Well, if it were true that he has been defeated, then news would have reached us."

"I'm not so sure," said Prince Andrei.

"As I told you, prince, the Austrians have taken us over, no good will come of it."

Prince Andrei smiled and stepped towards the door, but just at that moment, an Austrian general, obviously just recently arrived, with his head bandaged in a black kerchief and an Order of Marya-Theresa round his neck, hurried into the room, banging the door behind him. Prince Andrei came to a halt. The Austrian general's tall figure, his wrinkled, determined face and rapid movements were so strikingly consequential and disquieting that everyone in the room involuntarily rose to their feet.

"General-in-chief Kutuzov?" the new arrival said rapidly, with a harsh

German accent, glancing about on both sides as he walked without stopping across to the door of the study.

"The general-in-chief is busy," said Kozlovsky with the sombre briskness with which he always carried out his duties, and he approached the unknown general to block his way to the door. "How shall I announce you?"

The unknown general glanced down contemptuously at the short Kozlovsky, as if amazed that that anyone might not know him.

"The general-in-chief is busy," Kozlovsky repeated calmly.

The general's face turned sullen, his lips twitched and began trembling. He took out a notebook, dashed off something hastily with a pencil, tore out the page, handed it to Kozlovsky, walked quickly over to the window, hurled his body into a chair and looked round at everybody in the room as if asking why they were all looking at him. The general raised his head, stretched out his neck and half-turned towards Prince Andrei, who was standing closest of all to him, as though intending to say something, but immediately turned away again and made a strange sound, as though he were beginning to hum something nonchalantly to himself, but the sound immediately broke off. The door of the study opened and Kutuzov appeared on the threshold. In a moment the general with the bandaged head, ducking down as if fleeing from danger, moved swiftly across the room with long strides on thin legs which brought him close to Kutuzov's face. His own elderly, wrinkled face turned pale, and he was unable to prevent his lower lip from trembling nervously as he uttered the following words in badly pronounced French in a voice that faltered and was too loud:

"You see before you the unfortunate Mack."

For a few moments, as Kutuzov stood there in the doorway of his study, his broad face, disfigured by wounds, remained absolutely motionless. Then, like a wave, a frown rippled across his face and his forehead smoothed out again; he inclined his head respectfully, closed his eyes and, without a word, allowed Mack to go past him into the room, closing the door behind himself.

The rumour which had been spread earlier, concerning the defeat of the Austrians and the surrender of the entire army at the Ulm, proved to be correct. The members of headquarters staff related to each other the details of Mack's conversation with the commander-in-chief, which not one of them had been able to hear. Half an hour later adjutants had already been despatched in various directions with orders clearly indicating that the Russian forces, which had so far not seen action, were also certain to encounter the enemy soon.

"That half-crazy old fanatic Mack wanted to fight the greatest military genius since Caesar!" thought Prince Andrei as he went back to his room. "What did I tell Kozlovsky? What did I write to my father?" he thought. "Now it has happened." And despite himself he experienced a feeling of joyful excitement at thinking of arrogant Austria's disgrace and that perhaps in a week's time he would see and take part in an armed conflict between the Russians and the French, the first since Suvorov.

Once he got back downstairs to the room that he shared with Nesvitsky, Prince Andrei put the now unnecessary papers on the table and, holding his hands behind his back, he began walking to and fro across the room, smiling at his own thoughts. He feared the genius of Bonaparte, which might prove stronger than all the bravery of the Russian troops, yet at the same time he was unable to conceive of his hero being disgraced. The only possible solution to this contradiction was that he himself should command the Russian army against Bonaparte. But when could that be? In ten years – ten years that seem like an eternity when they amount to more than a third of one's life so far. "Ah! Do what duty requires, come what may," he said, rehearsing to himself the motto that he had chosen. He called for his servant, took off his uniform coat, put on his smoking jacket and sat down at the table. Despite life on the march and the cramped room that he shared with Nesvitsky, Prince Andrei, just as he had been in Russia, was as fastidious as a woman, careful of his own person, neat and tidy. Nesvitsky knew that nothing could make his room-mate more angry than disorder among his things, and Bolkonsky's two tables, one a writing-desk that was set, like his desk in St. Petersburg, with bronze writing accessories, the other arrayed with brushes, soap-dishes and a mirror, were always arranged symmetrically and without a single speck of dust. Since his departure from St. Petersburg and, most importantly, since parting from his wife, Prince Andrei had entered a new era of activity and seemed to be reliving his youth. He read and studied a lot. Campaign life gave him a good deal of free time, and the books he had acquired abroad opened up new interests to him. The greater part of these books were works of philosophy. Apart from its intrinsic interest, philosophy was for him one of those pedestals of pride which he loved to ascend in front of other people. Although he had many different pedestals from which he could look down on people – birth, connections, wealth – philosophy represented for him the one from which he could feel superior even to people such as Kutuzov, and feeling that was essential for Prince Andrei's peace of mind. He picked up Kant's latest work, which was lying on his table with half its pages cut, and began reading. But his thoughts were far away, and he constantly imagined that he saw before him his most cherished dream – the banner of the Bridge at Arcole.

"Well, brother, I owe you a bottle," said the immense, fat Nesvitsky as he entered the room, accompanied, as always, by Zherkov. "What do you make of this business with Mack?"

"Yes, he must have just spent an unpleasant quarter of an hour upstairs," said Prince Andrei.

(They had had a wager. Prince Andrei had asserted that Mack would be routed, so he had won.)

"I owe you a bottle," said Nesvitsky, unbuttoning his uniform coat, which squeezed his plump neck. "But what a dinner we'll have today, brother! Wild goat, I got a fresh one, and turkey with chestnuts."

"I told you Mack would get stuck in your teeth," said Zherkov, but his jest was not appreciated. Prince Andrei glanced round coldly at him and turned to Nesvitsky.

"What have you heard, when are they setting out?" he asked.

"They have sent for the second division to be moved," Zherkov said in his ingratiating manner.

"Ah!" said Prince Andrei, then turned away and began reading.

"Right, that's enough of your philosophising," cried Nesvitsky, throwing himself onto his bed and panting for breath. "Let's talk. How I laughed just now! Imagine it, we'd just come out, and there was Strauch walking along. You should have seen the capers Zherkov cut in front of him."

"That's all right, I was saluting an ally," said Zherkov, and Nesvitsky began laughing so hard that the bed creaked under him.

Strauch, the Austrian general sent from Vienna to oversee the supply of provisions to the Russian army, had for some reason become Zherkov's favourite victim. Zherkov mimicked him with deadly accuracy and every time he encountered him, Zherkov would stand to attention, pretending to be afraid of him, and at every opportunity he could find, he would begin speaking with him in broken German, making himself out to be a naïve fool, to Nesvitsky's great delight.

"Ah, yes!" said Nesvitsky, turning to Prince Andrei. "By the way, about Strauch. There's an infantry officer here who's been waiting a long time to see you."

"What officer?"

"Remember, they sent you to investigate the case, he stole a cow or something from the Germans."

"What does *he* want?" said Prince Andrei, frowning and twisting the ring on his small white hand.

"He's a pitiful sort, come to petition you. Zherkov, what was his name? Well, what was it he said?"

Zherkov pulled a face and began imitating the officer.

"I . . . didn't, not that, not at all . . . the soldiers . . . they bought the beast, because the owners . . . The beast . . . the owners . . . the beast . . ."

Prince Andrei got up and put on his uniform jacket.

"Yes, do hush it up somehow," said Nesvitsky. "My God, how pitiful he is."

"I do not wish either to hush it up or to be unfair to anyone. I was sent, and I reported what had happened. I never take pity on scoundrels nor do I laugh at them," he added, glancing at Zherkov.

He went out to speak with the officer, and explained haughtily that he had no personal business with him and did not wish to have any.

"But after all, you know yourself, your . . . prince," said the officer, evidently unsure about the right way to address this adjutant: he was equally afraid of abasing himself and of not being polite enough. "After all, you yourself know, prince, that we'd been on the march for days, the soldiers hadn't eaten, so how could I forbid it . . . judge for yourself . . ."

"If you require my personal conviction," said Prince Andrei, "then I can tell you that in my opinion, pillaging is always a serious offence, and there is no punishment severe enough for it in the country of one's allies. But above all, please understand that there is nothing I can do; my job is to report to the commander-in-chief what I have found. I cannot lie for you." And, with a smile at this odd idea, he bowed to the officer and left to return to his room. In the corridor, he saw General Strauch and the member of the Hofkriegsrat walking ahead of him. Nesvitsky and Zherkov were coming the other way, towards them.

There was enough space in the broad corridor for the generals to pass the two officers, but Zherkov, pushing Nesvitsky to one side with his hand, said in a breathless voice:

"They're coming! They're coming! Move over, make way! Please, make way!"

The generals were walking along with an air that suggested they wished to avoid bothersome expressions of respect. Zherkov's face was suddenly transformed by a stupid smile of joy, as if he were unable to restrain it.

"You excellency," he said in German, advancing and addressing the Austrian general. "Please permit me to congratulate you." He inclined his head and began scraping first one foot, then the other, in a clumsy fashion, like a child learning to dance.

The general who was a member of the Hofkriegsrat glanced sternly at him but, noticing the seriousness of the stupid smile, felt obliged to grant him a moment of attention. He lowered his gaze, to show he was listening.

"Allow me to congratulate you on General Mack's arriving quite unhurt, with only a little bump here," Zherkov went on, smiling radiantly and pointing to his own head.

The general scowled, turned away and began to walk on.

"*Gott*, how naïve!" he said angrily after a few steps. Nesvitsky embraced Prince Andrei with a laugh and pulled him towards their room. Ignoring the laughter, Prince Andrei followed Nesvitsky inside, and going over to where Zherkov's cap was lying on his table, he knocked it to the floor.

"Yes, did you see that face?" Nesvitsky said through his laughter. "It was marvellous! Just a little bump here . . . ha, ha, ha!"

"There's nothing funny about it," said Prince Andrei.

"Nothing funny? Why, his face alone . . ."

"Nothing funny. I am no great friend of the Austrians. However, there are proprieties that this *villain* may not be aware of, but which you and I should observe."

"Do stop that, he'll come in any moment," Nesvitsky interrupted, taking fright.

"I do not care. What a good light it shows us in to our allies, how very tactful it is! That officer who stole a cow for his company is no worse than your Zherkov. He, at least, needed that cow."

"Just as you wish, brother, it's all very pitiful, but it's funny nonetheless. If only you . . ."

"There's nothing funny about it. Forty thousand men have been killed and our ally's army has been destroyed, and you joke about it," he said in French, as though reinforcing his opinion. "It is forgivable for a contemptible little fellow like this gentleman whom you have made your friend, but not for you, not for you," said Prince Andrei in Russian. He had uttered "little fellow" with a French accent, on noticing Zherkov enter the room. He waited to see if the cornet would make any reply. But the cornet said nothing; he picked up his cap, winked at Nesvitsky and went out again.

"Come for dinner," shouted Nesvitsky. Prince Andrei had been watching the cornet intently and, when he had gone, he sat down at his table.

"I have been wanting to say something for a long time," he said to Nesvitsky, who was now looking at Prince Andrei with a smile in his eyes, as though for him any amusement was agreeable, and now he was rather enjoying listening to the sound of Prince Andrei's voice and what he was saying.

"I have wanted to say for a long time that it is your passion to be familiar with everyone, feed absolutely everyone and buy drink indiscriminately. This is all very fine, and even though I live with you, I do not find it awkward, because I know how to make these gentlemen aware of their place. And I am speaking not for myself, but for you. You can joke with me. We understand each other and we know the limits to jokes, but you should not be on such familiar terms with this Zherkov. His only goal is to be noticed in some way, to win some little cross for himself, and for you to give him food and drink for free; he sees nothing beyond that and is prepared to amuse you in any way necessary, without the slightest awareness of the significance of his own jokes, but you must not do this."

"Oh, come now, he's a fine fellow," interceded Nesvitsky, "a fine fellow."

"It is possible to give these Zherkovs drink after dinner and get them to perform their comedies, that I can understand, but no more that that."

"That's enough, now, brother, this is really too awkward . . . Well, all right, I won't do it again, just don't say another word," Nesvitsky cried, laughing and leaping up from the divan. He embraced Prince Andrei and kissed him. Prince Andrei smiled like a teacher smiling at a fawning pupil.

"It makes me sick to the stomach when these Zherkovs worm their way into your intimate friendship. He wishes to be elevated and cleansed through his closeness with you, but he will not be cleansed, he will only besmirch you."

# V

The Pavlograd Hussars Regiment was stationed two miles from Braunau. The squadron in which Nikolai Rostov was serving as a cadet was located in the German village of Salzenek. The squadron commander, Captain Denisov, known to the entire cavalry division by the name of Vaska Denisov, had been allocated the best quarters in the village. Cadet Rostov had been living with the squadron commander since he overtook the regiment in Poland.

On the 8th of October, the same day when, at general headquarters, everyone was spurred into action by the news of Mack's defeat, life at the squadron headquarters continued calmly in the same way as usual. Denisov, who had spent the entire night playing cards, was still asleep when Rostov returned on horseback early in the morning. In breeches and a hussar's jacket, Rostov rode up to the porch and, giving his horse a pat, flung one leg over its back with a fluid, youthful movement, standing in the stirrup for a moment, as though not wishing to be parted from his horse, before finally jumping down and turning his flushed, sunburnt face with its young growth of moustache to call to his orderly.

"Ah, Bondarenko, my good friend," he said to the hussar who came dashing headlong to his horse. "Walk him for me, dear friend," he said with that fraternal, jolly affection with which good-hearted young men address everybody when they are happy.

"Yes, your excellency," replied the Ukrainian, tossing his head merrily.

"Take care now, a good walk!"

Another hussar also dashed up to the horse, but Bondarenko had already brought the reins of the snaffle-bridle over the horse's head. It was obvious that the cadet tipped well and it was profitable to do him a service. Rostov ran his hand over the horse's neck, then its rump, and stood still by the porch.

"Glorious," he said to himself, smiling and holding his sabre down as he ran up the porch and clicked his heels and spurs together, as they do in the mazurka. The German landlord, in a quilted jacket and cap, holding the fork he was using for mucking out, glanced out of the cowshed. The German's face suddenly brightened when he saw Rostov. He smiled cheerfully and winked: "*Schön gut Morgen!* Fine, good morning!" he repeated, evidently taking pleasure in the young man's greeting.

"Already at work," said Nikolai, still with the same joyful, fraternal smile, which never left his animated face. "Hurrah for the Austrians! Hurrah for the Russians! Hurrah for Emperor Alexander!" he said to the German, repeating the words frequently spoken by the German landlord. The German laughed, and coming all the way out of the cowshed, he pulled off his cap, waving it over his head, and shouted:

"And hurrah for all the world!"

Just like the German, Rostov waved his forage cap over his head and shouted with a laugh: "And hurrah for all the world!" Although neither of them – not the German, who was mucking out his cowshed, nor Nikolai, who had taken a platoon to fetch hay – had any special reason for merriment, these two men looked at each other in transports of happiness and brotherly love, shook their heads as a sign of their mutual love and went their separate ways with a smile, the German back into the cowshed and Nikolai into the hut that he and Denisov occupied.

The previous day the officers of this squadron had gathered at the quarters of the captain of the fourth squadron in a different village and spent the whole night playing cards. Rostov had been there, but he had left early. For all his desire to be the complete hussar and comrade, he could not drink more than a glass of wine without feeling ill, and he fell asleep at cards. He had too much money, and did not know what to do with it, so he could not understand the pleasure of winning. Every time he placed a stake on the advice of the officers, he won money that he did not need and observed how disagreeable this was for the man whose money it was, but he was unable to help him. Even though the squadron commander had never reprimanded him in connection with his duties, Rostov had decided for himself that in military service the most important thing was to be conscientious in performing one's duty, and he had informed all the officers that he would regard himself as worthless trash if he ever permitted himself to skip his turn for a duty assignment or a mission. Subsequently he discovered for himself that the duties of serving as a non-commissioned officer, which no one had forced him to undertake, were onerous, but he remembered the incautious pledge that he had given and did not betray it. Having been given, as part of his duties as a non-commissioned officer, the order of the day by the sergeant-major the previous evening, he had accordingly given orders to be woken before dawn so as to take a platoon out to get hay. While Denisov was still sleeping, Rostov had already had a long talk with the hussars, taken a good look at a German girl, the daughter of the schoolteacher in Salzenek, started to feel hungry and arrived back in that happy state of mind in which all people are kind, lovable and agreeable. Quietly jingling his soldier's spurs, he walked backwards and forwards across the squeaking floor, glancing at Denisov sleeping with his head tucked under the blanket. He wanted to talk. Denisov coughed and turned over. Rostov went up to him and tugged on the blanket.

"Time to get up, Denisov! It's time!" he shouted.

Out from under the blanket popped a dark, hirsute, shaggy head with red cheeks and glittering pitch-black eyes.

"Time!" shouted Denisov. "What time? Time to get the hell out of this . . . kingdom of salami. Such bad luck! Such bad luck! It started the moment you left. I was cleaned wight out yesterday, bwother, like a weal son of a bitch! Hey there, some tea!"

Denisov leapt up on brown naked legs that were covered with black hairs as dense as a monkey's, and he screwed up his face, as if smiling, to display short, strong teeth, while with both hands he tousled his thick black hair and moustache, which were as curly and tangled as a forest. It was clear from Denisov's first words that he was feeling down-at-heart, that his body was weakened by wine and sleepless nights, and his cheery manner was not an expression of his feelings, but merely a habit.

"What devil made me go to that wat's place" (the officer was nicknamed "the rat") said Denisov, rubbing his forehead and face with both hands. "Can you believe that yesterday, after you left, he didn't give me a single card, not one, not even one card," Denisov went on, raising his voice to a shout and turning completely crimson in his excitement.

Denisov was one of those people who had his blood let regularly twice a year and who were called hot-headed.

"Now, that's enough, it's all over now," said Rostov, noticing that Denisov was about to fly into a passion at the mere memory of his bad luck. "Let's have some tea instead."

It was clear that Rostov had not yet grown accustomed to his position and he found it pleasant to speak so familiarly to such an old person. But Denisov was already getting carried away, his eyes turned bloodshot, he took the lighted pipe held out to him, squeezed it in his fist, struck it against the floor, scattering sparks, and carried on shouting.

"No, it's such devilish bad luck I have – he gives you the singles, then beats you on the doubles, gives you the singles, then beats you on the doubles."

He scattered sparks and broke the pipe, tossed it away and threatened the orderly with his hand. But by the time Rostov began speaking a moment later, the fit of fury had already passed.

"And I had such a glorious ride. We went past that park, where the teacher's daughter is, remember?" said Rostov, blushing and smiling.

"That's young blood for you," said Denisov, speaking calmly now, grabbing the cadet's hand and shaking it. "The youth is blushing, it's quite wepulsive . . ."

"I saw her again . . ."

"Wight then, brother, clearly I'll have to set about the fair sex – I've no money, that's enough gambling for me. Nikita, my fwiend, give me my purse," he said to the orderly whom he had almost struck. "Right then. What a blockhead, damn it! Where's that you're wummaging? Under the pillow! Wight, thank you, dear fellow," he said, taking the purse and tipping several gold coins out on to the table. "Squadwon money, fowage money, it's all here," he said. "There must be forty-five of fowage money alone. Ah no, why bother counting! It won't fix me up."

He pushed the gold coins aside.

"Never mind, take some from me," said Rostov.

"If they don't bwing the pay on Sunday, things'll be weally bad," said Denisov, not answering him.

"Well take some from me," said Rostov, blushing in the way that young men always do when it is a matter of money. The vague thought flashed through his mind that Denisov was already in his debt, together with the thought that Denisov was insulting him by not accepting his offer.

Denisov's face fell and became sad.

"I tell you what! You take Bedouin fwom me," he said seriously, after thinking for a moment. "I paid one and a half thousand for him in Russia myself, I'll let you have him for the same price. Nothing is sacred except the sabre. Take him! Let's shake hands on it . . ."

"I won't, not for anything. The finest horse in the regiment," said Rostov, blushing furiously again.

Bedouin really was a fine horse, and Rostov would have very much liked to own him, but he felt ashamed to admit it to Denisov. He felt as if he were to blame for having money. Denisov fell silent and again began tousling his hair thoughtfully.

"Hey, who's there?" he said, turning towards the door on hearing the footfalls of thick boots with jingling spurs and a short, respectful cough.

"The sergeant-major," said Nikita. Denisov frowned even more darkly.

"That's weally bad," he said. "Wostov, my dear fellow, count up how much is left there and chuck the purse under my pillow," he said, going out to the sergeant-major.

Rostov, already imagining himself having bought Bedouin and riding him as a cornet at the rear of the squadron, began counting the money, mechanically setting the old and new gold coins apart in equal heaps (there were seven old and sixteen new ones).

"Ah! Telyanin! Gweetings! They cleaned me out yesterday," Denisov's sad voice said in the next room.

"Where? At Bykov the rat's place? I knew it," said another thin voice, and then Lieutenant Telyanin, a foppish little officer from the same squadron, entered the room.

Rostov tossed the purse under the pillow and shook the moist little hand extended towards him. Before the campaign, Telyanin had for some reason or other been transferred from the Guards. He was disliked in the squadron for his stand-offish manner. Rostov had bought his horse from him.

"Well now, young cavalryman, how's my Grachik serving you?" he asked. The lieutenant never looked into the eyes of the person with whom he was talking; his eyes constantly shifted about from one object to another. "I saw you ride past today . . ."

"Well enough, a sound mount," Rostov replied in the serious tone of an experienced cavalryman, even though the horse that he had bought for seven hundred roubles had bad legs and was not worth half that price. "He's started limping a bit on his left foreleg . . ." he added.

"Is the hoof split? That's all right. I'll teach you how, I'll show you what kind of brace to put on."

Telyanin's eyes never settled, despite the fact that his entire small figure had assumed an indolently nonchalant pose and the tone of his speech was slightly superior and patronising.

"Would you like some tea? Yes, please do show me how to do that brace," said Rostov.

"I'll show you, I'll show you, it's no secret. And you'll thank me for that horse."

"I'll order the horse to be led round then." And Rostov went out to have it brought.

Out in the lobby Denisov, wearing a short padded kaftan, was sitting hunched over his pipe on the doorstep in front of the sergeant-major, who was reporting something.

Catching sight of Rostov, Denisov screwed up his face and, pointing back over his shoulder with his thumb into the room that Telyanin had entered, he frowned and shook his head in disgust.

"Oh, I don't like that fine fellow," he said, unembarrassed by the presence of the sergeant-major.

Rostov shrugged, as if to say: "Neither do I, but what can you do?" and, after giving his instructions, he went back to Telyanin.

Telyanin was sitting in the same indolent pose in which Rostov had left him, rubbing his small white hands.

"What a station – not a single house or a single woman since we left Poland," said Telyanin, standing up and glancing casually around himself. "Well then, did you tell them to bring the horse?" he added.

"Yes."

"Let's go then."

"But what about tea?"

"No, I don't want any. I only called in to ask Denisov about yesterday's order. Have you received it, Denisov?"

"Not yet. Where are you going?"

"I want to teach this young man how to shoe a horse," said Telyanin.

They went out through the porch and into the stable. The lieutenant showed him how to put on the brace and went back to his quarters.

When Rostov returned there was vodka and ham standing on the table and Denisov, now dressed, was walking backwards and forwards across the room with rapid strides. He looked into Rostov's face sombrely.

"It's not often I don't like someone," said Denisov, "but I find that Telyanin as repulsive as milk with sugar. He swindled you with that Grachik of his, that's for sure. Let's go to the stable. Take Bedouin anyway, cash in hand on the nail, and two bottles of champagne."

Rostov blushed fiercely again, like a girl.

"No, please, Denisov . . . I won't take the horse, not for anything. If you won't take money as a comrade, you'll offend me. Really. I have money."

Denisov frowned, turned away and began tousling his hair. He was clearly displeased by this.

"Well, have it your way!"

Rostov made to take out his money.

"Later, later, I still have some. Chuchela, send in the sergeant-major," Denisov shouted to Nikita, "I have to pay him back some money."

He went to the bed to get the purse from under the pillow.

"Where did you put it?"

"Under the bottom pillow."

"I'm looking under the bottom pillow."

Denisov threw both pillows on to the floor. The purse was not there.

"That's incredible!"

"Wait, perhaps you might have dropped it," said Rostov, picking up the pillows by turn and shaking them. He took off the blanket and shook it out. The purse was not there.

"Could I really have forgotten? No, I even had a thought that you kept your treasure under your head," said Rostov. "I put the purse here. Where is it?" he said, turning to the servant.

"I haven't been in here. It ought to be where you left it."

"But it's not . . ."

"You're always throwing things down somewhere and then forgetting. Look in your pockets."

"No, I wouldn't have had that thought about the treasure," said Rostov, "I remember putting it there."

Nikita rummaged through the entire bed, looking under it, under the table, rummaging through the whole room, but the purse was not there. Denisov, having turned out his own pockets, followed Nikita's movements without speaking, and when Nikita shrugged and spread his arms in amazement, saying it was not in his pocket, he gave Rostov a glance.

"Rostov, you're playing a schoolboy . . ."

He didn't finish. Rostov was standing there with both hands in his pockets and his head bowed. Sensing Denisov's gaze on him, he looked up and instantly lowered his eyes again. At that instant all of his blood, which had been locked somewhere below his throat, rushed up into his face and eyes. The young man was clearly unable to catch his breath. Denisov hastily turned away, winced and began tousling his hair.

"And there was no one in the room, apart from the lieutenant and you yourself. It's in here somewhere."

"Right, you devil's puppet, get cracking, look for it," Denisov suddenly shouted, turning crimson and rushing at the orderly with a threatening gesture. "I'll have that purse, or I'll whip you!"

Gasping for breath and avoiding looking at Denisov, Rostov began buttoning up his jacket. He fastened on his sabre and put on his forage cap.

"Come on, you devil. I tell you, find me that purse," shouted Denisov, senselessly shaking the orderly by the shoulders and pushing him against the wall.

"Denisov, leave him. I'll be back straightaway," said Rostov, walking to the door without looking up.

"Rostov! Rostov!" Denisov shouted so hard that the veins on his neck and forehead swelled up like ropes. "I tell you, you've gone crazy, I won't allow it." And Denisov grabbed Rostov by the arm. "The purse is here, I'll flay all the orderlies, and it will be here."

"But I know where the purse is," Rostov replied in a trembling voice. They looked each other in the eye.

"But I'm telling you, don't do this," Denisov shouted at the top of his voice, lunging at the cadet in order to hold him back. "I tell you, to hell with that money! This cannot be, I won't allow it. It's lost, so to hell with it . . ." But despite the resolute sense of his words, the captain's hirsute face now expressed indecision and fear. Rostov pulled his arm free and fixed his eyes directly and firmly on Denisov with as much malice as if he were his greatest enemy.

"Do you understand what you're saying?" he said in a trembling voice. "Apart from me, there was no one in the room. That means, if not . . ."

He couldn't finish what he was saying and ran out of the room.

"Ah, to hell with you and everybody," were the last words that Rostov heard.

He reached Telyanin's quarters.

"The master's not at home, he's gone to staff headquarters," Telyanin's orderly told him. "Why, has something happened?" the orderly added, surprised at the cadet's distraught expression.

"No, nothing."

"You only just missed him," said the orderly.

The staff building was located three *versts* from Salzenek. Without returning to base, Rostov took his horse and rode to headquarters.

In the village occupied by the headquarters there was an inn that was frequented by the officers.

Rostov arrived at the inn and he saw Telyanin's horse by the porch.

The lieutenant was sitting in the second room of the inn, with a dish of sausages and a bottle in front of him.

"Ah, you've called in too, young man," he said, smiling and raising his eyebrows very high.

"Yes," said Rostov, as though it cost him a great effort to pronounce the word, and sat at the next table.

Neither of them said anything, there was no one else in the room and all that could be heard were the sounds of the knife against the plate and the lieutenant's chomping. When Telyanin finished his breakfast he took a double purse out of his pocket, parted the rings with his little white fingers curved upwards, took out a gold coin and, raising his eyebrows slightly, handed the money to the servant.

"Be quick, if you please," he said.

The gold coin was new. Rostov stood up and approached Telyanin.

"Permit me to take a look at your purse," he said in a low, barely audible voice.

With his eyes shifting restlessly, but his eyebrows still raised, Telyanin held out the purse.

"It's a souvenir from a little Polish girl ... yes ..." he said and suddenly turned pale. "Take a look, young man," he added.

Rostov took hold of the purse and looked at it and the money that was in it, and at Telyanin. The lieutenant was glancing around himself in his habitual manner and he seemed suddenly to have become very jolly.

"When we're in Vienna, I'll get rid of it all there, but there's nothing to do with it now in these wretched little towns," he said. "Right, come on young man, I'll be going."

Rostov said nothing.

"Well, are you buying the horse from Denisov? A fine steed," Telyanin continued. "Give it back now." He held out his hand and took hold of the purse. Rostov let go of it. Telyanin took the purse and began lowering it into the pocket of his breeches, and his eyebrows rose carelessly, and his lips parted slightly, as if he were saying: "Yes, I'm putting my purse in my pocket, and it's nobody's business but mine."

"Well then, young man?" he asked with a sigh and looked into Rostov's eyes from under his raised eyebrows. A strange light leapt with the speed of an electric spark from Telyanin's eyes to Rostov's eyes and back, back and forth, back and forth, all in a single instant.

"Come here," said Rostov, grabbing Telyanin by the arm. He pulled him almost over to the window. "You are a thief!" he whispered into his ear.

"What? What? How dare you? What?" But these words sounded like a pitiful, desperate cry appealing for forgiveness. As soon as Rostov heard the sound of that voice, a heavy stone of doubt fell from his heart. He felt joy and at the same moment he felt so sorry for the miserable man standing before him that tears sprang to his eyes.

"There are people here, God knows what they might think," Telyanin muttered, snatching up his cap and walking towards a small empty room. "Explain yourself, what's wrong with you?"

When they entered the little room, Telyanin looked pale, grey and short, as though he had lost weight after a long illness.

"Just now you stole the purse from under Denisov's pillow," said Rostov, emphasising each word. Telyanin was on the point of saying something. "I know this, I shall prove it."

"I . . ."

The grey face had lost all of its attractiveness now, every muscle in it began trembling, the eyes shifted about in a different way from before, somewhere low down, not rising to look at the cadet's face, and Rostov could hear sobbing.

"Count! Do not ruin . . . a young man . . . Here is the miserable . . . money, take it . . ." He tossed it on to a table. "I have an old father, a mother!"

Rostov took the money, avoiding Telyanin's eyes and, without saying a word, walked out of the room. But at the door he stopped and turned back.

"My God," he said with tears in his eyes, "how could you do it?"

"Count," said Telyanin imploringly, approaching the cadet.

"Don't touch me," said Rostov, moving away from him. "If you need this money, take it." He tossed the purse to him. "Don't touch me, don't touch me!" And Rostov ran out of the inn, scarcely able to conceal his tears.

That evening there was a lively discussion between the squadron's officers in Denisov's quarters.

"And I tell you, Rostov, that you should apologise to the regimental commander," said a tall staff-captain with greying hair, immense moustaches and a wrinkled face with large features, addressing a crimson-faced, agitated Rostov. Staff-Captain Kiersten had twice been reduced to the ranks on a matter of honour and twice won promotion again. A man who did not believe in God would have been less odd in the regiment than a man who did not respect Staff-Captain Kiersten.

"I will not permit anyone to say that I am a liar!" exclaimed Rostov. "He told me that I was lying, and I told him that he was lying. That is the way it will remain. He can assign me duty every day and place me under arrest, but no one will make me apologise, because if he, as the regimental commander, regards it as unworthy of him to give me satisfaction, then . . ."

"Just you hang on, old man, you listen to me," the staff-captain interrupted in his deep bass voice, calmly stroking his long moustaches. "In the presence of other officers you told the regimental commander that an officer stole."

"I cannot be a diplomat, I do not know how, and I am not to blame that the conversation took place in the presence of other officers. That was why I went into the hussars, I thought there was no need for such niceties here, and he told me that I was lying . . . then let him give me satisfaction . . ."

"That's all very well, no one thinks that you're a coward, that's not the point. Ask Denisov, does it make any sense for a cadet to demand satisfaction from the regimental commander?"

Denisov was listening to the conversation with a morose air, biting on his moustache and clearly not wishing to join in. He replied to the staff-captain's question with a shake of his head.

"I told you," he said, addressing the staff officer, "judge for yourself, as best you can. All I know is that if I hadn't listened to you and I'd given this petty thief's head a good battewing a long time ago (I couldn't bear the sight of him from the vewy beginning), then nothing would have happened, there'd be none of this shameful business."

"Yes, but what's done is done," the staff-captain continued. "You tell the regimental commander about this filthy trick in the presence of other officers. Bogdanich" (Bogdanich was what they called the regimental commander) "put you in your place, you said a lot of stupid things to him and you ought to apologise."

"Not for anything!" cried Rostov.

"I didn't expect this of you," the staff-captain said seriously and sternly. "You don't want to apologise, but it's not only him you've offended, old man, it's the whole regiment, all of us, you've offended everyone. That's the way of it: if only you'd thought about it and taken some advice on how to deal with this business, but you blurted it straight out, and in the presence of officers. What can the regimental commander do now? Does he have to hand an officer over to trial and besmirch the entire regiment? Disgrace the whole regiment because of a single scoundrel? Is that what you think? It's not what we think. And Bogdanich did right to tell you that you were lying. It's not nice, but what's to be done, old man, you jumped in with both feet. And now that they want to hush the business up, out of some snobbish ideas of your own, you don't want to apologise, you want to tell the whole story. You're offended because you'll be on duty detail, but what's it to you to apologise to an old and honest officer? Whatever Bogdanich may be like, he's still an honest and brave old colonel, what if you are offended, don't you mind

184

besmirching the regiment?" The staff-captain's voice was beginning to tremble. "You've hardly even been in the regiment two minutes, old man, here today and tomorrow you've moved somewhere as a little adjutant, you don't give a damn that people will say there are thieves among the Pavlogradsk officers! But we do care. Isn't that right, Denisov? We do care?"

"Yes, brother, I'd let them chop off my right hand, if only this business had never happened," said Denisov, banging his fist on the table.

"Your snobbish ideas mean a lot to you, you don't want to apologise," the staff-captain continued, "but we old men have grown up in the regiment and, God willing, we'll die in it, so the honour of the regiment means a lot to us, and Bogdanich knows it. Oh, it means such a lot, old man! And this is not right, it's not right. You can take offence if you like, but I always tell the honest truth. It's not right."

And the staff-captain stood up and turned away from Rostov.

"It's true, damn it!" shouted Denisov, beginning to get worked up and glancing repeatedly at Rostov. "Come on, Wostov! Come on, Wostov! To hell with false shame, come on!"

Rostov, turning red and white by turns, looked first at one officer, then at the other.

"No, gentlemen, no . . . you, don't think . . . I do understand, you're wrong to think that about me . . . I . . . for myself . . . for the honour of the regiment . . . but what good is . . . ? I'll prove it to you in action, and for me the honour of the standard . . . all right, all the same, it's true, I'm at fault!" There were tears in his eyes. "I'm at fault, in every way! Well, what else do you want?"

"That's the way, count," cried the staff-captain, turning round and slapping him on the shoulder with a large hand.

"Didn't I tell you?" shouted Denisov, "devil take it, but he's a fine chap."

"It's the best way, count," repeated the staff-captain, as if rewarding him for his admission by beginning to use his title. "Yes sir, go and apologise, your excellency, do."

"Gentlemen, I will do anything, no one will hear a single word from me," Rostov said in an imploring voice, "but I can't apologise, honest to God I can't, no matter what! How am I going to apologise, like a little child asking for forgiveness?"

Denisov laughed.

"It'll be worse for you, Bogdanich never forgives, you'll pay for your stubbornness."

"By God, it's not stubbornness! I can't describe to you the kind of feeling it is, I can't . . ."

"Well, as you wish," said the staff-captain. "Tell me now, where's that rogue got to?" he asked Denisov.

"He's claiming to be sick and the instwuction's been given to dismiss him from the wegiment tomorrow. Oh, if he just cwosses my path," said Denisov, "I'll squash him like a fly."

"It's a sickness, there's no other way to explain it," said the staff-captain.

"Maybe it's an illness, maybe not, but I'd gladly shoot him," Denisov shouted in a bloodthirsty voice.

Zherkov came into the room.

"What are you doing here?" the officers all asked the new arrival.

"Action, gentlemen. Mack has surrendered with his entire army and all."

"You're lying!"

"I've seen him myself."

"What you saw Mack, alive? With arms and legs?"

"Action! Action! Give him a bottle for news like that. How do you come to be here?"

"They've sent me back to the regiment again, because of that devil Mack. An Austrian general complained. I congratulated him on Mack's arrival. What's wrong with you, Rostov, you look like you're straight out of the bathhouse."

"We've got a weal mess going on here, brother, it's the second day now."

The regimental adjutant came in and confirmed the news brought by Zherkov. The order was to advance the next day.

"Action, gentlemen."

"Well, thank God for that. We've been sitting here too long."

# VI

Kutuzov withdrew towards Vienna, destroying the bridges on the rivers Inn (at Braunau) and Traun (at Linz) behind him. On the 23rd of October the Russian forces crossed the river Enns. By the middle of the day the Russian transports, artillery and troop columns were extended right through the town of Enns, on both sides of the bridge. It was a warm, rainy autumn day. The great panorama that opened out from the elevation on which the Russian batteries were positioned to defend the bridge would suddenly be veiled by a muslin curtain of slanting rain, but then just as suddenly clear again to reveal distant objects shining brightly in the sunlight, as if coated with lacquer. The little town could be seen down below, with its white houses and red roofs, cathedral and bridge, with the massed throng of the Russian troops streaming along on both sides. In the bend of the Danube, ships and an island could be seen, and a castle with a park, surrounded by the watery confluence of the Enns and the Danube; the rocky, pine-clad left bank of the Danube could be seen with its mysterious distant expanse of green tree-tops and bluish ravines. The towers of monasteries could be seen, jutting up out of the apparently virgin, wild pine forest, and also, far ahead, on a mountain on the other side of the Rhine, could the enemy's mounted patrols.

Standing at the front, up among the artillery pieces on the elevation, were the commander of the rearguard, a general, and an officer of his retinue, who were examining the locality through a spy-glass. A short distance behind them Prince Nesvitsky, sent to the rearguard by the commander-in-chief, was sitting on the tail of a gun-carriage. The Cossack accompanying Nesvitsky had handed him a bag and a flask and Nesvitsky was now regaling the officers with pies and genuine Doppel-Kümmel. The officers gladly crowded around him, some kneeling, some sitting cross-legged on the wet grass.

"Yes, the Austrian prince who built a castle over there was no fool. A glorious spot. Why are you not eating, gentlemen?" said Nesvitsky.

"Thank you so much, prince," replied one of the officers, pleased to be talking to such an important staff official. "It is a fine spot. We marched right past that park and saw two deer, and the house is quite wonderful!"

"Look, prince," said another, who greatly wanted to take another pie, but felt too embarrassed, and therefore pretended to be surveying the locality, "look over there, see how far our infantry have already reached. And over there, on that little meadow beyond the village, three of them are dragging something away. They'll clean that palace right out," he said with evident approval.

"That they will," said Nesvitsky. "Yes, but what I should like," he added, chewing on a pie with his lovely, moist mouth, "is to get way over there." He pointed to a convent with towers that could be seen on the mountain. He smiled, his eyes narrowed and sparkled. "Now that would be good, gentlemen."

The officers laughed.

"If only to give those little nuns a fright. They say there are young Italian girls. Truly, I'd give five years of my life."

"They must be bored, too, prince," said one officer who was a bit bolder, laughing.

Meanwhile the officer of the retinue standing at the front was pointing out something to the general: the general was looking through the spy-glass.

"Yes, that's it all right, that's it," the general said angrily, lowering the spy-glass from his eye with a shrug of his shoulders, "that's it all right, they'll shoot at the crossing. But why are they dawdling like that?"

On the other side of the river, the enemy could be seen with the naked eye, and also his gun-battery, above which appeared a puff of milky-white smoke. Following the smoke there came the distant sound of a shot and they could see our troops begin to bustle at the crossing.

Nesvitsky got up, puffing and panting, and walked over, smiling, to the general.

"Would your excellency care for a bite to eat?" he said.

"A bad business," said the general, not answering him, "our people have delayed too long."

"Shall I go to them, your excellency?" asked Nesvitsky.

"Yes, do please go," said the general, repeating an order that had already been spelled out in detail, "and tell the hussars that they are to cross last and torch the bridge, as I ordered, and to inspect the combustible materials on the bridge."

"Very good," replied Nesvitsky.

He called the Cossack with his horse, ordered him to clear away the bag and flask, and swung his heavy body lightly into the saddle.

"I really will call in to see the little nuns," he said to the officers, who were looking at him with cunning smiles, and set off downhill along a winding little track.

"Right then, as far as it will reach, captain, give it a try," said the general, turning to the gunner. "Amuse yourself a bit, keep the boredom at bay."

"Man the guns!" the officer commanded, and a moment later the artillerymen came running from their campfires and loaded up.

"Fire number one!" came the command.

Gun number one recoiled sharply. The artillery piece gave a deafening metallic clang, a grenade flew, whistling, over the heads of our men below the hill and fell far short of the enemy, a puff of smoke showing the spot where it burst.

The faces of the officers and soldiers brightened at this sound: they all stood up and began observing the movements of our forces, spread out clearly below them, and, straight ahead, the movements of the approaching enemy. At that very moment the sun emerged completely from behind the clouds, and the beautiful sound of this solitary shot and the brilliance of the bright sunshine fused into a single cheerful, uplifting impression.

# VII

Two enemy shots had already flown over the bridge, and on the bridge itself there was a crush. In the middle of the bridge, dismounted from his horse, his fat body pressed against the railings, stood Prince Nesvitsky. He glanced back, laughing, at his Cossack, who was standing a few paces behind him, holding the two horses' bridles. No sooner did Prince Nesvitsky try to move forward than the soldiers and wagons bore down on him and squeezed him against the railings again, and there was nothing left for him to do but smile.

"Hey, you, little brother!" the Cossack said to a transport soldier with a wagon, who was trying to force his way through the infantry crowding close around his wheels and horse. "Look at you! Can't be bothered to wait to let the general through." But the soldier, paying no heed to the title of general, shouted at the soldiers who were blocking his way. "Hey there, brothers! Keep to the left, wait!" But his fellow countrymen, crowding shoulder to shoulder and interlocking bayonets in an unbroken line, moved along the bridge in a single compact mass. Glancing down over the railings, Nesvitsky saw the swift, turbid, low waves of the Enns pursuing and overtaking each other, fusing together, rippling and curving around the piles of the bridge. Glancing at the bridge, he saw the equally uniform, living waves of soldiers, the tasselled cords, shakos with hoods, knapsacks, bayonets and long guns, and under the shakos, faces with broad cheekbones, sunken cheeks and resignedly weary expressions, and feet moving through the sticky mud that had been dragged onto the wooden boards of the bridge. Sometimes among the uniform waves of soldiers, like a splash of white foam in the waves of the Enns, an officer in a cloak squeezed his way through the soldiers, with features that were different from theirs, sometimes, like a chip of wood swirling along the river, a hussar on foot, an orderly or a local resident was carried along the bridge by the waves of infantry, sometimes, like a log floating along the river, a company cart or officer's cart, loaded up to the top and covered with sheets of leather, floated along the bridge.

"Look at them, like a dam's burst," said the Cossack, coming dejectedly to a halt. "Are there many more of you over there?"

"A mellion, nigh on!" said a jolly soldier, winking, as he walked past in a torn greatcoat and was lost to view; behind him came another, old, soldier.

"Just watch how *he*" (*he* was the enemy) "starts peppering the bridge now," the old soldier said gloomily to his comrade, "that'll stop you scratching yourself." And the soldier passed on. Behind him came another soldier riding on a cart.

"Where the hell did you stick those puttees?" said an orderly, running after the cart and rummaging in the back of it. And he too passed by with the cart. He was followed by some jolly soldiers who were clearly tipsy.

"The way he let him have it, the darling man, smashed his musket-butt right in his teeth . . ." one soldier with his greatcoat tucked up high said gleefully, flinging his arms out.

"That's right enough, sweet, tasty ham," another chortled. And they passed on by, so that Nesvitsky never did find out who was hit in the teeth and what the ham had to do with anything.

"The rush they're in, because *he* fired one shot from a distance. You'd think they were going to kill everyone," a non-commissioned officer said in angry reproach.

"The moment that thing flew past me, uncle, that shot," a young soldier with a huge mouth said cheerfully, barely able to stop himself laughing, "I just froze. Really, honest to God, I was that frightened, it was terrible!" this soldier said, as though boasting that he had been frightened.

That soldier also passed by: following behind him came a cart unlike all those that had passed by so far. It was a German Vorspan with a pair of horses pulling a load that seemed to be an entire household: tethered behind the Vorspan, which was driven by a German, was a beautiful brindled cow with an immense udder. Sitting on feather mattresses were a woman with a babe-in-arms, an old woman and a young, healthy German girl with a crimson flush on her cheeks. Evidently these local evacuees had been allowed through by special permission. The eyes of all the soldiers turned to the women and while the cart was passing by, moving along step by step, all of the soldiers' remarks concerned only the women. All of their faces bore an almost identical smile of obscene thoughts about the one woman.

"What, a kraut clearing out as well."

"Sell me the missus," said another soldier, emphasising the last word, to the German who was walking with long strides, angry and frightened, with his eyes cast down.

"Just look how dolled up she is! Devils they are!"

"You ought to get billeted with them, Fedotov!"

"We've seen their kind, brother!"

"Where are you going?" asked an infantry officer who was eating an

RUSSIAN ARMY MARCHING ACROSS THE RIVER ENNS
*Drawing by M. S. Bashilov, 1867*

apple, also half-smiling as he looked at the beautiful girl. The German showed by closing his eyes that he did not understand.

"Take it if you like," said the officer, handing the apple to the girl. The girl smiled and took it. Nesvitsky, like everyone on the bridge, kept his eyes fixed on the women until they had driven past. When they had driven past, the same kind of soldiers walked by, with the same kind of talk until finally, everyone came to a halt. As often happens, the horses in a company wagon had baulked at the end of the bridge and the entire crowd had to wait.

"What are they stopping for? There's no order at all!" said the soldiers. "Where are you pushing? Damn you! Can't be bothered to wait. It'll be worse again when *he* sets fire to the bridge. Look, they've got an officer jammed in here too," the halted crowds said on all sides, looking each other over, and they all pressed forward towards the way out. Glancing at the waters of the Enns under the bridge, Nesvitsky suddenly heard another sound new to him, something drawing closer, something big that plopped into the water.

"Look how far he's flinging them!" a soldier standing close by said grimly, glancing round at the sound.

"He's encouraging us to get across quick," another said agitatedly. The crowd began moving again. Nesvitsky realised that it had been a shot.

"Hey, Cossack, give me my horse!" he said. "Right, you! Stand aside! Stand aside! Make way!"

With a great effort he managed to reach his horse. Still continuing to shout, he began moving forward. The soldiers squeezed together to make way for him, but then bore against him again so strongly that they squeezed his leg tight, and the ones closest to him were not to blame, because they were being crushed even more powerfully.

"Nesvitsky! Nesvitsky! You ugly pig!" a hoarse voice called out from behind at just that moment.

Nesvitsky glanced round and fifteen paces away, separated from him by the living mass of moving infantry, he saw Vaska Denisov, red-faced, black-haired and tousled, with his cap on the back of his head and a hussar's pelisse thrown dashingly across his shoulder.

"Order these devils to make way," shouted Denisov, evidently in the throes of a fit of passion, rolling his glittering eyes as black as coal in their inflamed whites and waving his sabre still in its scabbard, holding it in a naked little hand as red as his face.

"Hey! Vasya!" Nesvitsky replied happily. "What are you up to?"

"The squadron can't get through," shouted Vaska Denisov, baring his white teeth angrily, spurring on his beautiful black thoroughbred Bedouin, who, twitching his ears as he ran up against bayonets, was snorting and scattering spray around himself from his curb-bit, beating his hooves resoundingly on the boards of the bridge, and seemed ready to leap over the railings of the bridge, if his rider would allow him. "What's this? Like sheep! Exactly like sheep! Exactly . . . give way! Stop, over there, you, the cart, damn it! I'll slice you with my sabre . . ." he shouted, actually baring his sabre and beginning to wave it about.

The soldiers squeezed against each other with frightened faces, and Denisov joined Nesvitsky.

"Why aren't you drunk today, then?" Nesvitsky said to Denisov when he rode up to him.

"They won't even give you time to get drunk!" replied Vaska Denisov. "All day long, dragging the regiment this way and that way. Let's fight, if we're going to. But God only knows what's going on!"

"What a dandy you are today!" said Nesvitsky, examining Denisov's new pelisse and saddlecloth.

Denisov smiled, took a handkerchief that gave off a smell of perfume out of his flap pocket, and thrust it under Nesvitsky's nose.

"But of course, I'm going into action! I shaved, brushed my teeth and put on scent."

The imposing figure of Denisov, accompanied by the Cossack, and Denisov's determination, waving his sabre and shouting wildly, had such an effect that they managed to squeeze through to the other side of the bridge and halted the infantry. At the exit Nesvitsky found the colonel to whom he had to pass on the orders and, having carried out his assignment, set off back.

After clearing the way, Denisov halted at the entrance to the bridge. Casually restraining the stallion that was straining to get to its fellows and stamping its foot, he looked at the squadron moving towards him. The hollow echoing of hoof beats rang along the boards of the bridge, as though there were several horses galloping, and the squadron, riding four men abreast in each row, with the officers in front, stretched out along the bridge and began emerging on to the other side.

Handsome young Peronsky, the finest horseman in the regiment and a rich man, brought up the rear, weaving to and fro on his three-thousand-rouble stallion. The foot soldiers, forced to halt, jostled in the trampled mud by the bridge, watching the clean, dandified hussars riding past them in strict order with that special feeling of spiteful, derisive antipathy with which different kinds of troops meet each other.

"Fine smart lads! Just the thing for the Podnovinskoe Park!"

"What are they good for? They only keep them for show!" said another.

"Don't kick up the dust, infantry!" joked a hussar whose horse pranced and splashed mud on a foot soldier.

"If I put you through a couple of days' marching with a knapsack, your fancy laces would soon be looking tattered," said the infantryman, wiping the mud from his face with his sleeve, "perched up there like a bird, not a man!"

"And if they sat you on a horse, Zinkin, you'd manage really well," said a corporal, mocking the thin little soldier hunched over under the weight of his knapsack.

"Put a club between your legs, and that will be your steed," the hussar responded.

# VIII

The remaining infantry hurriedly crossed the bridge, funnelling in tightly at the entrance. Eventually the carts all got across, the crush became less heavy and the final battalion stepped onto the bridge. Only the hussars of Denisov's squadron were left at the other end of the bridge to face the enemy. The enemy, visible in the far distance from the facing mountain, could still not be seen from the bridge below, since the horizon of the depression along which the river flowed was bounded by the opposing elevation at a distance of no more than half a *verst*. Ahead of them lay a wasteland, across which a mounted patrol of our Cossacks was moving here and there in little clusters. Suddenly troops in blue coats and artillery appeared on the opposite elevation of the road. It was the French. The Cossack patrol withdrew downhill at a canter. All the officers and men of Denisov's squadron, although they tried to talk about something else and look somewhere else, could not stop thinking about what was up there on the hill, and they all kept glancing constantly at the spots of colour appearing on the horizon, which they recognised as enemy troops. After midday the weather had cleared up again, the sun was bright as it moved lower over the Danube and the dark mountains surrounding it. It was quiet, and occasionally the sounds of horns and the shouts of the enemy reached them from that mountain. There was no one left now between the squadron and the enemy soldiers, apart from small mounted patrols. An empty space, about three hundred *sazhens* across, separated them from the enemy, who had stopped firing, so that the stern, menacing, unassailable and imperceptible line that separates two hostile forces could be sensed even more clearly.

A single step across that line, which resembles the line separating the living from the dead, and there is the mystery of suffering and death. And what is over there? Who is there? There, beyond this field and village and roof lit up by the sunlight? Nobody knows, you want to know and at the same time you are afraid to cross this line, and you want to cross it, and you know that sooner or later you will have to cross it and learn what is over there, on the far side of the line, just as you will inevitably learn what is over there, on the far side of the death. And you are so strong, healthy, merry and excited and surrounded by such healthy and boisterously excited men. Although no one thinks this, every man senses it when he is within view of the enemy, and this feeling lends a particular brilliance and joyful clarity to the impressions of everything that takes place at such moments.

The smoke-puff of a shot appeared on a hillock beside the enemy and the shot whistled over the heads of the squadron of hussars. The officers, who had been standing together, each went to their own places and the hussars began painstakingly drawing the horses up in lines. Everyone in the squadron fell silent. They all kept glancing straight ahead at the enemy and the squadron commander, waiting for the command. Another shot, the third, flew past. It was obvious that they were firing at the hussars; but the shot flew past over the hussars' heads with a swift, uniform whistle and struck somewhere behind them. The hussars did

NAPOLEON IN 1807
*Engraving by Debucourt*

not look round, but every time there was the sound of a shot flying over, the whole squadron, with its faces that were all identical but different, and its trimmed moustaches, held its breath as if by command while the shot was in the air and, tensing the muscles of all its legs in their tight blue breeches, half-stood in the stirrups and then sank down again. Without turning their heads, the soldiers squinted sideways at each other, curious to spy out the impression made on their comrades. On every face, from Denisov to the bugler, the single common expression of the struggle between irritation and excitement appeared around the lips and the chin. The sergeant-major frowned, surveying the soldiers as though he were threatening them with punishment. The cadet Mironov bent down every time a shot flew over. Rostov, standing on the left flank on his mount Grachik, handsome but with the bad legs, had the happy air of a pupil called out in front of a large audience to answer an examination question in which he was certain that he would distinguish himself. He glanced round at everyone with a clear, bright gaze, as though asking them to notice how calmly he stood his ground under fire. But in his face also, even against his will, that same expression of something new and stern appeared around the mouth.

"Who's that bowing over there? Cadet Miwonov! That won't do, look at me!" shouted Denisov, who could not stay still and was whirling round on his horse in front of the squadron. Vaska Denisov's face, with its snub nose and black hair, and his entire stocky little figure with the short, hair-covered fingers of the sinewy hand in which he was grasping the hilt of his drawn sabre, was exactly the same as it always was, especially in the evening after he had drunk two bottles. He was only redder than usual and, throwing his shaggy head back and up as birds do when they sing, pressing his spurs mercilessly into the sides of his good Bedouin with his small feet and appearing to fall backwards, he galloped off to the other flank of the squadron and shouted in a hoarse voice that they should inspect their pistols. As he rode by he glanced at the handsome officer Peronsky in the rear and hastily turned away.

In his semi-dress hussar uniform, on his steed that cost thousands, Peronsky was very handsome. But his handsome face was as white as snow. His thoroughbred stallion, hearing the terrible sounds above its head, had entered into that fervent fury of the well-trained thoroughbred of which children and hussars are so fond. He kept snorting, jingling the chain and rings of his bit and striking at the ground with his slim, muscular leg, sometimes not reaching it and waving his foot through the air, or, turning his lean head to the right and the left as far as his bit allowed, he squinted at his rider with a black, bulging bloodshot eye. Turning fierily away from him, Denisov set off towards Kiersten. The staff-captain was riding at a walk towards Denisov on a broad, sedate mare. The staff-captain, with his long moustaches, was serious as always, only his eyes were gleaming more than usual.

"What is this?" he said to Denisov. "This action won't get as far as an attack. You'll see, we'll withdraw."

"God only knows what they're doing!" shouted Denisov. "Ah! Wostov!" he cried to the cadet as he noticed him. "Well, here you are at last." And he smiled approvingly as he looked at the cadet, evidently pleased for him.

Rostov felt perfectly happy. Just at that moment the commander appeared on the bridge. Denisov galloped towards him.

"Your excellency! Permission to attack! I'll thwow them back!"

"What do you mean, attack?" said the commander in a bored voice, frowning as though at some tiresome fly. "And why are you holding position here? Can't you see the flankers are withdrawing? Pull your squadron back."

The squadron crossed the bridge and moved out of range without losing a single man. They were followed across by the second squadron, which had been on the skirmish line, and the final Cossacks withdrew, clearing that side of the river.

## IX

After crossing the bridge, one after another the two squadrons of Pavlograd Hussars set off back uphill. The regimental commander, Karl Bogdanovich Schubert, came across to Denisov's squadron and rode at a walk not far from Rostov, not paying the slightest attention to him, even though this was the first time they had seen each other since the old clash over Telyanin. Rostov, feeling that at the front he was in the power of a man whom he now considered himself guilty of offending, kept his eyes fixed on the athletic back, blond head and red neck of the regimental commander. Sometimes it seemed to Rostov that Bogdanich was only pretending not to notice him and that his entire purpose now was to test the cadet's courage, and he drew himself erect and gazed around cheerfully: sometimes it seemed to him that Bogdanich was deliberately riding close in order to demonstrate his own courage to Rostov. Sometimes Nikolai thought that now his enemy would deliberately send the squadron into a reckless attack in order to punish him. Sometimes he thought that after the attack the commander would walk up to him and magnanimously offer him, now a wounded man, the hand of reconciliation.

Zherkov's high-shouldered figure, well-known to the Pavlograders, rode up to the regimental commander. After his banishment from the central headquarters staff, Zherkov had not remained in the regiment, saying that he was no fool, to go slaving away at the front, when he would be better rewarded at staff headquarters for doing nothing, and he had managed to obtain a place as an orderly with Prince Bagration. He had come to his former commanding officer with an order from the commander of the rearguard.

"Colonel," he said with grim seriousness, addressing Nikolai's enemy and surveying his comrades, "the order is to halt and fire the bridge."

"Who the ordered?" the colonel asked morosely.

"That I do not know, colonel, *who the ordered*," the cornet replied naïvely and seriously, "only that the prince told me: 'Go and tell the colonel that the hussars must go back quickly and fire the bridge.'"

Following Zherkov, an officer of the retinue rode up to the colonel of hussars with the same order. Following the officer of the retinue, the fat Nesvitsky rode up on a Cossack horse that was scarcely able to carry him at a gallop.

"What's this, colonel," he cried as he was still riding up, "I told you to fire the bridge; and now someone's garbled it, everyone's going mad up there and you can't make sense of anything."

The colonel unhurriedly halted the regiment and turned to Nesvitsky:

"You told me about the combustible substances," he said, "but you don't told me anything about setting fire to them."

"Come on now, old man," Nesvitsky said when he came to a halt, taking off his cap and straightening his sweaty hair with a plump hand, "certainly I told you to fire the bridge when you had put the combustible substances in place."

"I'm not your 'old man', mister staff officer, and you did not told me fire the bridge! I know military service, and am in the habit of following strictly orders. You told me they would set fire to the bridge. How by the Holy Spirit know can I . . ."

"There, it is always the same," said Nesvitsky with a wave of his hand. "What brings you here?" he asked, addressing Zherkov.

"Why, the same thing. But you have become all damp, allow me to wring you out."

"You said, mister staff officer . . ." the colonel continued in an offended tone.

"Colonel," the officer of the retinue interrupted, "you need to hurry, or the enemy will have moved his guns close enough to fire grapeshot."

The colonel looked without speaking at the officer of the retinue, at the fat headquarters staff officer, at Zherkov and frowned.

"I shall fire the bridge," he said in a solemn tone of voice as though, despite all the problems they were causing him, this was how he showed his magnanimity.

Striking his horse with his long, well-muscled legs, as if it were to blame for everything, the colonel rode out in front and commanded the second squadron, the very one in which Rostov was serving under Denisov's command, to go back to the bridge.

"So that's how it is," thought Rostov, "he wants to test me!" His heart faltered and the blood rushed to his face. "Then let him look and see if I'm a coward," he thought.

Again there appeared on all the jolly faces of the men in the squadron the same serious expression that they had worn when they were holding position under fire.

Nikolai kept his eyes fixed on his enemy, the regimental commander, wishing to discover some confirmation of his guesses in his face, but the colonel did not even glance at Nikolai once and he looked stern and solemn, as he always did at the front. The command rang out.

"Look lively, lively now!" said several voices around him. Snagging the reins with their sabres, jangling their spurs in their haste, the hussars dismounted, not knowing themselves what they were going to do. The hussars crossed themselves. Rostov was no longer looking at the regimental commander, he had no time for that. He was afraid, his heart was sinking in fear that he might somehow fall behind the hussars. His hand trembled as he handed his horse to the holder, and he could feel the blood pounding as it rushed to his heart. Denisov rode past him, lounging backwards and shouting something. Nikolai could not see anything apart from the hussars running around him, getting their spurs tangled and jangling their sabres.

"A stretcher!" someone's voice shouted behind him. Rostov did not think about what the demand for a stretcher meant, he ran, trying only to be ahead of all the others, but just at the bridge, not looking where he was putting his feet, he stepped into the sticky trampled mud, slipped and fell on to his hands. The others ran round him.

"On both sides, captain," he heard the regimental commander's voice say. The commander, having ridden forward, had stopped on his horse not far from the bridge with a triumphant, jolly expression.

Rostov, wiping his dirty hands on his breeches, glanced round at his enemy and started running further, assuming that the further forward he went, the better it would be. But Bogdanich, even though he had not been looking and did not recognise Rostov, shouted at him:

"Who's that running in the middle of the bridge? To the right side! Cadet, come back!" he shouted angrily.

Even now, however, Karl Bogdanovich did not pay any attention to him: but he did turn to Denisov who, flaunting his courage, had ridden on to the boards of the bridge.

"Why take a risk, captain! You should dismount," said the colonel.

"Eh! It'll hit whoever it likes," replied Vaska Denisov, turning round in the saddle.

Meanwhile Nesvitsky, Zherkov and the officer of the retinue were standing together, out of range, and watching either one or another of the small groups of men in yellow shakos, dark-green jackets decorated with tasselled cords and blue breeches fussing about beside the bridge, or watching the far side, where in the distance the blue coats were drawing nearer, and the groups with horses which could easily be taken for gun crews.

"Will they fire the bridge or won't they? Who'll be first? Will they get there and fire the bridge, or will the French get within grapeshot distance and kill them all?" Every one of the large number of troops who were standing above the bridge had his heart in his mouth and could not help asking himself this question, and in the bright evening light they watched the bridge and the hussars, and the far side where the blue hoods were advancing with bayonets and guns.

"Oh! The hussars are in for it!" said Nesvitsky. "They're within grape-shot range now."

"He shouldn't have taken so many men," said the officer of the suite.

"No, he really shouldn't," said Nesvitsky. "He could have sent two brave lads, it would have been all the same."

"Ah, your excellency," interjected Zherkov, keeping his eyes fixed on the hussars, but still speaking with that naïve manner of his, which made it impossible to guess whether what he said was serious or not. "Ah, your excellency! What a way to think! Send two men, then who's going to give us an Order of St. Vladimir with a ribbon? But this way, even though they'll take a drubbing, you can still present the squadron and get a ribbon for yourself. Our Bogdanich knows the ways things are done."

"Well," said the officer of the retinue, "that's grapeshot." He pointed to the French artillery pieces which were being uncoupled from their limbers and rapidly moving away.

"But he's wrong," continued Zherkov, "I'll be presented too, we were under fire as well."

At that moment a puff of smoke appeared again in the groups with the artillery pieces, then a second and a third and just as the sound of the first shot reached them, a fourth puff appeared. Two sounds one after the other, then a third.

"O-oh!" gasped Nesvitsky, as if from some searing pain, clutching at the arm of the officer of the retinue. "Look, one of them has fallen, he's fallen."

"Two, I think."

"If I were Tsar, I would never go to war. And why are they taking so long?"

They were hastily reloading the French field guns. Again, this time at even intervals, the puffs of smoke appeared, and the grapeshot rattled and clattered along the bridge. But this time Nesvitsky could not see what was happening there. Thick smoke rose from the bridge. The hussars had managed to set fire to it, and the French batteries were no longer firing at them simply in order to hinder them, but because the guns were trained and there was someone to shoot at. The French had time to fire three rounds of grapeshot before the hussars returned to the horse-holders. Two volleys were fired inaccurately and all the grapeshot carried too far, but the final shot landed in the middle of the group of hussars and felled three of them.

Nikolai Rostov, obsessed by his relations with Bogdanovich, stayed on the bridge, not knowing what he ought to do. There was no one to hack at (in the way that he had always imagined battle) and he could not help in firing the bridge either, because he had not brought a plaited twist of straw with him, as the other soldiers had done. He was standing there looking around when suddenly there was a rattling sound like nuts being scattered along the bridge and one of the hussars closest to him fell on to the railings with a groan. Nikolai ran over to him together with some others. Again someone shouted: "Stretcher!" Four men grabbed hold of the hussar and began lifting him up.

"Aaaagh! Leave me, for Christ's sake," cried the wounded man, but even so they lifted him and set him down. His cap fell off. They picked it up and threw it on to the stretcher. Nikolai Rostov turned away, as though looking for something, he began looking into the distance, at the water of the Danube, at the sky, at the sun. How good the sky looked, how blue, calm and deep! How bright and triumphant the descending sun was! How tenderly lustrous the gleaming water was in the distant Danube! And even better were the distant blue mountains beyond the Danube, the convent, the mysterious ravines, the pine forests filled up to the crowns of the trees with mist . . . it was quiet and happy there . . . "I wouldn't want anything, anything at all, if only I were there," thought Nikolai. "In just me and this sun there is so much happiness, but here . . . groaning, suffering, fear and this uncertainty, this haste . . . Now they're shouting something again and again everyone has gone running back somewhere, and I'm running with them, and there it is, there is death above me, around me . . . another instant and I shall never see this sun again, this water, this ravine . . ." At that moment the sun began moving behind the clouds; ahead of Nikolai another stretcher appeared. The fear of death and the stretcher, and love of the sun and life, all fused together into a single, painfully disturbing impression.

"Lord God Almighty! The One who is up there in this sky, save, forgive and protect me!" Nikolai whispered to himself.

The hussars ran up to the horse-holders, their voices became louder and calmer, the stretcher disappeared from view . . .

"Well, bwother, had a whiff of gunpowder?" Vaska Denisov's voice shouted in his ear.

"It's all over, but I'm a coward, I'm a coward," thought Nikolai, and, sighing deeply, he took his Grachik, who was holding one foot out to the side, and began to mount him.

"What was that, grapeshot?" he asked Denisov.

"The weal thing, all wight!" shouted Denisov. "We put up a fine show. And it was a foul job! An attack is pleasant work, you're all on fire, you forget yourself, but this is God knows what, they shoot at you like a target."

And Denisov rode off to a group of men that had halted not far away from Rostov: the regimental commander, Nesvitsky, Zherkov and the officer of the retinue.

"But it seems that no one noticed," Rostov thought to himself. And indeed, no one had noticed, because everyone was familiar with the feeling that the cadet new to fire had experienced for the first time.

"This will mean a report for you," said Zherkov, "they might even promote me to second lieutenant."

"Inform the prince that the bridge I have fired," the colonel said triumphantly and happily.

"And if they ask about our losses?"

"A mere trifle!" rumbled the colonel. "Two hussars wounded and one killed *outright*," he said with evident delight, unable to restrain a happy smile as he loudly snapped out the lovely word *outright*.

# X

Pursued by a French army of a hundred thousand men under the command of Bonaparte, met by an unfriendly local population, no longer trusting in their allies, suffering from a shortage of provisions and obliged to act outside all the anticipated conditions of warfare, the Russian army of thirty thousand, under the command of Kutuzov, hastily retreated downstream along the Danube, halting where the enemy closed in on it and defending itself with rearguard action only insofar as necessary to withdraw without loss of heavy equipment. There were actions at Lambach, Amstetten and Melk, but despite the courage and fortitude that were acknowledged even by the French against whom the Russians were fighting, the only consequence of these actions was even more rapid withdrawal. The Austrian troops who had avoided capture at the Ulm and joined with Kutuzov at Braunau, now separated from the Russian army and Kutuzov was left with only his own weak, exhausted forces. It was no longer possible even to think of defending Vienna. Instead of the offensive strategy of war, thoroughly considered according to the laws of the new science of military strategy, the plan for which had been transmitted to Kutuzov by the Austrian Hofkriegsrat while he was in Vienna, the only goal – an almost unattainable one – that now presented itself to Kutuzov was to unite with the forces on their way from Russia without destroying his army as Mack had done at the Ulm.

On the 28th of October Kutuzov and his army crossed to the left bank of the Danube and halted for the first time, having put the Danube between them and the main forces of the French. On the 30th they attacked Mortier's division on the left bank and routed it. In this action trophies were taken for the first time: a banner, guns and two enemy generals. For the first time, following two weeks of retreat, the Russian forces had halted and had not only been left holding the battlefield after the battle, but had also routed the French. Despite the fact that the troops were inadequately dressed and exhausted, with their numbers reduced by a third by stragglers and wounded, dead and sick, despite all this, the halt at Krems and the victory over Mortier raised the spirits of the troops significantly. Throughout the army and at its headquarters there circulated extremely joyful, but inaccurate rumours of columns supposedly approaching from Russia, of some victory won by the Austrians and of Bonaparte retreating in fright.

During the battle, Prince Andrei had been with the Austrian general Schmidt, who was killed in the course of the action. Bolkonsky's horse was wounded under him and he himself received a slight graze on the arm from a bullet. As a sign of the commander-in-chief's special favour, he was sent to carry the news of this victory to the Austrian court, at that time no longer located in Vienna, which was under threat from French forces, but in Brünn. On the night following the battle an excited but unweary Prince Andrei (who, despite his delicate appearance, could bear physical fatigue far better than the very strongest of men) arrived in Krems on horseback with a report from Dokhturov for Kutuzov, and that same night Prince Andrei was sent as a courier to Brünn. To be sent as a courier signified, in addition to awards, an important step towards promotion. Having received the dispatch, and letters and instructions from comrades, Prince Andrei set off at night, getting into a *britzka* by the light of a lantern.

"Well, brother," said Nesvitsky, embracing him as he saw him on his way. "I congratulate you in advance on the Order of Marya-Theresa."

"I tell you as an honest man," replied Prince Andrei, "if they were to give me nothing, it is all the same to me. I am so happy, so happy . . . that I am carrying such news . . . that I myself saw it . . . you understand me."

The exciting sense of danger and awareness of one's own courage that Prince Andrei had experienced during the battle had only been intensified by a sleepless night and the mission to the Austrian court. He was a different man, animated and affectionate.

"Well, Christ be with you . . ."

"Goodbye, my dear friend. Goodbye, Kozlovsky."

"Kiss the pretty hand of Baroness Seifer from me. And bring back at least a bottle of *Cordial* if you have room," said Nesvitsky.

"I'll bring the bottle and give the kiss."

"Goodbye."

The whip cracked and the postal *britzka* set off at a gallop over the dark mud road, past the lights of the troops. It was a dark, starry night, the road was black against the white snow that had fallen the previous day, the day of the battle. Whether reviewing his impressions of the battle that had taken place, or happily imagining the impression that he would produce with the news of victory, recalling how he had been seen off by the commander-in-chief and by his comrades, Prince Andrei experienced the feeling of a man who has been waiting a long time for the happiness he desires to begin and has finally achieved it. No sooner did he close his eyes than his ears were filled with the roar of muskets and artillery, which fused with the hammering of the wheels and the impression of victory. Sometimes he began to dream that the Russians were running, that he himself had been killed, but he came to hurriedly, with a happy feeling, as if discovering anew that none of that had happened and, on the contrary, it was the French who had run. He recalled once again all the details of the victory, of his own calm courage during the battle and, reassured, he fell into a doze . . . The dark, starry night was followed by a bright, cheerful morning. The snow was melting in the sunshine, the horses were galloping along briskly and a diverse sequence of forests, fields and villages passed by on the right and left alike.

At one of the post-stages he overtook a string of wagons carrying Russian wounded. Sprawling on the front wagon, the Russian officer leading the transport shouted something, abusing a soldier with coarse words. There were six or more pale, bandaged, dirty wounded jolting over the rocky road in each of the long German Vorspans. Some of them were talking (he could hear Russian speech), others were eating bread, the most seriously hurt silently watched the courier galloping past them with the meek, childish interest of the sick.

"The poor unfortunates!" thought Prince Andrei. "But they are also inevitable . . ." He ordered the driver to stop and asked a soldier in which action they had been wounded.

"The day before yesterday on the Danube," the soldier replied. Prince Andrei took out his purse and gave the soldier three gold coins.

"For everybody," he added, addressing the officer who had come up to him. "Get well, lads," he said to the soldiers, "there's still plenty of work to do."

"Well, mister adjutant, what news?" asked the officer, evidently wishing to strike up a conversation.

"Good news. Forward!" he called to the driver and galloped on. It was already completely dark when Prince Andrei drove into Brünn and found himself surrounded by tall buildings, the lights of shops, windows, houses and street lamps, beautiful carriages rattling along the roadway and all the atmosphere of a big, bustling town that a military man always finds so attractive after camp. Despite his rapid journey and sleepless night, as Prince Andrei drove up to the palace, he felt even more lively than the evening before, only his eyes now gleamed with a feverish glitter, and his thoughts revolved with exceptional rapidity and clarity. All the details of the battle appeared vividly to him again, no longer vague, but quite definite, in the condensed exposition which he was making to the Emperor Franz in his imagination. He vividly imagined the Emperor's face, and all the chance questions that might be put to him, and the answers he would give. He expected to be presented to the Emperor straight away. But at the main entrance to the palace, an official ran out to him and, recognising him as a courier, showed him to a different entrance.

"Turn right out of this corridor, your excellency, there you will find the duty aide-de-camp. He will take you to the war minister."

The duty aide-de-camp, after greeting Andrei, asked him to wait and went to the war minister. Five minutes later the aide-de-camp came back and, bowing with especial politeness and allowing Prince Andrei to precede him, showed the prince along a corridor to the study where the war minister was at work. The war minister apparently wished to employ his refined courtesy to protect himself against any attempt at familiarity by the Russian adjutant. Prince Andrei's jubilant exaltation faded significantly as he approached the door of the war minister's study. He felt insulted and, as always happened in his proud heart, at that very moment the feeling of offence expanded, unperceived by him, into a feeling of contempt that was entirely without any basis. In that same instant his resourceful mind also suggested to him the viewpoint from which he had the right to despise both the adjutant and the war minister. "No doubt it will seem to them very easy to win a victory, without smelling gunpowder," he thought. His eyes narrowed contemptuously, his arms slumped lifelessly at his sides and he walked into the war minister's study as if he could barely drag his feet along. This feeling grew stronger still when he saw the war minister sitting at a large desk paying no attention, for the first two minutes, to the man who had just come in. The war minister, whose bald head with its grey temples was bent over the papers which he was reading, in the light of two wax candles, and marking with a pencil, went on to complete his reading, refusing to raise his head, even when the door had opened and he heard footsteps.

"Take this and pass it on," the war minister said to his adjutant, handing him some papers and still ignoring the courier.

Prince Andrei sensed that, of all the affairs occupying the war minister, the actions of Kutuzov's army were those least capable of holding his interest, or so he wished to make the Russian courier feel. "But that is all the same to me," he thought. The war minister gathered up the rest of his papers, squared them together edge to edge and raised his head. He had an intelligent and distinctive face. But as soon as he addressed Prince Andrei, his intelligent and firm expression altered, in a manner that was clearly habitual and deliberate, and his face assumed a stupid, affected smile that did not attempt to conceal its own artificiality, the smile of a man who receives many petitioners one after another.

"From General-Field-Marshal Kutuzov?" he asked. "Good news, I hope? There has been a clash with Mortier? A victory? About time!"

He took the dispatch, which was addressed to him, and began reading it with a sad expression.

"Ah, my God! My God! Schmidt!" he said in German. "What a misfortune! What a misfortune!" After quickly looking through the dispatch, he laid it on the desk and glanced at Prince Andrei, evidently pondering something.

"Ah, what a misfortune! You say the action is conclusive? But Mortier has not been taken, even so." He thought for a moment. "I am very glad you have brought good news, although the death of Schmidt is a high price to pay for victory. His Majesty will certainly wish to see you, but not today. Thank you, take a rest now. Tomorrow be at the exit after the parade. However, I will let you know."

The stupid smile that had disappeared during the conversation appeared once again on the war minister's face.

"Goodbye, thank you very much. His Majesty the Emperor will probably wish to see you," he repeated and inclined his head.

Prince Andrei went out into the waiting room. There were two adjutants sitting there, talking to each other, evidently about something entirely unrelated to Prince Andrei's arrival. One of them stood up reluctantly and, with the same insolent politeness as before, asked Prince Andrei to write his rank, title and address in the book that he handed to him. Prince Andrei complied with his wish in silence and left the waiting room without even glancing in his direction.

As he emerged from the palace, he felt that all the interest and joy that victory had brought him had now been left behind in the indifferent hands of the war minister and the polite adjutant. His entire frame of mind had changed instantly and the battle now seemed to him like a distant memory from long ago: what now seemed most vital and significant to him were his reception by the war minister, the politeness of the adjutant and his forthcoming presentation to the emperor.

# XI

Prince Andrei went on to the house of the Russian diplomat, Bilibin. The diplomat's German servant recognised Prince Andrei, who had stayed with Bilibin when he visited Vienna, and chatted garrulously as he received him.

"Herr von Bilibin was obliged to leave his apartment in Vienna. That accursed Bonaparte!" said the diplomat's servant. "He has created so many misfortunes, so much loss and disorder!"

"Is Mr. Bilibin well?" asked Prince Andrei.

"Not entirely well, he's still not going out, and will be very glad to see you. This way, if you please. They will bring your things. Will the Cossack be staying here too? Look, here's the master, he has heard you."

"Ah, dear prince, no guest is more welcome," said Bilibin, coming out to greet his visitor. "Franz, put the prince's things in my bedroom. Well, here as a herald of victory? Excellent. But I am a house-bound invalid, as you see."

"Yes, a herald of victory," replied Prince Andrei, "but not, it would seem, a very welcome one."

"Well, if you are not too tired, tell me of your exalted feats over supper," said Bilibin and, putting his feet up on a chaise-longue, he settled himself by the fire to wait until Prince Andrei, washed and changed, emerged into the diplomat's luxurious study and sat down to the meal that had been prepared for him. "Franz, move the screen, or it will be too hot for the prince."

After his journey, and indeed after the entire campaign, throughout which he had been totally deprived of the comforts of cleanliness and a civilised life, Prince Andrei now felt pleasantly relaxed on being once more in the luxurious surroundings to which he had been accustomed since childhood. He also found it pleasant, after his reception by the Austrians, to talk, if not actually in Russian (for he and Bilibin spoke in French), then at least with someone Russian who, he knew, shared his own aversion (an aversion now felt with particular intensity) to the Austrians. The only thing that struck an unpleasant note was that Bilibin listened to his account with almost the same distrust and indifference as had the Austrian war minister.

Bilibin was a man of about thirty-five, a bachelor, from the same social circles as Prince Andrei. They had already been acquainted in St. Petersburg, but had become particularly close during Prince Andrei's last visit to Vienna with Kutuzov. Bilibin had told him on that occasion that should he ever come to Vienna, he must be sure to stay with him. Just as Prince Andrei was a young man who promised to go far in the military field, so Bilibin promised even greater things in the field of diplomacy. Though still young in years, he was not new to diplomacy, since he had entered the service at sixteen, and had been in Paris, in Copenhagen and now in Vienna where he held an important post. Both the chancellor and our envoy in Vienna knew and valued him. He was not one of those numerous diplomats who are expected to display purely negative qualities, doing nothing of great note and merely speaking French in order to be effective. He was, rather, a diplomat who loved his work and knew how to go about it and, despite his natural indolence, sometimes spent whole nights at his desk. Whatever the task, he always applied the same effort. It was not the question "why?" but the question "how?" that interested him. No matter what the content, it was the composing of a circular, a memorandum or a report with concise, deft elegance that gave him satisfaction. Aside from his writing, Bilibin's wider capacities were also greatly valued, in particular his ability to establish contact with the higher spheres of power and maintain dialogue at that level.

Bilibin loved conversation in the same way that he loved work, but only so long as it could be subtly witty. In company he was constantly alert for the chance to say something of note and he would only take part when he could do so. All Bilibin's talk was *spiced* with sharply original, well-turned phrases that appealed to everyone. These witticisms were expressly forged in Bilibin's internal laboratory to travel forth, so that lesser members of society might remember them with ease and bear them from one set of drawing rooms to another. And indeed, Bilibin's opinions had spread through all the drawing rooms of Vienna, being frequently repeated and frequently having influence on matters deemed important.

His thin, emaciated, unusually pale face was entirely covered with large, young wrinkles, which always looked as assiduously and scrupu- lously clean as the tips of one's fingers after a bath. The movements of these wrinkles were his physiognomy's main means of expression. Either his forehead would wrinkle into broad folds and his eyebrows would rise, or his eyebrows would be lowered and large folds would form on his cheeks. The gaze of the small, deep-set eyes was always direct and jovial.

Despite his refinement of dress, refinement of manners and the elegant French that he spoke so well, there were nevertheless still Russian traits discernible in his whole face, figure and the modulations of his voice.

Bolkonsky related the action in the most modest fashion, without once mentioning himself, and told about the reception by the war minister.

"They made me as welcome with this news as a dog at a game of skittles," he concluded.

Bilibin laughed and relaxed the folds in his skin.

"And yet, *mon cher*," he said, contemplating his own fingernail from a distance and again puckering the skin above his left eye, "for all my respect for the *Army of Orthodoxy*, I'm bound to say that your victory was not an altogether brilliant one."

He went on in the same vein in French, pronouncing in Russian only those words that he wished to emphasise with contempt.

"How could it be? You fell with the entire bulk of your army upon the unfortunate Mortier with his single division, and this Mortier slips through your hands? Where's the victory in that?"

"Come now, be serious," Prince Andrei replied, pushing away his plate, "we can still claim without bragging that it's somewhat better than the Ulm."

"Why did you not capture us a marshal, at least one?"

"Because not everything happens as expected, or as smoothly as at a parade. We had planned, as I told you, to approach the rear by seven in the morning, but we had not reached it by five in the evening."

"And why did you not arrive at seven in the morning? You ought to have arrived by seven in the morning," said Bilibin, smiling, "you really ought to have arrived by seven in the morning."

"And why did you not impress upon Bonaparte via diplomatic channels that it would be better for him to leave Genoa alone?" Prince Andrei asked in the same tone.

"I know," interrupted Bilibin, "you're thinking it's all very easy to capture marshals while sitting on a divan by the fireside. That is true, but even so, why did you not capture him? And don't be surprised that not only the war minister, but also the most august Emperor and King Franz will not be over-delighted by your victory and even I, a miserable secretary at the Russian embassy, do not feel any need to express my joy by giving my Franz a thaler and letting him take time off to go to the Prater with his girlfriend . . . although of course, there's no Prater around here."

BILIBIN
*Drawing by M. S. Bashilov, 1867*

He looked directly at Prince Andrei and suddenly released the gathered skin of his forehead.

"Now it is my turn to ask you 'why', *mon cher*," said Bolkonsky. "I must confess, I do not understand, perhaps there are diplomatic subtleties here beyond my feeble intellect, but I do not understand. Mack loses an entire army, the Archduke Ferdinand and the Archduke Karl show no signs of life and make mistake upon mistake, and finally only Kutuzov achieves a genuine victory and shatters the French spell, and the war minister is not even interested in knowing the details."

"That is precisely the reason why, my dear fellow. Take another piece of roast, there won't be anything else."

"*Merci.*"

"You see, *mon cher* – hoorah for the Tsar, for Rus, for the faith! – all that is fine and good but what interest, say I, have we, the Austrian court, in your victories? Bring us good news of a victory by Archduke Karl or Ferdinand – one archduke is as good as another, as you know – even if it's only over Bonaparte's fire brigade, and that is a different matter, we'll set the cannon roaring. But this only seems deliberately intended to mock us. Archduke Karl does nothing, Archduke Ferdinand covers himself in shame. You abandon Vienna and no longer defend it, as if you had said to us: God is with us, but you go with God – and take your capital with you. The one general we all loved, Schmidt, you lead into the path of a bullet and then you regale us with a victory! You have captured a couple of navvies dressed up as Bonaparte's generals. You are bound to admit that nothing more irritating than the news that you bring could possibly be imagined. As if you did it on purpose, quite on purpose. Apart from which, even if you did win a brilliant victory, even if Archduke Karl did win a brilliant victory, what would that change, in the general course of events? It's already too late, with Vienna occupied by the French."

"Occupied, you say? Vienna is occupied?"

"Not only is it occupied, but Bonaparte is in Schönbrunn and the count, your dear Count Vrbna, is on his way to receive his orders."

After the fatigue and impressions of the journey, the reception, and especially after the meal, Bolkonsky found it hard to grasp the full meaning of the words he had just heard.

"That is a quite different kettle of fish," he said, taking out a toothpick and moving closer to the hearth.

"This morning Count Lichtenfels was here," Bilibin continued, "and he showed me a letter which described the French parade in Vienna in detail. Prince Murat and the whole caboodle . . . You can see why your victory is not such a very joyous event and why you cannot be welcomed as saviour . . ."

"Really, it makes no difference to me, absolutely no difference," said Prince Andrei, beginning to understand that his news of the battle at

Krems really was of little importance in view of such events as the occupation of the capital of Austria. "But how was Vienna taken? What of the bridge and its famous fortification, and Prince Auersperg? We heard rumours that Prince Auersperg was defending Vienna," he said.

"Prince Auersperg is stationed on this side, our side, and defending us, defending us very poorly, I think, but nonetheless defending us. But Vienna is on the other side. No, the bridge has still not been taken, and I hope it will not be taken, because it is mined and orders have been given to blow it up. Otherwise we should have been in the mountains of Bohemia long ago, and you and your army would have spent a bad quarter of an hour caught between two fires."

"If that happens, the campaign is over," said Prince Andrei.

"That is what I think too. And the simpletons here think it as well, but they don't dare to say so. It will be just as I said at the start of the campaign, this whole business will be decided not by your skirmish at Dürenstein, and not by gunpowder at all, but by the people who dreamed it up," said Bilibin, repeating one of his *bons mots*, releasing the skin on his forehead and pausing for a moment. "The only question is, what will come of the Berlin meeting between Emperor Alexander and the King of Prussia? If Prussia joins the alliance, they will leave Austria no choice, and there will be war. But if not, then all that has to be done (take this pear, it is very good) is to agree on where to compose the initial articles of the new Campo Formio."

"But what exceptional genius this is!" Prince Andrei suddenly exclaimed, clenching his small hand and banging it on the table. "And what luck this man has!"

"Buonaparte?" enquired Bilibin, wrinkling his forehead to signal the approach of a *bon mot*. "Buonaparte?" he said, with special emphasis on the *u*. "I rather think that now he is dictating laws to Austria from Schönbrunn, he should be relieved of his *u*. I hereby declare an innovation, to call him simply Bonaparte. Wouldn't you like some more coffee? Franz!"

"No, joking apart," said Prince Andrei, "you are in a position to know. What do you think, how will all this end?"

"This is what I think. Austria has been left looking foolish, and she is not used to that, and she will repay the favour. And she has been left looking foolish because, in the first place, her provinces are ruined (they say the *Army of Orthodoxy* is terrible when it comes to plunder), her army is shattered, her capital is captured, and all this for his Sardinian Majesty's beautiful eyes."

"Is Emperor Alexander expected?" asked Prince Andrei.

"Any day. They will deceive us; my intuition tells me of diplomatic contacts with France and projects for peace, a secret peace, separately concluded."

"Wouldn't that be nice!" said Prince Andrei.

"Time will tell."

They paused.

Bilibin relaxed his brow again as a sign that this conversation was at an end.

"Did you know that during your last visit you made a total conquest of the Baroness Seifer?"

"What, is she still as enthusiastic as ever?" asked Prince Andrei, remembering one of the agreeable women among whom he had enjoyed great success during his visit to Vienna with Kutuzov.

"She is the only one who is a real woman, not just a lady," said Bilibin, making one of his jokes. "We shall go and see her tomorrow. For you and for her, I shall disobey my doctor. You must enjoy the days you spend here. Whatever the Austrian cabinet are like, the people, especially the women, are exceptionally charming, and I should wish for nothing better than to spend my entire life in Vienna. Ah yes, do you know who is a constant visitor in her drawing room? Our Hippolyte Kuragin. He is the most forthright fool I have ever set eyes on. You will see him here tomorrow. Our people meet at my house on Thursdays, and you will see them all. But anyway, go to bed, I can see that you are ready to drop."

When Prince Andrei reached the room prepared for him and lay down in his clean linen on the feather mattresses and fragrant warmed pillows, the battle of which he had brought news seemed far, very far, away. The Prussian alliance, Hippolyte Kuragin, the Baroness Seifer, the treachery of Austria, Bonaparte's new triumph, the parade and his reception by Emperor Franz the next day occupied his thoughts. He closed his eyes, but the moment he did so his ears were filled with the crackling of a cannonade, a volley of shots, the clacking of carriage wheels, and then there were the musketeers coming down the mountain once again, stretched out in a long, thin line and the French were firing, and he could feel his heart thumping as he rode out to the front beside Schmidt, and the bullets whistled merrily around him, and he experienced that feeling of a ten-fold joy in life that he had not experienced since childhood. He came to. "Yes, it all did happen! . . ." he said happily, smiling to himself like a child, and fell into a deep, youthful sleep.

# XII

The following morning he woke late. Reviewing his impression of the previous day, he first of all remembered that today he had to be presented to Emperor Franz, and then he remembered the war minister, the civil Austrian aide-de-camp, Bilibin and the previous evening's conversation. The memory of the battle seemed like something from long ago, something that had happened long ago and meant nothing. After attiring himself for the trip to the palace in full dress uniform, which he had not worn for a long time, he entered Bilibin's study fresh, poised and handsome, with his bandaged arm, in a mood more suited to high society and the court than to military matters. Already there, sitting, lounging and standing about in the study were several gentlemen of the diplomatic corps who were visiting Bilibin – the ones whom he had called *our people*. The majority were Russian, but there was one Englishman and one Swede. Bolkonsky was acquainted with many of them, as he was with Hippolyte: Bilibin introduced him to the others, calling Bolkonsky the herald of the victory of which the entire city was already aware.

*"Les plumes . . ."* said Bilibin, indicating his own people. *". . . et l'épée,"* he said, indicating Bolkonsky. "Gentlemen, allow me to present one of those people who possess the art of constant good fortune. He has always been loved by the prettiest of women, and possesses the prettiest wife and the handsomest exterior and has never been, nor will he ever be, wounded in the nose, the belly or anywhere even worse, like my acquaintance Captain Gnilopupov. What a wonderful name! Unfortunately, you foreign gentlemen" – he turned to the Englishman and the Swede – "cannot appreciate the full charm and euphony of this name. But gentlemen, explain to me if you can why Captain Gnilopupov always has to be wounded in the nose or simply killed, but a man like Bolkonsky is wounded in the arm, in order to render him even more attractive in the eyes of the women."

The guests who visited Bilibin – young, rich and jovial men of the world – made up, both in Vienna and here, a distinct circle which Bilibin, in his role as the head of that circle, called *our people – les nôtres*. Those within this circle, which consisted almost entirely of diplomats, evidently had their own interests in a higher sphere, which had nothing in common with war and politics, and concerned relationships with certain women and the formal side of official service. These gentlemen evidently accepted Prince Andrei quite willingly into their circle as *one of their own* (an honour which they extended to only a few). Out of politeness and as a pretext for engaging in conversation, they asked him a few questions about the army and the battle, and then the conversation reverted once more to disparate, inconsequential jokes and gossip. They all spoke in French. And yet despite their familiarity with that language and their lively mood, their conversation had the character of a pretence or imitation of someone else's merriment.

"But it is especially good," said one, relating the misfortune of a diplomatic colleague, "especially good that the chancellor told him bluntly that his appointment to London was a promotion and that was how he should regard it. You should have seen his face on hearing that! But worst of all, gentlemen, let me tell you Kuragin's secret: a man runs into bad luck, and this Don Juan, this terrible fellow, goes and takes advantage."

Prince Hippolyte was lying across a Voltaire armchair with his legs draped over one of the armrests; he laughed wildly.

"Go on, go on," he said.

"Oh, the Don Juan! Oh, the serpent!" said several voices.

"You may not know it, Bolkonsky," said Bilibin, addressing Prince Andrei, "but all the horrors of the French army (I almost said the Russian army) are as nothing compared with what this man has done among the women."

"Woman is the friend of man," Prince Hippolyte declared sententiously and began looking through his lorgnette at his raised feet.

Bilibin and *our people* laughed unceremoniously, glancing at Hippolyte. Prince Andrei realised that this Hippolyte, whose contact with his own wife had almost (it must be admitted) made him feel jealous, was simply a jester in light-hearted company.

"Yes, I must treat you to Kuragin," Bilibin said quietly to Bolkonsky. "He is delightful when he discusses politics: you should see how pompous he sounds."

He sat down beside Hippolyte and, gathering the folds on his forehead, began to discuss politics. Prince Andrei and the others clustered round them.

"The Berlin cabinet cannot express its opinion of the alliance," Hippolyte began, surveying them all meaningfully, "without expressing . . . as in its latest note . . . you understand . . . you understand . . . however, if His Majesty the Emperor does not swerve from the essential principle of our alliance . . ."

Even though *our people* were listening to Hippoplyte with amused faces, Prince Andrei stepped away in disgust: but Hippolyte grabbed him by the arm.

"*Attendez*, I haven't finished . . ." he went on, evidently wishing to inspire respect in the new arrival with his opinions on politics. "I believe intervention is more effective than non-intervention. And . . ." He paused. "One should not consider the matter concluded by the rejection of our despatch of the 28th of November. That is how everything will end up."

And he released Bolkonsky's hand, showing thereby that he had now quite finished.

"Demosthenes! I know you from the pebble hidden beneath your golden tongue," said Bilibin, his cap of hair shifting on his head in his pleasure.

And they all burst into boisterous laughter, which was provoked still more by Hippolyte's own way of laughing: he was evidently in difficulty and choking, but could not restrain the raucous laughter that convulsed his usually impassive face.

"Well, I tell you what, gentlemen," said Bilibin. "Bolkonsky is my guest, in my house and here in the town. And I wish to treat him, as far as I can, to all the delights of local life. If we were in Vienna, it would be easy, but here, in this dreadful Moravian backwater, it is difficult, and I ask you all to help. We have to show him Brünn. You deal with the theatre, I shall take on society; and you, Hippolyte, naturally, the women."

"We have to show him Amélie, she's so delightful!" said one of *our people*, kissing the tips of his fingers. "Come with me."

"And from there we'll go to the Baroness Seifer. For your sake I'll be going out for the first time today, but the night is yours, if you wish to make use of it. One of the gentlemen can guide you."

"Generally speaking," said someone, "this bloodthirsty soldier Bolkonsky should be converted to a more philanthropic way of thinking."

"Then let him fall in love with our Brünn and our darling Vienna!"

"I'm afraid it's time for me to go," said Bolkonsky, glancing at his watch. Despite the animated conversation, he had not for a moment forgotten his forthcoming presentation to the Emperor.

"Where are you going?"

"To the Emperor."

"Oh! Oh! Oh!"

"Well, goodbye, Bolkonsky! Goodbye, prince, do come to dinner early," said the voices. "We are taking you in hand."

"When you speak with the Emperor, do try to praise as highly as possible the fine organisation in the supply of provisions and choice of routes," said Bilibin, as he saw Bolkonsky out to the hallway.

"I would like to praise them but, from what I know, I cannot," Bolkonsky replied with a smile.

216

"Well, in general, say as much as possible. Audiences are his passion, but he does not like to speak himself and does not know how to, as you will see."

# XIII

The Emperor Franz approached Prince Andrei, who was standing in his appointed place among the Austrian officers at the reception, swiftly uttered several indistinct, but obviously well-disposed words to him and walked on. After the reception, the aide-de-camp from the previous day, who was now quite changed, a courteous and considerate individual, conveyed to Bolkonsky the Emperor's wish to see him again. Before he stepped into the study, the sight of the whispering courtiers and the respect that they now paid him upon realising he would be received by the Emperor, made Prince Andrei realise that he too was excited by the forthcoming meeting. But yet again in his heart this feeling of excitement was instantly transformed into a feeling of contempt for the conventional pomp and this crowd of whispering courtiers who were prepared to betray themselves and the truth in order to please the Emperor. "No," said Prince Andrei to himself, "no matter how difficult my position might be in this forthcoming meeting, I shall cast all other considerations aside and say nothing but the complete and unvarnished truth." But the conversation that took place between himself and the Emperor did not offer the chance to tell either truth or lies. The Emperor Franz received him standing in the centre of the room. Prince Andrei was astonished to see that before engaging in conversation, the Emperor looked embarrassed, not knowing what to say, and even blushing.

"Tell me, when did the battle start?" he asked hastily. Prince Andrei replied. That question was followed by others, equally simple: "Is Kutuzov well?", "How long ago did he leave Krems?" and so on. The Emperor's expression as he spoke suggested that his sole purpose consisted merely in asking a set number of questions. But it was only too obvious that the answers to these questions were of no interest to him whatever.

"At what time did the battle start?" asked the Emperor.

"I cannot inform Your Majesty at what time the battle commenced at the front, but in Dürenstein, where I was, the army began the attack at six in the evening," said Bolkonsky, more animated now as he imagined that this opportunity would allow him to present the truthful description he was holding ready in his head of everything that he knew and had seen. But the Emperor smiled and interrupted him.

"How many miles?"

"From where to where, Your Majesty?"

"From Dürenstein to Krems."

"Three and a half miles, Your Majesty."

"Did the French abandon the left bank?"

"According to the scouts' reports, the last ones crossed on rafts during the night."

"Is there sufficient fodder in Krems?"

"Fodder was not provided in the quantity . . ."

The Emperor interrupted him.

"At what hour was General Schmidt killed?"

Having asked this final question, which required only a brief answer, the Emperor said that he thanked Prince Andrei and bowed. Bolkonsky left the room and, without understanding why, for a minute or so, despite the incredible simplicity of the Emperor's bearing and manner, he felt not entirely sober. Upon emerging through the doors of the study he found himself surrounded on every side by eyes gazing at him endearingly, by smiles and endearing words. The courteous aide-de-camp from the previous day reproached him with endearments, asking why he had not stayed in the section for foreign couriers at the palace. The war minister came up, congratulating him on the Order of Marya-Theresa, Third Class, which the Emperor had awarded him. He did not know which question to answer first and took several seconds to gather his thoughts. The Russian envoy grasped him by the shoulder, led him over to the window and began talking. Contrary to his own expectations and Bilibin's, the presentation had been a complete success. A service of thanksgiving would be arranged. Kutuzov had been awarded the Grand Cross of Marya-Theresa and the entire army had been decorated. The Empress had expressed a wish to see Prince Bolkonsky and he was being showered with invitations to dinners and *soirées* from all sides.

On his way back from the palace Prince Andrei, sitting in the carriage, mentally composed a letter to his father about all the circumstances of the battle, the journey to Brünn and the conversation with the Emperor. Yet no matter what he thought about, the conversation with the Emperor – that superficial, that simply stupid, conversation – rose up time and again in his imagination with all the minutest details of Emperor Franz's expression and intonation. "At what hour was General Schmidt killed?" he repeated to himself. He had wanted so much to know the hour at which General Schmidt had been killed. Why had he not asked the precise number of minutes and seconds? What considerations of importance for the state would he deduce from this knowledge? "But even worse and more stupid than the question," thought Prince Andrei, "is

PRINCE ANDREI AND EMPEROR FRANZ
*Drawing by M. S. Bashilov, 1867*

the excitement I felt as I began that conversation. And the excitement of all those old men at the thought that he had spoken to me. Two days ago as I faced bullets, any one of which could have brought death, I did not experience even a hundredth part of the excitement which for some reason I felt in conversing with this simple, good-natured and absolutely insignificant man. Yes, one must be a philosopher," he concluded, and instead of going directly to Bilibin's house, he drove to a bookshop to stock up with books for the campaign. He delayed there, looking through philosophical works that he did not know, for more than an hour. When he drove up to Bilibin's porch, he was astonished to see a half-loaded *britzka* standing there and Franz, Bilibin's servant, who ran out to meet him with a distressed expression on his face.

"Ah, your excellency!" said Franz. "Disaster!"

"What's wrong?" asked Bolkonsky.

"We are moving further away, God knows where to. The villain is already close on our heels again."

Bilibin came out to meet Bolkonsky. Bilibin's always calm face was agitated.

"Yes indeed, you really must admit this is delightful," he said, "this business with the Tabor Bridge in Vienna. They have crossed it entirely unopposed."

Prince Andrei could not understand a thing.

"But where have you come from, if you don't even know what every coachman in the town already knows? Have you not come from the palace?"

"Yes, I have. I saw the Emperor too. Kutuzov has been awarded the Grand Cross of Marya-Theresa."

"This is no time for crosses. Do they really not know anything there?"

"Nothing, but perhaps they heard after I left; on the way back I called into some shops . . . but what's wrong?"

"Well, at least now I understand. What is wrong? That's wonderful! The French have crossed the bridge that Auersperg is defending, and they did not blow the bridge up, so now Murat is racing along the road to Brünn and will be here today or tomorrow."

"What do you mean, here? How could they fail to blow up the bridge, when it's mined?"

"I could ask you the same question. That is something that nobody knows, not even Bonaparte himself."

Bolkonsky shrugged.

"But if the bridge has been crossed, that means the army is lost as well, it will be cut off," he said.

"I think it will."

"But how did this happen?"

"That is the whole point, and the charm of it. Listen. The French enter Vienna, as I told you. Everything is fine. The next day, that is

220

yesterday, Messieurs Murat, Lann and Belliard mount their steeds and set out for the bridge. (Note that all three of them are Gascons.) 'Gentlemen,' says one of them, 'you know that the Tabor Bridge is mined and counter-mined and that we are faced with redoubtable fortifications and fifteen thousand troops who have been ordered to blow up the bridge and not allow us to pass. But our lord the Emperor Napoleon will be pleased if we take this bridge. So let us three go and take this bridge.' 'Let us go,' say the others and they set out to take the bridge, they cross it, and now with the entire army on this side of the Danube they are heading towards us, towards you and your lines of communication."

"Stop this joking."

"I am not joking in the least," Bilibin continued in response to Bolkonsky's impatient and distrustful gesture. "Nothing could possibly be truer or sadder. These gentlemen arrive at the bridge alone and raise white handkerchiefs, assuring everyone that there is a truce and that they, the marshals, are on their way to negotiations with Prince Auersperg. The duty officer allows them inside the bridge fortifications. They tell him a thousand pieces of Gascon nonsense, they say the war is over, that the Emperor Franz has set a meeting with Bonaparte, that they wish to see Prince Auersperg, and so on. The officer sends for Auersperg, these gentlemen embrace the officers, joke, sit about on the cannons, and meanwhile a French battalion advances onto the bridge unnoticed, throws the sacks of combustible materials into the water and approaches the bridge fortifications. Eventually the lieutenant-general himself arrives, our dear Prince Auersperg von Mautern. 'Our dear enemy! Flower of the Austrian army, hero of the Turkish wars! The hostilities are over, we can shake hands with each other. The Emperor Napoleon is consumed with desire to know Prince Auersperg.' In short, these gentlemen are true Gascons and they shower that turkey-cock so thickly with fine words, he is so flattered at having established intimate terms with the French marshals so rapidly, so blinded by the sight of Murat's cloak and ostrich feathers, that he sees nothing at all but this, blazing away, and entirely forgets that he was supposed to open fire against the enemy himself."

(Despite the animation with which he spoke, Bilibin did not forget to pause after these words, in order to allow time for them to be appreciated.)

"The French battalion runs on to the bridge fortifications, spikes the cannons, and the bridge is taken. Yes, but best of all," he continued, soothing his own agitation with the charm of his story, "is that the sergeant posted at the cannon which was to give the signal for the mines to be detonated and the bridge blown up, this sergeant, seeing that French troops were running on to the bridge, was about to shoot, but

Lann pulled his hand away. The sergeant, who evidently was more intelligent than his general, approaches Auersperg and says: 'Prince, they are deceiving you, the French are over there!' Murat sees that the game is up if the sergeant is allowed to continue speaking. Feigning amazement (a genuine Gascon) he turns to Auersperg: 'I do not recognise that Austrian discipline which is so highly praised throughout the world,' he says, 'when you permit a man of lower rank to speak to you like this.' A stroke of genius. Prince Auersperg feels insulted and orders the sergeant to be arrested. You must confess that it is delightful – this entire business with the bridge. It is not exactly stupidity, nor is it exactly cowardice."

"Perhaps it is treason," said Prince Andrei, evidently unable to share in the satisfaction that Bilibin took in the stupidity of the incident that he had related. This story instantly transformed the civil, high-society mood in which he had left the palace. He thought of the position in which Kutuzov's army had now been placed, and how, instead of peaceful days in Brünn, he now faced an immediate gallop to the army to take part in either a desperate struggle or a disgrace. And instantly his imagination conjured up the vivid picture of the grey greatcoats, the wounds, the gunpowder smoke and the sounds of guns firing. And again at that moment, as always when he thought about the general course of events, a powerful, proud patriotic feeling, fear of a Russian defeat, was strangely united in his heart with a feeling of triumph at the triumph of his hero. The campaign was over. All the forces of the whole of Europe, all their calculations, all their efforts had been destroyed in two months by the genius and luck of this unfathomable man of destiny . . .

"Not that either. It places the court in a most absurd position," Bilibin continued. "It is neither treason, nor cowardice, nor stupidity, it is the way it was at Ulm . . ." he seemed to ponder, seeking for the right expression. "It is *Mackness*. We have *Macked ourselves*," he concluded, feeling that he had uttered *un mot* and a fresh *mot* at that, the kind of thing that would be repeated. The tight folds that had thus far been gathered on his forehead rapidly dissolved, indicating his gratification, and he began inspecting his nails, smiling faintly.

"Where are you going?" he said abruptly to Prince Andrei who had risen to his feet without saying a word and set out for his own room.

"I'm leaving."

"Where to?"

"The army."

"But you were going to stay here for another two days."

"Well, now I'm leaving straight away."

Prince Abdrei gave instructions for his departure and went to his own room.

"You know what, my dear fellow," said Bilibin, coming into the room. "I've been thinking about you. What point is there in your going?" And in proof of the incontrovertibility of this argument, all the folds vanished from his face.

Prince Andrei looked at the other man enquiringly and said nothing.

"What is the point in your going? I know you think it your duty to gallop off to the army now when the army is in danger. I understand that, my dear fellow, and it is sheer heroism."

"Not in the least," said Prince Andrei.

"But you are a philosopher; so be one completely, look at things from the other side and you will see that it is your duty, on the contrary, to take care of yourself. Leave this business to others, to those who are good for nothing else. You have not been ordered to return, and you have not been released from here, which means you should stay and go with us wherever our miserable fate leads us. They say they are going to Olmütz. And Olmütz is a very pleasant town. And you and I will drive there calmly in my carriage."

"You're joking, Bilibin," said Bolkonsky.

"I speak to you sincerely, as a friend. Think it over. Where will you go now and what is the point, when you can stay here? One of two things awaits you" (he gathered up the skin above his left temple) "either you fail to reach the army and peace is concluded, or you face defeat and disgrace with the whole of Kutuzov's army."

And Bilibin released the folded skin, feeling that the dilemma he had posed was irrefutable.

"That is something I cannot even discuss," Prince Andrei replied coldly. "Before I am a philosopher, I am a man, and therefore I am going."

"*Mon cher*, you are a hero," said Bilibin.

"Not at all, I am simply an officer carrying out his duty, and nothing more," said Prince Andrei, not without a certain pride.

# XIV

That same night, having taken his leave of the war minister, Bolkonsky travelled to join the army, not knowing where he would find it, and apprehensive that on his way to Krems he would be intercepted by the French.

In Brünn, the entire population of the court was packing up and heavy things were already being despatched to Olmütz. What Bolkonsky's purpose was in setting out to join the army and not staying on in Brünn, what considerations had led him to do this, he could not have said. As soon as he had heard the terrible news from Bilibin, the coin of life, which he had been viewing from the bright side, had flipped over. He now saw only the bad side of everything and instinctively felt the need to be involved in all these bad things. "There can be no other outcome apart from disgrace and destruction for our forces in the conditions under which we are fighting against this fatal genius," ran his gloomy train of thought.

Tired, hungry and angry, having evaded the French on the previous day, Bolkonsky now approached the place where Kutuzov was rumoured to be. Close to Etzelsdorf Prince Andrei came out onto a road which the Russian army was moving along in extreme haste and utter confusion. The road was so tightly thronged with carts the carriage could not get through. Taking a horse and a Cossack from a Cossack officer, Prince Andrei rode up ahead, overtaking the transports, in search of the commander-in-chief and his carriage. Along the way he had heard the most ominous rumours about the army's situation, but the sight of the army fleeing in disorder only confirmed his conviction that the campaign was now a completely lost cause. He looked upon everything taking place around him with disdainful melancholy, like a man who no longer belongs to this world.

"This Russian army, which English gold has brought here from the other side of the world, will suffer the same fate, the fate of the army of the Ulm" – he recalled Napoleon's words to his army before the beginning of the campaign, and the emotions aroused in him now by these words were amazement at the genius of his hero and a sense of insulted pride in equal measure. "There is nothing left to do, but die," he thought. "Well, if it's necessary, so be it! I'll do it no worse than others."

The disorder and haste of the army's movement, increased by the incessantly repeated orders from the general staff to march as fast as possible, had reached an extreme. A few Cossack jokers, making fun of the orderlies asleep in the wagons, had shouted "The French" as they galloped past. The cry "The French" had rolled along the entire column, gathering size like a snowball: everyone had started hurtling along, knocking each other aside in the rush to get ahead, shots had even been heard and a fusillade from the infantry, who did not even know what they were firing at. A quarter of an hour later, those in charge of the column were still struggling to contain the chaos that had cost the lives of several men who had been crushed and another who had been shot.

Prince Andrei gazed with indifferent contempt at these endless confusing commands, carriages, artillery and again more carriages, carriages and carriages of every possible kind, overtaking each other and blocking the road, three or four rows deep. On all sides, as far as he could hear up ahead and behind, there was the clacking of wheels, the rumbling of wagons and gun-carriages, the tramping of horses, the crack of whips, and the yells of encouragement and obscenities from soldiers, orderlies and officers. Along the sides of the road he kept seeing fallen horses, some flayed and some not, or broken wagons with solitary soldiers sitting beside them, waiting, or soldiers who had been separated from their units, setting out in droves to the nearby villages or already returning with chickens, sheep, straw or sacks stuffed with items from the villages. On the uphill and downhill sections the crowds grew thicker and the shouting merged into one continuous groan. Sinking up to their knees in the mud, soldiers grabbed at guns and wagons with their hands: whips lashed, hooves slipped, traces snapped and men's chests were strained to bursting with shouts. The officers in charge of the column rode to and fro between the wagons. Their voices could just barely be made out above the general roar and it was clear from their faces that they despaired of being able to halt the confusion.

"*Voilà*, the distinguished Army of Orthodoxy," thought Bolkonsky, remembering what Bilibin had said.

Wishing to ask one of these people where the commander-in-chief was, he rode up to a wagon. Trundling along right next to it was a strange, one-horse vehicle, clearly knocked together by soldiers from whatever had come to hand and resembling a cross between a cart, a cabriolet and a barouche. There was a soldier driving this carriage and a woman sitting inside beneath the leather roof behind the apron, all bundled up in shawls. Prince Andrei rode up and had already addressed his question to the soldier when he heard the despairing cries of the woman sitting in the covered carriage. The officer supervising the convoy was beating away at the soldier sitting in the driver's seat for trying to overtake the others, and his whip kept striking against the apron of the carriage. The woman's shrieks were piercing. Catching sight of Prince Andrei, she hung out through the apron, waving her thin arms that had popped out from under a patterned shawl, and shouted:

"Adjutant! Mister adjutant! In the name of God . . . protect me . . . What's going to happen to us? I'm the doctor's wife from the Seventh Chasseurs . . . they won't let us through, we fell behind, we've lost our people . . ."

"I'll beat you to a pulp, get back!" the furious officer yelled at the soldier. "Get back with your whore."

"Mister Adjutant, protect me. What's happening?" screamed the doctor's wife.

"Kindly let this carriage pass. Can you not see that this is a woman?" said Prince Andrei, riding up to the officer.

The officer glanced at him and turned back to the soldier without replying.

"I'll give you it for overtaking . . . get back!"

"Let them through, I tell you," Prince Andrei repeated, pressing his lips together.

"And who are you?" said the officer, suddenly turning on him in drunken fury. "Who are you? Are *you*" (he pronounced the word with insulting derision) "in charge or something? I'm in charge here, not you. You, go back," he repeated, "I'll beat you to a pulp."

The officer had clearly taken a liking to that expression.

"He took that little adjutant down a peg, all right," said a voice behind Prince Andrei, who now realised that the officer was in that state of drunken frenzy in which people do not know what they are saying. He saw that his intercession for the doctor's wife in the covered carriage was fraught with the danger of the thing he feared most in all the world, what is known as ridicule, yet his instinct told him something else. Before the officer had even finished his final words, Prince Andrei, his face distorted in terrible fury, rode up to him and raised his whip.

"Be so good as to let them pass!"

The officer gave up and hurriedly rode away.

"This chaos is the fault of all these staff officers," he growled. "Do whatever you like."

Keeping his eyes lowered, Prince Andrei hastily rode away from the doctor's wife who was calling him her saviour and, recalling with revulsion the finest details of this humiliating incident, he galloped on towards the village where he had been told the commander-in-chief was to be found.

On riding into the village he dismounted from his horse and walked towards the first house with the intention of resting for at least a moment, and eating something while clarifying all these offensive thoughts that were tormenting him.

"This is a crowd of scoundrels, not an army," he was thinking as he approached the window of the first house, when a familiar voice called out his name.

He looked round and saw Nesvitsky's handsome face leaning out of a small window. Nesvitsky was waving his arms, calling Andrei over to him.

"Bolkonsky! Bolkonsky! Can't you hear me, or what? Come quick," he shouted.

On entering the house Andrei saw Nesvitsky and one other adjutant.

They asked Bolkonsky eagerly whether he knew anything new. In the expressions of their familiar faces Prince Andrei read alarm and anxiety. This expression was especially noticeable in Nesvitsky whose face was usually cheerful.

"Where is the commander-in-chief?" asked Bolkonsky.

"Here, in that house," replied the adjutant.

"Well, then? Is it true that there is a peace, and surrender?" asked Nesvitsky.

"That's what I am asking you. I know nothing except that I barely managed to get through to you."

"And things are terrible with us, brother! I should never have laughed at Mack, brother, for we are in a worse way ourselves," said Nesvitsky. "But sit down, do, have something to eat."

"Now, prince, you'll never find your carriage or anything else, and God knows where your Pyotr has got to," said the other adjutant.

"Where is general headquarters? Are we spending the night in Znaim?"

"And I had all the things I need bundled up so that two horses could carry them," said Nesvitsky, "and excellent bundles they were. I could bolt across the Bohemian mountains with them. Things are bad, brother. What's wrong, you must be unwell, why are you shaking like that?" asked Nesvitsky, noticing Prince Andrei shudder as though he had touched an electric Leyden jar.

"It's nothing," replied Prince Andrei.

Just at that moment he had recalled his recent encounter with the doctor's wife and the convoy officer.

"What is the commander-in-chief doing here?" he asked.

"I don't understand a thing," said Nesvitsky.

"Well, I understand one thing, that all this is vile, vile, vile," said Prince Andrei and he went to the house where the commander-in-chief was quartered.

Walking past Kutuzov's carriage, and the exhausted saddle-horses of the entourage and some Cossacks talking loudly among themselves, Prince Andrei entered the porch of the hut. As Prince Andrei had been told, Kutuzov himself was in the hut, with Prince Bagration and Weierother. This was the Austrian general who had replaced the now dead Schmidt. Little Kozlovsky was also there in the hall, squatting down on his haunches in front of a clerk. The clerk was writing at speed on an upturned tub, with the cuffs of his uniform jacket turned back. Kozlovsky's face looked exhausted – he had clearly also not slept all night – and more gloomy and worried than ever before. He glanced up at Prince Andrei and did not even nod to him.

"The second line . . . Have you written that?" he continued dictating to the clerk. "Kiev Grenadiers, Podolsk . . ."

"I can't keep up with you, your excellency," the clerk replied, glancing disrespectfully and angrily at Kozlovsky.

Meanwhile General Kutuzov's agitated and dissatisfied voice could be heard behind the door, punctuated by another, unfamiliar voice. The sound of those voices, the indifference with which Kozlovsky had glanced at him and the disrespectfulness of the exhausted clerk, the very fact that the clerk and Kozlovsky were sitting on the floor beside a tub so close to the commander-in-chief, that the Cossacks holding the horses were laughing loudly outside the window of the house, gave Prince Andrei the feeling that something important and disastrous was bound to happen. Nonetheless he questioned Kozlovsky insistently.

"One moment, prince," said Kozlovsky. "The disposition for Bagration."

"A surrender?"

"Far from it, all the instructions have been given for battle."

Prince Andrei walked towards the door behind which the voices could be heard.

But just as he was about to open the door, the voices in the room fell silent, the door opened and Kutuzov appeared in the doorway. Prince Andrei was standing directly opposite Kutuzov, but from the expression of the commander-in-chief's only seeing eye it was clear that he was so powerfully occupied by his own thoughts and concerns that they seemed to obscure his vision. He looked straight at his adjutant's face but did not recognise him.

"Well, have you finished?" he said to Kozlovsky.

"This very second, your excellency."

Bagration, a short, lean man with a resolute and immobile eastern type of face, who was not yet old, came out behind the commander-in-chief.

"I have the honour to report for duty," Prince Andrei repeated loudly, holding out an envelope.

"Ah, from Vienna? Good. Later, later."

Kutuzov went out on to the porch with Bagration.

"Well, prince, farewell! May Christ be with you. My blessings for your great feat of courage."

Kutuzov's face suddenly softened and tears appeared in his eyes. He pulled Bagration towards him with his left hand, crossed him in what was clearly a customary gesture with his right hand, on which there was a ring, and offered his plump cheek, but Bagration kissed him on the neck instead.

"May Christ be with you!" Kutuzov repeated and went across to the carriage.

"Get in with me," he said to Bolkonsky.

"Your excellency, I would like to be useful here. Allow me to remain in Prince Bagration's detachment."

"Get in," said Kutuzov, noticing Bolkonsky dawdling, "I need good officers myself, I need them myself."

They got into the carriage and rode along in silence for several minutes.

"There are many things, all sorts of things ahead of us," he said, speaking with an old man's perspicacity, as if he had understood what was going on in Bolkonsky's heart. "If one tenth of his detachment returns tomorrow, I shall thank God for it," Kutuzov added, as if he were talking to himself.

Prince Andrei glanced at Kutuzov and could not help being struck by the cleanly washed puckers of the scar on Kutuzov's temple, now an arm's length from him, at the point where the bullet had pierced his head at Izmail. "Yes, he has earned the right to talk so calmly about these men's death," thought Bolkonsky.

"That is why I ask to be posted to that detachment," he said.

Kutuzov did not reply. He seemed already to have forgotten what he had said, and sat there lost in thought. Five minutes later, swaying smoothly on the soft springs of the carriage, Kutuzov began speaking again. There was not a trace of agitation in his face. He questioned Prince Andrei with subtle humour about the details of his meeting with the Emperor and the opinions he had heard expressed at court about the Krems affair. It was clear that he had anticipated everything his adjutant told him.

## XV

On the 1st of November Kutuzov had received, via one of his scouts, the news that placed the army under his command in an almost hopeless position. The scout had reported that, after crossing the Vienna bridge, the French had set out in huge numbers towards Kutuzov's lines of communication with the troops coming from Russia. If Kutuzov had decided to stay at Krems, then Napoleon's one hundred and fifty thousand-strong army would have cut him off from all communications and would have surrounded his totally exhausted army of forty thousand men, and he would have found himself in the same position as Mack at Ulm. If

Kutuzov had decided to leave the road that led to communications with the troops from Russia, then he would have had to enter the unfamiliar region of the Bohemian mountains with no road to guide him while defending himself against an enemy with superior numbers, and having to abandon all hope of communication with Buxhöwden. If Kutuzov decided to withdraw along the road from Krems to Olmütz to join with the troops from Russia, then he would have risked reaching that road later than the French, who had crossed the bridge in Vienna, and so would have been forced to accept battle on the march, with all his heavy equipment and transports, against an enemy force three times greater in strength and surrounding him on both sides. Kutuzov chose this final solution.

The scout reported that the French, having crossed the bridge in Vienna, were now advancing in forced marches on Znaim, which lay on Kutuzov's line of retreat, more than a hundred *versts* ahead of him. Reaching Znaim before the French would have raised great hopes of saving the army; to allow the French to reach Znaim before him would probably be to condemn the entire army to a disgrace like that at the Ulm or to total destruction. But to arrive ahead of the French with the entire army was impossible. The road that the French had from Vienna to Znaim was shorter and better than the road that the Russians had from Krems to Znaim.

The night after he received the news, Kutuzov despatched Bagration's sixteen-thousand-strong avant-garde to the right, across the mountains from the Krems–Znaim road to the Vienna–Znaim road. Bagration was to make this crossing without any rest and halt facing Vienna with his rear towards Znaim, and if he had succeeded in arriving before the French, then he was to detain them for as long as he was able. Kutuzov himself set out for Znaim with all the heavy equipment.

Having covered forty-five *versts* with hungry, ill-shod soldiers, across mountains without any road, and having lost a third of his men as stragglers, Bagration arrived at Hollabrünn, on the Vienna–Znaim road, several hours ahead of the French, who were approaching Hollabrünn from Vienna. Kutuzov still had days to march with his transports in order to reach Znaim and therefore, in order to save the army, Bagration, with four thousand hungry, exhausted soldiers, had somehow to delay the enemy's entire army for twenty-four hours when he met it at Hollabrünn, which was obviously impossible. But a strange twist of fate made the impossible possible. The success of the deception which had delivered the Vienna bridge into the hands of the French without a battle prompted Murat to attempt to deceive Kutuzov in the same way. When Murat encountered Bagration's weak detachment on the Znaim road, he thought it was Kutuzov's entire army. In order to crush this army decisively, he waited a while for the troops who were lagging behind on the road from Vienna, and for this purpose he proposed a three-day truce on condition that neither of the two forces should change their position or move away. Murat assured his enemy that peace negotiations were already taking place and therefore he was proposing the truce in order to avoid useless bloodshed. The Austrian general Count Nostitz, who was occupying the advance posts, believed what Murat's truce envoy told him and fell back, exposing Bagration's detachment. Another truce envoy rode to the Russian line to announce the same news concerning peace negotiations and propose a three-day truce to the Russians. Bagration replied that he could neither accept nor reject a truce and sent his adjutant to Kutuzov with a report on the proposal that had been put to him.

A truce was the only way for Kutuzov to gain time, allow Bagration's exhausted detachment to rest and allow his transports and heavy equipment, the movement of which was concealed from the French, to cover at least one extra day's march towards Znaim. The proposal of a truce gave him a unique and unexpected opportunity to save his army. On receiving this news, Kutuzov immediately sent Adjutant-General Wintzengerode, who was attached to him, to the enemy camp. Not only was Wintzengerode to accept the truce, but also to propose terms of surrender, and in the meantime Kutuzov sent his adjutants back to hasten as far as possible the movement of the transports of the entire army along the Krems–Znaim road. Bagration's exhausted and hungry detachment had to cover the movement of the transports and the entire army by remaining stationary in the face of an enemy eight times as strong.

Kutuzov's expectations proved correct concerning both the idea that the proposals for surrender, which did not bind him to anything, might give part of the transports time to get through and the idea that Murat's mistake would be discovered very soon. As soon as Bonaparte, who was in Schönbrunn, twenty-five *versts* from Hollabrünn, received Murat's report and the proposal for a truce and surrender, he spotted the deception and wrote the following letter to Murat.

> *To Prince Murat. Schoenbrunn, 25th Brumaire 1805,*
> *at eight in the morning.*
> *I cannot find words to express my displeasure to you. You command only my avant-garde and have no right to conclude a truce without an order from me. You are causing me to lose the fruits of the entire campaign. Tear up the truce immediately and advance on the enemy. You will inform him that the general who signed this surrender had no*

*right to do so and that no one has that right, apart from the Emperor of Russia.*

*However, if the Emperor of Russia will accept the terms mentioned, I will also accept them, but this is nothing but a cunning trick. Advance, destroy the Russian army. You can take its transports and artillery.*

*The general is an adjutant of the Emperor of Russia . . . Officers mean nothing when they do not have official authority, and he also does not have any. The Austrians allowed themselves to be tricked at the crossing of the Vienna bridge, and you are allowing yourself to be tricked by this general – the Emperor of Russia's adjutant.*

*Napoleon*

Bonaparte's adjutant galloped as fast as his horse could carry him with this menacing letter to Murat. Bonaparte himself, not trusting his own generals, moved to the field of battle with his entire guard, afraid of missing an easy victim, and Bagration's detachment of four thousand men merrily lit campfires, dried themselves out and boiled up gruel for the first time in three days, and not one of the men in the detachment knew or gave a thought to what lay ahead.

# XVI

Between three and four in the afternoon Prince Andrei, having insisted on his request to Kutuzov, arrived in Grunth and reported to Bagration. Napoleon's adjutant had not yet reached Murat's detachment and battle had not yet commenced. In Bagration's detachment they knew nothing about the general course of events. They spoke of peace, but did not believe that it was possible, they spoke of battle and also did not believe that battle was near. Bagration, knowing Bolkonsky to be a favourite and trusted adjutant, received him with a commander's special distinction and favour, explained to him that there would probably be a battle that day or the next and offered him total freedom of choice either to stay with him during the battle or to supervise the order of retreat in the rearguard, "which was also very important".

"But there will probably not be any action today," said Bagration, as if trying to reassure Prince Andrei.

"If he is one of the usual staff dandies who are sent to win themselves a cross, he will get his decoration in the rearguard, but if he wishes to be with me, then let him . . . he will come in useful if he is a brave officer," thought Bagration.

Without giving any answer, Prince Andrei requested the prince's permission to ride round the positions and learn the disposition of the troops so that he would know where to go if he should receive an assignment. The detachment's duty officer, a handsome, foppishly dressed man with a diamond ring on his index finger, who spoke French freely but badly, volunteered to take Prince Andrei round.

The duty officer was staying in one of the ruined houses in the village of Grunth, and Prince Andrei called in while the horses were being saddled. A stove was burning behind a broken-down partition wall and in front of the stove there were gleaming-wet, wrinkled boots drying and a soaking-wet greatcoat steaming. Three officers were sleeping on the floor of the room and the air was thick.

"Have a seat, prince, try here," the staff officer said in French. "They'll bring me my horse in a moment. These are our gentlemen, prince. Two nights out in the rain, there was nowhere even to get dried off."

These officers were a pitiful and sad sight, and the entire village presented an equally mournful and chaotic sight when they mounted their horses and rode through it. On every side they saw soaking officers with sad faces, looking as though they were searching for something, while soldiers were dragging doors, benches and fencing out of the village.

"Look, prince, we can't get these people away from here," said the staff officer, indicating those men. "The commanders let them run loose. And over here" – he pointed across to where a camp-trader's tent was pitched – "is where they gather together and sit around. This morning I drove them all away, but look, there's a load of them back there again. I ought to go across, prince, and give them a fright. One moment."

"No, let's go in, I'll buy some cheese and a roll from him," said Prince Andrei, who had still not had time to eat anything.

"Why did you not say, prince?"

They dismounted from their horses and went into the camp-trader's tent. There were several officers with flushed and exhausted faces sitting at tables and eating.

"Now, what's this, gentlemen," the staff officer said in a reproachful tone, like a man who has already repeated the same thing several times. "You can't go absenting yourselves like this. The prince has given orders to keep everybody out of here. You, for instance, Mister Staff-Captain," he said, addressing a small, dirty, thin artillery officer without any boots (he had given them to the camp-trader to dry) who stood up in front of the new arrivals in just his stockings, with a smile that was not quite natural.

"You ought to be ashamed of yourself, Captain Tushin!" the staff

233

officer continued. "I'd have thought that as an artilleryman you would set an example, but you have no boots on. When they sound the alarm, you'll be in a fine state, with no boots." (The staff officer smiled.) "Please be so good as to return to your posts, gentlemen, all of you, all of you," he added imperiously.

Prince Andrei smiled despite himself when he also glanced at Staff-Captain Tushin. Smiling without saying a word, Tushin was stepping from one bootless foot to the other, gazing enquiringly with his big, intelligent, good-natured eyes at Prince Andrei and the staff officer by turns.

"The soldiers say: barefoot's more nimble," said Captain Tushin, smiling and growing timid, evidently hoping that his humorous tone would get him out of the awkward position that he was in; but even before he had finished speaking, he sensed that his joke had failed and been rejected. He grew embarrassed.

"Please be on your way," said the staff officer, trying to remain serious.

Prince Andrei glanced once more at the artilleryman's small figure. There was something distinctive about it, absolutely unmilitary, rather comical, but extremely appealing.

The staff officer and Prince Andrei mounted their horses and rode on.

Riding out of the village, constantly overtaking and meeting soldiers on foot and officers from various units along the way, they saw on their left the newly excavated, fresh red clay of fortifications under construction. There were several battalions of soldiers in their shirtsleeves, despite the cold wind, like white ants creeping about on these fortifications; spadefuls of red clay were being incessantly thrown up from behind the rampart by someone they could not see. They rode over to the fortifications, inspected them and rode on. Immediately behind the fortifications they came across several dozen soldiers running away from the fortifications and being continually replaced by others. They had to hold their noses and put their horses to a trot in order to escape from that poisoned atmosphere.

"There you have the pleasure of the camp, prince," said the duty staff officer.

They rode out onto the facing hillside. From this hillside the French could already be seen. Prince Andrei halted and began surveying them.

"No, we'll take a look later, prince," said the staff officer, for this was already an ordinary sight. He pointed to the highest point of the hill. "Our battery is up there," he said, "commanded by that odd fellow who was sitting there without his boots; you can see everything from up there; we'll ride up later."

"Actually, I'll go up on my own now," said Prince Andrei, wishing to get away from the staff officer's broken French, "please do not bother yourself."

But the staff officer replied that he had to go on to the dragoons and they rode to the right together.

The further forward they moved, and the closer they drew to the enemy, the more orderly and cheerful the troops appeared to become. The greatest disorder and despondency had been in that convoy close to Znaim which Prince Andrei had overtaken in the morning, and which was ten *versts* from the French. In Grunth too a certain alarm and fear of something could be sensed. But the closer Prince Andrei approached to the French line, the more self-confident the appearance of our troops became. The soldiers were standing drawn up in line in their greatcoats and a sergeant-major and company commander were counting the men, prodding the man at the edge of each section in the chest with a finger and ordering him to raise his hand; soldiers scattered all across the area were carrying firewood and brushwood and building shelters, laughing cheerfully and chatting; men clothed and unclothed sat beside campfires, drying shirts and leg wrappings or mending boots and greatcoats; they crowded round the cauldrons and the cooks. In one company, dinner was ready and the soldiers were gazing at the steaming cauldrons with greedy expressions while waiting for the quartermaster-sergeant, who was carrying a taster in a wooden bowl to the officer sitting on a log outside his shelter.

In another company, one of the luckier ones, since not all of them had vodka, the soldiers were crowding round a pock-marked sergeant-major with broad shoulders, who was tilting a small keg to pour liquor by turns into the canteen lids they held out to him. The soldiers raised the canteens to their mouths with pious faces, tipped them back, swilling the vodka round in their mouths and then, wiping their lips on the sleeves of their greatcoats, walked away from the sergeant-major with a contented air. All of their faces were as calm as if all this was taking place not in view of the enemy, before an engagement in which at least half of the detachment was bound to be left in this spot, but somewhere at home in Russia, in anticipation of a peaceful halt. Prince Andrei and the staff officer rode past a regiment of chasseurs and sprightly men from the ranks of the Kiev Grenadiers, all engaged in the same peaceful activities, but then, not far from the field commander's shelter, which was tall and different from the others, they came across a platoon of grenadiers standing in line, with a naked man lying in front of them. Two soldiers were holding him down and two were swinging supple birch withies and striking him on his bare back in a regular rhythm. The man being punished was screaming unnaturally, a fat major was walking up and down the line, speaking incessantly, paying no attention to the screams.

"It is shameful for a soldier to steal, a soldier must be honest, noble and brave, but if he has stolen from his brother, there is no honour in him, he is a scoundrel. More, more!"

And the sound of the swingeing blows and the desperate but somehow exaggerated screaming continued.

"More, more," the major kept saying.

A young officer whose face bore an expression of incomprehension and suffering moved away from the man being punished and glanced quizzically at the adjutants as they rode by. But the adjutants said nothing, they turned away and rode on.

The unnaturally desperate, affected screams of the man being punished mingled awkwardly with the sounds of the dance song that they were singing in the next company. The soldiers were standing in a circle and a young recruit was dancing in the middle, performing intensely rapid and ungainly movements with his feet and mouth.

"Go on, have a go, Makatiuk! Go on!" they were saying to an old soldier with a medal and a cross, shoving him into the circle.

"But I can't do it like him."

"Ah, come on!"

The soldier walked into the circle, keeping his hands in his pockets, with his greatcoat flung over his shoulders and the decorations dangling from it, and strode round the circle, shaking his shoulders slightly and screwing up his eyes. He glanced round and his eyes met the eyes of the adjutants riding by. It was clearly all the same to him whom he should happen to look at, although the expression of his eyes seemed to be intended for one particular friend, with whom he was sharing the joke that was recalled in his gaze. He stopped in the middle and suddenly swung round, dropped down into a squat, kicked out his feet twice, got up, swung back round and walked straight out of the circle, pushing aside the men who tried to stop him.

"Damn the lot of you! Let the young lads do the dancing. I'm off to clean my musket," he said.

Everything that Prince Andrei saw was etched into his memory.

At a company of dragoons the staff officer called in to see the regimental commander and Prince Andrei rode on alone along the front. On the left and right flanks our line and the enemy's ran far apart, but in the middle, at the spot where the truce envoys had passed through that morning, the lines came so close together that they could see each other's faces and talk with each other. As well as the soldiers occupying the line at that point, many curious onlookers had come up from both sides and were standing there laughing, as they examined the strange and alien-looking enemy.

Despite a prohibition on approaching the line, the officers had been trying to keep the curious away since early morning. The soldiers standing along the line like showmen displaying some rarity, were no longer looking at the French, but making remarks about those who had come up out of boredom, which they were now waiting to end. Prince Andrei halted to examine the French.

"Lookee, look," said one soldier to his comrade, pointing to a Russian musketeer who had approached the line with an officer and was speaking rapidly and heatedly with a French grenadier. "See how smartly he gabbles away! Even yer Frenchie can't keep up with him. You have a go, you, Sidorov!"

"Wait, listen. Ee, that's smart!" replied Sidorov, who was considered a master at speaking French.

The soldier whom they were pointing out as they laughed was Dolokhov. Prince Andrei recognised him and listened to his conversation. Dolokhov and his company commander had approached the line from the left flank, where their regiment was stationed.

"Go on, more, more!" Brykov urged him on with a fixed expression of naïve joy, leaning forward and trying not to miss a single word, though they were incomprehensible to him. "Quicker, please. What does he say?"

Dolokhov did not answer his company commander, he was absorbed in a passionate argument with the French grenadier. They were talking, as they were bound to do, about the campaign. The Frenchman was confusing the Austrians with the Russians and claiming that the Russians had capitulated and fled from the Ulm; Dolokhov, as always, was speaking with excessive and somewhat bombastic ardour. He was trying to prove that the Russians had not capitulated but withdrawn. And where they had chosen to stand their ground, they had routed the French, as at Krems.

"Our orders are to drive you back and we shall drive you back," said Dolokhov.

"Just you try, and see if you're not captured with all your Cossacks," said the French grenadier.

The Frenchmen watching and listening laughed.

"We'll make you dance the way you danced for Suvorov."

"What's that song he's singing?" asked one of the Frenchmen.

"It's ancient history," said another, guessing that the talk was about previous wars. "The Emperor will show this Souvara of yours and all the rest."

"Bonaparte . . ." Dolokhov began, but the Frenchman interrupted him.

"There is no Bonaparte, there is the Emperor, *sacré nom!*" he cried angrily.

"To hell with him!"

Dolokhov cursed crudely, in Russian, like a soldier and, shouldering his musket, he walked away.

"Let's go, Ivan Lukich," he said to his company commander.

"Now that's the way to talk French," said the soldiers in the line. "You have a go, Sidorov!"

Sidorov winked at them and began talking to the French, rapidly gabbling out incomprehensible words: "Kari, mala, musiu, paskavili, muter, kaska, moushchit," he gabbled, trying to pronounce the words with an expressive intonation.

"Ho, ho, ho! Ha, ha, ha, ha! Uh! Uh!" The soldiers broke into a roar of laughter so hearty and jolly that it was involuntarily communicated across the line to the French, after which it seemed that they all really ought to unload their muskets, blow up their ammunition and go back home as quickly as possible. But the muskets remained loaded, the loopholes in the houses and fortifications gazed forward as menacingly as ever and the cannon detached from their limbers remained facing each other just as before.

# XVII

"*Eh bien*," Prince Andrei said to himself, "the Army of Orthodoxy is not so very bad. It doesn't look bad at all . . . Not at all, not at all."

Having ridden round the entire line of the troops from the right flank to the left, he went up the hill to the battery from which, according to the staff officer who had been accompanying him, the entire field was visible. Here he dismounted from his horse and stopped at the first of four field guns detached from their limbers. An artilleryman on sentry duty was walking to and fro in front of the guns. He was about to stand to attention for the officer, but at the sign that was made to him he resumed his regular, boring pacing. Behind the guns stood the limbers, and behind them were the tethering post and the artillerymen's camp-fires. On the left, not far from the end gun, was a new shelter of woven branches from which the lively voices of officers could be heard.

The view from the battery did indeed extend right across almost the entire disposition of the Russian forces and the greater part of the enemy's. Directly opposite the battery, on the horizon of the opposite hill, the village of Schöngraben could be seen; further to the left and the right it was possible to distinguish, in three places, the massed French forces through the smoke of their campfires. A greater part of them was evidently located in the village itself and behind the mountain. To the left of the village, in the smoke, there seemed to be something like a battery, but it was not possible to make it out clearly with the naked eye. Our right flank was located on a rather steep elevation, which dominated the French position. Our infantry was disposed along it and the dragoons could be seen right at the very end. In the centre, at the location of Tushin's battery, from which Prince Andrei was surveying the position, there was the most shallow and direct descent and ascent from the stream that separated us from Schöngraben. On the left our troops were stationed along the edge of a wood, where smoke was rising from the campfires of our infantry, who had been cutting firewood. The French line was wider than ours and it was clear that the French could outflank us on both sides and attack; in the centre, behind our position, there was a steep-sided, deep ravine, along which it was difficult for artillery and cavalry to pull back. Leaning his elbow on the cannon and taking out his notebook, Prince Andrei sketched himself a plan of the disposition of forces. In two places he made pencil marks, intending, if he should have the chance, to inform Bagration, or at least an officer of his retinue, of his doubts concerning the correctness of the disposition. He proposed, firstly, to concentrate all the artillery in the centre and, secondly, to move the cavalry back, to the far side of the ravine. Prince Andrei, who had been constantly with the commander-in-chief, following the movements of the masses of troops and general dispositions and constantly studying historical descriptions of battles, could not help but conceive the course of the forthcoming military action also in general terms. He imagined only large-scale eventualities of the following kind: "If the enemy launches his attack against the right flank," he said to himself, "the Kiev Grenadiers and Podolsk Chasseurs will have to hold their position until the reserves from the centre reach them. In that case the dragoons can strike at the flank and drive it back. But in the case of an attack against the centre we advance the central battery on this elevation and under its cover we extend the left flank and withdraw to the ravine by echelons . . ." As often happens, all the time that he was beside the gun at the battery, he could constantly hear the voices of officers speaking in the shelter, but he could not understand a single word of what they were saying. Recalling Marshal Laudon, Suvorov, Friedrich, Bonaparte and their battles, and regarding the troop units which he knew and which were laid out before him as lifeless weapons, in his imagination he presumed various combinations and eventualities, anchoring his thoughts to French words. Suddenly he was struck so forcibly by the heartfelt and simple tone of the voices from the shelter that he involuntarily began to understand the meaning of their conversation and began listening to it. The officers were evidently engaged in a most heartfelt conversation and they were talking philosophy.

"No, my dear fellow," said a pleasant voice that seemed familiar to Prince Andrei, "I am saying that if it were possible to know what will come after death, then none of us would fear death. That's it, my dear fellow."

Another, younger voice interrupted the first:

"Fear it or not, you still can't escape it."

"But everyone's always afraid! Ah, you educated people," said a third, manly voice, cutting across both of them. "You being artillerymen and so very learned, you think you can take everything along with you, the vodka, the snacks and all."

And the owner of the manly voice, evidently an infantry officer, laughed. The artillerymen continued arguing.

"But everyone's always afraid," the first voice continued. "Afraid of the unknown, that's what. No matter what they say about the soul going up to heaven . . . we still know there is no heaven, there's just an atmosphere."

Again the manly voice interrupted the artilleryman.

"Right, treat us to some of your herb vodka, Tushin," he said.

"Ah, it's that captain, the one who was standing in the camp-trader's tent without his boots," thought Prince Andrei, delighted to recognise the pleasant, philosophising voice.

"Hey you!" cried the infantry officer. "Alyoshka! Go bring the snacks, brother, from the ammunition wagon."

"Go on, go on," the artilleryman's voice confirmed, "and get my pipe while you're at it."

Either one of them was ashamed of having asked for vodka and snacks, or the other was afraid he might be thought stingy, but they said nothing for a moment.

"Look at that, some even carry books with them," said the manly voice, laughing.

"Someone writing about Circassian women."

He began reading, barely able to restrain his laughter, of which he himself evidently felt ashamed, but he was still unable to restrain it.

"Circassian women are famed for their beauty and their fame is well deserved for the amazing whiteness . . ."

Just then there was a whistling sound in the air; closer, closer, faster

240

and louder, louder and faster, and as if it had not yet finished saying everything that it needed to say, the round shot slammed into the ground not far from the shelter, blasting a shower of earth up into the air with superhuman force. The ground seemed to gasp at the terrible blow. That very instant the little Tushin bounded out of the shelter ahead of everyone else with a pipe gripped in the side of his mouth; his kind, intelligent face was rather pale. He was followed out by the owner of the manly voice, an infantry officer, who ran off to his company, buttoning up his jacket as he went.

# XVIII

Prince Andrei halted his horse at the battery, surveying the French forces. He ran his eyes across the wide expanse of space. He could only see that the formerly motionless masses of the French had begun to stir and that there was in fact a battery on the left. The smoke above it had still not dispersed. Two French horsemen, probably adjutants, galloped across the hillside. A column of the enemy was clearly visible moving down the hill, probably to reinforce the line. The smoke of the first shot had still not dispersed when there was a second puff and a shot. Battle had commenced. Prince Andrei turned his horse and galloped back to Grunth to seek out Prince Bagration. Behind him he could hear the cannon-fire grow denser and louder. Evidently our men had begun to reply. Down below, at the spot where the truce envoys had passed through the lines, there was the sound of musket shot.

Lemarrois had just reached Murat at full gallop with Bonaparte's menacing letter, and the mortified Murat, wishing to atone for his mistake, had immediately moved up his forces into the centre and around the outside of both flanks, hoping to crush the pitiful detachment standing in front of him before evening and before the Emperor's arrival.

"It has begun! This is it!" thought Prince Andrei, feeling the blood beginning to pound through his heart. Riding between those same companies which a quarter of an hour earlier had been eating gruel and drinking vodka, everywhere he saw the same, quick movements of soldiers forming into ranks as they grabbed up their muskets, and on every face he recognised the same sense of agitation that was in his own heart. "It has begun! This is it! It's terrible but joyful!"

Before reaching the partially constructed fortifications, he saw, in the evening light of the overcast autumnal day, mounted men moving towards him. The leading rider, in a general's tailcoat, felt cloak and peaked astrakhan cap, was riding a white horse. It was Prince Bagration and his retinue. Prince Andrei stopped and waited for him. Prince Bagration reined in his horse and, recognising Prince Andrei, nodded to him. He carried on looking ahead while Prince Andrei told him what he had seen.

The expression "It has begun! This is it!" was there even on the firm brown face of Prince Bagration, with its half-closed eyes, which looked dull, as though he had not slept enough. Prince Andrei looked into this impassive face with anxious curiosity, he wanted to know whether this man was thinking and feeling, and what he was thinking and feeling, at that moment. "Is there anything there at all, behind this impassive face?" Prince Andrei wondered as he looked at it. Prince Bagration inclined his head as a sign of assent to Prince Andrei's words and said "Good" with an expression that suggested everything that was happening and being reported to him was exactly what he had already foreseen. Prince Andrei, gasping for breath after his fast ride, spoke quickly. Speaking with his eastern accent, Prince Bagration pronounced his words especially slowly, as though trying to emphasise that there was no need for haste. However, he set his horse at a trot in the direction of Tushin's battery. Prince Andrei and the retinue followed. Riding behind Prince Bagration came an officer of the retinue, Prince Zherkov's personal adjutant, an orderly, the duty staff officer riding a handsome bob-tailed horse, a civilian official, an auditor, who had asked to ride to the battle out of curiosity, and also lower ranks, Cossacks and hussars. The auditor, a plump man with a plump face, wearing a naïve smile of joy, looked all around him, trembling on his horse, looking odd seated in his camlet greatcoat on a convoy officer's saddle among the hussars, Cossacks and adjutants.

"There you are, prince, he wants to watch the battle," Zherkov said to Bolkonsky, pointing to the auditor, "but his heart's already in his mouth."

"Now, that's enough from you," said the auditor with a gleaming smile that was naïve and cunning at the same time, as if he were flattered to be the butt of Zherkov's jokes and was deliberately trying to appear more stupid than he really was.

"How amusing, *mon monsieur prince*," said the duty staff officer. (He had remembered that the title of prince was used in some special way in French but he simply could not get it right.)

By this time they were all approaching Tushin's battery, and a cannonball landed ahead of them.

"What was it that fell?" the auditor asked, smiling naïvely.

"French pancakes," said Zherkov.

"Is that what they fire, then?" asked the auditor. "How terrifying!"

He seemed to be blossoming with delight, but had barely finished speaking when there was another terrible whistle, terminating suddenly in a blow to something soggy and s-s-squelch – and the Cossack riding a little to the right and behind the auditor tumbled to the ground from his horse. Zherkov and the duty staff officer huddled down towards their saddles and turned their horses away. The auditor turned to face the Cossack and examined him with intense curiosity. The Cossack was dead, the horse was still thrashing about.

"Well? We ought to pick him up," he said with a smile. Prince Bagration glanced round, squinting, and seeing the reason for the distraction, turned away with indifference, as if to say: why waste time on nonsense? He halted his horse in the manner of a good rider, bent over a little and straightened up the sword that had snagged on his cloak. It was an old sword, not like the ones they wore then. Prince Andrei remembered the story of how Suvorov had given his sword to Bagration in Italy, and at that moment found the memory particularly pleasant. They rode up to the same battery beside which Bolkonsky had stood earlier, surveying the field of battle.

"Whose company?" Prince Bagration asked the artilleryman standing by the ammunition wagons.

He asked: "Whose company?" but in actual fact he was asking: "Are you not feeling scared up here?" And the artilleryman understood that.

"Captain Tushin's, your excellency," shouted the ginger-haired, freckle-faced man in a voice that was both fearful and cheerful.

"Good, good," said Bagration, thinking about something else, and rode past the limber and up to the last gun in the row. Just as he was coming up, a shot roared out of that gun, deafening him and his retinue, and in the smoke that had suddenly enveloped it, the artillerymen who had grabbed the cannon could be seen straining in their haste to roll it back in position. A huge soldier with broad shoulders, the number one artilleryman with the ramrod, leapt away towards the wheel, planting his feet wide. Another, number two, placed a shot in the barrel with a trembling hand. A small man with a stoop, the officer Tushin, ran out to the front, stumbling over the trail of the gun-carriage without noticing the general and gazing out from under his little hand.

"Raise it another two notches, that'll be just right," he shouted in a shrill voice to which he tried to impart a swagger ill-suited to his stature. "Number two!" he squeaked. "Let them have it, Medvedev!"

Bagration called the officer by name and Tushin walked up to the general, raising two fingers to the peak of his cap in a timid and awkward movement, not at all in the way that military men salute, more like the way priests give their blessing. Although Tushin's guns had been intended to bombard the hollow, he was firing incendiary balls straight ahead at the village of Schöngraben, out of which large masses of French troops could be seen advancing.

No one had ordered Tushin what to fire or where to fire it and, after consulting with his sergeant-major Zakharchenko, for whom he had great respect, he had decided it would be good to set the village alight. "Good!" said Bagration in reply to the officer's report, and he began surveying all the skirmishes that were breaking out in front of him, as if trying to reach some conclusion. The French had approached closest of all. A little below the elevation on which the Kiev Regiment was positioned, in the hollow with the little river, the heart-stopping, rumbling crackle of musket fire could be heard, and much further to the right, behind the dragoons, the officer of the retinue pointed out to the prince a column of French that was rounding our flank. On the left, the horizon was bounded by the nearby forest.

Prince Bagration ordered two battalions from the centre to move across to reinforce the right. The officer of the retinue was bold enough to remark to the prince that if these battalions shifted, the guns would be left without cover. Prince Bagration turned towards the officer of the retinue and looked at him with his dull eyes without speaking. Prince Andrei thought the officer's remark was correct and that nothing could actually be said against it. But just then an adjutant galloped up from the company commander who was in the hollow with the news that huge masses of French were moving along the bottom, that the regiment had broken ranks and was falling back towards the Kiev Grenadiers. Prince Bagration inclined his head as a sign of assent and approval. He rode at a walk to the right and sent the adjutant to the dragoons with the order to attack the French. But the adjutant who was sent returned half an hour later with the news that the dragoons regimental commander had fallen back behind the ravine since heavy fire had been directed against him and he was losing men pointlessly and had therefore moved his dismounted musketeers into the forest on foot.

"Good," said Bagration. As he was riding away from the battery, shots were also heard in the forest on the left, and since it was too far to the left flank for Prince Bagration to get there in time himself, he sent Zherkov to tell the senior general, the same one who had presented the regiment to Kutuzov in Braunau, to fall back as rapidly as possible behind the ravine, because the right flank would probably not be able to hold the enemy up for long. Tushin and the battalion covering him were forgotten.

Prince Andrei listened intently to Prince Bagration's conversations with his commanders and to the orders that he gave, and noticed to his amazement that absolutely no orders were given, but that Prince Bagration simply tried to give the impression that everything that happened through necessity, chance and the will of individual commanders actually happened, if not at his command, then in accordance with his intentions. Prince Andrei noticed that thanks to the tact which Prince Bagration showed, despite this chance, unconnected nature of events, his presence achieved a very great deal. The commanders who rode up to Prince Bagration with distraught faces became calm, the soldiers and officers greeted him cheerfully and their spirits improved in his presence and they clearly tried to flaunt their bravery before him.

# XIX

Prince Bagration, having ridden up to the very highest point of our right flank, now began moving down towards where the sounds of rumbling gunfire were coming from but where nothing could be seen through the powder smoke. The closer they descended to the hollow, the less they could see, but the more palpable became the closeness of the genuine field of battle. They began to encounter wounded men. One, with a bloody head and no cap, was being dragged along by two soldiers holding him under the arms. He was wheezing and spitting. A bullet had evidently hit him in the mouth or throat. Another that they met was walking along briskly on his own without a musket, groaning loudly and waving his arm about to fight the fresh pain as blood streamed from it onto his greatcoat as if from a bottle. His face seemed to express more fright than suffering. He had been wounded only a moment earlier. After riding across the road, they began descending steeply and on the descent they saw several men lying on the ground; they encountered a crowd of wounded among whom there were also some without wounds. The soldiers were walking uphill, breathing heavily and, despite seeing the general, talking loudly and waving their arms about. Ahead, in the smoke, the ranks of grey greatcoats were already visible and an officer, catching sight of Bagration, ran after the soldiers with a shout, demanding that they turn back. Bagration rode up to the ranks, in which, now here and now there, there was the brisk crackle of shots, drowning out speech and shouted commands. The air was thickly suffused with powder smoke. The soldiers' excited faces were all blackened with powder. Some were pushing home their ramrods, others were tipping powder onto their pans or getting rounds out of their pouches, while still others were firing right beside their ears. But the powder smoke, which the wind failed to disperse, made it impossible to see at whom they were shooting. And quite often the pleasant sounds of humming and whistling could be heard.

"What is this?" thought Prince Andrei, riding up to this crowd of soldiers. "It can't be a line, because they're all in a bunch! It can't be an attack, because they're not moving, it can't be a square, they're not standing as they should."

The regimental commander, a small, lean, weak-looking old man with an agreeable smile and eyebrows that covered more than half of his old eyes, giving him a mild appearance, rode up to Prince Bagration and greeted him like a host receiving a dear guest. He reported to Prince Bagration that there had been a cavalry attack on his regiment by the French and that, although the attack had been repulsed, the regiment had lost more than half its men. The regimental commander said that the attack had been repulsed, thinking up this military term for what had happened in his regiment, but in reality he himself did not know what had happened during that half-hour in the forces entrusted to his command, and he could not say with any certainty whether the attack had been beaten off or whether his regiment had been routed by the attack. All he knew was that at the beginning of the action, round shots and grenades had started flying at his regiment and killing people, and that then someone had shouted "cavalry" and our men had started shooting. And they had been carrying on shooting since then, no longer at the cavalry, which had vanished, but at the French foot soldiers who had appeared in the hollow and were shooting at our men.

Prince Bagration inclined his head as a sign that all this was entirely as he had wished and anticipated. Addressing the adjutant, he ordered him to bring down from the hill the two battalions of the Sixth Chasseurs Regiment past which they had just ridden. Prince Andrei was astounded at that moment by the change that had taken place in Prince Bagration's face. For the expression on that face was the intensely joyful resolution of a man about to plunge into water on a hot day, and who is making his final run at it. The somnolent, dull eyes and the feigned air of deep thought were gone: the round, resolute hawk's eyes gazed forwards rapturously and rather contemptuously, obviously not settling on anything, although his movements remained as slow and measured as previously.

The regimental commander spoke to Prince Bagration, asking him to go back, since it was too dangerous here.

"For goodness' sake, your excellency, for the love of God," he said, looking for support to the retinue officer, who was turning his face away from him. "Look, by your leave."

He drew their attention to the bullets that were constantly whining, singing and whistling close by them. He spoke in the same tone of entreaty and reproach with which a carpenter addresses a gentleman who has picked up an axe: "We're used to this work, but you'll give your hands blisters." He spoke as though he himself could not be killed by the bullets. And his half-closed eyes lent his words even more conviction. The staff officer joined in with the regimental commander's exhortations, but Prince Bagration did not answer them and only gave orders to stop shooting and form up in such a way as to make room for the two battalions approaching. While he was speaking, the pall of smoke concealing the hollow was drawn aside from right to left, as if by an invisible hand, when a gust of wind suddenly sprang up, and the hillside opposite with the French moving across it was exposed to their view. All eyes were involuntarily turned towards that French column, moving towards us and winding over the terraced terrain. They could already see the shaggy caps of the soldiers, they could already distinguish the officers from the privates, they could see the banner flapping.

"They march splendidly," said someone in Bagration's retinue.

The head of the column had already descended into the hollow. The clash would take place on this side.

Hastily forming up, the remains of our regiment that had been in the action moved away to the right; moving up from behind them, hurrying along the stragglers, came the two battalions of the Sixth Chasseurs. Before they had even drawn level with Bagration, the heavy, ponderous tread of this mass of men marching in time could be clearly heard. Marching on the left flank, closest of all to Bagration, was the company commander, a round-faced, imposing man with a stupid, happy expression on his face. It was clear that the only thing he was thinking about at that moment was that he would march past his commander in fine style. With an air of front-line smugness he trod lightly on muscular legs, as if he were gliding along, drawing himself erect without the slightest effort, this lightness contrasting with the heavy tread of the soldiers marching in time to his step. He was carrying a slim, narrow unsheathed sword close to his leg (a curved sword that did not look like a weapon) and glancing round, now at the commander, now backwards, but without losing step, flexibly turning his entire powerful figure. It was as if all the strength of his soul were directed towards marching past the commander in the finest possible manner and, sensing that he was performing this task well, he was happy. "Left . . . left . . . left," he seemed to be repeating inwardly at every other step, and the wall of soldiers' figures with faces that were all stern in their own various ways moved to this rhythm, burdened down with knapsacks

247

and muskets, as though inwardly at every other step every one of these hundreds of soldiers was repeating: "Left . . . left . . . left . . ."

A fat major, puffing and panting and falling out of step, walked round a bush that was in his way; a soldier lagging behind, gasping for breath, his face frightened at his own deliquency, chased after the company at a trot; compressing the air as it passed, a cannonball flew over the heads of Prince Bagration and his retinue and hit the column.

"Close ranks!" rang out the company commander's show-off voice.

The soldiers skirted in an arc round something at the spot where the cannonball had fallen and an old trooper, a non-commissioned officer who had dropped behind alongside the men who were killed, caught up with his line, adjusted his stride with a skip, fell into step and looked around angrily. "Left . . . left . . . left . . ." the word seemed to be audible behind the menacing silence and the unvarying rhythm of feet striking the earth in unison.

"Well done, lads!" said Bagration.

"For your ex–cy-cy-cy-cy-cy!" – the cry rang through the ranks.

A morose soldier marching on the left turned his eyes to Bagration as he yelled with an expression that seemed to say: "We already know that." Another, opening his mouth without looking round as if he were afraid of being distracted, shouted and walked past. The order was given to halt and remove knapsacks.

Bagration rode round the ranks that had marched past him and dismounted from his horse. He handed the reins to a Cossack, then took off his cloak and handed that to him, straightened his legs and adjusted his cap on his head. The head of the French column, with officers at the front, appeared from under the hill. But nobody saw them, they were all watching only this short man with the sheepskin cap set straight on his head, with his hands simply lowered and his eyes now gleaming.

"God be with us!" he said in a firm, clearly audible voice, turned for a moment to face the front and, swinging his arms slightly, stepped forward across the uneven field. Prince Andrei felt that some insuperable force was drawing him forward and at that moment he experienced a happiness that made him forget everything . . .

There then took place the attack of which Mister Thiers says: "The Russians conducted themselves valiantly and – a rare thing in war – two masses of infantry advanced resolutely one against the other, and neither of the two gave way until the very clash"; and Napoleon on the island of St. Helena said: "Several Russian battalions demonstrated fearlessness."

The French were drawing close now and Prince Andrei, walking beside Bagration, could clearly distinguish the bandoliers, the red epaulettes, even the faces of the French. (He clearly saw one old French officer wearing gaiters who was climbing the hillside with difficulty, his feet turned out sideways.) Prince Bagration gave no new order and carried on walking in silence ahead of the ranks. Suddenly the crack of a shot rang out among the French, a second, a third . . . and smoke spread and gunfire crackled right along all the enemy's broken ranks. Several of our men fell, including the round-faced officer who had marched along with such assiduous merriment. But the very moment that the first shot rang out, Bagration looked round and shouted:

"Hoorah!"

"Hoo-oo-ra-ah!" The long, drawn-out cry ran along our line and, overtaking Prince Bagration and each other, in an untidy but jolly and spirited crowd, our men ran downhill after the disordered French.

## XX

The attack by the Sixth Chasseurs made it possible for the right flank to fall back. At the centre, the action of Tushin's forgotten battery, which had succeeded in setting fire to Schöngraben, halted the movement of the French. The French tried to extinguish the fire, which was being spread by the wind and allowed time for us to fall back. Although the withdrawal across the ravine took place in hasty commotion, the troops fell back without their units mingling together. But the left flank, consisting of the Azov and Podolsk Foot and the Pavlograd Hussars Regiments, which was attacked simultaneously and outflanked by superior French forces under the command of Lannes, was broken. Bagration sent Zherkov to the general of the left flank with orders to fall back immediately.

Zherkov started his horse in sprightly fashion, with his hand still raised to his cap, and galloped off. While with Bagration he had behaved excellently, that is, with absolute bravery, but scarcely had he ridden off when his strength deserted him. He was afraid, invincibly afraid of being killed, and he could not go back again to where there was danger.

Having reached the forces of the left flank, he rode forward to where the firing was and began searching for the general and the officers in places where they could not possibly be, and therefore he failed to convey the order.

The command of the left flank belonged by seniority to the regimental commander from that same regiment that had been presented to Kutuzov near Braunau, and in which the soldier Dolokhov was serving. However, the command of the extreme left flank was reserved for the commander of the Pavlograd Regiment, in which Rostov was serving, and as a consequence a misunderstanding occurred. The two commanders were extremely annoyed with each other, and when there had already been action on the right flank for some time and the French had already begun their attack, the two commanders were still absorbed in negotiations, which they conducted via adjutants with the aim of insulting each other. The regiments, both cavalry and infantry, were completely unprepared for imminent action. Due to this strange circumstance, the men of the regiments, from common soldier to general, were not anticipating battle and were calmly engaged in peaceful pursuits, the cavalry in feeding their horses, the infantry in gathering firewood.

"Since, however, he outranks me," said the German, the colonel of hussars, flushing as he addressed the adjutant who had ridden up to him, "let him do as he wishes. I cannot sacrifice my hussars. Trumpeter! Sound the retreat."

But matters were coming to a head. The rumbling of a cannonade and musket fire, mingling together, could be heard from the right and in the centre, and the French hoods of Lannes's musketeers were already crossing the mill dam and lining up on this side only two musket shots away. The colonel of infantry approached his horse with his swaggering gait and after mounting and drawing himself up very straight and tall, rode off to see the Pavlograd commander. The regimental commanders met with polite bows and with hidden malice in their hearts.

"But even so, colonel," said the general, "I still cannot leave half my men in the forest. I *beg* you, I *beg* of you," he repeated, "to take up your *position* and prepare to attack."

"And I beg of you not to interfere in matters that are not your concern," the colonel replied, growing heated. "If you were a cavalryman . . ."

"I am not a cavalryman, colonel, but I am a Russian general, and if you are not aware of that . . ."

"I am perfectly well aware of it, your excellency," the colonel suddenly shouted, starting his horse and turning crimson. "If you will be so good as to visit the lines, you will see that this position is no good for anything. I do not wish to destroy my regiment for your satisfaction."

"You forget yourself, colonel. It is not my own satisfaction that I seek and I will not permit such things to be said to me."

Accepting the colonel's invitation to a contest of bravery, the general thrust out his chest, knitted his brows and rode off with him in the direction of the line, as if all their differences had to be settled there, in the line, facing the bullets. They rode into the line, several bullets flew over their heads and they stopped without speaking. There was no point in looking from the line, since even from the spot where they had been standing before, it was clear that the cavalry could not operate through the bushes and ravines and that the French were outflanking our left wing. The general and the colonel glared sternly and significantly at each other, like two cocks preparing to fight, waiting in vain for signs of cowardice. They stood the test. Since there was nothing to say and neither of them wished to give the other any excuse to say that he had been the first to ride away from the bullets, they would have stood there for a long time, testing each other's courage, if at that moment they had not heard the crackling of muskets and a dull, muffled shouting almost behind them in the forest. The French had attacked the soldiers who were gathering firewood in the forest. The hussars could no longer fall back together with the infantry. They were cut off from the line of retreat on the left by the French line. Now, no matter how inconvenient the terrain might be, they had to attack in order to clear the way for themselves.

The squadron in which Rostov was serving, having barely had time to mount its horses, was left facing the enemy. Once again, as at the Enns bridge, there was no one between the squadron and the enemy, but between, separating them, there lay that same strange line of uncertainty and fear, seeming like the line that divides the living from the dead. All the men could feel that line and were agitated by the question of whether or not they were going to cross it and how.

The colonel rode up to the front line, gave some angry answer to questions from the officers and gave some order, like a man desperately insisting on having his own way. Nobody said anything definite, but word of the attack ran through the squadron. The command to form up rang out, then there was the squeal of sabres being drawn from their scabbards. But still no one moved. The troops of the left flank, both infantry and hussars, sensed that the commanders themselves did not know what to do. And the indecisiveness of the commanders was communicated to the troops. They all looked impatiently at each other and at the commanders ahead of them.

"Why have you dropped your reins?" a non-commissioned officer shouted at a soldier not far from Rostov.

"There's the sergeant-major galloping up," said another soldier. "It must mean there's going to be action."

"Come on, get on with it," thought Nikolai, glancing now and again at the George Cross hanging on the lace of his jacket, which he had received two days before for the firing of the bridge at Enns. On this day Nikolai's customary happy state of mind was even more pronounced than ever. Two days ago he had been awarded the cross; he had completely made things up with Bogdanich and – the height of happiness!

– the time had finally come to experience the joys of the attack, about which he had heard so much from his fellow hussars and which he had been waiting so impatiently to experience. Nikolai had heard of an attack as something supernaturally thrilling. He had been told that when you go tearing into that square you forgot yourself completely, that the hussar's sabre is nobly stained with the enemy's blood, etc.

"No good will come of this," said an old soldier. Nikolai looked at him reproachfully.

"Well, God be with you, lads," said Denisov's voice. "At a twot, forward!"

The cruppers of the horses quivered in the front row. Grachik pulled on the reins and set off himself.

"Tear into the square," thought Nikolai, squeezing the hilt of his sabre. Ahead of him he could see the first row of his hussars, and still further ahead he could see a dark stripe which he could not make out, but took to be the enemy. There was not a single shot, it was, like before, a single clap of thunder.

"Faster, now!" came the command, and Nikolai felt his Grachik lower his flanks, breaking into a gallop. He anticipated the horse's movements in advance, and he was feeling happier and happier. He noticed a solitary tree past which the squadron had to ride. At first the tree was ahead, in the middle of that line which had seemed so terrible. And then they had passed that line and not only had nothing terrible happened, but he was feeling even happier and more excited. "Quickly, quickly. Let my sabre taste the flesh of the enemy," thought Nikolai. He saw nothing either below his feet or ahead of him except for the cruppers of the horses and the backs of the hussars in the middle row. The horses began to gallop, overtaking each other despite themselves. "If they could see me now in Moscow at this moment!" he thought.

"Hoo-oo-ra-rah!" voices roared.

"Now, whoever I come across," thought Nikolai, spurring Grachik on and, overtaking the others, he loosed him into a full gallop. Suddenly something lashed across the squadron like a broad birch broom. Nikolai raised his sabre, preparing to slash, but at that moment the soldier Nikitenko galloping ahead of him drew away from him and as if in a dream Nikolai felt that he was still hurtling along with unnatural speed and at the same time standing still. A hussar he knew, Bondarchuk, galloped into him from behind and gave him an angry look. Bondarchuk's horse shied away and he galloped past. Another galloped past, a second and a third.

"What is this? I am not moving? I've fallen, I'm dead . . ." Nikolai asked and answered in a single instant. He was already alone in the middle of an empty field. Instead of moving horses and hussars' backs he saw around him the motionless earth and stubble. There was warm blood under him. "No, I'm wounded, but my horse is dead." Grachik tried to get up on to his forelegs, but he fell and pinned down his rider's leg. There was blood streaming out of the horse's head. The horse flailed about but could not get up. Nikolai tried to get up and also fell. His sabre snagged on his saddle. Where our men were, where the French were, he did not know. There was no one anywhere nearby.

Extricating his leg, he got up. "Where, on which side was that line now, the one that had separated the two forces so sharply?" he asked himself and he could not answer. "Could something bad have happened to me? Do things like that happen and what should one do in such cases?" he asked himself as he got up. And then he felt that there was something superfluous dangling on his numb left arm. The hand felt as if it were not his own. He examined the arm, looking in vain for blood on it. "Well, there are people over there," he thought happily, spotting several men running towards him. "They'll help me." Running at the front of these men was one in a strange shako and a blue greatcoat, black-haired, sunburnt, with a hooked nose. Another two and many more were running behind him. One of them said something strange, not Russian. Standing at the back among the same kind of people in the same kind of shako was one Russian hussar. They were holding him by the arms; behind him they were holding his horse.

"It must be one of us taken prisoner . . . Yes. Will they really take me too? What kind of people are they?" Nikolai kept thinking, not believing himself. "Are they really the French?" He looked at the approaching Frenchmen and despite the fact that a second ago he had been galloping solely in order to reach these French and cut them down, their closeness now seemed so terrible to him that he could not believe his eyes. "Who are they? Why are they running? Surely not towards me? Surely they're not running towards me? But what for? To kill me? *Me*, whom everybody loves so much?" He recalled his mother's love for him, the love of his family, his friends, and it seemed impossible that the enemy could intend to kill. "But perhaps they do want to kill me." He stood for more than ten seconds without moving from the spot, not understanding his situation. The front Frenchman with the hooked nose had run so close that he could already see the expression on his face. And the agitated, alien features of this man who was running towards him so lightly with his bayonet held forward, holding his breath, frightened Rostov. He grabbed his pistol, and instead of firing it, threw it at the Frenchman and ran towards the bushes as fast as he could. He ran, not with the feeling of doubt and struggle with which he had walked on to the bridge at Enns, but with the feeling of a hare running from the hounds. A single, indivisible feeling of fear for his young, happy life possessed his entire being. Jumping quickly over the hedges, in the same impetuous manner as when he used to run when he played tag, he flew across the field, occasionally turning back his pale, kind, young face, and a chill of terror ran down his spine. "No, better not look," he thought, but running up to the bushes, he glanced round once more. The French had fallen behind and just at the moment when he glanced round, the leading one had just slowed from a jog to a walk and turned round and was saying something to a comrade behind him. "There's something wrong," he thought, "they can't have wanted to kill me." But meanwhile his left arm was as heavy as if a two-*pood* weight had been hung on it. He couldn't run any further. The Frenchman stopped too and took aim. Nikolai squeezed his eyes shut and ducked down. A bullet flew past him, humming, and then another. He gathered his final strength, took hold of his left hand with his right and ran as far as the bushes. In the bushes there were Russian musketeers.

# XXI

The infantry regiments, caught by surprise in the forest, were running out of the trees and companies were mingling with other companies and rushing along in disorderly crowds. In his fright one soldier uttered that senseless phrase so terrible in war, "cut off", and the phrase and feeling of fear associated with it were communicated to the entire mass of men.

"They've outflanked us! They've cut us off! We're done for!" shouted the panting voices of men on the run.

Without attacking from the front, the French had outflanked our left flank on the right and struck (as they write in reports) at the Podolsk Regiment, which was positioned in front of the forest, and a great part of which had been gathering firewood in the forest. "Struck" meant that, having approached the forest, the French had fired at the edge of the wood, where they could see three Russian soldiers chopping firewood. The two Podolsk battalions had mingled together and run into the forest. The woodchoppers had joined the fleeing men, increasing the disorder. Having run through the narrow forest and emerged into the field on the other side, they continued running in absolute disorder. The forest, located at the centre of our left flank disposition, was occupied by the French, so that the Pavlograd musketeers were split off, and in order to rejoin their detachment they had to move far to the left and drive back the enemy line that had cut them off. But the two companies located in our forward line, some of the soldiers located in the forest and the regimental commander himself were cut off by the French. They had either to move out onto the opposite elevation and flank the forest in full view, under French fire, or break through the French. As soon as the regimental commander heard shooting and shouting behind him, he realised that something terrible had happened to his regiment, and the idea that he, an exemplary officer guilty of doing nothing wrong in his twenty-two years of service, might be guilty of incompetence or negligence in the eyes of his superiors so astounded him that, forgetting even the rebellious cavalry colonel and his own general's dignity and, most importantly, completely forgetting about danger and his instinct for self-preservation, he instantly grabbed hold of the pommel of his saddle and, spurring on his horse, galloped towards his regiment through a thick hail of bullets, which fortunately missed him. He wanted only one thing: to find out what had happened and help to correct the mistake, no matter what the cost, if he was the one that had made it, and not be held to blame but remain an inconspicuously worthy, exemplary officer.

Having galloped safely through the French, he reached the field behind the forest, across which our men were running and disobeying orders by moving downhill. That moment of moral vacillation which determines the outcome of a battle had arrived: Would these disorderly crowds of soldiers heed the voice of their commander or merely glance round at him and continue running?

Despite the regimental commander's desperate shouting in that voice formerly so feared by the soldiers, despite the regimental commander's crimson face, transformed in its fury and the waving of his sword, the soldiers carried on running, talking, shooting into the air and disobeying orders.

The moral vacillation which determines the fate of battles had evidently been resolved in favour of fear.

"Captain Maslov! Lieutenant Pletnev! Lads, forward! Let us die for the Tsar!" shouted the regimental commander. "Hoorah!"

A small bunch of soldiers set off forwards after the general, but suddenly stopped again and began shooting. The general started coughing from the shouting and the powder smoke and halted in the middle of the soldiers. All appeared to be lost; but just then the French, who were advancing on our men, suddenly started running away from the edge of the forest as Russian musketeers emerged from the trees. It was Timokhin's company, the only one that had maintained its order and had waited in ambush in a ditch in the forest and attacked the French unexpectedly. Timokhin had hurled himself at the French with such a desperate scream and rushed at the enemy with such insane, drunken determination, with nothing but his sword, that the French had no time to gather their wits, but dropped their weapons and ran. Dolokhov, running almost alongside Timokhin, killed one Frenchman close up and was the first to catch hold of a surrendering officer by the collar. The fleeing men returned, the battalions reassembled and the French, who had been on the point of splitting the forces on the left flank into two parts, were forced back for the moment. Reserve units were able to get through and join the others, and those who had fled were sent back.

The regimental commander was standing by the bridge with Major Ekonomov, letting the companies go past as they fell back, when a soldier came up and, to draw attention to himself, unceremoniously grabbed hold of his stirrup and almost leaned against it. The soldier was wearing a bluish greatcoat of good-quality factory cloth, he had no knapsack or shako, his head was bandaged and he had a French ammunition bag thrown over his shoulder. He was holding an officer's sword in his hand. The soldier was red-faced, his blue eyes gazed insolently into the regimental commander's face, and his mouth was smiling. Although the regimental commander was busy giving orders to Major Ekonomov, he could not help paying attention to this soldier.

"Your excellency, here are two trophies," said Dolokhov, indicating the French sword and the bag. "I took an officer prisoner. I halted the company." Dolokhov was breathing hard from fatigue; he spoke haltingly. "Our men stabbed the officer later. The whole company can testify to it. I ask you to remember this, your excellency."

"Very well, very well," said the regimental commander, and turned to Major Ekonomov. But Dolokhov did not go away; he untied the kerchief, tugged on it and blood poured across his open, handsome forehead on to the hair that was matted with blood in one spot.

"Bayonet wound; I remained at the front."

The general rode away, not listening to Dolokhov. New columns of French were moving towards the mill.

"Don't forget, your excellency," shouted Dolokhov and, after bandaging up his head with the kerchief, he followed the soldiers who were falling back.

## XXII

Tushin's battery had been forgotten, and it was only at the very end of the action that Prince Bagration, who could still hear cannon-fire at the centre, sent off his duty staff officer, and then later Prince Andrei, to order the battery to fall back as quickly as possible. The covering force stationed beside Tushin's cannon had left on someone's orders in the middle of the action, but the battery had continued firing and had not been taken by the French only because, in the smoke, the enemy was unable to tell whether it had any cover or not and could not imagine that four cannon without protection would be bold enough to fire. On the contrary, from the energetic action of this battery, the enemy assumed that the Russians' main forces were concentrated here in the centre and twice launched an attack against this point, and both times were driven back by rounds of grapeshot.

Soon after Prince Bagration left, Tushin had succeeded in setting Schöngraben on fire.

"See how they're scrambling! It's burning! Look at that smoke! That's neat! That's grand! The smoke, the smoke!" said the gun hands, livening up.

All the guns kept on firing without orders in the direction of the flames. With each shot, as if they were urging it on, the soldiers cried out "That's neat! Yes, that's it! Oh yes . . . That's a grand one!" Spread by the wind, the fire expanded rapidly. The French columns that had advanced beyond the village withdrew again, but as if in retaliation for this failure, the enemy set up ten guns to the right of the village, by the mill on the very same knoll where Tushin's tent had stood the day before, and began firing towards Tushin.

In their childish delight at the fire and carried away by their success in shooting at the French, our gunners only noticed this battery when first two cannonballs and then four more landed among their guns and one felled two horses, while another tore off an ammunition wagon-driver's leg. However, once roused, their spirits did not flag, only the mood changed. The horses were replaced by others from the reserve gun-carriage, the wounded were taken away and the four guns were turned against the ten-cannon battery. One officer, Tushin's comrade, had been killed at the beginning of the action and in the course of an hour, seventeen out of forty gun hands were disabled, and one gun could no longer fire; but the artillerymen were as cheerful and lively as ever. Twice they noticed that the French had appeared below, not far away, and then they fired shrapnel at them.

The little man with the weak, awkward movements constantly demanded another pipe from his orderly "at the same time", as he put it, and scattered sparks from it as he ran out to the front and peered at the French from under his little hand.

"Hit them, lads" he kept repeating, catching hold of the guns by their wheels himself and turning the screws. In the smoke, deafened by the ceaseless shots that set his weak nerves shuddering every time, Tushin hobbled from one gun to another or to the ammunition wagons, always keeping his nose-warmer in his mouth, sometimes aiming a gun, sometimes counting shells, sometimes giving instructions for changing and reharnessing the dead and wounded horses, shouting in his weak, shrill, irresolute little voice. His face became more and more animated. It was only when men were killed or wounded that he frowned and wheezed as if in pain and, turning away from the dead man, shouted angrily at the other men, who as always hesitated to lift a wounded man or a body. The soldiers, fine handsome fellows for the most part (and, as always in a battery company, two heads taller than their officer and twice as broad across as he was), all looked to their commander like children in a difficult situation, and the expression on his face was always reflected on theirs.

As a consequence of this terrible din and commotion and the need to pay attention and act, Tushin did not experience a single unpleasant twinge of fear; the very thought that he could be killed or painfully wounded never even entered his head. On the contrary, he became jollier and jollier, and he became more and more certain that he could not be killed. To him it seemed that the moment when he had first seen the enemy and fired the first shot was a long time ago, almost as long ago as yesterday, and that the patch of the battlefield on which he was standing was his own home, a familiar place that he had known for a very long time. Even though he remembered everything, was aware of everything and did everything that the very finest officer could do in his position, the condition that he was in resembled a feverish delirium or the state of a man who is drunk.

Due to the deafening roar of his own guns on all sides, due to the whistling and explosions of the enemy's shells, due to the sight of the sweaty, red-faced gun hands bustling around the guns, due to the sight of blood – men's and horses' – due to the sight of the smoke-puffs of the enemy's guns on the other side, from where a cannonball came flying after each puff and struck the ground, or a man, or a gun or a horse, due to the sight of all these things, inside his head he constructed a fantastic world that was his alone, one in which he could take pleasure at just that moment. In his imagination the enemy's cannon were not cannon, but tobacco pipes, from which an invisible smoker puffed out smoke in sparse clouds.

"See, he's taken another puff," Tushin whispered to himself when a cloud of smoke shot up from the hill and was borne away to the left by the wind in a long streak, "now wait for the ball, you have to send it back."

"What are the orders, your honour?" asked a gunner standing close beside him who could hear him muttering something.

"Never mind, a grenade . . ." he replied.

"Come on now, our Matvevna," he said to himself. In his imagination Matvevna was the large cannon cast in the old style at the edge. He imagined the French beside their guns as ants. In his world, the number one hand of the second gun, a handsome drunkard, was *uncle*; Tushin looked at him more often than at the others and delighted in his every movement. The sound of the musket fire, fading away and then growing louder at the bottom of the hill, seemed to him to be someone's breathing. He listened closely to the ebb and flow of these sounds.

"There she's started breathing again, she has," he said to himself.

He imagined himself as an immensely tall and powerful man who was tossing the cannonballs at the French with both hands.

"Come on, mother Matvevna, don't let me down!" he was saying as he walked away from the gun, when he heard a strange, unfamiliar voice above his head.

"Captain Tushin! Captain!"

Tushin glanced round in fright. It was the staff officer who had thrown him out of Grunth. He was shouting to Tushin in a breathless voice.

"Have you lost your mind, dear sir? Twice you have been ordered to fall back, and you . . ."

"Why are they after me? . . ." Tushin thought to himself, looking at the officer fearfully.

"I . . . never . . ." he said, pressing two fingers to the peak of his cap. "I . . ."

But the colonel never finished what he wanted to say. A cannonball flying through the air close by forced him to bend lower in the saddle. He stopped talking and was just about to say something else when another shot stopped him. He turned his horse and galloped away.

"Pull back! Everyone pull back!" he shouted from the distance.

"You don't like me!" said Tushin. A minute later an adjutant arrived with the same order. It was Prince Andrei. The first thing he saw as he rode out into the open space occupied by Tushin's cannon was an unharnessed horse with a broken leg whinnying beside horses in harness. The blood was gushing out of its leg like a spring. There were several strange objects lying between the limbers. They were dead men. Prince Andrei's horse stepped on one of them and he could not help noticing that it had no head at all, but the hand with the half-curved fingers looked alive. One shell after another flew over his head as he rode up. And he felt a nervous shudder run down his spine. He was morally and physically exhausted. But the mere thought that he was afraid uplifted him again. "I cannot be afraid." He passed on the order but did not leave the battery. He had decided that he would have the guns removed from position in his presence and withdrawn in his presence. Prince Andrei dismounted from his horse and, stepping over the bodies, under terrible fire from the French, he and Tushin set about removing the guns.

"There was an officer here just now, but he soon cleared out," an artilleryman said to Prince Andrei, "not like your honour."

Prince Andrei and Tushin did not say a word to each other. They were both so busy it seemed as if they did not even see each other. When they had set the two guns out of the four that had survived on their limbers and set off downhill (one shattered cannon and a howitzer were left behind), Prince Andrei rode up to Tushin.

"Well goodbye," said Prince Andrei, extending his hand to Tushin.

"Goodbye, my dear chap," said Tushin, "dear fellow. Goodbye, my dear chap," said Tushin, with tears in his eyes.

Prince Andrei shrugged and rode away.

"Right-o, and a pipe at the same time," said Tushin.

# XXIII

The wind died down and black clouds hung low over the site of the battle, mingling with the powder smoke at the horizon. As it grew darker, the glow of fires in two places became all the more sharply visible. The cannon-fire had become weaker, but at the rear and to the right the crackle of musket fire could be heard closer and more frequently. As soon as Tushin and his guns, driving round or over the wounded, had moved out of range and descended into the ravine, he was met by the commander and his adjutants, including both the staff officer and Zherkov, who had twice been sent to Tushin's battery and twice failed to reach it. They were all interrupting each other, issuing and relaying orders on where to go and how, and they all reproached and rebuked him, asking why he had acted so thoughtlessly in not falling back for such a long time. Tushin did not give any orders and he rode along silently on his artillery nag at the back, afraid to speak because, although he did not know why, at every word he was on the point of bursting into tears. Although orders had been given to abandon the wounded, many of them dragged themselves along after the troops and asked to be allowed onto the guns. The same artillery officer who had been reading about Circassian women before the battle was put on a gun-carriage with a bullet in his stomach. At the bottom of the hill a pale-faced hussar cadet, supporting one arm with the other hand, approached Tushin and asked for a seat.

"Captain, for God's sake, my arm is crushed and bruised," he said timidly. "For God's sake, I can't walk. For God's sake." It was clear that this cadet had already asked for a seat somewhere else more than once and been refused everywhere. He asked in an indecisive and pitiful voice. "Order them to give me a seat, for God's sake . . ."

"Give him a seat. Sit down, dear fellow, sit down," said Tushin. "Put your greatcoat under him, uncle. But where's the wounded officer?"

"We took him off, he died," someone answered.

"Give him a seat. Sit down, dear fellow, sit down. Spread out your greatcoat, Antonov."

The cadet was Rostov. Holding one arm with the other hand, he was pale-faced and his lower jaw was trembling and shuddering feverishly. They sat him on the same gun from which they had taken off the dead officer. There was blood on the greatcoat spread beneath him and it stained Rostov's breeches and hands.

"What's this, are you wounded, my dear chap" said Tushin, approaching the gun on which Rostov was sitting.

"No, crushed."

"How come there's blood on the carriage?" asked Tushin.

"It was the officer as bloodied it, your honour," replied an artilleryman, wiping up the blood with the sleeve of his greatcoat as though in apology for the dirty condition that the gun was in.

With the help of the infantry they just barely managed to drag the guns up the hill and halted when they reached the village of Guntersdorf. It was already so dark that it was impossible to make out a soldier's uniform at ten paces, and the shooting had begun to die away. The shots already glinted in the dark. It was the final attack by the French, and the soldiers entrenched in the village houses replied. Once again everybody dashed out of the village, but Tushin's guns could not move and the artillerymen, Tushin and the cadet looked at each other without speaking, waiting to learn their fate. The shooting began to die away and soldiers full of lively talk spilled out of a side street.

"All right, Petrov?" one of them asked.

"We gave it them hot, brother. They won't go sticking their noses in now," said another.

"Couldn't see a blind thing. They blazed away at their own men! Too dark to see, brothers. Is there anything to get drunk on?"

The French had been beaten off for the last time. And under cover of the absolute darkness Tushin's guns once again began moving forward somewhere, framed by the droning infantry that surrounded them.

In the gloom it was as if there was a murky, invisible river flowing always in the same direction, humming with whispering and talking and the sounds of hooves and wheels. Among the general hum the clearest sounds of all were the groans and voices of the wounded in the gloom of the night. Their groans seemed to fill up the darkness that surrounded the troops. Their groans and the gloom of this night were one and the same. After some time, there was a disturbance in the moving crowd. Someone rode past on a white horse with a retinue and said something while riding by.

"What did he say? Where to now? Halt, is it? Did he thank us, then?" came the avid questions from all sides, and the entire moving mass began pressing into itself (clearly, those at the front had stopped), and the rumour spread that they had been ordered to halt. Everybody stopped just as they had been walking, in the middle of the muddy road.

Fires sprang up and voices could be heard more clearly. Captain Tushin, having given orders to his company, sent one of the soldiers to look for a dressing station or doctor for the cadet and sat down beside a fire built on the road by the soldiers. Rostov dragged himself across to the fire too. His entire body was trembling and shuddering from the pain, cold and damp. He felt an irresistible urge to sleep, but could not fall asleep because of the agonising pain in his arm that ached so badly he could not find a comfortable position. Sometimes he closed his eyes, sometimes glanced at the fire which looked like a red-hot glow to him, sometimes at Tushin's hunched, weak little figure sitting cross-legged beside him. Tushin's large, kind and intelligent eyes gazed at him with such great sympathy and compassion that he began feeling sorry for Tushin. He could see that Tushin wanted with all his heart to help him and was unable to do a thing.

On all sides they could hear the footsteps and talk of men walking and riding by and the foot soldiers settling in around them, the sounds of voices, footsteps and horses' hooves shifting in the mud, the crackling of firewood near and far fused into a single quivering roar.

Now the invisible river no longer flowed through the darkness as before, it was as if a dark, gloomy sea had settled back down after a storm, still quivering and swaying. Rostov watched and listened to what was going on in front of him and around him, making no sense of it. A foot soldier came up to the fire, squatted down, and held his hands out to the flames, averting his face.

"You don't mind, your honour?" he said directing his request to Tushin. "I got separated from my company, your honour; don't know where – terrible luck!"

An infantry officer with a bandaged cheek approached the fire to-

WOUNDED ROSTOV AT THE CAMPFIRE
*Drawing by M. S. Bashilov, 1867*

gether with the soldier and addressed Tushin, asking him to order the
guns to be moved up a bit, so they could get a wagon through. Two
soldiers came running up to the fire after the company commander.
They were cursing desperately and fighting, trying to pull some boot or
other out of each other's hands.

"Of course, you picked it up! That's real smart!" one shouted in a
hoarse voice.

Then a thin, pale soldier came up, with his neck bandaged in a
bloody leg-wrapping, and demanded water from the artillerymen in an
angry voice.

"Am I just supposed to die like a dog, or what?" he said. Tushin
ordered them to give him some water. Then up ran a cheery soldier,
asking for fire for the infantry.

"A little bit of hot fire for the infantry! Enjoy your stay, fellow
countrymen, thanks for the fire, we'll return it with interest," he said,
carrying the glowing red brand off somewhere into the darkness.

After that four soldiers walked past the fire carrying something heavy
on a greatcoat. One of them stumbled.

"Look, damn them, they've put their firewood on the road," growled
one.

"He's dead, what's the point of carrying him?" said one of them.

"Stop that!"

And they disappeared into the darkness with their load.

Just then two infantry officers and a soldier with his head bandaged and no cap came up from the other side.

"Fire, gentlemen. We can't find our own men, we could at least sit here."

The artillerymen made room for them.

"Gentlemen, have you not seen where the third battalion is, the Podolsk Regiment?" one of them asked.

No one knew. The soldier with the bandaged head sat at the fire and looked over the people sitting round it with a frown.

"Lads," he said, addressing the artillerymen, "haven't you got any vodka? A gold piece for two canteen lids of vodka."

He took out his purse. According to his uniform he was a private, but the greatcoat he was wearing was blue, with a torn sleeve. He had a French bag and sword hanging over his shoulder. His forehead and brows were covered in blood. An unnatural fold on the bridge of his nose between his eyebrows gave him a weary and cruel expression, but his face was strikingly handsome, there was a smile at the corners of his lips. The officers carried on with a conversation that they had clearly begun earlier.

"Didn't I hit them hard! How he shouted!" said one officer. "Yes, brother, your Frenchmen aren't up to much."

"All right, stop boasting," said the other.

Meanwhile the soldier drank both the canteen lids of vodka that the artillerymen had managed to find and gave them a gold piece.

"Yes, there'll be plenty of stories now," he said, addressing the officer scornfully, "but somehow no one saw them happen."

"Yes, well there's no one else like Dolokhov, right enough," said the officer, laughing timidly and turning to his comrade. "It's not enough for him to bayonet the French, he shot one of his own from the fifth company."

Dolokhov glanced round quickly at Tushin and Rostov, whose eyes were fixed on him.

"Well you shouldn't run, that's what I shot him for," he said. "I'd have stuck an officer, if he was a coward."

Dolokhov began stirring the fire and adding more wood.

"Why did you leave the guns for the French?" he asked Tushin. Tushin frowned, turned away and pretended he hadn't heard.

"How's it going? Does it hurt?" he asked Rostov in a whisper.

"Yes."

"And what guns are they firing with?" said Tushin with a sigh.

Just then they heard the footfalls of two horses close beside the fire, the shadows of the riders appeared and an officer's voice spoke sternly.

"You were ordered to march at the back of the column, so fall in at the back," said the angry voice, "and no discussions."

"I never heard his voice there, but here he is putting on airs again," Dolokhov said so that the men riding past could hear, and he stood up, straightened his greatcoat, adjusted the bandage on his head and walked away from the fire.

"Your honour, the general wants you. He is billeted there in the hut," said an artilleryman, walking up to Tushin.

"One moment, dear fellow."

Tushin stood up and walked away from the fire, buttoning his greatcoat and pulling it straight.

Not far from the artillerymen's fire, in the hut that had been made ready for him, Prince Bagration was sitting at his supper, conversing with several unit commanders who had gathered there. There was the old man with the half-closed eyes, greedily gnawing on a mutton bone, and the general who had served irreproachably for twenty-two years, red-faced after a glass of vodka and supper, and the staff officer with the signet ring, and Zherkov, anxiously surveying them all, and Prince Andrei, with his eyes narrowed indolently and contemptuously.

There was a captured French standard leaning against the wall in the corner of the hut and the auditor with the naïve face was feeling the fabric of the standard and shaking his head in incomprehension, perhaps because he was genuinely interested in the standard's appearance, or perhaps because he was hungry and found it hard to watch a supper at which he had been given no place. In the next hut there was a French colonel taken prisoner by the dragoons. Our officers were crowding round him, studying him. Prince Bagration thanked individual officers and asked them about the details of the action and their losses. The commander who had presented his regiment near Braunau reported to the prince that as soon as the action had begun he had fallen back out of the forest, collected the men chopping wood and, after letting the French past him, had charged them with bayonets with two battalions and overrun them.

"As soon as I saw, your excellency, that the first battalion had broken ranks, I halted on the road and I thought: 'I'll let these past and meet them with the fire of battle,' and that's what I did."

The regimental commander had wanted so badly to do this, and regretted so badly not having done it, that it seemed to him that everything had definitely happened that way. Yes, perhaps it really had happened? How could you possibly tell in that confusion what had happened and what had not?

"And moreover I must remark, your excellency," he continued, recalling Dolokhov's conversation with Kutuzov and his own last conversation with the demoted man, "that I saw the demoted private Dolokhov capture a French officer and particularly distinguish himself."

"At the same place, your excellency, I saw the Pavlograd Regiment's attack," Zherkov put in with bold politeness, although he had not seen his hussars that day, only heard about them from an infantry officer. "They scattered two squares, your excellency."

Several men there smiled at Zherkov's words, as always expecting a joke from him; but, observing that what he said was also conducive to the glory of our arms and the day, they assumed serious expressions, although many of them knew quite well that what Zherkov was saying was a lie, entirely without foundation. Prince Bagration frowned and turned to address the old colonel.

"Thank you all, gentlemen, all units fought heroically: the infantry, cavalry and artillery. How did two guns come to be left in the centre?" he asked, seeking somebody out with his eyes. (Prince Bagration did not ask about the guns on the left flank, he already knew that two cannon had been abandoned there at the very beginning of the action.) "I believe I asked you," he said, addressing the duty staff officer.

"One was disabled," the duty staff officer replied firmly and definitely. "As for the other, I cannot understand it, I was there all the time, supervising, and as soon I left . . . True, it was a hot spot," he added modestly.

Someone said that Captain Tushin was right beside the village and he had already been sent for.

"But you were there, Prince Bolkonsky," said Prince Bagration, turning to Prince Andrei.

"We seem to have just missed each other," said the duty staff officer, smiling pleasantly at Bolkonsky.

"I did not have the pleasure of seeing you," Prince Andrei said coldly, getting to his feet.

Just then Tushin appeared in the doorway, timidly making his way through from behind the backs of the generals. As he made his way round the generals in the cramped hut, embarrassed, as always at the sight of superior officers, Tushin failed to notice the shaft of the banner and stumbled over it. Several voices laughed.

"How did the gun come to be left?" asked Bagration, frowning not so much at the captain as at the laughing voices, among which the loudest of all was the voice of Zherkov. Only now, at the sight of his menacing commander did Tushin realise the full horror of his own guilt and disgrace in having remained alive and lost two guns. He had been so agitated that until this moment he had not got around to thinking about it. The officers' laughter confused him even more. He stood in front of Bagration with his lower jaw trembling, as if he had a fever or like a child about to cry, and scarcely managed to get his words out.

"I don't know . . . your excellency . . . there weren't any men, your excellency."

"Surely you could have taken some from the covering force?"

Tushin did not say that there had not been any cover, although it was the absolute truth. He was afraid that by doing so he would cause trouble for another officer and he kept his eyes fixed on Bagration's face and said nothing, the way a pupil who has lost the thread of his thought stands in front of the examiner.

The silence lasted rather a long time. Prince Bagration, evidently not wishing to be stern, could not think of anything to say; the others did not dare to interfere in the conversation. Prince Andrei screwed up his eyes, looking at Tushin.

"Your excellency," said Prince Andrei, interrupting the silence with his sharp voice, "you were good enough to send me to Captain Tushin's battery. I was there and I found two thirds of the men and horses killed, two guns destroyed. And no covering force whatever."

Both Prince Bagration and Tushin were now looking equally intensely at Bolkonsky as he spoke slowly through clenched teeth.

"And if you will permit me, your excellency, to express my opinion," he continued, "then we are indebted most of all for the success of the day to the action of this battery and the heroic endurance of Captain Tushin and his company," said Prince Andrei, indicating the amazed captain with a careless and dismissive gesture.

Prince Bagration looked at Tushin and, clearly not wishing to demonstrate any mistrust of Bolkonsky's strange judgement, while at the same time not feeling able to believe it entirely, he inclined his head and told Tushin that he could go.

# XXIV

"Who are they? Why are they here? What do they want? And when will all this end?" thought Rostov, watching the shifting shadows before his eyes when Tushin left him. The pain in his arm was growing more agonising. He felt an irresistible urge to sleep, there were red circles dancing in front of his eyes, and the impression of these voices and these faces, and the feeling of loneliness fused with the feeling of pain. They were the ones, these soldiers, wounded and not wounded; they were the ones, these officers, and especially that strange, restless soldier with the bandaged head – they were the ones who were squeezing and stretching and twisting the sinews and burning the flesh in his shattered arm and shoulder. In order to be rid of them, especially of him, the alarming soldier with that frozen smile, he closed his eyes.

He dozed for a moment, but in that brief period of forgetfulness he dreamed of a countless number of things: he saw his mother and her big white hand, he saw Sonya's slim shoulders, Natasha's eyes and laughter, and Denisov with his voice and his moustache, and Telyanin, and the whole business with Telyanin and Bogdanich. This whole story was the same thing as that soldier with the harsh voice, and it was this whole story and this soldier who were gripping his arm so agonisingly and relentlessly, squeezing it and pulling it in one direction all the time. He tried to get away from them, but they would not let him move a hair's breadth, would not let go of him, even for a second. It wouldn't hurt, it would be well, if only they didn't tug at it; but he couldn't get rid of them.

He raised himself up a little. The dampness rising up from the ground and the pain made him shudder as if he had a fever. He opened his eyes and looked upwards. The black shroud of night hung an arm's length above the light of the coals. There were specks of snow flying in that light. Tushin had not come back, the doctor had not come. He was alone, now there was only some little soldier sitting naked on the other side of the fire and warming his thin, yellow body.

"Nobody needs me!" thought Rostov. "There is nobody to help or pity me. But when I was at home I used to be strong, cheerful, loved." He sighed and could not help groaning as he sighed.

"Hurts bad, does it?" asked the little soldier, shaking his shirt over the flames and, without waiting for an answer he added with a grunt: "All those people damaged in one day, it's terrible!"

Nikolai was not listening to the soldier. He was watching the snowflakes swirling above the flames and remembering a Russian winter with a warm, bright house, a fluffy fur coat, a fast sleigh and a healthy body, with all the love and care of a family. "And why did I come here? Everything's finished now! I'm alone and I'm dying," he thought.

The following day the French did not renew their attack and the remnant of Bagration's detachment joined Kutuzov's army. Two days later Prince Anatoly Kuragin, Buxhöwden's adjutant, rode to Kutuzov with the news that the army coming from Russia was one day's march away. The armies united.

Kutuzov's retreat, despite the loss of the Vienna bridge, and this final battle at Schöngraben in particular, amazed not only the Russians and the French, but even the Austrians. They called Bagration's detachment "an army of heroes", and Bagration and his detachment were awarded great honours by the Austrians and the Russian Emperor, who arrived in Olmütz soon afterwards.

# PART THREE

# I

Prince Vasily did not brood over his plans, any more than he thought of doing harm to others to secure an advantage. He was merely a man of the world who had got on in society and made a habit of success. According to circumstance and his closeness to various people, he was constantly formulating different plans and ideas of which he himself was not even properly aware, but which made up the entire interest of his life. Usually he would have not just one or two of these plans on the go, but dozens, some of which were only just becoming clear to him, while others were coming to fruition and yet still others were being discarded. He did not say, for instance: "This man has influence at present, I must win his trust and friendship and through him request that I be issued a lump sum gratuity," nor did he say to himself: "So now I must entice him, marry him to my daughter and exploit his fortune, if only indirectly." But when he did encounter someone with influence, instinct immediately prompted the notion that this man could be useful, and Prince Vasily would become friends with him and, at the first opportunity, without premeditation, quite naturally and instinctively, he would flatter him, assume a familiar manner and speak of the matter about which he wished to ask him. It was not happiness that he found in this game of intrigue, but the entire meaning of life. Without it, life for him would not have been worth living. Thus when Pierre had been close at hand in Moscow, he had insisted on the young man going to St. Petersburg, and had borrowed thirty thousand roubles from him, while arranging for the young man to be appointed a Gentleman of the Bedchamber, at that time the equivalent in rank of a State Counsellor. Apparently acting absent-mindedly and without guile, without self-interest and yet at the same time with the unquestioning assurance that it had to be, he had done everything that was necessary in order to marry Pierre to his daughter. If Prince Vasily had been in the habit of preparing his plans, he could never have been so natural in his dealings or so direct and familiar with everyone. He had an instinct that always attracted him to people richer and more powerful than himself and also an instinct that dictated the best moment to take advantage of such people.

Following his father's death, Pierre, after his former solitude and inactivity, found himself so surrounded by people and so busy that his bed was the only place where he could be alone with himself. He had to sign documents, deal with official offices, the significance of which he did not clearly understand, ask his senior steward about things, travel to his estates and receive the quite immense number of people who had formerly not wished to know of his existence but who would now be offended and aggrieved if he did not wish to see them. All these various people – businessmen, relatives, acquaintances – were equally well-disposed and cordial towards the young heir – and all were obviously convinced beyond the smallest doubt of Pierre's exalted virtues. He continually heard the words: "With your exceptional kindness", or "With your fine heart", or "You yourself are so pure, count", "With your intellect", or "If he were as intelligent as you," and so forth, so that in the end he came to believe in his own goodness and his own intellect, especially since deep in his heart he had always felt that he was kinder and more intelligent than almost all the people he met. Even people who formerly had been spiteful and apparently hostile became tender and affectionate. The eldest of the princesses, who had been so spiteful, came to Pierre's room after the funeral and, lowering her eyes and constantly blushing, said that she greatly regretted the misunderstandings that had occurred between them and now felt she had no right to request anything more than to be allowed, following the heavy blow she had suffered, to remain for a few weeks in the house she had loved so much, and in which she had sacrificed so much. At these words she was unable to restrain herself and burst into tears. Pierre took her by the hand, told her not to worry and never to leave that house. And the princess thenceforth began knitting him a scarf, took care of his health and told him that she had simply been afraid of him and now was glad that he had allowed her to love him.

"Do this for me, *mon cher*, after all she did suffer a great deal for the deceased," said Prince Vasily, handing him some paper to sign in favour of the princess, following which the eldest princess became even more kindly. The younger sisters also became more kindly: in particular the youngest one, the pretty one with the mole, who often embarrassed Pierre with her own embarrassment at the sight of him. Soon after his father's death, Pierre wrote to Prince Andrei. In his brief reply from Brünn, Prince Andrei wrote: "It will be hard for you now, my dear fellow, to look clearly at God's world, even over the top of your spectacles. Remember that all that is base and sordid will now crowd up close, and all that is noble will stand aloof." "He would not have said that if he had seen their kindness and sincerity," thought Pierre. It seemed so natural to Pierre that everyone should like him, and so unnatural for anyone not to love him, that he could not help but believe in the sincerity of the people surrounding him. Only rarely, very rarely did he find time to read a little and think a little about his favourite subjects: about the ideas of the revolution, and about Buonaparte, and about strategy, which, as he followed the military events, had now begun to interest him passionately. He found no sympathy for these interests among those who now surrounded him.

He was constantly short of time. He constantly felt as if he were in a state of gentle and jolly intoxication. He felt he was the centre of some important general movement, that something was constantly expected of him, and that if he did not do that something, he would aggrieve many people and deprive them of what they expected but that if he did do it, that would be a good thing, even a very good thing. He did what they required of him, but that very good thing always remained somewhere out of reach.

During this first period the person who gained more control than anyone else over Pierre's affairs and Pierre himself was Prince Vasily. Since Count Bezukhov's death he had not let Pierre out of his hands. He had the air of a man heavily burdened with affairs, weary and exhausted but ultimately unable through sheer compassion to cast this helpless youth, who was his friend's son and had such an immense fortune, upon the mercy of fate and swindlers. During the few days he spent in Moscow following Count Bezukhov's death, he either summoned Pierre to see him or came to see him himself and instructed him on what had to be done in a tone of such weary certitude that each time it was as if he were repeating: "You know what a frightfully busy man I am, and that I'm helping you out of pure charity, but it really must end; and you know perfectly well that what I am proposing to you is the only thing that's feasible."

"Well, my friend, tomorrow we leave, at last," he said to Pierre one day, closing his eyes and patting Pierre's elbow lightly with his fingertips and speaking in a tone which suggested that what he was saying had been decided between them long ago and could not have been decided in any other way, despite the fact that Pierre was hearing it for the first time. "Tomorrow we leave, and I shall give you a place in my carriage. I am very glad. All our important business here is finished. And I should have left a long time ago. Look, I have received this from the prince. I petitioned him for you, and you have been enlisted in the diplomatic corps and made a Gentleman of the Bedchamber."

Despite the force of that tone of weary certitude that it could not have been otherwise, Pierre, who had been thinking about his career for so long, was on the point of objecting, but Prince Vasily interrupted him.

"*Mais mon cher*, I have done this for myself, for the sake of my conscience, and there is no need to thank me. No one has ever complained that he was too well loved, but then you are a free man – you can give it up tomorrow if you wish, once you have seen for yourself in St. Petersburg. And it is high time for you to leave these terrible memories behind." Prince Vasily sighed. "Indeed, indeed, my dear fellow. My valet can travel in your carriage. Ah, yes, I almost forgot," Prince Vasily added. "You know, *mon cher*, that the deceased and I had accounts to settle, well I have received money from the Ryazan peasants and so I'll keep it. You don't need it. You and I can settle up."

The money that Prince Vasily referred to as "from the Ryazan peasants" was several thousand roubles of quit-rent which he was keeping for himself . . .

In St. Petersburg, just as in Moscow, Pierre was surrounded by the atmosphere of affectionate, loving people. He was unable to refuse the position, or rather, title (since he did not do anything) that Prince Vasily had obtained for him, and there were so many people to meet, invitations and social engagements to fulfil that Pierre experienced even more than in Moscow that sensation of vague anxiety and constantly impending but never consummated good. Many members of Pierre's former bachelor circle were away from St. Petersburg. The Guards were on the march. Dolokhov had been reduced to the ranks and Anatole was in the army, in the provinces, so that Pierre was unable to spend the nights in the way he had previously liked. All his time was spent at dinners, balls and – predominantly – at Prince Vasily's house, in the company of the old, fat princess and the beautiful Hélène, in relation to whom, despite himself, he was seen by society in what was for him the unusual role of a cousin or brother, since they saw each other every day and they lived under one roof. But should Hélène wish to dance, she instructed Pierre openly to partner her. She sent him to tell her mother that it was time to leave, and to find out if the carriage had arrived, and in the morning, out walking, to fetch her gloves.

More clearly than anyone else, it was Anna Pavlovna Scherer who demonstrated to Pierre the change that had taken place in society's view of him. Formerly, as in the inappropriate conversation about the French Revolution that Pierre had struck up with her in the drawing room, he had constantly felt that the things he said were inept, that he was behaving improperly and tactlessly, and that even if Hippolyte said something stupid, it was *à propos*, while his own words, which had seemed so clever as he was preparing them in his imagination, sounded stupid as soon as he began speaking out loud, and this fatal awkwardness that he experienced in the company of Anna Pavlovna provoked him into defiance and particularly abrupt conversation. "What does it matter," he used to think, "if everything comes out awkwardly, I'll say it all anyway." And that was how he had reached the point of having conversations like the one about the vicomte. That was previously. Now, however, it was quite different. Whatever he might say turned out *charmant*. Even if Anna Pavlovna did not say so, he could see that she wanted to but refrained, while maintaining a deferential air.

Early in the winter of 1805–1806 Pierre received from Anna Pavlovna the usual pink note with an invitation, to which the following had been added: "You will find *chez moi* la Belle Hélène, whom one can never weary of admiring." Reading this part, Pierre sensed for the first time that there was some kind of connection between him and Hélène that was recognised by other people, and he felt frightened by this thought, as if obligations that he could not fulfil were being imposed on him, and yet at the same time pleased by such an amusing suggestion.

Anna Pavlovna's *soirée* was the same as the first one, except only that the novelty with which Anna Pavlovna regaled her guests this time was not Mortemart, but a diplomat who had arrived from Berlin and brought with him the very latest news of the Emperor Alexander's sojourn at Potsdam, and of the military action. Pierre was received by Anna Pavlovna with a hint of sadness which obviously referred to the young man's recent loss, the very same kind of sadness as that supreme sadness which was expressed at every mention of the most august Empress Maria Fedorovna. Without knowing why, Pierre felt flattered. Anna Pavlovna composed the circles in her drawing room with her customary artistry. The large circle, which included Prince Vasily and some generals, had the services of the diplomat. The other circle was by the tea table. Pierre had wanted to join the former but on seeing him, Anna Pavlovna, who was in the agitated state of a general on the battlefield when visited by thousands of brilliant new ideas which he barely has time to put into effect, had touched him with her finger: "Wait, I have something in mind for you for this evening." She glanced at Hélène and smiled at her. "My dear Hélène, do show some pity on my poor aunt, who absolutely adores you. Give her ten minutes or so of your time. And so that you will not feel too bored, here is a knight who will not refuse to accompany you."

The beauty set out towards the aunt, but Anna Pavlovna held Pierre back at her side with the appearance of having to give one final, essential instruction.

"She is truly delightful, is she not?" she said to Pierre, indicating the majestic beauty as she floated away. "And such comportment! Such tact for such a young girl, such elegant comportment! That comes from the heart! The man to whom she belongs will be a happy one. With her even the most unworldly husband will occupy a brilliant place in society despite himself, without the least effort. Do you not think so? I only wished to know your opinion." And Anna Pavlovna let Pierre go.

Pierre replied sincerely in the affirmative to Anna Pavlovna's question concerning Hélène's elegant comportment. If he had ever thought about Hélène at all, he had thought precisely about that exceptional, calm ability of hers to be agreeable in society.

The aunt received the two young people in her corner, but apparently wished to conceal her adoration of Hélène, preferring instead to express her fear of Anna Pavlovna. She kept glancing at her niece as if asking what she was supposed to do with these people. As she left them, Anna Pavlovna once again touched Pierre's sleeve with her finger and said: "I hope next time you will not say it is boring at Mademoiselle Scherer's."

Hélène smiled with an expression which stated that she could not even conceive of anyone possibly experiencing anything but rapturous delight at the sight of herself. The aunt cleared her throat, swallowed hard and said in French that she was awfully pleased to see Hélène. Then she addressed Pierre with the same greeting and the same expression.

In the middle of their dreary and halting conversation, Hélène glanced towards Pierre and smiled at him with that clear and beautiful smile with which she smiled at everybody. Pierre was so accustomed to this smile, it conveyed so little to him, that he also smiled, out of weakness, and looked away.

The aunt was just then talking about a collection of snuffboxes that Pierre's deceased father, Count Bezukhov, had owned. She opened her own snuffbox and Princess Hélène asked to see the portrait of the aunt's husband that had been painted on this snuffbox.

"It was definitely done by Vinès," said Pierre, naming a famous miniaturist, as he craned towards the table in order to pick up the snuffbox, listening to the conversation at the neighbouring table as he did so. He half-rose, intending to walk round, but the aunt handed him the snuffbox directly, behind Hélène's back. Hélène leaned forward to make space and glanced round, smiling. As always at *soirées*, she was wearing a dress that was extremely low-cut at both front and back, in the fashion of the time. Her bosom, which had always seemed to Pierre to be made of marble, was so close that even with his short-sighted eyes he could not help but discern the living charms of her shoulders and neck, all in such close proximity to his mouth that he only had to lean a little further in order to touch her. Pierre involuntarily leaned further over, then drew back in fright, suddenly feeling himself enveloped in the fragrant, warm atmosphere of the beautiful woman's body. He could sense the warmth of her body, smell the scent of her perfume and hear her corset rustling as she breathed. He did not see Hélène, the marble beauty who was all of a piece with her dress, as he had seen and sensed her before, but instead suddenly saw and sensed only her body, covered by clothing. And once having seen it, he could not see her in any other way, just as we cannot restore an optical illusion that we have seen through.

She glanced round, looked straight at him with her black eyes gleaming, and smiled. "So had you not noticed before how lovely I am?" she seemed to have said. "Had you not noticed that I am a woman. Yes, I am a woman. And also such a woman as can belong to anyone, even to you."

Blushing furiously, Pierre lowered his gaze and attempted once again to see her as that aloof, distant beauty, a beauty existing for her own sake, that he had previously imagined her to be. But he could no longer do it. He could not, just as a man who has been looking at a tall weed in the fog and sees it as a tree, can no longer, having once seen the weed, perceive it as a tree again. He looked and what he saw was a vibrant woman inside a dress that was simply covering her. More than that, in that very instant he felt that Hélène not only could be, but must be or already was his wife, and that it could not be otherwise. He knew this just as surely as if he had known it while standing beneath the wedding crown with her.

How it would happen and when, he did not know, he did not even know if it would be a good thing. He even had a feeling that for some reason it was not a good thing, but he knew that it would happen.

"*Bon*, I'll leave you in your little corner, I see you're quite happy there," said Anna Pavlovna's voice.

And Pierre, trying fearfully to remember whether he had done anything reprehensible, blushed and glanced around him, feeling that everybody knew as well as he did what had happened to him.

A little while later, when he moved to the large circle, Anna Pavlovna said to him: "They say you are decorating your Petersburg house." (It was true. The architect had shown that he needed to do it and so, without knowing why, Pierre was decorating his house in St. Petersburg.) "That's good, but do not move out of the prince's house," she said, smiling at Prince Vasily. "It is good to have a friend like the prince. I know a thing or two, do I not? But you? You need advice." She paused. "If you get married, well that is a different matter." And she linked them together in a single glance. Pierre did not look at Hélène, and she no longer held aloof from him, she was still as strangely close, all of her so close, with her lovely body, her smell, her skin and her bright flush of womanly passion. He mumbled something and blushed.

On returning home, Pierre was unable to get to sleep for a long time, thinking about what had happened to him. What had happened to him? Nothing. He had merely realised that a woman whom he had known as a child, whom he used to despise, about whom he had used to say without thinking, "Yes, she is beautiful" when they told him that Hélène was a beauty, he had realised that this woman could give him an entire world of pleasures about which he had never thought before. "But she's stupid, I've said myself that she's stupid," he thought. "This is not love at all, quite the opposite. But there is something vile in the feeling that she has aroused in me, something forbidden. How could she become mine? They say her brother Anatole is in love with her, and she is in love with him, which is the reason Anatole was sent away. Her brother is Hippolyte, her father is Prince Vasily. I must not love her," he reasoned, yet even as he reasoned in this way, his reasoning remained unresolved, he caught himself smiling and realised that there was a second string of thought emerging from behind the first, that at the same time as he thought about how trivial she was, he was also dreaming of how she would be his wife, how she could love him, how she could be quite different and how everything that he had thought and heard about her could be untrue, and again he no longer saw her as he had done previously, but only her neck, shoulders and bosom. "But then, why is it that this thought never occurred to me before . . ."

And again he told himself that it was impossible, that there was something vile and unnatural in this marriage. He recalled her previous words and glances and the words and glances of those who had seen them together. He recalled with horror the words and the glance of Anna Pavlovna when she was speaking to him about his house, he recalled hundreds of similar hints made by Prince Vasily and others, and he was overcome by horror that he might already have bound himself in some way to carry through this business, which would ruin his entire life. And he decided firmly to distance himself from her, to keep a careful eye on himself and to go away. But even while he was reciting this decision to himself, her image would appear at the other side of his heart and he would say: "To give myself to her, to forget everything, abandon everything – that is true happiness, and how blind I am for not having seen the possibility of this great happiness before."

In November 1805, Prince Vasily was due to travel to Moscow and four other provinces on a tour of inspection. He had arranged this commission for himself in order at the same time to visit his own disordered estates and the estates of his future son-in-law, the young Count Bezukhov and also, after collecting his son Anatole from where his regiment was stationed, to take him to call on Prince Nikolai Andreevich Bolkonsky, in order to marry this son to the daughter of the rich old man. But before his departure and this new business, Prince Vasily had to settle matters with Pierre, who, although he had recently been visiting Prince Vasily's house every day and spending entire days there, and was as odd, agitated and foolish in Hélène's presence as a man in love ought to be, had still not proposed.

"This is all very well," Prince Vasily said to himself one morning with a sigh of sadness, acknowledging that Pierre, who owed him so much (well, Christ be with him) was not acting entirely properly towards him. "Youth and frivolity, oh well, God be with him," thought Prince Vasily, taking pleasure in the feeling of his own kindness, "but there has to be an end to everything. The day after tomorrow is Hélène's name-day, I shall invite a few people. And if he does not understand what he must do, then it will be up to me. I'm the father."

For a month and a half after Anna Pavlovna's *soirée* and the sleepless, anxious night that followed it, during which Pierre had decided that marriage to Hélène would be the ruination of his life, that he had to avoid her and go away, every day since that decision Pierre had gone to Prince Vasily's home and been horrified to feel that every day he was linking himself with her more and more in other people's eyes, that he absolutely could not go back to his former opinion of her, nor could he tear himself away from her, that it would be a terrible thing, but he must link his life with hers. Perhaps he might have been able to hold back, but not a day passed without his receiving a note from the princess or from Hélène herself at her mother's instructions, in which they wrote to him that they were expecting him and if he did not come he would spoil the pleasure of the company and dash their hopes ... In those rare moments when Prince Vasily was at home, as he passed Pierre he would tug his hand downwards, distractedly proffer his cheek and say either "until tomorrow" or "I shan't see you till dinner", or "I'm staying in for you" and so forth. And all this despite the fact that when Prince Vasily stayed in for Pierre (as he said), he did not exchange as much as two words with him. Pierre did not feel strong enough to disappoint their expectations.

He visited them and each time he told himself the same thing: "I have to understand her at last and realise who she is. Was I mistaken before or am I mistaken now? No, she is not stupid, no, she is a beautiful woman," he said to himself. "She is never mistaken about anything, she will never say anything stupid. She says little, but what she does say is always simple and clear. So she is not stupid. She has never been embarrassed in company and she does not get embarrassed. So she is not a bad woman."

It often happened that he would start discoursing, thinking out loud with her, and every time she would reply to him either with short but aptly put comments indicating that this did not interest her, or with the silent smile and glance that demonstrated her superiority to Pierre most palpably of all. She was right to regard all arguments as nonsense in comparison with that smile. She always met him with a joyful, trusting smile meant only for him, which contained something more significant than the general smile that always adorned her face. Everything was fine. Pierre knew that everyone was only waiting for him finally to say one word, step across a certain line, and he knew that sooner or later he would step across it, but an incomprehensible terror overwhelmed him at the mere thought of this inevitable step.

Thousands of times in the course of this month and a half, during which he felt himself being drawn deeper and deeper into an abyss that terrified him, Pierre told himself: "But what is all this? I need energy. Do I really not have any?" And he tried to uplift himself morally, but felt to his horror that in this case he did not have the energy which he knew was in him and which really was in him. Pierre was one of those people who are only strong when they feel they are entirely pure. And since the day that his passionate nature had been overwhelmed by a feeling of desire which he had experienced when leaning over the snuffbox at Anna Pavlovna's, his energy had been paralysed by an unconscious sense of guilt over that urge. There was no one to help him, and he moved closer and closer towards taking that step that he was yearning to take.

On Hélène's name-day a small company of the very closest people, as the princess put it, took supper at Prince Vasily's home – relatives and friends. All these relatives and friends had been given to feel that on this day the fate of the name-day girl would be decided. The guests were sitting at supper. Princess Kuragina, a massive and imposing woman who had once been beautiful, sat at the head of the table. On both sides of her sat the most honoured guests, an old general, his wife and Anna Pavlovna Scherer. At the far end of the table sat the less elderly and honoured guests, and also sitting there like members of the household were Pierre and Hélène – side by side. Prince Vasily was not taking supper. He strode round the table in a most jovial mood, seating himself first with one, then with another of the guests, saying a casually agreeable word to each of them, with the exception of Pierre and Hélène, whose presence he appeared to ignore.

Prince Vasily buoyed everyone up. The wax candles burned brightly, the silver and crystal on the table, the ladies' fine outfits, the gold and silver of the epaulettes all gleamed, the servants in red kaftans scurried round the table: there were the sounds of knives, glasses and plates, and the sounds of animated speech in several conversations being conducted around this table. In one corner an elderly gentleman of the chamber could be heard assuring an elderly baroness of his passionate love for her and her laughter; on one side there was the story of Marya Viktorovna's failure, and on another – an invitation for the next day. At the centre of the table Prince Vasily was the focus of his listeners' attention and only his voice could be heard. He was telling the ladies, with a facetious smile on his lips, about the most recent session – on Wednesday – of the State Council, at which His Majesty Alexander Pavlovich's then-famous rescript to the army had been received and read by Sergei Kuzmich Vyazmitinov, the new military governor-general of St. Petersburg. In it the sovereign, addressing Sergei Kuzmich, had said that he was receiving assurances of the people's devotion from every side and that he thanked the inhabitants of St. Petersburg for their expressions of devotion which were reaching him, and that he took pride in the honour of being the head of this nation and would endeavour to be worthy of it.

"Well, so it never got any further than 'Sergei Kuzmich'?" one lady asked, laughing.

"Not a single hair's breadth," replied Prince Vasily. "Poor Vyazmitinov simply could not go any further. He tried several times to start the letter from the beginning, but as soon as he said Sergei . . . there were tears, and then Ku-uzmi-i-ch was drowned out by sobbing, and he could not go on, and out came the handkerchief again, and then 'Kuzmich' again and more tears . . . and so we asked someone else to read it."

"Kuzmich . . . and more tears . . ." someone else repeated.

"Don't be spiteful," said Anna Pavlovna, wagging her finger at them from the far end of the table, "he is such a fine man, our good-hearted Vyazmitinov."

Everyone joined in the conversation that had sprung up at the upper, honoured end of the table, everyone seemed to be cheerful and under the influence of the most diverse and lively sentiments; only Pierre and Hélène sat beside each other saying nothing, almost at the lower end of the table; both their faces shone with a restrained smile of bashfulness at their happiness, and no matter what the others said or how they laughed and joked, no matter with what gusto they all consumed Rheinwein and sauté and ice cream, no matter how hard they tried to avoid glancing at this couple, or how indifferent and inattentive to them the couple seemed, somehow, from the rare glances that were cast in their direction, it could be felt that the anecdote about Sergei Kuzmich and the laughter and the eating – all of this was merely dissembling and all the powers of attention of this entire company were focused only on Pierre and Hélène. Prince Vasily demonstrated Sergei Kuzmich's sobbing while at the same time running his glance over his daughter: and even while he was laughing, the expression on his face said: "Right, everything is going well, today everything will be decided." Anna Pavlovna rebuked him for our good-hearted Vyazmitinov, but in her eyes, which flickered briefly on to Pierre, the prince read congratulations on the happiness of his future son-in-law and his daughter. The old princess, sighing sadly as she offered wine to the lady beside her, shot a severe glance at her daughter, seeming to be saying with that sigh: "Yes, now there is nothing left for you and me to do, my dear, except drink sweet wine, now is the time for these young people to be so boldly and defiantly happy." The old general morosely and scornfully repeated the things his wife said and in doing so demonstrated their stupidity. "And why couldn't she be as beautiful and lovely as this beauty," he thought, "she's always talking nonsense." "And what sort of nonsense are all these things that I am telling them about the Viennese cabinet, as if I were even interested in it," thought a diplomat, glancing at the happy faces of the lovers, "now *that* is happiness!"

Among the paltry, petty, artificial interests which bound this company together, there had appeared the simple feeling of attraction to each other felt by a young man and woman, both handsome and healthy. And this serious human feeling suppressed everything else, hanging in the air above all their artificial babble. The jokes were not funny, the news was not interesting, the animation was obviously feigned. It seemed that not only they, but also the servants waiting at table could sense the same thing and they forgot the right order for serving as they gazed, lost in admiration, at Hélène's upright, well-formed marble figure and her radiant face, which had suddenly acquired a new meaning for everyone, and Pierre's fat, red face, languishing in restrained passion. The very flames of the candles seemed to be focused only on those two happy faces.

Pierre felt that he was the centre of everything and this position both delighted and embarrassed him. He saw nothing, remembered nothing, heard nothing. He was in the same state as a man absorbed in some task, when only very occasionally and unexpectedly is his soul briefly disturbed by thoughts and impressions of reality.

"So it is all over!" he thought. "But how did it all happen? So fast! Now I know that it is not for her alone, not for myself alone, but for everybody's sake that this must inevitably happen. They are all expecting it so eagerly, all so certain that it will happen, that I cannot, I cannot disappoint them. But how will it be? I don't know." And again he immersed himself in his own task, which absorbed all of his mental powers. Again he saw close up, to one side of him, that face, those eyes, that nose and the line of that brow, and the neck where her hair began and the bosom. Or he would suddenly feel ashamed of something. He felt awkward that he alone was occupying everybody's attention, that he was a fortunate man in other people's eyes, that he was the sybarite Paris taking possession of Hélène. But that is probably the way it always is, and the way it should be. And again he heard and saw and felt only her, her closeness, her breathing, her movements, her beauty. And it seemed to him that it was not she but he who was so lovely, and that was the reason why they were looking at him in that way and, happy at the general amazement, he thrust out his chest, lifted up his head and delighted in his happiness. Suddenly he heard some voice, the voice of someone he knew, from out of that pitiful, petty life in which he used to live, in which there was no beauty and self-forgetting, a voice saying something to him for the second time.

"I was asking you when you received the letter from Bolkonsky," said Prince Vasily's voice. "How distracted you are, my dear fellow."

Prince Vasily was smiling, and Pierre saw that everyone, absolutely everyone was smiling at him and at Hélène. "Well then, since you all know," Pierre said to himself. "Well then? It is true." And he himself smiled, exposing his bad teeth, and Hélène smiled.

"When did you receive it? From Olmütz?" repeated Prince Vasily, who needed to know this to settle an argument.

"How is it possible to talk and think of such trifles?" thought Pierre.

"Yes, from Olmütz," he replied with a sigh of sympathy for everyone who was not him at that moment.

From supper, Pierre led his lady after the others into the drawing room. The guests began going home and some left without saying good-bye to Hélène, as if they did not wish to distract her from some serious occupation; some approached her for a moment and quickly moved away, forbidding her to see them off. The diplomat was sadly silent as he emerged from the dining room. He was contemplating the absolute vanity of his diplomatic career in comparison with Pierre's happiness. The old general growled angrily at his wife when she asked him about his leg. "What an old crone," he thought. "Now Elena Vasilievna, she'll still be a beauty in fifty years."

"It would seem that I can congratulate you," Anna Pavlovna whispered to the princess and squeezed her hand firmly. "Were it not for my migraine, I would have stayed."

The princess did not answer: she was tormented by envy at her daughter's happiness.

While the guests were being seen off, Pierre remained for a long time with Hélène in the little drawing room, where they had sat down. In recent months he had often been left alone with Hélène and had never spoken to her of love, but now he felt that it was necessary, and yet he could not bring himself to take that final step. Even more than before, it still seemed shameful to him that he was here alone with this beautiful woman who attracted him so. As if here, beside Hélène, he were occupying someone else's place. "This happiness is not for you," some inner voice told him. "This happiness is for those who do not have what you have." But something had to be said, and he began speaking. He asked her if she was pleased with today's *soirée*. She replied, as always with her customary simplicity, that today's name-day celebration had been one of the most agreeable that she had known. And she began talking about the people who had been there, and she spoke well of everyone.

A few of the closest relatives were still there. They were sitting in the large drawing room. Striding indolently, Prince Vasily approached Pierre. Pierre stood up and said that it was already late. Prince Vasily gave him a severe, searching look, as if what he had said were so strange that he found it impossible even to make out. But following that, the prince's expression of severity changed and he tugged at Pierre by the hand, sat him down and smiled affectionately.

"Well, then, Lelya?" he said, immediately addressing his daughter in that careless tone of habitual endearment which is acquired by parents who are affectionate with their children from their childhood, but which Prince Vasily had acquired by means of imitation.

And he turned back again to Pierre:

"Sergei Kuzmich! Quite delightful, that, isn't it?"

Pierre smiled, but it was clear from his smile that he had understood that it was not the joke about Sergei Kuzmich which interested Prince Vasily at that moment; and Prince Vasily understood that Pierre had understood this. He suddenly became embarrassed, muttered something and left the room. The sight of this old, worldly-wise man's embarrassment touched Pierre, and he looked round at Hélène – she too seemed embarrassed and her look seemed to say: "Well, you have only yourself to blame."

"I absolutely must step across the line, but I can't, I can't," thought Pierre, and he began talking about something irrelevant, about Sergei Kuzmich, he asked what the point of the story had been, since he had not heard it. Hélène replied with a smile that she also did not know.

When Prince Vasily entered the drawing room, the princess was talking quietly about Pierre with an elderly lady.

"Of course, this is a brilliant match, but happiness, my dear . . ."

"Marriages are made in heaven," the elderly lady replied.

As if he were not listening to the ladies, Prince Vasily walked across to the far corner and sat down on a divan. He closed his eyes and seemed to be dozing. His head slumped slightly and he woke up.

"Alina," he said to his wife, "go and see what they are doing."

The princess approached the door, walked past it with an emphatically indifferent air and glanced into the other drawing room. Pierre and Hélène were still sitting and conversing in a dignified manner.

"Still the same thing," she told her husband.

Prince Vasily frowned, twisted his mouth over to one side, which gave him an angry expression, then suddenly shook himself and stood up, throwing his head back and assuming an expression of solemn happiness while he was still in the large drawing room, then striding resolutely past the ladies and into the small drawing room. He walked up to Pierre with rapid strides. The prince's face looked so exceptionally solemn that Pierre rose to his feet in fright on seeing it.

"And me? What about me?" Prince Vasily began. "My wife has only just told me. You come here too, Lelya." He embraced Pierre with one arm and his daughter with the other. "I am very, very glad." His voice began to tremble. "I loved your father, and she will be a good wife to you. May God bless you."

He embraced his daughter, then Pierre once again, and Pierre felt relieved and happy. The princess cried, and so did the elderly lady. They kissed Pierre. And he kissed the beautiful Hélène's hands. After the blessings they were left alone again. Pierre held her hand without saying anything and watched her bosom rising and falling.

"Hélène! I love you terribly," he said, and felt ashamed. He glanced into her face. She moved closer to him. Her face was red.

"Ah, take off those what-do-you-call-them . . ." she said, pointing to his spectacles.

Pierre took off his spectacles and in addition to that general strange look in people's eyes when they take off their spectacles, his eyes held a frightened, questioning look. He was about to lean down over her hand and kiss it when, with a sudden, quick movement of her head, she intercepted his lips and set them against her own. Her face at that moment astounded Pierre with its suddenly changed expression of unpleasant embarrassment. "Now it's too late, it's all finished, and anyway I love her," thought Pierre.

A month and a half later he was married and he and his wife moved into the large St. Petersburg house of the Counts Bezukhov.

# II

After Pierre and Hélène's wedding, the old prince Nikolai Andreevich Bolkonsky received a letter from Prince Vasily informing him that he would shortly be arriving with his son. ("I am going on a tour of inspection and, naturally even a hundred *versts* is no serious detour for me in order to visit you, my dearly respected benefactor," he wrote, "and my Anatole is accompanying me, travelling to the army, and I hope that you will permit him to express in person that profound respect which he, following his father, feels towards you.")

"There's no need even to bring her out, the suitors come to us themselves," the little princess remarked imprudently on hearing about this. Prince Nikolai Andreevich scowled and said nothing.

One evening two weeks after the letter was received, Prince Vasily's people arrived in advance and the following day he himself arrived with his son. Old Bolkonsky had always held a low opinion of Prince Vasily's character but in recent times, as Prince Vasily had climbed his way up in rank and honour, and especially after the old prince had surmised Prince Vasily's matchmaking intentions from the hints in the letter and those dropped by the little princess, this low opinion had turned into a feeling of hostile contempt. Whenever he mentioned Prince Vasily, he would snort. The day Prince Vasily was due to arrive, Prince Nikolai Andreevich was especially grumpy and ill-tempered. He might have been out of sorts because Prince Vasily was arriving, or perhaps he was displeased at Prince Vasily's arrival because he was out of sorts, but those who were used to dealing with him could tell, merely from his face and bearing, that he was in a bad mood and best avoided. As usual, he went out for a walk in his warm velvet coat with a sable collar and cap. The previous day deep snow had fallen. The prince went into the garden looking for something to find fault with, or so the steward assumed, but the path along which Prince Nikolai Andreevich walked to the conservatory had already been swept, and the tracks of the broom were visible on the scattered snow, while a spade was stuck into one of the loose banks of snow that ran along both sides of the path. The prince walked through the conservatories. Everything was in order. But at the building site he became angry with the architect because the roof of the new outhouse had not yet been completed and, even though he had known about this the day before, he scolded Mikhail Ivanovich roundly. He was now approaching the house, accompanied by the steward.

"Can the sleigh get through?" he asked. "For the princess to go for a ride?"

"The snow's deep, your excellency, but I've already given orders for the avenue to be swept."

The prince inclined his head in approval and mounted the porch.

"It was hard to get through earlier," added the steward. "But we had heard, your excellency, that a minister was coming to visit your excellency."

The prince suddenly swung round bodily towards the steward.

"What? What minister? And who ordered it?" the prince shouted in his harsh, piercing voice. "You didn't clear the avenue for my daughter, the princess, but you did for a minister. I'm not expecting any ministers."

"Begging your pardon, your excellency, I assumed . . ."

"You assumed!" shouted the prince, growing more and more furious until, having worked himself up into an extreme state simply with his own words, he struck Alpatych, something he would never normally do. "And who taught you to pay respects on my behalf to people that I do not even wish to know? It can't be done for my daughter, no, but it can for someone else." The prince simply could not bear the idea.

Before lunch was served, Princess Marya and Mademoiselle Bourienne stood waiting for the prince, knowing he was in a foul mood: Mademoiselle Bourienne wore a glowing expression which said, "I know nothing, I am the same as ever", while Princess Marya looked pale and fearful, with downcast eyes. What was hardest of all for Princess Marya was knowing that at times such as this she ought to behave like Mademoiselle Bourienne, but also knowing she could not. She thought: "If I act as though I don't notice (apart from the fact that I am unable to lie), he'll think I lack sympathy, but if I act as if I'm feeling low and depressed (which is true), he will say, as he always does, that I've lost heart, I'm sulking, and so on."

The prince glanced at his daughter's frightened face and snorted.

"Bah! What a fool," he said and turned towards Mademoiselle Bourienne.

"And the other one's not here, they've been telling her tales," he thought à propos the little princess, who was absent from the dining room.

"So where's the princess?" he asked. "Hiding?"

"She's not feeling well," answered Mademoiselle Bourienne with a bright smile. "She won't be coming. It's quite understandable in her condition."

"I can well imagine it," said the prince and sat down at the table.

His plate did not look clean; he pointed to a spot on it and tossed it aside. Tikhon caught it. The little princess was not feeling unwell; but she was so insurmountably afraid of the prince that, having heard he was in a bad temper, she had decided not to leave her room.

"I am afraid for the child," she had said to Mademoiselle Bourienne. "God only knows what a fright might do."

"To be sure, to be sure."

In general, living at Bleak Hills the little princess was in a constant state of fear and aversion; she was unaware of her own aversion for the old prince because her fear was so dominant that she could not feel it. The prince felt the same aversion, but in his case, it was stifled by contempt. The princess had taken an especial liking to Mademoiselle Bourienne, she spent the days with her, and asked her to sleep in her room at night too and often talked about her father-in-law, criticising him.

"We are expecting guests, *mon prince*," said Mademoiselle Bourienne, unfolding her white napkin with her pink hands. "His excellency the prince and his son, is that what I've heard?" she enquired.

"Hm! This *excellence* is a young lad that I once took up and found a place in a Collegium," the prince said in an outraged voice, as if Mademoiselle Bourienne had meant to humiliate him. "And why he should be bringing his son, I cannot fathom. Perhaps Princess Liseveta Karlovna and Princess Marya know; I don't know what he would bring that fop here for. I don't want it." He glanced at his red-faced daughter. "What's wrong with you? Are you unwell, is that it? From fear of the minister, as that blockhead Alpatych told me he was today."

"No, *mon père*."

"Go and fetch Alpatych."

Mademoiselle Bourienne's choice of a topic of conversation had been quite unfortunate enough, but even so, she did not stop there, and went on to chatter about the conservatory, saying how beautiful the new building was, and after the soup the prince softened, so it seemed to her, as a result of what she had been saying, although in actual fact it was because he had eaten some soup and his stomach had begun to absorb the food.

After lunch he went to see his daughter-in-law. The little princess was sitting at a small table and chatting with Masha, the maid. She turned pale on seeing her father-in-law.

"Yes, I'm feeling rather low."

She looked quite plain, her cheeks had sunk, her lip had lifted upwards, and under her eyes the skin was taut and drawn.

"Is there anything you need?"

"No thank you."

"Very well, very well." He went out and took himself to the servants' room.

Alpatych was now standing there with the look of a condemned man.

"Has the road been covered over again?"

"It has, your excellency. Forgive me, for God's sake, it was just a stupid . . ."

The prince interrupted him and laughed his unnatural laugh.

"Well, all right, it's all right." He extended his hand, which Alpatych kissed, and he went into his study.

That evening Prince Vasily arrived. He was met on the avenue by the coachmen and servants, who drove his carriages and sleigh through to the outhouse along the road now once again strewn with snow.

Prince Vasily and Anatole were allocated separate rooms. Anatole was perfectly calm and jolly, just as he always was. He regarded his entire life as one long party that someone should always provide for him, and he regarded his trip to see a bad-tempered old man and a rich, ugly heiress in precisely this way too. It might all turn out rather well and could even be amusing, he decided, if the dinners were good and there was wine and pretty women as well. "And why not get married, if she's very rich? That never does any harm." – So thought Anatole. He pinched the princess's pretty maid when she came running in and, laughing loudly, set about his toilet.

He shaved and scented himself with the foppish thoroughness that had become a habit and, with his innate expression of triumphant victory, thrusting out his chest and holding his handsome head high, he entered his father's room. Prince Vasily's two valets were bustling around as they readied him: he himself was gazing about brightly and nodded at his son as he came in, as if to say: "Yes, that's just the way I need you to look!"

"But joking apart, father, is she so very ugly? Eh?" he asked, as though continuing the conversation they had had more than once during the journey.

"Enough of that nonsense! The most important thing is – try to be respectful and rational with the old prince."

"If he gets quarrelsome, I shall walk out," he said. "I can't stand these old men. Eh?"

"My dear boy, I do not wish to hear your jokes on this subject. Remember that for you, everything depends on this."

Meanwhile in the maidservants' room not only were they already aware of the arrival of the minister and his son, but the appearance of both had already been described in detail. Princess Marya was sitting alone in her own room and vainly attempting to master her inner agitation.

"Why did they write, why did Lise tell me about it, surely it cannot be true," she said to herself, looking in the mirror. "How can I go into the drawing room? Even if I like him, I still could not be myself with him." And the mere thought of her father's mocking glance reduced her to terror.

Having extracted from Masha the maid, who had already encountered Anatole, all the necessary information about what a handsome, dark-browed man the minister's son was and how his old papa had barely managed to drag his feet up the staircase while the son had flown up behind him three steps at a time like an eagle, the little princess and Mademoiselle Bourienne proceeded to Marya's room. As they stepped into the corridor, the murmur of pleasant voices in animated conversation reached their ears.

"They've arrived, Marie, did you know?" said the little princess, waddling in with her large belly and collapsing into an armchair. She was no longer wearing the same blouse she had on at lunch, but had changed into a green silk dress that was one of her finest: her hair was carefully arranged and there was an expression of excitement on her face, which failed, however, to mask its pale, sunken features. In an outfit that she usually wore at social gatherings in St. Petersburg, it was even more noticeable how much she had lost her looks. There was also a noticeable improvement in Mademoiselle Bourienne's attire, but it made her pretty, fresh face still more attractive.

"So you're going just as you are, *chère princesse*?" she said. "Any minute now they'll be here to say the gentlemen are in the drawing room. We shall have to go down, and you haven't dressed yourself up at all."

The little princess raised her short upper lip above her white teeth, got up out of the armchair on her own, rang for the maid and in merry haste set about inventing and creating an outfit for Princess Marya. Princess Marya felt her sense of personal dignity affronted because the arrival of a potential suitor stirred her to the depths of her soul, yet she was ashamed of her feelings and tried to conceal them even from herself. But here were the others (with her sister-in-law already got up in her finery), telling her openly that she must do as they did, assuming this to be in the nature of things. Telling them how ashamed she felt for herself and for them would have meant betraying her agitation; and in addition, to refuse this dressing-up would have resulted in repeated jokes and persistent demands. She blushed, her lovely eyes dimmed, her plain face was covered with blotches, and with that unattractive expression of the victim that resided most often on her face, she surrendered herself to the authority of Mademoiselle Bourienne and Lise. Both women were quite sincerely concerned to make her beautiful. She was so plain that no thought of competing with her could ever have occurred to either of them; therefore they set about dressing her with perfect sincerity, with that naïve and firm conviction women have that clothes can make a face beautiful.

"No, really, *ma bonne amie*, that dress is not good," said Lise, "tell them to bring that maroon one you have. Really. This one is not good, the colour's too light, it's no good, really it isn't."

It was not the dress that was not good, but the princess's face and her entire figure. Mademoiselle Bourienne and the little princess did not sense this; they kept thinking that if they used a blue ribbon in her hair and combed it up and back, and draped a blue shawl over a brown dress and so on, then everything would be all right. But they forgot that the frightened face and the figure could not be changed and therefore, no matter how much they altered the frame and decoration around this face, the face itself ruined everything. After two or three changes, to which Princess Marya submitted meekly, when her hair was combed upwards (in a style that entirely changed and spoiled her face), and she was dressed in a blue shawl with a maroon formal dress, the little princess walked round her twice, adjusting a fold of the dress here and tugging the shawl down there with her little hand, and looked, inclining her head, first from one side and then the other.

"No, that won't do," she said firmly, throwing up her hands. "No, Marie, that definitely does not suit you. I like you best in your grey everyday dress, please, do this for me," she said to the maid, "bring the princess her grey dress, and just you watch, Mademoiselle Bourienne, how I shall arrange it," she said, smiling in anticipation of her artistic pleasure.

But when Katya brought the required dress, Princess Marya was still sitting motionless in front of the mirror, staring at her face and Katya saw that her eyes were brimming with tears and her mouth was trembling, ready to break into sobs.

"Come, *chère princesse*," said Mademoiselle Bourienne. "Just one more little effort."

Taking the dress out of the maid's hands, the little princess approached Princess Marya.

"Right, now we'll do it simply and prettily," she said.

Her voice and those of Mademoiselle Bourienne and Katya, who were giggling at something, merged into a jolly babbling that sounded like birdsong.

"No, leave me alone," said the princess.

And there was such a serious ring of suffering in her voice that the babbling of the birds ceased instantly. They looked at those large, lovely eyes, filled with tears and thoughts, looking back at them clearly and pleadingly, and they realised that it was pointless and even cruel to insist.

"At least change your hairstyle," said the little princess. "I told you," she said reproachfully, turning to Mademoiselle Bourienne, "that Marie has one of those faces that this kind of hairstyle doesn't suit at all. Not a bit. Do change it, please."

"No, leave me, leave me, none of this makes any difference to me at all," replied Princess Marya, scarcely able to restrain her tears.

They shrugged and gestured in astonishment, admitting that in this state Princess Marya looked extremely plain, worse than ever; but it was too late. She looked at them with that familiar expression, an expression of thoughtful sadness. This expression did not make them feel afraid of Princess Marya. (She did not inspire that feeling in anyone.) But they knew that when she wore that expression, she was low-spirited, untalkative and utterly resolute in her decisions.

"You will change it, won't you?" said Lise, and when Princess Marya promised, she left the room.

Once Princess Marya was left alone in her room, she did not keep her promise to Lise, she did not even look at herself in the mirror, but dropped her hands and her eyes helplessly and sat in silence, thinking. She imagined a husband – a strong, definite, incomprehensibly attractive being who belonged only to her. She imagined a child at her breast, her own little child like the one she had seen with the wet-nurse's daughter the day before, and again she imagined that husband embracing her. And she was looking at him in shamefaced joy.

"Please come down to tea. The prince will be out any minute," the maid's voice said from behind the door, and this voice aroused her.

Coming to her senses, she was horrified at what she had been thinking about. "This is too impossible," she thought. "This is a happiness that is not granted to me here on earth." Before going down, she stood up, went to the icon and, fixing her gaze on the black visage of the large image of the Saviour, she stood before it with clasped hands for several minutes, then sighed, crossed herself and went out.

Princess Marya's heart was tormented with doubt. Was the joy of love, earthly love for a man, possible for her? While thinking about marriage, Princess Marya also thought about family happiness, and about children, but her most important, most powerful and secret dream was earthly love. The more she attempted to conceal this feeling and appear to others, and even to herself, as if she had completely conquered it, the stronger it grew. "My God," she said, "how can I suppress these thoughts of the devil in this heart of mine? How can I reject evil thoughts once and for all in order calmly to obey Thy will?" And scarcely had she finished asking this question, before God answered her in her own heart: "Desire nothing for yourself, do not seek, do not fret, do not envy. Other people's future and your own fate must be unknown to you; but live so as to be prepared for anything. If it should please God to test you in the obligations of marriage, be prepared to obey His will." With this reassuring and joyful thought (and in the hope that her forbidden earthly dream would be fulfilled) Princess Marya sighed, crossed herself and went downstairs, not thinking about her dress, or about her hair, or about how she would enter the room and what she would say. What could all that mean in comparison with the intentions of God, without whose will not a single hair falls from a man's head?

When she entered, Prince Vasily and his son were already in the drawing room with the little princess and Mademoiselle Bourienne. As she entered with her heavy tread, striking hard with her heels, the men and Mademoiselle Bourienne rose and the little princess, gesturing towards the men, said: "This is Marie!"

Princess Marya saw everyone, and she took in every detail. She saw Prince Vasily's face freeze for a moment of serious thought at the sight of the princess before he smiled, and the little princess's face, curiously and fearfully reading on the old prince's face the impression that Marie would make on him. She also saw Mademoiselle Bourienne with her ribbon and her beautiful face and Mademoiselle Bourienne's glance, more animated than ever before, directed at *him*: but she could not see *him* – she could not bring herself to look, and if perhaps she did glance, she did not make anything out, apart from something very large, bright and handsome.

First she kissed Prince Vasily's bald head when it was lowered over her hand and replied to his words that, on the contrary, she remembered him very well. "I know that," she thought, catching the smell of tobacco and old age, "it is like father." Then Anatole also approached her. She felt the gentle hand that took firm hold of her, caught the smell of his perfume and pressed her lips lightly against the white forehead surmounted by the lovely, light-brown pomaded hair. She glanced at him and was astounded at his beauty. Anatole, with the thumb of his right hand behind the closed button of his uniform jacket, with his chest curving out in front and his back curving out behind, swinging one outstretched leg and inclining his head slightly to one side, looked cheerfully at the princess without speaking, evidently not thinking about her at all.

Anatole was one of the least sophisticated people in the world. He had never known how to begin or to maintain a conversation, or even how to say those few words that are necessary at the beginning of every new acquaintance; but in spite of this, he was socially acceptable, thanks to his absolutely unvarying confidence and composure, which is valued above all else in society. Let a person who lacks self-assurance fall silent at first acquaintance and betray an awareness of the impropriety of this silence and a desire to find something to say, and he will plummet in the opinion of high-society folk. Yet Anatole remained silent, swinging his leg and happily studying the princess's hairstyle, and it was clear that he could remain calmly silent in this way for as long as he wanted. "If anyone finds the silence awkward, then by all means make conversation, but I don't feel like it," his expression seemed to say. In addition, in his dealings with women, Anatole possessed that manner which most inspires curiosity, fear and love in women, a manner of contemptuous awareness of his own superiority. As though he were telling them with this air: "I know all about you, yes I do, why should I bother wasting time on you, acting like an old woman? Wouldn't you just love that!" It is possible, and even probable, that he did not *think* this when he met women (indeed it was probable, since he generally did not do much thinking of any kind), but such was his air and his manner. The princess sensed this, and as if wishing to show him that she would not dare to think of taking his time, she turned to the old prince.

Everyone joined in the conversation, which was lively, thanks to the little princess's squeaky little voice and dainty lip. She became very lively altogether. She greeted Prince Vasily in that jocular manner often employed by the garrulous and cheerful, which assumes the prior existence of certain mutual jokes shared by them alone and certain happy and amusing reminiscences not known to everyone present, even though no such reminiscences actually exist, and as indeed none actually existed between the little princess and Prince Vasily. Prince Vasily gladly accepted this tone. Into her reminiscing the little princess wove humorous incidents which had never taken place and which included Anatole, whom she hardly knew at all. Mademoiselle Bourienne also shared in these general reminiscences, and even Princess Marya was delighted to find herself drawn into the jolly reminiscing.

"Well, at least now we shall exploit you to the full, dear prince," said the little princess, naturally in French, to Prince Vasily, "this is not like our *soirées* at Annette's house, from which you can always escape. Do you remember our dear Annette?"

"Ah, but you will not set me to talk politics as Annette does!"

"And our tea table?"

"Oh, yes!"

"Why were you never at Annette's?" the little princess asked Anatole. "Oh! I know, I know," she said with a wink, "your brother Hippolyte told me what you get up to. Oh!" – She wagged her finger at him reproachfully. "And I know all about your pranks in the Champs Elysées!"

"And did Hippolyte not tell you," said Prince Vasily, turning towards his son and grasping the princess's hand, as if she had been about to run away and he had barely been quick enough to restrain her, "did he not tell you, how he pined for the lovely princess and how she drove him out of the house?"

"Ah! She is a pearl among women, princess!" he said to Princess Marya. And they began recalling Prince Andrei, when he was still a child at the Kuragins'.

For her part Mademoiselle Bourienne did not let slip this opportunity, at the mention of the "Champs Elysées", to join in the general reminiscing.

"Ah, the Champs Elysées," she said. "And the railings in the Tuileries, prince," she said to Anatole in the sad tone of nostalgia.

The sight of the pretty Bourienne reassured Anatole that there would be fun. "Ah, so you want the same thing too?" he thought, looking her over. "Well now, not bad-looking. She can bring this one with her when she marries me," he thought about the Princess Marya. "The girl's not bad."

The old prince was dressing unhurriedly in his study, gloomily brooding on what to do. The arrival of these guests angered him. "What do I want with Prince Vasily and this little son of his? Prince Vasily is an empty-headed chatterbox, and as for his son, he must be one of these modern dandies." None of this was of great consequence; but he was angered by the fact that their arrival raised in his heart a question that was constantly suppressed, a question concerning which the old prince always deceived himself. The question was whether he would ever bring himself to allow Princess Marya to experience the happiness of family life, whether he would ever part with her and give her away to a husband. This question lay buried in the very deepest depths of the old prince's mind, and he had never been able to pose it to himself directly, knowing in advance that he would answer, as always, in accordance with what was fair, and that fairness contradicted not only his feelings, but also the possibility of his entire life as he knew it. For Prince Nikolai Andreevich, life without Princess Marya, despite the fact that, while living with her, he tormented her with every means within his power, life without her was unthinkable for the old prince. While he did not ask himself the most important question, however, a host of related considerations were never far from his mind. "What would she get married for? She would probably be unhappy. Look at Lise married to Andrei, I suppose it would be hard to find anyone better nowadays, but is she happy with her lot? And who will take her for herself? She's ugly and clumsy. They'll take her for her connections, for her wealth, but not for happiness, why can't people just be left to live as they wish . . ." But Prince Vasily had openly brought his son, had openly stated his wish. The name and the social position were respectable and the question had to be faced. "Well then, I have nothing against it," the old prince told himself (although his heart fell at the mere thought of separation from his daughter), "but he had better be worthy of her. And we shall soon see about that."

"We shall see about that," he said out loud, and so saying, he twisted on the lid of his snuffbox, and set off for the drawing room. "We shall see about that."

As always, he entered the drawing room with a brisk step and quickly ran his eyes over everyone, taking note of the little princess's change of dress, and Bourienne's ribbon, and Princess Marya's ugly hairstyle, and Bourienne's and Anatole's smiles, and his princess's loneliness with her hairstyle. "She's done herself up like a stupid fool!" he thought, glancing furiously at his daughter. "She has no shame! And he doesn't want to know her!"

He went up to Prince Vasily.

"Well, hello my friend, I'm very glad to see you."

"For a dear friend seven *versts* is no distance," said Prince Vasily, speaking familiarly, as always, with Prince Nikolai Andreich. "This is my second son, I hope you'll make him very welcome."

Prince Nikolai Andreich looked Anatole up and down.

"Too fat, too fat!" he said, "otherwise he would be a fine fellow, well, come, kiss me," and he proffered his cheek.

Anatole kissed the old man and looked at him curiously and absolutely calmly, wondering whether he would soon start doing the funny things that his father had promised. When he said "Too fat, too fat", Anatole had laughed.

Prince Nikolai Andreich sat in his usual place in the corner of the divan, pulled an armchair up closer for Prince Vasily and began questioning him about political affairs and the news. He listened attentively, enjoying what Prince Vasily told him, but glancing all the while at Princess Marya.

"So that's what they write from Potsdam?" he said, repeating Prince Vasily's final words and then, suddenly rising, he went over to his daughter.

"Did you do your hair like that for our guests? Eh?" he said. "Lovely, very lovely. You have a new hairstyle for our guests, and I'm telling you in front of our guests from now on never again to dare to change your appearance without asking me."

"It is my fault, father," said the little princess.

"You, *madame*, are free to do entirely as you please," said Prince Nikolai Andreich, bowing elaborately to his daughter-in-law, "but there's no point in her disfiguring herself – she is ugly enough already."

And he sat back down in his place, apparently paying no more attention to his daughter, who was now reduced to tears.

"On the contrary. This style suits the princess very well," said Anatole, who made it a rule and a habit to take every opportunity to say something agreeable to women. The princess flushed with pleasure. She felt grateful to her father for the comment he had drawn from Anatole.

"Well, old fellow, the young prince, what's his name?" said her father, turning towards Anatole. "Come here, let us have a talk and get to know each other." There was kindness in Nikolai Andreich's voice, but Princess Marya and Mademoiselle Bourienne knew that this kindness concealed a threat. And indeed, what the prince wanted was to examine Anatole and try to exhibit him to his daughter in the most unfavourable light.

"This is when the fun starts," thought Anatole, and sat beside the old prince with a mocking, cheerful smile.

"Right, tell me, you have travelled a lot, my dear fellow, you were educated abroad, not taught to read and write by the sexton like your father and me, tell me, are you in the service at present?"

"In the Horse Guards." Anatole could scarcely prevent himself from smirking.

"You mean, you are in the ranks?"

"Yes, I'm still in the ranks."

"But why did you not go abroad with the regiment?"

"Well, I just didn't, prince."

"But my son did. I daresay you still miss Paris? That was where you had them educated, was it not? Prince Vasily? Eh?"

"But of course I miss it, prince," Anatole snorted in laughter.

"Well in my day I asked to come back from Paris to Bleak Hills. But everything's different nowadays. Well, let us go to my study." He took Prince Vasily by the arm and led him away.

In the study Prince Vasily, in his typical casual manner, managed to strike up a conversation on the business in hand.

"What do you think," the old prince said angrily, "that I am keeping her here, that I can't part with her? They imagine things!" he said angrily, although no one was imagining anything. "It can be tomorrow as far as I'm concerned! Only let me tell you that I want to know my son-in-law better. I shall ask her tomorrow in your presence whether she wants him, then let him stay on for a while. Let him stay on for a while, and I shall see." The prince snorted. "Let her marry, it is all the same to me," he shouted in the same shrill voice in which he had said goodbye to his son.

"I will tell you frankly," said Prince Vasily, in the tone of a cunning man who sees that cunning is no use in the face of such perspicacity. "You can see straight through people. Anatole is no genius, but he is an honest, good-hearted fellow, a fine son to his family. That is a fact."

"Well now, very well, we shall see."

As always happens with unattached women who have been living without men for a long time, at the arrival of Anatole, this fine, handsome, outgoing young fellow with his serene self-confidence, all three women in Prince Nikolai Andreich's house felt equally powerfully that life had been unreal until this young man had appeared. Each instantly sensed her inner capacity to think, feel and see intensify tenfold, as though life, lived until now in darkness, was suddenly illuminated by bright sunlight suffused with solemn significance.

Princess Marya forgot all about her face and hairstyle. The sight of the handsome, open face of this man who, perhaps, was going to be her husband, absorbed all her attention. He seemed so kind and brave to her, so resolute and manly and magnanimous. Of this she was certain. A thousand dreams of future family life kept flooding through her imagination. She drove them away, trying to let no one notice, while wondering how not to be too cold with him. "If I think about how I shall embrace him and how I shall ask him to love and understand my father as I understand him, if I think about that and imagine myself already so close to him, I cannot help lowering my eyes and trying to appear indifferent towards him but, after all, he does not know why that is, and he might think I am completely cold towards him, that I do not find him likeable at all, when it is not true and even quite the opposite." With these thoughts in mind, Princess Marya made an effort to be agreeable and simply sweet and trusting.

"A kind-hearted girl," Anatole thought about her.

Mademoiselle Bourienne, who also soared to a high level of excitement, thought quite differently. Of course, this beautiful young girl with no clear position in society, with no family or friends or even a country, was not intending to dedicate her entire life to serving Prince Nikolai Andreich, reading him books and being a friend to Princess Marya. Mademoiselle Bourienne had long been waiting for the Russian prince who would immediately appreciate her superiority over these unattractive, badly dressed, ungainly princesses, fall in love with her and carry her off; first he would take her away, and then, anything could happen when a man was in love. Mademoiselle Bourienne had a story, heard from her aunt, and augmented by herself, which she loved to repeat in her imagination. It was the story of how her poor mother, *"ma pauvre mère"*, appeared to her and reproached her for giving herself to a man outside marriage. Mademoiselle Bourienne had often been moved to tears as she told *him* this story in her imagination. And now *he*, a genuine Russian prince, had appeared. And yet Mademoiselle Bourienne was not guided by calculation, not for a single moment did she consider what she should do. She felt excited and elated. She hung on Anatole's every glance and every movement and she felt happy.

The little princess, like an old war-horse hearing the sound of the bugle, quite unconsciously, forgetting what an inappropriate time it was, readied herself for her customary gallop of coquetry, without any ulterior motive or struggle, but with a naïve, thoughtless gaiety.

Despite the fact that in dealing with women Anatole usually assumed the role of a man who is fed up with women running after him, he was susceptible to the vain satisfaction of feeling that women were in love with him. In addition, he was beginning to feel for the pretty and provocative Mademoiselle Bourienne that passionate, animal feeling that came over him with extreme rapidity and provoked him to the crudest and most reckless of actions.

After tea the company moved to the sitting room and Princess Marya was asked to play the clavichord. Anatole, standing next to Mademoiselle Bourienne, leaned against the clavichord on one elbow, facing Princess Marya, his eyes laughing with amusement as he looked at her. Princess Marya could not endure this look which agitated and tormented her. Even with her gaze lowered, she could still sense it. Her favourite sonata transported her into a most intimate and poetic world, and the look that she felt fixed on her made that world seem all the more poetic. But Anatole's look, while directed towards her, was not concerned with her at all but with the shuffling about of Mademoiselle Bourienne's little foot, which he was kneading and stroking with his own foot under the fortepiano. Mademoiselle Bourienne was also looking at the princess, and there was an expression in her lovely eyes that was also new to Princess Marya, an expression of startled delight and hope.

"How she loves me!" thought Princess Marya. "How happy I am now and how happy I could be with such a friend and husband! Could it really be?" And she looked over his chest, hands and figure, but did not dare to glance at his face, so long as she sensed that same look directed at her.

In the evening, when they began to retire after supper, Anatole kissed Princess Marya's hand. She did not know herself where she found the courage, but she glanced directly at the large, handsome face that had moved close to her short-sighted eyes. After the princess, he approached Mademoiselle Bourienne's hand (which was improper, but he did everything with such simple confidence), and Mademoiselle Bourienne flushed and glanced in fright at the princess.

"Oh the dear thing!" thought the princess. "She's afraid I might think that she wishes to make him like her." She went up to Mademoiselle Bourienne and kissed her hard.

When Anatole came to take the little princess's hand, she stood up and moved away.

"*Non, non, non*! Once your father writes to me that you are behaving yourself properly, then I shall let you kiss my hand. Not before." And, raising her little fingers in the air and smiling, she left the room.

Everyone went to their rooms and, apart from Anatole, who was at the centre of everything and who fell asleep the moment he got into bed, no one could get to sleep for a long time that night.

"Is he really my husband, this stranger, this handsome man," thought Princess Marya, and fear, of a kind she had almost never known, overcame her: she was afraid to look round, imagining there was someone standing behind the screens or in the dark corner. And that *someone* was the devil – and he was this very man with the white forehead and black eyebrows and red mouth. She rang for the maid and asked her to sleep in her room.

That evening, Mademoiselle Bourienne, smiling at her own thoughts, walked for a long time in the winter garden, waiting in vain for someone to come.

The little princess grumbled to her maid because the bed had not been properly made. She could not lie comfortably on either side. Everything felt heavy and awkward. Her belly hampered her, and she noticed it hampered her today more than ever before because Anatole's presence had transported her vividly back to a time when she had been without it and had been happy. Now she felt irritable, so she got angry with her maid. She sat herself in an armchair in her jacket and cap. Katya stood there drowsily in front of her without saying a word, shifting from one foot to the other.

"You should be ashamed of yourself, you might at least feel sorry for me!" said the little princess.

The old prince was not sleeping either. As Tikhon dozed, he could hear the prince angrily pacing to and fro, snorting. The old prince felt insulted for his daughter. The insult was the most hurtful, the most irreparable kind of insult, because it did not concern himself, but another person, and one whom he loved more than himself. He kept pacing about to calm himself down. With his usual passion he commanded himself to have self-control so he might think the whole matter through and decide what was right and what he should do, but instead of this, he only made himself all the more vexed.

"The first man to come along – and everything, even her father, everything is forgotten and she goes running off upstairs wagging her tail, quite unlike her normal self. She is delighted to abandon her father. And she knew I would notice . . . Frr . . . frr . . . frr . . ." he blew his nose furiously. "As if I couldn't see that that simpleton only has eyes for little Bourienne. I should throw her out. How can she have so little pride as not to understand? Not even for herself, if she has no pride, then for me, at least. I have to show her that this blockhead won't even give her a thought and only has eyes for Bourienne. If she has no pride herself, then it is my job to show her . . ." he told himself.

The old prince knew that by telling his daughter she was mistaken, that Anatole planned to seek Bourienne's favours, knew he would injure Princess Marya's pride, and his cause (the desire not to be parted from his daughter) would be won, and this thought calmed him. He called Tikhon and began getting undressed.

"What the devil do we want them here for!" he thought as Tikhon dropped the nightshirt over his dry old man's body. "I didn't invite them. They came to disrupt my life. And there is not much of it left. I should send them packing. Damn them," he said from underneath the shirt.

Tikhon knew the prince's habit of sometimes expressing his thoughts aloud and therefore his face remained unchanged as he stood there before the prince.

"Have they gone to bed over there?" asked the prince.

Tikhon, like all servants, intuitively knew the direction of his master's thoughts. He guessed that he had been asked about Prince Vasily and his son.

"They put the light out a long time ago."

"There's no point, there's no point . . ." the prince said quickly and, slipping his feet into his slippers and his arms into his dressing gown, he went into the bedroom.

Even though no words had been exchanged between Anatole and Mademoiselle Bourienne, they had understood each other perfectly, and knew that what they wanted to say had to be said in secret, and therefore in the morning both sought the chance to meet. When Princess Marya went to see her father at the usual hour, Mademoiselle Bourienne met Anatole in the winter garden. On this particular day Princess Marya approached the door of the study with greater trepidation than usual. Everybody seemed to know that her fate was being decided today, and they also seemed to know what she thought. She read it expressed in Tikhon's face, and in the face of Prince Vasily's valet, who met her as he was carrying hot water and bowed low. "Everybody knows how happy I am," she thought.

The old prince was extremely affectionate and attentive. Princess Marya knew this expression of attentiveness from her father only too well. It was the expression that his face wore at those very moments when his hands were clenched in annoyance, such as when Princess Marya failed to understand a problem in arithmetic, and, getting to his feet, he would walk away from her and repeat his words in a quiet voice. He began the conversation with his daughter in French, which he did only rarely.

"A proposition that concerns you has been made," he said, smiling unnaturally.

"I will translate. I think you have guessed," he continued, "that Prince Vasily did not come here and bring his ward with him" (for some reason Nikolai Andreich called Anatole a ward) "for the sake of my beautiful eyes. Yesterday I received a proposal concerning you. And as you know my rules, I have referred it to you."

"How am I to understand you, father?" said the princess, turning pale then red, feeling she had reached that solemn moment when her fate was to be decided.

"What is there to understand?" her father shouted angrily in Russian. "Prince Vasily finds you to his taste as a daughter-in-law and is proposing to make you a proposal for his ward. Well? Well?"

"I don't know, what do you think, father?" the princess said in a whisper.

"I? I? What have I to do with it? Leave me out of this business. I believe I am not the one getting married. What do you think? That's what I would like to know."

The princess could see that her father was ill-disposed towards this business, and realised at once that the fate of her life would be decided now and for ever. She lowered her eyes to avoid that glare under which she felt unable to think, but could only submit as usual, and said:

"I wish for only one thing, to do your will," she said, "but if I needed to express my wish . . ." She did not have time to finish. The prince interrupted her.

"Excellent!" he shouted. "He'll take you with the dowry and take Mademoiselle Bourienne into the bargain. Mademoiselle Bourienne will be the wife, and you will be the companion."

But the prince collected himself and curbed his involuntary outburst of irritation, having noticed the effect produced on his daughter by these crude words.

She staggered, grabbing hold of the armrest of the chair and burst into tears.

"Come, come. I'm joking, I'm only joking," he said. "Remember one thing, princess: I am observing the rules that give my daughter the full right to choose. And I give you complete freedom. Remember one thing. The happiness of your life depends on your decision. There's no need to worry about me."

"But I don't know . . ."

"There's nothing to be said! If he is told to, he will marry anybody at all, not just you; but you are free to choose . . . Go to your room, think it over and then come to me in an hour and tell me in the presence of Prince Vasily: yes or no. I know you will pray. Well, pray, by all means. Only you had better do some thinking as well. Off you go.

"Yes or no, yes or no, yes or no!" he shouted.

Staggering as if lost in a fog, the princess left the room.

Her fate had been decided, and it had been decided happily. But what he had said about Mademoiselle Bourienne – that hint had been terrible. Even assuming it was not true, it was still terrible, and she could not help thinking about it. She walked straight ahead through the winter garden, seeing nothing and hearing nothing, when suddenly Mademoiselle Bourienne's familiar whisper aroused her. She raised her eyes and literally two paces away saw Anatole, who was embracing the Frenchwoman and whispering something to her. Anatole looked round at Princess Marya with a bestial expression of excitement on his handsome face and for a moment he continued to hold Mademoiselle Bourienne, who had hunched up in fright and covered her face with her hands.

"Who's there? Why? Wait!" Anatole's face seemed to say. Princess Marya looked at them without speaking. She could not understand. Mademoiselle Bourienne cried out, tore herself free and ran away. Anatole looked at Princess Marya as assuredly as always and eventually bowed in recognition and smiled, as if inviting her to laugh at this strange incident. Princess Marya did not understand. She went on standing there, not a single feature of her face moving. Anatole walked away.

An hour later, when Tikhon came, the princess was sitting in her room with Mademoiselle Bourienne. Mademoiselle Bourienne was sobbing in her arms. Princess Marya was gently stroking her hair. Those lovely eyes were looking with all their former calm and radiance, with a feeling of boundless love and pity, at Mademoiselle Bourienne's pretty little face.

"No, princess, I have forfeited your goodwill for ever," said Mademoiselle Bourienne.

"I love you more than ever," said Princess Marya, "and I shall try to do everything in my power for your happiness."

"But you despise me, you are so very pure, you must despise me, you can never understand how it is to be carried away by passion."

"I understand everything," said Princess Marya, smiling sadly. "I shall go to father," she said and went out.

Prince Vasily was sitting with one leg crossed high, holding a snuffbox in his hands and seeming quite impossibly touched, as though regretting and laughing at his own sensitivity, sitting with his face set in a sweet smile. When Princess Marya entered, he hastily raised a pinch of tobacco to his nose.

"Ah, my dear, my dear," he said, getting up and taking hold of both her hands. He sighed and added: "My son's fate is in your hands. Decide, my dear, my dear, my sweet Marie, whom I have always loved like a daughter."

He stepped away. A genuine tear appeared in his eye.

"Frr . . . frr . . ." snorted the prince. "Say yes or no, do you wish to be the wife of Prince Anatoly Kuragin. You tell us: yes or no," he shouted, "and then I reserve the right to express my opinion as well. Yes, my opinion and my will," added Prince Nikolai Andreich, addressing Prince Vasily and answering his imploring glance. The old prince wished to leave himself a chance of salvation. "Yes or no? Well?"

"Father, your will above all."

"Yes or no."

"My will, father, is never to leave you, never to separate my life from yours. I do not wish to marry," she said, with a resolute glance from her lovely eyes at Prince Vasily and her father.

"Rubbish! Nonsense! Rubbish, rubbish, rubbish," cried Prince Nikolai Andreich, with a frown. He took his daughter by the hand, and without kissing it, pulled it roughly towards him, hurting her arm. She burst into tears.

Prince Vasily stood up.

"My dear, let me say that I shall never, ever forget this moment but, dearest one, grant us at least some slight hope of touching this heart, so kind and magnanimous. Say perhaps. The future is so vast. Say perhaps."

"Prince, what I have said is all that is in my heart. I thank you for the honour, but I shall never be your son's wife."

"Well then, of course, my dear fellow. Very glad to have seen you, very glad to have seen you. Go to your room, princess, go now," said the old prince.

"My calling is different," Princess Marya thought about herself, "my calling is to be unhappy alone, my calling is to be happy with a different kind of happiness, the happiness of sacrificing myself for others. And no matter what it might cost me, I shall secure poor Caroline's happiness. She loves him so passionately. She repents so passionately. I shall do everything possible to arrange her marriage with him. If he is not rich, I shall give her the means, I shall ask father, I shall ask Andrei. I shall be so happy when she is his wife. She is so unhappy, a foreigner, alone, helpless, and she loves him so passionately." A day later Prince Vasily and his son left, and life at Bleak Hills carried on as before.

# III

The Rostovs had had no news about Nikolai for a long time. Not until the middle of winter was the count handed a letter on which he recognised his son's hand. On receiving the letter, the count sped to his study in fearful haste, trying not to be noticed, and locking himself in, began to read. When Anna Mikhailovna, having learned of the letter's arrival (in the way she knew everything that went on in the house), entered the count's study with quiet steps, she caught him holding the letter in his hands, sobbing and laughing at the same time.

"My dear friend," Anna Mikhailovna said in a sad, questioning tone, prepared to sympathise in any way.

The count began sobbing even more.

"Nikolai . . . the letter . . . my little darling's wounded . . . he was . . . wounded . . . my little darling . . . the little countess . . . thank God . . . How can I tell the countess?"

Anna Mikhailovna sat down beside him, and then with her own handkerchief wiped away the tears from his face, then from the letter that was spattered with them, and then she wiped her own tears, read the letter, calmed the count and decided that she would prepare the countess at lunch and at tea, and then after tea she would tell her everything, with God's help. Throughout lunch Anna Mikhailovna spoke about the war news and about Nikolai, twice asking when the last letter from Nikolai had arrived, although she already knew, and remarked that there could quite easily be a letter today too. Every time the countess began to look worried and started glancing in alarm from the count to Anna Mikhailovna and back, Anna Mikhailovna unobtrusively diverted the conversation to trivial matters. Natasha, who of the whole family was the one most gifted with the ability to sense subtle shades of intonation, glance and facial expression, pricked up her ears from the beginning of lunch and knew that something was going on between her father and Anna Mikhailovna, something that concerned Nikolai. But she knew how sensitive her mother was to everything that concerned news of Nikolai and so, bold as she was, she could not bring herself to ask the question at lunch, but in her agitation she ate nothing and fidgeted on her chair, paying no attention to the rebukes of her governess. After lunch she dashed headlong to catch up with Anna Mikhailovna in the sitting room and flung herself on her neck at full pelt.

"Aunty, sweet darling, angel, tell me, *what* do you know?"

"Nothing, my friend."

"No my sweetheart, my darling, my dearest, my peach, I shan't love Borya if you don't tell, I shan't leave you in peace, I *know* you know."

Anna Mikhailovna shook her head.

"Ah, you're a little scamp, my child," she said. "But for God's sake, be careful; you know how badly it might affect your mama" – and in a few brief words she told Natasha the contents of the letter, making her promise not to tell anyone.

"On my most noble word of honour," Natasha said, crossing herself. "I won't tell a soul" – and she immediately ran into the nursery, called Sonya and Petya and told them everything. Natasha did not follow Anna Mikhailovna's example, however, but ran into Sonya's room, grabbed hold of her hand, and whispering "an important secret", she dragged her into the nursery.

"Nikolai! He's wounded, a letter," she said, triumphant and delighted at the strength of the impression she would make. Sonya suddenly turned as pale as a handkerchief, started trembling and would have fallen if Natasha had not grabbed hold of her. The impression produced by the news was stronger than Natasha had expected. She herself broke into tears as she calmed and comforted her friend.

"Just see, what cry-babies all you women are," said the tubby Petya, although he himself had been more frightened than anyone else by the sight of Sonya collapsing, "but I'm so glad, I'm really glad that Nikolai has distinguished himself like this. You're all just snivellers."

The girls laughed.

"You had genuine hysterics," said Natasha, clearly extremely proud of the fact, "I thought only old people could have hysterics."

"Have you read the letter?" asked Sonya.

"No, I haven't, but she said it was all over now and he was already an officer."

Petya began striding around the room in silence.

"If I had been in Nikolai's place, I should have killed even more of those French," he exclaimed suddenly, "they're so loathsome!" Sonya evidently did not want to talk and did not even smile at Petya's words but carried on staring at the dark window in silence.

"I should have killed so many, there'd be a great heap of them," Petya continued.

"Shut up, Petya, you're such a fool."

Petya took offence and everyone was quiet for a moment.

"Do you remember him?" Natasha asked suddenly.

Sonya smiled.

"Nikolai?"

"No, Sonya, I mean do you remember him so that you can remember him really well, so you remember everything about him?" Natasha said, gesturing emphatically, evidently wishing to lend her words the most serious possible expression. "I can remember like that, I remember Nikolai," she said, "but not Boris. I don't remember him at all."

"What? You don't remember Boris?" Sonya asked in amazement.

"It's not that I don't remember – I know what he's like, but I don't remember him the same way as Nikolai. I close my eyes and I remember Nikolai, but not Boris" (she closed her eyes) "there's nothing there."

"Oh no, I remember him very well," said Sonya.

"And will you write to him?" asked Natasha.

Sonya pondered. How to write to Nikolai, and whether she ought to write, and what to write, was a question that tormented her. Now that he was an officer and a wounded hero, would it be right on her part to remind him of herself and also, as it were, of the commitment that he had made to her? "Let him do as he wishes," she thought. "It is enough for me just to love him. But if he gets a letter from me, he might think I am reminding him about something."

"I don't know, I think if he writes, I'll write back," Sonya said, smiling happily.

"And won't you be ashamed to write to him?"

"No, why?" said Sonya, laughing, but not knowing why.

"Well, I'd be ashamed to write to Boris. And I shan't write."

"But why would you be ashamed?"

"I just am, I don't know why. It feels awkward, shameful."

"Well, I know why she would be ashamed," said Petya, still offended by Natasha's first remark, "it's because she was in love with that fat man in glasses" (that was what Petya called Pierre) "and now she's in love with that singer" (Petya meant Natasha's Italian singing teacher) "that's why she's ashamed."

"Oh, Petya, enough, aren't you ashamed, when we're all feeling so happy, to be quarrelling. Let's talk about Nikolai instead."

"Petya, you're stupid," said Natasha. "Yes, today he was so sweet, quite charming," she said, turning to Sonya (and speaking of the singing teacher). "He told me he had never heard a better voice than mine, and when he sings he gets this lump in his throat, it's so lovely."

"Ah, Natasha, how can you think about anyone else just now?" said Sonya.

"I don't know. I was just thinking, I probably don't love Boris. He's such a dear, I do love him, but not in the same way as you do. I wouldn't have had hysterics, like you did. Why is it I don't remember him?" Natasha closed her eyes. "I can't, I don't remember."

"But surely you can't be in love with Fezoni? Ah, Natasha, how funny you are," Sonya said reproachfully.

"Now Fezoni, and before that Pierre, and before that Boris," Natasha said fiercely. "But now it's Fezoni, and I do love him, I love him, and I'm going to marry him and be a singer myself."

The countess had indeed been well prepared by Anna Mikhailovna's hints during lunch. Going back to her room and sitting in an armchair, she fixed her eyes on a miniature portrait of her son mounted on a snuffbox and wept a little. Anna Mikhailovna, holding the letter, tiptoed to the countess's room and stopped.

"Don't come in," she said to the old count who was following close behind, "later." And she closed the door after her.

The count pressed his ear to the keyhole and listened.

At first he heard the sound of indifferent conversation, then the sound of only Anna Mikhailovna's voice delivering a long speech, then a screech, then silence, then again both voices speaking with joyful intonations, and then steps, and Anna Mikhailovna opened the door for him. The expression on Anna Mikhailovna's face was the proud, happy and relieved expression of a surgeon who has just completed a difficult amputation and is admitting the public so that it can appreciate his skill.

"All done," she said to the count, gesturing in triumph towards the countess, who was holding the snuffbox with her son's portrait in one hand and the letter in the other, and pressing her lips first against one, then against the other.

Catching sight of the count, she stretched her arms out towards him, embraced his bald head and then looked again at the letter and the portrait across the top of that bald head, and then again, in order to press them to her lips, she gently pushed the bald head away. The letter contained a brief description of the campaign and the two battles and said that he kissed his mama's and papa's hands, asking for their blessing, that he kissed Vera, Natasha and Petya and also asked them to kiss dear

310

Sonya, whom he often remembered, as he remembered all of them. In addition, he sent greetings to Mr Schelling and Madame Hubert, and his nanny, and everybody there. The postscript was about money.

This letter was read a hundred times, but those considered worthy of hearing it had to come to the countess's room. And so the tutors came, and the nannies, and the resident jester, and Mitenka, and several acquaintances, and the countess read it out again and again, taking fresh delight even for the hundredth time, as the letter's contents revealed new virtues in her Nikolai. How strange and unusually pleasing it was that her son – the same son who had stirred inside her twenty years before, the same son over whom she had quarrelled with the indulgent count, the same son who had learned to say *"chère maman"* so recently – that this son was now far away, in a foreign country, in foreign surroundings, a courageous man, braving death and writing letters. That age-old experience of children all the world over imperceptibly changing from the cradle onwards into men, simply vanished, and her son's entry into manhood was for her as extraordinarily joyful as if there had been millions upon millions of people who had grown up in precisely the same way. Just as she had never expected the tiny creature stirring in her womb to cry and suck at her breast, and start to talk, to understand and learn and become a man, a servant of his homeland and a model son and citizen, so now she could not believe that this same creature could be the strong, brave man, the model son and individual who, judging from this letter, he now was.

"He writes with such style! How charmingly he describes things!" she said, reading the descriptive part of the letter. "And such a soul! Nothing about himself, nothing! About some Denisov or other, when he himself is probably the bravest of them all. He writes nothing about his own sufferings. Such a heart! How very like him that is! And the way he has remembered everybody! He hasn't forgotten a single one!"

They spent more than a week in preparations, rough drafts were written and presented for the countess's consideration, and letters to Nikolai from the entire household were written out afresh. Anna Mikhailovna, a practical woman, had managed to arrange special protection for herself and her son in the army, even for purposes of correspondence. She was able to send her letters with a courier to the Grand Duke Konstantin Pavlovich, who commanded the Guards. According to the rumours, the Guards should already have joined Kutuzov's army by the time the letter reached them, and therefore it was decided to forward the letters and money to Boris via the Grand Duke's courier, and Boris would deliver them to Nikolai. There were letters from the old count, from the countess, from Petya, from Vera, from Natasha and from Sonya and, finally, there was money, the old count sent six thousand, which was an enormous sum for those times.

The count's affairs had already reached such a degree of confusion that he grimaced painfully when Mitenka suggested that he should check the accounts, and Mitenka had already acquired such a degree of confidence in his principal's cowardice towards the accounts that he would suggest looking at accounts that did not exist, while he gave the count the count's own money, saying that it was borrowed, and taking fifteen per cent of it for himself. The count knew in advance that if he demanded six thousand for fitting out Nikolai, Mitenka would tell him to his face that he did not have it, so the count cunningly said he needed ten thousand. Mitenka replied that with his revenues in such a sorry state, it was unthinkable to raise such a sum without mortgaging the estate and he offered him the accounts. The count turned away from Mitenka abruptly and, avoiding his gaze, began shouting that when he owned eight thousand souls, it was perfectly ridiculous not to have ten thousand to fit out his son, and he would have all the stewards sent to the army, that he had to have this money, there was no point in arguing, let the money be found, if not ten, then six, but let it be found. And so the money was indeed found, although the count had to sign a promissory note with immense interest.

# IV

On the 12th of November Kutuzov's active army, camped near Olmütz, was preparing for a review by the two Emperors – of Russia and Austria – the following day. The Guards, who had only just arrived from Russia, spent the night fifteen *versts* from Olmütz and the next morning moved straight to the field at Olmütz for the review at ten o'clock.

Nikolai Rostov had received a note from Boris informing him that the Izmailovsky Regiment had just arrived and was spending the night fifteen *versts* from Olmütz, and he requested Nikolai to come to see him and receive a packet of letters and money – those very letters that had been written with such anxiety and love, and the very money that had been acquired with such unpleasantness and anger.

Having informed Denisov, after lunch Rostov mounted the horse that was brought for him, the new one bought after the death of Grachik, and, accompanied by a hussar, set out for the Guards. Rostov was wearing a private's jacket, but there were epaulettes on the jacket and he had

an officer's sabre with a sword-knot. His arm, which was already beginning to heal, was supported by a black bandage, his weathered, matured
face was carefree and jolly. He would trot for two *versts*, standing up in
the stirrups and looking round at the hussar galloping after him, then
he would ride at a casual walk, singing a German song that had taken
his fancy in his resonant voice:

> *I know not what it is I lack,*
> *I'm dying with impatience*

with a new maturity in his voice. Two days earlier, one of the most
important events in a young man's life had happened to him:

"Well, brother, I've done all the reconnaissance, and today we're all
going together to see what the women are like in Olmütz: one Hungarian
girl, two Polish girls and one Greek girl – that's what there is . . ."

Rostov neither refused nor agreed to go at once, but he pretended
that this was a very ordinary thing for him and that he regarded it in
exactly the same way as Denisov; whereas in fact he felt that the crucial
moment he had thought about with hesitation and uncertainty a thousand times was now upon him, and he was barely able to utter a word
in reply to Denisov. He still did not know women, he imagined there
was something outrageous and offensive in intimacy with a strange
woman, bought and shared with Denisov and everybody else, but an
indefinable curiosity also drew him to experience this feeling. After all,
there was not a man there who had not known this feeling and who did
not regard it as a necessary and pleasant condition of sensual experience.
All who spoke about it had an air of innocent pleasure, only reinforced
by the fact that this pleasure was forbidden in some quarters.

He and Denisov went in Denisov's trap drawn by two horses. On the
way to Olmütz, Denisov chatted about irrelevancies, making his own
observations on the troops they drove past and recalling the past as
naturally, calmly and merrily as if they were simply out for a ride, and
not on their way to commit one of the most terrible, criminal and
irrevocable acts possible. They arrived in Olmütz and, at Denisov's command, the soldier who was driving them turned into one street, then
into another side street, and then another, and stopped at a small house.
As they entered, an elderly lady received Denisov like a friend and led
them into the drawing room. Two women, smiling pleasantly, greeted
Denisov.

At first Rostov thought they greeted Denisov that way because they
knew him, but they addressed Rostov in exactly the same affectionate
manner as well, as if he was an old friend. They laughed at each other
as they looked at him. It seemed to him that they were laughing at him

and he blushed, and watching what Denisov was doing, he tried to do the same. But he could not do it, he simply was not able to. Denisov took hold one of them – a plump blonde with a low, open neckline, and beautiful, although despite her youth and merriment, there seemed to be something old, tired, sad and wrongful about her. Denisov took her in his arms and kissed her. Rostov could not do that. He stood facing the plump, black-haired Greek girl, who was looking cheerfully at him with her lovely eyes and revealing her lovely teeth in a smile, apparently waiting, enjoying his indecision. Rostov could not take his eyes off her, he trembled in fear, feeling angry with himself, that he was taking an irreversible step in his life, that an illicit and terrible act was being committed at that very moment, and yet feeling that in some strange way it was the very charm of the illicit that drew him to her. One moment she seemed to him charming, especially charming in her strangeness, and the next moment something base and loathsome repulsed him. But the eyes, surrounded by black shadow, bored deeper and deeper into his own, and merged with him, and he felt himself drawn into their depths in some indefinable way that made his head spin. The sense of the forbidden was totally overwhelmed by this sense of intoxication.

"You've made a grand choice," shouted Denisov. "That Greek girl of yours and I got acquainted last night. Kiss the young man, will you!" shouted Denisov.

Rostov shuddered, tore himself away from her and ran outside, ready to leave, but five minutes later the passion of curiosity and the desire to overcome the fear of the forbidden and his revulsion drew him back again. He went back inside. There was wine on the table. The Greek girl had meanwhile been instructed by Denisov in how to treat a novice. She took hold of his hand, drew him to the table, sat him down and seated herself on his knees, pouring wine for herself and for him. Rostov drank, embraced her gently, then more forcefully, then more forcefully still; revulsion and passion and the desire to prove himself quickly, quickly, to crush this sense of purity that was still resisting inside him, fused into one and he felt with joy that he was losing himself.

The next morning, accompanied by the Greek girl (Denisov had left that evening, without waiting), he went out on to the porch, walked for a cab, and drove to the camp, then spent the day as usual, with his comrades, giving nothing away and behaving as though what had happened to him the day before was perfectly ordinary. In the evening, when he went to bed, all he could see in his mind's eye was the Greek girl, and he wanted to see her again as soon as possible. He fell into a sound sleep and dreamed of a battle and a crowd of people who were pursuing him, because he was the victor.

In his dream he stood on a swaying dais and told people everything that was in his heart and that he had not known before. His thoughts were fresh and clear, automatically expressing themselves in speech that was inspired and measured. He was surprised by what he said and delighted to hear the sound of his own voice. He could not see anything, but he sensed there were brethren that he did not know crowding around him. Close by he could distinguish their heavy sighs, in the distance the endless crowd murmured like the sea. When he spoke, a tremor of delight ran through the crowd like the wind through the leaves; when he fell silent, the crowd held its breath as one man. His eyes did not see them, but he felt the eyes of all the people on him, and these glances pressed onto him and delighted him. They moved him, just as he moved them. The painful delight burning within gave him power, and his power knew no bounds. A faint inner voice told him "this is frightening", but the speed of his movement intoxicated him and drew him onwards. Suppressed fear intensified the enchantment, and, still swaying, the dais on which he was standing raised him ever higher and higher.

Suddenly from behind he felt someone's free, solitary gaze which instantly dispelled all the preceding charm. The gaze drew him relentlessly to itself, and he was compelled to look round. He saw a woman and sensed the life of another being. He felt ashamed, and stopped. The crowd did not disappear and did not make way, but by some miracle the simple woman moved calmly through the midst of the crowd without becoming part of it. Who this woman was, he did not know, except that she was Sonya, and all who love were in her, and an irresistible force drew him to her sweetly and painfully. Meeting his eyes, she turned aside with indifference, and he could only dimly make out the contours of her half-turned face. Only her calm gaze remained in his mind, and it expressed mild mockery and loving regret. She did not understand what he was saying, but that was not what she regretted, her regret was for him. She did not despise either him, or the crowd, or our raptures, she was only filled with happiness. She needed nobody, and for this reason he felt he could not live without her. The quivering gloom remorselessly concealed her image, and in his dream he wept at the impossibility of being with her. He wept for a past happiness that was beyond recovery and for the impossibility of a future happiness. But the happiness of the present was already present in those tears.

He woke and continued to weep, crying tears of shame and repentance for his fall, which had separated him from Sonya for ever. But the bustle of the day dispersed this impression, and whenever his dream came to mind, he tried to drive it away, although it arose of its own accord. And now it kept arising more frequently and more powerfully as he rode to see Boris after learning about the letters from home.

It was already completely dark, the village where the Izmailovsky Regiment was stationed was frosty, moonlit and smoky when Nikolai rode up to it. He was told where the third battalion was stationed, but in the dark, the sentries refused to let him pass, so he was obliged to say he was an adjutant sent to the Grand Duke. But when they did let him through, he made a mistake, and instead of the third battalion, he found himself in the village where the Grand Duke himself was staying and he had to make his way back out again in fright. It was already late when, tired and impatient, he enquired from some soldier cooks where Boris was stationed.

"Where is Prince Drubetskoy stationed, ensign?" he asked.

The soldier inspected the hussar curiously and came up to him.

"No such person in our battalion. Ask in the fourth battalion, they have lots of princes, but we don't have any."

"Prince Drubetskoy! He is definitely here."

"Oh no, your honour, I ought to know . . ."

"And in the fourth company, isn't there a prince billeted with the captain?" another soldier responded.

"A prince, where, with Captain Berg?"

"Berg, Berg, that's the one, show me!" shouted Rostov, "a rouble tip."

The Guards had gone through the entire campaign as if they were out for a stroll, flaunting their handsome get-up and discipline. The day's marches were short, the men's knapsacks were carried on the carts, the Austrian command prepared excellent dinners for the officers at each halt. The regiments entered and left the towns to the sound of music; and throughout the entire campaign (the guardsmen were proud of this) the men marched in step and the officers marched in position on foot. During the entire campaign Boris had marched and been billeted with Berg, his company commander. For him the entire campaign had been a jolly festival. Berg and Boris, already rested after the march, were sitting in the clean quarters assigned to them at a round table, drinking tea and playing chess. Boris's fine-featured, intent face had become slightly sunburnt, but he was as fine and elegant in his dress as in Russia. Berg, even more at home on the march than in Moscow, was scrupulously neat and tidy, constantly admiring the cleanness and neatness of his own dressing gown and travelling cases, clearly inviting others to appreciate his neatness and praise him for it. Just as in Moscow, he was blowing out the neat smoke rings that seemed to be the emblem and motto of his life and, picking up the chess pieces by the head in his clean hands, he placed them precisely, repeating the same significant words over and over again, in the way people of limited thought tend to repeat their words.

"Well, there you are, Boris Sergeevich, well, there you are, Boris Sergeevich."

But before he could finish these last words, he heard a rumble and clatter on the porch and saw an officer of the hussars, whom he did not recognise at first, come running into the room.

"Ah you, damn you all," shouted the officer of the hussars, incomprehensibly making as much din and racket as if an entire squadron had come bursting into the room. "Berg's here too! Damned guards. Why, there are children here!"

"*Allez*, children, time for bed now," Boris said, taking up the theme, jumping up from his chair and running to meet Rostov. With that peculiar proud feeling of youth that scorns the well-beaten track and seeks to express feelings in its very own new way, imitating no one, especially not the often affected way of the older generation, both friends, who loved each other tenderly, ran together, grabbed each other by the shoulders, and shoved and pinched, saying: "Ah, damn you to hell, devil take you" – and they put their arms around each other, but did not kiss, and did not exchange a single tender word. Yet despite this absence of outward tenderness, their faces, especially Rostov's, expressed such happiness, excitement and love, that for a moment even Berg seemed to forget to admire his own comfortable arrangements. He smiled tenderly, even though he felt like an outsider between these two friends.

"Ah, you damned society dandies, all clean and fresh, just back from your stroll, not like us filthy army types," declared Rostov, proudly indicating his mud-spattered greatcoat, and shouting so loudly that the German landlady stuck her head in at the door in order to take a look at this terrible bawler. Questions left unanswered flew thick and fast from both sides.

"Well, tell me, when did you last see my folks, are they all well?" asked Rostov.

"What, are you an officer? What, are you wounded?" said Boris, pointing to his greatcoat and bandaged arm.

"Ah, so you're here too," said Rostov, not replying and turning to Berg. "Hello, my dear fellow." Formerly Rostov would have changed completely at the sight of a new face, especially one that he disliked as much as Boris certainly knew for sure he disliked Berg's, but now not only did Rostov not shrink away at the sight of this face that he disliked but, on the contrary, seemed almost deliberately to become even more carefree and familiar. Rostov pulled across a chair for himself, sat on it backwards and swept all the chess pieces onto the divan with his sleeve.

"Well, sit down, tell me," he said, tugging Boris towards him by the

317

arm, "do they know what we've been doing? Do they know that I've been promoted? We've been away from Russia for two months now."

"Well, and have you seen action?" asked Boris.

Without replying, Rostov slapped the soldier's George Medal hanging on the cording of his greatcoat and, indicating his bandaged arm with a smile, glanced at Berg.

"No, I haven't," he said.

"Oho," said Boris, still surprised, smiling quietly as he examined the change that had taken place in his friend. And it was really only now for the first time that Rostov, measuring himself against his old attitudes to life, felt how great was the change that had taken place in him. Everything that he would formerly have found difficult was now easy. However much he amazed Boris with his familiar manner, he was even more amazed at it himself. Falling into the tone of a dashing hussar in his desire to show off to the guardsmen, he discovered an unexpected freedom and charm in that tone. He was gratified to feel that, in contrast with the way things had previously been between himself and Boris, it was no longer Boris, but he who was setting the tone and direction of conversation. He was evidently amusing himself by shifting the subject of conversation at will: as soon as Boris began asking about the war and his promotion, Rostov changed the subject again, recalling Boris's old servant.

"And what about your faithful old dog, Gavrilo, is he with you?" he asked.

"Of course," replied Boris, "he's studying German with our hosts here."

"Hey there, you old devil," shouted Rostov, "come here." Anna Mikhailovna's venerable and imposing old servant appeared at his summons.

"Come here, kiss me, you old dog," Rostov said with a happy smile and embraced him.

"Allow me to congratulate you, your excellency," said old Gavrilo with good-natured respect, admiring Rostov's cross and epaulettes.

"Well then, give me fifty kopecks for a cab," Rostov shouted with a laugh, reminding the old servant of the way he used to borrow ten kopecks at a time in his student days. The amiable and good-hearted servant immediately found a reply:

"How could I not trust a decorated officer, your excellency," he said jokingly, pretending to take the money out of his pocket.

"Off you go then, you Guards creature," said Rostov, slapping the old man on the back, "how glad I am to see him, how glad, and I'll tell you what," he said suddenly, "send him to get some wine."

Although Boris did not drink, he willingly took out his slender purse from under the clean pillows and ordered wine to be brought.

"By the way, I have to give you your money and letter."

"Come on then, you rotten swine," shouted Rostov, slapping Boris on the shoulder as he bent over a chest, clicking the English lock inside and taking out the letters and money.

"You've put on weight, for sure," said Rostov and, grabbing the letters from him and tossing the money on to the divan, he propped both of his elbows on the table and began reading. He read several lines, his eyes dimmed and his entire face changed, assuming nobler, less childlike contours. He read more, and his gaze became even stranger, and an expression of tenderness and repentance appeared on his lips, which began trembling. He glanced angrily at Boris and, meeting his gaze, hid his face behind the letters.

"They certainly sent you plenty of money," said Berg, looking at the heavy purse that had sunk into the divan.

"I'll tell you something, Berg, dear chap," said Rostov, "when you receive a letter from home and meet a close friend that you want to ask about everything, and I'm there – I'll clear off at once to get out of your way. Listen, do go away, please, somewhere, anywhere . . . to the devil!" he shouted and then immediately grabbed Berg by the shoulder and looked amiably into his face, evidently trying to soften the rudeness of his words, and added: "You know I'd only speak from the heart to a good old friend of the family."

"Ah, by all means, count, I understand perfectly," said Berg, getting up and speaking in a muffled, guttural voice.

"Go to our hosts, they invited you," said Boris. Berg put on a supremely clean frock coat, without a single stain or speck of dust, fluffed up the hair at his temples in the mirror, in the way that Alexander Pavlovich wore it, and having confirmed by glancing at Rostov that his frock coat had been noticed, left the room with a pleased smile.

"I'm a swine," said Rostov, looking at a letter (just then he was reading Sonya's note added in French. He seemed to see her black plait and thin shoulders before his very eyes and, most importantly of all, he saw and knew what was happening in her soul when she was writing this letter, as if it had all happened in his own. He could feel how she hesitated to write too little or too much, and felt how strongly and how well she loved him).

"Ah, what a swine I am! Look what they write," he repeated, blushing at the memory of the previous night's dream and, when Boris bent down, not showing him the lines that agitated him so much.

He read him the following piece from his mother's letter: "To think that you, my dearest, adored, incomparable Coco, are there amid all the horrors of war, and stay calm and think of anything else at all is more than I am capable of. May God forgive me for my sin, but you alone, my most precious Coco, are dearer to me than all my children." With his sensitivities heightened by all that had happened to him in recent days and now by Sonya's note, he could not read this letter from his mother without tears. He wept, grew angry with himself and laughed self-consciously.

Inserted among the letters from his family there was also a letter of recommendation to Prince Bagration, which the old countess had obtained through acquaintances on Anna Mikhailovna's advice and sent to her son, asking him to deliver it as addressed and make use of it.

"No, bother it," said Rostov, tossing the letter aside. "I'm happy enough in the regiment."

"What, surely you won't throw that letter away," Boris asked in astonishment.

"Naturally."

"You shouldn't," said Boris, "it doesn't put you under any obligation, and it could improve your position."

"But I don't want a better position."

"Yes, you're still the same as ever," said Boris, shaking his head and smiling. "How can you judge whether a position is better or worse until you've tried it? Take me, for instance, I am also perfectly satisfied with my position in the regiment and the company, but my mother gave me a letter to a certain adjutant of Kutuzov's, Bolkonsky. They say he is a very influential man. And so I went to see him and he promised to obtain me a position at headquarters. I don't see anything wrong with it: once you've embarked on a career of military service, then strive as far as possible to make it a brilliant career. What, do you not know this Bolkonsky, have you not met him?" asked Boris.

"No, I don't want to know that general staff trash," Rostov replied morosely.

"But he was going to call to see me this evening," said Boris. "He is with the Tsarevich at present, sent from your commander-in-chief."

"Ah," said Rostov, becoming thoughtful. After pausing for a few seconds, he looked into Boris's eyes brightly and tenderly.

"Well, why are we talking about this nonsense?" he said. "Tell me properly about everybody at home. How is papa? How is my dear Natasha? Petya?" He asked about everyone, but he could not bring himself to ask about Sonya. Nor did he speak with Boris about his friend's relations with Natasha, as though he now recognised them as childish folly that ought to be left behind.

Old Gavrilo brought the wine and, since all the intimate talk was already over or, rather, since nothing intimate had been said and it obviously would not be, Boris suggested sending for the banished Berg so that he could share in the bottle that had been brought.

"Well, how is the old kraut?" Rostov asked with a contemptuous expression before Berg had returned. "Still the same mean creature, full of his accounts?"

"No," said Boris defending his friend, "he is a fine fellow, honest and humble."

Once again Rostov was struck by the fundamental, rather than incidental difference between his own views and his friend's.

"Yes but give me someone who may not be so very honest and neat, but is at least alive, and not such a limp rag as this little German."

"He is a very, very good, honest and pleasant person," said Boris.

Rostov looked hard into Boris's eyes and sighed, as if saying farewell for ever to his former friendship and simple relations with his childhood companion. "We are absolutely, absolutely different," thought Rostov.

Berg returned and over the bottle of wine the conversation between the three officers became lively. The guardsmen told Rostov about their campaign, about how they had been fêted in Russia, Poland and abroad, they told him about what the Grand Duke had said and done, anecdotes about his kindness and irascibility. Berg, as usual, said nothing when the subject did not concern him personally, but in connection with the anecdotes about the Grand Duke's irascibility, he took delight in telling how he had had occasion to talk with the Grand Duke, who was touring the regiments and was furious at the irregular way in which they were moving. Choking on his satisfaction and scarcely restraining a broad smile, he told how the Grand Duke had ridden up to him in fury, shouted: "Albanians" ("Albanians" was the Tsarevich's favourite expression when he was in a temper), and as Berg repeated this expression, he was clearly choking from happiness.

"'Albanians, Albanians,' the Grand Duke shouted, and demanded to see the company commander. 'Where's that rogue, the company commander'" – Berg took pleasure in repeating the Grand Duke's words. "I stepped forward more dead than alive," said Berg, "and all he did was scold me and scold me and scold me, and it was 'Albanians' and 'damn' and 'off to Siberia'," said Berg, with a subtle, astute smile. "I kept quiet. 'Well then, are you dumb, or what?' The way he suddenly shouted it out: 'Albanians'. I kept quiet, what could I say? The next day it wasn't even in the orders! That's what it means not to lose your head! So there you are, count," said Berg, blowing his perfect smoke rings.

Boris noticed that Rostov did not entirely like these stories. He turned the conversation to the military action and how and where he had been wounded. In the presence of Berg, whom he did not like, Rostov once again assumed his former tone of hussar bravado and became inspired, telling them his Schöngraben experience in precisely the way that people who have taken part in battles usually tell others about them, that is, as they would have liked it to be, as they had heard it told by others, as it was more beautiful to tell, but entirely unlike the way that it actually happened. Rostov was a truthful young man, he would never have deliberately told an untruth for anything, he began his story with the intention of telling everything exactly as it had happened, but imperceptibly to himself, involuntarily and inevitably he slipped into fantasy, into falsehood and even into bragging. How was he really supposed to tell his story? Surely he was not supposed to tell his listeners, who like himself (he knew this very well), had already heard stories about attacks on numerous occasions and had formed their own definite understanding of what an attack was, and were expecting precisely such a story – to tell them something different, the truth, and so shatter their previous understanding? Either they would not have believed him or, which was even worse, they would have thought it was Rostov's own fault that what usually happened to people who tell the story of a cavalry attack had not happened to him. He could not simply tell them that they all set off at a trot, that he fell off his horse, sprained his arm and ran into the forest as fast as he could to get away from a Frenchman.

They were expecting him to tell them how in a blaze of fury, completely beside himself, he flew at the square like a storm, sliced into it, slashed to the right and the left, fell in exhaustion and so forth. So that was the style in which he told his story, and they were satisfied, and he failed to notice that everything that he said was far from the truth.

In the middle of his story the Prince Andrei whom Boris was expecting entered the room. The previous day, when Boris had handed him the letter from Pierre, which Anna Mikhailovna had persuaded Pierre to write to his friend and in which the young Count Bezukhov told Bolkonsky that the person tendering this letter was a remarkably likeable young man, Bolkonsky, flattered that he was being petitioned for protection, had looked closely at young Boris, and taken a great liking to the youth. Furthermore, for Prince Andrei the most agreeable form of relations with people were the relations of a patron to a likeable man who would defer to his authority. Such were his relations with Pierre himself, and the same kind had now been established with Boris. As for Boris, with his innate tact he had managed at their first meeting to let Prince Andrei feel that he was quite prepared to defer to his authority. Bolkonsky had called in to Boris now in order to rest before his departure for headquarters and to discuss, as he had promised, what steps to take in order to fulfil Boris's wish for a transfer to General Headquarters. On entering the room and seeing an army hussar who was sitting backwards on a chair and relating his military adventures to the novice guardsmen ("lies, no doubt," thought Prince Andrei, who had already heard hundreds of such tales), Prince Andrei frowned, screwed up his eyes and, with a brief bow, sat down wearily and indolently on the divan. He was displeased that he had fallen into bad company. Even though Boris introduced Count Rostov to him, he did not change either his opinion or his contemptuous expression.

"Pray do continue," he said in a tone following which it was impossible to continue. Despite Prince Andrei's unpleasant, mocking tone, despite the general contempt that Rostov felt from his field combatant's point of view for all these little General Staff adjutants, of whom the new arrival was obviously one, Rostov felt embarrassed and he could not continue. He blushed, turned away and fell silent, but he could not help following closely all the movements and facial expressions of this tired, weak and lazy little man who forced his words out between his teeth as though he were doing a favour to the person with whom he was talking. This man interested and agitated him, inspiring him with an involuntary respect. Rostov blushed and thought in silence, looking at the new arrival. Berg was fawning on him so obsequiously that it was indecent. Boris, like a clever hostess, tried to draw the two of them into general conversation. He asked what news there was and what, without being indiscreet, had been heard about our intentions.

"It seems likely they will advance," Bolkonsky replied, evidently not wishing to say more in front of outsiders.

Berg availed himself of the opportunity to ask with especial politeness whether they would now be issuing, as he had heard, double forage money to army company commanders. To this Prince Andrei replied with a smile that he could not opine on such important state instructions, and Berg laughed merrily.

"Concerning your business," Prince Andrei said to Boris, "we shall talk some time later" – and he glanced at Rostov, as if to show him that he was not needed. Rostov blushed suddenly in silence. Bolkonsky continued: "Come to see me after the review and we'll do whatever can be done."

And in order, finally, to say something before leaving, he turned to Rostov, whose state of insuperable childish embarrassment bordering on bitter fury he had not deigned to notice, and said:

"I believe you were talking about the Schöngraben action? Were you there?"

"I was indeed," said Rostov bitterly, as if he wished to insult the adjutant with his words.

323

Bolkonsky noticed the hussar's state of mind, and he found it amusing. He smiled scornfully.

"Yes, there are many stories about that business."

"Yes indeed, stories!" Rostov said loudly, staring straight at Bolkonsky with furious, wide-open eyes. "Yes, there are many stories, but ours are the stories of those who were right under the enemy's fire, our stories have weight, not like the stories of those fine fellows at headquarters who receive honours for doing nothing."

"Of whom you assume I am one?" said Prince Andrei, smiling calmly and cheerfully.

At that moment a feeling of resentment and respect for this individual's composure mingled strangely in Rostov's heart.

"I am not speaking about *you*," he said, "I do not know you, and I confess that I do not wish to know you. I am speaking about staff officers in general."

"Let me tell you something," Prince Andrei interrupted him with calm authority in his voice. "Perhaps you wish to insult me, and I am willing to agree that it is very easy to do so, if you are lacking in respect for yourself; but you must agree that the time and place for doing so have been chosen very badly. In a few days we shall all have to attend a far greater, and far more serious duel, and furthermore Drubetskoy, who tells me he is your old friend, is in no way to blame that my character has had the misfortune to provoke your dislike. However," he said, getting up, "you know my name and you know where to find me: but do not forget," he added, "that I do not consider either myself or yourself insulted in the least, and my advice to you, as a somewhat older man, is to let this matter drop. So I'll be expecting you on Friday after the review, Boris, goodbye" – and he went out.

Rostov only remembered how he ought to have answered when the prince had already left the room. Boris knew that the more he asked Rostov to drop the matter, the more obstinate he would become, and therefore did not say a word about it. Rostov also said nothing and half an hour later he ordered his horse to be brought and left. He left with doubts about whether Boris was still his friend, or whether he must accept that they had already grown far apart for ever. His other doubt concerned whether he should ride to General Headquarters the next day and challenge this affected adjutant or really let this matter drop. One moment he thought spitefully what great satisfaction he would get from calling this small, weak and proud man up to the barrier and the next he felt with surprise that of all the people he knew, there was no one whom he would have been so glad to make his friend.

# V

The day after Boris's meeting with Rostov, there was a review of the Austrian and Russian forces, both those who were freshly arrived from Russia, and those who were back from the campaign with Kutuzov. Both of the Emperors, the Russian with his heir the Grand Duke, and the Austrian with the Archduke, took this review of the eighty-thousand-strong allied army.

From early morning the troops, all spic and span, began drawing up on the fortified site. First came thousands of feet and bayonets with their fluttering banners moving and halting at the officers' command, then wheeling round to form up at intervals, close to other similarly massed infantry all in different uniforms. Then came the ringing, regular hoof beats and jangling sabres of the spruce cavalry in their blue, red and green embroidered uniforms, with the elaborate bandsmen at the front, mounted on black, chestnut and grey horses. Next, with polished bronze cannons clanking and gleaming as they trundled along shaking on their carriages and reeking of linstocks, a long line of artillery crawled between the infantry and the cavalry and into position. Not only the generals in full-dress uniform, with their fat and thin waists belted in impossibly tight and their red necks, propped up by their collars, with their scarves and full decorations, and the pomaded, smartly dressed officers, but every single soldier, with his face freshly shaved and washed and his equipment polished till it could shine no more, every horse, so thoroughly groomed that its coat gleamed like satin, and with every hair in its damp mane perfectly in place – they all felt that something truly serious, solemn and significant was taking place. Every general and every soldier felt like a single tiny drop in this sea of humanity, felt his own insignificance as an individual yet at the same time was proudly aware of the strength and grandeur that he drew from the massive whole with which he felt himself to be indivisibly linked.

The strenuous bustle and effort continued from dawn until ten in the morning and at last everything stood in due order.

With the ranks drawn up across the immense open field, all that could be seen were the strict, regular lines of infantry, artillery, cavalry, the Guards with their gleaming white bandoliers, Kutuzov's army – distinguished by its irregular battledress – and the Austrian army with its white-clad generals.

An excited whisper, like the wind in leaves, rustled through them, and from various directions floated the strains of the generals' march. It seemed as if it was the entire army, in its joy at meeting its sovereign, that was making these triumphant sounds, that it was not the wind gently stirring the unfurled banners fluttering at the centre of the battalions, but the army itself expressing, through this gentle movement, its joy at the approach of the sovereigns. One single voice was heard and then, like cocks at dawn, voices repeated the cry on all sides. The army stood to attention, and everything went quiet. In the deathly silence there came the hoof beats of hundred horses in the Emperors' retinue. Then a single gentle, young voice, the Emperor Alexander's voice. And the army let out such a terrible, deafening, prolonged, joyful shout that the men themselves were terrified by the power and mass of which they were part.

In Kutuzov's army Rostov stood in his place and felt the same feeling as every man in that army felt, self-forgetfulness and a powerful, superhumanly proud awareness of might and passionate loyalty to the person who was the cause of this triumph.

He felt that a single word from that man could make this entire mass (and him too, as one insignificant atom linked to it) go through fire or water, commit a crime or go to its death, and therefore he trembled and his heart stood still at the sight of that word drawing closer.

"Hoorah! Hoorah! Hoorah!" came the roar from all sides and, moving to the regular, deafening sound of these voices, riding casually, asymmetrically and – above all – freely between the motionless rectangular masses of the troops, that seemed to have turned to stone, there came the hundreds of riders of the retinue, with two men riding at their head – the Emperors. The undivided attention of this entire mass of men was focused on them.

The handsome young Emperor Alexander in his Cavalry Guards uniform, with a three-cornered hat worn with the peak forward, with his pleasant face and soft, resonant voice attracted all the attention.

Rostov was seeing the Emperor for the first time. He was enchanted by the simple charm of his appearance in conjunction with the magnificence of the setting.

Halting opposite the Pavlograd Regiment, the sovereign said something in French to the Austrian Emperor and smiled.

On seeing that smile, Rostov felt at that moment that he loved his sovereign more than anything in the world. He did not know why, but it was true. The sovereign summoned the German regimental commander Usach and said a few words to him. Rostov envied him with all his heart.

The sovereign also addressed the officers:

"I thank you all, gentlemen" – Rostov heard every word as if the sound were coming from the heavens – "from the bottom of my heart." (How happy Rostov would have been if he could have died for his Tsar then and there!) "You have earned your standards of St. George and you will be worthy of them."

The sovereign said something else that Rostov could not make out and the soldiers, straining their hussars' chests, shouted, "Hoorah!"

Rostov shouted too, with all the strength he could muster, bending down into the saddle, wishing he could wound himself with this shout, but only to express completely his joy in his sovereign.

The sovereign stood for several seconds as if in indecision.

"How could the sovereign be in indecision?" thought Rostov, finding this indecision even more sublime. But the indecision lasted for a moment only. The sovereign's foot touched the groin of the beautiful bob-tailed bay horse that he was riding with the narrow, pointed toe of his boot: the sovereign's hand in its white glove gathered up the reins, and it all moved away and was concealed behind the sea of adjutants that swayed along irregularly yet gracefully.

When the review was over, the singers started up, and the officers rode together into groups and began talking about decorations, about the Austrians and their uniforms, with mocking banter as Kutuzov's men met friends in the Guards, and talk about Buonaparte and what a bad time he would have of it now, especially when the Essen corps arrived and Prussia took our side.

But above all they spoke about their sovereign Alexander, passing on every word he said and every movement he made, and delighting in them. All everybody wanted was to move against the French as soon as possible under the command of their sovereign. After the review, everyone was more certain of victory than they could have been after already winning two battles.

# VI

The day after the review Boris, dressed up in his best uniform and seen on his way with wishes for success from his comrade Berg, went to Olmütz to see Bolkonsky, wishing to profit by his kindness and obtain the best possible position for himself with some person of importance, a prospect which he found particularly alluring in the army. An inner voice advised against his intentions and at times it seemed shameful to him to bow down to anybody at all.

"But that is not so," he told himself, "these are merely the echoes of Rostov's childish, chivalrous fantasies inside me. It's time to drop all that. It's all very well for him, whose father sends him ten thousand roubles at a time. (I do not envy him and I love him.) But I, who have nothing except my own head, have to make a career for myself."

He crushed this feeling of false shame, as he thought it, within himself and set out resolutely for Olmütz. He did not find Prince Andrei at headquarters on that day, but the brilliance, the signs of power and the festive, ceremonial manner of life which he saw in Olmütz, where Central Headquarters was located, together with the diplomatic corps and both Emperors with their retinues of courtiers and attendants, only further reinforced his desire to belong to this superior world.

He knew no one, and despite his fancy Guards uniform, all these courtiers and military men darting along the streets in their fancy carriages, plumes, ribbons and decorations stood so far above him that they did not wish to acknowledge his existence and were not even capable of doing so. At Kutuzov's headquarters, where he enquired after Bolkonsky, all these adjutants, and even the orderlies, looked at him as if they wished to impress on him that there were many, very many officers like him hanging about here and they were heartily sick of them all. But despite that, or rather as a consequence of it, after lunch on the following day, the 15th of the month, he once again entered the large house in Olmütz occupied by Kutuzov and asked for Bolkonsky. He was in, and Boris was led to a large hall, in which people had probably once danced, but which now contained five beds and miscellaneous pieces of furniture: tables, chairs and a clavichord. One adjutant, not far from the door, was sitting at a table in a Persian dressing gown and writing. Another, red and fat, was lying on a bed with his hands under his head and laughing with an officer who had sat down beside him. A third was playing a merry waltz on the clavichord, a fourth was reclining on the clavichord and singing along. Bolkonsky was not there. None of these gentlemen stirred on noticing Boris. The one who was writing, whom Boris addressed, looked up in annoyance and told him that Bolkonsky was on duty and he should go through the door on the left, into the reception room, if he wished to see him. In the reception room, besides the duty adjutant, there were the constant comings and goings of at least five or so men, now a quartermaster-general, now an artillery commander, now a senior lieutenant, now the commander of a detachment, now an Oberproviantmeister, now the head of the personal chancellery, now an adjutant-orderly, now an aide-de-camp, and so on and so forth. Almost without exception, they all spoke in French.

Just when Boris entered, Prince Andrei, his eyes narrowed in contempt and with that peculiar air of highly courteous weariness which says quite clearly that, were it not my duty, I should not waste a moment talking to you, was listening to an old Russian general with decorations, who was standing to attention, almost on tiptoe, wearing an obsequious soldier's expression on his crimson face that was propped up by a tight collar, and reporting something to Prince Andrei.

"Very well, be so good as to wait for a moment," Bolkonsky said to the general and, noticing Boris, he paid no more attention to the general, who ran after him, imploring him to hear something else he had to say, but Prince Andrei turned to Boris with a cheerful smile and a nod. His face assumed the childishly gentle expression that was so enchanting for those to whom he was speaking.

At this moment Boris finally realised, more clearly than ever before, that in addition to the line of seniority and discipline that was prescribed in the regulations that they knew in the regiment and he knew, there was another, more fundamental line of seniority, the one that made this tight-laced general with the crimson face wait respectfully while Prince Andrei, a captain, found it more convenient for his own immediate pleasure to converse with Drubetskoy, a warrant officer, and Boris determined more resolutely than ever that henceforth his career would not follow the line of seniority that was inscribed in the regulations, but would observe this unwritten one. He now felt that, simply by being recommended by Prince Andrei, he had already become senior to the general who, in different circumstances, in the ranks, could have crushed a warrant officer of the Guards like him. Prince Andrei came up and shook his hand.

"I am so sorry you did not find me here yesterday. I spent all day fussing about with the Germans. I went with Weierother to check the dispositions. Once the Germans start getting precise it goes on for ever!"

Boris smiled, as if he understood what Prince Andrei was hinting at and it was something everyone knew about. But this was the first time he had heard the name Weierother, or even the word "dispositions".

"Well then, my dear fellow, do you still want to be an adjutant? I've given some thought to you in the meantime."

"Yes, I was thinking," said Boris, involuntarily blushing for some reason, "of asking the commander-in-chief. He has had a letter about me from Prince Kuragin: I only wanted to ask," he added, as if apologising, and still feeling that involuntary shame, "because I am afraid that the Guards will not see any action."

"Very well! Very well! We shall talk it all over," said Prince Andrei, "only let me report about this gentleman, and then I shall be all yours."

While Prince Andrei went to report about the crimson-faced general, the general himself, who evidently did not share Boris's notions concerning the unwritten line of seniority, began staring with such bloodthirsty ferocity at the insolent warrant officer who had prevented him from finishing what he was saying to the adjutant, that Boris began to feel uncomfortable. He turned away and waited impatiently for Prince Andrei to come back from the commander-in-chief's office.

"Well now, my dear fellow, I've been thinking about you," said Prince Andrei after they walked through to the large hall with the clavichord. (The adjutant who had formerly greeted Boris so coldly was now attentive and amiable with him.) "There's no point in your going to Kutuzov," said Prince Andrei. "He will say any number of polite things to you, he will tell you to come and dine with him" ("which would not be so bad for the unwritten rules of seniority," thought Boris) "but nothing further will come of it: there will soon be an entire battalion of us adjutants and aides-de-camp. But I'll tell you what we shall do: I have a good friend, the Emperor Alexander's adjutant-general and a fine fellow, Prince Dolgorukov; and although you could not know this, the point is that now Kutuzov and his staff and all of us no longer mean a thing: everything now is focused on the sovereign; so let's go to Dolgorukov, I need to see him anyway, I've already mentioned you to him; and then we shall see whether he can find you a place with himself or somewhere else, closer to the sun."

It was already late in the evening when they walked into the palace at Olmütz which was occupied by the Emperors and their retinues.

# VII

That very day there had been a council of war in which all the members of the Hofkriegsrat and both Emperors had taken part and at which, in opposition to the opinion of the old men, Kutuzov and Prince Schwarzenberg, it had been decided to advance immediately and give full-scale battle to Bonaparte. The council of war had just concluded when Prince Andrei, accompanied by Boris, arrived at the palace to seek out Prince Dolgorukov. Everybody at headquarters was still under the spell of the Olmütz review and also, on that particular evening, intensely affected by the council of war. The voices of those who wished to delay and had advised waiting for something else before advancing had been so unanimously stifled and their arguments refuted by such manifest proofs of the advantages of an attack, that what had been spoken about at the council – the future battle and, of course, certain victory – no longer seemed to be the future, but the past. All the advantages were on our side. Immense forces, undoubtedly superior to those of Napoleon, had been concentrated in one single place. Bonaparte, evidently weakened, was not undertaking any action, while our troops, inspired by the presence of the Emperor, were eager for action: the strategic position for operations was already familiar, right down to the smallest of details, to the Austrian General Weierother who was commanding our forces (by a lucky coincidence, the Austrian forces had carried out manoeuvres in the previous year in those very fields in which the battle with the French was now to be fought) while the adjacent locality was also known down to the smallest detail and shown on the maps.

Dolgorukov, one of the most passionate advocates of an attack, had only just returned, wearied and exhausted, from the review, but enlivened and proud at the victory won in the council. When Prince Andrei and Boris went upstairs to see him, Prince Andrei introduced his protégé officer, but Prince Dolgorukov, shaking him politely and firmly by the hand, said nothing to him and, clearly unable to resist expressing the thoughts that were most fully occupying him at that moment, addressed Prince Andrei in French.

"Well, my dear fellow, what a battle we have won! May God only grant that the battle that ensues will be equally victorious. Well, my dear fellow," he said, speaking with brusque eagerness, "I must admit I've been unjust to the Austrians and especially to Weierother. Such precision, such detail, such knowledge of the locality and foresight for all the conditions in prospect. Yes, indeed, my dear fellow, you couldn't possibly imagine more propitious conditions than those in which we find ourselves, even if you tried. A combination of Austrian precision with Russian valour – what more could you wish for?"

"So an attack has definitely been decided on?" asked Bolkonsky.

"And you know, my dear fellow, I think Buonaparte has definitely lost his bearings. D'you know, a letter to the Emperor was received from him today."

"Was it now! What does he write?" asked Bolkonsky.

"What can he write? Tra-diri-dira and suchlike, all to no purpose except to gain time. I tell you, he's within our grasp, that's for sure! But the most amusing thing of all," he said, suddenly laughing good-naturedly, "is that they simply couldn't think how to address the reply to him. If not to the consul and, of course, not to the Emperor, then to General Buonaparte, or so it seemed to me."

"Well what did they decide on, in the end," asked Bolkonsky, smiling.

"You know Bilibin, he's a very clever chap, he suggested addressing it to 'the usurper and enemy of mankind'. " Dolgorukov laughed merrily.

"But still, that Bilibin does have a good head, and he did find a title for the address."

"What was it?" asked Bolkonsky.

"To the Head of the French Government," said Prince Dolgorukov with serious satisfaction. "He won't like it. My brother knows him, he dined with him in Paris and he says you could not imagine a man more skilled in diplomatic subtlety. Indeed, Count Markov was the only one who knew how to deal with him. Do you know the story of the handkerchief? Quite delightful."

And the talkative Dolgorukov, turning now to Boris, now to Prince Andrei, told them approvingly how Buonaparte, wishing to test Markov, our ambassador, deliberately dropped his handkerchief in front of him and halted, looking at it, probably expecting Markov to assist him, but Markov immediately dropped his own handkerchief beside the first and then picked up his own, without touching Buonaparte's.

"Yes, that is excellent," said Bolkonsky, still smiling in the same way. "But listen, prince, I have come to you as a petitioner with this young man here. You see . . ."

But Prince Andrei had no time to finish before an adjutant entered the room and summoned Prince Dolgorukov to the Emperor.

"Ah, what a pity!" said Dolgorukov, rising hastily to his feet and shaking hands with Prince Andrei and Boris. "You know, I shall be very glad to do everything in my power, both for you and for this dear young man." He shook Boris's hand again with an expression of good-natured, sincere and animated levity.

Boris could not help but be excited by the idea of being as close to the supreme power as he felt he now was. He was aware that here he was in contact with the springs that controlled all those immense movements of the masses of which he, in his regiment, had felt merely a small, submissive and insignificant part. Following Prince Dolgorukov out into the corridor they saw a young man coming out of the same door through which Dolgorukov was going in. He had a remarkably handsome and proud face with a sharp line to his forward-jutting jaw which, instead of spoiling his features, lent them a distinctive expression of lively resourcefulness. This short man nodded to Dolgorukov as if he knew him well and fixed Prince Andrei with an intensely cold glare as he walked directly at him, evidently expecting Prince Andrei to bow or make way. Prince Andrei did neither: his face took on an expression of fierce anger, and the young man, turning aside, walked past and along the corridor.

"Who is that?" asked Boris.

"That is a most remarkable man, and one I most dislike. He is Polish,

Prince Czartorysky. Such are the people," Bolkonsky said with a sigh which he could not repress, as they made their way out of the palace, "such are the people who decide the fate of a nation."

Boris looked at him in puzzlement, uncertain whether this had been said with contempt, respect or envy. But he could read nothing in the dark, sallow face of the small man walking beside him. It had been said simply because it was so.

The next day the troops set out, and until the Battle of Austerlitz, Boris had no time to visit either Bolkonsky or Dolgorukov, and he remained in the ranks.

# VIII

On the 15th of November the allied army advanced from Olmütz in five columns under the command of generals, not one of whom bore a Russian name. These names were: first – Wimpfen, second – Count Langeron, third – Przebyszewsky, fourth – the Prince of Lichtenstein and fifth – Prince Hohenlohe. The weather was frosty and clear, and the men marched merrily. Although no one, apart from the top commanders, knew where the army was headed and why, they were all glad to be on the march after the idleness of camp at Olmütz. On command, the columns set out to music and with banners flying. For the entire day's march they had to march smartly, as if on parade, keeping in step the whole time. Between eight and nine o'clock in the morning the sovereign, riding on horseback with his retinue, caught up with the Guards to join Przebyszewsky's column. The soldiers kept shouting a cheery "Hoorah", and for the entire length of ten *versts* over which the force of eighty thousand men on the move was spread, the sounds of military marches and soldiers' songs rang out, clashing disharmoniously in adjacent units. The adjutants and convoy leaders darting between the regiments all wore cheerful, self-satisfied expressions on their faces. As evening approached General Weierother, in sole command of the forces' movement, watched the troops pass by as he stood at the side of the road with several officers of the retinue and Prince Dolgorukov, who had ridden up. The general had the satisfied air of a man who has successfully carried out a set exercise. As each unit walked past, he asked the commander where they had been allocated quarters, and the commanders' statements matched the forecasts he had made to Dolgorukov standing beside him.

"There, you see, prince," he said, "the Novgorodians are stationed in

Rausnitz, just as I said, behind them come the musketeers, who are going to Clausewitz" – he checked his notebook – "then the Pavlograders and then the Guards marching along the high road. Excellent. Wonderful. I cannot see," he said, recalling an objection made to him by the old Russian generals, "I really cannot see why they assume that the Russian troops cannot manoeuvre just as well as the Austrian ones. You see, prince, how strictly and precisely everything can be carried out according to dispositions, so long as the dispositions are thorough . . ."

Prince Dolgorukov was barely listening to the Austrian general; he was preoccupied with the question of whether it would be possible, and if so how, to attack a French detachment that Russian troops had come across that evening in front of the small town of Wischau.

He put this question to General Weierother. Weierother replied:

"This business can only be decided by the will of Their Majesties. However, it might well be possible."

"We cannot leave this French detachment right in front of our nose," said Dolgorukov, and with those words he set off to the two Emperors' quarters. A scout from the advance guard, sent by Prince Bagration, had already reached their headquarters, and reported that the French detachment at Wischau was not strong and had no reinforcements.

Half an hour after Prince Dolgorukov's arrival it was decided to attack the French at dawn the next day and thereby disregard the Emperor Alexander's arrival in the army and his first campaign.

Prince Dolgorukov was to command the cavalry taking part in this action.

The Emperor Alexander submitted with a sigh to the representations of his retinue and decided to remain with the third column.

# IX

Before dawn the next day, Denisov's squadron, in which Nikolai Rostov was serving and which was in Prince Bagration's detachment, advanced from its night's lodgings and, after covering about a *verst* behind the columns, was halted on the high road.

Rostov saw Cossacks, the First and Second Squadrons of Hussars and infantry battalions with artillery march past him, and the generals with their retinue ride past. All the fear that he had felt in the face of action, just as the previous time, the entire internal struggle through which he had overcome that fear, all his dreams of how he would distinguish himself in true hussar fashion in this action – all had been wasted. Their squadron was left in the reserve, and Nikolai Rostov spent a dull and miserable day. Between eight and nine in the morning he heard the sound of shooting ahead of him, and shouts of "hoorah", he saw the wounded (there were not many) being led back and, finally, he saw an entire detachment of French cavalrymen being led in the middle of a squadron of Cossacks. The action was obviously over, and the action had obviously been successful. The men walking back past him spoke of a brilliant victory, the taking of the town and the capture of an entire squadron.

It was a clear, sunny day after a deep night frost, and the cheerful gleam of the autumn day was in keeping with the news of victory, which was conveyed not only through what was said, but also by the joyful expressions on the faces of the soldiers, the officers, the generals and the adjutants riding back and forth past Rostov's squadron. Nikolai Rostov's heart ached all the more painfully, he had suffered all the fear that precedes a battle in vain and spent this happy day in solitary inactivity.

Denisov was gloomy and taciturn for the same reasons. He saw his squadron being left in the reserve as deliberate intrigue by that scoundrel of an adjutant and was planning to teach him a lesson.

"Wostov, come here, let's dwink to dwown our misewy," shouted Denisov, who had sat down at the side of the road with a flask and some snacks spread in front of him. Rostov took a drink without speaking, trying not to look at Denisov; he was sick of the abuse of the adjutant, and apprehensive lest it be repeated.

"There they are, bringing another one," said one of the officers, pointing to a captured French dragoon whom two Cossacks were leading along on foot. One of them was leading the high, handsome French horse taken from the prisoner by its reins.

"Sell the horse!" Denisov shouted to the Cossack.

"By all means, your honour."

The officers stood up and surrounded the Cossacks and the French prisoner. The French dragoon was a young fellow, from Alsace, who spoke French with a German accent. He was breathless with excitement, his face was red and, on hearing the French language, he immediately began talking to the officers, addressing first one, then another. He said they wouldn't have caught him, he wasn't to blame for them catching him, the corporal was to blame, he'd sent him to grab some horse-cloths, and he'd told him the Russians were there already. And at every word he added: "But don't you do anything bad to my little horse," and he stroked the horse affectionately. It was clear that he did not understand very well where he was. One moment he apologised for being taken, the next, imagining that he was facing his officers, he strove to demonstrate his soldierly discipline and zeal in the service. He brought with him into our rearguard all the freshness of the atmosphere of the French army, which was so foreign.

The Cossacks let the horse go for two gold pieces, and Rostov, the richest of the officers, bought it.

"But don't you do anything bad to my little horse," said the Alsatian ardently to Rostov when the horse was handed over to the hussar.

Rostov, smiling, reassured the dragoon and gave him the money.

"Allay, allay!" said the Cossack, starting to move. And just then someone shouted: "The sovereign!"

Everyone started running and bustling about, the two words: "The sovereign! The sovereign!" were heard being repeated with eager excitement, and Rostov saw several riders with white plumes on their hats coming along the road behind him. In an instant everyone was in place and waiting.

Nikolai Rostov could not remember how he had run and mounted his horse. His regret at not having been involved in the action and his state of habitual boredom in the face of company that he knew only too well were gone in an instant, all thoughts of himself instantly disappeared, and he was totally absorbed by a feeling of happiness and the nearness of the Emperor. In this nearness alone he felt himself rewarded for the loss of that day. He was as happy as a lover when the time for a long-awaited rendezvous has come. Although not daring to glance round in the ranks, he could sense *his* approach with an ecstatic intuition. And he could sense it, not only from the hoof beats of the horses in the approaching cavalcade, he could sense it because as *he* approached everything around him became brighter, more joyful and significant.

Closer and closer approached Rostov's sun, scattering around itself rays of mild and majestic light, and then he could already feel himself engulfed by these rays, he could hear *his* voice – that kindly, calm, majestic voice that was yet so simple.

Just as Rostov felt it should, a deathly silence fell, and in this silence the sounds of *his* voice were heard.

"The Pavlograd Hussars?" the voice enquired.

"The reserve, sire," replied a different, coarse, carnal voice, so very human after that transcendent voice that had said: "*Les hussards de Pavlograd?*"

The sovereign drew level with Rostov and halted. His face was even more handsome than at the review three days earlier. It shone with such great gaiety and youthfulness, youthfulness so innocent that it seemed like the playfulness of a fourteen-year-old boy and yet at the same time was still the face of a majestic Emperor. By chance, looking over the squadron, the sovereign's eyes met Rostov's eyes and lingered on them for no more than two seconds. Whether or not the sovereign understood everything that was happening in Rostov's heart (to Rostov it seemed that he did), he looked into Rostov's face for about two seconds with his blue eyes (the light poured out of them, soft and gentle and bright), then he abruptly raised his brows, struck his horse with a sharp movement of his left foot and set off ahead at a gallop. Rostov could scarcely catch his breath from joy.

Hearing shooting in the avant-garde, the young Emperor could not resist the desire to be present at the battle and, despite all the representations of his retainers, at twelve o'clock he left the third column and galloped off to the avant-garde. Before he reached the hussars, several adjutants met him with news of the happy outcome to the action. The battle was represented as a brilliant victory over the French and therefore the sovereign and the entire army believed, especially before the powder smoke hanging over the field of battle had dispersed, that the French had been defeated and had retreated against their will. Several minutes after the sovereign had ridden by, the Pavlograd division was ordered to advance, and in Wischau itself Rostov saw the sovereign again. Several dead and wounded, whom there had not yet been time to collect, were lying in the city square, where there had been a rather intense exchange of fire. The sovereign, surrounded by his retinue of military men and civilians, among whom the elegant figure of Adam Czartorysky particularly caught the eye, was seated on his bob-tailed mare, leaning over to one side, holding a gold lorgnette up to his eyes with a graceful gesture and looking through it at a soldier lying face downwards with a bloodied head without a shako. The wounded soldier was so coarse and repellent, so foul that Rostov was offended by his closeness to the sovereign. Rostov saw the sovereign's rounded shoulders shudder as if a chilly frost had run across them, saw the sovereign's left foot begin spasmodically beating its spur against the side of the horse, which was looking round indifferently and did not stir from the spot. Dismounting from their horses, adjutants grasped the soldier under the arms and starting setting him down on a stretcher that had appeared. The soldier groaned.

"Gently, gently, can't you be gentler!" the sovereign said, evidently suffering even more than the dying soldier, and he rode away. Rostov saw the tears that filled the sovereign's eyes and heard him say in French to Czartorysky as he rode away: "What a terrible thing is war, what a terrible thing."

Forgetting himself, Rostov started his horse and set off after the sovereign, only coming to his senses when Denisov called his name.

*

The forces of the avant-garde were stationed in front of Wischau, in view of the enemy line, which had politely fallen back before us with the minimum exchange of fire throughout the whole day. The sovereign's gratitude was conveyed to the avant-garde, honours were promised and a double ration of vodka was issued to the men. The bivouac campfires crackled and the soldiers' songs resounded even more merrily than on the previous night. On this night Denisov celebrated his promotion to major, and Rostov proposed a toast to the health of the sovereign, not, however, to "the health of His Majesty the Emperor", as they say at official dinners, but to "our sovereign, a good, enchanting and great man".

"We drink to his health and to certain victory over the French. I don't know," he said, "but if we fought before and gave the French no quarter, as at Schöngraben, then what will happen now, when *he* himself is in the lead, we will all die, we will gladly die for him. Right, gentlemen? Perhaps I am not saying this right, I have drunk a lot, yes, but that is how I feel, and so do you. To the health of Alexander the First. Hoorah!"

"Hoorah!" boomed the fervent voices of the officers. Old man Kiersten shouted enthusiastically and no less sincerely than the enamoured boy Rostov. When Rostov proposed his toast Kiersten, in just his shirt and breeches, went across to the soldiers' campfires with his glass in hand, his long grey moustaches and the greying hair on his chest peeping out from under his open shirt, and stood in a magnificent pose, one arm swept up high, in the light of a campfire.

"Lads, to the health of His Majesty the Emperor! To victory over our enemies! Hoorah!" he shouted in his dashing old hussar's baritone.

The hussars crowded together and replied in unison with a loud shout.

Late that night, when everybody had dispersed, Denisov patted his favourite Rostov on the shoulder with his small, short hand.

"There's no one to fall in love with during the campaign, so he fell in love with the Tsar," he said.

"Denisov, don't make a joke of it," Rostov shouted angrily. "It's such an exalted, such a beautiful feeling."

"I believe you, I believe you, my friend, and I share it and understand."

"No, you don't understand," said Rostov, and he got up and went off to wander between the campfires, dreaming about what happiness it would be to die, not even saving his sovereign's life (he did not dare to dream of that), but simply to die in front of his sovereign's eyes. He really was in love with the Tsar, and with the glory of Russian arms, and with the hope of triumph to come, and he was not alone in experiencing this feeling in those memorable days that preceded the defeat at Auster-litz. At that time, nine out of ten men in the Russian army were in love, although less ecstatically, with their Tsar and the glory of Russian arms.

# X

The following day the sovereign remained at Wischau. His physician-in-ordinary Doctor Villier was summoned to see him several times. At General Headquarters and among the closest troops the news spread that the sovereign was unwell. He did not eat and had slept badly that night. According to his retainers, the cause of this indisposition lay in the intense impression produced on the sovereign's sensitive soul by the sight of the wounded and the dead.

At dawn on the 17th of November, a French officer who had arrived with a flag of truce, demanding a meeting with the Russian Emperor, was sent through from our advance positions. This officer was Savary. The sovereign had only just fallen asleep, and therefore Savary was obliged to wait.

At midday he was admitted to the sovereign's presence and an hour later he rode off with Prince Dolgorukov to the advance positions of the French army.

Rumour had it that the purpose in sending Savary had been to propose a truce and also to propose a meeting between the Emperor Alexander and Napoleon. The latter proposal was rejected and, instead of the sovereign, Prince Dolgorukov, the victor at Wischau, was sent with Savary to negotiate with Napoleon if, contrary to expectations, such negotiations had as their goal a genuine desire for peace.

In the evening Dolgorukov returned, and to those who knew him, the change that had taken place in him was remarkable. Following his conversation with Buonaparte he carried himself like a prince of the blood, and refused to discuss what had happened at the meeting with any of the royal retinue. Upon returning, he went straight through to the sovereign himself and spent a long time alone with him.

Despite this, however, rumours spread at headquarters that Dolgoru-kov had behaved worthily with Buonaparte, and that, in order to avoid calling him Your Majesty, he had deliberately not addressed him by any title at all and, in declining the proposal for a truce made by Buonaparte, he had actually rebuked him. Dolgorukov himself said the following to the Austrian General Weierother, in the presence of others:

"Either I understand nothing," said Prince Dolgorukov, "or what he fears most at the present moment is a general engagement. Otherwise what was his purpose in demanding this meeting, conducting negotiations and, most significantly, retreating without the slightest delay, when retreat is so repugnant to his entire method of waging war? Believe me, his hour will come and very soon. And we would be fine fools to listen to the so-called experienced old men, Prince Schwarzenberg and so forth. Regardless of my total admiration for the services they have rendered, we would be fine fools to wait for something to happen and so give him the chance to get away from us or trick us in one way or another, when now he is surely within our grasp. No, we should not forget Suvorov and his rules: do not put yourself in the position of the attacked, but be the attacker yourself. Believe me, in war the energy of young men often shows the way forward more reliably than all the experience of the old eccentrics."

On the 17th, 18th and 19th of November the troops moved forward and, after brief exchanges of fire, the enemy's advance outposts hastily retreated.

At the highest levels of the army a certain powerful, bustling, agitated activity began at midday on the 19th and continued until the morning of the following day, the 20th of November, on which the memorable battle of Austerlitz was fought. At first, the activity (animated conversations, running to and fro, the despatching of adjutants) was centred in the General Headquarters of the two Emperors, then, in the early evening, this activity was transmitted to Kutuzov's General Headquarters, and from there it spread to every corner and every unit of the army, so that in the gloom of the November night the troops rose from their night-quarters and started buzzing with talk as the words of command were given and, in the darkness, the eighty-thousand-strong mass of troops began fluttering and transmitting its movement like a sheet of canvas ten *versts* long. And these masses of troops moved and fought throughout the whole of the memorable 20th under the influence of the impetus that had been imparted between three and four in the afternoon on the previous day by the intense movement at the Central Headquarters of the two Emperors. This intense momentum, which provided the impetus for all that followed, was like the first movement of the main wheel in a great tower clock. One wheel moved slowly into motion, a second was turned, then a third, and they all began turning faster and faster, big wheels and bigger wheels, pulleys, gears, drums, large bells and small bells, the chimes began to sound, figures began popping out, the clock moved and struck and the hands went round slowly and evenly, displaying the final result of all this activity. Just like the movement of a clock, the movement of fate is likewise inexorable and likewise independent of the first cause that gives the first impetus to movement in the main wheel. In the same way the wheels closest to those that are already moving, although impassively silent and still a moment before the transmission of momentum, fall in submissively with the movement as soon as it reaches them, and the wheels whistle on their axles, their cog-teeth engage, the spinning pulleys hiss in their rapid movement, while the next wheel still stands calm and motionless, as if willing to remain in this motionless state for a hundred years, yet when the moment arrives, the lever has caught and the wheel, submitting to the movement, creaks as it turns and merges with the single unified action.

Just as in a clock the result of the incalculably complex movement of the parts is the slow but regular movement of a hand that tells the time, so the result of the complex movements of these hundred and sixty thousand Russians and Frenchmen, all the passions, desires, remorse, humiliations, pride, sufferings, fears and ecstasies of these men is defeat in the battle of Austerlitz, the so-called battle of the three Emperors, that is, the slow movement of the hand of world history on the clock face of the history of mankind.

The two Emperors and their retinues were agitated by hope and apprehension about the outcome of the following day, afraid above all that Buonaparte might trick them by retreating at a rapid march into Bohemia, thus depriving them of the sure success that everything appeared to promise. The people thinking specifically about the next day's battle (there were not many of them) were: the sovereign himself, Prince Dolgorukov and Adam Czartorysky. The mainspring of the entire movement was Weierother, his aide being charged with the details.

He rode to the advance positions to survey the enemy, dictated the dispositions in German, rode to Kutuzov and then to the sovereign and indicated the proposed disposition and movement of the troops on a plan. Like a man who is too busy, Weierother even forgot to be respectful with crowned sovereigns. He spoke rapidly and unclearly, without look-ing into the face of the other man, he did not answer the questions put to him, he was spattered with mud and had a presumptuous and proud air that was at the same time embarrassed. He felt he was at the head of a movement that had begun and had already become irresistible. He was like a horse in harness that has started running fast down a steep hill. He did not know whether he was pulling or being driven, but he was rushing headlong as fast as he possibly could, with no time to think about what his movement would lead to. Most of the people in the headquarters of the two emperors were occupied with quite different interests. In one place the talk was that while it was desirable to appoint General N.N. commander of the cavalry, it was awkward because the

Austrian General N.N. might be offended by it, and he had to be accommodated, since he was in the Emperor Franz's good favour, and therefore it was proposed to give N.N. the title of commander of the cavalry of the extreme left flank. In another place there were stories and jokes told in confidence about how Count Arakcheev had refused his appointment as commander of one of the columns of the army.

"Well now, that at least is frank," someone said about him, "he said openly that his nerves could not stand it."

"Frank and naïve," said another. Yet somewhere else an old, offended general was trying to prove his right to command a separate unit.

"I'm not asking for anything particular, but having served for twenty years, I feel offended at being left without an appointment and being under the command of a general younger than myself." The old general asserted with tears in his voice that there was only one thing that he desired – to have an opportunity to prove his zeal to His Majesty the Emperor and indeed, it was impossible to consider offending the old fellow, after he had gone petitioning through this person and that, and an entirely new, quite unnecessary appointment was finally made for him.

The reasoning and discussions among the Austrian generals concerned how things might be arranged so that the artillery commanders did not come under the command of the Russians so that the glory of the next day's victory could not be claimed by the presumptuous Russian barbarians. They tried to arrange things so that the Russians were sent to the difficult, inconspicuous places, where no brilliant action was anticipated, while the Austrians were kept for those spots where the fate of the battle ought to be decided. In yet another place there was talk of the need to restrain the Emperor Alexander from his expressed intention and desire, so in keeping with his chivalrous character, to take part in the battle in person and expose himself to danger. Hundreds of headquarters staff members petitioned to be granted places in the retinue of the Emperors the following day: some only because there was likely to be less danger wherever the Emperor was, some from the calculation that more honours would be awarded close to the Emperor than anywhere else. People were already conjecturing where the troops would next proceed after the victory.

Between seven and eight in the evening, old man Kutuzov himself arrived at the General Headquarters of the two Emperors and his conversation with Count Tolstoy, the Chief High Marshal, was repeated with approval in a certain circle. "The Emperor will heed you, tell him we shall lose the battle," Kutuzov supposedly said, in order to protect himself in advance against any reproaches and to shift all the guilt in case of defeat on to someone else's shoulders. But it was not permitted, it was wrong to foresee failure, and therefore Count Tolstoy's reply was highly approved: "*Eh, mon cher général,* I am busy with rice and chicken, you should busy yourself with military matters."

# XI

After nine in the evening Weierother moved on with his plans to Kutuzov's headquarters, where something less than a council of war and more a final issuing of instructions for the next day had been arranged. All the commanders of columns were summoned to the commander-in-chief and all made an appearance with the exception of Bagration, who was out of sorts and refused to attend on the pretext of the remote position of his detachment. He grumbled that the sausage-eaters had muddled everything up and said that the battle would be lost.

Kutuzov was occupying a small nobleman's castle close to Ostralitz. The members of the council of war had gathered in the large drawing room, which had become the commander-in-chief's office, and were drinking tea when Bagration's orderly, Rostov, arrived with the news that the prince could not be present.

"Since Prince Bagration will not be here, we can begin," said Weierother, rising hastily from his seat and approaching the table, on which a huge map of the environs of Brünn and Austerlitz was laid out.

Kutuzov, his uniform unbuttoned so that his fat neck bulged over the collar as if suddenly released, was sitting dozing in a Voltaire armchair, with his plump old man's hands placed symmetrically on the armrests, when Prince Andrei entered. He opened his only eye with an effort and said through his dribbling saliva:

"Yes, yes, please, it's already late." He nodded his head and, leaving it to droop, he closed his eyes again.

If at first the members of the council of war thought Kutuzov was pretending to be asleep, then the sounds that he emitted through his nose during the reading that followed proved that the commander-in-chief was concerned at that moment with a far more important question than the desire to demonstrate his contempt for the dispositions or, indeed, for anything else: he was concerned with the irresistible urge to satisfy a human need – sleep. He really was sleeping. Weierother, with the gesture of a man too busy to waste even a minute of his time, began reading the dispositions for the following day in a brusque, loud, monotonous tone of voice, under the title, which he also read out: "Dispositions for an attack on the enemy's positions at the rear of Kobelnitz and Sokolnitz, 20th November 1805."

The dispositions were very complicated and difficult. In the original dispositions it said: "Since the enemy's left wing abuts on hills covered with forest, and his right wing extends along Kobelnitz and Sokolnitz, at the rear of the ponds located there, while we, on the contrary, outflank his right wing with our left, it is advantageous for us to attack this latter wing of the enemy, especially if we occupy the villages of Sokolnitz and Kobelnitz, thereby placing ourselves in a position to attack the enemy's flank, and pursue him across the plain between Schlapanitz and the Thürassa Forest, avoiding the defiles between Schlapanitz and Bellowitz, which cover the enemy's front. For this purpose it is essential . . . The first column marches . . . The second column marches . . . The third column marches . . ." and so it went on, sprinkled with an incalculable number of names which General Weierother reeled off each time he stopped reading to point out all the various places on the map spread out before them. The generals appeared to listen to the dispositions with great unwillingness and lack of curiosity. The tall, light-haired General Buxhöwden stood there, leaning back against the wall, with his eyes fixed senselessly on a burning candle, seeming not to be listening and not even to wish it to be thought that he was listening. Directly opposite Weierother, gazing at him with glittering eyes wide open, sat the ruddy-faced Miloradovich in a militant pose, with his moustaches curved up and his shoulders braced high, hands on knees with elbows sticking out. He kept stubbornly silent, looking Weierother in the face and only taking his eyes off him whenever the Austrian commander stopped speaking. At those times Miloradovich looked round significantly at the other generals. But it was impossible to grasp the meaning of this significant glance. It was impossible to know whether he agreed or disagreed, was pleased or displeased with the dispositions. Sitting closest of all to Weierother was Count Langeron, his southern French face set in a subtle smile that did not leave it throughout the reading, during which he stared at his own delicate fingers that were rapidly rotating a gold snuffbox, decorated with a portrait, by its corners. In the middle of one of the longest sentences of all, he halted the rotary motion of the snuffbox, raised his head and, with an unpleasant politeness playing at the corners of his thin lips, he interrupted Weierother with an objection, but the Austrian general waved his hands angrily without interrupting the reading, as if to say: later, you may tell me your thoughts later, but for now be so good as to look at the map and listen. Langeron raised his eyes with an expression of perplexity and glanced round at Miloradovich as if seeking an explanation, but on encountering Miloradovich's significant but unfathomable glance, he lowered his eyes sadly and once again set to rotating the snuffbox.

"A geography lesson," he said, as if to himself, but loudly enough to be heard.

Przebyszewsky, inclining his ear towards Weierother with respectful but dignified politeness, had the air of a man engrossed. The short Dokhturov sat directly opposite Weierother with an assiduous, conscientious, modest air, obviously ignoring the awkwardness of the situation while conscientiously studying the dispositions and the unfamiliar locality on the outspread map. Several times he asked Weierother to repeat words that he had not heard clearly, and Weierother obliged.

When the reading, which lasted for over an hour, was concluded, Langeron, again halting his snuffbox's rotation, but avoiding Weierother's eyes, raised a number of objections, but it was apparent that the sole purpose of these objections lay in the desire to show General Weierother, who had read his dispositions with such great self-confidence, as if to pupils in school, that he was not dealing with a set of fools, but with men who could teach him a thing or two about military matters. When the monotonous drone of Weierother's voice fell silent, Kutuzov opened his eyes, like a miller awakening when the soporific sound of the mill-wheels is interrupted, listened to what Langeron was saying, then hastily dropped his head again, even lower, as if to say: "Ah, you're still talking about that nonsense . . ."

Attempting to insult Weierother's pride as a military author as caustically as possibly, Langeron tried to demonstrate that Bonaparte could quite as easily attack instead of being attacked and could, as a consequence, render all these dispositions absolutely pointless.

"If he could attack us, he would have done so today."

"You would appear to think he is helpless?" said Langeron.

"He cannot have more than forty thousand troops," Weierother replied, with the smile of a doctor to whom a nurse is trying to suggest a means of treatment.

"In that case, he is inviting his own ruin by waiting for our attack," said Langeron, with a smile of subtle irony, once again glancing round at Miloradovich, who was closest to him, for confirmation.

But obviously at that moment the last thing on Miloradovich's mind was what the generals were arguing about.

"*Ma foi!*" he said. "We'll see everything tomorrow on the field of battle."

Weierother smirked again, with a smile that said *he* found it amusing and strange to encounter objections and to have to demonstrate something of which he himself was only too well convinced, and of which he had also convinced Their Majesties the Emperors.

345

"The enemy has put out his fires and a constant commotion can be heard in his camp," he said. "What does this mean? Either he is withdrawing, which is the only thing we should fear, or he is changing his position." He smirked. "But even if he takes up a position in Thürassa, he will only spare us a good deal of bother, and all the orders, down to the minutest detail, will remain the same."

Kutuzov woke up, cleared his throat hoarsely and glanced round the generals.

"Gentlemen! The dispositions for tomorrow, or in fact for today, because it is already past midnight, cannot be changed," he said. "You have heard them, and we shall all do our duty. But before a battle nothing is more important than to get a really good sleep."

He made as if to get to his feet. The generals took their leave and departed.

# XII

It was after one in the morning when Rostov, sent to the commander-in-chief by Bagration, finally received the next day's dispositions, which had now been translated and copied out for delivery to Bagration, and he set out at a trot, accompanied by several hussars, for Posorzitz, our right flank.

The previous night Rostov had not slept at all, being in the skirmishing line of the avant-garde, and having been appointed Bagration's orderly only earlier that evening, he had been once again unable to get any sleep. He managed to doze while the dispositions were being written out and was distressed to be woken and told he could set off. He only came to properly when already sitting on his horse.

The night was dark and cloudy, the almost full moon was now hidden, now exposed, revealing all around him the cavalry and infantry, in which preparations were obviously in progress. Several times he was met by galloping adjutants and officers on horseback who took him for someone else and asked him what news or orders he was bringing. He told them what he knew and asked what they knew, in particular about the sovereign, whom he thought he might meet at any moment.

Having covered several *versts*, he attempted to cut his route short, lost his way and rode into the middle of the infantry's campfires. He rode up to one to ask his way.

The soldiers were not sleeping, and there was a large crowd sitting and standing around the brightly blazing campfire.

"Come on, brother, the Austrian will get everything I own anyway," said one soldier, hurling a painted chair into the flames of the fire.

"No, brother, wait, let me sit in style for a bit," said another soldier, grabbing the chair out of the fire and seating himself on it in a pompous pose, propping himself up on its sides. "Right, brother, tell me now, what do you make of me like this?"

"Lads, how can I get to the third division?" asked Rostov. (He did not ask directions by place-names, but by the names of the army units, since the army covered his entire route.)

The soldiers told him what they knew. One young soldier, after an obvious struggle with hesitation, said to him:

"Is it true, your honour, the battle will be tomorrow?"

"Yes, it's true. Why, do you feel keen? The sovereign himself will be in command," Rostov said joyfully, but his news did not bring any great joy. The soldiers said nothing. Moving a few steps away, Rostov stopped to listen to what they would say.

"What's up, don't he have enough generals, then?" said one soldier.

"Plenty, everyone knows."

"That's it, little brother, that time we went over the mountains with Suvorov," an old, hoarse voice began saying, "and, would you believe, little brother, we came up to the edge of a cliff, and there your Frenchie was swarming down below, and we grabbed our guns, sat on our arses and slid all the way down to him on the snow, and we thrashed away. Gave him a good hiding that time. That was all the same Bonaparte, that was."

"That one was even nastier, they say," said another voice. "Dunno where they'll put him when they catch him."

"As if there's not plenty of space in Russia," remarked another.

"Lookee, they're harnessing the wagons, must be time to move out soon."

The soldier sitting on the chair stood up and tossed it into the blazing campfire.

"That's right, don't let anyone have it. When the lieutenant comes out, I'll take his shelter apart too."

Rostov started his horse and rode on. After he had ridden two *versts* through a solid mass of troops who were still assembling in some places, and already on the move in others, a German officer, a convoy leader, rode up to him in the middle of the infantry regiment into which he had ridden, and asked politely if he knew German and, on receiving a positive reply, asked him to translate for the battalion commander with whom he was dealing. The battalion commander laughed when Rostov and the Austrian rode up and, without heeding Rostov, immediately addressed the Austrian, shouting at him as loudly as he could and repeating certain words of which he was obviously very fond: "*Nicht verstehen*, German, I don't understand sausage language, German." Rostov translated what the Austrian officer said, but the battalion commander, still laughing, repeated his favourite phrase to the German several times more and at the end told Rostov that he had known about the order the Austrian convoy leader was passing on a long time before, and it had already been carried out. The battalion commander also asked for news, and Rostov repeated what he had heard about the sovereign being in personal command.

"So that's it," said the battalion commander. "They're real swines, aren't they?" he said to Rostov. "Really, swines. Isn't that right, Mr Officer of the Hussars?"

"It's a wonder they don't get confused, there are so many of them," thought Rostov. He rode on. Instead of riding along the ranks of the troops, as he was already approaching the avant-garde, he moved further forward and rode along the front line. It was shorter that way. After galloping for about a *verst*, he let his horse take a rest and thought about his favourite subject for reflection – the sovereign and the possibility of getting to know him better. "What if I'm riding in the dark and he suddenly says: 'Go and find out what's happening there!' – I'd go anywhere, I'd go and find out and bring back the information. If he says . . ."

"Who goes there, speak or I'll kill you," he suddenly heard a sentry shout.

Rostov started in fright.

"Georgii, Olmütz, beams," he replied automatically, giving the password of the day. "They're so dull, it's strange they don't get them confused." He looked round and strained his eyes especially hard to the left, where the enemy was, and where he wanted to go, but it was impossible to see anything and that made him feel even more frightened.

The moon went behind the clouds.

"Where am I? Could I have ridden beyond the line?" thought Rostov. He began to feel afraid, he wanted to ask the hussar and he was ashamed. "They'll kill me and they won't give a damn. If they don't kill me today, they'll kill me tomorrow. Oh, that's bad. But I'm so sleepy, so terribly sleepy." He opened his eyes with an effort.

The moon came out from behind the clouds. On his left side he could see a shallow incline lit up and facing it a black hillock that looked as steep as a wall. On this hillock there was a white patch that Rostov simply could not make out: was it a clearing in the forest, illuminated by the moon, or a lingering patch of snow, or white houses? He even thought he saw something move across this white patch. But the moon hid again. "Someone will shoot from over there and kill me. I shouldn't have come," thought Rostov. "They'll kill me, damn it, if not today, then tomorrow, they'll do it. If only I could go to sleep, and see the sovereign. It must be snow, that patch – *une tâche, tâche*," thought Rostov. "But look, that's no *tâche*. Natasha, my sister, black eyes. Na – tashka . . . Won't she be surprised, when I tell her how I saw the sovereign! Natashka – take my sabre – *tâche. Nicht verstehen*, German, no." And he lifted back up the head that had sunk down on to the mane of his horse. "Yes, what was that I was thinking? I mustn't forget. They'll kill me tomorrow, no, not that, that's later. Yes. At – tack the *tâche*, attack. Attacking us. Who? Us hussars. But they'll kill me anyway. Ah, hussars and mous – taches. This hussar was riding along Tverskaya Street with a moustache, I thought about him too, right opposite Guriev's house . . . Old man Guriev. Am I really going to be an old man, nasty, nasty old man, little old man . . . But they'll kill me here, still young, anyway. Just as long as the sovereign doesn't stop loving me for that. But this is all nonsense. The important thing now is that the sovereign is here. The way he looked at me, and he wanted to say something, but he didn't dare . . . No, it was me who didn't dare. It's a pity they're going to kill me. I would have told him everything. The soldiers didn't say anything, they only burned the chair. But it's true, they'll kill me anyway. But that's all nonsense, and what's important is not to forget what that important thing was I was thinking. Yes at – tack the *tâche*. Yes, yes, yes. That's good." And his head slumped almost right down on to his horse's neck. Suddenly it seemed to him that he was being shot at and stabbed.

"What? What? Have they attacked, then? Slash them? What?" Rostov said, waking up and seeing a bright-red light before him the very instant he opened his eyes, and hearing the drawn-out cries of a thousand voices, which for the first moment seemed to be only ten paces away from him in the direction of the enemy.

"Must be getting his courage up," said the soldiers, pointing to the left. Far away, much further than it had seemed to Rostov at first, at the same spot where he had thought there was something white earlier, he saw lights spreading out along a single line and heard the drawn-out distant shouts of probably several thousand French voices.

"What do you think that is?" said Rostov, trying to calm himself and turning to the hussar.

"It's nothing, they're just celebrating, your honour."

The lights and the shouting continued for about a quarter of an hour.

"What on earth could that be?" thought Rostov, "are they attacking, or trying to frighten us, or do they think they've already defeated some-one? Strange! Damn them anyway. Now, what was that the sovereign was saying to me? Yes, yes. At – tack that *tâche*."

"Your honour, here's the general," said the hussar.

Rostov awoke and saw Bagration, who had also ridden out, with Prince Dolgorukov and his adjutants, to look at the strange phenomenon of the lights and hear the shouting of the enemy army, and Rostov met them there at the advance position and delivered the document to his commander.

"Believe me, prince," said Dolgorukov, "this is nothing more than cunning, he has retreated and ordered his rearguard to set fires and make noise in order to trick us."

"What business is it of theirs," thought Rostov, dropping with sleep, "it makes no difference."

"Well, perhaps," said Prince Bagration, "but we'll soon find out." And Prince Bagration ordered a Cossack squadron to be sent a long way round to the right of the burning lights. "If the noise and the fires are only in the rearguard that's been left behind, then the area to the right, where I am sending my Cossacks, should already be empty."

After a wait of ten minutes, during which the shouting and the fires continued on the enemy side, several rifle shots were heard in the quiet of the night in the area into which the Cossacks had ridden down and the Cossack squadron, which had been ordered to withdraw at once if it encountered the enemy, came riding uphill at a trot.

"Oho, so that's the way it is," said Prince Bagration, when he heard a shot. "No, they have clearly not all gone, prince. Till tomorrow. Tomorrow morning, we'll find out," he said, and set off back towards the house that he was occupying.

"Until tomorrow, tomorrow," thought Rostov, following the generals. "Tomorrow we'll see if they'll kill us or not, but today we'll sleep." And barely having dismounted from his horse, he fell straight asleep on Prince Bagration's porch, without even taking off his cap, with his head resting on the railings.

Had Nikolai Rostov's gaze been able to pierce the gloom of the autumn night in the direction of the enemy's glowing lights as he was riding along the front line, then at one point in the French advance positions, which were no more than a thousand paces away, he would have seen the following: stacks of infantry muskets standing in the darkness with no bivouac fires, but with sentries walking to and fro beside them, and behind the stacks, lying on the bare earth or on straw, French soldiers wrapped in their cloaks, and a tent standing behind the group of soldiers. Beside the tent stood a saddle-horse and a cavalryman. A young French officer emerged from the tent and called a sergeant. He was followed out by another Frenchman in an adjutant's uniform. The corporals called the men to muster, the sleeping soldiers stretched and stood up, and five minutes later they were clustered round the two officers.

"Soldiers! An order from the Emperor!" declaimed an officer, moving inside the close circle formed by the company.

A foot soldier held a tallow candle, shading it with his hand, to light the sheet of paper. The flame fluttered, flickered and went out. The officer cleared his throat as he waited for the candle. The soldier knotted a bunch of straw, attached it to a stick, lit it at the campfire and raised it above the officer's head, to give him light. As soon as one bunch of straw started to fade, another was lit, and the officer was able to read the whole of the Emperor's famous order without breaking off. While the soldier was knotting his bunch of straw, an adjutant spoke to the officer holding the order:

"That's where they are, right there, but there's no way of finding out what's happening over there," he said, pointing towards the Russians.

"The Emperor finds out everything," replied the infantry officer. "Attention!"

And he started reading the order with a certain bombast, as they do in the theatre.

During the reading, three mounted men rode up and halted behind the ranks of soldiers who were listening to the order. At the end of the reading the officer waved the sheet of paper above his head and shouted: "Long live the Emperor!" and the soldiers took up the triumphant cry in unison. Then one rider, wearing a three-cornered hat and a grey greatcoat, moved forward into the circle illuminated by the burning bunch of straw. It was the Emperor. Most of the soldiers saw his face. And despite the black shadow cast across his upper face by the three-cornered hat, they recognised him immediately and pressed round him, breaking ranks.

The shouting grew so strong it was impossible to understand how so few soldiers could shout so loudly. One of the soldiers had the idea of lighting another two bunches of straw in order to light the Emperor's face more clearly, and others followed the example of the first soldier until bunches of straw were bursting into flame along the entire line. The soldiers of the neighbouring companies and regiments ran towards the spot where the Emperor was standing, and the light of burning bunches of straw spread further and further along the line as the shouts fused together and spread further afield.

These, then, were the shouts and the lights which that night had so astonished not only Rostov, Bagration and Dolgorukov, but all the forward regiments of the Russian army that were already stationed on the field of Austerlitz.

We were seeking Napoleon and expecting to find him in full retreat. We were afraid we would not be able to catch up with him in time. Our army was moving in a hasty and disorganised fashion (but it proved far from possible to carry out in reality what had been thought through in such detail on plans and a map): and therefore at the beginning of the day, when we encountered the French before we had managed to occupy the position we were supposed to occupy, we had no position at all, apart from the one in which the dawn found us. But Napoleon, either having received information from traitors about our intentions or having guessed them, chose the best position in front of Brünn and, instead of retreating as we had assumed, he advanced the entire mass of his forces to the very line of his forward positions.

Those lights and shouts that had amazed our men the previous day were shouts of greeting to the Emperor and bunches of lighted straw held by the soldiers running after him as he made a tour of the forward positions, readying his regiments for battle.

On the eve of the battle in which we had thought to take him by surprise, the following order from Napoleon was read out throughout the French forces:

> Soldiers! The Russian army is advancing against us in order to avenge the Austrian army of the Ulm. These are the same battalions that you crushed at Hollabrunn and which you have pursued constantly since then to this place. The positions which we occupy are very strong, and while they march to pass me on the right, they will expose their flank to me! Soldiers! I myself shall command your battalions. I shall remain far from the fire if you, with your customary courage, inspire disorder and dismay in the ranks of the enemy; but if the victory is in doubt for even a moment, you will see your Emperor expose himself to the first blows of the enemy, for there can be no hesitation in victory, especially on the day when the point at stake is the honour of the French infantry, which is so necessary to the honour of its nation.
>
> Do not break ranks under the pretext of taking away the wounded. Let every one of you be imbued with the thought that we have to defeat these mercenaries of England who are inspired by such hatred of our nation! This victory will conclude our campaign and we can return to our winter quarters, where we shall be joined by new French forces which are assembling in France; and then the peace that I conclude will be worthy of my people, of you and of myself.
>
> Napoleon

And thus there was a double advantage of surprise on his side. Anticipating the advantages of our own position and our own surprise attack, we met his unexpected attack with no position at all. All this did not mean that the plan of attack drawn up by the Austrians was not very good, or that, by carrying it out to the letter, we could not have shattered Napoleon's right wing, held the centre and driven him back into the mountains of Bohemia, cutting him off from the Vienna road. All this could indeed have happened, if on our side we had had not only a certain number of troops, not only the very newest and most deadly ordnance, not only great order in provisioning the troops, and even the skill of our military commanders, but if we had also had on our side something that it is impossible to weigh, count or quantify but which everywhere, under all possible conditions of inequality, has always decided, still decides and will continue to decide the outcome of any battle – and that is the spirit of our army raised to its highest possible pitch.

It was a dark, cloudy night, with the moon occasionally showing its face, and the campfires blazed all night in both camps at a distance of five *versts* from each other. At five o'clock in the morning it was still completely dark, the forces of the centre, the reserves and the left flank were still standing motionless when there was the first stirring of movement on the right flank amid the columns of infantry, cavalry and artillery which were due to be the first to descend from the heights, attack the French left flank and drive it back into the mountains of Bohemia. Smoke from the campfires, on which things that were no longer needed were being thrown, made the men's eyes smart. It was cold and dark. The officers hastily drank tea and breakfasted. The soldiers chewed on rusks, beating out a tattoo with their feet to keep warm and huddling together round the campfires on which anything made of wood had been thrown, to warm themselves and have a smoke.

The Austrian convoy leaders scurried about among the Russian forces, for some reason provoking mockery, and served as heralds of the advance; as soon as an Austrian appeared beside a regimental commander, everything started moving. The soldiers left the campfires at a run to form ranks, stuffing their pipes into the tops of their boots, the officers walked round the ranks, the transport drivers and orderlies harnessed the wagons, loaded them, tied the loads in and at the command they set off, crossing themselves. There was the tramping of a thousand feet and the columns moved, not knowing where, and unable, because of the men surrounding them and the thickening fog, to see the new terrain they were entering.

A soldier moves along in his regiment like a sailor on his ship. No matter how far he might go or what strange and dangerous latitudes he might enter, the soldier always has the same comrades, ranks, bayonets and officers surrounding him, just as the sailor is surrounded by his own familiar decks, masts and cables. A soldier is rarely interested in knowing the latitudes in which his ship as a whole is located. But on the day of a battle, God knows how or from where, in the moral world of every soldier the same stern note sounds, resonant with the approach of something decisive and significant. The soldiers excitedly try to move beyond the interests of their own regiment, they listen, look and ask eagerly about what is going on around them. The fog became so thick that, even though day was dawning, you could not see ten paces ahead. Bushes looked like huge trees, level ground seemed like steep ravines and cliffs. Everywhere, on all sides, you might run into the enemy, invisible at ten paces. But the columns carried on moving through this same fog for a long time, moving down and up hills, passing gardens and fences, over new, obscure terrain, not encountering the enemy anywhere. On the contrary, now ahead and now behind, on all sides they were made aware that our Russian columns were moving in the same direction. It gave every soldier a warm feeling to know that there were many, many others going where he was, that is, somewhere into the unknown.

"Look, that was the Kurskies marched past," said voices in the ranks.

"It's mighty fine, little brother, the numbers of our troops as has gathered! Last evening I looked at the fires they'd lit, they went right on up, way out of sight. As good as Moscow!"

Although none of the column commanders approached the ranks or spoke to the soldiers (the column commanders, as we have seen at the council of war, were out of sorts and displeased with the action that was being taken, therefore they only carried out their orders and took no trouble to cheer the soldiers, despite the fact that the soldiers were marching merrily, as they always do going into action, especially offensive action). But after walking continuously through thick fog for about an hour, the greater part of the army was obliged to halt and an unpleasant awareness that disorder and confusion were taking hold ran through the ranks. Exactly how this awareness spreads it is very hard to say: but it is without doubt conveyed with exceptional steadiness, spreading rapidly, stealthily and irresistibly, like water across a hollow. If the Russian army had been alone, without allies, then perhaps much more time would have passed before this awareness of disorder became a universal conviction; but now, naturally taking special pleasure in attributing the cause of disorder to the muddle-headed Germans, everyone was convinced that there was an immense muddle going on and the sausage-eaters had caused it.

"What we stopped for? Have they blocked us off, then? Or have we run up against the French?"

"No, can't hear anything. They'd have started shooting."

"They wanted us to move out in a hurry, and we did – and here we are stuck like fools in the middle of a field – those damned Germans are always confusing things. Damned muddle-heads."

"What I'd have done is let them go in front. But they're probably pressing up behind. So we just stand here hungry."

"Well now, it won't be too soon. They say the cavalry's blocked off the road," said an officer.

"Agh, damned Germans, don't even know their own country."

"Which division are you in?" an adjutant shouted, riding up to them.

"The eighteenth."

"Then what are you doing here? You should have gone up in the front ages ago, you'll not get through now until evening."

"It's those stupid orders; they don't know what they're doing themselves."

Then a general rode by and angrily shouted something that wasn't Russian.

"Tafa-lafa – no way of telling what he's muttering about," said a soldier, when the general had gone past. "I'd shoot the lot, the scoundrels!"

"Orders were to be in place before nine, and we haven't even got halfway. There's orders for you!"

The cause of the confusion lay in the fact that in the course of moving, the Austrian cavalry, travelling on the left flank, had been ordered to cross over to the right. Several thousand cavalrymen were already moving across at the head of the infantry, and the infantry had to wait.

Up ahead a confrontation took place between an Austrian convoy leader and a Russian general. The Russian general screamed and shouted himself into a wild fury, demanding that the cavalry be stopped. The Austrian tried to prove it was not he who was at fault, but the top command. Meanwhile the troops stood there, feeling listless and losing heart. Finally, after an hour's delay, the troops moved forward and began walking downhill. The fog, which was dispersing on the hill, only spread still more thickly in the lower regions into which the troops descended. Ahead, in the mist, there came a shot, then another and, in the hollow of the river Goldbach, the action began.

Not expecting to encounter the enemy down there by the river, and having come across him accidentally, hearing no word of encouragement from their top commanders, and with the awareness that had spread through the troops that they had run out of time and, above all, being unable to see anything ahead or around them in the thick fog, the Russians moved forward, exchanging shots with the enemy haphazardly and sluggishly, then halted again, having received no immediate orders from their commanders and adjutants, who, being also caught in fog on unfamiliar terrain, were unable to locate their own units within the army.

Thus began the action for the first, second and third columns, which had gone down the hill. The fourth, where Kutuzov himself was, was positioned on the Pratzen Heights. Down below, where the action had commenced, there was still thick fog, while higher up it had turned clear, yet still nothing could be seen of what was happening up ahead. Whether all the enemy's forces were ten *versts* away from us, as we had presumed, or he was here, in this strip of fog, no one discovered until after eight o'clock.

# XIII

It was nine o'clock in the morning. The fog extended below in an unbroken sea, but high up at the village of Schlapanitz, where Napoleon was seated on his horse surrounded by his marshals, it was perfectly clear. The sky above him was a clear blue, and the immense sphere of the sun floated on the surface of the milky sea of fog like a hollow crimson ball. Neither Napoleon himself nor any of the French forces were any longer on the far side of the villages of Sokolnitz and Schlapanitz, beyond which we had intended to take up position and move into action; instead they were all on this side, and so close to our troops that Napoleon could distinguish cavalry from infantry among our forces with his naked eye. Napoleon was a little ahead of his marshals, sitting on the same grey horse, in the same greatcoat and hat he had worn the day before at the advance positions. That same impassive, unconcerned and majestic face was now illuminated by the bright light of morning. He gazed for a long time into the hills that rose out of the sea of fog, with the Russian troops moving across them in the distance, and listened to the sounds of shooting in the hollow. His suppositions had proved correct.

One part of the Russian force had already descended into the hollow towards the ponds and lakes, while another part was moving out of the Pratzen Heights, which he intended to attack and regarded as the key to his position. On that island consisting of two hilltops surrounded by the fog, with the village of Pratzen lying in the depths between them, he saw, both in the ravine ahead and on both sides of the village, gleaming Russian bayonets all moving in the same direction, towards the hollows, and disappearing into the sea of fog. From information received during the night, from the sounds of wheels and footsteps heard in the night at the advance positions, from the disorderly manner in which the Russian troops moved, from all his own suppositions, he could clearly see that the allies believed he was far ahead of them, that the columns moving near Pratzen constituted the centre of the Russian army, and that the centre was already sufficiently weakened for it to be attacked successfully. But still he did not start the battle.

For him this was a day of celebration, the day of his coronation. Just before morning he had fallen into a doze for a few hours and he had mounted his horse and ridden out into the field feeling well, cheerful and fresh, in that happy state of mind in which everything seems possible and everything is successful. He sat without moving, looking at the heights that could be seen beyond the fog, and his twenty-eight-year-old face bore that special hint of confident, well-deserved happiness that is seen on the face of a sixteen-year-old boy who is in love and happy. The marshals stood behind him, not daring to distract his attention. He gazed at the Pratzen Heights, then at the sun emerging from the fog. Once the sun had completely emerged from the fog and scattered its blinding brilliance over the fields and fog, as if he had been waiting just for this to begin the battle, Napoleon removed his glove and gave a sign to the marshals with his elegant white hand. They moved up to him, and he gave the order to commence the action. Accompanied by their adjutants, the marshals galloped off in various directions and a few minutes later the main forces of the French army moved rapidly towards those Pratzen Heights, which were being left ever more empty by the Russian troops moving down to the left and into the hollow, where the pointless exchange of fire was blazing ever more furiously.

Kutuzov rode out to Pratzen at the head of the fourth column, the very one that was due to take the place of Przebyszewsky and Langeron's column, which had already descended the hill. He exchanged greetings with the men in the forward regiment and gave the order to move, thereby indicating that he intended to lead this column himself. Having reached the village of Pratzen he halted, surveying the future field of battle.

Prince Andrei, one of the immense number of individuals who made up the commander-in-chief's retinue, stood behind him. That night Prince Andrei had had so many thoughts and experienced so many different feelings that he had not shut his eyes once and was now surprised at his own composure. This morning he sensed that his mental capacity could not exceed the bounds of observation and physical activity (he could see, note and remember everything without drawing any

BATTLE OF AUSTERLITZ ON 2 DECEMBER 1805
*Engraving by Bosque after the drawing by Charles Vernet*

rational conclusions, and he was capable of doing everything, but no more than that), and therefore he felt himself especially prepared for absolutely everything that a man can do.

It was after eight in the morning, the air was cold, but dry and sharp,

although there was no wind. On the heights, all that remained of the
night's fog was a hoar frost, turning to dew, but in the depressions it
remained spread out in a milky-white sea. Nothing could be seen in the
hollow to the left, into which our forces had descended, and where the
sounds of musket shot could be heard. The sky above the heights was
deep and clear and behind him on his right the immense sphere of the

sun was emerging from the fog. The sun seemed like a great hollow, crimson, spherical float, bobbing as it drifted on the sea of fog. Far ahead, on the other shore, where the enemy's army supposedly stood, the forest-clad hills could be seen rising out of the sea of fog. On the right, the Guards could be seen advancing into the region of fog, with their hoof beats and rumbling wheels and gleaming bayonets; on the left, similar masses of cavalry, infantry and artillery approached the sea of fog and bit by bit disappeared into it. Close beside him Prince Andrei could see the familiar and uninteresting figures of Kozlovsky, Nesvitsky and others. Ahead of him, on a low horse he could see Kutuzov's bent, stooping back.

On this day Kutuzov seemed to Prince Andrei quite different from the man he had known in his good moments. That covert lack of concern, that calm, quiet strength of an old man's disdain for other people and faith in himself which Prince Andrei loved in him were just not there. Today the commander-in-chief seemed jaded, downcast and irritable.

"Will you tell them at last to form up into battalion columns and march around the village," he said angrily to a subordinate general. "Can you really not understand, your excellency, that you cannot extend your line and defile through the village street when we are advancing on the enemy?"

"I was intending to deploy the front beyond the village, your excellency," the general replied. Kutuzov laughed bitterly.

"Won't you look fine, deploying the front in view of the enemy, very fine indeed!"

"Your excellency, according to the dispositions we still have to go three *versts* to reach the enemy line."

"The dispositions . . ." Kutuzov exclaimed bitterly. "Who told you that? Please be so good as to do as you are ordered."

"Yes, sir!"

"Well, *mon cher*," whispered Nesvitsky, who was standing there with his constant carefree, fleshy and amiable air, to Prince Andrei, "the old man's in a really foul mood."

An Austrian officer in a white uniform with a green plume galloped up to Kutuzov and asked on behalf of the Emperor if the fourth column had advanced into action.

Kutuzov frowned and turned away without answering and his glance fell by accident on Prince Andrei standing beside him. Noticing Bolkonsky, Kutuzov softened the angry, caustic expression in his eyes, as if acknowledging that this adjutant was not to blame for what was being done. And, without replying to the Austrian adjutant, he spoke to Bolkonsky:

"You go, *mon cher*, find out whether the marksmen have been posted," he said. "What are they doing, what are they doing!" he said to himself, still not answering the Austrian.

They had indeed forgotten to scatter marksmen ahead of the column, and on behalf of the commander-in-chief, Prince Andrei ordered the nearest officer to make good this omission.

The fog had already dispersed completely. It was now well after eight in the morning, and more than a quarter of an hour had already passed since Napoleon, whom we had believed to be ten *versts* away, but who had all the time been here, with his entire army, in this sea of fog spread all around us, gave his marshals the order to attack. The firing in the hollows on the left flank was already growing stronger, more frequent and distinct, and Kutuzov's horse and those of his retinue pricked up their ears and listened. But the commander-in-chief, his stout body slumped over his saddle in senile debility and his puffy cheeks hanging loose, sat there saying nothing, with his head lowered, and still he did not give the order for the fourth column that he was with to advance.

At around this hour, sometime after nine, the sounds of regiments greeting someone's arrival were heard in the distance behind Kutuzov and rapidly began to travel down the entire extended line of advancing Russian columns. It was clear that the person they were greeting was moving fast. When the soldiers in the regiment at whose head Kutuzov was standing also began to shout, he shifted a little to one side and looked round. Galloping along the road from Pratzen came what looked like a squadron of riders dressed in various colours. Two of them were riding side by side ahead of the others: one was in black uniform with a white plume, on a chestnut horse, the other in white uniform, on a black horse. These were the two Emperors with their retinue. Kutuzov, affecting the manners of an old campaigner in the ranks, ordered his troops to attention and saluted the Emperor. His entire bearing and manner changed. He assumed the air of an obedient, unreasoning subordinate. With an affectation of habitual refinement and respect, which obviously struck the Emperor Alexander disagreeably, he rode up, saluted and made his report.

An expression of displeasure flitted across the Emperor's young, happy face, like the barest wisps of fog in the clear sky. After his illness he was somewhat thinner today than he had been on the field at Olmütz, where Bolkonsky had seen him for the first time abroad; but there was still the same enchanting combination of majesty and meekness in his lovely grey eyes, the same capacity for different emotions on his thin lips with an overriding expression of good-natured, innocent youth.

At the Olmütz review he had been more majestic, but here he was more cheerful and energetic. He was somewhat flushed after galloping these three *versts* and, having halted his horse, he gave a restful sigh and glanced round at the equally young, equally animated faces of his retinue. Here were the handsome monkey Czartorysky, and the distinctive figure of Novosiltsev, and Prince Bolkonsky, and Stroganov – all handsome, elegant, richly dressed young men on beautiful, well-groomed, fresh horses that had barely broken into a sweat. The Emperor Franz, a ruddy-cheeked, round-faced young man holding his head, body and legs straight on his exceptionally beautiful black stallion, had a calm and handsome air. He looked around himself, saying nothing and holding his head high. He asked something of one of his white-clad adjutants with a significant air. "He must be asking at what time they set out," thought Prince Andrei, with a smile that he could not restrain, observing his old acquaintance with curiosity. Dashing young orderlies, Russian and Austrian, had been selected for the retinue of the two Emperors from Guards and line regiments. In the middle of them the Tsar's reserve horses, in embroidered horse-cloths of exceptional beauty, were led by riding-masters.

Like the sudden scent of fresh air that wafts in from the fields when a window is opened in a stuffy room, a scent of youth and energy and confidence in success arrived with these brilliant young men as they galloped up. Or so it seemed to Prince Andrei as he looked at them. There seemed to be such a powerful impulse in this glittering galaxy of youth, it was as if nothing could stand against it. Turning away from Kutuzov, the Emperor Alexander glanced across the field of battle, his gaze lingering especially at the spot from which musket shots could be heard, and he said something in French, with a smile of regret, to one of his retainers. Prince Andrei was certain, although he was out of ear-shot, that the Emperor had voiced regret that his position deprived him of the chance of being there, in the thick of the fire, where the fate of the battle was being decided, the place to which he was drawn by his inner feelings.

"Why do you not begin, Mikhail Larionovich?" the Emperor asked Kutuzov with a cordial smile, at the same time glancing courteously at Emperor Franz.

"I am waiting, Your Majesty," Kutuzov replied, leaning forward respectfully.

"We are not on Empress Meadow, Mikhail Larionovich, where the parade doesn't start until all the regiments have arrived," the sovereign said in mild reproach, again glancing courteously into the eyes of Emperor Franz, as if inviting him, if not to take part, then to heed what he said; but the Emperor Franz, continuing to look around, nodded his head.

"That is why I am not beginning," said Kutuzov, and a wrinkle of annoyance rippled across his face, "I am not beginning, sire," he said in a harsh, resounding voice, "because we are not on parade and not at Empress Meadow."

All the faces in the sovereign's retinue instantly exchanged glances and assumed an expression of displeasure and reproach. "No matter how old he is, he ought not, he absolutely ought not to speak like that," said those faces.

The sovereign looked into Kutuzov's eyes intently, amiably and considerately, waiting to see if he would say anything else.

"However, since you order it, Your Majesty," said Kutuzov, assuming once again his former tone of an obtuse, unreasoning but obedient general.

He started his horse and gave the order to advance.

The army began forming up, and two battalions of the Novgorod Regiment and a battalion of the Apsheron Regiment set off ahead past the sovereign.

Just as the Apsheron Battalion was marching past, the strange figure of a little general, quite striking in its pompous mobility, with no greatcoat, a uniform with decorations and a hat with an immense plume, worn askew, its corners to the front and back, bounded forward at a quick march and, with a dashing salute, reined in his horse before the sovereign. Bolkonsky did not immediately recognise this bellicose general with the glittering eyes and upraised face as Miloradovich, who had been striving so conscientiously not to fall asleep at the council of war the previous evening.

"God be with you, general," the sovereign said to him.

"*Ma foi, sire*, we shall do everything that is in our possibility to do," he replied in a cheerful, bold and triumphant tone, nonetheless provoking the gentlemen of the retinue into mocking smiles with his bad French. Miloradovich swung his horse around sharply and halted a little behind the sovereign.

The men of the Apsheron Battalion, excited by the sounds of firing and the presence of the sovereign, marched past their commander with a dashing, brisk stride.

"Lads!" Miloradovich cried in a loud, confident and jolly voice, evidently elated to such a degree by the sounds of gunshots, the anticipation of a battle and the sight of the gallant Apsherons, who had also been his comrades on the Italian campaign under Suvorov, that he forgot the sovereign was present. "Lads! This isn't the first village you have had to take," he shouted and, urging his horse forward, he galloped headlong away, again saluting the Emperor.

The sovereign's horse shied in surprise. (This horse, which had carried the sovereign at reviews in Russia, carried its rider here on the field of

Austerlitz, enduring the unthinking blows from his left boot and pricking up its ears at the sounds of shots in exactly the same way as it had done on the Field of Mars, without understanding the meaning either of the shots that it heard or of the closeness of the Emperor Franz's black stallion, or of anything that was said, thought or felt on that day by the person riding it.)

The sovereign smiled approvingly at Miloradovich's act of bellicose impropriety, and at what one of the Apsheron soldiers marching on the flank did. On hearing the general's shout, this soldier started and was about to shout: "We'll do our best", but then he evidently changed his mind, abandoned the idea and winked gallantly at Miloradovich as he galloped by. Bolkonsky last saw the Emperor with that smile on his face.

Kutuzov, accompanied by his adjutants, set off at a walk after the carabineers.

Having ridden about half a *verst* at the tail of the column, Kutuzov halted in front of Pratzen beside a solitary abandoned house (probably a former inn) at a fork in the road. Both roads went down the hill. Although the fog was already drifting over the depression in wisps and the sun was flooding the fields with bright, slanting light, the enemy could still not be seen, and the troops and officers were moving without haste, in anticipation of a clash. Kutuzov sent part of the Novgorod Regiment along the road to the left and a smaller part of the Apsheron Battalion to the right. He was talking with the Austrian general.

Prince Andrei, standing somewhat further back, observed the generals, Russian and Austrian, surrounding him, and the adjutants. Not one of them had a natural manner: he knew all of them, they all tried in exactly the same way to assume either a shrewd or a bellicose or casual manner, but not a natural one. One of the adjutants had a telescope and he looked through it.

"Look, look," he cried, "it's the French."

Two or three generals or adjutants began grabbing at the telescope, tearing it out of each other's hands, and all their faces suddenly changed, all of them becoming natural, assuming expressions of fright and bewilderment. Prince Andrei could see in their faces what was happening ahead, as if it were reflected in a mirror.

"It's the enemy ... No. Yes, look. It's them. It must be. But what is this?" voices said.

Kutuzov looked through the telescope and went across to the Austrian general.

Prince Andrei looked ahead and, down below to the right, he could see with his unaided eye a column of French ascending to meet the Apsheron Battalion that was no more than eight hundred paces away from him. The gun battery trundling at the front was removed from its carriages and opened fire, rapid musket fire was heard up ahead, and for an instant everything was hidden in smoke.

The memory of the brilliant attack at Schöngraben rose vividly in Prince Andrei's imagination. The French troops, in their blue coats and gaiters, had advanced in exactly the same way then and the Kiev Grenadiers had moved against them in exactly the same way as the Novogorod men and gallant Apsherons were doing now, closing on the French after their march past the sovereign. Prince Andrei could not imagine this attack having any different outcome from the one he had witnessed at Schöngraben and he waited confidently for the opening volley from the French, a cry of "hoorah" and then the French flight with our pursuit. But now everything was shrouded in haze, and the firing fused into a single sound, and it was impossible to make anything out. There were Russian foot soldiers running forward past the inn. That continued for no more than a few minutes. But then the firing ahead began drawing closer instead of moving away and to his great surprise Prince Andrei saw Kutuzov make what he felt was a gesture of despair. One wounded soldier ran past the inn with a scream of pain, a second, a third, and a crowd of soldiers ran past after him, sweeping Kutuzov and his retinue off the road. Increasingly large crowds of Russians and Austrians mixed together ran back to the spot where five minutes before the troops had marched past the Emperor. Bolkonsky looked around, not understanding, and not able to understand what was happening in front of him.

He tried to catch sight of Kutuzov's face, hoping to receive some explanation of what was happening in front of him. But Kutuzov, standing with his back to Bolkonsky, was saying something, speaking rapidly, with gestures, to a general standing nearby. Nesvitsky, who had been sent forward, looking flushed and beside himself, was shouting with a furious expression on his face that the troops were running back and imploring Kutuzov to get back himself, claiming that if the commander did not heed him, in twenty minutes he would be captured by the French, who were only two hundred paces away down the hill. Kutuzov did not answer and Nesvitsky turned to Prince Andrei with an air of fury such as the prince had never seen before and could never even have imagined him capable of.

"I don't understand," he shouted, "everyone's running, and so must we, or they'll kill us all, or take us like sheep."

Prince Andrei, scarcely able to control the trembling of his lower jaw, rode closer to Kutuzov.

"Stop them," shouted the commander-in-chief, pointing to an officer of the Apsheron Regiment who had gathered up his cloak and was running back at a trot with a crowd that was growing bigger and bigger with every moment. "What is this? What is this?"

Prince Andrei galloped after the officer and, overhauling him, shouted:

"Did you not hear, my dear sir, that the commander-in-chief orders you to come back?"

"Yes, well if you're so very clever, you try poking your head in there," said the officer rudely, clearly abandoning all notions of rank or lines of superiority in the grip of panic and fear. Just then one man from a group of soldiers ran at Prince Andrei and struck his horse in the chest with a musket-butt, clearing the way for himself and the crowd, that was still swelling as it continued to career on towards Pratzen, to the spot where the two Emperors were standing with their retinue.

The troops ran in such a dense crowd that, once caught in the middle, it was hard to get out. One man yelled: "Get out of it! Why are you blocking the way?" Another, turning on the spot, fired into the air. Someone else struck the horse that Prince Andrei was riding. Bolkonsky soon realised it was pointless even to think of halting these fleeing men and all he could do was get himself out of this crush, where at any moment he could be knocked off his horse, or crushed or shot, and join the commander-in-chief, with whom he might hope to die a worthy death. Forcing his way with enormous effort out of the deluge of men, he galloped round to the left through the bushes beside the road and, spotting the plumes of Kutuzov's retinue up ahead in the middle of an infantry battalion, he went to join them.

During his five minutes of absence everything in Kutuzov's retinue had changed. Dismounted from his horse, Kutuzov was standing with his head lowered slightly to the right of the road, beside the Novgorod Battalion which had not yet broken ranks, and he was giving an order to a general who was seated on a horse in front of him with his hand to his peak.

"Everyone you can catch, get them all here. Off you go! Tell General Miloradovich!" shouted Kutuzov. The adjutant galloped off towards the general without hearing these final words.

Surrounding Kutuzov were the gentlemen of his retinue, their numbers reduced by more than half. Some were on foot, some on horseback. They were all pale-faced and muttering among themselves, staring up ahead and constantly appealing to the commander-in-chief, begging him to leave. The eyes of every one were trained above all on a Russian battery that stood ahead of them to the left, firing on its own, with no covering force against the French, who were now no more than a hundred and fifty paces away. Just as Prince Andrei rode up, Kutuzov was remounting his horse with difficulty, assisted into the saddle by a Cossack. Once he was seated on the horse, Kutuzov's appearance underwent a change, he seemed to wake up, his thin lips folded together expressively, and his single eye glittered with an intense, clear gleam.

"Take them into a bayonet charge. Lads!" Kutuzov shouted to the colonel standing beside him and he set his own horse moving forward. The cannonballs flew incessantly over the heads of Kutuzov and his retinue with a strange whistling and, just as he set off forward, bullets came flying through the battalion and the retinue like a flock of birds, hitting a number of men. Kutuzov glanced at Prince Andrei, and this glance was flattering to Bolkonsky. In the brief glance that Kutuzov cast at his favourite and preferred adjutant, Bolkonsky read joy at seeing him at this decisive moment, and advice to take heart and be ready for anything, and something like regret for his youth. "For an old man like me this is easy, I can enjoy it, but for you, I feel sorry," Kutuzov's glance seemed to say. All this was undoubtedly only in Prince Andrei's imagination, which was teeming with a thousand subtle thoughts and feelings of unparalleled clarity, and yet he was only observing what was happening and not, at that moment, thinking about the very thing that he had thought about for so long and so agonisingly, about the moment having arrived for him to do something great or die young and unknown.

The battalion set off and, after waiting a few moments, Kutuzov set off after it, at a gallop. But before he had reached the battalion, Prince Andrei saw him clutch at his cheek with one hand, blood flowing out from under his fingers.

"Your excellency! You are wounded," said Kozlovsky in his dour, unpretentious manner, still riding alongside Kutuzov.

"The wound is not here," said Kutuzov, halting his horse and taking out a handkerchief, "but over there." He pointed ahead to all the advancing columns of French and the battalion, which had come to a halt.

In the same volley that had wounded Kutuzov, the battalion commander standing at the front had been wounded and several soldiers and the sub-ensign carrying the banner had been killed. The battalion commander had fallen from his horse. The banner swayed but its fall was broken by the guns of the soldiers next to it. The front rows stopped and several shots that were not ordered were heard in the ranks. Kutuzov pressed the handkerchief, reddened with blood, against his wounded cheek.

"Aaagh," Kutuzov bellowed as if from the pain. He struck his horse with his spurs and galloped into the centre of the battalion.

The only men still behind him at this point were Prince Andrei and Kozlovsky.

"For shame, lads, for shame," Kutuzov shouted with an involuntary note of suffering in his voice, letting his handkerchief drop.

But the soldiers only looked round in puzzlement.

"Forward! Lads!"

The soldiers were firing without shifting position, no longer advancing towards the battery, which had ceased firing and from which the French up ahead and our men behind were at an equal distance of no more than a hundred paces. But the French were advancing, and our men were standing still, shooting. It was obvious that the fate of the battle depended on who would make the more determined dash for those cannons.

"Ooogh," Kutuzov bellowed again with a note of despair and, glancing mechanically at his bloody handkerchief, he suddenly straightened up as if recalling his young days and his storming of Izmail and, his single eye glinting, he galloped forward. "Hoorah!" he shouted in a voice that obviously, owing to his weakness and the hoarseness of an old man's throat, did not express all the energy of his mood. Hearing his own voice and sensing his own physical powerlessness, he glanced round at the adjutants with the glittering downcast pupil of his good eye and a ferocious expression on his totally changed face, as if looking for help.

Kozlovsky was the first to reach him. Suvorov glanced past him and looked at Prince Andrei.

"Bolkonsky," he whispered in an old man's voice trembling at the awareness of his own powerlessness. "Bolkonsky," he whispered, pointing at the broken ranks of the battalion and at the enemy. "What is this?"

But before he had finished these words, Prince Andrei, also feeling tears of shame, fury and exaltation rising to his throat, had already moved forward in order to do what Kutuzov expected of him, the thing for which he had been preparing for so long. He started his horse, galloped round Kutuzov and, coming upon the fallen standard, he leapt down from his horse without himself knowing how, and raised the standard high.

"Lads, forward!" he shouted in a childishly shrill voice. The horse, sensing freedom, gave a whinny and with its tail held high, broke into a proud trot away from the ranks of the battalion. No sooner had Prince Andrei seized hold of the banner's shaft than ten bullets instantly flew humming past him, but he was unhurt, although several soldiers fell beside him.

"Hoorah!" shouted Prince Andrei, and he ran forward in the absolute certainty that the entire battalion would run after him. And he did indeed run only a few steps on his own. First one, then another soldier started moving until the entire battalion ran forward with a cry of "hoorah".

No one who knew Prince Andrei would have believed now, looking at his brisk, resolute run and his happy face, that this was the same Prince Bolkonsky who had dragged his feet and his conversations round the drawing rooms of St. Petersburg with such indolence, yet it really was he, the genuine Bolkonsky, experiencing at that moment the greatest joy he had ever experienced in his life. A non-commissioned officer from the battalion ran up and took the banner that was swaying in Prince Andrei's hands, but he was immediately shot down. Prince Andrei picked up the banner again, and setting it against his shoulder, ran forward, refusing to let the soldiers overtake him. Prince Andrei was now only twenty paces from the guns, running forward with his battalion under extremely intense fire from the French, running past the fallen all around him, but even now, at this moment, he did not think of what lay ahead, and all the surrounding impressions were only imprinted involuntarily in his imagination in clear, bright colours. He saw and remembered the minutest of details of the figure and face of a redheaded gunner, pulling on one end of a cleaning rod while a French soldier pulled on the other. A little beyond that soldier, in the middle of the four guns, he saw the same Tushin who had so astounded him at Schöngraben, standing there with a guilty and confused air. Tushin apparently failed to understand the significance of the moment and was smiling a stupid, pitiful smile, exactly the same smile as he had smiled while standing without his boots in front of the duty staff officer in the camp-trader's tent in the village of Grunth, as if he were amused by the comic nature of his position, and now he stood watching the French soldiers moving towards him with muskets held menacingly forward. "Surely they won't kill him before we can get there?" thought Prince Andrei. But that was the last thing that Prince Andrei saw and thought. Suddenly one of the soldiers closest to him struck him on his left side as if he had swung a stout stick at him with all his might. It was a little painful, but most of all it was annoying, because the pain distracted him from his observations, which had been so interesting just then. But then came something strange: his feet were getting stuck in some kind of hole, his legs were giving way and he was falling. And suddenly there was nothing at all apart from the high sky – the high sky with the grey clouds creeping across it – nothing apart from the high sky. "Why did I never see this high sky before?" thought Prince Andrei. "I would have thought differently then. There is nothing apart from the high sky, but even that does not exist, there is nothing except silence, peace and quiet."

When Prince Andrei fell, the battalion grew confused again and drew back, adding to the disarray of those at the rear. The crowd dashed up against the Emperors and their retinue, sweeping them away with it to the other side of the Pratzen Heights. No one could halt this flight, nor even discover its cause from the men who were fleeing. In the retinue of the two Emperors this panic-stricken terror, intensified yet more by uncertainty, reached such a pitch that within five minutes, out of this entire glittering retinue, there was no one left with Alexander except his physician-in-ordinary Villier and horse-master Ainet.

# XIV

The plan for the Battle of Austerlitz had been drawn up as follows: the Russian forces, with the fourth column – the one that the Emperors were with – at the centre, Buxhöwden's forces on the left wing and Bagration's detachment on the right, were supposed, by advancing their left flank and turning to the right, to form a right angle, one side of which would have consisted of the first, second, third and fourth columns, and the other of Bagration's detachment. The intention of the allies was for the enemy forces to be trapped within this right angle and attacked. But instead of waiting for the allies to attack en masse, Bonaparte forestalled them by attacking the very angle that was formed by the two lines of allies where they met on the Pratzen Heights and thus, by breaking through that angle, split the army in two, the greater part of which – our left wing – was located in the hollows, among the pools and streams. The attack made by our left wing was weak, uncoordinated and lacking in vigour, because, due to unforeseen circumstances, the columns had been delayed on the march and arrived several hours later than the time estimated. (It is always the case that the more shamefully a battle has been lost, the greater the number of unforeseen circumstances.) The result of all of these regularly repeated unforeseen circumstances was that these twenty-five thousand Russians were held up for two hours by Friant's single division of six thousand men, which gave Napoleon the opportunity to direct all his forces against the single point that seemed to him more important than any other, that is, against the Pratzen Heights.

At the centre, where all the Guards were located, the Austrian cavalry and the Guards reserve should have been stationed further to the right, but owing to unforeseen circumstances, the Austrian cavalry was not stationed in its correct position, and the Guards found themselves in the front line. The Guards advanced at the appointed time in impossibly ideal order with flying banners, music and incredibly impeccable dress. The massive drum-majors, twirling their sticks around and tossing them high in the air, walked ahead of the band of musicians, the cavalry officers pranced on their horses, each worth thousands of roubles, and the infantry marched modestly in their places, exactly as all soldiers do, maintaining step throughout the entire regiment and beating out a single rhythm. The Grand Duke Konstantin Pavlovich rode at the front of the Horse Guards in his white Cavalry Guards collar and gleaming gold helmet.

The Guards forded a brook at Valk-Mülle and halted after covering about a *verst* in the direction of Blasowitz, where the Prince of Liechtenstein ought to have been positioned. Troops could be seen ahead of the Guards, and our side initially took them for the Prince of Liechtenstein's column. The Tsarevich drew up the Guards infantry into two lines along an extended front: the Preobrazhensky and Semyonovsky Regiments stood in the first line, with the Grand Duke Mikhail Pavlovich Artillery Company ahead of their centre, and the Izmailovsky Regiment and Guards Chasseurs Battalion stood in the second line. On the right flank of each battalion there were two field guns. Located behind the infantry were the Life Hussars and the Horse Guards. According to the dispositions, the Austrian cavalry should have been stationed ahead of the Guards. Then suddenly a cannonball came flying from the direction of the forces that could be seen ahead and had been taken for the Austrians, throwing the Life Hussars and Horse Guards into confusion, and together with them the entire Guards detachment and its commander, the Grand Duke. The forces that could be seen ahead belonged not to us, but to the enemy, and he was not only firing, but advancing directly on the Guards, who were psychologically unprepared for action. Here at the centre those very same inevitable and yet unforeseen circumstances had forced the Austrian cavalry, which ought to have been stationed ahead of the Guards, to move away, since the area in which it had been positioned was criss-crossed with pits and gullies and it was quite impossible for cavalry to operate there; the consequence of *this* was that the Guards suddenly found themselves involved in the action without any warning and, as the military historians tell us, despite brilliant attacks by the Preobrazhensky Regiment and the Cavalry Guards, they were obliged to retreat in the greatest haste in the same direction that was being followed by other columns retreating from Pratzen.

According to the dispositions Bagration, with his right flank, ought to have been the last to strike at the enemy and complete his defeat, but after only a very short time it was observed that not only had the enemy not been crushed at all the other points, he was actually advancing, and therefore Prince Dolgorukov limited his actions to defence and retreat. As he had done at Schöngraben, Prince Bagration rode slowly in front of the rows of troops on his white horse; just as he had done there, he gave very few orders or instructions, and just as had happened there, the actions of his right wing saved the entire army, and he retreated in perfect order.

# XV

At the beginning of the battle Prince Bagration, reluctant to accede to Dolgorukov's demand to commence combat, suggested sending his duty orderly Rostov to clarify the question with the commander-in-chief. Bagration knew that the distance of almost ten *versts* separating one flank from the other meant that even if Rostov was not killed, which he was very likely to be, and he then found the commander-in-chief, which was extremely difficult, he could not get back before evening.

"And if I meet the Emperor before the commander-in-chief?" said Rostov, holding his hand to the peak of his cap.

"You may give the message to His Majesty," said Bagration hastily, before Dolgorukov could reply.

Rostov galloped off without thinking about the danger, beside himself with happiness. Having managed to grab a few hours' sleep before first light, he was feeling cheerful, bold and resolute, his movements were fluid and he felt confident in his own good luck: he was in that mood in which everything seems possible and easy. For the moment, he was not thinking about his previous night's dreams of being close to the Emperor, but they had been so vivid that they had left traces of an actual event in his imagination. Nor was he thinking at this moment of his own danger, or of his failure to approach the Emperor, and even less of the possibility of the general collapse of our forces. The sovereign was with his troops, it was a bright, cheerful day and his heart was filled with joy and happiness. "They sorted things out after all, they didn't get muddled up together," he thought, galloping round Uvarov's precisely drawn-up cavalry squadrons, which had not yet gone into action. He could hear shooting ahead of him in the distance, rending the fresh morning air at irregular intervals, two or three shots at a time, but they sounded like the irregular rhythm of threshing flails and did not arouse any unpleasant or frightening feelings. They were cheerful sounds. He could see masses of infantry on the move ahead of him. And just as yesterday night everything had seemed to be confusion, today he firmly believed that all of this had been thoroughly thought through, that every man knew his place and his job and no matter what might happen, everything would turn out well. The further he rode, the clearer the sound of shooting became and the less he could see ahead of him. As he approached the Guards, he noticed several riders who had split off and seemed to be galloping towards him. "The sovereign and Kutuzov must be near here," he thought, and set his horse in the direction of the riders. They were our Life Guards, returning from the attack in broken ranks, carrying something on a horse, something dead and bloody.

Rostov swung his horse to the left and galloped as hard as he could. "That is no concern of mine," he thought. "I have to find the commander-in-chief quickly, as quickly as possible." Before he had ridden even a few hundred paces a huge mass of cavalrymen appeared on his left, cutting across him and stretching right across the field, riding on grey and black horses, in white uniforms, armour plates, cuirasses and helmets, riding straight towards him at a brisk pace. It was an attack on the French cavalry by two squadrons of the Cavalry Guards. Rostov put his horse to full gallop in order to get out of the path of these squadrons, which were trotting faster and faster, and at full gallop could have crushed him. He could already hear the rumbling and jingling, the terrible rumbling and jingling that sound like a hurricane, of cavalry approaching, the Cavalry Guards were already more than half-galloping, scarcely restraining their excited horses. Rostov could see their flushed red faces, and the command "Full gallop!" rang out as he just managed to scrape past them. The Cavalry Guard on the extreme flank, a man of immense size, with broad cheekbones and a grim expression, raised his sword in a frenzy, as if to slash at him too. That cavalryman would certainly have felled Rostov and his Bedouin (Rostov himself seemed so small and weak in comparison with these huge men and horses), had Rostov not been sufficiently quickwitted to flick his whip in the eyes of the other man's horse. The heavy, dappled-grey, sixteen-hand horse, which seemed as confused and excited as its rider, shied away, flattening its ears, but the pock-marked Cavalry Guard swung his immense spurs and sank them into its flanks and the horse flicked its tail, stretched out its neck and dashed on even faster. The Cavalry Guards had barely passed Rostov when he heard their shout of "Hoorah!" and when he looked round, he saw their front ranks already mingling with enemy cavalrymen in red epaulettes who must be the French.

This was that brilliant Cavalry Guards attack that amazed even the French, and Rostov was horrified to hear later that out of that entire body of huge, handsome men, out of all those brilliant, rich young men on horses worth thousands of roubles, those officers and cadets, all so full of beauty, strength and life – out of the entire squadron only eighteen men were left after the attack.

Although he had barely avoided being trampled, Rostov nevertheless envied the Cavalry Guards. He envied them yet at the same time realised how many dangers still lay ahead of him and what great happiness he might and probably would feel (of that he was certain) when he spoke with the sovereign, and he galloped on without looking back, towards the left flank where he hoped, from what he had heard, to find the supreme command. As he passed the Guards infantry, he was not even thinking about his friend Boris, when he heard a voice calling him by name and asking how things were going in his detachment.

"It's a long time since I left, I think everything's all right," Rostov shouted back, reining in his horse.

"We ended up in the front line, though, brother," said Boris with an ambivalent smile on his flushed face.

"And did it go well?" asked Rostov.

"We beat them back," shouted someone else.

Rostov galloped on in high spirits.

After he had ridden past the Guards, he heard firing ahead of him on the road, at a spot where the enemy could not possibly be, the spot where our rearguard was located. "What could that be?" thought Rostov. "It's not the enemy. It can't be. They know what they're about," he thought, meaning the command in general. However, it cost him a serious effort to ride into that mass of troops where he could still hear shouting and see continuous gunfire.

"What's happening? What's happening?" asked Rostov as he drew level with the mixed crowds of Russian and Austrian soldiers running across his path.

"What's happening? What's happening?" The crowds of running men answered him in Russian, German and Bulgarian, not understanding what was happening there any more than he did.

"They fired at the Austrians," one man shouted. "Damn them, the traitors."

"You try sticking your head in. Got beaten? To hell with it."

The curses and shouts drowned each other out. Rostov had been ordered to look for Kutuzov at the village of Pratzen, and the hill at Pratzen and the German churches had been pointed out to him from the right flank. Now as he stood facing the church, he could not believe his own eyes as he looked at the French guns and troops standing round it.

Having learned from an officer that the Pratzen Heights had been taken by the French, whose battery he could see with his unaided eye, Rostov attempted to gallop round the running men and come out onto the line of retreat. When he emerged on to the main line of retreat, or flight, of the centre of the Russian army, he saw a picture of even greater confusion and disorder. Carriages and coaches of every sort, Russian and Austrian soldiers, troops of all kinds, wounded and dead – they were all creeping along in a tangle to the dismal sound of cannonballs flying through the clear sunny noon from the French batteries set on the Pratzen Heights.

"Where is the sovereign? Where is Kutuzov?" Rostov asked everybody, but could get no answer from anyone.

"Hey, brother! They're already long gone up ahead, they scarpered off quick," a soldier said to Rostov, laughing at something. Another man, obviously the orderly or horse-master of some important individual, informed Rostov that the sovereign had been carried along this road in a carriage at full speed about an hour earlier, and that the sovereign was seriously wounded.

"That's not possible," said Rostov, "it must be someone else."

"I saw it myself, your honour," said the orderly with a self-assured laugh. "I ought to know the sovereign by now, I think, the number of times I've seen him this close in Petersburg. He was sitting in his carriage as pale as could be, and Ilya Ivanich was sitting on the coachbox. He set those four blacks going and, my goodness, didn't they go thundering past us. I think I should know the Tsar's horses and Ilya Ivanich by now too, Ilya doesn't drive anyone else but the Tsar."

Rostov rode on in despair, shattered by the officious orderly's claims, hoping to find one of the commanding officers and, through him, Kutuzov. The news related by the orderly did have some foundation. The Tsar's coachman Ilya had indeed been seen hurtling past with someone pale in his carriage, but it was not the Tsar, it was the Knight Marshal Count Tolstoy, who had driven out, like the others, to admire the victory over Bonaparte.

"The commander-in-chief's dead," a soldier said in reply to Rostov's question. "No, it was that other one, what's his name, and Kutuzov went over that way to the village." The soldier indicated the village of Gostieradek, and Rostov galloped off in that direction, where he could see a tower and a church in the distance. What point was there in hurrying? What did he have to say now to the sovereign or Kutuzov?

"Don't go through that village, your honour, go straight over that way," a soldier shouted to him. "They'll kill you this way."

"Oh! What are you saying," said another. "How can he go that way? This way's shorter."

Rostov pondered and galloped in the direction that was shorter and more dangerous. "Ah, it's all the same now," he thought. He rode into an area where more men had died fleeing from Pratzen than anywhere else. The French had not yet occupied that area and the Russians – those of them who were still alive or only lightly wounded – had left it long ago. There were dead and wounded lying there in the field, ten or fifteen of them on every *desyatina* of ground, like stooks on good plough land. The wounded had crawled together into groups of two or three and the distressing screams and moans, which sometimes sounded feigned to

Rostov, grew louder as he approached them, as if they wished to arouse his pity. Some implored him to help them and asked for water, some screamed and swore, some groaned and wheezed hoarsely. Rostov noticed several soldiers who were not wounded removing the boots from dead men (boots are a precious item to soldiers) and running off at a trot, away from that terrible field. Rostov did not stop, not only did he not help, he did not even look at all the suffering men as his horse avoided them, squinting sideways. He was too fearful for himself, not for his life, but for the courage he needed, and which he knew could not bear the sight of these unfortunates. He was not afraid but, as happens with all men at war, an inner instinct forced him to pay no heed their sufferings, even to feel indifferent towards them, and that instinct also hid from view everything that surrounded him, so that he felt less sympathy for the death and suffering of these thousands of men than for a comrade's toothache in a calm moment.

The French, who had stopped firing at this field scattered with dead and wounded once there was no one left moving there, saw the adjutant riding across and, probably as a joke or simply to pass the time, aimed a gun at him and fired a few cannonballs. For Rostov the impression of those terrible whistling sounds and the dead men all around him fused into a single sensation of horror and pity for himself. He recalled his mother's last letter. "How would she feel," he thought, "if she could see me here now, in this field, and with the guns trained on me." However, not a single shot hit him and he completed his gallop to Gostieradek without mishap. There were indeed Russian forces there, jumbled together, but in very good order, and the French cannonballs could no longer reach him, and the sound of firing seemed to come from a distance. Here everyone could see that the battle had been lost and said so.

"The battle has been lost, but at least I am alive and unharmed," thought Rostov. "Thank God. But I still have to carry out my assignment." Whoever he asked, no one could tell him where the Tsar was, or where Kutuzov was, but they advised him to ride to the left behind the village, they had seen some of the top command there. After riding another three *versts* or so and passing the last Russian troops, Rostov saw two riders standing near a ditch that surrounded a vegetable garden on his left. One, with a white sultan on his hat, looked like a general, and for some reason Rostov thought that he knew him. The other rider, whom he did not know, on a beautiful chestnut horse, rode up to the ditch, urged the horse on with his spurs, releasing the reins, and jumped easily across into the vegetable garden. The earth merely scattered down the embankment under the horse's hind hooves. Swinging his horse round sharply, he jumped back again and turned politely to the rider with the white sultan, obviously suggesting that he should do the same. The rider, whose figure seemed familiar to Rostov and who completely engrossed his attention, shook his head and waved his hand in a gesture of refusal, and from this gesture Rostov instantly recognised his idol, his adored sovereign. Surely it could not be him, alone in the middle of this empty field. But just at that moment Alexander turned his head and Rostov recognised the beloved features that had etched themselves so sharply into his memory. The sovereign was pale, his cheeks were hollow and his eyes were sunken, but it seemed to Rostov that the charm and meekness of his features were only all the greater as a result. Rostov was happy to know for certain that the rumour about the sovereign's wound was untrue. He was happy that he had seen him and that he could, even must, approach him and speak to him, which was the supreme object of his desires. But just as a youth in love quakes in fearful joy when the longed-for moment has arrived and he stands facing her, alone, and does not dare to speak of the thing that he dreams about at night, glancing around in fright, looking for help or a chance to put the matter off and flee, so Rostov, having attained the goal that he desired more than anything in the world, did not know how to approach his sovereign or dare to do it, imagining thousands of reasons why it was inappropriate, improper and impossible.

"How can I! As if I am glad to take advantage of the fact that he is alone and dejected. Perhaps it is distressing and painful for him to show himself to someone he does not know at this moment of sadness and then, what can I say to him now, when the mere sight of him makes my heart sink and my mouth go dry?" Rostov had forgotten all the innumerable speeches he had made to the sovereign in his imagination, in the nocturnal solitude of his life in camp, ever since he had been smitten by a passion for him. But those speeches had for the most part been made under different conditions, they had for the most part been spoken at moments of victory and triumph and primarily on Rostov's death bed from the wounds he had received, while the sovereign thanked him for his heroic deeds and, as he died, Rostov had expressed to his sovereign the love that had already been confirmed in action. "And then, what am I going to ask the sovereign about his orders for the right flank, when I have ridden so far that I won't be able to get back before night? No, I definitely must not approach him. It might seem like a pretext for bothering him. Better to die a thousand times than receive a bad glance from him, or have him think badly of me." And with his heart full of sadness, almost despair, Rostov rode off at a walk, constantly looking back. Rostov had not taken into account the fact that there was one thing more important than all his reasoning, and he had not done that thing. The sovereign was exhausted, sick, downhearted and alone. He simply needed help, if only in order to cross the ditch that he could not bring himself to make his horse jump, or to send someone to look for his carriage and his adjutants.

While Rostov was reasoning in this way and sadly riding away from his sovereign, the Lithuanian German Count von Toll, the same man who had translated the dispositions on the eve of the battle, happened by chance to arrive at the same spot and, without considering any arguments at all, rode straight up to the sovereign, offered him his services, helped him to cross the ditch on foot, led his horse across and halted beside him when the sovereign felt tired and sat down under an apple tree. Rostov watched from a distance, with envy and remorse as Toll spoke ardently and at length to the sovereign about something, he saw the sovereign evidently break into tears, cover his eyes with his hands and press Toll's hand. "It could have been me in his place," Rostov thought to himself, and he galloped on in absolute despair, not knowing where he was going or why. His despair was all the greater for feeling that his own weakness was the cause of his grief. He could have, he not only could have, but he should have ridden up to the sovereign. It had been his only chance to demonstrate his devotion to him. And he had not taken it . . . "What have I done," he thought and, turning his horse, he galloped back to the spot where he had seen the Emperor. But there was no longer anyone there. There were only carts and carriages driving along . . .

He learned from a horse-master that Kutuzov's headquarters were located in the village to which the transports were going. Rostov rode after them. The horse-master walked in front of him, leading his horses. There was a cart following the horse-master, and an old man with bandy legs, probably a cook, waddling after the cart.

"Tit, hey Tit," said the horse-master.

"What?" the cook replied absent-mindedly.

"Are you feeling fit?"

"Ah, you fool. Pah!"

After they moved along for a little more time in silence, the same joke was repeated yet again.

# XVI

By five o'clock in the evening the battle had been lost at all points. Przebyszewsky and his corps had already laid down their arms. After being surrounded on all sides by the enemy, the Perm Regiment had been completely annihilated: its dead, wounded and captured amounted to five staff officers, 39 subalterns and 1,684 members of the lower ranks, and it had lost six field guns. The confused remnants of Langeron's and Dokhturov's forces were clustered around the pools and sluices and banks at Augest. By six o'clock, however, that was the only point at which intense heavy gunfire could still be heard, coming almost entirely from the French, who had posted numerous batteries on the slopes of the Pratzen Heights with the single aim of causing as much damage as possible, and were firing unerringly at the solid mass of Russians crowded around the pools over an area of more than four square *versts*. The Russians offered little response: most of their field guns had hurried forward, getting bogged down on the dykes and falling through the weak ice. In the rear guard Dokhturov gathered a battalion together, returned fire and withstood the attacks of the French cavalry so stoutly and successfully that those attacks soon ceased, especially as the day was declining into evening, dusk was falling, and it was impossible to win the battle any more completely. The full horror of the day was not seen either on the Pratzen Heights, which were scattered with uncollected wounded and dead, or in Przebyszewsky's column, where soldiers with tears of fury in their eyes, surrounded by their own dead and wounded, laid down their arms on the orders of the French, or in the hearts of men who had lost more than half of their comrades, or even in the soul of the Emperor who, humiliated, tormented by remorse and compassion, and physically ill, left alone with only his horse-master, had come to a helpless halt with a fever burning in his body, unable to travel further, so oppressed was he by the relentless impression of death and suffering, and stopped at the village of Urzhits where he lay down on the straw in a peasant hut in the vain anticipation of physical relief for his torments, at the very least a drop of wine, which could not be obtained for him, and which he was refused by the court retinue of Emperor Franz, who was in the same condition. It was not here that the full horror of the day was seen. The horror of the day was seen in full on the narrow mill dam of Auguest, where for so many years an old German in a cap had sat peacefully fishing with his grandson, who rolled up his shirtsleeves and ran his fingers through the silver fish quivering in the watering can – on that mill dam across which for so many years Moravians in shaggy caps and blue jackets dusted with flour had peacefully driven up in their two-horse carts loaded with wheat, leaving with their white loads of flour across that same dam, which was now so tightly hemmed in by cannons and soldiers that there was not a single space beside a wheel or under a horse's strapped girth into which a soldier had not crawled, and there was not a single face that did not express a degrading disregard of all human feelings and laws, and the awareness of nothing but a sense of egotistical self-preservation. Appalling things happened on this mill dam. At the rear, by the entrance to the dam, an officer's voice was heard shouting with such imperative determination that no one nearby could help but pay attention to him. The officer was standing on the ice of the lake and shouting that the guns and the soldiers must move on to the ice, that the ice was holding – and the ice was indeed holding him.

At that very moment the same general who had presented the soldiers for review near Braunau, and who was now sitting on his horse by the entrance to the dam, raised his arm and opened his mouth, when suddenly one of the cannonballs whistled so low above the heads of the crowd that everyone ducked: there was a plopping sound, the general gave a gasp and fell in a puddle of blood. No one even glanced at the general, let alone thought of picking him up.

"Onto the ice! Onto the ice! Come on! Turn round! Don't you hear! Come on!"

Suddenly, after the shot that had hit the general, innumerable voices were raised, as always happens in a crowd of people who have no idea what they are shouting about or why. One of the field guns moving on to the dam at the rear turned on to the ice, and crowds of soldiers instantly went scattering onto the ice from the dam. The ice cracked under one of the soldiers at the front and one of his feet slipped into the water. He tried to recover his balance and fell through up to his waist, the soldiers closest to him faltered in confusion and the gun driver stopped his horse, but they were still shouting from behind: "Onto the ice, why have you stopped, go on!" The soldiers surrounding the field gun waved their hands at the horses and beat them to make them move. The horses set off. A huge sheet of ice gave way and some of them started dashing forwards and some backwards, pushing each other under with desperate screams that no one could hear.

"Brothers! Dear lads! My own fathers!" cried an old infantry officer with a bandaged cheek, spitting out water after he had sunk in over his head and re-emerged on the surface. He grabbed hold of the edge of the ice, supporting himself on it with his elbows and chin, hoping to scramble out in a moment, but a soldier came running at the officer and stepped on his shoulders, then tried to drag him out and went under himself. And then other soldiers came running up and fell through and pushed each other under ruthlessly as they tried to scramble out. And still from the rear there was the same sound of shots that had been heard all day long, and cannonballs flew across the lake and high over the lake, adding to the confusion and horror.

# XVII

Prince Andrei was lying on Pratzen Hill, still at the same spot where he had fallen with the banner in his hands, losing blood and uttering faint, plaintive, childish moans, unaware that he was doing it. Some sound moved past close to him. He opened his eyes, surprised that he had the strength to do it, heard his own moaning and stopped it. He saw the legs of a grey horse right in front of his face. Glancing upwards with an effort, he saw a man towering over him in a three-cornered hat and a grey tailcoat, with an expression that was happy, yet at the same time devoid of feeling. The man was peering forward intently. Prince Andrei looked in the same direction and saw the pools at Augest, and beyond them the scene of the Russians moving across the dykes and the ice, which appeared from the hill like some beautiful, moving panoramic painting. The man was Bonaparte. He gave an order to his artillery officers and looked down to his right. Prince Andrei followed the movement of his glance. Bonaparte was looking at a dead Russian soldier, looking attentively at this single dead body, wearing the same unemotional expression with which he had looked at the living, as if he wanted to ask the dead man something, but he said nothing, merely examined him intently and even moved a little closer to him. The Russian soldier had no head, only red shreds of flesh extending from his neck, and the withered grass was drenched with blood: the soldier's hand was holding a button on his greatcoat in a strangely calm gesture, with the fingers bent. Napoleon looked away from him, back to the field of battle.

"A splendid death, a handsome man," he said, gazing at the Augest dam and turning back to the corpse. "Tell the twentieth battery to fire nothing but round shot." One of his adjutants galloped away to carry out the order. Napoleon glanced to his left and saw Prince Andrei lying there with the staff of the banner abandoned beside him. Some French soldier had picked up the banner and was carrying it off as a trophy.

"There is a young man who died well," said Napoleon, even though his mind was still on other things, and he immediately gave the order to tell Lannes to move Friant's division up to the stream.

Bolkonsky heard everything Napoleon said as he sat over him on his horse, he heard the praise Napoleon gave him, but he felt no more excited than if a fly had been buzzing above him: his chest was on fire, he could feel he was losing blood, and he could see the distant, eternal sky high above him. (At this moment he was thinking about his own life with a clarity that his thoughts had not possessed since his wedding.) He knew this was Napoleon, his hero, but at that very moment the person of Napoleon seemed utterly insignificant compared with what was happening between him, his soul and that high, eternal sky with the clouds racing across it. At that moment he did not care in the least who it was standing over him, whatever they might say about him – he was glad that these people had halted above him and wished for only one thing, for them to help him and return him to the life that he understood so differently now, the life he loved so much now and which he was determined to put to good use, if only destiny would give him the chance; he summoned his remaining strength to make some small movement and managed to move one foot feebly, which forced a groan of pain from his lips.

"Pick up this young man and take him to the dressing station," said Napoleon, and rode on further to meet Marshal Lannes, who was riding towards him, congratulating him on his victory.

Prince Andrei remembered nothing after that, he lost consciousness from the appalling pain of being placed on the stretcher, the jolting as he was moved and the treatment of his wound at the dressing station. He only came round later, at the end of the day, when he was carried off to the hospital, together with other wounded and captured Russian officers. The first words he heard when he came round were spoken by the officer of the French escort, who was speaking rapidly:

"We have to stop here. He will ride past in a moment, and it will give him pleasure to see these captured gentlemen."

"There are so many prisoners this time, almost the entire Russian army, he's probably sick of it already," said another officer.

"Oh, come now!" said the first officer. "They say this one is the commander of all Emperor Alexander's Guards." He pointed to a Russian officer in a white Cavalry Guards uniform, whom Bolkonsky immediately recognised as Prince Repnin, a man he had met in St. Petersburg society. Standing beside him was another young man, a Cavalry Guards officer. They were both wounded and both clearly trying to maintain a dignified and serious air. "As if it even mattered," thought Prince Andrei, glancing at them. Just then Buonaparte came riding up, smiling as he said something to the general riding beside him.

"Ah," he said, catching sight of the prisoners. "Who is the senior officer here?" He was told it was a colonel, Prince Repnin.

"You are the commander of Emperor Alexander's Horse Guards?" Napoleon asked him.

"I commanded a squadron," Prince Repnin replied.

"Your regiment did its duty with honour," said Napoleon.

"Praise from a great general is a soldier's best reward," was the reply.

"It is my pleasure to give you it," Napoleon responded and asked: "Who is this young man beside you?"

Prince Repnin said it was Lieutenant Sukhtelen, who was little more than a mere youth.

Napoleon looked at Sukhtelen and said with a smile: "He is too young to think of crossing swords with us."

"Youth is no hindrance to courage," Sukhtelen answered with bold animation.

"A fine answer," said Napoleon. "Young man, you will go far."

To complete the triumphant display of prisoners, Prince Andrei had also been displayed in the front rank for the Emperor to see, and could not have failed to attract his attention. Napoleon clearly recognised him.

"Well, and you, young man," he said to him, "how are you feeling?"

Even though five minutes earlier Prince Andrei had managed, with great effort, to utter a few words, he now gazed directly at Napoleon and remained silent. He thought again about the high sky he had seen when he fell. Everything that was happening seemed so insignificant to him at that moment. Those pompous, unnatural things Repnin and Sukhtelen had said seemed so stupid, even his own hero seemed so petty and insignificant, seen from close up, stripped of his vague aura of mystery, he seemed so insignificant with his petty vanity, compared with that high sky. In fact, everything seemed pointless and insignificant compared with the rigorous and exalted train of thought prompted by the weakness he felt from the loss of blood, the pain he had endured and the expectation that death was near. He thought about the insignificance of greatness, the pettiness of life, the meaning of which no one could understand, and the even greater pettiness of death, the meaning of which none of the living could understand or explain. That was what Prince Andrei thought about as he looked into Napoleon's eyes without speaking. The Emperor turned away without waiting for an answer, addressing one of his senior officers as he rode off.

"Let these gentlemen be cared for and taken to my bivouac. Let my doctor Larrey examine their wounds. *Au revoir*, Prince Repnin," and he started his horse and galloped off, his face beaming with the happy joy of a thirteen-year-old boy in love.

When the soldiers who carried Prince Andrei had come across the little gold icon hung round his neck by Princess Marya, they had taken it off him, but having seen how genteelly the Emperor had spoken to the prisoners, they hastily returned it. Prince Andrei did not see who put the icon on him or how, but suddenly it was there again, on its familiar fine gold chain, lying on his chest.

"How good it would be," thought Prince Andrei, glancing at the icon that his sister had hung round his neck with such heartfelt reverence, "how good it would be, if only everything were so clear and simple as it seems to dear, poor, kind Princess Marya. How good it would be to know where to turn for help in this life and to know that its meaning had been explained correctly to us, and to find succour even in death, in the firm knowledge of what we shall find there, beyond the grave. But for me, even now when I am dying, there is nothing certain in all this, except for the pettiness of all that I understand and the greatness of something else, something incomprehensible but supremely important."

The stretchers set off, and with every jolt he again suffered excruciating pain, his fever intensified and he became delirious. His feverish visions were rooted in dreams of a quiet family life, his father, his wife, his sister and the son he would have, the remorse he felt towards his wife and the tenderness he had felt on the night before the battle. But just as a quiet life and calm domestic happiness in Bleak Hills beckoned to him and he had achieved this state of tranquillity, Napoleon's little figure would suddenly appear, with its cold, condescending gaze, happy at the misfortunes of others, and Bolkonsky's chest burned, tormenting and nagging at him, robbing him of all the tranquillity and happiness he had been feeling.

Soon all these dreams blurred and fused together into the dark gloom of unconscious oblivion which, in the opinion of Doctor Larrey, was more likely to end in death than recovery.

"He is a nervous and bilious man," said Larrey. "He will not recover."

# XVIII

At the beginning of 1806, Nikolai Rostov went home on leave. He arrived by post relay sleigh during the night to find the house on Povarskaya Street still lit up. Nikolai had persuaded Denisov, who was also going on leave, to travel with him and stay at his father's house, and Denisov was sleeping in the sleigh after a heavy drinking session on his last night.

"Soon now, will it be soon? Oh, I can't bear all these streets, shops, bakery signs, street lamps and cabs," thought Nikolai, straining forward in the sleigh as if in that way he were helping the horses along. "Denisov, we're here! He's asleep. There's the corner now, and the crossroads where Zakhar the cabby stands, and there's Zakhar himself, with the same old horse. And there's the shop where we used to buy spice cakes. Soon, will it be soon? Come on!"

"Which house is it?" asked the driver.

"That house, the big one. Surely you can see? It's our house. Denisov!"

"What?"

"We're here."

"Oh, that's good."

"Dmitri," Nikolai said to the servant sitting on the box, "are there lights on in our house?"

"In your father's study. He hasn't gone to bed yet."

"Now, don't you forget to get out my new hussar's jacket. There might be visitors." Rostov felt his moustache. It was all in order. "All right, everything's fine. Right, get going. They've no idea we've arrived yet."

"They're bound to start bawling, your excellency," said Dmitri.

"Yes, well you can have a three-rouble tip. Off you go. Get going then!" he shouted at the driver. "Oh, wake up, will you, Vasya," he said to Denisov, who had slumped over again. "Go on then, three roubles for your trouble, go!"

Nikolai jumped out of the sleigh, he was already walking into the dirty porch of the mansion, but the house was as silent and unwelcoming as ever. Nobody knew, nobody had come to meet him. There was old Mikhaila in his spectacles, sitting weaving bast sandals out of narrow strips of bark.

"My God! I hope everything's all right! Good grief, it's too much, I can't breathe," thought Nikolai, stopping to catch his breath. "Mikhaila! What are you doing?"

"Oh Lord! By all the saints!" Mikhaila cried out loud when he recognised the young master. "Lord Jesus Christ, what's going on?" He began trembling in excitement and dashed to the door, then came back and fell on Nikolai's shoulder.

"Is everyone well?"

"Yes, thank God. They've just finished supper."

"Show me through."

Nikolai ran into the large dark hall on tiptoe. Everything was still the same, the same card tables, the same cracks in the walls, the same dusty chandelier. One servant girl had already seen Nikolai, and before he could reach the drawing room, something came rushing furiously out of one of the side doors and embraced him. Then another, and another. More kisses, more tears, more shouts.

"And I didn't know . . . Coco! My friend Coco! Here he is . . . Our very own . . . How he's changed! Candles, tea!"

"Denisov is with me."

"Excellent."

"Give me a kiss too."

"My dear. Mama. Prepare the countess."

Sonya, Natasha, Petya, Anna Mikhailovna, Vera and the old count embraced him, the menservants and the maids exclaimed and gasped. Petya clung to his legs.

"And what about me?"

Natasha had first pressed him against herself and kissed him all over the face, then jumped back from him, still clutching the flap of his hussar's jacket, and bounced up and down on the spot like a goat, squealing all the time. He was surrounded by loving eyes gleaming with tears of joy, all around him there were lips waiting to be kissed. Sonya, flushed scarlet, was also holding on to his hand, quite radiant as she gazed deeply, blissfully into this eyes. But above and beyond all of them, he was waiting for someone else. And then there was the sound of footsteps in the doorway, steps that were surely too quick to be his mother's. But it was her, in a new, unfamiliar dress that must have been sewn while he was away.

She ran, stumbling as she went, and fell against her son's chest. She could not lift her face and simply pressed it against the cold braid of his hussar's jacket.

Denisov, who was standing there unnoticed, began rubbing his eyes, which must have started watering from the cold.

"Papa, my friend Denisov."

"You're most welcome. I've heard all about you."

All the happy, exultant faces turned towards Denisov, with his shaggy hair and black moustache, and surrounded him.

"Dear Denisov!" squealed Natasha, who was still passionately excited. "Thank God." And the moment Denisov was pointed out, she dashed over to him, put her arms round him and kissed him. Everybody was embarrassed by Natasha's behaviour, even Denisov. But Natasha was so enraptured that she did not realise how improperly she had acted until much later.

Denisov was led off to the room he was to sleep in, but it was a long time before the Rostovs went to bed. They sat in a tight circle round Nikolai, gazing at him lovingly, rapturously, hanging on his every word, movement and glance. The old countess clutched his hand the whole time and constantly kissed it. The others argued as they tried to steal the places nearest to him from each other and fought over who should bring him tea, a handkerchief, a pipe . . .

The next morning the new arrivals slept until ten. Their room was stuffy and untidy, and the ante-room was a jumble of sabres, bags, sabretâches, open trunks and dirty boots. Two newly cleaned pairs with spurs had just been set by the wall. Their servants brought them wash-stands, hot water and freshly cleaned clothing. The room smelled of tobacco and men.

"Hey, Grishka, a pipe!" Denisov cried in a hoarse voice. "Wostov, get up!"

Nikolai rubbed his eyes, struggling to open them, and raised his tousled head from his hot pillow.

"Why, is it late?" and then he heard the rustling of crisp dresses in the next room and the whispering of fresh girls' voices and, through the gap of the slightly opened door, he caught a glimpse of something pink, ribbons, black hair, white faces and shoulders. It was Natasha and Sonya, who had come to enquire if Rostov was up yet.

"Get up, Coco!" he heard Natasha's voice say.

"Stop it, don't," whispered Sonya.

"Is that your sabre?" shouted Petya. "I'm coming in." And he opened the door.

The girls jumped back. Denisov hid his shaggy legs under the blanket with a startled look in his eyes, staring round at his comrade for help. The door closed again, and again there was the sound of steps and voices babbling outside it.

"Coco, come out here in your dressing gown," shouted Natasha.

Rostov went out.

"Why, how fresh and clean and smart you all are," he said.

"Yes, yes, it's mine," he replied to Petya, who was pestering him with the question about the sabre. Sonya had run away when Nikolai came out, but Natasha grabbed him by the arm and led him into the next room.

"Was that Sonya who just ran away?" asked Nikolai.

"Yes, she's so funny. Are you glad to see her?"

"Why, of course."

"I mean, very glad?"

"Very glad."

"No, tell me, really. Come on over here and sit down." She sat him down and sat beside him, looking him over from every side and laughing at every word he spoke, unable to remain calm and contain her joy.

"Oh, how good it is," she said. "Really good. Listen!"

"Why do you ask if I'm glad to see Sonya?" Nikolai asked, and under the influence of those warm rays of love, he felt his face relaxing for the first time in a year and a half into the pure, childlike smile that he had not smiled even once since he left home. Natasha did not answer his question.

"No, listen," she said, "you're a real man now, aren't you?" she said. "I'm terribly glad you're my brother. And you're all so . . ." She touched his moustache. "I want to know what you're like. Are you the same as we are?"

"Why did you ask . . ."

"Yes, there's a whole story to that. How are you going to talk to Sonya? Will you be informal with her or polite?"

"However it comes out," said Nikolai.

"Talk to her politely, please, I'll tell you why later."

"Why, what's the matter?"

"All right, I'll tell you now. You know that Sonya's my friend. She's such a great friend, I'd even burn my arm for her. Here, look." She pushed up her muslin sleeve and showed him a red mark on the soft skin of her long, slim arm, up near the shoulder (in a spot concealed by a ball gown).

"I made that burn to show I love her. I just heated up a ruler in the fire and pressed it against me."

Sitting there in his old familiar classroom, on the divan with the padded armrests, and looking into Natasha's recklessly excited eyes, Nikolai found himself back in the little domestic world of his childhood, and burning arms with a ruler to prove one's love did not seem absurd to him, he understood it and he was not surprised at all.

"So what are you saying?" was all he said.

"We're such great friends, such great friends! It's nothing, that ruler, it's nonsense; but we're friends for ever, and I know that if she's ever unhappy, then I shall be too. If she falls in love with someone, then it's for ever; but I don't understand that. I'll forget straightaway."

"Well then, what are you saying?"

"Well then, she loves me and you." Natasha smiled in that gentle, affectionate, radiant way of hers. "You know, you remember, before you went away . . . Well, she says you'd better just forget it. She said: 'I shall love him for ever, but let him be free.' That really is excellent, it is, isn't it, excellent and noble?" cried Natasha.

"I do not take back my word," said Nikolai.

"No, no," cried Natasha. "We've already talked about that. We knew you would say that. But that won't do, you see, because if you refuse to change your mind, then it's as if she said it on purpose. And then it turns out you're marrying her because you have to, so it all turns out wrong."

Nikolai was at a loss how to answer his little sister, they had thought the whole thing through so cleverly.

"Even so, I can't go back on my word," he said, but the tone in which he said it showed that he had gone back on it long before. "Ah, how glad I am to see you," he said. "Well, and haven't you been unfaithful to Boris?" he asked.

The discord between the two childhood friends, that had been expressed so clearly at their meeting during the campaign, the condescending, didactic tone that Boris had taken with his friend and also perhaps, just a little, the fact that Boris, who had only seen action once, had been awarded more decorations than Rostov and outstripped him in rank, all meant that, without actually admitting it to himself, Rostov now felt a dislike for Boris that was all the stronger for his former friendship. And furthermore, if Natasha and Boris were to part, for him that would be like a justification of his betrayal of his own relationship with Sonya, which he had found burdensome because it was a promise and a constraint on his freedom. He asked this question smilingly, as if he were joking, but he watched the expression on his sister's face carefully. But to Natasha nothing in life seemed complicated and difficult, especially the things that concerned her personally.

She answered merrily, without the slightest hesitation:

"Boris is a different matter," she said, "he's a firm character, but as far as he's concerned, I'd still say it was a childish thing. He could fall in love again, and I . . ." She paused for a moment. "And I could still fall genuinely in love. I fact, I am in love."

"You were in love with Fezzoni, weren't you?"

"No, what nonsense. I'm fourteen now, at my age granny was already married. Tell me, is Denisov a good man?" she suddenly asked.

"Yes, he is."

"Well, goodbye then. You get dressed. But how ugly your friend is!"

"Vaska?" asked Nikolai, wishing to show his closeness to Denisov by using his pet name.

"Yes. But is he a good man?"

"Very good."

"Come quickly and we'll have some tea. All together."

When he met Sonya in the drawing room, Nikolai blushed. He did not know how to treat her. The day before they had kissed, but now they felt they should not have done so, and he could sense that all of them, his mother and his sisters, were watching him quizzically and waiting to see how he would treat her now. He kissed her hand and addressed her formally, but their eyes spoke to each other lovingly, with no anxiety, but with happiness and gratitude. With her glance she asked his forgiveness for using Natasha as a messenger to remind him of his promise and thanked him for his love. With his glance he thanked her for the offer of freedom and said that whatever happened he would not stop loving her, because it was impossible not to love her. To Rostov's amazement, in the company of ladies Denisov was more lively, jolly and polite than he had ever thought he could be. The old hussar charmed

389

everyone in the household, especially Natasha, whom he openly admired in front of everyone, calling her an enchantress and saying that his hussar's heart had been wounded more deeply by her than it had been at Austerlitz. Natasha jumped up and down, teased him and sang him some wonderful romances, of which he was extremely fond. He wrote her poems and amused the entire household, and especially Natasha, with his jesting infatuation for the jolly fourteen-year-old girl, which in his heart of hearts was perhaps not entirely a jest. Natasha glowed with happiness, and the praise and flattery quite obviously excited her, making her more and more attractive.

On his return to Moscow from the army, Nikolai Rostov was greeted by his family as the best of sons, a hero, the beloved Coco, by his relatives as a dear, likeable and respectful young man, by his acquaintances as a handsome lieutenant of hussars, a decent singer, an excellent dancer and one of the most eligible bachelors in Moscow. The whole of Moscow society was acquainted with the Rostovs, and in that year the old count was not short of money, because the forest had been sold and the estate remortgaged, and therefore when Nikolai returned home, having acquired his own trotter and his own fashionable breeches, boots and new pelisse embroidered with silver, which was the thing he was fondest of, when he measured his new life against the old, he experienced a fine sense of satisfaction. He felt he had matured and grown a great deal. He recalled the doll's wedding with Boris and the secret kisses with Sonya with scorn. He was preparing his trotter for a race now. The toes of his boots were pointed, only three other military men in Moscow had boots like that. He had a certain lady acquaintance on one of the boulevards, where he went late in the evening. He conducted the mazurka at the Arkharovs' ball, talked about the war with Field-Marshal Kamensky, was on familiar terms with Moscow's old fast-set.

He was occupied most of the time with his trotter and its fashionable horse-cloth, with boots and gloves in the latest fashion and ever new acquaintances with people who were always glad to get to know him. His passion for the sovereign had now abated, since he had not seen the sovereign nor had any occasion to see him. But the memories of that passion and his impressions of Wischau and Austerlitz were among his very strongest, and he often spoke of the sovereign and his own love for him, giving the impression that he was leaving something unsaid, that there was something else in his feeling for the sovereign that not everyone could understand. But then, at that time so many others shared Rostov's feeling that he could not possibly have forgotten it, and he often repeated the name given to Alexander I in Moscow – "The angel incarnate".

His most frequent sensations during the time he spent in Moscow were the feeling of tight-fitting new, lacquered hussar boots on his legs and new suede gloves on his freshly washed hands, the smell of the fixative on his growing moustache, and the sensation of haste and the anticipation of something very jolly, then of this expectation failing to come to anything, and then a new set of expectations. When he stayed at home, he frequently thought what a sin it was for him, with all his charms, to waste his time in this way, denying anyone the chance to enjoy them, and he was always hurrying to go somewhere. And when he missed a dinner, a party or a bachelor spree, he thought the place where he ought to have been was the very place where the especially happy event that he was supposedly anticipating would happen. He danced a lot, drank a lot, wrote a lot of verse in ladies' albums and every evening he wondered if he was in love with this one or that, but no, he was not in love with anyone, least of all with Sonya, whom he simply loved. And the reason he was not in love with anyone was that he was in love with himself.

# XIX

The following day, the 3rd of March, after one o'clock in the afternoon, the two hundred and fifty members of the English Club and fifty guests were expecting as their dear guest for dinner the hero of the Austrian campaign, Prince Bagration. When the news of Austerlitz was first received, Moscow had lost heart a little, but at that time the Russians were so accustomed to victories, they could not believe the terrible news coming from the army and they sought explanations in some exceptional circumstances that must have been responsible for this strange event. All of the nobility that had definite information and influence used to gather in the English Club, but in December, immediately after the news was received, nothing was heard there. Those who gave opinions, such as Count Rostopchin, Prince Yury Vladimirovich Dolgorukov, Valuev, Markov and Vyazemsky, did not appear at the club, but gathered together at each other's homes, in their own circles, evidently discussing the news that had arrived, while the Muscovites who repeated what others said, one of whom was Count Ilya Rostov, were left for a short while without any definite opinions on the matter of the war. They said nothing about it to each other, dismissed it with a joke, or timidly recounted the rumours. But after a little while the bigwigs had reappeared, like jurymen emerging from their conference room, to give their opinion in the club, and once again everything was stated clearly and distinctly. Reasons were found for that incredible, unprecedented and impossible event of the Russian defeat, and these reasons were invented, analysed, and amplified in every corner of Moscow. These reasons were: Austrian treachery, bad provisions, betrayal by the Pole Przebyszewsky and the Frenchman Langeron, and Kutuzov's incompetence, and, they also said in secret, the youth and inexperience of the sovereign, who had put his faith in bad and worthless men: but the army had been exceptional and performed miraculous feats of courage. The men, the officers and the generals were heroes. And the hero of all heroes was Prince Bagration, who had won fame and glory in the action at Schöngraben and in the retreat from Austerlitz, where he alone had not been routed. The choice of Bagration as the hero by Moscow was facilitated by the fact that he had no connections in Moscow, he was a stranger. In his person, due honour was paid to the simple fighting Russian soldier, with no connections or intrigues, the Russian soldier still linked by memories of the Italian campaign with the name of Suvorov, and the granting of such honours to him was the best possible way of expressing dislike and disapproval of Kutuzov.

"If Bagration did not exist, he would have to be invented." No one spoke about Kutuzov, and several even whispered that he was an old court intriguer and satyr. Dolgorukov consoled himself by discovering a reminiscence of former victories in our defeat and his words, "Your luck's bound to run out some time" were repeated all over Moscow, together with Rostopchin's statement that the French soldier had to be roused to battle with bombastic phrases and the Germans needed to be convinced by logical argument that it was more dangerous to flee, but the Russian soldiers only needed to be restrained and asked to go easy. On every hand there were ever new stories to be heard about individual examples of the courage of our soldiers and officers – this one had saved a banner, that one had killed five of the French, another one had loaded five cannon. People who did not know Berg said that when he was wounded in the right arm, he had grasped his sword in his left hand and marched onward. No one spoke about Bolkonsky, and only those who knew him well regretted that he had died young, leaving a pregnant wife and an eccentric father.

After one o'clock on the 3rd of March, all the rooms of the club were filled with the hubbub of voices in conversation, and like bees in a spring swarming, the club's members and their guests in their uniforms and frock coats, some still even wearing powdered wigs and kaftans, darted to and fro, sat, stood, met and parted. Powdered lackeys in livery with stockings and shoes stood at every door, straining to catch every movement of the especially important members. Most of these were venerable old men with broad, self-confident faces and sure movements.

The young men were especially noticeable in the corners, with officers including the slim, handsome hussar Rostov and Denisov. They were talking with their new acquaintance Dolokhov, whose Semyonovsky Regiment epaulettes had been returned to him. The young men's faces, especially those in the military, expressed that feeling of scornful respect for the old men which says that the future is ours, after all. Nesvitsky was there, as an old member of the club, and Pierre was there, grown stouter and haggard-faced, standing with a weary, almost miserable, indifferent air in the very middle of the room, apparently having forgotten to move off to one side. He was surrounded, as he was wherever he went, by the aura created by people who worshipped him and his wealth, but he treated them with contempt, as a man accustomed to ruling others. According to his age, he ought to have been among the young but, probably because of his wealth, he associated more with the old men. The most important old men stood at the centre of groups which even strangers approached respectfully in order to listen. The biggest groups were centred around Count Rostopchin and Count Naryshkin. Rostopchin was telling everyone how the Russians had been trampled by fleeing Austrians and forced to clear themselves a path through the fugitives with their bayonets.

"Ah, there he is," he said, turning to Dolokhov and beckoning to him. Dolokhov confirmed what Rostopchin had said.

In another place it was confidentially reported that Uvarov had been sent from St. Petersburg in order to discover the Muscovites' opinion about Austerlitz. In yet another, Naryshkin told everyone about the session of the Austrian council of war at which Suvorov had crowed like a cock in reply to the stupid things the Austrian generals had said. Shinshin was standing there and he tried to make a joke, saying that Kutuzov had clearly failed to learn even this simple art – crowing like a cock – from Suvorov, but the old men looked at him severely, making it clear that even on this day it was improper to speak of Kutuzov in such a way here.

Count Ilya Andreevich Rostov trotted about anxiously in his soft boots, from the dining room to the drawing room and back, greeting the important and unimportant in exactly the same rushed manner, but not forgetting to glance joyfully all the while at his slim young son. He went up to Dolokhov, shook his hand with a laugh, recalling the incident with the bear.

"Please do come and visit us, you know my young hero . . . you were there together, heroes together . . . Ah! Vasily Ignatievich . . ."

Just at that moment a servant with a frightened look on his face came dashing up to the count.

"He's arrived!"

Bells started to ring, the senior members rushed to the front: the guests who had been scattered throughout the various rooms drew together in a single heap, like rye shaken on a shovel, in the large drawing room, by the doors of the hall.

Bagration walked ahead of everyone else, wearing neither hat nor sword, according to the club's tradition, without his astrakhan cap or the whip across his shoulder, as Nikolai Rostov was used to seeing him, but in a new, tight uniform jacket with the Star of St. George and with his hair short at the temples (evidently trimmed only recently, for it altered his features for the worse), pomaded and awkward, as if he were more accustomed to walking across a ploughed field (as he had walked in front of the Kursk Regiment at Schöngraben), than across a parquet floor. There was something naïvely festive about his face that combined with his firm, manly features to lend them a rather comic expression. Bekleshov and Count Alexei Uvarov walked behind him, politely ushering him ahead as a guest. Bagration hesitated, reluctant to take advantage of their courtesy, and finally walked through. The senior members greeted him with a few words about Moscow's hearty welcome for their dear guest and so forth, and then, as if they had now taken possession of him, they calmed down and turned to lead him into the drawing room, but it was impossible to get through the doors because of the numbers who had crowded there, crushing each other and peering over each other's shoulders at the hero, as if he were some rare animal. Count Ilya Andreevich, laughing more vigorously than everyone else and repeating, "My dear fellow", pushed a way through the crowd and led the guests in. They were given seats and then surrounded by the bigwigs. Count Ilya Andreevich pushed his way through the crowd again, making his way round the guests, and a minute later appeared with another senior member, carrying a large silver platter, which he presented to Prince Bagration. There was a poem lying on the platter. When he saw the platter, Bagration glanced round in fright, as if he were seeking rescue or assistance, but on seeing there was none to be had, he grasped the platter firmly with both hands and gave the count an angry, bitter look, as if to say: "And what else do you want from me? Torturer!" Someone obligingly removed the platter from Bagration's hands (it seemed as if otherwise he would have held on to it until evening and taken it with him to the dinner table) and drew his attention to the poem. "Well then, I'll read it," Bagration seemed to say, and he began reading with the same expression of serious concentration with which he read regimental reports. The author, Nikolev, took the poem from him and started reading it himself. Prince Bagration inclined his head and began listening in the same way as people listen to "Lord, have mercy on us" in church.

> Be thou the pride of Alexander's reign,
> Preserving our dear Titus on his throne.
> Be thou our doughty champion, our firm stay,
> Our country's guiding light, a Caesar in the fray.
> Napoleon, enamoured with his fame,
> Has learned to fear the bold Bagration's name,
> And dares not to rouse the Russian foe again.

Before Nikolev had finished the poem a stentorian footman announced: "Dinner is served!" The door opened, and from the dining room there came the rumbling strains of "Let victory's thunder now resound; rejoice, oh fearful Russian", and Count Ilya Andreevich shot an angry look at Nikolev when he carried on reading. Everyone stood up, indicating that dinner was more important than poetry, and again Bagration led the way to the table. Bagration was seated in the top place, between two Alexanders – Bekleshov and Naryshkin, which was a significant reference to the name of the sovereign. The three hundred men found their places in the dining room as naturally as water flows to the lowest spot. Those who were most important sat closest to the guest of honour.

Before dinner Ilya Andreevich introduced the prince to his son, who, he was firmly convinced, was more of a hero than Prince Bagration, and Bagration, recognising him, said a few awkward words, like all the other words he spoke that day. Count Ilya Andreevich beamed as he looked round, certain that everyone was as pleased as he was at this event, which he regarded as the most important of the day.

On that day Nikolai Rostov met Dolokhov, and this strange man astounded and attracted him, as he did everyone. Nikolai never left his side and, thanks to the introduction to Bagration, the two of them sat close to the centre of the table. Sitting opposite them were Pierre and his retinue and Prince Nesvitsky. Count Ilya Andreevich was sitting with the other senior members opposite Bagration and regaling the prince with food, acting as the very embodiment of Moscow hospitality. His efforts were not wasted. The dinners here were magnificent even during the church fasts, but even so he could not feel completely calm until dinner was over. During the second course the servants already began popping corks and pouring champagne. Count Ilya Andreevich exchanged glances with the other senior members. "There'll be a lot of toasts, it's time to get started!" he whispered, then took his glass in his hand and rose to his feet.

"The health of our sovereign the Emperor!" he declared, and instantly his kind eyes were suddenly moist with tears, the meaning of which he himself did not understand. Everybody got to their feet and they started playing "Let victory's thunder..." again, and everybody cried out "hoorah", and Bagration cried "hoorah" in the same voice that had sounded over the battlefield at Schöngraben. Nikolai's rapturous voice could be heard above all the other three hundred. He was almost crying. He drained his glass in a single gulp and dashed it to the ground. Many followed his example. No sooner had the voices of the guests died away and the servants picked up the broken glass, and everyone begun to resume their seats, talking with the far end of the table, smiling even as they shouted, than Ilya Andreevich rose to his feet again and proposed a toast for the health of the hero, Prince Bagration, and his eyes became even more moist. They cried "hoorah" again and instead of the orchestra there was the sound of the choir, singing the Pavel Ivanovich Kutuzov cantata:

> No hindrance bars the Russian's path,
> Courage brings victory in the field.
> Bagrations inspire in us our faith,
> And all our foes shall kneel and yield.

Immediately the choir finished singing, there followed more and more toasts, at which Count Ilya Andreevich shed more and more tears, and there was yet more breaking of glasses and shouting. They drank for the health of Bekleshov, Naryshkin, Uvarov, Dolgorukov, Apraksin and Valuev, for the health of the senior members, for the health of the master of ceremonies, for the health of all the members of the club.

Pierre sat opposite Dolokhov and Nikolai Rostov, and in his heart Nikolai could not help laughing at this rich young man's strange appearance. When he was not eating, Pierre sat there, squinting and frowning at the first face he happened to see and picking his nose with a perfectly absent-minded air. He had never had the air of a smart young man, but at least previously he had been benevolent and jovial, whereas now his face expressed apathy and weariness. In Rostov's eyes he looked like an idiot.

While Nikolai watched Pierre, amazed at the stupid figure he cut, Pierre was arguing that the battle of Austerlitz had been conducted wrongly and the right flank ought to have been attacked. At the same moment Rostov, speaking with the man next to him, said: "No one saw the battle of Austerlitz better from every side than I did."

"Tell me," Pierre suddenly said to him, "why on earth, after our centre had been breached, were we not able to catch the enemy in a crossfire?"

"Because there was no one to give the order," said Dolokhov, answering for Rostov. "You'd do very well in a war," he added.

Rostov and Dolokhov laughed. Pierre hurriedly turned away from them. When they drank the health of the sovereign, he was so deep in thought that he failed to stand up, and his neighbour nudged him. He drained his glass and stood up, looking around. He waited for everyone to sit down, then sat down himself, glanced at Dolokhov and flushed. After the official toasts Dolokhov proposed a toast for beautiful women to Rostov and turned to Pierre with a serious expression, but with a faint smile in the corners of his mouth. Pierre drank absent-mindedly without looking at Dolokhov. The servant who was distributing the words of the Kutuzov Cantata set a sheet in front of Pierre, as one of the more honoured guests. He was just picking it up when Dolokhov grabbed it out of his hand and began reading it. Pierre leaned his entire corpulent body across the table.

"Give me it. That's impolite," he shouted.

"Let it be, count," whispered Bezukhov's neighbour, who knew Dolokhov to be a duellist. Dolokhov looked at Pierre in surprise, with the same smile but quite different eyes – bright, merry and cruel – as if he were saying: "Now that I like."

"I won't," he said quite clearly.

Pierre suddenly started breathing noisily, as if sobs were choking his throat.

"You . . . you . . . blackguard! I challenge you," he said, and neither Nesvitsky nor the man on his other side could restrain him. He got up from the table. Right there and then in the club, Rostov, who had agreed to be a second, settled the terms of the duel with Bezukhov's second, Nesvitsky. Pierre went home, but Nikolai and Dolokhov sat in the club until late in the evening, listening to the gypsy singers.

"He has nothing to gain anyway," Dolokhov said to Rostov. "He has an income of three thousand a year; there'll be a scandal in any case, and I'll end up with the excellent widow. Goodnight, till tomorrow at Sokolniki. But my instinct tells me I'll kill him."

## XX

The following day at Sokolniki Pierre, as absent-minded as ever, scowling and discontented, looked around him at the melting snow and the circles round the bare trees and the seconds, who were intently measuring out the paces. He had the air of a man absorbed by certain thoughts entirely unconnected with what was about to happen. And indeed, early that morning he had spread out his maps and devised plans for a new battle of Austerlitz, in which Napoleon was routed. Not only had he not taken his leave of his wife or anyone else, he had followed his usual habit of engrossing himself in intellectual activity, trying to forget about the present, only at rare moments recalling that today he was fighting a pistol duel with a famous shot, a duellist, and he himself did not even know how to shoot. When Nesvitsky arrived, he briskly reminded Pierre of what was about to happen and repeated what he had said the day before, trying to persuade Pierre that he had been wrong and, more importantly, rash in challenging a marksman like Dolokhov and giving him the first shot.

"I don't wish to interfere, but this is all very stupid," said Nesvitsky.

"Yes, terribly, terribly stupid," said Pierre, frowning and scratching his head.

"If you will only permit me, I will arrange things," the peaceably inclined Nesvitsky said with eager joy.

"What will I arrange?" asked Pierre. "Ah, yes, the duel. No, there's no point anyway," he added, "they've already made their preparations."

When the seconds made the final, classical attempt at reconciliation at the site of the duel, Pierre said nothing, he was thinking about something else.

"You just tell me where I should walk and how, and which way I should shoot."

When they told him he said, with a good-natured, absent-minded smile, "You know, I've never done this before." And he began asking them about how to press the trigger and admiring Schneller's clever invention. He had never held a pistol in his hands before. Dolokhov smiled cheerfully with his mouth, but there was a bright, harsh, insolent gleam in his handsome blue eyes.

"I don't want the first shot," he said, "what's the point of just shooting him like a chicken? Everything's already on my side as it is."

As an inexperienced second, Rostov agreed, delighted at his new friend's magnanimity.

They were given their pistols and told to advance to a distance of fifteen paces from each other before the count of twenty, each shooting when he wished.

"So I can already fire now?" asked Pierre.

"Yes, as soon as you reach the barrier."

Pierre took the pistol in his big, plump hand with timid caution, apparently afraid that he might kill himself, adjusted his spectacles and set off towards a tree. As soon as he reached it, he raised the pistol without aiming, fired and shuddered bodily. He even staggered a little at the sound of his own shot, then smiled at his own response. Dolokhov fell, dropping his pistol.

"Damned stupid bullet," he grunted through his teeth, pressing one hand against his side, which was bleeding.

Pierre ran over to him. "Ah, my God," he said, going down on his knees in front of him. Dolokhov glanced round at Pierre, frowning and pointing to his pistol: "Give me that." Rostov gave it to him. Dolokhov sat up on his backside. His left hand was covered in blood; he wiped it on his frock coat and propped himself up on it. "If you please," he said to Pierre. "If you please, go to the barr . . ."

Pierre moved across, hurrying in a courteous desire not to make Dolokhov wait, and stood directly opposite him, ten paces away.

"Sideways, cover your chest with the pistol, your chest," shouted Nesvitsky. Pierre stood there, peering at Dolokhov over his spectacles with a vague smile of regret. Dolokhov raised his pistol. The corners of his lips were still smiling and his eyes were glittering with spite and the effort of summoning his final ounces of strength. Nesvitsky and Pierre squeezed their eyes shut. They heard the shot and Dolokhov's despairing shout at the same moment.

"Damn that hand, it shook! Take me away! Take me away!"

Pierre turned and was about to approach Dolokhov, but then he changed his mind and went to his carriage, his face a wrinkled grimace. He muttered something all the way home, but he gave no answers to Nesvitsky's questions.

# XXI

Recently Pierre had only seen his wife at night or in the company of guests, of whom they frequently had a full house in both St. Petersburg and Moscow. On the night of the 4th of March he did not go to his wife's room to sleep, but stayed in his father's immense study, the same room in which the old count had died. He lay down, but could not sleep, and spent the whole night walking to and fro across the study. In his mind's eye he saw Dolokhov's face, suffering, dying, spiteful, but still with the affectation of some kind of bravado, demanding, implacably demanding that he must stop and think about the significance of that face and the part it had played in his life, and about all of his preceding life. The memories of the past that he recalled started from the time of his marriage, and his marriage had followed so soon after the death of his father (at a time when he was still very far from coming to terms with his new situation), that it seemed to him the two things had happened together.

"What happened?" he asked himself. "What did I do wrong? Yes, how terrible it is to remember how I said those stupid words after the dinner at Prince Vasily's: 'I love you.' I could feel it, even then I could feel it was wrong. And that's how it's turned out." He recalled the honey-moon, and he felt ashamed, as he had been ashamed at the time and all through that early period. And he found one vivid memory especially humiliating and shameful, of the time shortly after he was married, when he had gone into his study after eleven in the morning, wearing his silk dressing gown, and come across his senior steward, who had respectfully got to his feet, looked at Pierre's face and his dressing gown and smiled gently, as if he wished to express his respectful understanding of his principal's happiness. Pierre blushed every time the vivid memory of that glance came to him. He remembered it now and gasped. He recalled that he had still seen her as beautiful, that she had astounded him with her pride and composure, her ability to move quite naturally and elegantly in the highest spheres. That he had been astounded by her skill in managing a house while remaining a grand lady and setting the house on an aristocratic footing. Then he recalled how, having grown accustomed to the forms of elegance in which she arrayed herself and her home with such great skill, he had begun seeking for the content, and not found it. There was nothing behind the brilliant forms, they were her goal. And all the time her coldness had increased. He recalled how he had narrowed his own moral vision in order to find a point of view from which he could see something good, some kind of content, but there had been nothing and no one there. And she had felt no frustration at this lack. She had been satisfied, content in her fine damask drawing room, with pearls at her lovely throat. Her brother Anatole came to see her to borrow money and kissed her naked shoulders. She drove him away as if he were a lover. Her father jokingly tried to provoke her jealousy: she said with a calm smile that she was not so stupid as to be jealous and Pierre could do as he wished.

Pierre had once asked if she did not feel any signs of pregnancy. She had laughed scornfully and said she was not such a fool as to wish to have children and she would not have children by him.

Then he recalled the crude clarity of her thoughts and the vulgarity of the expressions she used: "I'm no fool; clear off", despite her upbring-ing in the highest aristocratic circles. Often, when he beheld the success she enjoyed in the eyes of men and women, both old and young, Pierre was baffled and could not understand why he did not love her. As he tried to recall himself during all this time, the only things Pierre could remember feeling were the blind numbness with which he had carried on, refusing to allow himself to be controlled, a feeling of surprise, indifference and dislike for her, and a constant feeling of awkwardness, of being out of place in the stupid position of a fortunate man who possessed a beautiful woman, even when he met his own valet as he came out of his wife's bedroom, wearing the bright, silk-embroidered dressing gown that she had given him. Then he recalled how, imperceptibly and independently of his own will, the conditions of his life had changed, how he had been drawn into the life of a young gentleman, an idle aristocrat, which he, having been nourished on the ideas of the French Revolution, had formerly condemned so strictly. Everyone, on all sides, took money from him, they demanded money from him and accused him of something. All of his time was occupied. The most frivolous things were required of him – a visit, a trip, a dinner – but the demands followed each other without interruption. And these demands were made so simply, with such assurance that this was how things ought to be, that the idea of refusing could not possibly have occurred to him. But then in St. Petersburg he had received an anonymous letter saying Dolokhov was his wife's lover, that Pierre's spectacles were clearly of no help to him. He had thrown the letter on the floor, then burned it, but he had thought about it constantly. Dolokhov really was closer to his wife than anyone else. When Pierre had come to Moscow, the very next day he had seen Dolokhov at dinner at the club – and now there was Dolokhov sitting on the snow in front of him, forcing himself to smile as he died with a curse on his lips.

Pierre was one of those people who, despite the appearance of what is called weakness of character, do not seek a confidant for their grief. He suffered his own grief alone, holding it inside. "Everything, she was to blame for everything, with no passion, no feelings, no intelligence, she was to blame for everything," he told himself. "But what difference does that make? Why did I get involved with her, why did I say those words 'I love you' to her, when it was a lie and something even worse than that?" he asked himself. "I am to blame and I must bear . . . bear what? The shame to my name, a life of unhappiness? Ah, it's all nonsense," he thought. "Louis XVI was executed because he was a criminal without honour. Then they executed Robespierre. Who is right, who is wrong? Nobody. If you're alive, then live. Tomorrow you will die, as I could have died an hour ago, as that Dolokhov will die, and is it worth suffering, when you have only a single second of life left, in comparison with eternity? I don't need anything. I'm content with just myself. What should I do?" And again the question came to him: "Why did I get involved with her? He recalled Molière's words: "*Que diable allait-il faire dans cette galère?*" and smiled.

In the morning, when his valet entered the study and was surprised to observe that the count had not gone to bed, Pierre, now calm, was lying on the ottoman and reading.

"The countess instructed me to enquire if you are at home," said the valet. But even before he had finished speaking, the countess herself, in her dressing gown of white satin embroidered with silver and her hair in simple Russian style (two immense plaits ran twice round her lovely head, forming a diadem), entered the room with an air of grand composure, but her lovely, marble-white forehead was wrinkled in fury. With her customary tact, that could endure anything, she did not speak in front of the valet. She knew about the duel and had come to talk about it. She waited until the valet had set out the coffee and then pointed him to the door with a grand gesture. Pierre looked at her timidly over the top of his spectacles, like a schoolboy caught misbehaving. In order to create a familiar situation, he began eating, although he did not want to. She did not sit down.

"How could you dare to do this?" she asked.

"I? What have I . . ." said Pierre.

"To do what? To compromise your wife. Who told you that he is my lover?" she said in French, in her coarse manner enunciating the word "lover", which turned Pierre's stomach, just as if it were any other word. "He's not my lover, and you're a stupid fool. Now I'm the laughing stock of the whole of Moscow because, when you were drunk and out of your mind, you challenged a man who had done nothing to you to a duel."

"I know . . . but . . ."

"You don't know anything. If you were cleverer and more amusing, then I would spend time with you, and not with him, but naturally I find it more amusing to be with an intelligent man than with you. You couldn't think of anything better than to go and kill a man who's a thousand times better than you."

"Stop," said Pierre, flushing and moving away from her. "That's enough. What do you want?"

"Yes, better than you. And it's a rare wife who would not have taken a lover, with such a husband."

"For God's sake, say no more, *madame*, we had better separate," Pierre said in a imploring voice.

"Yes, separate – so that I am left with nothing but the shame of being abandoned by my husband? No one knows what that husband is like."

Hélène was red, with an expression of malice in her eyes that Pierre had never seen before.

"Separate?" she continued. "We can, by all means, but only if you give me the whole fortune. I'm pregnant. And not from you."

"A-agh! Go away, or I'll kill you!" Pierre shouted. His face suddenly became entirely his father's, and with a strength he had never known before, he grabbed the marble slab off the table, took a step forward and brandished it at her. Hélène suddenly began sobbing. Her face contorted, she turned and ran. Pierre dropped the slab, seized hold of his hair and began walking round the room. A week later Pierre gave his wife power of attorney to manage all the estates in Russia proper, which amounted to more than half of the entire fortune, and set out to St. Petersburg on his own.

## XXII

Two months had passed since Bleak Hills received news of the battle of Austerlitz and the death of Prince Andrei. Despite all the searches, his body had not been found, and despite all the letters sent via embassies, he had not been found listed among the prisoners. Worst of all, there was still some hope that he might have been picked up on the battlefield by local people and be lying somewhere, recovering or dying alone among strangers, unable to pass on any news about himself. The newspapers, from which the old prince had first learned about the defeat at Austerlitz, had written in an extremely brief and vague manner that the Russians had been obliged to retreat, but had retreated in good order. However this official report had been enough for the old prince to realise what had happened, and although he still knew nothing about his son, he had been shattered by the news. He had not left his study for three whole days and Tikhon had seen him writing letters every day, all day long, and sending heaps of envelopes to the post, addressed to everyone who was of any importance. He went to bed at his usual time, but when the diligent Tikhon rose from his thick felt mat in the servants' room and stole across to the door of the study, he could hear the old prince rummaging about in the darkness and walking around in his room, grunting and muttering something to himself.

A week after the newspaper that had brought the news of the battle of Austerlitz, a letter arrived from Kutuzov, who had not waited to be asked before informing the prince of the fate that had overtaken his son.

"Before my eyes," Kutuzov wrote, "your son fell, holding the banner in his hands, at the head of the regiment, a hero worthy of his father and his fatherland. As yet, despite all the measures I have undertaken, I have not been able to discover whether he is alive or not. I flatter myself and you with the hope that that he is alive, for if that were not so, he would have been among the officers found on the battlefield, a list of whom was sent to me via the truce envoys."

After receiving this news late in the evening, when he was alone in his study, the old prince did not say anything to anyone. The following day, as usual, he went for his walk, was taciturn with the steward, the gardener and the architect, and although he appeared angry, did not speak to anyone. When Princess Marya came into his room at the usual time, he was standing at the lathe, turning something, but, as usual, he did not look round at her. He began to turn his head towards her, but then seemed to change his mind.

"Ah! Princess Marya!" he suddenly said in an unnatural voice and put down his chisel. The wheel carried on spinning by inertia. Princess Marya remembered that dying squeak of the wheel for a long time afterwards, for it became fused with what followed. Princess Marya moved towards him and saw his face, and suddenly something inside her collapsed completely (it was her happiness, her interest and love of life – it was all gone in an instant) and a dark veil obscured her vision. She saw from her father's face, a face that was not sad, not crushed, but angry and struggling unnaturally to control itself, that a terrible misfortune was hanging just above her head and it would crush her, the worst misfortune in life, that she had not yet experienced, an irreparable, incomprehensible misfortune – the death of a person you love.

"Father! Andrei!" the inelegant, awkward princess said with such inexpressibly elegant and eloquent sadness and self-renunciation that her father could not bear her glance and turned away.

"He is gone," he shouted in a shrill voice, as if he wished to drive the princess away with this shout.

The princess did not fall, she did not faint. She was already pale, and when she heard these words, her face changed, but it did not change to express the worst thing – suffering – on the contrary, something began shining out through her beautiful, radiant eyes, as if some exalted joy had overwhelmed the powerful sadness that she felt. She forgot all her fear of her father (the strongest feeling in her soul). She went up to him, took him by the hand and pulled him towards her, raising her other arm to embrace his dry, sinewy neck.

"Don't turn away from me, let's cry together." There were tears in her eyes.

The old man pulled away from her angrily.

"The villains! The scoundrels!" he shouted. "To destroy an army, to destroy the men! For what? Go, go and tell Lise."

"Yes, I'll tell her."

Too weak to stand, the princess sat down in an armchair and cried without wiping away her tears. She visualised Andrei just as he was taking his leave of herself and Lise with that scornful air of his. She saw him putting on the little icon with an air of gentle mockery. "Did he believe? Did he repent of his disbelief? Is he there now?" she wondered.

"Father, tell me, how did it happen?" she asked through her tears.

"Go, go; he was killed in a battle in which the best of Russian men and Russian glory were led to the slaughter. Go, Princess Marya."

She stood up and went. But, mindful of her sister-in-law's condition, she suffered torments, trying to find a way to start and trying to conceal everything and unable to do either. Before dinner the prince sent Tikhon to the princess with a note to ask if the announcement had been made. When he received a reply in the negative, he went to her himself.

"For God's sake, father," cried Princess Marya, rushing at him, "do not forget what she is carrying inside her now!"

The prince looked at her and his daughter-in-law and went out. But he did not go to his own room, he closed the door of the small sitting room where the two women were and began walking backwards and forwards across the drawing room.

Princess Marya could not bring herself to tell Lise that morning, precisely because she had never seen Lise so subdued, kind and sad before.

When Princess Marya came back from her father, the little princess was sitting at her needlework, and she looked at Princess Marya with that special expression of inner, calm happiness that pregnant women have.

"Marie," she said, moving away from the sewing frame and slumping backwards, "give me your hand." She took hold of Princess Marya's hand and put it on her belly. Her eyes smiled in anticipation, the little lip with the little moustache rose and stayed there in such a childishly happy fashion. "He's stopped, you have to wait . . . there he is . . . do you feel it? How is he in there, the tiny little thing? If only I weren't so afraid, Marie. But I'll love him anyway. I'll love him very, very much. What is it? What's wrong with you?"

Marie fell on her knees and sobbed. She said she was suddenly feeling very sad about Andrei, yet still she could not bring herself to tell the truth. Several times during the morning she began to cry. These tears, the cause of which Marie did not explain, alarmed Lise, even though she was so unobservant. She did not say anything, but kept glancing around anxiously, as if she were looking for something. And when the old prince, of whom she had always been so afraid, came in, with the agitated, angry expression that he was wearing now, she understood everything. She threw herself at Marie, no longer asking her what was wrong, but asking her, begging her to say that Andrei was alive, that it wasn't true, but Princess Marya could not tell her that. Lise cried out and fell down in a faint. The old prince opened the door, glanced at her and then, as if he was convinced that the operation was over, he withdrew to his study, and after that only emerged in the mornings for his walk, but did not go to the drawing room or the dining room. The lessons in mathematics continued. Tikhon could hear that the prince was not sleeping, and his strength suddenly deserted him. He lost weight, turned yellow and seemed to start puffing up somehow, and in the mornings he began to suffer more often from moments of fury, when he did not realise what he was doing, and he would go running to his room, accompanied by nobody but Tikhon, whom he beat more often than previously, but who was the only person he spoke to in the evenings, ordering him to sit down and tell him what was going on among the servants and in the village. The old prince did not want to hope, he informed everyone that Prince Andrei had been killed, he ordered a gravestone for his son and selected a spot in the garden for it, but he was still hoping nonetheless, and he sent a state official to Austria to search for traces of Prince Andrei. He waited and he hoped, and therefore he suffered more than everyone else. Princess Marya and Lise each suffered her grief in her own way. Although Lise was physically unharmed by her suffering, her spirit was broken and she said she knew she would die in childbirth.

Princess Marya prayed to God, looked after Lise and tried to set her father on the path of religion and tears, but it was all in vain.

Two months had passed since the news had arrived. The old prince was visibly pining away, despite all his efforts to take up his old life. The little princess's time was approaching. Princess Marya reminded her father of Prince Andrei's request concerning an obstetrician and a messenger was sent to Moscow with orders to bring the best there was.

## XXIII

"*Ma bonne amie*," the little princess said after breakfast on the morning of the 19th of March, and her lip with the little moustache rose, following her old habit, but now, in the same way as all the smiling and speaking and even walking in this house had been filled with sadness since the day the terrible news had been received, so the little princess's smile only served as an even more forceful reminder of the general sorrow.

"My little friend, I am afraid that today's 'frustik', as Foka calls it, might have disagreed with me."

"Why, what's wrong with you, my darling? You look pale. Ah, you are very pale," Princess Marya said in fright, running across to her sister-in-law with soft, heavy steps.

"Your excellency, should we send for Marya Bogdanovna?" said one of the maids who was present (Marya Bogdanovna was a midwife from the nearest town, who had been living there for over a week).

"Yes indeed," Princess Marya agreed eagerly, "perhaps, in fact definitely. I'll go. Don't be afraid, *courage, mon ange!*" She kissed Lise.

"Oh, no, no!" The pallor and physical suffering in the little princess's face were overlaid by the fear of inescapable despair. "No, it's my stomach . . . Marie, tell me it's my stomach . . ."

But when she saw the little princess begin wringing her hands and crying, Marya hurried out of the room.

"My God! My God! Oh!" she heard behind her, but even so she did not go back and ran for Marya Bogdanovna.

And there was Marya Bogdanovna already walking towards her, rubbing her small, plump hands, with a serious, calm face.

"It's all right, princess, don't be alarmed," she said.

Five minutes later from her room Princess Marya heard something heavy being carried along. She glanced out and saw some servants carrying a leather divan into the bedroom for some reason. There was something solemn and still in all their faces. The princess stayed alone in her room for a long time, opening the door or sitting down in her armchair, or picking up her prayer book, or going down on her knees in front of the icon case. But to her surprise and distress, she did not feel her prayer calming her agitation. She was tormented by the thought of how Prince Andrei had died, how he had ceased to exist and how and when the new prince, Nikolai Andreevich, would start his life. (Like everyone in the house, she was certain the child would be a son.) She sat down in her armchair again, opened her psalm book and began reading Psalm 104.

In every corner of the house, everyone was filled with the same feelings that possessed Princess Marya as she sat there in her room. Following the common belief that the fewer people who know about the sufferings of a woman giving birth, the less she suffers, everyone tried to pretend they did not know and nobody spoke about it, but nonetheless in all these people, above and beyond the usual staid and respectful manners that were the rule in the prince's house, there could be observed a single common concern, a softening of the feelings and an awareness that something great and incomprehensible was taking place at that moment. The old nanny, the old prince's wet-nurse and now a hundred years old, shouted angrily at the barefooted girl who served her for running into the room so quickly. Then she took out the young prince's wedding candle, told the girl to light it in front of the icons, closed her eyes and whispered something. A different nanny went into Princess Marya's room.

"It's all right, my angel, don't torment yourself, God is merciful," she said, kissing the princess's shoulder. "Pray. I'll sit with you." And she sat beside the princess.

There was no laughter to be heard in the large maidservants' room. In the menservants' room all the men sat in silent readiness for something. The old prince heard the bustle and sent Tikhon to Marya Bogdanovna to ask what was happening. Marya Bogdanovna came out of the room where screams could be heard, gave the messenger a serious look and said:

"Inform the prince that the birth has begun."

Tikhon came and reported to the prince.

"Good," said the prince, and after that, no matter how hard he listened, Tikhon could not hear even the tiniest sound in the study. Even though there was a candle burning, Tikhon went into the study, as if he was going to trim the candles, and saw the prince lying on the divan. Forgetting his fear, Tikhon looked at the prince's downcast face and shook his head, then moved closer to him without saying anything, kissed him on the shoulder and went out without trimming the candles or even saying why he had come. In the servants' rooms they burned torches of splinters and candles until late at night and did not sleep. The mystery, the most solemn in the world, continued to unfold. The evening passed and night began. And the feeling of anticipation and softening of the heart in the face of the ineffable grew not weaker, but stronger. Nobody slept. The prince emerged from his study and walked past everybody in the servants' room with his head lowered, into the dining room and then the sitting room and halted in the darkness. He heard distant groans from some door that was opened at that moment. He turned, walked back to his room with rapid steps and ordered the steward to be sent for. That very day they were expecting the obstetrician. The prince walked around his study, stopping all the time to listen for the sound of a bell. But he could hear nothing except the howling of the wind and the rattling of the window frames. It was one of those March nights when the winter seems to demand its due and pours down its final snowfalls and blizzards in reckless spite. The prince sent men on horseback with lanterns to meet the obstetrician and carried on walking to and fro. Princess Marya was sitting in silence, with her radiant eyes fixed on the flame of the icon lamp, when suddenly a wild gust of wind flung itself against one of her window frames (the princess removed the second frames every day very early in the morning), forced open the badly closed catch and set the curtain fluttering, bringing a chilly breath of white snow that blew out the candle. The Princess came to herself. "Yes, all that was lacking was the full horror of death," she thought. She stood up in fright. The nanny dashed to lock the window.

"Princess, dearest, there's someone driving down the avenue," the nanny said when she stuck her head out to catch the frame that had been thrown open, "with lanterns, it must be the doctor . . ."

Princess Marya threw on a shawl and ran to meet the travellers. When she came out on to the porch, a carriage with lanterns was standing at the entrance. A crowd of menservants on the lower platform separated her from the person who had arrived. Tikhon said something, sobbing as he spoke:

"Little father, Andrei Nikolaevich, and we'd already buried you."

And then suddenly the voice of the buried man – Prince Andrei's voice – replied and, horror of horrors, it sounded cheerful.

"No, we'll live for a little while yet, Tikhon. Is my father well, and my sister and my wife?" said the voice, quavering slightly. When Tikhon whispered into his ear and answered that the princess was in labour, Andrei shouted to his coachman to move away. The carriage he had come in belonged to the obstetrician, whom he had met at the last station and then travelled on with him. When the menservants saw Princess Marya behind them, they began bustling about and let her through. She looked at her brother in fright. He walked up and put his arms around her. She needed to believe that it was really he. Yes, it was he, but pale and thin, with a strangely changed expression on his face, softer and happy.

"Did you not get my letter?" he asked and, without waiting for a reply, which he would not have received because the princess was unable to speak, he turned back, ran quickly up the steps with the obstetrician and went to his wife. As he walked along the corridor, he did not even notice when the old man in a white dressing gown thrust his head out of the doorway of the menservants' room and gaped at him with wide, terrible eyes until he had gone past. Without listening to anyone, Prince Andrei walked straight to his wife.

"Well? What?" he asked anxiously.

She was lying on the pillows wearing a white cloth cap (the pains had only just released her, there were braids of her black hair curling on her inflamed, perspiring cheeks and her lovely pink little mouth with the moustache on the upper lip was open) and she was smiling with a childlike joy. Her gleaming eyes gazed like a child's, seeming to say: "I love you all, but why am I suffering, help me!"

Prince Andrei kissed her and began to weep.

"My little darling," he said, using a word he had never spoken before. She looked at him questioningly, with childlike reproach. "I was expecting help from you, and nothing came at all, even from you." She was not surprised that he had come. The pains began again, and they led him out of the room. The obstetrician stayed with her. Prince Andrei set off to see his father, but Princess Marya stopped him, saying his father had told her to say Andrei should not go to him, but stay with his wife. He and his sister spoke for a while, but the conversation constantly faltered. They waited and listened.

"Go, *mon ami*," said Princess Marya and ran away herself. Prince Andrei was left alone, he could hear the sound of the wind at the windows and he felt afraid. Suddenly there was a terrible cry – not her cry, she could not scream like that – in the next room. He ran to her door and the screaming stopped, but then he heard a different cry, a child's cry. "Why have they brought a child here?" Prince Andrei thought in amazement. The door opened and the obstetrician came out without his frock coat, with his sleeves rolled up and his forehead quivering. Prince Andrei turned to him, but the obstetrician glanced angrily at the prince and walked away without saying a word. A frightened woman came running out and halted in confusion in the doorway when she saw Prince Andrei. He ran into his wife's room. She was lying dead in the position in which he had seen her only five minutes earlier and even though her eyes were staring blankly and her cheeks were pale, there was the same expression on that lovely, childlike, timid face with the lip covered in little black hairs. "I loved you all and I did nothing bad, and what have you done to me! Ah, what have you done to me!"

In the corner of the room something small and red grunted like a piglet in Marya Bogdanovna's white hands.

Two hours later it was still just as dark and the wind was still howling. Prince Andrei walked quietly into his father's study. The old man already knew everything. He was lying on the divan. Prince Andrei went closer to him. The old man was asleep or pretending to be asleep. Prince Andrei sat down beside him on the divan. The old man's eyelids quivered.

"Father . . ."

Without speaking, the old man embraced his son's neck with arms like a vice and began sobbing like a child.

The little princess's funeral was held three days later. Prince Andrei stepped up on to the platform of the coffin and saw that face once again, although this time its eyes were closed. "Ah, what have you done to me!" And he felt that something in his soul had been torn apart, that he was guilty and his guilt could never be redeemed or forgotten. He could not cry. The old man also went up and kissed her hand, and to him also she said: "Ah, what have you done to me, and why?" And for the second time in his life the old man began sobbing and weeping.

Five days later they christened the young prince Nikolai Andreevich.

# XXIV

The impression of the first war with Napoleon was still fresh when the second began, ending in the Treaty of Tilsit. In early 1806 and in 1807 the feeling of hostility towards Buonaparte, as they called him, sank deeper into the hearts of the Russian people than in 1805. The conscription of half a million men, with two intakes in a single year, and the curses pronounced in all the churches on the enemy of mankind and Antichrist Buonaparte, and the rumours that he was approaching the Russian border, set all classes of society bristling against him.

After the unfortunate duel in which he had taken a part, Rostov took the wounded Dolokhov home. Rostov knew Dolokhov from his bachelor life with the gypsies, but he had never been at his home and had never even thought about what kind of home Dolokhov might have. Rostov had assumed that, if Dolokhov had a home, it was probably some smoky, dirty little room full of bottles and pipes, with a dog, where he kept his trunks and occasionally spent the night. But Dolokhov told him that he lived in his own house beside the Church of the Miraculous Apparition St. Nicholas with his old mother and two unmarried sisters.

Dolokhov did not speak during the journey, evidently struggling to prevent himself from groaning, but just before the house, when he recognised Arbat Street, he raised himself up a little and took hold of Rostov's hand, with an expression of passionate, intense despair that Rostov would never have expected from him.

"For God's sake, don't take me straight to my mother, she'll never be able to stand it . . . Rostov, leave me here, run to her and prepare her. That angel won't be able to stand it."

It was a nice, clean little house with flowers and floor rugs. Marya Ivanovna Dolokhova was a respectable-looking old lady. She ran out in fright to meet Rostov in the hallway.

"Fedya! What's happened to Fedya?" she exclaimed as soon as Rostov told her Dolokhov had sent him and was not entirely well.

"Is he dead? Where is he?" She fainted and fell. The sisters, plain young women, ran out and held their mother from both sides. One of them asked Rostov in a whisper what had happened to Fedya, and he told her that Dolokhov had been wounded, but not seriously. Rostov was unable to bear the heartbreaking sight of the mother's and sisters' despair and he carried Dolokhov in, then left on the pretext of going for a doctor, sparing himself the sight of the meeting between mother and son.

When Rostov returned with the doctor, Dolokhov had already been laid on a bearskin on the floor in his own study, which was hung with carpets and expensive weapons, and his mother was sitting on a little bench at his head, paler than her own son. The sisters were busy doing something in the back rooms or in the corridor, but they did not dare to enter the room. Dolokhov bore the pain of the probing of his wound and the extraction of the bullet as he had borne the injury itself. He did not even wince, and even smiled as soon as his mother came into the room. All his efforts were clearly intended to reassure the old woman. The better Rostov got to know Dolokhov, the more attached he felt to him. Everything about him was unusual, from his habit of lying on the floor to the vain pride he took in his own evil proclivities and his secrecy about his good ones. It was all so unusual, so different from other people, all so decisive and clear. At first Marya Ivanovna regarded Rostov with hostility, associating him with her son's misfortune, but when Dolokhov noticed this and told her in so many words: "Dearest mama, Rostov is my friend, and I ask you to love him", Marya Ivanovna really did start to love Nikolai, and Nikolai began visiting the little house beside the Miraculous Apparition of St. Nicholas every day. Despite the jokes of his family and the reproaches of his society acquaintances, he spent entire days with the convalescing patient, conversing with him and listening to his stories, hanging on his every word, movement and smile, and always without fail agreeing with him about everything, and sometimes talking with Marya Ivanovna Dolokhova about her son. He learned from her that Fedya supported her and his sisters, that he was the best son and brother in the world. Marya Ivanovna was convinced that her Fedya was a paragon of all the perfections in the world. (Rostov shared this opinion, especially when he listened to Dolokhov and could see the man himself.) She did not even accept that it was possible to have any other opinion of her son.

"He is too noble and exalted," she would say, "his heart is too pure for our modern, depraved society. Nobody loves virtue, it sets everyone's teeth on edge. Tell me, count, is this right, is this honest on the part of this Bezukhov, when Fedya in his nobility loved him and even now will not say anything bad about him? Those pranks in St. Petersburg – they played a joke on some policeman – they did all that together. Then why did Bezukhov get away with it, but Fedya had to bear the entire burden on his shoulders? And the things he had to suffer! Very well, so they gave him back his rank, but how could they possibly not give it back? I doubt if there were many brave sons of the fatherland like him out there. And now why this duel? Do these people have any feelings and honour? Challenging him to a duel and killing him, knowing that he is an only son. Thankfully God has been merciful to us. And what was it for? Who doesn't have affairs nowadays? Well, if he really is so jealous, I understand, but he could have made it clear sooner – it had been going on for a year. And then he challenged Fedya to a duel and assumed he wouldn't fight because he was in his debt. How despicable! How disgusting! I know you have understood Fedya, my dear count, that is why I love you with all my heart. Believe me, it is a rare thing for anyone to understand him, he is such a lofty, divine soul . . ."

While he was recovering at his own home, Dolokhov was often quite rapturously humble. Nikolai felt almost in love with him when this courageous man of iron, enfeebled now by his wound, turned his bright blue eyes and handsome face towards him, smiled faintly and spoke of his friendship for Rostov.

"Believe me, my friend," he said, "there are four sorts of people in the world: one sort loves nobody and hates nobody – they are the happiest people. Others, who hate everybody, are all scoundrels like Cartouche. The third sort love anybody who happens to be around them at that the moment and are indifferent to everyone else – there are more of those in Moscow than you could count, and they're all fools. And then there are those like me. If I love anyone, I love them so much that I will give my life for them, and I will crush all the rest if they get in my way or the way of those I love. I have a mother beyond all price whom I adore, my sisters, two or three friends, including you, and I hate all the rest, I'd chop them all up in order to help my select few." He smiled and squeezed Rostov's hand. "Yes, my dearest fellow," he went on, glancing affectionately at Rostov again, "I have met men who are loving, honest, noble and exalted, but as for women – countesses or cooks, it makes no difference – all women without exception are low, venal creatures. They do not have a pure heart capable of loving purely, as Karamzin's poor Lise loved Erast. If I found such a woman, I would give my life for her. But these . . ." He gestured scornfully. "Do you know why I challenged Bezukhov, that is, forced him to challenge me? I am fed up with her. She's a fish. She didn't love me, she was afraid. And I felt curious. Love is the supreme bliss, but I have not yet been granted it."

Most of the time he was meek and humble, but only Rostov saw him in that paroxysm of rage in which he would do such terrible things. His illness was already at its end. He took off his bandage and ordered a servant to give him a fresh one, but there was no fresh one, and the servant went running to the laundress, who began ironing bandages. Dolokhov was waiting for about five minutes. He sat on the bed, gritting his teeth and frowning, then he half stood, took hold of a chair and moved it towards him. "Egorka!" he began shouting, stopping and waiting at regular intervals. Rostov tried to distract him, but Dolokhov would not answer. Rostov went for Egorka and brought him back with the bandages. But as soon as Egorka came in, Dolokhov threw himself upon the servant, knocked him down and began beating him with the chair. The blood spurted from Dolokhov's wound. His mother and sisters came running, but despite all the efforts Rostov and they made, they were unable to free Egor until Dolokhov himself collapsed from exhaustion and loss of blood.

# XXV

Despite the sovereign's strict attitude to duellists at that time, the families of both Hélène and Rostov hushed the matter up and no one was punished. Dolokhov was still weak and could hardly walk when his new friend Nikolai introduced him to his parents' house. At the Rostovs' house everyone was welcomed with open arms, but Dolokhov was received even more cordially than usual, firstly because of his friendship with Nikolai and secondly for his fearsome and brilliant reputation. They waited in vain for his visit for several days. The countess felt rather timid and the young ladies were excited, even though Sonya was totally engrossed in her love for Nikolai and Vera in her love for Berg, who had come back on leave and gone away again, while Natasha was entirely satisfied with her admirer Denisov. Not one of them would have wanted Dolokhov to fall in love with her, but they all asked Nikolai about him in detail and when they spoke to each other about him, they laughed in a way that was obviously intended to conceal their excitement and fear.

On the third day of their wait, a carriage drove up. The young ladies ran across to the windows and then away from them when they recognised Dolokhov, and Nikolai led his friend in. Dolokhov was courteous. He spoke little (what he did say was original) and looked intently into the women's faces. Everybody was expecting something exceptional from him, but he did not say or do anything exceptional. The one thing about him that was not entirely ordinary was that his manner betrayed not a single trace of the awkwardness and embarrassment that can always be observed, no matter how carefully they are concealed, in a young bachelor's manner in the company of young ladies. On the contrary, Dolokhov exploited the advantage conferred by his injury and the weakness it presumably caused, sprawling at his ease in the Voltaire armchair that he was offered and accepting the small services that were done for him. Everyone in the Rostov household liked him. Sonya saw him as a friend and, believing this to be very important, she did everything she could to make him comfortable in his friend's house. She asked how he liked his tea, played him a piece that he liked on the clavichord, and showed him the pictures in the large hall. Vera reasoned that he was a man unlike any other, and therefore must be good. For the first two hours of the meeting Natasha never took her curious, quizzical eyes off him (the old countess even whispered to her several times that it was impolite of her). After dinner Natasha sang, obviously for him, and Vaska Denisov even said that the sorceress was forgetting her dwarf (as he called himself) and wished to enchant a new prince. She laughed, but when she finished singing her song in the hall, glancing anxiously towards Dolokhov all the time, she went back into the drawing room where he was sitting and sat down quite close, trying to read in his face what impression she had made, while keeping her eyes fixed on him and waiting for praise. Dolokhov did not pay the slightest attention to her, he was telling Vera and Sonya something, for the most part addressing his words to the latter. Natasha's agitation and desire to be praised were so evident that the old countess exchanged glances with Nikolai, smiling and indicating Natasha and Dolokhov with her eyes. They understood what it was she wanted.

"Do you like music?" the countess asked Dolokhov.

"Yes, very much, but I must confess I have never heard anything to compare with the gypsy songs and in my opinion no Italian singer can compare with Akulka."

"Did you hear how I sing," Natasha suddenly asked, blushing. "Was it good? Better than Akulka the gypsy?"

"Ah, yes, very good," Dolokhov said with cool, gentle courtesy, as if he were talking to a child, smiling his radiant smile.

Natasha turned round quickly and walked away. From that moment on Dolokhov was less of a man for her than the servant serving her food.

That evening, as often happened, the countess called her favourite to her room and laughed with her, with the irrepressible, rippling laughter that kind old women only rarely use.

"What are you laughing at, mama?" Sonya asked from behind the screen.

"Dolokhov's not to her taste," the countess said to her, launching into an even more powerful fit of laughter . . .

"You laugh, but he really isn't to my taste," Natasha responded, trying to feel offended, but unable to restrain her own laughter.

"What a divine creature your cousin Sophie is," Dolokhov said to Nikolai when they met the next day. "Yes, it's a lucky man who will call that heavenly creature his friend. But let's not talk about that."

They did not speak about Sonya any more, but Dolokhov began visiting every day and Marya Ivanovna Dolokhova would sometimes sigh and secretly ask Nikolai about his cousin Sonya.

The question that all members of a family ask in the case of a close acquaintance with a young man was quickly answered by everyone in the household: Dolokhov came to see Sonya and he was in love with her. Nikolai provided Dolokhov with opportunities to see Sonya with a feeling of proud complacency and confidence, firmly convinced that Sonya, or any woman who loved him, could not possibly be unfaithful to him. He once said to Sonya that it would be a good match. Sonya burst into tears:

"You're a wicked man," was all she said to him.

The old count and the countess joked with Sonya, but they also said, quite seriously: "Well, it's not a bad match – when he marries, he'll change." Sonya merely looked at them and Nikolai and Dolokhov himself in reproachful surprise, as if she could not make up her mind, although she was flattered by Dolokhov's attention and waited with intense curiosity to see what would happen.

A month after the young ladies made Dolokhov's acquaintance, their maid, who was combing out Sonya's huge plait, waited until Natasha had left the room and said in whisper:

"Sophia Alexandrovna, don't be angry with me, a certain person asked me . . ." and she started taking something out of the front of her dress with one hand.

It was a love letter from Dolokhov. Startled and delighted, Sonya grabbed the letter with a catlike movement and went into her bedroom, blushing even more brightly than the maid. There she began thinking whether she ought to open the letter or not. She knew that it was a declaration. "Yes, if I were *maman*'s daughter" (that was what she called the countess), "I should show her the letter, but God only knows what's in store for me. I love Nikolai and I will be his wife or no one's, but I am not her daughter, I am a solitary orphan and I cannot reject this Dolokhov's love or friendship."

She opened the letter and read: "Sophie, my adored one, I love you as no man has ever loved a woman. My fate is in your hands. I do not dare to ask for your hand. I know that you, a pure angel, will not give it to me, a man with a reputation that I have deserved. But from the moment I first met you, I have been a different man, I have seen heaven. If you love me even a hundredth part as much as I love you, then you will understand me, Sophie, give yourself to me and I will be your slave. If you love me, write 'yes', and I will find the moment for us to meet."

Natasha came across Sonya reading the letter and realised what was happening. "Ah, how lucky you are," she cried. "How will you answer him?"

"I don't know what I should do, I can't see him now."

For a week Dolokhov received no reply to this letter and Sonya avoided being left alone with him. Then Dolokhov arrived at the Rostovs' house early in the morning, asked to see the countess and said he wished to ask for Sophia Alexandrovna's hand. The countess gave her provisional consent and sent for Sonya. Sonya, flushed and trembling, exchanged hugs with Natasha and walked into the room where Dolokhov was waiting, past the curious eyes of the servants, who already knew what was going on and were happily anticipating the young lady's wedding. Curious heads were immediately pressed against the doors that closed behind her. Dolokhov blushed as soon as Sonya entered, now looking frightened and blushing even more brightly. He went up to her, took hold of her hand, which she was too afraid to take away. "How can it possibly be true that he loves me?" she thought.

"Sophia Alexandrovna, I adore you, need I say any more? You already understand what you have done to my heart. I was wanton, I was benighted until I knew you, my adored one, my incomparable Sophie. You are the angel who has lit up my life. Be my star, be my guardian angel." His fine, resonant voice began trembling when he spoke to her, and he embraced her, trying to press her against him.

Sonya was trembling with fear and seemed confused, beads of sweat stood out on her forehead, but as soon as he touched her, the little cat came to life and put out its claws. She leapt back and away from him. None of the things she had prepared to say to him were said. She felt his attraction and his power over her and she was horrified. She could not be anyone's wife but Nikolai's.

"Monsieur Dolokhov, I cannot . . . thank you . . . ah, go away, please."

"Sophie, remember that my life, my future is in your hands."

But she pushed him away in horror.

"Sophie, do you already love someone? Who? I'll kill him."

"My cousin," said Sonya.

Dolokhov frowned and strode quickly and firmly out of the room and across the hall, wearing the special expression of spiteful determination that his face sometimes assumed.

The old count met Dolokhov in the hall and held out both arms to him. "Well, shall I congratulate . . ." he began, but did not finish what he was saying, horrified by Dolokhov's angry expression.

"Sophia Alexandrovna has refused me," Dolokhov said in a trembling voice. "Goodbye, count."

"I didn't expect it, I didn't, I would consider it an honour to call you my nephew. Well, we'll have another talk to her, my dear fellow. I know that my Coco . . . since they were children the two cousins . . . wait . . ."

"Yes," said Dolokhov, "you think Sophia Alexandrovna is not worthy of your son, and so does he. But she thinks I am not worthy of her. Yes, that's all in order. Goodbye, and thank you for this" – and he went out. When he met Nikolai he did not say a word and turned his face away from him.

Two days later Nikolai received the following note from Dolokhov: "I shall not be at your family's house any more, and you know why. I am leaving tomorrow and you are going soon, so I have heard. Come this evening and we shall bid farewell to Moscow with a true hussars' party. I am celebrating at the Yar inn."

Rostov arrived at Dolokhov's place from the theatre after ten o'clock and found him in a hallway filled with cloaks and fur coats. Through open doors he heard the rumble of men's voices and the sounds of gold being tossed about. The three small rooms that Dolokhov occupied were beautifully arranged and brightly lit. The guests were sitting sedately at the tables, gambling. Dolokhov walked between them and greeted Rostov cordially. Not a word was spoken about the proposal or about Rostov's family in general. He was more serene and calm than usual, but Rostov noticed the same cold glint and insolent stubbornness in his eyes as when he had challenged Bezukhov at dinner at the club. Rostov had not gambled at all while he had been in Moscow, his father had asked him not even to take a card in his hands. Dolokhov laughed several times and told him: "Only a fool trusts to luck playing cards, you should only gamble on a certainty."

"Would you really gamble on a certainty?" Rostov asked him. Dolokhov smiled strangely at these words and said: "Perhaps."

Rostov was reminded of this conversation after supper, when Dolokhov seated himself on the divan between two candles, pulled a bag of gold coins out of the desk, opened a pack of cards with his wide-boned, muscular hands and glanced round at everybody there with a challenging expression in his handsome eyes. His glance met Rostov's. Rostov was afraid Dolokhov might think he was remembering their earlier conversation about gambling on a certainty, and he racked his brains in vain for a joke that would prove he wasn't, but before he could find one Dolokhov fixed his steely gaze on Rostov's face and, speaking with slow emphasis so that everyone could hear him, said:

"You remember we were saying only a fool would trust to luck, you should only gamble on a certainty? Well, I'd like to try."

"Trusting to luck or gambling on a certainty?" thought Rostov.

"Or are you afraid of me? Well, better not play then," Dolokhov added. He flicked an opened pack and said: "The bank, gentlemen!" He pushed the money forward and prepared to deal.

Rostov sat down beside him and did not play at first. Dolokhov kept glancing at him scornfully.

"Why aren't you playing?" he said.

And strangely enough, Nikolai felt he had to take a card, bet a considerable sum on it and start playing.

Dolokhov paid not the slightest attention to how his friend was doing and asked him to keep count himself. But not one of Rostov's cards won.

"Gentlemen," said Dolokhov, after dealing for a while, "please put the money on the cards, otherwise I get my figures confused."

One of the players said he hoped that he could be trusted.

"Oh, of course," Dolokhov replied and then added, without looking at Rostov:

"Go ahead, we'll settle up later."

The game continued . . . A servant served champagne continuously. Rostov refused the third glass poured for him, because at that precise moment he was engaged in placing a large bet on a card. All his cards were beaten, and he was already noted down as owing eight hundred roubles. He almost placed eight hundred roubles on one card, but as he was being served champagne, he changed his mind and wrote down his usual bet of twenty roubles again. Although Dolokhov was not looking at him, he saw his indecision.

"Leave it," he said, "you'll win everything back sooner. I'm giving the others good cards and beating you. Or are you afraid of me?" he added.

Rostov hastily restored the eight hundred roubles he had first written down and set down the seven of hearts with its corner folded over. Afterwards he remembered it very well. He set down the seven of hearts, writing "eight hundred" above it with a broken piece of chalk in round, vertical figures; he drank the glass of warm champagne proffered to him, smiled at what Dolokhov had said and, with his heart in his mouth for the first time in the game as he anticipated a seven, began impatiently watching Dolokhov's hands holding the pack.

On Sunday the week before, Count Ilya Andreevich had given his son two thousand roubles and, although he did not like to talk about money problems, told him that this was the last money until May and therefore asked his son to be a little thriftier this time. Nikolai had laughed and said he gave his word not to take any more money until the autumn.

Now one thousand two hundred roubles remained of that money. And so the seven of hearts might mean not only a loss of one thousand six hundred roubles, but that he would be forced to go back on his word. With his heart in his mouth, he watched Dolokhov's hands and thought: "Come on, quick, give me that card and I'll take my cap and go back home to sing with Denisov and Natasha, and I'll definitely never pick up a card again." And at that moment the delights of singing and being at home with Denisov, Natasha and Sonya, of making conversation and even of his quiet bed in the house on Povarskaya Street were borne in on him so powerfully that he could not believe stupid, blind chance, simply by placing the first seven on the right and not on the left, could steal all his happiness and plunge him into an abyss of uncertainty and misery, such as he had never experienced before. It could not happen, but still he waited with his heart in his mouth for Dolokhov's hands to move. The hands calmly set down the pack of cards and took the glass and pipe that were being proffered to them.

"So you're not afraid to play with me," Dolokhov repeated. He set down the cards as if he were intending to tell a funny story and, leaning back on his chair, he smiled and began unhurriedly:

"Well, gentlemen, I gather there are rumours going around Moscow that I am a card-sharp, therefore I advise you to be wary of me."

"Come on, deal!" said Rostov. Dolokhov picked up the cards with a smile. The seven that he needed was already lying on the top, the first card in the pack.

"Don't get too carried away," he said to Rostov and carried on dealing.

An hour and a half later most of the players were no longer taking their own game seriously. The entire game was focused on Rostov. Instead of one thousand six hundred roubles against his name, there was a long column of figures that he had counted up as far as ten thousand, and assumed to be more than fifteen thousand, but which was actually more than twenty thousand. He had decided to carry on playing until the account reached forty-two thousand. He had chosen that number because forty-two was the sum of his age and Sonya's.

Rostov rested his head on both hands, seeing nothing and hearing nothing. "Six hundred roubles, ace, a bent corner, nine . . . impossible to win it all back, I could have been enjoying myself at Elena's place . . . the knave of . . . no that's impossible . . . So why is he doing this to me?" Sometimes he placed a large bet, but Dolokhov refused to play it and set the bet himself. Nikolai gave way to him, praying as he did so as he had prayed on the battlefield at the bridge of Enns, and either guessing that the first card to come into his hand under the table would be the one to save him, or counting up how many galloons there were on his jacket and trying to place his entire losses on a card with the same number of pips, or looking round, appealing to the other players for help, or peering into Dolokhov's cold face and trying to fathom what lay behind it. "After all," Nikolai said to himself, "he knows what this loss means to me. He can't want me to be completely ruined. But it's not his fault either: how can he help it if he's lucky, and it's not my fault," he told himself. "I haven't done anything bad. How have I deserved such terrible misery? And when did it begin? Only a little while ago, when I came to this table with the idea of winning a hundred roubles and going to see Elena, I was so happy, even though I didn't appreciate that happiness. But when did it end and when did this terrible new state begin? What were the signs of the change? I was sitting here in the same way, in the same place at the table, choosing and placing the cards in the same way; when did it happen, and what was it that happened? When I am healthy and strong and still the same, and still in the same place. No, it's not possible, and it will probably all come to nothing." He was red-faced and soaked in sweat, although the room was not hot. And his face was made especially frightening and pathetic by his helpless struggle to appear calm.

The account reached the fatal figure. Rostov readied the card that was to be played with its corner marked at three thousand roubles, a sum he had just been given, when Dolokhov tapped the pack on the table, put it down, picked up the chalk and began quickly adding up Rostov's account. At that moment, Nikolai realised all was lost; but he said indifferently, as if what interested him most of all was the fun of playing the game:

"What, are you not going to carry on? I have a wonderful card ready."

"It's all over, I'm done for," he thought. "Now all that's left is a bullet in the forehead." And at the same time he said in a cheerful voice:

"Come on, just one more card."

"All right," Dolokhov replied, concluding his addition, "all right! For the twenty-one roubles," he said, indicating the figure twenty-one at the end of the round sum of thousands. He picked up the pack and prepared to deal. Rostov submissively bent down the corner of the card and wrote twenty-one instead of the six thousand he had intended.

"It's all the same to me," he said, "I'm only interested in seeing whether you'll beat me or give me that ten."

Without smiling, Dolokhov satisfied his curiosity. The ten was given.

"That's forty-two thousand you owe, count," he said, stretching, and got up from the table. "It's really tiring to sit for so long," he said.

"Yes, I'm tired too," said Rostov.

Dolokhov interrupted him, as if reminding him that it was unseemly for him to joke now.

"When would you like to give me the money, count?"

Rostov cast an enquiring glance at him.

"Tomorrow, Mr. Dolokhov," he said and then, after spending a few seconds with the other guests, he went out into the hallway to go home. Dolokhov stopped him and called him into another little room with a door opening on to the hallway.

"Listen, Rostov," said Dolokhov, grabbing hold of Nikolai's hand and glowering at him with a fearsome expression. Rostov sensed that Dolokhov was not really angry, it was more that he wished to appear frightening just at that moment.

"Listen, you know that I love Sophie so much that I'd give the whole world for her. She's in love with you, and you're holding her back, give her to me and we're quits for the forty-two thousand you can't pay me."

"You're insane," said Nikolai, not even offended, because what had been said was so unexpected.

"Help me to carry her off and make her mine, and we're quits."

Rostov suddenly felt the full horror of his position. He realised what a blow he would be forced to deal his father by asking him for this money, and the full extent of his shame, and he realised what happiness it would be to be rid of all of this and be quits, as Dolokhov put it, but even as he realised all this, his blood boiled.

"You are a blackguard if you can say that," he shouted, and threw himself at Dolokhov in a wild fury. But Dolokhov grabbed both his arms.

"Go, calm down."

"All the same I shall slap your face and I challenge you."

"I won't fight you, she loves you."

"Tomorrow you will receive the money and the challenge."

"I shan't accept the challenge."

It was not difficult to say "tomorrow" and maintain a decorous tone, but to come home alone with the terrible memory of what had happened, to wake up the next day and remember, to go to his generous, gentle father whose affairs were in such a tangle, to confess and ask for the impossible – that was terrifying. He was not thinking about the duel. He would have to pay first, fighting was easy.

Nobody was asleep yet at home. As he entered the hall, he heard Denisov's loud, hoarse voice laughing and women's voices laughing with it.

"If my goddess so demands, I cannot refuse," Denisov shouted.

"Marvellous, excellent," the female voices shouted.

They were all standing round the grand piano in the drawing room.

There were two tallow candles burning in the room, but Natasha could not have looked more brilliant by the light of a thousand wax candles. Her silver laughter could not have rippled more brilliantly.

"Ah, here's Nikolai!" the voices cried. Natasha came running over to him.

"How clever of you to come back early! We're having so much fun! Monsieur Denisov stayed for me, and we're amusing him."

"Well, all right, all right," cried Denisov, winking at Nikolai and not noticing how downcast he was. "Natalya Ilinichna, you owe us a barcarolle. Nikolai, sit down and accompany her – and then he'll do everything I tell him to do."

Nikolai sat down at the piano and no one noticed that he was miserable. In fact, it was hard to notice anything because even he had not yet fully grasped what he had done and what was in store for him. He sat down and played the prelude of his favourite barcarolle. This was a barcarolle, recently brought from Italy by the Countess Perovskaya, that had only newly been studied and learned in the Rostov house. It was one of those musical pieces that are so irresistibly attractive, they inveigle their way into the ear and the feelings and for a while displace all other musical memories. When you go to bed and when you wake up, the same musical phrases ring in your ears and everything else seems like pale, boring nonsense in comparison with those phrases. When a good voice starts singing the melody, the tears come to your eyes, everything else seems so facile and insignificant, and happiness seems so close and so possible. Of course, melodies like this barcarolle soon cloy and become as unbearable as they were once irresistible.

Nikolai played the first chord of the prelude and wanted to get up.

"My God, what am I doing?" he thought. "I'm disgraced, I'm a dead man. A bullet in the forehead is all that's left for me. What should I do? How can I get out of this? There is no way out. And I want to sing with them."

"Nikolai, what's wrong?" asked the gaze that Sonya directed at him. She was the only one who could see that something bad had happened to him. He turned away angrily. He felt unworthy of her sympathy, it demeaned her. He felt he had fallen so low that he had shamed everybody who loved him.

Natasha, with her sensitive nature, had also instantly noticed her brother's state of mind. She had noticed it, but she was enjoying herself so much at that moment, she was so far from feelings of grief, sadness or reproach, that she deliberately deceived herself, as young people often do. "I'm too happy just at the moment, and there is too much pleasure in store for me for me to spoil it by sympathising with grief," she felt, and she told herself: "No, I must be wrong, he must be in just as good a humour as I am."

"Right, Nikolai," she said, and walked out into the very centre of the hall, where she thought the acoustics were best. First she raised her head proudly, lowered her arms gracefully, shifted briskly from her heels to her tiptoes, walked around the centre of the room and stopped.

"Look, this is me!" she seemed to be saying. "Well now, who will remain indifferent to me? We'll see." It was all the same to her whether there were two people looking at her or three. She challenged the entire world with that look. Denisov's kind, admiring glance met hers. "Well now, what a villainous little flirt you will be," said his glance. "Yes indeed," her glance and smile replied. "But is that really so very bad? Well?"

Nikolai played the first chord mechanically. "How stupidly they are all behaving," he thought, "singing, when there's someone here – me – who is dying. I shouldn't be thinking about this, but about how to save myself. This is all stupid childishness and old Denisov's repulsive courting."

Natasha caught the first note, her throat expanded, her chest lifted, her eyes took on a serious expression. She was no longer thinking about anyone or anything at that moment, and the sounds poured out of her mouth that was shaped into a smile, sounds that can be produced with the same intervals of time and pitch by anyone, but will leave you cold a thousand times, only to make you tremble and weep on the thousand and first time. Nikolai's entire world was instantly concentrated in the anticipation of the next phrase, everything was divided into the triple time in which the aria she was singing was written. One, two, three, one, two, three, one . . . "Ah, how foolish our life is," thought Nikolai. "It's nothing but misery – Dolokhov, and spite, and money, and the debt, and honour – it's all nonsense . . . but this is genuine . . . Now, Natasha, how will she take this B . . . Excellent." And he instinctively filled his chest to sing the second and third beats of the high note – one, two, three, one . . .

It was a long time since Nikolai had taken such delight in music as he did that day. But time passed, and again he remembered and was horrified. The old count arrived from the club, cheerful and content. Nikolai did not have the courage to tell him that evening.

The following day he did not leave the house, but he could not bring himself to inform his father about his losses. Several times he approached the door of the study and then fled from it in terror. But there was no way out of the situation. Whether he went back on what he had said to Dolokhov, or took his own life, as he repeatedly thought of doing, or told them everything, there was no way to avoid dealing a heavy blow to his old parents. He went to his father just before lunch, and instead of telling him what he ought to have, without knowing why, he began talking with a jolly expression about the latest ball. Finally, when his father took him by the arm and led him off to drink tea, he suddenly told him in the most casual tone of voice, as if he were asking for a carriage to go to town:

"Papa, I came to you about something serious. I almost forget. I need some money."

"I see," said his father, who was in a particularly jovial mood. "I told you it wouldn't be enough. How much?"

"An awful lot," Nikolai said, blushing, with a stupid, casual smile that he was unable to forgive himself for a long time. "I lost a bit," he said, "I mean a lot, an awful lot, forty-two thousand."

"What? No more of that, it's not possible . . ."

When his son told him everything that had happened and, most importantly, that he had promised to pay that very evening, the old man clutched his head in his hands and without a thought of reproaching his son or complaining, dashed out of the room, muttering to himself: "Why on earth didn't you tell me sooner," and went to his aristocratic acquaintances to try to raise the money that was needed. When he returned after eleven with his valet close behind, carrying the money, he found his son in the study, lying on the divan, sobbing like a child.

The following day Denisov took the money and the challenge to Dolokhov, but his challenge was refused.

Two weeks later Nikolai Rostov left to join his regiment, subdued, thoughtful and sad, without saying goodbye to any of his brilliant acquaintances, after spending his last days in the three young ladies' drawing room, filling their albums with poems and music. Soon after his son's departure the old count left for his country estate, taking the teachers and governesses with him. He thought his presence was required there because his affairs were in such a poor state, primarily owing to this latest, unforeseen debt of forty-two thousand.

# XXVI

Two days after clarifying things with his wife, Pierre went to St. Petersburg, intending to obtain a passport and go abroad, but with the declaration of war, passports were not being issued. Instead of staying at his own house, or with his father-in-law, Prince Vasily, or with any of his numerous acquaintances, he lived at the Hotel Angleterre, staying in his room the entire time and informing no one of his arrival. He spent whole days and nights lying curled up on the divan reading, or striding around his room, or listening to Mr. Blagoveshchensky – the only person he saw in St. Petersburg. Blagoveshchensky was a wily, servile and stupid man of business who had managed various matters for the late Count Bezukhov. Pierre had sent for him to commission him to obtain a passport, and after that he came every day and sat in front of Pierre without speaking for days at a time, in the belief that sitting in the count's room like this was an extremely cunning manoeuvre on his part, and one which ought to prove very profitable to him. Pierre became accustomed to this stupid, craven individual and paid no attention to him at all, although he liked him sitting there.

"Come again," he would say as they said goodbye.

"Very good, sir. Still reading, are you, sir?" Blagoveshchensky would say as he came in.

"Yes. Sit down, some tea," Pierre would say.

Pierre lived in this way for more than two weeks. He did not know what date or day of the week it was, and every time he woke up he wondered whether it was the evening or the morning. Sometimes he ate in the middle of the day, sometimes in the middle of the night. During this time he read all the novels of both Madame de Souza and Anne Radcliffe, Montesquieu's *The Spirit of the Laws* and the tedious volumes of Rousseau's correspondence, which he had not read previously, and he found everything equally good. As soon as he was left alone without a book or with Blagoveshchensky telling him about the advantages of serving in the Senate, he began thinking about his own position and each time that he returned to the same oppressive thoughts, tracing the same path already taken a thousand times before, which led yet again into a cul-de-sac of hopeless despair and contempt for life, he would say aloud to himself in French: "Ah, what does it matter anyway. What is the point of thinking about this, when the whole of life is such brief folly?"

It was only at odd moments when he was reading or listening to Blagoveshchensky, that his earlier thoughts would come back to him, about how stupid Blagoveshchensky was to believe that being a senator was the height of glory, when even the glory of the hero of Egypt was not a pure glory; or, as he read about the love of some Amélie, he would imagine himself being in love and how he would devote himself to the love of a woman; or, as he read Montesquieu, he thought about how one-sidedly the writer reasoned concerning the reasons for the spirit of the laws and how, if he, Pierre, took the trouble to think a little, he would write a different and better book on this subject, and so on.

But as soon as he dwelt on this thought, everything that had happened to him came back into his mind, and he told himself that this was all nonsense and it didn't matter, and the whole stupid business of life wasn't worth the effort of doing anything. It was as if the thread had been stripped away from the screw that held his entire life in place.

"What am I, what am I living for, what is going on around me, what should I love and what should I despise, what do I love and what do I despise, what is bad, what is good?" – these were the questions which came to him and received no answer. And in his solitary search for answers, despite his limited study of philosophy, he personally travelled along the same paths of thought and arrived at the same doubts as the classic philosophy of all mankind. "What am I, what is life, what is death, what force controls everything?" he asked himself. And there was only one single, illogical answer to all these questions that satisfied him. This answer was: "Only in death is tranquillity possible." Everything within himself and in the world around him all seemed so tangled, senseless and ugly, that the one thing he feared was that people might drag him back into life, that they might draw him out of the contempt for everything that was the only thing in which he found temporary calm.

One morning, he was lying with his feet up on the table, with a novel open in front of him, but engrossed in this oppressive, hopeless train of thought, turning and turning the worn screw of his thought that went on rotating without biting on anything. Blagoveshchensky was sitting in the corner, and Pierre was looking at his neat and tidy figure the way people look at the corner of the stove. "You can't discover anything, you can't invent anything," Pierre told himself. "Everything's disgusting, everything's stupid, everything's the wrong way round. All the things people struggle over aren't worth a farthing. The only thing we can know is that we don't know anything. And that's the greatest extent of human wisdom. That allegory about not tasting the fruit of the tree of the knowledge of good and evil is far from stupid," he thought.

"Zakhar Nikodimych!" he said, turning to Blagoveshchensky. "How did your teachers in the seminary explain the meaning of the tree of the knowledge of good and evil?"

"Oh, I've forgotten, your excellency, but the professor was a highly intelligent man . . ."

"Well, tell me . . ." But just at that moment Pierre heard his valet's voice in the entrance hall, refusing to admit someone, and the quiet but firm voice of the visitor, saying: "It's all right, my friend, the count won't throw me out, and he'll be grateful to you for admitting me."

"Close the door, close it!" Pierre shouted, but the door opened and in came a short, thin old man in a powdered wig, stockings and shoes, with grey, almost white eyebrows that stood out very distinctly on his clean old face. There was an agreeable assurance in the man's manner, the civility of a man of the highest society. Pierre leapt up in confusion from the divan and turned to the old man with an awkward smile of enquiry. The old man smiled sadly at Pierre, glanced round the untidy

427

room and gave his non-Russian name – one that was well known to Pierre – in a quiet, steady voice, and explained that he had something to talk about with Pierre, *tête-à-tête*. As he said this, he glanced at Blagoveshchensky in a manner that only people with power possess. When Blagoveshchensky went out, the old man sat down beside Pierre and gazed intently and amicably into his eyes for a long time without saying a word.

Pierre was surrounded by papers, books and clothes that were scattered across the floor and on chairs. The remains of his breakfast and tea still lay on the table. Pierre himself was unwashed, unshaven and tousle-headed, and his dressing gown was dirty. The old man was so cleanly shaven, the high jabot fitted round his neck so neatly, the powdered wig framed his face and the stockings outlined his skinny legs so precisely, it seemed he could not possibly have looked any different.

"*Monsieur le Conte*," he said to Pierre, who was gaping at him in surprise and wrapping his dressing gown round himself. "Despite your entirely legitimate surprise at seeing me, a stranger, here in your room, I was obliged to disturb you. And if you would be so kind as to grant me a brief audience, you will learn what the matter is."

Pierre peered at the old man over the top of his spectacles with involuntary respect and said nothing.

"Have you ever heard, count, of the Brotherhood of Freemasons?" the old man asked. "I have the good fortune to be a member, and my brothers have instructed me to come to see you. You do not know me, but we know you. You love God, that is, the truth, and you love the good, that is, your neighbour, your brothers, and you are in a condition of misery, despondency and grief. You are under a delusion, and we have come to help you, to open your eyes and guide you on to the path that leads to the gates of the restored Eden."

"Ah, yes," said Pierre, with a guilty smile. "I'm most grateful to you . . . I . . ." Pierre did not know what to say, but the old man's face and words had a pleasant, calming effect on him. The old man's face, which had lit up and assumed a lively expression when he began talking about Freemasonry, once again became formal, restrained and polite.

"I'm most grateful . . . but leave me in peace," said the old man, completing Pierre's phrase for him. He smiled and sighed, staring insistently into Pierre's embarrassed eyes with a steady, energetic gaze and, strangely enough, Pierre sensed a hope of peace in that gaze. He sensed that for this old man the world was not a hideous confusion, unilluminated by the light of truth but, on the contrary, an elegant and sublime whole.

"Ah, no, not at all," said Pierre. "On the contrary, I'm only afraid,

428

from what I have heard and read about Freemasonry, that I am very far from understanding it."

"Fear not, my brother. Fear none but the almighty Creator. Speak out all your thoughts and doubts plainly," the old man said in a calm, stern voice, then once again abandoned his courteous tone for an inspired one. "No one can attain to the truth alone and unaided, only stone by stone, with everyone taking part, through millions of generations from our forefather Adam down to our time is the Temple of Solomon built, the temple that must be a worthy dwelling-place for the great God. If I know something, if I, a mere worthless slave, dare to come to the help of my neighbour, then it is only because I am a part of a great whole, because I am a link in an invisible chain, the beginning of which is lost in the heavens."

"Yes . . . I . . . well why not?" said Pierre. "I would like to know what genuine Freemasonry consists of. What is its goal?" he asked.

"Its goal? The erection of the Temple of Solomon, the knowledge of nature. The love of God and love of one's neighbour." The old man paused with an air suggesting that his words required long, careful consideration. Neither of them said anything for about two minutes.

"But that is the goal of Christianity," said Pierre. The old man did not reply. "And what is the knowledge of nature? And by which means have you managed to realise your threefold goal of love of God, of one's neighbour and of the truth in this world? It seems to me that this is impossible."

The old man nodded as if he approved of everything that Pierre said. At the last statement he stopped Pierre, who was becoming intellectually aroused and over-excited.

"But surely you can see that in nature these forces do not devour each other, and when they collide, they produce harmony and good."

"Yes, but . . ." Pierre began.

"Yes, but in the moral world," the old man interrupted him, "you do not see this harmony. You see that elements come together in order to produce growth, that growth serves to nourish the animal, and animals devour each other aimlessly, leaving no trace. And man, it seems to you, destroys everything around him for the satisfaction of his lust, and ultimately still does not know the goal he is living for and why he is alive."

Pierre felt ever-increasing respect for this little old man who guessed his thoughts and expressed them.

"He is alive in order to understand God, his creator," the old man said, once again falling silent to emphasise what he had said.

"I . . . don't think it's just because it's fashionable . . . I don't believe, no, it's not that I don't believe ... I don't know God," Pierre said regretfully, with an effort, feeling a need to tell the whole truth and frightened that he was telling it.

The old man smiled, as a rich man holding thousands of roubles in his hand might have smiled at a poor man who had told him that he didn't even have five roubles and felt it was impossible to get them anywhere.

"Yes, you do not know Him, count," said the old man, changing his tone of voice as he calmly sat down and took out his snuffbox. You do not know Him, and that is why you are unhappy, that is why for you the world is a heap of scattered ruins collapsing on each other."

"Yes, yes," said Pierre, in the tone of a beggar confirming a rich man's assertion that he is poor.

"You do not know Him, count, you are very unhappy, but we know Him, and we serve Him, and in this service we attain supreme bliss not only in the life beyond the grave, but also in this world. Many say that they know Him, but they have not even set foot on the first rung of that knowledge. You do not know Him, but He is here, He is in my words, He is in you, and even in those blasphemous things you said just now," the old man said in a trembling voice. He paused. "But it is hard to come to know Him. We work for this knowledge and in this work we find the supreme earthly happiness on earth."

"But what does it consist of, this work?"

"You said just now that our goal is the same as the goal of Christianity. To some extent that is correct, but our goal was determined before the incarnation of the Son of God. There were masters of our order among the Egyptians, Chaldeans and ancient Jews."

Even though what the old man said was strange, even though previously in his heart Pierre had laughed at Masonic arguments of this kind when he had heard them, with their references to the Chaldeans and the mysteries of nature, now his heart stood still as he listened to the old man, and he did not question him, but believed what he said. He did not believe in the rational arguments in what the old man said, he believed, as children believe, in the note of sincere conviction in his voice. He believed in that trembling of the voice in which the old man expressed his regret that Pierre did not know God, he believed in those bright eyes that had grown old in that conviction, he believed in the calmness and good cheer that shone out of the old man's entire being and struck him all the more forcibly by contrast with his own depression and hopelessness. He believed in the strength of that immense association of people connected through the centuries by the single idea that the old man himself had upheld for so many years.

"It is not possible to reveal the mystery of our order to a layman. It is not possible, because the knowledge of this goal is only attained through works that slowly advance the true Mason from one level of knowledge to the next, higher, level. To comprehend everything means to comprehend all the wisdom possessed by the order. But we have been watching you for a long time, despite your pitiful ignorance and the darkness shrouding the light of your soul. We decided to choose you and save you from yourself. You say that the world consists of ruins tumbling over and crushing each other. And that is correct. You yourself are this ruin. What are you?" And the old man began recounting the whole of Pierre's life to him, his situation and his personal qualities, speaking plainly and forcefully, without glossing over anything. "You are rich, ten thousand people depend on your will. Have you seen them, have you learned about their needs, have you concerned yourself, thought about their physical and spiritual condition, have you helped them, as was your direct and sacred duty, to find their way to the comprehension of the Kingdom of God? Have you dried the tears of the widows and orphans; have you loved them in your heart for even a single moment? No. While profiting from the fruits of their labours, you have abandoned them to the will of self-seeking, ignorant people, and you say the world is a collapsing ruin. You married, taking upon yourself the responsibility of guiding a young and inexperienced being, and what did you do, thinking only of satisfying your own pleasures?"

As soon as the old man mentioned his wife, Pierre flushed scarlet and began breathing hard through his nose, trying to interrupt him, but the old man would not allow it.

"You did not help her to find the path of truth, instead you plunged her into an abyss of lies and depravity. A man offended you, and you killed him, or tried to kill him. Society, and your fatherland, have given you a most fortunate and exalted position in the state. How have you repaid it for these favours? Have you tried to uphold the side of justice in the courts or become close to the throne of the Tsar in order to defend the truth and help your neighbour? No, you have done none of this, you have given yourself over to the most paltry of human passions, surrounded yourself with absolutely despicable flatterers, and now that misfortune has revealed to you the absolute worthlessness of your life, it is not yourself that you accuse, but the all-wise Creator, whom you do not acknowledge, in order not to fear Him."

Pierre said nothing. Having painted Pierre's past life in gloomy colours, the old man went on to describe the life that Pierre ought to have led and how he ought to have arranged it, if he had wished to follow the precepts of the Masons. He ought to make a tour of his immense estates and introduce material improvements for the peasants in all of them; almshouses, hospitals and schools ought to be established everywhere. His immense financial resources ought to be employed to spread enlightenment in Russia, publish books, educate the clergy, amass libraries and so forth. He himself ought to occupy a prominent position in the state service and assist the virtuous Alexander to eradicate extortion and falsehood in the courts. His home ought to be a place of meeting for all likeminded individuals striving to achieve the same goal. Since he possessed a propensity for philosophical study, his time that was not taken up by state service and managing his property ought to be used in acquiring knowledge of the mysteries of nature, in which the supreme masters of the order would not refuse him their assistance.

"And then," the old man concluded, "the knowledge of Him who would guide you in leading such a life, Whose help and blessing you would feel at every moment, then this knowledge would come of its own accord."

Pierre sat facing him without speaking, and there were tears in his large, intelligent, attentive eyes. He felt completely renewed.

"Yes, all these thing that you tell me were my only desires, my dreams," said Pierre. "But never in my life have I seen a single man who would not have laughed at such thoughts. I thought it was impossible, if only . . ."

The old man interrupted him.

"Why have these dreams not been realised?" the old man asked, evidently keen to engage in a dispute to which Pierre had not challenged him, but which he had often been offered in other cases. "Let me give you an answer to the question you asked me earlier. You said that Freemasonry teaches the same thing as Christianity. Christianity is a teaching, Freemasonry is a force. Christianity would not have supported you, it would have turned away from you in disgust as soon as you pronounced those blasphemous words that you have spoken in my presence. We do not recognise differences of faith, just as we do not recognise differences of nation and class; we regard all as equal to their brothers – all who love mankind and the truth. Christianity did not and could not come to your aid, but we have saved and are still saving worse criminals than you. You are tormented by the thought of Dolokhov. Then know that our brother, a master of our order, with profound knowledge of the mystery of healing the human body, was sent by us to the man you believe you have killed, and this is what he writes to us."

The old man took out a letter in French and read it aloud. The letter described Dolokhov's condition, which had been almost hopeless, as no longer posing any danger. The writer added that, unfortunately, his attempts at the moral healing of this soul deep-rooted in darkness had been completely ineffective.

"That is the difference between Christianity and us."

The old man stopped speaking, took a sheet of paper and drew a square on it with a pencil, adding two crossed diagonals, and at each side of the square he wrote a number from one to four.

Against the number one he wrote – "God", against the number two – "man", against the number three – "flesh", and against the number four – "conjoined". Then he pondered for a moment and pushed the sheet of paper towards Pierre.

"We do not know everything, count, I am therefore showing you just how much cannot be understood or revealed to the uninitiated. There, that is Freemasonry. Man must strive to be the centre. The sides of this square contain everything . . ."

The old man stayed in Pierre's room from midday until late in the evening. They spoke about everything. Pierre noticed that the old man did not accept his lack of faith, as if he were saying he was sure this momentary aberration would soon pass.

Bezukhov's admission into the St. Petersburg lodge was arranged for a week later.

# XXVII

The matter between Pierre and Dolokhov was hushed up and, despite the sovereign's strict attitude to duels at that time, neither of the opponents or their seconds suffered any consequences. But the story of the duel, confirmed by Pierre's split with his wife, was broadcast throughout good society and reached the ears of the sovereign himself. Pierre had been regarded with protective condescension when he was still an illegitimate son, and received with kindness and praise when he was the most eligible bachelor in the Russian Empire, but after his marriage, when potential brides and their mothers could no longer hope for anything from him, his reputation in society had suffered badly, especially since he did not know how and had no desire to curry general favour and approval. Now he was accused of being entirely responsible for what had happened, it was said that he was a foolish and jealous man, liable to the same fits of bloodthirsty fury as his father. Prince Vasily, having learned from his daughter's letters that his son-in-law was in St. Petersburg, sought Pierre out and wrote him a note, inviting Pierre to visit him. Pierre did not answer and he did not go. Prince Vasily himself came to see Pierre soon after the Freemason's visit. All this time Pierre had seen no one, apart from the first Italian Freemason and his new friends, the Masons, and he spent entire days reading their books, making the transition from a state of apathy to a passionate curiosity to learn what this Freemasonry was all about. He was accepted as a member of the Society, he went through the trial, he made contributions, he listened to speeches, and although he could not clearly understand what they wanted, he felt peace in his heart and a hope of self-improvement and, most important of all, submission to something and someone unknown and liberation from his own unfettered will. He was only waiting for the outcome of the Thursday meeting of the lodge, when he was to read his proposals for work to be carried out at his country estates, and making plans to go and put them into effect. He was busy with writing out the clean copy of his speech when Prince Vasily entered the room.

"My friend, you are deluded" – these were the first words he spoke as he entered. "I have found out everything and I can tell you with certainty that Hélène is as guiltless before you as Christ was before the Jews." Pierre tried to reply, but the prince interrupted him. "I understand everything, I understand everything," he said, "you acted as becomes a man who cherishes his honour; perhaps too hastily, but let us not go into that. But understand one thing, the position in which you put her and me in the eyes of all society and even the court," he added, lowering his voice. "Enough, my dear fellow," he said, tugging Pierre's hand downwards, "any sin can be forgiven; be the same good fellow that I knew before. Write a letter with me here and now, and she will come here, and all these rumours will end, or, let me tell you, you could very easily suffer for it, my dear fellow. I have learned from reliable sources that the Dowager Empress is taking a lively interest in this whole matter. You know, she was very fond of Hélène before she married."

Several times Pierre tried to speak but, on the one hand, Prince Vasily would not give him a chance, hastily interrupting, and, on the other hand, Pierre was afraid he might not speak in the tone of decisive rejection and disagreement in which he had firmly decided to reply to his father-in-law. He frowned and blushed, stood up and sat back down, trying to make himself do what he found most difficult of all in life – to say something disagreeable to someone's face, not to say what that person was expecting, whoever he might be. He felt that now his destiny depended on the first word he spoke. He was so accustomed to obeying Prince Vasily's tone of casual self-assurance that even now he felt he lacked the strength to resist it. But he also felt that his entire subsequent destiny would depend on what he said now: it would determine whether he continued along his former path, or followed the new one which had been pointed out to him so enticingly, on which he firmly believed he would find resurrection to a new life.

"Now, my dear fellow," said Prince Vasily in a jocularly confident tone, "just tell me 'yes' and I'll write to her, and we'll kill the fatted calf . . ." But before Prince Vasily could finish his joke Pierre spoke in a quiet whisper, not looking the other man in the eyes, but with an expression of fury that really was like his father.

"Prince, I did not invite you here, go, go!" He leapt up and opened the door for the prince. "Go, I said!" he repeated, unable to believe what he was doing and delighted by the expression of confusion and fear that appeared on Prince Vasily's face.

"What's wrong with you? You're not well."

"Go!" the menacing voice said once again. And Prince Vasily had to leave without receiving any explanation.

The following day Pierre received a note from Anna Pavlovna Scherer, saying that he must come to visit her between seven and eight o'clock in the evening of the same day to discuss very important matters and to receive some happy news concerning Prince Andrei Bolkonsky. Pierre and everyone else in St. Petersburg believed Prince Andrei had been killed.

The note also contained a postscript saying they would have a *tête-à-tête* alone. From this postscript, Pierre guessed that Anna Pavlovna already knew about the meeting with his father-in-law the previous day, that the purpose of today's meeting was only to continue yesterday's and the news about Prince Andrei was merely intended to lure him, but he convinced himself that in his new life he need not be afraid of people and that there was probably some truth in the mention of news concerning Prince Andrei. He shaved for the first time since his duel, put on his frock coat and went out visiting. He had an air of reserved good-humour, as if he knew the truth and was mocking everybody.

A lot of time had passed since that first evening when Pierre had so inappropriately defended Napoleon in Anna Pavlovna's drawing room. The first coalition had been destroyed, hundreds of thousands of men had died at the Ulm and Austerlitz. And Buonaparte, who had so outraged Anna Pavlovna with his insolence in annexing Genoa and placing the crown of the kingdom of Sardinia on his own head, since then this Buonaparte had made his two brothers kings in Europe, dictated laws to the whole of Germany, been recognised as Emperor by all of the European courts except for Russia and England, destroyed the Prussian army at Jena in two weeks, entered Berlin, taken the sword of Frederick the Great because he took a liking to it and sent it to Paris (this latter circumstance irritated Anna Pavlovna more than all the others), then declared war on Russia, and was now promising to destroy its new army just as he had destroyed the army at Austerlitz. On her free days Anna Pavlovna was still holding the same kind of *soirées* at her home as before, making fun of Napoleon and raging in uncomprehending fury at him and all the European sovereigns and generals who, as it seemed to her, had deliberately agreed to indulge Napoleon, in order to cause her and the Dowager Empress this moral suffering and distress. But Anna Pavlovna and her exalted patroness considered themselves above such provocation. "All the worse for them," they said, but they nonetheless expressed their real thoughts concerning this matter to their intimate acquaintances.

That evening, when Pierre stepped up on to Anna Pavlovna's porch, he was met by the same court footman as before, who opened the door with the same significant and solemn air as before and announced Pierre's name as he walked over the carpet into the same dark-crimson velvet drawing room, where the silent aunt was sitting in the same armchair with the same indifferent air, with all her features and her entire pose expressing a placid and devoted sadness at Buonaparte's godless successes.

Anna Pavlovna, as firm and definite in her manner as ever, came out to meet Pierre and offered him her yellow, dry hand with especial affection.

"Oh, how you have changed!" she told him. "And for the better, significantly for the better. I'm most grateful to you for coming. You will not regret it, but before I tell you the news that is sure to delight you, I must read you a sermon."

"Is he alive?" Pierre asked impatiently, and his face assumed an expression of young love and happiness that it had not worn since his marriage.

"Later! Later!" Anna Pavlovna said jocularly. "If you are responsive to my sermonising, then I shall tell you the news."

Pierre frowned. "I cannot make a joke of this," he said. "You do not know what this man means to me. Is he alive?"

"Your Pilades is alive," Anna Pavlovna said with gentle derision, "just remember the condition on which I tell you that, and I shall tell you about him in detail. You must listen to me like a confessor and follow my advice, but I hope that you are not so terribly argumentative as you used to be. I have observed that marriage is a highly formative influence on people's characters, and I hope it has affected you in that way, especially knowing our dear Hélène's character."

To his own surprise, Pierre felt unusually firm and calm in the face of the admonitions to come. It was the knowledge that he had a goal and hopes in his life that gave him this firmness. For the first time since he had been accepted into the brotherhood, he measured himself against the everyday circumstances of life and felt that he had grown quite substantially. He was not afraid of Anna Pavlovna's influence on him, and moreover, he was delighted and excited by the unexpected news of his friend's return to life.

At the same time Pierre was wondering how the court lady Anna Pavlovna would bring up the forbidden duel, when duels were so strictly condemned at court. He was surprised that Anna Pavlovna could talk with him in such a mild and friendly fashion after he had acted in a manner so unacceptable at court. He still did not understand that, although Anna Pavlovna knew every last tiny detail about his duel, she ignored them all, that is, she regarded this duel as never having taken place. She only spoke about Pierre's relations with his wife. When Pierre incautiously remarked to her that he was prepared to suffer all the consequences of his actions, but that it would not change his decision to separate from his wife, she looked at him in quizzical incomprehension, as if she were asking him what actions he was talking about, and added hastily: "We women cannot and do not wish to know about any actions apart from those that are taken concerning us."

Despite all Anna Pavlovna's touching admonitions and arguments about how crushed Prince Vasily was, as an old father, about how a young wife abandoned by her husband was left at the whim of destiny and her inclinations, and the damage being caused to his reputation by this separation, which could not be permanent, because Hélène would make him come back to her, Pierre, blushing and smiling uncertainly, gave the single, decisive answer that it was not possible for him to alter his decision and he would not.

Restrained as he was by his innate respect for this woman, which was combined with a certain disdain for her, Pierre could not lose his temper, but he was beginning to find things difficult.

"Let us drop this conversation, it won't get us anywhere."

Anna Pavlovna became thoughtful.

"Ah! Think, my friend," she said, raising her eyes to heaven. "Just think how certain individuals, especially women, and very highly placed ones, suffer and how they bear their suffering," she said, assuming the mournful expression she always wore when speaking about royal ladies.

"If only you could see, as I can, the entire lives of certain women or, rather, heavenly angels, who suffer but do not complain about the unhappiness of marriage." Tears welled up in her exultant eyes. "Ah, my dear count, you have a gift for rousing my feelings," she said, repeating the words she spoke to everyone when she wished to show them special affection, and held out her hand to him. "God only knows what I'm saying," she said, as if laughing at her own ardour and recovering her senses. Pierre promised her that he would think and not make his separation public, but he implored her to tell him everything she knew about his friend. Lise Bolkonskaya's relatives had received news that he had been wounded and treated for his wounds in a German village, and now he was completely recovered and on his way to his father's country estate. Pierre was especially delighted by hearing this news at a time when, having been resurrected to a new life, he had nonetheless been repeatedly saddened by the loss of his best friend, with whom he would so much have liked to share his new thoughts and views on life. "It couldn't have been otherwise," he thought. "A man like Andrei couldn't have been killed. He had so much still ahead of him."

Pierre wanted to take his leave, but Anna Pavlovna would not let him go and she made him move out of the isolated corner in which their conversation had taken place and go with her to join the guests, who were gathered into three groups, two of which were clearly made up of anybody at all, while one, by the tea table, was the focal point at which everyone higher and more important was grouped. Here there were starry decorations, military epaulettes and an ambassador. In the first group Pierre found mostly elderly people, one of whom, a man he did not know, was making his voice heard more than the others. Pierre knew everyone else, and they all greeted him as if they had seen him only the day before. Anna Pavlovna introduced Pierre to the man he did not know, mentioning a foreign name and whispering: "A man of very great and profound intellect."

The subject of discussion was the commander-in-chief Kamensky's application for retirement, which had just been received in St. Petersburg.

"Kamensky has completely lost his mind," the people there said. "Bennigsen and Buxhöwden are at daggers drawn, and God is the only one left in control of the army. Things could hardly be better! This is what he writes to the sovereign: 'I am too old for the army, I can scarcely see, I can hardly ride a horse but for me, unlike others, this is not due to laziness. I am quite unable to find places on the maps, and am not familiar with the region. I make so bold as to offer for your consideration a tiny part, consisting of six pages, of the correspondence which I have had to deal with in a single day, and which I cannot manage much longer, for which reason I make so bold as to request that I be replaced.' And this is the commander-in-chief."

"But who was there to appoint?" Anna Pavlovna interrupted, as if she were being attacked and defending herself. "Where are our men?" – as if the lack of men were yet another of the provocations directed against Maria Fedorovna. "Kutuzov?" she asked, and her smile annihilated Kutuzov for all time. "He's shown what he's capable of. Prozorovsky? We don't have any men. Who's to blame for that?"

"When God wishes to destroy someone, he makes him mad," said the man of profound intellect. "We have many reasons for not having any men," he said. "Some are too low in rank, others are too low by birth, and others have not yet managed to obtain the sovereign's favour, but over there, on the other side, the finest forces are called into service by the revolution."

"So you say," Anna Pavlovna put in, "that the forces of the revolution are bound to triumph over us, the defenders of the old order."

"God forbid that I should think that," replied the wise man, "but it could well be that the significance of Buonaparte, which still remains unclear to us, will be clearer to posterity. Perhaps he is called to destroy those kingdoms which have not been pleasing to God and show us clearly how vain the greatness of this world is." And then the man of profound intellect began speaking of the prophecies of Jung Stilling concerning the significance of the apocalyptic number four thousand, four hundred and forty-four, and how the Book of the Revelations specifically foretold the appearance of Napoleon, and how he was the Antichrist.

"I have not arrived at this through books, "Anna Pavlovna objected, "I understood first through my feelings that he is not a man, and in my freethinking way I often wondered whether the rite of cursing him did not contradict Christian teaching, but now I feel the entreaties and curses of my heart fusing with the curses that are now prescribed reading in the churches; yes, I do believe he is the Antichrist, and when I think that this appalling creature has had the insolence to suggest that our Emperor should become his ally and correspond with him, like a dear brother . . . Only one thing I ask of God in my prayers, that if it is not given to Alexander to crush the head of this dragon like St. George, then at least may we never stoop so low as to acknowledge him as our equal. I know that I, at least, could never bear that." And with those words and a nod, Anna Pavlovna walked across to another group, primarily diplomatic, in which Pierre recognised Mortemart, now wearing a Russian Guards uniform, Hippolyte, recently arrived from Vienna, and Boris, the same fellow he had taken such a liking to for his frank declaration in Moscow.

During his time in military service, thanks to Anna Mikhailovna's efforts and the traits of his own agreeable and moderate character, Boris had managed to situate himself most advantageously for his career. He had been with Prince Volkonsky for a while, and now, after being sent to the army, he had just returned as a courier. He had a rather more mature, but even more agreeable, calm air about him. He had evidently completely mastered that unwritten line of subordination that had so greatly appealed to him, according to which an ensign might stand substantially higher than a general. And now here, in Anna Pavlovna's drawing room, surrounded by people of high rank and importance, despite his own low rank and young age, he conducted himself in an exceptionally simple and dignified manner. Pierre greeted him gladly and began listening to the general conversation. The subject was the latest news received from Vienna, and the Viennese cabinet, which, having refused to assist us, was now being showered with reproaches.

"Vienna finds the basic aims of the proposed agreement to be so far beyond the possible that they could not be achieved, even by a series of brilliant successes, and it doubts that the means exist by which these successes could be achieved. That is the true opinion of the Viennese cabinet," said the most imposing member of the diplomatic group, the Swedish chargé d'affaires. "This doubt is flattering," he said with a subtle smile.

"It is essential to distinguish between the Viennese cabinet and the Emperor of Austria," said Mortemart. "The Emperor could never have thought that, it is only what the cabinet says."

"Ah, my dear vicomte," said Anna Pavlovna, feeling compelled to intervene. "Europe will never be our sincere ally. The King of Prussia is our ally only temporarily. He reaches out one hand to Russia, and with the other he writes his famous letter to Bonaparte, asking him if he was satisfied with the reception he received in the palace at Potsdam. No, reason can make no sense of this, it is beyond belief."

"Everything is still the same as two years ago," thought Pierre, and even though he wanted to tell Anna Pavlovna his opinion on this matter, the fact that the tone and point of the conversations were still the same held him back. Laughing inwardly to himself, he turned towards Boris, wishing to exchange smiles with someone, but Boris seemed not to understand his glance and did not smile back at Pierre. He was listening attentively to his elders' conversation, like a pupil in school.

As soon as the phrase "the King of Prussia" was pronounced, Hippolyte began grimacing and became agitated, preparing to say something and then stopping.

"But he is our ally," someone said.

440

"The King of Prussia?" asked Hippolyte and laughed.

"Here is a young man who saw what was left of the Prussian army with his own eyes, he can tell you there was nothing left of it," said Anna Pavlovna, indicating Boris. With all eyes turned towards him, Boris calmly confirmed what Anna Pavlovna had said, and even held everybody's attention for a moment by telling them what he had seen when he was sent to the fortress at Glogau.

The conversation faltered for an instant. Anna Pavlovna had just begun saying something, when Hippolyte interrupted her and then apologised. She gave him the floor, but he apologised again, laughed and said nothing.

"It is the sword of Frederick the Great . . ." Anna Pavlovna began, but Hippolyte interrupted her again with the words, "the King of Prussia", and then apologised again. Anna Pavlovna turned to him resolutely and asked him to finish what he wanted to say. Hippolyte laughed.

"No, it's all right, I just wanted to say . . ." he said and laughed as he repeated a joke he had heard in Vienna and had been trying to put in all evening, "I wanted to say that we are fighting imprudently."

Pierre frowned: Hippolyte's stupid face reminded him so painfully of Hélène. Someone laughed. Boris smiled cautiously, so that his smile could be taken for mockery or approval of the joke, depending on how it was received.

"Oh, how wicked that Prince Hippolyte is!" said Anna Pavlovna, wagging a small, yellow finger at him. She moved across to the most important group, leading away Pierre, whom she was keeping at her side. Pierre had not been in society for a long time, and he was interested to find out what was going on now. He had learned many interesting things from the conversations in the first two groups, but as he approached the third, central, group and observed how intensely the conversation in it was being conducted, he was hoping to hear all the most important and interesting things.

"They say that Hardenberg received a snuffbox decorated with diamonds, and Count N. received an Order of St. Anne, First Class," one man said.

"Forgive me, but a snuffbox with the Emperor's portrait is an award, not a distinction," said another.

"The Emperor takes a different view," a third man interrupted sternly. "There have been examples in the past, I can name Count Schwarzenberg in Vienna."

"But a count, it's not possible," yet another man objected.

"Yes, that's quite true," Anna Pavlovna put in sadly, taking a seat, and everyone suddenly started speaking passionately at the same time. Just then Pierre was overcome by one of those delusions of the senses when you think you are asleep and everything that is happening is a dream and you only have to open your eyes for everyone to disappear, and you can test whether it is a dream or reality by doing something extraordinary – by hitting someone or shouting out in a wild voice. He tried to shout out, and the loud beginning of his shout brought him to his senses. He converted the shout into a cough without attracting any particular attention to himself, stood up, wishing to convey his mood of jocose mockery to someone else, and glanced round the lively gathering. "Either they're all freaks, or I'm a freak, but we are certainly different," he thought. Young Boris Drubetskoy was sitting with a dignified and respectful air a little behind the ambassador, smiling gently and cautiously at his jokes. Pierre vividly recalled his own argument in this drawing room two years before, and found he liked himself as he had been then. He also recalled Andrei as he had been at that time, their friendship and the evening they had spent over supper. "Thank God he's alive. I'll go home and write to him."

He left the room quietly, unnoticed. And all the time in the carriage he smiled gently at his own life, now so full of joy and interests.

# XXVIII

In 1807 Pierre finally set off on a tour of his country estates with a goal that was absolutely clear and definite: to improve the lot of his twenty thousand peasant serfs. This goal was subdivided into three sections: 1) liberation of the serfs, 2) improvement of their physical welfare: almshouses and hospitals, 3) improvement of their moral welfare: schools, improving the clergy. But as soon as he arrived in the countryside and saw how things were on the spot and talked with his steward, he saw that the project was impossible, and it was impossible primarily because of a lack of financial means.

For all of Count Bezukhov's great wealth, all the estates were mortgaged, and therefore it was impossible to set all the serfs free as he had been intending to do. It was impossible to pay off the debt, since the six hundred thousand roubles of his annual income were all expended and, in addition, each year he felt the need to borrow more. He now felt far less rich than when he used to receive his ten thousand roubles from the deceased count. In general terms, he was vaguely aware of the following budget.

Eighty thousand from all the estates was paid to the Guardian Council. Salaries paid to the stewards of all the estates – thirty-two thousand. Two hundred thousand given to Prince Vasily. A huge number of petty debts. Maintaining the Moscow house and the two princesses – thirty thousand. The house outside Moscow – seventeen thousand. Pensions – sixteen thousand. Charitable institutions and personal requests – ten thousand. To the countess abroad – one hundred and sixty thousand. Interest on debts – seventy-three thousand. Building a church, already begun – one hundred and fifteen thousand. He did not know how the other half of his income, a huge half of three hundred thousand roubles, was spent. Just as he had in the Moscow house, on all the estates he found old people with large families who had been living at his father's expense for as long as twenty years and regarded their own longevity as a service rendered. It was impossible to change this situation. Wishing to reduce the size of his stables in Moscow, he saw the old, long-serving coachman who had been with the deceased count during the Turkish War.

"I have too many horses, what do I need them for?" Pierre said, assuming that the coachman would support his plans for simplicity. But the coachman only said respectfully: "Whatever you say," and "Can I go now?" And his face expressed bitter reproach and annoyance with the illegitimate juvenile who did not know how to uphold his own dignity, appreciate the value of people and maintain the honour of the house of Count Bezukhov. It was the same with his gardener, the princesses, his butler. Pierre frowned, bit on his nails and said: "Very well. I'll think about it." Everything – the stables, and the garden, and the conservatory, and the princesses – everything remained as it had been and carried on living in the same way as before, independently of the count's will, costing Pierre half his income. At first they were afraid he might change something, but then they understood him and only tried to display their distress and readiness to accept the misery into which he was undeservedly plunging them, and they knew he would leave everything as it had been.

When he arrived at his main estates in Orlov, with a completed plan, approved in the lodge and by the Benefactor (that was what they called the grand master of the lodge) for the liberation of the serfs and the improvement of their physical and moral existence, Pierre summoned his chief steward and all the stewards of the estates, read them his project and expounded his ideas in a long, clever speech. He told them measures would be taken immediately for the complete liberation of the peasants from the bondage of serfdom, that until then the peasants must not be overburdened with work, that women with children must not be sent to work, that the peasants must be given assistance, that verbal chastisement must be employed instead of physical punishment, that hospitals, orphanages and schools must be established on every estate, and so on. Some of the stewards (there were also peasant bailiffs present) were frightened by what they heard, imagining that the young count was displeased with their threshing and their concealment of grain, while others, after the initial fright, found Pierre's lisping speech and the new words they had never heard before amusing, and yet others simply took pleasure in hearing the young count speak, but the cleverest among them, including the chief steward, realised from this speech that the master could be managed.

After his speech to everyone, Pierre *busied himself* every day with the chief steward. But, to his surprise, he felt that his efforts did not move matters one single step forward. He felt his efforts were taking place independently of the business in hand, that they failed to take any purchase on matters and force them to move. On one hand, the steward painted matters in a very dark light, trying to demonstrate to Pierre the need to carry on paying his debts and undertake new works, using the male serfs as manpower, to which Pierre did not agree: on the other hand, Pierre demanded that the work of liberation must be begun, to which the steward opposed the need first to pay off the debt to the Guardian Council, which made it impossible to proceed rapidly. The steward did not say that Pierre's goal was completely impossible. In order to achieve it he proposed selling off the forests in the Kostroma province, the estuarine lands and the estate in the Crimea; but the steward described all these operations as involving such complicated procedures in order to remove distraints and obtain permits and so forth, that Pierre grew confused and simply told him: "Yes, yes, do that."

Two weeks went by and the cause of liberation had not advanced by a single step. Pierre hustled and bustled, but he vaguely sensed that he did not have the practical tenacity required in order take hold of the business and set the wheels turning. He began growing angry, threatening the steward and making demands. The steward, regarding all the young count's initiatives as near-insanity, damaging to the interests of the count, the steward and the peasants, made a concession. While continuing to represent the liberation of the peasants as impossible, he gave instructions for large buildings to be constructed on all the estates for schools, hospitals and orphanages – and he prompted the peasants to come to their master and express their gratitude for his bounties. Pierre spoke with the peasants a few times, asked them about their needs and became even more convinced of the necessity for the reforms that he was undertaking. In the words they spoke, he discovered the confirmation of all his plans, while in those same words the steward found condemnation and proof that all the count's plans were pointless. But

Pierre did not know that the ambivalent words of the simple people are like the words of an oracle, in which it is possible to discover confirmation for anything, and he was very happy when the peasants told him they would pray to God for him and his hospitals and schools for ever. When Pierre drove round his villages in the Orlov province, he saw the brick walls of new school and hospital buildings rising before his very eyes.

"Look how far the life breathed into me by our sacred brotherhood has reached and see how it teems," he thought joyfully as he watched the masons and carpenters bustling about beside the new buildings. Pierre saw the steward's reports on husbandry service, with the figures reduced (in actual fact the volume of work had increased, since everywhere the construction of hospitals and schools using estate manpower had been added to the husbandry service). The steward told Pierre the people blessed him and the quit-rent serfs, whose rent had been reduced, were now building a chapel dedicated to his angel. The steward exhorted the count to abandon his plans for liberation, since now the peasants already had twice as many benefits as they had had before, and when Pierre firmly demanded that the forests and the estate in the Crimea must be sold in order to make a start with repayment of the debt, he promised to do everything in his power to carry out the count's will.

# XXIX

After his three-week sojourn in the country, concerning which he sent a report to the lodge, Pierre set off back to St. Petersburg, happy and contented, but before reaching Moscow, he made a detour of a hundred and fifty *versts* in order to visit Prince Andrei, whom he had still not seen. On learning that Prince Andrei was living at Bogucharovo, the village forty *versts* away from Bleak Hills that his father, the old prince, had assigned to him, Pierre drove directly there to see him.

The estate, the house, the garden, the courtyard and the outbuildings were all as completely new as the first blades of grass and the first leaves on the birch trees in spring. The house had not been plastered yet, carpenters (serfs) were building the fence. Dirty, tattered peasant men brought sand in single-axle carts and barefooted women spread it out on the instructions of the gardener (a German). The dirtiness of the peasants contrasted sharply with the cleanness and elegance of the courtyard, the façade of the house and the flowerbeds. The peasant men hastily tugged off their caps and moved aside as Pierre's *dormaise* carriage drove in. He was not met by the servants dressed in the knee-length coats of the average estate owner, or wearing the powdered wig and stockings of the old style still followed at his own estates, but by a footman wearing a frock coat, in the new English fashion.

"Is the prince at home?"

"He is taking coffee on the terrace. How should I announce you?" the footman said politely. There was something about Pierre that inspired respect, despite his awkwardness or, rather, as a consequence of it.

Pierre was struck by the contrast between the elegance of everything around him (which must have been carefully considered) and his concept of how crushed and distraught his friend must be. He hurried into the clean, brand-new house smelling of pine timber that had not yet been plastered, but was elegant in every tiny detail and finished in exceptional taste. He walked through the study and approached the door of the terrace, through the window of which he could see a white tablecloth, china and someone's back in a velvet smoking jacket.

It was one those hot, early-April days when everything is growing so fast, it makes you afraid that this spring joy will pass too soon.

He heard a harsh, unpleasant voice from the terrace:

"Who is it, Zakhar? Show them into the corner room." Zakhar halted, but Pierre walked round him, panting hard as he strode out on to the terrace and caught hold of Andrei's arm from below so swiftly that the expression of annoyance had still not left the prince's face before Pierre was already kissing him and peering at him from close up with his spectacles raised.

"It's you, my dearest fellow," said Prince Andrei, and at these words Pierre was struck by the change that had taken place in the prince. The words were affectionate, Prince Andrei's lips and face were smiling, but his eyes were dull and dead, and even though he clearly wished to, Prince Andrei could not make them shine with joy and happiness. As Pierre asked questions and talked about things that had happened, he was constantly observing the amazing change that had taken place. It was not simply that Prince Andrei had grown thinner and paler, and looked older; that look in his eyes and that wrinkle on his brow, indicating an exclusive concentration on one single thing continued to astound Pierre for a long time until he grew accustomed to them.

As is always the case when people meet after a long separation, it took some time for the conversation to settle; they asked questions and gave short answers about things that they knew needed to be spoken about at length. Eventually the conversation began to dwell briefly on things that had already been mentioned in desultory fashion, on questions of the past campaign, the Prince's wound and illness, his plans for the future (Andrei did not speak about his wife's death), on the prince's questions about Pierre's marriage and separation, the duel and Freemasonry. (They had not written to each other, they had not known how to. How could Pierre write just half a page to Prince Andrei? Only once had Pierre written a letter of recommendation for Dolokhov.)

The intense, distraught look that Pierre had noticed in Prince Andrei's eyes became even more emphatic as the prince expressed his opinions, which were often alloyed with a sad mockery of everything that had made up his former life – his desires and hopes of happiness and glory. Pierre began to feel that in Prince Andrei's company enthusiasm, dreams and hopes of happiness and good were improper. He felt ashamed to describe all his new Masonic ideas and actions, and he restrained himself.

"I shall never serve in the army again," said Prince Andrei. "Either I am not suited to our service, or our service is not suited to me, I don't know which, but we're not a match. I really think I'm not suited." He smiled. "Yes, my dear friend. We have changed a lot, such a lot since those days. You'll find no pride in me now. I am resigned. Not to people, because for the most part they are worse than me, but I am resigned to life. Plant trees, raise my child, amuse myself by toying with some intellectual game, if it manages to amuse me somehow. Look, see, I'm reading Montesquieu and making notes. What for? It's the way I kill the time. The men over there" – he pointed to the peasants – "they're doing the same thing with the sand, and that's good."

"No, you haven't changed," Pierre said after a moment's thought. "You may not have the pride of ambition, but you have the same pride of intellect. And that pride is both a vice and a virtue."

"What pride is this, my friend, when I feel guilty and useless and, feeling this, not only do I not grumble, I am content?"

"Why guilty?" They were already in the study now. Andrei pointed to a wonderful portrait of the little princess, gazing at him as if she were alive.

"That's why," he said, moved to feeling by the presence of a person dear to him: his lip began to tremble and he turned away.

Pierre realised Andrei bitterly regretted that he had not loved his wife enough, and understood how this feeling could have grown so terribly strong in Prince Andrei's heart, but at the same time he could not understand how it was possible to love a woman. He said nothing.

"Well, I tell you what, dear fellow," Prince Andrei said to change the subject. "I'm only camping here. I just came to take a look. Today I go back to the old man and my little boy. He's at home with my sister. I'll introduce you to him. We'll go after lunch."

At lunch they began talking about Pierre's marriage and the whole story of the separation. Andrei asked him how it had happened. Pierre blushed scarlet, as he always did at this subject, and said hurriedly:

"Later, later, I'll tell you some time." He choked as he said it. Andrei sighed and said what had happened should have been expected, it was fortunate that things had ended that way and Pierre had managed to keep at least some faith in people.

"Yes, I feel very, very sorry for you."

"Yes, well it's all over now," said Pierre, "and how fortunate I am not to have killed that man. I would never have forgiven myself for that."

Prince Andrei laughed.

"Ah, in war they kill men all the time," he said. "And everyone finds it very just. And killing a vicious dog is really a very good thing. What is just and what is not is not given to people to judge. People constantly make mistakes, they always will, and never more so than in what they consider just or unjust. You just have to live your life so that you have no regrets. Joseph Maistre was right when he said: 'There are only two genuine misfortunes in life: pangs of conscience and illness. Happiness consists of no more than the absence of these two evils.' To live for myself, simply avoiding those two evils, that is all my wisdom now," Prince Andrei said and fell silent.

"No, I lived only for myself," Pierre began, "and in doing so I merely destroyed my life. No, I cannot agree with you. No, only now am I beginning to understand the full meaning of the Christian teaching of love and self-sacrifice."

Andrei looked at Pierre with his dull eyes, smiling in gentle mockery.

"Let's go straight away to my sister, to Princess Marya, you'll get on well with her. So, my dear heart, that is the difference between us," he said, "you lived for yourself and almost destroyed your life and only discovered happiness when you began to live for others, and my experience has been the diametrical opposite. I lived for glory, and what, after all, is glory? The same love of others, the desire to do something for them, the desire for their praise. So I lived for others and did not almost destroy my life, I destroyed it utterly, and I have only become calm since I have been living for myself."

"Not for yourself alone, what about your son, your father, your sister?" said Pierre.

"Ah, they are all me, not other people," Andrei continued. "But other people, my neighbours, le prochain, as you and Princess Marya call this source of error and evil – they are the Orlov peasants you left behind when you came here, the ones you wish to do good for." He gave Pierre a mocking, challenging glance. As a man who was not yet entirely convinced of his own new views and had not had any opportunity to express them, Andrei was clearly challenging Pierre.

"You're joking – how can you say that?" said Pierre, growing enthusiastic. "What error and evil can there be in these unfortunate people – our peasants, people just the same as us, who grow up and die with no concept of God and the truth apart from an icon and a meaningless prayer – learning about consoling truths, beliefs about the future life, retribution, reward, consolation? We might think differently, but things are different for them. But what evil and error it is that people are dying from disease, from giving birth without any help, when it is so easy to give them material support, and I shall give them a doctor and a hospital, and shelter for the old? And surely it is a tangible, manifest good when someone knows no peace by day or night, and I give him rest and leisure?" said Pierre, growing excited and lisping. "And I have done this. And not only will you not persuade me that this is not good, you will not persuade me that you yourself do not think so."

Andrei carried on smiling without speaking.

"And the most important thing," Pierre continued, "is that the pleasure of doing this good is the natural happiness of life."

"Yes, that's a different matter," Prince Andrei began. "I build an arbour in the garden, you build hospitals. Both of these can serve as a way of passing the time. But as for judging what is just and what is good, leave that to the One who knows everything, that's not for us. You say schools," he said, bending down one finger to count, "studying and so forth, that is, you wish to remove the peasant from his animal condition and give him moral needs. But it seems to me that the only possible happiness is the happiness of the animal, and that is what you wish to take away from him. I envy him, and you wish to make him into me, but without giving him my intellect, or my feelings, or my resources. Then, another thing you say is: make his work easier. But, in my opinion, for him physical labour is as much a requirement, as much a condition of his existence, as mental labour is for you and me. You cannot help thinking. I go to bed after two, thoughts come to me and I cannot get to sleep, I toss and turn and do not sleep until the morning because I think and I cannot help thinking; in the same way he cannot help ploughing and reaping; if he doesn't he'll go to the tavern. Just as I could not tolerate his terrible physical labour, so he could not tolerate my physical idleness, he would grow fat and die. Thirdly . . . what else was it that you said?"

Prince Andrei bent down a third finger.

"Ah, yes. Hospitals, medicine. He's had a stroke, he's dying, and you've let his blood and cured him, and now he'll carry on as a cripple for another ten years, a burden to everyone. It's much less trouble, much simpler for him to die. Others will be born, there are too many of them anyway. If only it was because you regretted the loss of one more worker, but you want to cure him out of love for him. But he doesn't need that. And then, what sort of fancy is it that medicine has ever cured anybody . . ."

Prince Andrei expressed his disenchanted thoughts with especial ardour, like a man who has not talked for a long time. And the more hopeless his opinions were, the livelier his glance became. He contradicted Pierre about everything, but seemed as he did so to hesitate over what he was saying, and he was glad when Pierre countered his arguments forcibly.

"I just don't understand how it is possible to live with such thoughts," said Pierre. "I've had moments like that, it happened just recently, in St. Petersburg, but then I sink so low that I'm not even alive, everything is so disgusting, myself most of all – I don't wash, I don't eat . . . so how can you . . ."

"Yes, the same thoughts, but not quite the same," Prince Andrei replied. "I see that's how things are, that everything's senseless and disgusting, but I'm still alive – and I'm not to blame for that; it seems that somehow I'll have to carry on living as best I can, without bothering anyone, until I die."

"But what makes you keep on living? With thoughts like that you'll just sit there without moving, without undertaking . . ."

"That's what's so annoying, that life won't leave me in peace. I'd be glad not to do anything, but then, in the first place, the local nobility honoured me by electing me their marshal: I barely managed to get out of it. They couldn't understand that I don't have what they need, I don't have that certain good-natured vulgarity that the position requires. And then there's this house, which had to be built so that I would have my own little corner where I can be at peace. And now there's the home guard, and they won't leave me in peace over that either."

"Why don't you serve in the army?"

"After Austerlitz!" Prince Andrei said gloomily. "No, I promised myself I wouldn't serve in the active Russian army again. And I won't. Even if Bonaparte were encamped on our doorstep, at Smolensk, threatening Bleak Hills, even then I wouldn't serve in the Russian army. Well, as I was saying," said Prince Andrei, calming down and continuing, "now there's the home guard, my father's been appointed commander-in-chief of the third district, and the only way I can avoid serving is to become his assistant."

"And will you do that?"

"Yes, I've already been approved." He paused briefly. "And that's how everything is done, my dear fellow," he went on, smiling. "I could have got out of it, but do you know why I took that position? You'll tell me I confirm your theories about doing good. I took it – I'll be honest with you – because my father is one of the most remarkable men of his time, but he is getting old, and he's not exactly cruel, but his character is too inflexible. What makes him terrifying is that he is accustomed to un-limited power, and now he has the power conferred by the sovereign on the home guard commanders-in-chief. If I'd arrived two hours later two weeks ago, he'd have hanged the registrar in Yukhnovo. Well, I took the post because I'm the only person who has any influence on my father, and there will be times when I'll be able to save him from some action that would torment him afterwards."

"Ah, so now you see . . ."

"Yes, but it's not what you think," Prince Andrei continued. "I didn't wish to do the slightest good for that rascally registrar who had stolen some boots or other from the men in the home guard; I would actually have been very pleased to see him hanged, but I feel sorry for my father – that is, for myself once again."

Now, after lunch, Prince Andrei livened up for the first time since Pierre's arrival. His eyes sparkled merrily as he tried to demonstrate to Pierre that what he had done had nothing whatever to do with com-passion or the desire to do good for his neighbour.

"Well then, you wish to liberate the peasants," he went on. "That's very good. But not for you, not for me, and least of all for the peasants. I don't think you have ever had anyone flogged or sent to Siberia. If they are beaten, flogged and sent to Siberia, they are none the worse for that. In Siberia they still live like cattle, and the weals on their bodies heal, and they're as happy as they were before. But it *is* necessary for those people who are suffering a moral death, who build up remorse, then suppress that remorse and grow coarse because they have the opportunity to execute people, justly or unjustly. They are the people I pity, and for their sake I would like to liberate the peasants. Perhaps you have never seen it, but I have seen how, with the years, good people raised in these traditions of unlimited power grow irritable and become cruel and coarse and, knowing this, they cannot restrain themselves and become more and more miserable."

Prince Andrei said this with such ardour that Pierre could not help thinking these thoughts must have been inspired by his father. He did not answer the prince.

"So you see whom and what I feel sympathy for: human dignity, a tranquil conscience, a pure heart, and not their backsides and their foreheads – no matter how often they are flogged or shaved, they'll always be just backsides and foreheads."

"*Vrai*, that's right, that's right," cried Pierre, who liked this new angle on the matters that were occupying his mind.

That evening Andrei and Pierre got into a carriage and set out for Bleak Hills. Prince Andrei kept glancing at Pierre, occasionally breaking the silence with exclamations that showed he was in a very good mood.

"How glad I am to see you! So glad!" he said.

Pierre remained gloomily silent, replying in monosyllables, as if engrossed in his own thoughts.

"Are you fond of children?" the prince asked after one of these silences. "Be sure to tell me the truth now, say if you like him or not." Pierre curtly promised.

"How strange you are, you've changed," said Prince Andrei. "And for the better, greatly for the better."

"And do you know why I've changed?" said Pierre. "I'll never find a better time than this to talk to you about it." He suddenly swung round bodily inside the carriage and said: "Give me your hand." Pierre gave Andrei the Masonic handshake, but Andrei's hand did not respond. "Are you really a Mason?" he asked.

"If you believe in something that is higher than this . . ." Pierre began.

"Stop, don't go on, I used to think the same way. I know what Freemasonry is, in your eyes."

Pierre still didn't say anything. He was thinking that he ought to reveal Masonic teaching to Andrei; but as soon as he started thinking what he would say and how he would say it, he sensed that Prince Andrei would demolish his teaching with a single word, a single argument, and he was afraid of exposing his beloved holy of holies to the danger of mockery.

"But why do you think that?" Pierre suddenly began, lowering his head like a bull charge. "Why do you think like that? You mustn't think like that."

"What are you talking about?"

"About life, about man's purpose in life, about the kingdom of evil and disorder. That things have to be like that. I used to think that way, and do you know what saved me? The Masons. No, don't smile, Freemasonry isn't a religious sect or set of rituals, as I used to think, but it is the best, the only expression of the finest, the eternal aspects of humanity." And he began expounding Freemasonry to Andrei as he understood it, in a manner with which his brother Masons would hardly have agreed. He said that Freemasonry was the teaching of wisdom, the teaching of Christianity, freed from the fetters of the state and religion, a teaching that recognised the primacy in man of his ability to perfect himself, to help his neighbour, to eradicate all evil and spread this teaching of equality, love and knowledge.

"Yes, that's all very fine, but it's Illuminism, and it's prosecuted by the government, and being well known, it's therefore powerless."

"I don't know where Illuminism ends and Freemasonry begins," said Pierre, lapsing into that state of verbal ecstasy in which he was oblivious to everything else, "and I don't wish to know. I know that these are my convictions and I enjoy the sympathy of fellow thinkers, whose numbers are countless in the present and in the past, and to whom the future belongs. Only our sacred brotherhood has any real meaning in this life; all the rest is a dream," he said. "You must understand, my friend, that everything apart from this alliance is full of lies and falsehood, and I agree with you that there is nothing that an intelligent and good man such as yourself can do, except live out his life trying not to harm others. But accept our basic teachings, join our brotherhood, give us your hand, allow yourself to be guided, and immediately you will feel, as I did, that you are a part of this immense, invisible chain with its beginning lost in the heavens."

Prince Andrei looked straight ahead without responding, as he listened to what Pierre was saying. Several times, when he could not catch something because of the noise of the carriage, he asked Pierre to repeat the words he had lost. From the special glow that was kindled in Andrei's eyes and his silence, Pierre could see that his words were not in vain and that Andrei would not interrupt him. He no longer felt afraid of any derisive or cold rebuff, and only wished to know how his words were being received.

When they reached the river, they had to cross on the ferry, because it had burst its banks. While the carriage and horses were being loaded, they walked on foot onto the ferry and stood, leaning their elbows on the railing. Prince Andrei looked out across the flood waters sparkling in the setting sun, and still did not say a word.

"Well, what do you think? Why don't you say anything?"

"What do I think? I'm listening to you. Everything you say is right. But you say: join the brotherhood and we'll show you the meaning of life and the purpose of man and the laws that govern the world. But who are *we*? Mere men. How is it that your brotherhood knows everything, and I don't, and you, just one man, do not know what you are."

"How do you mean, I don't know?" Pierre exclaimed ardently. "I do know. I feel in my very soul that I am part of that immense, harmonious whole. I certainly feel that I am one of a countless number of beings that is the manifestation of the divine being – a higher power, whatever you like – that I am a single link, a single step up from the lowest being to the highest! If I can clearly see this ladder that leads from the plant to man, then why should I assume that this ladder, to which I can see no end below me – it is lost among the plants and the polyps – why should I assume that this ladder breaks off with me, and does not lead on further to higher beings? You have read Herder. He is a truly great philosopher and sage. He says . . ." and Pierre began expounding Herder's entire doctrine, which was still completely new at the time, a doctrine with which Pierre had become intimately familiar and understood profoundly.

The carriage and the horses had been led out onto the other bank and harnessed together, the sun was already half-hidden, and the evening frost was covering the puddles by the river-crossing with glittering stars but, to the astonishment of the servants, coachmen and ferrymen, Pierre went on standing there, waving his arms about and talking away in his lisping voice, while Prince Andrei stood there rooted to the spot, listening with his eyes gazing forward at the red reflection of the sun on the blue flood water.

"Yes, my friend," Pierre concluded, "there is a God in heaven and good on earth."

Prince Andrei sighed like a child and cast a radiant glance, as gentle as a child's, at Pierre's face, which was flushed with enthusiasm, although he still looked bashfully at his superior friend.

"Yes, if only it were so!" said the prince. "But let's get into the carriage." As he walked off the ferry, Prince Andrei glanced up at the high, clear sky, and for the first time since Austerlitz he saw the same high, eternal sky he had seen as he lay on the battlefield, bleeding to death. Recognising this sky, he recalled his entire state of mind and his thoughts at that time, and was amazed at how he could have slipped back afterwards into the old rut of life's petty cares and forgotten all of this. Pierre had not convinced him. All Pierre's logical arguments had only impressed him with their cool reason, but the passionate devotion with which Pierre clung to his convictions, as if to some plank of wood that would save his life, and his evident desire to share with his friend the happiness that these convictions brought him and, above all, Pierre's diffidence in adopting a didactic tone for the first time with someone with whom he had always agreed about everything – all of this, in combination with the marvellous April evening and the stillness of the water, made Prince Andrei aware once again of the high, eternal sky and the heightened sense of his own being, still pulsing with the forces of young life which he had thought already exhausted.

"Why not?" Prince Andrei replied to the insistent demand to introduce him into the Masonic lodge. "Why not? It is no trouble to me, and it will bring you great pleasure."

# XXX

In 1807 life at Bleak Hills had changed little, except that there was now a nursery where the little princess's quarters had been, and instead of her, the little prince lived there with Mademoiselle Bourienne and his English nanny. Princess Marya had completed her lessons in mathematics and only went to her father's study in the mornings to greet him when he was at home. The old prince had been appointed one of the home guard's eight commanders-in-chief for the whole of Russia and he had recovered so much of his strength since his son's return that he felt he had no right to refuse the position, to which he had been assigned by the sovereign himself. He was still the same as he had always been, except that recently, before he had eaten anything in the mornings, and shortly before lunch, he was visited more frequently by those moments of wild fury that made him terrifying to his subordinates and unbearably difficult with members of his household.

In the cemetery at the church there was a tall new monument standing on the little princess's grave, a chapel with a marble statue of a weeping angel. The old prince had entered this chapel once, begun blowing his nose angrily and come back out. Prince Andrei did not like to look at this monument either, it seemed to him – as it probably did to his father – that the face of the weeping angel resembled the princess's face, and was saying the same thing: "Ah, what have you done to me! I gave you everything that I could, and what have you done to me?" Only Princess Marya visited the chapel willingly and frequently; she took her little nephew with her, trying to transmit her own feelings to the child but frightening him with her tears.

The old prince had only just returned from a trip to the provincial capital on matters of state service and, as usually happened, the activity had enlivened him. He had returned in a cheerful mood and was particularly pleased when his son arrived with a guest; although he had not met Pierre in person before, he had heard about him from Pierre's father, with whom he had been friends. Prince Andrei led Pierre into his father's study and immediately left to visit Princess Marya's rooms and see his son. When he came back, the old man and Pierre were arguing, and Andrei was glad to see, from the lively look in his father's old eyes and his loud voice, that the old man had taken a genuine liking to Pierre.

They were arguing, as was only to have been expected, about Bonaparte, on whom Nikolai Andreevich so to speak examined every new arrival. The old man was still not able to stomach Buonaparte's reputation, and tried to demonstrate that he was a poor tactician. Pierre's opinion of his former hero had greatly changed, but he still considered him a man of genius, despite accusing him of betraying the ideas of the revolution. The old prince could not understand this point of view at all. He only judged Buonaparte as a general.

"What then, you think it was clever of him to take up a position with his back to the sea?" said the old man. "If it wasn't for those Kuxhevens" (which was what he called Buxhöwden), "he would have come off badly."

"That is precisely his strength," Pierre objected, "that he despises military traditions and does everything in his own way."

"Yes, and he got caught in a crossfire in his own way at Austerlitz . . ."

But just at that moment Prince Andrei came in and the old prince stopped talking.

He never spoke of Austerlitz in his son's presence.

"Still talking about Bonaparte," Prince Andrei said with a smile.

"Yes," replied Pierre, "remember how we regarded him two years ago."

"And now," said Prince Andrei, "now, it is clear to me that all this man's strength is based on his contempt for ideas, and on lies. You only have to convince all your men that you always win, and you will win."

"Tell us about that puddle at Arcole, Prince Andrei," the old man said, laughing in anticipation.

The old man had heard this story a hundred times, and still he made Andrei tell it again. It concerned the details of the taking of the bridge at Arcole in 1796. While Prince Andrei was a prisoner, he had heard it from an eyewitness, a French officer. At that time Bonaparte's imagined feat of heroism, when he was still only commander-in-chief, was even more famous and widely known than it is now. The story was repeatedly told by word of mouth and in print and pictures of how the French forces were hesitating on the bridge when they were raked with grapeshot and Bonaparte grabbed the banner and dashed forward on to the bridge and the troops, inspired by his example, followed him and took the bridge. The eyewitness had told Andrei that none of this had happened. It was true that the troops had hesitated on the bridge and fled several times after being sent forward; it was true that Bonaparte had ridden up and dismounted from his horse to inspect the bridge. However, he did not dismount at the head of the troops. The troops who were ahead of him had come running back and knocked little Bonaparte off his feet, and in his efforts to escape the crush, he had ended up in a trench full of water, getting muddy and soaked to the skin. It had taken quite an effort to get him out, seat him on someone else's horse and take him away to be dried off. The French had not taken the bridge that day, but the next, when they set up gun batteries that knocked out the Austrian ones . . .

"That's the way the French acquire their glory," the old man said, laughing in his irritating way, "and he ordered them to write in despatches that he carried the banner on to the bridge."

"But he has no need of this glory," said Pierre, "his greatest glory is the suppression of the Terror."

"Ha-ha-ha. The Terror . . . Well, enough of that." The old man stood up. "Well, brother," he said, turning to Andrei, "your friend's a fine fellow. I've taken a real liking to him. He fires me up. Some people say clever things the whole time, and I still don't want to listen, but he's always wrong and I just can't resist arguing with him. And he's brought back the old times for me, when I was in the Crimea with his father. Go along, then," he said. "Perhaps I'll come to supper. We'll have another argument. Off you go, my friend. Be good to my little fool, Princess Marya."

Prince Andrei took Pierre to see Princess Marya, but she was not expecting them so early and was still in her room with her favourite guests.

"Come on, let's go and see her," said Prince Andrei. "She's hiding away in there now with her godly people, serve her right, she'll be embarrassed, and you'll see the godly people. It's amusing, it really is."

"But exactly what are godly people?" asked Pierre.

"You'll see."

Princess Marya was indeed greatly embarrassed and came out in red blotches when they entered her cosy little room with the icon lamps standing in front of the icon cases. A young boy with long hair, dressed in a monk's habit, was sitting beside her on the divan in front of the samovar. Sitting near them in an armchair was an old woman with a black shawl covering her head and shoulders.

"Andrei, why didn't you warn me?" she said in meek reproach, moving to stand in front of her wandering pilgrims like a nesting bird facing up to a black kite. "I'm glad to see you, very glad," she said to Pierre as he kissed her hand. She had known him as a child, and now his friendship with Andrei, his misfortune in marriage and, above all, his kind, reticent face, endeared him to her. She looked at him with her beautiful, radiant eyes and seemed to be saying: "I love you very much, but please don't laugh at *my people*."

"Ah, Ivanushka's here again," said Andrei, indicating the young pilgrim with a smile while his sister was speaking to Pierre.

"Andrei!" Princess Marya said imploringly.

"You know, *c'est une femme*, he's a woman," Andrei said to Pierre.

"Andrei, for God's sake," Princess Marya repeated her appeal. It was clear that Prince Andrei's mocking attitude to the pilgrims and Princess Marya's ineffective intercession for them were their usual, well-established manner of speaking to each other.

"But *ma chère, ma bonne amie*," said Prince Andrei, "you ought to be grateful to me for explaining your intimate friendship with this young man."

"Really?" Pierre asked with serious curiosity (for which Princess Marya was especially grateful to him), peering at Ivanushka's face over the top of his spectacles. Meanwhile Ivanushka-the-woman, realising that he was being talked about in French, was running his cunning glance over everyone there.

Princess Marya had no need at all to feel embarrassed for *her people*. They were not in the least bit timid. The old woman got into conversation with Prince Andrei, speaking in the special inward, sing-song voice she used when she talked about holiness. Ivanushka-the-woman, also un-embarrassed, sipped his tea and tried to speak in a bass voice as he replied to Prince Andrei's questions.

"So have you been in Kiev?" Prince Andrei asked the old woman.

"I have, father. Father Amfilokhii gave me his blessing. He's grown very weak, little mother," she said, turning to Princess Marya. "I think he's seeking salvation already in this world. He's as thin as thin can be, and when you approach to be blessed, his hand smells of funeral incense. I went to the caves. It's easy to get in the caves nowadays. The monks know me. They just give me the key and I go and kiss the saints, I pray to them all, glory be to Thee, Lord."

Everybody else was silent as the pilgrim spoke in her calm, steady voice.

"And where else have you been?" asked Prince Andrei. "Have you been to see the Mother?"

"That's enough, Andrei," said Princess Marya. "Don't tell him about it, Pelageyushka."

"No, it's all right, little mother, why shouldn't I tell him? You think he's laughing at me. No, he's kind and god-fearing, a benefactor, he gave me ten roubles, I remember. I was in Kalyazin. In Kalyazin, little mother. The Holy Virgin revealed herself to me, I was able to see the miraculous icon. It's a miracle, father, chrism flows out of her cheek."

"All right, all right, you can tell me later," said Princess Marya, blushing.

"If I may ask her something," said Pierre. "How do you mean, chrism?"

"Myrrh – it just flows out, my darling, out of the Holy Mother's cheek, such a sweet fragrance, father."

"And you believe that?" said Pierre.

"How couldn't I believe it?" the pilgrim asked, startled.

"But it's a trick."

"Ah, father, what are you saying!" said Pelageyushka, horrified, turning to Princess Marya for protection.

"Oh, come on, he's speaking the truth," said Prince Andrei.

"Lord Jesus Christ," said the pilgrim, crossing herself, "you too. Oh, don't say that, father. There was one gen'ral as didn't believe, he said: 'It's a trick of the monks', and the moment he said it, he went blind. And then he had a dream that our Mother the Holy Virgin came to him and said: 'Believe in me and I will cure you.' And so he started begging them: take me to her, take me. It's the honest truth I'm telling you, I saw it with my own eyes. They took the blind man straight to her: he walked up, fell down before her and said: 'Heal me! I give everything the Tsar's bestowed on me to you,' he said. I saw it myself, they pinned his star decoration on her. And then he could see!" she said, turning to Princess Marya.

Princess Marya blushed. Ivanushka glowered at everyone with his cunning eyes.

Prince Andrei simply could not help laughing – he was used to teasing his sister in this loving fashion.

"So the Holy Mother was promoted to the rank of general."

"Father, father, that's a sin, you have children," the pilgrim said in a voice that was suddenly angry and frightened. Her face was bright red and she kept glancing round at Princess Marya. "It's a sin, what you just said. May God forgive you." She crossed herself. "Lord, forgive him. Little mother, what's going on?" She stood up, almost crying, and began gathering her little bag together. She was obviously afraid of a person who could have said such a thing, and pitied him, and felt ashamed of having accepted charity in a house where it could be said. Princess Marya did not need to ask Andrei again. This time both he and Pierre, especially Pierre, attempted to calm the pilgrim and convince her that no one really thought that, it had just been a slip of the tongue. The pilgrim calmed down, and then spent a long time telling them about the happiness of wandering alone through the caves, about Father Amfilokhii's blessing and so forth. Then she started singing a chant.

Princess Marya let her visitors go to their beds for the night and took her brother and his guest to drink tea.

"You see, count," said Princess Marya, "Andrei refuses to agree with me that a life of pilgrimage is a great thing. To leave everything behind, all your ties, all the joys of life and go off through the world, relying on nothing but charity, praying for everyone, for your benefactors and your enemies."

"Yes," said Prince Andrei, "if you did it, it would be a sacrifice, but for them it's a career."

"No, you don't understand. Just listen to what they say."

"I have listened, and I hear only ignorance, delusion and wanderlust, but you hear everything you want to hear, everything that is in your heart."

"Well, I agree with the princess," said Pierre. "It's just that I find these superstitious delusions pitiful."

"Oh, you would agree with Princess Marya about everything, you're exactly the same."

"And I'm very proud of that."

When Pierre had left Bleak Hills, all the members of the family, apart from Mademoiselle Bourienne, gathered together and began discussing him in the way people always do, but most unusually, this time everyone only had good things to say. Even Mikhail Ivanovich kept praising him, knowing this would give pleasure to the old prince. Princess Marya often asked about him and requested Andrei to write to him more often. Although Andrei rarely spoke about him, Pierre's visit proved a turning point. Without any discussion, he began encouraging on his own estate all of Pierre's suggestions, all of those dreams he had almost laughed at and disputed in conversation with him. At Bogucharovo an outbuilding was assigned as a hospital, the priest was given instructions and money to teach the children, the burden of corvée labour was reduced, and a request was forwarded for the Bogucharovo peasants to be granted their liberty.

*

It happened on the 26th of February. The coachmen who had driven the old prince to the town returned, bringing documents and letters for Prince Andrei. His valet, failing to find him in the study, went to Princess Marya's room, but he was not there either, and the valet was told he had gone to the nursery.

"Pardon me, your excellency, Petrusha's come with some papers," said one of the nanny's young helpers to Prince Andrei, who was seated on a little child's chair and, with trembling hands and a frown, was just then counting drops of medicine into a glass half-filled with water which, on pouring in too many drops, he angrily tipped all over the floor, demanding more water.

"My friend," said Princess Marya from the little bed where she was standing, "why don't you wait a little, later . . ."

"Ah, I beg you, please, you're always talking nonsense, you kept on waiting, now see what things have come to," he said peevishly, clearly wishing to pique his sister.

"My friend, it really would be better not to wake him, he's fallen asleep."

Prince Andrei tiptoed across uncertainly with the glass.

"Or perhaps you're right when you say not to wake him," he said. Princess Marya pointed out the girl who was calling him out of the room. Prince Andrei went out, muttering as he went: "Why the hell did these have to come?" He snatched the envelopes and his father's letter out of the hands that proffered them, and went back into the nursery. The old prince had written on blue paper in his own large hand with elongated letters, using headings here and there, as follows: "I have received most joyful news just this moment by courier, if it is not lies. Bennigsen has supposedly won a total victory over Buonaparte at Pultusk. Everybody in St. Petersburg is exultant and countless numbers of decorations have been sent to the army. Even though he is a German, I congratulate him. I cannot fathom what the Korcheva marshal of the nobility, a certain Count Rostov, is doing: the additional men and provisions have still not been delivered. Gallop over there immediately and tell him I'll have his head if everything is not here in a week's time. I have just received a letter about Pultusk from Petenka – it is all true. As soon as there is no interference from those who have no business interfering, a German has beaten Napoleon. They say he is fleeing in great disorder."

In earlier times this letter would have been an extremely heavy blow to Prince Andrei but, having received it, read it through rapidly and grasped its essential meaning, which was, firstly, that fate was continuing to play its tricks on him by arranging for Napoleon to be defeated while he was sitting at home feeling, entirely without reason, ashamed for the defeat at Austerlitz and, secondly, that his father required him to leave immediately for Korcheva to see some Rostov or other, he remained absolutely indifferent to both points.

"Damn them all, and their Pultusks and Bonapartes and decorations," were his thoughts about the first point. "No, I'm sorry, I won't go now, not while Nikolenka is still in this condition," was his response to the second point, and he went back into the nursery, holding the open letter in his hand, and looked around for his sister.

It was the second night neither of them had slept because they were caring for the boy, who was burning up with fever. All this time, because they did not trust their own household doctor, they had tried one medicine and then another while they waited for the doctor who had been sent for from the town. Exhausted by lack of sleep, in their alarm and anxiety they had been reproaching each other and quarrelling. As Prince Andrei went back into the room, holding the letter in his hand, he saw the nanny hide something from him with a frightened look on her face and noticed that Princess Marya was not by the little bed.

"My friend," he heard Princess Marya say behind him, in a whisper of what he thought was despair. As often happens in moments of fearful anticipation, he was overcome by a sudden, groundless fear.

"It's over, he's dead," he thought, his heart broke and the cold sweat stood out on his forehead. He walked across to the bed with his thoughts in turmoil, certain that he would find it empty, but the pretty, rosy-cheeked child was lying there, sprawled in it. Prince Andrei leaned down and felt with his lips, as his sister had taught him to do, to see if the child had a fever. The tender forehead was moist: he touched it with his hand, and even the hair was wet. He could see some kind of shadow beside him under the curtains of the little bed, but he did not look round, he was so happy, looking at the child's face and listening to his regular breathing. The dark shadow was Princess Marya, who had approached the bed with silent steps, raised the curtain and lowered it behind herself. There was a dense half-light under the muslin curtain, and the three of them seemed to be isolated from the entire world.

"He's broken into a sweat," said Prince Andrei.

"I went to find you and tell you that."

Prince Andrei looked at his sister with his kind eyes and smiled guiltily. The tears of happiness in Princess Marya's radiant eyes made them glow even more brightly than usual. Quietly, so as not to wake the child, they clasped each other by the hand, and in making this gesture the awkward Princess Marya caught the edge of the coverlet of the bed. They wagged their fingers at each other and stood there for a little longer in the dense light behind the curtain, as if they felt sorry to leave this pure, separate world that was filled with such love, until eventually they emerged, sighing and with ruffled hair, and closed the curtain behind them.

The next day the boy was perfectly well, and Prince Andrei went to Korcheva to carry out his father's instructions.

# XXXI

Although the final debt of forty-two thousand, taken on to pay for Nikolai's losses, was an insignificant sum relative to the entire fortune of Count Rostov, it was the little one-pound weight that finally tipped the scales already loaded with hundredweights. This was the final sum borrowed by the count against his good word, and paying it back finally undermined the Rostov family's affairs. In autumn the promissory notes and requisitions of the Guardian Council would fall due for collection, and there was nothing with which to pay them, without selling off estates. But the old count, with the conviction of a gambler engrossed in the game, paid no attention to the banker and carried on believing. Mitenka, fishing in troubled waters, made no attempt to clarify matters. On the pretext of reducing their outgoings, the count and his family went to the country, intending to spend the winter there as well. But living in the country brought the count no closer at all to mending his affairs. He lived at his estate of Otradnoe, which had five hundred souls and produced no income at all, but had a splendid garden and a park with a conservatory, a huge pack of hunting dogs, a choir with musicians and a stud farm. Unfortunately, that year there had been two conscriptions and the establishment of the home guard, which had ruined many landowners in Russia; they also completed his ruin. Every third working man was taken from his estates for the home guard, so that in the arable provinces, the area of plough land had to be reduced, and in the quit-rent provinces, which were his major sources of income, the peasants did not pay and could not pay their arrears. In addition to that, he had to hold back tens of thousands of roubles for equipment and provisions. But the count never deviated even slightly from either his cordial joviality or his hospitality, which assumed an even greater scale in the countryside after he was unanimously elected marshal of the nobility. In addition to the immense reception and amusements to which he treated the gentry of his district, he paid with his own money for some of the poorest among them and stood up for them with every means he could muster, against the commander-in-chief, Prince Bolkonsky, despite the commander's reputation for great severity. This was why his district was responsible for the omissions that had made Nikolai Andreevich so furious and which he had sent his son, Prince Andrei, to put right.

Mitenka and his family lived in a large separate building in Otradnoe village, and everyone who had any business with the count knew it was here, in Mitenka's house, that all matters were decided. A crowd of peasant headmen in new kaftans and clean boots, and tattered peasants and women with petitions all clustered around his porch. Mitenka came out in his smoking jacket, cheeks flushed, and with a vague, distracted manner.

"Well, what do you want?"

The head man of the village began explaining that the home guard recruiting officer had come again, demanding men for training tomorrow, and the fallow land wasn't yet ploughed.

"What shall we do?"

Mitenka frowned.

"The devil only knows what they're up to. Might as well abandon the entire estate. I told him to write," he muttered to himself. "And what's this?"

It was a document from the district police superintendent, demanding money on the orders of the commander-in-chief. Mitenka read it.

"Say he's not here, he's going to town now. I'll tell him later. Well, what do you want?"

An old peasant fell at his feet.

"Father! They've taken Vanka, at least let them leave Matiushka! Order them to cancel it!"

"They've told you it's only for while."

"How's that, for a while, father? They're saying they'll take everyone."

A woman petitioning for her husband threw herself at his feet.

"Well now, yours should have been taken long ago for being such a boor."

Another dozen men, also clearly supplicants, appeared from round the corner.

"Look, I can't listen to all of you. The Tsar has ordered . . ."

"Father . . . Little father . . ."

"Look, go to the master, will you . . ."

"Father, protect us."

At that moment a huge carriage with six well-fed greys harnessed in pairs went thundering past the steward's porch. At the back stood two plump, well-fed servants in silver embroidered livery. The fat, red-faced coachman with a pomaded beard started yelling at the people, and the nearest colt began prancing. "Keep his rein short, Vaska." The carriage drove up to the colonnaded entrance between the rows of shrubs that stood in tubs in front of the huge Otradnoe house. The count was going to town for his meeting with Prince Andrei, but he knew he would be back the next day, since the day after that was his name-day, a day of celebration, and there would be a reception. A household theatre had been under construction for some time in the large hall as a surprise for that day – and despite the noisy thudding of the axes as they constructed the stage, the count was not supposed to know about it. Many visitors from Moscow and the provincial town had already started gathering for the day.

Mitenka dismissed the crowd of people, saying the count had no time and nothing could be changed, because it had all been decided in the count's name.

Prince Andrei was spending his second day in the district town, he

464

had carried out all the necessary instructions with the authority granted to him by his father and was only waiting for his meeting with the marshal of the nobility, which was set for that evening, before leaving. It hardly need be said that, despite the change which, he flattered himself to hope, had taken place in him, the prince could not possibly associate with anyone in the town, not even the local mayor or the judge. He strolled about, as if he were walking through a desert.

One morning he went to the market and, captivated by the beauty of a certain young woman selling bread, he gave her five roubles to start her trade; the next day a peasant came to him, complaining of his daughter's disgrace. They were taunting her for being the mistress of the commander-in-chief's son. Prince Andrei changed a note and the next day, he went to the bazaar and handed out five roubles to each and every one of the girls there. When Ilya Andreevich arrived in the town and changed his clothes at the judge's house, he learned what young Bolkonsky had done and was greatly delighted by it. He entered Prince Andrei's room, hurrying as he always did, with a jovial air, even more jovial than usual.

The old count possessed that great advantage of good-hearted people that he did not need to alter his behaviour for anyone, important or unimportant. He could not be more affable than he already was with everyone.

"Well hello, my dear prince! I'm very pleased to make your acquaintance. I've met your father, but he probably doesn't remember me. Aren't you ashamed to be staying here? You could have come straight to me, it's only a stone's throw away, my drivers would have got you there in no time, and you and your servants would have had peace and quiet, and we could have talked about business, and I expect you haven't even been able to find anything to eat; my little countess and my children would all be heartily glad to see you. Come with me now, you can stay the night, stay as long as you wish, the day after tomorrow is my patron saint's day, pray don't disdain my hospitality, prince. Wait a little while with the business, I'll just call my secretary and we'll arrange everything in a moment. I have the money ready; I know, little father, that duty comes before all else."

Perhaps it was because the count and his secretary really had presented adequate reasons for the delay in fulfilling certain demands and provided Prince Andrei with every satisfaction that it was possible to provide, or perhaps because the prince was won over by the old count's manner of open-hearted goodwill, behind which there lay nothing more than a general attitude of generous benevolence towards everybody without exception, but Prince Andrei felt in any case that all his official

465

business had been concluded and, if it had not been concluded, then the hindrance was by no means the old count's reluctance to oblige the government, the prince's father and everybody else in the world.

"Well, prince, that was a fine joke you played on the market girls! I like that, it was lordly." And he slapped the prince genially on the shoulder.

"Now, please, prince, do not refuse to be my guest for a while, say, just for a week," he said, as if he had no doubt that the prince would certainly go to his home. Prince Andrei was in a particularly good mood following the happy outcome of his son's illness, a mood rendered jovial by the episode with the market girls, and he felt he could not refuse the old count, especially since he belonged to that category of people who were so different from the prince that he never measured them against himself and found them especially likeable.

"Well, not for a week," he said, smiling.

"We'll see about that," the old count replied with a beaming, joyful smile. "You'll see, the day after tomorrow, there'll be a play at my place, it's my girls' idea. Only it's a secret, a surprise, be careful not to let it slip!"

The old count seated the prince in his carriage, telling the prince's carriage to follow, and brought the prince home for evening tea at Otradnoe. The dear old man chattered away merrily the whole time and this chatter made the young Bolkonsky warm to him even more. He spoke with such love and respect of his son, whom Prince Andrei remembered having seen once abroad; he spoke so cautiously about his daughters, trying hard not to praise them (Prince Andrei understood this was the innate delicacy of a father of marriageable girls mentioning them to an eligible single man); he took such a simple view of all relations between people and was so unlike all those proud, restive and ambitious individuals, of whom the prince himself was one, and whom he so disliked, that the prince felt a particular liking for him.

"So this is my little shack," the count said with a certain pride as he led the prince up the broad, shallow stone steps decorated with potted plants, and into the large hallway, where more than a dozen grubby but cheerful servants leapt to their feet. The old man took him straight through to the ladies on the drawing-room balcony, where they were all sitting at the tea table. Prince Andrei found in the Rostov family, just what he had expected to find: an old Moscow lady who made meaningless, vacuous conversation in French; the prim young lady Vera, trying to appear casual while she studied every last tiny detail of a potential bridegroom; the modest, blushing ward, Sonya; and the boy's German tutor, who constantly pestered the boy with his rebukes, only in order to demonstrate to the parents and – especially – the guest that as a good German he remembered his job, and that you, mister guest, could take him into your own home if you had need of a good German, and I would gladly go with you, because here, after all, they do not know how to appreciate me properly; and there were members of the noble gentry – guests on their best behaviour at the marshal's house. All of this was just as it ought to be. There was nothing unexpected, but for some reason all of this, with its banal insignificance, touched Prince Andrei to the depths of his heart. He did not know if the reason lay in his mood, painting everything in a tender, poetic light just at that moment, or if everything around him had combined to produce this mood in him, but it all touched him, and everything he saw and heard was stamped vividly in his memory, as happens at important moments in our life.

The little old man in his soft boots hurried across to his wife, kissed her as he took her hands and indicated their visitor with his glance as they said to each other the sort of things that only a husband and wife understand. Vera, whom the prince had immediately thought disagreeable, seated herself beside the guest (he regretted that she was not as good-natured as her father). Sonya, with her high-coloured complexion, her faithful, doglike eyes and thick black plaits coiled round on her cheeks like a gun dog's ears, and the old servant, smiling as he watched the introduction of a new face, and the huge old birch tree with its branches hanging down motionless in the warm evening light, and the sound of hunting horns and yelping of hunting dogs that could be heard from the kennels behind the hill, and the horseman on the lathered thoroughbred stallion in the gilded droshky drawn up in front of the balcony in order to let the count see his favourite stallion, and the sun going down, and the short grass along the edge of the path, and the gardener's watering can standing on it – these were all engraved in his memory as the attributes of happiness. The new place, the new people, the quiet of the summer evening, the mood of calm reminiscence and a certain new, benign view of the world with which the old count had infected him during their journey, made him aware of the possibility of a new, happy life. He glanced briefly at the sky and saw it afresh once more, as at the battle of Austerlitz, he saw the high, infinitely high sky, but now there were no clouds creeping across, it was blue, clear and infinite. There was a noise at the window, like the noise of a bird that had flown into the room and was fluttering against the window that opened on to the balcony, and a desperately merry voice called out:

"Open up, I've catched myself out, mama! I've catched myself out!"

cried a figure that Prince Andrei took for a boy standing on the windowsill, laughing and crying. Catching sight of him, the boy – a delightful boy – tossed his black curls, blushed, covered his face with his hands and jumped down off the windowsill.

It was Natasha. She was wearing her male costume for the rehearsal of the play, and when she learned that her father had brought back a guest, she had come to boast and show herself off, but when she grabbed hold of the window catch, she had thought up the phrase "catched myself out" and, wishing at one and the same time to make a joke of this phrase and open the long window, which would not budge, and show herself to this new person in her male costume, which she knew suited her very well, she had started fluttering at the window like a little bird, not really knowing what she was doing herself, because, as always with her, all these thoughts had suddenly flooded into her head at the same moment, and she wanted to act on them all at once.

"Well, I'll go and take a look at Polkan," said the old count, winking and smiling at his wife to show that he hadn't seen anything and didn't know about the surprise, and walked down the balcony steps to Polkan, who was impatiently stamping his foot and whisking away the flies with a movement that rocked the summer droshky from side to side.

"That's my younger daughter, they're rehearsing a play for my husband's name-day," said the old countess.

Prince Andrei said with a smile that he already knew all about it.

"But who from?" cried the voice of that earlier head at the window (Natasha was fifteen now, she had matured and become prettier that summer). "From papa?"

"No, I found everything out here," he said with a smile.

"Ah!" said the little voice, reassured. "Mama, come here and see if this looks good." The old countess went out and Prince Andrei heard her trying to persuade her daughter to show everybody, since they would see her in that costume anyway. Meanwhile Vera explained in detail that this costume was part of the preparations for the play, that the old count really knew, but was pretending he didn't, in short, everything that Prince Andrei had understood from the first hint.

The old count was talking with the horseman about how fast Polkan could go. The sound of a balalaika came from one side, near the kitchen, and the sounds of a herd of cattle being driven home came from beyond the pond. Prince Andrei heard all these sounds, but they were only the accompaniment to the voice of the girl-boy, who was agreeing to show herself to the visitor. The old countess had persuaded her. The door suddenly swung open, and Natasha ran out onto the balcony. She was wearing moose-skin trousers, little hussar's boots and a velvet jacket embroidered with silver, open at her chest. Slim and graceful, with long curled locks reaching down to her shoulders and rosy cheeks, excited and self-assured, she was about to take a few steps forward, but suddenly she was overcome with embarrassment, covered her face with her hands and slipped back out through the door, almost knocking her mother off her feet, and all that could be heard was the squeaking of her little hussar's boots retreating rapidly across the parquet floor.

That evening Natasha, who was not usually very shy, did not come to supper.

"Why won't you go?" they asked her.

"I won't, I feel embarrassed."

The countess herself had to go up to fetch her. But when Natasha heard her mother's steps, she suddenly started to weep.

"What are you crying for? What's wrong?" the countess asked, stroking her.

"Oh, it's nothing, it annoys me that you're making so much out of nothing. Go, go on, honestly, I promise I'll come," she said and crossed herself. And in she came just before supper was served, wearing a woman's dress that was as long as the grown-ups' dresses, but with her hair still in the same style. Blushing, she curtseyed to Prince Andrei.

Although it was clear that she would still grow a lot more, she had a good figure and was already as tall as a full-grown woman. She was both pretty and plain. The features of the upper part of her face, the forehead, eyebrows and eyes, were delicate, fine and quite exceptionally beautiful, but her lips were too thick and her chin was too long and irregular, almost merging into a sturdy neck that was too powerful for the tenderness of her shoulders and breasts. But the shortcomings of her face could only have been analysed in a portrait or bust of her, all this could not be analysed in the living Natasha because the moment her face lit up, the regular beauty of the upper part of her face merged together with the rather sensual and animal expression of the lower part to form a vision of brilliant and constantly changing delight. And she was always bright and lively, even when she was not speaking, but listening or thinking. At supper she peered attentively into the new face with her keen, curious eyes, not joining in the grown-ups' conversation. Noticing how quiet she was, the old count winked merrily at Andrei, glanced sideways at his favourite daughter and said:

"There's one thing I miss about Moscow, prince: there are no theatres here, I'd give anything to see a play. Ah, Natasha!" he said, turning towards her. Prince Andrei, following his glance, also looked at her.

"You know, my daughter's a singer," said the old count.

"So you sing?" asked Prince Andrei. He spoke these simple words, looking directly into the fifteen-year-old girl's beautiful eyes. She looked at him too and Prince Andrei could not believe it when suddenly, without the slightest reason, he felt the blood rush to his face and his lips and eyes felt awkward and he realised that he had simply blushed in embarrassment, like a boy. Natasha seemed to have noticed his reaction, as had the others.

Later that evening, the old countess, now in her knitted bed-jacket, let her daughter into her room again. Natasha was especially lively following her attack of shyness and she sat there on a heap of pillows, dressed up in another of the old woman's knitted jackets and her mob cap, and held forth.

"Yes. This one's to my taste," she said.

"You know a good thing when you see it," said the countess.

Prince Andrei did not stay on, but left the next morning. Riding alone in his carriage he kept on thinking about his dead wife. Her face appeared to him as clearly as if she were alive. "What have you done to me?" the face kept saying, and his heart felt sad and heavy.

"Yes, hope and youth do exist," he told himself, "but I've had my time, I'm finished, I'm an old man," he said to himself, as he was approaching the house at Bleak Hills and passing the birch grove close to the house. When he was on his way out to Korcheva this grove had already broken into leaf, but an oak tree standing at its middle was still bare, and he had begun thinking about that oak. It was early spring, the streams of melted snow had already gone, everything was green, the birch trees were already drowning in sticky, sappy, fluffy greenery, the forest had a warm, fresh smell. Standing right beside the road, with one crooked arm stretched clumsily out above, was this old oak with a double trunk, its bark broken away on one of them. The entire old tree, with its awkward, naked arms, hands and fingers, with its hundred-year-old bark overgrown with moss, with its scabs and naked, protruding limbs, seemed to speak of old age and death. "There you go, up to the same old nonsense again," it seemed to be saying to the nightingales and the birch trees, "playing at some joy of spring or other, babbling the same old boring, stupid stories about spring, about hope, about love. It's all rubbish, all stupid nonsense. Just look at me: I'm awkward and crooked, standing here the way I was made, but I'm strong, I don't pretend, I don't ooze sap and put out young leaves (they'll only fall off), I don't play with the winds, I stand here, and I'll carry on standing here, naked and crooked, for as long as I can."

Now, on his way back, Prince Andrei remembered the oak tree which had matched his thoughts about himself, and he glanced ahead along the road, looking for the old man with his naked, battered arm stretched out in reproach to the laughing, amorous spring. But the old man was no longer there: the heat of the spring sunshine had warmed everything, the earth had softened, and the old man had been unable to resist, he had forgotten his reproaches and his pride – all the limbs that had been naked and frightening were now clad in luscious young leaves that fluttered in the breeze, young leaves had emerged from the trunk, from the gnarled bumps of tough bark, and the obstinate old man was celebrating spring and love and hope more completely and magnificently and with more feeling than anyone else.

# XXXII

The sovereign was in residence at Bartenstein. The army was stationed at Friedland.

The Pavlovsky Regiment, located in the section of the army that had been through the campaign of 1805, had arrived too late for the earliest action because it was being brought up to strength in Russia, and was now stationed in a ruined Polish village. Denisov, despite his well-known bravery, was not one of those officers who prosper in the service; he was still in command of the same squadron of hussars and, even though more than half of its number had changed, the new men, like the old ones, were not afraid of him, but felt a childish fondness for him. Nikolai was still a subaltern in Denisov's squadron, although now he was a lieutenant.

When Nikolai returned from Russia on the post-chaise he found Denisov in his campaign jacket, with his campaign pipe, in a hut with his things thrown all over the place, as dirty, shaggy and jolly as he used to be, quite different from the pomaded individual Nikolai had seen in Moscow, and the two of them embraced, realising that the affection they felt for each other was genuine. Denisov asked Nikolai about his family, and especially about Natasha. He did not try to hide his love for the sister from her brother. He said frankly that he was in love with her, but immediately (nothing was ever vague with Denisov) he added:

"Only it's not for me, it's not for an old stinking dog like me to call such a charmer my own. My job is fighting with cold steel and drinking. But I love her, I love her, that's all there is to it, and she'll have no more faithful knight until I'm killed. I'd hack anyone to death for her, for her I'd go through hell and high water."

Nikolai smiled and said:

"Why not. What if she loves you."

"Rubbish, not with my ugly mug. Wait, brother, listen. I've been living on my own here – it's so boring! So I wrote her a poem."

He read it out:

> Enchantress, say, what can this power be
> That draws me to my long-forsaken lyre?
> Why does my heart glow with enthralling fire,
> Why do my fingers thrill with ecstasy?
>
> How long have I, rapt in my deep despair,
> In bitter sadness secretly repining,
> Spurned your love with a cold heart, unfeeling,
> Rejected your pure gift with a disdainful air?
>
> But now, in cherished dreams of sweet enchantment
> Imagination has revealed a magic world,
> And roused the urge to sing my song out loud
> And fire these strings with joyous merriment.
>
> Fancies are born within my ardent breast,
> Thoughts hover in a swarm above my head,
> Swirl, flutter, vanish, reappear again,
> All is forgotten . . . sleep, and food, and rest.
>
> My blood's ablaze with fervent inspiration,
> By day and night this rapture kindles me.
> I sing a song of frenzied ecstasy,
> Consumed within by this sweet conflagration.

Ashamed of his most recent exploit at home, Nikolai had arrived in an exalted state, with the intention of serving and fighting, and not taking a single kopeck from home to make amends. With this in mind, he was particularly receptive to Denisov's friendship and all the charm of the squadron's isolated, reflective and monastic life, with its enforced idleness, despite the vodka and the cards, and he immersed himself in it with relish.

It was April, the time of thaw, mud and chill, the frozen rivers had broken up, the roads were submerged and they received no provisions for several days at a time. Men were sent round the local inhabitants to find potatoes, but there were no potatoes to be found, nor any inhabitants either. Everything had been eaten and everybody had fled. Those local people who had not fled were worse off than beggars, and either

472

they had nothing for the taking, or even soldiers completely lacking in compassion did not have the heart to take what they had. The Pavlovsky Regiment had seen hardly any action, but it had been reduced by half simply through starvation. Men were so certain of dying in the hospitals that soldiers sick with fever and swelling preferred to remain on duty and drag their exhausted legs to the front line. With the arrival of spring the soldiers, ever canny and resourceful, found a root pushing up through the ground, which for some reason they called Masha's sweet root, and they wandered over meadows and fields in search of this sweet root (which was actually very bitter), digging it up with their sabres and devouring it in spite of orders against eating this particular plant. The soldiers' hands, feet and faces began swelling up, and it was assumed that the root was to blame. The soldiers had still eaten the root despite the prohibition because, after having been promised provisions for more than a week now, they had only received a single pound of rusks per man. The horses had also been feeding off the roof-coverings of the houses for more than a week, and were now on the last of the straw that had been brought from three miles away. They were all skin and bone, and still covered with clumps of their winter coat. Denisov had won at cards and he gave more than a thousand roubles of his own money for feed and borrowed everything that Rostov had, but there was no feed to be bought anywhere.

Yet even despite this terrible disaster, the soldiers and officers lived in exactly the same way as they always had done: they lined up for roll-calls, turned up for cleaning duty, kept their equipment in proper order, and even did training, while in the evenings, they told stories and played knucklebones. But the dashing hussars had become rather ragged, and all their faces were more yellow and their cheekbones more prominent than usual. The officers gathered together in the same way, and sometimes they drank, but more often they gambled for high stakes, since a lot of money had been issued for buying provisions that could not be bought. All this money was in circulation – in the game.

"Well, brother, saddle up," Denisov cried one evening, soon after Rostov's arrival. Denisov had been to see the regimental commander for instructions. "We're taking two platoons straight away and we're going to take a supply convoy. Hell and damnation, the men can't just die like dogs!" He gave the sergeant-major the order to saddle up and he dismounted.

"What convoy? An enemy one?" asked Rostov, who had been lying on his bed in solitary boredom in their room.

"One of our own!" Denisov cried, clearly still in the grip of the impulsiveness with which he had spoken to the regimental commander.

"Look, there I am, riding along, I meet a supply convoy and I think it's for us, so I ride up and ask for some rusks. No, he tells me again. They're taking this lot to the infantry. Wait another day: I've requested it, I've written, I've written seven times, he says, there's no roads. Well, come what may, now I'm going to take any convoy we meet. We can't let the men die," Denisov continued. "They can try me later, if they like."

Still in the same irritated state of mind, Denisov mounted his horse again and set off. The soldiers knew where they were going, and they could not have supported their commander's instructions more willingly. They were in a gay mood, making fun of each other and the horses that kept stumbling and falling. Denisov looked at the men and turned away.

"What a disgusting sight," he said, and set off at a trot down the road along which the convoy would be travelling. Not all the horses could move at a trot; some were falling to their knees, but they were clearly struggling with their final strength not to fall behind the others. They eventually caught up with a supply convoy. The soldiers of the convoy were on the point of resisting, but Denisov beat the senior non-commissioned officer black and blue with his whip and turned the convoy round. Half an hour later, two infantry officers – an adjutant and a regimental quartermaster – galloped up on horseback to demand an explanation. Denisov didn't say a word in reply to their representations and just shouted to his own men:

"Keep going!"

"You will answer for this, captain; this is riotous conduct, looting from your own side, our men haven't eaten for two days. It's highway robbery. You'll answer for it, my dear sir," and the officer rode off, quivering on his horse the way infantry officers do when they ride.

"A dog on a fence, a live dog on a fence!" Denisov shouted after him, and this cavalryman's supreme insult for mounted infantry set the entire squadron laughing.

They duly handed out as many rusks as the men wanted, and even shared with the other squadrons, and when the regimental commander found out about everything, he set his open fingers over his eyes, squinted through them and said:

"This is how I regard this business, but I'm not responsible and I know nothing."

However, a day later, in response to complaints received from the infantry commander, he summoned Denisov and advised him to ride over to headquarters and at least go to the provisions department and sign for the receipt of a certain amount of provisions, because the requisition had been listed for the infantry regiment. Denisov went, and he came back to Rostov bright red with fury, he was so hot and flushed that he had to have blood let the same day; not until a deep bowl of black blood had been let from his shaggy arm was he capable of telling anyone what had happened to him. But even then, when he reached the dramatic part, he grew so furious that the blood started flowing from his arm and it had to be bandaged up.

"I get there, and do you think they're as badly off as we are? Not a bit! I look and I see those quartermaster kikes all squeaky clean and in high old spirits. Well, where's your commanding officer, I ask. They showed me in. I waited a long time. That was enough to make me furious. I cursed and swore at them all and told them to announce me. I've got army business to deal with, I've come thirty *versts*. All right, out comes the head-thief and says: you go to the commission secretary and sign there, and your actions will be reported to higher authority. Don't you teach me what to do, old man, I said. Just don't keep me waiting for three hours. Permission to leave.

"I cursed him out, and then I went. I get to the place and I'm passed from one official to another, and then another, they egg each other on, they're all dandy dressers, I tell you, I started getting really furious. I finally get to that secretary in the commission. Very well, he's dining, just a moment. I look, and I see them bringing porter, and turkey. Well, I think, I'm not going to wait for that. I go in and there's his lordship eating . . . And who is it? Can you imagine!" (At this point the bandage came unwound and the blood spurted out.) "Telyanin!"

"'So you're the one who's starving us to death!' I give it to him, left and right, across the face! Ah . . . !" (he uttered a coarse invective). "If they hadn't jumped on me, I'd have beaten him to death . . . Fine fellows, eh? Fine fellows?"

"Stop shouting, will you, calm down," said Rostov. "Otherwise they'll have to let your blood again."

*

[Some weeks later, on the 14th of June 1807] the battle of Friedland took place: the two Pavlogradsky squadrons that Denisov was command-ing were positioned on the left flank to cover the artillery, as instructed by the regimental commander the evening before. The hussars came under appallingly heavy fire as soon as action began. Ranks upon ranks were mown down and no one ordered them either to retreat or change position. As always, Denisov was scented and pomaded for battle, but he was in low spirits and gave orders to remove the dead bodies and the wounded in an angry voice. Catching sight of a general riding by not far away, he galloped up to him and explained that the entire division was going to be wiped out without it doing any good to anyone at all. The horses were so weak they couldn't go into the attack, and even if they could have done, the area was too pitted and rutted and, in conclusion, there was no need to stay where shots were falling, when they could just as well move further away. The general turned without hearing him out and rode off.

"Speak to General Dokhturov, I'm not in command here."

Denisov found Dokhturov, who told him that yet another general was in command, and the other general told him the first general was in command.

"The devil take the lot of you," thought Denisov and galloped back. Kiersten had already been killed and Rostov was now the officer-in-charge. There were so many dead that the men were becoming confused and losing formation. Denisov decided it was his duty to gather them back together. But at that very moment the infantry came running into the squadron, and threw it into confusion again.

"What was the point of getting half the squadron killed!" said Denisov. "Damnation!" But just then grapeshot struck him in the back and flung him off his horse, unconscious. Rostov, who was already accustomed to coping with the sense of fear that always came in action, tried his best to gather the squadron together as they ran, but the men simply fled in disorder.

# XXXIII

Boris had found himself a position with the Emperor's staff at the end of the last campaign, and his army career was going extremely well. He was listed with His Majesty's own Preobrazhensky Battalion, and consequently received a far higher salary and was now in the Emperor's eye. Prince Dolgorukov had not forgotten him, and had introduced him to Prince Volkonsky. Prince Volkonsky had recommended him to another extremely important individual, to whom the young Drubetskoy was attached (while continuing to receive his pay for His Majesty's own Preobrazhensky Battalion) as an adjutant. Boris was liked by everyone, especially important people, for what they called his forthright and elegant manners, modesty, appropriate conduct, conscientiousness in carrying out instructions and his precise and refined manner of expression. The Guards moved from one celebration to another, as they had in the first war; throughout the whole campaign their knapsacks and even some of the men were carried on carts. The officers rode in carriages with all the comforts of life. All of the Guards lived this way on the move, but His Majesty's own battalion lived even more luxuriously. Berg was already the senior company commander in the battalion and a Knight of St. Vladimir, very well regarded by his superiors. At Bartenstein, when Boris reported to an important individual for whom he had a note from Prince Volkonsky, he was taken on as an adjutant and so parted from Berg, since he could see a better future ahead. His hopes were justified. In the palace at Olmütz he had only seen the magnificence of the imperial court from the corridor, but here he saw it from inside the hall. He was invited to one of the balls held by the Prussian minister Hardenberg, which both the Emperor Alexander and the Prussian King graced with their presence. Boris was a fine dancer, and at that ball he was noticed. He even happened to be dancing with the Countess Bezukhova when the sovereign spoke to her. Boris was paired with the countess for the écossaise when the sovereign approached to say a few words to her after which, as he departed, he directed a genial smile at her partner, for they were all waiting to start the dance. While the Tsar had been talking with the countess, Boris had stepped away so as not to overhear them. Although no one had taught him to act that way, he knew that was what he should do. As soon as he realised, however, who this beauty was to whom the sovereign had been paying attention, he asked a lieutenant aide-de-camp that he knew to make a formal introduction. Hélène beamed her dazzling smile at Boris, the same smile she had beamed at the Tsar, and just as she had done when the Tsar had approached her to speak, so now she extended her hand towards Boris. In his opening conversation, Boris exploited his acquaintance with Prince Vasily, but, with innate tact, he avoided all mention of her husband (somehow instinctively sensing, without knowing the details, that he should do so).

Boris was constantly with the sovereign, that is, in the towns and villages where the sovereign was, and the main interest of his life was everything that was happening at court. He was at Junsburg when the terrible news of the Friedland defeat was received. He was sent to St. Petersburg and then he was on our side of the river Niemen in Tilsit for the meeting between the two Emperors. Since the individual to whom Boris was attached was not actually with the sovereign in Tilsit while both Emperors were there, but the Preobrazhensky Battalion was, Boris frankly stated that he would like to witness the event and asked his superior to allow him back to the front temporarily, and permission was granted.

In July he arrived at his battalion and was well received by his comrades, with whom he got on as well as he did with his superiors. No one

THE MEETING OF THE TWO EMPERORS AT TILSIT ON 25 JUNE 1807
*Engraving by Couché fils after the drawing by Zwiebach*

was passionately fond of him, but everyone considered him a pleasant young man. He arrived during the night – the password that had been set was: "Napoleon, France, bravery", in response to the password set by Napoleon the previous day: "Alexander, Russia, glory". That was the first news that Berg told him, with great delight. Berg showed him the house where Napoleon was, and he felt a strange thrill of joy at being so near to a man whose nearness had previously been so frightening. Boris had seen all the festivities and was hoping to get a closer look at Napoleon, when Rostov came to see him.

The next morning the officers gathered at Berg's quarters and Boris, who had witnessed the meeting two days earlier, told them about it in detail. Boris spoke with his unvarying smile, which signified either mild mockery or a gentle affection for what he had seen, or delight that he was able to tell others about it. He related events as few are able to do – with such power in his voice that they could not help but feel everything he said was the exact truth, something that he had really seen himself, and he spoke with such moderate embellishment and such a lack of personal judgements, that they listened in silence. They could feel that he was stating the facts, and avoiding expressing his own opinions.

"I was at the meeting with Napoleon," he began. "We set out early in the morning. The sovereign was riding beside the King of Prussia. The sovereign was in Preobrazhensky uniform, with a scarf and the ribbon of the Order of St. Andrew. You know the village of Ober-Mamenschek Kruk, there's an inn there not far from the river bank. The sovereign entered the inn, sat down beside the window and set his hat and gloves on the table. The generals also entered the inn and everyone stood around the door, as if they were waiting for something. The sovereign as was calm as ever, but a little thoughtful. I was standing by the window, and I could see everything. We were there for about a quarter of an hour and no one, neither the sovereign nor the King of Prussia, nor any of the generals, spoke a single word. I walked to the river bank and since, as you know, the river is not wide, not only could I make out the pavilion on rafts, with the huge monograms 'A' and 'N', I could see the whole of the opposite bank, which was completely covered with crowds of spectators. On the right I could see the Emperor Napoleon's Guards" (Boris called the former Buonaparte "Napoleon", despite not yet knowing that in the army it was now strictly forbidden to call Napoleon "Buonaparte"; his natural instinct told him this was what he should do), "and I could see similar preparations on the other bank. You understand," Boris said with a subtle smile, "just how much thought was required to arrange matters so that neither of them arrived before the other, so that our Emperor did not have to wait for Napoleon or vice versa. And in all fairness it must be said that everything was arranged splendidly, splendidly," he repeated. "It was definitely one of the most magnificent sights in the world. The moment we heard Napoleon's Guards on the other bank shout 'Long live the Emperor! . . .'"

"Then their shout's a lot better than our stupid hoorah," said one of the officers.

"Yes, and in general, the organisation of their Guards is quite exceptional! Two officers of the French Imperial Guards have promised to join us for lunch today. But continue, Drubetskoy."

"Well then, as soon as we heard the shouting on the other bank and saw the Emperor Napoleon galloping on his white horse, our aide-de-camp went dashing headlong into the inn, saying: 'He's coming, Your Majesty!'

"The sovereign came out, put on his hat and gloves very calmly and walked to the boat. They both pushed off at almost exactly the same time, but the Emperor Napoleon's boat reached the raft first. He rode standing, with his arms crossed on his chest. I must admit, he's very grand, despite being so short. But everyone was astounded by our sovereign's appearance. It was quite exceptional," Boris said with feeling, "and in general, that moment was so magnificent and touching, that no one who saw it all will ever forget it.

"The Emperor Napoleon stepped onto the raft first and hurried across to the other side so that, just as our sovereign was getting out of his boat, he could give him his hand." At this point Boris stopped with a subtle smile, as if he wished to give his listeners time to appreciate the full, profound significance of this circumstance.

"But is it true," one of his listeners asked, "that as the Emperors entered the pavilion, a French boat full of armed soldiers put out from their side and halted between our bank and the raft?"

Boris frowned, as if trying to convey that this particular circumstance, which actually had taken place and which he himself had seen, ought not to be mentioned.

His intuition had told him there was something wrong about it. Whether Napoleon really had intended, if the negotiations had ended inauspiciously, to intimidate the Emperor Alexander by saying that he had him in his power, or whether it was simply a part of the ceremonial (although no boat had moved out to the other side from our own bank of the river), it was in any case not something that ought to be mentioned, and even though he had seen the boat quite clearly and even wondered about it himself, he said:

"No, I didn't notice that," and carried on with his story. "They were in the pavilion," he said, "for exactly one hour and fifty-two minutes. I kept an eye on my watch. Then from the bank we saw them summon the gentlemen of their retinues and introduce them to each other. Then the sovereign returned by the same route, got into his carriage and went back to Amt Baublen with the King of Prussia. And so, in this, gentlemen," Boris continued, "you see the true magnificence of our sovereign, whom we cannot help comparing with the King of Prussia," Boris concluded. But the other officers seized on the subject:

"They say the King of Prussia was quite unable to control himself during the meeting: he was like a madman: he rode along the river bank aimlessly, first to the right, then to the left, as if he was trying to listen to what they were saying in there and finally he rode straight into the water, just like a madman, he probably wanted to drown himself. They say he rode into the water up to his horse's belly and stopped. Did you see that, Drubetskoy?"

"No, I didn't notice that."

"But his position really is terrible," said another young officer, "they say his wife, Queen Amalia, has come here too."

"How lovely she is! Yes, I saw her yesterday," said Berg. "I think she is even better than Maria Fedorovna. She dined yesterday with the Emperor Napoleon."

"If I were Napoleon, I would not refuse her anything."

"Yes, as long as she did not refuse him anything, either," said another officer.

"Well, that goes without saying."

All the officers laughed, apart from Boris.

"If I were in the King of Prussia's place, I would have ridden into the river out of grief too. Things are bad for him."

Boris frowned slightly, indicating with this expression that he considered such talk about an ally and a crowned lady improper, even among comrades, and he hastily changed the subject.

"Yes, gentlemen," he said, "greatness of soul does not come with a crown. I think the Friedland disaster was just as heavy a blow for our sovereign Alexander as it was for the King of Prussia, but you should have seen the courage and resolve with which he bore it."

Then Boris told his attentive listeners about the impression produced in Junsburg by the news about Friedland, and from what he said it was clear that the entire interest of this event was focused in the impression it produced on the Emperor Alexander, an Emperor who had borne so many sacrifices and made so much effort, in the confident assumption that his army was in a brilliant position, that he had been expecting news of victory; who had sacrificed his own personal glory by removing himself from command simply for the success of the cause and then, suddenly, instead of news of victory, had received news of a total defeat, for which the senior commanders and the officers and the soldiers were all to blame, and which, by denying the sovereign all the fruits of his labours, had changed all his plans and wounded him to the depths of his heart. What had the sovereign done? In his angelic meekness and greatness of soul he had not ordered all the criminals to be punished. He had simply been distressed and, after considering his position, taken new measures. Boris said all this with such genuine conviction that he made his listeners share in his conviction completely. Just then Nikolai Rostov arrived to see Boris. The appearance of an army hussar in civilian clothes, who had obviously travelled to Tilsit in secret, was badly received by the officers. But Boris greeted his old comrade hospitably. He refrained from any outpouring of feelings, but asked if Rostov would like to take tea, dine or sleep. The officers left.

## XXXIV

After the Friedland disaster, Nikolai Rostov had been left as the senior officer in the squadron, which was a squadron only in name, since he had only sixty men. They were stationed not far from the Niemen, and news of the peace had already reached them. Provisions were now adequate and the officers were already talking about a withdrawal to Russia.

At first Rostov was engrossed in the responsibilities of his new rank and managing the squadron's housekeeping. He managed it with such diligence that he even won the approval of his former enemy, now his direct superior, the regimental commander. He enjoyed receiving the squadron's rations, greeting the men, giving orders to the sergeant-major and saying "in my squadron".

He also enjoyed thinking the war was over and there were no more dangers ahead, that soon he would be able to go back to Russia and see his family. Like all the frontline officers, the very last thing he thought about was the inglorious way in which this campaign had ended.

A German proverb says: you can't see the wood for the trees. And it is true that military men who take part in a war, never see or understand the significance of that war. The war's over, you have provisions, you're on your way to Russia, or you've retreated into Poland and you're stationed with the little Polish ladies, they say there's a truce. Well, thank God for that. But how the war ended and what its result was – that will be discussed and decided by those who took no part in it. The serving soldier only becomes keenly aware of the general outcome when he meets his former enemies after the peace and sees their triumph and joy.

This is what had happened to Nikolai Rostov on the [17th] of June, when he rode to Bennigsen's headquarters to receive his orders, and on the same day met the French captain Périgord, who had come from Napoleon for the beginning of the Tilsit negotiations. At Bennigsen's headquarters Rostov stayed with his former comrade Zherkov, who was now attached to the commander-in-chief's staff. The two of them had just dropped into a camp-trader's shop when there was a movement in the street, with everyone running to look at something. Rostov and Zherkov followed the general movement and saw a handsome officer of the French Guards in a bearskin cap riding along the street, accompanied by a bugler. It was the truce envoy, Périgord. The French officer had such a contemptuous and haughty air, that Rostov suddenly felt the shame of the defeated. He hastily turned away and walked back the way he had come.

Périgord reached the commander-in-chief's headquarters during dinner and was invited to the table. Setting aside the various rumours about how haughtily this Périgord behaved and the things he said at dinner that were offensive to the Russians, eyewitnesses said that he walked in, sat down and never took off his bearskin cap the whole time he was in the commander-in-chief's headquarters. Rostov, who was obliged to wait until the evening for his documents, said nothing when he heard these rumours. He could not speak for all the indignation, shame and anger that were seething inside him so furiously. He could not help wondering whether the French were entitled to despise the Russians so greatly, and whether he and his comrades and his soldiers were not to blame for the contempt shown by this Frenchman. But no, whenever he recalled Kiersten, Denisov and his own hussars, he knew this was insolent behaviour on the part of the Frenchman and low cowardice on the part of the Russians who tolerated it.

He was standing with Zherkov and other officers on the porch of one of the houses occupied by the staff officers. Zherkov was joking, as usual.

"He must have got sweaty under that cap, I should think," he said and turned to Rostov. "Everybody's correctly dressed, but you can recognise the devil from his cap! Isn't that right, eh, Rostov?" This phrase drew Rostov out of his state of concealed fury and he said in great agitation:

"I do not understand, gentlemen," he said, raising his voice higher and higher, "how you can joke and laugh at such things. It turns my stomach: if some rubbishy French cobbler" (Rostov was mistaken: Périgord-Talleyrand was a member of the old French aristocracy) "dares to keep his cap on while he sits opposite our commander-in-chief, then what are we worth after that? How will any Frenchman feel free to treat me, a Russian officer, after that? I'm a lieutenant of hussars and I would have knocked the cap off his head with the flat of my sabre, because I'm not some Courland German, and Russian honour is dear to me."

"Come, come!" the officers said, looking around and trying to turn the whole business into a joke. There was a group of generals standing quite near, but Rostov was only exhilarated by the danger and grew even more agitated.

"Are we some kind of Prussians?" he said. "What right do they have to treat us like that? I'd have thought Pultusk and Preussisch Eylau would have shown them, but the fact that we have God knows who for our senior commanders . . ."

"That will do, that will do," said the officers.

"God knows who, Germans, sausage-eaters, madmen and possessed." Most of the officers walked away from Rostov, but as they did so, one of the generals standing nearby – a tall, thickset, grey-haired man – broke away from the group and walked up to the young hussar.

"What's your name?" he asked.

"Count Rostov, the Pavlogradsky Hussars Regiment, at your service," said Nikolai, "and I am prepared to repeat what I have just said even in the presence of His Majesty the Emperor, let alone in your excellency's presence, although I do not have the pleasure of your acquaintance."

Still frowning and looking at Rostov sternly, the general took hold of his hand.

"I share your opinion entirely, young man," he said, "entirely, and I am very glad to make your acquaintance, very glad."

At that moment the shaggy cap that had stirred up such fury in Rostov's soul appeared at the entrance to the commander-in-chief's quarters. He was leaving. Rostov turned away in order not to see him. Despite the pleasure he took in commanding the squadron and the imminent return to Russia, the feeling of shame in defeat aroused by this incident, the constant remorse he had suffered for his losses at cards in Moscow and, above all, his sadness at the loss of Denisov whom he had come to love so dearly of late and who had been rumoured to be lying in hospital, poised between life and death – all of this made his life extremely sad during the festivities in Tilsit.

Halfway through June, although it was difficult, Rostov had asked the regimental commander for leave to ride the forty *versts* to see Denisov in hospital.

The little Prussian village where the hospital was located had been devastated twice, once by the Russian army and then by the French, and precisely because it was now summer and the countryside looked so fine, its broken roofs and fences, filthy streets, tattered inhabitants and drunk or sick soldiers made a dismal sight. The hospital was set up in a stone house whose window frames and glass panes had mostly been smashed, and whose adjoining courtyard was surrounded by the broken remnants of a fence. Several pale-faced soldiers in bandages were walking about and sitting in the sun in this yard. As Nikolai had walked in through the door, he was engulfed by the stench of rotting flesh and the smell of a hospital. Just at that moment, a body was being carried along the corridor by its arms and legs – whether it was alive or dead, he couldn't tell. A Russian military doctor came out to meet him with a cigar in his mouth, accompanied by a medical assistant who was trying to report something.

"I can't be in two places at once," the doctor said, "come to the burgomaster's house this evening, I'll be there." The medical assistant asked him something else.

"Eh! Do what you think best, what difference will it make?" he answered and walked on, then was astonished to notice Rostov.

"And what are you doing here, your honour?" he said in that jocular tone peculiar to doctors, clearly not in the slightest bit embarrassed that Rostov had overheard what he said to the medical asssistant.

"What are you doing here? The bullets missed you, so you want to get typhus instead, is that it? This is a leper house, my good man, it's death for anyone who enters. The only ones still on their feet are me and Makeev (he pointed to the medical assistant). We've had five doctors die here already: set foot in here, and a week later you've had it. We've tried sending for Prussian doctors, but our allies don't care for it here" – and the garrulous doctor laughed in a way that showed he never felt like laughing normally, and especially not just now.

Rostov had explained to him that he would like to see the hussars major who was a patient there.

"We don't have any wounded here, my good man. Even if a man's wounded, he immediately becomes a typhus case here, and you can't know them all. Just think about it, I have three hospitals all to myself, over four hundred patients. Thank goodness, the Prussian ladies send us coffee and two pounds of lint each, or we'd be finished. I discharge the dead, no hold-ups there with the help of the typhus, and they keep sending me new men. Four hundred of them, aren't there, eh?" he asked the medical assistant.

"Yes, sir," replied the assistant, who had obviously been wanting his lunch for a long time and was waiting with irritable impatience for the garrulous doctor, who had been so delighted at the appearance of the new person, to go away.

"Major Denisov," Rostov repeated, "he was wounded at Moliten."

"He died, didn't he?" the doctor asked the medical assistant impassively. The medical assistant didn't know.

"Is he lanky and ginger-haired?" the doctor asked. Rostov described Denisov's appearance.

"Yes, yes," the doctor said in apparent delight, "I'm sure that one died, but anyway I'll check, I had the lists. Have you got them, Makeev?"

Despite all the doctor's efforts to persuade Rostov not to walk round the wards, which he called ruined sheds, where the sick men were lying on the floor, and all his threats that Rostov was bound to catch typhus, Rostov took leave of him, went upstairs with the medical assistant and walked round all the patients. When he saw the condition of the patients (mostly ordinary soldiers), Rostov was immediately convinced that Denisov could not be here. But even so he walked round them all. Some strange feeling told him: it is disgusting and frightening for you to see this, but look, you must, you must see this. And so Rostov walked round all the wards. He had never seen anything so terrible as what he saw in that house.

Only the first floor was occupied. The house was built like all mansion houses: a hallway, a large hall, communicating drawing rooms, a sitting room, a bedroom, a girls' room and the hallway again. There was no furniture at all. From the first room to the last of this entire circuit there were soldiers lying in two rows with their heads towards the wall, leaving a path in the middle. Some lay on torn paliasses, some on straw, some on their greatcoats on the bare floor. The smell and the ordure were terrible, the flies were clustered so thickly on the patients that they had stopped trying to brush them off. Some were dying, and their wheezing was the only sign they were still alive, others were thrashing about in a fever, jostling each other, and others gazed with their weak, feverish eyes at the healthy, fresh, clean man walking past them. There were five healthy soldiers here as orderlies, and they distributed scoops of the water that was what the sick men asked for more than anything. Denisov was not among them, and in the medical assistant Makeev's lists it said that Denisov had been registered in this hospital, but had moved to an old estate house and was being treated there by a Prussian doctor.

After a great deal of trouble, Nikolai finally found him. Denisov was recovering from his wounds, but was suffering greater inner distress from the correspondence that had followed from the incident of the convoy that he had taken by force and the beating he had given the provisions officer Telyanin. Barely acknowledging Rostov's presence and taking not the slightest interest in his talk about Périgord and Tilsit and the horrors of the hospital, Denisov was interested in only one thing, and that was the correspondence and his replies to the enquiries from the provisions department, in which he reviled all provisions officers as thieves: he revelled in the eloquence of his own writing, laughing and banging his fist on the table as he recited the jibes he had directed at the provisions department. The latest letter, which he thought extremely subtle, ironic and devastating, concluded with the words: "If the gentlemen of the commissariat acted as efficiently to supply the army's needs as they do to supply their own, then the army would never know the meaning of hunger." He handed this letter to Rostov, asking him to be sure to take it to Tilsit and hand it in to His Majesty's personal chancellery.

It had been the desire to carry out this wish that had brought Nikolai to Boris's quarters on the 27th of June.

*

"Well, I'm very glad you came just now. You'll see a lot of interesting things. Did you know that the Emperor Napoleon dined with the sovereign today?"

"Bonaparte?"

"Ah, you ignorant yokel, the Emperor Napoleon, not Bonaparte,"

Boris said with a smile. "Surely you know there's peace now, that they've had a meeting?"

"I don't know anything. Did you see it?"

"But of course, I was here."

Rostov felt awkward with his former friend. He dined and went to bed. The next morning both young men went to the review.

Rostov had arrived in Tilsit on a day that could not have been less convenient for talking with his friend Boris and submitting Denisov's letter. He could not do it himself, since he was dressed in a frock coat and had come to Tilsit without permission from his commanding officer, but neither could Boris, whom he asked, do it on that particular day, the 27th of June. From early in the morning word spread that peace had been concluded, that the Emperors had exchanged decorations – the Order of St. Andrew and the Légion d'Honneur – and that there would be a dinner for the Preobrazhensky Battalion, as the guests of the French Guards Battalion. Rostov set out to wander round the town. Between ten and eleven he came out on to a square between the two streets, where the Emperors were staying. The Preobrazhensky Regiment and the French Guards were standing on the square. A signalman came running out of the next street and the battalion began forming up. Galloping towards him Rostov saw the familiar figure that he loved so passionately of the Emperor Alexander, looking happy and in good spirits. Wearing the star of the Légion d'Honneur, the Emperor Alexander was looking straight ahead and smiling. Rostov was confused at first and thought the Emperor was smiling at him, and for an instant he felt happiness, but the Emperor was looking past him. Rostov looked round in the direction of his glance and saw another man galloping along in a hat with no feather, wearing a colonel's uniform and the Order of St. Andrew. He guessed this was Napoleon. It could not have been anyone else, this small, hook-nosed man riding at the head of a retinue, holding his hat in his hand as he rode towards Alexander. But Rostov could not believe this was Napoleon Bonaparte, the victor of Austerlitz, whom he was seeing so close up, for he was such an ordinary man, and he was seated on his horse and rode it so very badly (as was all too obvious to a cavalryman). Where was the magnificence? A mere man, like the rest of us mortals . . . But as he was thinking this, Rostov was almost knocked off his feet by the gendarmes driving back the crowd. He barely managed to get through to the Preobrazhensky Battalion, where the crowd was standing, and if Boris had not intervened to rescue him, he would have been pushed away. Boris led him out of the crowd and stood him beside the front rank of the troops with two other civilian gentlemen who were standing there. One was a diplomat, the other an Englishman.

All the time he was being pushed and shoved into position, he kept looking at his hero, following the way he behaved with Bonaparte, in surprise and agitation. For Nikolai he was still "Buonaparte", and even more Buonaparte after the sight of Périgord.

Rostov saw them talk for a while then shake each other's hand with a smile (he was insulted that Napoleon should shake the hand of our sovereign – he still felt that Napoleon and indeed any Frenchman could only ever be a teacher or an actor). Napoleon's smile was unpleasantly affected, Alexander's was genial and radiant. They rode towards the Preobrazhensky Battalion, moving directly towards the group of civilians, who moved back upon unexpectedly finding themselves so close to the Emperors, that they felt uncomfortable, especially Rostov, who began to tremble for fear that he might be recognised and charged for being absent without leave. His eyes met the eyes of the sovereign yet again, and Nikolai hastily averted his gaze. He felt unworthy of the radiant gleam in the sovereign's eyes. (Perhaps he felt this because he was feeling irked by everything, including his own awkward situation and his youth.) As he turned away, his eyes involuntarily came to rest on the figure of the nearest soldier of the Preobrazhensky Regiment, at the end of the rank. He was a big, strapping, ginger-haired man with a red, stupid face and eyes the colour of tin. At that moment not only his body, but the features of his face, his eyes and even, it was clear, the thoughts of his very soul were poised like a hunting dog pointing, that is, they were completely engrossed in the effort of standing to attention and looking into the sovereign's eyes.

Three steps away from him, Rostov heard a sharp, precise, agreeable voice speaking in French:

"*Sire*, I request your permission to award the Order of the Légion d'Honneur to the bravest of your soldiers."

Rostov glanced round – it was Bonaparte speaking. Alexander inclined his head with a faint smile.

"To the man who has conducted himself more courageously than anyone else in this war," Napoleon added, surveying the ranks.

"Permit me, Your Majesty, to ask the opinion of the colonel," said Alexander, starting his horse and moving towards Colonel Kozlovsky. Bonaparte meanwhile dismounted from his horse and dropped the reins. An adjutant – another French teacher – hurriedly dashed forward. "Giving himself airs," Nikolai thought spitefully.

"Who shall we give it to?" the Emperor asked Kozlovsky quietly in Russian.

"Whoever you say, Your Majesty."

The sovereign frowned at that, glanced round and said:

"But we have to give him an answer."

Kozlovsky glanced along the ranks with a decisive air, his gaze taking in Rostov.

"Surely it can't be me," thought Rostov.

"Lazarev!" the colonel said in a firm, steady voice, calling out the first, tallest soldier in the rank, the one whose stupid face Rostov had been looking at.

Lazarev stepped out smartly and handsomely, but his face was twitching like the face of a soldier who has been called out in front of the ranks to be punished.

Bonaparte took off his glove, exposing his plump little hand (a hairdresser, thought Rostov). He only had to turn his head slightly for the members of his retinue, who had guessed that very second what was required, to spring into action and start passing the decoration and its ribbon from one hand to another until one finally leapt forward to pass it to him, without keeping the little hand he had extended backwards waiting for even a second. He clearly knew that it would not be otherwise. He extended his hand, curved his finger and thumb together without even looking, and they closed on the decoration. He walked up to Lazarev, looked up at that impassive face without his own expression either darkening or brightening – his face was not capable of change – glanced round at the Emperor Alexander to indicate that this was for *him*, and the hand with the decoration touched the soldier Lazarev's button, probably hoping and expecting that the decoration would adhere to the soldier Lazarev's button of its own accord. He was aware the whole point was simply that his hand, Napoleon's hand, had deigned to touch the chest of a Russian soldier, and that soldier was now a sacred object. The cross did indeed adhere, because obliging Russian and French hands vied with each other in their haste to hook it on. Meanwhile Lazarev, with all the powers of the world hovering around him, stood rigidly to attention, gazing directly into the Emperor Alexander's eyes and occasionally squinting downwards at Bonaparte and glancing round at Alexander as if he were asking the sovereign if he should carry on standing there, or would they order him to do something else, should he kill this Bonaparte or shouldn't he, or should he stay as he was? But nobody gave him any orders, so he stayed as he was.

The sovereigns mounted their horses and rode away. The men of the Preobrazhensky Regiment proceeded to dinner and Russians sat down with the French at tables standing all around, set with silver cutlery, and began to eat.

Lazarev sat in the place of honour. The faces of the men and even the officers looked as happy as if they had just got married. The soldiers exchanged shakos, caps and jackets, slapping each other on the shoulder and the belly. The word "bonjour" was heard more often than any other. Officers, both Russian and French, strode around, sometimes acting as interpreters for the soldiers, and also embracing and declaring their love and eulogising each other's courage. Rostov walked through the streets, watching this scene from a distance, then went to Boris's quarters to wait for him.

Boris and Berg came back in the evening, also happy and ruddy-faced.

"What a lucky fellow that Lazarev is – a pension of one thousand two hundred roubles for life," Berg said as he came in.

"Yes," replied Boris. "Why didn't you join us?" he asked, turning to Rostov. "Everything was superb. We've heard that the sovereign has sent an Order of St. George to the bravest man in the French Guards as well," he said. "Well, you were fortunate to be here and see all this celebration."

"I don't think it's a celebration, it's a cheap farce," Rostov said gloomily.

"How you love to contradict."

"A farce, pure and simple, nothing more . . ." Rostov began again, but Boris did not let him finish.

"Anyway, I have to go to Saussure, he's sent for me."

"Off you go, then."

Boris went off and Rostov departed for his squadron without saying goodbye, but leaving the following note for Boris: "I left because I have nothing more to do; and I didn't wait to see you because I think our views have grown so different that it is much simpler for us to part, and not pretend. Go your own way, and I wish you success. Please hand on Denisov's letter."

# PART FOUR

# I

---

No one mentioned *"Buonaparte"*, the Corsican upstart and Antichrist, any longer: he was not Buonaparte, he was the great man Napoleon. For two years we had been allied with this genius and great man – the Emperor Napoleon. For two years his envoy Caulaincourt had been fêted like no other ambassador in St. Petersburg or Moscow. In 1809 the Emperor Alexander travelled to Erfurt for a new meeting with his new friend and all the talk in high society – the society of Anna Pavlovna – was of the grandeur of this solemn meeting of the two rulers of the world and the genius of the Emperor Napoleon, the former Corsican Buonaparte and Antichrist, who a year earlier, under the terms of an imperial manifesto, had been anathematised in all Russian churches as an enemy of the human race. In 1809 the friendship between the two rulers of the world, as Napoleon and Alexander were called, even reached the point at which there was talk of Napoleon marrying one of the Emperor Alexander's sisters, and when Napoleon declared war on Austria, the Russian army moved abroad in order to support their former enemy Napoleon and fight against their former ally, the Emperor of Austria.

In Russian society, however, it was generally felt that we would take no serious part in this war, and there was little concern. The attention of society was focused above all on the internal reforms then being put through by the Emperor in every section of the state administration. It was that early period of a reign following a long preceding one (the reign of Catherine), in which all that has gone before suddenly seems outmoded and unsuitable and, in addition the urge to change what has grown irksome and permit free play to younger forces, and the fact that the old order's defects are obvious while its advantages are obscure, countless other reasons are also found for the need to throw out the old and usher in the new. Everything was being changed, just as a new owner inevitably changes an apartment that has been occupied for many long years by his predecessor. It was that young period of a reign that every nation passes through five times in a century – the revolutionary period, distinguished from what we call revolution only by the fact that in such

493

revolutions, power remains in the hands of the previous government, and not a new one. In these revolutions, as in all others, there is talk of the spirit of a new age, of the requirements of this age, of the rights of man, of justice in general, of the need for rationality in the ordering of the state, and under the pretext of these ideas, the most irrational passions of man are brought into play. When time and inclination have passed, the former innovators will cling to what was once new, but now is old, in exactly the same way, defending their furnishing of the apartment against the young people who have grown up in the meantime and once again feel the desire to satisfy their need to try their own strength. And in exactly the same way as before, both sides use arguments against each other that they believe to be the truth: some speak of the new spirit of the age, the rights of man and so forth, others of the law sanctified by time, the advantages of what is familiar and customary and so forth, and both sides strive only to satisfy the needs of different ages of man.

As always, the innovators in 1809 had an example that they strove to imitate. And this example was partly England, and partly Napoleonic France.

The decree abolishing the old collegiums and establishing a Council of State and ministries had been issued a long time before, there had been a decree abolishing the privileges of court ranks, and still other, even more important, even more highly rational reforms were in preparation, reforms that frightened the old men, who knew that they would not live to see the fruits of these seeds, and delighted the young, because youth loves what is new. As always, both of them were merely satisfying their own instinctive need, believing they were adducing arguments, and thinking they were following the dictates of thought founded on rationality – but both of them were only satisfying their own instinctive need. And exactly as always happens, the dispute led both to forget even their own specious arguments and follow the dictates of nothing but passion.

"Ah, so you say the nobility was the bulwark of the throne, well then, perhaps the fifty-year-old Court Counsellors would like to take an examination?" said the reformer Speransky.

"Ah, so you say the new spirit of the age is better, well I shall prove to you that the Russians were happier under Ivan the Terrible than they are now," said Karamzin and the opponents of reform.

Both sides thought that the fate of humanity, and certainly of Russia and all Russians, depended on the outcome of their argument and the implementation or non-implementation of the decree on ministries and examinations. And as always, this was precisely where they were most mistaken. Nobody, apart from those who had discovered their happiness in life in arguing about the subject, had any interest at all in ministries, or examinations, or the liberation of the peasants, or the introduction of law courts and so forth. Life, with its essential interests of health and sickness, wealth and poverty, the love of a brother, sister, son, father, wife or lover, with its interests of work and leisure, desire, passion, thought, knowledge, music and poetry, continued above and beyond any decrees about ministries and collegiums, as it always follows its course above and beyond any possible governmental instructions.

## II

With the exception of a short visit to St. Petersburg, when he was accepted into the Masons, for two years after Tilsit Prince Andrei lived in the country without leaving it once. All the initiatives that Pierre had launched on his estates and then abandoned because he lacked the strength to overcome his stewards' resistance and his own indecision and inefficiency, all of these initiatives were carried through without any apparent effort by Prince Andrei. He possessed in the highest degree that practical tenacity which Pierre lacked, and which, without the least stress or strain and the smallest of movements on his part, set the wheels closest to him moving in the right way, just as they should. The thousand serfs on one of his estates were granted their freedom, on others the corvée was replaced by quit-rent. At Bogucharovo there was a vaccinator for smallpox and a qualified midwife. That was the most important thing for Prince Andrei. He read a lot, studied a lot and corresponded a lot with his Masonic brothers. He followed the course of Speransky's reforms and started to become increasingly frustrated with his own quiet, steady, fruitful activity, which seemed to him like idleness in comparison with the struggle and the collapse of everything old which, as he understood things, was about to take place in St. Petersburg, the centre of governmental power.

In both springs of these two years he observed the gnarled oak in the birch grove, putting out its leaves every spring and outshining the birch trees, whose spring happiness it had mocked so morosely before, with its own beauty and happiness. He had thoughts that were vague and indefinite, that he could not put into words even for himself, that were as secret as a secret crime (Prince Andrei blushed when he was alone, like a little child, at the very idea that anyone might discover these thoughts), and these vague thoughts about the oak tree were the very essence of the problem that was being resolved in Prince Andrei's soul, and the entire interest of his life. All his practical and intellectual work merely filled up the time that was empty of life, but the problem of the oak tree and the thoughts it provoked *were* life.

"Yes, he was obstinate," Prince Andrei thought with a smile about the oak, "he was obstinate for a long time, but he couldn't hold out once he was warmed, warmed by the warmth of love, he couldn't hold out, he softened and began to serve what he had mocked, and now he is trembling in delight, covered in succulent greenery. Yes, yes," he said, smiling and hearing Natasha's resonant, fervent, frolicsome voice, as if it were singing right beside him, and seeing her light in front of his eyes. He would get to his feet, walk across to the mirror and gaze for a long time at his own handsome, lean, thoughtful, intelligent face. Then he would turn away and look at the portrait of his deceased Lise, who stared at him affectionately and cheerfully out of the golden frame, with her curls fluffed up in the Greek fashion. She looked at him cheerfully, but even so she said: "What did I do to you? I loved you all so much!"

And Prince Andrei would clasp his hands behind his back and walk around the room for a long time, now frowning, now smiling, going over his thoughts about the oak tree in relation to Speransky, and glory, and Freemasonry and his future life. And at such moments, if anyone entered his room, he was especially dry, severe, firm and, in particular, disagreeably logical.

"My dear friend," Princess Marya might say when she entered at such a moment. "Coco can't go for a walk today – it's very cold."

At such moments Prince Andrei would look at his sister and say:

"If it were warm, he would have gone in just his blouse, but since it is cold, he needs to be dressed in warm clothing, which was invented for this purpose, and that is all that follows from the fact that it is cold, it does not follow that the child ought to stay home, when he needs air," he said with emphatic logicality, as if he were punishing someone for all that secret, illogical mental work on the oak. In such instances, Princess Marya thought that Prince Andrei was occupied with intellectual work and noted how dry this intellectual work made men.

In the winter of 1809 the Rostovs, whom Prince Andrei had visited occasionally after his first visit in 1807, left for St. Petersburg (the old count's affairs had reached such a state of disarray that he went to look for positions in the state service). In the spring of that same year, Prince Andrei had begun to cough. Princess Marya had persuaded him to see a doctor, and the doctor had shaken his head solemnly and advised the young prince to take more care and not to neglect this illness. Prince Andrei had laughed at his sister's preoccupation with medicine and gone back to Bogucharovo, where he spent a week on his own and carried on coughing. At the end of the week he went to see his father, firmly convinced that he did not have long left to live, and then, as he was driving past the oak in full leaf, he finally resolved beyond all doubt the mysterious problem that had been occupying him for so long. Yes, I have been wrong, he thought. Happiness, and love, and hope – all of these do exist, they must exist, and I have to use what is left of my life for them. Perhaps Prince Andrei resolved this problem so clearly because he was convinced, as people about thirty years of age often are, that his death was near. Sensing that his youth was coming to an end, Prince Andrei believed his life was ending, and firmly believed that death was near. Naturally, Prince Andrei did not tell anyone about his presentiment of death, which was a continuation of his secret thoughts, but he became more attentive, more active, kinder and more affectionate with everyone and soon left for St. Petersburg.

# III

On arriving in St. Petersburg in 1809, Prince Andrei ordered his driver to take him straight to Bezukhov's house, on the assumption that if – as was only to be expected – Pierre was not occupying the entire Moika Canal house that was known to the whole of St. Petersburg all on his own, then at least there the Prince would be able to find out where Pierre was living. Having driven through the gates, he noticed that the house was occupied and enquired if anyone was home, certain that this question could only refer to Pierre, since Andrei knew that the countess had been living separately, and had recently been staying in Erfurt with the rest of the court.

"The countess has gone out," the yard-keeper replied.

"Then I presume Count Pyotr Grigorievich does not live here?" asked Prince Andrei.

"The count is at home, by all means."

Prince Andrei was so surprised by this news that he scarcely managed to restrain himself from expressing his bewilderment to the yard-keeper. He followed a servant to Pierre's rooms. The house was large, and the apartments were on the top floor, in small, low-ceilinged rooms. Pierre was sitting at his desk writing, with his shirt hanging out of his trousers and his fat, bare feet in slippers. The low room was cluttered with heaps of books and so smoky that it was dark even in the afternoon.

Pierre was clearly so absorbed in what he was doing that at first he did not notice the noise of the two men entering. He glanced round at the sound of Prince Andrei's voice and looked straight into Bolkonsky's face, but clearly still did not recognise him. Pierre's face looked unhealthy, puffy with a yellowish pallor, and there was an expression of obsessive vexation in his eyes and on his lips. "He's unhappy again," thought Prince Andrei, "and it could not be otherwise, if he is together with that woman again."

"Ah, it's you," exclaimed Pierre. "Thank God, at last." But the former childish delight and joy were absent from Pierre's tone of voice. He embraced Prince Andrei, then immediately turned back to his notebooks and started arranging them in a pile.

"Ah, I haven't even washed, I was so preoccupied . . . naturally, you'll stay with me, there's nowhere else . . . Thank God," said Pierre, and as he said it, Prince Andrei noticed the new wrinkles on his puffy face more clearly than before, and especially the general expression of superficial preoccupation that usually conceals some uncertainty in the essential conditions of life.

"So, you didn't receive my last letter?" asked Prince Andrei. "The one in which I wrote about my illness and my visit?"

"No . . . ah, yes, I did. What's wrong with you? Surely you're not really ill? No, you look well."

"No, you and I are in a bad way, my friend. We are getting old," said Prince Andrei.

"Old?" Pierre echoed in fright. "Oh, no," he laughed in confusion. "On the contrary, I have never been so completely alive as I am now," he said. But his tone of voice seemed to confirm what Prince Andrei had said. Pierre turned back to his desk, as if he were accustomed to seek escape from life in his papers on that desk.

"Do you know what you found me doing? I am writing a project for the reform of the courts . . ."

Pierre did not finish, because he noticed that Prince Andrei, who was tired after his journey, was taking off his travelling coat and giving instructions to the servant.

"But what am I saying, we'll have time enough for that. Ah, how glad I am to see you! Well, how are Princess Marya and your father? You know, my stay at Bleak Hills left me with the very best of memories."

Prince Andrei smiled without speaking.

"Don't think that," said Pierre, responding to the smile as firmly as if Prince Andrei had expressed in words the thought that the smile signified. "No, don't imagine everything in this house is dominated by formality and outward show. No, we receive some remarkable people. The Grand Master is here now. He is a remarkable man. I was talking to him about you . . . Oh, how happy I am, how glad," said Pierre, gradually beginning to recover his former natural animation. Just then a ruddy-faced footman with gleaming new livery entered the room in boots that squeaked slightly and gave a dignified, respectful bow.

Pierre looked up, narrowing his eyes in a frown, and even before the servant start to speak, he began to nod his head gently in approval, confirming every word the servant was about to say.

"Her Excellency Countess Elena Vasilievna has ordered me to inform your excellency," the footman said in a clear, agreeable voice, "that she has learned of the arrival of Prince Andrei Nikolaevich and asks whether you will instruct the princely apartments downstairs to be assigned to him."

"Yes, good, good, yes, yes, yes, yes," Pierre rattled off hastily. Despite the sympathy he felt for his friend's fate, Prince Andrei could not help smiling.

Prince Andrei felt Bezukhov would find it unpleasant if he asked how he had been reunited with his wife, but it would also have been disagreeable to pass over this news in silence.

"Has the countess been back long?" he asked when the servant left. Pierre smiled feebly, and that smile told Prince Andrei everything he wanted to know. With that smile, Pierre said, firstly, that he had been worn down with talk, confused and outmanoeuvred in order to be reunited with his wife against his will; and, secondly – which was Pierre's fundamental belief – that life was so short and stupid it wasn't worth refusing to do something that others wanted so badly, it wasn't worth believing, or not believing, in anything whatsoever. But what he said, in French, was as follows:

"You want the key to the riddle? *Eh bien, mon cher*, I confess to you that I was too obstinate, and I was wrong. And then, essentially, she is not such a bad woman in herself . . . She has her faults, but who does not? And then, although I have no love for her (and there is none between us), she is my wife, and then . . . well, so you see . . ."

Pierre's explanation became totally confused and he walked across to the desk, picked up his notebook and began talking about what he was writing.

It was now perfectly obvious to Prince Andrei which thoughts Pierre was seeking refuge from in his work on an essay about the old Russia and the new, and it was clear why Pierre's face had become so puffy and developed wrinkles so early, less from age than from neglect.

"Look, you see? I began telling you about my essay. I believe that constitutional reform alone and ministerial responsibility are not enough, a complete range of reforms is required, and what can be . . ."

Prince Andrei knew what was being done by Speransky in the most minute detail, and he had his own particular opinion about it. He thought the entire existing order a total disgrace, he despised and hated all the figures in the government so heartily that he found Speransky's revolutionary activity, demolishing everything, very much to his liking. He had never seen Speransky and imagined him to be something like a civilian Napoleon. He was delighted at his elevation and the humiliation of previous state officials, and he could see beyond the reforms that were being made to the general, fundamental idea of those reforms. He could see the liberation of the peasants, the chambers of deputies, the openness of the courts and the limitation of the power of the monarch. Speransky interested him as an expression of new ideas and a protest against old ones. He agreed entirely with Pierre's idea, but just at the moment that did not concern him much.

"So you are greatly interested in Speransky?" said Pierre. "Did you know he is a Mason? I can introduce you through my wife."

"Yes, he is a remarkable man," said Prince Andrei.

# IV

Prince Andrei was a novelty in St. Petersburg. His claim to fame lay in the fact that he, an interesting widower, had abandoned everything and devoted himself to his son, and, having mended his ways and turned on to the true path, he was now doing much good in the countryside and, most important of all, he had liberated the peasants.

Countess Elena Vasilievna Bezukhova had previously held one of the foremost salons in St. Petersburg but now, following her arrival from Erfurt where, so it was said, she had been vouchsaved the favours of a certain highly important personage, and especially after rejoining her husband (a husband – precisely such a husband as Pierre – was an essential condition for the completely fashionable woman), the Countess Bezukhova and her salon were undoubtedly at the forefront of St. Petersburg society. Prince Andrei, by virtue of his former reputation as a fashionable young man about the town of St. Petersburg, and also because of his position in general and in particular because he was a young man (Hélène preferred the company of men), he was considered by the countess to be not unworthy of certain efforts. The day after his arrival he was invited downstairs, to the countess's apartments, to dine and spend the evening.

Prince Andrei could not possibly refuse, and so Pierre, who normally did not care to dine in his wife's apartments (he usually dined at the club), accompanied his friend downstairs.

"I ought to tell you, *mon cher*, that my wife's salon is the most important salon in St. Petersburg. All the eminent diplomats come to her, especially from the French embassy. Caulaincourt comes."

Prince Andrei merely narrowed his eyes and smiled gently as he listened.

Shortly after five in the evening (following the latest fashion) the countess, wearing a simple black velvet dress (it had cost eight hundred roubles) with equally simple black lace, received Prince Andrei in her drawing room, which was also simple (it had cost sixteen thousand to decorate). The countess was already surrounded by the varied court of her male retainers, including all ranks and uniforms, with the French predominating. The only person there known to Prince Andrei was Boris, who immediately made an unpleasant impression on Prince Andrei by the manner in which he behaved with the Bezukhovs, husband and wife, a manner that others failed to notice, but which was as clear as day to the prince. Boris was now a Guards captain and N.N.'s adjutant, but his most prominent characteristic was still that same agreeable and impressive composure, although it was clear from the subtle smile lingering in his eyes and on his lips that this was a composure that concealed a great deal. Naturally, as he entered the drawing room, Prince Andrei had been prepared to seek signs of poor Pierre's misfortune in everything, but he was especially struck by the particular air of rather sad, considerate deference with which Boris greeted Pierre, standing before him in silence, with his head bowed. Of course, it was no more than Prince Andrei's imagination, but imagination often reveals the truth more accurately than the very clearest of proofs. Prince Andrei imagined that Boris's expression as he greeted Hélène's husband was meekly shamefaced and fatalistic, as if he were saying: "I respect you and I have wished you no harm; but our passions and the passions of women are not in our power to control. If I have done you harm out of passion, and you consider it harm, then I am in your hands and willing to bear full responsibility for my situation. But if, in fact, you know nothing and do not suspect," the mocking glint in his eyes said at the same time, "then so much the better for you, my dear friend."

Prince Andrei merely imagined this but, strangely enough, all of his subsequent observations of Boris and Hélène, which he was unable to refrain from making, confirmed his first impression. Boris did not sit among the men surrounding the countess; he kept to one side, amusing the guests, like a man accepted in the house, like a man who is content with what actually belongs to him and therefore no longer feels the desire to display what he has. Then Prince Andrei noticed the countess ask Boris to hand her something with an especially cold glance. Then he noticed their fleeting glances when they were not talking to each other and, finally, he noticed Boris turn to the countess in conversation and say *countess*, but from the tone in which it was said, it was quite obvious to Prince Andrei that when they were alone, Boris did not say *countess* to her, but spoke to her more intimately, and that Boris very probably had been, still was or would be the lover of her heart, whereas it was that most highly important individual whose liaison with Hélène was well-known to everyone, who was her acknowledged lover.

In society, in his wife's drawing room, Pierre was as lively in conversation and provocatively argumentative as always. He was the same with everyone and seemed only to be interested in discovering everyone's thoughts. It was clear that he forgot himself in society in the same way as he did in his work. There were not many ladies: two or three whom Prince Andrei did not know and Anna Pavlovna, whom Hélène, with her exceptional high-society tact, had invited as a friend of Bolkonsky's deceased wife and seated beside him at dinner.

Countess Bezukhova received all her guests, including Prince Andrei, with that special ease and confidence in her own irreproachability that virtuous women never possess. She had become even more lovely in the time since Prince Andrei had last seen her. She was very full-figured, but not fat, and exceptionally white-skinned – there was not a single wrinkle on her lovely face. Her hair was unusually long and thick. Her sable-black brows, which seemed to be painted on, contrasted with her prominent forehead, as smooth as marble. And there was still that same smile on those rubicund lips, saying either a great deal or nothing at all, but lighting up her face. She was an acknowledged beauty not only in St. Petersburg, but also abroad, and everyone in the stalls turned their back on the stage when she entered her box. Napoleon had said of her: She is a magnificent animal.

She knew this and the knowledge made her even more lovely. Prince Andrei had never particularly liked her, he would never have chosen her as his wife, but now even he found himself involuntarily under the sway of this beauty and elegance and this carousel of society life. He did not like *her*, but he saw in her the goal that all held to be desirable, towards which all were striving, and he too wanted to take his place in this tournament and try to conquer all. And furthermore, after his renaissance, he felt so keenly inclined to enjoy the pleasure he had not experienced for so long of finding himself in an elegantly furnished society setting, that he did not even notice how he sat beside the countess and paid her several more than usually courtly compliments and looked at her more than was necessary. Already he was forgetting his wife, and Pierre, and everything else. The countess was gratified. Andrei was especially handsome now, and he was behaving with such free abandon in the drawing room that any woman would have taken pleasure in unsettling him: in mid-conversation she suddenly turned to face him and fell silent, her lovely eyes narrowed and began to glitter behind the long lashes, the same eyes that had looked at Pierre when she kissed him on the day of their betrothal, so brazen, ardent and vile that Prince Andrei came to his senses and his liking for her disappeared again. He turned away and replied to her question in a cold tone.

Anna Pavlovna greeted Prince Andrei as her neighbour at dinner cordially, but with a subtle nuance of reproach for his having served as adjutant to Kutuzov, who had distressed the sovereign so badly at Austerlitz.

The general conversation mostly concerned the meeting at Erfurt, which was the news of the day. Four years after his last society *soirée* with Anna Pavlovna, Prince Andrei now found himself listening to enthusiastic talk about Napoleon, the very same man who had formerly been showered with curses. Now no amount of rapturous and deferential respect could suffice to speak about this genius.

The countess spoke about the festivities at Erfurt, mentioning in the course of her conversation the most remarkable individuals in Europe as her close acquaintances. "There were a lot of us, Duke such-and-such . . . Count so-and-so . . ."; or "Duke Louen made me laugh."

"How can they listen to her, and how can she pretend so skilfully that she understands all this, and that she's not a fool," Pierre thought as he listened to his wife. The countess was talking about the famous gala performance in which Talma had played Racine and both Emperors had sat on a special platform in front of the stage, on two armchairs placed there just for them, and saying how – as Talma had said then – "the friendship of a great man is a gift from God . . ."

"The gods, countess, if you will permit me to restore Racine," a gentleman from the French embassy corrected her.

"Oh, I do not profess monotheism," said the countess.

"And from whom did she learn that word and then remember it?" thought Pierre, pouring himself some wine, "and how did she think of saying it? I don't understand. But I do know she's a fool and she doesn't understand a single thing she says."

Prince Andrei noticed that Pierre was drinking a lot. The countess continued with her story, which was about how, when Talma pronounced these words, "the Emperor Alexander – we all saw it – took the Emperor Napoleon's hand and squeezed it. You cannot imagine the impression it made on us. Everyone held their breath."

Prince Vasily completed his daughter's phrases and hemmed significantly, as if he were saying: "Well now, a great man, a genius. Well now, I have never denied it."

Anna Pavlovna took part in these conversations and did not deny His Majesty the Emperor of the French, as she now called him, her gentle enthusiasm and profound admiration, but her enthusiasm was tinged with a certain melancholy that was intended to refer to the particular view taken by her exalted patroness of Russia's new alliance. She acknowledged that Napoleon was a genius who had done great service to the revolution and had recognised the advantages to himself of an alliance with Alexander, but she still mourned the destruction of the old order and was still a convinced supporter of strict principles. One thing in which she was completely at one with the countess was her passionate enthusiasm for the French in general.

"It is the chief of all the nations. To be French and belong to the nobility," she said.

As he always did in a drawing room, Prince Andrei initiated conversations and maintained them by cheerfully and sardonically contradicting his partners. He, who had always been so willing to scold the Russians, could not resist making several remarks that displeased Anna Pavlovna, to the effect that in that case it would be better to become subjects of Napoleon and never fight against the French.

"Yes, that would be much better," Anna Pavlovna said emphatically.

Pierre joked and, despite his disadvantageous position as a husband in his wife's drawing room, he occasionally caught people's attention with his brilliant French repartee. "Yes, never mind, pay no attention, he's my husband," the countess's expression said when that happened.

# V

In the evening, after leaving the countess's drawing room, Pierre drove to the club, and when he got back Prince Andrei was already asleep. The following day Andrei went out early on business, lunched with his father-in-law, spent the evening in the house where they had promised to acquaint him with Speransky, and only returned late in the evening to enter Pierre's low, smoky rooms after they had not seen each other for an entire day.

"How good to find you at home," said Prince Andrei, after unbuttoning his coat, reclining on the ottoman and rubbing his face with his hands.

Pierre knew this expression on Andrei's face, he knew it and loved it. He put down his notebooks, lit a pipe and seated himself more comfortably opposite his friend.

"You know, my dear chap, I am staying in St. Petersburg – I have received offers that I cannot refuse. And indeed, these are such times, such immense changes, when everything is seething, everything rotten and old is cracking apart, that it is impossible to hold back and not take a hand."

"So that's it? How glad I am," said Pierre. "But where?"

"Kochubei requests me to join the commission for drafting the laws, then they are offering me a place in the Crimea."

"No, stay here," said Pierre. "We haven't seen each other since yesterday evening," he continued. "I think all this has had a strange effect on you, all these eulogies of Napoleon. How differently everybody has begun to speak of him. It seems to me that even if I still thought the same about Napoleon as I used to, I ought to change my ideas simply in order not to agree with this crowd."

"Yes," said Prince Andrei, smiling, "what you and I thought and felt four years ago is what they have only just realised now. But they could not understand Egypt, the Italian campaign, the liberation of Italy, the first consul: in order to breach the walls of their minds, it required the pomp and ceremony of Tilsit and Erfurt, which can provoke only mockery and revulsion. As Goethe says, they are like an echo, but there are no voices. And, like an echo, they come late and they all distort the tune. They never sing in time. When the new is already drawing close, they still believe in the old, when the new becomes the old, outdated banality and progressive minds can already see the new, they are only just beginning to chew over the old, that is, what they have been arguing against all the time. That's how it is now with Napoleon. If I could still admit the existence of great men as I did four years ago, I would have become disenchanted with Bonaparte long ago, even without Austerlitz."

"Ah," put in Pierre, "then you are of the same opinion about Bonaparte. I think he is a nonentity, an empty space, approaching his own destruction. He is a man who has not maintained his position and has crumbled."

"But of course, of course," said Prince Andrei, nodding his head as if what Pierre was saying was a common truism, although there were scarcely one or two people in St. Petersburg who thought so.

They paused and exchanged glances. They found it pleasant to think that, even though living apart, they had advanced so uniformly in their thoughts, that after such a long period of time, much further on down the road of life, they had found each other again. By a natural association of ideas, Prince Andrei moved on from this coming together to his memories of Boris, to whom he had taken such a liking in 1805. He sensed that he and Boris had grown very far apart in this time.

"Remember, I was talking to you about Boris Drubetskoy, whom you recommended to me. I liked him a great deal. I was very much mistaken. I met him again today. I do not like him."

Again their opinions coincided. In exactly the same way, Pierre had formerly been greatly taken with this young man and then disappointed, but because of the suspicions he harboured about Boris, he did not express his thoughts frankly.

"No, he is a very fine young man. And he is getting on very well in society and in the army."

"Yes, yes, he will go very, very far. And that is what I do not like about him. He attaches great weight to success in society and his career. That is what is so pitiful about him. He is cleverer than all of them. And that is not hard. But he has the tact to hide his superiority, so as not to offend them, and he pretends to be their equal. That is the basic recipe for success, but the truly regrettable thing is that he is not clever enough to see that it is not worth the effort. It seems to him that all this is very important – he is blowing his soap bubble with painstaking care, and it will be the worse for him when the bubble bursts."

Pierre changed the subject.

"You still haven't told me if you saw Speransky. Well?"

Prince Andrei sighed.

"That's one error less," he said. "Not that I agree with you. There are many things that can and should be done, but not with the unclean hands of a priest's son."

"Ah, my dear fellow, the spirit of caste . . ."

"Spirit of caste or not, I simply cannot bear the tone of a priest's son with such dogmatism and the polish of some courtier's Jacobinism. A priest's son is a special breed. No, I do not agree. His concept is good, but the measures taken are wrong."

"But think, this is the only man who is capable . . ."

"And then," Prince Andrei interrupted, "these men cannot under-stand freedom, because they are used to looking up from below."

# VI

The Rostovs' financial affairs had not been restored during the two years that they spent in the countryside. Despite the fact that Nikolai stuck firmly to his intentions and continued to serve in the thick of the army, spending relatively little money, the course of life at Otradnoe and, in particular, the way in which Mitenka managed the family's affairs, meant that the debts mounted up relentlessly every year. The only obvious remedy that the old count could think of was state service, and he came to St. Petersburg to look for a position. To look for a position and also at the same time – as he put it – to amuse the girls one last time. And perhaps even marry one of them off, he thought, as all fathers of eligible young women think. And indeed Berg, now the commander of a Guards battalion, decorated with the Order of St. Vladimir and a Gold Sabre for bravery, a moral, modest, handsome young man, already launched upon a brilliant career, proposed to Vera, carrying out the decision on which he had firmly resolved four years earlier.

"Well, you see," he said, virtuously blowing smoke rings as he spoke to a comrade whom he called a friend, simply because he knew that everybody had friends. "Well, you see, I've thought it all through, and I wouldn't marry if I hadn't considered everything and if it was awkward for any reason. But now things are quite different. My papa and mama are provided for, I've rented this place for them in the Ostsee District, and with my salary and my wife's fortune, she and I can live in St. Petersburg. I'm not marrying for money, I consider that dishonourable, but a wife should make her contribution and a husband should make his. I have my army career, and she has her small fortune and connections. In our times that means something, does it not? And the most important thing is that she is a respectable girl and she loves me . . ." Berg blushed and smiled.

"You will come round and see us . . ." he was going to say "for dinner", but he changed his mind and said "to take tea", and then he blew a round little smoke ring, puncturing it quickly with his tongue to create the perfect embodiment of his dreams of happiness.

At first Berg's proposal was received with an incomprehension that was rather unflattering to him. At first it was deemed strange that the son of an obscure Lifland noble should make a proposal, but Berg's most fundamental personal quality was such a naïve and good-natured egotism that the Rostovs could not help thinking it might be a good thing, if he was so firmly convinced that it was really so very, very good. And then Vera explained in the most thorough manner possible that Berg was a baron, that he was making a good career for himself, that there was not the slightest mismatch involved in marrying him and society had many examples of such marriages, which she then listed. Agreement was given. After their puzzlement, the feelings of the parents changed to joy, but not a genuine joy, only an external one. When they spoke about this union, confusion and embarrassment could be detected in the parents' feelings, as if they felt ashamed of not having loved Vera enough and were now simply getting her off their hands. The most embarrassed of all was the old count. He probably could not have put a name to the reason for his embarrassment, but this reason was his own financial affairs, which in recent times had become fused with all his household and family affairs. He simply did not know how much he had, how many debts he had, and how much he would be able to afford to give for Vera's dowry. When his daughters were born, three hundred souls had been appointed to each of them as a dowry, but one of those villages had already been sold, and another had been mortgaged and the payments were so overdue that it would soon have to be sold too. Berg had already been a fiancé for more than a month, and only a week remained to the wedding, but the count had still not made up his mind what he was going to give Vera, and he had not spoken about it with the countess, who felt sorry for her husband and had promised herself never to talk about money matters. A week before the wedding all this had still not been resolved, and the count's sense of shame and torment had reached such a level that he would have fallen ill, if Berg had not drawn him out of this situation. Berg requested a private conversation with the count and with a virtuous smile respectfully asked his father-in-law what would be given away with Vera. The count felt so guilty and so embarrassed at this long anticipated question that he gave the first unconsidered answer that came into his head.

"I love her, and have taken care, I love you, and you will be content," he said, then slapped Berg on the shoulder and stood up, wishing to put an end to the conversation. But Berg said with a pleasant smile that if he did not know for certain how much Vera had, and did not receive it in advance, then, for all his love, he would not marry her.

"Because, judge for yourself, count, if I allowed myself to marry now, without having any definite means to support my wife, I would be acting basely . . ."

The conversation ended with the count, who wished to appear grand and not be subjected to further requests, saying that he would give a promissory note for eighty thousand, but Berg, after thinking for a moment, said that he could not take a promissory note alone and requested forty thousand in cash and a promissory note for forty.

"Yes, yes, all right," the count agreed hastily, "only forgive me, my dear friend, I'll get the forty thousand and give it to you, but in addition I'll give you a promissory note for eighty thousand. There now, kiss me."

A little while later the count obtained the money at a usurious rate of interest and gave it to Berg. The count's conversation with Berg was a secret kept from everyone in the house. The only thing that was remarked, however, was that the count and the fiancé were especially cheerful.

Nikolai continued to serve in his new regiment, stationed in Poland. On receiving the news of his sister's marriage, he sent a cool letter of congratulation, but did not come himself on the pretext of service business.

Soon after the Peace of Tilsit he came home on leave and gave everyone in the household the impression of being greatly changed. His father thought him far more mature and steady. He took only a little money, did not play cards and promised to retire from the army in two years, marry and come to the country to manage the estate.

"It's still early yet, let me at least reach the rank of captain."

"He's a fine chap, very fine," said his father.

The countess was also pleased with her son, only to her mother's eye it was noticeable that Nikolai had grown coarser, and she would have liked to marry him off. But when she hinted at a rich fiancée, specifically Julie Kornakova, she saw that her son would not do it. She saw that something in her son had changed for the worse, and she could not understand it. For the first time she experienced that maternal feeling of joyfully believing in her child's every forward step, but not in any decline such as she herself might suffer. Vera was perfectly content with her brother, she approved of his moderation in expenditure and his staid attitude. During this visit Sonya was hoping more than ever to be Nikolai's wife. He said nothing to her about love or marriage, but he was gentle, affectionate and friendly with her. Sonya still loved him as truly as ever and she promised to love him whether he married her or someone else. Sonya's love was so true and so firm, that Natasha said:

"I can't even understand how it's possible to love like that: as if you've ordered yourself to do it and now you can't change."

Natasha was the only one dissatisfied with her brother. She gasped at his completely grown-up ways, at his brown neck, at his manner of holding his pipe between his fingers, and she kept tugging at him and pestering him, jumping up on to him and making him carry her round the rooms, and seemed constantly to be searching for something in him that she could not find.

"What's wrong with you," she said. "Well! Well! Where are you?" she kept pestering him, as if she were trying to find that bright diamond of vitality within him that others had not noticed and she alone had loved, and which had grown significantly duller in recent times.

# VII

---

Natasha, having lived in solitude in the country for the last year, had formed her own definite ideas about everything, which frequently contradicted the opinions of the members of her own family. This last year in the country had been boring because everyone, apart from herself and Sonya, had spoken of nothing but how there was too little money and they could not go to Moscow and bewailed the poor young ladies, and every day they had heard Vera's comments about how very hard it was to marry in the country, that you could die of boredom, that a place should be found in St. Peterburg, and so forth. Natasha rarely joined in these conversations, and if she did join in she attacked Vera resentfully and claimed that it was much more fun in the country than in Moscow. In the summer, indeed, Natasha arranged her life in such a way that she could have said without the slightest pretence that she was extremely happy. She rose early in the morning and went off with the servant girls and the governess and Sonya to gather mushrooms, berries or nuts. When it grew hot, they moved to the river and bathed in the bathing hut that had been set up there. Natasha was happy and proud to have learned how to swim. Then she would sing, have lunch and set out on horseback with just Mitka the huntsman to her favourite places, the fields and meadows. Every day she could feel herself growing stronger, plumper and prettier, swimming better and better, riding and singing better. She was always happy out in the open and out of the house. And when she heard that talk about the boredom of the country and poverty again over dinner or evening tea, she felt even happier when she was out in the field, in the forest, on her horse, in the water, or on her windowsill on a moonlit night. She was not in love with anyone and did not feel the slightest need to be. Sonya was part of her life, but in Natasha's very best moments she felt no matter how much Sonya wanted to, she could not keep up with her, just as she could not keep up in the forest, in the water, on a horse. One hot June day, when she and Sonya, the governess and seven girls had gone to the river and the bathing hut, Natasha undressed, tied up her hair with a white headscarf, and crouched down on the front bench wearing nothing but her shift and, with her slim arms clasped round her lithe legs, she gazed long into the water, her eyes lost in thought. Everybody else splashed about for a long time, shouting wildly. In the water the girls all called out to one another freely, making no distinction between masters and servants.

"Come on, girls, come on, to the other side!" they cried with that herd-like bravado of Russian girls bathing. But Natasha went on sitting and looking at the water and the birch tree opposite her. She was thinking, seriously thinking for the first time in her life: "Why go to Moscow? Why not live here all the time? It's good here, isn't it? Oh, how good it is. And how content I am, and how happy! And then, everyone says we're poor. How can we be poor, when we have so much land, so many people and houses? Look at Nastya there, she has nothing apart from that pink dress, and she's so pretty, and so jolly, and her plait's so wonderful. How can we be poor? Why do we need so many teachers, and musicians, and two jesters? We don't need all that. Papasha's content with everything, and so is mama, and so am I. Sell everything we don't need and live with two maids in one wing, and how jolly everything will be! I'll definitely go and tell papa," she decided to herself.

Just then a whirlwind raising dust on the ploughed land ran across the field, down the road to the river and along the river, rippling the water, and straight into Nastya's face as she was swimming. Nastya was frightened and choked, then she giggled, and Natasha laughed too, ran into the bathing hut and flung herself into the water at last. When she returned home from bathing, tanned and in high spirits, with her hair still tied up in a scarf, Natasha ran into her father's study and recounted her philosophy, as she called it, with impressive seriousness. Her father laughed, kissed her and said in a condescendingly affectionate tone that it would be a good thing if only it were so easy to do everything. But Natasha did not give in quickly – even though she was still a young girl and he was an old man, she felt that what she was saying was right.

"But why not?" she said. "So there are debts. Then let's live so that living only costs half as much."

Natasha did not trust her father's condescendingly affectionate smile and her mother's jokes, she knew what she was saying was right, and from that time on she began thinking and believing in her own thoughts and having her own opinion about everything. In St. Petersburg she did not approve of her father's search for a position and said it was all nonsense, that they were rich anyway. She very much approved of Berg's marriage, because Vera would be suited where she would not. She was glad, however, of the opportunity to have fun in St. Petersburg and, despite being prepared to live in the country all the time, she was dissatisfied with the manner of life that her family led in St. Petersburg. Everything seemed wrong to her, insufficiently *comme il faut*, too provincial. How could she have known the right way to live in the highest society? But her instinct guided her correctly, and her feeling for elegance and vanity was offended by the fact that the rooms were not arranged in the correct manner, the servants were grubby, the carriage was ancient and the table was not set correctly. She not only dressed herself, but also the old countess, who placed herself entirely in her hands, and she dressed her beautifully. She instantly guessed all those minor nuances of manners and toilette that constitute the tone of the highest society, and in the Rostovs' house, which seemed rather funny, provincial and Muscovite in St. Petersburg, Natasha astounded everyone with the irreproachable manners of the very highest elegant society.

She was sixteen years old. Some said she was very lovely, others said she was merely pretty, they said she was shallow, that she was a flirt, that she was spoilt, but everyone said she was very sweet.

However, during the month following the Rostovs' arrival in St. Petersburg, Natasha received two proposals from rich bridegrooms, one of them most advantageous, yet she rejected both. Natasha laughed and flirted so gaily that proposing to her would never even have occurred to anyone with the least powers of observation. She seemed to be not of this world. It was strange to think that she might suddenly wish to choose herself a husband who would wear a dressing gown in her company, out of all these hundreds of men, who could all be her husbands when she wanted them to be. They were all prepared to court her, pick up her handkerchief, dance with only her and write poems in her album. She did not allow that men had any other function. And the more there were of that kind, the better it was.

Pierre immediately won Natasha's approval, not so much because she had once imagined herself to be in love with him, and not so much because she immediately included him among the people of the very highest society, as because he was cleverer and more sincere than everybody else. On learning that he was a Mason, she asked what that was, and when he told her the goal of Freemasonry in general terms, she stared at him wide-eyed for a long time and said that it was beautiful.

When he left, the old countess asked her what they had been talking about so ardently.

"I can't tell you, mama."

"I know, I know he's a farmason," said the countess.

"A Freemason, mama," Natasha corrected her.

With regard to men, her feeling was like that of the master of the hunt inspecting the guns to check they are loaded. If it's loaded, and the trigger works and there's powder on the pan – good. Then wait until we want to fire a volley with all the guns or just one. Whichever, all of them, every one, must be loaded.

Natasha was sixteen years old, and it was 1809, the very year that she had counted up to on her fingers with Boris after the two of them had kissed. Since then she had not seen Boris even once.

In front of Sonya and her mother, whenever the conversation turned to Boris, she said quite frankly, as if the matter had been decided, that everything that had happened before was childishness and not even worth talking about and had been forgotten long ago; but this girl possessed in the highest degree the cunning female gift of lending any tone she wished to her words, of concealing and deceiving, and in the most secret depths of her soul the question of whether her undertaking to Boris was a joke, a forgotten piece of childish foolishness, or an important, binding promise, tormented her painfully. On the one hand, it would have been fun to get married now, and especially to Boris, who was so sweet, handsome and *comme il faut* (and especially great fun, because she would have shown Vera that she had nothing to be so proud of just because she was already grown-up and getting married, as if she were the only one who could do it, and she would have shown her the right way to get married, not to that little German Berg, but to Prince Drubetskoy); on the other hand, the thought of an obligation that would bind her and deprive her of her greatest satisfaction – fancying that any man she met might become her husband – was one she found oppressive.

In 1809, when the Rostovs arrived in St. Petersburg, Boris came to their house and was immediately received like everyone else, with an invitation to dinner and supper every day. When Natasha learned that Boris had arrived, she flushed and told Sonya in a trembling voice:

"You know, he's come."

"Who, Bezukhov?" asked Sonya.

"No, the earlier one," said Natasha, "Boris." And after taking a look in the mirror and tidying herself up, she went into the drawing room.

Boris had expected to meet a changed Natasha, but in his imagination he still carried the image he cherished of a black-haired girl with eyes that glittered from under her ringlets, with little red lips and a childish, reckless laugh. He had felt quite agitated on his way to the Rostovs' house. Boris's memory of Natasha was his most powerful poetic memory. But his brilliant career in society, one of the most important conditions of which was his freedom, and the news that the Rostovs' affairs were in disarray, which he had heard from his mother, had led him to take a final decision to blot out and forget those childish memories and promises. However, he knew the Rostovs were in St. Petersburg, and so he could not avoid coming to see them. If he had not come, in that way he would only have demonstrated even more clearly what he thought of the past. He decided to go as a good old acquaintance, treating his past with Natasha in the same forgetful manner in which many shameful and amorous memories are covered up in society. But he felt confused when Natasha entered with a glowing smile that was more than affectionate, in all the charm of her newly unfolded sixteen-year-old beauty. He had not expected to see her like that at all. He blushed and hesitated.

"Well, do you recognise your old naughty little friend?"

Boris kissed Natasha's hand and said he was amazed at the change that had taken place in her.

"How lovely you have become!"

"I should think so!" replied Natasha's glowing eyes.

"And has papa grown older?" she asked.

Natasha sat down and listened without speaking to Boris's conversation with the countess, who treated him like a grown-up. She looked him over in the finest detail without saying a word, and he could feel the delighted pressure of her insistent, impolite gaze on him. Natasha watched Boris closely and noted in him a condescending courtesy that seemed to say he remembered his former friendship with the Rostovs and because of it, and only because of it, he would not put on airs, even though he no longer belonged to the Rostovs' circle. During this first visit Boris referred tactfully, but, Natasha could tell, not by chance, to a palace ball he had attended and invitations to visit N.N. and S.S., naming members of the highest aristocracy. He sat there, adjusting the skin-tight glove on his left hand with his soft, white, right hand; his uniform, spurs, tie and hairstyle were all in the latest fashion and absolutely *comme il faut*. Natasha sat without saying a word, glowering at him with blazing, offended eyes.

\*

He was unable to stay for dinner, but he came several days later. He came again and stayed from dinner until supper. He had not even wanted to come, and certainly not to stay so long, but he could not do otherwise. Although he had decided to give up Natasha, although he told himself it would be dishonourable – he still could not help going. He fancied it was necessary to explain himself to Natasha, to tell her that all the old things must be forgotten, that despite everything . . . she could not be his wife, that he had no fortune and they would never give him her hand. He came, and that day the countess and Sonya noticed that Natasha seemed to be in love with Boris in the way she used to be. She sang him his favourite songs, showed him her album, made him write in it, and would not let him mention the past, letting him see how wonderful the present was: and late in the evening he went away in a haze, not knowing himself what he had done and why he had come, and without having said what he had intended to say. The following day Boris came again, and the next day, and the day after that.

He received notes from the Countess Bezukhova and spent whole days at the Rostovs' house.

In the evening of the fourth day, when the old countess, in her night cap and knitted jacket, without her false curls, with just a single wisp of grey hair escaping from under her calico cap, was gasping and groaning as she made the low bows of evening prayer on her rug, her door squeaked and Natasha ran in with her slippers on her bare feet, also in a knitted jacket and paper curlers. The countess glanced round, frowned and counted out the bows of her final prayer: "Surely this bed shall not be my coffin." Natasha was flushed and excited, but when she noticed her mother at prayer, she suddenly stopped in full flight, squatted down and stuck out her tongue, shaking her finger at herself. Seeing her mother continue with her prayer, she ran across to the bed on tiptoe, quickly brushed one little foot against the other, shaking off her slippers, and jumped on to the bed that the countess was afraid would be her coffin. It was a high feather bed with five pillows, each smaller than the one below. Natasha leapt up, sank into the feather mattress, tumbled over towards the wall and began jumping and squirming under the cover, kicking her legs about as she settled down and laughing quietly, first pulling the cover up over her head and then peeping out at her mother. The countess approached the bed with a stern face and smiled her kind, weak smile when Natasha's head was covered over and she could not see her.

"Now, now, now," she said.

"Mama! A conference, may we?" said Natasha, "Just one special kiss." And clasping her mother's face in her hands she planted a kiss in her favourite spot just under the chin. Natasha appeared outwardly to be rough in the way she treated her mother, but she was so sensitive and deft that, no matter how she seized hold of her mother, she always managed to do it without hurting or annoying or embarrassing her.

"Well then, what about today?" asked her mother, settling on her pillows and waiting for Natasha to finish kicking her legs about as she rolled this way and that before at last lying quietly beside the countess under the covers, working her hands free and assuming a serious expression. (These nocturnal visits of Natasha's, which were made before the count's return from the club, were one of the mother and daughter's very best-loved pleasures.)

"What about today? Well, I have to tell you . . ."

Natasha put her hand over her mother's mouth.

"About Boris . . . I know," she said gravely. "That's what I came for. Don't tell me – I know. No, do tell me." She lowered her hand. "Tell me, mama, is he nice?"

"Natasha, you're sixteen, at your age I was married. You say Boris is nice. He is very nice, and I love him like a son. But what is it you want . . . what are you thinking, you've completely turned his head, I can see that . . ."

As she said this, the countess looked round at her daughter. Natasha was lying straight and still, looking straight ahead at one of the carved mahogany sphinxes on the corners of the bedstead, so the countess could only see her daughter's face in profile. And it astounded the countess that this face was capable of an expression of such intense seriousness. Natasha was listening and thinking.

"You've completely turned his head, but what for? What do you want from him? You do know, don't you, that you cannot marry him?"

"Why not?" asked Natasha, without changing her position.

"Because he's young, because he's poor, because he's family . . . and it's not what you want yourself."

"But how do you know that?"

"I know that it is not good, my little friend, and I wanted to ask you if you love him . . ."

"You know who I love, why are you talking nonsense . . ."

"No, I don't know. Bezukhov, perhaps, or Denisov, or someone else, or . . ." the countess said, and her laughter prevented her from finishing.

Natasha pulled the countess's large hand over to herself and kissed it on the back, then on the palm, then turned it over again and started kissing it on the top knuckle of one finger, then in the gaps between the fingers, then on a knuckle again, intoning in a whisper: "January, February, March, April" and so on.

"Talk to me, mama, why don't you say anything? Talk to me," she said, glancing at her mother, who was contemplating her daughter with a look of tender rapture and in her meditation seemed to have forgotten everything she had wanted to say.

"I've already told you it is no good. Firstly, because not everyone will understand your childhood connection, and seeing him so close to you might harm you in the eyes of other young men who come to see you, but more importantly, it is a distraction and a torment for him. Perhaps he might have found a match for himself – someone rich – and now he's going crazy."

"Is he?" Natasha asked.

"I can tell you from my own experience, I had one cousin . . ."

"I know, Kirila Matveich, but he's an old man."

516

"He wasn't always an old man. But I'll tell you what, I'll have a little word with Borya. He shouldn't come visiting so often . . ."

"Why shouldn't he, if he wants to."

"Because you say yourself that you won't marry him."

"What of it if I won't marry him, as if I had to marry all of them. No, mama, don't you talk to him, don't you dare talk to him. What non-sense," said Natasha, in the tone of someone who is being deprived of a personal possession. "What if I won't marry him, let him come visiting, if he enjoys it and I enjoy it." Natasha looked at her mother with a smile. "Not for marrying, just like that," she said.

"How do you mean, my little friend?"

"Just so. Just like that. Well, and if it's so important I don't marry him – then I won't, just like that."

"Just like that," the countess repeated, with her kind, surprising, old-woman's laughter that set her entire body shaking.

"Enough laughing, stop it," shouted Natasha. "You're shaking the whole bed. You're so terribly like me, we're just a pair of gigglers . . . Wait." She grabbed both of the countess's hands, kissed one knuckle of her little finger – "June" – and carried on kissing – "July, August" – on the other hand. "Mama, is he very much in love? What do you think? Were men ever in love with you like that? He is very nice, very, very nice. Only not exactly to my taste – he's so narrow somehow, like the dining-room clock – don't you understand? . . . Narrow – you know, grey, light-coloured. Bezukhov, now – he's blue, dark-blue and red, and he's square. And did you see the way he snorted and got jealous this evening? He's wonderful. I'd marry him, if I didn't love anyone else and he wasn't married."

"Little countess," the count's voice said outside the door, "are you asleep?"

Natasha leapt out of bed in her bare feet, picked up her slippers and ran off into her room, where it was a long time before she could fall asleep, still thinking about the fact that no one could possibly under-stand everything that she understood and knew inside her. "Sonya," she thought, looking at the sleeping girl curled up like a cat with her huge plait. "No, how could she possibly! Even mama can't understand. It's amazing how clever I am and . . . what a darling she is," she continued, speaking of herself in the third person and imagining it was some very clever, extremely clever and extremely good man talking about her . . . "Everything, she has everything," the man continued, "she is clever – exceptionally pretty – and then she is lovely, exceptionally lovely, nimble, and her voice!" She sang her favourite musical phrase from Cherubini's opera, threw herself about the bed and laughed at the joyful thought that now she would fall asleep. She shouted to Dunyasha to put out the candle, and before Dunyasha had even left the room, she had already crossed over into a different, even happier world of dreams, where everything was as light and lovely as in reality, but even jollier, because it was different . . .

The following day Boris again came to the Rostovs' house, and the countess called him into her room, took him by the hand, pulled him towards her and gave him a kiss.

"Boris, you know I love you like a son."

The countess blushed, and Boris blushed even deeper.

"You know, my friend, that maternal love has its own eyes that see what others do not. My dear friend, you are a fully grown young man, decent and sober-minded. You know that a young girl is all fire, and that a young man ought not to visit a house where . . ." The countess hesitated. "You are an honest young man, and I have always thought of you as a son . . ."

"*Ma tante*," Boris replied, understanding the meaning of the countess's mysterious words as clearly as if they had been set forth according to all the laws of logic. "My dear aunt, if I have offended anyone, then let it not be you. I shall never forget how much I am indebted to you, and if you should tell me not to visit your house, no matter how hard it might be for me, I shall never set foot here again."

"No need for that, but just bear it in mind, my dear."

Boris kissed the countess's hand and from that day on he only visited the Rostovs for balls and dinners and spent no time alone with Natasha.

# VIII

Prince Andrei arrived in St. Peterburg in August 1809. At this period, Speransky's emerging power and the energy of the reforms he was undertaking were at their apogee. That same August, while out riding, the sovereign was thrown from his carriage and injured his leg, thus he remained at Peterhof for three weeks, and during this time he met with Speransky every single day and received no one else. Two famous decrees were just then in preparation and these were sending shocks of alarm through all society – one was on the elimination of court titles and the other on the introduction of examinations for the state service ranks of collegiate assessor and state counsellor – but there was also in preparation an inclusive state constitution that was designed to change the existing judicial, administrative and financial systems by which Russia was then governed and make a switch from a State Council to smaller, rural district administrations. All those vague and indefinite liberal dreams were now being realised and put into practice, dreams with which the Emperor Alexander had ascended the throne and which he had initially striven to realise with assistance from Czartorysky, Novosiltsev, Kochubei and Speransky, whom he himself would jokingly refer to as the committee for social salvation.

Now all of them had been replaced by Speransky on the civilian side and Arakcheev on the military. Soon after his arrival, Prince Andrei attended the court to be presented as a gentleman of the chamber.

The sovereign enquired about his wound. Until now, Prince Andrei had always thought the sovereign held a dislike of him, that the sovereign did not like his personality, his entire being. And in the few words spoken to him at the presentation, Prince Andrei now discovered in that dry, alienating glance, stronger confirmation of this assumption. In view of his service record and his connections, he might have been given a more cordial reception, yet the actual reception was precisely as he had expected. The courtiers saw in the sovereign's dryness a rebuke to Bolkonsky for no longer serving in the army, and this is how they explained it.

"I know quite well how little we can control our likes and dislikes," thought Prince Andrei, "so it's pointless to think of presenting my project to the sovereign in person and expecting thanks from him. But the matter will speak for itself." There and then at the presentation, he handed his project to an old field-marshal who was a friend of his father. The field-marshal duly gave him an appointment, received him cordially and promised to report on the matter to the sovereign. A few days later Prince Andrei was asked to report to the war minister, Count Arakcheev.

At nine o'clock in the morning on the appointed day, Prince Andrei arrived at Count Arakcheev's reception room. Prince Andrei knew Count Arakcheev from what he had heard from artillery guardsmen, from the story of his pulling out soldiers' sideburns with his bare hands, and from the eve of the Battle of Austerlitz, when the entire general staff knew that Arakcheev had refused to command a column in action on the pretext of bad nerves. This reputation had been confirmed in the campaign of 1807 in the Finnish War, when Count Arakcheev had commanded the army from a distance of one hundred *versts*. Prince Andrei did not know him personally and had never had dealings with him, but nothing he already knew inspired great confidence. "But he is the war minister, the authorised deputy of our sovereign the Emperor, and his personal qualities should not be of concern, and since he has been entrusted with my project, only he can put it into effect" – this was how Prince Andrei reasoned while waiting in Count Arakcheev's ante-chamber, along with numerous other individuals, both important and unimportant. During his long service as an adjutant, Prince Andrei had been inside many reception rooms and at many receptions, and all were familiar in their wide variety. Count Arakcheev had a quite special kind of reception room.

The unimportant faces all bore the same common expression of unease, masked by false familiarity and self-mockery, mockery of their own person and the person they were waiting for. Some were walking thoughtfully back and forth, some were whispering and laughing, and Prince Andrei heard Arakcheev's nickname "the power of Andreich" and the words "uncle will give you something". One man, an important individual, evidently offended at having to wait so long, sat there crossing and uncrossing his legs and smiling derisively to himself. But the very instant the door opened, there was only one expression on all faces – fear. Prince Andrei astonished one of the functionaries on duty by asking to be announced for a second time but even so, he still had to wait, while hearing from behind the door the low rumble of a rude and disagreeable voice, before a pale-cheeked officer emerged and, with trembling hands, clutched his head in his hands as he made his way through the reception room.

When his turn arrived, Prince Andrei was led up to the door and the functionary said in a whisper: "On the right, near the window."

Prince Andrei found himself facing a lean, dark-complexioned man of forty with his brows knitted in a frown over dull eyes, who turned his head irritably without looking at him directly.

"What is your request?" asked Arakcheev.

"I have no request," Prince Andrei declared, speaking quietly and slowly. The eyes turned to look at him and blinked, and the lips twitched briefly.

"Sit down," said Arakcheev. "Prince Bolkonsky?"

"I have no request to make, but His Majesty the Emperor has deigned to forward to your excellency a note that I submitted."

"Be so good as to understand, my very dear man, I have read your note," Arakcheev interrupted, speaking only the first words in a cordial tone, after which he stopped looking at Prince Andrei and withdrew further and further into his peevishly contemptuous tone. "You propose new military laws? There are many laws, and no one to apply the old ones. Nowadays everyone is writing laws, it's easier to write than to do."

"I have come on the instructions of the sovereign to enquire how your excellency intends to proceed with the note I submitted," said Prince Andrei.

"I have added a resolution to your note and sent it to the committee, but you should know that I do not approve," said Arakcheev, getting to his feet and taking a piece of paper from the desk. "Here," he said, handing the paper to Prince Andrei.

The words on the paper were: "Superficially drafted, an imitation copied from the French military regulations and departing unnecessarily from the articles of war."

"To which committee has the note been sent?" asked Prince Andrei.

"To the committee for military regulations, and I have recommended your honour's appointment to that committee without salary."

Prince Andrei smiled.

"I do not desire one."

"Without salary," Arakcheev repeated. "Pleased to meet you. Hey there, call the next one," he shouted out, bowing to Prince Andrei.

His reception by Count Arakcheev failed to cool Prince Andrei's ardour for his project. While he waited for notification of his appointment to the committee, he renewed old acquaintances and made several visits, especially to those individuals whom he knew to be in positions of power and able to support him and those who, his society instincts informed him, were now at the head of the government and intent on preparations. In St. Petersburg he now felt just as he had on the eve of battle, when he had languished in a state of uneasy curiosity and felt a vague attraction to the higher sphere, where the fate of millions hung on what was being planned. He sensed from the bitterness of the old men, from the curiosity of those who were in the know and the reticence of those who were not, from the anxious bustling of everyone, and from the countless numbers of new committees and commissions that he learned about every day, that here and now, in St. Petersburg in 1809, preparations were under way for some immense civil battle, in which the commander-in-chief was a mysterious individual whom he did not know, but who seemed to him to be a genius – Speransky. And he was so passionately interested in the process of transformation about which he had only the haziest notion, and so interested in Speransky, its chief mover, that his own business concerning the military regulations soon assumed merely secondary importance in his own mind.

Prince Andrei was in the most advantageous of positions, being gladly welcomed into all the highest social circles in St. Petersburg of the day. The party of reformers welcomed him cordially and sought to attract him, firstly because he had a reputation for being intelligent and very well read and, secondly, because by liberating his peasants he had already earned himself a reputation as a liberal. The party of the old and disgruntled appealed to him as his father's son, for sympathy with their condemnation of the reforms. Female society and high society accepted him cordially because he was a rich, noble, eligible, single man and an almost new face with an aura of romantic history surrounding his own falsely reported death and the tragic death of his wife. In addition, in the general opinion of all who had known him before, he had changed greatly for the better during those five years, having mellowed and matured, cast off his old pride and mocking attitude, and having acquired the calm that comes with the years. People talked about him and took an interest in him, and everyone wished to see him.

# IX

The day after his visit to Count Arakcheev, Prince Andrei spent the evening at Count Kochubei's house. He told the count about his meeting with "the power of Andreich", as Kochubei called him with the same ambiguous mockery that Prince Andrei had noticed in the war minister's reception room.

"My dear fellow," said Kochubei, "even in this matter you will not get round Mikhail Mikhailovich. He is a great doer. I'll tell him. He promised to come this evening..."

"What does Speransky have to do with the military regulations?" asked Prince Andrei.

Kochubei smiled and shook his head, as if amazed at Bolkonsky's naïvety.

"He and I were talking about you a few days ago," Kochubei continued, "about your free tillers of the earth."

"So you're the one who let your serfs go," said an old man from Catherine the Great's time, glancing at Bolkonsky derisively.

"The small estate wasn't making money," replied Bolkonsky.

"You're afraid of being late," said the old man, looking at Kochubei. "There's one thing I don't understand," he continued. "Who's going to plough the land if we give them their freedom? Writing laws is easy, but it's hard to govern. But just you tell me now, count, who is going to lead departments when everyone has to take examinations?"

"The ones who pass the examinations," replied Kochubei, crossing one leg over the other and glancing round the room.

"Well, I've got Pryanichnikov working for me, a wonderful man, worth his weight in gold, but he's seventy years old, and if you think he'll sit examinations..."

"Yes, that is difficult, with education not so widespread, but..."

Count Kochubei did not finish what he was saying, but got to his feet and took Prince Andrei by the arm across the room to meet the man who was just entering. He was a tall, fair-haired but balding man of about forty, wearing a blue tailcoat with a cross hanging from his neck and a star decoration. He had a large, expansive forehead and an unusual, elongated face that had a strange white pallor. This was Speransky. Prince Andrei recognised him at once from his highly distinctive bearing which was quite unique. Amid all the clumsy, ungainly movements of the social world that he inhabited, Prince Andrei had never encountered such composure and self-assurance, such a direct and, at the same time, gentle glance from half-closed and slightly watery eyes, such firmness in a smile that was so meaningless, such a high, modulated, quiet voice and, above all, such soft whiteness of the face and especially the hands, which were rather broad, but unusually puffy, soft and white. Prince Andrei had only seen that whiteness and softness of the face in soldiers who had spent a long time in hospital.

Speransky did not run his eyes from face to face as people involuntarily do when entering a large company, and he took his time when speaking. He spoke quietly, confident that he would be listened to, and looked only at the person he was addressing.

Prince Andrei followed Speransky's every word and movement closely. As often with those who, like Prince Andrei, judge others harshly, meeting someone new who is already known by reputation, and especially meeting someone like Speransky, he expected to find in him the perfection of all human virtue.

Speransky told Kochubei he was sorry to have been unable to come earlier, but he had been delayed at the palace. He did not say that the sovereign had detained him, an affectation that was noted by Prince Andrei. As Kochubei was introducing Prince Andrei, Speransky slowly turned his gaze to Bolkonsky and looked at him in silence, still smiling.

"I am very pleased to make your acquaintance, I have heard so much about you, as has everyone," he said.

Kochubei told Speransky about Bolkonsky's project and his reception by Arakcheev. Speransky smiled more broadly.

"The director of the commission is my old friend Magnitsky," said Speransky, "if you wish, I shall introduce you to him, and I am sure you will find him entirely sympathetic to everything reasonable."

A circle quickly formed round Speransky, and the old man who had already mentioned his official, Pryanichnikov, raised the same question with Speransky.

Prince Andrei automatically followed all this man's movements. He was astounded by the exceptional, contemptuous calm with which

Speransky withstood attacks, the way he smiled from time to time, saying that he could not judge the advantage or disadvantage of something that was pleasing to the sovereign. After talking for a while, Speransky stood up and walked over to Prince Andrew. It was clear that he thought it necessary to pay Bolkonsky attention.

"I have not had time to speak with you, prince, during all this lively discussion," he said with a sardonic smile, as if acknowledging with this smile that they both understood the insignificance of such conversations. Prince Andrei could not help feeling flattered by this attention. "I have known of you a long time, prince, firstly from what you have done with your peasants, it is our first example, and one we would very much like to see followed by others, and, secondly, because you are one of those gentlemen of the chamber who feel they have been insulted by the new decree."

"Yes," said Prince Andrei. "My father did not wish me to take advantage of that right; I began my service from the lower ranks."

"And yet this measure is being condemned."

"There are, I believe, some grounds for condemnation."

"Grounds for personal ambition, maybe . . ."

"And partly for the state as well."

"How so?"

"I am an admirer of Montesquieu," said Prince Andrei. "And his idea, that monarchy is founded on honour, appears to me indisputable. I see the various rights and privileges of the nobility as a means of maintaining this sense of honour."

The smile on Speransky's white face faded, which much improved his face. He must have found Prince Andrei's idea diverting.

"If you regard the matter in that way . . ." he began in badly pronounced French, speaking even more slowly than in Russian, but perfectly calmly. Honour, he said, could not be maintained by privileges that obstructed good service, for honour was either the negative concept of not committing reprehensible actions, or a long-standing source of rivalry for obtaining approval and the rewards that express it. His arguments were concise, simple and clear. The institution that supported this kind of honour was Napoleon's Legion of Honour, which did not impede but promoted good service, but not the privilege of class or court.

"However, it still attempts to achieve the same purpose," said Prince Andrei.

"But you yourself did not wish to take advantage of it, prince," said Speransky, with a smile on his face again. "If you will do me the honour of visiting me on Wednesday," he said, "then I shall have had a word with Magnitsky, and will tell you something that may interest you and also, in addition, I shall have the pleasure of conversing with you in greater detail." He closed his eyes, bowed and left the hall in the French manner, without saying goodbye and trying to attract no attention.

In St. Petersburg, Prince Andrei soon realised that his entire way of thinking had undergone a change. Yet perhaps his way of thinking, his view of life developed in isolation, had not so much changed but rather had earlier been stifled, obscured by all the petty concerns that had so preoccupied him at first in St. Petersburg. Now, each evening when he returned home, he noted down the appointed times for four or five essential visits or meetings in his memorandum book. The workings of his life and the arrangement of his day were such that simply getting everywhere on time took up a large part of his energy. It was only right that during this first visit he got nothing done, did not even think hard about anything and had no time for thinking deeply, for all he did was talk, and talk successfully, telling people what he had had time to think about earlier on in the country, although after several days he noticed with some dissatisfaction that he was repeating the same thing in different company on the same day. But he was so busy for whole days at a time that he had no time even to think about the fact that he was not getting anything done. Of his former interests in life, only the vague thoughts about the oak tree in leaf, himself and women still came to mind in St. Petersburg just as frequently as before.

Both at their meeting at Kochubei's house and later on Wednesday, when Speransky received Bolkonsky *tête-à-tête* and spoke with him confidentially at some length, Prince Andrei liked Speransky in the way that only the very arrogant can like new people. Regarding such an immense number of people as despicable, insignificant creatures and wanting so strongly to discover in someone the living ideal of that perfection towards which he himself strove, Prince Andrei believed he had found in Speransky the reassuring ideal of a man who was capable of understanding him entirely and whom he was prepared to respect and to love with that strong kind of love and respect that he withheld from others. Had Speransky been from the same society as Prince Andrei, with the same upbringing and mental outlook, then Bolkonsky would soon have discovered his weak, human, unheroic sides, but now that strange and unfamiliar manner of thought only inspired still greater respect. And in addition, either because Speransky appreciated Prince Andrei's abilities, or because he wished to acquire him for his own, Speransky flirted with Prince Andrei, flaunting the dispassionate, calm reason that he advanced as the sole motive for his actions, and flattering Prince Andrei with that subtle form of flattery which, combined with conceit, consists in the tacit acknowledgement of the other as the only man capable of seeing the full stupidity of *everybody* else and the full meaning of one's own ideas.

During their long conversation on that Wednesday Speransky repeated several times: "*With us* anything beyond the old rut of tradition is scrutinised . . ." or, with a smile: "But *we* want the wolves to be content and the sheep left unharmed . . ." or: "*They* cannot understand that . . ." and all this with an expression that said: "*We*, you and I, *we* understand what *they* are and who *we* are." This first long conversation with Speransky merely reinforced the feeling of respect and even admiration Prince Andrei had felt on first meeting him. He saw in him a virtuous, rational, clear-thinking man of immense intellect who had achieved power through energy and persistence and was using it solely for the good of Russia. In Prince Andrei's eyes, Speransky was precisely the man he himself wished to be, a man who explained all the phenomena of life rationally, recognising as real only what was reasonable and applying reason to everything. In Speransky's exposition, everything appeared so simple, clear and – most importantly – rational, that Prince Andrei could not help but agree with him in everything. If he objected and argued, it was only because he stubbornly wished to be independent, and the sight of Speransky's hands picking up a snuffbox or a handkerchief irritated him. Everything was right, everything was good, there was just one thing that disturbed Prince Andrei, and that was Speransky's plump, white soft hand, which Prince Andrei could not help watching, as we usually watch the hands of people who have power, and for some reason this hand irritated Prince Andrei.

Prince Andrei found the excessive contempt for people that he observed in Speransky unpleasant, as well as the variety of devices and proofs he adduced to confirm his opinion. He deployed every possible weapon of argument, apart from simile, and switched from one to the other too boldly, or so it seemed to Prince Andrei. First he would take his stand as a man of practical action and condemn dreamers, then switch his stance to that of satirist, ironically mocking his opponent, then become strictly logical, suddenly soaring up into the regions of metaphysics. (This latter weapon of proof he employed the moment Prince Andrei expressed disagreement with his views.) He transposed the question to the heights of metaphysics, moved on to definitions of space, time and thought and, deducing therefrom his refutation, descended once more to the grounds of the argument.

The most salient feature of Speransky's mind, and one that had most impressed Prince Andrei, was deference to reason and the unquestioning faith in it that is common to all upstarts. It was clear that an idea quite normal for Prince Andrei – namely, that not everything can be put into words, and that what is said or believed in could conceivably be nonsense – would never occur to Speransky. These were the features, or rather, impressions, that Prince Andrei vaguely observed in the course of their talk, yet on emerging, Prince Andrei nevertheless felt a strange sense of respect for Speransky, similar to what he had once felt for Bonaparte. The fact that Speransky might be despised, as many foolish people did despise him, simply for being a priest's son, made Prince Andrei treat his feelings for Speransky with especial delicacy and unconsciously strengthened them within him.

Their conversation began with Prince Andrei's peasants, whom he had transformed into free workers of the land. With a trust that Prince Andrei found especially flattering, Speransky informed him of the sovereign's thoughts on the subject of the abolition of slavery. From this subject the conversation naturally moved on to the need for reforms to be simultaneous, and so on and so forth.

Concerning the project for new military regulations, Speransky said only that Magnitsky had promised to review it with Bolkonsky's assistance, but had not yet had time to do so.

As their conversation was drawing to a close, Speransky asked Prince Bolkonsky why he was not in government service and offered him a place in the commission for the drafting of the legal code. The legal commission, observed Speransky ironically, had already existed for a hundred and fifty years, it had cost millions and done nothing, and all Rozenkampf had done was merely file and label the articles of comparative legislation.

"And that is all. We wish to grant new judicial power to the Senate, but we have no laws. And therefore, prince, it is a sin for people like yourself not to be serving now."

Prince Andrei said that would require a legal education, and he did not have one.

"Why, no one has one, so what is to be done? It's a vicious circle that we have to break out of."

*

A week later Prince Andrei was a member of the commission for the drafting of military regulations and also – something he had not at all expected – the chairman of the commission's section for drafting laws. And at Speransky's request, he took the first part of the civil code that was being drafted and, with the help of the Napoleonic Code and Code of Justinian, worked on the section on the rights of individuals.

Prince Andrei lived in this way until the New Year of 1810, on the first day of which the entire new constitution was due to come into effect and the first session of the State Council was due to be held. He passed on to Speransky the work he had been working on all this time. But a few days later, he learned that his work had been handed on yet again to Rozenkampf, to be rewritten. Prince Andrei was offended that Speransky had not mentioned this and had passed on his work for rewriting to the very man for whom Speransky had repeatedly expressed total contempt. Although this offended Prince Andrei, it did not in the least undermine his high opinion of Speransky or the love and respect he felt for him. With the obstinacy of a man who despises a great deal, Prince Andrei clung to his feeling for Speransky. He visited his house some six times during this period, always seeing him alone and each time speaking with him at length, and thereby confirming his opinion that Speransky's mind was exalted, quite special and utterly out of the ordinary. In contrast, he did not like Magnitsky, with whom he dealt on the commission for military regulations. He recognised in this man that unpleasant type of French mind which quite lacked good-natured French frivolity, something that always struck him unfavourably. Magnitsky spoke beautifully, he often spoke very intelligently and could recall a frightening number of things, but to that secret question we always ask ourselves when we listen to clever words: Why is this man saying this? – to that question there was no answer in what Magnitsky said. One day shortly before the New Year, Speransky invited Prince Andrei to dine with a circle of friends.

Prince Andrei found the entire company of this circle of friends already assembled at five o'clock on the parquet floor of the house beside the Tauride Gardens – a house of outstanding cleanliness (resembling the cleanliness of a monastery). There were no ladies, apart from a small daughter with a long face, disagreeably reminiscent of her father, and a governess. Gervais, Magnitsky and Stolypin were there. From the hallway Prince Andrei had heard loud voices and peals of clear, mirthless laughter. Laughter like the laughter that actors use in the theatre. Gervais's voice rang out distinctly – ha-ha-ha – and so did Speransky's own. Magnitsky was speaking rapidly. He was telling funny stories about the stupidity of one of the high officials with whom he had been dealing, and telling them very wittily, but the laughter that rang out on all sides did not sound funny to Prince Andrei. Speransky proffered Prince Andrei his white, soft hand as he chewed on a piece of food and continued to laugh. They sat at the table, and the conversation did not stop for a moment. Nor did the laughter, the false note of which grated on some sensitive string in Prince Andrei's soul. The huge, fat Stolypin stuttered as he spoke about his serious dislike of a certain person, and although Stolypin's voice sounded sincere, he was still met with the same laughter.

Speransky himself was quiet here, as always. It was clear that he wanted to rest after his labours and enjoy himself in the company of friends; that he had heard that people enjoyed themselves making jolly conversation at dinner, and wished to do the same himself: but it all felt awkward. The thin sound of his voice jarred unpleasantly on Prince Andrei's ears. The topics of conversation were mostly jibes at people who had already been thoroughly ridiculed long before and, worst of all, the laughter was joyless. Prince Andrei did not laugh and feared he might be too solemn for this company. But no one noticed that he was out of tune with the general mood.

After dinner the daughter and the governess stood up, Speransky stroked his daughter with his white hand and kissed her. Yet to Prince Andrei that too seemed false.

The men remained at the table in the English manner and drank port after the wine. There was no talk on anything serious, indeed it was jokingly forbidden to mention such matters. One had to joke, and everybody joked. On several occasions Prince Andrei tried to escape from his awkward situation by joining in the conversation, but each time whatever he said was thrown back out, like a cork tossed up out of the water, and he was unable to join in. They seemed to him like deaf people who had taken up chamber instruments which they had learned to play purely by observation, and that was how they played all evening. There was nothing bad or inappropriate in what they said, quite the opposite, all of it was clever and could have been funny, but that special something that is the essential zest of merriment was not only lacking, they did not even know that it existed.

Magnitsky recited a poem he had written on the subject of Prince Vasily. Gervais immediately improvised a reply, and the two of them presented a scene with Prince Vasily and his wife. Prince Andrei wished to leave, but Speransky detained him. Magnitsky dressed up in women's clothes and declaimed Phèdre's monologue. Everybody laughed. Prince Andrei took his leave of the guests early and left.

Speransky's enemies in the old party upbraided him, saying he was a thief and a bribe-taker, that he was a mad Illuminist or an ignorant youth. And they did not say this to insult Speransky or blacken his character, but because they were sincerely convinced of it. In Speransky's circle, as Prince Andrei had now heard, they said the people of the old party were thieves, liars and fools, and they sneered at them. And also not because they wished to blacken their characters, but because they sincerely believed it. Prince Andrei found this offensive. What did Speransky, who was doing such great things, need with censure, personal insults and petty spite? And then there was that precise, humourless laughter that was constantly ringing in Prince Andrei's ears. As Prince Andrei grew disappointed with Speransky, he grew more enthusiastic, if that were possible, for his own work and his participation in the general reform. Having finished his work on the civil code, he was now writing a project for the liberation of the peasants and excitedly awaiting the opening of the State Council, before which the foundations of the constitution were due to be laid. Prince Andrei's own past was already linked to this work, bound up with it through personal connections and his personal sense of distaste and he gave himself to the task wholeheartedly, with never a moment's doubt about its importance.

# X

There were many reasons that had led Pierre to this reunion with his wife, but one of the most important, indeed almost the only one, had been that Hélène, and her relatives and friends all regarded the reunion of the married couple as a matter of great importance for themselves, whereas there was nothing in life that Pierre regarded as a matter of any great importance, he did not even regard as such his own freedom or his own obstinacy in punishing his wife. The argument that had vanquished him, even though no one, not even he himself, had expressed it, was: it costs me nothing, but it will bring them great pleasure.

For the Countess Elena Vasilievna and her position in society it was essential to live at home with a husband, and with precisely such a husband as Pierre, and therefore on her part, and on the side of Prince Vasily, use had been made, with the insistence so typical of stupid people, of every possible means of cunning and pressure to persuade Pierre. The primary means had been to act through the Grand Master of the lodge, who held great influence over Pierre. As a man who accorded no importance to anything worldly, Pierre had soon agreed, especially because after two years the painful wound inflicted on his pride had already healed into a scar. The Grand Master of the lodge, whom the Masons knew only by the title of the Benefactor, lived in Moscow. At each and every difficulty in life, the Masons turned to him and he, like a confessor, gave them advice that was accepted as instruction. In the present case he had told Pierre, who had come to Moscow specially for a meeting with him: 1) that in marrying he had taken upon himself the obligation to guide a woman and therefore had no right to abandon her to her own devices; 2) that his wife's crime had not been proven, and that even if it had been proven, he would not have the right to reject her; 3) that it is not good for a man to be alone and, since he needed a wife, he could not take any other wife than the one he had. Pierre had concurred. Hélène had returned from abroad, where she had been living all this time, and the reconciliation had taken place at Prince Vasily's house. He had kissed his smiling wife's hand and a month later moved into the large St. Petersburg house with her.

The two years had changed Hélène. She was now even more beautiful and composed. Before meeting her again, Pierre had thought he could forge genuine relations with her, but when he actually saw her he realised it was impossible. He had declined her explanations, gallantly kissed her hand and established his own separate quarters in the low-ceilinged rooms up on the third floor of the house that they occupied together. Sometimes, especially when there were guests, he went downstairs to dine, and was often present at his wife's *soirées* and balls, at which the most notable sections of the very highest St. Petersburg society gathered. On these occasions, as always, despite the fact that they all gathered at court and at large balls, high society divided up into various circles, each with its own nuance. There was a small, but clearly defined circle of those who disliked the alliance with Napoleon, a circle of the legitimists Josephe Maistre and Maria Fedorovna (to which circle Anna Pavlovna, naturally, belonged). There was M.A. Naryshkina's circle, characterised by social elegance and no political allegiance. There was the circle of practical activists, mostly male and liberal: Speransky, Kochubei, Prince Andrei; and there was the circle of the Polish aristocracy, Adam Czartorysky and others; and finally there was the French circle, the circle of the Napoleonic alliance – of Count Rumyantsev and Caulaincourt – and in this circle Hélène was one of the most prominent centres. The gentlemen from the French embassy came to her, as did Caulaincourt himself, and a large number of people known for their intelligence and polite manners who belonged to this tendency.

Hélène had been in Erfurt during the famous meeting between the Emperors and from there she had returned with connections to all the Napoleonic celebrities of Europe. In Erfurt she had been brilliantly successful. Napoleon himself had noticed her in the theatre and publicly remarked on her beauty. That she was more elegant and lovely than before did not surprise Pierre, but what did surprise him was that during these two years his wife had managed to acquire the reputation of a charming woman who was as intelligent as she was beautiful. The secretaries of the embassy and even the ambassador confided diplomatic secrets to her and in a certain sense she was even a social force. The well-known Duc de Lignes wrote her letters eight pages long. Bilibin saved up his witticisms in order to utter them for the first time in the company of Countess Bezukhova. To be accepted into the salon of Countess Bezukhova was regarded as a diploma of intellect, and young people read books before one of Hélène's *soirées* in order to have something to talk about in her company. Whenever Pierre attended one of her *soirées* and heard the talk about politics, poetry and philosophy, he felt, knowing that she was very stupid, a strange mixture of puzzlement and fear that at any moment the deception would be discovered. At these *soirées* he felt like a conjurer who constantly expected his trickery to be exposed. But either because the operation of such a salon requires no more than stupidity, or because those who were being deceived took pleasure in their own deception, the deception was not unmasked, and Elena Vasilievna's reputation as a charming and intelligent woman had become firmly established.

Pierre was precisely the kind of husband that this brilliant society woman needed. He was that absent-minded eccentric, the important gentlemanly husband for receptions, who was a hindrance to no one and, far from spoiling the general impression, was actually an advantageous foil for his wife because he provided such a contrast with her elegance and tact. Pierre had matured after marriage, as all people do, but he had matured even further as a result of his constant, intense study of the higher Masonic teachings, and in society that did not interest him he had unconsciously adopted that tone of casual indifference, which cannot be acquired artificially, and inspires involuntary respect. He entered his wife's drawing room as if it were a buffet. He was acquainted with everyone and tried to pass the time he spent at home in the least boring way possible. Sometimes he joined in a conversation that caught his interest, and then, mumbling, he expressed his own opinion, sometimes very tactlessly. But his reputation as the eccentric husband of the most remarkable woman in St. Petersburg was already so well established that no one took his outbursts seriously. He had suffered so badly two years before, when he learned of the humiliation inflicted on him by his wife, that now he protected himself against the possibility of any humiliation, firstly, by not living as her husband and secondly, by unconsciously turning his back on everything that might make him think of any such humiliation, and he was firmly convinced that his wife had become a bluestocking and therefore could not become infatuated with anything else.

Boris Drubetskoy had already made great advances in his career and been at Erfurt. When the court returned from Erfurt, he was a regular visitor in the Bezukhovs' home. Hélène called him "my page" and treated him like a child. The smile she gave him was the same as she bestowed on everyone, but sometimes she would look at him without smiling. At rare moments, the thought would sometimes occur to Pierre that there was something unnatural about this patronising friendship for a spurious child, who was already twenty-three years old, but afterwards he would rebuke himself for this lack of trust. For Hélène behaved so naturally and openly with her page. From the first moment, Boris's own behaviour had struck Pierre as unpleasant. Since arriving in St. Petersburg and becoming an intimate of the household, Boris had behaved towards Pierre with a quite distinctive, dignified and sober politeness. "This nuance of politeness probably alludes to my new position," Pierre thought, and tried not to take any notice of it, but, strangely enough, Boris's presence in his wife's drawing room (which was almost constant) had a physical effect on Pierre. It shackled all his limbs, destroying the spontaneity and freedom of his movements. "Such a strange antipathy," thought Pierre, and began staying at home less often.

In the eyes of society Pierre was a great gentleman, the husband of a famous wife, a good fellow, a clever eccentric who, although he did nothing, at least did no harm to others. But all this time in Pierre's own soul the complicated and difficult work of internal development was continuing, revealing many things to him, leading him to many spiritual joys and doubts. In the autumn of that year he had gone to Moscow for a meeting with the Grand Master of the order, Iosif Alexeevich Pozdeev, who was revered and respected by the Masons and known to them simply as the Benefactor.

The meeting with the Benefactor, in the course of which Pierre had been persuaded to be reunited with his wife, had had a great influence on Pierre in other respects and revealed many sides of Freemasonry to him. Following that meeting, Pierre had made it a private rule to keep a regular diary, and he wrote:

*Moscow, 17th November.*

*I have just returned from the Benefactor and hasten to write down everything that I experienced during the visit. Knowing Iosif Alexeevich from the letters and speeches read at our meetings, from the great title that he enjoys among us and the general reverence in which he is held, I travelled in the expectation of seeing a sublime old man, the very image of virtue, and what I saw was even more exalted than what I had expected. Iosif Alexeevich is a short, thin old man with extremely broad bones, with a wrinkled, sullen face and large, grey eyebrows with fiery eyes gazing out from beneath them. He lives in poor and dirty conditions, he has been suffering for several years from a painful disease of the bladder, and yet no one has ever heard a single groan or word of complaint from him. From early in the morning until late at night, with*

533

the exception of the hours when he eats the very simplest of coarse food, he works, composing epistles and reports, and working on the science of self-knowledge. He received me graciously, was good enough to say he knew of me, and made me sit beside the bed where he was lying. When we spoke about my family affairs, he told me: 'The true Mason's primary obligation is to improve himself. And we often think that by removing all the difficulties of our life, we shall achieve this goal sooner – on the contrary, my dear sir,' he said to me, 'it is only in the midst of worldly woes that we can achieve the three major goals: 1) self-knowledge, for man can only know himself through comparison; 2) self-improvement, since it is only achieved through struggle, and 3) most important of all – the love of death. Only the vicissitudes of life can demonstrate its vanity to us and promote our innate love of death or rebirth to a new life.' These words are all the more remarkable because, for all his terrible physical suffering, Iosifovich Alexeevich is never weary of life, but he loves death, for which he feels himself as yet insufficiently prepared. Then our conversation turned to the actions of our lodge, and Iosif Alexeevich voiced his disapproval of our latest actions. He said there was a tendency in the newest lodges to be obsessed with social activity, whereas the main goal should be the attainment of wisdom and the erection of the Temple of Solomon within oneself. He explained to me in full the meaning of the great square of the universe and pointed out that the numbers three and seven are the foundation of everything. He advised me to devote myself first of all to improving myself, and for this purpose he gave me a notebook, the very one in which I am now writing and in which I shall in future write all my actions that deviate from the seven virtues.

St. Petersburg, 23rd November.

I am living with my wife again. Yesterday we moved into our house, I settled into the upper rooms once again and experienced a happy feeling of renewal. I told my wife that the past is forgotten, that I would never remind her of it, that I ask her to do the same and I have nothing to forgive. I felt glad to say all this. May she never know how hard it was for me to forgive her. Following the regime I have drawn up for myself, I rose at eight, read the Holy Scriptures, then went to my job (Pierre was serving on one of the committees), came back for lunch, ate and drank moderately and after lunch copied out articles for my brothers. In the evening I told a funny story about B. and only remembered it was something I ought not to have done when everyone laughed loudly. I go to bed in a happy, calm mood. Great Lord, help me to follow in Thy steps: 1) To conquer the wrathful part of me with

534

*calmness and deliberation, 2) Lust – with abstinence and disgust, 3)*
*to hold aloof from vanity, but not to become alienated from: a) the work*
*of the state – service, b) from family concerns, c) from friendly relations*
*and d) economic activity.*

The following dates in Pierre's diary indicate that with only slight devi-
ation, he maintained his vows for about a week and during that time he
experienced a state of happiness and even bliss, which made him reflect
at night, so that he had *dreams in the* thoughts of the same kind in
dreams, some of which he noted down. Thus, on 28th November, the
following was noted:

> *I had a dream in which Iosif Alexeevich was sitting in my house and*
> *I was very glad and wished to offer him refreshments. I was chattering*
> *incessantly with strangers and suddenly remembered he would not like*
> *that, and I wished to approach him and embrace him. But as soon as I*
> *came close to him, I saw his face had changed and become young, and*
> *he was saying something to me out of the teachings, very, very quietly,*
> *so quietly that I could not make it out. Then we all went out of the*
> *room and something strange happened. We were sitting or lying on the*
> *floor. He was saying something to me. But I wanted to show him how*
> *sensitive I was and, without listening to what he was saying, I started*
> *to imagine the condition of my inner man and the grace of God that*
> *had illuminated me, and tears appeared in my eyes, and I was glad that*
> *he had noticed this. But he glanced at me in annoyance, jumped to his*
> *feet and broke off what he was saying. I became shy and asked if what*
> *he had said had not applied to me, but he did not reply and gave me*
> *an affectionate look. And afterwards we were suddenly in my bedroom,*
> *where the double bed is. He lay down on the edge of it and I, ablaze*
> *with the desire to caress him, lay down right beside him. And he asked*
> *me: tell me truly, what is the main weakness you have? Have you*
> *recognised it? I think you have recognised it. Embarrassed by this ques-*
> *tion, I replied that laziness was my main weakness. He shook his head*
> *in disbelief. And then, even more embarrassed, I replied that, although*
> *I lived with my wife on his advice, it was not as the husband of my*
> *wife. To this he objected that I ought not to be ashamed of this, and*
> *suddenly everything vanished. And I woke up and discovered in my*
> *thoughts the text of the Holy Writ:* 'Life was the light of man, the
> light shineth in darkness, and the darkness comprehended it
> not.' *Iosif Alexeevich's face was youthful and radiant. That same day I*
> *received a letter from the Benefactor in which he wrote about the*
> *obligations of marriage.*
>
> *Another dream. I saw myself walking in the darkness and suddenly*

surrounded by dogs (who bit me on the legs), but I walked on without fear, when suddenly one small dog seized me by the left thigh with its teeth and would not let go. I began pushing it off with my hands. And scarcely had I torn it away, than another, larger one, gripped me by the chest, I tore that one off too, but a third, even larger one, began gnawing at me. I started to lift it, but the higher I lifted it, the bigger and heavier it grew. And suddenly brother A.I. came, and led me by the arm to a building that had to be entered by crossing a narrow plank. I stepped onto it, the plank bent and gave way, and I began climbing up the fence, which I could barely reach with my hands. After great effort, I pulled my body up so that my legs were dangling on one side and my trunk on the other. I glanced round and saw that brother A.I. was standing on the fence, pointing out to me a broad avenue and a garden, in which stood a large and beautiful building. I woke up. Lord, Great Architect of nature, help me to tear from myself the dogs of my passions, especially this last, which combines all the power of the others, and help me to enter into the temple of virtue, a vision of which I attained in my dream.

30th November.

I rose late and, once awake, lay in bed for a long while, indulging my laziness. My God! Help me and give me strength, that I may follow Thy paths. I read the Holy Writings without proper feeling. Then brother Urusov arrived and we talked about the vanities of the world. He told me about the sovereign's new plans. I was about to condemn them, but recalled my rules and the Benefactor's words that the true Mason must be zealously active in the state when his participation is required and contemplate calmly those things he is not called upon to do. My tongue is my enemy. Brothers G.,V. and O. visited me and we had a preparatory discussion for the initiation of a new brother. They are laying the obligations of the orator on me. I feel weak and unworthy. Then we began talking about the explanation of the seven pillars and degrees of the shrine: the seven sciences, the seven virtues, the seven sins, the seven gifts of the Holy Spirit. Brother O. was very eloquent. The initiation took place that evening. The new arrangement of the premises greatly enhanced the magnificence of the spectacle. Boris Drubetskoy was initiated. I proposed him and I was the orator. I was disturbed by a strange feeling all the time I was alone with him in the dark chamber. I discovered in myself a feeling of hatred for him, which I strove in vain to overcome. And for that reason I wished I could truly save him from evil and lead him on to the path of truth, but the bad thoughts about him did not leave me. It seemed to me that his purpose in joining the

536

*brotherhood consisted only in the desire to become close to the important men who happen by chance to be members of our lodge. Apart from the fact that he asked several times whether N.N. and S.S. are members of our lodge (to which I cannot give him an answer), and apart from the fact that, as I have observed, he is not capable of feeling any respect for our holy order and is too occupied and content with his own external man in order to wish to improve the spiritual one, I had no reasons for doubting him; but he seemed to me insincere, and all the time I was standing alone with him in the dark chamber, I felt that he was smiling derisively at what I said, and I felt the urge really to stab his naked chest with the sword I was holding pressed against it. I could not be eloquent and I could not sincerely communicate my doubt to the brothers and the Grand Master. Great Architect of Nature, assist me in finding the true paths that lead out of the labyrinth of falsehood.*

*At dinner I was intemperate, I refused one dish, but drank too much. And so I rose from the table heavy and sleepy.*

After that three days were missed, and then came the following:

*I have had a lengthy and instructive conversation tête-à-tête with brother I. Many things were revealed to me, unworthy as I am. Adonai is the name of him, who created the world. Elohim is the name of him who rules over all. The third name is the unspeakable name, with the meaning of ALL. My conversations with A. strengthen, refresh and confirm me on the path of virtue. With him there is no place for doubt. The difference between the poor teaching of worldly knowledge and our sacred, all-embracing teaching is clear to me. The human sciences split everything up in order to understand, kill everything in order to scrutinise. In the sacred science of the Order all is one, everything is perceived in its totality and its life. The trinity is the three elemental principles of matter – sulphur, mercury and salt. The property of sulphur is unctuous and fiery; when combined with salt its fiery nature arouses craving in the salt, which draws in the mercury, seizes and holds it and in combination they produce yet other substances. Mercury is a fluid, volatile, spiritual essence – Christ, the Holy Spirit, He.*

*I am still as lazy and gluttonous as ever. I remembered the rule of abstinence at the end of dinner, when it was too late. I looked at Marya Mikhailovna with lustful thoughts. Lord, help me.*

4 December.
*There was instruction for fellow Masons at the lodge. And a description of the sufferings of our father Adoniram. As I listened I was overcome by doubt, as I had been the first time. Did Adoniram ever*

*exist, is he not an allegory that has its own meaning? I explained my doubts to brother O. He told me I must wait patiently for the revelation of further mysteries which will explain many things. I spent this evening with the countess (my wife). I cannot overcome my inner revulsion for her. I became carried away by a conversation with N.N. about vanity and insignificance and mocked the senators spitefully. I ate an immoderate supper, so that I had bad dreams all night long.*

*7 December.*

*I was entrusted with the arrangements and chairmanship of the dining room at the lodge. With God's assistance, I arranged everything satisfactorily. I persuaded Prince Andrei to join us. I see him so little and cannot keep track of him. He is engrossed in the worldly battle, and I confess that I often envy him, although my lot ought to appear preferable to me. He called to see me and told me proudly about his success. He is proud, and in his success he is as glad of the good that has been established as of his victory over those he regards as his enemies. I tried to prepare him for the solemnity of today's session, but although he listens to me meekly and pays attention, I feel I do not touch his soul, as the Benefactor touches mine when he speaks with me. Prince Andrei is one of the cold but honest Masons. According to my observations, Masons fall into four categories. The first includes those rare luminaries such as the Benefactor, who have entirely assimilated the holy truths, who have travelled the long road that confirms them in their undertaking to travel the remaining road ahead, for whom there are fewer mysteries than knowledge, and who have fused their lives with the holy teaching to serve as examples to humanity. They are few. The second category includes us, the seekers – hesitating, erring and repenting, but nonetheless seeking the true light of self-knowledge and the building of the inner temple. The third group includes men like my dear friend Bolkonsky and O. and B., and of these there are many. These Masons regard our works with indifference, they do not expect success from them, although they do not doubt. They are men who only give a small part of their soul to our cause. They, like Prince Andrei, join because they are invited and, although they cannot see the full light of Zion, they see nothing but good in Freemasonry. They are faithful, but lax brothers. The fourth and final category includes those who, alas, join the holy brotherhood only because there is a fashion for it and in the lodge they make contacts with rich and titled people, whom they need for their worldly ends. There are many of these, and young Drubetskoy is one.*

*The lodge meeting passed off with proper solemnity. I ate and drank a lot. After dinner in my speech of response I was unable to speak as clearly as I should have done, which many noticed.*

*12 December.*

 *I woke late. Read the Holy Scripture, but was unmoved. Afterwards I went out and walked around the hall. I wanted to think and think, but instead of that I found myself recollecting an event that took place four years ago. After my duel, the French vicomte had the impudence to take leave of me, saying he wished me health and spiritual peace. At the time I did not answer. Now I have recalled all the details of that meeting and in my heart I have spoken the most spiteful and barbed words in reply. I only came to my senses and abandoned this thought when I saw myself in the dissolution of wrath, but I did not repent of this enough. Afterwards Boris came and started telling me about various adventures, but from the moment he arrived I felt annoyed by his presence and said something disagreeable. He objected. I flared up and said many unpleasant and even rude things. He fell silent, and I did not realise what I had done until it was too late. My God, I simply cannot bear to be with him. The reason for this is pride. I set myself above him, and therefore make myself far worse than him, for he is tolerant of my rudeness, while I, on the contrary, feel contempt for him. My God, in his presence rather let me see my own vileness and act in a way that will be helpful to him.*

 *After dinner I fell asleep, and as I was dropping off, I quite clearly heard a voice say in my left ear: 'Your day.' I had a dream, after which I woke with my soul illuminated and my heart trembling. I saw myself in Moscow, in the large sitting room in my own house, and Iosif Alexeevich walked in from the drawing room. I saw at once that he had completed the process of rebirth, and rushed towards him. I kissed him and kissed his hand and he said: 'Have you noticed that today I have a different face?' I looked at him, continuing to embrace him, and seemed to see that his face was young, but he had no hair on his head and his features were completely different. And I said to him: 'I would have known you if I had met you by chance' – but at the same time I was thinking: 'Did I tell the truth?' And suddenly I saw him lying there like a dead body, then he gradually came round and went into the large study with me, holding a large book written in his own hand. He put the book down and began to read. And I said: 'I wrote that.' And he answered me by inclining his head. And I read many things in that book. And everything that I read was a definition of the goal. From these thoughts that came to me in the dream, I have composed the following speech, which I am going to read in the lodge."*

*26 December.*

*It is a long time since I have glanced into this notebook or my own soul. I have devoted myself entirely to vanity and to all of my vices, which I had flattered myself that I had eliminated. Yesterday, suddenly realising what an abyss of evil this heedlessness had led me into, I felt horrified and determined to come to my senses. My old Moscow acquaintances, the Rostovs, have arrived in St. Petersburg. The old count is an extremely kind man, and on meeting me at N.'s house he invited me to visit, and I have been at the Rostovs' every day for two weeks now, but only yesterday did I realise why I was doing it. The younger daughter, Natasha, has a lovely voice and charming appearance. I have taken music to her, listened to her singing, made her laugh and even discussed exalted matters with her. This girl understands everything. But yesterday evening her elder sister said jokingly that when I was at their estate near Moscow five years ago the younger daughter, Natasha, fell in love with me. When I heard that, I felt so embarrassed I blushed and even felt tears in my eyes. I could not think of anything to say and got up, noticing, however, that she had also blushed. This incident forced me to examine my feelings and feel horrified at what I had exposed myself to. Last night I had a dream. In it someone showed me a large book in Imperial format. And there were beautiful drawings on all the pages of the book. And I knew that these pictures represented the amorous adventures of the soul with its beloved. And on these pages I saw a beautiful image of a maiden in transparent clothing and with a transparent body, reclining on the clouds. And I knew that this maiden was none other than the younger Countess Rostova, and at the same time I knew that this was an image of the Song of Songs. And as I looked at these pictures, I felt that I was doing wrong and yet I could not tear myself away from them.*

*Lord, help me. My God, if this Thine abandonment of me is Thy doing, then Thy will be done, but if I myself have caused it, then teach me what to do. I shall perish from my depravity, shouldst Thou abandon me entirely.*

During the final days of December, at a formal session of the second degree lodge, Pierre read his speech *On the means for the dissemination of the pure truth and the triumph of virtue.* This speech not only made a strong impression, it provoked agitation in the lodge. Bezukhov himself was so strongly agitated as he read his speech, he spoke with such feeling and passion, almost with tears in his eyes, that his feeling was communicated to many of the sincere brothers and frightened many of them, who saw dangerous intentions in this speech. It was a long time since there had been such a stormy meeting. Factions were formed. Many argued against Pierre, accusing him of Illuminism, but many supported him. The Grand Master, who was chairing the lodge, concluded the debate by deciding to forward the speech to the highest levels for consideration and in the meantime to set it aside and proceed with usual matters. Pierre himself had simply not realised he carried such convictions until he read out his speech and encountered opposition. The brothers were amazed to observe a passion and energy in Bezukhov that they had never seen before and had never expected of him. He forgot the ritual formalities, grew red in the face, shouted and interrupted everyone, and hugely enjoyed his own state of enthusiasm. The Grand Master rebuked Bezukhov for his hotheadedness and for being guided in the argument not by love of the virtues alone, but also by the ardour of the struggle, to which Pierre was obliged to admit.

Instead of going home, Pierre went straight from the lodge to visit Prince Andrei, whom he had not seen for a long while. At the meeting Pierre had been struck for the first time by the infinite variety of human minds, which means that no truth is perceived identically by any two people. For all the power of his own conviction, Pierre had not succeeded in totally convincing a single man of his ideas: each had understood in his own way, with limitations and changes; and yet the main requirement of a thought is that it should be communicated to someone else exactly as you yourself understand it. Prince Andrei was at home, working. He listened attentively to what Pierre told him about the meeting of the lodge, made a few comments and, when Bezukhov had finished, stood up and started walking around the room.

"All this is very fine, my friend, all this is the truth, and I should be a zealous brother if I believed all this were possible," he began, looking at Pierre with his eyes glowing, "but none of this will happen, in order to make such a transformation, power is required, and power is in the hands of the government! And rather than paralysing it, we need to help it, especially a government like ours."

"Yes, but that is coincidental," said Pierre, "while the power and the actions of the order are eternal. It is coincidental that there is a man like Speransky now."

"Not Speransky," said Prince Andrei, "the sovereign and, above all, the time, education."

"Why do you speak so disparagingly of Speransky?" asked Pierre.

"Speransky. One error the less, my dear fellow," said Prince Andrei. "Speransky is a jumped-up priest's son, who is just a little, one hair's breadth, cleverer than the common crowd."

"My dear fellow!" Pierre exclaimed reproachfully. "The spirit of caste . . ."

"No, it is not the spirit of caste. I have seen what he is. I have not told this to anyone else nor shall I. Better him than Arakcheev, but Speransky is no hero of mine. No, of course he is not. You see, it is not Speransky who can achieve anything, but the institutions which take time and are created by people, by all of us. We do not understand the times that we are living through. This is one of the greatest events of history. The sovereign himself is curbing his own power and granting rights to the people. The old men cannot understand this properly. But how can we fail to sense what is happening just now? This is far better and greater than any feats of military heroism. In a few days' time the State Council will be opened as a constituent element of state. Ministers will give their reports in public. Financial matters will be openly declared to the people. Today or tomorrow the bill to liberate slaves will be passed. What else could you want, what else is needed?"

"Yes, that is all well and good," said Pierre, "but you must agree that there is another side to the soul that is not satisfied by this, that only our sacred brotherhood supports and enlightens, I do not understand how you can be so indifferent as a brother."

"I am not indifferent, especially now. Your order, I know, is one of the finest institutions in the world, but that is not enough in life."

Pierre paused for a moment.

"Why don't you marry?" he said. "I have been thinking about you, you ought to get married."

Prince Andrei smiled but said nothing.

"Oh, never mind me," Pierre responded, "what kind of example am I? I was a boy when I married, and anyway . . . Hélène's not really such a bad woman, not really . . ."

Prince Andrei gave a meek smile of joy, went up to Pierre and patted him gently on the back.

"It's such a terrible pity we've seen so little of each other," he said. "I don't know why you always have such an uplifting effect on me. One look at your face is enough to make me feel young and cheerful."

"Marry," Pierre repeated, looking at Andrei with a radiant smile. And at that very moment it came to him whom Prince Andrei ought to marry. Only one girl, better than any other he knew, was worthy of his best friend. It was Natasha Rostova. Pierre somehow felt he had thought this before, and it was the only reason he had fallen so much in love with her himself. "You ought to get married, and I know just who to," he said.

Prince Andrei blushed strangely. His memories of the oak tree and his thoughts about it had suddenly come back to him.

"Marya is already marrying me off," he said. "Her friend Julie Korna-kova is here. You know her."

"Yes, I know, but she's not the right one," said Pierre. "I don't want you to marry for logical reasons, I want you to come back to life, and I know . . ."

"No, my friend, we must not think about this, and I do not think about it. What kind of husband am I, so sickly and weak? A few days ago my wound reopened again and Villiers is sending me abroad."

"Will you be at Lev Kirillovich's ball the day after tomorrow?" asked Pierre.

"Yes, I shall."

# XI

On the 31st of December, the eve of the New Year of 1810, during the season of Epiphany, a ball was held at the home of Lev Kirillovich Naryshkin, a grandee from Catherine the Great's time. The ball was due to be attended by the diplomatic corps, Caulaincourt and the sovereign. The grandee's renowned house on the English Embankment was resplendent with countless points of light. There were policemen posted at the brightly lit entrance with its red carpet, and not merely gendarmes, but the chief-of-police and dozens of police officers standing around the porch. As carriages drove away, new ones constantly drove up with servants wearing feathers in their hats. Out of the carriages emerged men in uniform, decked in stars and ribbons: ladies in satin and ermine stepped lightly down from the footboards, and for a moment the crowd glimpsed the light, graceful forms of their movements.

Each time a new carriage approached with its shimmering servant, a murmur ran through the crowd and hats were doffed.

"The sovereign? . . . No, a minister, a prince, an ambassador. Can't you see the feathers?" – said a voice in the crowd. Someone in the crowd apparently knew everyone by their hats, and was identifying the most distinguished grandees of the day by name.

Eventually there was a lot of hustle and bustle, the police chief raised his hand to his hat and the sovereign's lacquered boot and spur stepped down lightly out of a carriage onto the brightly lit red carpet. Hats were doffed, and the young and handsome figure of the sovereign that the people knew so well, with his hair combed back from his high temples and tall epaulettes visible under his greatcoat, walked quickly through into the main entrance and out of sight. The sovereign was carrying a hat with a plume in one hand and he said something in passing to the chief-of-police who was standing to attention, inclined rigidly towards him.

From inside the windows came the harmonious sounds of a large, fine orchestra, and the shadows of men and women began moving back and forth across the brightly lit windows in front of the watching crowd. The ballrooms were already full of people. Speransky was there, and Count Kochubei, and Saltykov, and the Vyazmitinovs, and their wives and daughters, and the whole of St. Petersburg society, and all the court nobles, and the diplomatic corps, and visiting dignitaries from Moscow, and unknown Guards officers, dancers and absolutely everyone. Prince Vasily was also there, as were Prince Andrei, and Pierre, and Boris, and Berg and his wife, and old man Rostov, and the countess in a toque selected to Natasha's taste, and Sonya and Natasha in white dresses and with roses in their hair.

Natasha was attending her first big ball. There had been a great many discussions and preparations for this ball, many fears that no invitation would be received, that the gowns would not be ready and things would not be done properly. The Rostovs were being accompanied by a friend and relative of the countess who was a maid of honour at the old court, Marya Ignatievna Peronskaya, a skinny old maid. It was she who had arranged everything for the Rostovs, and at ten o'clock in the evening the Rostovs were to call for her at Tauride Gardens. When it came to swimming, Natasha put all her strength into swimming to the other side faster than everyone, when it came to gathering mushrooms, then she gathered more mushrooms and better ones than anyone else, and meanwhile anything that did not concern mushrooms or swimming seemed of no consequence. Now, however, when it was a matter of a ball, everything else seemed sheer nonsense, and the entire happiness of her life depended on everybody – mama, Sonya and herself – being turned out as finely as possible. Sonya and the countess placed themselves entirely in her hands. The countess was to wear a gown of dark-red velvet, with the two young girls in white muslin frocks with roses on the bodice and in their hair, styled in the Greek manner.

They had no time to think about what would happen at the ball and what awaited them there. There was only a feeling of anticipation of something great and festive, but there was no time to think about what it would be like. Natasha fussed over everybody and she was therefore the last to be ready. She was still sitting in front of the mirror with her peignoir thrown over her thin little shoulders when Sonya was ready and putting in her ribbon.

"Not that way, Sonya, not like that," shouted Natasha, twisting Sonya's hair arrangement and pulling the hair so hard that it hurt. "You don't want a bow like that. Come here." Sonya sat down and Natasha tied her ribbon.

"I beg your pardon, young miss, that's not the right way."

"Well, what's to be done with it . . ."

"Will you be long?" the countess's voice asked, "it's a quarter to ten."

"*Maman*, are you ready?"

"I just have to pin on my toque."

"Don't do it without me," shouted Natasha, "don't you dare!"

Naturally, as always, they were late. Natasha's skirt was too long; it was sewn up by two maids, who hastily bit off the threads with their teeth. Another maid with pins between lips and teeth ran backwards and forwards between the countess and Sonya and Natasha. All the important things had already been done: feet, hands, necks and ears – even though already clean – had been carefully washed, scented and powdered; but there was still so much left to do. Natasha, her hair already done and wearing her evening shoes, but still in her mother's dressing jacket, ran from Sonya to the countess to the maids. Finally at ten o'clock, the count entered the room in blue tails, stockings and shoes, all pomaded and scented.

"Are you going to be much longer? Here's your perfume. Peronskaya will be worn out with waiting."

"*Papa*, how fine you look, so lovely!" cried Natasha, who was now dressed in her frock, with the two maids still on their knees raising the hem (the whole skirt was too long).

"Papa, we're going to dance the Daniel Cooper," said Natasha. The countess came out, walking coyly, with especially cautious steps.

"Oh, my beauty!" said the count. "Lovelier than all the rest . . ."

"Mama, the toque should be more to the side. I'll pin it." Natasha suddenly rushed forward, too quick for the maid sewing her hem to move with her, so that a little piece of muslin tore.

"Never you mind, I'll just tack it up, no one'll see."

The young ladies' nanny came to look at them and gasped.

"'My little beauties, all stolen away,'" she said.

One more glove got ripped, then at last everyone climbed into the carriage and set off. Peronskaya was not yet ready. Despite her age and plain looks, exactly the same things had been going on at her house as at the Rostovs', although not with the same haste (as was only to be expected), but the old, unlovely body was still scented, washed and powdered in exactly the same way, just as carefully washed behind the ears, and exactly as at the Rostovs', an aged maid admired her mistress's finery with delight when she entered the drawing room in a yellow gown embroidered with her monogram. Peronskaya complimented the Rostovs on their outfits: "*Charmant, délicieux!*"

The Rostovs complimented her in turn and then, carefully protecting their hairstyles, they got into the carriages and set out. For Natasha, the preparations and making-ready had already begun the day before, but since this morning she had not had a single moment of freedom, nor had she once had time to think about what lay in store. In the damp, cold air and the semi-darkness of the cramped, swaying carriage, Natasha imagined for the first time what awaited her there at the ball, in the brightly lit halls, among hundreds of gorgeous women – music, flowers, the sovereign; but she could not believe it was really going to happen. It all fitted so ill with the sensations of the cold and cramped darkness inside the carriage. She only came to think about what lay ahead after walking up the red carpet at the entrance, entering the hallway, slipping off her fur coat and proceeding in front of her mother up between the flowers lining the brightly lit stairway. It was only then that she remembered the way she was meant to behave at a ball and tried to assume the grand manner that she regarded as correct for a girl at a ball. But to her good fortune, at that very moment she felt her pulse starting to race at a hundred beats a minute, and she was unable to assume that manner, which would have made her look ridiculous, but instead simply walked along with her heart fluttering in joyful excitement, trying as hard as she could to conceal it. And this was precisely the way that suited her best. Ahead of them and behind, guests in their finery were all arriving and greeting each other in the same subdued manner. All the way up the staircase, the mirrors reflected ladies in white and blue gowns, with their diamonds and pearls and bare throats and shoulders. Natasha could scarcely recognise her own reflection among them. As she stepped into the first hall, the rhythmic hubbub of voices, footsteps and rustling of dresses deafened her, while the light and the glitter blinded her still more. The host and hostess, who had been standing by the door for half an hour uttering the same words over and over as people came in, to wit: "So pleased to see you," greeted the Rostovs and Peronskaya in precisely this same manner.

The two girls in their white dresses, with identical roses in their dark hair, curtseyed in an identical manner; but it was to the slim figure of Natasha that the hostess's gaze was drawn despite herself and she looked at her with a special smile, different from her hostess's smile. Perhaps she was reminded of her own first ball and the irrecoverable golden days of her girlhood. The host too watched as Natasha moved away and asked the count whose daughter she was.

"*Charmant!*" he said.

People standing in the hall were all crowding around the door, waiting for the sovereign. But they made room for the countess and she stood at the front of the crowd.

Natasha could hear several voices asking about her and she sensed people's eyes on her. At such moments she could not see or take anything in, yet she showed not the slightest trace of embarrassment in her face. So as not to stand there in silence, she said a few words to her mother. She looked unhurriedly all around, keeping her curiosity well concealed. Nearby was an old ambassador with a full head of silver-grey curls, who was holding a snuffbox and laughing as he made the ladies around him laugh. A tall, full-figured lady of exceptional beauty was smiling calmly as she addressed a small group of men. This was Hélène. Natasha was filled with intense admiration and thought sadly of her own insignificance in comparison with such beauty. Pierre waddled through the crowd with his arms dangling idly, looking as if he were wandering round a market, shaking hands with everyone to left and right. Before reaching Natasha, whom he had noticed from a distance even with his short-sighted eyes, he grabbed some young cavalry officer by the arm and told him: "Go and look after my wife," indicating Hélène. Some old general came up to Peronskaya, but soon left her again, then a young man began talking with her quietly. Natasha sensed that they were talking about her. Boris came up to them and spoke with the countess. Two young blonde girls arrived with their mother, who was decked out in immense diamonds. Prince Andrei Bolkonsky came in wearing a colonel's uniform, impressing Natasha with his confidence and elegance. She remembered seeing him somewhere before. People did not move or talk much as they waited for the sovereign to arrive, and Natasha had time to make her observations. She observed everything: the hairstyles and the uniforms and how people behaved with each other. From their demeanour and glances she worked out for herself who belonged to the highest society, to high society and to ordinary society, and amused herself by trying to place them all. Of the men who had so far arrived and were standing about nearby, she identified four from high society: Pierre, Prince Andrei, the secretary of the French embassy and another exceptionally handsome Cavalry Guard, who entered after the others and took up a position almost at the centre of the hall, his hands tucked behind the buttons of his uniform in a disdainful manner. When Pierre spotted Natasha, he left his young officer and began moving through the crowd towards the Rostovs, but just at that moment everyone surged forward together, then surged back again and burst into chatter, the music struck up and the sovereign entered between the two rows that had parted, followed by the host and hostess. The sovereign walked rapidly, bowing to the right and left, as if trying to get this first moment of meeting over with as quickly as possible.

Then the polka began to play, there was a general stirring, and some young man with a busy expression asked Natasha to move aside. Several ladies went rushing forward, their faces showing that they had completely forgotten all the rules of good society. The men began approaching the women and lining up in pairs for the polka. Everyone parted to make way and the sovereign entered again, now from the other room, smiling as he led the hostess by the hand, walking out of time. He was followed by the host with Marya Antonovna Naryshkina, then the ambassador, the ministers and the generals, one of whom Peronskaya called across, since she had not been taken for the polka. Natasha felt humiliated, left with her mother and Sonya with the few other women not asked to dance, and if she was going to be left like that for the entire ball, simply taking up space, then that fine frock that her nanny had so greatly admired would be completely wasted, and she would end up feeling extremely unhappy. She stood there with her slim little arms lowered, clutching her fan, holding her breath so that her barely formed bosom rose and fell regularly, and staring straight ahead of her with her brilliant, startled, agate eyes, like a bird that has been winged, with an expression of readiness for immense joy or immense grief. She was not the least bit interested in all the important faces, or the sovereign, when Peronskaya pointed them out, only one thought occupied her mind: "Could it really be that no one will come up to me, am I really not going to be among the first to dance, are all these men really not going to notice me, they don't even seem to see me now, or if they do look at me, then their expression seems to say: 'Oh, not that one, no point in looking at her.' No, it cannot be possible," she thought. "They must know how much I want to dance, how wonderfully I dance and how much they would enjoy dancing with me."

The sounds of the polka had been going on for ages and now they began to sound like some sad memory in Natasha's ears. She felt like crying. Pierre went by with some grand lady, mumbling something and not even noticing Natasha. Prince Andrei, whom she had noticed, went by with the beautiful Hélène, smiling indolently as he spoke to her. Another two or three young men that she had noticed and assumed were from high society, and were therefore people she would have liked to dance with, went by, but no one even so much as glanced at her. The handsome Anatole had not joined in the polka and was smiling sardonically as he talked to the young men surrounding him. (Natasha noticed that he too was a celebrity of a kind.) Natasha sensed that he was talking about her as he looked in her direction, which was alarming. Peronskaya pointed him out and said to the countess:

"You know, that's the well-known rake Kuragin. See how handsome he is!"

Boris went by twice and looked at Natasha without making the slightest sign to her. Natasha stopped liking him altogether. Berg and his wife, who were not dancing, walked across. That was even worse. Here at the ball Natasha felt this family connection was utterly humiliating.

Finally the sovereign came to a halt beside his latest partner (he had danced with three). The music stopped and a nervous adjutant ran at the Rostovs, asking them to move aside and widen the circle. From the music-stalls there rang out the clear, gentle and seductive rhythm of a waltz. The sovereign glanced around the hall with a smile. A minute went by and still no one had begun. The master of ceremonies approached Marya Antonovna and invited her to take a turn at the waltz. She raised her hand to set it on his shoulder. She was exceptionally lovely. The adjutant danced beautifully. In the large circle of the hall, watched by hundreds of eyes, they set off into a glissade, without turning, then swung round smoothly, and as the adjutant swung Marya Antonovna round, the regular clinking of the spurs on his quick, deft feet could be heard above the sounds of the music that was growing faster and faster. As she watched them, Natasha was ready to weep at not being the one dancing the first round of the waltz. She did not notice that Bezukhov and Bolkonsky were now approaching and looking at her. Prince Andrei loved a ball with its crowds, flowers, music and dancing. He had been one of the best dancers of his time, before the war, but this was the first ball he had been to during this visit. He knew everyone, almost everyone knew him, and everyone desired his company. But during the five years he had been absent from this world, the young, dancing, merry-making society had changed. Those who had been society girls in his day were now ladies, and the brilliant ladies of that time had been eclipsed by others. He was greeted with a question about the latest decree, about the political news. Old men and women wanted to remember the past with him, but that was not what he wanted. He loved a ball, with its movement – the waltz – at a ball he loved to be an actor, not an observer. The moment he entered the ball he was caught up with this poetry of brilliant, elegant gaiety and, separating himself from the ladies and men who wished to engage him, he strode forward, feeling an unexpected inner excitement. He felt just as he used to feel, that he was handsome and attractive, and for no apparent reason he felt happy. Pierre stopped him by the arm.

"How lovely Rostova is, remember, I told you."

"You never told me, and I don't know her, but who is that, over there?" He asked, also indicating Natasha Rostova. "I'll bet it's her first ball."

"That's her. Come, I'll introduce you."

"Ah, I know: her father is that stupid marshal of the nobility in Ryazan, let's go over."

Bolkonsky and Pierre thus approached from the other side, when Natasha's head was turned away. And Prince Andrei invited her to a round of the waltz. That glazed expression of readiness for despair or ecstasy suddenly lit up with a happy, grateful, childish smile. "I've been waiting for you so long," this little girl seemed to be saying with this smile that shone through the tears, with her slim, bare little shoulders, as, frightened, happy and hesitant, she raised her hand to Prince Andrei's shoulder.

They were the third couple to enter the circle. And Natasha was noticed at once. It was quite impossible not to notice her now. There was such an ecstatic glow streaming from her eyes, such a childlike, innocent grace in her bare arms and neck. Her exposed body was not beautiful when compared with Hélène's shoulders, for her shoulders were thin, her bosom unformed, her arms slim, but Hélène seemed already to be painted with the varnish of the thousand glances that had already slid over her body, while Natasha seemed like a little girl who had been displayed in public for the first time and might have felt highly ashamed, had she not known that this was how things always had to be. Prince Andrei had started dancing because he had wanted to choose her, because out of all the debutantes whom he wished to lead out, she had been introduced to him first, but no sooner had he put his arms round this slim, agile, trembling figure, and this bare-shouldered girl had begun moving so close to him and smiling so close to him, than the wine of her charm went straight to his head. During the waltz he told her how beautifully she danced. She smiled. Then he said he had seen her somewhere before. She did not smile, but blushed. And then suddenly Pierre on the ferry, the oak, the poem, spring, happiness – all of these memories were suddenly resurrected in Prince Andrei's soul. Pierre was standing beside the countess, and when she asked him who the lady in the diamonds was, he answered: "The Swedish ambassador." For he heard nothing and saw nothing, so avidly was he following every movement of that couple, the rapid, regular movements of Andrei's feet, Natasha's little shoes and her devoted, grateful, happy face leaning so close to the face of Prince Andrei. He found it painful and joyful at the same time. He moved away in the other direction and saw his wife in all the magnificence of her beauty, standing in front of some tall individual who had bestowed the favour of his conversation upon her.

"My God, help me!" he said, and his face clouded with gloom. He walked round the hall like someone who had lost something, and that evening he particularly surprised his acquaintances with his muddle-headed absent-mindedness.

He returned to Natasha and started telling her more about Prince Andrei, about whom he had already talked so often. After Prince Andrei, Boris was next to approach Natasha to invite her to dance, and then came more and more young men, and Natasha, now happy and flushed, did not stop dancing all evening.

Chosen time after time for the cotillion, Natasha repeatedly accepted with a smile, even though she was still breathing hard. Prince Andrei, who was dancing not far from her, suddenly had the notion that before this girl had danced away half the winter she would be married, and he felt somehow fearful. As the ball was nearing its end and Natasha was crossing the room, Prince Andrei caught himself thinking something strange and utterly unexpected: "If she goes up to her cousin first and then to her mother, then this girl will be my wife," he said to himself. She went up to her cousin first. "What can I be saying? I've gone crazy," thought Andrei.

Prince Andrei danced the last dance, the mazurka, with Natasha and led her in to supper. The old count came up in his blue tailcoat, reminded Andrei of Otradnoe and invited him to visit again, then he asked his daughter if she was enjoying herself.

Natasha did not answer but simply smiled in a way that said reproachfully: "How could you even ask?"

"More than I ever have in my whole life," she said, pulling the scented glove from her slender white arm. Natasha was happier than she had ever been before. She was at that extreme degree of happiness when someone becomes entirely kind and good and loves everyone equally, and regards everyone as equal. His Majesty Alexander Pavlovich seemed delightful to her, and if she had needed to, she would have gone up to him and told him he was delightful, just as simply as she had said it to Peronskaya. She wanted everyone to be cheerful and happy. Sonya was dancing, but when she was left without a partner, Natasha said to some young men she did not even know:

"Go over and ask my cousin" – and it was all so simple that no one was surprised.

Peronskaya did not dance, and sat on her own. It occurred to Natasha that she ought not to have powdered her neck like that, but she took comfort in the fact that for Peronskaya it didn't matter. She went up and kissed her anyway. Prince Andrei, Pierre, the other dancers – she felt the same about all of them, and they were all simply delightful.

# XII

The following day Prince Andrei woke up and smiled, without even knowing why. The whole of his preceding life in St. Petersburg appeared to him in a new light. He recalled the previous day's ball, but his thoughts did not dwell on it for long: "Yes, it was truly a brilliant ball. And I can still take great pleasure in such delights. And also – yes – Rostova was very sweet. There's something fresh and special about her, not from St. Petersburg, it marks her out." That was all that he thought about the previous night's ball. But he began recollecting things from much earlier, he began thinking over the whole of his life in St. Petersburg. And these four recent months came to him in an entirely new light, as if he had never thought about them before now. He recalled his bustling activity and searching, the story of his project for the military regulations, which had been accepted for consideration by the committee, and which they had attempted to suppress solely because some other piece of work had already been completed and, even though it was no good, presented to the sovereign. He recalled the story of his notes on the liberation of the peasants, which Speransky had constantly avoided discussing, not because the paper was not composed logically, or it was not necessary to take this measure, but because now was not the right moment to take up the sovereign's time with it. He remembered his legislative work, his resentment when his work had been handed over to Rozenkampf, and he felt like laughing and also felt somehow ashamed. He vividly recalled Bogucharovo and his peasants there, Dron the village headsman and the servants, and when he tried to apply to them the articles on the rights of the individual that he had divided up into all those paragraphs, he realised how funny it was that he could have engaged in such pointless work.

He was discovered thinking these thoughts by a young man of his acquaintance, Bitsky, who served on various commissions and appeared in all the social circles of St. Petersburg, a passionate admirer of the new ideas and of Speransky, and a compulsive St. Petersburg tattler. One of those people who choose their allegiance, like their clothes, according to fashion, but who therefore seem to be the most ardent partisans of their tendencies. He had barely even removed his hat, when he came hurrying in to Prince Andrei, whom he regarded as one of the bulwarks of the liberal party, and immediately started airing what was on his mind. He had just learned the details of the famous opening session of the State Council, which had been inaugurated by the sovereign, and which he described in rapturous terms. The sovereign's speech had been exceptional, it had been one of those speeches that are only made by the constitutional monarchs of England. The sovereign had said in so many words that the Council and the Senate stood at the heart of the state, he had said that the rule of law should be based not on *arbitrary will* but on *solid principles*, said Bitsky, emphasising his words and opening his eyes wide as he reported that state finances were to be reformed and accounts made public.

"Yes, today's event marks a turning point, a truly great turning point in our history," he concluded.

Prince Andrei listened to his story about this opening of the State Council, which he himself had been awaiting with such impatience and to which he had attached so much importance, and was surprised to discover that not only did this event fail to touch him, but it actually seemed utterly insignificant.

He listened to Bitsky's ecstatic narrative with a smile of quiet, kind, concealed mockery and a very simple thought kept occurring to him: "What has it got to do with me, and what has it got to do with Bitsky, what the sovereign saw fit to say in the Council?" Prince Andrei began to find Bitsky's conversation boring. He begged his pardon and said that he had to make several important visits. They went out together. And when Prince Andrei found himself alone, he wondered where it was he needed to go. Ah yes, he needed to pay a visit to the Rostovs. Courtesy required it.

Natasha was wearing a different dress from yesterday, a blue one, in which she looked even lovelier. The entire family, whom Prince Andrei had formerly judged so harshly, now seemed in his opinion to consist of fine, straightforward, good people. The hospitability and good-nature of the old count, which seemed especially pleasant here in St. Petersburg, were so striking that Prince Andrei could not refuse to stay for lunch. They were all kind, wonderful people who naturally did not have the slightest understanding of the treasure they possessed in Natasha. Yet they were all good people who provided the finest possible setting to display this exceptionally charming and delightful girl who was absolutely brimming with life. In Natasha, Prince Andrei sensed the presence of a special world entirely alien to him, filled with joys unknown to him – that special world that had so astounded him when he first rode up the avenue to Otradnoe. This mystery was what fascinated him most of all about the young Rostova. After lunch she sang. At first Prince Andrei half-listened while chatting to her mother, then both of them fell silent, and then Prince Andrei suddenly felt a lump of emotion rising in his throat, something he had never known he was capable of. He was happy, but at the same time he also felt very sad.

He had absolutely nothing at all to cry about, yet he was ready to cry. About what? About his former love? About the little princess? About his disappointments? Yes and no. It was some strange opposition between something infinitely great and indefinable that was inside him and some narrow, corporeal thing that was himself. That was what both oppressed and delighted him while she was singing. As soon as she finished singing, she ran up to him and asked if he had liked it. He looked at her and smiled. She smiled too.

He left late in the evening and went to bed as usual, but soon felt no need to sleep. He lit a candle and sat up in bed, then got up, lay down again, yet without feeling at all burdened by insomnia: his heart was filled with such a joyful, new feeling. Just before dawn he fell asleep for about two hours, yet when he woke he felt as fresh as he ever had in his life. In the morning he received a letter from Marya in which she described their father's poor state of health and could not help expressing her annoyance with Mademoiselle Bourienne; then a colleague of his from the committee arrived and complained about their work having been spoiled. Prince Andrei tried to calm him down. "Why can't they understand that all this is trivial, that everything will be all right?" he thought.

He went to the Rostovs' again, and again did not sleep at night, and then once again he went to the Rostovs'. On the evening of the third day, as he was sitting in the Rostovs' drawing room talking with them, laughing and making them laugh at Pierre's absent-mindedness, he suddenly felt someone's stubborn, serious glance fixed on him. He looked round. It was the sad, stern and at the same sympathetic gaze of the countess, which she was directing at both of them, as if she was both blessing them and expressing her fear of deception on his part and already regretting parting with her favourite daughter. The countess immediately changed her expression and said she was surprised she hadn't seen Count Bezukhov for so long, but Prince Andrei understood her words to mean something else. He realised she was reminding him of the responsibility he was taking on himself now with this increasing intimacy, and with this thought in mind he looked at Natasha again, as if he were wondering whether she was worth all that responsibility: "At home," thought Prince Andrei, "I'll think that over at home too."

That night again he could not sleep and the whole time was thinking and wondering what he was going to do.

He tried to forget, to dismiss from his mind the memory of Natasha's face, her hands, her walk, the sound of her voice, the last words she had spoken, trying to decide in spite of this memory whether he would marry her and when. He started weighing things up: "There are family reasons against it, my father would probably be displeased, I would be abandoning the memory of my wife, and she is so young to be little Coco's stepmother . . . Stepmother, stepmother. Indeed, but the most important thing is, what am I to do for myself?" He imagined her already as his wife. "I cannot help it, I cannot do otherwise, I cannot be without her. Yet I cannot tell her I love her, I cannot, it is too soon," he thought.

The terrible thought of making a mistake in such a state of excitement, of enthralling her then failing to keep even some unspoken promise, of acting dishonourably, frightened him so much that on the fourth day he decided not to see her but to try to think everything through and decide for himself. He did not go to the Rostovs', but went to talk with other people and hear their talk of meaningless concerns, these people who did not know what he knew, that it was all impossible.

That night Natasha, her eyes staring wide in excitement or in fright, lay in her mother's bed for a long time, asking what it could mean, and telling her mother how he had complimented her, how he had asked where they were going to be and when they were going to the country.

"I just don't know what he's found in me. And you said I'm silly. If I always feel scared when he's there, what does that mean? Does it mean I'm in love? Yes, does it? Mama, you've gone to asleep."

"No, my darling, I'm scared myself," her mother replied. "Now, off you go."

"I shan't sleep anyway. It's so stupid to sleep. And to think . . ." And again she started saying what she had already said ten times ". . . that I would love him and he would love me. And then imagine it, he came here to St. Petersburg, just as we did."

She said all this like a gambler who cannot get over drawing his first high card, which he has just played. It now seemed to her that she had fallen in love with him that first time she saw him at Otradnoe. She was almost frightened by the strange, unexpected happiness that the one whom she had chosen (she was sure of that now) had also chosen her. It gave her a feeling of exceptional happiness and flattered her immense vanity that she had been chosen by him, and because of this feeling she did not know if she felt love for him. She had been surer that she loved him previously, but now if she had found the strength to ask herself this question, she would not have known how to answer.

"Mama, what's he . . . when will he propose? Will he?"

"That's enough, Natasha, pray to God. Marriages are made in heaven."

"Dearest darling mamasha, I do love you so," Natasha shouted, hugging her mother with tears of happiness in her eyes.

# XIII

For four days Prince Andrei did not go to the Rostovs' or anywhere where he might possibly meet them. But on the fourth day he could hold out no longer and, deceiving himself, because he was really hoping vaguely to see Natasha, he went to visit the young Bergs, who had been at his house twice and had invited him to them for that evening.

Every time Berg met Prince Andrei, however, and wherever it might be, he always insisted that Bolkonsky should come to visit him in the evening, and yet when it was announced to him in his neat and revoltingly clean apartment on Vladimirskaya Street that Bolkonsky had arrived, Berg was surprised and flustered. When Bolkonsky was shown in, he was sitting in his new study, clean and bright, decorated with busts and pictures and new furniture all so precisely arranged that it was difficult to live in, for its sole purpose seemed always to be in perfect order, so that even the very slightest everyday use of this room would cause a disruption. He had been sitting there in the study with his new uniform jacket unbuttoned, impressing on Vera, who was sitting near him, that one always can and should have acquaintances who are superior to oneself, because only then is there any benefit from the acquaintance. "You can pick things up, you can ask about things. Just look at the way I got on with the top ranks." (Berg did not count his life in years, but by the awards he had received from the Emperor.) "My colleagues are nothing now, but I am in line for regimental commander, and I have the happiness of being your husband" (he stood up and kissed her hand, but on his way across to her he straightened the corner of a carpet that had flipped over). "And how did I achieve all this? First and foremost by knowing how to choose my acquaintances. It goes without saying that one has to be virtuous and conscientious . . ." Berg smiled in the awareness of his superiority over this weak woman and paused to consider that his dear wife was, after all, indeed a weak woman and incapable of comprehending all that constituted worthiness in men. In being a man. Vera smiled at the same time in the awareness of her own superiority over her virtuous, good husband, who nonetheless, like all men (as Vera saw things) had a mistaken understanding of life. In her opinion he did not understand that the most important thing in life was in fact an art that Vera believed she possessed in the highest degree, the art of managing people with subtle diplomacy and being fixed in one's desires. "If I had not possessed this art, I would still be an ageing maid in the home of parents who are gradually being ruined, and not the wife of a good, honest husband making a brilliant career, and one, moreover, in whose future success I shall play a part." Berg thought that all women were only good for marriage and were as limited as his own wife. Vera thought, judging from her husband alone, and then extending this opinion to everyone, in the way that limited people always do, that all men were proud and merely believed in their own intelligence, while in fact they understood nothing. And they were both quite content with their destiny.

Berg stood up, embraced his wife carefully in order not to crease the lace cap that he had spent a lot of money on buying for her, and kissed her directly on her lips.

"Just one thing, we shouldn't have children so soon," he said, following an unconscious train of thoughts.

"Yes," replied Vera. "I don't want that at all. However," she said, smiling at the care with which Berg removed her expensive cap (through her husband she liked to feel her superiority to any kind of man), "however, I do hope we shall have someone visiting us today," she said, moving away from her husband, again following an unconscious line of thoughts. "Are the candles lit in the drawing room?"

"Yes. The Princess Yusupova was wearing one just like it," said Berg with a happy, kind smile, indicating the cap.

At this moment the arrival of the honoured and long-desired guest, Prince Andrei, was announced, and the two spouses exchanged self-satisfied smiles – each of them ascribing the honour of this visit to themselves. "That's what knowing how to make acquaintances means," thought Berg. "That's what it means to know how to conduct oneself!" thought Vera.

In visiting the Bergs, Prince Andrei compromised with his decision not to see Natasha for two days, since he was vaguely hoping to see her at her sister's. He was accepted into the new drawing room, where there was nowhere to sit without disrupting the symmetry, cleanliness and order, and therefore it was perfectly understandable and not at all strange that Berg, magnanimously offering to disrupt the symmetry of an armchair or a divan for his dear guest, should find himself in a state of painful irresolution on this matter and suggest that his guest should decide the question. Prince Andrei did not at all mind Berg and his naïve, egotistical stupidity (probably because Berg represented the most acute contrast possible to his own character) and now in particular Berg was the very best conversation partner he could have. As he listened at length to Berg's voice talk about promotions, about his plans, about making a home, Prince Andrei enjoyed dreaming about just one thing. Vera sat there putting in a word from time to time, in her heart disapproving of her husband, not because he always spoke of nothing but himself (in her opinion, this could not be otherwise) but for talking too carelessly. Prince Andrei also found Vera's company pleasant because of the involuntary connection that existed between her and Natasha in his memory. Vera was one of those decent, inconspicuous individuals whom one comes across so frequently in the world that you never think seriously about them, and Prince Andrei had always considered her a good, insignificant creature who was now especially close to him because of her closeness to Natasha.

Berg begged Prince Andrei's pardon for leaving him alone with Vera (Vera's glance told Berg how improper this apology was) and left the room, in order to send his orderly out quickly to buy the same biscuits for tea that he had eaten at the Potemkins', which he considered to be the height of society chic and which would therefore be sure to amaze Prince Andrei when they were served in the silver basket sent to Berg as a wedding present by his father.

Prince Andrei was left alone with Vera, and he suddenly felt uncomfortable. Vera spoke just as much as her husband, but while she was speaking it was not possible to think independently because she had the habit, which her husband lacked, of addressing questions to her interlocutor in the middle of what she was saying, as if she were examining him: "Do you understand?" Prince Andrei was therefore obliged to follow her conversation, and in addition, as soon as her husband went out, she began talking about Natasha.

Like everyone else who lived in the Rostovs' house or visited it, Vera had noted Prince Andrei's feelings for Natasha and drawn her own conclusions from them. She did not precisely feel it *necessary* to inform Prince Andrei of her own ideas about Natasha's character and her previous partialities and enthusiasms, but she did so anyway, for in conversation with such a precious guest from high society she felt it essential to apply her spurious art of diplomatic expression, tactful comment and pointless cunning. She needed to be piercingly subtle, and the most convenient and best pretext for that was Natasha, so it was to her that she applied this art. Having directed the conversation to her own family, Prince Andrei's last visit and Natasha's voice, she dwelt on the discussion of her sister's qualities.

"I believe, prince, that you have often been surprised by this strange ability of Natasha's to switch her attachments. She used to love French music, now she cannot bear it. And it's the same all the time with her.

She is capable of become attached to everything and then *just as quickly* forgetting . . ."

"Yes, I think she feels very strongly," said Prince Andrei in a tone suggesting that the matter of Natasha's personal qualities could not possibly be of any interest to him.

"Yes," said Vera with a subtle smile. "But you, prince, are so perceptive and you understand people's characters straight away. What do you think of Natalya? Can she love one man constantly?"

Prince Andrei did not like this turn in the conversation.

"I have no reason to think anything but good of your sister."

"And I think, prince, that when she really falls in love . . ." Vera said with a significant air, as if implying that Natasha was in love at the moment (throughout this conversation Vera thought that she was trying to do good for Natasha.). "But these days," she continued, mentioning "these days" in the way that limited people in general like to, assuming that they have discovered and analysed the distinctive features of our time, and that people's qualities change with time, "these days a girl has so much freedom that the pleasure of having admirers stifles this feeling, and it must be admitted that Nathalie is very sensitive to this."

Prince Andrei had no idea what to expect next, but as he listened to Vera's tactless and clumsy comments, he felt an inner suffering similar to what a musician must feel when he sees his servant mimicking him and playing with a pompous air on an instrument that he does not know. Such was the smug way in which Vera played the instrument of subtle drawing-room conversation.

"Yes, I know," Andrei replied drily, "were you at Catalani's latest concert?"

"No, I was not, but to come back to Nathalie, no one was ever courted more than she has been, but until very recently she has not taken a real liking to anyone, even our own dear cousin Boris, who found it very painful to renounce her."

Prince Andrei cleared his throat, frowned and said nothing. He was feeling a certain hostility for Vera, and he would not have refrained from expressing it, were she not a woman. She did not notice this.

"You are friends with Boris, are you not?" she said.

"Yes, I know him . . ."

"I'm sure he has told you of his childhood love for Nathalie. Recently he was very touching, very much in love and if he had been rich . . ."

"Did he make a proposal to her?" Andrei asked, annoyed.

"Well, you know, it was a childhood love, you know, between cousins, such intimacy frequently leads to love. But, you know, age and circumstances . . ."

"Did your sister refuse him or did he refuse her?" asked Prince Andrei.

"Well, you know, these were intimate childhood relations, which were very charming, when they were children. But, you know, cousinhood is a dangerously close relationship, and mama set everything right. And so much the better for Natasha, do you not think?"

Prince Andrei made no reply and nodded politely. Something inside him had snapped. Something as natural and even as inevitable – with Natasha's character – that she had loved someone, that she had kissed her cousin (as Prince Andrei himself had hugged and kissed his own cousin in his boyhood) – such a thing had never even entered Prince Andrei's head. Whenever he thought about her his thoughts had always been associated with the virginal purity of the freshly fallen snow. "What nonsense to have thought I was in love with this girl," was the first thing that Prince Andrei thought. And just as a traveller who has lost his way in the night looks around in amazement at the place where he finds himself at dawn, Prince Andrei could not immediately understand how on earth he had come to be sitting drinking tea with these young, naïve Bergs. What had he to do with Natasha, and her sister, and this naïve German who was telling him how well they make silver baskets for bread and rusks in Finland? But just as a traveller who has wandered into an unfamiliar area takes a long time in order to find his old road and go on his way, so Prince Andrei sat in the Bergs' house for a long time without listening or answering, surprising and eventually even wearying them with his presence.

But once Prince Andrei had left the Bergs' house and found himself on his own, he felt that he could not go back to his old road, that he loved her and was jealous of her, and afraid of losing *her*, despite *everything*, even more than before. It was not yet late. He told his driver to go to Pierre's place, realising with surprise that he had not seen him during these last few days. There were carriages standing at the illuminated entrance to the Bezukhovs' house. The countess was holding a reception, the French ambassador was there, but Pierre was alone in his rooms upstairs.

Pierre was sitting in his low, smoky room with his shirt hanging out, copying out the original principles of the Scottish lodge when Prince Andrei came in.

Since the ball Pierre had sensed the approach of an attack of depression and was desperately attempting to combat it. Once again everything seemed insignificant to him in comparison with eternity, again he was facing the question: what for? And he was forcing himself to work by day and night, hoping to keep the evil spirit at bay by his labours.

"Ah, it's you," he said to the prince with a joyless, absent-minded air. "And here I am at work," he said, indicating his notebook as if it were some form of salvation from the misfortunes of life, in the way some unfortunate people regard their work.

"I haven't seen you in ages, dear fellow," said Andrei. "The Rostovs have been asking after you."

"Ah, the Rostovs." Pierre blushed. "You've been there?"

"Yes."

"I have no time, I'm leaving, and I'm finishing this work . . ."

"Where to?" asked Prince Andrei.

"Moscow." Pierrre suddenly sighed deeply and slumped down heavily at full length on the divan near Andrei. "To tell you the truth, the countess and I are not suited to each other. The experiment has been made and . . . Yes, yes, I married too young, but for you, for you, this is the very time."

"You think so?" asked Prince Andrei.

"Yes and I'll tell you to whom," said Pierre, blushing again.

"The younger Rostova," Andrei said with a smile. "Yes, and I'll tell you too that I really could fall in love with her."

"Then fall in love, and marry, and be happy," said Pierre with particular passion, jumping to his feet and beginning to stride around. "This is what I've always thought. That girl is such a treasure, such a . . . She's a rare girl. My dear friend, I implore you – don't philosophise over this, don't have any doubts. Marry, marry, marry."

"Easily said! In the first place, I'm getting on," said Prince Andrei, looking into Pierre's eyes for an answer.

"Rubbish," Pierre cried angrily.

"And even if I were within a hundred miles of marrying, then there's my father . . . who has told me that my marrying again would be the only grief that could hurt him."

"Rubbish!" shouted Pierre. "He'll love her as well. She's a wonderful girl. Marry, marry, marry, and let us talk no more about it."

And Pierre promptly drew his notebooks closer and began explaining the founding articles of the Scottish lodges to Prince Andrei, but Prince Andrei did not hear the explanation of the articles, he did not even guess at Pierre's hidden, envious suffering, and he started talking once again about the Rostovs and marriage. Now where were his languor, his contempt for life, his disenchantment? He was dreaming like a boy, making plans and living entirely in the future. Pierre was the only person he could ever dare to express his feelings to, and now he was opening his heart, setting forth plans naïvely, like a boy, while sometimes laughing at himself.

"Yes, if I married now," he said, "I'd be in the best of circumstances.

561

All my ambition is buried for ever. I have learned how to live in the country. I'd take back a tutor for Nikolushka. Masha, whose life is so miserable, could stay with me. I'd come to Moscow for the winter. I really feel as if I were seventeen."

They talked on into the night and Pierre's parting words were: "Marry, marry, marry!"

# XIV

The morning after her bed-time discussion with her mother, when it had been decided that Prince Andrei should make a proposal, Natasha waited for him, fearful that the decisive moment was about to arrive that was going to deprive her of her greatest pleasure – the hope and anticipation of love from all the men she met, and the tests that she loved to put every man through to make him love her. The time would come when there would be other joys – to be a lady, to attend court and so on, and then she would have to abandon all her former, customary pleasures and delights. She was afraid that this Prince Andrei, who was indeed the one she liked best of all men, was going to come and propose to her. But he did not come, and the following day she waited for him with intense impatience, now afraid that he was not going to come. If she had been able to understand her own feelings, she would have seen that her impatience sprang not from love, but from a fear of appearing foolish and deceived in her own eyes, her mother's, and Pierre's, as well as – so it seemed to her – in the eyes of the whole of society, which already knew, or would soon discover, what had happened and what high hopes she had entertained. All that day she was subdued and shamefaced. Everyone seemed to know all about her disappointment and was either laughing at her or feeling sorry for her. That evening she came to her mother's bed and burst into sobs, like a child. At first her tears were the tears of an offended and insulted child, who is trying to find out what he has done wrong, and when he cannot find out, asks what he has been punished for, but then she grew angry and told her mother that she didn't love Prince Andrei at all and never had loved him and wouldn't marry him now, no matter how much he asked her. But would he ask her now? That was the question that was always in her mind, and she went to bed with that unsolved question tormenting her.

"He's so strange, so different from all the others. He could do anything," she thought. "But even so, of course, I'm not going to think about him any more, and tomorrow I'll put on papa's blue name-day dress, Boris's favourite, and then I'll be happy all day."

But despite her firm decision to forget everything and go back to her former life, despite papa's blue dress, the stripy one with the lace which always brought happier feelings, Natasha could no longer fit back into her former way of life. Every one of her admirers visited over those days . . . Boris, and all the others, every one of them looked into her eyes in the same way and admired her, but none of it was any fun, and while they were there she only thought about Prince Andrei even more vividly, and was constantly flushed and irritable: it constantly seemed to her that they *knew* and were pitying her. The idea of possibly getting married and the serious view her mother took of all this had changed her completely without her even being aware of it. She could no longer feel the same kind of joy in her heart as she used to.

When the countess began consoling Natasha one evening, telling her it was perfectly natural for Prince Andrei not to come, that he must have a lot to do and think about before such an important decision, that he probably needed his father's consent, Natasha first listened to what her mother was saying and then suddenly interrupted her.

"Stop it, mama, I'm not thinking about it and I don't want to think about it. He came for a bit, and then he stopped, he stopped." Her voice began to tremble and she almost started to cry, but she pulled herself together again and carried on cheerfully. "But anyway, I don't want to get married at all. And I'm scared of him. I'm perfectly, perfectly calm now . . ."

The day after this conversation Natasha, wearing the same blue dress that she liked so well for the joy it brought her in the mornings, was strolling about the large ballroom, which she particularly liked for its resounding echo, and glancing into each of the mirrors as she walked past, halting in the middle of the hall and repeating a single musical phrase that she particularly liked from the end of Cherubini's chorus and listening delightedly to the charming manner (which seemed to surprise her every time) in which these trilling sounds filled the entire space of the hall and then slowly faded away. She stopped, smiled triumphantly and continued with her stroll, not walking across the echoing parquet in the ordinary way, but switching from heel to toe at every step (she was wearing her favourite new shoes), listening to this regular click of the heel and squeak of the toe: tuk-cheep, tuk-cheep, as joyfully as she did to the sounds of her own voice. And again, she glanced into a mirror as she passed it. "That's her, that's me!" the reflection of her face seemed to say at the sight of her. "That's good." A servant wished to enter in order to clear something out of the hall but she would not let him in and after she closed the door behind him, she continued with her stroll again.

That morning she was once again in her favourite, habitual state of love and admiration of herself. "How delightful this Natasha is," she told herself again in the words of some collective male third party, "attractive ... that voice ... young, and she never bothers anyone, just leave her in peace. Such good tone – to-to-to," she sang and then, once again, like a refrain, she began tapping her heels and squeaking her toes. She felt so happy she couldn't help laughing out loud in her joy.

Just then the front door in the entrance hall opened, someone asked: "Is she at home?" and there was the sound of footsteps.

Natasha was looking into the mirror, but she wasn't seeing herself. She was listening to the sounds in the hallway. When she did see herself, her face was pale and then suddenly flushed. It was *him*, the real *him*. She knew that for certain, although she could barely hear the sounds from behind the closed doors.

She went into the drawing room.

"Mama, Bolkonsky's come," she said. "Mama, it's terrible, it's intolerable. I'll end it all," she said bitterly. "I don't want to suffer."

"Very well, show him in," the countess said with a sigh to the servant who had followed Natasha in and confirmed her news.

Prince Andrei entered the room, kissed the ladies' hands with a calm expression and began talking about Mademoiselle Georges. Prince Andrei said all these things more calmly than he did in other drawing rooms. He looked at Natasha, and his glance was as cool and calm as when he looked at Anna Pavlovna. In his worldly experience Prince Andrei had managed to acquire the essential art of speaking with only his mouth and looking without seeing – the art that we apply unawares when our gaze becomes firmly fixed on one object and we do not see it, or when we speak words we have learned off without thinking about them, the art that is deliberately applied when we wish, without frightening ourselves, to look at something terrible or pronounce touching words without our voice trembling – the art that consists in the apparent disconnection of two mechanisms – outward appearances and the inner, spiritual life – so that the roller, piston or belt, the transmission mechanism which in normal circumstances exists between these two mechanisms, exists no longer. Prince Andrei deliberately disconnected these two mechanisms when he looked and spoke, and he felt that if he restored this connection, he would not be able to look and speak as he was doing, and then God alone knew what would happen. This was why he carefully did not allow the wheel of external appearances to connect with his inner life and why he was so disagreeably simple and calm. Natasha realised immediately that there was something unnatural and mysterious here, and she gazed with a stubborn, impolite curiosity at Prince Andrei's face, never taking her eyes off him for a moment. The countess was listening to Prince Andrei, she did not understand what he was saying to her (she did not even hear him say that he was going away). She flushed repeatedly, like a young girl, and glanced at her daughter. During the last week, in her thoughts and feelings, the countess had dwelt so much on this imminent proposal, that all she could think about now was whether it could really have come already, was this already the terrible moment now and ought she to stand up and go away on some pretext, leaving them to declare their feelings. After chatting about the theatre for a little, the countess got up.

"I'll go and call my husband," she said. "He's busy, but he'd be so sorry to miss you."

When her mother stood up to go out, Natasha glanced at her with frightened, imploring eyes, and Prince Andrei felt that, against his will, the disconnected mechanism had reconnected itself, and now he was not capable of saying a single calm word, and his eyes were now transmitting the full force of the girl's influence on him.

"Do you know why I came here?"

"Yes . . . No . . ." she said hastily.

"I came to learn my fate, which depends on you."

Natasha's face lit up, but she did not say anything.

"I came to tell you that I love you and my happiness depends on you. Do you wish to unite your life with mine?"

"Yes," said Natasha, very, very quietly.

"But are you aware that I am a widower, that I have a son, that I have a father whose consent I should wish to receive?"

"Yes," said Natasha in the same way.

He glanced at her, and the serious passion of her expression frightened and surprised him. He wanted to go on looking at her, but he was overcome by such happiness in this new love, that he could not. He smiled and kissed her hand.

"But time is needed. Give me a year . . ." he said.

"I really don't know, I don't understand, not anything . . . I'm just . . . I'm very happy. I . . ."

"Will you give me a year? You won't fall out of love with me?"

Natasha was unable to answer. All the inward effort she had made had exhausted her. She sighed loudly once, then again, then more and more rapidly and finally she burst into sobs. She could not say a word.

"Well, so be it," said her eyes, gazing with childish tenderness into Prince

Andrei's face. She sat down. Prince Andrei took her fine slim hand and pressed it to his lips.

"Yes?" he said, smiling. She smiled too through her tears, leaned over his bowed head and thought for a second, as if she were wondering if it were possible, and kissed him.

"No, tell me . . ."

Prince Andrei asked to see the countess and repeated everything again. He requested her daughter's hand. But since the daughter was still young and had had an attachment to her cousin, since Prince Andrei needed to receive consent from his father (who would, of course, said Prince Andrei, consider family connection with the Rostovs an honour), and since he, Andrei, needed to undergo treatment abroad, he requested a waiting period of one year, for which period he bound himself, but did not bind Natalia. In a year's time, if he were alive, with or without his father's consent, he would request them to make him a happy man by giving him Natalia's hand. But if Natalia should fall in love with another during this time, he requested her only to write him a single word. Natasha smiled as she listened to him, and out of all that he said she understood only that she, the little girl Natasha, the child who so recently was taking umbrage at the governess Marya Emilievna, at whom Nikolai used to laugh when she tried to argue, this little girl was being spoken to so seriously as an equal, as a superior and beloved being – and by whom? By Prince Andrei, this knight, this intelligent man, who was so adult and yet so kind. It was flattering, it made her happy and frightened all at the same time. Frightened because Natasha could tell that this was now no joke, she could not play at life any longer. For the first time she felt she was grown-up and she also bore responsibility for every word she said from now on.

"It is up to the countess to decide whether to announce this commitment or keep it a secret."

Prince Andrei would have preferred for his father's sake not to make it public. The countess agreed to keep it a secret. But that very day the whole family was informed, in secret.

Prince Andrei was happy, not as happy as he had expected, but still he was happy. He walked across to the window with Natasha.

"You know, I have loved you since that time you visited us at Otradnoe," she said.

The old count pretended that he knew nothing, but he was especially cheerful and affectionate with Prince Andrei. The Rostovs had been about to leave, but they stayed on for a while for Natasha and Prince Andrei. Bolkonsky visited every day, and as a friend of the house he sat with his jacket unbuttoned at the little chess table, drew in albums, played ball with Petya and enlivened their family circle with his simple good-natured merriment. At first there was a certain awkwardness in the way the family treated him. They spoke of him and thought of him as learned. He seemed like a man from another world; but then they grew used to him and discussed domestic affairs in front of him without embarrassment and talked to him about unimportant trifles, in which he took part, like everyone else. At first he seemed arrogant and rather studious, but they soon realised that he could talk about everything. He could talk about the estate with the count and about clothes with the countess and Natasha. They spoke to him trustingly about Nikolai, about his decision not to accept much money from his father and about his loss at cards.

"It is very fortunate that he lost once and badly," said Prince Andrei. "That's the best way for a young man. It happened to me too." And he told them how, when he had not been in the army long he had been cleaned out in St. Petersburg and how he had wanted to shoot himself. Natasha looked at him.

"It's amazing how he already knows about everything!" said Natasha. "He knows everything and everybody, he's experienced everything, it's even rather off-putting."

"Why?" asked Prince Andrei, smiling.

"I don't know, it just is."

"Then I won't tell you any more."

"No, do, I like it."

Sometimes even in Prince Andrei's presence the Rostovs expressed surprise at how this had all happened and how there had quite obviously been omens. They saw omens everywhere: in Prince Andrei's visit to Otradnoe, and their coming to St. Petersburg, and the resemblance between Natasha and Andrei, which the nanny had noticed during Prince Andrei's first visit, and the clash in 1805 between Andrei and Nikolai, and the fact that all this had been decided on St. Hadrian's and Natalya's day – or Andrei's and Natasha's, as they called them.

The house, however, was full of that poetic tedium and silence that always surround a bride and groom. They often sat together in silence. Sometimes the others would get up and go out, and the bride and groom would still not speak yet did not feel bored. The old count embraced and kissed Prince Andrei, asked his advice on Petya's education or Nikolai's army service. The old countess sighed as she looked at them. Sonya looked joyfully from Prince Andrei to Natasha and back. Natasha was both alarmed and happy. But the happier she was, the more she felt there was something missing. When Prince Andrei spoke – he spoke so well on so many things – she listened to him with pride: when she spoke she was both scared and delighted to notice him looking at her intently and quizzically. And she asked herself in puzzlement: "What is he searching for in me? What is he trying to find with that glance?" Sometimes she fell into her crazy, happy mood, and then she particularly enjoyed listening and watching as Prince Andrei laughed. He rarely laughed, but when he did, he devoted himself completely to his laughter, and every time this laughter made her feel closer to him.

On the day before their departure Prince Andrei brought Pierre with him. Pierre seemed confused and embarrassed. He spoke with her mother. Natasha went and sat at the chess table with Sonya, inviting Prince Andrei to come over to join her. He walked across to them.

"You've known Bezukhov for a long time," he said. "Do you like him?"

"Yes, he's lovely, but terribly funny."

And as always when they spoke about Pierre, they started telling anecdotes about his absent-mindedness, some of which had even been specially invented about him.

"You know, I tell him everything," said Prince Andrei. "I've known him since we were children. He has a heart of gold. I want to ask you one thing, Nathalie," he said, suddenly serious. "I am going away. God knows what might happen. We might fall out . . . Well, I know I am not supposed to talk like that. But one thing, though, no matter what might happen to you while I am away . . ."

"But what could happen?"

"No matter what sorrow you might suffer," Prince Andrei continued, "I beg you, Nathalie. No matter what happens, go to no one but Pierre for advice and help."

At the end of February the Rostovs left, and soon afterwards, having been granted retirement, Prince Andrei also went abroad, only calling in for four days to Bleak Hills, to which the old prince and his daughter had just returned after spending that winter in Moscow.

## XV

Prince Nikolai Andreevich Bolkonsky and his daughter spent that winter of 1809 and 1810 in Moscow. The old man had been granted permission to visit the two capital cities, and he wished to make use of it, but could not bear life in Moscow for more than three months and returned to Bleak Hills during Lent. The prince's health and character had deteriorated greatly during the last year, after his son had left. He had become even more crotchety than before and for the most part the eruptions of his persistent wrath were directed at Princess Marya. He seemed to make a point of seeking out all her very sorest spots in order to subject her to the cruellest moral torment possible. Princess Marya had two passions, and therefore two joys: her nephew Nikolushka and religion, and both were favourite targets for attack and mockery by the prince. No matter what topic they might start off with, he would turn the conversation to the superstitions of old maids or the overindulgence of spoilt children. "You want to turn him" (Nikolushka) "into an old maid just like yourself, but you shouldn't, Prince Andrei needs a son," he would say; or he would turn to Mademoiselle Bourienne and ask her in front of Princess Marya how she liked our priests and icons, and make jokes about them . . .

Although he painfully insulted Princess Marya the whole time, it cost his daughter no effort to forgive him. How could she blame a sick, weak, old man for what he said, and how could her father, who (as she knew, after all) did love her, how could he be unjust towards her? And what was justice in any case? The princess never thought about this lofty word – justice. All of humanity's complicated laws and opinions were concentrated for her in one simple and clear law – the law of love and self-sacrifice granted to us by Him who suffered lovingly for humanity, for he was God. What concern of hers was the justice or injustice of other people? She herself had to suffer and love, and she had done so.

In the early spring Prince Andrei came to Bleak Hills. He had taken leave and would now travel abroad to have treatment for his wound which had reopened and also to find a Swiss tutor for his son – one of those philosophical mentors and virtuous friends that rich parents used to bring home for their children in those days. Prince Andrei was more cheerful, gentle and affectionate than Princess Marya had seen him for a long time. She sensed that something had happened to him, but he did not breathe a word about his love to Princess Marya. Before leaving, he talked for a long time with his father, and Princess Marya noticed that just before his departure they both seemed displeased with each other.

Following the news of his son's supposed death, then Andrei's return and the death of his young wife, and especially following the difficulties he had suffered over the home guard, the old prince had aged greatly. His moral decline was particularly marked after his son's departure. It was expressed primarily in a state of irritability that was only interrupted by rare moments of calm and a strange partiality that would appear out of the blue (when Princess Marya saw it, she could not believe her eyes) for Mademoiselle Bourienne. Only she could talk and laugh with him without irritating him, only she could read aloud to him in a way that gave him satisfaction and she provided him with a steady example to hold up to his daughter for imitation. Princess Marya was constantly found wanting for not being so jolly or not having such a healthy complexion, or not being as nimble as Mademoiselle Bourienne. Much of the talk at dinner with Mikhail Ivanovich turned on the subject of education, with the aim of demonstrating to Princess Marya that she was spoiling her nephew with her indulgence, that women were capable of nothing more than producing children, and that had there been old maids in Rome, they would probably have been forced to jump off a cliff; or else the conversation with Mademoiselle Bourienne turned on the subject of religion as an occupation for idle folk, with the only intelligent thing her fellow countrymen had done in '92 being to abolish God. Weeks would go by without his saying a single affectionate word to his daughter, while he persistently sought out all her sore spots in order to inflict some hurt. Sometimes (this occurred most frequently before breakfast, when his mood was at its very worst), he would come into the nursery, the nannies and nurse-maids would flee in alarm, and he would find fault with everything there, it was all was systematic spoiling of the child, he threw the toys about and broke them, abused and sometimes even pushed Princess Marya and then departed hastily.

In the middle of the winter the prince locked himself in his room without giving any reason, refused to see anyone except Mademoiselle Bourienne and even refused to receive his daughter. Mademoiselle Bourienne became very lively and jolly, while things started being gathered together in the house for some sort of move. The Princess knew nothing. She suffered for two nights without sleeping, and eventually resolved to ask her father to explain what was going on. Princess Marya went to see her father, requesting to see him for the necessary explanation, but imprudently chose the hour before dinner. Driven by her feelings of indignation at this unfair treatment in her own home, for once she overcame the fear that she habitually felt. So greatly agitated was she by this thought that she even allowed herself to suspect Mademoiselle Bourienne of deliberately setting her father against her. But she alone was at fault for choosing such a bad time for the explanation. Had she but asked Mademoiselle Bourienne, *she* would have explained to the princess when and when not to speak with the prince. But Princess Marya entered the study with her clumsy, heavy tread and with prominent red blotches all over her face and, afraid that if she hesitated she would not summon up her courage again, she went straight to the heart of the matter.

"Father," she said, "I have come to say one thing, that if I have done something bad, tell me, punish me, but do not torment me. What have I done?"

The prince was in one of his very worst moments. Lying on the divan, listening to Bourienne reading, he snorted derisively and looked at her without uttering a word for several seconds and then said with an unnatural laugh:

"What do you want? What? What a life – not a moment's peace!"

"Father . . ."

"What do you want? I don't want a thing. I have Bourienne, she reads well, and Tikhon is a good butler. What else do I need? Well, just carry on," he told Mademoiselle Bourienne and lay down again.

Princess Marya burst into tears and ran out, but once in her room she fell to the floor in a fit of hysterics.

That evening, the old prince called her to him and met her at the door – he had clearly been waiting – embracing her immediately she entered the room and making her read to him while all the time he walked about, stroking her hair. He did not summon Mademoiselle Bourienne that evening, and he would not let Princess Marya leave for a long time. As soon as she wanted to go, he invented some new piece of reading and carried on walking around again. Princess Marya knew that he wanted to talk to her about the scene that morning, but did not know how to begin. She found it inexpressibly painful and shameful that her father should be feeling guilty towards her and she could not help him because she did not dare. Finally, the third time she stood up to leave, he turned his face, softened and illuminated with a childishly timid glance and with a childish smile on its wrinkled cheeks, directly towards her . . . He seized her hand with a rapid movement and, despite all her efforts to pull it away, he kissed it. He had never done that before in his life. He put both his palms around it, kissed it again, looked into his daughter's eyes with that same timid smile, then suddenly frowned, swung her round by the shoulders and shoved her towards the door.

"Go on, off you go," he said. He was so weak as he swung her round that he staggered, and the voice that said "Go on, off you go", which was meant to sound menacing, was a weak, old man's voice.

How could she not forgive him everything after that?

But the old man's moment of tenderness passed, and the next day life went on in the same way as before and the old man's feeling of subdued hatred for his daughter, expressed in the constant insults that he seemed to make even against his own will, made themselves felt just as before.

From that time on a new thought began to enter Princess Marya's head. For Princess Marya, this was a thought as dark and as intimate, as much the very essence of her life, as Prince Andrei's thought about the oak tree. It was the thought of taking the veil, or, not so much of taking

571

the veil as of constant pilgrimage. For three years already Princess Marya had made it a habit to travel twice a year to the Serdobsk Hermitage to fast, to talk with the abbot there, Father Akinfii, and make confession to him. She had entrusted this secret to no one save Father Akinfii, and at first he had tried to dissuade her, but finally he had given his blessing. "To leave family, relatives, one's social position, all concern for the good things of the world in order to cling to nothing, to wear a hempen shirt, wander under a different name, doing no harm to people and praying for them. To pray for those who protect you and for those who persecute you. There is no truth and life higher than this truth and this life," thought Princess Marya. "What could be better than such a life? What could be purer, more exalted and happier?" Often, as she listened to the tales of the wandering pilgrims she was so excited by their simple, plain talk that she could have abandoned everything there and then and run out of the house (she already had an outfit prepared), but afterwards, when she saw her father, and especially little Coco, she would quietly weep, cursing her weakness, feeling she was a sinner who loved them more than God. The princess was horrified and terrified to discover in her own soul things that were even worse (to her opinion and way of thinking): fear of her father, envy of Bourienne, regret at the impossibility of linking her own life to such a simple, honest and kind man as Rostov had seemed to her. And then again and again she returned to her favourite dream of seeing herself with Pelageyushka the pilgrim, in a coarse shirt, or striding alone along a dusty road with a stick and a knapsack pursuing her wanderings without joy, without human love, without desires, from one saint to another and eventually to the place where there is no sadness, nor any sighing after eternal joy and bliss. "No, I have completely thought this over, I must carry it through," thought Princess Marya, as she sat at her desk, chewing on the same pen she had used all last year in 1809 to write her customary Thursday letter in French to her friend Julie.

*Sorrows are evidently our common lot, my dear and tender friend, who seems more unhappy, the more I love her," wrote the princess. "Your loss after the misfortunes inflicted on you by the war is so terrible that I cannot explain it in any other way than a special mercy from God, who wishes to test you in His love for you and your excellent mother. (Princess Marya's letter was a letter of condolences on the occasion of the death of a third brother of Julie's from fever, after two had been killed, one in the campaign of 1805, the other in 1807, so that now out of Nastasya Dmitrievna's four sons, only one remained.) Ah, my friend, it is religion and only religion that can – I will not say console* us – but can free us of despair, only religion can explain to us that without its help man cannot understand why, for what purpose, good, exalted beings capable of finding happiness in life, who not only do no harm to others, but are essential for their happiness, are called to God, while others who are evil, useless and vicious, a burden to themselves and others, are left to live. The first death I saw and which I shall never forget, the death of my sweet sister-in-law, made an immense impression on me. You ask fate why your beautiful brother had to die, and in just the same way I asked why this angel had to die – Lise, who had never done any harm to anyone, nor ever had any but kind thoughts in her heart. But now, my friend, five years have passed since then and with my paltry intellect I am already beginning clearly to understand why she had to die, and in what way this death was merely an expression of the infinite mercy of the Creator, all of whose actions, although for the most part we do not understand them, are only manifestations of His infinite love for His creation. I often think that perhaps she was too angelically innocent and not strong enough to bear all the responsibilities of a mother. She was irreproachable as a young wife, perhaps she could not have been such a good mother. Now, in addition to having left us, and Andrei in particular, the purest feeling of regret and reminiscence, where she is she will probably receive the place which I do not dare to hope for for myself.

But, to speak of the others as well as her, this early and terrible death had a most beneficial effect, despite all the sadness, on me, on Andrei and on my father. Then, at the moment of loss, these thoughts could not come to me. I would have driven them away in horror, but now it is so clear and obvious. I am writing all this to you, my friend, only in order to convince you of the truth of the gospel, which has become the rule of my life: not a single hair shall fall from our head without His will, and His will is guided only by His boundless love for us, and therefore whatever might happen to us, it is all for our good. You ask if we shall come to Moscow, and soon? Much as I long to see you, I do not think so and do not wish to come. You will be surprised to learn that the reason for this is Buonaparte. And this is why. My father's health is clearly declining, and this is particularly expressed in his nervous irritability. This irritability, as you know, is primarily directed at political matters. He cannot bear the thought that Buonaparte manages affairs as an equal with all the sovereigns of Europe and especially with ours, the grandson of the Great Catherine.

As you know, I am absolutely indifferent to political matters, but, from what my father says and his conversations with Mikhail Ivanovich, I know everything that is going on in the world, and especially all the honours heaped on Buonaparte, who would seem to be accepted as a great man and the Emperor of France throughout the whole world, except here at Bleak Hills. And my father cannot stand this. It seems to me that my father speaks so unwillingly of a trip to Moscow primarily as a consequence of his view of political matters, and in anticipation of the conflicts he will have as a result of his manner of expressing his opinion freely in front of anyone. All the gains he will make from treatment, he will lose as a result of arguments about Buonaparte, which are inevitable. We saw an example of that last year. In any case, it will be decided very soon. Our family life continues as before, with the exception that Andrei is here. As I have already written to you, he has changed greatly in recent times. Following his grievous loss he has only fully recovered morally this year. He has become the way I knew him as a child: meek, kind and affectionate. It seems to me he has realised that life is not yet over for him; but together with this moral change, he has become very weak physically. He has become thinner than before, more nervous. I am very much afraid for him, and glad that he has undertaken this trip to St. Petersburg. I hope it will do him good. He went to St. Petersburg, where he has to finalise matters with his father-in-law, and also because he promised the Rostovs to attend their eldest daughter's wedding. She is marrying someone called Berg. But I hope that this trip will in any case liven him up. I know that Prince Razumovsky wrote to Andrei, inviting him to take up some important position in the state service. Andrei said no, but I hope he will change his mind. He needs activity. My father greatly approved of Andrei's trip. He wants Andrei to serve. No matter how he abuses and despises the present government, and although he does not show it, nonetheless these five years of Andrei's inactivity and the fact that many of his colleagues have overtaken him in the service have greatly upset my father; the government is despised, but he wants Andrei to occupy a prominent place and be in the sovereign's eye, and not remain a retired colonel for ever. And just recently I have seen that while Andrei may not exactly find his inactivity burdensome, he has never been idle, and he cannot be, with his immense abilities and his heart. It is impossible to list all the good he has done for everyone here, from his peasants right up to the nobles and so on, and while he may not feel restless in his inactivity, he feels so ready for any important state work in the military or the civil sphere, that he is sorry to see his ability going to waste and places that belong to him by right being occupied by other, insignificant people. I know that he is upset by this.

And so he left, thin, unwell and coughing a little, but moved and affectionate. He did not hide it like before, when he considered it shameful to show sadness, he cried a little as he said goodbye to me, our father and little Coco. I am amazed at the manner in which rumours reach Moscow from the country at all, especially such incorrect ones as the one you write to me, rumours about Andrei marrying the young Rostova girl. It is true that recently Andrei has only been out in company at the Rostovs, and it is true that on their way from the country to St. Petersburg, the whole Rostov family called to see us and spent the entire day here, and it is true that Nathalie Rostova is one of the most enchanting girls that I have ever seen, it is true that Andrei is very affectionate towards her, with the affection of an old uncle to his niece, it is true that he loves her charming little voice, which even raised my father's spirits, but I do not think that Andrei has ever thought of marrying her, and I do not think it could happen. And this is why. Firstly, I know that although Andrei rarely speaks of his deceased wife, the sadness of that loss has taken too deep a root in his heart for him ever to give her a successor and our little Coco a stepmother. Secondly, because this Nathalie does not fall within the category of women that Andrei tends to like. She is attractive, enchanting, but she lacks what is called depth. After she has enchanted you and you are looking at her, smiling without any reason, you cannot help asking: 'What is so good in her, why have I been captivated by her?' – and you can find no answer. She enchanted me and all of us so thoroughly that it was two days before I could gather my thoughts in order to consider her character. She has two immense faults: vanity, a passion for praise and flirting without any limits or purpose. I have never seen anything like it. She flirted with everyone: with Andrei, with me, with her own brother and, above all, with my father. She had evidently heard about his character and decided to defeat him – and she did: after just two hours she had reached the stage of taking such liberties with him as no one else, I think, has ever dared. I do not think Andrei would choose her as his wife, and I can say frankly that I do not wish it.

As for Nikolai, I may say frankly that I like him very much and confess that as I looked at him, I dreamed of you being happy with him. How glad I should be to see such a dear man as the husband of best friend.

But I have got carried away. I am finishing my ninth page. Goodbye, my dear friend, may God preserve you beneath his mighty veil. My dear friend Bourienne sends you a kiss.

# PART FIVE

# I

The Biblical tradition has it that the absence of labour – idleness – was a necessary condition of the bliss enjoyed by the first man until his fall. The love of idleness has remained unchanged in fallen man, but the curse still hangs over him, and not only because we must earn our daily bread – we simply cannot be idle and be at peace. Some little worm gnaws away at us, telling us that we must feel guilty for being idle. If man could find a condition in which, while being idle, he could feel he was being useful and fulfilling his duty, then he would have discovered one aspect of primordial bliss. And, in fact, within every well-organised state such a condition of compulsory and irreproachable idleness is indeed constantly enjoyed by one large estate – the estate of the military. It is this compulsory and irreproachable idleness that constitutes the bliss and the attraction of military service. After 1807 Nikolai Rostov continued to serve in the Hussars Regiment on a peace footing, experiencing this bliss to the full.

Denisov was no longer in the regiment; he had moved on. Rostov would rise late in the morning, with no need to go anywhere in a hurry, drink his tea, smoke a few pipes and chat with the sergeant-major, and then the officers would come and tell him about some impressive prank played by N.N., or how some new thug needed to be put in his place, or about a black stallion sold for a song or about where to go that evening. Rostov did not play cards, fulfilled his duties efficiently, had once fought a duel, always had money, drank a lot without getting drunk and was generous with his hospitality. He had become a rather coarse good chap, whom his Moscow acquaintances would have regarded as being rather *mauvais ton*, but he was respected by his comrades and had the reputation of a good sport and fine fellow even at division level.

He was a daring horseman and was constantly changing, selling and buying horses. He also broke them in himself, riding them and running them on a lunging rein. He dined at home and everyone knew that if they had no dinner, they would always find a place set and a ready welcome at Rostov's place. After dinner he took a nap, then summoned the singers and trained them himself. He also visited the Poles and dallied with the Polish ladies, but he affected the part of a crude hussar, not a ladies' man. When he was alone he rarely picked up a book and if he did, he forgot things as soon as he had read them.

In recent times, that is in 1809, in his letters from home he had found an increasing number of complaints from his mother that the state of their financial affairs was becoming ever more precarious, that something had to be done and it was time for him to come home. Reading these letters disturbed Nikolai, making him afraid that they wanted to extract him from this secure and familiar shell of military service in which he lived so quietly and calmly, having cut himself off from the whole tangled muddle of outside life. He sensed that sooner or later he would have to step back into that whirlpool of life, with its collapsing and mending of financial affairs, with accounts drawn up by stewards (to which his father had alluded on his previous visit), with society connections, with Sonya's love and his promise to her. This was all terribly difficult and complicated, and he replied to his mother's letters with cold, correct letters, never saying when he intended to come. He replied in a similar manner to the letter informing him about Vera's wedding. No one wrote to him about Prince Andrei's engagement, but from Natasha's letters alone he could tell that something had happened to her and that they were concealing something from him. This troubled him. He loved Natasha more than anyone else at home.

But in late 1810 he received a despairing letter from his mother, written in secret from the count. She wrote that if Nikolai did not come and take matters in hand, the entire estate would be auctioned off and they would all be left homeless. The count was so weak, he had come to trust Mitenka so completely and was such a good man, and everyone deceived him so badly, that everything was going from bad to worse. "For God's sake, I implore you, come immediately, if you do not wish to bring misery on me and your whole family," wrote the countess. This letter produced its effect on Nikolai. He already possessed a common sense or instinct of behaviour that told him what *must* be done.

And now what *must* be done was to go, taking leave, or even retirement. Why, he did not know, but when he had taken his nap after dinner, he ordered them to saddle up the grey, Mars, a terribly bad-tempered stallion, who had not been ridden for a long time, and when he returned home with the horse lathered, he told his Danila to start packing and declared that he was taking leave and going home. It was difficult and painful for him to think that he would go away and would not hear from headquarters the news that particularly interested him – whether he would be promoted to captain or awarded the Order of St. Anne for the latest manoeuvres; it was strange to think he would go away without having sold to Count Golukhovsky the threesome of roans that the count was bargaining for, and which Rostov had wagered he would sell for two thousand; it was strange that he would not be there for the ball that the Hussars were about to hold for Panna Przizetska in order to pique the Uhlans, who were holding a ball for their own Panna Brzozowska, yet he knew that he had to leave this good, straightforward world and go to a place where there was nothing but nonsense and confusion.

A week later his leave was granted, his fellow hussars from the regiment and even the brigade held a dinner for Rostov for a subscription of fifteen roubles each – two orchestras played and there were two choirs of singers. Rostov danced the trepak with Major Basov. The young men had all keeled over by eight o'clock. Everybody was drunk, they tossed Rostov in the air and hugged him. He kissed his own soldiers. The men tossed him in the air once again, and he remembered nothing after that until he woke the following morning at the third coach station in a bad mood and with a headache, and found some reason to give the yid who was the station-keeper a good beating. As always happens, until halfway through the journey, until Kremenchug or Kiev, all Rostov's thoughts remained with the squadron and what lay behind him, but after the halfway mark, the threesome of roans, his sergeant-major and Panna Brzozowska began to fade and he began wondering anxiously how he would find things at Otradnoe. The closer he came, the stronger his thoughts of home became, constantly growing more powerful, as if his emotions were subject to the law of the acceleration of falling bodies in inverse proportion to the square of the distance. At the last station but one, he gave a beating to a coachman who had bad horses, at the final station before Otradnoe he paid three roubles for vodka, and finally he was running, panting, up to the porch of the house, like a boy.

After the raptures of the meeting and that strange sense of disappointment in comparison with what he had been expecting (they are all the same, why was I in such a hurry?), Nikolai began to readjust to his old home world. His father and mother were the same, they had only aged a little, but there was a new air of anxiety and sometimes discord about them, which, as Nikolai soon learned, was caused by the poor state of their affairs. Sonya was already nineteen. She had already stopped growing prettier, and did not promise to become any better than she already was, but that was quite good enough. She positively radiated happiness and love from the moment Nikolai arrived, and this girl's faithful, unshakeable love gave him a joyful feeling.

Nikolai was surprised and shocked when he saw Natasha and he laughed at her.

"You're completely different."

"Why, am I less pretty?"

"Quite the opposite. But such dignity."

On the very first day of Nikolai's arrival, Natasha told him in secret about her romance with Prince Andrei and showed him the latest letter. Nikolai was very surprised and not very pleased. For him Prince Andrei was a stranger from a different and higher world.

"Well then, are you glad?" Natasha asked.

"Very glad," Nikolai replied. "He is an excellent man. And are you very much in love?"

"How can I put it," replied Natasha. "I feel calm and secure. I know that people better than him do not exist, and I feel so sure and peaceful now. Not at all like it used to be . . ."

Petya astonished him most of all. He was a really big chap now.

For a while after his arrival Nikolai was in a serious, even irritable mood. He was tormented by the imminent need to become involved in these stupid matters of accounts and the whole business of non-military life. In order to shrug off this burden as rapidly as possible, on the evening of his first day (he arrived in the morning), he ignored Natasha's enquiry as to where he was going, set off with an angry frown and walked into Mitenka's outhouse, where he demanded accounts of *everything*. But just what these accounts of everything might be, Nikolai knew even less than the terrified and puzzled Mitenka did.

The conversation and the accounting with Mitenka did not last long. A bailiff, a peasant elder and a country clerk who were waiting in the hallway of the outhouse were frightened and delighted to hear the young count's voice start roaring and bellowing, growing ever louder and louder; they heard abusive and terrible words following one after the other in rapid succession: "Bandit, ungrateful wretch. I'll cut you down like a dog . . . not dealing with my papa now . . . robbed us, you rogue . . ."

Then these men were equally delighted and frightened to see the young count, flushed bright red and with bloodshot eyes, drag the staid Mitenka outside by his collar and deftly pound his backside with one foot and a knee in the pauses between his words as he shouted: "Get out, clear out and stay out, you scoundrel." Mitenka went hurtling headlong down the six steps and ran into the *border*. (This border was a well-known hiding place for criminals at Otradnoe. Mitenka himself, when he came home drunk from town, would hide from his wife in the border. And many inhabitants of Otradnoe were familiar with the sanctuary offered by the border when they were hiding from Mitenka.) Mitenka's wife and sisters-in-law peered out into the hallway with frightened faces from the doors of a room where a bright samovar was boiling and the steward's high bed towered up under its patchwork quilt. Paying no further attention to Mitenka, the young count, out of breath, strode purposefully past them with his spurs jangling, and went back into the house.

When the countess learned straightaway from the servant girls what had happened in the outhouse, on the one hand she felt reassured – in the sense that now their situation was bound to improve – but on the other, she was concerned how Nikolai would take it and several times she crept up to his door on tiptoe and listened as he smoked one pipe after another.

The next day the old count called Nikolai aside and told him with a smile:

"You know, my dear boy, you shouldn't have got so carried away. Mitenka has told me everything."

Nikolai blushed, which was something he had not done for a long time. "I knew," he thought, "that I would never understand anything here, in this stupid world."

"You got annoyed because he hadn't included those seven hundred roubles. But he has them down as transport, and you didn't look at the next page."

"Papa, he's a scoundrel and a thief, that I do know. And I have done what I have done. But if you don't want me to, I shan't say another word to him."

"No, you know, my dear boy." The count was embarrassed too. He sensed that he had been a poor manager of his wife's estate and had let down his children, but he did not know how to put it right. "No, you know, he is a loyal man. I want to ask you to take on our affairs, I'm old, I . . ."

At the sight of his father's embarrassed face Nikolai forgot about Mitenka and everything else, he did not know what to say and almost burst into tears. It was so terrible to think that his old, good, kind father could think of himself as guilty of anything.

"No, papenka, you forgive me if I've done anything to upset you, I understand less than you do, forgive me, I won't interfere again, not for anything."

"To hell with it, with all this transport business, and the peasants and the money and all that rubbish," he thought. And from that time on he never interfered in business matters and his only dealings with Mitenka – who was especially pleasant and polite with the young count – concerned the arrangements for the old count's pack of hunting dogs, which was huge and neglected. The only financial decision he took at this time was when the countess once informed him in secret that she had a promissory note for twelve thousand from Anna Mikhailovna and asked Nikolai what he thought she ought to do with it.

"This," Nikolai replied, recalling Anna Mikhailovna's poverty, his own past friendship and present dislike for Boris (it was this last circumstance above all that made him act in the way he did). "This!" he said. "You said it is up to me, then do this!" And he tore the note into pieces, making his old mother sob and weep tears of joy.

Nikolai began hunting very actively, since it was autumn and the finest hunting season of all. Natasha was a bold horsewoman, she had hunting in her blood and she loved and understood hunting like a man. Thanks to the hunt, those two autumn months that Natasha and Nikolai spent at Otradnoe in 1810 were the happiest of such times in their entire lives, and they later enjoyed recalling them more than any others. Sonya did not know how to ride and she stayed at home, so that Nikolai saw less of her. His relationship with her was simple and friendly, he loved her but considered himself completely free. Natasha, who had stopped taking her lessons and had no one she could flirt with, did not find her solitude a burden, for she was sure of her future marriage with Prince Andrei, and since she was not waiting too impatiently for the time to come, she too felt herself completely free, as never before, and with the passion with which she did all things, she devoted herself to hunting and friendship with her brother. Thanks to her, Nikolai became more cheerful and even here, in this world that had been such a fearful tangle, he discovered his own little world, centred on friendship with Natasha and hunting.

## II

It was the 12th of September. There were already early morning frosts that bound hard the soft ground moistened by the autumn mist. The great, healthy green stripes of the thickly clumped shoots of winter crops contrasted with stripes of pale yellow winter-crop stubble and the brownish summer-crop stubble trampled by the cattle and cut through by red stripes of buckwheat. The hills and woods, which in late August had still been green islands among the black winter fields and the fields of stubble in which stooks were still standing, were now dark brown islands of wet fallen leaves with highlights of gold and bright-red, amid the bright-green winter crops. The grey hare had already half-changed the colour of his breeches and the saddle on his back. The fox's colour had faded a little and this year's cubs were beginning to wander away. The young wolves were already larger than a harrier, the dogs of the keen young huntsman Rostov had already run in to reach good hunting form and, at the general council of hunters, it was decided to give the dogs three days' rest and take them out on the 14th of September, beginning with the oak grove, where there were wolves.

That was the way things stood on the evening of the 11th of September. All that day the hunt had stayed at home, and it was frosty and sharp, but with the evening it became overcast and a little warmer, it started to drizzle and there was not a breath of wind at all, and when Nikolai woke early the following day and glanced out of the window in his dressing gown, he beheld the best hunting morning that any hunter could ever wish to see, it was as if the sky was melting and sinking on to the earth. If there was any movement in the air, it could only have been downwards from above. The drops hanging on the naked branches were light-grey, the earth in the vegetable garden was as shiny black as poppy seeds; something between rain and mist was falling from out of a grey infinity. Nikolai went out on to the porch, where there was a smell of wet leaves and dogs, who were already there under the awning. When the black and brindled, broad-beamed borzoi bitch Milka, with the delightful bulging black eyes, spotted her master, she stood up, stretched out her hindquarters and lay down like a hare, then suddenly leapt up and licked her master on the nose and moustache. Milka's litter-mate, the red Rugai, spying his master from the garden path that he had been walking along and feeling jealous of Milka, hunched up his back and bounded straight for the porch, then halted hard with his tail hoisted high and began rubbing himself against Nikolai's legs.

"Ahoy! Halloo!" a hunter's call rang out just at that moment, that inimitable call which combines the deepest bass with the most subtle tenor, and round the corner came Danila, a grey-haired huntsman with a wrinkled face and hair cut square in the Ukrainian style, holding a curved, lead-weighted crop in his hand and wearing that special expression that only huntsmen have, of independence and scorn for everything in the world. He doffed his Circassian cap to his master, and in his gesture there was contempt for his master, but contempt that was a compliment because, after all, Nikolai knew that this Danila who scorned and looked down on everything was still his man.

"Danila!" said Nikolai, smoothing his moustache and smiling, sensing himself already in the grip of that indefinable hunting feeling, in which a man forgets his entire past and future, and all his previous intentions, like a man in love who is in the presence of his beloved.

"What can I do for your excellency?" Danila asked in a voice like a protodeacon's bass, grown hoarse from hallooing to the dogs, and he shot his master a sly glance from a pair of brilliant black eyes when Nikolai said nothing in reply. "Well, are you going to give in, then?" that pair of eyes seemed to say.

"A fine day, eh? The chase, and the gallop, eh?" said Nikolai, scratching Milka behind the ears.

Danila said nothing and just blinked his eyes.

"I sent Uvarka to listen," his deep bass said after a moment's silence, "at dawn. He said she'd moved them to the Otradnoe reserve." This meant that the she-wolf they both knew about had moved, together with her cubs, into the Otradnoe Wood, which was only two *versts* from the house.

"Well, are we going to go, then? You bring Uvarka to me."

"As you wish," said Danila and disappeared round the corner.

"Wait though, don't feed them."

"Very well."

Five minutes later Danila and Uvarka were standing talking in the large study. Nikolai's study was certainly big, but it was shocking to see Danila inside a room. Although not a tall man, in a room he looked like a horse or a bear standing there among the pieces of furniture and the accoutrements of human life. Danila himself felt this even more keenly than anyone else. Usually when he came inside he stood there stock still with his legs like stone pillars and tried to talk as quietly as possible. He had the constant fear that he might accidentally smash and spoil everything, and he was always in a great hurry to get out from under the ceiling into the space under the open sky. When he had finished asking about the dogs and learned that they were in good order (Danila himself was desperate to go) and then had decided on a route, Nikolai ordered them to saddle up the horses. But just as Danila was about to leave the room, Natasha came rushing in with quick steps, wrapped in her nanny's large shawl with birds depicted on its black centre, and her hair still uncombed.

Natasha was so excited that she could barely stop herself from throwing open the shawl and waving her bare arms about in front of the huntsmen. In fact, she did partly do just that.

"No, this is beastly, it's horrid," she shouted. "He's going, he's ordered his horse to be saddled, and he didn't tell me . . ."

"But you can't go. Mamenka said you can't go."

"And you chose the time to go so very well." She could hardly stop herself crying. "But I shall go, I'm definitely going. No matter what mama wants, I'm going. Danila, tell them to saddle up my horse, and have Sasha ride out with my leash of dogs," she said to the master of hounds.

586

Danila was already suffering badly enough from the impropriety of being inside a room, but he did not know the first thing about addressing a young lady while there. He lowered his eyes and hurried out, as if all this had nothing to do with him, simply trying not to accidentally hurt the young lady somehow.

Even though Natasha had been told she could not go, that she would catch a chill, there was nothing to prevent her from doing just what she wanted to do, and she got herself ready and went.

The old count, who had always maintained an immense hunt and only occasionally ridden out into the field himself, had now handed over its entire management to his son. But on that day, the 12th of September, being in a cheerful mood, he was intending to ride out as well, and he sent his wife, and Sonya, and the governess and Petya to ride in the brake . . .

An hour later the entire hunt was at the porch. Without waiting for anyone, Nikolai, with a stern, serious expression on his face to show that he had no time for trifles, walked straight past Natasha, who was being helped to mount her horse by her groom Sasha, inspected every section of the hunt, sent the pack and the hunters on ahead to cut off the game's retreat, mounted his chestnut Don stallion and, whistling to the dogs of his leash, set off across the threshing floor into the field leading to the Otradnoe reserve. The old count's horse, a sorrel gelding called Viflyanka, was led by the count's groom. He himself was supposed to drive straight out in the little droshky to the best trail, which had been reserved for him. The Rostovs had a total of eighty harriers in their hunt. All of the same old Rostov breed of Kostroma dogs, set low on their legs, lean, strong runners with loud barks, and black coats with reddish markings. But many of the dogs were worn out, so that only fifty-four of them were led out in the pack. Danila and Karp Turka rode at the front. At the back there were three whippers-in. There were four of the Rostovs' huntsmen with leashes of borzois: the old count's, with eleven dogs and two grooms, the young count's (Nikolai's) with six dogs, and Natasha's with four rather poor dogs (not expecting much from her, they had given her the worst there was) and Mitenka with his leash. In addition, there were another seven leashes of borzois. And so about a hundred and fifty dogs and twenty-five mounted huntsmen went out into the field. Every dog knew its master and its call, every huntsman knew his job, his place and his purpose. Once outside the fence, this chaotic mass of squealing dogs and yelling hunters that had assembled in the courtyard of the house drifted off smoothly and calmly, without any noise or talk, across the field. All that could be heard was occasional whistling, the snort of a horse or squeal of a dog, the quiet tread of the horses, as if they were walking on a soft-pile carpet, and the jangling of the clasp on a dog-collar. No sooner had they ridden beyond Chepyzh than another five hunters with borzois and two with harriers appeared, riding towards the Rostovs' pack.

"Ah, uncle!" said Nikolai to the handsome old man with large grey moustaches who rode up to him.

"I knew it," said the uncle (he was actually a distant relative, a neighbour with a small estate, who devoted his entire life to hunting), "impossible not to, and it's a good thing you're going too, weather like this, no nonsense, forward march" (that was the uncle's special saying). "Better take the reserve now, my Girchik tells me the Ilagins are out with their hunt at Karniki, no nonsense, forward march, and they'll snatch that litter from under your nose."

"That's just where I'm going. Well then, shall we combine the packs?" asked Nikolai. They put the hounds together, especially because the uncle claimed that without his Voltor, no nonsense, forward march, there was no point in hunting wolves, and the gentlemen rode side by side. Natasha also came riding up to them at a gallop, wrapped and bundled and swaddled in a clumsy, ugly fashion in shawls that still could not conceal her easy, confident seat on the horse and her excited, happy face with its glowing eyes peering out from under a shawl and a man's cap. And as well as everything else, she was carrying a horn, a dagger and a leash.

"Nikolai, what a darling Trunila is, he recognised me," she said. "Good morning, uncle." Nikolai, absorbed in his thoughts and plans, did not reply, feeling the full responsibility for the expedition on his shoulders as he surveyed his army. The uncle bowed, but did not say anything, and frowned at the sight of a skirt. He did not like to see amusement combined with a serious business like hunting. Nikolai felt the same way and he shot a severe glance at his sister, trying to make her feel the distance that ought to separate them at this moment, in the way that Henry IV made it clear to Falstaff that whatever friendship they might have shared previously, there was now a gulf between the king and his subject.

But Natasha was feeling too exuberant to notice this.

"Nikolai, just look how thin my Zavidka's got, I'm sure they're not feeding her properly." She called to Zavidka, a really old, mangy bitch with rough lumps on her rump. "Just look."

Nikolai had given this bitch to Natasha because he did not know what else to do with her, and now he felt ashamed for the uncle to see that he had a dog like this in his pack. "Time she was hanged," he said brusquely, and gave an instruction, which a groom on a sorrel horse went galloping off to deliver, splashing mud over Nikolai, Natasha and the uncle. But Zavidka's sad condition failed to abash Natasha. She turned to the uncle, showing him another of her dogs and boasted about him, although this other dog was also a very poor specimen. But the island of the Otradnoe reserve was already visible only a hundred *sazhens* away, the riders were already approaching it.

After deciding with the uncle which particular spot to set the dogs onto, Nikolai showed Natasha her place and confirmed where her groom should stand, while he himself set off for what was regarded as the second best trail for tracking a mature wolf, a point above the ravine from which he planned to close in. The very best trail, in the strip of growth leading to the large forest, had been left for the old count.

"Nikolai," shouted Natasha, "I'll slaughter it myself . . ."

Nikolai did not answer and merely shrugged his shoulders at his sister's lack of tact.

"If you come across an old one, he'll slip past you," said the uncle.

"We'll see," answered Nikolai. "Karai, here boy," he shouted, answering the uncle's words with this summons. Karai was a huge, loose-jowled hound, not like a dog at all, solemn and ugly, and famous for having taken a mature wolf on his own.

They all went to their places.

The old count, knowing his son's hunting fever, made sure not to delay, and before the whippers-in had even reached the spot, Ilya Andreich, jolly and flushed after breakfast, with his cheeks quivering, drove up on his blacks across the green winter crops to his spot on the trail and, after straightening his fur coat and donning his hunting gear, clambered up onto his Viflyanka, a sleek, well-fed, docile, good-tempered horse as grey-haired as the count himself. He sent the horses and droshky away. Although Count Ilya Andreich Rostov was not a hunter in his soul, he knew the laws of hunting through and through, and he crept into the edge of the wood beside which he was standing, held his reins wide, adjusted his coat and glanced around with a smile. Beside him on his horse was his valet, an old horseman, now grown fat and heavy, Semyon Chekmar, holding three spirited wolfhounds, also as fat as their master and his horse, on a leash. Two other old, clever dogs lay down without any leash. Further along just inside the edge of the wood stood another groom, the short, red-faced, permanently drunk coachman Mitka Kopyl, a daring horseman and passionate hunter. Following his old habit, before the hunt the count had drunk a silver goblet of hunter's spiced brandy followed by a bite to eat and half a bottle of his favourite Bordeaux. Ilya Andreich was rather flushed from the drink and the riding, his eyes were moist, with a bright gleam to them, and as he sat there straight in the saddle, bundled up in his fur coat, glancing around and smiling, he looked like a child who had been got ready for a walk.

Semyon Chekmar, who did his drinking in hard bouts, was thin with sunken cheeks, and had a menacing air, but he kept his eyes fixed on his master, with whom he had lived for thirty years on the best of terms and, seeing what an agreeable mood he was in, anticipated an agreeable conversation. A third person rode up cautiously (he had clearly been warned) from round the edge of the wood and halted behind the count. This person was an old man with a grey beard, wearing a woman's gown and a tall pointed cap. He was the household jester Nastasya Ivanich.

"Listen here, Nastasya Ivanich," the count said to him with a wink, "you just frighten off the game and Danila will give you what for."

"I wasn't born yesterday."

"Ss-sh-sh," the count hissed and turned to Semyon.

"Have you seen Natalya Ilinichna?" he asked Semyon. "Where is she?"

"She stopped over by the Zharovs' bushes," Semyon replied with a smile. "She's that keen to hunt down that wolf . . ."

"Aren't you amazed, Semyon, the way she rides . . . eh?" said the count.

"As good as any man."

"Where's Nikolasha? Up on Lyadovsky Height, is he?" the count asked, still speaking in a whisper.

"That's right, sir. He knows how it's done. He knows his hunting so well, there's times it amazes Danila and me," said Semyon, knowing how to please his master.

"He rides well, eh? And looks well on a horse, eh?"

"A real picture. The way as he drove that fox out of the Zavarzins' thickets the other day – what a sight: the horse is worth a thousand, but the rider's priceless. Where would you find a fellow to match him."

"Where would you . . ." the count repeated, evidently regretting that Semyon had not gone on to say more. "Where would you?" he said, turning back the flaps of his fur coat to take out his snuffbox. Semyon dismounted, freed the snuffbox and handed it to him.

"The other day, when Mikhail Sidorich . . ." Semyon started and stopped when he clearly heard the sound of no more than two or three hounds giving tongue in the still air. He hastily grabbed hold of his stirrup and began to mount, groaning and muttering something.

"They've caught the litter's scent . . ." he began, "there she is, that's her howling, hear how she's howling. But they've led her straight on to Lyadovsky Height."

Forgetting to remove the smile from his face, the count looked

590

straight ahead along the strip of forest, holding the snuffbox in his hand but not sniffing any tobacco. What Semyon had said was true. They could hear the cry for a wolf on Danila's low-sounding horn. The pack had come upon the litter, they heard the harriers begin to bay with that special quavering note that indicates a wolf-chase, they could hear the whippers-in hallooing in a different tone, and Danila's voice soaring over all the others, sometimes low and growling, sometimes steely and piercing, too loud for these two hundred *desyatines* of forest, so that it escaped and echoed across the open field. After listening for a few seconds, the count noticed that the hounds had split into two packs: the first, a large one, which was baying especially keenly, began to move away (that was this year's new cubs), while the other part of the pack went dashing along the edge of the forest, past the count, and that was the pack with which Danila's hallooing could be heard. The sound of the two chases mingled and mixed together, but they were both moving away. Semyon sighed and leaned down to adjust his leash, in which a young dog had become entangled. The count also sighed and, noticing the snuffbox in his hand, unthinkingly opened it and took a pinch.

"Back," Semyon cried in a whisper at that moment to his dog, who had stepped out of the edge of the wood. The count started and dropped the snuffbox.

Semyon was about to dismount to pick it up, but he changed his mind and winked at the jester. Nastasya Ivanich dismounted and as he walked towards the snuffbox, he stumbled on a branch and fell.

"Just tipped over." Semyon and the count laughed.

"If only he's run into my Nikolasha," said the count, continuing the interrupted conversation. "He'll have fun with him, Karai will take him . . ."

"That dog's got a real death-grip . . . Come on, give it here," said Semyon, reaching out his hand for the count's snuffbox and laughing at Nastasya Ivanich handing back the snuffbox with one hand and picking up the tobacco from the dry leaves with the other. The count and Semyon were both watching Nastasya Ivanich. The hounds still seemed to be coursing as far away as before. Suddenly, as often happens, the sound moved nearer in an instant and they could heard the chase as if the dogs' barking mouths were right there in front of them, and they heard Danila's hallooing, as if he was about to crush them, galloping along on his brown gelding. They both glanced round anxiously, frightened, but there was nothing ahead of them. The count glanced to the right at Mitka and was horrified. Pale and bleary, with eyes popping out of his head, Mitka was looking at the count with his cap raised, pointing forward to the edge of the wood opposite.

"Watch out!" he cried in a voice that made it clear that the words had been stuck painfully in his throat for a long time. Mitka set off at a gallop towards the count, loosing the dogs. The count and Semyon, without even knowing why, galloped out of the wood and about thirty paces to their left they saw a large-headed grey wolf with a fine, full belly, loping quietly past them with a clumsy, rolling movement towards the very spot at the edge of the wood where they had been standing. The furious dogs snarled and snorted and, tearing themselves off their leash, moving in bounds across the springy, soft stubble, they tore towards the wolf like arrows, past the horses' legs. The wolf was already at the edge of the wood; he paused in his run, turned his grey head awkwardly towards the dogs, in the way someone sick with angina turns his head and, with the same gentle rolling movement, leapt once, then again and the last thing they saw was his tail disappearing into the wood. At the very moment that the count, realising his mistake, began hallooing after the wolf in a wailing voice, at that very moment first one, then a second, then a third hound came dashing in confusion out of the opposite wood with a howl that sounded like keening, and then the entire pack rushed headlong across the open field, along the line that the wolf had followed. That would have been all right, but after the hounds the hazelnut bushes parted and out flew Danila's brown horse, so soaked in sweat that it looked black. Danila was hunched close over its long back, slumped forward, with no cap, with his grey hair tousled above his red, sweaty face (one moustache was pointing comically upwards).

"Halloo-oo-oo," Danila cried once more in the field. "Look out . . . you stupid ass," he shouted, hurtling at the count at full tilt with his crop raised. But even when he recognised the count he did not change his tone.

"You lost the bloody wolf. Hunters!" And, as if not considering the count worthy of further conversation, he lashed the rapidly heaving, wet flanks of his brown gelding with all the fury he felt for the count and, hallooing so loudly that it hurt the count's ears, went flying after the hounds. The count stood there as if he had been thrashed, looking around and trying with a smile to arouse some sympathy for his position at least in Semyon. But Semyon, having seen the wolf's full belly, had realised there was a chance to out-gallop him, and was rushing through the bushes, trying to cut the wolf off from the Zaseka forest. The men with the borzois also tried to cut the beast off from both sides. But the wolf went through the bushes and not a single hunter managed to cut him off.

Half an hour later Danila returned to the first island from the other side with the hounds, to add them to the section of the pack that had split off and was still chasing the cubs.

There were still two one-year-olds and four cubs left in the island. One cub was hunted down by the uncle, another was caught by the hounds and slaughtered by the whippers-in. A third was hunted down by the owners of the borzois on the edge of the wood, the fourth was still being pursued. One of the one-year-olds slipped through the gully towards the village and got away unhurt, the other one-year-old set off along the Lyadovsky ravine, above which Nikolai was waiting.

With a hunter's instinct (which is unconscious and impossible to define), Nikolai sensed, from the approach and retreat of the chase, from the sound of the voices of the dogs that he knew, from the approach, retreat and increased loudness of the voices of the whippers-in, what was going on in the island, that there were cubs and mature wolves, that the hounds had split up, that in places they were in pursuit and that something had not turned out well. At first he listened with pleasure to the sound of the massed pack that hurtled past him twice on the edge of the forest, at first he froze still, straining his eyes and gathering himself in the saddle, ready to cry out the desperate halloo that was already at the top of his throat. He held that cry in his mouth in the way someone holds water in his mouth, preparing to release it at any second. Then he despaired, grew angry, hoped, prayed to God several times in his heart for the wolf to come out his way – prayed with that passionate and guilty feeling with which people pray at moments of powerful excitement produced by some trivial cause. "Well, what bother is it to you," he said to God, "do it for me. I know that you are great and it is a sin to ask for this, but for God's sake make that old wolf come out to me and let Karai clamp his jaws tight on his throat in front of uncle, who's watching from over there." But the wolf did not come running out. A thousand times in that half-hour Nikolai ran his dogged, tense and anxious glance across the edge of the forest with its two isolated oaks above the aspen copse, and the ravine with the eroded edge and, just barely visible above a bush on his right, the uncle's cap, and Natasha and Sasha, who were standing on his left. "No, no such luck for me!" thought Nikolai. "And what would it have cost him? I shan't have the luck, I always have bad luck in everything, there's no point in even looking." And even as he thought this, he strained his tired eyes, his entire vision and hearing, looking round to the left and again to the right.

Just as Nikolai glanced to the right again, he saw, running along the gully of the Lyadovsky Height, about thirty paces from the edge of the wood, what he thought was a mature wolf, his whitish-grey colour standing out against the grey foliage of the slope of the ravine. "No, it can't be!" thought Nikolai with a deep sigh, the way a man sighs in relief after some long-awaited event has finally occurred. His greatest piece of luck had come after all, and so simply, without any clamour or drama – the grey beast was skipping along as if simply going about its own business, not too fast and not too slow, peering all around. Nikolai could not believe his eyes: he glanced round at his groom. Bent down to the saddle, Prokoshka was holding his breath, focusing not only his bulging eyes, but the entire inclined trunk of his body in the direction of the wolf, like a cat waiting for a mouse running carelessly towards it. The dogs were lying or standing there, not seeing the wolf, understanding nothing. Old Karai himself had his head turned away as he reached back, baring an old, yellow fang and clacking his teeth to search angrily for a flea in the forest of hair that hung like tangles of wool on his haunches.

Pale-faced Nikolai looked at them sternly, but they failed to understand his glance. "Hall-oo-oo!" he whispered to them, pouting his lips. Jingling the rings of their leashes, the dogs leapt up and pointed their ears. Karai, however, first finished scratching his thigh and only then got up, pointing his ears and giving a brief wag of his tail, hung with its strings of matted hair. "All right, now I'm ready, what is it?" he seemed to say.

"Shall I loose them or not," Nikolai kept wondering to himself, as the wolf moved towards him and further away from the wood. But suddenly the wolf's entire expression changed: noticing the human eyes fixed on him, he started, hunched down and wondered whether to go back or go on – then without a backward glance he darted forwards with his gentle, loose, skipping movement, as if he had said to himself: "Ah, what's the difference! Let's see how they're going to catch me."

"Ah! So that's your way! Right, you're for it!" And Nikolai let out a halloo and set his good horse moving full tilt downhill from the Lyadovsky Height, to intercept the wolf. Nikolai was only looking at the dogs and the wolf, but he also saw Natasha hurtling towards him in her fluttering riding-habit, overtaking Sashka with a piercing squeal, and the uncle hurrying along behind him with his two leashes of dogs.

The wolf flew along the gully, without changing direction. The first to reach it was black-and-brindled Milka. But, horror of horrors, instead of speeding up as she got close to him, she began slowing down, raised her tail and dug in her front paws. The second dog there was Liubim. He grabbed the wolf by the haunches on the run, but the wolf stopped, looked round and bared his teeth. Liubim let go. "No, this is impossible. He'll get away," thought Nikolai.

"Karai!" But Karai was galloping along slowly and heavily beside his horse. One dog and then another reached the wolf. The dogs from Natasha's leash were there as well, but not one of them took him. Nikolai was already only twenty paces from the wolf. Three times the wolf stopped, sat down and snarled, shaking off the dogs grabbing at his back

594

legs and setting off again with his tail between his legs. This all took place in the middle of the height connecting the Otradnoe reserve with the huge state forest of Zaseka. If he got through to Zaseka, the wolf was lost to them.

"Karai, old fella'," shouted Nikolai. The ancient, mutilated monster Karai was a little ahead of the horse, and with a regular, steady skip, holding his breath and keeping his eyes on the target, he was coming up on the wolf just as it had hunched down again for a moment. In its inexperience a long thin, young, maroon dog from Natasha's leash flew at the wolf from in front and tried to grab hold of it. More quickly than could have been expected, the wolf lunged at the inexperienced dog and snapped its teeth together, and the bloodied dog went dashing off with its side torn open and its tail between its legs, yelping in pain and distress. The wolf got up and set off again, hiding its tail between its legs. But while this clash had been going on, Karai, with the clumps of matted wool dangling on his thighs and his brows knitted in a frown, was already within five paces of the wolf, still not changing his even skipping run. But then he seemed to be charged with a sudden surge of energy: all Nikolai could see was that something had happened to him. In two reckless bounds Karai was on top of the wolf and the two of them went tumbling over. The moment Nikolai saw the wolf's head with its open jaws raised up, snapping and catching nothing, the moment he saw the wolf's entire figure on its side for the first time, struggling to catch at the earth with its broad paws in order not to fall on its back, that was the happiest moment of Nikolai's life. Now Nikolai was standing over them and had already swung back his leg to dismount and slaughter the wolf. Karai fell across the wolf himself. His coat was bristling, he was shuddering all over and he was making desperate attempts to get up and shift the grip of his worn-down teeth from the back of the neck to the throat. But his teeth were clearly no longer good. In one of these attempts the wolf broke free and righted itself. Karai fell and let go. As if finally realising that this had to be taken seriously, the wolf took off at full pelt and began to get away from the dogs.

"My God! Why?" Nikolai shouted in despair.

The uncle, an old huntsman, galloped across to cut the wolf off from the Zaseka, met it again and held it back. But not a single dog took a firm hold. Karai had been left far behind. The hunters, Nikolai and his groom, the uncle and his groom, Natasha and her dogs were all circling round the beast, hallooing and shouting, not hearing each other, getting ready to dismount the moment the wolf sat down. But each time the wolf shook himself free, and moved gradually closer to the Zaseka, which would be his salvation.

At the start of this chase Danila, having heard the hallooing, had galloped to the edge of the wood, and since it was not his business and he had no hounds, he had stopped to watch what would happen. He saw Karai take the wolf and expected that now they would finish it off. But when the hunters did not dismount and the wolf shook itself free, Danila grunted.

"He'll get away," he said and set his brown horse moving. Not towards the wolf, but in a straight line towards the Zaseka, towards the point where he knew the wolf would enter the Zaseka. By taking this route, he was approaching the wolf just as it was being stopped for the second time by the uncle's dogs, and before Karai had managed to reach the wolf for the second time. Danila galloped on in silence, grasping his naked dagger in his left hand and lashing his crop like a flail across the lean flanks of his brown horse. Nikolai neither saw nor heard Danila until the brown horse shot past him, panting heavily, nor did he see Danila vault over the head of his horse into the middle of the dogs, on to the back of the wolf. But in the very same instant the same dogs who had failed to take a grip, grabbed at the wolf by the haunches with a snarl and Danila rolled as he fell and then ran as far as the halted beast and, as if he were exhausted and lying down to rest, dropped with his full weight on to the wolf, grabbing hold of it by the ears. Danila would not let them slaughter the wolf, but sent a groom to cut a stick, stuck it across the wolf's mouth and bound the jaws together with a leash, hoisting the wolf onto his horse. When all was done, Danila said not a word. He merely doffed his cap and congratulated the young count on a fine kill and smiled under his moustache with that childishly gentle, broad, meek smile of his.

They called the hounds and everybody gathered, wanting to talk: under the pretext of telling each other everything that had happened, they told each other all sorts of things that had not happened, and then moved on. The old count joked with Danila about the wolf that had been missed.

"My, brother, but you've a temper," said the count.

At that Danila merely smiled his amiable smile. The old count and the brake set off home. Natasha ignored all arguments and demands, and stayed with the hunt. What Nikolai wanted most of all was to reach the Zybinskaya Rise before the Ilagins, who were now not far off, and so he went further than he had been expecting.

The Zybinskaya Rise was a deep, water-rutted hollow, overgrown with aspen thickets, in the winter fields, where there were always foxes. No sooner had they let the harriers loose than they heard the horns and the chase of the Ilagin hunt in the next island of forest and saw one of

Ilagin's huntsmen with borzois, standing off the Zybinskaya Rise. Just as a fox ran out ahead of Rostov's hounds onto the strip of forest running from the Ilagin wood, the hunter rode to cut it off. Both sides began to give chase, and Nikolai saw the red, low, bushy fox flatten itself against the green shoots of the winter corn and move round in circles between the dogs, these circles growing tighter and tighter, as it waved its fluffy brush this way and that until finally a white dog attacked, followed by a black one, and everything became jumbled up together and the dogs formed a star-shaped ruck with their backsides sticking out, trembling slightly, and two huntsmen came riding up – one of them Nikolai's, in a red cap, the other one theirs, in a green kaftan. Neither huntsman hung the fox on his saddle immediately, they stood on the ground – their horses on the rein, with their saddles jutting up, and their dogs beside them – and threw their arms about and one of them, waving the fox, began to shout.

"They're fighting," said the groom to Nikolai.

Nikolai sent for his sister to come and then rode at a walk to the site of the fight. From the other side a fat landowner, also on a fine horse and dressed unlike the other men, rode out to meet Nikolai, accompanied by two grooms. But before the gentlemen reached one another, one of the hunters who had been fighting rode up to the count with the fox hanging on his saddle. He raised his cap at a distance and tried to speak respectfully, but he was as pale as a sheet and panting and clearly in such a state of fury that he did not know what he was doing. One of his eyes was bruised, but he still had the proud air of a victor.

"What right has he to kill from under our hounds, and it was my fawn bitch who caught it. Take me to court if you like. He grabbed at the fox, and I gave him a swipe with it. He says, let me hang it on my saddle. Perhaps you'd like this instead," said the hunter, pointing to his dagger and probably imagining that he was still speaking to his enemy.

Without saying a word, Nikolai, who was also agitated, rode on to meet the huntsman's master. The victorious huntsman rode into the rear ranks where, surrounded by sympathetic and curious listeners, he told them about his heroic feat. Instead of an enemy, Nikolai found Ilagin to be a good-hearted, personable gentleman who particularly wished to make the young count's acquaintance. He explained that he had given strict orders for the huntsman to be punished, was very sorry for what had happened, offered the count his friendship and the use of his hunting land, and gallantly doffed his beaver cap to Natasha, paying her a number of mythological compliments, comparing her to Diana. In order to atone for his guilt, Ilagin insistently requested Nikolai to ride through to his upland, which he had been keeping for himself, and where there was an abundance of foxes and hares. Nikolai, flattered by Ilagin's courtesy and wishing to boast to him about his own hunt, agreed and was drawn even further off his route.

To get to Ilagin's upland meant riding a long way through bare fields, in which there was little hope of finding hares. They rode in a line and kept going for three *versts* without finding a thing. The gentlemen gathered and rode together. Everybody kept glancing at each other's dogs, trying to do this furtively, without the others noticing, and anxiously seeking out among these dogs rivals for their own. If the talk was of the dogs' speed, then usually each of them spoke particularly casually of his own dog's virtues, which – when he was talking to his own huntsman – he could never find words enough to praise.

"Yes, she's a good dog, she gets them," Ilagin said in an indifferent voice about his own red-dappled Erza, for whom he had given three families of house serfs to his neighbour two years earlier. This Erza particularly bothered Nikolai, she was exceptionally fine. Thoroughbred, slim and narrow, but with muscles that looked like steel and that precious energy and vivacity that hunters call heart. A dog does not run with its legs, but with its heart. All the hunters were dying to try their dogs against each other, every one of them had a dog he had hopes for, but none would admit it. Nikolai whispered to his groom that he would give a rouble to anyone who spotted game, and Ilagin gave the same instruction.

"You have a fine fawn dog, count," said Ilagin.

"Yes, not bad," Nikolai replied.

"I don't understand," said Ilagin, "the way other hunters are so envious over game and dogs. Let me tell you about myself. You know, I enjoy taking a ride, chasing a bit . . . and then you meet up with a company like this . . . What could be better . . ." Again he doffed his beaver cap to Natasha. "But all this counting who's brought home the most pelts, I couldn't care less about that."

"Quite so, indeed."

"And why should I take offence if someone else's dog gets the catch, and not mine – I can only admire it – isn't that right, count, to my way of thinking . . ."

The huntsmen were moving along a ravine in a line. The gentlemen were riding on the right in the centre.

Just then one of Ilagin's borzoi huntsmen let out a prolonged cry: "Sick him!" He had earned a rouble by spotting a grey hare.

"Ah, I think he's spotted something," Ilagin said casually. "Well, shall we course it, count?"

"Yes, let's go closer . . . and why not together?" replied Nikolai, looking hard at Erza and the uncle's red dog, unable to conceal his excitement that the moment had almost arrived to compare his dogs with someone else's, especially with Ilagin's, which were famed for their speed. This was something he had never done before.

"Well, and what if they outrun my Milka?" he thought.

"An old one?" asked Ilagin, moving towards the spot, looking around with some excitement and whistling to Erza . . . "And what about you, Mikhail Nikanorovich?" he asked, turning to the uncle.

The uncle was riding along with a sullen expression.

"What chance have I got, when your dogs cost a village apiece? Rugai, here, here," he shouted. "Rugaiushka," he added, unwittingly expressing through this affectionate form of the name all of his fondness for the red dog and the hopes he placed in him. Natasha felt the same way as the others and made no attempt to conceal her excitement. She already felt and even expressed her loathing for all the dogs who would dare to catch the hare instead of her Zavidka.

"Which way is its head pointing? Move away, take the harriers away," someone shouted: but before they could carry out these instructions the grey hare, sensing frost in the air, couldn't stand it a moment longer and leapt up, at first with one ear held flat. The harriers on their leashes, pursued by the whippers-in, went dashing after it. The borzoi hunters released dogs from all sides. Staid and calm, Ilagin started his horse downhill. Nikolai, Natasha and the uncle flew along, not knowing why or where, seeing only the dogs and the hare and afraid of nothing except losing sight of them for even an instant. The hare proved to be experienced and fast. He had been lying among stubble, but ahead there were green winter crops, which were soft for running on. The impatient Natasha was closest of all to the hare. Her dogs had been the first to catch sight of it and set off. But she was horrified to see her dependable Zavidka beginning to swerve to one side. Two young dogs had begun gaining on her, but were still a long way from catching up with her, when the red-dappled Erza shot out from behind them, coming within a dog's length of the hare and starting to weave after it, threatening to seize it at any instant. But this only lasted a moment. Liubim drew level with Erza and even got his nose ahead of her.

"Liubimushka! Old fella'!" Nikolai cried out triumphantly. Natasha merely squealed but said nothing. It looked as though Liubim would strike first and then the others would pick it up but Liubim caught up with the hare and went rushing on past. The hare squatted down and doubled back, the beautiful Erza overtook the hare again and stuck to its tail, stuck right there, as if she were taking aim so as not to miss grabbing the hare by its back thigh.

"Erza! Old girl!" Ilagin called out in a changed, imploring voice.

But Erza did not heed his entreaties. On the very edge of the winter crops she gained on the hare, but only slightly, and the hare swerved and skidded into the winter crops; again, like a pair of harnessed horses, Erza drew level with Liubim and began racing after the hare, although not as swiftly as in the stubble.

"Rugai, Rugaiushka! No nonsense, forward march," a voice cried out at that moment and Rugai, a heavy, ponderous red dog, sinking up to his knees, bounding at full stretch with his back arched, began to pull ahead of the first two, overtook them, and with a great spurt of speed threw himself right on the hare, after which all that could be seen was him rolling over, his back coated with mud, and then the star-shaped ruck of dogs that surrounded him. A moment later they were all standing over the hare. The only happy one, the uncle, dismounted, and after cutting off the hare's feet and shaking it so that the blood would drip out, he glanced around, his eyes restless with excitement and, not knowing where to put his hands and feet, said, without knowing who he was speaking to:

"There's a dog for you . . . see how he outran them – no nonsense, forward march." He was gasping for breath as if he were abusing someone, as if they were all his enemies, as if they had all offended him and now he had been proved right. "So much for dogs that cost thousands, no nonsense, forward march. Rugai, here's a paw," he said, tossing the dog a foot with earth still sticking to it. "You've earned it, no nonsense, forward march. Well, did you miss, then?"

"He wore himself out, ran it down three times on his own," said Nikolai, also not listening to anyone else and not concerned about whether they were listening or not, having forgotten to try to appear calm and indifferent. "Cutting across sideways like that, eh?"

"Why, once she missed it like that, any mongrel could chase it down," Ilagin was saying at the same time, red-faced and breathless from galloping.

Natasha was squealing at the same time, without stopping to draw breath, so that their ears were ringing. She could not help squealing every time they coursed a hare when she was present. She squealed in this way as some kind of ritual. With this squealing she expressed everything that the other hunters expressed by all speaking at the same time. The uncle himself flung the hare deftly and neatly across his horse's back, as though he were reproaching everyone else with this movement, and with the air of not even wishing to speak to anyone else, rode off. The others, sad and humiliated, also left. It took a long while for them to recover their former pretence of indifference, and for a long time afterwards they kept glancing at the red dog Rugai, trotting along beside the feet of the uncle's horse, with the calm air of a victor, his hunched back smeared with earth and his collar quietly jangling.

"Well, of course, I'm the same as everyone else, except when it comes to coursing. But then watch out, I'll make fools of them all."

Much later on, when the uncle rode up to Nikolai and simply started talking to him, Nikolai was flattered that, after all that had happened, the uncle would still deign to speak with him.

They did not find much in the upland, and in any case it was already late. The hunts went their separate ways, but Nikolai had so far to go to get home that he accepted the uncle's invitation to stay with him in his village of Mikhailovka, which was only two *versts* from the upland.

"Why don't you come to my place, no nonsense, forward march, look at the wet weather," the uncle said, becoming especially lively, "you'd get some rest, and take the countess home in the droshky."

The hunt reached Mikhailovka, and Nikolai and Natasha got down from their horses in front of the uncle's little grey house, almost hidden in its overgrown garden.

# III

About five male house serfs, both big and little, came running out onto the front porch to meet their master. Dozens of women, both big and little, peeped out from the back porch to look at the hunters as they arrived. The presence of Natasha, a woman, a lady, on a horse had the same effect as it did in all the unfamiliar places that Natasha rode through, raising their curiosity to such a height of astonishment, that many of them, unabashed even by her live presence, walked right up to her, glancing into her eyes and at the same time passing comments, as if she were not a human being but some wonder on display, incapable of hearing and understanding them.

"Arinka, lookee, she's sitting all to one side, with her skirt a'dangling. And d'you see that little horn. Holy saints, and a knife . . . Must be a Tatar woman." "How'd you manage not to come tumbling off, then?" said the boldest of them, speaking to her directly and then running back a bit.

The uncle dismounted by the porch and, glancing round at his household, shouted imperiously that those who weren't needed should go away and that everything should be done at once to receive his guests and the hunt, repeating several times over what had to be done. Everyone ran off and set about their tasks. Natasha, who, despite her tiredness or, perhaps even because of it, was in that elated and happy state of mind in which the mirror of the soul is especially bright and reflects every impression brilliantly, and she was observing and taking note of the smallest of details. She noticed how the uncle's face was transformed at home, becoming calm and confident.

They sent to Otradnoe for the brake and went into the house. The hallway smelt of fresh apples and was hung with wolf and fox skins. It was not very clean – there was no sign that the goal of the people who lived here was to make sure there were no dirty stains anywhere, but nor were there were any signs of neglect. The parts that were lived in were washed and swept, but in other corners they only cleaned on church holidays. The house had unplastered walls and plain board floors. There was a small hall and a drawing room with a round table and a divan. But these rooms were not much used. The room that was lived in was the study, with its tattered divan and tattered carpet, a portrait of Suvorov and Greek goddesses, and the smell of Zhukov tobacco and dog. Rugai ambled into the study with his back still dirty, lay down on the divan and started cleaning himself with his tongue and teeth. Milka and Zavidka were also brought in. There was a corridor leading from the study that was hung with torn curtains and full of whispering. That was obviously the beginning of the women's quarters – secret women's quarters, since the uncle was not married.

Natasha and Nikolai took off their coats, glancing around, and sat down on the divan (the uncle had left them alone, obviously having gone to make preparations). Their faces were burning, they were hungry and very happy, and to the end of their lives they would recall with a melancholy pleasure every single moment of the hour that they spent at the uncle's house, even though nothing particularly joyous happened that day, just as they would recall many of the moments during this same period when they were living at Otradnoe. They glanced at each other (after the hunt, inside in the room, Nikolai no longer felt it necessary to put on airs in front of his sister). Natasha winked at her brother and it was not long before they both gave way and broke into loud peals of laughter.

They laughed without even needing to invent an excuse for laughter. The uncle soon entered, wearing a short kaftan with hook fastenings, blue trousers and short boots. And Natasha felt that this outfit, which she had regarded with astonishment and derision when she had once seen the uncle in it at Otradnoe, was just the right outfit here and that frock coats and tailcoats were ridiculous, so naturally and nobly did the uncle wear this outfit. The uncle was in a cheerful mood too, not offended in the least by the brother and sister laughing (it could never even enter his head that they could be laughing at his life), in fact he himself joined in their laughter.

"I tell you, young countess, no nonsense, forward march, I've never seen the like of you," he said, handing one pipe to Nikolai and filling another with an accustomed gesture, holding it with three fingers. "Rode all day long, as well as any man, and it seems like nothing to you. Let me tell you, my lady, if there'd been one like you in my time – no nonsense, forward march – I'd have married her straight away."

Natasha did not reply, but simply broke into peals of laughter and, speaking through her laughter, said:

"How delightful this uncle is!"

Not long after the uncle's return, a young girl who, from the sound of her footsteps, was obviously barefoot, opened the door and a woman of about forty came in, a full-breasted, stout, ruddy-cheeked, brown-haired beauty with a double chin and full, red, smiling lips, a pleasant appearance and a welcoming look in her eyes and in every movement. Despite her exceptional stoutness, which obliged her to thrust her belly out and hold her head back, this woman (the uncle's housekeeper) had an extremely light step. With very deft, plump, white hands she set down the tray she was carrying, bowed respectfully and cordially, and set out the bottles, plates of food and treats on the table, then stepped aside with a smile on her face and stood there. "I am the one, now you understand the uncle," she seemed to say.

How could they not understand? Not only Nikolai, but also Natasha understood the uncle and the meaning of those knitted brows and the happy, self-contented smile that had gently wrinkled his lips when Anisya Fedorovna entered the room.

On the tray there were liqueurs and infusions, mushrooms, flat cakes of rye flour and buttermilk, honey on the comb, sparkling mead, apples, nuts raw and roasted and nuts in honey. Then Anisya Fedorovna also brought in jam with honey and with sugar, and ham, and a freshly roasted chicken. All of it had been grown, gathered, cooked and prepared by Anisya Fedorovna. All of it smelled and tasted of Anisya Fedorovna, all of it was redolent of the mellowness, the impeccable cleanliness, the whiteness of her and of her pleasant smile.

"Eat, my lady countess," she said, handing Natasha first one thing, then another.

Afterwards Natasha always said that she had never, anywhere, ever seen or tasted buttermilk flat cakes with such a fragrant range of jams, honey and nuts as she ate that time with Anisya Fedorovna.

Anisya Fedorovna went out. Nikolai and the uncle, trying first one liqueur then another, talked about the last hunt and the next hunt, about Rugai and the Ilagins' dogs. Natasha, having drunk some mead, also joined in the conversation. After one of those chance silences that almost always happen when people receive acquaintances as guests in their own home for the first time, the uncle said, probably responding to his guests' thoughts:

"So this is how I'm living out my days. When you die, no nonsense, forward march, there'll be nothing left. So what's the point in sinning?"

The uncle's face was very expressive and even beautiful as he said this, and Nikolai could not help recalling all the good things he had heard about the uncle from his father and the neighbours. Throughout that district of the province, the uncle had the reputation of a very high-minded and impartial eccentric. He was asked to settle family disputes, he was made the executor of wills, he was trusted with secrets, he was appointed a judge and to other posts, but he stubbornly refused everything. He spent the autumn and the spring out in the fields on his cream gelding, the winter sitting at home and the summer lying in his overgrown garden.

"Why aren't you in the service, uncle?"

"I was, but I gave it up. I'm not suited, I can't understand a thing about it. That sort of thing's for you. But I'm not clever enough. But hunting, now, that's a different matter. Open the door there," he shouted. "Why have you closed it!" The door at the end of the corridor (which the uncle called a collidor) led into the huntsmen's room. The door was opened and the sounds of a balalaika clearly emerged, obviously being played by some master. Natasha had been listening to the sounds for a long time and now she went out into the corridor to hear them more clearly.

"That's my Mitka, the coachman. I bought him a good balalaika, I like it," said the uncle. It was a habit of the uncle's to listen to the sounds of the balalaika from the menservants' room when he came back from hunting.

"Excellent, superb, charming," said Nikolai and Natasha. They had thought the mushrooms, honey and liqueurs the best in the world, and now they thought the same of this dashing rendition of "*Barinya*".

"More, more," Natasha shouted through the door. The uncle was sitting and listening, with his head to one side and a smile that seemed to say, here I am, an old man sitting here peacefully with my pipe, but I can do that too, I certainly can. The tune of "*Barinya*" was repeated a hundred times. The player tuned his instrument several times and then the same sounds jangled out, but the listeners did not get bored, they only wanted more and more. Anisya Fedorovna came in and leaned her corpulent body against the doorpost.

"Yes, hear that, do, little countess," she said to Natasha with a smile that seemed to say, like the uncle's, that she could do it too, "he's a wonderful player."

"He's doing something wrong in that stretch," the uncle said, with an energetic gesture which showed very clearly indeed that he could do it. "The notes should be more scattered there – no nonsense, forward march."

"Can you really play?" asked Natasha. The uncle smiled without answering her.

"Anisushka, see if the strings are broken on the guitar, I haven't touched it in ages, I gave it up, no nonsense, forward march."

With obvious delight, Anisya Fedorovna set off with her light tread to carry out her master's instructions and brought in the guitar.

Without a glance at anyone, the uncle blew the dust off, tapped the top with his bony fingers, tuned the strings and then, clearly having forgotten about everything and everyone who was there in the room, adjusted his position in the armchair, took hold of the neck of the guitar high up (with a graceful, rather theatrical gesture), winked at Anisya Fedorovna and began to play, but not *"Barinya"*. He struck a single resonant, pure chord and gently, calmly but firmly began performing *"Down along the pavement . . ."* with a quiet rhythm. Both doorways were crowded with the faces of house serfs. *". . . the maiden went for water."* Immediately the tune filled Nikolai's and Natasha's hearts with a sedate merriment (the same sedate merriment that was radiated by Anisya Fedorovna's entire being). Anisya Fedorovna blushed bright red, covered her face with her kerchief and left the room, laughing. The uncle carried on playing the song precisely and carefully, with a firm energy, still casting inspired glances at the spot where Anisya Fedorovna had been. There was just a hint of a smile in his face, on one side, under his grey moustache, especially when the song grew stronger and stronger, the tempo quickened and something was revealed in the places with flourishes. It made them expect the uncle to get up and dance.

"Wonderful, charming, superb, uncle! More, more," cried Natasha, jumping up, embracing the uncle and kissing him, beside herself with joy, and glancing round at Nikolai as if she were asking him: what is this? Nikolai was delighted too. The uncle began to play the song a second time. Anisya Fedorovna's smiling face reappeared in the doorway, with other faces behind it. *". . . For the cold spring water . . . maiden wait, he cries . . ."* sang the uncle, making another flourish, then he broke off and jerked his shoulder in an energetic fashion.

"Oh, oh, uncle darling," Natasha groaned in such an imploring voice, as if her life depended on it. The uncle stood up, and it was as if there were two people inside him – one of them smiling seriously at the

NATASHA DANCING AT THE UNCLE'S HOUSE
*Drawing by M. S. Bashilov, 1860s, Tretyakov Gallery, Moscow*

merrymaker, and the merrymaker who had played a naïve but purely comic prank.

"Come on, niece!" he cried, clearly quite carried away, and he struck a chord with his hand, then waved it towards Natasha.

Natasha threw off the shawl that was lying across her shoulders, ran out in front of the uncle, thrust her hands against her sides, made a movement of her shoulders and stood there.

Where, how and when this young countess, educated by an émigré Frenchwoman, had absorbed these movements from the Russian air that she breathed, how she had kept them (when the *pas de châle* ought to have driven them out long ago), who could say, but as soon as she stood there and smiled and moved her shoulder, the initial fear that Nikolai and everyone present had felt, the fear that she, a lady, would not do this right, vanished and they began admiring her. She did everything so well, so precisely and completely, that Anisya Fedorovna immediately handed the young countess the kerchief she needed for her dance. Anisya Fedorovna wept a little as she watched this slim, gracious countess, who had been raised in silk and velvet and was so different from her, but could still understand everything that there was in Anisya and in Anisya's father and aunt and mother, and in every Russian person.

"Well, countess, no nonsense forward march," the uncle said with a happy laugh as he finished the dance. "Well done, niece! You ought to choose yourself a fine young man, no nonsense, forward march!"

"He's already chosen," Nikolai said with a laugh.

"Oh?" said the uncle, astonished, looking quizzically at Natasha.

Natasha nodded with a happy smile.

"And what a man too!"

"That's grand! No nonsense, forward march!"

After *"Along the pavement"* the uncle played several more songs at his niece's insistent request and sang her his favourite hunting song:

> *In this morning's early light*
> *Fine snow has fallen, shining bright*

The uncle sang in the same way as the people sing, in the total conviction that everything that is important in a song lies in the words while the air is only there to hold them together, and that made the spontaneous tune sound exceptionally good on his lips. The uncle sang well and Natasha was delighted. She decided there and then that she would not learn the harp any more, but only the guitar, and she immediately started learning how to select chords. However, they had already come to fetch Natasha. As well as the brake, the droshky and three men on horses had been sent to look for her. The count and countess did not know where she was, they were concerned and worried to the point of despair. Natasha said goodbye to the uncle and got into the brake. The uncle wrapped Natasha up warmly and said goodbye to her with an entirely new feeling of affection. He accompanied them on foot as far as the bridge and told the hunters to ride on ahead with lanterns.

"Goodbye, dear niece!" called his old man's voice, warm with feeling, out of the darkness.

The night was cold and damp. The horses sloshed through the invisible mud.

As they drove through one village, there were little red lights.

"How delightful this uncle is," said Natasha after they had set off.

"Yes," said Nikolai. "Are you not cold?"

"I feel good, really, really fine. I feel so good," Natasha said with a special feeling of happiness: and then she fell silent.

God alone knows what was happening in that pure, childishly receptive soul that caught all the infinitely varied aspects to life, or how it all arranged itself inside her. But she was very happy.

As they were approaching the house, she suddenly began to sing the tune of the song *"In this morning's early light"*, which she had been trying to recall all the time they were travelling and had now finally caught.

607

"Excellent," said Nikolai.

"What were you thinking about just now?" asked Natasha. They liked to ask each other that.

"I . . ." said Nikolai, pondering, "well, you see, first I was thinking that Rugai, the red dog, is like uncle, and that if he were a man, then he would keep uncle, for his good physique. He is really well-built, uncle, isn't he?" He laughed. "Well, and what about you?"

"I wasn't thinking anything, all the way I was just repeating to myself 'My dear Pumpernickel. My dear Pumpernickel,'" she said, and laughed even more loudly. "You know," Natasha suddenly said, "I know that I'll never be so happy or at peace again as I am, now."

"That's nonsense, it's stupid, and you're wrong," said Nikolai, and he thought: "How delightful my Natasha is, I don't have any other friend and companion like her and I never shall."

"My Nikolai is so delightful," thought Natasha.

"Ah, there's still a light in the drawing room," she said, pointing to the windows of the Otradnoe house, glowing beautifully in the damp darkness of the night.

"Well, now you'll be for it. Mama told you . . ."

# IV

---

In the late autumn another letter was received from Prince Andrei, in which he wrote that his health was very good now, that he loved his dear fiancée more than ever and was counting the hours until the happy moment of their meeting, but there were certain circumstances, which were not worth mentioning, that prevented him from returning sooner than the appointed time. Natasha and the countess deduced that these circumstances were his father's consent. He implored Natasha not to forget him, but repeated with a sinking heart that it was still the case that she was free and could still reject him if she stopped loving him and fell in love with someone else.

"What a fool!" exclaimed Natasha, with tears in her eyes.

He enclosed a miniature portrait of himself with the letter and told Natasha: "Only now, after six months of separation have I realised how strong is the passion with which I love you. I do not forget you for a single minute, there is no joy which does not make me think of you."

For a few days Natasha walked about with rapture in her eyes, spoke about nothing but him and counted the days until the 15th of February.

But it was too hard. The more strongly she loved him, the more passionately she devoted herself to the small joys of life.

She forgot again and, as she told Nikolai, never in her life, earlier or later, did she feel the freedom, the interest in life that she felt during those eight months. Knowing that the question of marriage, of her life's happiness, of love was decided, realising (although she did not deliberately think about it) that there was a man, the best of men, who loved her, she completely lost her former anxiety and alarm at the sight of any man and her need to make every one her own emotional property, and the whole world, no longer overshadowed by this coquettish alarm, opened up to her, with its countless joys.

Never before had she felt the beauty of nature, or music, or poetry, or the charm of family life and friendship with such clarity and simplicity. She herself felt simpler, kinder and more intelligent. She rarely thought about Andrei and did not abandon herself to thoughts about him, although she had no fear that she might forget him, so deeply did this feeling seem to have taken root in her heart. With her brother's arrival, an entirely new world had opened up for her, a world of equality and comradeship, of friendship, hunting and all things fundamental, natural and wild that are associated with that way of life. The old widower Ilagin, captivated by Natasha, began visiting and made her a proposal through a matchmaker. Formerly Natasha would have found this flattering, she would have found it amusing and laughed over it, but now she felt insulted for Prince Andrei. "How dare he?" Natasha thought.

Count Ilya Andreevich had resigned as marshal of the nobility because the expenses involved in this post were too great and, since he had stopped hoping to find a position, he remained in the country for the winter. But the state of his affairs still did not improve, Natasha and Nikolai frequently observed their parents in secret, anxious conversation and heard rumours about the sale of their rich family house in Moscow and the estate outside Moscow. Their closest acquaintances and neighbours went away to Moscow and, with the count no longer marshal, there was no need to entertain on such a large scale so life at Otradnoe was quieter than in previous years, which made it still more enjoyable. The huge house and the outhouse were still full, and more than twenty people still sat down to dinner, but they were all members of the household, people who belonged there, almost members of the family. They included the musician Dimmler and his wife, Yogel and his family, the young lady Belova, who lived in the house, and others.

There were no staying guests, but life went on in the same way, since the count and countess could not imagine any other life. The hunt was still there, enlarged by Nikolai, there were the same fifty horses and fifteen coachmen in the stables, the same blind storyteller told the countess stories before bed, the same two jesters in gold-fringed costumes came to the dinner table and the tea table and were given finger-bowls of tea, with a rusk, and declaimed the supposedly funny speeches they had learned off by heart, at which the masters smiled charitably. The same teachers and tutors for Petya, the same expensive presents for each other on name-days and festive dinners for the entire district. The same whist and boston sessions at which the count spread out his cards like a fan so that everyone could see them and allowed his neighbours to win hundreds of roubles from him every day – they regarded the right to play with Count Ilya Andreevich as a highly profitable business. With every post Berg wrote insistently, with cold courtesy, that they were in difficulties and needed to receive all the moneys against the promissory note that they held. The count wandered through his affairs as if he were caught in a huge net, trying not to believe that he was entangled, while growing ever more entangled with every step and feeling unable either to tear the tangle apart or set to untangling it cautiously and patiently. The countess would have been quite unable to say what she thought of this state of affairs, but she felt with her loving heart that her children were being ruined, that the count was not to blame, that he could not be any different, that he himself was suffering, although he was hiding it. The countess sought remedies and from her woman's point of view could find only one, namely that Nikolai should marry. In her apathetic and lackadaisical manner she searched, worried, wrote letters, consulted with the count and eventually found someone she thought a highly advantageous match for Nikolai in every respect, feeling that nothing better than this could possibly be found, and if Nikolai refused, they would have to abandon for ever the idea of putting their affairs to rights.

This match was Julie Kornakova, known to the Rostovs since she was a child and from an excellent family, the daughter of a beautiful and virtuous mother and now a rich young woman owing to the death of the last of her brothers. The countess wrote a letter to Anna Mikhailovna in Moscow and received a positive reply and an invitation for Nikolai to go to Moscow from Anna Mikhailovna. On that side of things everything was all right, but the countess realised intuitively that with his character Nikolai would indignantly reject marriage for money and therefore she exercised to perfection all her ability as a diplomat and spoke to Nikolai several times, with tears in her eyes, about her only desire being to see him married and told him she would lie easy in her grave if that happened and what a lovely girl she had in mind. In other conversations she praised Julie and advised Nikolai to go to Moscow for the holidays and enjoy himself. (Nikolai very quickly guessed where these conversations were leading, he asked her to be frank, and when she told him that the only hope of setting their affairs in order lay in his marrying, he asked his mother, with a cruelty that he himself did not understand, whether, if he loved a girl with no fortune, she would require him to sacrifice his feelings and his honour for the sake of a fortune. At that time Nikolai had been experiencing the same feeling as Natasha, of calmness, freedom and relaxation in the uncomplicated circumstances of his life. He was so content that he did not wish to change his situation for anything, and was therefore less able than ever to think calmly about marriage.) His mother did not answer and burst into tears.

"No, you don't understand me," she said, not knowing what else to say or how to justify herself.

"Mama, don't cry, just tell me what it is that you want, and you know that I'll give my whole life, everything, to stop you worrying," said Nikolai, but although the countess believed him, she felt that her entire plan had collapsed.

"Yes, perhaps I do love a poor girl," Nikolai told himself, and from that day onwards, although he remained as indifferent to Sonya as ever, he began moving closer and closer to her.

"I can always sacrifice my feelings for the sake of my family," he told himself, "but I cannot force my feelings if I fall in love with her."

After the hunt, the long winter evenings drew in, but Nikolai, Natasha and Sonya were never bored. In addition to wolf-hunting for Nikolai, their time was occupied happily and completely with troika rides, sleigh rides, sliding down the hills, and then plays, music, friendly conversation and reading aloud (they read *Corinne* and *La Nouvelle Héloïse*). In the mornings Nikolai sat in his smoke-filled study with a pipe and book, although there was no reason for him to be on his own, but he did it just because he was a man. And the young ladies sniffed the smell of tobacco respectfully and discussed this separate, man's life of his, which he spent either reading or lying down, smoking, and thinking, sometimes about his future marriage, sometimes about his former career in the army, sometimes about Karai and his future pups and a horse with a thick mane, sometimes about Matryosha, the hall maid, sometimes about the fact that Milka was pigeon-toed after all. But then their life together was all the jollier when he joined them, and especially when they stayed up until after midnight at the fortepiano or simply sitting in the sitting room with a guitar, making conversation that only made sense to them. Usually Natasha had a new saying or joke every day, something they simply had to laugh at, either "lead cylinder", or "the Isle of Madagascar", which she pronounced with a special intonation. Afterwards, when they parted for the night, she would leap on to Nikolai's back and demand that he carry her upstairs to bed like that, and she would detain him there, bringing him close to Sonya and occasionally glancing at their lovers' whispering through sleepy, half-closed eyes.

# V

The Yuletide season arrived. Besides the festive liturgy, at which for the first time Natasha, Nikolai, the sexton and the huntsmen sang the church songs that they had learned, and all the solemn and boring congratulations from the neighbours and the house serfs, there was nothing special to mark the season. The first, second and third days of the holidays passed quietly and cheerlessly. But everything – the air, the sunshine, the windless Christmas frost, the cold moonlight, the snowflakes, the emptiness of the entrance hall and the female servants' room, with people having asked permission to go out walking and later coming in at a run from the servants' quarters, panting and red-faced, bringing the frost with them – all of this expressed the poetic necessity to celebrate the holiday that makes silence at a time of feasting so sad.

After dinner Nikolai, who had been to visit neighbours in the morning, fell into a doze in the sitting room. Sonya went in and walked out again on tiptoe. No candles were lit and the moonlight from the windows cast distinct shadows across the room. Natasha sang and sat with her dozing father after dinner, then she set off to walk around the house. There was no one in the female servants' room except the old women. She sat down with them and listened to a story about fortune-telling and how someone's future husband was going to the bathhouse and when a cock crowed he flew to pieces, then she went to the Dimmlers' room. The musician was reading something by the light of a candle, with his spectacles on his nose, and his wife was sewing. As soon as they moved up a chair for her and said how pleased they were to see her, she stood up and went out, saying with an emphatic intonation: "the Isle of Madagascar, the Isle of Madagascar." The Dimmlers were not offended. Nobody took offence at Natasha. Then she went to the entrance hall and sent one servant to get a cock, another to get some oats, and a third for some chalk, but as soon they brought all of this to her, she said she did not want it and told them to take it back. The servants, even the staid old men whom the count treated gently, were never angry with Natasha, even though Natasha was constantly ordering them about and tormenting them with errands, as if she were wondering: "Well, will he get angry, will he sulk at me? Will he dare?" The maid Dunyasha was the most unfortunate of them all: her young mistress never gave her a moment's peace, if she was not demanding one thing or another, she was unravelling Dunyasha's plait or spoiling her dress instead of giving her another one, but despite this Dunyasha would have died of boredom without her, the way she had felt once when she fell ill and spent two weeks in the servants' quarters without her young mistress and came back to work when she was still weak and unwell. From the entrance hall, Natasha went to the sitting room, where she found her mother with the old lady Belova, sitting at the round table, setting out a game of patience. She mixed up her cards, kissed her on her beauty spot and went off to order the samovar to be brought in, although it was not the right time at all. They ordered the samovar to be taken away again.

"Oh that young mistress," said Foka as he carried the samovar away, quite unable to feel angry. Natasha laughed and glanced into Foka's eyes, and no one was angry with her for laughing.

"Nastasya Ivanich, what kind of children will I have?" she asked as she walked past the jester.

"You'll have fleas, dragonflies and crickets," the jester replied. Natasha had asked the jester, but she didn't listen to his answer, she rarely laughed at the jester and did not like talking to him. As if she was making the rounds of her kingdom and making sure that everyone was loyal, Natasha went into the hall, picked up the guitar, sat down in a dark corner and began plucking at the strings, playing a phrase she had remembered from a certain opera. Anyone else listening to her play the guitar would have heard nothing more than a "twang twang" sound that made no sense at all, but in her mind the "twang twang" gave rise to an entire series of memories. She sat in the corner with a serious smile and her eyes staring, listening to herself and remembering – she remembered everything. She was in a state of remembering. First the sounds of the thick string reminded her of a whole number of experiences from the past, but when she had run through everything from that time, she had nothing left to remember, but she still wanted to remain in this half-sad state of remembering. And suddenly she imagined that she was remembering the present: that her sitting in the corner now with the guitar, with the light falling through the crack of the door of the pantry, that this had happened before, and already happened before that, and she was remembering that it had happened. Sonya walked through into the pantry at the end of the hall to get something. And it was precisely the same as it had been before.

"Sonya, what's this?" Natasha shouted, making her "twang twang" sound on the thick string. Sonya came over to her and listened.

"I don't know," she said, feeling shy, as she always did when Nikolai and Natasha had one of their unfathomable conversations on various strange, subtle points that she did not understand. And it was particularly painful for her when Nikolai was there, since she could see that he particularly valued these incomprehensible conversations. "I don't know," she said timidly trying to guess, afraid of guessing wrong. When these conversations began, Sonya always sensed that Nikolai and Natasha were experiencing a quite special poetic pleasure. She did not understand what pleasure it was they found in these conversations and in music, but she felt and believed that something good was happening here, and with her beloved Nikolai and Natasha, she tried to imitate their feelings. "There, she smiled in exactly the same timid way *then*, when this happened before," thought Natasha, "and then it was all exactly the same . . ."

"Why, it's a choir, can't you hear it: 'tweet, tweet'?" And Natasha sang as well, in order to make it clear. "Where were you going?" she asked.

"To change my painting water, I'm copying a pattern for mama." Sonya was always busy with something.

"And where's Nikolai?"

"I think he's asleep, in the sitting room."

"Go and wake him up," said Natasha. "I'll come in a minute."

She sat there for a moment, wondering what it meant that all this had happened before, and, failing to answer this question, but without the least regret, she thought: "Ah, I wish he would come soon, I'm so afraid that it won't happen! The worst thing is, I'm getting older, that's what it is. All these things that I am just now . . ." She stood up, put down the guitar and went into the drawing room. The entire household was sitting at the tea table, and uncle was there as a guest. There were servants standing round the table. Natasha walked in and stopped.

"Ah, there she is," said Ilya Andreevich.

Natasha looked around.

"What do you want?" her mother asked.

"I want a husband. Give me a husband, mama, give me a husband," she shouted in her chesty voice, through a barely noticeable smile, exactly the same voice in which she used to demand a cake at dinner when she was a child.

Just for a second everybody was confused and frightened by these words, but the doubt only lasted for a second. It was funny, and everybody, even the servants and the jester Nastasya Ivanich, burst into laughter. Natasha knew, and she even abused the fact that she knew, that she would not be liked and admired because she did one thing or another, but everything would be liked, no matter what it was, as soon as she did it or said it.

"Mama, give me a husband. A husband," she repeated, "everybody has husbands, and I don't."

"My dear, just choose one," said the count.

Natasha kissed her father's bald spot.

"No, it's all right, papa." She sat down at the table (she never drank tea and could not understand why people pretended that they like tea) and talked rationally and simply for a while with her father and the uncle, but soon left and went into the sitting room, to her and Nikolai's favourite corner, where the intimate conversations always began. She brought her brother a pipe and some tea and sat down with him.

Nikolai smiled as he stretched and looked at her.

"I had an excellent sleep," he said.

"Do you ever feel," Natasha began, "that nothing is going to happen, nothing. That everything good has happened already. And you don't feel bored exactly, but sad?"

"I should say so!" he said. "I've had times when everything was fine, everybody was happy, and I suddenly got it into my head that nothing was going to happen and everything was nonsense. Especially sometimes in the regiment, when I used to hear music in the distance."

"That's it! I know, I know," Natasha said eagerly. "When I was still little, that used to happen to me. Remember, I was punished once for stealing plums. And you were all dancing, and I was sitting in the class-room and crying. I'll never forget the way I cried. I felt sad and sorry for everyone, and myself, and absolutely everyone."

"I remember that," said Nikolai.

Natasha thought some more (she was still in her state of remembering).

"And do you remember," she said with a thoughtful smile, "once, a long, long time ago, when we were still little, papa called us into the study, still in the old house and it was dark, and when we got there, suddenly there was . . ."

"A blackamoor," Nikolai finished what she was saying with a joyful smile. "How could I not remember that? I still don't know if it really was a blackamoor or we dreamed it or made it up."

"He was grey, remember, with white teeth – standing there and looking at us . . ."

"Do you remember, Sonya?" asked Nikolai.

"No, I don't," Sonya answered shyly.

"I asked papa and mama about that blackamoor, you know," said

Natasha. "They say there wasn't any blackamoor. But you remember him."

"Of course, I remember his teeth so well, I can see them now."

"How strange it is, as if it was a dream. I like that."

"And do you remember, we were rolling eggs in the hall and suddenly there were two old ladies and they began spinning round on the carpet? Did that happen or not? Do you remember how good it was . . ."

"Yes, and do you remember when papa fired a musket?"

They smiled as they ran through their memories with new enjoyment – not sad, old people's memories, but poetically youthful memories, from the same distant past where dreams mingle with reality, and they laughed quietly in sad joy at something. As always, Sonya was left behind, although the memories were common to them all. She only joined in when they remembered the time Sonya first arrived. Sonya said she had been afraid of Nikolai, because he had cording on his jacket and the nanny had said they would sew her up in cording too.

"And I thought you'd been found in a cabbage, they told me . . ."

Dimmler came into the sitting room, where there was only a single burned-down tallow candle lit, and walked over to the harp standing in the corner. He took off the cloth cover and the harp resounded tunelessly.

"Edward Karlich, please play my favourite nocturne by Field," the old count's voice said from the drawing room.

Dimmler struck a chord and, turning to Natasha, Nikolai and Sonya, he said: "The young people are sitting so quietly."

"Yes, we're philosophising," said Natasha, glancing round for a moment before carrying on with the conversation, which was now about dreams. Natasha was telling them that before, she often used to fly in her dreams, but now it only happened rarely.

"How did you fly, with wings?" asked Nikolai.

"No, just with my legs. You just have to make a bit of an effort with your legs."

"Oh, yes. Oh, yes," Nikolai said with a smile.

"Like this," Natasha said, promptly leaping up on to the divan. She put an expression of effort on her face, stretched her arms out in front of her and tried to fly, but only jumped down to the floor. Sonya and Nikolai laughed.

"No, wait, that's not right, I will fly, I will," said Natasha.

But at that moment Dimmler began to play. Natasha jumped to her feet, picked up the candle and carried it out, but soon came back again and sat down quietly in her place. It was dark in their corner, but the cold, frosty light of the moon fell on the floor through the large windows.

"You know, I think," said Natasha in a whisper, moving closer to

Nikolai and Sonya after Dimmler had finished and was still sitting there, gently running his fingers over the strings, clearly undecided whether to stop or to begin something new, "I think that when you remember and remember and remember everything, you remember so far back that you remember what happened even before you ever existed."

"That's metempsychosis," said Sonya, who had always been a good student and remembered her history. "The Egyptians believed that our souls have been in animals and they will go back into animals again."

"I know what your soul will go into."

"What?"

"A horse?"

"Yes."

"And Sonya's?"

"She was a cat, but she'll turn into a dog."

"No, you know, I don't believe we've ever been in animals," Natasha continued in the same whisper, even though the music had now ended, "but I believe and know for certain that we have been angels somewhere else and here too, and that's why we remember everything . . ."

"May I join you?" asked Dimmler, who had walked across to them quietly and sat down nearby.

"If we used to be angels, then why have we ended up lower now? No, that can't be right," said Nikolai.

"Not lower, who said we're lower . . . How should I know?" Natasha objected ardently. "Well, you yourself said that souls are immortal."

"Yes, but it's hard for us to imagine eternity," said Dimmler, who had sat down with a condescending smile but now, somehow, without knowing how himself, felt he had come under the influence of the sitting room and was taking the conversation seriously.

"Why is it hard? There'll be today, then there'll be tomorrow, there always will be! I just don't understand how it got started . . ."

"Natasha, now it's your turn, sing something for me," they heard the countess's voice say. "Why are you huddled up in there like conspirators?"

"Mama, I don't feel like it, really," said Natasha, but at the same time she stood up.

None of them wanted to leave, not even the old, cynical Dimmler, who had discovered some new, fresh feeling in this corner. But Natasha stood up and went. Nikolai sat at the fortepiano and she began to sing, standing in the centre of the hall, as she always did, selecting the best spot for resonance. She had said she did not feel like it, but she had not sung as she sang that evening for a long time before and she would not sing like it again for a long time to come. Count Ilya Andreich heard her singing from the study, where he was talking with Mitenka, and he got his words confused, like a pupil hurrying to finish his lesson, and fell silent. Mitenka gave a smile now and then. Nikolai kept his eyes fixed on his sister and took breaths when she did. Sonya listened to her in horror, thinking what an immense difference there was between herself and her friend and how it was impossible for her to be loved. The old countess sat with a smile of sad happiness on her face and tears in her eyes, shaking her head occasionally and thinking that soon she would have to part with Natasha and how good, and at the same time sad, it would be to give her away to Prince Andrei.

Dimmler sat beside the countess, closed his eyes and listened.

"No, say what you will, countess," he said after a while. "That is a European talent, she has nothing more to learn . . . such gentleness, tenderness, strength . . ."

"Ah, I am so afraid for her, so afraid!" said the countess, forgetting who she was talking to. Her mother's instinct told her that there was too much of something good in Natasha, and she should feel afraid for her.

Her maternal feelings did not deceive her. Before Natasha had finished singing, the rapturously excited eleven-year-old Petya came running into the room with the news that the maskers had arrived. Natasha stopped abruptly.

"Fool," she shouted at her brother then ran over to a chair, fell onto it and began to cry. But she immediately leapt up, kissed Petya and ran to meet the maskers: bears, goats, Turks, gentlemen and gentlewomen, frightening and funny figures. House serfs with a balalaika crowded into the hall and then it all began: singing, dancing, roundelays and fortune-telling songs. Half an hour later new figures appeared among the maskers: an old lady in a hooped skirt (Nikolai), a witch (Dimmler), a hussar (Natasha), a Circassian (Sonya) and a Turkish woman (Petya). It had all been thought up and arranged by Natasha. She had got up the costumes and drawn the moustaches and eyebrows with burnt cork. Now she was merrier and livelier than usual. After the expressions of indulgent surprise, the pretence that they were unrecognisable and the praise from those who were not dressed up, the young people felt their costumes were so good they ought to show them to someone else. Nikolai, who wanted to take everyone for a ride along the excellent road on his troika, suggested taking six of the house serfs in costume with him to call on the uncle, who had only just gone home. Half an hour later four troikas with bells and jingles were ready, and in the still, frosty air suffused with moonlight, the troikas with the maskers set off for the uncle's house across the snow that squeaked and whistled in twenty degrees of frost.

# VI

Natasha was the first to set the tone of Yuletide merriment that now blazed up in everyone, even in Dimmler, who was dancing with his broomstick in the costume of a witch. The merriment was transmitted from each one of them to the next, growing stronger and stronger, especially when they all went out into the frost and got into the sleighs, talking and calling to each other, laughing and shouting.

There were two fast troikas: one was the old count's with an Orlov trotter in the lead position, the other was Nikolai's own troika with his low, shaggy black in the lead. Nikolai was in a very jolly mood. In his old woman's costume, over which he had belted on a hussar's cloak, he stood in the middle of his sleigh with the reins gathered. It was so light that he could see the horses' harness plates and eyes gleaming in the moonlight and they looked round in fright at the riders clamouring by the porch in the mysterious light of the moon.

Nikolai was joined in his sleigh by Natasha, Sonya, two servant girls and the nanny.

"Forward, Zakhar," he shouted to his father's coachman, so that he could race with them. One troika set off ahead, with a whistle of runners and jingling of bells that were too loud for that still night. The trace horses pressed against the shafts, their feet sinking in the firm snow and throwing it up, so that it glittered like sugar.

"Now, my darlings," Nikolai shouted like a coachman, forgetting about his hooped skirt, and set off after them, first at a trot along the narrow road past the garden. The shadows from the naked trees lay thick across the road and obscured the bright light of the moon. But then they came out onto a snowy plain as white as sugar with a bright glint of violet, and then a hump in the road hit the lead sleigh – bang, bang – and then hit the ones that were following in exactly the same way.

"There's a hare's track, lots of tracks!" Natasha's voice rang out in the frost-bound air.

"How clear everything is!" said Sonya's voice.

Nikolai glanced round at them and bent down to inspect some completely new face, with eyebrows and a moustache, peeping out from under a sable coat. "That used to be Sonya," he thought. He looked closer into her face and smiled.

"What is it, Nikolai?"

"Nothing," he said, and turned back to the horses who, after emerging onto the well-trodden high road over the slippery snow, marked all over by the tracks of spikes, had begun to pull. The left trace horse was already tugging in leaps on his braces. The lead horse was swaying, but holding back, as if asking: "Shall we start? Or is it still too soon?" Zakhar was speeding away up ahead, already a long way in front, his black troika clearly visible against the white snow, jingling his bell and shouting, and the sound of house serfs squealing and Dimmler talking and laughing could be heard from his troika.

"Come on, you sweet darlings," shouted the old woman in the hooped skirt, tugging on the reins from one side and swinging his other hand that held up the whip. It was only from the wind, which seemed to have grown stronger, and the jerking of the trace horses, which were pulling hard and constantly lengthening their stride, that they could tell how swiftly the troika was flying along. Nikolai glanced back. The other troikas were falling behind, with shouting and shrieking and whips lashing the horses on. The lead horse was swaying firmly under the yoke, but still not thinking of slowing down, promising to go even faster if need be. Holding back a little, they drew level with the first troika.

"Right, Zakhar, let's see who's fastest."

Zakhar turned to him, his face covered with frost up to the brows.

"Just hang on, master."

The troikas rushed on, but Zakhar took the lead. Nikolai began creeping up on him.

"No you don't, master," Zakhar shouted, and began squeezing him to the right. The right trace horse was galloping in fresh snow and spraying the riders with fine, dry powder.

Nikolai could resist no longer, and he set the full troika to a gallop. After going about a *verst*, he came to a halt and glanced round again; there were strangers sitting in the sleigh, with moustaches and jolly faces.

"Look, his moustache and his eyelashes are all white," said one of the strangers with a moustache.

"That must be Natasha," thought Nikolai.

"Feeling the cold?" Dimmler shouted something funny from the other sleigh. They didn't catch what he said, but they laughed anyway.

God only knew if the uncle was pleased at all this merriment – at first he even seemed embarrassed and awkward, but his visitors did not even notice it. After the dancing and singing, the fortune-telling began. Nikolai took off his hooped skirt and put on the uncle's short kaftan, the ladies remained in their costumes and each time Nikolai looked at them with their moustaches and eyebrows drawn in burnt cork, he had to remind himself that they were Sonya and Natasha. Sonya in particular astonished him and, to her joy, he kept looking at her with loving attention. It seemed to him that he had only come to know her for the first time today, thanks to her moustache and eyebrows. "So that's what she's like, and I'm a fool," he thought, looking at her flashing eyes and the rapturously happy smile beneath her moustache, making dimples in her cheeks that he had never seen before.

After the games with the rings and the cock, Anisya Fedorovna suggested the ladies should go to the barn to listen. The barn was right beside the house, and Anisya Fedorovna said that in the barn you really could always hear them pouring things or tapping, and once a voice had been heard speaking there. Natasha said she was afraid.

Sonya laughed as she threw her fur coat over her head and then peeped out from under it with a smile.

"See, I'm not afraid of anything, I'm going right now."

And again Nikolai saw that unexpected smile from under the cork moustache.

"What a charming girl she is!" he thought. "And what have I been thinking about, fool that I am?" And as soon as Sonya went out into the corridor, Nikolai went on to the front porch for a breath of fresh air (it was hot in the little house). Outside there was still the same cold calm and the same moon, only brighter than ever. Its light was so strong that it dimmed the stars and with so many sparkling stars on the snow, he had no desire to look at the sky, which was black and boring, but only at the earth which was festive and happy.

"I'm a fool, a fool. What have I been waiting for until now?" thought Nikolai and, without knowing why, he ran down off the porch and went round the corner of the house along the path that led to the back porch. He knew that Sonya would go that way. Halfway along the path there was firewood stacked in seven-foot lengths, They were covered in snow and the shadow that they cast wove in with the other shadows that fell across them before spreading across the snow and the path. The path led to the barn. The wall of the log-built barn glittered in the moonlight as if it were carved out of some rare precious stone. Everything was absolutely still. A tree cracked in the garden and then everything was quiet again. Nikolai's chest seemed not to be breathing air, but some eternally youthful strength and joy.

Suddenly there was the clatter of feet on the steps in the women's porch, with a loud creak on the bottom one, which was covered with snow, and Anisya Fedorovna's voice said:

"Straight over there, my lady. Only don't look round."

"I'm not afraid," answered Sonya's voice, and feet in thin shoes squeaked and crunched through the snow along the path towards Nikolai.

"Yes, it's her. Now what should I do?" thought Nikolai. "I don't know. But she is charming."

Sonya was only two steps away now, and she saw him. She also saw him not as the person she knew and had always been slightly afraid of. He was wearing the uncle's kaftan, his hair was tangled, his eyebrows were painted black and there was a happy smile on his face that was new to Sonya. Sonya felt frightened at what was about to happen and ran up to him quickly.

"Quite different and yet the same," thought Nikolai, looking at her face, completely illuminated by the moonlight. He put his hands in under the fur coat covering her head, hugged her, pulled her close and kissed the lips that smelled sweetly of cork from the moustache above them. Sonya kissed him full in the centre of his lips, bringing out her little hands to enfold both his cheeks.

"Sonya, I see you're waiting for your destined husband," said Nikolai. "There's no point listening in the barn. Let's go, they'll see us." They ran across to the barn and then each went back through their own porch.

When they were going back home Natasha, who always saw everything and noticed everything, got into the sleigh with Dimmler and put Sonya in with Nikolai. Nikolai drove steadily, no longer racing, looking round all the time at Sonya in the strange moonlight, seeking under those eyebrows and that moustache in this constantly changing light for the former Sonya and the present one, the one from whom he had decided never to be separated. He looked and he looked, and when he recognised first the one and then the other and remembered that smell of cork mingled with a kiss, he turned away without speaking, or sometimes he simply asked: "Sonya, are you happy?" and carried on driving.

Halfway there, however, he gave the horses to the coachman to hold and ran across to the Dimmlers. He ran up to Natasha's sleigh and sat on the running board.

"Natasha," he whispered to her, speaking in French, "you know, I've made up my mind about Sonya."

"Have you told her?" asked Natasha, suddenly all aglow with joy.

"Ah, how strange you look with that moustache and those eyebrows. Natasha! Are you glad?"

"I'm so glad, so very glad! I was beginning to feel angry with you. I didn't say anything, but you haven't been treating her nicely. She has such a fine heart, Nikolai, and I'm so glad! I might be moody, but I'd feel guilty being happy if Sonya wasn't," Natasha went on. "And now I'm really glad. Well, run back to her."

"No, wait, oh, how funny you look!" said Nikolai, still gazing at her and finding in her too something that was new and unusual, something

622

he had never seen in her before. What he had never seen before was precisely this heartfelt seriousness which had become so apparent when she told him, with that moustache and those eyebrows, just what he ought to do.

"If I'd ever seen her the way she is now, I'd have asked her what to do ages ago and I'd have done just what she told me, and everything would be all right."

"So you're glad, and I've said the right thing?"

"Oh, absolutely the right thing! You know, a while ago I quarrelled with mama over this. Mama said she was trying to catch you. How could she say such a thing? I argued with mama. And I'll never let anybody say or think anything bad about her, because there's nothing but good in her."

"Good, then," said Nikolai, peering once again at the eyebrows and the moustache in order to be sure that it was true, then his boots squeaked in the snow as he jumped down and ran back to his own sleigh. That happy, smiling Circassian with the moustache and glowing eyes was still sitting there, looking out from under a sable hood.

*

"Natasha, I saw a big room and he was sitting there, writing," Sonya said.

After Sonya, Natasha took a turn, but no matter how much her eyes watered from the strain of peering into that mirrored perspective of candles, she still did not see anything, and declared that she had not seen a thing.

Soon after Yuletide the old countess began insistently demanding that her son should marry Julie, and when he confessed his love and the promises he had made to Sonya, the old countess began reproaching Sonya in front of her son, calling her ungrateful. Nikolai implored his mother to forgive both himself and Sonya, even threatening that if they harassed her, he would marry her in secret at once, and he left for his regiment barely on speaking terms with his father and mother, promising Sonya that he would put his affairs in the regiment in order and return in a year to marry her.

Soon after his son's departure, Ilya Andreevich made ready to go to Moscow to sell the house. Natasha contended that Prince Andrei had probably returned already and begged her father to take her with him. After much discussion and hesitation, it was decided that the countess would stay at Otradnoe and the father would take the two girls to Moscow for a month to stay with their aunts.

# VII

The love between Prince Andrei and Natasha and their happiness was one of the main reasons for the change that had taken place in Pierre's life. He was not envious, he was not jealous. He was glad of Natasha's happiness and his friend's, but after this his life fell into total disarray. All his interest in Freemasonry suddenly evaporated. All his efforts at self-knowledge and self-improvement had been wasted. He went to the club. From the club he went with some old friends to visit women. And from that day on, he began to lead such a life that Countess Elena Vasilievna felt it necessary to rebuke him severely. Without informing her, Pierre packed and left for Moscow.

In Moscow, as soon as he had moved into his immense house with the withered and withering princesses, with its huge staff of servants who were fed but always idle, and as soon as he drove around the city and saw the Iverskaya Chapel with its candles, the square with its smooth, unmarked snow, the cabbies, the hovels on Sivtsev Vrazhek Street, the old Moscow men, who swore the whole time, wanting nothing and hurrying nowhere, just living out their lives, and as soon as he saw the old women, the Moscow ladies and the English Club, he felt he was at home, back in a calm haven. There in Moscow he did not open his diary once, nor did he visit his brother Masons, but gave in once more to his ruling passions, those he had confessed when being received into the lodge and he was, if not content, then at least cheerful and no longer morose. He would not simply have been horrified, but would have turned away and refused to listen to anyone who had tried to tell him, seven years ago, before Austerlitz, when he had just returned from abroad, that he had no need to search for anything or think up new ideas, that his path had been determined since the beginning of time, his way long since laid out for him. Marry a beautiful woman, live in Moscow, hold dinners, play boston, run down the government a little, sometimes carouse with young people and belong to the English Club.

He had wanted to set up a republic in Russia, he had wanted to be Napoleon, he had wanted to be a philosopher, he had wanted to down a bottle of rum in a single gulp on a window-ledge, he had wanted to be a tactician, the conqueror of Napoleon, he had wanted to change the sinful race of man and make himself perfect, he had wanted to found schools and hospitals and set the peasants free, and instead of all of this he was the rich husband of an unfaithful wife, a retired gentleman of the chamber and a member of Moscow's English Club who loved to eat and drink, unbutton his jacket and abuse the government a bit. He was all of this, but even now he could not have believed, he would not have been able to believe, that he really was that retired Moscow gentleman of the chamber, the kind of man that he had so thoroughly despised seven years earlier. To himself he seemed to be an entirely different person, someone special, and the others, those vulgar, stupid people, were quite different from him, for even now he was still constantly dissatisfied, wanting to do so much for mankind. It would have been too painful for him to imagine that all those retired gentlemen of the chamber were really struggling in the same way, searching for some new path in life and that they, just like him, had been brought here to Moscow, to the English Club, to mild opposition to the government and retirement as gentlemen of the chamber, by the force of circumstance, by society and by birth, by that natural force that makes potato shoots grow towards the light.

He still thought that he was a different person, that he could not stop here, that this way of life was just for the time being (in just the same way that thousands of people, for the time being, have entered the English Club in Moscow with all their teeth and hair and left it toothless and bald) and that any time now he would start to act . . . In this view of life, he and his friend Prince Andrei were strangely opposite. Pierre had always wanted to do something, believed that life without a rational goal, without a struggle, without activity is not life at all, and he had never been able to do what he wanted to do, but simply lived, causing harm to no one and bringing pleasure to many. Prince Andrei, on the contrary, had regarded his own life as finished since early youth and said that his only desire and goal was to live out the rest of his days causing no harm to anyone and no nuisance to his near and dear ones, and yet at the same time, without even knowing why, everything he took up he had seized with a tight practical grasp, inspiring himself, and inspiring others to action.

After living there for a year, Pierre became the complete Moscow resident. Moscow began to feel calm, warm, natural and comfortable, like worn old clothing which there is no good reason to change, no matter how threadbare it has become. Alien as his wife's house had been to him, unpleasant as Hélène's constant nearness had been, it was perhaps the constant, bitter resentment he felt for her that had driven him on and kept him going. When, at the end of April, Hélène had gone away to Vilnius when the court moved there, Pierre had felt strangely sad and confused, but above all else he felt confused. Allowing for the difference in age and experience, he had now fallen back into almost the same state in which he had been seven years earlier in St. Petersburg.

In his heart an awareness of the love of goodness, of justice, of order, of happiness rose up once again with all its former strength, and when he measured his own life and other people's against this awareness he was baffled by the insubstantiality of life and he tried, but could not, close his eyes to the hopeless muddle that seemed so outrageous to him. "What has been done to the world?" he wondered constantly, clinging in his heart to an ideal of justice, happiness, order and purpose in life. "What is being done to the world? I hate and despise this woman. And I am bound to her for ever, like a convict bound by a chain with the ball of honour and reputation attached to it, and I bind her too. Her lover Boris abandons her in order to find some stupid, boring woman to marry and casts aside his feelings to become an inferior to his wife (she will be rich, he poor). Old Bolkonsky loves his daughter yet still he torments her, and she loves the good, but her misery has turned her to stone. Speransky was a practical, useful man, and they send him off to Siberia. The sovereign was a friend of Napoleon, and now they tell us to curse him. The Masons take vows of love and charity and withhold their dues and hatch intrigues to set Astrei against the Seekers of Manna, squabbling over the apron of a Scottish lodge. And yet I understand this whole tangle. I see that there are innumerable knots all tangled together, but how to untangle them, I do not know. No, not only do I not know how to do it, I know that there is no way to untangle them."

In this state, Pierre was especially fond of taking the newspapers and reading the political news. "Lord Pitt talks about grain, but it's not what he thinks. Why does Napoleon talk about friendship – they all lie, but do they even know why? But what about me, what can I do with myself?" thought Pierre. He could feel the misfortune of many people, and especially of Russian people – the ability to see and believe in the possibility of good and truth and to see the falsehood and evil of life too clearly. And therefore the intellectual salvation from this torment – activity and work – was denied him. In his eyes every sphere of work was connected with evil and deception. If he tried to be a philanthropist and a liberal in government service, he soon found the falsehood and the evil repellent. And yet at the same time Pierre, like everyone else, needed work and a special profession, for two reasons. On the one hand – for the sake of justice – a man who enjoys the benefits of society must also work himself, in order to repay to society what he takes from it: while on the other hand, work and a profession are a personal necessity, because a man who is not busy *doing* will look at the entire confused, ugly tangle of life and go mad or die from looking at it. Like the men taking cover under the flying cannonballs that Prince Andrei had told Pierre about, everybody was occupied – everybody was weaving little baskets out of dry grass, or building, or putting up fences round their little houses, or mending boots. It was too frightening not to be doing anything with cannonballs overhead, too terrible, with life hanging over your head, not to be doing anything. Pierre too needed to be doing something.

And he did do something. Having retained from Freemasonry only the mysticism, he read mystical books, and he rested from his reading and his thoughts with the idle chatter in the drawing rooms of his club, and usually after dinner in the evening he drank a lot. Pierre's need to drink wine was another expression of the coincidence of two opposite causes leading to the same result. Drinking wine became more and more of a physical necessity for him. He tipped it into his large mouth, without noticing what he was doing, swallowing glasses of Château Margaux (his favourite wine) in a single gulp, and he felt good, despite the fact that the doctors had warned him against wine on account of his corpulence. Besides, it was only after he had drunk a bottle or two that the terrifying, tangled knot of life no longer seemed so terrible to him. As he chatted, listened to conversations or read after dinner or supper, in his own mind he constantly caught glimpses of one side or another of that knot. And he told himself: "That's all right. I'll untie that – I've got my explanation ready here – but I don't have the time just now, I'll think it through later – it's clear enough." But this "later" never arrived. And Pierre was more afraid than ever of loneliness.

He took refuge from life in wine, company and reading. Sometimes he thought over what Prince Andrei had said about the soldiers assiduously keeping themselves busy with the cannonballs overhead, and he imagined all people as soldiers, likewise taking refuge from life: some took refuge in ambition, some in cards, some in writing laws, some in women, some in games with horses and hunting. "Anything not to see *it*, that terrible *it*," thought Pierre.

This was the person Pierre was for himself in the mysterious depths of his own soul, in the sufferings that he never spoke about to anyone, the existence of which no one ever suspected within him, but for others, for society – especially Moscow society, in which everyone, from the old women to the children, had accepted him as their friend, as a long-awaited guest whose place was always ready and never taken – for others Pierre was the dearest, kindest, cleverest, jolliest, most generous eccentric, a gentleman of the old school, free and easy, soulful and Russian. His purse was always empty, because it was open to all. If kind people had not been found who, while exploiting his wealth with a smile and treating him like a child, had taken him under their care in financial terms, he would have been destitute long before. Benefit performances, bad paintings, statues, charitable societies, schools, churches, books – nothing was ever refused, and were it not for his two friends, who had borrowed a lot of money from him while taking him under their tutelage, he would have given everything away. There was never a dinner or a *soirée* at the club without him. As soon as he slumped into his place on the sofa after two bottles of Margaux, he was surrounded, and the arguments, discussions and jokes began. When people quarrelled, he brought them together with nothing but his kind smile and a well-chosen joke. At balls he was everywhere; if a partner was needed, he danced. He bantered with the old women and made them laugh. He was witty and courteous with the young ladies, and no one was better than he was at telling funny stories and writing amusing things in albums. In the rhyming verse competitions with V.L. Pushkin and P.I. Kutuzov, his rhymes were always finished first and always more amusing than the others. "He is delightful. He is sexless," the young ladies said about him. The Masons' lodge dinners were boring and insipid if he was not there. It was only in the most secret depths of his soul that Pierre explained his dissolute life by telling himself that he had become like this, not because his nature had led him to it, but because of his ill-fated love for Natasha, the love that he had suppressed within himself.

Life in Moscow was very jolly in the winter of 1810–1811. Just as he knew everyone in St. Petersburg, Pierre knew the whole of Moscow society and he visited the most various social circles there, enjoying himself in all of them, and in all of them people were glad to see him. He went out visiting the old men and women, who all loved him, and into high society, to the balls, where he was generally considered to be an erratic, eccentric individual, highly intelligent but funny, and he got together with his old carousing buddies to go into Moscow and visit the gypsies and so on. His comrades in these excursions were Dolokhov, with whom he had become friends once again, and his brother-in-law, Anatole Kuragin.

# VIII

At the beginning of winter, Prince Nikolai Andreevich Bolkonsky and his daughter arrived in Moscow once again. Because of his past, because of his sharp wit and originality, and especially because at this time the rapturous delight with the reign of Alexander I had ebbed somewhat and Moscow was in the grip of a patriotic mood that was hostile to French influence, Prince Nikolai Andreevich quickly became the object of the Muscovites' special respect and devotion, and the focus of the Moscow opposition to the government.

That year the old prince had aged a good deal, both in his outward appearance and in those saddest symptoms of old age: waking unexpectedly, forgetting the immediate past, recalling events from long ago and, most significantly, assuming the role of head of the Moscow opposition and accepting the ovations of Moscow with a puerile vanity. And yet despite the fact that the old prince came in for tea wearing a coat and powdered wig, especially in the evenings, and the fact that, whatever subject anyone brought up, he would begin talking in an abrupt, fragmentary fashion about the past, or passing even more abrupt and harsh judgements on the present, it was impossible not to be amazed at the freshness of his mind, his memory and his exposition.

To visitors, this entire old house presented a pleasantly majestic spectacle, with its immense pier glasses and pre-revolutionary furniture, servants in powdered wigs and the energetic old man himself, with his meek daughter and the pretty Frenchwoman, who were both in awe of him. But the visitors forgot that, in addition to the two or three hours for which they saw the inhabitants of the house, there were another twenty-one hours in the day when the mysterious, internal domestic life of the house followed its own course. And in recent times this internal domestic life had become so painful for Princess Marya that she no longer tried to conceal the painfulness of her position from herself, but admitted it and prayed to God to assist her. If her father had made her spend entire nights bowing down to him, if he had beaten her, forced her to carry firewood and water, the idea that her position was painful would never have entered her head, but this loving tormentor was driven to his greatest cruelty by his very love for her, and with the deliberate cunning of spite, he knew how to put her in a position that required her to choose between two equally intolerable situations.

He knew that her current main concern was to obtain his consent for Prince Andrei to marry, especially since the day of Andrei's return was drawing near, and so he directed all his blows at this sorest point with all the perspicacity of love and hate. He saw how painfully Princess Marya was affected by the joke that had recently occurred to him, that if Andrei was to be married, then he would be married as well, to Mademoiselle Bourienne, and recently he had stubbornly and deliberately (or so it seemed to Princess Marya) displayed especial affection for Mademoiselle Bourienne and pursued his plan of displaying dissatisfaction with his daughter through his love for Mademoiselle Bourienne. Once, in Moscow, Princess Marya saw him kiss Mademoiselle Bourienne's hand (it seemed to Princess Marya that her father had deliberately done this in her presence). Princess Marya had blushed violently and rushed out of the room. A few minutes later Mademoiselle Bourienne had come into her room and asked her to go to the prince. When she saw Mademoiselle Bourienne, Princess Marya had hidden her tears, jumped to her feet and accused her French friend of all sorts of things, shouting at her to get out. The next day the servant Lavrushka, who had failed to serve the Frenchwoman her coffee on time, was despatched to the police station with a demand that he be exiled to Siberia. The many incidents of this kind made Princess Marya recall Prince Andrei's words about who was really harmed by the order of serfdom. The old prince told Princess Marya that he could not expect his servants to respect his friend Amélie Evgenievna if his daughter permitted herself to forget her manners in her presence. Princess Marya apologised to Amélie Evgeni-evna in order to save Lavrushka. She no longer drew any consolation from the monastery and the wandering pilgrims. She no longer had a friend. Julie, to whom Princess Marya had written for five years, had proved to be quite alien to her when they finally came to meet. Julie, having now become, through the death of her brothers, one of the richest marriageable young women in Moscow, was absorbed in the full round of high society pleasures. She was surrounded by young men who had known her for many years but had only now, or so she thought, come to appreciate her merits. Julie was at the stage of an ageing society lady who senses that her last chance at married life has arrived – and it is now or never.

Every Thursday Princess Marya would recollect with a sad smile that she now had no one to write to, since Julie – the Julie whose actual presence brought her no joy – was right here and she saw her every week. She recalled the story of some old émigré who had refused to marry the lady with whom he had long spent his evenings since, if he did, "where would he then spend his evenings?" Society life did not exist for Princess Marya. (Everyone knew that her father would not let her out and they did not invite her.) She told people that she could not leave her sick father. Everyone admired her loving devotion; many people sent matchmakers for their sons, since she and Julie were now the richest marriageable young women in Moscow. But since they had been in Moscow, Prince Nikolai Andreevich had seen off more than one young man who had come to his house and he mocked them so cruelly that nobody came any more.

The worst thing of all was that her brother's commission had not only not been carried out, but the whole business had been completely spoiled, and the very mention of Countess Rostova infuriated the old prince. It was particularly hard for Princess Marya because only very,

very rarely, in her most difficult moments, did she allow herself to think that she was not to blame for her own distressing situation, for the most part she was firmly convinced that she herself was bad and evil and therefore the guilty one. She thought this firstly because recently, especially here in Moscow, when she had been expecting her brother to arrive any day, she had always been in such a state of anxious agitation that she could no longer find it in herself to think about the future of life as she used to do, or to love God as she used to do. She could not pray with her soul as she used to do, she felt that she was merely performing a ritual. Secondly, she felt guilty because in her relations with Coco, who had been entrusted to her, she was horrified to discover signs of her father's irritable character within herself. Again and again she had told herself that she must not let herself get angry while teaching her nephew, but almost every time, when she sat down with a pointer and a French primer, she wanted so badly to transfer her knowledge to Coco's light-haired head as quickly and easily as possible that, although she shone the loving, radiant light of her eyes on the child, he was already afraid that aunty was about to get angry. Coco did not understand and she winced, tried to hurry, grew angry, sometimes raised her voice and tugged at his hand; if she stood him in the corner, she herself collapsed on the divan, covered her face with her lovely hands and sobbed, she sobbed at her wicked, bad nature and Coco would start sobbing too, walk over to her and pull her wet hands away from her face. But she felt her own depravity and culpability most strongly at those times when her father, whom she occasionally reproached, suddenly began looking for his spectacles when she was there, fumbling close beside them and failing to see them, or when he forgot what had only just happened, or took a faltering step with his weak legs and looked around to see if anyone had noticed or, the worst thing of all, when he suddenly fell into a doze at dinner, dropping his napkin and letting his trembling head droop. Yes, he was old and weak; he was not to blame, she was. How she longed to support his head, lower it on to the high armrest of the armchair and gently kiss his pock-marked, wrinkled forehead, but she did not dare even to think of it – Mademoiselle Bourienne did it, and Princess Marya could only quake in fear at the thought that her father might notice that she had seen it. She tried, but she was unable either to conceal or to express what she wanted, and she hated and despised herself for that.

# IX

In 1811 a French doctor acquired rapid fashionability in Moscow. He was immensely tall and handsome and courteous, as a Frenchman should be, he was exceptionally learned and everyone in Moscow pronounced him a doctor of exceptional skill. Métivier was welcomed in the homes of the highest members of society, not as a doctor, but as an equal.

Prince Nikolai Andreevich, who had always laughed at medicine, had recently begun to allow doctors to see him, primarily in order, it seemed, to laugh at them. In recent times Métivier had also been called, and he had seen the prince twice and attempted, as he did everywhere, to move beyond his position as a doctor and enter into the family life of his patient. On St. Nicholas Day, the old prince's name-day, the whole of Moscow society was at the entrance to his house, but he received no one and gave Princess Marya a list of those who were to be invited to dinner. Métivier, who had come like the others to offer his congratulations, felt it was proper for him, as a doctor, to defy the order by force, as he put it to Princess Marya, and went inside to see the prince. On that morning, the morning of his name-day, the prince was having one of his very worst spells. He had driven Princess Marya out of his room and thrown an inkwell at Tikhon and was lying in a doze on his Voltaire armchair, when the handsome Métivier, with his black topknot of hair and charming ruddy face, entered his room, congratulated him, took his pulse and sat down beside him. As if he had not noticed the prince's bad mood, Métivier chatted freely, shifting from one subject to another. The old prince frowned without opening his eyes, as if he had not noticed the doctor's over-familiar, jolly mood, and remained silent, occasionally mumbling something incomprehensible and hostile. Métivier spoke with respectful regret about the latest news of Napoleon's setbacks in Spain and expressed conventional regret at the Emperor's infatuation with his own ambition. The prince said nothing. Métivier touched on the shortcomings of the continental system. The prince said nothing. The doctor began speaking about the latest news of the introduction of Speransky's new code of laws. The prince said nothing. Métivier began speaking with a solemn smile about the East, saying that French policy ought to be directed to the East, conjointly with Russian policy, that the Mediterranean should be made a French lake once again . . .

The prince could not put up with this and he began talking on his favourite theme of the significance of the East for Russia, about the views of Catherine the Great concerning the Black Sea. He spoke willingly and at length, occasionally looking at Métivier.

"From what you say, my prince, all the interests of both empires lie in alliance and peace."

The prince suddenly fell silent and fixed the doctor with a gaze from eyes half-hidden by his eyebrows.

"You're making me talk. You want me to talk," he suddenly shouted at the doctor. "Get out, you spy!" The prince flew into a rage and leapt up off the armchair, and the resourceful Métivier could think of nothing better to do than leave the room with a smile and tell Princess Marya, who came running towards him, that the prince was not entirely well – "bile and a rush of blood to the head. Don't be concerned, I will call tomorrow" – and then he put a finger to his lips and walked out, because he had heard the prince's footsteps as he approached the sitting room in his slippers. The entire force of his rage was vented on Princess Marya – she was to blame for admitting the spy to see him. He could never have a moment's peace with her, he could not even die in peace.

"We have to part, you know that," he told his daughter. And as if he were afraid that she might manage to console herself somehow, he turned back to her, trying to assume an air of calm, and added: "And don't you imagine I said that in a moment of anger, I am calm, and I have thought about it, and it will happen." But then he gave way and, with the bitterness that can only be felt by someone who loves, he shook his fists in the air, clearly suffering himself, and shouted at her: "If only some fool would marry her!"

He slammed the door, summoned Mademoiselle Bourienne and lay there, coughing occasionally, while she read him *Amélie de Mansfeld*.

(After that day a rumour that Métivier was Bonaparte's spy spread throughout Moscow, and was half believed.)

At two o'clock, the six select individuals gathered for dinner and Prince Nikolai Andreevich, wearing his powdered wig, kaftan and star decoration, entered and greeted his guests, as magnanimously gracious and calm as always. The guests were: the famous Count Rostopchin, Prince Lopukhin and his nephew, General Chatrov, an old comrade of the prince's, and from the young generation, Pierre and Boris Drubetskoy. Boris, the adjutant of an important personage and a captain of the Guards who occupied a notable position in St. Petersburg, had arrived in Moscow on leave a few days earlier and, on being introduced to Prince Nikolai Andreevich soon thereafter, had managed to behave in his presence so cleverly, respectfully and with such independent patriotism that for him the prince had made an exception to his rule of never receiving young bachelors in his house. The prince's house was not exactly part of what is know as "society", it was a small circle and nothing was heard of it in the city, but to be accepted into it was regarded as the highest flattery. Boris had understood this a week earlier, when he had overheard the commander-in-chief saying to Rostopchin that he hoped to see him at his house on St. Nicholas Day, to which Rostopchin had replied that it was not possible:

"On that day I always go to kiss the walking relic of Prince Nikolai Andreevich."

"Ah, yes, yes," the commander-in-chief had said.

The dinner was prim and proper, but there was constant conversation, and interesting conversation at that. The tone of this conversation required the guests to report to Prince Nikolai Andreevich, as if on trial in the supreme court, about all the stupid and disagreeable things they were doing at the highest levels of government. It was as if Prince Nikolai Andreevich were taking all these things into his personal consideration. Everything was reported with emphatic objectivity and in heroical style, and everybody stated the facts, abstaining from judgements, especially when the matter could touch on the person of the sovereign. Only Pierre sometimes transgressed this tone, trying to draw conclusions from facts that demanded conclusions to be drawn and thereby crossing a boundary, but each time he was prevented. Everyone had clearly been waiting for Rostopchin, and when he began to speak, everyone turned towards him, although he only struck his best form after dinner.

"A State Council, a Ministry of Religion. They could at least think up something for themselves, the traitors," shouted Prince Nikolai Andreevich. " 'Sovereign power' . . . We have autocratic power," said the prince, "the power that is ordering us to make these changes."

"The ministers should be whipped into action," said Rostopchin, mostly in order to provoke an argument.

"Responsibility! They don't know what they're talking about. Who appoints the ministers? The Tsar, and he'll change them all about and give them a roasting, and exile them to Siberia, but he won't tell the people that I have ministers who can beggar you with their taxes and that they're the ones to blame.

"Fashion, fashion, fashion, French fashion, that's all it is. Like the fashion for ladies to go around as naked as the signboard in the public baths, it's cold and it's shameful, but they still expose themselves. That's what we have now. Why should power limit itself? What kind of idea is it to show Russia on the coins instead of the Tsar? Russia and the Tsar are the same thing, and they're the same thing when the Tsar wants to be the Tsar completely."

"Prince, have you read Karamzin's essay on the old and new Russia?" Pierre asked. "He says . . ."

"An intelligent young man, I would like to know him."

Champagne was served with the roast. Everyone stood to congratulate the old prince. Princess Marya walked up to him too. He presented his cheek to her, but he had not forgotten a thing, and he gave her a look to show her that he still remembered their clash that morning and was still feeling as bitter towards her as ever.

The conversation flagged for a minute. The old general, a senator, found the silence oppressive and decided to speak.

"Have you heard about the latest event at the review in St. Petersburg?"

"The new French ambassador" (this was Lauriston, who followed Caulaincourt) "was with His Majesty. His Majesty drew his attention to the Grenadiers division and the ceremonial march, and he supposedly said that they don't pay any attention to such trivia in their country. They say that at the next review the Tsar never deigned to speak to him even once," said the general, as if he were abstaining from judgement and merely stating a fact.

"Have you read the note sent to the royal courts in defence of the rights of the Duke of Oldenburg?" Rostopchin asked with the exasperated air of a man who sees that a matter he used to manage well is now being handled badly. "In the first place, it is weak and poorly written. But we can and we should make a bolder protest, with an army of fifty thousand."

"Yes, with an army of fifty thousand it's surely not so difficult to write in good style."

Pierre noticed that in all their judgements these old men halted at the boundary line where censure might apply to the sovereign himself, and they never crossed this boundary.

Rostopchin stopped for a moment and borrowed a phrase of Pierre's to liven up his speech.

"I ask you, what laws can we write for our own state, what justice can we demand when Bonaparte treats Europe as if he were a pirate with a captured ship . . ."

"There won't be any war," the prince interrupted curtly and sententiously. "There won't, because we have no people. Kutuzov's old, and what he was doing in Rushchuk, I don't understand. But what about the count, how is he bearing up in his situation?" he asked Rostopchin, who had been with the Duke of Oldenburg in Tver a few days earlier. Prince Nikolai Andreevich had deliberately changed the subject; recently he had been unable to talk about Bonaparte, because he was constantly thinking about him. He was beginning to feel he did not understand this man: following Napoleon's marriage to the daughter of the Austrian Kaiser the year before, the old prince had no longer been able to despise him with confidence, but nor could he believe in his strength either. He could not understand, he was mystified and confused when people spoke about Bonaparte.

"The Duke of Oldenburg is enduring his misfortune with steadfast and dignified resignation," said Rostopchin, and then continued talking about Bonaparte. "Now things are reaching as far as the Pope," he said. "We adopt absolutely everything! Our gods are the French, our heavenly kingdom is Paris," he said to the young men, Boris and Pierre. "French clothes, French thoughts, French feelings. Oh, when I look at our young people, I want to take Peter the Great's old cudgel out of the Kunstkamera museum and give them a good old Russian thrashing. Well, goodbye, your excellency. Now keep well, don't get downhearted."

"Goodbye, dear fellow, what sweet chanting – how I love to listen to him," said the old prince, holding him back by the hand and presenting his cheek to be kissed. The others stood up together with Rostopchin. Pierre was the only one left, but the old prince ignored him and went to his room. As Boris took his leave, he told Princess Marya how he had always regarded her father with sacred reverence, adored listening to him and could not get enough of his company, then he left the room with the others, having asked permission to visit her.

Throughout the men's conversation, Princess Marya had sat silently in the drawing room listening to the gossip and newsmongering about highly important affairs of state, understanding nothing of what was said, and thinking, strangely enough, only about whether they noticed her father's hostility towards her. With this query in her eyes she turned to Pierre who, before he left, had flung his fat body down into an armchair beside her. "Did you not notice anything?" she seemed to be asking. But Pierre was in a pleasant after-dinner state of mind. He looked straight ahead and smiled.

"Have you known that young man for long, Princess Marya?" he said, indicating Boris as he was leaving.

"I knew him as a child, but it is long time since . . ."

"Well, and do you like him?"

"Yes, why not?"

"Well, would you marry him?"

"Why do you ask that?" asked Princess Marya, blushing, although she had long since abandoned all thoughts of marriage.

"Because when I go into society, not when I come to you, but in society, I amuse myself by making observations. And now I have made the observation that usually the only purpose with which a young man with no fortune comes from St. Petersburg to Moscow on leave is to marry a rich woman."

"I see," said Princess Marya, still thinking about her own concerns.

"Yes," Pierre continued with a smile, "and this youth's behaviour is designed to ensure that wherever there is a rich prospect, he is there too. I can read him like a book. He is undecided now as to whom he should besiege: you or Mademoiselle Julie Kornakova."

"Really?" asked Princess Marya, but she was thinking: "Why should I not make him my friend and confidant and tell him everything? I would feel better. He would give me advice."

"Would you marry him?"

"Ah, my God, there are moments when I would marry anyone," Princess Marya said in a tearful voice, surprising even herself. "Ah, if you only knew, my friend," she continued, "how hard it is to love someone near and dear to you and to feel there is nothing you can do for them, except to grieve, when you know that you cannot change things. When the only thing to do is to go, but where can I go?"

"What do you mean, princess?"

But the princess burst into tears without finishing what she was saying.

"I don't know what's wrong with me today," she said, recovering her self-control. "Don't listen to me, let's talk about Andrei instead. Will the Rostovs be here soon?"

"I've heard they'll be here any day now."

In order to forget her own woes, Princess Marya told Pierre about her plan to try to make friends with the future bride, without telling her father about it, as soon as the Rostovs arrived, so that "he would grow used to her and come to love her".

Pierre wholeheartedly approved of this plan.

"One more thing," he said as he was leaving, looking into her eyes with special affection, "about what you said about yourself, remember that you have a devoted friend in me." And Pierre took her by the hand.

"No, God only knows what I was saying, forget it," said the princess. "But do let me know when the Rostovs arrive."

That evening as usual she sat in her father's room with her needle-work. He was grunting angrily as he listened to a book being read. Princess Marya looked at him without speaking. She thought a thousand angry thoughts about him: "He hates me, he wants me to die." She looked up at him again. His lower lip was drooping and he was dozing in senile exhaustion.

# X

Pierre's suppositions concerning Boris were correct. Boris could not make up his mind in the choice between the two richest marriageable women in Moscow. He found Princess Marya, plain as she was, more attractive than Julie; however, he was afraid and felt that it would be hard for him to accomplish his aims with her, so he chose Julie. He began calling on the Akhrosimovs every day. Marya Dmitrievna was as erect as ever, but she had been shattered by the loss of her sons and in her heart she despised the daughter who was so much like herself and was only waiting impatiently for a chance to be rid of her. Julie was twenty-seven years old. She thought that she was now not only as attractive as ever, but perhaps even more so. And indeed she really was, firstly because she was rich, and secondly because, the older she grew, the less danger she posed for men, and the more freely she behaved with them. She received visitors herself and went visiting in a kind of mob cap.

A man who ten years earlier would have been afraid to go every day to a house where there was a young lady of seventeen, because he might compromise her, now boldly came to her house for supper (such was her manner). She knew how to receive guests and imitate every possible style of conversation; depending on the people present, she was a demure aristocrat, a lady-in-waiting, or a simple-hearted Moscow woman, or simply a jolly young lady, or a poetic, melancholic, disenchanted maiden. This last style, which she had mastered in her youth and used when she was flirting with Nikolai, was her favourite. In fact she adopted these styles so superficially that her imitations shocked and repulsed people who were genuinely melancholic or simply in a jolly mood, but since most people only pretend and do not actually live, most people crowded round her and held her in high regard. Her friends included Karamzin, who had formerly been poor, and Vasily Pushkin, and Pyotr Andreevich Vyazemksy, who wrote poems for her. Everyone enjoyed simply talking to her without heeding the consequences. Boris was one of the admirers whom she liked the most, she cherished him, and felt it was right to adopt her favourite tone of melancholy with him. While Boris was still undecided, he had laughed and been jolly, but when he firmly decided to choose her, he suddenly became sad and melancholic, and Julie realised that he was surrendering himself to her. Julie's entire album was covered with aphorisms in his hand above little pictures of gravestones, such as: "Death is salvation, and in the grave there is peace.

There is no other refuge from our woes." Or: "Ancient trees, your dark branches inspire me with gloom and melancholy. There is refuge for melancholy in the grove. I wish to rest in its shade like a hermit." Or: "The closer I draw to the final boundary, the less it frightens me . . ." and so on. Julie played Boris the saddest marches on the harp. Boris sighed and read "Poor Lise" to her out loud. But after two weeks this state of affairs started to become wearisome. They both knew they had to abandon the anticipation of death, love of the coffin and disdain for life. Julie had to do so in order to become an aide-de-camp's wife. Boris had to do so in order to acquire three thousand souls in the Penza province from his melancholy bride. The transition was painful, but they had to go through it and one day Boris confessed that he dreamed of more than heavenly love: he had made up his mind to declare his feelings that day, and he proposed. To the horror of old Countess Rostova and the annoyance of Natasha (who still regarded Boris as her own property), the proposal was accepted. And the following day neither player in the game any longer considered it necessary to employ the tactic of melancholy and they began to go out visiting, appear in theatres and at balls, as an engaged couple, and in the mornings they went to the shops, buying everything for the wedding. The firm arrangements for Julie and Boris's wedding were already major, fresh news in society when Ilya Andreevich Rostov arrived in Moscow at the end of winter to sell his house, bringing Natasha with him to give her some amusement.

## XI

The Rostovs arrived in early February. Natasha had never been so excited, so ready, so ripe for love and therefore so lovely as a woman as she was when she arrived in Moscow. Before they left Otradnoe, she had dreamed that Prince Andrei met her in the drawing room and said: "Why don't you come? I've been back a long time." Natasha wanted this so passionately, her need to love a man, not just in her imagination, was so strong, the waiting to see her fiancé had become so hard, that when she arrived in Moscow she was firmly convinced that her dream would be true and she would find Prince Andrei already there.

They arrived in the evening. The following morning notification was sent to Pierre, Anna Mikhailovna and Shinshin. The next morning Shinshin came before anyone else and told them all the Moscow news. The main gossip concerned two young men here, Dolokhov and Kuragin, who had driven all the young ladies of Moscow crazy.

"Are those the ones who tied up the bear?" asked the count.

"The very ones," replied Shinshin, "I don't mind Kuragin, why, his father's a famous man, and he's a really handsome fellow, but who's this Dolokhov? 'Dolokhov the Persian' – that's what the young ladies call him."

"But where did he come from?" asked the count. "He disappeared three years ago."

"He just turned up; apparently he was a minister for some influential prince somewhere in Persia, he had a harem and he killed the Shah's brother. Well, all our young Moscow ladies are crazy about him. Why of course – if he's Dolokhov the Persian! And he's a card-sharp and a thief. But there's never a dinner here without Dolokhov, they always invite Dolokhov – that's the way it is.

"And the most amusing thing of all . . ." Shinshin continued. "You remember Bezukhov fought a duel with him, well now they're bosom pals. He's the count's most important guest, and Countess Bezukhova's too."

"Is she here as well?" the count asked.

"Certainly, she arrived a few days ago. Her husband ran away from her and she followed him here. And she is lovely, really lovely, I understand that . . ."

"What do I care about them?" Natasha thought as she listened absent-mindedly.

"And is Bolkonsky here?" she asked.

"The old man is, but I'm afraid the young prince isn't, my dear cousin, there's no one to flirt with," Shinshin replied sarcastically, but with an affectionate smile.

Natasha did not even smile at Shinshin's reply, she barely managed to prevent herself from crying.

Then Anna Mikhailovna arrived and told them with tears in her eyes about her joy, about her son marrying Julie.

"Best of all, she has a heart of gold. And my Borya loves her so passionately. Ever since they were children," said Anna Mikhailovna who, having now grown rather old, repeated the phrase that she said to everybody before she realised that this phrase should have been changed for the Rostovs.

Natasha blushed on hearing this news and she got up and walked out without a word. But as soon as she was out of the room, she realised how inappropriate her annoyance was. Why should it matter to her what Boris did, when she was already engaged, and to Prince Andrei, the very best man in the world? But even so, she felt hurt and annoyed and still more annoyed for having shown her annoyance.

Pierre, who was going to tell her the latest news about Andrei, had still not arrived. He had been carousing long into the previous night, so he had not got up until after two. He arrived in time for dinner. When Natasha heard he had arrived, she went running to him from the back rooms, where she had been sitting in thoughtful silence.

On seeing Natasha, Pierre blushed like a child and felt stupid for blushing like that.

"Well, any news?" said Natasha, drawing back her hand as he kissed it. "Are there any letters? Dear count, everyone is so repulsive except you. There are? Do give them to me," she said and led Pierre by the hand to her own room, beside herself with joy.

"Will he be coming soon?"

"It should be soon, he writes about a passport for the tutor he has found."

"Show me, show me," said Natasha, and Pierre handed her the letter. It was a curt, efficient letter, in French. Prince Andrei wrote that his final piece of business had been concluded. Laborde, an intelligent, educated Swiss, and an ideal tutor, was travelling with him, and a passport had to be obtained for him. Prince Andrei had written the letter in a dry and businesslike manner, but from that Pierre concluded that he was on the way.

"Well, and what else?" Natasha asked.

"There is nothing else," Pierre said, smiling.

Natasha pondered.

"All right, let's go into the drawing room."

Pierre also told her about Princess Marya's wish to see her, saying that the princess would come to visit the Rostovs and that it would be nice for her to make the acquaintance of the old man who would be her father-in-law. Natasha agreed to everything, but she was very taciturn and withdrawn.

The following day Ilya Andreevich and his daughter went to see the old prince. Natasha was frightened and dismayed to observe that her father had only reluctantly agreed to this visit and he was quailing as he entered the front hall and asked if the prince was at home. Natasha also noticed that after they were announced there was a commotion among the servants, that two of them were whispering about something in the hall, that a maid came running out to them, and then after that they were told that the prince could not receive them, but the princess requested them to come to her. The first person they met was Mademoiselle Bourienne. She was emphatically polite, but she greeted the father and daughter coldly and then led them to the princess. The princess greeted her guests with an agitated, frightened expression and red blotches on her face and tried in vain to appear welcoming and at her ease. Apart from her insuperable antipathy and envy of Natasha, the princess was even more upset by the fact that when the Rostovs' arrival was announced, the prince had shouted that he didn't want to see them, that Princess Marya could receive them if she wished, but they were not to be shown through to him.

Princess Marya had decided to receive the Rostovs, but at every moment she was afraid that the prince might create a scene. Princess Marya knew about the proposed marriage, and Natasha knew that Princess Marya knew, but they did not mention it even once.

"Well, you see, dear princess, I have brought you my singer," the count said, "she wanted so much to see you . . . It is a shame, a shame, that the prince is still unwell." And then, after uttering a few commonplaces, he stood up.

"If you will permit me, princess, to leave my Natasha with you for a quarter of an hour, I will go just a couple of steps along Konyushennaya Street to call on Anna Dmitrievna and come back for her . . ."

Ilya Andreevich had thought up this piece of diplomatic cunning in order to give the future sisters-in-law the opportunity to get to know each other. The princess said she would be very glad and her only request was that the count stay longer at Anna Dmitrievna's.

Despite the anxious glances that Princess Marya gave her, Mademoiselle Bourienne did not leave the room and firmly maintained a thread of conversation about the pleasures of Moscow and its theatres.

Natasha felt insulted and annoyed but, although she was not aware of it, with her calm dignity she inspired respect and fear in Princess Marya. Five minutes after the count had left, the door of the room opened and the prince entered in his white cap and dressing gown.

"Ah, my lady," he said, "my lady the Countess Rostova, if I am not mistaken . . . I beg your pardon, I really do . . . I didn't know, my lady. As God is my witness, I didn't know that you had honoured us with a visit, I beg your pardon," he said, speaking in such an unnatural and unpleasant voice that Princess Marya stood there with her eyes lowered, not daring to glance at either her father or Natasha, while Natasha, having stood up and sat down again, was also at a loss as to what she ought to do. Mademoiselle Bourienne was the only one smiling pleasantly.

"I beg your pardon. I beg your pardon," the old man muttered and went out. Mademoiselle Bourienne was the first to recover after this intrusion and she began talking about the prince's ill health, but five minutes later Tikhon came in and informed Princess Marya that the prince had ordered her to visit her aunt. Princess Marya blushed bright red and almost cried, and told Tikhon to say that she had guests.

"Dear Amélie," she said, turning to Mademoiselle Bourienne, "go and tell my father that I will not be going this morning. Please," she added in the tone that Mademoiselle Bourienne recognised as peremptory, a tone that indicated Princess Marya had been pushed to the limits of her patience and would not give way. Mademoiselle Bourienne went out. Left alone with Natasha, Princess Marya stood up, took her by the hand and sighed heavily, preparing to speak.

"Princess," Natasha suddenly said, also getting up. "No, do go, princess, please do go," she said with tears in her eyes. "I wanted to say, it would be best to leave everything . . . it would be best" – and she burst into tears.

"Stop, do stop, my darling," said Princess Marya, also breaking into tears and starting to kiss her. The old count returned to find them like this, and after receiving the princess's promise to visit his house the following evening, he led his daughter away.

# XII

That evening the Rostovs went to the theatre. Natasha had been taciturn and distracted all day long, and she dressed for the theatre without taking the slightest pleasure in it.

That evening a benefit performance was to be given by the favourites of the Moscow public and Count Ilya Andreevich had managed to obtain tickets to take his ladies. Natasha went reluctantly, only because she had to pass the time somehow, but when she was dressed and went into the hall to wait for her father, and she looked in the big mirror, she saw that she was looking lovely, very lovely, and she felt even sadder, but with the sweet sadness of love. "My God! If only he was here. I would simply hug him, not like before, stupidly and timidly, but in a new way, I'd press myself to him, make him look at me with those searching, curious eyes and then make him laugh, as he laughed then, with his eyes too – I can see those eyes so clearly," thought Natasha. "And why should I worry about his father and his sister, I love him, only him, with that face and those eyes and that smile, so manly and childish all at once. No, it's better not to think about him, not to think, to forget, to forget completely just for the time being. Or else I won't be able to bear this waiting, I shall start crying straight away." And she walked away from the mirror in order not to start crying. "How can Sonya love and wait so calmly and steadily?" she thought, looking at Sonya, who had just entered, also dressed for the theatre and holding her fan. "Yes, she is quite different . . ."

Having removed her furs, Natasha entered the brightly lit lower box as the orchestra was playing her favourite overture, and the brilliant sounds and the light made her feel even sadder and more in love. She was not thinking about Prince Andrei, but she felt just as she did in his company. She was full of tender feelings. She wanted to fall into someone's arms, to snuggle up against them and love them. She sat in the seat she was shown, at the front, placed her hand on the frame of the footlights and turned to gaze around the stalls and the boxes along the sides. She did not notice her little gloved hand involuntarily opening and closing rhythmically in time to the overture and crumpling her programme. The two remarkably pretty girls, Natasha and Sonya, who had entered the theatre with Count Ilya Andreevich, who was known to the whole of Moscow society, but had not been seen for a long time, attracted a lot of attention. In addition, everyone had heard vague rumours about her engagement to Prince Andrei, one of the city's most eligible bachelors, and they knew that since the engagement she had lived in the country, a circumstance that heightened interest in her still further. All this attention was focused especially on Natasha, who on that evening, thanks to her melancholy, poetic mood, was looking especially lovely. The sight of a girl so full of life and beauty but so indifferent to everything around her was particularly striking.

"Look, there's Alenina," said Sonya, "she's with her mother, I think."

"Good Lord! Mikhail Kirillich has got even fatter," said the old count. "Look what a toque our Anna Mikhailovna is wearing! Boris and Julie are there too. Now you can see they're an engaged couple."

Natasha looked in the same direction as her father and saw Julie wearing a low-cut dress, with diamonds around her plump red neck (Natasha knew it was sprinkled with powder), seated beside her mother with a happy air. Behind them she could see Boris's handsome, smoothly combed head bent down with one ear to Julie's mouth. He gave the Rostovs a sideways glance and said something with a smile.

"They're talking about us," Natasha thought. "And he's probably reassuring his fiancée, telling her she has no need to be jealous of me." Anna Mikhailovna was sitting behind in her green toque, wearing an expression of happy celebration and devotion to the will of God. Their box was suffused with the special mood of an engaged couple, a mood that Natasha knew and loved so well. She sighed and began looking round at the other faces, familiar and unfamiliar. Dolokhov was standing at the front of the stalls, in the very centre, leaning with his back against the footlights, with his immense, thick head of curly hair combed upwards in a strange style and wearing Persian costume. He was standing in full view of the entire theatre, knowing he was attracting the attention of everyone in the hall, as casually as if he were standing in his own room. Crowding around him were Moscow's most brilliant young people, and he himself was clearly the most brilliant among them. Since the incident with Nikolai, Dolokhov no longer greeted the Rostovs. He looked into Natasha's eyes with impudent amusement. Natasha turned her head away in disdain. Count Ilya Andreevich laughed as he nudged the blushing Sonya and pointed to her former admirer.

In the next box at the lower level, just two steps away from her, Natasha could see a lady standing with her back towards her, with delightful, completely bare shoulders and a pampered neck and hairstyle expressive of elegance of the highest degree. Natasha had always loved beauty and grace in everything, especially in women, and she glanced back several times at this neck with its pearls, the naked shoulders and the hairstyle, and she seemed to recall having already admired this beauty somewhere before. The lady was sitting alone. As Natasha was gazing at her yet again, the lady glanced round, her eyes met Count Ilya Andreevich's and she nodded and smiled to him. She was quite exceptionally lovely, and Natasha remembered that she had indeed already seen her and admired her somewhere. Once Ilya Andreevich, who knew absolutely everyone, began speaking to the lady after their exchange of glances, Natasha remembered that she was the Countess Bezukhova, Pierre's wife.

"Have you been in Moscow long, countess?" he began. "Let me come, let me come and kiss your hand. I've come here on business, and I've brought my girls with me. They say Semenovna's acting is quite superb. But where's your husband?"

Countess Bezukhova smiled her delightful smile and said:

"So glad to see you, my husband was supposed to come," she said and turned away from the count.

"What a beauty," the count said in a whisper.

"She's wonderful!" said Natasha, profoundly impressed, as always, by female beauty.

At that moment the final chords of the overture sounded, the conductor tapped his baton, the people who were standing sat down, others made their way to their places, and the curtain rose.

There were level boards in the centre of the stage and sheets of cardboard at the side, painted green, supposedly to represent trees. Men in frock coats and a few girls were sticking their heads out from behind the sheets of cardboard, and at the back there was a very poorly painted town – the kind you always see in the theatre, but which doesn't exist in reality. Sheets of canvas were stretched over the top of everything. There were young ladies in red bodices and little white skirts sitting on the boards and one in a white silk dress who was sitting apart from the rest, all of them dressed in a way that people never are in reality, but always are in the theatre. And they were all singing something. Then the maiden in white walked over to a little hut, and a young man in skin-tight silk breeches (he had fat legs), with a feather in his hat and a dagger at his side, walked up to her and began trying to persuade her of something, clutching at her bare arm, running his fingers along the arm and singing. As usual, Natasha knew that all this would happen, and she took no interest in what was happening on the stage. She was not very fond of the theatre in general, and now, after living in the country, and being in such a serious mood, she found all this boring and uninter-esting. In one of the quiet moments, when the lover in the tight breeches was running his fingers along the arm of the maiden in the white dress, obviously waiting for the right beat in order to start, the door of the stalls creaked open and there was the sound of someone walking in slightly squeaky boots across the carpet on the same side of the hall as the Rostovs' box.

Hélène turned and gave the person who had entered a friendly smile. Natasha involuntarily looked in the same direction as Countess Bezukhova. Walking towards them was Anatole Kuragin, the very same handsome cavalry guardsman whom Natasha had noticed that time at the ball in St. Petersburg. Now he was wearing an adjutant's uniform with a single epaulette and aiguillettes. He walked with a rapid, valiant, dashing stride that would have been funny were he not so good-looking and his face not wearing an expression of good-natured satisfaction and amusement. As well as Hélène and Natasha, many of the ladies and gentlemen turned to glance at him as he walked at a leisurely pace along the carpeted slope of the corridor, with his boots squeaking slightly and his spurs and sabre jangling.

Although the performance had already begun, he took his time to look all around before taking his place and on noticing Natasha, at whom he took a second look, he walked over to his sister and gave her a brief nod, walked past again and then, leaning over her and pointing to Natasha, he asked. "Who's she?" Natasha heard him say this, and she heard, or saw from the movement of his lips, that he said: "Delightful!" Then he made his way to the front row and sat down beside Dolokhov.

"How alike the brother and sister are," said the count. "A pair of thoroughbreds!" he said.

During the interval everyone in the stalls stood up again, came to-gether in a jumble and began walking around and going in and out of the hall. Boris came into the Rostovs' box in a very simple and polite manner in order to receive their congratulations and, raising his eyebrows, passed on to Natasha and Sonya his fiancée's invitation for them to attend the wedding. Several other men entered the Rostovs' box and went out again. Hélène's box was crowded and she was surrounded by men of the highest noble rank and intelligence, and Natasha caught snatches of the most refined conversation.

Anatole Kuragin, who interested Natasha insofar as any man who possesses the reputation of a rake interests a woman, stood at the front by the footlights throughout the interval, looking at the Rostovs' box as he talked to Dolokhov, and Natasha knew he was talking about her.

In the middle of the rows of seats, Natasha noticed the large, fat figure of a man with spectacles who was standing there, naïvely surveying the boxes. It was Pierre. When his eyes met Natasha's he nodded to her with a smile. And at the same moment Natasha saw Anatole walking towards Pierre, moving through the crowd as if he were parting the foliage of bushes before as he went. Anatole reached Pierre and began to say something, looking at the Rostovs' box. "I bet he's asking Pierre to introduce him to us," thought Natasha. But Natasha was mistaken. Anatole walked out of the stalls and only returned when people had already taken their seats once again. As he walked past their box, Anatole casually turned his handsome head to look directly at her, and she thought she saw him smile. Then she heard his voice in his sister's box, whispering something.

During the second act all the sheets of cardboard depicted monuments of some kind and there was a hole in the canvas, representing the moon, while the shades were raised over the footlights, and the trumpets and double basses began rumbling as people began walking around in black robes, and then lots of people appeared from the left and the right, and they started waving their arms around again, and they had things in their hands that looked like daggers, and then some other people came running in and began dragging the maiden away, but they did not drag her away immediately and she sang with them for a long time, and then they did drag her away, and someone in the wings banged on a saucepan three times, at which everyone was very frightened and went down on their knees and they all started singing a lovely prayer once again.

During this act, every time Natasha glanced into the stalls, she saw Anatole Kuragin with his arm thrown over the back of his chair, looking at her: his gaze was beginning to make her feel anxious and uneasy.

As soon as the act was over, Hélène got up, turned towards the Rostovs' box, beckoned the old count to come to her with a single gloved finger and began talking to him with a polite smile, paying no attention to the other people who had entered her box.

"Do introduce me to your charming daughters," she said, "the entire city is clamouring about them, and I don't know them."

Natasha sat there, blushing. She was glad to be introduced to this brilliant beauty and be praised by her.

"Now I want to be a Muscovite too. And aren't you ashamed of yourself for burying such prize pearls in the country?" Hélène's reputation for being enchanting was justified. She could say something she didn't really believe, especially if it was flattering, in the most simple and natural manner.

"Yes, my dear count, do allow me to take your daughters in hand. I haven't been here long, but neither have you, and I shall try to keep your girls amused." Countess Alena Vasilievna asked about Prince Andrei Bolkonsky, thereby subtly hinting that she knew of his relationship with them and asked if one of the daughters could stay in her box for the rest of the performance so that she could become better acquainted with her, so Natasha moved to Hélène's box.

In the third act they showed a very brightly lit castle with pictures of knights with little beards, painted particularly badly, worse than anywhere else except in a theatre, and two people who sang very badly, probably a queen and a king, sang something at the sides of the stage and then sat down on a throne. Both of them were poorly dressed and very sad. But there they sat. Some men with bare legs came out from the right, and some women with bare legs too, and they all began dancing together, swirling around, and then the violins began to play and one woman walked off into the corner, adjusting her bodice with her thin hands and began jumping in the air and beating her fat legs against each other rapidly.

At that moment Natasha noticed Anatole watching the woman through a spy-glass and clapping and shouting. Then one man stood in the corner, the dulcimer and trumpets began playing louder, and this man with bare legs began jumping very high, all on his own (this man was Duport, who received sixty thousand silver roubles a year for his art), fluttering his feet, and everyone began clapping and shouting, and the man began smiling stupidly and bowing. Then the others danced again, and then one of the kings shouted something in time with the music and they began to sing. But then, naturally, there was a storm, of course, and everybody ran off and they dragged someone away again. All of this was barely over when there was a sudden breath of cold air in the box as the door opened and Pierre came in and the handsome Anatole came in behind him, smiling, stooping down and trying not to nudge anybody. Natasha was glad to see Pierre, and she turned to Kuragin with the same happy smile; when Hélène introduced him, he came up to Natasha, bent his scented head down low towards her and said he had wished to have this pleasure ever since the Naryshkins' ball in 1810.

Anatole Kuragin spoke in a simple, cheerful fashion, and Natasha was strangely and pleasantly surprised that, not only was there nothing frightening in this man about whom so much was said, but, well, on the contrary, his smile was perfectly naïve, jolly and good-hearted.

Anatole Kuragin told her about a medieval tournament that was being arranged in Moscow and asked her to take part in it.

"It will be great fun."

"How do you know?"

"Please, do come, really," he said.

He spoke in an extremely easy and simple manner, clearly not thinking about what effect his words would have. He looked at Natasha's face, her neck and her hands with a smile constantly playing in his eyes. She found this very amusing, but she began feeling hot and bothered and a little breathless. When she was not looking at him, she could feel him looking at her shoulders and she naïvely caught his glance, so that he would look at her eyes instead. But as she looked into his eyes, she was terrified to realise that they were not separated by the barrier of modesty that she had always felt between herself and men. She herself could not understand how in five minutes she had come to feel intimately familiar with this man. When she turned away, she was afraid that he would take hold of her bare arm from behind or kiss her on the neck. They talked about the very simplest things, and she felt that they were intimately close, although she had never been with a man. And she found it strange that he was not even bashful, he was not even trying to understand anything but, on the contrary, he seemed to be caressing her, approving her. Natasha kept looking round at Pierre and her father in the way a child looks round when nanny says its time to go, but they were not looking at her. One of the questions that Natasha asked Anatole out of politeness was how he liked Moscow. As she asked, Natasha blushed: she felt all the time that she was doing something improper in talking to him. Anatole smiled.

"At first I didn't like it much, because it is the women that make a town agreeable, the pretty women. But now I like it enormously," he said, smiling the whole time and looking at her.

"Will you go to the ball? Please, do let's go," he said and then, reaching out a hand to her bouquet, he lowered his voice and said: "Give me this flower." Natasha did not know what to say, and turned away as if she had not heard. But no sooner had she turned away than she had the horrifying thought that he was there behind her and right up close, and now he was embarrassed and angry, and she had to put that right.

She could not stop herself looking round. He picked up a leaf that had fallen off her bouquet and glanced at her with a smile. Natasha could not tell if she wanted to be angry or not, she looked him straight in the eyes, and his closeness and self-assurance and his good-natured, affectionate smile conquered her. She smiled too, just as he was smiling, still looking straight into his eyes. "My God, what am I doing? Where am I?" she thought, but as she looked at him, submitting to him and smiling, she felt that there was no barrier between them.

The curtain rose again, and he left. In the third act there was some kind of devil who sang and waved his arms around until they opened the boards underneath him and he dropped down, but Natasha did not hear or see any of this, she wanted to follow every movement that Anatole was making, but she could not. As he walked past their box again, he smiled, and she smiled back at him. When they left the theatre, he saw her to her carriage, put her in it and squeezed her arm above the elbow.

"My God! What is this?" Natasha thought all the rest of the evening and the next morning, when she could not help recalling Anatole and the liberties he had taken. "I've never felt this before. What is this? I don't want to think of him but I can't help it. Perhaps this is what they call sudden love? No, I don't love him, but I can't help remembering him, thinking about him every moment. What is this? What is this fear that I feel for him?" The old countess was the one and only person Natasha could tell all her thoughts to, in bed at night. Sonya, with her stern view of life would, she knew, only be horrified by her confession, and she did not tell her.

## XIII

In the year of 1811, life in Moscow was very merry. The tsars and leaders of the young bachelors were Dolokhov and Anatole Kuragin. Prince Andrei had still not returned. The old prince had gone back to the country. Pierre was afraid of Natasha and did not visit the Rostovs.

Dolokhov had only just reappeared in Moscow this year, after disappearing from the city shortly after he had fleeced Rostov. They said that in the same year he had also fleeced a merchant and when the merchant declared the following morning that he had been given drugged drink and did not intend to pay, Dolokhov said nothing to him, but called his servants, told them to put promissory note-paper and some salted herrings in an empty room and then locked the merchant in it.

"He can stay as my guest like that, then perhaps he'll decide to sign."

They said that after three days, during which the merchant was not given anything to drink, the promissory note was signed and the merchant was released. But the merchant had filed a complaint and, despite the powerful protection that Dolokhov managed to find for himself, he was exiled from Moscow and faced demotion to the ranks if he did not go back to the army. Then he had joined the Finnish army as a captain. His regiment in Finland was not in action, and owing to his unfailing ability to maintain contact with people of higher rank and position than himself, he lived with Prince Ivan Bolkonsky, Andrei's cousin. They were both quartered with a pastor, and they both fell in love with his daughter. Dolokhov, while pretending only to be in love, had in fact long been the daughter's lover. When Bolkonsky discovered this, he began upbraiding Dolokhov. Dolokhov challenged him to a duel and killed him. That same evening the pastor's daughter came to him with reproaches and threats. He threw her out and beat her badly. Two new court cases were immediately begun. And that was when Dolokhov had disappeared, and for two years no one had heard anything about him. The latest news received from him had been a letter to his mother, mysteriously delivered by one of Dolokhov's underlings and gambling accomplices during his brilliant life in Moscow. The letter was brief, but deeply affectionate, like all Dolokhov's letters to his mother, expressing the way he had always felt about her ever since he could first stand.

Marya Ivanovna Dolokhova drove around Moscow showing this letter to everyone and asking for protection and mercy for her adored son Fedya. Written in Finland, the letter ran as follows:

"My beloved guardian angel, dearest mother. Cruel fate continues to persecute me. Fatal circumstances are bearing me off into the stormy torrent of life. Again I am unfortunate, again I am accused in court. The truth is known to the true God, the just God. I have fled. But I am not thinking of myself. The only grief that torments me is for you, my angel, my dearest; I embrace you, my beloved, and implore you not to pine, and to save yourself for better days. I shall not come to grief. I can feel that I shall yet see again those clear eyes filled with love, a mother's love, which means more than all the world to me, and I kiss those eyes and those hands. The divine nature speaks louder in me than all other voices. Farewell, my angel, I am sending you what I can and implore you to be patient. Your adoring son F. Dolokhov."

There were five thousand roubles with the letter. Dolokhov wrote that he did not need anything.

Marya Ivanovna Dolokhova watered this letter with her tears, accused the entire world of being unjust to her noble son, and Bezukhov for his cruelty, and Rostov for his slander, and that repulsive, base little merchant who had lost to a noble man, and that impertinent Finnish slut, and the cruel government.

Three years went by without any news until eventually, in the autumn of the year 1810, a man with reddish, weathered skin and a big thick beard, dressed in strange Persian clothes, appeared in Marya Ivanovna's little house and threw himself at her feet. It was Dolokhov. They said that all this time he had been in Georgia as a minister of some sovereign prince, that he had fought against the Persians there, and had his own harem, killed someone, done some service to the government and been brought back to Russia. Despite his past, which Dolokhov made no effort to hide – on the contrary, he liked to dwell on it, cynically – not only was he gradually accepted back into all of Moscow highest society, he actually behaved as if he were doing a special favour to anyone he visited. They held dinners for him in the best houses of Moscow and invited guests to see Dolokhov the Persian. Numerous young men were consumed by the desire to make friends with Dolokhov and felt ashamed of their own pasts, which contained no episode to compare with Dolokhov's.

No one knew what he lived on in Moscow, but he lived like an exceedingly rich man. He continued to wear his Persian costume, which suited him well, and ladies and young women vied with each other to flirt with him. But during his latest period in Moscow, Dolokhov had assumed the style of a contemptuous Don Juan in his relations with women, and that especially excited the married ladies. In Moscow they repeated his well-known words to Julie Kornakova who, like all the others, had been keen to tame this bear. Why, she had asked him at a ball, did he not marry.

"Because," Dolokhov had replied, "there is not a single woman, and still less a girl, whom I trust."

"How could a girl prove her love to you?" Julie had asked.

"Quite simply: by giving herself to me before the wedding – then I would marry. Would you like to do that?"

This year Dolokhov had made gypsy choirs fashionable for the first time, and he often entertained his friends with them, saying that there was not one young lady in all Moscow who was worth Matryoshka's little finger.

Anatole was the other brilliant man of this season in Moscow, although among somewhat different society, but he was Dolokhov's friend and associate.

Anatole was twenty-eight years old. He was at the brilliant peak of his strength and beauty. He had spent all of the five years since 1805, with the exception of the Austerlitz campaign, in St. Petersburg, in Kiev – where he had been an adjutant – and in Gatchina in a Cavalry Guards regiment. Not only did he not seek active service, in fact he always avoided it, yet in spite of this he always secured conspicuous, comfortable positions that did not require him to do anything at all. Prince Vasily considered it one of the conditions of his own respectability that his son should be in state service, and therefore no sooner had his son managed to make a mess of one position, than he was already appointed to another. Anatole regarded this as a necessary condition of life and, when he became an adjutant, he had acted as if he were doing everybody a favour by accepting the position. In fact he did not even act in this way deliberately. His health was always too robust and he was always too jolly and good-natured to make a pretence.

Anatole regarded money in the same way. He was instinctively convinced, with his entire being, that he could not possibly live in any other way than he did, that is, running through about twenty thousand a year, and that this was one of the natural conditions of his life – as water is to a duck. His father complained and rebuked him (although not often: Prince Vasily understood what his son was like and could see there was no point in saying anything), but he gave him the money, denying himself in the process, so that he was obliged to solicit the sovereign for more. Anatole felt all the more convinced that he simply needed his twenty thousand, and did not have any bad habits. He was not a gambler, he did not spend large sums on women (he was so spoilt by women that he could not understand how anyone would pay them for what they themselves wanted so much), he was not ambitious (he had vexed his father a hundred times by ruining his own career and he scorned all honours), he was not miserly and he did not hoard money, on the contrary, he scattered it around wherever he could and was in debt on all sides.

How could he possibly not have two valets, not have a race horse if he took it into his head to ride for prizes, not have a carriage, not run up accounts of around a thousand a year with tailors, perfumiers, suppliers of epaulettes and so on? How could he even think about letting his uniforms become worn? And above all, how could he not share a bottle with a friend, not treat his friends to dinner or supper? He could not see how he was doing anybody any harm in this way. He had to send a bouquet and a bracelet to a pretty woman when he parted from her, to thank her for her attentions. High livers, those male equivalents of female Magdalenes, have an obscure sense of their own innocence, based, exactly like Magdalenes, on the same hope of forgiveness. "She will be forgiven everything, because she loved so much. And he will be forgiven everything because he made merry and harmed no one." That is what high livers think, or rather, feel deep in their hearts, and Anatole felt it too, despite his inability to think. And Anatole felt it more strongly than anyone, because he was an entirely sincere high liver who sacrificed everything for good-hearted amusement. He was not like other high livers, not even Vaska Denisov, to whom the doors of ambition, high society, wealth and married happiness were closed and who therefore exaggerated his carousing, nor was he like Dolokhov, who always bore his own advantage and disadvantage uppermost in mind – genuinely wishing to know nothing other than the satisfaction of his own fancies, chief among which were women and making merry. This was why he believed so firmly that someone else had to take care of his interests and find him positions and that there should always be money available to him. And this was why he believed so firmly that life is always like this, because it truly always had been. In recent times he had run up such large debts in St. Petersburg and Gatchina, that his creditors had abandoned the special tolerance with which they had treated him and begun to pester him. (Previously his creditors had been disarmed by his handsome, open face and his handsome figure with the barrel chest, when he told them with a smile: "Honest to God, I don't have it, what can I do?") But now they had begun to press him. He had gone to his father and said: "Papa, all this needs to be settled. They won't give me any peace."

Then he had called on his sister.

"What's happening? Give me some money."

His father had droned on a little and then in the evening had come up with an idea:

"You go to Moscow, I'll write a letter and they'll give you a position there, and you can live in Pierre's house – that won't cost you a thing."

Anatole had gone and begun living merrily in Moscow, becoming friends with Dolokhov and with whom he pursued his womanising with a kind of Masonic zeal.

At first Pierre had been reluctant to take Anatole in, on account of the memories of his wife that the sight of him reawakened, but then he had grown accustomed to him, occasionally went out with him on binges to the gypsies, lent him money and had even come to like him. People could not help liking this man once they got to know him better. He did not have a single bad trait – neither concupiscence, nor vanity, nor ambition, nor envy, let alone any hatred of anyone. (Anatole never spoke badly or thought badly of anyone.) "Just as long as things aren't boring" – that was all that he needed.

The company he kept in Moscow was different from Dolokhov's.

Anatole's main circle was high society, with its balls and its French actresses, especially Mademoiselle Georges.

He went out to society gatherings and danced at balls and took part in the medieval tournaments in knight's costumes that were held in high society in those days, and he even acted in people's private theatres, but Prince Vasily's plans for him to make a rich marriage were far from being realised. Anatole's most enjoyable moments in Moscow were when he went from a ball, or even from Mademoiselle Georges, with whom he was very close, either to Talma, or to Dolokhov, or home, or to the gypsies, where he would take off his uniform jacket and get down to business: drinking and singing and hugging some gypsy woman or an actress. In such cases a ball or high society served to stimulate him, like a forced constraint before his nocturnal debauch. The strength and stamina with which he endured these sleepless, drunken nights astonished all his comrades. After such a night, he would arrive at a society dinner looking as fresh and handsome as ever.

Anatole's relations with Dolokhov were based on a naïve and pure comradely friendship, insofar as he was capable of experiencing any such feeling, but on Dolokhov's side they were based on calculation. He kept the dissipated Anatole Kuragin close at hand and played any tune on him that he wanted.

He needed Kuragin's unsullied name, noble connections and reputation for his own kind of society and for his gambling schemes, since he had begun gambling once again, but most of all he needed to be able to direct Anatole and control him as he wished. This very process of controlling another person's will was a pleasure, a habit and a necessity for Dolokhov, for it was only in the rare moments of his fits of violence and cruelty that Dolokhov forgot himself, otherwise he was always a cool and calculating man who loved more than anything else to despise people and force them to act according to his own will. He had controlled Rostov in this way, and now he controlled Anatole, among so many others, sometimes merely amusing himself with this control to no particular purpose, as if he were simply keeping his hand in.

Natasha had made a strong impression on Kuragin. He himself did not know why this was so, or why he trailed around after her.

He did not visit the Rostovs at their aunt's house, where they were staying, firstly because he was not acquainted with her, and secondly because the old count, who was extremely starchy when it came to his girls, regarded it as improper to invite such a well-known rake, and thirdly, because he did not like to visit a house where there were young ladies. He was at home in a ball, but in a narrow domestic circle he felt cramped and awkward.

Anatole was not capable of thinking, and so he did not think about what would come of his courting of Natasha.

Three days after the theatre he went to his sister's house for dinner – she had recently arrived from St. Petersburg.

"I'm in love. Love is driving me insane," he told his sister. "She's a delight," he said. "But she doesn't go out anywhere. And how can I go visiting them? Then what – get married . . . Eh? No, you have to arrange it for me. Invite them to dinner or, I don't know, hold a *soirée*."

Hélène listened to her brother with gleeful mockery and teased him. She genuinely loved people who were in love and loved to follow the course of love.

"Now you're caught!" she said. "No, I won't invite them. They're boring."

"Boring!" Anatole retorted, horrified. "She's so delightful. She's a goddess."

Anatole was fond of that expression. At dinner he didn't speak and sighed. Hélène laughed at him. When Pierre left the drawing room (Hélène knew he would not approve of this), she told her brother that she was prepared to take pity on him, that the next day she was having a *soirée* at which Madamoiselle Georges would declaim and she would invite the Rostovs.

"Only make sure you don't get up to any of your pranks. I'm taking responsibility for her and they say she's engaged," said Hélène, who really did want her brother to play one of his pranks.

"You are the best of women," Anatole shouted, kissing his sister on the neck and shoulders. "What a sweet little foot she has. Did you see it? Delightful."

"She's delightful, delightful," said Hélène, who genuinely admired Natasha and sincerely wished to amuse her.

The next day Hélène's grey trotters took her to the Rostovs' house and she entered the drawing room fresh from the frost, with her smile beaming brightly from her sables, and walking with rapid, lively steps.

"Why, this simply will not do, my dear count. How can you live in Moscow and not go out anywhere? No, I will not let you off: this evening Mademoiselle Georges is at my house, and if you do not bring your two beauties, who are far better than Georges, I shall not wish to know you any more."

Left alone with Natasha, she had time to say:

"Yesterday my brother dined with me. We were dying of laughter. He doesn't eat a thing and he sighs over you, my delightful girl. He's going mad, but mad, with love for you."

Natasha blushed. "Why is she telling me this!" she thought. "What business is it of mine who sighs, when I have my own chosen one?"

But Hélène seemed to guess Natasha's doubts and she added:

"You absolutely must come. You'll enjoy yourself. Just because you love someone, it doesn't follow at all that you have to live like a nun. Even if you are engaged, I'm sure your fiancé would prefer you to go out into society while he is away, rather than die of boredom."

"What is this: she knows, and yet she speaks to me of Anatole's love? She talked and laughed about this with her husband, Pierre. And she is such a grand, fashionable lady, so kind, and she obviously loves me with all her heart." (Natasha was not mistaken about that: Hélène did sincerely like Natasha.) "She knows best," Natasha thought. "Who can forbid anyone to fall in love? And why shouldn't I enjoy myself?"

# XIV

The brightly lit drawing room at the Bezukhovs' house was full. Anatole was there, clearly waiting by the door for Natasha to enter, and when she did, he immediately approached her and did not leave her side for the entire evening. As soon as Natasha saw him, she was overcome once again by that same disturbing feeling of fear at the absence of barriers. Mademoiselle Georges threw a red shawl over one shoulder, stood in the centre of the drawing room, glanced around her audience sternly and sullenly, and began the monologue from *Phèdre*, raising her voice in some places, whispering in others and holding her head high in triumph. Everybody whispered: "How delightful, divine, how wonderful."

But Natasha heard nothing and understood nothing and saw nothing good apart from Mademoiselle Georges's lovely hands, which, however, were too plump. Natasha was seated almost at the back, and with Anatole sitting right behind her, she waited in alarm for something to happen. Occasionally her eyes met Pierre's, which were always fixed firmly on her and were always lowered when they encountered her glance. After the first monologue the entire company got to its feet and surrounded Mademoiselle Georges, expressing their delight.

"How lovely she is!" said Natasha, in order to say something.

"I don't think so, looking at you," said Anatole. "And she's fat now, but have you seen her portrait?"

"No, I haven't."

"If you'd like to see it, it's in that room over there."

"Ah, do take a look," said Hélène as she walked by. "Anatole, show the countess the picture."

They got up and made their way into the adjacent picture gallery.

Anatole lifted his triple bronze candlestick to light the inclined portrait. Standing beside Natasha and holding the candles high in one hand, he leaned his head down, looking into Natasha's eyes. Natasha tried to look at the portrait, but she felt ashamed to pretend, she had no interest in the portrait. She lowered her eyes, then glanced up at Anatole. "I'm not looking, I'm not interested in looking at the portrait," her glance said. Without lowering the hand holding the candlestick, Anatole put his other arm round Natasha and kissed her on the cheek. Natasha tore his arm way in horror. She wanted to say something, she wanted to say that she was insulted, but she could not, she did not know what to say. She was ready to cry and she hurried out of the room, flushed and trembling.

"One word, just one word. For God's sake," Anatole said, following her.

She stopped. She needed so badly for him to say the one word that would explain what had happened.

"Nathalie, one word, just one," he kept repeating. But at that moment there was the sound of steps and Pierre came in with Ilya Andreevich and a lady to look at the gallery.

As the evening went on, Anatole Kuragin found the opportunity to tell Natasha that he loved her, but he was the unluckiest of men, for he could not visit their home (he did not say why, and Natasha did not ask him). He implored her to visit his sister, so that they could at least see each other occasionally, and Natasha looked at him in fright and did not answer. She herself did not understand what was happening to her.

"Tomorrow, I'll tell you tomorrow."

After the *soirée* Natasha did not sleep all night and when morning came she had decided for herself that she had never loved Prince Andrei and she loved only Anatole, and she would tell everyone so – her father, and Sonya and Prince Andrei.

The inner workings of the psyche, fitting rational reasons to accomplished facts, had led her to this conclusion: "If, after that, I could return his smile as we said goodbye, if I could allow that to happen, then it could only be because he is noble and handsome and I have always loved him from the very first moment, and I have never loved Prince Andrei." But she felt herself overcome by fear when she thought about how she would tell people this. The following evening, one of the maids passed on to her a passionate letter from Anatole, in which he asked her to answer his question: did she love him, should he live or die, was she willing to trust him and, if she was, he would wait at her back porch the next evening and carry her away to marry her in secret, and if not, he could not carry on living.

All of these old words, learned off by rote and copied from novels, seemed new to her, and she thought they only applied to her. But although she felt that everything was already decided in her heart, she gave no answer and told the maid not to say anything to anyone.

But first, first of all, she had to write to Prince Andrei. She locked herself in her room and began to write.

"You were right when you told me that I might fall out of love with you. I cannot help falling out of love with you. The memory of you will never be erased from my heart. But . . . I love another, I love Kuragin, and he loves me." At this point Natasha stopped and began thinking. No, she could not finish writing this letter, this was all stupid – it was wrong. She carried on thinking for a long time.

The tormenting doubt, her fear, the secret that she had not shared with anyone and a sleepless night had broken her strength. After receiving the letter from Kuragin she had sent the girl away, and now she collapsed onto the divan, dressed as she was, and fell asleep with his letter in her hands.

Sonya entered the room, not suspecting anything, tiptoed across to Natasha like a cat, took the letter out of her hands and read it.

As she read Kuragin's letter, Sonya could not believe her eyes. She read and peered at Natasha's sleeping face, as if she were seeking for an explanation there. She did not find any. It was a dear, gentle face. Clutching at her chest so that she would not choke, Sonya quietly put down the letter, sat down and began to think.

The count was not at home, the aunt was a devout old woman who could not offer any help. Sonya was afraid of talking to Natasha: she knew that being contradicted only made her all the more determined in her intentions. Pale and trembling all over with fear and agitation, Sonya tiptoed away, went to her own room and broke into floods of tears. "How could I not have seen anything? How could it have gone so far? Yes, it's Anatole Kuragin. And why doesn't he come visiting? Why this secrecy? Could he really be a deceiver? Could she really have forgotten Prince Andrei?" And the most terrible thing of all: if he was a deceiver, how would Nikolai, her dear, noble Nikolai react when he found out about this? "So that was why her expression was so agitated, and determined and unnatural today," thought Sonya. "But there's no point in conjecture, I have to act," thought Sonya. "But how, what can I do?" As a woman, and especially a woman with her character, Sonya immediately started thinking of roundabout cunning means: wait, follow her, win her confidence and intervene at the decisive moment. "But perhaps they really do love each other. What right do I have to get in their way? Should I send word to the count? No, the count must not know a thing. God only knows what this news would do to him. I could write to

Anatole Kuragin and demand an honest, truthful explanation from him, but who will make him come to me if he is a deceiver? Should I turn to Pierre, the only person I could trust with Natasha's secret? But it's so awkward, and what would he do?" But no matter what, Sonya felt that the moment had now arrived when she could and should repay all the good that the Rostov family had done for her by saving them from the disaster that threatened them. She wept tears of joy at this thought, and bitter tears at the thought that Natasha was intending to inflict such misery on herself.

After long hesitation, she reached a decision. She remembered what Prince Andrei had said to her about whom she should turn to in case of any misfortune, and she returned to the room where Natasha was sleeping, took Kuragin's letter and wrote Bezukhov a note from herself, into which she put the letter that Natasha had begun to write back to him. She implored Pierre to help herself and her cousin to clarify things with Anatole and discover the reason for this secret liaison and what his intentions were.

When Natasha woke up and did not find the letter, she dashed to Sonya's room with that tender determination that comes at the moment of awakening.

"Did you take the letter?"

"Yes," said Sonya.

"Oh, Sonya, I can't bear it. I'm so relieved," said Natasha. "I can't hide it a moment longer. You know, we love each other. He told me, Sonya, my darling. He writes . . . Sonya."

Sonya was gazing wide-eyed at Natasha, as if she could not believe her ears.

"What about Bolkonsky?" she said.

"Ah, Sonya, that wasn't love, I was wrong about that. Ah, if only you could know how happy I am. How I love him."

"But Natasha, how could you possibly exchange Bolkonsky for him?"

"Oh yes, I can. You don't know how he loves me. See what he writes."

"But Natasha! Can *that* really be all finished now?"

"Ah, you don't understand a thing," Natasha said with a blissful smile.

"But my dearest, how will you refuse Prince Andrei?"

"Oh, my God! Did I ever promise?" Natasha said angrily.

"But my darling, my dearest, think. What are you exchanging for what? Does this one love you?"

Natasha merely smiled derisively.

"Then why doesn't he come to the house? Why this secrecy? Think what kind of man he is."

"Ah, how funny you are. He can't announce it to everyone now, and he asked me not to tell."

"Why?"

"Why? Why? He doesn't want to, I don't know. It must be his father. But Sonya, you don't know what love is . . ."

But Sonya was not convinced by the expression of happiness glowing on her friend's face, and Sonya's own face expressed fright, dismay and determination. She carried on questioning Natasha sternly.

"What can it be that prevents him from declaring his love and asking your father for your hand," she said, "if you no longer love Bolkonsky?"

"Ah, don't talk nonsense!" Natasha burst out.

"How can his father stand in his way, why is our family any worse than his? Natasha, this isn't right . . ."

"Don't talk nonsense, you don't understand a thing, not a thing," said Natasha, smiling, for she was certain that if only Sonya could talk to him as she had talked to him, then she would not ask such stupid questions.

"Natasha, I can't leave it like this," Sonya continued in a frightened voice. "I won't let it go so far, I'll have a talk with him."

"Why not, why not? By all means, do that," shouted Natasha, blocking Sonya's way as if she might do it that very moment. "You want me to be unhappy, you want him to go away, you want him . . ."

"I'll tell him that an honourable man . . ." Sonya began.

"All right, I'll tell him myself, I'll tell him this evening, it will be a vile thing for me to do, but I'll talk everything through with him, I'll ask him about everything. You think he's a dishonourable man? If only you knew," said Natasha.

"No, I don't understand you," said Sonya, paying no heed when Natasha suddenly burst into tears.

Their conversation was interrupted by the call to dinner. Afterwards, Natasha started asking Sonya for the letter.

"Natasha, you can be angry with me if you like, but I wrote to Count Bezukhov and sent him the letter, asking him to clarify things with Kuragin."

"How stupid, how mean of you," Natasha shouted angrily.

"Natasha, either he'll declare his intentions or he'll refuse . . ."

Natasha burst into sobs. "He'll refuse, and I can't live without him. And if you're going to be like this," she shouted, "I'll run away from home, and that will be worse."

"Natasha, I don't understand what you're saying. If you have already stopped loving Prince Andrei, think about Nikolai and what it will do to him when he finds out about this."

"I don't want anyone, I don't love anyone, except him. How dare you say he's dishonourable? Don't you know that I love him?" Natasha shouted.

"Natasha, you don't love him," said Sonya. "When people love, they become kind, but you're angry with everyone, you have no pity for anyone, not for Prince Andrei and not for Nikolai."

"No, my darling Sonya, I love everyone, I feel sorry for everyone," said Natasha, weeping kind tears, "but I love him so much, I'm so happy with him, I can't be parted from him."

"But it has to be done properly. Let him declare his feelings. Think of your father and mother."

"Ah, don't say that, don't, for God's sake, don't."

"Natasha, you want to destroy yourself. Bezukhov says he's a dishonourable man too."

"Why did you talk to him, nobody asked you to. And you can't understand all this. You're my enemy – for ever."

"Natasha, you'll destroy yourself."

"I will destroy myself, I will, I'll do it so you won't pester me any more. If I end up in misery, then abandon me." And, weeping angrily, Natasha ran off to her room, taking the letter she had begun to Prince Andrei. After adding: "I am in love, goodbye and forgive me", she gave it to a maid and told her to take it to the post. She then wrote another letter to Anatole, in which she begged him to come for her that night and take her away, because she could not live at home.

The next day there was no news from either Anatole or Pierre. Natasha stayed in her room and said she was ill. That evening, Pierre arrived.

# XV

---

After his first meeting with Natasha in Moscow, Pierre had felt that he was not calm or at ease with her and decided not to visit the Rostovs. But Hélène had brought Natasha into their house and Pierre had suffered with all the sensitivity of a man in love as he watched their relations develop. But what right had he to interfere in this matter? Especially since he felt that he was not impartial. He had decided not to see either of them.

When Pierre received Sonya's letter, his first feeling, ashamed as he would have been to admit it, was one of gladness. He was glad that Prince Andrei was not happier than himself. This fleeting feeling passed, and then he felt sorry for Natasha, who could fall in love with a man whom Pierre despised as greatly as he despised Anatole, then he felt that he could not understand it, and then he felt afraid for Prince Andrei and then afraid above all of the responsibility that had been placed on him in this matter. Instantly, as consolation, the dark thought came to him that everything was pointless and transitory, and he tried to feel disdain for everyone, but no, he could not just let this go. Natasha's betrayal of Prince Andrei hurt him as much as his own wife's betrayal of himself, in fact it hurt him more. Just as when he had learned of his own wife's betrayal, he now felt mild disgust for the person for whose sake another had been betrayed, and bitter resentment for the betrayer. He hated Natasha. But he had to decide what to do: he ordered the carriage to be harnessed and went to look for Anatole.

Pierre found him with the gypsies in a merry mood, looking handsome, without his frock coat and with a gypsy girl on his knees.

They were singing and dancing in the low-ceilinged room, there was shouting and uproar. Pierre walked up to Anatole and asked him to come with him.

"I've come from the Rostovs," said Pierre.

Anatole blushed in embarrassment.

"What, what? Eh?"

But Pierre was even more embarrassed than Anatole and he did not look at him.

"My dear fellow," he began, "you know that my friend, Andrei Bolkonsky, is in love with this young girl. I am a friend of the family and I should like to know your intentions . . ."

Pierre glanced at Anatole and was surprised at the agitated and embarrassed expression that appeared on Anatole's face.

"What do you know, what?" said Anatole. "Ah, it's all so stupid. It was Dolokhov who put me up to it."

"What I know is that you took the liberty of writing this letter and it fell into the hands of members of the family."

Anatole grabbed at the letter and tore it out of Pierre's hand.

"What's done is done, that's all there is to it," he said, turning crimson.

"That's all very well, but I have been requested to find out what your intentions are."

"If they want to force me to marry her," said Anatole, tearing up the letter, "then let me tell you that they won't make me dance to their tune, and she is free, she told me so herself. And if she loves me, so much the worse for Bolkonsky."

Pierre heaved a heavy sigh. His metaphysical doubts about the reality of justice and injustice, that screw stripped of its thread, had already surfaced, and then, he envied and despised Anatole so much at the same time that he tried to be especially gentle with him. "He's right," he thought, "she is to blame and he is right."

"Well, give me a straight answer anyway, that's what I came here for," Pierre said in a whisper, without raising his eyes. "What am I to tell them, do you intend to ask for her hand?"

"Of course not!" said Anatole growing bolder as Pierre became more timid.

Pierre stood up and went into the room with the gypsies and their guests. The gypsies knew Pierre and they knew his generosity. They started calling out his name. Ilyushka danced across and handed him a guitar with a flourish. Pierre put some money down for him and smiled at him. Ilyushka was not to blame for any of this, and he danced excellently. Pierre drank the wine that was handed to him and stayed with the gypsies for more than an hour. "He's right, it's her fault," he thought, and he arrived at the Rostovs' with this thought in his head. Sonya met him in the hall and told him that a letter had been written. The old count complained that there was some trouble with the girls and he could not understand what was wrong with Natasha.

"But papa, you don't understand, I told you," said Sonya, glancing towards Pierre. "Kuragin proposed. Well, she refused him, and the whole business has upset her."

"Yes, yes, that's so," Pierre confirmed.

After talking for a while, the count went to the club. Natasha did not come out of her room but she did not cry, she sat there, staring straight ahead without speaking and did not eat or sleep or talk. Sonya begged Pierre to go and talk to her.

Pierre went to Natasha. She was pale and trembling and Pierre felt sorry for her. She gave him a cold look and did not smile. Pierre did not know where to begin or what to say. Sonya began first.

"Natasha, Pyotr Kirillovich knows everything, he has come to tell you . . ."

Natasha glanced at Pierre with curiosity, as if enquiring whether he was her friend or her enemy where Anatole was concerned. He did not exist for her in his own right. Pierre could sense that. When he saw this changed expression and her strained face, Pierre realised that she was not to blame, he realised that she was ill and he began to speak.

"Natalya Ilinichna," he said, lowering his eyes, "I have just seen him and spoken with him."

"So he hasn't gone away?" Natasha exclaimed joyfully.

"No, but that is of no account for you because he is not worthy of you. He cannot be your husband. And I know you would never wish to make my friend unhappy. This was just a passing fancy, a momentary aberration, you are not capable of loving a bad, worthless man."

"For God's sake, don't speak badly of him to me."

Pierre interrupted her.

"Natalya Ilinichna, think, your happiness and my friend's depend on what you decide. It's still not too late."

Natasha laughed at him, thinking: "How is this possible, and why should I think of Bolkonsky as he wants me to?"

"Natalya Ilinichna, he is a contemptible, bad man . . ."

"He's better than all of you," Natasha interrupted again. "If only you hadn't got in our way! Oh, my God, what is all this, what has happened? Sonya, why did you do it? Go away!" She burst into sobs, sobbing with the kind of despair felt only by those who feel they have brought it all on themselves.

Pierre was about to speak, but she shouted: "Go away, go away!"

And it was only then that Pierre began to pity her with all his heart, as he realised that she was not to blame for what had been done to her.

Pierre went to the club. Nobody was aware of what was happening in Pierre's soul and in the Rostovs' house, and that seemed strange to Pierre. Everybody was sitting in their usual places, playing cards, and they all greeted him. A servant brought a candle to Pierre's usual place and informed him that the count was in the dining room (the servant knew who Pierre's acquaintances were). But Pierre did not read, or talk, or even take supper.

"Where's Anatoly Vasilievich?" he asked the doorman as he returned home.

"He hasn't come back yet. A letter was delivered from the Rostovs and left here."

"Tell me when he arrives."

"Yes, sir."

Until late in the night Pierre strode round his room like a lion in a cage, unable to lie down. He did not notice the time passing until three o'clock, when his valet came to say that Anatoly Vasilievich had arrived back. Pierre paused to draw breath and then went to him. Anatole was sitting on the divan, half-undressed; a servant was pulling off his boots and he was holding Natasha's letter and smiling as he read it. He was red, as he always was after drinking, but his speech was clear and he was steady on his feet, he was only hiccupping. "Yes, he's right, he's right," Pierre thought as he looked at him, then walked over to sit down beside him.

"Tell him to go away," he said, meaning the servant.

The servant left.

"Now, yet again, I ask you," said Pierre. " I would like to know."

"What are you interfering for?" said Anatole.

"I'm sorry, my dear fellow, but you have to give me that letter. That's the first thing."

"I won't tell you anything and I won't show you this."

Pierre grabbed the letter, recognised the handwriting, crumpled it up, put it in his mouth and began to chew.

Anatole tried to object, but he was too late and, seeing Pierre's mood, he fell silent. Pierre gave him no chance to speak.

"I shan't use force, don't be afraid."

He stood up, however, picked up the sugar-tongs from the table and began convulsively bending and breaking them.

"The second thing is that you must go away this very night," he said, chewing the paper and breaking the tongs.

"Now listen here," Anatole said, but timidly.

"It may be discourteous of me, but you must not only leave this place, my house, you must leave Moscow today. Yes, yes. And the third thing is that you must never say a word about what happened between you and this unfortunate . . . and you must never show your face to her again."

Anatole frowned and said nothing, with his eyes downcast. Then he glanced timidly at Pierre.

"You're a good, honest fellow," Pierre said in a voice that had suddenly begun to quaver, in answer to that timid glance. "But you must do this. I won't tell you why, but you must, my dear fellow."

"Why are you doing this?" said Anatole.

"Why," Pierre shouted. "Why? Who is she, a whore, or what? This is vile. You amuse yourself and you bring misery on a whole family. But I forgive you."

It was not the words, but their tone, that convinced Anatole. He kept glancing timidly at Pierre.

"Yes, yes," he said. "I told Dolokhov. He was the one who egged me on. He wanted to abduct her. I told him that afterwards . . ."

"The scoundrel!" said Pierre. "He . . ." He was going to say something else, but he stopped and began breathing loudly through his nose, glaring at Anatole with wild eyes. Anatole knew this mood of his, he knew his terrible physical strength, and he moved away from him.

"She's delightful, but if that's what you say, then of course."

Pierre carried on breathing heavily, like inflated bagpipes, and said nothing.

"Yes, yes, you're quite right," said Anatole. "We won't talk about it. And let me tell you, my dear chap, that I wouldn't make this sacrifice for anyone except you. I'm going."

"Do you give me your word?" asked Pierre.

"I give you my word."

Pierre went out of the room and sent a servant to Anatole with money for his journey.

The next day Anatole took leave and left for St. Petersburg.

# PART SIX

# I

In the spring of 1812, Prince Andrei was in Turkey, in the army which Kutuzov had been appointed to command after Prozorovsky and Kamensky. Prince Andrei, whose views on army service had greatly changed, had declined the posts at headquarters which he had been offered by Kutuzov and gone to the front, as a battalion commander in an infantry regiment. After their first action he had been promoted to colonel and appointed regimental commander. He had achieved what he wanted – activity, that is, relief from the awareness of his own idleness and at the same time solitude. Even though he thought himself greatly changed since the battle at Austerlitz and the death of his wife, and even though he really had changed a great deal since then, to other people, his colleagues, his subordinates and even his superiors, he appeared to be the same proud, unapproachable man as before, but with one difference, that his pride was no longer insulting. His subordinates and comrades knew that he was an honest, brave, truthful man and special, in that he disdained everything equally. (Nothing provokes disdain like inequality and its reverse, firmness.)

In the regiment he was more isolated than in his own village, more even than he could have been in a monastery. Pyotr, his valet, was the only man who knew his past and his sorrows; all the others were soldiers, officers – men you'd just met, and you fought with them, but you'd probably never see them again when you left the regiment. They looked at you, and you looked at them in the same way – without any idea of a past or a future, and therefore in an especially simple, friendly, human way. In addition, the regimental commander's position set him apart. They loved him and called him *our prince*, but not because he was calm-tempered, caring and brave, they loved him primarily because they were not ashamed to obey him. He – "our prince" – was so obviously superior to them. The adjutant, the billeting officer, the battalion commander, quailed as they entered his tent, always so meticulously clean and tidy, where he sat, always clean, cool and calm, to report to him on the needs of the regiment, as if they were afraid of distracting him from his important reading or thoughts. They did not know that the reading was Schiller and the thoughts were dreams of love and family life. He commanded the regiment well and he did it well precisely because his main energies were directed to his dreams, and he gave the army only his insignificant, casual, mechanical attention, without excessive zeal, and this produced good results, as it always does.

On the 18th of May 1812 his regimental headquarters were located at Oltenitsa on the bank of the Danube. After inspecting a newly arrived battalion in the morning, he went for a ride, as usual, and after riding about six *versts*, he came upon the Moldavian village of Budsheta, where they were celebrating a holiday. The southern villagers, well-fed and full of wine, were lounging about in festive mood in their new hempen shirts. The girls were singing and dancing in a ring, they glanced at him and carried on with their fun. The complex tune was jolly and melodic. There was a happy-looking gypsy girl there who had a pock-marked face and high, firm breasts under her white hempen shirt with a pock-marked gypsy, a smart-looking fellow. The soldier's presence made them awkward and they held each other closer. He bought them some nuts, but they refused to take them. He was enjoying himself, he was smiling. But he felt sad that they were afraid of him. He was in the same state of clear perception that he had experienced on the battlefield at Austerlitz and at the Rostovs' house. He rode into the forest: young oak leaves, fluttering light and shade, warm, scented air. The officers thought he was inspecting the position. He could not understand what was happening to him. He sent his guide away and left as quickly as he could, so no one would see him. He wanted to weep.

"They do exist," he thought, "truth and love and the true, happy path through life. But where is it? Where is it?" He dismounted from his horse, sat down on the grass and burst into tears. "The warm, scented forest. The gypsy girl with the breasts, the high sky and the power of life and love, and Pierre, and mankind – and Natasha. Yes, Natasha – I love her more than anything in the world. I love silence, nature, thought." And suddenly, although he had just been wondering what to do with himself, he hurriedly stood up and set off back home, cheerful and happy. Back in his quarters, he sat down and wrote two letters, one on postal paper, the other on a plain sheet. One was an application to resign, the other was a letter to Count Rostov, in which he formally requested his daughter's hand in marriage, enclosing a note to Natasha in French: "I love you, you know that. Until now I have not dared to offer you my broken heart, but my love for you has so revived it, that I can feel within myself the strength to devote my entire life to our happiness. I await your reply."

To Prince Andrei's way of thinking, both of these decisions were sacrifices. To leave the army, when he had been proposed for promotion to general and had been offered a post as acting general, and when he had such a fine reputation with the men, was a deprivation and a renunciation of his entire past, but that only increased the pleasure he felt when he thought why he was abandoning it all. Because of an idea at which he had often laughed when he heard it from Pierre, that war is an evil in which only stupid, mindless weaponry can participate, but not independent, thinking people. He was sacrificing this for humanity. All this had lain inside him, but it had suddenly emerged, simply because of the impression made on him by the gypsy woman for whom he had bought the nuts and the warm, trembling shade of the leaves: so let it be. The other sacrifice was becoming involved in a life of family squabbles. If only she were here, like the gypsy woman, there would be none of this self-sacrifice.

He was terrified by the future, but he had firmly decided to go through with it. To endure his relatives' banality, his father's displeasure. He imagined her crying and flirting with Pierre. "No, I cannot, I cannot live without her," he thought. And the gypsy woman in the hempen shirt was somehow connected with all these decisions.

A number of officers always dined with him. Today's conversation revolved around war with the French. After dinner several pieces of post arrived. About repairing wagons. About promotions.

"I congratulate you, gentlemen."

"But we should congratulate you, your excellency."

"Why should we, prince?"

"An appointment to general."

"What, are you going to leave us?" said a battalion commander, trying to seem sad.

"I would have left you anyway," said Prince Andrei. "Try to make sure this envelope is despatched. Excuse me." He began reading a letter that related the story of Speransky's downfall, together with all the plans for a constitution and spoke of war ahead in 1812.

"Napoleon is approaching the Niemen, war is inevitable. Who is to be in command? This is no longer a joke. They will not take Moscow, of course, but I cannot imagine what is going to happen. You are fortunate to be serving in the army. Whereas I do nothing. I have not seen the Rostovs, they are in the country, but I am still hoping to."

This letter upset Prince Andrei so badly that he began to sigh. Was he really not going to take part in the action that would determine the fate of his fatherland, the action fought against that little corporal? No, he must rise above it. He had obligations to himself. He went to Bucharest and found Kutuzov at a ball, fastening a moldavian woman's shoe.

He said a chilly farewell, took his leave and left. They would not allow him to resign.

## II

---

The count was in despair. He wrote to send for his wife and the two of them cared for Natasha as if she were ill. Doctors came to see her, but they said in so many words that the illness was psychological. Natasha hardly ate or slept and sat in one spot in her room, doing nothing, occasionally saying something trivial. Whenever she was reminded of Prince Andrei or Anatole, she burst into angry tears. She liked being with her brother Petya better than anything else and occasionally was heard to laugh with him. The other person with whom she sometimes came to life was Pierre. He spent whole days at the Rostovs' house and treated her with a gentleness and tact that Natasha deeply appreciated.

During Holy Week, Natasha fasted and prayed, but she did not want to pray with everyone else in the parish church. She and her nanny asked to be allowed to pray separately in a special church that the nanny knew, the Church of the Assumption on the Mound. According to the nanny, there was a special priest there, who led a very strict and moral life. The nanny was a trustworthy person, and so they allowed Natasha to go with her. Every night at three o'clock the nanny woke Natasha from a deep sleep and she leapt up in fright, afraid she had overslept, and washed, feeling chilly, and dressed, took her patterned shawl – "the spirit of resignation", Natasha reminded herself every time – and tied it around herself. And they went to matins in a cart drawn by one horse, or sometimes they went on foot, through the dark streets and along the icy pavement. At the Assumption on the Mound, where the deacons and the priests and the parishioners already knew Natasha, she stood before the icon of the Mother of God set into the back of the choir and illuminated by the bright light of the little candles, and as she looked into the face of the Mother of God, crooked and black and yet full of heavenly meekness and calm, she prayed for herself, for her misdeeds, for her future life, for her enemies and for the whole of humankind, and especially for the man whom she had hurt so cruelly.

Sometimes common men from the lower classes of society would push and shove their way through to the icon in front of which Natasha was standing, despite the angry efforts of the nanny, who lacked Natasha's resignation. The parishioners had great faith in the icon, and these men did not recognise Natasha as a lady, with their candles they tapped her on her shoulders covered with the patterned shawl and whispered: "little mother", and Natasha would joyfully and resignedly set the warmed-through candle in place with her thin fingers and modestly hide her ungloved hands under the patterned shawl, as house serfs did. When they read the psalms and prayers, Natasha listened attentively to the prayers and tried to follow them in her soul. When she did not understand, which happened most often when the words were about transgressions and profanation, she thought up meanings for these words, and at those moments her soul was filled with tender meekness at the thought of her own vileness and the goodness of the ineffable God and his saints. When the deacon with the long brown hair that he was always tugging out from under his chasuble, reaching in as far as he could with his thumb, the deacon that she knew like a good friend, read "we pray to the Lord for the world", Natasha felt glad that she was praying for the world with everyone, in exactly the same way, and she followed every word about those travelling by sea and by land (and here every time she recalled Prince Andrei clearly and calmly, simply as a man, and she prayed for him). At the words about those who love us and hate us, she recalled her family – "those who love us" – and Anatole – "those who hate us". She felt especially glad to pray for him. She knew now that he was her enemy.

She had always lacked enemies for whom she could pray. She included among them all their creditors and everyone who did business with her father. Later, when they prayed for the royal family, each time she had to overcome a feeling of doubt within herself: why should they pray so much especially for them, and bow down and cross themselves – but she told herself that this was pride, and they were people too. She prayed with the same fervour for the Holy Synod, telling herself that she also loved the officiating and ruling Synod. When they read the Gospel, she felt glad and rejoiced as she pronounced the words that preceded the reading: "Glory be to Thee, Oh Lord", and she felt happy when she heard these words, each of which had a special meaning for her, but when they opened the sanctuary doors and the people around her whispered piously: "The doors of mercy", or when the priest came out with the offerings, or she could hear the mysterious exclamations of the priest behind the sanctuary gates and they read the credo, "I believe", Natasha hung her head in joyful terror at the majesty and ineffability of God, and tears streamed down her cheeks that had grown so thin. She did not miss a single matins or vespers. She prostrated herself at the words "The light of Christ shines through you" and thought in horror that someone might look up sacrilegiously at that moment and see what was happening above their heads. Many times a day she asked "God, the

Lord of her life" to take away from her the spirit of idleness . . . and give her true spirit . . . She followed the sufferings of Christ in horror as they took place before her very eyes. Holy Week, or Passion Week, as her nanny called it, the passions, the Holy Shroud, the black chasubles – all of this was reflected vaguely and unclearly in Natasha's soul, but one thing was clear to her: "Thy will be done." "Take me, Oh Lord," she said with tears in her eyes, when she lost her way in the complexity of all these joyful impressions.

On Wednesday she asked her mother to invite Pierre, and on that same day she locked herself in her room and wrote a letter to Prince Andrei. After several drafts she settled on the following: "As I prepare myself for the exalted sacrament of confession and communion, I need to ask your forgiveness for the harm that I have done to you. I promised not to love anyone except you, but I was so wanton that I fell in love with another and betrayed you. For the sake of God, for this day, forgive me and forget one who is not worthy of you." She gave this letter to Pierre and asked him to give it to Prince Andrei, whom she knew to be in Moscow.

She asked her mother, who was surprised and frightened by her daughter's religious passion, to allow her not to make her confession at home, but to Father Anisim at the Assumption on the Mound. She confessed there behind the screens beside the choir, between a coachman and a merchant with his wife. The priest Anisim, tired from all his hard work, gave Natasha a casually affectionate glance, covered her head with a scarf and listened sadly to her sobbing out her admissions of guilt. He absolved her with a brief and simple exhortation to sin no more, which Natasha understood as if every single word came straight from heaven. She walked home and for the first time since that day in the theatre, she fell asleep calmly and happily.

The next day she came home happier from communion and after that the countess was overjoyed to see that Natasha was coming back to life. She took part in the family's life, she sometimes sang, she read many of the books brought to her by Pierre, who had become almost a member of the Rostov family, but she never recovered her former vitality and gaiety. Whoever she was with, she always had the air and the manner of someone who was guilty, for whom everything was better than it ought to be according to what she had done.

The incident of Natasha and Anatole shook Pierre badly. Apart from his love for Andrei and his feelings of something more than friendship for Natasha, apart from the strange confluence of circumstances that constantly obliged him to become involved in Natasha's life and his involvement in their engagement, he was struck by the thought that he was to blame for this clash, that he had not foreseen what Anatole would do. But how could he have foreseen it? In his mind, Natasha was such an exalted, heavenly being, who had given her love to the best man in the world – Prince Andrei – and Anatole was a stupid, coarse, dishonest brute.

For several days after the incident, Pierre had not visited the Rostovs, but had diligently gone out into society, and especially to see the gossips, that is, the very widest circle of society. And indeed, people there were talking about Natasha with joyful regret, and Pierre was astonished with all the force of his faculties at how people could invent nonsense that had no basis whatever and talk calmly about how his brother-in-law had fallen in love with Natasha Rostov and how his proposal had been refused. When he visited the Rostovs again for the first time, he was especially jolly with the members of the family and Natasha. He pretended not to notice her tearful eyes and sunken cheeks and he stayed to dinner. At dinner, he spoke in front of everyone about how people in Moscow were saying that Anatole had proposed to Natasha and Natasha had refused him, and Anatole was grief-stricken and had gone away. He paid no attention to the fact that Natasha's nose began to bleed as he said this and she got up from the table, or the tender, devout way that Sonya looked at him for saying it. He stayed for the evening and came again the next day. And he began visiting the Rostovs every day.

With Natasha he was jolly and humorous, as he had been before, but with that special subtle tone of reticent politeness that sensitive people adopt in the face of unhappiness. Natasha often smiled at him through the tears that always seemed to be in her eyes, even though her eyes were dry. For the good that he was doing to her friend, Sonya now loved Pierre more than anyone in the world after Nikolai, and she told him so in secret.

He did not talk about Anatole with Natasha at all, or about Prince Andrei, he simply talked to her a lot and began to bring her books, including his favourite *La Nouvelle Héloïse*, which Natasha enjoyed and began to discuss, saying she did not understand how Abélard could have loved Héloïse.

"I could have," said Pierre (it seemed strange to Natasha that Pierre could talk about himself as a man who was also capable of loving and suffering). "Once when I was talking to a friend, we decided that a woman's love purges the whole past, that the past is not . . ." He looked at Natasha though his spectacles.

Sonya deliberately moved away from them. She had been waiting and hoping for some clear speaking.

Natasha suddenly burst into tears.

"Pyotr Kirillovich," she said. "Why should we pretend? I know what you're saying. It can never, never be ... not on his side, nor on mine. I loved him too much to cause him such suffering."

"Tell me one thing, did you love ..." (he did not know what to call Anatole, and he blushed at the very thought of him) "... did you love that bad man ..."

"Yes," said Natasha, "and don't call him bad, you're insulting me. But now, I don't know anything, anything at all. Now," she said and burst into tears again, "I just don't understand anything."

"Let's not talk about it, my friend," said Pierre.

The gentle tone he used with her, like a nurse, suddenly seemed very strange to her.

"Let's not talk about it, my friend," he repeated, "but I ask one thing of you, to regard me as your friend, and if you need help, advice or if you simply need to pour out your heart to someone – not now, but when things are clear in your heart – remember me."

He kissed her hand, then took his handkerchief out of the pocket of his frock coat and began wiping his spectacles. Natasha was happy at this offer of friendship and she accepted it. It never even entered her head that Pierre was also a man, that friendship could develop into something else. It could, but not with dear, kind Pierre. She felt this way because the moral barrier, which in Anatole's case she had felt so painfully to be absent, seemed insuperable with Pierre. Pierre had visited the Rostovs every day, especially in recent times and it had continued right until spring, when during Holy Week he received the note Natasha had written before her confession, and the request to pass it on to Prince Andrei.

Prince Andrei had not come to Pierre's house, he had put up in a hotel, from where he wrote a note to Pierre, asking him to come.

Pierre found him still the same as ever. He was rather pale and morose and he was walking back and forth across the room, evidently waiting. He smiled feebly when he saw Pierre, but just with his mouth. And he interrupted Pierre as soon as he could, to prevent him from speaking humorously or lightly, when the clarification that was to come was neither light nor humorous. He led him into the inner room and closed the door.

"I would not have called in here" (this was how he spoke of Moscow), "I am on my way to Kutuzov and the army in Turkey, but I need to give you my response to this letter here." He showed Pierre a scrap of grey paper with Natasha's scribble on it (the scribble had reached its intended destination). "It says there: 'You told me that I was free and I should write to you if I love again. I have fallen in love with another. Forgive me. N. Rostova.'"

It was clear that the letter had been written in a moment of mental aberration and its laconic rudeness was therefore forgivable, but only all the more painful.

"Forgive me if I am causing you any difficulties, but I am also in some difficulty" – his voice trembled. "I have received a refusal from Countess Rostova and rumours have reached me that her hand has been sought by your brother-in-law or something of the kind. Is this true?" He wiped his forehead with his hand. "Here are her letters and her portrait."

He took the portrait out of the desk and glanced at it as he handed it to Pierre. His lip began to tremble as he handed it over.

"Give this back to the countess . . ."

"Yes . . . No . . ." said Pierre. "You are upset, Andrei, I cannot talk with you now, I have a letter for you, here it is, but first I must tell you . . ."

"Ah, I am perfectly calm, just allow me to read the letter." Andrei sat down, read the letter and gave a cold, angry, unpleasant laugh, like his father's.

"I did not know that it had gone so far and that Mr. Anatole Kuragin did not think fit to offer his hand to Countess Rostova." Prince Andrei snorted through his nose several times. "Well, I see, I see," he said. "Tell Countess Rostova that I am most grateful to her for remembering me so kindly, that I share her feelings entirely and wish her all the very best. This is impolite, but forgive me, my dear friend, I shall not be able to . . ." he broke off without finishing and turned away.

"Andrei, surely you can understand this girlish infatuation, this madness. She is such a charming, honest creature."

Prince Andrei interrupted him and laughed angrily.

"What, ask for her hand again? Forgive, be magnanimous and so forth. Yes, all very noble, but I'm not capable of following in the steps . . . Ah yes, now, as a friend. Where is this . . . gentleman now . . . Where is this . . . well . . ." And a terrible light glinted in Prince Andrei's eyes. "Go, Pierre, go away, I beg of you."

Pierre did as he asked and went away, it was all too painful for him, and he saw that he could not help. He went outside and ordered the coachman to go to the Rostovs', without even knowing what for, but he simply wanted to see Natasha, without telling her anything, and to come back again, as if the sight of her could teach him what to do. But he did not find the Rostovs at home and so went back to Prince Andrei.

Bolkonsky was sitting at the table, absolutely calm, and eating breakfast alone.

"Well, sit down, now we can have a proper talk," he said.

Prince Andrei did not notice it, but he was incapable of talking himself nor did he let Pierre talk. Whatever subject they touched on, Prince Andrei responded to it with some brief, mocking, hopeless remark which, for Pierre, who was already close to hopelessness himself, served to undermine his whole interest in life, bringing to mind in all its dreadful nakedness the terrible knot of life that it was impossible to untangle. Words and thoughts of this kind could only be produced by a soul steeped in the poison of despair, even if they were sometimes amusing.

Andrei began talking about his father and he said:

"What can be done, he loves Princess Marya, but he torments her. Clearly that's how things should be – for the spider to devour the fly, and for my father to devour Princess Marya's life. And she is content. She will eat her God with wine and bread no matter how much our father might humiliate and torment her. Clearly that's how it should be."

He talked about himself too:

"I would only have to put on a general's epaulettes for everyone to assume that I am a general and I understand something, but I'm no good for that at all, and the others are even worse. Yes, everything is for the best in this best of all possible worlds. So, shall I have the pleasure of meeting your dear brother-in-law in Vilnius? That's good. And your dear wife too, my dear friend, you are doing so well, although a good wife would be living with you. And that's even worse. Well then, goodbye. Or will you stay for a while?" he said as he stood up and went to get dressed. Pierre could not think of anything to say. He was almost in more pain than his friend. Pierre had not really been expecting Prince Andrei to take this business so much to heart, but seeing the way he had taken it did not surprise him.

"But I am to blame, for everything, for every single thing, and I must not leave it like this," he thought, remembering how easy he had thought the reconciliation would be, and how impossible it seemed now. "But I must do everything that I was going to do." He remembered the speech he had prepared in advance and went to deliver it to Prince Andrei, no matter how bad a moment it might be. As he entered Prince Andrei's room, Bolkonsky was sitting and reading some letter and a servant was packing his things on the floor. Bolkonsky looked at Pierre angrily. But Pierre determinedly began what he had intended to say.

"Do you remember our argument in St. Petersburg?" he said. "Do you remember about *La Nouvelle Héloïse*?"

"Yes, I remember," Prince Andrei replied hastily. "I said that a woman who falls should be forgiven, that was what I said, but I did not say that I can forgive. I cannot."

"Andrei," said Pierre.

Prince Andrei interrupted him:

"If you wish to be my friend, do not speak to me about . . . about all this. Well, goodbye. Is it ready?" he shouted at the servant.

"Not yet, sir."

"But I told you it had to be ready, you scoundrel. Get out. Goodbye, Pierre, forgive me." Then straight away he turned to Bezukhov, embraced him and kissed him farewell. "Forgive me, please forgive me . . ." And he showed Pierre out into the hallway.

Pierre did not see him again and he did not tell the Rostovs about his meeting.

That spring the Rostovs spoke constantly of leaving Moscow, but did not go because the sale of their house had not been settled. Pierre, also still living in Moscow, visited the Rostovs every day.

# III

"My brother sovereign!" Napoleon wrote in the spring of 1812 to the Emperor Alexander. "The Count de Norbonne has delivered Your Majesty's letter to me. I am happy to see that Your Majesty remembers Tilsit and Erfurt . . ."

"My brother sovereign!" Alexander wrote on the 12th of June, after Napoleon's army had crossed the Niemen. "I have been informed that, despite my frankness . . . If Your Majesty is not inclined to spill the blood of our subjects over such a misunderstanding . . . An agreement between us will be possible.

"Your Majesty still has an opportunity to spare mankind the calamity of a new war.

Alexander"

These were the last two letters, the last two expressions of the relations between these two individuals.

But clearly, although Napoleon appealed twice in his letter to the memories of Tilsit and Erfurt, and despite the implicit promise that he would remain as charming as he had been at Tilsit and Erfurt, despite this desire to penetrate through all the complicated international and diplomatic subtleties of relations to the very heart of things, to personally dear memories of friendship with Alexander (in the way a woman who was once loved says, to pacify the callous lover who has cooled towards her: "Do you remember that first moment of confession, do you remember that moment of self-abandonment – that night in the moonlight?") despite all of that, it is clear that what had to happen was going to happen, and Napoleon crossed the Russian border, that is, he was bound to cross it, as inevitably as an apple falls from the branch when it is ripe.

It is usually thought that the more power a man has, the greater his freedom. Historians, describing world events, say that such and such an event took place because it was willed by one man – Caesar, Napoleon, Bismarck and so on – although to say that a hundred thousand people were killed in Russia, that they killed each other because one or two men wanted it to happen, is as meaningless as saying that a hill weighing millions of *poods*, which has been undermined, collapsed because the last workman Ivan dug his shovel in under it. Napoleon did not bring Europe into Russia, it was the people of Europe who brought him with them and made him lead them. In order to be convinced of this, one has only to ponder the fact that they ascribe to this single man the power to force a hundred thousand men to kill each other and die. Clearly, there might be a zoological human law, similar to the zoological law of bees, that compels them to kill each other and forces one male to kill another, and even history confirms the existence of this law, but to say that one man ordered millions of others to kill each other is senseless – it is impossible to understand and it is not possible. This is why we do not say that Attila led his hordes, we already understand that there was a movement of peoples from the east to the west. But in modern history we do not yet wish to understand this. It still seems to us that the Prussians beat the Austrians because Bismarck is very clever and cunning, whereas in fact all of Bismarck's cleverness was only fitted to a historical event that inevitably had to happen.

This deception occurs for two reasons: firstly, because of the psychological habit of retrospectively fitting intellectual reasons to what takes place inevitably, just as we fit a dream we have been having to a fact that occurs at the moment of awakening; and secondly, in accordance with the law governing the coincidence of a countless number of causes in every spontaneous event, according to which every fly can justifiably regard itself as the centre of the universe and its needs as the goal of the universe; and according to which man thinks the fox tricks dogs with its tail, when the tail only functions as a balance for turning. Fatalism is as rational in history as it is irrational in the individual. It is no accident that Solomon's saying – the king's heart is in God's hand – became proverbial. The king is the slave of history, of the spontaneous event, and has less free will than other people. The greater the power, the greater the tie to other people, and the less free will there is. There are involuntarily actions that form part of the instinctive life of man, and there are voluntarily actions, no matter what the physiologists might say and how precisely they might study the nervous system.

One irrefutable argument against them is that at this moment I can choose to raise my hand or not to raise it. I can continue to write or I can stop. There is no doubt about this. But can I know what I will say when I am at sea, can I know what I will do in a war, in a clash with some other person, whoever it is, can I ever know, in an action where I myself am not the subject of my activity, can I know what I will do? No, I cannot. There I act according to the instinctive, involuntary laws of humanity. And the greater my power, the greater the ties to other people, the less freedom I have. In acting upon himself the scientist, the artist, the thinker is free, in acting upon other people the general, the king, the minister, the husband, the father is not free, he is subject to instinctive laws and as he submits to them, with the assistance of imagination and intellect, he unconsciously manufactures his idea of freedom and from the innumerable causes that coincide to produce any spontaneous event, he selects those which seem to him to confirm his freedom. This is where the misunderstanding lies. Despite the fact that now, more than ever, it seemed to the Emperor Napoleon that it depended on him whether or not the blood of his peoples would be spilt, he had never been more subject than he was now to the inevitable laws which forced him (while assuming that he was acting according to his own free will) to do what had to come about. He could not stop, he could not act otherwise. Countless complex historical causes were leading towards what had to take place, and he was their false front, he was like a horse in a mill wheel, while thinking that he was running forward for his own purposes, he was moving the mechanism attached to the horse's wheel. The immense armies gathered together at a single centre were gathered for instinctive, involuntary reasons. This force required action. The first pretext that naturally presented itself was Russia, and according to the law of the coincidence of causes, a thousand tiny reasons were found: reproaches for failure to observe the continental system, the Duke of Oldenburg, a moment of irritability and an outburst in which Napoleon said he knew not what to Kurakin, the Russian ambassador in Paris. Then the army moved into Prussia in order to support the threat. If the threat was not to be a joke, serious preparations had to be made. In making serious preparations, the person who was making them got carried away. When a large number of preparations had been made, a sense of false shame required that they should not be wasted – a need was felt to apply them in action. There were negotiations which, in the eyes of contemporaries, were undertaken with sincere intentions, and were intended to achieve peace, but which only wounded the pride of both sides and made conflicts inevitable. Neither Alexander's will, nor the will of Napoleon, still less the will of the peoples and, even less than that, the continental system, the Duke of Oldenburg or the intriguing of England were the cause, it was a countless number of circumstances coinciding with each other, any of which could have been called the cause, that led to what had to happen, to war and bloodshed, to what is repellent to humanity itself and therefore cannot occur simply because humanity wills it.

When the apple has ripened and it falls, why does it fall? Is it because it is drawn towards the earth, is it because the stalk dries out, is it because it is dried by the sun, because it grows heavy, because the wind shakes it, because the boy standing underneath it wants to eat it? Not one of these is the reason. They are all no more than the coincidence of those conditions under which one of life's organic, spontaneous events occurs. And the botanist who thinks that the apple falls because the cellular tissue . . . and so on, will be just as right and just as wrong as the boy standing underneath the apple who says that it fell because he wanted to eat it. Just as the person who says that Napoleon went to Moscow because he wanted to, and was destroyed because Alexander wanted him to be, will be both right and wrong.

In historical events, great people are the labels that give a name to an event, but just like labels, they have least of all to do with the actual event itself.

# IV

On the 11th of June at eleven o'clock in the morning, Colonel Pogovsky, stationed on the Niemen with his regiment of Uhlans, saw a carriage driving fast directly towards him, accompanied by the imperial retinue. The Emperor Napoleon was sitting in the carriage, in his Old Guards hat and uniform. He was talking with Berthier. Pogovsky had never set eyes on the Emperor before, but he recognised him immediately and gathered his whole command to greet him.

That morning Napoleon was in the same mood that he had been in on the memorable morning of the Battle of Austerlitz. He was in that fresh, clear morning mood in which everything that is difficult naturally becomes easy and in which, precisely because a person believes in himself, he can do everything, even more than he believes he can – he does not have a single moment of doubt, as if some external force that is independent of him is making him act. Napoleon had been in this mood since early morning, and it had been strengthened still further by a fifteen-*verst* ride with fast horses and soft springs along an excellent road running through countryside that was still wet from the night rain, fields of sprouting rye and the green foliage of the forests in all its June glory.

He had set out (or so he thought) in order to review places for crossing the Niemen. In his own mind he still had not settled the question of whether he would cross the Niemen now or wait there for Lauriston's reply but, in reality, he had gone because on that morning he was the agent of the inescapable will of Providence. It was a beautiful morning, he was in that Austerlitz morning mood, in which he absolutely had to do something, and he was amused by the thought that, despite his great majesty, despite his latest visit to Dresden, during which kings and emperors had made up the court awaiting his appearance, the appearance of the man who had flattered the royal house of Austria by marrying its princess, despite all this he, *himself*, was going to review the places for the crossing of the Niemen and give the necessary orders. After greeting the Polish Uhlans, he got out of his carriage, keeping his eyes fixed on the tight bend of the Niemen at that spot, and gestured to his officers to move closer. Sukhorzevsky was one of the first and Napoleon asked him questions about the roads to the Niemen and the locations of the advance outposts. Without listening to the end of what Sukhorzevsky was saying, Napoleon lowered the spy-glass through which he had been looking and said to Berthier that he intended to survey the Niemen himself. Berthier hastily asked the officers whether such reconnaissance involved any danger to the Emperor from Cossacks, and on being told that it did, he reported to the Emperor that his person and his hat were too well known to the whole world and it would be imprudent for him to expose himself to fire from the Cossacks. An awareness of his own short height had always annoyed Napoleon and the tallness of others disconcerted him. But this was a happy morning, as the morning is always happy for those who are in a happy mood. Either the officers happened to be short, or Napoleon only noticed the short ones, and he said with a smile that he would put on a Polish uniform.

Several officers of appropriate height hastened to remove their uniforms, including Sukhorzevsky himself. But before he could expose his shoulders, a stern glance from a member of Napoleon's retinue stopped him. Like Paris with his apple, Napoleon surveyed the officers who had undressed and, perhaps because Pogovsky was the most senior officer, or because Pogovsky's underwear was the cleanest revealed by the removal of the uniforms, the Emperor chose him and, after removing his grey tailcoat with the ribbon, which was immediately seized on as a relic, he put on Pogovsky's tailcoat and peaked cap. Behind him, Berthier also hastily dressed up as a Polish Uhlan and gave orders for the Emperor to be given the calmest horse, since Bonaparte was a timid and uncertain horseman. Accompanied by Berthier and Major Sukhorzevsky, Napoleon rode to the village of Aleksoten and from there to the Niemen, on which five years earlier the Treaty of Tilsit had been concluded, and beyond which in the distance he could see Russian Cossacks.

When he saw this Niemen, on which the peace of Tilsit had been concluded five years earlier and, more importantly, this Niemen on the other side of which there began a vast Scythian state like the one that Alexander the Great had entered, and beyond which there ruled this other Alexander, who had insolently demanded the withdrawal of French troops from Pomerania at a time when the whole of Europe was bowing down before him, the ruler of France, this Niemen beyond which there lay the Asiatic city of Moscow with its innumerable churches and Chinese pagodas, when he saw this Niemen and this beautiful sky, and the green fields stretching into the distance, after having put on Polish uniform and exposed himself to shots from the Russian advance outposts – he could not help but decide in his own mind that he would advance the next day. As they rode back to the village of Nogarishky, Sokhorzevsky, who was riding behind, heard the great man start to sing out of tune: "*Marlborough s'en va-t-en guerre . . .*", and he saw the brilliant, bright, cheerful look that took in everything impartially and indifferently and expressed the great man's happy, easy mood at that moment. Instructions were sent ahead to Nogarishky to move Central Headquarters there, and it was there that Napoleon dictated the disposition for the crossing of the Niemen and the advance. In addition, it was in Nogarishky that the Emperor Napoleon was first shown examples of the false Russian bank notes, of which a hundred million roubles' worth had been produced, compared them with real ones and approved them, and also signed the sentence to death by shooting of a Polish sergeant who had spoken insolently to a French general.

# V

The Russian Emperor and his court had already been living for about a month in Vilnius, where the Central Headquarters of the Russian army was located. After many balls and celebrations held by the Polish magnates, the courtiers and the sovereign himself, in June one of the Polish adjutants-general had the idea of holding a dinner and a ball for the sovereign, hosted by his adjutants-general. This idea was approved by everyone. The sovereign expressed his consent, the adjutants-general collected money by subscription and a female individual whom the sovereign was most likely to find pleasing was invited to be the hostess of the ball. Bennigsen offered his country house and the dinner, ball, boating and fireworks were planned for 11th of June. On the very same day when Napoleon gave the order to cross the Niemen and his advance forces pushed back the Cossacks and did cross the Niemen, the Russian sovereign spent the evening at Bennigsen's dacha, at the ball held by his adjutants-general.

In the evening of the following day there was a jolly and brilliant celebration at the Countess Lovich's. It was particularly merry and lively.

Among the Polish beauties, the Countess Bezukhova upheld the high reputation of Russian beauties and she was noticed. Boris Drubetskoy was also at this ball, having received an invitation through Hélène Bezukhova.

They were still dancing after eleven o'clock. The sovereign, strolling about in front of the dancers, delighted first some, then others with those amiable words that only he knew how to say. Boris who, like everyone else at the ball, was favoured with the imperial presence, felt drawn with all his heart to the sovereign and was with him in his heart, although he danced and conversed with the ladies. At the beginning of the mazurka, he saw Balashov go up to the sovereign, who was saying something to a Polish lady, and halt beside the sovereign in a manner not done at court. This meant something. The sovereign gave Balashov a quizzical glance but realised that he had only acted in this way because he had important reasons to do so, that he needed to speak with the sovereign. Bowing briefly to the lady to indicate that the audience was over, the sovereign turned to Balashov, took him by the arm and began to walk with him through the crowd, unaware that a path three *sazhens* wide cleared for him as people on both sides drew back. Boris looked at the coarse and basely devoted face of Arakcheev, who had noticed the sovereign conversing with Balashov and moved out of the crowd, but did not dare approach any closer. Boris, like most decent people, felt an instinctive dislike for Arakcheev, but the favour shown to this man by the Tsar made Boris doubt the correctness of his feelings. Balashov told the sovereign something with an extremely serious expression on his face. The sovereign drew himself erect rapidly, like a man who has been insulted and surprised, and continued listening in his amiable, calm manner. Boris, although he realised quite clearly that what was being said was very important, although he wanted desperately to find out what was the matter, realised that if Arakcheev did not dare move any closer, then he could not even think of it, and he also moved aside. Quite unexpectedly the sovereign and Balashov veered directly towards him (he was standing by the door that led out into the garden). Before he could move out of the way, he heard the sovereign, speaking with the agitation of a man who has been personally insulted, say the following words:

"I shall only make peace when not a single armed enemy remains on my land."

As he said these words, the sovereign noticed Boris and gave him a proud and determined look, and it seemed to Boris that the sovereign enjoyed saying those words – he was pleased with the form in which he had expressed his thoughts and was even pleased that the respectful Boris had heard him and been delighted.

"No one must know," the sovereign added (Boris realised that this was meant for him).

And the sovereign walked by.

The news that Balashov gave the sovereign at the ball was that, without any declaration of war, Napoleon and his entire army had crossed the Niemen only one day's march away from Vilnius. This unexpected news was all the more unexpected for coming after a month of fruitless waiting and being delivered at a ball. For a moment the sovereign was outraged and agitated by the news, and under the influence of that fleeting mood he had found the words that he liked so much, which completely expressed his feelings and later became a famous saying. When he returned home from the ball at two in the morning, the sovereign sent for his secretary Shishkov and told him to write to the military governor of St. Petersburg and the army, insisting that the letter absolutely had to include his words about not making peace while even one armed enemy remained on Russian land.

The following day the letter cited earlier was written, the one beginning with the words "My brother sovereign!", and Balashov was sent to Napoleon for a final attempt at reconciliation. The day after that, the news that Balashov had brought was known to everyone. The imperial quarters moved one station further back, to Sventsian, and the whole army fell back.

# VI

---

As he despatched Balashov, the sovereign repeated yet again his words about not making peace as long as a single armed enemy remained on Russian land and told him that he must repeat them to Napoleon, although the sovereign had not written them in the letter, probably because, with his innate tact, he felt it was rather awkward to repeat these words at the very moment when a final attempt at reconciliation was being made, which was why he told Balashov to say them, that is, he felt a personal need to express them.

Balashov set out at night and by morning he had arrived at the advance positions and been stopped by French cavalry sentries. The hussars in crimson uniforms would not let him through, impolitely failing to salute him as they should have done and speaking sullenly among themselves in his presence, and they sent him to an officer. It seemed extraordinarily strange to Balashov, who had long been accustomed to high honours in his work and close proximity to the ultimate seats of power and majesty – only three hours before he had been talking to the sovereign – that he should encounter this hostile and, above all, disrespectful, attitude towards himself here on Russian soil. But the thought naturally occurred to him that these people were worthless nonentities, that even though they appeared to be men like himself, with arms and legs, with memories and thoughts, and even though they were blocking his way by crude force – their relationship to him was the same as that of a mere grain of hulled wheat to one of the main grindstones of a mill. He did not even deign to look at them while waiting inside the cordon. He did not have to wait for long. The French Colonel of Hussars Julner rode out to him on a beautiful, well-fed grey horse with the same air of prosperity and neatness that the soldiers in the cordon possessed. This was the early stage of the campaign, when the troops were still neat and tidy, it was almost like sentry duty in peacetime, except that there was a hint of that cheerful excitement and adventure that always accompany the start of a campaign. The soldiers preen themselves and play the dandy, as if they do not know that all too soon they will have no time, not only for combing their horses' tails, but even their own hair, as if they do not know that soon there will no merriment, but instead there will be fear, suffering and death.

Colonel Julner was restrained, dignified and polite, evidently understanding the full significance of Balashov's message. He led Balashov past his soldiers and smiled pleasantly as he began conversing with him.

They had not gone even a hundred paces when the King of Naples appeared, riding towards them, that same Murat who had taken the bridge at Vienna single-handedly with such impertinent ease, and whom Napoleon had long ago made the King of Naples for his services. When Julner indicated the brilliant group with Murat riding at its head in a red cloak covered with gold and precious stones, and said that this was the King of Naples, Balashov inclined his head slightly as a sign of humility and respect, and rode to meet Murat, who was now a king, more majestic and impressive than he had been in 1805 on the Vienna bridge, where he and Belar had tricked the other half of Vienna with their cunning. This was the Murat who was now called the King of Naples, and everybody sincerely believed that he was. This was the Murat who, on the eve of the day he had left Naples to join his army at Napoleon's command, had strolled arm-in-arm with his wife and the members of his court through the streets of Naples; and when two Italian piemen leapt up from their seats and sought to amuse themselves after their boring day's work by shouting: "Long live the King!", Murat had said with a sad smile, which, like any king's smile, was immediately reflected on the faces of his courtiers:

"The poor fellows! I feel sorry for them ... They do not know that I am leaving them tomorrow."

Like an old horse that has put on a bit of weight but is still nonetheless ready to serve, he rode on his Arabian stallion, decorated with gold and precious stones, cheerful, radiant, enlivened by the old familiar business of war. He rode to meet Balashov, raised his hand to his gold-embroidered hat with the ostrich feather and greeted the Emperor Alexander's adjutant-general cheerfully. He rode up close and put his hand on the withers of Balashov's horse. His good-natured face with its moustache glowed with self- satisfaction as Balashov spoke to him, constantly honouring him with "Your Majesty, Your Majesty" – in every grammatical case – this repetition an inevitable affectation on the part of one for whom the title was still a novelty.

Perhaps Murat took a liking to Balashov's face, or he was in a good mood and inclined to be cheerful because of the beautiful morning and after his ride, but in any case he dismounted from his horse, took Balashov by the arm and entered into a tone of conversation that was not at all kingly or hostile, the tone of good-hearted, cheerful servants of quarrelling masters, servants who will remain good friends, whatever the relations between their principals might be.

"Well then, general, it looks as though things are leading to war?" asked Murat.

Balashov admitted that this was indeed the case, but he observed that His Majesty Alexander did not desire war and that his message served to prove that.

"Then you do not think that the Emperor Alexander is the instigator of the war?" Murat asked with a good-natured smile through his moustache.

After talking a little about the reasons for war, Murat said something that he had probably not wanted to say, but he said it because of his cheerful mood:

"I wish with all my heart that the Emperors would put an end to this matter between them and that a war, started against my will, would end as soon as possible.

"I will not detain you further. I am glad to have made your acquaintance, general," Murat added, and Balashov bowed and took his leave of His Majesty and rode on assuming, as Murat had told him, that he would very soon meet Napoleon himself.

But instead of soon meeting Napoleon, Balashov was detained once again, this time by the sentries of Davout's infantry corps, and the commander's adjutant who was summoned took him to Marshal Davout himself.

# VII

The gloomy soldier Davout was the complete opposite of Murat.

He was the Emperor Napoleon's Arakcheev – an Arakcheev who was not a coward, but no less punctilious and cruel, and incapable of expressing his devotion in any way other than through cruelty. Such people are necessary in the mechanism of the body of the state, just as wolves are necessary in the organism of nature, and they are always there, they always appear and they stay, no matter how incongruous their presence and their closeness to the head of the government might seem. If it were not for this organic necessity, how could the cruel, uneducated, uncourtly Arakcheev, who personally plucked out grenadiers' moustaches and whose nerves could not tolerate danger, have maintained a position of such power under someone with the chivalrous, noble and gentle character of Alexander? But it had to be so, and so it was.

Balashov found Marshal Davout in a shed, sitting on a barrel, engaged in clerical work (he was checking the accounts). It would have been possible to find better premises, but Marshal Davout was one of those characters who deliberately locate themselves in the grimmest of conditions in order to have the right to be grim themselves. For this same reason they are always stubbornly engaged in urgent work: "How can I give any thought or attention to the happy and loving, human side of life, when you can see for yourself that I'm sitting on a barrel in a dirty shed and working?" It gives these people the greatest pleasure and fulfils one of their most fundamental needs, whenever they encounter life lived with youthful, positive gusto, to fling their gloomy, stubborn activity in its face. Davout permitted himself this pleasure when Balashov was led in to see him.

He immersed himself even more deeply in his work when the Russian general entered and, glancing over his spectacles at the face that was cheerful and dignified owing to the lovely morning and the conversation with Murat, he scowled even more darkly and laughed.

"Here's another dandy with pleasantries," he thought. "I've no time now for pleasantries. I was against this war, but since the war has already begun, I have to work, not exchange pleasantries." Observing the unpleasant impression reflected in Balashov's face, Davout addressed him sternly and coldly with a rude question: what did he want? Assuming that he could only be given such a reception because Davout did not know he was the Emperor Alexander's adjutant-general and even his representative to Napoleon, Balashov hurriedly informed him of his rank and his mission.

Contrary to his expectations that this news would instantly transform Davout's tone and attitude to one of great respect, as usually happens with rude people, Davout became even sterner and ruder after what Balashov had told him.

"Where's your package?" he asked. "Give it to me, I'll send it to the Emperor."

Balashov said that he had personal instructions to hand the package to the Emperor himself.

"The orders of your Emperor are carried out in your army," Davout said rudely, "you must do as you are told." And as if to make the Russian general even more aware that he could not resist coercion, Davout stuck his head out of the shed and called the sentry.

Balashov took out the envelope that contained the sovereign's letter and put it on the table without looking at Davout (the table consisted of a door with the hinges torn out of the wall still protruding from it, set on two barrels).

Davout took the envelope and read the inscription.

"You have a perfect right to show me respect or not," said Balashov, "but permit me to remark that I have the honour to bear the title of His Majesty's adjutant-general . . . Where can I wait for a reply?"

Davout looked at him in silence. He was clearly wondering whether he had not really made a mistake by indulging too far his need to show that he was a worker and not a charmer.

"You will be provided with what is necessary," he said and put the envelope in his pocket as he walked out of the shed. A minute later an adjutant came in and showed Balashov to the room that had been prepared for him.

That day Balashov dined with the marshal, in the same hut, on the same crude door on barrels, and he spent another three days at Davout's headquarters, advancing with it in the direction of Vilnius, without seeing the marshal again, although his own adjutant – a French general – was always at his side.

# VIII

After Balashov had spent four days in solitude, boredom and the awareness of his own dependency and insignificance, which he felt especially keenly after the sphere of power which he had left so recently, a carriage was sent for him, and he was driven past the French troops who occupied the entire locality, to Vilnius, to the same gates from which he had ridden out four days before. And to the very same house, the finest in Vilnius, in which he had received his final instructions from the Emperor Alexander. Four days earlier there had been sentries from the Preobrazhensky Regiment in front of this house, now there were two French grenadiers with their blue uniform jackets open, wearing shaggy caps. In front of the porch there was a bustling crowd of generals and local officials, several of whom recognised Balashov and turned away from him. Also standing by the porch were the French Emperor's horse, his pages, the Mameluke Rustan and a brilliant retinue of adjutants. They were probably waiting for Napoleon himself to come out.

In the first room Berthier greeted Balashov politely, then left him and went through to Napoleon. Five minutes later he came out and announced that the Emperor would be glad to receive him now.

Napoleon was waiting for Balashov with the excitement he always felt when the business in hand concerned relations with aristocrats of royal blood, of whom he regarded Alexander as the most brilliant of all, in both his physical and mental qualities. He knew that every word he said and every movement he made, the entire impression, would be related to Alexander. He had chosen the time most advantageous to himself, the morning, and, in his opinion, his most majestic costume: an open uniform jacket with the ribbon of the Legion of Honour over a white piqué waistcoat and the thigh-boots that he used for riding. The composition of the brilliant retinue at the entrance had also been deliberately calculated. Napoleon had decided to receive Balashov as if he were about to go riding, and he received him in his study. He stood by the window of the room, leaning on a little table with his small white hand toying with a snuffbox. He inclined his head slightly in reply to Balashov's bow.

"I shall be calm and majestic. The proper expression of an awareness of strength is calmness," Napoleon was thinking at that moment. "I shall leave him to say everything and that will show him my power. I shall show him how insolent it was to demand the withdrawal of my forces from Pomerania and that they have been punished for this insolence by my forces entering their territory." For a number of reasons, at the moment when the demand to clear Pomerania had been received, Napoleon had found it especially insulting: it had reached him when he was in a bad mood, and an hour earlier he had been telling Berthier that Russia would now propose terms for peace, and the memory of this now threatened to reawaken his feeling of insult. But he immediately told himself: "That will not happen. Now, since I occupy the city of Vilnius, from which this adjutant-general was sent, I must demonstrate my strength to him through calmness alone."

"Well, you see me, do not be embarrassed, gather yourself, calm down and tell me what you wish to say," his glance said.

"Your Majesty! The Emperor, My Sovereign . . ." Balashov began, a little embarrassed, but speaking with his characteristic ease and elegance. He told Napoleon everything he had been instructed to say. He told him that the Emperor Alexander was surprised by the entry of French soldiers into Russian territory, that it was not Alexander who was starting a war and that he did not desire one, but Prince Kurakin had demanded his passports without the Emperor Alexander's knowledge, that there were no relations between Russia and England and that the Emperor Alexander desired peace, but would only accept it on the condition that Napoleon's forces withdrew beyond the Niemen. He said on the condition *that French forces withdrew beyond the Niemen*, but he did not say the phrase which the Emperor Alexander obviously liked so very much, which he had written in a letter, which he had ordered to be included in a decree to the army, and which he had ordered Balashov to repeat to Napoleon. Balashov remembered about those words – "while even a single armed enemy remains on Russian land" – but that inexplicable, complex feeling called tact, held him back; he could not utter those words, looking the man in the eye, even though he wanted to do so. The sense of personal insult was too clear in those words, and it was probably instinct, that is, not the intellect alone, but the totality of all the faculties, that forbade Balashov to say them. Napoleon listened to everything calmly, but these final words stung him, even though they had been softened. They stung him all the more because he heard in them the memory of the earlier demand to leave Pomerania, "the demand that led to my entering Russia," he thought.

"I desire peace no less than the Emperor Alexander," he began. "For eighteen months I have been doing everything to achieve it. For eighteen months I have been waiting for an explanation." But he had begun to speak and already, independently of his will, the words drove each other on, and the memory of the demand to leave Pomerania, which had ended with his entry into Russia, came bursting out of him and was immediately expressed in words.

"But in order to begin negotiations, what is required from me?"

"The withdrawal of your forces beyond the Niemen."

Napoleon pretended not to have heard that and continued:

"But in order for there to be negotiations, you must not have any connections with England."

Balashov expressed the Emperor Alexander's assurance that there were no connections with England.

Napoleon drew out a repetition of the demand to withdraw beyond the Niemen, and only beyond the Niemen. He needed this demand. It was both insulting and reassuring to him. Instead of the demand of four months earlier to withdraw from Pomerania, now they were demanding that he withdraw beyond the Niemen and meanwhile their alliance and his enmity with England would continue.

"Yes, that is how I understand it," thought Napoleon, and he was about to say that the current demand to withdraw behind the Niemen would soon be followed by a demand for him to withdraw from Moscow. "But no, I will not say anything excessive, I will not break for his sake (that is, for Alexander, via Balashov) this impression of calm awareness of strength." But he had already begun to speak, and the more he spoke, the less he was able to control his speech. All the insulting memories of the demand to withdraw from Pomerania, of the refusal to acknowledge him as Emperor in 1805 and 1806, of the refusal to grant him the hand of a grand duchess – all these memories were revived within him as he spoke, and together with and opposed to each memory of these humiliations, there rose up in his imagination the memory of the price paid for his humiliation, the triumphant celebrations such as those at Tilsit and Erfurt and his recent visit to Dresden. "They're all just people, worthless people," he thought and carried on speaking, rejoicing in the offensive logicality of his words, which to him seemed undeniable. He had abandoned his pose long ago, sometimes folding his arms across his chest, sometimes holding his hands beside his back.

"Suggestions such as withdrawal from the Oder and Wislau can be made to the Prince of Baden, not to me. Even if you were to give me St. Petersburg and Moscow" (the Asiatic city of Moscow that was there, in Scythia!) "I would not accept these terms. And who joined his army first? The Emperor Alexander, not I. Even though he has nothing to do in the army. I am a different case, I am doing my job. And what a

wonderful reign his reign could have been," he said, as if he were expressing regret that a boy had misbehaved and did not deserve a sweet. "I
gave him Finland, I would have given him Moldavia and Wallachia.
They say you have concluded a peace?"

Balashov confirmed this news, but Napoleon would not let him say
any more, and especially not something that he found unpleasant (and
this was very unpleasant). He wanted to speak himself, on his own, to
prove that he was right, that he was good, that he was great, and he
carried on speaking with the intemperate eloquence of the irritability to
which spoilt people are inclined in general and the eloquent intemper-
ance and irritability with which he had spoken to the English ambassador in 1803 and recently to Prince Kurakin.

"Yes," he continued, "I promised and I gave him Moldavia and Wallachia, and now he will not have these beautiful provinces. He could
have annexed them to his empire and in a single reign he would have
expanded Russia from the Gulf of Bothnia to the mouth of the Danube.
Catherine the Great could not have done that," said Napoleon, growing
more and more heated, walking around the room and repeating almost
exactly the same words to Balashov as he had spoken to Alexander
himself in Tilsit. "For all of this he was obliged to my friendship . . . Oh
what a wonderful reign, what a wonderful reign the reign of the Emperor
Alexander *could have been*!" He looked at Balashov regretfully, and as
soon as Balashov tried to make some comment, he hastily interrupted
him again. At that moment Napoleon was bitterly resentful in his
inability to understand how Alexander could have departed from the
programme sketched out for him by Napoleon, which was so brilliant
(or at least it seemed so to Napoleon).

"What could he have desired and sought that I would not have found
in my friendship? But no, he felt it better to surround himself with others
– and with whom?" Napoleon continued, interrupting Balashov. "He
summoned the Steins, Armfeldts, Wintzengerodes, Bennigsens. Stein,
who was driven out of his own homeland," Napoleon repeated spitefully, and the colour rushed to his pale face.

The memory of Stein was particularly insulting to him because he
had been mistaken about Stein in the beginning, regarding him as a
worthless individual, but recommending him to the King of Prussia:
"Take Stein, he is a clever man" – and later, when he learned of Stein's
hatred for France, he had signed a decree in Madrid, confiscating all of
Stein's estates and demanding his extradition. But for Napoleon the most
humiliating memory connected with the name of Stein was of how he
had ordered Stein's innocent sister to be arrested and brought to Paris
for trial. Napoleon could not forgive any of this, and so he continued,

growing even more irritated and even less in control of his own tongue.

"Armfeldt is a libertine and an intriguer. Wintzengerode is a fugitive French subject, Bennigsen is a bit more of a soldier than the others, but he is still an incompetent who was unable to do anything in 1807 and who must have aroused terrible memories in the Emperor Alexander . . . Let us assume, if they were competent, they could be used," Napoleon continued, his words barely able to keep pace with the ideas that constantly arose to demonstrate to him that he was right, "but even that is not so, they are no good, either for war or for peace. They say Barclay is more efficient than the rest of them, but I would not say so, judging from his first movements. And what are they doing? What are they doing?" said Napoleon, growing even more agitated at the thought that the Emperor Alexander had allowed into his most intimate sphere, the sphere that Napoleon had valued so highly, individuals whom Napoleon despised more than anything else in the world and would have hanged immediately if they had fallen into his hands.

"Pfuhl makes proposals, Armfeldt argues, Bennigsen reviews the situation and Barclay, who is supposed to act, does not know what to decide, and time passes without anything being done. Bagration is the only soldier among them, he is stupid, but he has experience, a good eye and he is decisive . . . and what role does your young sovereign play in this outrageous crowd? They compromise him and lay the responsibility for everything that happens on his shoulders."

He fell silent for a moment and started striding about with an air of majesty.

"The sovereign should only be with the army if he is a general!" he said, obviously appealing directly to the Russian sovereign with these words of magnanimous advice. Napoleon knew how desperately the Emperor Alexander wanted to be a general.

"It is a week since the campaign began and you have failed to defend Vilnius, you have been cut in two and driven out of the Polish provinces. Your army is discontent . . ."

"On the contrary, Your Majesty," said Balashov, barely able to remember everything that had been said to him and following this firework display of words with difficulty, "the army is burning with desire . . ."

"I know everything," Napoleon interrupted him. "I know everything and I know the number of your battalions as well as I know my own. You have less than two hundred thousand troops, and I have three times that number, I give you my word of honour," said Napoleon, forgetting that his word could not possibly have any meaning. "I give you my word of honour that I have five hundred and thirty thousand men on this side of the Visla. The Turks are no help to you, they are good for nothing

697

and have proved that by making peace with you. The Swedes are fated to be ruled by insane kings. Their King was insane and they replaced him with another who immediately went insane" (Napoleon laughed at his own joke), "because only a madman can conclude a treaty with Russia."

Balashov had objections that he wished to raise to everything that Napoleon said and he kept making the gestures of a man who wishes to speak, but Napoleon kept interrupting him.

For instance, concerning the insanity of the Swedes, Balashov had wished to say that Sweden was an island, but Russia was behind it, but he was no longer trying to say this, because he could tell, not just with his reason or intellect, but with his entire being, that Napoleon was now in that state that everyone falls into when their nerves are agitated, and was feeling the need that results from that state to talk and talk and talk, simply in order to prove that he was right. On the one hand, Balashov was glad to see this state of agitation; he saw that Napoleon was behaving badly by telling him everything as he had done. (He could see this most clearly of all from the resigned indifference on the face of Berthier, who evidently did not approve of Napoleon's words.) On the other hand, Balashov was afraid of harming the dignity of the Emperor who had sent him and he was prepared at any moment to respond.

"What do your allies mean to me? *My* allies are the Poles. There are eighty thousand of them and they fight like lions. And there will be two hundred thousand." ("Where will those two hundred thousand come from?" Berthier wondered and sighed sadly.)

"They also wrote a protest about the Duke of Oldenburg," thought Napoleon and, recalling this past insult, he continued:

"If you sway Prussia against me, know that I shall wipe it off the map of Europe," he said, growing more and more heated, with an energetic gesture of his little hand. "Yes, I shall throw you back beyond the Dvina and the Dnepr, and restore the barrier against you that Europe was criminally blind to allow to be destroyed. Yes, that is what will happen to you, that is what you have won by distancing yourselves from me," Napoleon concluded, after having begun talking to Balashov with the firm intention of discovering the Emperor Alexander's views on the state of the war and achieving a genuine peace.

He halted facing Balashov and, feeling the need somehow to conclude his odd speech, which at its end had reached the intensity of Italian rapture, he repeated with taunting regret: "What a wonderful reign your sovereign might have had, *might* have had . . ."

In response to the arguments put forward by Balashov, who tried to prove that on Russia's side things did not appear as gloomy as they seemed to Napoleon, that the generals and their allies expected the very best from the war, Napoleon tossed his head condescendingly, as if to say: "I know it is your duty to say that, but you yourself do not even believe it . . ."

"Assure the Emperor Alexander in my name," he interrupted, evidently not even hearing what Balashov was saying, "that I am as devoted to him as formerly, I know him perfectly and greatly appreciate his exalted qualities.

"What the devil made him turn in that direction?" he then asked, returning to his regret that Alexander had ruined his career, but making it obvious that he was really only thinking about himself.

"My God, My God, what a wonderful reign your sovereign *might have had* . . . I will not detain you any further, general, you will receive my letter to the Emperor," and Napoleon strode off resolutely in his thigh-boots, preceded by his pages, to mount his horse and go for his ride.

Balashov presumed that they had said goodbye, but shortly after three he was invited to the Emperor's table. At this dinner Bessier, Caulaincourt and Berthier were present, and Balashov was more on his guard, trying to respond to every one of Napoleon's questions with a long, subtle diplomatic riposte that would rebuff Napoleon's haughty tone. And he did manage to produce two such diplomatic ripostes – one was his reply to Napoleon's question about Moscow, in which he asked about the city with all the amiable curiosity of a traveller who intended to visit it in the near future.

"How many inhabitants, how many houses, what are these houses like? How many churches?" Napoleon asked. And when he was told that there were more than two hundred churches, he remarked that the large number of churches and monasteries he had seen in Poland was a sign of the backwardness of the people. Balashov was delighted to have found a point to insert his diplomatic riposte and he politely permitted himself not to agree with the French Emperor's opinion and remarked that there were two countries in Europe where civilisation could not wipe out the religious spirit of the people. "These countries are Russia and Spain," said Balashov, tossing his bouquet and making his point. But, much as this diplomatic bouquet was appreciated – according to Balashov – among Napoleon's enemies, it was not appreciated at the dinner table and it passed without remark. It was clear from the blank and uncomprehending expressions on the faces of the marshals that they had failed to appreciate the wit or take the point at which Balashov's intonation had hinted. "If there was a point, then we did not understand it, or it was not witty in the least," said the expressions on the faces of the marshals. The other riposte, which also went unappreciated, was Balashov's reply to Napoleon's questions about the roads in Moscow, in which he said that, just as all roads led to Rome, so all roads led to Moscow and that from his various possible routes, Charles the XII had chosen the road to *Poltava*. But this was also not considered witty, since Caulaincourt had already gone on to talk about the difficulty of the road from St. Petersburg to Moscow and his memories of that time.

After dinner they moved on to drink coffee in Napoleon's study, which for four days had been the Emperor Alexander's study. Napoleon sat there, toying with his Sèvres coffee cup and indicated that Balashov should take the chair next to him. There is a certain after-dinner mood that is stronger than any rational impulse and makes a man feel contented with himself and regard everyone as his friends. Napoleon was in this mood. He felt that he was surrounded by people who adored him. He even felt that after dinner Balashov must be his friend and admirer.

This is not an error. It is simply unnatural for a man who has sat at dinner with another, to think him of him as his enemy. Forgetting who Balashov was, Napoleon turned to him with a pleasant, friendly smile and said:

"I've been told that this is the room in which the Emperor Alexander lived. Strange."

Balashov replied briefly in the affirmative, with his head lowered sadly.

"Four days ago Wintzengerode and Stein were deliberating in this room," said Napoleon, suddenly irascible again because he felt insulted by the tone of Balashov's reply. "One thing I cannot bear," he said, "is that the Emperor Alexander has made my personal enemies his close advisers. Have you not thought that I could do the same? Yes. I'll drive all his relatives out of Germany – the nobility of Württemberg, Baden, Weimar, yes, I'll drive them out . . ." Napoleon began walking around again, just as he had that morning. "Let him prepare to give them sanctuary in Russia."

Balashov stood up and made it clear from his manner that he wished to take his leave. Napoleon paid no attention to him and continued:

"And why has he assumed command of the army, what is the point of that? War is my trade, but his job is to rule and not to command armies. Why has he taken such a great responsibility upon himself?"

He fell silent, walked round the room several times in silence and suddenly went up to Balashov and smiled gently as he raised his hand with rapid, simple confidence, as if he were not only doing something important but also conferring some boon, and touched Balashov gently on the ear. In the French Empire it was regarded as an honour to have your ear tweaked by the Emperor.

"Well, why do you not say anything, admirer and courtier of the Emperor Alexander? Are the horses ready for the general?" he added and inclined his head slightly in response to Balashov's bow. "Give him mine, he has a long way to go."

The letter that Balashov brought was the last one from Napoleon that Alexander ever read. All the details of the conversation were reported to the Russian Emperor and the war began.

## IX

After his meeting with Pierre in Moscow, Prince Andrei went to St. Petersburg, hoping to meet Prince Kuragin there. He felt he had to meet him. But in St. Petersburg he learned that Kuragin had departed for the Moldavian army on the instructions of the minister of war. During his stay in Petersburg, Prince Andrei also learned that Kutuzov, the Kutuzov who had always been well-disposed towards him, had been appointed to the Moldavian army as an assistant to Field-Marshal Prozorovsky. Prince Andrei submitted an application to serve with Field-Marshal Prozorovsky in the Moldavian army and, after being appointed to the General Headquarters, he left for Turkey.

After Prince Andrei had spent about a year in the army in Turkey, early in 1812, when Kutuzov had already been living in Bucharest for two months with his Wallachian lover without once leaving the city while he conducted peace negotiations, rumours reached Prince Andrei of an impending war with the French and he requested a transfer back to the Russian army. With Kutuzov's patronage, he was attached to the headquarters of the minister of war, Barclay de Tolly.

Kuragin had gone back to Russia shortly after Prince Andrei arrived in Turkey, and Prince Andrei had not managed to meet him. Prince Andrei regarded it as inappropriate to write to Kuragin to challenge him. Until he could provide another reason for the duel, Prince Andrei considered that a challenge from him would compromise Natalya Rostova, and he therefore waited for a meeting in person, at which he intended to find a different pretext for a duel.

Even though more than a year had passed since his return from abroad, Prince Andrei's resolution had not changed, just as his general mood had not changed. No matter how much time might pass, if he met him, he would have to issue a challenge, just as a hungry man cannot help throwing himself on food. And no matter how much time might pass, he could not see anything in life except a combination of vices, injustices and stupidities, which could only interest him because of the disdain that they provoked in him. His physical wound was completely healed, but his emotional wound was still raw. It was not his fiancée's infidelity that had disenchanted him with life, his fiancée's infidelity had simply been the last of his disappointments. His only pleasure in life now was a proud disdain for everything and everyone, and he liked to demonstrate this disdain most often to those who could not understand it, whom he disdained just as much as all the others. He had become a witty, but idle and spiteful, gossip, as men who are unmarried and idle often are. His son did not require his support and active love – he had the *instituteur* Monsieur Laborde, who had been brought from Switzerland, and his aunt, Princess Marya. And then what could this boy become, even in the very best of educational circumstances? Either one more deceiver or one more dupe, like all men living and acting in this world, or an unhappy man who saw the stupidity of this world all too clearly and despised everything in it, like his father. That was how Prince Andrei thought about him. In Turkey he had occasionally received letters from his sister, his father, Laborde and little Nikolushka, who could already write on lined paper. It was clear that Princess Marya loved Nikolushka passionately, and that Laborde adored Princess Marya, while his father was still the same as ever.

Before travelling to the army, which was encamped by the Drissa river in May, Prince Andrei called in to Bleak Hills, which, being only three *versts* off the Smolensk high road, lay close to his route. There had been so many changes in Prince Andrei's life during the previous three years, he had thought so much, felt so much, seen so much (having travelled widely in the west and the east) that he was strangely and unexpectedly surprised when the Bleak Hills that he drove into was still exactly the same, down to the tiniest details, and the order of life there was still the same. He drove through the stone pillars of the gates, and along the avenue of the Bleak Hills house as if he were entering a castle wrapt in enchanted slumber. The same staid manners, the same cleanliness, the same quietness were still there in the house, the same furniture, the same walls, the same stains and marks and the same timid faces, only a little bit older. Princess Marya had put on weight, but her eyes had dimmed and rarely lit up with their former bright radiance, and she seemed to have reconciled herself to her life. Bourienne had also grown plumper and prettier and more sure of herself, or so it seemed to Prince Andrei. Laborde was dressed in a tailcoat of Russian cut and he spoke to the servants in mangled Russian, but he was still the same intelligent but limited, educated, virtuous and pedantic educator. The only noticeable change in the old prince was that he was missing a tooth from the side of his mouth. Only little Nikolushka had grown, changed, become ruddy-cheeked and sprouted a head of dark, curly hair, and when he laughed and was happy, he unconsciously lifted the upper lip of his pretty little mouth in exactly the same way as the late little princess used to do. He was the only one who did not obey the law of immutability in this enchanted sleeping castle.

Prince Andrei had intended to stay for a week, but he only stayed three days. From the very first glance he noticed that, although externally everything had remained the same, the internal relations had changed. The members of the family were divided into two alien and hostile camps, which had only come together while he was there, changing their usual way of life for his benefit. The old prince, Mademoiselle Bourienne and the architect belonged to one camp, and Princess Marya, Laborde, Nikolushka and all the nannies and nurse-maids belonged to the other.

In the evening of the first day, when the valet Pyotr had put his master to bed and was standing there holding a candle, he told Prince Andrei that the prince did not usually go to the dining room for meals, he and Amélie Karlovna and the architect were usually served in the study, while the princess ate alone and never saw her father for weeks at a time.

In fact, ever since Prince Andrei's engagement the old prince had drawn Mademoiselle Bourienne closer to him, jokingly at first and then quite seriously. She read aloud to him, and he had become less and less able to tolerate his own daughter's presence. Everything about her irritated him and made him act unfairly, which he felt and became even more upset. It was precisely because he loved Princess Marya that he could not tolerate her. He wanted her to be perfect and he saw that he could not change her, but neither could he accept her as she was. Bourienne was merely a pleasant object to him, her soul and her qualities were no concern of his. If she flattered and pretended, that was also of no concern to him, so long as he enjoyed it. He loved his grandson, but he did not approve of his upbringing and therefore tried not to see him. His only occupation now, apart from reading, was building. As soon as he had finished building the conservatory, he started a huge summer house in the Greek style in the new garden, where he was having ponds dug and trees planted. It was only when he spoke about this future park with the summer house, which would not be ready for another fifty years, that the old man became as lively as he used to be. He did not speak much now about general political matters, and he did so not so much unwillingly as with restraint. Prince Andrei noticed several times that when he tried to rouse his father by talking about the Turkish War and the future campaign against Bonaparte, the old man would listen and ready himself to say something, but then he seemed to change his mind, as if he knew something that reduced all the interest of these matters to nothing and it was not worth his saying what he knew, because no one could understand it.

During Prince Andrei's visit to Bleak Hills all the members of the household dined together, but everybody felt awkward, and he felt that he was a guest for whom they were making an exception, that his presence was a hindrance to them. Because he could not help feeling this, Prince Andrei was taciturn at dinner, and the old prince, noticing his unnatural mood, also fell into a gloomy silence and went to his room. When Prince Andrei came to see him the following day, the old prince unexpectedly began talking to him about Princess Marya, condemning her for her superstition and her dislike of Mademoiselle Bourienne, who was genuinely devoted to him.

Naturally, Prince Andrei could not say anything to help him. But the old prince spoke so that his son could listen in silence. The old prince felt in the depths of his heart that he treated his daughter badly, that he tormented her as badly as it was possible to torment any living creature, but he could not help tormenting her, and so she ought to be tormented, and he was right to torment her, and there were reasons for it. And he found these reasons. He had a vague feeling that Prince Andrei did not approve of the way he was acting. Prince Andrei clearly did not understand, and so he had to explain to him, and he would have to listen. So the old prince began to explain. But in his present state of mind, Prince Andrei could not listen calmly. He also needed to fight, and argue, and make other people unhappy. "Why should I feel sorry for him?" thought Prince Andrei. "He is my father only so long as he is fair, 'Plato is my friend, but the truth is more dear.'"

"If you ask me," said Prince Andrei, not looking at his father (this was the first time in his life that he had censured his father), "I was not going to say anything, but if you ask me, then I would say: quite the contrary, I do not know any creature more gentle and kind than Princess Marya and I cannot understand why you keep her at a distance. If you ask me," Prince Andrei continued, growing irritated, because he was always on the point of irritation in recent times, and did not realise what he was saying, "then I can only say that I feel sorry for Princess Marya, in any case. She is such a very kind and innocent creature, she should be pitied and cherished, and so . . ." Prince Andrei was unable to finish what he was saying, because the old man first gaped wide-eyed at his son, then he began laughing in an unnatural, sardonic manner, and the laugh revealed the gap of the missing tooth, which Andrei was unable to get used to.

"So I ought to leave her free to torment me, and your son, with her nonsense . . ."

"Father, I cannot be the judge of everything, but you asked me to speak, and I said, and I always will say, that it is not so much you who are to blame, as that Frenchwoman."

"Ah! He has condemned her! Well, good, good. Very good," the old prince said in a quiet voice, then he suddenly jumped to his feet and, pointing to the door with a vigorous gesture, he shouted: "Out! Out! Never let me see you here again . . ."

Prince Andrei walked out with a sad smile. "All this is how things should be in this world," he thought.

When Princess Marya learned about Prince Andrei's quarrel with their father, she began to reproach him for it.

Prince Andrei wanted to leave immediately, but Princess Marya persuaded him to stay for one more day. During that day Prince Andrei saw his father again. He did not mention the quarrel, but the old prince spoke to him in an exceedingly formal manner and gave him a very generous amount of money with emphatic courtesy. The next day Andrei ordered his things to be packed and went to his son's rooms. The affectionate boy with his mother's curly hair sat on Prince Andrei's knees. The prince began to tell him a story about Blue Beard, but before he had finished he grew thoughtful and turned to Laborde.

"So you get on very well with the princess?" he asked him. "I'm very glad that you share the same views on his upbringing . . ."

"How could anyone not agree with the princess?" Laborde said, clasping his hands together rapturously. "The princess is a model of virtue, intelligence and self-sacrifice. If Nikolai does not grow up to be a fine person it will not be the fault of the people around him," he said with naïve self-praise.

Prince Andrei noted that, but, as in his previous conversations with Laborde, he also observed his genuine admiration of the princess.

"Come on, tell me the story," Andrei's son said.

Without answering him, the prince spoke to Laborde again.

"Well, and in the matter of religion, how well do you agree with her?" he asked. "After all, you are a champion of Protestantism."

"I see only one thing in the princess: the purest essence of Christianity without any attachment to forms, and in religion, as in everything else, she is perfection."

"And her wandering pilgrims and monks, have you seen them?" Prince Andrei asked with a smile.

"No, I have not seen them, but I have heard of them. The princess noticed that the prince did not like her to receive them, and she stopped."

In actual fact, in recent times the princess had become passionately attached to her plan to become a wandering pilgrim, but knew she could never put it into action until after her father's death. The thought that she might desire that death had so horrified her, she had given away her pilgrim clothes to Fedosiushka and abandoned her dream.

In the middle of Andrei's conversation with Laborde, Princess Marya came into the room with a frightened look.

"What? Are you leaving?" she said. When her brother said he was, she took him to her room to talk.

As soon as she began speaking about things, her lips began to tremble and tears welled up in her eyes. Prince Andrei realised that, contrary to her words, which said she was happy, these tears said that he had guessed correctly about how much she was suffering and she was grateful and loved him more than ever (if that were possible) for his intervention.

"Let us not talk of it any more, it will pass. I will try to calm him down." (She knew that this was impossible, that following the hostile parting, everything would fall on her.) "But there is something I wanted to tell you." She took hold of him by the elbow with a gracious feminine gesture of her gentle hand and moved him closer to her, and her eyes, which were still filled with tears, lit up as they looked straight into her brother's face, radiating love, pure love. She had already forgotten about herself. Just as in 1805 she had needed to hang the icon round Andrei's neck, now she needed to give him some advice, to soothe and console him in his grief. She knew about everything from Julie Drubetskaya's letters (Drubetskaya as she now was), but she had never spoken to her brother about it. "No man could ever fully understand and appreciate the delightful inner charm of this girl," Prince Andrei thought as he looked at her. "And she will die like this, crushed and persecuted by an old father who is turning senile."

"Andrei, there is one thing I want to ask you, to implore you to do. If you are in grief, do not think that people have created this grief of yours. People are His instruments." She looked just over the top of Prince Andrei's head in the same confident way that people look at a familiar portrait on the wall. No doubt she could see Him as she said this.

"Grief is sent by Him, and not by people. People are His instrument – they are not to blame. If it seems to you that someone is guilty towards you, forget it and forgive. For God's sake, Andrei, do not take revenge on anyone. We do not have the right to punish. We ourselves are punished."

The moment he saw that gaze of hers, Andrei understood everything, he realised that she knew everything, that she knew he wished to meet Kuragin, who was in the main army, and challenge him, and that was

706

what she was talking about. He wanted to believe her. He could feel how exalted her feelings were, how he wanted to move towards her . . . "Forgive what?" he asked himself. "The sensuous kisses of the woman whom I loved more than anything? Forgive whom? That . . . No, I cannot tear this out of my heart."

"If I were a woman, I would do it, Marie. It is a woman's virtue, but if a man is struck in the face, he must not forgive it, he cannot."

"Andrei . . ."

"No, my darling, no, my dear friend Masha, I have never loved you more than I do now. Let us not talk about this." He put his arms around her head, burst into tears and began to kiss her.

They heard the steps of Nikolai and his nanny. The brother and sister straightened up and stepped apart. Andrei sat Nikolasha on his knees.

"Come with me," said Prince Andrei.

"No, I won't come. I'm going to the garden tomorrow with aunty to collect cones, you know what cones are, and I'm going to make a house out of the cones, and everyone will go riding down the high road. You know, the high road . . .;"

Nikolasha had still not finished his story, which had no meaning except that it used his new words (Nikolasha was learning to talk properly), when Prince Andrei stood up, picked up Nikolasha and, with tears in his eyes again, pressed his lips against his pretty little face. Prince Andrei was ready to go and he sent to ask his father if he could come to say goodbye to him. The messenger returned with the news that the prince said they had already said goodbye and he wished Andrei a good journey. Princess Marya implored Andrei to wait one more day, saying she knew how unhappy their father would be if Andrei left without making peace with him, but Prince Andrei reassured her that he would probably come back from the army again soon and he would definitely write to their father, but the longer he stayed now, the more bitter the conflict would become.

"It will all pass, it will all pass," said Prince Andrei.

"Goodbye, goodbye. Remember that sorrows come from God and that people are never to blame," Princess Marya shouted as the carriage set off. And the last words he heard Princess Marya's tearful voice say were "the right to punish".

"This is how it should be," thought Prince Andrei. "She is a delightful creature and she is left behind to be devoured by a fine old man who is losing his mind. I know that what she says is right, but I will do the opposite. My little boy wants to catch a wolf, and I am going to the army. What for? That's how it has to be. And it doesn't matter, it does not matter."

# X

Prince Andrei reached army Central Headquarters on the 13th of July. Although he took little interest now in the general progress of the war, he knew that Napoleon had crossed the Niemen, taken Vilnius and cut the Russian army in two, but our forces had withdrawn to the fortified camp on the Drissa, and there had been a small amount of action during the withdrawal, solely for the purpose of saving the army and reuniting it. Reunification had not yet been achieved, and it was said to be a dubious prospect. Prince Andrei knew from rumours that the Emperor Alexander was commanding the armies himself, while it was Pfuhl who was running the campaign – this same Pfuhl who, with other learned Prussians, had drawn up the plan of the Prussian campaign at Jena and who enjoyed the sovereign's full confidence. The following were now with the army: the Chancellor Rumyantsev, the former Minister of War Arakcheev, the new Minister of War Barclay de Tolly, Bennigsen (without appointment), the Swedish General Armfeldt, the former Prussian Minister Stein, Paulucci (an acquaintance of Prince Andrei's from Turkey) and in general, a huge number of foreigners within a complex apparatus of headquarters positions. But no one had given a thought to the danger of an invasion of the Russian provinces.

Prince Andrei was appointed to serve on the staff of Barclay de Tolly, and Kuragin was supposed to be there, also on the same staff. Prince Andrei found Barclay de Tolly beside the Drissa. The forces had arranged themselves in the fortified camp according to a plan drawn up by Pfuhl. Since there was not a single large village or small town in the vicinity, the immense number of generals and courtiers had been quartered within a distance of ten *versts* in the best houses in the small hamlets, on both sides of the river. Barclay de Tolly was quartered four *versts* from the sovereign. He received Bolkonsky coolly and said in his German accent that he would inform the sovereign so that his appointment could be confirmed. Then Prince Andrei learned, although he did not ask, that Anatole Kuragin was with Bagration's army. He had been sent there and had remained. Prince Andrei was pleased by this news. He did not intend to go looking for Kuragin and he was in no hurry to carry out his decision, for he knew it would never change.

Here in the camp, despite his total indifference to life, he was drawn into the interests of the controlling centre of an immense war. Wherever he went during the four days before he was required anywhere, Prince

Andrei learned from conversations with headquarters staff that the confusion in the army command was so great that even Prince Andrei who, in his present mood, felt that every outrage was the way things ought to be, found it impossible to imagine. When the army was still at Vilnius, it had been split in two. The 1st army came under the command of Barclay de Tolly, the 2nd under the command of Bagration. The sovereign was with the 2nd army. The relevant decree had not stated that the sovereign would be in command, only that he would be with the army. Furthermore, the sovereign did not have any commander-in-chief's personal staff, but an imperial headquarters staff, which included the head of his imperial highness's headquarters, Prince Volkonsky, and his officials, generals and aides-de-camp, together with a large number of foreigners, but no military central staff. And thus they had to carry out Prince Volkonsky's orders in the knowledge that sometimes they came from the sovereign, and sometimes not. Then there were several people with the Tsar who did not hold formal posts: Arakcheev, a full general, Bennigsen, senior to everyone, and the Grand Duke. Although these individuals did not hold official posts, by virtue of their position they wielded influence, but a corps commander was often unsure of the capacity in which Bennigsen or the Grand Duke or the commander-in-chief asked him questions or gave him advice. These, however, were merely the superficial arrangements; the real significance of the sovereign's presence together with all these other individuals was perfectly obvious to those in the court (and in the presence of the sovereign, everybody becomes a courtier). It was as follows: the Tsar had not assumed the title of commander-in-chief, but was in control of both armies. Arakcheev was a faithful servant of the sovereign and guardian of interest and order, who might be required at any moment. Bennigsen, a local, i.e. Vilnian, landowner, was essentially a good general, useful for advice and a possible replacement for Barclay. The Grand Duke was here because he wished to be here. Minister Stein was here because he could offer useful advice and because he was an honest, intelligent man whom Alexander valued. Armfeldt was a bitter enemy of Napoleon and a general who was confident of himself, which always impressed Alexander. Paulucci was here because he was a bold and decisive speaker. The adjutants-general were here because wherever the sovereign was, they were always there too, and, finally and most importantly, Pfuhl was here because, having drawn up a plan of war against Napoleon and made Alexander believe in its suitability, he was running the entire war. With Pfuhl was Woltzogen, who expressed Pfuhl's ideas in a more accessible form than Pfuhl himself was able to do, but Pfuhl was an abrasive, academic theoretician, arrogant to the point of despising everything.

Since he had no personal interests of any kind, Prince Andrei was in an excellent position for observation, and in all the great diversity of ideas and voices within this vast, brilliant, proud and teeming realm, he distinguished several clearly defined factions and parties.

The first party was Pfuhl and his followers, the military theoreticians, who believed in a science of war, a science that has its immutable laws, the laws of movement, of outflanking, and so on, and who demanded a withdrawal into the heartland of the country, according to the precise laws prescribed by this unreal theory of war, and they saw nothing but barbarity, ignorance or malice in any departure from this theory. These people included Woltzogen, Armfeldt and others, primarily Germans.

As always happens, where there was one extreme, there were representatives of the opposite extreme. These were the people who, since Vilnius, had been demanding an advance into Poland and freedom from any forward planning. In addition to being proponents of bold action, the members of this second party were also representatives of a single nationality, and this led them to be even more one-sided in their arguments. They were Russians: Bagration, Ermolov and others. It was at this point that Ermolov's famous joke spread throughout the army, in which he claimed to have asked the sovereign for a special favour – to be promoted to be a German. These men, thinking of Suvorov and Rumyantsev, said that what was needed was not to think, not to stick pins into a map, but to do battle and to keep on fighting, not to allow the enemy into Russia and not to let the army lose heart.

The third party, to which the sovereign himself appeared to belong, consisted of members of the court who brokered deals between the first two factions. These men thought and said what people usually think and say when they have no firm convictions but wish to look as if they do, especially since they appeared to stand above both extremes, deliberating and reconciling their differences – they said there was no doubt that war, especially with a genius like Bonaparte (he had become Bonaparte again), required profound thinking and a profound knowledge of science (and in this matter Pfuhl was a genius); but at the same time there was no doubt that the theoreticians were one-sided, and therefore we should also listen to those who demand energetic action, and then we put it all together to produce . . . a fine mess, said their opponents, but they said: a fine result.

The fourth faction was the tendency that found its most eminent representative in the Grand Duke and heir to the throne, who could not forget his disappointment at Austerlitz, where he had ridden out in front of the Guards in helmet and cavalry jacket, as if he were on parade, expecting to crush the French in valiant style, and unexpectedly found himself in the front line, barely managing to withdraw in the general disarray. The opinions of these men possessed the quality of sincerity, but this was a shortcoming. They were afraid of Napoleon, they regarded him as strong and themselves as weak, and they openly said as much. They said: "Nothing but grief, shame and destruction will come of all of this. Look, we have abandoned Vilnius, we have abandoned Vitebsk, we will abandon the Drissa too." "All Germans are swine," the Grand Duke said succinctly and clearly. "The only sensible thing we can do now is to conclude a peace, and as soon as possible, before we are driven out of St. Petersburg." This point of view, which was widespread at senior levels in the army, also enjoyed support in St. Petersburg, and from the Chancellor Rumyantsev, who was in favour of peace for other reasons of state.

The fifth faction consisted of supporters of Barclay de Tolly, not so much as a man, but as the minister of war and commander-in-chief. They said: "Whatever else he might be" (they almost always began like that), "he is an honest, practical man, there is no one better. Give him a chief-of-staff and give him the authority, because the war cannot proceed successfully without unity of command. And if not Barclay," they said, "then not Bennigsen either, he has already demonstrated his incompetence in 1807, but give us somebody, and let them have authority, things can't go on like this."

The sixth faction, Bennigsen's supporters, said, on the contrary, that there was no one more practical and experienced than Bennigsen and whichever way you looked at things you always came back to him. Let them make mistakes now, the more mistakes they made the better: at least they would understand sooner that things could not go on like this. And what was needed was not some Barclay, but a man like Bennigsen, who had already shown what he could do, to whom even Napoleon had given his due, and whose authority people would willingly acknowledge.

The seventh faction were those people who are always found close to sovereigns, especially young ones, and the Emperor Alexander had an especially large number of them – individuals among the generals and aides-de-camp who were passionately devoted to the sovereign, not as an emperor, but as a man, who adored him, as Nikolai Rostov had adored him in 1805 and saw in him not only all the virtues, but every human quality. These individuals admired the sovereign's modesty, and yet they also regretted it and wished for only one thing – that their adored sovereign would abandon his needless mistrust of himself and openly declare that he was taking command of the army, set up his own general staff and, consulting as necessary with experienced theoreticians and practitioners, lead his forces himself, which fact alone would induce highest possible inspiration.

The eighth faction was the largest group, it included such a huge number of people that its ratio to all the others was 99 to 1, and it consisted of those who wanted neither peace nor war, neither offensive nor non-offensive tactics, nor a camp on the Drissa or anywhere else, nor Barclay, nor the sovereign, nor Pfuhl, nor Bennigsen, but who wanted only one thing, and the most important thing – the greatest possible advantages and satisfactions for themselves. In the murky waters teeming with intersecting, entangled intrigues at the sovereign's General Headquarters, it was possible to get ahead in ways that would have been unthinkable at other times. A man who wished to maintain his favourable position would agree with Pfuhl one day, and with his enemy the next, and the day after that he would claim that he had no opinion on a certain subject, simply in order to avoid responsibility. Another who wished to acquire some favour attracted the sovereign's attention with his prodigious argumentation, shouting loudly in a council meeting, and thumping himself on the chest and challenging those who disagreed with him to a duel, thereby demonstrating that he was prepared to sacrifice himself for the general good. A third simply requested, on the quiet, in the interval between two council meetings and in the absence of any enemies, a lump-sum gratuity for his faithful service. A fourth would repeatedly appear dejectedly before the Tsar, burdened down with work. A fifth achieved a goal he had long desired – dinner with the Tsar – at which he tried to prove, through more or less powerful arguments, that Pfuhl was right, or perhaps not right.

Most were fishing for roubles, decorations and ranks and in their fishing the only direction they followed was that set by the weathercock of the Tsar's favour, and no sooner did they notice that the weathercock had swung in a certain direction, than this entire population of drones began blowing in that direction, which made it all the harder for the sovereign to turn it in another direction. In this indeterminate situation, which threatened the army with serious danger and lent the general atmosphere an air of alarm, amid this whirlwind of intrigue, pride, conflicts, multiplicity of views and feelings, complicated by the different nationalities of all these various individuals, this eighth party of people, preoccupied with their own personal interests, contributed a substantial element of confusion and anxiety to the general cause. No matter what question was raised, this swarm of drones abandoned its trumpeting of the previous one and flew across to the new subject, drowning out all the sincere voices in the argument with its buzzing.

In addition to all these parties, just when Prince Andrei reached the army, another party, the ninth, was beginning to emerge. This was the party of old, reasonable men with experience of statecraft who were able, without siding with any particular faction, to look objectively at everything that was happening at headquarters and consider the means of escape from this indeterminacy, indecision, confusion and weakness. The men of this party thought and said that all these bad things resulted from the presence of the sovereign and his military court; that the shifting, conditional, fluid and precarious nature of relations that was apropriate at court had been transferred to the army, where it was harmful; that the sovereign should reign and not command the army; that the only way out of this situation was for the sovereign and his court to leave the army; that the very presence of the sovereign paralysed the fifty thousand soldiers needed to keep him secure, that even the very worst independent commander-in-chief would be better than the very best under the constraint of the sovereign's presence and authority.

# XI

While Prince Andrei was living on the Drissa with nothing to do, the State Secretary Shishkov, who was one of the chief members of this last party, wrote a letter to the sovereign that both Balashov and Arakcheev agreed to sign. In this letter, taking advantage of the permission granted them by the sovereign to discuss the general progress of the war, and under the pretext of the need for the sovereign to give the people of the capital inspiration for the war, they respectfully suggested that the sovereign should leave the army.

This letter had not yet been presented to the sovereign when Barclay told Bolkonsky, over dinner, that the sovereign had requested to see Prince Andrei in person to ask him about Turkey, and that Prince Andrei should report to Bennigsen's quarters at six in the evening. That same day the sovereign's headquarters received news of a new movement by Napoleon which could pose a military danger. Meanwhile, that same morning, as Michaud was riding round the Drissa fortifications with the sovereign, he had tried to prove to him that this fortified camp, organised by Pfuhl and regarded as a tactical masterpiece designed to destroy Napoleon, was a piece of nonsense and would be the ruin of the Russian army.

Prince Andrei arrived at General Bennigsen's quarters in a former landowner's house right on the bank of the river. Neither Bennigsen nor the sovereign was there, but Chernyshev, the sovereign's aide-de-camp, received Bolkonsky, informing him that the sovereign had gone with General Bennigsen and the Marquis Paulucci to inspect the Drissa camp fortifications for the second time that day, since serious doubts had arisen concerning their suitability.

Chernyshev was sitting by the window of the first room with a French novel. In former times this room had probably been the hall, and it still contained an organ, on which some carpets or other had been piled up, and the folding bed of Bennigsen's adjutant in one corner. The adjutant was there too. Obviously exhausted by bingeing or working, he was slumped on the unfolded bed, dozing. Two doors led off from the hall: one straight ahead into the former drawing room, the other into the study on the right. Behind the first door there were voices talking in German with an occasional burst of French. At the sovereign's request, several people had gathered in the old drawing room because he wished to hear their opinion concerning the impending difficulties. This was not a council of war, but something like a council of the select few for the clarifying of certain matters for the sovereign himself. It included the Swedish General Armfeldt, the aide-de-camp Woltzogen, Wintzengerode, Michaud, Toll, Count Stein – who was not a military man at all – and, finally, Pfuhl himself, who, as Andrei could hear, was the mainspring of the entire business. Prince Andrei had the opportunity to take a good look at him, since he arrived shortly after the prince and walked through to the drawing room, halting for a moment on his way to have a word with Chernyshev.

At first glance Prince Andrei thought that Pfuhl, in his poorly made Russian general's uniform that sat on him rather badly, as if he were in fancy dress, looked somehow familiar, although he had never seen him before. The prince could see in him Weierother, and Mack, and Schmidt, and many other German generals and theoreticians whom he had seen in 1805. Pfuhl was the most typical of them all. Prince Andrei had never encountered another who combined so clearly the general features of all of them.

Pfuhl was short in height, but broad-shouldered, with a crude, strong figure, but very thin, with a wide pelvis and bony shoulder-blades. His face was very wrinkled, with deep-set, bright, intelligent eyes. His hair at the front and on the temples had been hastily smoothed down with a brush, but at the back in stuck up in naïve clumps. He looked around anxiously and angrily as he came in, as if he were afraid of everything in this large room. He turned to Chernyshev, holding his sword with an awkward gesture, and asked in German where the sovereign was. He clearly wished to walk through this first room as quickly as possible, sit down in his place and get down to work. He nodded his head rapidly in response to what Chernyshev said, smiling sardonically as he heard that the sovereign was inspecting the fortifications. "There are those who should inspect the fortifications, and those who should only go with them," he seemed to be saying, "since I laid them out." He said something abrupt in a deep bass voice, in the way self-confident Germans speak, and muttered to himself: "The stupid fathead" or "Damn this whole business", or "Something outrageous will come of this . . ." or "Where on earth will this end?" – Prince Andrei could not make it out. Chernyshev introduced Prince Andrei to Pfuhl, remarking that Prince Andrei had come from Turkey, where the war had ended so well. Pfuhl threw a brief glance not so much at Prince Andrei as through him, and said with a smile: "That was bound to be the right thing – it was a tactical war," and with a sneering laugh, he went on to the room from which the voices could be heard.

Evidently Pfuhl, who was constantly on the edge of sarcastic ill-temper, was especially irritated on that particular day by the fact that they had dared to inspect his camp and discuss it without him. From this one brief encounter Prince Andrei was able, after his experience at Austerlitz, to compose his own clear character portrait of Pfuhl.

Pfuhl was one of those Germans who are eternal, hopeless martyrs to their own self-confidence, he was the kind of man only a German can be, precisely because only Germans build their self-confidence on the basis of an abstract idea – on theoretical or real science. A Frenchman is self-confident because he thinks he possesses irresistible charm of both intellect and body for men as well as women, and that makes him amusing. An Englishman bases his self-confidence on being a subject of the best organised state in the world and as an Englishman, he always knows what he should do, and therefore knows beyond all doubt that everything he does as an Englishman is good. An Italian is self-confident because he is excited and easily forgets his own dignity and that of others. A Russian is self-confident precisely because he knows nothing and does not wish to know anything. A German's self-confidence is worse than all the rest and stronger than all the rest because he knows the truth, a science that he himself has invented, but which to him is the absolute truth. Pfuhl was evidently such a man, he had his science – the theory of oblique movement, which he had derived from the wars of Frederick the Great, and everything that he encountered in modern history which did not fit with this theory, he regarded as barbaric nonsense. In 1806 he had been one of the people who drew up the plan that ended in Jena and Austerlitz: but he had not learned a single lesson from the outcome of that war; on the contrary, minor deviations from his theory had apparently been the cause of the entire debacle, and he had said with his typically gleeful sarcasm: "Did I not say the whole thing would end in hell?" Pfuhl was one of those theoreticians who are so in love with their theory, they forget that its object is to be applied in practice: his love of theory made him hate all practice and he wished to know nothing about it. He was even glad of failure, because to him failure, resulting from the inevitable departure from theory in practice, proved to him that the theory was correct.

He said a few words to Prince Andrei with the expression of a man who knows in advance that everything will turn out badly and is not actually displeased by this. The uncombed tufts of hair sticking up on the back of his head and his hastily brushed temples confirmed this with especial eloquence.

He walked through into the room like a martyr going to his execution, and the prince heard the deep, querulous sounds of his voice from behind the door.

Prince Andrei had only just watched Pfuhl go out when Bennigsen entered the room and walked straight through into the study without stopping, giving instructions to his adjutant on his way. The sovereign was travelling behind him, and Bennigsen had hurried ahead to make preparations to receive him. Chernyshev and Prince Andrei went out on to the porch. The sovereign was already dismounting from his horse, looking tired but resolute. The Marquis Paulucci was saying something to the sovereign. The sovereign did not notice Prince Andrei and listened with his head inclined to one side as Paulucci spoke with distinct passion. The sovereign said something and moved away, evidently wishing to end the conversation, but the flushed, agitated Italian followed him, ignoring the proprieties and continuing to speak:

"As for the question of who counselled the Drissa camp . . ." Paulucci was saying, as the sovereign, walking up the steps, noticed Prince Andrei and nodded to him, and then frowned at what the Italian was saying.

"And, *sire*," Paulucci continued desperately, as if he could not stop, "as for the matter of who counselled the camp on the Drissa – I see no other option for him but the madhouse or the gallows."

The sovereign had stopped listening and did not appear to hear what the Italian was saying. He addressed Bolkonsky graciously:

"I am very glad to see you, go through to where the others are already gathered and wait for me." The sovereign walked through into the study. Prince Volkonsky and Count Stein followed him in, and the door closed behind them. With the sovereign's permission, Prince Andrei and Paulucci, whom he knew from Turkey, went into the drawing room where the council was gathered.

Prince Volkonsky came in to them from the sovereign, bringing maps which he then fixed to the wall, and recited to the assembled gentlemen the questions on which the sovereign wished to hear their opinion. During the night news had been received (news which later proved to be false) that the French were on the move to bypass the Drissa camp. The sovereign wished them to discuss this subject calmly in his absence, and he would join them later.

The discussion began. General Armfeldt began first, unexpectedly proposing a completely new position beyond the roads leading to St. Petersburg and Moscow, for no other reason than to show that he too could have an opinion. This was one of millions of suggestions that could have been made, each with as much justification as the others, with no idea what kind of war would ensue. It was disputed and defended with great thoroughness. Then Toll, a young colonel, read his note, which also proposed a new plan with extreme thoroughness. Then Paulucci proposed a plan of attack and began arguing very loudly and angrily about it with Prince Volkonsky. He argued so fiercely that it was almost like a duel. Throughout all these arguments Pfuhl and his interpreter Woltzogen (his bridge in relations with the court) said nothing. Pfuhl merely snorted derisively and turned away to show that he would not even stoop so low as to object to the nonsense that he was hearing at that moment. But when Prince Volkonsky asked him to express his opinion, all he said was:

"Why bother asking me, gentlemen. General Armfeldt has proposed an excellent position with an open rear, or there's the attack of this Italian gentleman, very good! Or a retreat. Very good! What's the point of asking me?" he said. "You all know better than me anyway."

However, when Volkonsky frowned and said he was requesting his opinion in the name of the sovereign, Pfuhl stood up and began speaking with sudden inspiration:

"You have spoiled everything and confused everything, you all thought you knew better than me, and now you have come to me. How to put things right? There is no point in making adjustments. You need to carry out everything precisely according to the principles that I have expounded. Where is the difficulty? It's just nonsense, childish games." He walked over to the map and began talking quickly, poking at the map with his skinny finger and trying to demonstrate that no unforeseen eventuality could require revision of the Drissa camp, that everything had been provided for and if the enemy really did try to bypass it, then he would be destroyed.

Paulucci, who knew no German, began questioning him in French. Woltzogen came to the assistance of his principal and began translating, barely able to keep up as Pfuhl, with his naïve temples and tufts of hair, rapidly tried to demonstrate that everything, every single thing, not just what had happened, but also what might have happened, everything had been foreseen, and it was only the failure to carry everything out precisely that was to blame. Laughing sardonically throughout his demonstration, he finally abandoned it with contempt, in the way a mathematician gives up checking the correctness of a result by different methods after it has already been proved by one. Woltzogen took his place, continuing the exposition in French and occasionally interjecting: "Is that not so, your excellency?" Pfuhl, like a man who strikes at his own side in the heat of battle, shouted angrily at Woltzogen:

"Yes, yes, what's the point of any more talk?"

Paulucci and Michaud both attacked Woltzogen in French and Armfeldt fell upon Pfuhl in German. Toll explained everything to Prince Volkonsky in Russian. Prince Andrei listened and watched without saying a word.

Of all these individuals, the one who provoked the greatest sympathy in Prince Andrei was the furious, determined and foolishly self-confident Pfuhl. From the tone in which he addressed the courtiers, from what Paulucci had taken the liberty of saying to the Emperor but, most importantly, from a certain desperation in Pfuhl's own expression, it was clear that his downfall was near. And despite his self-confidence and querulous German irony, he was pitiful, with his hair brushed at the temples and sticking up on the back of his head. Of all those present, he alone wanted nothing for himself, harboured no enmity for anyone and desired only one thing – to put into action a plan derived from a theory that he had spent years developing – and his one and only chance was slipping away from him. He was absurd, his sarcastic attitude made him disagreeable, but at the same time he inspired an involuntary respect with his absolute dedication to an idea, and he was pitiful.

In addition to this, everyone who spoke, apart from Pfuhl, shared a single common feature, which had been absent from the council of war in 1805 – and this was panic-stricken fear of the genius of Napoleon, which they tried to conceal, but which was expressed in every objection. They assumed that for Napoleon anything was possible, they expected him from every direction and they used his fearsome name to demolish each other's surmises. Only Pfuhl seemed to regard him as just one more barbarian like all the others.

Prince Andrei listened and watched in silence. He enjoyed being present at this multilingual muddle of incoherent talk, and even shouting, just a few paces away from the Emperor, who sat in a room that he himself could enter at will. This was all the way things ought to be, it suited his morose mood and, like Pfuhl, who was rejoicing in something

718

that was bad, he even felt glad that everything was a real mess. The thoughts that had come to him at various times during his military service that there was not, and could not be, any science of war, and therefore any so-called military genius, had now acquired the evident nature of manifest truth.

"How could there be a theory and science in an activity, the circumstances of which are unknown and cannot be determined, in which the strength of the participants in a war is even more difficult to determine. No one could or can know what the situation of our army or the enemy's will be in one day's time, and no one can know the strength of one division or another. Sometimes, when the man at the front is not a coward who shouts: 'We're cut off!' and runs away, but is a cheerful and courageous fellow, then a division of five thousand men is worth thirty thousand, as it was at Schöngraben, and sometimes fifty thousand men will run from eight thousand, as they did at Austerlitz. How can there be any science in a matter in which, as in any practical business, nothing can be determined in advance and everything depends on countless conditions, the meaning of which is determined at any one moment, a moment whose timing is known to no one? Armfeldt says our army is cut off. But Paulucci says we have trapped the French army between two lines of fire; Michaud says the fatal feature of the Drissa camp is that it has the river behind it. Toll proposes one position, Armfeldt proposes another: all are good, and all are bad, but the advantages of any one position only become evident at the moment the event takes place.

"And why does everyone say: a military genius? Is a man a genius because he gives the order to ship in the rusks in good time and tells this man to go right and that man to go left? It's only because men of war have an aura of brilliance and power and crowds of scoundrels flatter power, lending it a quality of genius that it does not possess. In fact, on the contrary, the best generals that I have known are stupid or vague. The best is Bagration, as Napoleon himself has acknowledged. He has a stupid, smug face. I remember Napoleon's face at Austerlitz. A good general does not need genius or special qualities of any kind, on the contrary, what he requires is the absence of the very finest, highest human qualities – love, poetry, tenderness, philosophical, enquiring doubt. He has to be limited and firmly believe that what he does is very important, otherwise he will not have the patience for it. Only then will he be a good general. God forbid that he should be a man who falls in love with anyone, feels sorry for anyone, or starts thinking about what is just and what is not. The theory of genius was clearly invented to describe such people in olden times, because they possessed power."

This was what Prince Andrei was thinking as he listened to the talk, and he only came to himself when Paulucci was summoned to the sovereign and everybody left.

At the review the next day, the sovereign asked Prince Andrei where he wished to serve, and Prince Andrei damned his prospects in the world of the court for ever by not asking to remain near the person of the sovereign and instead requesting a regiment. Two days after the council, Bolkonsky left headquarters and the sovereign left the army.

# XII

Before the start of the campaign, when the regiment was already on the march and they were expecting the sovereign to join the army, Rostov received a letter from his parents, imploring him to resign and come home. They wrote briefly about the break-up between Natasha and Andrei, explaining simply that Natasha had refused him. Nikolai knew nothing of what had happened. He did not even try to request leave, but wrote back to his parents saying things there might yet be put right, but if he were to depart now from this great war that was brewing, then he would be dishonoured for ever in his own eyes, and that could never be put right. To Sonya he wrote separately: "Adored friend of my heart. This year of separation will be the last. Wait patiently and believe in my eternal, unchanging love. After this war I shall abandon everything and take you, if you still love me, and we will hide ourselves away in quiet solitude, living only for love and each other. This is my last letter. The next time, we shall meet, and I shall press you to my ardent breast as my bride." The old hint of romanticism was still there in Nikolai's tone (although not in his character), but he wrote what he genuinely believed.

He was very content in the regiment, even more content than before, but he could already see that he could not live his entire life this way. The autumn and winter at Otradnoe, with its hunting and Yuletide festivities, had opened up the alluring prospect of a quiet country life with all its peaceful pleasures. "A wonderful wife, children, a good pack of hounds, ten or twelve grand leashes, and I'd manage the estate and give elected service," he thought. "But that is all afterwards. For now, I am quite content here and cannot leave – we have a campaign."

Shortly after Nikolai's return from leave and the joyful welcome by his comrades, he was sent to acquire horses for remounting and returned from Little Russia with an excellent set of steeds. In his absence he had been promoted to captain and was soon given a squadron.

He was now more absorbed in regimental life than before, although he knew that sooner or later he would have to abandon it. But now the campaign was beginning, the regiment was moving to Poland, they were being given double pay, there were new officers arriving, and new men and horses, and, most importantly of all, that mood of cheery excitement that always accompanies the beginning of a new war had spread right through the regiment and Nikolai, aware of his advantageous position within the regiment, devoted himself entirely to the pleasures and interests of military service.

The army was retreating from the very border, and not once until the 12th of July was the Pavlograd Regiment involved in any action, but the constant retreating did not make the hussars feel even slightly despondent. On the contrary, this long march, at the very best time of the summer, with adequate provisions, became an occasion of continuous jollity. They could lose heart, feel anxious and intrigue at Central Headquarters, but out in the army they did not even wonder where they were going and why, they had heard vague talk about the camp on the Drissa but they only regretted the retreat because they had to move out of familiar, comfortable quarters or leave a pretty Polish girl behind. If the notion that things were going badly should occur to anyone, then he would try all the harder, as a good soldier should, to stay cheerful and not dwell on the general course of events.

On the 12th of July, the night before action, there was a strong storm. (That summer was generally remarkable for its storms.) Two squadrons of the Pavlograd Regiment were bivouacked behind the village occupied by the command, in the middle of a field of ripe yellow rye that had been totally flattened. The rain poured down in torrents, and Rostov and three officers, all soaked to the skin, were huddling under a hastily improvised shelter of branches. One officer with long moustaches that stretched out over his cheeks and who liked to lean right into the face of whoever he was talking to, was telling Rostov the news about the battle at Saltanov that he had heard at headquarters.

Rostov shrugged his shoulders as water ran down his back and puffed on his pipe while half listening, occasionally smiling at the young officer Ilin, who was huddled up beside him and pulling faces. This sixteen-year-old officer had only joined the regiment recently, and now he was to Nikolai what Nikolai had been to Denisov seven years earlier. Ilin tried to imitate Rostov in every way and was in love with him, like a woman.

The officer with the long moustache, Zdrzhinsky, was telling them that the dam at Saltanov was Thermopylae, that what General Raevsky had done on that dam was worthy of antiquity. In his Polish accent and with Polish fervour, Zdrzhinsky told them about Raevsky's brave feat in leading his two sons out on to the dam under fearsome fire and going into the attack with them beside him. Rostov listened to the story without saying a word to support Zdrzhinsky's rapture, on the contrary, he had the air of a man who is discomfited by what he is hearing, although he will not object. After the Austerlitz and Prussian campaigns, Rostov was a genuinely experienced soldier. He knew from his own life that when men tell stories of what happens in war, they always lie, just as he himself had lied, and he was also sufficiently experienced to realise that in war everything happens quite differently from the way we think or talk about it, so he did not care for the story that Zdrzhinsky was telling. "Firstly, everything must have been so crowded and confused on the dam they were attacking that even if Raevsky did take his sons out on to it, it couldn't have made any difference to anybody, apart from the ten men who happened to be right there beside them. The others could not even have seen it. But even those who did see it could not have been really inspired, because what would they care for Raevsky's tender parental feelings when they were concerned with saving their own lives? And then the fate of the fatherland did not depend on whether the Saltanov dam was taken or not, in the way that Thermopylae is described, so what was the point of making such a sacrifice? And then why involve your children in war. I wouldn't bring Petya, my brother, I'd even try to protect this nice boy Ilin in some way or other," thought Nikolai. But he did not utter these thoughts aloud: knowing that the story glorified our army, he was obliged to pretend he did not doubt it. And that is what he did. "I can't take this any more," Ilin said with a smile. "My stockings and my shirt, and under my backside, everything's soaking. I'm going to look . . ."

Five minutes later Ilin ran back to the shelter, splashing through the mud.

"Hoorah! Rostov, come quick. I found something. Right here, just twenty paces away, a tavern, and it's excellent. And Marya Genrikhovna's there."

Marya Genrikhovna was the regimental doctor's wife, a pretty young German woman the doctor had married in Poland. Either because he had no money, or because he could not bear to be parted from his young wife so early in their marriage, the doctor took her with him everywhere the hussars regiment went, and the doctor's jealousy had become a regular subject for jokes among the officers.

Rostov was doubly pleased to be rid of the man who leaned into his face as he talked and to have a chance to get dry, and he set off with Ilin through the puddles of water in the pouring rain and the dark evening which was occasionally illuminated by flashes of lightning.

"Where are you going?" asked Zdrzhinsky.

"To the tavern." And Ilin and Rostov ran off, dashing through the puddles, chatting to each other as they went:

"Rostov, where are you?"

"Here. What lightning!"

The doctor's hooded cart was standing outside the tavern, and inside there were twelve officers from the two squadrons. Several were playing cards in one corner, but most were sitting around the pretty, flushed Marya Genrikhovna, who was wearing a dressing gown and night cap. Her husband, the doctor, was sleeping on the broad bench beside her. Rostov and Ilin were greeted by laughter as they entered the room – the water was streaming off them. Marya Genrikhovna lent them her skirt to use as a curtain, and Rostov and Ilin got changed and dried themselves behind it with the help of Lavrushka, who had brought their kitbags. They set a fire in the broken stove. They found a plank, set it across two saddles and covered it with a horse-blanket, and then got the doctor's little samovar, the provisions hamper and half a bottle of rum, and asked Marya Genrikhovna to play the hostess as they all crowded round her. Someone offered her a clean handkerchief to wipe her hands, someone put a hussar's jacket under her feet so she would not feel the damp, someone hung a cloak across the window that was letting in a draught, and someone wafted the flies off her husband's face so he would not wake up.

"Leave him alone," Marya Genrikhovna said with a happy smile. "He's sleeping very soundly after his sleepless night."

"That's not right, Marya Genrikhovna," one officer replied with a gloomy smile, "I have to get on the right side of the doctor. Anything might happen, and perhaps he'll take pity on me when he starts cutting off my leg or arm."

There were only three glasses and the samovar only held enough water for six glasses, but the tea looked strong because it was made with murky rain water, and it was all the more enjoyable to take turns by rank and receive your glass from the pretty white hands of Marya Genrikhovna. On that evening all the officers seemed to be genuinely in love with her. Even the officers who were playing cards in the other corner soon gave up their game and came across to the samovar, joining in the general mood and courting Marya Genrikhovna. They were all very jolly, and Marya Genrikhovna was glowing with happiness, even though she tried hard not to show it.

There was more sugar than anything else, but there was only one spoon, so they didn't have enough time to stir it in properly, and therefore it was decided, at the suggestion of Rostov, who was the ringleader in this courting of Marya Genrikhovna, that she would stir in the sugar for each of them. When Rostov received his glass and poured in some rum without any sugar, he asked Marya Genrikhovna to stir it.

"But you haven't got any sugar!" she said, smiling the whole time as if everything she or the others said was very funny and had a double meaning.

"I don't want sugar, I just want you to stir it with your pretty hand." Marya Genrikhovna consented and began looking for the spoon.

"Use your finger, Marya Genrikhovna," said Nikolai, "that will be even nicer."

"It's too hot," said Marya Genrikhovna, smiling even more happily. When he heard that, Ilin picked up a bucket of water, poured a few drops of rum into it and asked Marya Genrikhovna to stir it with her finger.

"This is my cup," he said.

After tea, Nikolai took the cards from the men who had been playing and suggested a game of King with Marya Genrikhovna. They drew lots to see who would play the game with Marya Genrikhovna. Rostov was allowed to play without drawing lots. The rules proposed by Rostov were that whoever was king had the right to kiss Marya Genrikhovna's hand, while the dirty rascal had to put the samovar on again for the doctor when he woke up.

"And what if Marya Genrikhovna's king?" Ilin asked.

"She's already a queen! And her word is law!"

Everyone was really enjoying themselves. But in the middle of the game, the doctor's tousled head appeared from behind Marya Genrikhovna's back. He had not been asleep for a long time, he had been listening to what they were saying and evidently found nothing cheering, funny or amusing in what they were saying and doing. His face looked sad and glum. He said hello to all the officers, scratched his head, excused himself to go outside for a moment and when he came back he told Marya Genrikhovna, who had stopped smiling so happily, that the rain had stopped and they ought to go and sleep in the cart, or everything would be stolen.

"I'll send an orderly . . . two," said Rostov.

"I'll stand guard myself," said Ilin.

"No, gentlemen, you've all had a night's sleep, but I haven't slept for two days," the doctor said and sat gloomily beside his wife, waiting for the game to end. The officers grew merrier still, and many were unable to restrain their laughter, hastily seeking a respectable pretext.

The sound of jolly, innocent, unforced laughter, without the help of wine, since there was nothing to drink that evening, continued into the night until three o'clock in the morning. Some of the men lay down, but did not sleep, and either made conversation and laughed as they recalled the doctor's fright and the jolly doctor's wife, or they frightened the cornet with cockroaches, or played at charades. A happy mood had descended on these young men. Several times Nikolai snuggled down and tried to fall asleep, but then some remark made by one of the others would amuse him, and the conversation would start up again, and they would laugh like children.

It was after two, and still nobody was asleep, when the sergeant-major arrived with an order to advance to the small town of Ostrovno. The officers began hastily preparing, still talking and laughing in the same way: they set the samovar to heat again with dirty water. But Rostov went back to his squadron without waiting for tea. It was already getting light: the rain had stopped and the clouds had parted. It was damp and cold, especially in clothes that had not yet dried out. As they came out of the tavern, Rostov and Ilin both glanced at the doctor's cart, still glinting wetly in the twilight. They saw the doctor's feet protruding from under the flap and his wife's night cap in the middle and heard someone whistling in their sleep.

"Well, are you in love?" Rostov asked Ilin as they stepped outside.

"Not in love, it's just interesting," Ilin answered.

Rostov left the tethering post to give some instructions and half an hour later an adjutant rode up and gave the order: "Mount up!" The soldiers crossed themselves, Rostov did likewise, and the two squadrons set off in a line, four men abreast, along the broad road lined with birch trees, following some infantry and a gun battery.

The ragged lilac-blue clouds were turning red in the dawn as the wind drove them quickly along across the sky. It was growing lighter and lighter. They could already clearly see the curly grass that always takes hold along country roads, still wet from yesterday's rain: the hanging branches of the birches, also wet, swayed in the wind. The faces of the surrounding soldiers became clearer and clearer. Nikolai rode with Ilin, who kept close to him, at the edge of the road, between the two rows of birch trees, and did not dwell even for a moment on the fact that he had a battle ahead, but simply rejoiced in the morning, the stride of his good horse and the grand martial spectacle of his squadron moving along beside him. On a campaign Nikolai allowed himself the liberty of riding a Cossack horse instead of a front-line horse. A lover and connoisseur of horses, he had recently obtained a fast Don steed, a large, good-natured liver-chestnut, on which no one had been able to outrace him. Riding this horse was a real pleasure for Nikolai. He thought about the horse, the morning, the doctor's wife and he did not give a thought to the danger. In the past he had spoiled things for himself with his anxiety, but now he was quite different. The cornet admired his casual, calm, elegant air and every movement he made, whether plucking leaves off the bushes of broom, or touching his horse's loins gently with his foot or handing the pipe he had finished smoking to the hussar riding behind, without even looking round. The sun had just begun to emerge from behind the clouds into the clear sky when the wind fell, as if it did not dare spoil this charming summer morning following the storm. Drops of moisture were falling, but everything went quiet and the birds began to sing, and Nikolai pointed to a snipe that was cackling somewhere high in the sky.

"If we make a halt here, I'll have to take a look at that bog," said Rostov. "What a wonderful morning this is!"

The sun came out, hung briefly on the horizon and disappeared. Although they could no longer see it, everything became bright and sparkling. And, as if in response to the light growing stronger, the sound of field-gun shots rang out ahead of them.

Before Nikolai had time to think and determine how far away the shots were, Count Osterman-Tolstoy's adjutant came galloping up with an order to proceed along the road at a trot. Rostov happily rode across to his squadron and gave the command. His Don steed, begging the reins, set off at a full trot at the head of the squadron. They overtook the infantry, encountered some wounded, rode downhill and through a village, and then rode uphill again. The horses began lathering up, the men became flushed.

"Halt, form up!" they heard the division commander order ahead of them and then they were led at a walk, left shoulder forward, along the line of the army, where the field guns were firing, releasing puffs of blue smoke, and out into a hollow on the left flank. Ahead of them they could see our front line, throwing up puffs of gun-smoke and gaily exchanging crackling gunfire with the invisible enemy.

. These sounds, which Nikolai had not heard for four years, made him as happy as the jolliest of music. "Crack-cra-crack!" two or three shots sounded together, then there was silence for a moment, and then they started up again, like the sound of chains flailing grain. Nikolai started looking round: standing on his right was a dense column of our infantry – that was the reserves – on his left, on a hill on the very horizon, in the clear air and the bright, slanting morning light, he could see our cannon with men creeping around them, half-obscured by smoke, and ahead of him our dense front line was exchanging fire with the enemy, who were moving closer and had come into sight.

Count Osterman rode past behind the squadron with his retinue, stopped to speak to the commander of the regiment and rode off towards the cannon on the hill. Rostov's squadron was in the second line. They still had the Uhlans ahead of them. After Osterman had spoken to the regimental commander the command rang out for the Uhlans to form up into a column to attack. And Nikolai noticed that the infantry ahead had doubled up its platoons to let the Uhlans through. The Uhlans set off with the flags on their lances fluttering, and after that the hussars were moved up on to the hill to provide cover for the battery. Nikolai was no longer in the fog that once used to prevent him from observing what was going on in front of him. On the contrary, he was following everything very closely. The Uhlans went to the left to attack the enemy's cavalry and just as the hussars were taking position, bullets flew at them from the front line, squealing and whistling but hitting nothing. This sound, which he had not heard for so long, made Nikolai feel even more happy and energetic than the earlier sounds of gunfire. He straightened up and surveyed the view of the battlefield from the hill. The Uhlans galloped close to the French dragoons, something got tangled up in the smoke and five minutes later the Uhlans and the dragoons went hurtling together towards the hollow where the hussars had just been positioned. The Uhlans were running. The dragoons mingled with them from in front and from behind, flourishing their sabres. Rostov galloped towards the colonel to request permission to attack. The colonel rode towards him.

"Andrei Sevastyanich, give the order . . ."

The colonel began saying that he had no instructions, but a bullet struck him in the leg and he gasped and clutched at the neck of his horse. Rostov turned his horse, moved to the front of the squadron at a trot and gave the command to advance, Rostov himself did not know how and why he did it. He did everything as he did when hunting, without thinking, without conscious deliberation. He saw that the dragoons were close, that they were galloping out of formation; he knew they could not withstand an attack, that he had only one moment and it would not come again if he missed it. The bullets were whining so excitingly, whistling all around him, his horse was pressing so passionately to go forward, and most important of all he knew that in one more moment, especially if there was another sight like that of the colonel screaming desperately and clutching at his leg, the fear that was already near would take over. He gave the command and started his horse, and instantly heard the sound of his squadron deploying behind him. Glancing round at them, he shouted: "At a gallop, forward," and gave his horse its head.

As he looked round, he glimpsed Ilin's frightened face and, without knowing why, he said to himself: "He'll be killed for sure." But he had no time to think, the dragoons were already close. Those at the front spotted the hussars and began turning back, those at the back slowed down. With the same feeling as when he was dashing to cut off a wolf, Rostov galloped to cut off the broken lines of the French dragoons. One Uhlan stopped, one man on foot dropped to the ground to avoid being crushed, one riderless horse got caught up with the hussars. As the dragoons began to turn round and gallop back, Nikolai chose for himself one man mounted on a grey horse who was probably an officer, and set off after him. On the way he ran into a bush; his good horse carried him through it and Nikolai barely managed to stay in the saddle, then just five paces away he saw his officer, who had just begun galloping back after his dragoons. A moment later Nikolai's horse rammed its chest into the hindquarters of the officer's horse and almost knocked it off its feet, and at that, without knowing why he was doing it, Nikolai grabbed the officer's shoulder-belt and knocked him off his horse, somehow at the same time leaning against him to stay on his own horse. The officer tumbled off his horse and got caught in a stirrup. He looked up at Rostov, screwing up his eyes in fear, as if expecting death at any second. His face was pale and his dusty hair was glued together by sweat. But he was young and fair-haired, with a dimple in the chin and bright-blue eyes – his face wasn't a face for the battlefield, it was a perfectly ordinary drawing-room face. Before Nikolai had even decided what he was going to do with him, probably drawing the word from old childhood memories, he shouted: "Surrender." The officer would have been glad to, but he could not untangle himself from the stirrup and reach his sabre, which was caught between the two horses, in order to hand it over. Some hussars galloped up and took the captured officer away and Rostov looked around at what was happening. On all sides there were hussars scuffling with dragoons, one was wounded, but even with his blood-streaked face he would not leave his horse, another was sitting on the crupper of a hussar's horse with his arms round him. A third was dismounting, supported by a hussar. Several dragoons had been captured, the others had galloped away.

Ahead of them the French infantry was running forward, firing. The hussars turned and set off back. It was only as he was riding back up the hill that Rostov remembered with horror that he had attacked the enemy without orders, and he was terrified to see Osterman riding towards him. "This is trouble," thought Rostov. "What the devil made me do it, I should have stayed put." But in addition to this fear, Rostov also had a different unpleasant feeling, something unclear and confused that had been revealed to him as he captured the officer, something he could not explain to himself. Count Osterman-Tolstoy not only congratulated

Rostov, but said he would report his daring act to the sovereign and request the George Cross for him, and bear him in mind as a brilliant and brave officer. Unexpected as this praise was, Rostov found it very pleasant. But there was still something bothering him. Where was Ilin?

"Where's the cornet?" he asked.

"Wounded," the hussar Topchinko replied.

"What a pity," Rostov thought. But that still wasn't it, there was something else bothering him, something that he simply could not explain to himself. He rode over and looked at the officer with the dimple in his chin and the blue eyes, had a word with him and noticed his feigned smile, and still there was something he could not understand. All that day and on the days that followed Rostov's friends and comrades noticed that, although he was not bored or angry, he was taciturn, thoughtful and distracted. He was reluctant to drink, tried to stay on his own and seemed constantly preoccupied with something.

Rostov kept thinking about this brilliant feat of arms which, to his great surprise, had made him very famous (for that was what happened) and earned him the George Cross, but he still could not understand anything. "So they're even more afraid of us," he thought. "I was afraid of them. What kind of nonsense is this, it's far more dangerous to be at the back than at the front. So that's all there is to what they call a feat of heroism for the faith, the Tsar and the fatherland. And did I really do it for the fatherland? And how is he to blame, that one with his dimples and blue eyes? He was so frightened! He thought I was going to kill him. But what would I want to kill him for? And why the George Cross, after that, who knows what kind of career I could make? No, I don't understand anything, not a single thing!"

But while Nikolai was wrestling with these questions in his mind, still unable to grasp clearly what it was that had upset him so much, the wheel of fortune, as often happens, turned in his favour, advancing his career. He was promoted and given a battalion of hussars, he was trusted with advance outposts, and there he became even more convinced that the closer you were to the enemy the safer it was and the more favourable to an army career. And Nikolai gradually entered into his role as a famous, brave hero and no longer discussed all the things that had bothered him at first. Forgetting even these doubts, he enjoyed the consolations of his gratifying new situation.

# XIII

More than a year had passed since Natasha had rejected Andrei and moved from a life of constant happiness and joy to one of dull despair that was mitigated, but not dispelled, by religion.

The Rostovs spent the summer of 1811 in the country. Otradnoe brought back painfully vivid memories of the time when Natasha had felt so carefree and happy there, so open to all the joys of life. But now she did not go out walking or riding, she did not even read, she just sat in silence for hours at a time on a bench in the garden, or on the balcony or in her room.

Ever since that terrible moment when she had written her letter to Prince Andrei and realised just how badly she had acted, she had avoided all the outward circumstances conducive to pleasure, she had not laughed once without the tears being evident behind her laughter, and she could not sing. As soon as she began to laugh or sing, tears choked her – tears of repentance, tears for the memory of that pure time, now gone for ever, tears of regret that she had destroyed her own young life for nothing, when it could have been so happy. Laughter and singing seemed like blasphemy against her past grief.

She did not even think of flirting with anyone. She never even had to restrain herself. She said – and it was absolutely true – that for her all men were like the jester Nastasya Ivanovna.

Some internal jailor strictly forbade her all joy. And she no longer felt within herself any of her old interests that belonged to that carefree, girlish life so full of hopes. She recalled so often (indeed, most of the time) those autumn months she had spent hunting with Nikolai, months when she was engaged to be married. She would have given anything to bring back just one of those days. But all that was gone for ever now. Her premonition at that time had not deceived her when it foretold that this state of freedom and openness to every joy would never return. But she had to go on living. And that was the most terrible thing of all. For a time her life was filled with religion, to which she had come through the humility and resignation that it preached, although she had been so remote from it in her former life.

In early July the rumours spreading in Moscow about the course of the war became ever more alarming: people spoke of an appeal to the people by the sovereign, of the sovereign himself leaving the army and coming to Moscow. And since the manifesto and the appeal had still not been received by the 11th of July, exaggerated rumours circulated about them and about Russia's situation. People said that the sovereign was leaving the army because it was in danger, they said Smolensk had been surrendered, that Napoleon had a million troops and only a miracle could save Russia.

The manifesto was received on Saturday the 11th of July, but it had still not been printed, and when he was at the Rostovs', Pierre promised to come to dinner the following day, Sunday, and bring the manifesto and the appeal, which he would obtain from Count Rostopchin. On that Sunday the Rostovs, as usual, went to mass in the Razumovsky family church. It was a hot July day. At ten o'clock, when the Rostovs climbed out of the carriage in front of the church, everything – the hot air, the cries of the hawkers, the bright, colourful clothes of the crowd, the dusty leaves of the trees on the boulevard, the rumble of the roadway, the sounds of music and the white trousers of the battalion that had come to mount guard, the brilliant sunshine – everything was redolent of that summer languor, that satisfaction and dissatisfaction with the present, that need to desire the impossible that is felt with especial keenness on a clear, hot day in the city. The entire nobility of Moscow was in the Razumovskys' church, all of the Rostovs' acquaintances (that year, as if they were expecting something to happen, many rich people who usually went to their country houses had remained in the city). As she walked with her mother behind the liveried servant who was parting the crowd, Natasha heard the whispering as people pointed her out to each other.

"That's Rostova – you know the one . . ."

"How beautiful she is!"

She heard, or she thought she heard, the names Kuragin and Bolkonsky mentioned. But then, she was always imagining this. It always seemed that when people looked at her, all they thought about was what had happened to her. Suffering agonies in her soul, as she always did in a crowd, in her lilac silk dress with the black lace, Natasha walked in that way that women have – the more pain and shame she felt in her heart, the more calmly and majestically she bore herself. She knew, and she was not wrong, that she was beautiful, but that brought her no joy as it once used to do. On the contrary, recently it had been more a cause of torment than anything else, and especially on this hot summer day in the city. "Another Sunday, another week," she told herself, remembering that she had been here last Sunday, and that this was the same life without living, in exactly the same conditions in which life had once been so easy. "I am pretty and young, and I know that I am not bad," she thought, "and the best years of my life are being wasted, utterly wasted." She stood in her usual place and exchanged a few words with people she knew standing nearby. As usual, Natasha looked at what the women were wearing and in her mind criticised their way of holding themselves and unseemly manner of crossing themselves with such small movements, but at the first sounds of the service, she recalled the sin of judging others and her own spiritual wickedness and, enveloped in old memories of tender feelings, she began to pray. Only rarely, even during the best moments of the last Lenten fast, had she ever felt such a state of tender devotion as she did on this day. All these familiar, incomprehensible sounds and even less comprehensible solemn gestures were exactly what she needed. She tried to understand and was happy when she understood a few words: "We pray to God for the world," or: "We shall dedicate ourselves and each other to Christ the Lord." She understood these words in her own fashion. "For the world" meant together with everyone, with the whole world – "I am not asking for myself, we are all asking Thee, O God." "We shall dedicate ourselves to God" she took to mean the rejection of all will and desires and an entreaty to God to guide our thoughts and desires. But when she listened and did not understand, she found it even sweeter to think that to wish to understand was pride, that she should not understand, she should only believe and surrender herself. She crossed herself and bowed discreetly, trying not to draw attention to herself, but the old countess, who kept glancing at her stern, intense, immobile face with its brightly sparkling eyes, sighed and turned away, sensing that something important was taking place in her daughter's soul, and regretting that she could do nothing to help with this inner turmoil, she prayed to God to help her poor, innocent, unhappy young daughter and bring her consolation. The choir sang beautifully.

The meek, gentle old man conducted the service with that meek solemnity that has such a majestic and calming effect on the souls of people at prayer. The Holy Doors were closed and the curtain was slowly drawn across; a mysterious, quiet voice said something from behind them. Tears that Natasha herself did not understand flooded her breast and the feeling of agonising joy choked her.

"Teach me what I should do, what I should make of my life," she thought.

The deacon came out on to the ambon and read about those who labour and are oppressed, about all people and once again read those comforting words that affected Natasha so powerfully: "We shall dedicate ourselves and our lives to Christ the Lord."

"Yes, take me, take me," said Natasha, with impatient yearning in her soul, no longer crossing herself, with her thin hands lowered in helpless devotion, as if she expected that at any moment some invisible power would take her and free her from herself, from all her regrets, desires, self-reproaches and hopes.

Suddenly in the middle of the service, departing from the order of service that Natasha knew so well, the sexton brought out a little bench, the one on which the genuflectory prayers were read on Trinity Sunday, and set it in front of the Holy Doors. The priest came out in his lilac velvet skull cap, brushed back his hair and went down on his knees. Everybody did the same, although they were rather surprised. It was a prayer that had just been received from the Synod, a prayer for the salvation of Russia from invasion by its enemy.

The priest read in a clear, modest, meek voice, the voice which only Slavonic church readers use and which has such an irresistible effect on the Russian heart.

Natasha repeated the words of the general prayer with all the strength of her soul, praying for the same thing as everyone, but, as often happens, even as she listened and prayed, she could not help thinking at the same time. When the priest read the words: "Create in us a pure heart and renew the true spirit within us; strengthen us all in our faith in Thee, confirm our hope, inspire us with true love for each other" – in a flash an idea came to her about what was needed to save her homeland. Just as in the matter of her father's debts the idea had occurred to her of putting everything right by the simple, clear means of living more moderately, she now imagined a clear, simple means for defeating the enemy. This consisted in everyone genuinely uniting with each other in love, casting aside self-interest, spite, ambition and envy and loving and helping each other, like brothers. Everyone simply had to be told: "We are in danger, let us cast aside all former things, let us give up all that we have – the pearl necklace (like in the story *Martha the Mayoress*), we won't begrudge anyone – let Petya go to the army, since he wants to – and we will all be humble and good, and no enemy will be able to harm us, but if we all wait for help, if we argue and quarrel like Shinshin and Bezukhov did yesterday, then we will be destroyed."

This seemed so clear, simple and undeniable to Natasha that she was amazed it had never occurred to anyone before, and she rejoiced in her soul at the thought that she would tell Pierre about this thought when he came. "Only Bezukhov won't understand. He's so strange. I can't understand him at all. He's better than anyone else, but he's strange."

# XIV

As promised, Pierre came to dinner straight from Count Rostopchin's house, where he had copied the manifesto and the appeal. The Rostopchins had told him the positive news that the sovereign would arrive in Moscow the next day. Pierre, who had grown even fatter over the last year, panted as he started up the steps. His coachman no longer asked if he should wait, he knew that when the count was at the Rostovs' house, he would be there until after eleven. The Rostovs' servants came rushing joyfully to take his cloak. Following his habit from the club, Pierre always left his hat and stick in the entrance hall. In the main hall he was met by a handsome, broad-shouldered, fifteen-year-old boy who looked like Nikolai. It was Petya. He was preparing to go to university, but recently he and his friend Obolenksy had secretly decided to join the hussars. Petya had come darting out to his namesake in order to discuss this business. He had asked him to find out if they would take him as a hussar.

"Well, Petrukhan," said Pierre, merrily displaying his bad teeth and tugging the boy's hand downwards. "Am I late?"

"Well, what about my business, Pyotr Kirillich? For God's sake. You're my only hope," said Petya, blushing.

"I'll tell you everything today. I'll arrange it," Pierre answered. As soon as Sonya saw Pierre, she sat beside him and said:

"Pierre, Natasha's in her room, I'll go and call her."

Pierre was a close family friend, but he was primarily the friend of one member of the family – Natasha – and everyone knew this.

"Well, my dear fellow, well, have you got the manifesto?" the count asked. "The countess was at mass in the Razumovskys' church, she heard a new prayer. It's very good, she says."

Pierre patted all his pockets and could not find the piece of paper, and carried on patting his pockets as he kissed the countess's hand.

"Honest to God, I don't know where I put it," he said.

"Oh, you're always losing everything," said the countess.

Sonya and Petya smiled as they looked at Pierre's perplexed face. Natasha came in, wearing the same lilac dress. Despite his concern over the piece of paper, Pierre immediately noticed that something special had happened to Natasha. He looked at her more intently.

"Honest to God, I'll go back for it . . . I've left it at home. Yes, I'll go."

"Oh, you're already late for dinner."

"Ah, and the coachman's gone."

Everybody started looking and they finally found the paper in Pierre's hat, where he had carefully slipped it inside the lining.

"Well is it all true?" Natasha asked him.

"Yes. This is a serious business . . . Here, let's read it."

"No, after dinner," said the old count, "afterwards."

But Natasha asked for the paper and went off, flushed and excited, to read it, saying she did not want any dinner.

Pierre gave his arm to the countess and they went into the hall.

At dinner Pierre told them the news from the city, about the withdrawal from the camp on the Drissa, about the illness of the old Princess Gruzinskaya, about Métivier's disappearance from Moscow and about how someone had brought a German to Rostopchin and said he was a *champignon* – Count Rostopchin himself had told Pierre about it – and Rostopchin had ordered them to let the *champignon* go, saying that he was just an old German mushroom.

"They take people, they take people," said the count, chewing on a pie. "I've even told the countess to speak less French. Now's not the time for it."

"That's right," said Pierre. "Prince Golitsyn has hired a teacher of Russian and he's studying Russian. It really is getting dangerous to speak French in the streets."

"Well, then, is the appeal really very well written?" the count asked, anticipating the pleasure of the reading after dinner. "Well, Natasha, is it?"

Natasha gave no answer from the drawing room.

"My dear Natasha is ecstatic about the prayer," said the countess.

"Well count, when they start setting up the home guard, even you'll have to get up on a horse," the old count said to Pierre.

Pierre laughed:

"What kind of soldier am I? I can't get up on a horse, and they're not allowed to sleep after dinner . . ." he said.

Natasha came into the dining room and flared up again. "I don't understand it," she said passionately. "Why do you joke about it? It's not a joke. I know you'll be the first to sacrifice everything, why do you joke? I simply can't understand you."

Pierre smiled and thought for a moment, then he looked at Natasha affectionately and intently and said:

"I don't understand it myself! I simply don't know, my tastes are so far removed from military matters, and I think it is so easy for man, as a rational being to, to manage without war . . ."

"No, please, don't joke like that," said Natasha, smiling affectionately at Pierre and sitting down at the table, although she did not want anything to eat.

"What a patriot . . . Eh?" said the old count. The countess merely shook her head.

After dinner coffee was served. The count settled calmly into an armchair and with a smile on his face he asked Sonya, who was famous for her skill in reading, to read: *"The enemy has entered Russia. He comes to ravage our dear fatherland."*

The count interrupted the reading several times and asked for something to be repeated. When they read the part about the titled nobility, the count said:

"I see, I see."

During the reading Natasha sat erect, looking searchingly straight at her father or at Pierre, seeking in their faces for some expression of the feeling that she had inside her.

"Yes of course, we'll give up everything, everything, and we'll all go," the count shouted at the end of the reading: "Of course, this is really frightening!"

Natasha unexpectedly jumped up, put her arms round her father and started kissing him. "How wonderful! What a delightful papa he is!" she said with her former vivacity. Natasha's rapture made the count even livelier. He put on his spectacles and read the appeal again, breaking off several times and breathing heavily through his nose, as if someone were holding a bottle of strong *sal volatile* under it.

No sooner had the count finished than Petya, who had already stood up and was waving his clenched fists about, walked up to his father, flushing bright red, and said in a voice that was sometimes gruff, sometimes squeaky, but nonetheless firm:

"Now, papa, I am telling you definitely, and mama too, say what you like – I am telling you definitely that you will allow me to serve in the army, because I cannot . . . well, that's all . . ."

The countess merely shrugged her shoulders in horror and said nothing, but the count, recovering from his agitation, immediately turned to Petya:

"Come, come," he said. "No more of this nonsense."

"It's not nonsense, papa. Fedya Obolensky is younger than me and he's going to, and anyway, the main point is, I can't study anything anyway, and now when . . ." Petya stopped and blushed so hard that he began to sweat, but he said it: ". . . when the fatherland is in danger."

"Enough, no more of this nonsense."

"No, I've told you. And Pyotr Kirillich will tell you, and Natasha will tell you."

"And I tell you that it's nonsense! My heart's already worn out worrying about one son, and now the child, with the milk still wet on his lips . . . Come now, I tell you." And the count walked towards the door, taking the papers with him, probably so that he could read them again before his rest.

"Pyotr Kirillich, let's go and have a smoke . . ." Bezukhov got up, shaking his head thoughtfully. Petya ran out after him, grabbed hold of his hand and whispered to him:

"Dear Pyotr Kirillich, you persuade him, for Christ's sake."

But Petya received a decisive refusal. He went to his room alone, locked everyone out and cried bitterly. Everybody pretended not to have noticed anything when he came for tea silent and gloomy, with tearful eyes.

After tea, as usual when Pierre stayed at the Rostovs' for the evening, he and Irina Yakovlevna played a hand of cards with the countess. Pierre went to the Rostovs to see Natasha, but he very rarely spent time with her or spoke to her alone. He only needed the calm joy that he felt because he was there and he could look at her and listen to her. She knew this and she was always wherever he was when he visited them. She herself felt most at ease in his company. He was the only one who reminded her of those dark times in a way that was not painful, but on the contrary, comforting.

After the game Pierre stayed at the table, tracing shapes on it. He had to leave. And always, precisely when he had to leave, Pierre felt how happy he was in this house. Natasha and Sonya came up to him at the table.

"What are you drawing?"

Pierre did not answer.

"Well now," he said to Natasha, "you are seriously concerned with the war. I am glad." Natasha blushed. She realised that Pierre was glad of her enthusiasm, because this enthusiasm would overshadow her grief. "No," said Pierre, answering her thought, "I like to observe the way women deal with men's matters, they make everything clear and simple."

"Why, what could possibly not be clear, count?" Natasha said in a lively voice. "When I was listening to the prayer today, everything became so obvious to me. We simply have to accept things and put others first and not begrudge anything, and then everything will be all right."

"But you begrudge Petya."

"No, I don't. I wouldn't send him for anything, but I wouldn't hold him back for anything either."

"It's a pity I'm not Petya, you don't mind sending me," said Pierre.

"You, of course not. And you'll go."

"Not for anything," Pierre replied and, seeing Natasha's kind, doubtful smile, he went on: "I can't think why you have such a good opinion of me," he said. "You think I can do everything well, that I know everything."

"Yes, yes, everything. And now the most important thing is the defence of the fatherland" – Natasha hesitated over the word "fatherland" too, and she hastily justified her use of it. "I don't really know why myself, but I think about what's going to happen to us day and night and I'll never submit to Napoleon, not for anything."

"Not for anything," Pierre repeated seriously and began writing. "Do you know this?" he asked as he wrote a sequence of numbers. He explained that all numbers have the meaning of letters and according to this way of calculating if you wrote 666 it meant *L'empéreur* and 42. And he told them about the prophecy of the Apocalypse. Natasha stared hard at these numbers for a long time and checked their meaning.

"Yes, how frightening," she said, "and the comet too." Natasha was so agitated that Pierre regretted having told her about this.

## XV

On the twelfth the sovereign arrived in Moscow and from early in the morning of the thirteenth, the bells were ringing in all the churches and there were festive crowds walking along Povarskaya Street and past the Rostovs' house on their way to the Kremlin.

Several of the house serfs had asked permission to go and look at the Tsar. After the talk with his parents, Petya still had a hurt, secretive look. That morning he took a long time getting dressed on his own, combing his hair and trying to arrange his collars the way grown-ups wore them. He frowned into the mirror, made gestures, shrugged his shoulders and after all this, without saying a word to anyone, he put on his hat, went out through the back porch and, trying not to be noticed, ran out of the house into the street. Petya had made up his mind to go directly to the Tsar, talk to some usher of the chamber (Petya thought the Tsar was always surrounded by ushers of the chamber) and explain to him that he, Count Rostov, wished to serve the fatherland, and that youth could not be an obstacle to devotion. And Petya had prepared plenty more fine words while getting ready, convinced that the fact that he was a child would decide the success or failure of his appeal to the Tsar (Petya even thought about how surprised everyone would be that he was so young), but at the same time he wanted to appear like an adult, he arranged his clothes and his appearance to that effect, and he walked along the street with slow steps and a very stern, sedate air, but the further he walked, the more he was distracted by the constantly expanding crowd of people at the Kremlin. Then he started worrying about being jostled and stuck his elbows out determinedly on both sides with a menacing air. But at the Troitsky Gates the people, who probably didn't know the patriotic intention that had brought him to the Kremlin, hemmed him in so tightly that he had to give way and stay there while the carriages drove in through the gates. Standing beside Petya were a woman with a servant, two merchants and a retired soldier. The woman's freckled face, and the soldier's wrinkled face with its grey moustache, and the face of a thin official with hunched shoulders all wore the same expression of festive anticipation as they talked about where the sovereign was, which none of them knew.

After standing at the gates for a while, Petya wanted to go on further ahead of the others and began working determinedly with his elbows, but the first person he drove his elbows against, the woman immediately opposite, shouted at him angrily:

"What are you shoving for, young master, you can see everyone's standing and waiting. Stop pushing, will you!"

Petya was astounded that this woman, who only a minute earlier had been talking in such a tender voice, wondering "if our little father hasn't already gone through", could immediately turn on him so querulously. He stopped, unable to get his handkerchief out in the crush and he wiped away the sweat covering his face with his hands and straightened the sweat-soaked collars that he had arranged so presicely at home. Petya no longer felt that he looked so presentable, and feared that if he went to the ushers of the chamber looking like this, they wouldn't let him see the sovereign. But the crush made it impossible to tidy himself up and move to another spot. The worst thing of all was that when some general or other with a plume on his hat drove in through the gates with a rumble that echoed under the vaults of the roof, Petya was squeezed into a stinking corner. Petya recognised one of the generals and wanted to ask him to help, but he decided that would be unmanly. He smiled ironically at what the people around him said as they mistook the general for the sovereign.

But then the crowd surged forward, sweeping Petya with it into the square, which was suddenly crammed full of people. Everywhere – not just in the square, but even on the roofs of the arsenal and on the cannons – there were colourful figures and heads, heads, heads, and more heads. No sooner did Petya find himself in the square than all the heads suddenly opened their mouths and everyone went dashing forward, and Petya was squeezed so tight that he couldn't draw breath and everyone started shouting: "Hoorah, hoorah, hoorah!" Petya stood up on tiptoe, but all he could see were crowds of generals walking along and one plume, which he took to be the sovereign's head.

The woman who had been so angry with Petya at the gate was standing beside him, sobbing, and the tears were streaming out of her eyes.

"Father. Angel. Our little father. Hoorah!" everyone was shouting and many of them were crying. Beside himself now, Petya gritted his teeth, put on a fierce glare and dashed forwards, working with his elbows and shouting "hoorah" as if he were prepared to kill himself and everyone else at that moment, but on both sides there were equally fierce faces with the same cry of "hoorah" shoving from all sides.

"So that's what the sovereign's like," thought Petya. "No, I can't put my petition to him myself. That would be too bold." Petya stopped trying to move, but then the crowd swayed back (at the front the gendarmes were shoving back people who had moved too close to the procession). The sovereign was walking from the palace to the Cathedral of the Assumption. Petya was suddenly struck such a hard blow to his ribs and crushed so tightly that he squealed in pain and the priest or sexton standing beside him took pity and grabbed him by the arm.

"You crushed the young master," said the sexton. "Go easy, will you."

The crowd evened out again, and the sexton led Petya, pale and scarcely breathing, out to the cannons. Several people took pity on Petya and the entire crowd suddenly turned to him and started crushing each other around him. Those who were standing the closest danced attendance on him, unbuttoning his frock coat, sitting him on a cannon and reproaching those who had crushed him.

"Someone could get squashed to death like that. How could you. It's murder. Look friend, he's gone as white as a sheet," the voices said.

Petya soon recovered. The colour came back into his face, the pain passed, and for his momentary discomfort he had been given a place on a cannon, from where he would definitely be able to see the sovereign on his way back. Petya was no longer considering making his petition. If he could only just see him, then he would count himself happy.

During the service in the Cathedral of the Assumption – a combined prayer service to mark the sovereign's arrival and service of thanksgiving for the conclusion of peace with the Turks, the crowd spread out a little and ordinary, everyday conversations could be heard. One merchant's wife showed people her torn shawl and told them what a lot of money she had paid for it; another woman replied that all silk materials had become expensive nowadays. The sexton who had saved Petya talked to an official about who was talking the service with his eminence, the

740

Patriarch. Two young men from the lower middle class joked with some house serf girls who were eating nuts. All these conversations, especially the joking with the girls, had a particular attraction for Petya, in view of his age, but he had no interest in any of them: he sat in his exalted position on the cannon, still feeling excited at the thought of the sovereign and his love for him. The coincidence of the pain and fear he had felt when he was crushed and his feeling of rapturous adoration intensified his awareness of the importance of this moment.

From his cannon, Petya was able to see the sovereign when he came out of the church, although his tears prevented him from seeing the sovereign's face properly, and when he saw him he shouted out "hoorah" in a frenzied voice and resolved that tomorrow he would be a soldier, no matter what. Although it was already late and Petya had not eaten anything, and the sweat was pouring off his face, he did not go home, but stood in front of the palace with the crowd, which was now smaller and thinner, but still huge, gazing lovingly up at the windows, waiting with a thrill of happiness for something and envying equally the dignitaries driving up to the entrance – for the sovereign's dinner – and the servants serving at the table, whom he glimpsed occasionally through the windows. Twice the sovereign's head appeared at the window and they raised a shout of "hoorah".

At the sovereign's dinner, Valuev glanced round at the window and said:

"The people are still hoping to see Your Majesty."

The dinner was coming to its end. The sovereign got to his feet and, still finishing his biscuit, went out on to the balcony. The people, with Petya in the middle – for it seemed to Petya that the people were indeed surrounding him – rushed towards the balcony.

"Angel! Father! Hoorah! Our father!" shouted the people and Petya, and again the women and some of the weaker men, including Petya, had tears in their eyes. The sovereign ordered someone to hand him a plate of biscuits and he began throwing the biscuits from the balcony. The blood rushed to Petya's head as he was fired by the danger of being crushed and he dashed for the biscuits. He did not know why, but he did know he had to get at least one biscuit from the hands of the Tsar, and he could not be beaten. He dashed forward, knocking over an old woman who was catching a biscuit. But the old woman did not consider herself defeated, although she was lying on the ground (she tried to catch the biscuits with her hands, but missed). Petya knocked her hand aside with his knee and grabbed a biscuit and then, as if afraid of missing his chance, he shouted "hoorah" again, in a voice that was already hoarse.

The sovereign went back in and after that most of the crowd began to go home.

"You see, I said we should wait a bit longer – and I was right," people in the crowd were saying happily on every side.

Petya was profoundly happy, but he felt sad that he had to go home, knowing that all the enjoyment of the day was over. Although he was utterly exhausted, he did not go straight home from the Kremlin, but went to see his friend Obolensky, who was also fifteen and also trying to join a regiment. When he finally came home, Petya declared with firm determination that if they did not let him go, he would run away. And the following day, although the count had not yet surrendered completely, he went to find out how Petya could be found a place that was not too dangerous.

On the morning of the fifteenth, three days later, an immense number of carriages stood outside the Slobodsky Palace, and Petya was there again, in the middle, only this time with Sonya and Natasha, and his heart was at ease.

The halls were full. The first was full of nobles in uniform, the second was full of merchants with medals and beards, wearing blue kaftans. There was noise and movement in all the halls. There were groups gathered around the tables, but people were mostly walking about in the halls. The nobles, who were chiefly old men, toothless, bald and half-blind, flabby and fat – the same ones that Pierre saw every day of the week in the club or in their houses – were in their uniforms, most of which were from the time of Catherine the Great, and this common uniform lent a rather strange appearance to familiar faces, as if some joker had wrapped all sorts of different goods from a cheap novelty shop in the same kind of paper. The old men were the most striking in this respect. For the most part they sat there without speaking, but if they walked about and talked, they attached themselves to someone rather younger. Petya had seen this same expression on all the faces in the square, but the most striking feature of the faces here was the opposite of the earlier unquestioning anticipation of something solemn and special – here it was the expression of something ordinary, like a game of boston, or Petrushka the cook, Zinaida Dmitrievna's health or French tobacco.

Pierre had been in the halls since early morning, squeezed into an uncomfortable noble's uniform which had become too tight for him. He was feeling agitated: this unusual gathering of the nobility and the merchantry had brought back a whole series of thoughts he had abandoned long ago, but which were etched deep into his soul, about the "Social Contract" and the French Revolution. He walked about, looking closely at people, listening to the talk, but nowhere did he find anything that fitted his current thoughts.

The sovereign's manifesto had been read out and everyone had straggled away, talking. Apart from everyday interests, he heard talk about where the marshals of the nobility should stand, when to hold a ball for the sovereign and occasional comments about the general state of military matters, the advantages and disadvantages of a militia. But wherever talk touched on the subject of the war, which was why the nobility had been gathered together, it was vague and indecisive. Everybody wanted to listen rather than speak.

A stout, manly, handsome middle-aged man in the uniform of a retired naval officer was talking in the corner of the hall, and people had crowded round him. Pierre walked over to the circle that had formed around the voluble speaker and began listening. Count Ilya Andreevich, who had been walking around in his kaftan from Catherine's reign, smiling pleasantly at all these people, all of whom he knew, also made his way across to this group and began listening with his kindly smile, in the way he always listened, nodding his head to indicate agreement with the speaker. The retired sailor was speaking boldly. (Pierre could tell that from the look of the faces of his listeners and because the men Pierre knew to be the most humble and quiet went off in disapproval or stepped forward to contradict him.) Others came to join the group. The man who was speaking was obviously a liberal, and therefore Pierre squeezed through to get closer and listen. The sailor turned out to be a reckless, fiery individual who spoke energetically, and a liberal, but in a quite different sense from what Pierre had thought. He spoke with that special, resonant, singing baritone of the noble class that has a special way of pronouncing certain words. He spoke with the habit of debauch and power in his voice.

"What if the Smolensk nobility have offered a home guard to the sovereign? Do we have to do what those in Smolensk do? If the nobility of the province of Moscow feels it should, then it can express its devotion to the sovereign by other means. Surely we haven't forgotten the home guard of 1807? The priests' sons and thieves simply made a fortune out of it."

Count Ilya Andreevich smiled sweetly and nodded his head in approval.

"And what good did the home guard do anyway, it only ruined our estates. Better recruit from another conscription, or else what we'll have will be neither soldier nor peasant, but pure depravity. The nobles don't begrudge their own lives, we'll all join the levy ourselves, we'll send more recruits, you just give us the call, suver" (that was the noble way he pronounced the word "sovereign"), "we're all ready to die for him," added the orator, becoming inspired.

Ilya Andreevich gulped in delight and nudged Pierre, but Pierre wanted to speak as well; he moved to the front, with no idea what he was going to say. But a senator standing nearby, completely toothless, but with an intelligent face, intervened before Pierre. Clearly accustomed to the manner of formal discussion, he said quietly, but loudly enough for people to hear:

"I do not believe we were summoned here to discuss what is presently most appropriate for the state – conscription or a home guard. We were summoned so that the sovereign could favour us with a statement of the position in which the state currently finds itself, and he wishes to hear our response ... As for deciding what is more appropriate, conscription or a home guard, we will leave that decision to the supreme authority ..." And without finishing, the senator turned and left the circle.

Pierre, however, suddenly resented the senator's introduction of this tone of correctness and his narrow viewpoint on the forthcoming task of the nobility, and he spoke out against him. Not knowing what he was going to say, he began in a lively tone, occasionally breaking into French and expressing himself bookishly in Russian.

"I beg your pardon," he began, "but I do not agree with the gentleman ... whom I do not have the honour of knowing, but I suggest that the estate of the nobility, besides expressing its sympathy and rapturous adoration" (Pierre had taken a liking to that phrase), "has also been summoned to discuss the measures we can take to assist the fatherland. I believe," he said, growing inspired, "that the sovereign himself would be displeased to find we were nothing more than the owners of the serfs that we give him or the cannon-fodder that we make of ourselves, and to receive no counsel from us at all."

Many people moved away from the circle, seeing the senator's disdainful smile and noticing that Pierre was talking out of turn; only Ilya Andreevich was pleased, as he was always pleased, whoever was speaking.

"I suggest that before discussing these questions, we should ask the sovereign, as most loyal subjects of His Majesty, to tell us how many troops we have, what is the condition of the troops and the army, and then ..."

But before Pierre could finish what he was saying, he was attacked from three sides. The person who attacked him most fiercely was an old acquaintance who had always been well-disposed towards him and an agreeable man to play boston with, Stepan Stepanovich Apraksin. Stepan

Stepanovich was in uniform and either because of that, or for some other reason, Pierre saw a quite different person before him now. An expression of senile fury suddenly erupted on Stepan Stepanovich's face and he shouted at Pierre:

"In the first place, I can inform you that we have no right to ask the sovereign about such things, and in the second place, even if the Russian nobility did have such a right, the sovereign could not give us an answer. The troops move in accordance with the movements of the enemy – troops leave and new ones come . . ."

Another voice – from a middle-aged man of about forty whom Pierre had also seen at the gypsies' place and knew as a good card-player, and who had also changed now that he was in uniform – interrupted Apraksin.

"And this is not the time for discussion . . ." said that voice, which Pierre had often heard singing along gaily with the gypsies and shouting as he raised the stake. The voice smelled of wine. "This is not the time for discussion, we need to act: there is war in Russia, our enemy is coming to destroy Russia, to desecrate the graves of our fathers, to carry off our wives and children" – the nobleman struck himself on the chest – "and we will all arise, and every last one of us will go, for our father the Tsar!" Some people turned away, as if they could sense the ineptness of these words.

Pierre had begun yet he had been unable to say anything. He simply felt that the sound of his words, regardless of their sense, was less audible than the words this man was shouting.

Ilya Andreevich approved. Beyond the circle several men swung their shoulders towards the orator at the end of each phrase and said:

"Right, that's right! that's right!"

Pierre wanted to say that he had nothing against making sacrifices, whether it was money, or serfs, or himself, only one needed to know how things stood in order to help improve them, but he was unable to get a word in. There were so many voices shouting and speaking all at the same time that Ilya Andreevich could not even nod at all of them; and the group expanded and broke up and came together again, moving as a single body, buzzing with talk, into the hall, to the governor's table. Many young and inexperienced men were moved to reverent respect as they looked at this agitated crowd. The men in it were deciding the fate of Russia. Not only was Pierre not allowed to speak, he was rudely interrupted and jostled away, with people turning their backs on him as if he were the common enemy. They did not do this because they were displeased by what he said – they had already forgotten it after all the speeches that had followed – but for a crowd to become animated, it needs to have a palpable object of love and a palpable object of hate. Pierre had become the latter. Many orators spoke, all in the same vein as the bon vivant who smelled of wine, and many of them spoke elegantly and with originality.

The publisher of the *Russian Herald*, Glinka, who was recognised ("a writer, he's a writer," said voices in the crowd), said that he had seen a child smile at flashes of lightning and peals of thunder, but we would not be that child.

"Yes, yes, at peals of thunder!" they repeated approvingly in the rows at the back, assuming that the thunder referred only to Napoleon.

The crowd approached the governor's table, at which seventy grandees were sitting – old men with grey hair or bald heads, in uniforms covered with ribbons – almost all of whom Pierre saw regularly in their homes with their jesters and in the clubs, playing boston. The crowd approached them, still buzzing. One after another, sometimes two at a time, they came up to the table, pressed from behind by the crowd which pushed them up against the high backs of the chairs, and spoke. The men standing behind noticed what the current orator had left out and hastened to add what had been omitted. In the heat and the crush, others searched in their heads for some idea and hastened to say it. The old men whom Pierre knew sat there looking around first at one man, then another, and the expression on most of their faces said only that they felt very hot. Pierre, however, was in a state of agitation, and this general feeling of a desire to say that we weren't worried at all, which was expressed more in the sound of men's voices and their expressions than in the sense of what was said, was communicated to him as well. He had not disavowed his ideas, but he somehow felt guilty and wished to justify himself.

"I only said it would easier for us to make donations if we knew what was needed . . ."

The closest old man threw a glance at him, but was distracted by the shouting that began on the other side of the table.

"Yes, Moscow will be surrendered. She will be the sacrifice," one man shouted.

"He is the enemy of mankind!" shouted another. "Permit me to say . . . Gentlemen, you are crushing me . . ."

At that moment Count Rostopchin entered, wearing his general's uniform with its sash across his shoulder and, with his chin outthrust and his eyes darting sideways, walked rapidly past the nobles who had moved aside to let him through.

"His Majesty the Emperor will be here soon," said Count Rostopchin, "I have just come from there. I presume that there is nothing requiring much discussion in the situation in which we now find ourselves. The sovereign has deigned to gather us together with the merchantry," said Count Rostopchin. "Millions will be poured in from that side, and our job is to provide the home guard and not spare ourselves . . . What is your opinion, gentlemen?"

Quiet consultations began and very quickly concluded with a proposal from Count Rostopchin to give every tenth man, to which everyone agreed, and to kit them out, which was also declared acceptable, with some brief comments from several individuals who wondered who would be entrusted with this matter and how the abuses that had crept into the previous home guard could be avoided. These remarks were set aside by Count Rostopchin, who said they would consider that at a later stage. The entire process of consultation was more than just low-key, it even seemed sad, after all the hubbub that preceded it, to hear the old voices speaking one after the other, one saying merely "agreed", another saying, for the sake of variety: "I am of the same opinion" and so on.

Count Rostopchin ordered the secretary to write the nobility's resolution. And the gentlemen who had been sitting in session stood up as if relieved, clattering back their chairs to walk around the hall and stretch their legs and taking other men by the arm as they conversed.

"The sovereign, the sovereign" – the words suddenly flew round the halls, and the entire crowd went scurrying to the door, but the sovereign went to the merchants' hall first. He spent about ten minutes there. Pierre and the others saw the sovereign come out of the merchants' hall with tears of tender emotion in his eyes. As they learned later, the sovereign had only just begun his speech to the merchants when the tears had gushed from his eyes and he had finished it in a wavering voice. When Pierre glimpsed the sovereign, he was emerging from the hall, accompanied by three merchants. Pierre recognised two of them, the fat one was a tax-farmer, and the other, with a thin, sallow face and narrow beard, was a guild chairman. Both were weeping. The thin one had tears in his eyes, but the fat tax-farmer was sobbing like a child and kept repeating: "Take my life and all my property, Your Majesty."

The crowd flowed back and carried Pierre with it into the hall of the nobility. And as soon as the sovereign entered, his handsome face was suffused with emotion and tears sprang to his eyes, every face in the hall changed. Pierre heard sobs behind him. He was standing too far away to hear what Rostopchin said to the sovereign (as Rostopchin informed him of the nobility's resolution), but he could hear the sovereign's voice, so attractively human in its emotion, as it said:

"I have never doubted the zeal of the Russian nobility. But on this day it has exceeded my expectations. I thank you in the name of the fatherland. Gentlemen, let us act – time is more precious than anything . . ."

"Yes, more precious than anything . . . the Tsar's word," Pierre heard Ilya Andreevich's voice say behind him with a sob.

Pierre felt nothing at that moment beyond the desire to show that nothing held any meaning for him any longer and he was prepared to sacrifice everything. He sensed that the constitutional tendency of his outburst was being held against him and he searched for the chance to make amends. On hearing that Count Mamonov would contribute a regiment, Bezukhov immediately told Count Rostopchin he would contribute a thousand men, as well as the money to maintain them. Old Count Rostov was unable to tell his wife what had taken place without shedding tears and he immediately gave in to Petya's request, deciding to take him to Mamonov to join his future regiment.

The sovereign left the following day. All the nobles who had been gathered together took off their uniforms, settled into their houses and clubs again and groaned as they gave their stewards instructions for raising the home guard, amazed at what they had done.

Pierre was a member of the committee for receiving contributions. Petya had put on a Cossack uniform. The old count had finally decided to sell the entire house with its contents, which were exceedingly valuable, and was only waiting for Razumovsky to arrive.

# PART SEVEN

# I

What had to happen was bound to happen. Just as Napoleon thought that he started the war with Russia because he wanted a universal monarchy, but really started it because he could not help coming to Dresden, could not help being blinded by honours and accolades, could not help putting on Polish uniform and surrendering to the adventurous impulse of a June morning and setting out across the Niemen, so did Alexander think that *he* was waging a desperate war in which he would never accept a truce, even if he retreated as far as the Volga, whereas in fact he was only doing so because he could not act otherwise.

A horse set on the slope of the wheel in a barley-hulling mill thinks it is walking entirely freely, stepping with its left or right leg at will, raising and lowering its head, because it keeps wanting to go uphill, and in precisely the same way, all those innumerable individuals who took part in this war, who were afraid, vain, excited, or indignant, thinking they knew what they were doing, were in fact only horses, trudging along on the huge treadmill of history, performing work hidden from them but known to us. Such is the invariable fate of all practical people, and they are less free, the higher they stand in the human hierarchy; the higher they are, the more they are bound, the steeper the slope of the wheel, the quicker and less freely the horse walks. Once you step onto this wheel, there is no freedom, no comprehensible activity, and the more time that passes, the faster the wheel moves, so there is even less freedom until you get off it.

Only Newton, Socrates and Homer act consciously and independently, and only these people possess the free will which, despite all the evidence of the functioning of the nervous system, is demonstrated by the raising and lowering of my hand.

It is not the argument between materialists and idealists that interests me here. What is their argument to me? For that same argument takes place within me, within you, within each and every person. Do I have freedom of will – this old concept, so dear to me – or does it not exist, and is everything that I do brought about by the action of inescapable laws? Someone says that my nerves are affected in such a way that I cannot help making this movement; but, apart from the fact that this someone was himself confused when he came to explain the concept, from which nobody could understand anything, he did not answer, and no one can answer, the main argument, which is as simple and indisputable as Columbus's egg: I am sitting and writing, beside me lie a gymnastic weight and a dog. Can I or can I not stop writing now? I tried it – I can; and can I now continue writing? – I can. So there is free will. But I go on to ask myself, can I lift the weight and make a movement like this and this? – I can. But can I now drop the weight on the dog from the height of my hand? I tried – no I can't. At some other time it might be possible – but not now – because of a thousand considerations: it's stupid to do it, I feel sorry for the dog, I can use a different experiment. But no, I can't do it.

Ah! Then there are actions, like waving my hand in all directions and like writing or refraining from writing, that I can do, and there are those that I cannot do.

Let me continue my experiment. Can I go and kiss my sleeping child? Can I go and play a game of bezique with my aunt? I can. Can I go and strike a servant, can I go and kiss the cook? No, I cannot, now I cannot. Can I not sleep tonight? Could I not have brushed that fly off my eye? No, I cannot and I could not have. I have asked others to answer the same questions for me, and they have all given the same answers. There are things which one can choose to do or not do (naturally, within the realm of the physically possible). There are things which one cannot do and things one cannot help doing. This much is clear. And even if this person does not grow confused, as he has done so far with his proofs that there is nothing but nerves, when he does not even know what nerves are, even if he should prove this to me as clearly as $2 \times 2 = 4$, I still will not believe it, because at this moment I can reach out my hand or not reach it out.

The main source of human error consists in seeking out and defining the causes of the phenomena of human life – those organic phenomena of life which derive from the totality of a countless number of inevitabilities. I believe Voltaire said that there would not have been any St. Bartholomew's Night if the King had not been constipated. This is correct to exactly the same degree as the fact that if none of the disturbances that preceded St. Bartholomew's Night had occurred, the King's bowels would have been in better order. And it is also equally correct that the cause of St. Bartholomew's Night was medieval fanaticism, that it was a Catholic intrigue, and so on and so forth, which can be verified in all the history books. The fact of St. Bartholomew's Night is one of those phenomena of life which occur inevitably according to eternal laws intrinsic to humanity: to kill the excess number of people in one's environment and to justify this by adjusting your own passions appropriately.

The statistics of crime demonstrate that a man who thinks he kills his wife because she has been unfaithful to him, is only following a general law, which requires that he must be added to the number of murderers in the statistical report. A suicide who takes his own life for the most complex of philosophical reasons is merely following that same law. This applies to the individual person. But human society, the whole of mankind, in addition to the laws governing individuals, is also subject to laws that govern societies and groups of humanity (groups that are defined not on the basis of states – so that Baden does not constitute a separate group – but according to the principles by which they are governed) and the whole of mankind.

These societies have just as great a need for large-scale murders – wars – as individuals have for murders; and exactly the same thing happens in societies as with the suicide and the murderer – in part the intellect and imagination of man manufacture causes, in part circumstances coincide and are taken for causes.

Man, like the bee and the ant, cannot be regarded only as an individual. Only human societies are complete organisms, subject to the same laws as the organism of the hive and the anthill. In order to understand this more clearly, take a look at small human societies, standing at a low level of development (it is easier to see clearly there because the conditions are less complex and further away from us, and consequently we can regard them with a more independent eye). Take a look at any village. Every house, yard, hut, shop, icon, cup, knife, piece of clothing, item of food – everything is arranged in exactly the same way for one person as for another. On a spring day, from one yard and another you see the peasants emerge on their carts with exactly the same tools to go sowing. They have not conspired, they have not thought about this, but exactly as one bee is followed by another from another hive, as if saying: "to work lads", and the bees fly out and fly back with pollen, in exactly the same way the menfolk drive out and drive back, and the women go to take their linen cloths and wash themselves for a holiday. After the 19th of February how hard all we landowners strove to fathom the new circumstances of life, questing and searching, in the belief that it is only by way of reason that we are able to adapt to new circumstances. And what came of it? People from the Penza province met with people from the Tula province and all said the same things, interrupting each other as they spoke, like sons who have all by chance given their mother an umbrella as a present. Everybody said we must be more demanding at meetings, and certainly not too generous – that the best way was to share crops equally with the peasants, that paying hired hands was ruinous, that the area of tillage had to be reduced and so on and so forth. All this is the ant side, the herd side of life.

To understand fully the possibility of erring through the failure to recognise these general laws of instinct governing mankind, it is essential to understand the general characteristics of man.

1. The law of the mind's adjustment, with a speed that defies the very concept of time, to inescapable necessity; complex intellectual arguments which convince us that what we do is always done in accordance with our free will.
2. The law that prevents man, at the moment when he takes an elemental, spontaneous action, from seeing its spontaneous nature and the need to see his own personal advantage (church holidays and fasts), and
3. The law of coincidence between the external phenomena of life and the inner, moral or intellectual phenomena that correspond to them.

You are asleep and you have a dream that you've been hunting and you see the long sequence of events preceding the hunt; eventually, the quarry flies up, you shoot and you wake up. The sound of the shot was a real sound, the sound of a shutter slamming in the wind. Your imagination manufactured the entire story of the hunt at the moment of waking. A madman is not surprised by anything. They put him in a carriage and take him away, he does not know where to or what for. Not only is he not surprised but, depending on his specific mania, he explains why he expected this and tells the entire story leading up to why they had to come for him.

Some children are sitting still, they have not been allowed to run for the whole day. They sit and play a quiet game, playing the parts of a sick mother, a doctor, and a husband and a nanny. Suddenly they are allowed to run around. The servant runs round the table thirty times to get the medicine, and so does the husband, and the sick woman too. In order to satisfy the need for movement, the imagination has instantly manufactured them the pretext of sending for the doctor. A child is sleepy or hungry. He cries and grows angry, he is always crying or getting angry about something.

These are examples (and there are millions more like them) of the action of the imagination where the mind is weak and too slow to select the products of the imagination and provide a rational context for them. But the process is still the same.

You are the owner of an estate, you are in a bad mood, you go there and find something that could give you reason to be angry, and you are genuinely convinced that it is not you who have chosen the estate as the cause, but the estate that is troubling you, that were it not for the estate, you would feel at ease. Following the laws of nature, you need to believe; you have had a dream and you manipulate the future to match it and lie, deceiving yourself when you do not to admit this to yourself. The table-turning that everyone in the world used to do and all the arguing and talking and writing about magnetism were all due to a law of nature – the desire to see into the future. "All right, you do not believe in homeopathy, but this man recovered after taking belladonna, and I can help everyone without exception," says the healthy and learned allopath who possesses the human capacity for logic. You felt shivers down your spine while reading a book – you have had this feeling when something in a book touched your feelings and you were moved. You try to remember, but there is nothing to remember, and then you try to remember what it was you were trying to remember. Bismarck is convinced that his complicated, cunning and profound considerations of state gave rise to the latest victorious war. The members of "Vaterland" think that it came about through patriotism. The English think they outwitted Napoleon, but everything that they all think was invented for them by the imagination with the help of the mind – invented to satisfy European society's need for bloodletting. The same kind of need as the need that yellow and black ants have to exterminate each other and build their anthill according to the one, eternally familiar, form.

It would still be possible to dispute man's dependence on general and involuntary causes in some other area of social activity, but not in the military field, because war is one of the activities most directly opposed to another aspect of man – the moral aspect. We are used to speaking about war as an extremely noble business. Kings wear military uniform. Men of war are given the same title as the benefactors of the human race – geniuses – and glorified just as much, or more, incomparably more than Socrates and Newton. War is a boy's dream. The highest honour is military honour. And what is required to wage war successfully? In order to be a genius, you need:

1. Provisions – organised theft.
2. Discipline – barbaric despotism, the extreme restriction of freedom.
3. The ability to acquire information – spying, deceit, betrayal.
4. The ability to employ military tricks and deceit.
5. What is war itself? – Murder.

6. What are a soldier's activities? – Idleness.
7. Military morals are depravity and drunkenness.

Is there a single vice, a single bad side of human nature, that is not one of the conditions of military life? Why is the military calling respected? Because it is the supreme power. And power has flatterers.

So that is why war is subject above all to the inescapable ant laws that govern mankind, and why war increasingly excludes all personal will and knowledge of one's aims the closer the involvement of the individuals concerned with the general course of events. Just as the final transmission wheel revolves faster, the more levels of transmission there are below it. Those who turned the wheels of 1812 have left their posts long ago, the wheels have been destroyed and transformed, but we have the results before our eyes, and therefore it is clear to us that no single man (neither Napoleon nor Alexander), no matter how high he stood, ever had the slightest intimation of what was going to happen, nor that what did happen was what had to happen. After Vilnius, Napoleon kept expecting peace, and Alexander could not imagine that Smolensk would be surrendered, let alone Moscow. It is clear to us now what the reason was for our success in 1812. I think no one will dispute that our success relied on luring Napoleon into the heart of Russia, on burning towns and inciting hatred of the enemy. And not only did nobody see these measures for what they were. (I am not talking about various hints in a letter from Alexander to Bernadotte and various hints made by contemporaries who, naturally, in retrospect, select from everything that was thought and said, and forget that there is only one of these hints for all the hundred thousand that contradict them, and they do not mention the contradictory ones, but speak only of hints that confirm what actually happened. This is the method that is used to justify and confirm premonition and prophecy.) . . .

. . . And so, not only did no one see this at the time but, on the contrary, every effort was made to prevent it from happening – that is, the enemy reaching the heart of Russia and the incitement of national hatred. But, without being aware of it, the forces directed to prevent this proved to be useful. Napoleon enters Russia with an army of five hundred thousand men. He is dangerously skilled in inflicting decisive defeats. We split up our weaker army into little parts and stick to Pfuhl's plan. Our armies are separated. We attempt to combine them and in order to do this we are obliged to retreat. And unwittingly, by forming a narrow angle between the two armies, we lead Napoleon to Smolensk. We intend to give battle in front of Smolensk but are ourselves outflanked and obliged to defend Smolensk. We defend Smolensk, but not so intensely as to expose the army to danger, and not intensely enough to deceive the citizens who are dying within the walls of Smolensk, and Smolensk is set on fire. All of this is done in defiance of instructions from above, all of this results from the extremely complex interaction of intrigues, goals, plans and desires opposed to each other, which fail to divine what must happen and where the only salvation lies. Pfuhl departs, mouthing abuse, saying that the whole of history is going to the devil and he cannot understand the nonsense of first splitting up the armies in accordance with his plan and then abandoning this plan. The Emperor leaves the army following a letter from Shishkov, Arakcheev and Balashov, in which as a convenient pretext they seize upon the need to inspire the capital with his presence. And herein lies the very essence of the matter. The generals are in despair because their army is fragmented and there is no unity of command, because Bagration is the senior officer and Barclay is minister of war, but out of this confusion there emerges indecision and the avoidance of battle, which would have been impossible to avoid if the army had gathered together. The appointment of a non-Russian, the negligible Barclay, as commander-in-chief seems to be a mistake and a disaster, yet it is this that saves the army and rouses the national spirit . . .

All this is done for a goal that is obvious to us later generations, but hidden like the millstone from the horse who is treading in a circle. And for the achievement of this goal the invisible mechanic makes use of everything and takes everything into account: vices and virtues and passions and weaknesses and strength and indecision – everything, while seeming to strive towards its own immediate goal, leads only to the overall goal.

Following the sovereign's departure from the army the situation in the army command became still more confused, impossible as that might have seemed. Before, if only vaguely and indistinctly, everyone had felt there was a centre of power. Now even that was gone. Barclay could perhaps (although it is doubtful whether he would) have issued orders in the name of the sovereign, but Bagration was independent of him and outranked him, and was in a position not to obey him: in precisely the same way, Chichagov and Tormasov had to be asked to do things. The entire swarm of superfluous and therefore harmful men – adjutants-general and aides-de-camp, who discussed everything and confused everything – were the same. Pfuhl left, and so did Armfeldt, but Bennigsen, the senior general, and the Grand Duke, the heir to the throne, were with the army. The Grand Duke returned to Smolensk from Moscow and expressed his hatred for Barclay, and now, when it was already too late to speak of peace, and the brother he had contradicted was not there, he contradicted Barclay in everything. Barclay insisted on caution, the Grand Duke hinted at treason and demanded a general engagement. Liubomorsky, Branitsky, Vlodsky and so on amplified this clamour so that Barclay was obliged to entrust to them documents for delivery to the sovereign in St. Petersburg and he was also preparing essential documents for Bennigsen and the Grand Duke. Everyone, even those who did not directly contradict the commander-in-chief, had his own plan and project and did everything possible to prevent the success of his opponent's plan. One proposed battle, another supposedly went out on reconnaissance and instead of carrying out reconnaissance, he visited the corps commander nearby, then said that he had inspected the area and declared it unsuitable, whereas to his opponent it seemed the only possible choice. Witticisms, jokes, jibes and quarrels criss-crossed like small-shell fire. Bagration's army did not join the other for a long time, despite it being the main goal of all the commanders, since it seemed to Bagration that if he made that march he would place his army in danger and it would give him greater advantage to retreat further to the left and the south, harassing the enemy from the flank and the rear, and bringing his army up to strength in Ukraine. That was what he thought, but in fact he was only thinking up impossibilities and inventing advantages in order not to obey the hateful foreigner Barclay, whom he outranked.

Eventually the armies did unite at Smolensk. Bagration rode up to the house occupied by Barclay in a carriage. Barclay (for which his rare admirers praised him) put on his scarf and came out to meet Bagration and report to him. Bagration was satisfied and accepted Barclay's command. But, having accepted it, he agreed with him even less than before. Bagration sent personal reports to the sovereign. And when the two commanders met, they seemed to have reached agreement, but the swarm of Branitskys, Wintzengerodes and so forth poisoned their relations even more, and the result was even less unity. They wanted to attack, they were preparing, but they were obliged to accept battle unexpectedly at Smolensk, in order to save their own lines of communication. It had to be.

The supreme mechanic forced Bagration to trudge in his treadmill so that he would join the army nowhere but at Smolensk, and so that Smolensk would be burned and smashed. This was necessary so that the people would arise.

From the first days of August we sought a battle in front and to the right of the approach to Smolensk, the army moved there and back twice, but throughout all our indecision and quarrelling, we were unaware that the French wanted to outflank us on the right, take Smolensk and cut us off from the Moscow road. Entirely unexpectedly, on the 3rd of August the Neverovsky Division came upon the French and was attacked by Murat's entire avant-garde and forced to retreat, and as it retreated, fighting the whole day long, it led the French right up to Smolensk. A day before these events nobody could have thought of allowing the French to approach the town, let alone of surrendering it to them. Raevsky's corps was sent to defend Smolensk. The battle continued throughout the 4th of August, but the French did not fire on the town; on the 5th Dokhturov and Evgeny Württemberg's corps was sent to relieve Raevsky and on the 5th Napoleon said: "This little town will be taken or their entire army will be destroyed there" – and the cannonade from a hundred and fifty field guns began against the Russian forces and the town, thus beginning the French attacks. But the little town was not taken, and neither was the army destroyed. The following day Barclay de Tolly ordered Dokhturov to retreat, and Bennigsen and the Grand Duke promptly went to Barclay to impress upon him that the army was discontent and he should give battle, and suddenly at this point, documents were discovered in Barclay's headquarters which were so important that the commander-in-chief could not entrust them for delivery to St. Petersburg to anyone except the sovereign's brother himself.

## II

After Prince Andrei's departure, the old Prince Bolkonsky's daughter observed him growing weaker with every day, although in the eyes of indifferent servants and acquaintances, he seemed even more virile and energetic than ever. He began changing all his habits.

The night after his son's departure he walked around in his study for a long time, then some time after ten he opened the door into the servants' room and began walking about in the drawing room. He sat down beside a small cupboard in the hall, opened the window and looked out into the garden, then ordered a candle to be brought and sat there reading and then ordered Tikhon to set up his camp bed right there in the drawing room. The following afternoon he slept and walked about a lot, continually giving instructions. That evening and night he began walking round the rooms again, and again ordered his bed to be set up, but this time in the gallery, not in the drawing room. He lived in this way, continually changing the place where he slept, obviously not knowing what he was going to do next or when or where, but in constant haste, never able to think everything through and get everything done. In all this time there were no quarrels at all with Princess Marya, but he was permanently cold towards her. Princess Marya explained this to herself by his sense of decorum. It was awkward for him to switch from his former spite to affection. Princess Marya believed he would like to but was too proud to allow himself. In late July he received a letter about the taking of Vitebsk and the battle at Ostrovno. After reading the letter he drank a lot of tea with Princess Marya and Bourienne and spoke animatedly about the battle on the Danube. At the end of the conversation, apropos of something or other, he remarked how quickly Prince Andrei's letter had reached him from the border. When Princess Marya took the letter and examined it, she read: "the village of Gradnik, Vitebsk province."

"They must be close to Vilnius now. Bonaparte will move to the left. Ah, no one thinks about anything."

The count got up, ordered Tikhon to spread out the maps and began making calculations about the enemy's movement in the environs of Vilnius. He ran his gnarled old man's hands over the map and called the architect. Everything he said was well considered, but it all referred to the past. He had failed to understand, he could not understand, that Napoleon was already in Vitebsk. Princess Marya had noticed some time before that the prince had ceased to understand what was said to him, that he was thinking his own thoughts, and if he asked or enquired about something, he adapted what he was told to fit those thoughts. Princess Marya tried to remind him about Vitebsk, but he gave her such a self-assured, angry contemptuous look that she began to wonder whether she might be mistaken. While he was busy with the maps Alpatych came in. After marking spots on the map with pins, the prince hurried into his study and sat down at the secretaire. Alpatych was being sent on business, there were so many instructions he had to be given, and the prince thought no one could take his place.

"Letter paper. Make sure it's this kind, gilt-edged – here's a sample, it has to be the same. Then to the registrar, tell that scoundrel to give me back all the records." "They'll get everything muddled up without me," he thought. "Bleak Hills will fall apart." Then there was canvas that had to be bought for a portrait, then a wicker box had to be ordered to keep his will in. Alpatych accepted the instructions, but he was surprised: the prince had never dealt with everything in such petty detail and in such haste before. After letting Alpatych go, the prince opened his will, which he had taken out to measure its size, put on his spectacles and began reading. "Ah, yes, I still have to add a point about what to do if my grandson has no offspring." In his seclusion, the prince now felt tired and he began rereading the old text and rewriting it. The will was very extensive and detailed, and it reassured the prince to deal with matters that would come into effect when he was no longer there. He imagined everything would be clear and calm at that time, and thinking of it gave him especial satisfaction. It was already late when the prince got up from the desk and he was feeling sleepy, but he knew that he would not fall asleep for the very worst thoughts came to him in bed. Then he remembered another errand for Alpatych – to buy a horse for Kolya's name-day. He called Alpatych and described in detail what kind it had to be.

After that, he walked round the rooms for a while, checking every corner to see if it would be good to sleep there. Nowhere seemed any good to him – worst of all was his usual divan in the study – that divan was terrible, horrible, probably because of the painful thoughts he had thought while lying on it. There was nowhere that was good, but nevertheless, the corner in the sitting room, behind the fortepiano, was best, he had not slept there yet. Tikhon brought the bed from the servants' room and began setting it up.

"Not like that, not like that," the prince shouted and moved it himself a few inches away from the wall and then back closer to the wall again. "At last, I've done everything. Now I can have a rest," thought the prince. But the moment he lay down, the bed suddenly began to sway forwards and backwards underneath him, as if it were breathing heavily and shifting about. He opened the eyes he had only just closed.

"That's painful, it hurts! No rest for the body and the spirit hurts far, far more. I can't, I just can't understand and remember everything I need to. Yes, and there was something nice, something very nice I brought to bed with me for the night. Lemonade? No, what was it, there was something in the drawing room. Princess Marya got something wrong. Something in my pocket . . . I can't remember – Tishka! what were we talking about over dinner?"

"About Prince Mikhail."

"O, shut up, shut up." The prince slapped his hand against the side pocket of his sleeveless jacket. "I know, Prince Andrei's letter. Princess Marya said something about Vitebsk, I'll read it now."

He took out the letter and put it on the little table with the lemonade and a curled stump of wax candle that had been moved up against the bed. He began to get undressed. My God, my God, how hard it was to bend his exhausted, emaciated, seventy-year-old shoulders as Tikhon was taking off his kaftan, how hard it was for him to sit down on the bed, how reluctantly his foot lifted for the shoe to be taken off and how thin, dry and yellow it was as it fell downwards. And he still had to lift them up and move over on the bed. "Oh, how hard it is, oh let all these hardships be over soon, soon, when will you all release me," he thought. Pursing his lips, he made the effort for the twentieth time and lay down with the letter in his hand. His son's letter was recorded in his memory as something comforting and pleasing, but it had the opposite effect. It was only now, in the still of the night, having read the letter by the weak light coming from under the green shade, that he understood its full meaning. "What's this? The French in Vitebsk. Then they could reach Smolensk in four days' march. Perhaps they're already there? What is this? No, I have to do something."

He twirled his rattle. Tikhon jumped up. "Send Alpatych to me. Give me my dressing gown and put light in the study." He had to impress on Alpatych how to behave if he met the enemy, he had to lay in weapons and powder (he had plenty of muskets and blunderbusses) in case they were attacked by marauders. He let Alpatych go at two o'clock in the morning, but no sooner had he let him go than he remembered other essential arrangements that he still had not made. He needed to write a letter to his son, here, in Bleak Hills he needed to give instructions for setting up pickets on the roads, he needed to fortify the estate, to instruct the peasants, to write to the marshal of the nobility. Prince Nikolai Andreich stayed up until the dawn, still wearing his dressing gown. In the morning he dressed, went into the study and sent for his daughter and some tea. But when they arrived, he was asleep in the armchair, slumped over one of its arms, and the drink was carried away on tiptoe.

Like the days that preceded them, the three days of Alpatych's absence passed in unrelenting anxiety and bustle and every day, all day long, Prince Nikolai Andreich supervised the sewing of military clothing for all the house serfs and their training in shooting, which he entrusted to the architect.

Bleak Hills, the estate of Prince Nikolai Andreevich Bolkonsky was located sixty *versts* from Smolensk, to the rear of the town, and only thirty *versts* from the Moscow road. It was on the second day of the month, after the Festival of the Holy Life-Giving Tree, that Yakov Alpatych set out for Smolensk on the prince's instructions.

Despite, or perhaps precisely because of the fact that Yakov Alpatych had frequently had the honour and the pleasure of receiving blows from the old prince's gnarled stick, in the circles in which he had been active for thirty-six years he held the position of a powerful grandee of the kind that is now, perhaps, only be found in the Orient, the kind of grandee that Cardinal Richelieu used to be, the general, plenipotentiary favourite of an autocratic ruler. Above and beyond the district town, Smolensk also lay within the orbit of Alpatych's power. In Smolensk

Alpatych associated with the provincial secretary and the postmasters as if they were his equals or even inferiors, and the merchants vied with each other for the honour of a visit from him. As a boy Alpatych had fought at Ochakovo with the prince and therefore he had the somewhat militant and punctilious air of an old soldier. When it came to war, he regarded himself as no less infallible a judge than his master, and just like the prince, he believed that what happened at Ochakovo had been real war, and everything that they called war nowadays was mere child's play. "They're just pretending – we can fight too!" Alpatych would say. Like all people who repeat what somebody else says, Alpatych was even more certain of this than the prince himself.

Having received all his instructions the evening before, at first light on the 2nd of August, a beautiful summer day, after drinking his fill of tea, Alpatych, accompanied by the members of his household, wearing a white felt hat – a present from the prince – and carrying a stick, just as the prince did, went out to get into the leather-hooded cart, harnessed to a threesome of well-fed bays. The carriage bell was tied so that it would not ring, and the little bells were muffled with paper. The prince never allowed anyone to ride with a bell in Bleak Hills, and one police superintendent had been beaten for it by him in person. But Alpatych liked bells on a long journey. Alpatych's courtiers – the clerk, both cooks, (kitchen cook and serving cook), two old women, a boy-servant, the coachmen and various house serfs – saw him off. A maid came running up to ask him to do her a kind favour and buy her some needles exactly like the one she had. His daughter brought down pillows in cotton covers to go under him and at his back. His old sister-in-law furtively thrust a little bundle into his hands (Alpatych didn't like these gaggles of women), the coachman helped him in by the arm.

"Well, well, gaggles of women. Women, women," Alpatych panted, exactly as the prince used to say, as he got into the cart. He gave his final instructions about work to be done to the clerk and then, no longer imitating the prince, took the hat off his bald head and crossed himself three times.

"If anything happens, now, you come back Yakov Alpatych, for Christ's sake, have pity on us," his wife shouted to him, hinting at the rumours of war and the enemy.

"Women, women, gaggles of women," Alpatych said to himself and set off in the chill of the dawn, glancing around at the fields covered in dew and thinking about his arrangements for sowing and harvesting and wondering if he had forgotten any of the count's instructions. Alpatych not only spoke and acted like his master, his face even resembled that of the old prince.

In the evening of the second day of the month Alpatych arrived in the town and went to stay with the Ferapontovs. The Ferapontovs were merchants, five brothers, with whose father Yakov Alpatych had stayed thirty years before, playing draughts with him, just as he now played with the eldest brother in the flour shop.

Along the way Alpatych had met and overtaken military transports and troops, but in the town all was still quiet. The Ferapontovs told him that some foolish people were packing up to leave Smolensk because they were afraid.

"But with our business how can you just pack up, and the governor himself has announced that there's no danger and our army's a long way in front of the town."

Ferapontov also told Alpatych some news of the war, how Matvei Ivanovich Platov was giving the French a sound beating and how he had drowned eighteen thousand Frenchmen in a single night along the Marina river (although there was no river with any such name). Yakov Alpatych listened to Ferapontov's tales without paying much attention. Like the prince, he despised womanish gossip and was sure that no one knew how things were going more accurately than the prince did, even though he was sixty *versts* away. The next day Alpatych put on his camisole, which he only wore in the town, and went about his business. Everybody knew him, everybody greeted him cheerfully. He called into shops, the post office and the government offices, where he spent a very long time. Alpatych regarded himself as a great master at dealing with official business and writing applications with sentences in which the verb stood far, far away from all the substance and circumstances, right at the very end.

The business in the government offices was quite trifling, submitting the census lists, but Yakov Alpatych and his friend the registrar discussed the subject at length in subtle detail and decided to make everything as complicated and cunning as possible, although there was no need for cunning at all. Then Alpatych drank some dry Madeira with the registrar, talked a little about politics and came back a little red in the face to Ferapontov in his shop. (Yakov Alpatych was a great exception for those times: he was so strict about drinking that when he did drink, he did not conceal it from the prince and at times he would say to him: "Permit me to inform your excellency that I do not drink as such, except that occasionally I may take some dry Madeira with the clerk, I like it.")

After playing a few games and beating the coachman who, as always, had got drunk in the town, Yakov Alpatych went to bed early, as was his habit, on the hay in the yard. But no sooner had he fallen asleep than fat Ferapontov, wearing nothing but his shirt, adjusting his belt with the key, came to him and told him that there was bad news. Shots could be heard not far outside Smolensk and they said the enemy was already close. Alpatych laughed and, as a military man, explained to the merchant that this was women's talk, that they would tell lies about anything, that the shots could be training and they would never let the enemy reach Smolensk come what may, and went to sleep. But Ferapontov had not been mistaken: that day, the 3rd of August was when Neverovsky was attacked and fell back to Smolensk. Early the following morning Alpatych woke the drunken coachman he had beaten and, after harnessing the horses and packing to leave, went out on to the porch. There really were soldiers marching along the street. Alpatych's threesome of bays had only just driven out when one officer on horseback pointed to the cart and said something. Two soldiers jumped into the cart and ordered it to go to the Petersburg suburb for a wounded colonel. Alpatych politely but sternly removed his hat, waved to the coachman to tell him not to go and approached the officer, wishing to explain his mistake to him.

"Your honour, mister quartermaster," he said, "both the cart and the horses, and the coachman, and I myself," he said with a smile, "belong to his excellency the general-in-chief Prince Bolkonsky, like myself, and therefore . . ."

"Get going, get going," the officer shouted to the soldiers . . . "Follow them, they're going the same way." And the officer galloped off, clattering over the stones of the road.

Alpatych stopped dead in bewilderment.

"Well, that's nice!" he said ironically, once again repeating what his master said. He shrugged his shoulders. "Unload the things," he shouted to the coachman.

The coachman carried out his instruction, and Alpatych went back to Ferapontov with his bundles and cushions and immediately set about composing a complaint against an officer "of unknown name and rank, but probably reduced to frenzy by drink, who took a covered cart which is not mine, but belongs to his excellency the general-in-chief Prince Bolkonsky". Having composed his complaint and written it out neatly and drunk his fill of tea, Yakov Alpatych set off to take it to the commander-in-chief. Having learned that the senior general Raevsky was in the town, on the other side of the river, he went to him. As he walked through the streets, Yakov Alpatych saw troops marching everywhere, and before reaching his destination, he heard an exchange of fire close by. Raevsky was on the other side of the bridge and would not receive Alpatych. He waited. They were carrying wounded on the other side of the bridge. The streets were packed with people and a number of them advised Alpatych to turn back. An officer from whom Alpatych thought he should ask advice laughed in his face and said he would never find Raevsky now. Alpatych went back. On his way back he heard a cannonade not far away, and some soldiers walking by explained to him that the French were attacking the walls. Alpatych stopped several times to look at the wounded men or prisoners who were led past him and shook his head disapprovingly.

When he got back, the Ferapontovs confirmed the bad rumours, but they invited him to lunch in any case, since it was after midday. At lunch, during which the glass rattled in the windows, Alpatych, as an honoured guest, began talking about the war at Ochakovo and told them in detail what he had seen there and what the prince had done and how he had captured three thousand Turks. The Ferapontovs listened to him attentively, but as soon as he had finished, they began telling him, as if what they were saying was a reply to what he had said, that some people were leaving, that greedy peasants were charging three roubles in silver for a ride, that the merchant Selivanov had been lucky on Thursday and sold flour to the army for seven roubles a sack, and that even Marya, the woman who sold spice cakes, had sat on the bridge with kvass and taken six roubles from the soldiers for kvass in one day. And the kvass had gone bad in that heat.

By evening the shooting had quietened down. Some said the French had been driven away, others said that the next day there would be another big battle outside the town. The eldest Ferapontov brother left the yard. The brothers walked around the yard and the shops, bemused. Alpatych stayed on the bench by the gates, where he had sat in the evening, saying nothing and watching the soldiers walking by. Alpatych's cart had not come back. He did not lie down to sleep. All through the short summer night he sat on the bench, talking with the cook and the yard-keeper, asking the soldiers who continually walked by about what was going on, listening carefully to what they were saying as they went, and other sounds. In the next house they were packing in order to leave. The eldest Ferapontov came back. He also did not lie down to sleep and in the morning they began packing.

During the night the cart returned. The coachman said they had made him drive across the bridge, that the carnage was terrible and they wouldn't let him go. The horses needed to be fed. At dawn Alpatych immediately went to the cathedral and there found other people who could not sleep. They were offering prayers one after another before the Virgin of Smolensk. After Alpatych ordered a prayer for himself, he and a merchant he knew went up the bell tower, from where, he had been told, the French could be seen. The French could be seen quite clearly on the other side of the Dnepr. They were all moving, coming closer. Before Alpatych reached the bottom of the tower, the cannonade started up again on the other side of the Dnepr, but no cannonballs fell in the town.

"What's going to happen?" Alpatych thought on his way back to the house. He could not understand anything.

He met even more soldiers than the day before, walking through the town with anxious, exhausted faces towards the spot where there was shooting. Yakov Alpatych looked out for the young prince among them, but did not find him. One officer told him that the Pernovsky Regiment was already there – he pointed towards the area from which they could hear the constant confused buzzing of shots and from which they were carrying a constant stream of wounded. Yakov Alpatych sighed and crossed himself. Yakov Alpatych needed to leave. As a servant who faithfully carried out the prince's will, he knew what distress his absence was causing the prince, but he was unable to leave. He listened to the terrible rumbling of the field guns, sniffed the smell of gunpowder carried right into the town on the wind, looked at the wounded and stood still on one spot. The sight of countless numbers of our soldiers walking past him to the site of the battle delighted Alpatych. He smiled tenderly as he watched them but still he did not move from the spot.

He crossed himself, facing them and bowing from the waist.

Three carts drove close past him, full of wounded and dead, and one cart with a young officer in it stopped opposite Alpatych. The officer was shouting that they should let him off, that he would not last the journey. The officer was beating his head on the cart and shouting: "Take me! Take me!"

Alpatych went up to him.

"My dear fellow!" he said, and was about to help him get out, but the carts set off again. There were soldiers marching towards him again. Alpatych's heart was suddenly moved. He began crossing himself, bowing to the soldiers walking by and intoning:

"Fathers, dear friends, defend our Orthodox Russia."

Several of the men walking by glanced round at this respectable-looking old man and carried on without changing the stern expression on their faces. There were several carts driving in the opposite direction. Local inhabitants were leaving. Alpatych remembered that he also needed to leave, and he went to the house. Before reaching the house, he heard a familiar whistling sound that he had heard in Turkey; it was a cannonball that had flown into the town. Then there was a second, and a third, and cannonballs began falling on the street, on the roofs, on the gateways. In the courtyards and houses there was the sound

SMOLENSK, 20 AUGUST 1812
*Lithograph*

of women screeching and running feet. Alpatych began walking faster in order to reach the Ferapontovs' house in time. In front of the convent the nuns were packing their things; a woman selling kvass was still sitting at the crossroads: a man ran out of a house and shouted: "Stop thief!"

Two drunks walked past him. He reached the house. One Ferapontov brother was in the house, packing up in haste, the others were in the cellar with the women. The coachman told him that in the courtyard next door a woman had been killed and asked if it was not time to be loading up. But Alpatych did not answer him and sat down again on the bench by the gates. The cannonballs were still flying and striking on the other side of the street. It began to get dark. The bombardment began to slacken off, but in two places he could see the glow of fires. There were women in the next courtyard.

The Ferapontovs all came up out of the cellar and bustled about, fastening and packing things and running hastily from the house to the carts. Soldiers in various uniforms, all with timid or insolent expressions, ran around the streets and courtyards like ants from a smashed antheap. Two soldiers ran past him from out of the Ferapontov house, with sacks and a yoke. The Ferapontov women rode out of the yard.

People came flooding along the street and there was the sound of religious singing.

"They've brought out the Virgin of Smolensk!" a woman shouted.

Alpatych walked out into the crossroads and saw priests in chasubles carrying the icon along and a thin crowd following them. Some regiment or other was marching back from the outskirts of the town.

"Permit me to enquire of your honour," said Alpatych, baring his bald head, "has the enemy been defeated?"

"They're surrendering the town," the officer replied curtly and immediately turned to shout to the soldiers. "I'll teach you to go running round the yards!" he shouted at some soldiers who were running out of the ranks and turning into the Ferapontovs' courtyard. However, the soldiers slipped through into the yard anyway, and some others went into the shop.

Alpatych went into the courtyard, ordered the coachman to drive out and saw one of the Ferapontovs, who had gone up to the open doors of the shop and stood there. In the shop about ten soldiers were pouring rye flour and sunflower seeds into sacks and knapsacks.

Ferapontov went into the shop and was about to shout something, but suddenly stopped, seized hold of his hair and began laughing and sobbing.

"Take it, take it all, lads. Don't let the devils have it!" he shouted.

Some soldiers took fright and ran out, others carried on pouring.

The regiment was still moving along the Ferapontovs' street. It was already completely dark, and the stars had begun shining in the clear sky. There was a small bunch of soldiers loitering at the corner of the Ferapontov house, by the granary. It was beginning to get brighter, as if the dawn was beginning. The soldiers had lit a charge of gunpowder. Alpatych went closer to take a look. The corner of the granary caught fire because the soldiers had set boards around it. Ferapontov came running out to the burning corner.

"Burn it all, take everything, everything . . . everything. That's all it's good for now!" shouted Ferapontov, fanning the flames with a heavy coat. More and more people gathered round the fire.

"That's grand. It's caught now. Look, it's caught," voices said.

"To hell with all of it!" shouted Ferapontov's voice.

Alpatych watched the fire, unable to tear himself away from the sight for a long time, standing in his own spot, not in the crowd. A familiar voice called his name:

"Alpatych!"

"Your excellency," replied Alpatych, recognising the voice of Prince Andrei. Prince Andrei, wearing a cloak, was sitting on a grey horse at the crossroads, looking at Alpatych with a lively expression.

"How do you come to be here?"

"On his excellency's instructions. I'm just on my way back. Your excellency, what's happening, are we really done for?"

Without replying, Prince Andrei took out a notebook and, lifting one knee, began writing with a pencil on a torn-out page. He was writing to his sister. "Smolensk has been taken," he wrote. "Bleak Hills will be taken by the enemy in a week. Leave and go to Moscow immediately. Reply to me as soon as you have left by sending a courier to Gorki." When he had finished writing and handed the piece of paper to Alpatych, he told him how to arrange the departure of the old prince, the princess and the little prince with his tutor and how and where to send him an immediate reply. Before he had finished these instructions a mounted staff officer accompanied by his retinue galloped up to him.

"You, colonel?" the staff officer shouted with a German accent in a voice that was familiar to Prince Andrei. "They're setting fire to houses right in front of you, and you just stand there? This is disgraceful! You'll answer for it," shouted Berg, who was now chief-of-staff with the deputy commander of the left flank of the infantry.

Prince Andrei looked at him curiously and said nothing.

"Tell them," he continued, speaking to Alpatych, "that I expect an answer before the tenth, and if I don't have news on the tenth that everyone has left, I will drop everything and come to Bleak Hills myself."

"I only say that, prince," said Berg, trying to justify himself because he had recognised Prince Andrei, "because I must carry out my instructions, because I am always punctil . . ."

"Rarara!" the crowd roared when the roof of the granary collapsed, releasing a smell of pancakes from the burnt grain. The flame flared up brightly, lighting up Prince Andrei's thin, sallow face with its flashing eyes. Ferapontov was holding his arms in the air and shouting louder than anyone else.

"That's the owner himself, your excellency," said Alpatych.

"Well, all right. On your way, on your way!" said Prince Andrei. He bowed to Berg and set his horse moving after the regiment, which had almost gone past him.

Rumours about the battle at Smolensk had reached Princess Marya and she had concealed the news from her father, but Alpatych's arrival with a letter from Andrei and his demand that they leave and go to Moscow could not be hidden from him. The prince listened to Alpatych calmly. "Yes, yes, all right, all right," he repeated to everything that the princess and Alpatych said and then, having let them go, he immediately fell asleep in his armchair. When he woke in the evening, he ordered Princess

Marya to be sent for. She already spent all her time in the servants' room, listening at his door.

"Ah, what? Your old fool of a father's lost his mind! Eh? Is that it?" was how he greeted his daughter. "What did I say? Eh?"

"Yes, you're right, father, but . . ." Princess Marya tried to say that they had to leave, but she was not allowed to finish.

"Right, now listen, Princess Marya," (the prince seemed especially fresh that day), "listen, now's the time, there's no time to lose. We have to act. Sit down and write."

Princess Marya saw that she had to resign herself to doing as he said and she sat down at his desk, but could not find a good pen.

"Write, this is to the plenipotentiary commander-in-chief: 'Your excellency . . .'"

But the princess had still not found a pen. He shook her by the shoulder.

"Come on, you fish. 'Your excellency, having been informed . . .' Wait, once and for all – I have been bad, spiteful and unjust to you. Yes, yes," he said angrily, turning away from the frightened face that she had turned towards him. "Yes, yes." And he stroked her hair in his awkward manner. "Well, I am old, I am tired of living and against my will, I am spiteful and unjust. Please forgive me, Princess Marya," the prince cried, "once and for all I beg of you to forgive me, I beg, beg, beg of you, hoo-oo, hoo-oo," he cried out and coughed roughly at the same time.

"Well now, write: 'having been informed of the proximity of the enemy . . .'" and, walking about the room, he firmly dictated an entire letter, in which he said that he would not leave Bleak Hills, where he had been born and would die, that he would defend himself there to the absolute limit and that, if the government was not afraid of the shame of one of Russia's oldest generals being captured by the French, let them not send anybody, but otherwise he requested only a company of artillery and three hundred militia with a regular non-commissioned officer.

"Mikhail Ivanich," he shouted. "Seal it, and get it there quick. Princess Marya, write another. To the governor of Smolensk: 'Dear baron . . . Having been informed . . .'"

In the middle of the dictation of this letter, Mademoiselle Bourienne entered the room, stepping softly and smiling sympathetically, to ask if the prince would like some tea . . .

"*Madame*! I thank you for your services, I do not consider it possible to detain you any further. Be so good as to go to the governor in Smolensk."

"Princess," said Mademoiselle Bourienne, turning to Princess Marya.

"Out, out!" shouted the prince. "Mikhail Ivanich, call Alpatych and arrange for her to be sent to the town immediately."

He walked across to the secretaire, took out some money and painstakingly counted it.

"You can give this to her . . . Now write: 'Having been informed, dear baron, that the enemy . . .'"

He stopped again, trying to recall something and again walked up to Princess Marya. "Yes, once and for all, I was cruel to you, Princess Marya, unjust. Please I beg, I beg, I beg you – now write, write . . ."

Having written another two and a half letters and probably having forgotten that he had already said what he wanted to say to Princess Marya, he repeated it several times again: "Please, once and for all . . ." In the middle of the fourth letter he stopped, sat down in an armchair, said "go" and instantly fell asleep.

Afraid as she was that he might wake up, Princess Marya kissed him on the forehead, and then became even more frightened because he had not woken up and his sleep seemed so strangely deep.

It was already after midnight. Princess Marya went to her room, but on the way she met Alpatych, who, for the very first time in her life, asked her for advice and instruction. He requested clarification of the extent to which the prince's instructions should now be carried out.

"In my doubt I make so bold as to seek your excellency's advice and ask, will you instruct me to send the Frenchwoman away and send to Bogucharovo for men, as his excellency Prince Nikolai instructed, or? . . ."

That was what Alpatych said, but Princess Marya understood something quite different. She understood now for the first time that her father, the father for whom she had endured so much, this father had died or would die soon, that soon he would no longer be there. Princess Marya was dumbfounded and looked at Alpatych questioningly, with an expression almost of horror.

"Your excellency, if it was not necessary, I would not have dared to speak these words to your excellency. But Prince Andrei Nikolaevich explained most insistently the danger of staying here at the estate and ordered us to go to Moscow and inform him when we did so."

"I don't know," said Princess Marya. "But one thing is certain – Amelia Fedorovna" (Bourienne) "must not be sent to Smolensk, you yourself said . . ."

"Will you not instruct me, your excellency, to send her to Bogucharovo and instruct Dronushka there to show her every courtesy, but not to let her out of the house. And conceal this business from the prince for the time being. But what instructions will you give about sending the prince himself and yourself to Moscow? The horses and the carriages are ready. And in the present situation the prince will probably not give his assent; therefore, for the time being . . ."

"Yes, yes, please, I'll talk with you tomorrow," said Princess Marya, whose presence of mind had been finally undermined by the phrase "for the time being" and she walked away with her heavy tread, first to her own room, and then to Mademoiselle Bourienne, whom she could not forget because she was the one who had done most harm to her in her life. She walked into the room where the Frenchwoman was weeping and, like the guilty party, begged her forgiveness and implored her to go to Bogucharovo. Some time after one o'clock Princess Marya, walking silently, returned to her room and looked at the icons, but could not pray. She felt that now she was being called by a different, difficult world, the world of everyday activity, which was completely opposed to the moral world of prayer, she felt that by devoting herself to the latter, she would lose her final power to act. She could not pray and she did not try to. As she went through to her room, she heard her father's steps in the gallery. She had just undressed when these steps began moving closer to her, closer to her door, and then stopped. Then the prince moved again and stopped again. He was listening. He wanted to come in and did not dare to. Princess Marya cleared her throat. He entered her room, something that Princess Marya could never remember happening before.

"I just keep walking about, I can't sleep," the old man said in a weary, tormented voice that he tried to make sound casual. He sat down in an armchair under the icons. "I was unable to sleep like this once in the Crimea. The nights are warm there. I kept thinking all the time. The Empress sent for me . . . I was given an appointment . . ." He glanced round at the walls. "Yes, they wouldn't build like that now. I began building as soon as I came here. There was nothing here. You don't remember how they burned. No, how could you. They wouldn't build like that, nowadays it's just slam-bang and there's your ship. If I live a bit longer, I'll run the gallery round from here, and that will be Nikolasha's rooms. Where my daughter-in-law lived – she was a good little woman, she was, good good. But I'll have to send him away – I'll have to, and you as well . . . Ah, I forgot, I forgot, my memory's going. Well, sleep, sleep."

He went out. The princess heard his rattle and his footsteps and only stopped hearing them when she fell asleep. She woke late.

From her first glance at the maid's face, she realised that something had happened in the house. But she felt so afraid that she did not ask. She dressed hurriedly and went downstairs. Alpatych, standing in the servants' room, gave her a look of curious sympathy. Princess Marya did not stop to ask him anything, she walked straight up to the door of the study. Tikhon put his head out of the door. Princess Marya noticed that the curtains were closed.

"Karl Ivanich will come out in a moment," said Tikhon. Karl Ivanich was the doctor. He walked out on tiptoe.

"It's all right. Calm down, princess, for God's sake," said the doctor, "a mild stroke on the right side."

Princess Marya took a deep, heavy breath. She did so as if she had already known everything.

"Can I see him?"

"A bit later would be better," said the doctor, and made to close the door, but Princess Marya was afraid of being left alone, she beckoned to him to come out and led him into the sitting room.

"It was bound to happen. He took everything to heart so, he suffered so much inwardly that his strength gave out. This morning, after he received letters from the governor and Prince Andrei Nikolaevich, he went to inspect the serf militiamen, he showed them everything himself. He was about to go, and the carriage was harnessed and suddenly something happened to him . . ."

Princess Marya did not cry.

"Can he travel as far as Moscow?" she asked.

"No. In my opinion, it would be better to go to Bogucharovo . . ."

"Can I see him?"

"All right, come along."

Princess Marya walked into the warm room and at first she could not see anything in the darkness, then she made out something on the divan. She went closer. He was lying on his back with his legs bent up, covered with a blanket. He was so very small and thin and weak. She leaned down over him. His face was pointing directly at the opposite wall, his left eye obviously could not see, but when the right eye caught sight of Princess Marya's face, his entire face trembled, he lifted his right hand and took hold of her arm and the right side of his face twitched. He said something that Princess Marya could not understand and, realising that she could not understand, he began breathing heavily and angrily. Princess Marya nodded her head and said "yes", but he carried on snorting angrily, and the doctor led Princess Marya away.

"For so long we did not understand each other," thought Princess Marya, "and it is the same now."

After consulting the doctor and the mayor of the town, Princess Marya decided that instead of Moscow she would take her sick, paralysed father to Bogucharovo, which was forty *versts* off the road, and would send Nikolushka to his aunt in Moscow with Laborde. In order to reassure Andrei, she wrote to him that she was going to Moscow with her father and nephew.

Our forces continued their retreat from Smolensk. The enemy followed them. On the 10th of August the Pernovsky Regiment passed along the high road through the Bleak Hills estate. It had been hot and dry for more than three weeks. Every day fluffy clouds passed across the sky, occasionally obscuring the sun, but by evening the sky had cleared again and the sun set in a reddish-brown haze. And only the heavy dew refreshed the earth at night. The grain left on the stalk and the grass burned up. The bogs dried out. The cattle bellowed in hunger on the trampled fallow fields and after-grass. It was only cool at night because of the dew and in the woods, while the dew lasted. But on the road, the high road that the soldiers were marching along, even that coolness was absent. The dew was insignificant on the sandy dust of the road, that had been ground several inches deep. As soon as it began to get light, movements began. The transports and artillery moved soundlessly, sunk up to their wheel hubs, and the infantry walked up to their ankles in the soft, stifling, hot dust which had not cooled overnight, and now swirled up and hung in a cloud, getting into their eyes, their hair, their ears, their nostrils and, worst of all, their lungs. The higher the sun rose, the higher the cloud of dust rose too, and they could look directly at the sun through this fine hot dust: it looked like a crimson ball.

Prince Andrei was in command of a regiment, and like the soldiers smoothing their ramrods, he passionately smoothed his own – the organisation of the regiment. The welfare of his men, the improvement of the officers, preparedness for battle. After Smolensk he applied himself even more keenly. He began to forget his own problems. He was meek and kind with his officers and men. They called him "our prince", they were proud of him and they loved him. However, while he was kind and meek with the men of his regiment, with Timokhin and the others, and with people who were completely new or from a different circle, who could not know or understand his past, as soon as he encountered one of his former acquaintances from among the staff officers, his hackles immediately rose and he became spiteful, derisive and contemptuous. Everything that linked his memories to the past was repellent to him, and therefore with regard to this former world the most he could do was strive not to be unjust and to perform his duty. The word and the concept of duty were stronger than his pain now, and he was afraid of betraying it somehow under the influence of his bitterness. Earlier everything had appeared to Prince Andrei in a dark light – especially after they had left Smolensk and his father had been obliged to flee to Moscow and abandon Bleak Hills, which he had loved so much, which he had built, and created. But now despite that, and thanks to his command, Prince Andrei had something else to think about, completely independent of his problems – his regiment.

On the 10th of August the column that included his regiment was passing Bleak Hills. Two days earlier, Prince Andrei had received news that his father, son and sister had gone to Moscow. (That was the deceitful letter that Princess Marya had written to reassure him before she left for Bogucharovo.)

"Yes, I have to go," thought Prince Andrei, although he very much did not want to, "it is my duty to see that the estate is in order or at least to take a look." He ordered two horses to be saddled up and rode off with Pyotr. When they rode through the village, everything was the same as ever, but only the old men were at home, all the others were out working, the men were ploughing, the women were washing their laundry in the pond, and they bowed low in fright. Prince Andrei arrived at the house. There was no one in the lodge by the stone gateposts and the door was unlocked. The paths in the garden were already overgrown and there were calves and horses wandering about in the English park. A woman and a boy saw him and started running across the meadow. Pyotr went to the servants' quarters. Prince Andrei rode to the conservatory: the panes of glass were broken and some of the trees in tubs had been knocked over, some had withered. He called for Taras, the gardener. There was no response. Rounding the corner of the conservatory on to the ornamental garden, he saw that the timber fence was all smashed and whole branches of fruit had been torn off the plum trees. An old peasant was sitting on some little green seat and weaving a birch-bark sandal. He was deaf and did not hear Andrei riding up. He was seated comfortably on a tub, and the bast strips were hung very neatly around him on the branches of the broken and withered magnolias. He was sitting there as indifferently as flies walk across the face of a loved one who is dead. Prince Andrei rode up close to him. Several lime trees in the old garden had been cut down, there were horses walking about between the rose bushes. The shutters of the house were closed and barred. One window downstairs was open. Alpatych came running out of the house in his spectacles, buttoning up his coat. Alpatych had sent his family away and stayed in the house alone. He had been sitting in the house and reading the *Lives of the Saints*. He ran up to the prince and burst into tears without saying a word, kissing Prince Andrei on the knee. Then he turned away, angered by his own weakness and, after inviting the prince to dismount, began recounting the state of affairs to him. Everything precious and valuable had been taken to Bogucharovo, and nearly six hundred bushels of grain had been taken too but the hay and this year's harvest had been cut while still green by the troops in battle green. The peasants were ruined, but some of them had gone to Bogucharovo, and only a few had stayed behind. Without waiting for him to finish, Prince Andrei asked when his father and sister had left, meaning when they had gone to Moscow. Alpatych replied that they had left on the seventh, and then returned to talking at length about the affairs details of managing the estate, asking for instructions. Prince Andrei interrupted him again with a question about his father's health, at which Alpatych explained to Prince Andrei about the old prince's illness.

"Will you instruct me to issue oats to the foragers against a receipt? We still have more than three and a half thousand bushels left," asked Alpatych.

"What should I say?" thought Prince Andrei, gazing sadly at the old man's bald head gleaming in the sun and reading in Alpatych's expression his awareness of the untimeliness of his own questions, which he was only asking in order to stifle his own grief.

"If your excellency has noticed the disorder in the garden," said Alpatych, "that was impossible to prevent – three regiments came and spent the night here, especially dragoons, I wrote down ranks and titles in order to submit a complaint."

"Well, what are you going to do? Will you stay if the enemy takes the place?" Prince Andrei suddenly asked him.

Alpatych turned his face towards Prince Andrei and looked at him. And suddenly he raised his hand, pointing upwards in a solemn gesture:

"He is my protector. His will be done."

A crowd of peasants and house serfs with bare heads came walking across the meadow, approaching Prince Andrei.

"Farewell, old friend!" said Prince Andrei, embracing Alpatych. Alpatych pressed his face against his shoulder and burst into sobs. "Leave, all of you, and burn the house and the village," Prince Andrei said in a quiet voice. "Good day, lads. I've given Yakov Alpatych here all my orders. Do as he says. But I have no time, I have to go. Farewell."

"Father, father," said their voices.

He set his horse to a gallop and rode down the avenue. The old man was still sitting there in the arboretum and tapping on the last of his sandal, and two little girls carrying plums in their skirts walked across his path.

Prince Andrei felt a little fresher, having left the area of the high road along which the troops were marching. But not far from Bleak Hills he came out on to the road again and caught up with his regiment at a halt beside the dam of a small pond. It was shortly after one in the afternoon.

The heat of the sun, a red ball through the rising dust, was unbearable, it burned his back through the dark tailcoat, and the air was buzzing with the talking of the soldiers at the halt, where the dust hanging in the air was a bit less thick. There was no wind. As he rode over the dam, Prince Andrei caught a whiff of green slime and coolness from the pond. He suddenly wanted to get into the water. No matter how dirty it was. He heard shouting and laughter and glanced round at the pond. The level of the small, murky, slimy pond had clearly risen by about a foot overflowing the dam, because it was full of men, the white bodies of naked soldiers with brick-red hands, faces and necks wallowing in it. All this naked, white human flesh laughed and chortled as it wallowed in this dirty puddle, like carp crammed into a watering-can. This wallowing was full of carefree merriment, and that made it especially sad. One young, light-haired soldier with a strap round his ankle from the third company – a man that Prince Andrei knew – covered himself with one hand and crossed himself with the other as he stepped back to take a good run up and plummet into the water. Another, a non-commissioned officer whose dark hair was always tousled, stood up to his waist in the water, happily flexing the muscles of his torso, snorting joyfully and pouring water onto his head with hands that were black up to the wrist. There were the sounds of men slapping each other, and shrieks and hoots. Another company was undressing and climbing in as well. On the other side there were cavalrymen bathing. On the banks, on the dam, in the pond – everywhere there was white, healthy, muscular flesh. The officer Timokhin with his red nose was drying himself off on the dam and he felt ashamed when he spotted the prince, but decided to address him anyway:

"It's really good, your excellency sir, you ought to try it," he said.

"It's dirty," said Prince Andrei, with a frown.

"We'll soon clean it up for you." And, still not dressed, Timokhin ran off to clear the pond. "The prince wants to try." – "What prince?" – "*Our* prince," voices started saying, and everybody started hurrying so eagerly that Prince Andrei was barely able to calm them down . . .

# III

Among the countless categories of all the phenomena of life, a clear distinction can be drawn between those in which content, and those in which form, predominates. Unlike village, rural, provincial or even Moscow life, the life of St. Petersburg, and especially its salons, can be included in the latter category. This life is immutable. Since 1805 we had been making peace and quarrelling with Bonaparte, we had made constitutions and unmade them, but Anna Pavlovna's salon and Hélène's salon were exactly the same as they had been, in the first case seven, and in the second case five years before. At Anna Pavlovna's they still spoke in exactly the same puzzled fashion about Bonaparte's success and saw in everything the single goal of upsetting the Empress Marya Fedorovna, and likewise at Hélène's salon, which Rumyantsev himself had honoured with a visit since he regarded her as a highly intelligent woman, they spoke with a sigh of regret about the sad rift with a great nation and a great man.

In recent times, since the sovereign's return from the army, there had been a certain agitation in these opposed circles and there had even been certain demonstrative outbursts, but their divergent tendencies had remained the same. In the circle that centred on Marya Fedorovna, as if in proof of how terrible Bonaparte was, orders were given for the court and female institutions under the patronage of the Dowager Empress to pack up their heavy things and prepare to leave for Kazan and the only Frenchmen to be received were inveterate legitimists, while patriotism was expressed in refraining from attending the French theatre, based on the notion that the cost of maintaining the company was as great as that of maintaining an entire army corps. The events of the war were followed eagerly, and rumours that showed our army to best advantage were spread about. In Hélène's circle and the Rumyantsev-French circle, a distinctive calm confidence was expressed while rumours of the cruelty of the enemy and the war were rejected. In general the whole business of the war was regarded as an empty show which would very soon end in peace, and the dominant opinion was that of Bilibin, who was now in St. Petersburg and an habitué of Hélène's salon (every intelligent person had to visit Hélène's), that it was not the gunpowder, but the people who had invented it who would decide the matter. In this circle, with cutting irony and great wit, but also with great caution, they mocked the rapturous mood of Moscow, news of which had arrived in St. Petersburg together with the sovereign.

In Anna Pavlovna's circle they were delighted by these raptures and spoke of them much as Plutarch speaks of the ancients; Prince Vasily, who still occupied the same important posts, was the connecting link between the two circles. He visited both his good friend Anna Pavlovna and his daughter's diplomatic salon and frequently, in his constant moves back and forth between the two camps, he grew confused and said things at Anna Pavlovna's that ought to have been said at Hélène's, and vice versa.

Soon after the arrival of the sovereign, Prince Vasily got into conversation with Anna Pavlovna about the war, harshly condemning Barclay de Tolly yet finding himself at a loss as to who ought to be appointed commander-in-chief. One of the guests, known under the title of "a person of great qualities", told everyone that he had seen Kutuzov that very day, chairing the government chamber for army recruitment, and had heard rumours that this was the man who ought to be appointed.

Anna Pavlovna smiled sadly and remarked that Kutuzov had brought the sovereign nothing but trouble.

"I spoke and I spoke about it in the assembly of nobles," Prince Vasily interrupted, "but they refused to listen. I said the sovereign would not be pleased by his appointment to the General Staff of the home guard. They would not listen to me."

"It's all some kind of anti-monarchic mania. And for whom? And it's all because we wish to ape the stupid raptures of Moscow," said Prince Vasily, growing confused for a moment, but immediately correcting himself. "Well, it's indecent that Count Kutuzov, the oldest general in Russia, presides in the chamber. His efforts get him nowhere! How is it possible to appoint a commander-in-chief who cannot even sit on a horse, who falls asleep in meetings, a man of the very worst morals! He showed himself in a fine light in Bucharest. I am not speaking of his qualities as a general, but is it really possible at such a moment to appoint a man who is decrepit and blind – simply blind. A blind general would be a fine thing. He can't see a thing. Playing blind man's buff . . . he can't see a single thing."

Nobody objected to this.

On the 4th of August this was perfectly correct. On the 10th of August, Kutuzov was granted the title of prince. But the title of prince could have meant that they wished to get rid of him, and therefore Prince Vasily's opinion continued to be correct, although now he was not so quick to express it. But on the 15th of August, the very day of the Battle of Smolensk, a committee was convened consisting of Field-Marshal-General Saltykov, Arakcheev, Vyazmitinov, Lopukhin and Kochubei, in order to discuss the progress of the war. The committee decided that the failures were the result of divided command and proposed the appointment of Kutuzov as commander-in-chief. And on that day, Kutuzov was appointed plenipotentiary commander of the army and the whole area occupied by our forces.

On the 17th of August at Anna Pavlovna's, Prince Vasily once again met the man of great qualities, who was currying favour with Anna Pavlovna out of a desire to be appointed trustee of the Empress Marya Fedorovna's educational institution for young women. Prince Vasily entered the room with the air of a happy victor, a man who has attained the goal of his desires:

"Well now, you know the great news. Prince Kutuzov is Field-Marshal. All the disagreements are over. I am so happy, so glad!" said Prince Vasily. "At last, that is the man!"

The man of great qualities, despite his desire to acquire a position, could not resist reminding Prince Vasily of what had been said before. (This was discourteous to Prince Vasily in Anna Pavlovna's drawing room and also to Anna Pavlovna, who had greeted this news with equal joy; but he was unable to resist it.)

"But they say he is blind, prince," he said.

"Ah, nonsense, he can see well enough," said Prince Vasily in a low, quick, throaty voice, the voice with which he resolved all difficulties. "Ah, nonsense, he can see well enough," he repeated, and paying no more attention to this, he continued: "And what makes me really glad is that the sovereign has given him complete authority over all the armies, over the entire region – an authority that no other commander-in-chief has ever had. He is a second autocrat."

"God grant him success," said Anna Pavlovna. The man of great qualities, still a novice in court society, wishing to flatter Anna Pavlovna by bringing up her former opinion in this discussion, said:

"They say the sovereign granted this authority to Kutuzov reluctantly. They say that he blushed like a young lady who has read Joconde when they said to Kutuzov: 'The sovereign and the fatherland reward you with this honour.'"

"Perhaps his heart was not entirely in it," said Anna Pavlovna.

"Oh no, no," Prince Vasily interceded ardently. He could not surrender Kutuzov to anyone now. Not only was Kutuzov himself fine, but everybody adored him. "No, that cannot be so, because the sovereign previously appreciated him just as greatly."

"God grant only," said Anna Pavlovna, "that Prince Kutuzov really does take control and does not allow anyone to put a spoke in the wheel."

Prince Vasily immediately understood who that *anyone* was. He whispered:

"I know for certain that Kutuzov stipulated as an absolute condition that the Grand Duke should not be with the army. He said: 'I cannot punish him if he does something bad or reward him if he does something good.' Oh, he is a very clever man, Kutuzov, such character. Oh, I've known him a long time."

"They even say," said the man of great qualities, who still lacked courtly tact, "that he made it an absolute condition that the sovereign must not come to the army."

As soon as he said that, Prince Vasily and Anna Pavlovna turned away from him in the same instant, glancing at each other sadly, and heaving a sigh at his naïvety.

# IV

While this was taking place in St. Petersburg, the French had already passed Smolensk and were moving closer and closer *to* Moscow. In his history of Napoleon, Thiers claims, in an attempt to justify his hero against the accusations of all other historians, that Napoleon was led to the walls of Moscow against his will. He is just as correct as the other French historians who seek explanations for events in the will of a single man, and he is just as correct as the Russian historians who claim that Napoleon was attracted to Moscow by the skill of the Russian generals. Here, in addition to the law of retrospective interpretation, which sees the entire past as preparation for an accomplished fact, there is also an interconnection that confuses the whole issue. A good player who has lost at chess is genuinely convinced that his defeat was the result of a mistake that he made, and he searches for that mistake in the beginning of the game, but he forgets that every move he made throughout the entire course of the game contained the same mistakes (not a single move was perfect), but he can only see the mistake because his opponent took advantage of it. How much more complex is this game of war, which takes places under specific historical conditions, in which it is not just one will that controls lifeless automatons, but everything results from the innumerable conflicts of various wills.

Everything that happens in a matter in which many people act together does not happen according to these people's will, but according to various zoological laws, and it is not given to man to foresee their outcome.

After Smolensk, Napoleon sought to give battle beyond Dorogobuzh at Vyazma, and then at Tsarevo-Zaimishche, but due to the conjunction of innumerable circumstances, it turned out that the Russians were unable to join battle until Borodino, sixty *versts* from Moscow. It was after Vyazma that Napoleon gave the order to move directly on Moscow.

*Moscou, la capitale asiatique de ce grand Empire d'Orient, la ville sacrée des peuples d'Alexandre, Moscou avec ses innombrables eglises en forme de pagodes chinoises!* This Moscow gave Napoleon's imagination no rest. On the march from Vyazma to Tsarevo-Zaimishche, Napoleon rode his bob-tailed cream ambler, accompanied by the Guards, a bodyguard, pages and adjutants. Berthier dropped back in order to interrogate a Russian prisoner taken by the cavalry. He galloped to catch up with Napoleon and reined in his horse with a cheerful expression on his face.

"Well, what?" said Napoleon.

"He's one of Platov's Cossacks, he says that Platov's corps is joining a large army, that Kutuzov has been appointed commander-in-chief. He's very knowledgeable and a great chatterbox."

Napoleon smiled and gave orders for the Cossack to be given a horse and brought to him. He wished to speak with him himself. Several adjutants galloped off, and an hour later a Russian serf in an orderly's jacket, seated on a French cavalry saddle, with a roguish drunken, jolly face, rode up to Napoleon. Napoleon ordered him to ride beside him and began asking him questions.

"Are you a Cossack?"

"I am, your honour."

"The Cossack, not knowing the company in which he found himself, because there was nothing in Napoleon's simplicity that could reveal to the oriental mind the *presence* of a sovereign, spoke with exceptional familiarity about the circumstances of the war," says Thiers in his account of this episode. In fact, this Lavrushka, Denisov's servant, who had been inherited by Rostov, having got drunk the previous evening and left his master without any dinner, had been whipped and sent to loot a village, where he had been taken by the French. Lavrushka was one of those coarse, insolent servants who has been around a bit, who regard it as their duty to do everything in a base and cunning manner, who are prepared to do any service for their master and who are cunning enough to guess their master's bad thoughts, especially those that are vain and petty.

Having found himself in the company of Napoleon, whose person he recognised very well and very easily, Lavrushka was not in the least embarrassed and merely strove wholeheartedly to serve his new gentlemen. He knew perfectly well that this was Napoleon himself, and the presence of Napoleon could not intimidate him any more than the presence of Denisov or the sergeant-major with his birch rods, because he had nothing that either the sergeant-major or Napoleon could take from him. He told him all the gossip that was discussed among the orderlies. Much of this was the truth. But when Napoleon asked whether the Russians thought they would defeat Bonaparte or not, Lavrushka screwed up his eyes and pondered. He saw subtle cunning in this question (as profoundly depraved people always see cunning in everything) and he frowned cunningly and said nothing for a moment. What he said then was a cunningly woven, vague, sarcastic peasant quip:

"It's like this: if there's a battle, that means your side will soon win it. That's for sure, see, but if three days go by after that there date, then that means it's in God's hands."

This was translated to Napoleon as follows.

"If a battle takes place within three days, then the French will win it, but if it's after three days, then God knows what will happen," the interpreter said with a smile. But Napoleon did not smile, even though he was clearly in a very cheerful mood. Lavrushka noticed this and to amuse him, he dissembled and said he did not know who he was.

"We know you've got Bonaparte, he's beaten everybody in the world, but we're a different kettle of fish . . ." he said, not knowing himself how or why the boastful patriotism had slipped into his words at the end. The interpreter translated these words to Napoleon without the ending, and Bonaparte smiled.

"The young Cossack made his mighty interlocutor smile," says Thiers. After riding in silence for a few steps, Napoleon turned to Berthier and said he wished to see what effect the news that he was the Emperor himself would have on this child of the Don.

The news was relayed. And Lavrushka, realising that this was being done in order to flabbergast him and Napoleon thought he would be frightened, immediately pretended to be overwhelmed, goggled at Napoleon and made the face he usually wore when he was being taken to be flogged.

"No sooner did Napoleon's interpreter tell the Cossack this than the Cossack, overcome by some kind of stupefaction, did not say another word and carried on riding along with his eyes fixed on the conqueror whose name had reached him even across the oriental steppes. All his loquacity was suddenly gone, replaced by a naïve and wordless feeling of ecstatic awe. Napoleon rewarded the Cossack and ordered him to be given his freedom, like a bird who is returned to his native fields."

"In three days Moscow, the oriental steppes . . ." thought Napoleon as he moved towards Vyazma.

Let me not be reproached with selecting trivial details to describe the actions of people who are acknowledged as great, like this Cossack, like the bridge at Arcole, and so on. If there were no accounts attempting to portray the most banal details as great, then my descriptions would not exist either. In a description of Newton's life, the details of his food, the fact that he stumbled, cannot have the slightest impact on his significance as a great man – they are extraneous; but in this case the opposite is true. God knows what would be left of great men, rulers and warriors if all of their actions were translated into ordinary, everyday language.

# V

"The bird returned to its native fields" galloped to the left, reached the Cossacks, asked where the Pavlograd Regiment, which was included in Platov's division, was, and by the evening he had already found his master, Rostov, stationed at Yankovo, where he had only just mounted his horse in order to take a ride to Boucharovo. He gave Lavrushka a different horse and took him along with him.

Boucharovo was not an entirely good choice as a refuge from the French. However, the old count's health was so bad that he would not have reached Moscow. At Boucharovo, despite the doctor's help, the prince remained in the same condition for more than two weeks. There was already talk about the French, the French had already appeared in the surrounding area, and a regiment of French dragoons was stationed twenty-five *versts* away at the estate of a neighbour, Dmitri Mikhailovich Telyanin. But the prince did not understand any of this, and the doctor said he should not travel in his condition.

On the third night after he arrived in Boucharovo, the prince was lying, as he had on the preceding days, in Prince Andrei's study. Princess Marya spent the night in the next room. She had not slept, spending the whole night listening to his groaning and shifting about with the help of the doctor and Tikhon, but she had not dared to go in to him. She had not dared because all these days, as soon as the evening arrived, the prince had begun to show signs of irritation and driven her out with gestures, saying: "I want to sleep, I'm all right . . ." During the day he allowed her in and with his sound left hand he held her hand and squeezed it and became calm until something reminded him that he had been driven out of Bleak Hills. Then, despite all of the doctor's remedies, he began to shout, wheezing, and thrash about. He was clearly suffering greatly, both physically and mentally. The princess suffered no less than he did. There was no hope of recovery.

He suffered . . . "Would not the end have been better – the final end," Princess Marya sometimes thought. And strange as it may seem, as she watched him day and night, almost without sleeping, she often watched him, not in order to find signs of improvement, but watched him hoping to find signs of the approach of the end, of a great grief, but also relief. After a fourth sleepless night spent at his door in tense listening and dry-eyed waiting (Princess Marya did not cry, she was surprised at herself because she could not cry) she went into his room in the morning. He was lying propped up high on his back, with his small, bony hands on the blanket and his eyes staring forward fixedly. She went up to him and kissed his hand and his left hand squeezed hers so tightly that it was obvious he did not want to let go of her for a long time.

"What kind of night did you have?" she asked.

He began speaking (this was what Princess Marya found most terrible), controlling his tongue with a comical effort. He spoke better today, but his face had become like a bird's face and its features had become very small, as if it had dried up or melted away.

"A terrible night," he said.

"Why father? What was bothering you especially?"

"Thoughts! Russia is finished . . ." he began to cry.

Fearing that this recollection would make him furious again, Princess Marya hastily led him on to a different subject.

"Yes, I heard you tossing and turning . . ." she said. But today he did not grow angry as he had done before at the memory of the French. On the contrary, he seemed peaceful, and that astonished Princess Marya.

"Anyway, it's the end now," he said, and then, after a moment's pause: "You didn't sleep? You?"

Princess Marya shook her head: unconsciously imitating her father, she now spoke as he did, trying to say more with signs and also seeming to control her tongue with difficulty.

"No, I could hear everything," she said.

"Dear heart" (or "dearest" – Princess Marya could not make it out but, yes, strange as it seemed, from the look in his eyes it was probably a term of tender affection) "why didn't you come in to me?"

Princess Marya suddenly recovered the ability to cry and sob. She leaned her head down to his chest and burst into tears. He squeezed her hand and gestured with his head for her to go to the door.

"Should we send for the priest?" Tikhon asked in a whisper.

"Yes, yes."

Princess Marya turned back to her father. Before she had time to say anything, he said: "Priest, yes."

Princess Marya went out, sent for the priest and ran into the garden. It was a hot August day, the same day on which Prince Andrei visited Bleak Hills. She ran out into the garden and ran, sobbing, down towards the pond along the paths with young lime trees planted by Prince Andrei.

"Yes, I, I, I. I wanted his death. Yes, I wanted it. And now it's come. Be glad. It's come (I know it has), be glad, you'll have peace," thought Princess Marya, falling down on the withered grass and pressing her hands to her bosom to restrain the convulsive sobs escaping from it. But she had to go back.

She poured water on her head and went on to the big porch. The priest entered her father's room with her. She left and came back when they were wiping his mouth. He looked at her and, when the priest had gone, he indicated the door to Princess Marya again and closed his eyes. She went out into the dining room. The table was laid for breakfast. Princess Marya went up to his door. He was groaning. She went back into the dining room, walked over to the table, sat down, put a rissole and some potatoes on a plate and began eating and drinking water.

Tikhon came in through the door and beckoned to her. Tikhon was smiling in an unnatural way. He was clearly trying to conceal something with this smile.

"He wants you," he said.

Without hurrying, Princess Marya walked across to the door, still chewing her rissole. She stopped at the door to swallow it and wipe her mouth. Finally she took hold of the handle and opened the door with a squeak. He was still lying in the same way, only his face had melted away even more. He looked at her in a way that made it clear he had been waiting for her. And his hand had been waiting for her hand. It clutched it tightly . . . At first it was his hand, it was his face, but a few minutes later, it was not his face lying there on the pillows, and not his hand that was holding hers, it was something strange, terrible and hostile. And Princess Marya became aware of this change suddenly, at the moment when the doctor, no longer walking on tiptoe, but stepping on his full foot, went across to the window and opened the curtains. It was already evening. "I've probably been sitting here for more than two hours," thought Princess Marya. "No, it's not right, what am I afraid of? It is him." She got up and kissed him on the forehead. He was cold. "No he's not here any more. He's gone, and here, at the very same spot where he was, there is some terrible, horrifying mystery . . ."

In the presence of the doctor and Tikhon the women washed what had been him, bound the head so that the open mouth would not stiffen, and bound the parted feet with another shawl, dressed him in his uniform with decorations and set him on the table in the drawing room, covered with brocade. Just as horses shy away and then crowd round and whinny over a dead horse, the crowd of people, members of the household and outsiders, all with a glazed expression in their eyes, crossed themselves and fussed over the fir branches that they scattered on the floor, the brocade, the candles, the funeral headband . . .

Princess Marya sat on the trunk in her room, Prince Andrei's former bedroom, with her dry eyes gazing fixedly straight ahead and thought in horror that she had wanted this . . .

Mademoiselle Bourienne, who had not put in an appearance until now and had been living in the bailiff's house, came into the house again and Princess Marya heard her sobbing and the word "benefactor" and saw her looking at him with a frightened expression and crossing herself in the Catholic manner with her full hand.

Many people came to the funeral: the mayor, the district police officer, neighbours, even strangers who wished to pay their respects to the remains of the general-in-chief. These neighbours included Telyanin. The police captain respectfully informed Princess Marya that it was dangerous to stay any longer and she should leave quickly, because French marauders had begun appearing in the district. But Princess Marya did not understand him at all.

Among those gathered at the funeral was Alpatych, who had come from Bleak Hills that day. It gave the greatest comfort to Princess Marya, in these moments of grief, to see Alpatych and Tikhon, the two men who had been closer than any others to the deceased, who had endured more from him and were more shattered by grief than anyone else. She was especially touched by Alpatych, with his imitation of the old prince's manners. He stood there during the service, holding himself erect and frowning, clearly wishing to preserve a respectful dignity, but then his face suddenly fell, as if the springs supporting it had snapped, and he began shaking his head and sobbing like a woman. The burning of Smolensk, and the ruin of Bleak Hills, occupied by French dragoons, and Prince Andrei's fleeting visit, and now the death of the old prince – all had followed so rapidly one after the other – and all after thirty years of staid, regular life, that sometimes Alpatych could feel his reason beginning to fail. The one thing that supported his strength was the princess, but he could not look at her (he turned his eyes away from her). He felt he was needed by her and all his steadfastness was needed by her. As soon as they came back from the cemetery and Princess Marya saw the empty study where he had lain during his illness, and the empty room where he had lain when he was dead, as always happens, she felt for the first time the full gravity, the full significance of her loss and at the same time the demands of life, which had not stopped, despite the fact that he was no longer there.

The guests gathered for the wake. Alpatych quietly opened the door and went into Princess Marya's room. Several times in the course of that morning Princess Marya had begun to cry and then stopped, had started to do something and then abandoned it. When Alpatych entered, she had been reading, at long last, the letter that Alpatych had brought her before the funeral. It was from Julie, who wrote from Moscow, where she lived alone with her mother, since her husband was in the army. Of the hundreds of letters that Princess Marya had received from her, this was the first one written in Russian and it was filled with news of the war and patriotic phrases.

"I am writing to you in Russian, my kind friend," wrote Julie, "because I possess hatred of all the French and likewise of their tongue, which I cannot endure hearing or speaking . . . We in Moscow are all rapturous with enthusiasm for our adored Emperor. My poor husband suffers hard labour and hunger in the Yiddish inns of Poland, but news I have inspires me more still. You must have heard of Raevsky's heroic feat, when he embraced his two sons and said: 'I shall die with them, but we will not waver.' And indeed, though the enemy was twice stronger than us, we wavered not. We have been passing the time as best we can, war is war. Princess Alina and Sophia sit with me for whole days at a time, and we unfortunate widows of living men produce beautiful conversations over the lint, and only you, my friend, are missing," and so on.

Princess Marya did not know Russian any better than her friend Julie, but her Russian intuition told her that something in this letter was not right. She had stopped reading and was pondering on this when Alpatych came in. The sight of him made the sobs rise in her throat again. Several times she stood up, facing him and holding back the tears, waiting for what he would say, several times he cleared his throat with a frown, trying to begin, and every time they both broke down and began to cry.

Eventually Alpatych gathered his strength.

"I make so bold as to inform your excellency that according to my observations, the danger of remaining in this estate is growing more acute, and I would suggest that your excellency should go to the capital."

Princess Marya looked at him.

"Ah, let me gather my thoughts."

"Because it is necessary, your excellency."

"Well, do as you know best. I will go, I will do everything you say."

"Yes, your excellency. I shall make arrangements and come for your instructions this evening, your excellency."

Alpatych went out, summoned the elder, Dronushka, and gave him instructions to make ready about twenty carts for moving things out of the house, with the princess's beds and the maids.

The estate of Bogucharovo had always had an absentee master until Prince Andrei moved into it, and the Bogucharovo peasants had a quite different character from those at Bleak Hills. They differed from them in their speech, and their clothing, which was coarser, and their manners, and their mistrust and hostility towards the landowners. At Bleak Hills they had been called steppe men and the old prince used to praise them for their stamina in work when they came to help out with the harvest at Bleak Hills or dig ponds and ditches, but he did not like their drunkenness and crude manners. The last period Prince Andrei had spent at Bogucharovo, when he had introduced his innovations – the hospitals and schools – and reduced the burden of quit-rent, had only increased their mistrust of the landowners, as such things always have done and always will do. Rumours circulated among them that they were going all to be registered as Cossacks, or about a new faith to which they were going to be converted, or about some proclamations from the Tsar or other, or about the oath to Pavel Petrovich in 1796, which many of them remembered, believing that he had been about to give them freedom, but the masters had taken it away. For thirty years Bogucharovo had been governed by the elder Dron, whom the old prince had called Dronushka, and who used to bring back Vyazma spice cakes every year after his visit to the fair at Vyazma. Princess Marya could remember him from her childhood: the image of Dronushka, this tall, handsome thin man, with a Roman nose and an exceptionally firm and solid figure, was linked in her mind with the pleasant taste of spice cakes. Dronushka was one of those physically and morally strong peasants who grow a big beard as soon as they come of age and then live in the same way, without changing, until the age of sixty or seventy, without a single grey hair or missing tooth, as erect and agile at sixty as they are at thirty.

Twenty-three years earlier, when Dron was already the village elder, he had suddenly started to drink: he had been strictly punished and replaced as elder. After that Dron had run away and disappeared for about a year. He had walked round all the monasteries and hermitages, been to the lavras and the Solovetsk monasteries. On returning from these places, he had made no attempt to hide. He had been punished again and set to work on a plot of land, paying the full rate of tax. But he did not work and immediately disappeared. Two weeks later, exhausted and thin, barely able to drag himself along, he had come back to his hut and lain down on the stove. Then they had discovered that Dron had spent those two weeks in a cave that he himself had dug out on a hill in the forest and inside which he had sealed himself with rocks plastered with clay. He had spent nine days in that cave without food or drink in the desire for salvation, but on the ninth day he had been overcome by the fear of death and he had dug himself out with a struggle and come home. From that time on Dron had stopped drinking and swearing, been made elder again, and in this position he had never once been drunk or ill, had never been tired by any work or by going two nights without sleep, had never forgotten how many haycocks there had been on any *desyatina* of land for the last twenty years, or a single *pood* of flour that he had issued, and he had spent twenty-three irreproachable years as elder. Never hurrying anywhere, never getting round to anything too late, without haste and without rest, Dron had governed an estate of a thousand souls as deftly as a good coachman manages a three-in-hand.

In response to Alpatych's instruction to gather seventeen carts for Wednesday (it was Monday), Dron said that it was impossible, because the horses were being used for government carts and the others were wandering the bare fields without any feed. Alpatych looked at Dron in amazement unable to grasp the boldness of his refusal.

"What?" he said. "From a hundred and fifty households you can't find seventeen carts?"

"No," Dron answered in a quiet voice, and Alpatych was bewildered by the sight of Dron's downcast, scowling gaze.

"What are you thinking of?" asked Alpatych.

"I'm not thinking anything. Why would I be thinking?"

Following the method used by the old prince when he thought it inconvenient to waste too many words, Alpatych took hold of Dron by his neatly closed coat and began to speak, shaking him from side to side.

"No," he began. "No, just you listen. I'll be back this evening, if the carts aren't ready for tomorrow morning, you've no idea what I'll do to you. Do you hear?"

Dron swayed his body forwards regularly and submissively, trying to anticipate the movement of Alpatych's hands, without any change in the expression of his senseless downward gaze or the submissive position of his arms. He gave no answer. Alpatych shook his head and went off to fetch the Bleak Hills horses, which he had brought with him and left fifteen *versts* away from Bogucharovo.

# VI

Between four and five in the evening that day, long after Alpatych had left, Princess Marya was sitting in her room and, since she lacked the strength to do anything, reading the Psalter, although she was unable to understand what she was reading. Pictures of the recent past – the illness and death – constantly came into her mind. The door of her room opened and Mademoiselle Bourienne, the person she desired to see least of all, entered, wearing a black dress. She walked up to Princess Marya quietly, kissed her with a sigh and began talking about sadness and grief, about how, at such times, it was difficult to think about anything else, especially about oneself. Princess Marya looked at her in fright, sensing that this speech was the prologue to something else. She waited for the real point to come up.

"Your position is doubly difficult, my dear princess," said Mademoiselle Bourienne. "I am not thinking of myself, but you ... Oh, this is terrible! Why did I start this?"

Mademoiselle Bourienne burst into tears.

"Coco?" cried Princess Marya. "Andrei?"

"No, no, calm yourself, but you know that we are in danger, that we are surrounded, that today or tomorrow the French will be here."

"Ah," said Princess Marya, reassured. "We shall leave tomorrow."

"But I am afraid it is too late. In fact I am certain it is too late," said Mademoiselle Bourienne. "Look," and she reached into her reticule and showed Princess Marya a declaration from the French General Rameau, printed on unusual non-Russian paper, which said that the local inhabitants must not leave their homes and that they would be afforded due protection by the French authorities.

Princess Marya broke off before she had read it all and fixed her eyes on Mademoiselle Bourienne. The silence lasted for about a minute.

"And so you wish me to ..." Princess Marya began, blushing bright red, getting to her feet and approaching Mademoiselle Bourienne with her heavy stride, "... to accept the French in this house, to ... No, go away, ah, go away, for God's sake."

"Princess, I say this for your sake, believe me."

"Dunyasha!" the princess called. "Go away," she said.

Dunyasha, a ruddy-cheeked, dark-blonde young woman two years younger than the princess, and her god-daughter, came running into the room. Mademoiselle Bourienne was still saying that it was hard, but there was nothing else to be done, that she asked the princess to forgive her, that she knew ...

"Dunyasha, she won't go away. I'll come to your room." And Princess Marya walked out of the room and slammed the door behind her. Dunyasha, the nanny and all the young women were quite unable to convince her that Mademoiselle Bourienne had been right. Alpatych had not returned. Princess Marya went back to her room, which Mademoiselle Bourienne had now left, and walked to and fro with dry, glittering eyes. Dronushka, whom she had sent for, entered the room and stood fixedly by the doorpost with an expression of obtuse distrust.

"Dronushka!" said Princess Marya, seeing him as an undoubted friend, that same Drona who used to bring special spice cakes from Vyazma and smile when he gave them to her. "Dronushka, is it true what they tell me, that I cannot even leave?"

"And why can't you go?" Dronushka said suddenly with a note of kind humour in his voice.

"They say there is danger from the French."

"Nonsense, your excellency."

"You go with me, please, Dronushka, tomorrow."

"Yes, your excellency. Only Yakov Alpatych ordered the carts for tomorrow afternoon so it just won't be possible, your excellency," said Dron, still with the same kind smile. This quite involuntary smile appeared on his lips when he looked at and spoke with the princess, whom he had known and loved as a little girl.

"Why is it impossible, Dronushka, my dear?" asked the princess.

"Ah, little mother, it's these times, you must have heard yourself. I think God has punished us sinners. They've taken all the horses for the army, and they've trampled all the grain there was, killed it in the field. Never mind feeding the horses, we could even die of hunger ourselves. People haven't eaten these three days. There isn't anything, they've completely ruined us . . ."

"Oh, my God!" said Princess Marya. "And here I am thinking about my grief," she thought and, glad to have been presented with a pretext for concern that would allow her to forget her grief without feeling guilty, she began questioning Dron about the details of the peasants' disastrous situation, searching in her mind for some means to help them.

"Well, don't we have grain, couldn't you give some to the peasants?" she said.

"What's the point of giving it out, your excellency, it will all go the same way. We've angered God."

"Well you give them what grain there is, Dronushka. Try to prevent them from being ruined. Perhaps I should write to someone, I'll write."

"Very well," said Dron, clearly reluctant to carry out the princess's instructions, and he tried to go. The princess called him back.

"But how, when I go, how can the peasants stay here?" she asked.

"Where can they go to, your excellency," said Dron, "when there are no horses and no grain?"

Princess Marya remembered Yakov Alpatych had told her that the Bleak Hills peasants had almost all gone to a village outside Moscow. She told Dron.

"What's to be done?" she said with a sigh. "It's not just us, you all get yourselves together and we'll go, and I, I . . . I'll give everything I have, just as long as you are all saved. You tell the peasants we will go together. Yakov Alpatych will bring the horses now, I'll order him to give ours to anyone who doesn't have one. You tell the peasants that. No, I'd better go to them myself and tell them. Tell them that."

"Very well," Dron said with a smile and went out.

Princess Marya was so taken with the idea of the peasants' misery and poverty that she sent several times to find out if they had come and she asked the servants for advice about what she should do and how. Dunyasha, the second maid, a lively young woman, asked the princess not to go to see the peasants and not to have anything to do with them.

"It's all lies," she said. "Yakov Alpatych will come and we will go, your excellency, but, by your leave, don't you . . ."

"What lies? How can you? . . ."

"But I know, only listen to me, for God's sake." But the princess would not listen to her. Remembering the people who were closest to her, she summoned Tikhon as well.

The talk with Tikhon was even less reassuring than the talk with Dron. Tikhon, the best valet in the world, who had developed the art of guessing the prince's desires to an extraordinary degree of perspicacity, once he was removed from his own area of activity, was no good for anything. He could not understand anyone or anything. He came to the princess with a pale, exhausted face and answered all her questions with the words "as you wish" and tears.

Despite Dunyasha's attempts to dissuade her, Princess Marya put on her hat with the wide brim and went to the barn, where the peasants had gathered. Precisely because they had tried to dissuade her, the princess set out for the village with a special joy, her clumsy feet getting tangled in her skirt as she walked. Dron, Dunyasha and Mikhail Ivanich walked behind her. "What calculation can there be here?" thought Princess Marya. "I have to give everything away, but I must save these unfortunate people entrusted to me by God. I shall promise them a monthly ration from the Moscow estate and accommodation, no matter what it costs us. I'm sure Andrei would have done even more in my place," she thought as she drew closer.

The crowd opened out into a semi-circle, everybody took their caps off, exposing bald, black, ginger and grey heads. Princess Marya walked up to them with her eyes lowered. Standing directly in front of her was an old, stooped, grey-haired peasant, leaning on a stick with both hands.

"I have come, I have come," Princess Marya began, unable to look anywhere but at the old man and addressing him. "I have come . . . Dron has told me that the war has ruined you. This is our common sorrow, and I shall spare nothing in order to help you. I myself am going, because it is already dangerous here and the enemy is close, because . . . and I advise you to go, my friends . . . and I ask you to collect all the best things you own and go with me, and we will all go together to the Moscow estate and there you shall have everything from me. And we shall share our poverty and grief. If you wish to stay here, stay – that is your choice, but I ask you in the name of my dear departed father, who was a good master to you, and for my brother and his son, and for myself. Do as I say and let us all go together." She paused. They were silent too, and nobody was looking at her. "Now, if you are in need, I have ordered grain to be given out to you, and everything that is mine is yours . . ."

She fell silent again, and again they were silent, and the old man standing in front of her stubbornly avoided her gaze.

"Do you agree?"

They were silent. She glanced round at the twenty faces standing in the front row, not a single pair of eyes was looking at her, they all avoided her gaze.

"Do you agree? Come now, answer, will you?" Dron's voice asked from the back.

"Do you agree?" This time the princess asked the old man.

He worked his lips, turning away angrily from Princess Marya's gaze as she tried to catch his gaze.

Finally she did catch his gaze and, as if this had angered him, he dropped his head low and said:

"Why should we agree? Why should we just leave everything?"

"We don't agree," she heard a voice say at the back. "We don't consent. You go, on your own . . ."

Princess Marya started saying that they must have misunderstood her, that she was promising to settle them, to recompense them, but their voices drowned out what she was saying. A ginger-haired peasant at the back shouted louder than the others, and a woman was shouting something. Princess Marya glanced at these faces, and again she could not catch anyone's gaze.

She felt strange and awkward. She had come with the intention of helping them, of doing good for the peasants who had been so devoted to her family, and suddenly those same peasants were looking at her with hostility. She stopped speaking, lowered her head and walked out of the circle.

"See that, how clever she spoke, follow her and slave for her," she heard voices in the crowd say. "Strip the houses and put on chains. Of course! And I'll give you grain, she says," the old man with the stick said with an ironic laugh.

That night Alpatych arrived and brought a dozen horses. But when he sent for Dron, he was told the elder was in a meeting that had been convened again early in the morning and he had told the messenger to say: "Let him come himself." From people who were loyal to him, especially from Dunyasha, Alpatych learned that not only had the peasants refused to provide the carts, but they were all shouting at the inn that they wouldn't let the gentlefolk go, because they'd been told they'd be ruined if the gentlefolk left. However, the horses were ordered to be harnessed, and Princess Marya sat in the drawing room, pale-faced, in her travelling clothes.

The horses had still not arrived at the porch when a crowd of peasants approached the master's house and halted outside on the common.

They had concealed the peasants' hostile intentions from Princess Marya but, even though she pretended to herself that she did not know what was wrong, she understood her own position. Yakov Alpatych, with his face pale and distraught, and also dressed for the road – in trousers and boots – came into her room and cautiously suggested that since they might encounter the enemy on their way, perhaps the princess would wish to write a note to the Russian military commander at Yankovo (fifteen *versts* away), asking for an escort to come.

"Knowing your excellency's status, they cannot refuse."

Princess Marya realised that the escort was needed to dispel the peasants.

"Not for anything, not for anything," she said with ardent determination, "tell them to bring the carriage and we will go."

Yakov Alpatych said: "As you wish" – but he did not go.

Princess Marya walked to and fro across the room, occasionally glancing out of the window. She knew that her retinue, the Bleak Hills house serfs, had weapons, and what she was most afraid of was bloodshed.

"What are they standing out there for?" Princess Marya asked Alpatych in a flat, inexpressive voice, pointing to the crowd.

Yakov Alpatych prevaricated.

"I can't say. Probably they want to say goodbye," he said.

"You should tell them to go away."

"As you wish."

"And then have the carriage brought."

It was after one o'clock in the afternoon, and the peasants were still standing on the common. Princess Marya was informed that they had bought a barrel of vodka and were drinking it.

The priest was sent for to try to persuade them. They could be seen through the front window. Princess Marya sat in her travelling clothes and waited.

"The French, the French," Dunyasha suddenly began shouting, running up to Princess Marya. Everybody dashed to the window and saw three cavalrymen, one on a liver-chestnut horse, two on chestnut horses, ride up to the crowd of peasants and stop.

"The finger of the Almighty!" Alpatych said solemnly, raising his hand with one finger extended. "Officers of the Russian army."

The cavalrymen were in fact Rostov and Ilin, with the newly returned

Lavrushka. They had ridden into Bogucharovo, which for the last three days had been between the two lines of the opposed armies, so that either the Russian rearguard or the French avant-garde could have reached it with equal ease. Men from the French avant-garde were already appearing, in advance of the army's arrival, having already given out false documents for provisions and declared all serfs free and they were demanding that no one should move out, which was what had stirred up the Bogucharovo peasants.

Nikolai Rostov and his squadron had halted fifteen *versts* away, in Yankovo but, unable to find sufficient feed in Yankovo and wishing to take a ride on a beautiful summer day, he had set out with Ilin and Lavrushka to look for more oats and hay even in Bogucharovo, which was rather dangerous, given the present situation of the army. Nikolai Rostov was in a very cheerful mood. On the way he had questioned Lavrushka about Napoleon, made him sing what was supposedly a French song, and he and Ilin had sung and laughed at the thought they would have fun in the large estate house at Bogucharovo, where there should be a lot of servants and pretty girls. Nikolai did not know and did not suspect that this was the estate of that same Bolkonsky who was his sister's fiancé.

They rode up to the barrel on the common and stopped. Some of the peasants doffed their caps in embarrassment, some who were bolder and realised that the two officers were not dangerous, did not bother to doff their caps, and some, who were drunk, did not doff their caps but carried on talking and singing. Two old, lanky peasants with wrinkled faces and sparse beards, came out of the crowd and walked up to the officers, doffing their caps with a smile, swaying and singing some kind of tuneless song.

"Well done, lads!" Rostov said, laughing.

"And they look exactly the same," said Ilin.

"Joll-oll-olly con-ver . . . con-vers . . ." the peasants sang out with happy smiles. Rostov called across a peasant who he thought looked more sober than the others.

"Tell me, brother, do your masters have any oats and hay we can have for a receipt?"

"Oats – plenty," he replied. "Hay – God only knows."

"Rostov," said Ilin, speaking French, "look how many persons of the fair sex there are in the master's house. Look, look, that one's mine, now don't you try to take her away from me," he added, spotting Dunyasha coming towards him, red-faced but determined.

"She'll be ours," Lavrushka said to Ilin with a wink.

"Well my lovely, what can we do for you?" he said to her, smiling.

"The princess told me to ask what regiment you're from and your names."

"This is Count Rostov, squadron commander, and I am your humble servant. Such a pretty one," he said, taking hold of her chin.

"Ai, Dun . . . yu . . . shka . . aa," the two peasants carried on singing, smiling even more happily as they watched Ilin talking with the girl. Alpatych followed Dunyasha out to Nikolai, doffing his hat at a distance. He had already recognised his name.

"May I make so bold as to bother your excellency," he said with deference, but with disdain for the youth of this officer. "My mistress, the daughter of general-in-chief Prince Nikolai Andreevich Bolkonsky, finding herself in some difficulty, owing to the ignorance of these persons" – he pointed to the peasants – "requests you come into the house . . . Would you mind moving away a little," Alpatych said with a sad smile, "it is rather inconvenient with . . ." Alpatych indicated the two peasants, who were capering about close behind him, smiling and singing even more cheerfully and repeating:

"Eh, Alpatych? Eh, Yakov Alpatych? Grand, eh?"

Nikolai looked at the drunken old men and smiled.

"Or perhaps your excellency finds this amusing," Yakov Alpatych said with a staid air, standing with one hand set on the front of his jacket and indicating the old men.

"No, there's not much amusement in that," said Rostov and moved away a little. "Tell her I'll be there in a moment," he said to Alpatych and, after ordering Lavrushka to find out about the oats and hay and giving him his horse, he walked towards the house.

"Well, shall we do a bit of chasing?" he said, winking at Ilin.

"Look there, how delightful," said Ilin, pointing to Mademoiselle Bourienne, who was looking out of a different window. "A man could end up staying the night here. As long as this delightful princess provides rissoles, like yesterday at the mayor's place, I've got hunger cramps."

Bantering like this, they entered the porch and went into the drawing room, where the princess, flushed and frightened in her black dress, met them.

Ilin, having immediately decided that the mistress of the house was not very interesting, glanced at the crack of the door, through which he knew the pretty Dunyasha's eye was probably peeping. Nikolai, on the contrary, as soon as he saw the princess, with her deep, soft, sad eyes and heard her gentle voice, immediately changed completely (although he had not remembered that she was Prince Andrei's sister), expressing a gentle deference and timid sympathy in his pose and the expression of his face. "My sister and my mother could be in the same situation tomorrow," he thought, listening to the timid beginning of her simple explanation. She did not say that the peasants would not let her go and would not give her any carts, but she told him that she had been detained owing to the death of her father and now she was afraid of falling into the hands of the enemy, especially since there were disturbances among the people.

When she started telling him that all this had happened on the day after her father's funeral, her voice began to tremble and tears sprang to her eyes.

"There, that is my situation, and I hope that you will not refuse to help me."

Nikolai immediately stood up and bowed respectfully, in the way people bow to ladies of the royal blood, and declared that he would count himself fortunate if he were able to be of service, and was setting out immediately to carry out her instructions.

Through his respectful tone Nikolai seemed to indicate that, even though he would regard it as his good fortune to make her acquaintance, he did not wish to exploit the occasion of her misfortune as a pretext for familiarity. Princess Marya understood this tone and appreciated it.

"Our steward sees everything in a very dark light, do not take too much notice of him, count," the princess told him. "All I wish is that these peasants would go away and let me leave without seeing me off."

"Princess, your wishes are my command," said Nikolai, bowing like a marquis at the court of Louis XIV, and left the room.

"I do not know how to thank you."

On his way out, Nikolai thought about the two peasants who had sung songs to him and about the others who had not doffed their caps. He flushed, pursed his lips and issued hurried instructions, refusing the tea and lunch that he was offered. In the hallway Alpatych gave Rostov the gist of what was happening.

"Well, brother, why did you go away like that?" asked Ilin. "I managed to give that girl a good squeeze, after all . . ." But, glancing at Nikolai's face, Ilin fell silent. He could see that his hero and commander was in a quite different frame of mind.

"See what unfortunate creatures there are," Nikolai said with a frown. "These rogues . . ." he called Lavrushka, ordered him to give the horses to the princess's coachmen, and set off with him towards the common.

The two jolly peasants were lying one on top of the other, the one underneath snoring and the one on top still smiling good-naturedly and singing.

"Hey! Who's your elder here?" Nikolai shouted, striding rapidly into the crowd and stopping there.

"The elder?" said one peasant. "What do you want him for?" But before he had even finished speaking, his cap went flying and his head jerked to one side from a powerful blow.

"Caps off, you traitors!" Nikolai roared in a strong voice. All the caps leapt off all the heads and the crowd bunched closer together.

"Where's the elder?"

Dronushka, with his stern Roman face and firm glance, removed his cap respectfully, but with dignity, at a distance and walked towards Rostov with an unhurried stride. "I'm the elder, your honour," he said.

"Your mistress asked for carts. Why didn't you give her any? Eh?"

All eyes were on Dronushka, and Nikolai was not completely calm as he spoke with him. Dron's own dignity and calm were very impressive.

"The horses are all away with the army, you can look round the yards, your honour."

"Hm. Yes. All right. Then why are you all here, on the common, and why did you tell the steward that you won't let the princess out?"

"I don't know who said that. How is it possible to talk to gentlefolk like that?" Dron said with a laugh.

"Then why the gathering, and the vodka? Eh?"

"It's just the old men gathered for the village council."

"All right. But all of you, listen to me." He turned to the peasants. "Quick march back home right now, and make sure this man" – he pointed to Lavrushka – "gets a cart from five of the yards straight away. Do you hear me, elder?"

"How could I not help hearing you?"

"Right, quick march." Nikolai turned to the nearest peasant: "Quick march, bring a cart here."

The ginger-haired peasant looked at Dron. Dron winked at the peasant. The peasant stayed put.

"Well?" shouted Rostov.

"I'll do as Dron Zakharych says."

"Seems like we've got someone new giving the orders here," said Dron.

"What?" shouted Nikolai, going up to Dron.

"Eh, there's no point talking about it," Dron said, turning away from Rostov with an abrupt wave of his hand. "No more idle chattering. Let it be the way the elders have decided."

"Let it be," roared the crowd, beginning to stir. "There's too many of you giving orders round here. It's decided, nobody's moving out."

Dron turned away and was about to walk off.

"Stop!" Nikolai shouted at Dron, turning him back to face him. Dron frowned and started moving menacingly towards Nikolai. The crowd

800

started roaring more loudly. Ilin, pale-faced, ran up to Nikolai, reaching for his sabre.

The peasants were grabbing at the reins of the horses, and Lavrushka went dashing over to them. Dron was a head taller than Nikolai and it looked as if he could crush him. Closing his fist in a gesture of contempt, or determination, or menace, he drew his right hand back. But at that very moment Nikolai struck him in the face once, twice, three times, knocking him off his feet, and without stopping for an instant, dashed at the ginger-haired peasant.

"Lavrushka! Tie up the ringleaders!"

Leaving the horses, Lavrushka grabbed Dron from behind by the elbows, took off his belt and began tying him up.

"Come on, we didn't hurt anyone. We just didn't think, y'know," voices said.

"Quick march for those carts. Everyone go home."

The crowd moved off and started to scatter. One peasant started trotting and others followed his example. The only ones left on the common were the two drunks lying across each other and Dron with his hands tied, still with that stern, imperturbable expression on his face.

"Your excellency, give the order!" Lavrushka said to Rostov, indicating Dron. "Just give the order, and I'll give this one and the ginger one such a hiding, hussar-style, we'll have to fetch Fedchenka."

But Nikolai did not respond to Lavrushka's request, he ordered him to help pack up inside the house, while he went to the village with Alpatych to drive the carts out, and sent Ilin for some hussars. When Ilin brought a platoon of hussars an hour later, the carts were standing in the yard, with the peasants taking especial care as they loaded the things from the manor house, painstakingly packing hay into the corners of the carts and under the ropes so that nothing would get lost.

"Don't put it down that stupid way," said the same ginger-haired peasant who had shouted more menacingly than all the rest at the meeting, as he took a box out of the hands of a maid. "It costs money too, y'know. You can't just toss it on like that, it'll get lost. I don't like doing things like that. I like everything done proper, according to the rules, like this, cover it with sacking and then it's just grand. Lovely!"

"Ee, all these books, these books," another peasant muttered good-humouredly as he carried out the bookshelves of Prince Andrei's library. "Don't you grab. But they're heavy, lads. These books are some weight."

"Yes, someone was writing instead of enjoying himself," said a third peasant, pointing to the thick lexicons lying on top. Dron, who had initially been locked in the barn, but then let out at Princess Marya's request, was helping Alpatych with his careful supervision of the loading and despatch of the carts.

Nikolai Rostov, having reported Princess Marya's situation to his immediate superior, was given permission to escort her with his squadron to Vyazma and there, having set her on a route occupied by our forces, he respectfully took his leave of her, for the first time taking the liberty of kissing her hand.

## VII

On taking command of the armies, Kutuzov remembered Prince Andrei and sent him an order to report to central headquarters. Prince Andrei arrived in Tsarevo-Zaimishche on the same day and at the same time as Kutuzov was taking his first review of the troops. Prince Andrei stopped in the village, at the priest's house where the commander-in-chief's team was billeted and sat on a bench at the gates, waiting for His Serene Highness, or His Serenity, as Kutuzov was now known to everyone. In the distance he could hear the sounds of regimental music alternating with the roar of vast numbers of soldiers' voices, shouting "hoorah!" to Kutuzov. Two orderlies, a Cossack, a courier and a butler were standing there at the gates, taking advantage of Prince Kutuzov's absence and the fine weather. A small swarthy lieutenant-colonel of hussars, with shaggy moustaches and sideburns, rode up to the gate and asked if this was where His Serenity was quartered and would he be back soon.

It was Vaska Denisov. He was not acquainted with Prince Andrei, but he went up to him, gave his name straight away and got into conversation. Prince Andrei knew of Denisov from what Natasha had told him about her first admirer, and this bitter-sweet memory suddenly brought him back to angry and painful thoughts that had not occupied his mind for a long time. Having been through so many different, sombre experiences – the abandonment of Smolensk, his visit to Bleak Hills, the recent news of his father's death – these memories had not bothered him in a long while, and if they did occur, they did not affect him with anything like their former strength.

"Are you waiting for the commander-in-chief too?" said Denisov. "They say he's approachable. Thank God. Those sausage-eaters are a disaster. Ermolov was right when he asked to be made a German. Now maybe the Russians will be able to get a word in. The devil only knows what they were doing. You saw all the retreats, I suppose."

"I have had the pleasure," replied Prince Andrei, "not only of taking part in the retreat, but also of losing in that retreat everything that was dear to me, my father, who died of grief . . . I'm from Smolensk province."

"Ah! You're Prince Bolkonsky. Very pleased to make your acquaintance," said Denisov, shaking Bolkonsky's hand and looking into his face kindly and intently. "Yes, I heard, this is a real Scythian war. It's all very good, except for those who have to take the strain . . . So you're Prince Bolkonsky." He shook his head. "I'm very glad, prince, very glad to make your acquaintance," he added again with a sad smile, pressing Prince Andrei's hand.

But for Denisov too the sequence of memories aroused by the name Bolkonsky was now the distant past, and he immediately moved on to his passionate and, as always, exclusive preoccupation of the moment. This was a plan of campaign that he had thought up while serving on the outposts during the retreat, a plan that he had presented to Barclay de Tolly and now intended to present to Kutuzov. The plan was based on the fact that the French line of operation was too extended and the idea that instead of, or in addition to acting from the front and cutting off the French forces' advance, we should move against their lines of communication.

"They can't hold the whole of that line. It's impossible. I'll undertake to break them. Give me five hundred men and I'll break them. That's a certainty. One system – partisans – remember."

Denisov stepped closer to Bolkonsky, wishing to try to prove his idea to him, but at that moment they heard more shouting from the army at the review – less disciplined now, more extensive and mingled with music and songs.

"The review's over," said the Cossack. "Here he comes."

And there was Kutuzov approaching the gates, followed by a crowd of officers running after him with shouts of "hoorah". The adjutants galloped through in front of him and dismounted from their horses, waiting. Prince Andrei and Denisov also went in through the gates in order to meet Kutuzov when he dismounted. Kutuzov halted at the gates, taking his leave of the generals who had accompanied him.

Since Prince Andrei had last seen him, Kutuzov had grown even fatter, flabbier and more swollen. The familiar white eye and the old wound were the first things to catch the prince's eye. Kutuzov was dressed in a uniform tailcoat with a whip on the strap over his shoulder and a white cavalry forage cap. He heaved and swayed ponderously on the white horse that carried him at a brisk pace.

"Phew, phew, phew . . ." he whistled barely audibly as he rode up to the house with an expression of joyful relief on his face, the expression of a man intending to relax in simple surroundings after a formal engagement. He took his feet out of the stirrups and swung his right leg over with an effort. He adjusted his uniform, glancing round with his eyes screwed up and, clearly not recognising Prince Andrei, strode towards the porch with his plunging gait.

"Phew, phew, phew," he began to whistle again in a homely manner, but then he glanced round and, recognising Prince Andrei, called him across. "Ah, hello, prince, hello, my dear fellow, come on, I'm tired." He walked into the porch, unbuttoned his tailcoat and sat down on a bench. "Well, how's your father?"

"Yesterday I received news of his death," said Prince Andrei. "All this was too much for him to bear."

Kutuzov gave him a frightened look, then took off his cap and crossed himself.

"God rest his soul! That's sad." He sighed heavily with his entire chest and said nothing for a while. "A great pity. I loved him and respected him and I feel for you with all my heart." He embraced Prince Andrei and pressed him close. When he let go, Prince Andrei noticed tears in his eyes.

"Come on, come inside, we'll have a talk," added Kutuzov, but just then Denisov, no more timid when facing his commander than when he was facing the enemy, despite the fact that the adjutants at the porch tried to stop him with an angry whisper, walked boldly up to Kutuzov, clattering his spurs on the steps of the porch, gave his name and declared that he had something to communicate to His Serenity of great importance for the good of the fatherland. Kutuzov looked directly at Denisov with an indifferent, weary expression, waved his hand in a gesture of annoyance and repeated:

"For the good of the fatherland? Well, what is it? Tell me."

Denisov blushed like a girl (it was strangely touching to see the colour on that old face with a moustache), and began boldly expounding his plan for cutting the enemy's line of operations between Smolensk and Vyazma. Denisov had spent a month and a half in that region and he knew the terrain, and his plan undoubtedly seemed good, especially owing to the ring of conviction that he put into his words. Kutuzov looked down at his feet and occasionally glanced into the yard, towards the next house, as if he were expecting something from that direction. And soon an officer with a briefcase under his arm did appear out of the house that he was looking at and made his way towards the porch.

"What, done already?" Kutuzov shouted to the officer with an air of annoyance. And he shook his head, as if to say: "How can one man manage to do so much?"

Denisov was still talking, giving the honest, noble word of a Russian officer that he would break Napoleon's lines of communication.

"Subaltern Kirill Andreevich Denisov, who is he to you?" Kutuzov interrupted.

"My uncle, Your Serenity."

"Oh, we were friends! Very well, very well, dear fellow. Stay here at headquarters, I'll have a word with you tomorrow." And he stretched out his hand for the papers that his duty general had brought for him.

"Would Your Serenity not like to come inside?" asked the duty general. "You have to sign the papers, review the plan . . ."

"Everything's ready, Your Serenity," said an adjutant. But Kutuzov evidently only wished to go inside when he was free.

"No, tell them to bring a table here, dear fellow, I'll look at them here," he said. "Don't you go away," he added, speaking to Prince Andrei. For quite a long time Prince Andrei silently observed this old man whom he had known for so long and on whom all of Russia's hopes now rested. He stayed while the papers were signed and the duty general reported. One of the most important themes of this report was the choice of a position for battle and criticism of the position chosen by Barclay de Tolly at Tsarevo-Zaimishche.

During the report Prince Andrei heard a female voice whispering and silk rustling inside the front door. Several times, glancing in that direction, he saw a woman behind the door, plump, ruddy-cheeked and beautiful, dressed up in a pink dress of fine wool and a lilac silk shawl, and holding a dish. Kutuzov's adjutant explained to Prince Andrei that she was the mistress of the house, the priest's wife, who was intending to greet His Serenity with bread and salt. Her husband had greeted him with the cross in church, and she was greeting him at the house. "A very fine-looking woman," the adjutant added.

Kutuzov listened to the duty general's report and the criticism of the position at Tsarevo-Zaimishche in the same way as he had listened to Denisov. He listened only because he had ears that could not help hearing; but it was obvious that nothing they could tell him could surprise or even interest him, but that he knew everything they were going to say to him and he only listened to it all because he had to listen through to the end, as one has to listen through to the end of a prayer service when it is sung. Everything that Denisov had said had been practical and intelligent. What the duty general was saying was even more practical and intelligent, but it was obvious that Kutuzov despised knowledge and intelligence and knew something else that would decide the matter, something else that was independent of intelligence and knowledge. Prince Andrei watched his face attentively, and the only expression he could find there was one of boredom, the need to observe decorum, and curiosity about the significance of the female whispering behind the door, the rustling and the brief glimpses of the pink dress. It was obvious that Kutuzov despised intelligence, and learning, and even the patriotic feeling that Denisov had shown, but he clearly despised them with his own inner intuition and knowledge, because he made no effort to show them. He despised them because of his desire to relax, to have a joke with the priest's wife and fall asleep, he despised them because of his age, his experience of life and his knowledge that what had to happen would happen.

"Is that all now?" asked Kutuzov as he signed the final document and, rising heavily to his feet and adjusting the folds of his plump white neck, he moved towards the door.

The blood rushed to the face of the priest's wife as she seized the dish which, despite having spent so long preparing herself, she still hadn't managed to present at the right moment, and offered it to Kutuzov with a low bow. Kutuzov screwed up his eyes and smiled, took her chin in his hand and said:

"And such a beauty! Thank you, my sweetheart!"

He took several gold coins out of his pocket and put them on the dish. The priest's wife smiled, making dimples on her ruddy-cheeked face, as she followed her cherished guest into the room. Prince Andrei remained on the porch, waiting. Half an hour later he was called to Kutuzov again. Kutuzov was lying reclining in an armchair in the same unbuttoned coat, but in a clean shirt. He was holding a French book in his hand and when Prince Andrei came in, he marked his page with a knife and closed it. Prince Andrei saw from the cover that it was a novel by Madame de Genlis.

"Well, sit down, sit down here, let's talk," said Kutuzov. "It's sad, very sad. But remember, my friend, that I am your father, your second father. I summoned you in order to keep you with me . . ."

"I thank Your Serene Highness," replied Prince Andrei, "but I am afraid . . . that I am no longer fit for staff work," he said with a smile that Kutuzov noticed and which made him look quizzically at the prince. "But even more important, I have grown used to the regiment, and I've come to love the officers and the men. If I decline the honour of being at your side, then believe me . . ."

An expression of kind, subtle intelligence lit up Kutuzov's face. He interrupted Bolkonsky.

"I'm sorry to lose you, but you're right, you're right. It's not here that we need the good men. There are always plenty of advisers, but no good men. The regiments wouldn't be any different with all the advisers serving in them. I remember you at Austerlitz . . . I remember, with the banner." Kutuzov pulled him closer by the hand and kissed him, and once again Prince Andrei noticed tears in his eyes. Although he knew that Kutuzov grew tearful easily and that he was being particularly affectionate now on account of his loss, Prince Andrei was still gladdened and flattered by this reminder of Austerlitz.

"Go your way and God be with you. Well, tell me about Turkey, about Bucharest . . ." he said, suddenly changing the subject. After talking about Wallachia and asking about the Caliphate, in which he was particularly interested, Kutuzov returned to the subject of advisers, as he called the staff officers. He was clearly concerned about them.

"There were just as many advisers there. If I'd listened to them, we'd still be fighting in Turkey now. They all want to do things as fast as possible. But what's done fast simply doesn't last. If Kamensky hadn't died, he'd have been finished anyway. He used to storm fortresses with thirty thousand men. It's not hard to take a fortress, but it's hard to win a campaign. And what's needed for that is not storming and attacking, but patience and time. Kamensky sent soldiers against Rushchuk, but all I applied was patience and time, and I took more than that, and the Turks were eating horse meat. And so will the French."

"Battle will have to be accepted, however," said Prince Andrei.

"It will have to be, if that's what everybody wants, and then . . . There's nothing stronger than those two warriors, patience and time, they'll do everything, but the advisers won't hear of it, that's the problem. Well, goodbye, dear friend; remember that I share your loss with all my heart, and to you I am not a His Serene Highness or a commander-in-chief, but a father. Farewell."

How and why it happened, Prince Andrei could not explain at all, but after this meeting with Kutuzov he returned to his regiment feeling reassured about the general course of events and the person to whom the conduct of the war had been entrusted. The more he observed the absence of all human interests in this old man, who retained only the habits of passions, the more sure he felt that this was the man that was needed. He would not have any personal interests and he would not undermine the common cause. He would remember everything, listen to everything, calculate everything, he would be afraid of making a mess of things and losing the command, which amused him, and he would inadvertently do everything necessary for the common cause . . . He was that heavy carthorse, broken-down and old, who would not run in the treadmill, would not jump off, would not move in fits and starts and break the wheel, but would walk steadily at the same pace as the wheel moved downwards, and that was what was needed. This feeling, which was experienced more or less vaguely by everyone, was the basis of the unanimity and general approval that accompanied Kutuzov's appointment as commander-in-chief.

Prince Andrei had been feeling very gloomy and sad on that day. Only the day before, he had received the news of his father's death. The last time he had seen his father, he had quarrelled with him. He had died a sudden and painful death. His sister, his son and his son's tutor, a sensitive person and ideal friend for the child, but quite useless for providing help and support in Russia, had been left alone with no protection. How ought Prince Andrei to act? His first emotional response prompted him to abandon everything and go galloping to them, but then he clearly pictured to himself the solemn grandeur of the situation in which he found himself and decided to submit to that situation and stay. The fatherland was in danger, all hopes of personal happiness had been destroyed, he had no use for his life, the one person who had understood him, his father, had died in misery. What else that was dear to him was in danger? What else could he do? Flee from the army like a coward to try to help his loved ones but avoiding danger and deserting his duty, or seek death in the obscure ranks of the army, doing his duty and defending the fatherland? Yes, he had to choose the latter. Duty and death. After visiting Kutuzov and declining Kutuzov's invitation, his mood as he immersed himself once more in the obscure ranks of the army was gloomier than ever.

## VIII

On the 24th of August the French Emperor's chamberlain, de Beausset, and Colonel Fabvier arrived, the former from Paris and the latter from Madrid, at Napoleon's headquarters at his camp at Borodino. Having changed into his chamberlain's uniform, Beausset ordered a box containing a portrait that he had brought for the Emperor to be carried in ahead of him as he entered the reception room of the house occupied by the Emperor. This was the house of the Mozhaisk district landowner. I.G. Durov. The Emperor Napoleon was sleeping in Durov's former study, which still had plates decorated with gigantic ears of rye and a vase standing on the windowsills, and a portrait of Durov's father in a gold frame.

The military courtiers were already jostling in the reception room, the former hall. The newly arrived Monsieur de Beausset replied jokingly to questions about the ladies of Paris. Colonel Fabvier talked about how things were going in Spain and enquired about the progress of the Moscow campaign. Several men laughed as they spoke about the eccentricities of the Muscovites, one general by the window informed him in a whisper that the campaign was taking too long, their lines were over-extended, that there were disturbances in the army, the transports were immense and the day before yesterday at Gzhatsk many of the marshals had suggested to Napoleon that they needed to halt and spend the winter in Smolensk, but fate had evidently decided otherwise. The Emperor had said, as if he were fortune-telling: "If the weather tomorrow is bad, I shall listen to your advice and stay in Smolensk, if the weather is good, then we march on," and the weather was excellent, *et nous voilà aux portes de Moscou.* "God only knows, God only knows, what will come of this," said the generals, who saw everything in a bad light, but just then another of Fabvier's acquaintances came up to him and, as a jolly joke, told him what had happened the day before to the wagons of the commander of the avant-garde.

The Emperor had several times ordered that there should not be any superfluous carriages, and the day before he had come across a fine carriage crammed with things belonging to General Jouber. A charming little Polish carriage, which the general was sending to Vilnius. "And just imagine, my dear fellow, the Emperor ordered the carriage to be burned, with all the clutter in it . . . You should have seen the poor general's face . . . Well, *mon cher,* it was really comical."

At this time, Napoleon, concluding his toilet, was in shoes and short stockings that fitted tightly over his fat calves, but without a shirt. His fat stomach was exposed, with the breasts like a woman's hanging above it. One valet was spraying eau-de-cologne on the fat, pampered body, and another was massaging His Majesty's back with a brush. His short hair was wet and tangled on his forehead. Napoleon snorted and said: "More of that.

"Tell Monsieur de Beausset and Fabvier as well to wait for me."

The two valets rapidly dressed His Majesty and he emerged, cheerful and lively, walking with firm, quick steps. Monsieur de Beausset, with the help of the other gentlemen, made haste to tear open his package. It was a portrait of the Emperor's son, the King of Rome (the title that people were so fond of repeating in connection with Napoleon's son and which had probably become inseparable from him because it was totally meaningless), painted by Gérard. It was supposed to have been set up on the chairs (the same chairs on which Durov's children had played horses), directly facing the door through which the Emperor would enter.

But the Emperor had dressed with such unexpected speed that the courtiers were afraid they would not get it unpacked in time. Napoleon was in a very good mood. As he emerged, he noticed what they were doing, but did not wish to deprive them of the satisfaction of giving him a surprise. Acting as if he had not seen anything, he turned to Fabvier, called him over and began questioning him about the details of the battle of Salamanca. Napoleon listened with a frown, without speaking, to what Fabvier told him about the bravery and devotion of his forces who were fighting at the other end of Europe and who had but one thought – *to be* worthy of their Emperor – and one fear – of failing to please him. The battle had turned out badly. "It could not have been otherwise, without me," he thought. "Never mind. We will set this right from Moscow."

"*Au revoir*," he said to Fabvier and called Beausset.

Beausset gave a low bow, the kind of French courtly bow that only the servants of the Bourbons knew how to make, approached Napoleon and handed him an envelope. Napoleon was in a good mood, because the Russians were obviously accepting battle, and he felt as cheerful as a man who has been waiting biding his time for a chance to play a good card. In addition, the battlefield itself was on the banks of the river Moscow. Moscow, with its countless churches; Moscow, where Napoleon knew he was going to be. He knew it. Napoleon turned happily to Beausset and tweaked his ear.

"And you managed to get here. I am very glad to see you. Well, what has Paris to say?"

"Paris regrets your absence," de Beausset replied as he ought to. But Napoleon already knew this, it was not worth talking about.

"I am very sorry to have made you travel so far."

"I expected nothing less than to find you at the gates of Moscow, Your Majesty," said de Beausset.

Napoleon smiled and held out his hand. One of the leading adjutants jumped forward with a gold snuffbox and placed it in the hand. Napoleon took a pinch and sniffed it.

"Yes, it has turned out well for you," Napoleon joked. "You like travelling, and in three days you will see Moscow . . ."

De Beausset bowed in gratitude for this special attention.

"Ah, what is this?" said Napoleon, noticing that all the courtiers were looking at a brightly coloured portrait of the King of Rome that looked like one of Murillo's boys combined with Raphael's Christ, with a little something from the face of the boy from whom it had been painted. Napoleon wished to talk more with de Beausset and boast to him of his campaign and the conquest of Moscow, that Asiatic city with its countless churches. But he could not, everyone was waiting to see the effect of the

810

surprise. Napoleon had to turn his attention to the portrait, and with the typical Italian ability to change his expression at will, he walked up to the portrait and assumed an air of contemplative affection. He felt that whatever he would say and do now was history. He felt that the best thing he could do now – he, the great Emperor, with his grandeur, his great army, the pyramids, Moscow and her steppes – the best thing he could do was to display a feeling which is the opposite of grandeur – plain, simple fatherly affection. His eyes clouded over, he took a step and glanced at a chair, the chair slid under him and he sat down on it, facing the portrait. A single gesture from him, and everybody tiptoed out of the room, leaving him alone with the feelings of a great man. After sitting there for a while, without knowing why he reached out and touched the rough highlights, then got up, rang the bell and went to have breakfast. Over breakfast, as always, he received people and issued orders.

After breakfast he went for a ride and invited Fabvier and de Beausset, who loved to travel, to join him on his excursion.

"Your Majesty, you are too kind," said Beausset, who wanted to sleep. He did not know how to ride and was afraid to.

Napoleon rode out on to the field of Borodino.

The Russian forces were visible on the other side of the river and in the redoubt at the village of Shevardino. Napoleon did not need to give any instructions. The Russian forces had set themselves out in the open field without the slightest cunning, working on their fortifications and waiting for battle. It was already too late to start the battle that day. And furthermore, his forces had not all gathered yet, and the order for them to move up had been given a long time before. There was nothing he had to do and no orders he had to give. The question of how to attack the Russians – from the front, from the flank or by encircling them had not been decided and could not have been decided yet in Napoleon's mind, since he still did not have reliable information about the Russian positions and their strength, and therefore there were no orders to be given and nothing could be begun that evening, but everybody was awaiting orders. Many put forward their own opinions, which Napoleon encouraged them to do. The weather was excellent and Napoleon's mood was good. He looked at the Shevardino redoubt and said:

"That redoubt will not be hard to take."

"You only have to give the order, Your Majesty," said Marshal Davout and Napoleon, glancing round at de Beausset and seeing adoration in his eyes, immediately gave the order to attack the redoubt and dismounted in order to admire the spectacle more calmly.

# IX

The Shevardino redoubt was attacked on the evening of the 24th and about ten thousand men were killed or wounded on both sides. When it began to get dark, a page gave Napoleon his horse and another held the stirrup, and he rode at a walk back to Durov's house to have supper.

On the 24th there was a battle at the Shevardino redoubt. On the 25th, neither side fired a single shot. On the 26th there was the Battle of Borodino, which historians call a great event – the great battle at Moscow, the anniversary of which is now celebrated, for which at the time prayers of gratitude were offered up in both the Russian and the French armies, thanking God for their having killed many men – and concerning which Kutuzov wrote to his sovereign that he had won the battle, while Napoleon declared to his army and his people that he had won it, the battle concerning which the argument continues to this day about whose instructions were better and displayed the greater *genius* (they are especially fond of this word). But to us, the generations who have followed after these events, it all seems just as sad an event as a single murder, and more interesting only to the extent that eighty thousand murders committed in a single day at a single spot are more interesting than one, and an event for which we do not see any reason either to thank or reproach God, like any other inevitable event, such as spring, summer and winter. We see this event as an inevitable phenomenon that could not have been produced by the wills of the individuals Kutuzov and Napoleon, and in which their wills played no more part than the will of each soldier, an event that these generals not only did not create, they did not foresee it, they did not control it and they did not understand it. As is always the case in war, their actions – the actions of these geniuses – were as meaningless as the actions of that soldier who fired point-blank at another, foreign, soldier he did not know.

We would not have dwelt on the analysis of the actions of the generals, had the conviction that these general were geniuses not become so engrained.

The actions taken by Napoleon and Kutuzov at the Battle of Borodino were involuntary and meaningless. Why, in the first place, was battle given at Borodino? It did not make sense for either the French or the Russians. The immediate outcome of this murder for the Russians was, and had to be, that they moved closer to the destruction of Moscow, which they feared more than anything else in the world, while the French moved closer to the destruction of their army, which was also what they feared most in all the world. If the generals had been guided by rational considerations, then surely it ought to have been clear to Napoleon that, after travelling two thousand *versts* into Russia and losing a quarter of his army, by accepting battle he was sealing his own doom. And it ought to have been equally clear to Kutuzov that by accepting battle, he was sure to lose Moscow. This was mathematically clear, as clear as the fact that if, in a game of draughts I have fewer draughts and I exchange pieces one for one, I am sure to lose, and therefore I should not exchange pieces. When my opponent has sixteen draughts and I have fourteen, I am only weaker than him by one eighth, but if I swap thirteen pieces, then he will be three times as strong as me. This would seem to be clear, but neither Napoleon nor Kutuzov saw it, and there was a battle.

Before the Battle of Borodino, the ratio of our forces to those of the French was 5 to 6, but after the battle it was 1 to 2, i.e. before the battle it was a hundred and three thousand to a hundred and thirty thousand, and afterwards it was fifty thousand to a hundred thousand. And Moscow was surrendered. Napoleon acted with even less genius, losing some of his army and extending his line even further.

If it is said that, by taking Moscow he thought to put an end to the campaign, as he did by taking Vienna, then there is a great deal of evidence that this is not so. Napoleon's historians themselves tell us that from Gzhatsk onwards he already wanted to accept the advice to turn back and he knew how dangerous his extended position was: he knew, in addition, that the occupation of Moscow would not be the end of the campaign; from Smolensk onwards he saw the condition in which all the Russian towns were left to him, and in Smolensk he himself had told Tuchkov that if the taking of Moscow did not decide the fate of the campaign, then the Russians' losses would be irreparable, he said, in his vulgar manner of thinking, that the occupation of a capital by the enemy was like a girl losing her virginity, once it has been lost it cannot be recovered.

By giving and accepting battle at Borodino, Kutuzov and Napoleon acted involuntarily and senselessly. But the historians later adjusted their cunningly woven arguments of the foresight and genius of the commanders to fit the accomplished facts. Of all the involuntary instruments of world events, the commanders were the most servile and involuntary participants.

The ancients left us models of heroic poems in which the gods controlled the actions of the heroes, decided their fate, wept over them, interceded for them, and we have continued this form of poetry for a long time, even though everyone has long ago ceased to believe in the heroes. The ancients also left us models of heroic history, in which the entire interest of history is focused on various Romuluses, Xerxeses, Caesars, Scaevolas, Mariuses, and we still cannot accustom ourselves to the fact that history of that kind has no meaning for our own times.

# X

After the sovereign left Moscow, when that first moment of rapture had past, the life of Moscow continued in its former, customary manner, the course of this life being so ordinary that it was difficult to remember those earlier days of exaltation, and difficult to believe that Russia really was in danger and that the members of the English Club were also sons of the fatherland and prepared to make any sacrifice for it. The only reminder of the mood that had existed during the sovereign's presence in Moscow was the demand for contributions of men and money which, as soon as they were made, were clad in legal, official form. Old men hemmed and hawed as they gave instructions for recruits to be handed over for the army and the home guard, and for the breaches which these sacrifices made in the economies of their estates to be repaired. The danger from the enemy and patriotic feelings and pity for the dead and wounded, and sacrifices, and fear of the enemy's approach – in the ordinary life of society, all of this lost its stern and serious significance, and in the conversations at boston tables or in a circle of ladies who sat tweaking lint with their white hands, it assumed an insignificant character and was often the subject of arguments, jokes or boasting.

And with the approach of the enemy and danger, people's view of their own situation did not become more serious, but even more frivolous, as always happens with people who see danger approaching. At the approach of danger, two voices speak with equal strength in a man's soul: one says very reasonably that man invented the very nature of the danger and also the means of ridding himself of it; the other says, even more reasonably, that it is too difficult and painful to think about danger, since it is not in man's power to foresee and save himself from the overall course of events, and therefore it is better to turn one's back on what is difficult and painful until it has already happened and think only of pleasant things. As an individual, man – for the most part – heeds the first voice, but as a member of society, on the contrary, he heeds the second. That was now the condition of the inhabitants of Moscow.

The news that our army had retreated one day's march closer to

Moscow and that another battle had taken place was related together with the news that Princess Gruzinskaya had become very unwell and had driven away all the doctors, and was being treated by some wonder-worker, and that Katish had finally managed to catch a fiancé, and Prince Pyotr was in a very bad way. The proclamations on leaflets by Count Rostopchin that the sovereign had instructed him to make a big balloon, in which one could fly anywhere one wished, with the wind and against the wind, and that he was now well, that he had had trouble with one eye, but now he could see with both, and that the French were a puny people, that one woman could toss three Frenchmen with a pitchfork, and so on, such announcements were read and considered with the same interest as the latest rhyming verse from P.I. Kutuzov, V.L. Pushkin and Pierre Bezukhov. Some people liked these proclamations and in the club, in the corner room, they gathered to read them and laugh at the puny French. Some people did not approve of this tone and said it was banal and stupid. They talked about the fact that Rostopchin had sent all French people and even all foreigners out of Moscow, that there were spies and Napoleon's agents among them; with the same effort not to forget a single detail they related how, as Rostopchin despatched them on the barge he had said: "I hope that this boat will not become Charon's boat for you", they said that all the government offices had already been sent out of Moscow and immediately added Shinshin's joke that for that alone Moscow ought to be grateful to Napoleon. They said that Mamonov's regiment would cost him eight hundred thousand, that Bezukhhov had spent even more on his battalion, but the best thing about what Bezukhov had done was that he himself was going to put on uniform and ride at the head of the battalion, and he wouldn't charge people who watched him anything for their places.

"*Vous êtes* never nice to anyone," said Julie Drubetskaya, gathering up and squeezing together a heap of tweaked lint with her slim fingers covered in rings. "Bezukhov is so good, so kind. Where's the pleasure in being so *caustique?*"

"A forfeit to help the wounded, for being *caustique*," said the man whom she had accused.

"And another forfeit for using a Gallicism," added someone else. "You're never nice to anyone – you mean: you never show anyone any respect."

"I'm guilty of saying *caustique*," Julie replied, "I'll pay, and for the satisfaction of telling you the truth I am prepared to pay again, but I refuse to feel guilty for using Gallicisms, I do not have the time, as Prince Golitsyn does, to take a teacher and study Russian."

For Pierre the arrival of the sovereign, the meeting in the Slobodsky

Palace and the feeling he experienced there had been a turning point in his life. What was a terrible misfortune for the majority of people in his circle, this danger, this disruption of the usual course of things and the threat of ruin, made Pierre feel happy, refreshed and regenerated.

"But I am glad and happy," he thought, "that the time has come when this regular rhythm of life that has taken hold of me and of which I am so weary, will change, and that the time has come for me to show that it is all nonsense, inconsequential triviality." Pierre, like Mamonov, had begun straight away to assemble and equip a battalion of infantry, one which would cost more than Mamonov's, and even though Pierre's steward attempted to prove to him that, with his affairs in such disorder, he would be ruined by this undertaking, he replied: "Oh, just do it. Does it really matter?" The worse the state of his affairs became, the more he liked it. Pierre had a joyful, restless feeling that at last this false but all-powerful way of life that had shackled him was changing. He either sat in his room or drove around the city, eagerly collecting news and appealing, with all the strength of his heart, for that triumphant moment when everything would collapse to come as soon as possible, that moment when he would be able, not actually to celebrate, but simply abandon, not only his wealth but his entire life, which he needed as little as his wealth.

Even though Pierre had told all his acquaintances the same thing, blushing as he said it – that he would never command his own battalion and in fact he would not even go to war for anything in the world, that, owing to his corpulence he presented too large a target and was too clumsy and heavy – he had in fact been agitated for a long time by the idea of going to the army and seeing with his own eyes what war was like.

On the 25th of August, having been informed by Raevsky's adjutant of the approach of the French and the likelihood of a battle, Pierre wanted even more to go to the army and take a look at what was happening there, and with this goal in mind, he went to Rostopchin to free himself by giving up his place on the war contributions committee. As he drove across Bolotnaya Square, he saw a crowd at the execution site and stopped to get out of his droshky. It was the flogging of a French cook accused of spying. The flogging was only just over, and the flogger was untying a fat man with ginger sideburns wearing blue stockings and a green camisole from the wooden frame. The man was groaning pitifully. Another criminal, skinny and pale, was also standing there.

With a pained, frightened expression like that on the face of the thin Frenchman, Pierre pushed his way through the crowd, asking: "What's this? Who? What for?" but received no answer. The crowd of officials, ordinary people and women was watching eagerly and waiting. When the fat man was untied and could not help bursting into tears and crying, in the way that sanguine adults cry, angry with himself because he could not help it, the crowd started talking, as it seemed to Pierre, in order to smother its own feeling of pity, and he heard what the voices said:

"That's made him sing," said one man standing beside Pierre, probably a gentleman's coachman, and he himself began singing with a French accent: "Fathers, faithful people, I won't do it again . . ."

"Well, *monsieur*, obviously the Russian sauce is too sour, it's set the Frenchman's teeth on edge," said a clerk, continuing the coachman's joke. Pierre looked, shook his head and frowned, then turned round and walked back to the droshky. He decided he could not stay in Moscow a moment longer and was going to the army.

Rostopchin was busy and sent an adjutant to say it was quite all right. Pierre drove home and gave instructions to his all-knowing, all-powerful, highly intelligent butler Evstratovich to prepare for him to go and join the army at Tatarinova.

Early in the morning of the 25th, Pierre left without telling anyone, and in the evening he reached the army in his droshky, having changed horses along the way. There were horses waiting for him at Knyazkovo. Knyazkovo was full of soldiers and half ruined. On his way Pierre had learned from officers that he had arrived at just the right time, and that day or the next there would be a general engagement. "What am I to do? It's what I wanted, after all," Pierre told himself. "I can't go back now."

His cart was standing by ruined gates with a coachman, a horse-master and saddle-horses. Pierre was about to drive past his own people, but the horse-master recognised him and called to him, and Pierre was glad to see familiar faces after the countless numbers of strange soldiers' faces that he had seen on his way there. The horse-master was standing in the middle of an infantry regiment with the horses and the cart.

In order to change his appearance so as to attract less attention, Pierre had been intending to put on the uniform of his own regiment at Knyazkovo, but when he reached them and realised that he would have to change on the spot, in the open air, in front of the soldiers and officers who were looking in astonishment at his fluffy white hat and his fat body in a tailcoat, he changed his mind. He also refused the tea that the horse-master made for him and which the officers looked at enviously. Pierre was in a hurry to move on quickly. The further he travelled from Moscow and the deeper he plunged into this sea of soldiers, the stronger his anxiety became. He was afraid of the battle that was about to take place and even more afraid that he would be too late for that battle.

The horse-master brought two horses, one a bob-tailed chestnut and the other a black stallion. It was a long time since Pierre had ridden a horse, and he was terrified of getting up on one. He asked which of them was quieter. The horse-master thought about it.

"This one's gentler, your excellency."

Pierre chose the one that was gentler and when it was led up to him, he glanced round timidly to see if anyone was laughing at him, and seized its mane with a force that suggested he would never let go of that mane for anything in the world and climbed up, wishing he could adjust his spectacles, but unable to take his hands off the saddle and the reins. The horse-master looked disapprovingly at his count's bent legs and huge body bent forward against the pommel and, mounting his own horse, prepared to accompany him.

"No, don't, stay here, I'll go alone," muttered Pierre. He did not wish, firstly, to have behind him that reproachful stare at his seat, and, secondly, to expose the horse-master to the dangers to which he was determined to expose himself. Biting his lip and bending forwards, Pierre struck both of his heels against the horse's belly and then, clinging to the horse with those heels, he pulled on the gathered reins, tugging them unevenly to one side and, without loosening his grip on the horse's mane, set off along the road at an uneven gallop, commending his soul to God.

After galloping for two *versts*, scarcely able to stay in the saddle, Pierre was so nervous, he stopped his horse and rode on at a walk, trying to make sense of his situation. He had to make up his mind where he was going and what for, and to whom. He had been driven out of Moscow by the emotions that had assailed him in the Slobodsky Palace during the sovereign's visit, the agreeable awareness that everything that constituted people's happiness, the comforts of life, wealth and even life itself were all nonsense that it was a pleasure to cast aside, in comparison with . . . with something. With what?

Pierre could not really explain to himself, and he did not even try to clarify who or what it was that had led him to discover a special charm in sacrificing all his property and his own life. He was not concerned why he wanted to sacrifice them, but for him the feeling of sacrifice itself was new, joyful and revitalising. As a result of that feeling he had now come from Moscow to Borodino in order to take part in the forthcoming battle. In Moscow *taking part* had seemed to him a perfectly simple and clear business, but now, having seen these masses of men, all divided into different categories and bound to a strict hierarchy, each one immersed in his own job, he realised that it was not possible simply to arrive and take part in the battle, in order to do that he had to attach himself to someone, to subordinate himself to someone, be given something more specific to do than just taking part in the battle in general.

Pierre slowed his horse to a walk, and looked around on both sides of the road, seeking familiar faces, and everywhere he encountered only soldier's faces that he did not know from the various kinds of forces, all gazing with the same astonishment or derision at his white hat and green tailcoat. After riding through two villages that had been destroyed and abandoned by their inhabitants, but were now full of soldiers, he was approaching a third, when he finally met a man he knew and eagerly appealed to him for advice about what he should do with himself. This acquaintance was one of the army's senior doctors. He was riding in a light carriage, sitting beside a younger doctor, and on drawing close, he recognised Pierre and told the Cossack sitting on the coachbox instead of a coachman to stop.

"Your excellency, how do you come to be here?" the doctor asked.

"Why, I just wanted to take a look..."

"Yes, yes, there will be plenty to look at..."

Pierre dismounted and stood there. He fell into conversation with the doctor, asking him for advice on what he should do and who he should turn to and where he could find the Pernovsky Regiment that was commanded by Prince Andrei. The doctor was unable to answer this last question, but replied to the first by advising Bezukhov to go straight to His Serene Highness, Kutuzov.

"You wouldn't wish to find yourself God knows where during the battle, with no help at hand and no one knowing where you are," he said, exchanging glances with his young companion, "but His Serenity knows you and he will receive you graciously... You do that, old chap," said the doctor.

The doctor seemed to be tired and in a hurry, and Pierre was astonished by the familiar way in which he spoke to him, so unlike the affectedly respectful manner in which he had spoken to him in the past.

"When you get into this village – Burdino, I think it's called, Burdino or Borodino, I don't recall – at that spot, you see, where they're digging, take the road to the right, straight to Tatarinova, and you'll reach His Serenity's headquarters."

"But perhaps he has no time."

"He didn't sleep all night – he's preparing, it's no joke thinking through this great heap – I was there. But he'll receive you."

"So, you think..."

But the doctor cut him short and set off towards the carriage.

"I would show you the way, I'd consider it an honour – I would indeed – but I'm up to here." The doctor indicated his throat. "I'm galloping over to the corps commander. After all, as you know, count, tomorrow we have a battle with a hundred thousand men. I have to expect twenty thousand wounded at the very least, and we don't have enough stretchers, or beds, or medical assistants or doctors for six thousand. You do as you wish . . ."

The strange idea that out of those thousands of healthy, living men, young and old who had gazed at his hat in jolly amazement, twenty thousand were probably doomed to be wounded or killed (perhaps the very men that he had seen) struck him so powerfully that he did not say another word to the doctor, or reply when he said goodbye, but carried on standing there with a fixed expression of suffering and fright on his face.

With the assistance of a helpful transport soldier who held his horse while he remounted it, Pierre rode on into the village ahead of him, which the doctor had thought was called either Burdino or Borodino. The small street of this village, like that of the other one, with its roofless houses and a well in the street, was full of peasants in shirts with crosses on their caps and spades across their shoulders, who talked loudly as they came walking towards him. At the very end of the street more peasants like them were building some kind of hill, carrying earth along planks in barrows. Two officers were standing on the hill and giving instructions to the men. Pierre was enveloped by a choking, repulsive stench of men as soon as he rode close to this fortification that was being built by home guard militia.

"Excuse me," Pierre said to one officer, "can you tell me what village this is?"

"Borodino!"

"And how can I get to Tatarinova?"

The officer, clearly glad of a chance to talk, came down from his high position, pinching his nose shut as he ran past the militiamen working in their sweat-soaked shirts.

"Phew, damnation," he said, going up to Pierre and leaning his arm against his horse. "You want to get to Tatarinova? Then you need to go back – this way, you were going straight towards the French. You can see them over there."

"With the naked eye."

"That's right, that's right."

The officer pointed with his hand past the horse at the black masses. Neither of them said anything.

"Yes, there's no knowing who'll be alive tomorrow. There'll be plenty of men missing. Well, God be praised, we all end up the same way." A non-commissioned officer came up to say that someone had to go for baskets to be filled with earth as shields against bullets.

"Right, well send the third company again," the officer said reluctantly. "And who are you?" he asked. "Not one of the doctors?"

"No, I just happen to be here," replied Pierre.

"Well then, back along the street and the second turning to the left, where you can see the well with the handle."

Pierre set off, following the officer's instructions, and before he was even out of the village, he saw infantry marching smartly towards him along the road that he needed to follow, with their shakos off and muskets pointing down at the ground. He heard the sound of religious singing from behind the infantry and soldiers and home guard militiamen overtook him at a run, on their way to meet the marching men.

"They're carrying the Holy Virgin round the army!"

"The Mediatrix of Iversk."

"The Virgin of Smolensk," another soldier corrected him. The militiamen talked as they ran, both the ones who had been in the village, and the ones who had been working on the battery; dropping their spades, they ran to meet the church procession. Behind the battalion that was marching at the front there were priests in chasubles, one with a black veil on his hat, carrying a cross, with the choristers, and behind him came soldiers and officers carrying a big icon with a black face set in a metal cover, and there were crowds of soldiers walking after the icon, in front of it and around it, running and bowing their bare heads down to the ground. The icon halted in the village, the priests lit their censer again and the prayers began.

Dismounting from his horse and removing his hat, Pierre stood there for a while and then rode on.

All the way along the road on the right and the left he saw the same soldiers with the same intense faces that took on the same expression of astonishment at the sight of him. "And these ones, these ones are also among the twenty thousand for whom they are readying the stretchers and beds for tomorrow," he thought as he looked at them. Several adjutants and generals rode towards and past him. But they were all strangers. They looked him over with curiosity and rode past. At the turn into Tatarinova he came across two droshkies each harnessed to a pair of horses, carrying two generals, accompanied by a large number of adjutants. It was General Bennigsen, who was on his way to review the positions. The retinue riding behind Bennigsen included many acquaintances of Pierre. They immediately surrounded him and began asking him about Moscow, and why he was there and, to his surprise, they were hardly surprised at all to learn that he had come to take part in the battle. Bennigsen, halted by a fortification that was under construction,

821

noticed him standing there and, wishing to make his acquaintance, suggested he should ride along the line with him.

"It will be interesting for you," he said.

"Yes, very interesting," said Pierre.

"As for your wish to take part, I think it would be best for you to tell His Serenity, he will be very glad . . ."

Bennigsen said no more to Pierre. He was obviously too agitated about something and fretful on that day, as were most of the people around him. Bennigsen inspected the entire front line of our forces' disposition, made several comments, explained some things to the men with him and a general who came riding up to him, and occasionally gave orders. As he listened to him, Pierre strained all of his mental capacity to understand the nature of the forthcoming battle and the advantages and disadvantages of our position; but he could understand nothing of what he saw and heard. He could not understand because he was used to looking for something subtly profound and brilliant in the disposition of forces before a battle, and could see nothing of the kind here. He saw, quite simply, that certain men were standing here, certain others were standing there, and over here were troops who could just as usefully have been set further to the right or further to the left, closer or further away. And because it seemed so simple to him, he suspected that he did not understand the essence of the matter and listened attentively to what Bennigsen and the men around him said. They rode back along the front, through Borodino, surrounded by its breastwork, where Pierre had already been, then onto a redoubt which as yet had no name, but later became known as Raevsky's redoubt, where they were installing cannon. Pierre paid no attention to this redoubt (they were building them the same everywhere). He did not know that this spot would become the most memorable place on the field of Borodino. Then they went to Semenovsky, where the soldiers were dragging away the final beams from the huts and the drying barns. They then drove downhill and uphill through rye that had been trodden down and smashed as if by hail, along the new road made by the artillery across the hummocks of the plough land, on to the redan fortifications, which were also still being constructed then, and which Pierre only remembered because there he dismounted from his horse and breakfasted with Kutaisov in a trench, as guests of a colonel who offered them meatballs.

Bennigsen halted on the redans and began looking at the enemy, who was facing them, in the Shevardino redoubt that had been ours the day before, about one and a half *versts* away, and the officers assured Pierre that the group of men there was gathered round Napoleon or

Murat. When Pierre went back to Bennigsen, he was saying something, criticising the disposition of the spot:

"You should have moved further forward."

Pierre listened carefully, still chewing his meatballs.

"I don't think this is very interesting for you," Bennigsen suddenly said to him.

"Oh, on the contrary, it's very interesting," said Pierre, repeating the phrase he had uttered twenty times that day, every time not entirely truthfully. He could not understand why it was the redans that needed to be further forward, so that they could be fired on by Raevsky's battery, and not Raevsky's battery that should be further forward, so that it could be fired on from the redans.

"Yes, that's very interesting," he kept saying.

Eventually they reached the left flank, and here Bennigsen confused Pierre's understanding even more with his dissatisfaction at the position of Tuchkov's corps, which was supposed to protect the left flank. The overall position at Borodino appeared to Pierre as follows: the front line, curving outwards somewhat, extended for three *versts* from Gorki to Tuchkov's position. Almost at the centre of the line, slightly closer to the left flank, was the steep-banked river Kolocha, dividing our entire position into two.

Forward points on the line from right to left were 1) Borodino, 2) Raevsky's redoubt, 3) the redans 4) the end of the left flank – a forest of young birch as thick as cartshafts – where Tuchkov was stationed.

The right flank was strongly protected by the river Kolocha, the left flank was weakly protected by the forest, beyond which ran the old Kaluga road. Tuchkov's corps was stationed almost under a hill. Bennigsen decided that this corps was badly sited and ordered it to move one *verst* forward.

Why was it better to stand further forward, without fortifications, why were the other forces not moved up, if the left flank was weak, why did Bennigsen tell the colonel who was with him that this instruction of his should not be reported to Kutuzov, and why did he himself not tell Kutuzov? Afterwards, when Bennigsen met Kutuzov, Pierre heard him say in so many words that he had found everything in good order and not felt it necessary to change anything – Pierre could not understand this, but he found it all even more interesting.

Some time after five o'clock Pierre and Bennigsen arrived in Tatarinova, where Kutuzov was stationed, occupying one large hut with three windows. Beside it there was a board nailed to a wicker fence: "Central Headquarters Chancellery". Facing it was the hut in which Bennigsen was living, with wagons at the entrance.

Just before the village, Pierre was overtaken by his acquaintance Kutaisov, riding back from somewhere with two officers. Kutaisov greeted Pierre in a friendly manner, unable to restrain himself from running a mocking glance all over Pierre's figure, and he smiled at Pierre's question about how he should ask the commander-in-chief for permission to *take part* in the battle.

"Come along with me, count. Prince Kutuzov is probably in the garden under the apple tree. I'll take you to him. Well, how's Moscow, worried?" And without waiting for a reply Kutaisov rode up to a general who was coming towards him in a droshky and said something ardently in French. "The position is unreliable . . . You'd have to be mad," Pierre heard him say.

"Who is that?" asked Pierre.

"That's Prince Evgeny on his way to the left flank to inspect a position that is impossible. They want the artillery to fire from under a hill . . . Oh, yes, that's of no interest to you . . ."

"Oh, on the contrary . . . I find it very interesting. I've looked at everything."

"Ah," said Kutaisov, and he rode across to the fence to which the board was nailed. Kutaisov dismounted and ordered a Cossack to take Pierre's horse. He told Pierre which way to go and where to find his horse later.

In the shed there was an officer sleeping on the hay, covered with a shirt to keep the flies away, and another by the door dining on baked pies and water-melon.

"Is His Serenity in the garden?" asked Kutaisov.

"Yes, he is, your excellency."

Kutaisov walked through the shed into a peasant's apple orchard with the dappled light and shade that is only found in dense apple orchards. It was cool in the orchard, and in the distance he caught a glimpse of tents set up, a carpet and uniform collars and epaulettes. The apples were still on the trees, and by the wicker fence a barefooted boy had climbed into a tree and was shaking it. A little girl was gathering up the apples beneath it. They froze in fright when they saw Pierre. To them it seemed as if the sole purpose of every single person, and therefore of these two as well, was to stop them picking apples. Kutaisov could be glimpsed between the trees, as he walked on towards the gleaming carpet and epaulettes. Pierre, not wishing to distract the commander-in-chief, stayed behind.

"Very well, you take yourself back and send him to me."

Kutuzov, laughing to himself, stood up and set off towards the hut with his swaying, plunging gait, his hands clasped behind him. Pierre went towards to him. But before he got there the commander-in-chief stopped in front of a militia officer whom Pierre knew. It was Dolokhov. Dolokhov was saying something heatedly to Kutuzov, who nodded over his head at Pierre. Pierre came up. Dolokhov was saying:

"All our battles have been lost because of weakness on the left flanks. I have inspected our position, and the left flank is weak. I decided that if I informed you, Your Serene Highness might throw me out, but perhaps you know what I am reporting about and I'll have lost nothing."

"I see, I see."

"But if I am right, then I will have done a service to the fatherland for which I am prepared to die."

"I see, I see."

"And if Your Serene Highness has need of a man to enter the enemy's army and kill Napoleon, then I am ready to be that man."

"I see, I see . . ." said Kutuzov, laughing and looking at Pierre with his eyes narrowed, then he spoke to Tol, who was following him. "I'm coming – I can't be in two places at once."

"Very well, my dear fellow, I thank you," he said to Dolokhov as he let him go. Then he spoke to Pierre:

"You want to sniff the smell of gunpowder? Yes, well it's a pleasant smell. I have the honour of being an admirer of your wife. Is she well? My camp is at your disposal." And Kutuzov walked through into the hut.

After dining with Kutaisov, Pierre asked him for a horse and a Cossack and went to see Andrei, with whom he intended to relax and spend the night before the battle.

# XI

On that clear evening of the 25th of August, Prince Andrei was lying on a carpet spread out in a broken-down shed in the village of Knyazkovo. This shed was on the outskirts of the village, above the slope of the common on which the soldiers of his battalion were stationed. The roof of the shed had been completely removed and one side of it, looking out over a steep descent, had been broken away, so that Prince Andrei had before him a distant and lovely prospect, enlivened by the sight of the troops, horses and columns of smoke rising on all sides from cauldrons. In a space near the shed the remains of a drying barn could be seen, and between the drying barn and the shed there was a strip of aspens and thirty-year-old birches, from which branches had been cut off; one had been cut down and several had been hacked. Prince Andrei had found his soldiers cutting down this little wood or garden, which had evidently been planted by its diligent peasant owner, and forbidden them to cut it, suggesting they should take the sheds and the beams. The birch trees above his head were still covered in jaunty green leaves, with bright-yellow leaves here and there. Not a single leaf was stirring in the quiet of the evening. Prince Andrei felt compassion and love for all living things and he rejoiced as he looked at the birch trees. There were yellow leaves strewn on the spot around him, but they had fallen earlier, and nothing was falling now. They glowed in the bright light that broke through the clouds – a brilliant light. Sparrows flew from the birches to the remaining stretch of the fence and back again.

Prince Andrei lay there with his head propped on one hand and his eyes closed. His instructions had all been given, tomorrow there would be the battle. He had already seen the commanders of his columns, dined with the company commander and battalion commander – and now he wished to be alone and think – think as he had done on the eve of the battle at Austerlitz. No matter how much time had passed since then, no matter how much he had experienced since then, no matter how boring and unnecessary and painful his life seemed to him, he was still feeling excited and his nerves were on edge, just as they had been seven years earlier, on the eve of this battle, the terrible battle that he would see the next day, and just as he had then, he felt a need to sum up his own life and ask himself: What am I and why do I exist?

There was no similarity between the person he had been in 1805 and the person he was in 1812. None of the charms of war existed for him any longer. Continually casting aside his former errors, he had reached a point at which war seemed to be a very simple and straightforward affair, but terrible. Several weeks earlier he had told himself that war was only understood and fought with dignity in the ranks of the soldiers, where there was no expectation of honours or glory – fighting in the company of the Timokhins and Tushins, whom he had despised so profoundly before, and whom he had still not come to respect, but whom he nonetheless preferred to the Nesvitskys, Kutaisovs and Czart-oryskys and so forth, on the grounds that, although the Timokhins and Tushins were almost animals, they were honest, truthful, simple animals, but the others were deceivers and liars, who left the dirty work to others and earned their crosses and ribbons, which they did not even need, through the death and suffering of other people.

But now Prince Andrei could see even this most simplified form of war in all of its horrific pointlessness. His nerves were agitated, he wanted to think, he felt that he was in one of those moments when the mind is so acute that it can cast aside everything unnecessary and confusing and penetrate to the very essence of things, and precisely because of this he was afraid to think. He tried to stop himself, but he did think nevertheless. He tried to summon up the same sequence of thoughts that he had been following earlier, but nothing of the kind stirred within him. "What is it I want?" he asked himself. "Glory, power over people? No, what for? I wouldn't know what to do with it. Not only would I not know what to do, I know for certain that people should not desire anything, there is nothing to strive for." He watched a flock of sparrows fly from the fence to the common, and smiled: "But anyway, what can people decide? Everything follows the same ancient laws that made that sparrow fall behind the others and catch up later. So what is it that I want? What? To die? To be killed tomorrow? Not to exist – for all this to exist, but without me?"

He vividly pictured his own absence from this life with this wicker fence (he had broken off a stick) and the smoke of the cauldrons, and a cold shiver ran down his spine. "No, I don't want that, I'm still afraid of something. What is it that I want? Nothing, but I live because I can't help living and I'm afraid of death. All these men," he thought, watching two soldiers standing by the pond with their bare feet in the water and quarrelling loudly as they tried to tug out of each other's hand a plank that they wanted to stand on to wash their underwear, "these men and that officer who is so pleased at having galloped up on his horse, what do they want, what are they striving for? They think that plank, and that horse of his, and this battle that's going to happen – they think it's all very important, and they go on living . . . And somewhere my Princess Marya and Nikolushka are feeling afraid, and fussing over things, and God knows who is better off – them or me. And until recently I used to believe in everything, like them. How could I have made poetic plans about love, about happiness with women?"

"Oh, my dear boy!" he said angrily, speaking aloud. "How could you? I believed in some kind of ideal love that was supposed to remain true to me while I was absent for a whole year. Like the gentle dove in the fable, she was supposed to pine away in her separation from me and not love another. How afraid I was that she would pine away out of longing for me." The colour rushed to his face. He got to his feet and started walking quickly.

"But it is all much simpler. She's a female, she needs a husband. The first buck she came across was good enough for her. And I don't understand how it is possible not to see such a clear and simple truth. My father also builds at Bleak Hills, and thinks it is his place, his land, his air, his peasants, and then along came Napoleon and, without knowing that my father even exists, he shoved him aside, like sweeping a splinter of wood out of his way, and destroyed his Bleak Hills and his entire life. And Princess Marya says it is a test sent down from above. What is this test for, when he is no longer here and never will be again? And I shall also think that I have been sent a test. A very fine test. That it is preparing me for something. And tomorrow I shall be killed, and not even by the French, but by one of our men, the way that soldier discharged his musket right beside my ear yesterday, and the French will come and grab hold of me by the head and feet and fling me into a pit so that I don't stink under their noses, tomorrow they will reach Moscow and put their horses in the Cathedral, as they did in Smolensk, and tip oats and hay on to the Saviour's shrine, and the horses will be very calm . . . For whom is that a test? For a man who still does not understand that he is being mocked. It's stupid when you don't understand, and vile when you do understand the whole joke."

He walked into the shed, lay down on the carpet, opened his eyes and stopped thinking clearly. Images came to him, and were replaced by others. He lingered for a long time over something in one of them, and then was distracted by a very familiar, lisping voice speaking outside the shed: "Yes, it's not Pyotr Mikhailovich I'm looking for, but Prince Andrei Bolkonsky." Prince Andrei paid no more attention to the voice and began wondering what he had been thinking about so happily for so long: "What was I thinking about last? Yes, what was it? I walked in through the back door of our room. Natasha was sitting in front of the mirror, combing her hair. She heard my steps and looked round. She turned round, holding the locks of her hair in her hand, covering her fresh, rosy cheek with them and looked at me in happiness and gratitude. And I was her happy husband, and she was, yes, she was Natasha. Yes . . . Perhaps that man kissed her on those very cheeks, on those very shoulders. No, no, clearly I shall never forgive that, and I shall never forget."

Prince Andrei felt his tears choking him. He sat up and rolled over onto his other side. "And it could never have happened. Yes, there is one thing I want, that I still want. To kill that man, to see him.

"But why did he not marry her? He would not stoop so low. Yes, what for me was the very pinnacle of my desires, was something he despised. To such men belongs the kingdom of earth. But what is left to me? There is something, and yet I do not wish to be like them."

He heard steps and voices at the door. He knew it was the battalion commanders coming to drink tea with him, but in addition to them there was a familiar voice that said: "Oh, damn!" Andrei glanced round. It was Pierre in his fluffy hat, who had failed to bend down as he entered with the officers and banged his head against a thick pole that had been left across the top of the shed doors.

From his very first glance at his friend, Pierre could tell that, if he had changed at all since their last meeting, the only change during that time was that he had moved even further along his path of gloom and bitterness.

Andrei greeted Bezukhov with a smile that was mocking, even hostile. Prince Andrei did not generally like seeing people from his own world now, and especially Pierre, with whom he always somehow felt a need to be candid, and even more so because the sight of Pierre reminded him more vividly than anything else of their last meeting and threatened him with a repetition of the admissions that had been made at that last meeting. Without knowing why, Prince Andrei felt uncomfortable looking him straight in the eye (this awkwardness was instantly communicated to Pierre, who felt afraid of staying there alone with the Prince).

"So here you are," said Prince Andrei, going up to Pierre and embracing him. "What brings you here? I'm very glad to see you."

But even as he said this, the expression of his eyes and the whole of his face was more than cool – it was hostile, as if he were saying: "You're a very good man, but leave me alone, you make me suffer."

Their last meeting had been in Moscow, just after Andrei had received Natasha Rostova's letter.

"My dear fellow. I came . . . well . . . you know . . . I came because I'm interested," said Pierre, blushing. "My regiment is still not ready."

"Yes, yes, and what do you brothers the Masons say abut the war, do they talk of how to prevent it?" said Andrei with a smile.

"Yes, yes."

"Well, and how is Moscow? Have my family reached Moscow at long last?" asked Prince Andrei.

"I don't know. Julie Drubetskaya says she received a letter from Smolensk province."

"I don't understand what they're doing. I don't understand. Come in, gentlemen," he said, addressing the officers, who had seen his visitor and were hesitating at the entrance of the shed. The officer at the front was red-nosed Timokhin who, despite the fact that the shortage of officers had already made him a battalion commander, was still the same kind, timid soul as ever. He was followed in by an adjutant and the regimental treasurer. They seemed sad and serious to Pierre. The adjutant respectfully informed the prince that there had not been enough bread loaves sent from Moscow and one battalion had received none at all. He also passed on some army information to Timokhin.

They greeted Pierre when Prince Andrei introduced him, then sat on the floor around the samovar that had been brought in, and the most junior of them began pouring the tea. The officers observed Pierre's immense, fat figure with some surprise as he told them about Moscow and the dispositions of our forces, and how he had toured them. Prince Andrei said nothing, and his expression was so unpleasant that Pierre spoke more to the good-natured battalion commander Timokhin.

"So you understood the complete disposition of our forces?" Prince Andrei interrupted him.

"Yes, that is, how can I put it," said Pierre. "As a non-military man I can't say I completely understood everything, but I still understood the general disposition."

"Well in that case, you understand more than absolutely anyone else," said Prince Andrei.

"How do you mean?" Pierre asked, puzzled, peering at Prince Andrei over the top of his spectacles.

"I mean that nobody understands anything, and that's the way it should be," said Prince Andrei. "Yes, yes," he replied to Pierre's astonished gaze.

"What do you mean to say by that? There are laws, after all. For instance, on the left flank I myself saw Bennigsen decide that the troops were standing too far back to provide mutual support and move them forward."

Prince Andrei gave a cold, unpleasant laugh,

"He moved Tuchkov's corps forward, I was there, I saw it."

"But do you know why he moved them forward? Because there was nothing more stupid he could do."

"Oh but surely not," Pierre objected, avoiding his former friend's glance, "they all discussed the matter. And I'm sure no one would be so irresponsible at such a moment."

Prince Andrei laughed in the same way his father used to laugh.

Pierre was struck by the similarity.

"At such a moment," repeated Prince Andrei. "For those people with whom you toured the position, that moment was a moment in which they could undermine their enemies and win themselves another useless little cross or star. There is no point in siting and resiting anything, because no disposition at all makes any sense, but since they are paid for doing it, they have to pretend to be doing something."

"But the success or failure of a battle is always explained by incorrect orders," said Pierre, looking round at Timokhin for confirmation and finding in his face just as much agreement with his opinion as Prince Andrei found when he happened to glance at him.

"And I tell you that this is all nonsense, and if anything depended on the orders from headquarters, then I would be there giving those orders, instead of which, however, I have the honour of serving here in the regiment with these gentlemen, and I believe that tomorrow will genuinely depend on us, and not on them . . ."

Pierre said nothing.

The officers drank their tea without following the conversation and left.

"It's hard to explain to you the depth of this abyss of lies, the immense distance between the idea of war and the reality. I understand it: firstly, because I have experienced war in all its forms, and secondly, because I am not afraid of being called a coward – I have proved myself there. Well, let's start from the fact that a battle, with armies fighting, never happens, nor will it happen tomorrow either."

"I don't understand that," said Pierre. "They advance on each other and they fight."

"No, they advance, fire and *frighten* each other. Golovin, the admiral, says that in Japan the entire art of war is based on painting pictures of horrors and dressing up as bears on the ramparts of the fortresses. To us that seems stupid, knowing they are dressed up in costumes, but we do the same thing. 'He threw back the Russian dragoons . . . their bayonets clashed.' It never happens and it cannot happen. Not a single regiment has ever slashed with its sabres or stabbed with its bayonets, it has only pretended that it wants to stab, and enemies have taken fright and fled. The whole purpose of tomorrow for me is not to stab and kill people, but simply to prevent my soldiers from running away on account of the fear that they and I will feel. My goal is only for them to advance together and frighten the French, and for the French to take fright before we do. It has never happened and it never does happen, that two regiments clash and fight, and it cannot happen (they wrote about Schöngraben that we clashed with the French in that way. I was there. It's not true: the French ran). If we had clashed, we'd still be stabbing now, until everyone was killed or wounded, and that never happens. To prove it, I can even tell you that the cavalry only exists in order to frighten the enemy, because it is physically impossible for a cavalryman to kill an infantryman with a musket. And if they strike at an infantryman and he takes fright and runs, then they still can't do anything, because not a single soldier knows how to slash, and the very best slashers armed with the very best sabres will never kill a man even if he doesn't defend himself. All they can do is scratch him. And they only stab men lying on the ground with bayonets. Go to the dressing station and look. For thousands of injuries from bullets and balls, you'll only find one made

831

by cold steel. It is all about not taking fright until after the enemy does, frightening the enemy first. And the whole point is for as few as possible of your men to run away, because everyone is afraid. I was not afraid, when I advanced, holding the banner, at Austerlitz, I actually felt happy, but you can only do that for half an hour out of the twenty-four. And when I stood facing fire at Smolensk, I was barely able to stop myself abandoning the battalion and running. It's the same for everyone. And so everything they say about the bravery and courage of the army is all nonsense.

"And now for the second thing: no commander-in-chief ever gives orders in a battle, and it's not possible to, because everything is decided in an instant. No calculations can be made because, as I told you, I cannot be sure that tomorrow my battalion will not run after the third shot or that they will not make an entire division run from them. There are no orders here, but there is a certain cunning on the part of the commander-in-chief: to lie at the right time, to feed his men at the right time and, once again, most importantly of all, not to take fright, but to frighten the enemy and, most importantly, not to despise any means, including deception, betrayal and killing prisoners. It is not virtues that are required here, but the absence of honest qualities and intelligence. What is needed is to be like Frederick and attack defenceless Pomerania and Saxony. What is needed is to kill prisoners. What is needed is to kill the prisoners and leave everything to the flatterers, who will discover greatness in everything that has happened and brought them power, just as they have discovered an ancestry for Napoleon. Just note who Napoleon's generals are, they assure us that they are all geniuses: his brother-in-law, his stepson, his brother. As if the combination of family connection and military talent could be coincidental. It's not a coincidence of family connection, it is simply that, in order to be a commander, you have to be a nonentity, and there are many nonentities. You might just as well toss a dice."

"Yes, but how have such contradictory opinions come about?" asked Pierre.

"How have they come about? In the same way that any of the lies by which we are surrounded come about and, clearly, the worse the matter that serves as their pretext, the more powerful they have to be. And war is the most disgusting business, and therefore, everything that is said about war is lies and nothing but lies.

"How many hundreds of times have I seen men who fled in battle (it always happens) or have hidden themselves away, expecting disgrace, and then suddenly learned that according to reports they were heroes and they *broke through*, *threw back* or *crushed* the enemy, and afterwards

832

they firmly believed with all their hearts that it was true. Others have fled in fear and then come across the enemy, and the enemy has fled from them, and then they have come to believe that, driven by the natural courage of the sons of Russia, they threw themselves against the enemy and crushed him. And then both enemies offer up prayers of thanks because they have killed so many men (the number of which they also exaggerate) and declare victory. Ah, my dear fellow, recently I have found it hard to go on living. I see that I have begun to understand too much. And man should not eat from the tree of knowledge of good and evil."

They were walking about in front of the shed now, the sun had already set and the stars were coming out above the birch trees, the left side of the sky was covered with long, dark clouds and a light wind was rising. All around them on every side they could see the fires of our troops, and in the distance the fires of the French, looking particularly close in the night.

The hooves of three horses were clattering along the road not far from the shed and they heard the guttural voices of two Germans. They were riding close by, and Pierre and Andrei could not help hearing the following phrases:

"The war must be expanded into a wider area. I cannot praise this view highly enough."

"Why not, even as far as Kazan," said another voice.

"Since the goal is to weaken the enemy, we cannot take into account the losses of private individuals."

"Quite right," said a deep, self-confident German voice, and Klausewitz and another German, both important people at headquarters, rode by.

"Yes, expanded into a wider area," Prince Andrei repeated with a laugh. "I left my father in the wider area, at Bleak Hills, and my son and my sister. It's all the same to him."

"They're all Germans, and at headquarters they're all Germans," said Pierre.

"It's a sea with occasional islands of Russians. They've handed him the whole of Europe and then they come here to teach us, these wonderful teachers. The one thing I would do if I had the power is not take prisoners. What is the point of prisoners? It's chivalry. They are my enemies, they are all criminals, from my point of view. They should be executed. If they are my enemies, they cannot be my friends, no matter what Alexander Pavlovich may have said at Tilsit. That one thing would change war completely and make it less cruel. But we have been playing at war, that is what is so disgusting, being magnanimous and so forth.

All this magnanimity is because we do not wish to see how the calf is slaughtered for us, so that we can eat it with sauce. They talk to us about rights, chivalry and parliamentarianism, sparing the unfortunate and so on. It's all rubbish! I saw chivalry and parliamentarianism in 1805! We've been had, we've been had. They rob other people's homes, they circulate false money, and worst of all – they kill my children, my father, and talk about rules and rationality. The only rationality lies in understanding that in this business all that's required from me is brutality. And basing everything on that. Anyone who is prepared to take no prisoners, as I am prepared now – that man is a soldier, but if not, then stay at home and visit Anna Pavlovna's drawing room for conversation."

Prince Andrei halted, facing Pierre, and fixed him with the strangely glittering, exalted gaze of eyes that gazed far off into the distance.

"Yes, the war is a different matter now. Now that the action has reached Moscow, our children, our fathers, every one of us is ready, from myself to Timokhin. No one needs to send us. We are ready to slaughter. We are insulted" – Prince Andrei stopped, because his lip had begun to tremble. "If it had always been like that: if it meant going to certain death, there wouldn't be any war because P.I. offended M.I., as there is now. And if there was a war, like now, then the number of troops would be fewer than it is now. We would be going to our death, and they wouldn't like the taste of that – the Westphalians and Hessians and what have you. And we would never have fought in Austria at all. The key to everything is to cast aside all the lies, and let war be war, and not a game. Alexander Pavlovich is not sending me, I'm going on my own account. But you're asleep on your feet, go and lie down," said Prince Andrei.

"Oh no!" Pierre replied in a frightened voice, staring at Prince Andrei with pity in his eyes.

"Lie down, lie down, before a battle you need to get a good night's sleep," Prince Andrei repeated.

"And you?"

"I'll lie down too."

And Prince Andrei did lie down, but he was unable to fall asleep, and as soon as he heard the sound of Pierre snoring, he got up and carried on walking around in the shed until dawn. He woke Pierre shortly after five.

Prince Andrei's regiment, which was in the reserve, formed up in ranks. Ahead of them they could hear and see intense movement, but the cannonade had not yet begun. Pierre, who wished to see the entire battle, took his leave of Prince Andrei and rode forward in the direction of Borodino, where he hoped to meet Bennigsen, who had offered to include him in his retinue the previous day.

# XII

At six o'clock it was light. It was a grey morning. "Perhaps they won't start at all, it won't happen," thought Pierre as he rode along the road. Pierre rarely saw the morning. He rose late and the impression of the cold and the morning were associated in his mind with something terrible. As he rode along he felt as if he had still not woken up yet, as if he were still lying on the Turkish carpet with Prince Andrei and talking and listening to him talking and seeing those eyes flashing in terrible rapture and listening to those hopeless, restrained, rational words. He could not remember anything that Prince Andrei had said, he only remembered his eyes, glittering radiantly, gazing somewhere into the far distance, and out of everything he had said, just one introductory sentence had remained vivid in Pierre's memory. "War is a different business now," he had said, "now when it has reached Moscow, no one needs to send us, every one of us, from Timokhin to me, is prepared to slaughter at absolutely any moment. We are insulted." And Prince Andrei's lip had trembled as he said it. Pierre rode on with his shoulders hunched over against the coolness of morning, recalling those words. He had already passed Borodino and halted at the battery where he had been the previous day. There were foot soldiers, who had not been there then, standing there, and two officers gazing ahead and to the left. Pierre also looked in the direction of their gaze.

"There it is," said one officer.

A puff of smoke appeared ahead of them and the intense sound of a solitary shot rang out and faded away in the general silence. Several minutes passed and the soldiers standing there did exactly as Pierre did, staring at that puff of smoke and listening to that sound and staring at the movements of the French forces. A second shot, and a third, shook the air, a fourth and a fifth rang out close by and, seemingly as a result of this last shot, something bounced solemnly close by Pierre on his right and the soldiers moved up in a body, hiding the battery from view. The sound of these shots had still not died away when more rang out, and then more, the sounds fusing together and overlaying each other. It was no longer possible to count them or to hear them separately. It was no longer the sound of shots, but the thundering rumble of immense carts on every side, spreading bluish smoke around themselves instead of dust. Only occasional loud, sharp sounds stood out above the regular howling, as if something was shaking one of these invisible carts.

Pierre's horse began to get excited, pricking up its ears and hurrying. The same thing happened to Pierre. The rumble of the field guns, the hasty movements of the horse, the crowding of the regiment that he had ridden into and, above all, all these faces, stern and thoughtful – everything fused together inside him into a single general impression of haste and fear. He asked everyone where Bennigsen was, but no one answered him, everybody was concerned with his own work, work that could not be seen, but the presence of which was visible to Pierre.

"What's this here, riding in the white hat?" he heard a voice behind him say. "Go wherever you want, but don't come jostling people here," someone told him.

"Where's General Bennigsen?" asked Pierre.

"Who knows?"

After emerging from the regiment, Pierre galloped to the left, towards the spot where the cannonade was most intense. But no sooner had he emerged from one regiment than he found himself in another, and again someone shouted to him: "What are you doing riding in front of the line?" And again everywhere he saw the same preoccupied faces, concerned with some invisible but important work. Pierre was the only one with no work to do and no place of his own. The smoke grew thicker and the rumbling of the shots grew louder. If there were cannonballs flying over his head, Pierre did not notice, he did not know this sound and he was so alarmed that he could not understand the causes of the various sounds. He was in an ever greater hurry to get somewhere and find himself some work to do.

He did not see any wounded or dead (at least, that was what he thought, although he had already ridden passed hundreds of them). The action had begun with a cannonade directed against Bagration's redans, followed by an attack on them. Pierre was riding towards them, feeling with horror that he was falling deeper and deeper into the grip of anxious, pointless haste. Everything in front of his eyes had merged into a haze of smoke and shooting, in which he occasionally ran across oases of human faces, and all these faces bore the same imprint of concern and irritation, and reproach for the fat man in the white hat who had ridden in here without any job to do.

Pierre was riding away from Borodino across the field towards the redans, assuming that the battle would only take place there. But just as he came within two hundred paces of the redans and saw a general come galloping forward out of the smoke with his retinue (it was Bagration), and saw masses of soldiers in blue advancing with bayonets fixed, he suddenly heard the shooting and the cannonade start up behind him in Borodino, which he had just left. He set off at a gallop towards the spot

836

where he had seen the general with his retinue; but the general was no longer there, and again an angry voice shouted at him:

"What are you doing here, wandering around in all the shooting?"

And it was only now that Pierre heard the sound of the bullets whistling all around him. Pierre stopped, looked for a place to run to, lost his bearings and, not knowing where our men were and where the enemy was, set off forward at a gallop. But the bullets that he had not noticed before came whistling at him from all sides and he was overcome by horror.

Pierre was so certain that every bullet would hit him that he halted and leaned right down to his saddle, blinking and hardly even opening his eyes. But suddenly our cavalrymen came galloping at him from in front and his horse turned round and galloped with them. He could not remember how long he galloped, but when he stopped, he noticed that he was no longer surrounded by the terrible sounds of flying bullets, and he was trembling all over and his teeth were chattering.

All around him Uhlans were dismounting from their horses, There were a great many of them, wounded, and covered in blood. One, just two paces from Pierre, fell out of his saddle and his horse snorted and ran away from him. The faces of these men were terrible to look at. He could not hear any bullets, but the cannonballs were still flying over their heads. Pierre shuddered at the sound of every shot: it seemed to him that every one was aimed at his head. He rode up to the man who had fallen from his horse and saw that his arm had been ripped off above the elbow, that there was something bloody dangling from twitching ligaments and he heard the Uhlan crying and begging for vodka.

"There's no time to sort things out here, take them to the dressing station," a stern, angry commander's voice said behind him.

"Fathers! Good fellows!" the Uhlan called, weeping. "I'm dying. Don't let me die."

"Colonel," said Pierre to the officer giving orders, "tell them to help this one."

"That one's done for. I've got to get these to the dressing station, and I don't even know where it is."

"Can I be of any help?" asked Pierre.

The colonel ask him go and find the dressing station, which ought to be over on the right, by the grove of trees. Pierre set off in that direction, still listening to the continual firing with his heart in his mouth. He searched for the dressing station for a long time, and after many encounters with various people who gave him contradictory news about the course of the battle, he eventually found it, but he could no longer find the spot where the Uhlans were. As he was looking for them, Pierre rode along the narrow strip of space that separated the front line

THE BATTLE OF BORODINO
*Lithograph by Albrecht Adam*

from the reserves at Borodino. Suddenly the musket fire and cannonade behind him intensified to the point of frenzy, like a man straining and shouting out with his final ounces of strength. A crowd of soldiers, both wounded and unhurt, came flooding towards Pierre and the officers and troops that he had been facing galloped past him – the reserves had begun to advance.

Moving towards him at a trot there were cannons and crates covered all over with soldiers, with other soldiers clutching at them, jumping off and running round them, with an officer galloping at the front. It was Prince Andrei . . .

Prince Andrei recognised Pierre.

"Go away, go away, this is no place for you. Don't fall behind!" he shouted in a piercing voice to his own soldiers who were hanging on to the guns and running around them.

# XIII

Prince Andrei was in the reserves, who had been firing cannonballs without moving from one spot for more than two hours before they set off towards Raevsky's battery. Prince Andrei, who had grown weary and anxious from facing danger in inactivity, was now gasping in excitement and joy as he moved forward.

Yes, no matter how stupid the war might be, he felt exhilarated, happy, proud and content now, as the sounds of the bullets and cannon shots came ever more often, now, when he glanced round at his soldiers and saw their lively eyes fixed on him, and heard the cannonballs strike, felling his men, and felt those sounds and those cries stiffen his back still further and raise his head still higher and lend a strange joy to his movement.

"More of this," thought Prince Andrei, "come on, more, more." And at that moment he felt a blow above his nipple.

"That's nothing, damn it," he told himself in the first second after the blow. His spirits rose even higher, but suddenly his strength failed him and he fell.

"This is real death. This is the end," he told himself at that moment. "A shame. What now? There was still something, still something good. It's annoying," he thought. Some soldiers picked him up.

"Leave me, lads. Don't break ranks," said Prince Andrei, not knowing himself why he said it, but at the same time desperate to make them carry out his command. They disobeyed him and started carrying him.

"Yes, there was something I still had to do," he thought.

The soldiers carried him to a wood where there were long carts, the place where the dressing station was.

The dressing station consisted of three tents standing with their flaps rolled and tied up on the edge of a birch grove. The carts and horses were standing in the birch grove. The horses were eating oats out of nosebags and the sparrows were flying backwards and forwards to them, picking up what they spilled, as if there were nothing special in what was happening around the tents. Lying around the tents, covering more than two *desyatinas* of ground, were the bloodied bodies of the living and the dead; standing around the bodies lying on the ground there were crowds of military stretcher-bearers, who refused to be driven away from that place. They stood there, smoking pipes and leaning on stretchers. There were several officers in charge of proceedings, with eight

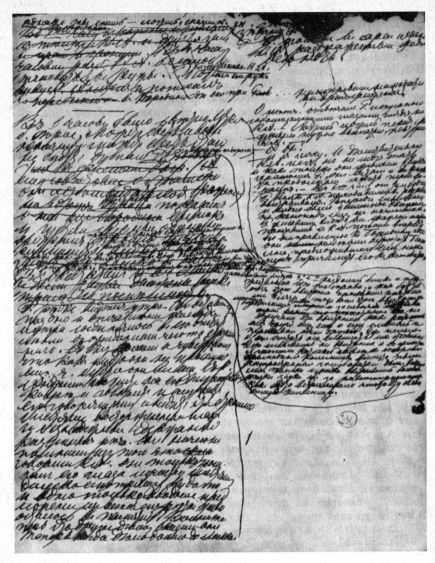

A SHEET OF MANUSCRIPT 107
*Autograph*

medical assistants and four doctors bandaging and cutting in the two tents. As they waited their turn for more than an hour, the wounded wheezed, groaned, screamed, swore, begged for vodka and raved deliriously. Prince Andrei was brought here too and, as a regimental commander, he was carried straight through the wounded who had been bandaged, closer to the tent and set down right beside it. He was pale and shuddering all over, his teeth were clenched and he did not speak, gazing around him with bright, wide-open eyes. He did not know why, perhaps because the battle had been lost, perhaps because he wanted to live or perhaps because there were so many men suffering here, but he felt like crying – not tears of despair, but kind, tender tears. There was something pitiful and childishly innocent in his face and probably that was why a doctor who had still not finished the operation he was working on glanced round at him twice.

It was some time before they got around to Prince Andrei. There were six doctors in aprons working there, drenched in blood and sweat. An officer was driving away the soldiers who had brought wounded.

"Was does it matter anyway?" thought Prince Andrei. "And perhaps . . ." – and he looked at the man the doctor was cutting into just ahead of him. The soldier was a Tatar, his brown back was uncovered and they were cutting a bullet out of it. (Prince Andrei recalled the meat he had seen in the river.) The Tatar was screaming terribly. The doctor let go of his arms, covered him with a greatcoat and walked over to Prince Andrei. They exchanged glances, and both of them understood something. Prince Andrei felt ashamed and cold when they took off his trousers as if he were a little child, and when they began probing him to remove the bullet, he felt a new feeling, the chill of death, that was stronger than the pain.

They laid him on the ground. The doctors who released patients exchanged glances and said he needed to rest before he could be taken to Mozhaisk. One of them, with a kind face, wanted to say something to Prince Andrei, but just then someone was carried past him on a stretcher, straight through the wounded, just as Prince Andrei had been carried earlier. Looking up at the stretcher Prince Andrei could see a head with soft, black, wavy hair on one side, and on the other, a feverishly twitching leg with blood trickling down and running off it. He stared indifferently at this new wounded man, simply because he was the first person to pass in front of his eyes.

"Put him down here!" shouted the doctor.

"Who's this?"

"An adjutant, some prince or other."

It was Anatole Kuragin, wounded by shrapnel in the knee. When they lifted him off the stretcher, Prince Andrei heard him crying like a woman, and he caught a glimpse of his handsome face, crumpled and soaked with tears.

"Oh God! Kill me! Oh! Oh! . . . Oh! . . . It's not possible! Oh, God, *mon Dieu, mon Dieu. Mon Dieu! Mon Dieu!* . . ."

The doctor frowned in disapproval at this womanish howling, but it roused pity in Prince Andrei. The doctors examined Anatole and said something. Two medical assistants came running up and carried him, writhing and hoarse from screaming, crying like a child, into the tent. From inside there was the sound of admonitions in quiet voices, for a moment everything went silent, then suddenly there was a terrible scream, expelled from Anatole's chest; but a scream like that could not last for long, and it faded. Prince Andrei gazed fixedly at the other wounded and heard them sawing through the bone. Finally, all at once, Anatole's strength was exhausted, he could scream no longer and the job was finished. The doctor's threw something on the ground and the medical assistants picked Anatole up and carried him away. His right leg was missing. Anatole was pale and only sobbed occasionally. They put him beside Prince Andrei.

"Show it to me," said Anatole. They showed him a beautiful white leg. He covered his face with his hands and began to sob.

Prince Andrei closed his eyes, and he wanted more than ever to weep tender, loving tears for people, for himself and for his mistakes. "Love, compassion for one's brothers, for those who love and hate us, yes, the love that was taught by God on earth, that Princess Marya tried to teach me – that is what would remain to me if I were to live."

They carefully lifted him up, carried him along and put him into an infirmary cart.

Shortly after four Pierre realised that all this wandering from place to place had made him tired, physically and mentally. His horse was injured and would not move from the spot. He got down and sat on an abandoned axle. He felt completely drained of strength and could neither move, nor think, nor understand anything. The same exhaustion, despondency and doubt about what they had done were visible in the faces of everyone he saw, walking towards the battle or coming back from it. He could not hear musket fire any more, but the cannonade was still continuing, although it too was beginning to slacken off.

The clouds gathered and a fine rain began falling on the dead, the wounded, the frightened, the exhausted and the doubters, as if to say: "Enough, enough, you people, stop, think, what are you doing?" But no, although by the evening of the battle the men had already felt the full horror of what they had done, although they would have been glad to stop, having already exhausted their need for battle, yet the initial impulse still continued to drive this terrifying movement, and although they were soaked in sweat, covered in gunpowder and blood and stumbling from fatigue, the one in three artillerymen who were left still carried charges up to the guns, charged them, aimed them, applied the fuses, and the cold, malicious cannonballs went flying across from both sides, splattering human bodies. The Russians had retreated from half of their positions, but were still standing firm and firing their remaining charges.

Napoleon, with his nose red from a cold, rode out of Shevardinsky's redoubt on his cream Arabian horse.

"They're still holding," he said, frowning and wiping his nose as he looked at the dense columns of Russians.

"They want more – well, give it to them then," he said, and the three hundred and fifty field guns continued firing, tearing the arms and legs and heads off the Russians, who stood there without moving.

Pierre sat on his axle with the skin on his temples twitching, and looked at the men without recognising them. He heard that Kutaisov had been killed, Bagration had been killed, Bolkonsky had been killed. He tried to talk to an adjutant he knew who rode by, but his tears prevented him from speaking. His horse-master found him there in the evening, slumped against a tree with his eyes staring. Pierre was taken to Mozhaisk, and there he was told that Prince Andrei was lying wounded in the next house, but Pierre did not go to him, because he wanted to sleep too badly. He lay down in his carriage, with his feet up on the coach box, and he would have slept until the next evening if they had they not woken him with the news that the army was moving out. Pierre woke up to see the continuation of what had been happening the day before. It was still the same war.

## XIV

After the Battle of Borodino, immediately after the battle, the truth was realised immediately – Moscow would be abandoned to the enemy.

The general course of events, which consisted firstly, of the fact that, despite the self-sacrifice of the soldiers who blocked the enemy's way, he could not be halted, secondly, of the fact that throughout the long retreat to Moscow there had been hesitation over the question of whether or not to give battle and, thirdly and finally, of the fact that it had been decided to surrender Moscow – this general course of events was reflected correctly in the minds of the people of Moscow without the need for any direct reports from the commander-in-chief.

Everything that happened flowed from the essential nature of the matter itself, and the masses are fully aware of that essential nature.

From the 29th of August onwards, every day a thousand or more wounded were brought to Dragomilov Gate. And every day a thousand or more carriages and carts left through the other gates, carrying away the city's inhabitants and their property,

On the same day that the army bunched more tightly together and the council of war took place at Fili and the ugly mob went to Three Hills to wait for Rostopchin, thirty-six carts came to Count Ilya Andreevich Rostov's address to remove the rich contents of the house on Povarskaya Street, which had still not been sold. The carts arrived this late, firstly because the count had been hoping for a sale until the very last day, secondly, because the count, relying on his universal range of acquaintances, had paid no heed to the general opinion but believed Count Rostopchin, whom he had visited every day to make enquiries. And thirdly, and most importantly, because the countess had refused to hear of moving out before her son Petya returned. He had been transferred to Bezukhov's regiment and was expected in Moscow any day from Belaya Tserkov, where his former regiment, Obolensky's Cossacks, had been formed.

On the 30th of August Petya arrived, and on the 31st the carts came.

Natasha's slim figure, with her black hair tied up in a white handkerchief, could be seen in the immense courtyard and on the street. Earlier there had been many people there watching the wounded, but there were so many wounded and everyone was so preoccupied with their own business that it never entered their minds to help anyone in any way; but as soon as Natasha and a volunteer began carrying the wounded into the house, giving them food and drink, people came pouring out of all the houses and out of the crowd and followed her example.

When Count Ilya Andreevich and his wife saw Natasha, she was replacing a cap that had slipped backwards on the head of a soldier whom Matiushka and Mitka were carrying into yard in their arms; she was walking behind, not looking round at anyone else, and gesturing with her arms as if she were maintaining the wounded man's balance for him, so that he would feel better. When he saw her, the count began breathing heavily through his nose, the way a dog sniffs intuitively at a strange smell and stared hard out through the window, not turning back to the countess. But the countess was feeling the same thing as the count, she did not wait for him, but tugged him towards her by the sleeve of his camisole. The count looked round and his glance met the guilty look in her moist eyes. He rushed to her, pressed his chin into her shoulder and burst into sobs behind her back.

"My dearest – we have to . . ." said the countess.

"It's true . . . the eggs are teaching the chickens . . ." the count said through tears of happiness. "And we thank them . . . Now, let us go . . ."

"My dear girl," the count shouted loudly and happily. "Throw all those things, damn them, off the carts, and put the wounded men on."

Sonya was overjoyed. She had no need, not a jot, for the wounded, or Moscow, or the fatherland. She needed the happiness of a family, a home in which she could live. She felt like laughing and jumping for joy. She ran into her room, ran about and started spinning, faster and faster, then sat down with her dress ballooning out, and began laughing quietly. After that, her need satisfied, she ran to Natasha and began helping her, understanding exactly what was required and doing it all much better than Natasha herself.

As if trying to redeem themselves for not having started sooner, the entire family set about the same task with especial ardour. The wounded kept arriving and they constantly took the opportunity to take this and that thing off and give the carts over to them. None of the servants found this odd.

The following day yet more wounded arrived, and again they stopped in the street outside. This latest transport included many officers, and one of the officers was Prince Andrei.

"We can take another four," said the butler, "I'm letting my cart go, but then where shall we put them?"

"Oh, give them the one with my wardrobe," said the countess. "Dunyasha can come in the carriage with me."

The cart that had carried the countess's wardrobe was handed over, and that happened to be the one in which they put Prince Andrei and Timokhin. Prince Andrei was lying unconscious. When they began to transfer them, Sonya glanced into the face of a man who seemed to be dead. It was Prince Andrei. Sonya's face turned as pale as that of the wounded man and she went running to the countess.

"Mama," she said, "we can't. Natasha won't be able to bear it. Who would believe it, such a trick of fate."

The countess did not reply, she only raised her eyes to the icons and prayed.

"God moves in mysterious ways," she told herself, feeling that the almighty hand that had been hidden from human eyes was beginning to show its terrible power in everything that was happening now.

"Clearly, this is how it must be, my friend. Tell them to take him into the billiard room, in the wing, and don't tell Natasha."

They stayed for the whole day without moving out. As young ladies, Natasha and Sonya did not go into the wing where the wounded officers had been put, because that would have been improper so Natasha did not know who was lying there, dying, so close to her.

On the 30th, Pierre awoke to find everything around him in his own house being packed up. He sat up and began calculating the figure 666, for l'Empéreur Napoleon, and le Russe Bezukhov was 666 too. He sat there a long time, pondering and pondering, and when he got up, he had made his mind up quite firmly to stay in Moscow and kill the Emperor Napoleon, who was responsible for all these outrages. "Everyone is suffering and has already suffered, apart from me . . . It's too late to leave now, so my butler and my servants can stay, and so can I. Bonaparte alone is the cause of all this misery. I must sacrifice everything for the same cause for which others have sacrificed . . . 666 . . . I shall stay in Moscow and kill Bonaparte," Pierre decided.

He summoned his butler, told him not to pack anything or hide anything or make any preparations, that he was staying in Moscow, and then he ordered horses to be harnessed to his droshky and set off round Moscow to find out how things stood. Failing to find anyone apart from a crowd at Count Rostopchin's house, he set off home and, as he drove along Povarskaya Street, he saw the carriages standing outside the Rostovs' house.

"There's nothing left of the old times now, and now when I am sure I shall never see her again, I must call on them," he thought.

He went into the Rostovs' house.

"Mademoiselle Nathalie, I need to talk to you, come here."

The two of them went into the hall.

"*Eh bien*," he began, speaking in French, "I know that I shall never see you again, I know . . . the way things are . . . I don't know why, I never thought I would tell you this, but the way things are now we are all standing on the edge of the grave, and I find the proprieties too restrictive. I love you, I love you madly, as I have never loved any woman. You have brought me the greatest happiness I have ever experienced. You should know this, you may find it pleasant to know it, goodbye."

Before Natasha had time to answer, he had already fled. Natasha told Sonya what Pierre had said to her and, strangely enough, in this house crammed full of wounded men, with the enemy at the gates of Moscow, with the uncertainty about her two brothers, for the first time in ages they fell into the intimate kind of conversation they used to have in the old days. Sonya said she had noticed it a long time ago and was astonished that he hadn't spoken out earlier, that now he was like a madman.

Natasha did not answer. She stood up.

"Where is he now?" she asked. "God grant him happiness and have mercy on him."

She meant Andrei. Sonya realised this but, with her capacity for concealment, she merely said calmly:

"If he had been wounded or killed, we would know."

"You know, Sonya, I never loved him with all my heart and soul – I didn't love that other one at all, that was something different – but I didn't love him, and that is the most important thing I am guilty of before him. If only I knew that he was happy, I could carry on living, but now there is no . . . Everything is black, the whole world is black. Goodnight, go. You're sleepy. Yes, you are."

# XV

The following day Napoleon stood on Poklonnaya Hill and looked at Moscow, that Asiatic city with its countless number of churches and said:

"And so, at last, this famous city . . . It is high time for them to bring the boyars out to me." And, dismounting from his horse, he looked at this city, which the next day would be taken by its enemy, and become like a girl who has lost her virginity, in his own expression.

This narrow mind perceived nothing except the city, the spoils and his own greatness as a conqueror – Alexander the Great and so on – and he looked at the city with a vulgar, predatory joy, checking the details of the city on a map spread out in front of him.

"Yes," says the bandit as he prepares to rape a woman, "just as they told me: beautiful, yes, and the plaits and the breasts, everything just as they told me."

The boyars did not come, and his forces went dashing in through the Dragomilov Gate, with a clanking and a clamour and cries of: "Long live the Emperor!"

At that moment Pierre was walking across the deserted Virgin's Field, wearing a long peasant's coat and boots of fine leather, which he had forgotten to take off, feeling the pistol under the skirt of his coat and staring fixedly down at his own feet without his spectacles. Pierre had burnt his boats and crossed the boundary of the territory occupied by our forces, and he was hurrying to cross the boundary into French territory. He was experiencing a new, happy, feeling of independence, like the feeling of a rich man when he leaves behind all the whims of luxury and sets off into the Swiss mountains with a rucksack. "What do I need? Here I am, alone, and I have everything, the sunshine, and my strength," he thought. This feeling of his had been intensified still further by what had happened to him at Alsufiev's house on the Virgin's Field. He had heard shouting and singing in the house and walked in through the gates. A drunken soldier had stuck his head out of the window of the sitting room.

"You're too late, brother . . . would you like some? Well, damn him for coming and hearing us."

Another man, obviously a house serf, stuck his head out.

"What are you swearing at?" he asked, then glanced at Pierre and, after coming downstairs, staggered up to Pierre and grabbed hold of him by his coat. "Well, the times we've lived to see, just look!" And he shook two full bags that he was holding in his hands. "Come on. I love you, friend." And he tugged at Pierre. Pierre tried to get away and pushed him. "Who are you shoving? Hey look, Petro, a gentleman. I swear, a gentleman – those boots."

Another three men surrounded Pierre.

"The gentleman's gone crazy. Dressed himself up as a peasant. Your house, is it?" one of them asked, staring insolently into his eyes.

"Out of the way, you good-for-nothings," Pierre shouted, pushing the one in front. They all stepped back and he walked on, intending to shoot Napoleon immediately. But soon after that he encountered some troops and hid from them in the gateway of a house, and they forced him over to the left side of the Virgin's Field, as Napoleon came across the Dragomilov Bridge.

All this time the shops in the Gostiny Dvor and the square were filled with the frenzied shouting of soldiers pilfering goods, and officers trying to bring them to order. Further on, in the streets leading to the Vladimir Gate, carts carrying goods and wounded were jostling for space. On the bridge over the Yauza the carts were jammed so close together that the artillery moving behind them could not get through. The leading carts was harnessed to a pair of horses, with a mountain of things heaped up, a child's chair and an eiderdown sticking out, and a woman sitting on the top, holding saucepans; at the back there were four borzois in collars squeezed between the wheels. Right beside this cart, with its wheels locked to it, there was a peasant cart with a small wardrobe, wrapped in sackcloth, and an orderly sitting on it, and this was followed by a carriage, and three large merchant's carts. A cuirassier was overtaking them on one side.

"Well, dear man, is there anything coming up from behind?" asked the woman.

"How lovely my sweet darling was," the cuirassier suddenly shouted out, trying to sing, and striking his thin horse with his short sword and swaying as he galloped past.

"Stop him!" someone shouted from behind, and two Cossacks galloped by, laughing, holding a fur coat in their hands.

"That will soon get you warm. I grabbed it off a cart. So what? He's worse than a Frenchman. Get a move on, will you."

Suddenly the crowd came pushing through blindly from behind: they're going to start shooting. Panic. Some went under the bridge, some went over the parapet. It was Ermolov, who had ordered the artillery to make it clear they would shoot to clear the bridge.

Elsewhere Rostopchin galloped up to Kutuzov and angrily began telling him all sorts of things.

"I have no time, count," replied Kutuzov and drove off, but then he stopped in his droshky, rested his old head on his arm and silently watched the troops go by.

Outside Moscow, on the Tambov road, the carriages stretched out in long trains two or three abreast. The nearer these trains were to Moscow, the denser they were, and the further they were from the city, the sparser they became. Once they were ten *versts* away, people began to recover from the fear, the congestion and the shouting that had filled the city and began talking to each other, looking things over to see if anything had been broken, and began to breathe in the air that was not less dusty. One of these lucky trains included the Rostovs' carriages. They had escaped from the city, but were still moving at a walking pace. Six carts carrying wounded had been sent off separately from their house. The wounded in the carts that they had given up from their own personal train were travelling with them. There were two of these, one of which was carrying Prince Andrei and Timokhin. This cart was travelling in front. Behind these two carts came a large carriage in which the countess, Dunyasha, the doctor, Natasha and Sonya were sitting, and behind that came the count's carriage – with the count and his valet – then a light carriage with a maid and servants. Suddenly the carts at the head of the train came to a halt and when Sonya and Natasha stuck their heads out of the windows, they saw some sort of bustling going on around the front carriage with the officers. Sonya heard one of the servants say: "It's over. He's going to die now." Trembling for fear lest Natasha had heard it as well, she pulled her head back into the carriage and began saying something to Natasha. But Natasha had heard it, and with her usual quickness, she opened the door, put down the step, ran out and then forward. In the front carriage Prince Andrei was lying on a calico cushion, face upwards, with his eyes closed, opening and closing his mouth like a fish, gulping in air. The doctor was already standing on the step, taking his pulse.

Natasha grabbed hold of the wheel of the cart, feeling her knees knocking together. But she did not fall.

"What do you think you're doing here, countess?" the doctor asked angrily. "Please be so good as to leave, it's perfectly all right!"

She meekly began walking away.

"Better ask the count whether he can spare a sprung carriage."

Natasha set off to see her father, but Count Ilya Andreevich was already there walking towards her, and she told him what the doctor had said. They transferred the sick man to a carriage, and Natasha got into the other carriage without saying a word. Both Sonya and her mother tried not to look at her. All her mother said was:

"The doctor said he will live."

Natasha looked at her and then turned away again to look out of the window. At the coaching station a man was sent on ahead to hold places at the inn for the Rostovs. They stopped there for the night, all of them sharing one room and giving the other room, which was better, to the wounded officers. It was already dark when they sat down to dinner. The doctor came from the wounded men and announced that Bolkonsky was better, he could well recover and complete the journey. The important thing was to complete the journey.

"Is he conscious?"

"He is fully conscious now."

The doctor went away to sleep by his patient, the count went to his carriage. Natasha shared a bed with her mother. When the candles were put out, she pressed herself against her mother and burst into sobs.

"He's going to live . . ."

"No, I know he's going to die . . . I know it." They cried together and said nothing more. Sonya raised her head several times from her straw bed on the floor, but she could hear nothing except the weeping. The cocks had already crowed several times nearby in the yard and everybody else had fallen asleep, but Natasha was not sleeping. She could not sleep but she could not just lie there either. She got up quietly and, without putting any shoes on, she slipped on her mother's fur-lined jacket, stepped over the sleeping girl on the floor and went into the entrance hall. There were several men sleeping in the hall and they muttered at the sound of the door opening. She found the handle of the other door and pushed it open. The room was lit by a tallow candle, already well burned down. Something stirred; it was Timokhin with his red nose, who had propped himself up on one elbow and was looking at the countess with a frightened expression in his eyes. Recognising the young lady, he began shyly covering himself with his cloak, gazing at her all the while. There was another wounded man lying on the bed opposite him, with a white hand hanging over the edge. Natasha went over to him, walking quietly in her bare feet, but he heard her, opened his eyes with an effort and suddenly smiled joyfully, like a child. Natasha did not speak, she went down on her knees without a sound, took hold of his hand, pressed it to her lips, which were swollen from crying, and tenderly pressed her cheek against it. He made a movement with his fingers, he wanted something. She realised that he wanted to see her face. She raised her wet face, childishly contorted by her sobbing, and looked at him. He was still smiling joyfully. Timokhin, shyly covering his head and yellow arm, tugged at the doctor who was sleeping beside him and the startled doctor and Timokhin looked, without moving, at Natasha and Andrei. The doctor began coughing, but they did not hear him.

"Can you forgive me?"

"Everything, everything," Andrei said in a quiet voice. "Go now."

The doctor began coughing more loudly and stirring in his bed. Timokhin, expecting her to turn round, covered everything up to his chin, although one bare leg was still exposed.

Natasha heaved a sigh and walked lightly out of the room.

# XVI

The two princesses (the third had married long ago) had been sent away from Pierre's house and many things had been taken away. What exactly, Pierre did not really know. He had begun supervising the clearing of the picture gallery, but when he saw how many precious things there were, how few means of transport and how little time, he had left the whole business to his butler and not interfered any more. He did not want to go anywhere, primarily because he felt ashamed of imitating all the weak men and the women who were leaving. He no longer believed in a final, desperate battle like the defence of Saragossa, but then, there had been so little time left when it was learned that there would be no battle, it was too late for him to act in any other way. He had had a vague idea about the number 666 and his own name, Pierre de Besouhoff, but the most important thing was his desperate desire to show that he couldn't give a damn for all this, to confirm the feeling he had expressed in the Assembly of Nobles. The strongest of all his feelings was the Russian one that makes a carousing merchant smash all the mirrors – a feeling that expresses a higher judgement on the truth of life, on the basis of some other, vaguely perceived, truth. There was one thing that Pierre did not think about, but which he understood instinctively, and that was a question that had been decided as soon as he conceived the idea of remaining in Moscow – he would not keep his own name and title of Count Bezukhov, the son-in-law of one of Russia's most important grandees, but would take the part of his own yard-keeper.

He moved his bed and his books into an outbuilding and settled in behind a partition in the room occupied by the butler and his old mother-in-law, wife and sister-in-law, who was a slender, lively, pretty widow. She had been Pierre's first lover and had later experienced many reverses of fortune and joys in her life and been intimately acquainted with many of Moscow's richest young people. She was no longer young, she wore a headscarf and plaits, and had cheeks that were ruddy from consumption, and strong, muscular, thin limbs and beautiful eyes that always glowed merrily. Their intimate relationship, which had been concluded most satisfactorily for Mavra Kondratievna, was now forgotten as far as Pierre was concerned. Mavra Kondratievna was familiar but respectful with Pierre and amused their entire circle with her ready wit and energy.

She dressed Pierre up in Styopka's heavy kaftan (after steaming it first), then dressed up in some of her finery and went with Pierre to meet the French. In the tavern there was a shout, they were stopped and asked, via a Polish interpreter: "Where do you live? Who is he? What is this church?" (pointing to the cathedral). Mavra Kondratievna laughed and advised Pierre to be more amiable with them.

Pierre was frightened and delighted to think that he was in the thick of things and his boats were already burnt. He walked around, looking at the various kinds of troops and saw people's faces from close up – kind, tired, suffering – faces that roused his pity and sympathy. They were shouting "Long live the Emperor!", and there were moments (after a while) when it seemed to Pierre that this was how things should be and they were right. He even felt like shouting along with them.

They found out that Napoleon was staying in the Dragomilovo suburb and went home. Mavra Kondratievna, in a pink dress and lilac silk headscarf, went off on her own, not feeling in the least bit intimidated, winking at the French.

Pierre set off alone to Staraya Koniushennaya Street to see the Princess Gruzinskaya, an old, old Muscovite, who he knew had not left Moscow. Pierre went to her because he had nowhere else to go, and he was glad that he did. The moment he walked into her entrance hall, he caught the familiar old musty smell, mixed with the smell of dogs, and saw an old servant, a servant girl and a female jester, he saw the plants on the windowsills and the parrot – everything the way it used to be – and he began to feel like a Russian again.

"Who's there?" an old woman's shrill, peevish voice asked, and Pierre wondered briefly whether the French would dare to enter if she shouted like that. "Queen!" (that was what the female jester was called) "Go out to the entrance hall."

"It's me, princess. May I come in?"

"Who's me? Bonaparte, is it? Well now, hello there, darling, why haven't you run away? Everybody's running, my dear man. Sit down, sit down. What's all this, who are you dressed up as, or is it Yuletide already, ha, ha? Queen, come and take a look . . . Why, what would they do to you? They wouldn't do anything to you. Well, have they come yet?" she asked, in exactly the same way as she asked if the chef had come from Okhotny Ryad. Either she did not understand, or she did not wish to understand. But strangely enough, her self-assurance was so strong that, looking at her, Pierre felt certain that nobody could do her any harm.

"My neighbour, Marya Ivanovna Dolokhova, left yesterday – her son persuaded her to go, he was dressed up just like you, he tried to persuade me to go too, said he was going to burn the house down. And I said: you burn it down and I'll have the police put you in jail."

"But the police have left."

"But we can't do without police! I expect they have their own. I don't think we can get along without any police. How can they go burning people like that? Let them go, all the better for me: I've moved my washing into their yard, I've got more space now . . ."

"You mean, they haven't come to you yet?"

"One came, but I didn't let him in."

At that moment there was a knock at the gate and shortly afterwards a hussar came in. Very politely, apologising for the inconvenience, he asked for something to eat. Princess Gruzinskaya looked at him and as soon as she realised what he wanted, she ordered him to be taken to the entrance hall and fed there.

"You go, darling, and make sure they've given him everything – there were some good waffles left over from lunch, but you know what they're like, they'll eat them all up themselves . . ."

Pierre walked up to the Frenchman and began talking to him.

"Count Pyotr Kirillich, come here," the old woman shouted, but the Frenchman had just called Pierre into the entrance hall and was showing him his filthy shirt and blushing as he asked Pierre to give him a clean one, if he could. Pierre went back to the old woman and told her.

"All right, give him ten *arshins* of linen, and tell I'm giving him it out of the kindness of my heart. And tell him to tell his superior that I, the Princess Marfa Fedorovna Gruzinskaya, live without causing anyone any harm and they mustn't cause me any bother, or else I'll make them answer for it. Or better still, send his superior to me. All right, all right, God be with you," she said to the Frenchman, who was standing in the doorway of the drawing room, taking his leave and thanking the kind lady . . .

As he was leaving the princess's house, Pierre came face to face, in the darkness, with a man in a kaftan exactly like his own.

"Ah, Bezukhov!" said the man, whom Pierre had immediately recognised as Dolokhov. Dolokhov took hold of his hand, as if they had always been friends. "I tell you, it's good that you've stayed. I've already set fire to Karetny Ryad, and my lads will set fire to everything, but what am I to do about the old woman? I feel sorry for her; but I'm going to set fire to my mother's house."

At that moment Pierre also forgot that Dolokhov had been his enemy and he answered him without any preamble.

"You can't, why do you want to burn her?" he said. "And who gave the order to burn everything?"

"Fire!" Dolokhov replied. "Are you going to set fire to your house?"

"It's better than entertaining the French in it," said Pierre, "but I'm not going to set fire to it myself."

"Well, I'll help you out. I'll come visiting tomorrow with the red cockerel," said Dolokhov. He moved his face close to Pierre's, laughed and walked away. "If you need me, ask Danidka under the Moskvoretsky bridge."

On his way back home to the outhouse, Pierre met French soldiers everywhere; some asked him who he was and when they were told: "the yard-keeper from such and such a house," they let him pass. There were sentries standing outside his house and he later learned that an important French commander was billeted in the house. They had set up a bedroom in the gallery and rearranged everything. They kept asking where the master of the house was and flirting with Mavra Kondratievna. There was also talk about the fires.

The next day Pierre went out to walk around again and without thinking, he followed the crowd to the shops at Gostiny Ryad, which were on fire. Then he walked away from the smoke towards the river, and right by the river he came across a crowd gathered round a five-year-old boy. Nobody knew whose child he was, and nobody was willing to take him. Pierre took him and set off for home. But Pokrovka Street was already on fire, and so was his house. There were crowds of people and soldiers rushing around the city, looting. At the entrance to his house he came across Mavra Kondratievna, running and shouting that everything had been burned and looted. They walked to the church together. On the way they saw an Uhlan kill a merchant with his pike. There was nothing to eat in the church. Mavra Kondratievna went out to hunt for something and found tea and sugar and vodka, then exchanged the vodka for bread.

Pierre went out to hunt for food, but on the way he was stopped by a soldier who took his kaftan off him and ordered him to carry a sack. On their way they called into Podnovinskoe Polye, and there Pierre watched as the soldier ordered the yard-keeper, an old man, to sit down and take off his boots. When the old man started crying, the looter gave him his boots back and walked off. Then he let Pierre go. When Pierre, still hungry, got back to the church, he fell asleep.

In the morning, two officers came to the church. One walked up to Pierre and asked who he was. Pierre gave him the Masonic sign but the officer did not understand and responded by asking what he wanted. Pierre explained his situation. Taking the foundling, they went to the Frenchman's quarters in the Rostovs' house, where they had dinner and a drink. Pierre told the Frenchman about his situation and his love, as if he were talking to his confessor. The Frenchman was a likeable, intelligent man.

In order not to cause the Frenchman any trouble, Pierre gave him his word to come back, and went to see the Princess Gruzinskaya. There was an officer at her house, he had sent her some coffee. Outside it was quiet, there were children pretending to fire at the French with sticks. There had been an event in the yard next door: the cook had been killed for collaborating, she had washed a pair of trousers with money in the pocket. Pierre went to look for Dolokhov in order to find some means of getting away. After he found him, they went down into a basement. Dolokhov suddenly stabbed a Frenchman with a knife and hit him with a pistol and escaped. Pierre was caught and they led him off to Davout at the Virgin's Field. Five people were shot right in front of his eyes. He was imprisoned in a chapel – for them the chapel was just like any other place.

# XVII

In St. Petersburg, after the sovereign's arrival from Moscow, many possessions were packed up and got ready to be sent away. In the highest circles of society the struggle between the opposing factions continued with greater fervour than ever: the party of Rumyantsev and the French, the patriotic party of Maria Fedorovna, who had taken offence at the sovereign himself, and the muddle-headed party of the Grand Duke, the heir to the throne. This struggle was alternately drowned out and intensified by the trumpetings of the idle drones; but the old calm, luxurious, vain and superficial life, concerned only with externals, carried on in the same old way, and because of the inertia of this life, it required great effort to realise what a dangerous and difficult situation the state was in. Girls still came out, even at balls, there was the French theatre, the interests of the court, the petty intrigues of the service and trade. Only in the very highest circles was the effort made not to forget the position that the state was in.

And so, on the 26th of August, the very day of the Battle of Borodino, Anna Pavlovna held a *soirée*, the highlight of which was intended to be the reading of a letter from Bishop — who had sent the sovereign an icon of St. Sergius. This letter was regarded as a model of patriotic religious eloquence. It was to be read out by Prince Vasily himself, who was famed for his skill in the art of reading – he had even read for the Empress. And the art of reading was considered to consist in delivering the words in a loud, warbling voice, manoeuvring between a desperate wail and a low, gentle rumble, gushing the words out, entirely without regard for their meaning, that is, it made absolutely no difference which word was wailed and which was rumbled. Like all of Anna Pavlovna's *soirées*, this reading had a political significance. There were many people gathered for the occasion, including certain individuals who had to be shamed for visiting the French theatre, and inspired anew.

Anna Pavlovna could still not see everyone she wanted to see in the drawing room, and so she wound up the springs of general conversation. At one end of the room they were talking about Hélène's illness and expressing sympathy for her. She had had a miscarriage, and the doctors had despaired of her recovery. Spiteful tongues whispered that it was strange for her to miscarry now, when she had been separated from her husband for some nine months.

"Well, let's simply say," another individual was saying, "that that is an open secret." He named a very important personage, who spent most of his time in the army. But the point was that she had not remained faithful to this individual either, and when he returned unexpectedly, arriving to find the other man, a young hussar, here, that was what had given her a such a fright.

"It's a shame. An exceptionally intelligent woman!"

"Ah, you are speaking of the poor countess," said Anna Pavlovna as she approached them. "Ah, how sorry I feel for her. She is not just an intelligent woman, she has such a good heart! And how remarkably she developed. She and I have argued a lot, but I cannot help loving her. Can there really be no hope? It is quite terrible. Useless people live, while the cream of our society . . ." She broke off and turned to Bilibin, who was in a different circle. He was talking about the Austrians, and had puckered up the skin of his face and was evidently about to release it in order to utter a *bon mot*.

"I find it charming," he was saying about a message, according to which the Austrian banners captured by Wittgenstein (the hero of Petropol) had been sent back to Vienna.

"What, how can that be?" Anna Pavlovna asked him, provoking a silence so that others would listen to the *bon mot* (which she already knew).

"The Emperor is returning the Austrian banners, the friendly banners that he found after they had strayed from their true path," Bilibin concluded, releasing his folds of skin.

"Charming, charming," said Prince Vasily, but just at that moment there arrived the insufficiently patriotic individual for whom Anna Pavlovna had been waiting in order to convert him, and she invited Prince Vasily to the table, placed two candles and the manuscript in front of him and asked him to begin. Everyone fell silent.

"Most gracious sovereign and Emperor," Prince Vasily declaimed austerely and glanced round his audience, as if asking whether anyone had anything to say against that. But no one said a word.

"The first capital city of Moscow, the New Jerusalem, will receive its *own* Christ," he read, laying abrupt emphasis on the word *own*, "as a mother receives her sons into her embrace and, foreseeing through the deepening gloom the resplendent glory of your realm, sings in ecstasy: 'Hosanna, blessed is he that cometh'," he howled, and glanced round at everybody. Bilibin was studying his nails intently while many others were clearly quailing, as if wondering what they were guilty of. Anna Pavlovna repeated the words in advance, like an old woman at communion: "Let the insolent and presumptuous Goliath . . ."

"Charming! Such power!" voices exclaimed in praise of the reader and the author. Inspired by this speech, Anna Pavlovna's guests talked at length about the situation of their fatherland and put forward various conjectures concerning the outcome of the battle that was expected to be fought any day now.

"You will see," said Anna Pavlovna, "that tomorrow, on the sovereign's birthday, we shall receive news. I have a positive premonition."

Anna Pavlovna's premonition proved to be correct. The following day, during the litany held in the palace to mark the occasion of the sovereign's birth, Prince Volkonsky was called out of the church and received an envelope from Prince Kutuzov, who wrote that the Russians had not retreated a single step, that the French losses were much greater than his, that he was writing in haste from the field of battle, before he had been able to gather the latest news. And so, it was a victory. And as soon as people emerged from the church, thanks were expressed to the Creator for his help and for victory.

Anna Pavlovna's premonition proved to be correct, and all that morning the mood in the city was joyful and festive. Far away from the action, in the midst of court life, it is extremely difficult for the full force and significance of events to make themselves felt. The general course of events tends to be focused around a single incident. Thus, the main cause of joy now was that we had been victorious, and the news of the victory had arrived precisely on the sovereign's birthday. It was like a successful surprise treat, Kutuzov's communication also only mentioned the Russian side's losses, including in their number Tuchkov, Bagration and Kutaisov. In the world of St. Petersburg, the sad side of events was involuntarily focused around a single event – the death of Kutaisov. Everybody had known him. The sovereign had loved him, he was young and interesting. On that day everyone greeted each other with the words:

"What an amazing thing! During the actual service! But what a loss Kutaisov is! Oh such a shame!"

"What did I tell you about Kutuzov," Prince Vasily said with the pride of a prophet.

But the next day no news came from the army and the common voice acquired a note of concern, while the courtiers began to suffer on account of the sovereign's suffering at the lack of news.

"Such a difficult situation for the sovereign," everybody said. They reproached Kutuzov, and Prince Vasily now kept silent about his protégé. In addition, early that evening yet another sad event for the city was added to their sorrows, when they learned that Hélène had died suddenly, and thus two days after the battle, the general talk was of three sad events: the sovereign's state of uncertainty, the death of Kutaisov and the death of Hélène. Eventually a landowner from Moscow arrived and the news of Moscow's surrender spread throughout the city. It was appalling! Such a difficult situation for the sovereign! Kutuzov was a traitor, and when people visited Prince Vasily to express their condolences he asked (he could be forgiven for forgetting in his grief what he had said before) what else had they expected from a blind old man with no morals.

Finally the Frenchman Michaud arrived to see the sovereign, and they had the famous conversation in which Michaud employed a play on words, saying that he had left the Russians in a state of fear, not fear of the French, but fear that the sovereign would conclude a peace, and thereby provoked the sovereign into making his famous pronouncement that he was prepared to grow his beard this long (he indicated the length) and eat no vegetable but potatoes, but he was not prepared to conclude a peace.

# XVIII

On the 1st of October, on the feast of the Intercession of the Holy Virgin, the bells of the convent in the Virgin's Field were rung, but they were not rung in the Russian manner. Pierre emerged from a rough shack built on the Virgin's Field and glanced at the bell tower. Two French Uhlans were ringing the bells.

"Is good?" one of the Uhlans asked Pierre.

"No, terrible," said Pierre, and added in French that you needed a proper knack for ringing bells.

"How's that, he speaks French, this man, fancy that now . . ."

But the sentry on duty at the hut, passing by with a rifle, said without turning his head: "Get back." And Pierre went back into the hut, where about fifteen Russian prisoners were sitting and lying round the walls.

"Uncle," said a boy of about fifteen, pushing against his leg, "get off it."

Pierre lifted his foot. He had accidentally stepped on a rag that the boy had spread out. Pierre lifted his foot and looked down at it. His feet were bare, protruding from a grey pair of trousers that had belonged to somebody else and were now tied round with twine at the ankles on the advice of one of his comrades in captivity, a soldier. Pierre set his bare feet down side by side and began staring thoughtfully at their dirty, chubby big toes. Contemplation of these bare feet seemed to give Pierre great satisfaction. He smiled to himself several times as he gazed at them, and then he went over to his greatcoat, on which lay a block of wood and a small knife, and began carving. The soldier next to him shifted away, but Pierre pulled up the greatcoat to shield him. To another old man, evidently a functionary, who was sitting beside him and sewing something, Pierre said:

"Now then, Mikhail Onufrievich, is it going well?"

"How could it, my hands are turning numb now."

"Oh well, never mind, it will pass – all will be well in the end," said Pierre, smiling and biting on his tongue, which he had the habit of doing when working, and set about carving the future doll.

The boy came over. Pierre took out a piece of white bread and sat the boy down on the greatcoat.

Pierre had not seen himself in a mirror for a long time and if he had done, he would have been greatly surprised, for he was now quite unlike his old self, and had changed much for the better. He was now consider-

860

ably thinner, especially in the face, but his shoulders and limbs nonetheless showed the strength inherited from his forebears. His hair which, through some attempt at originality and a fear of seeming to take trouble over himself, he had cut into a fringe, which spoiled his looks, had now grown long, curling just like his father's had done. A beard and moustache now covered the lower part of his face, and in his eyes there was a freshness, contentment and vitality that had never been there before. He was wearing a shirt, a remnant of former glory, made of fine cloth but torn and dirty, and over it a fur coat, probably a woman's, thrown like a hussar's pelisse across his shoulders, and the grey soldier's trousers tied in at the ankles, while his feet, at which he kept glancing with joy, were bare and calloused.

During this month of captivity in Moscow, Pierre had gone through a great deal. Although he might seem to have suffered, he felt he had enjoyed himself hugely and come to know both himself and other people in a way he had never done before in his entire life. And everything that he had learned was connected in his mind with the idea and the sensation of bare feet. It appeared that, while both boots and stockings needed constant changing, with bare feet one felt less constrained, more agile and more comfortable: "At least I know they are my feet." Although Pierre already felt very content, he would not have said so now for, on the contrary, he never for one moment stopped thinking about the happiness to come when he would escape this captivity and he wished for it with all the strength of his heart.

Yet deep in his heart, as he glanced at his bare feet, he did feel content. And this had come about primarily because for the very first time he had been deprived of the total freedom and unnecessary luxuries that he had enjoyed all his life – never before had he experienced the simple joys of eating and keeping himself warm; secondly, he had something to wish for; thirdly, he sensed, thanks especially to the young boy who had come his way, that within those narrow confines of freedom within which he now acted, he had behaved in the best manner possible; fourthly, because in observing the dejection of all this crowd that surrounded him, he had decided there was no point in feeling dejected, and he genuinely did not feel dejected, but rejoiced in those joys of life that no one could take away from him; fifthly, and most importantly, what great freedom he now felt with his bare feet, what a great weight of prejudice had slipped from his shoulders, when he had always imagined he had none, how distant and alien to him were the concepts of war, military commanders, heroism, state, government, administration and philosophical science, and how dear to him were the concepts of human love, compassion, joy, sunshine and song.

He had spent some five hours inside the chapel, and those were the most difficult moments of his captivity. He could see that everything was on fire outside, that everyone was leaving and that they had forgotten him. He began to feel physically afraid and, sticking his head out through the bars, he had shouted:

"If you intend to burn me alive, then say so, but if it's by accident, then I would like to remind you of my presence."

An officer who was walking by said nothing, but soon they came and took him out and after putting him with the others, led them across the city to the Pokrovsky guardhouse. Then they took him twice to some house, where he was interrogated about his involvement in the fires and then they took him back to the Virgin's Field. There he was brought to Davout. Davout was writing, and turning round he looked intently at Pierre and said:

"I know this man, I have seen him before. Have him shot."

Pierre turned cold and began speaking in French.

"You could not know me, because I have never seen you before."

"Ah, so he speaks French," said Davout, and looked again at Pierre.

For a moment they looked at each other, and this glance saved Pierre. This glance, which rose above all the circumstances of war and ordeals of life, forged a human link between the two men. In this one single instant they both vaguely experienced an infinite number of things and ideas: that they were both children of mankind, that each of them had, or used to have, a mother, that they had been loved and had loved, that they had been enthralled and had done evil and good, and had been proud and boastful, and had repented. Pierre realised that his salvation lay in the difference between this second glance and the first. In the first glance he had seen that, for the Davout who had just raised his head from army corps reports, in which human affairs and lives were accounted in numbers, for the Davout who followed strict method in his work and who was cruel, not because he loved cruelty, but because he loved precision in work and loved to demonstrate, glorying with vanity in his love of duty, that all the tender impulses of compassion were as nothing in comparison with duty – Pierre had realised that *that* Davout, after the first glance, would have had him shot without taking the evil deed on his own conscience, but now he was dealing not with him at all, but with the human being.

"Why did you not say that you knew our language?"

"I did not feel it was necessary."

"You are not what you say you are."

"Yes, you are right. But I cannot say who I am."

At this point Davout's adjutant entered the room and Davout ordered

Pierre to be taken to the execution. The way in which it was said was unclear. Pierre thought it could be understood to mean either that he should be shot or that he should be present at the execution, preparations for which he had been hearing about. But he himself was unable to ask. Turning his head, he saw the adjutant asking something.

"Yes, yes," said Davout.

But what "yes" meant, Pierre did not know.

Two sentries led him to the very edge of the river, where there was a crowd of people gathered around a post and a pit. The crowd consisted of a small number of Russians and a large number of Napoleon's troops out of formation, as well as Germans and Italians and Spanish, who startled him with their strange speech. To the right and the left of the post, ranks of French troops were standing to attention. Two platoons with five Russians at their middle approached the post. These were condemned arsonists. Pierre stopped beside them.

The commander of one platoon asked sadly: "This one as well?" with a quick glance at Pierre. (Pierre could not understand how his life, the life of Count Bezukhov, could weigh so light in these men's scales.)

"No," said the adjutant, "he's only going to watch."

And they began talking in whispers. They began beating the drums and the Russians were moved forward.

Pierre examined all of them. For him, a Russian, each of them had some meaning – he recognised now from their faces and figures what they all were. Two of the men were the kind who had inspired horror in Pierre since his childhood: they were shaven-headed convicts, one tall and thin, the other dark, shaggy and brawny with a nose squashed flat; the third was a factory hand, a sallow, thin fellow about eighteen years old wearing a dressing gown; the fourth was a peasant, very handsome, with a broad, thick, light-brown beard and black eyes; the fifth was either a functionary or a domestic serf, about forty-five years old with greying hair and a plump, well-fed body.

Pierre heard the French conferring about whether they should shoot two at a time and regretting that there was an uneven number. But even so he could see how repugnant they found this duty and were only concerned to finish the whole business as fast as possible. A French official in a scarf went up to the post and read out the sentence in French and in Russian.

The shackled prisoners gazed around them in silence, their eyes blazing brightly, the way a wounded animal watches the approaching hunter. One crossed himself, another scratched his back and folded his strong, gnarled hands across his belly. Eventually the official moved aside, they began blindfolding them and the marksmen came running out – twelve of them. Pierre turned away in order not to see, but the shots, which seemed very loud, made him glance round. There was smoke and Frenchmen with pale faces and trembling hands were doing something beside the pit. Then they led up another two in the same way, and these two looked at everybody there, vainly, silently begging for protection with their eyes alone and clearly not understanding or believing what was going to happen. They and they alone knew what their life had meant to them, and that was why they did not understand and did not believe it could be taken away. Pierre decided not to look again, but once again, like some appalling explosion, the shot forced him to look. He saw the same thing: smoke, blood, pale, frightened faces, and his agitation was further reinforced by reading all around him, on the faces of Russians and on the faces of the French soldiers and officers – on all of them without exception – a great fright, horror and inner struggle. "But who is doing this, after all?" thought Pierre. "Even Davout, even he, I saw, felt sorry for me, and everyone here is suffering just as I am."

"Marksmen of the 86th, forward!" someone shouted.

They led out the fifth man. It was the factory worker in the dressing gown. As soon as they touched him, he leapt back in terror and shouted out in a wild voice, but they grabbed hold of him by the arms and he suddenly fell silent. It was as though he had suddenly understood something. Either he had realised that it was pointless to cry out, or realised what he had been told by the fear that had seized him – that they could not possibly kill him. He went just the same as the others, looking around with gleaming eyes like a wounded animal. Pierre could no longer force himself to turn away and close his eyes. With this fifth killing the curiosity and excitement that he himself felt and the crowd also felt reached its highest peak. Just like the others, this fifth man seemed calm, holding his cap in his hand, pulling his loose robe around him, walking steadily, only looking and questioning. When they began blindfolding him, he adjusted the knot at the back of his neck himself, obviously it was too tight for him, then when they pushed him up against the bloody post, he leaned backwards and felt uncomfortable, so he adjusted his position, planting his feet evenly and then calmly leaned back again. Pierre was still gazing avidly at him, unwilling to miss the slightest movement. There must have been a command and after the command the report of twelve rifles, but as he later discovered, no one, including himself heard the slightest sound of a shot, they only saw the factory hand slump in his bonds, blood appear in two places and the ropes themselves come untied under the weight of the sagging body which hung there with its head drooping unnaturally and its legs buckled under it. Someone shouted out, pale faces ran up to him. The jaw of one was trembling as he untied him, and they dragged him in a terribly clumsy, hasty manner behind the post and began to push him into the pit, like criminals concealing the traces of their crime. Pierre glanced into the pit and saw the factory hand lying there with his knees up close to his head and one shoulder higher than the other. That shoulder was spasmodically rising and falling. But spadefuls of earth were already showering down onto the shoulder. The sentry shouted angrily, viciously and nervously at Pierre to come back. He heard the footfall of the troops leaving. The twelve marksmen ran to join the regiments as they were filing past. They had already taken their places, but one young, blond-haired soldier, a marksman in a shako that had fallen to the back of his head, had lowered his rifle helplessly and was still standing facing the pit at the spot from which he had fired, with his mouth and his eyes wide open in horror, staggering a few steps forwards and a few steps backwards like a drunk in order to hold up his falling body. He would have fallen if a corporal had not run out of the ranks, caught him by the shoulders and dragged him into the regiment.

Everyone began leaving with their heads bowed and shame in their faces.

"We'll teach them to set fires," said someone, but it was obvious that he only said it in order to bolster his courage, and that he was horrified and upset just like everyone else, and felt shamed by what had been done.

From that day on, Pierre had been kept in captivity. At first he was given a separate room and fed well, but later, in late September, he was transferred to the common hut and they evidently forgot about him.

Here in the common hut Pierre had given away all his possessions and his boots to the others and lived in anticipation of rescue, in the condition in which he now found himself, on the 1st of October. Although Pierre did nothing special here, all the prisoners would naturally turn to him for help. Apart from the fact that he spoke French and German (some of the guards were Bavarian), and the fact that he was terribly strong, and the fact that he was highly respected even by the French – no one knew why, neither the prisoners, nor he himself, nor the French: they called him the hairy giant – there was not a single man among his comrades who was not indebted to Pierre for something: he had helped one with his work, given clothing to another, he had lifted one person's spirits and had taken up the cause of another with the French. His chief virtue lay in being always calm and cheerful.

Before he had finished whittling his stick of wood, Pierre lay down in his corner and fell into a doze. No sooner was he dozing than there came a voice outside the door:

"The big cheery one. We've nicknamed him the hairy giant, it must be that one, captain."

"Show me which one, corporal," said a gentle, feminine voice. Bending his head, the corporal came in with an officer, a small handsome dark-haired man with fine, heavy-lidded, melancholy eyes. It was Poncini, a clandestine friend of Pierre's. Having learned about Pierre's captivity and situation he had finally managed to reach him. Poncini had brought a bundle, which the soldier was carrying. Poncini surveyed the prisoners as he went over to Pierre, sighed heavily, nodded to the corporal and began waking Pierre. As soon as Pierre was fully awake, the expression of tender compassion suddenly vanished from Poncini's face, for he was clearly fearful of insulting Pierre with it. Poncini embraced him with warmth and kissed him.

"*Enfin*, I have found you, *mon cher Pilade*," he said.

"*Bravo!*" cried Pierre, leaping to his feet, and grasping Poncini under the arm with the same self-assured gesture he used for promenading at balls, he began walking round the rooms with him.

"Well, why didn't you let me know?" Poncini reproached him. "It's terrible, the situation you are in here. I lost sight of you, I've been looking for you. Where have you been, what have you been doing?"

Pierre cheerfully recounted his adventures, his meeting with Davout and the execution at which he had been present. Poncini turned pale as he listened. He stopped, squeezed Pierre's hand and kissed him, like a woman, or rather, like the handsome man he was, who knew that his kiss was always a reward.

"But we must put an end to all this," he said. "It's terrible." Poncini looked at Pierre's bare feet.

Pierre smiled.

"If I survive, believe me, this will have been the best time of my life. How much kindness I have known and how strongly I have come to believe in kindness and in people. And I would never otherwise have got to know you, my dear friend," he said, patting Poncini on the shoulder.

"It takes someone of your strength of character to bear all this in such a way," said Poncini, glancing again and again at the bare feet and the bundle that he had put down. "I heard you were in terrible conditions, but I did not imagine they were as bad as this . . . You will have to tell me more, but now, look . . ."

Poncini glanced in embarrassment at the bundle and fell silent. Pierre understood him and smiled, but went on talking about something else.

"Sooner or later it will be over – one way or another the war will end, and what are two or three months compared with a whole life . . . Can you tell me how things are going, is there any sign of a peace?"

"Yes. No, I'd better not say anything now, but here are my plans. Firstly, I cannot bear to see you in such a state, although you do look well. You do look in such fine form! And I would so love you to be seen in this state by her . . . But look, I'll . . ." – and Poncini glanced once more at the bundle and fell silent. Pierre understood him, grabbed him under the arm, pulled him closer and said:

"All right, let me have your charity bundle. I am not ashamed to accept boots from you, after I know who seized at least eight million francs-worth of property from me in my houses," he said, unable to restrain himself, but with a benevolent and cheerful smile that softened the meaning of his words, which could have sounded like a reproach to the French. "Just one thing, as you can see," he said, directing Poncini's attention to the hungry eyes of the prisoners, which were fixed on the bundle as it was being untied, revealing loaves of bread, ham, boots and clothes. "I shall have to share with my comrades in misfortune, and since I am stronger than they are, I have the least right to all of this," he said, not without a certain proud satisfaction at seeing the delighted amazement on Poncini's melancholy, kind, dear face. To prevent the question of the bundle interfering with the conversation which they both valued so highly, Pierre handed out the contents of the bundle to his comrades, and having left himself two white loaves with slices of ham, one of which he set about eating immediately, he went out into the field with Poncini to walk about in front of the hut.

Poncini's plan consisted of the following. Pierre had to declare his name and title, and then not only would he be freed, but Poncini guaranteed that Napoleon himself would wish to see him and would very likely send Pierre to St. Petersburg with a letter. This had already happened before . . . But, observing that what he was saying was not welcome, Poncini simply asked Pierre to agree.

"Don't ruin my entire past," said Pierre. "I decided I wanted no one to know my name, and I will not do it."

"Then some other means will be necessary; I would make a petition, but I fear my requests will be useless. I'm glad I know where you are. You may be sure that I'll send so many bundles, you will even keep enough for yourself."

"Thank you! Tell me, what of the princess?"

"She is perfectly well and calm . . . Ah, my dear friend, what a terrible thing war is, what a senseless, evil thing."

"But inevitable, eternal," said Pierre, "and one of the finest means for revealing the goodness in mankind. You speak of my misfortune, but I feel happy so often these days. For the first time, I have come to know myself, to know people, to know my love for her. Tell me, have you had any letters?"

"Yes, but can you believe that my mother still will not hear of my marrying, yet I do not care."

Talking until evening, the friends did not part until the moon had already risen. Poncini wept as he took leave of Pierre and promised to do all he could to save him. He walked away. Pierre remained and, staring at the distant houses in the moonlight, he continued for a long while to think of Natasha, about how in the future he would devote his whole life to her, and how happy he would be that she was there and how little he had been able to appreciate life before.

The next day Poncini sent a cartload of things and Pierre received a pair of felt boots.

The day after that all the prisoners were gathered up and led out along the Smolensk road. During the first day's march one soldier fell behind, and a French soldier, who fell back with him, killed him. An escort officer explained to Pierre that they had to keep moving and with so many prisoners, anyone who would not walk would be shot.

# XIX

In the middle of September the Rostovs and their transport of wounded arrived in Tambov and occupied a merchant's house that had been prepared for them in advance. Tambov was crowded with people fleeing from Moscow, and new families arrived every day.

Prince Andrei's servants had arrived to join him, and he had lodged in the same house as the Rostovs and was gradually recovering. The two young ladies of the Rostov household took turns at his bedside. The main reason for the sick man's anxiety – the uncertainty of the situation of his father, his sister and his son – had been ended. A letter had been received from Nikolai and one from Princess Marya with the very same messenger, in which Prince Andrei was informed that she was travelling to Tambov with Coco, thanks to Nikolai Rostov, who had rescued her and was a most affectionate friend and brother to her.

The Rostovs had cleared another section of their house, crowding in together and doing without a drawing room, and were expecting Princess Marya any day.

On the 20th of September Prince Andrei was lying still confined to bed. Sonya was sitting and reading *Corinne* to him aloud.

Sonya was well known for reading well. Her melodious voice rose and fell evenly. She was reading about the sick Oswald's declaration of love and, involuntarily comparing Andrei with Oswald and Natasha with Corinne, she glanced at Andrei. Andrei was not listening.

Recently Sonya had acquired a new reason for concern. Princess Marya had written (Andrei had read the letter aloud to the Rostovs) that Nikolai was her friend and her brother, that she would retain for ever a tender gratitude to him for his concern and assistance during the difficult times she had endured. Nikolai had written that he had made the acquaintance of Princess Bolkonskaya by chance on a march and endeavoured to be of assistance to her, insofar as he was able, which had been an especial pleasure for him since, despite her plain appearance, he had never met a sweeter and more agreeable young woman.

Comparing these two letters, the countess, as Sonya observed (although the countess said nothing on the subject), had drawn the conclusion that Princess Marya was the very bride, rich and lovable, whom her Nikolai needed in order to set his affairs to rights. The state of Natasha's relations with Andrei remained unknown to the entire family. They seemed to be as much in love with each other as ever, although Natasha declared to her mother, in reply to the question of what was to come of it, that their relations were merely friendly, that Natasha had refused him, had not altered her refusal, and had no reason to alter it.

Sonya knew this, and she knew that the countess therefore secretly cherished the idea of marrying Nikolai to Princess Marya, which was why she bustled so joyfully over the arrangements for her accommodation. This very plan gave Sonya fresh reason for concern. She was unaware, and did not dwell on the fact that she wanted to marry Andrei to Natasha as soon as possible, principally so that it would then no longer be possible for Nikolai to marry Princess Marya because they would be related; she thought she desired it purely out of love for Natasha, her friend, but she wished for it herself with all her might and acted with feline cunning in order to bring it about.

"Why do you look at me like that, Mademoiselle Sophie?" asked Andrei with a kind, sickly smile. "You are thinking of similarities with your friend. Yes," he continued " – except that Countess Natasha is a million times more attractive than this boring blue-stocking Corinne . . ."

"No, I am not thinking anything of the kind, but I do think it is very hard for a woman to await the declaration of a man she loves and to see his waverings and doubts."

"But, *chère* Mademoiselle Sophie, there are, as in the case of Lord Neville, certain considerations that are higher than one's own personal happiness. Can you understand that?"

"I? Well, how am I to take your meaning?"

"Could you, for the happiness of a man whom you love, sacrifice your own possession of him?"

"Yes, probably . . ."

With a weak movement Andrei picked up Princess Marya's letter, which was lying on the small table beside him.

"But do you know, my poor Princess Marya seems to be in love with your cousin. She is such a transparent soul. Not only is she quite direct when she talks face-to-face, but I see everything clearly in her letters. You do not know her, Mademoiselle Sophie."

Sonya blushed painfully and said:

"No. Oh, but I feel I'm getting a migraine," she said, and rising quickly to her feet, scarcely able to hold back her tears, she left the room, passing Natasha on the way.

"How is he, asleep?"

"Yes." She ran to her bedroom and fell on to the bed, sobbing. "Yes, yes, that is what I should do, it is necessary for his happiness, for the happiness of the household, our family. But how have I deserved this? No. I do not want happiness for myself. I must . . ."

That same day everybody in the house began bustling about and went running to and fro, to Prince Andrei's room and the porch. The immense, princely carriage in which he usually travelled to town drew up at the entrance, with two *britzkas*. Princess Marya, upon seeing the countess, blushed, and although this was their first meeting, she rushed into her open arms and burst into sobs.

"I am doubly indebted to you, for Andrei and for myself," she said.

"My child!" said the countess. "In these present times how fortunate are those who are able to help others."

Ilya Andreevich kissed the princess's hand. He introduced Sonya to her. "This is my niece."

But Princess Marya was looking about anxiously for someone else. She was looking for Natasha.

"And where is Natasha?"

"She is with Prince Andrei," said Sonya.

The princess smiled and turned pale, casting an enquiring glance at the countess. But the reply to her enquiring glance, asking whether former relations had been renewed, was a mysteriously sad smile.

Natasha came running out to greet the princess, almost as quick, lively and cheerful as she had been in the old days. She surprised and astonished the princess, like everyone else, with her simplicity and charm. The princess gave her a look that was affectionate, but too unintentionally piercing, and began to kiss her.

"I have loved you and known you for so long," said Princess Marya.

Embarrassed, Natasha moved away without a word, and began paying attention to Coco, who understood nothing of what was going on, except that she, Natasha, was jollier and nicer than everyone, and he liked her best of all.

"He is on the way to a complete recovery," said the countess as she showed the princess through to Prince Andrei. "But you, my poor girl, how much you have suffered."

"Ah, I cannot tell you how hard it was," said Princess Marya (still rosy-cheeked and animated from the cold and her joy. "She is not at all so plain," thought the countess). "And your son saved me, quite decidedly saved me, not so much from the French as from despair."

Tears appeared in Princess Marya's beautiful, radiant eyes when she said this, and the countess realised that these tears expressed love for her son. "Yes, she will be his wife, this charming creature" – and she embraced Princess Marya, and they both wept a little more out of happiness, then smiled, wiping away the tears as they prepared to go in to see Prince Andrei.

Prince Andrei was sitting up in the armchair, and he greeted Princess Marya with an emaciated, altered, shame-filled face, the face of a pupil begging forgiveness, saying he will never do it again, the face of a prodigal son who has returned home. Princess Marya wept and kissed his hands and brought his son over to him. Andrei did not weep, he said little, his face was simply transformed and beaming with happiness. He spoke little about his father and his death. Every time they stumbled upon the memory of that, they tried to pass over it in silence. To talk of it was too hard. They each inwardly thought: "Later, later." But they did not know that later they would never speak of it. There was only one thing that Princess Marya could not help recounting – his final words, when she had sat by his door at night, on the eve of his death, not daring to enter, and how the next day, after she had told him about it, he – the austere Prince Nikolai Andreevich – had said to her: "Why did you not come in *my dearest! Yes, my dearest!* – I felt so terrible."

On hearing this, Prince Andrei turned away, his entire lower jaw began twitching and he rapidly changed the subject. He asked her about her journey and about Nikolai Rostov.

"A worthless fellow, apparently," said Andrei with a cunning twinkle in his eye.

"Ah, no!" the princess cried out in fright, as if she had suffered physical pain. "You should have seen him as I did during those terrible moments. Only a man with a heart of pure gold could have behaved as he did. Oh no."

Prince Andrei's eyes glowed even more brightly.

"Yes, yes, this has to be, it really must happen," he thought. "Yes. This is it, this is the thing that was still left in life, the thing I kept regretting as I was being brought here. Yes, this is it. Not one's own happiness, but other people's."

"So he's a dear chap! Well, I am very glad," he said.

Princess Marya was called to lunch, and she went out feeling they had failed to discuss the most important thing: she had not found out how things now stood with Natasha, yet somehow, as if from guilt, she felt afraid to ask. Now after lunch her brother spared her the trouble.

"You seem surprised, I think, my friend, at my relations with Miss Rostova?"

"Yes, I wished . . ."

"What went before is all forgotten. I am a petitioner who has been refused, and I do not pine. We are friendly and we shall always remain friendly, but she will never be anything to me but a younger sister. I do not suit at all."

"But how charming she is, Andrei! Although I do understand," said Princess Marya, inwardly reflecting that Prince Andrei's pride could not have allowed him to forgive her completely.

"Yes, yes, indeed," said Prince Andrei, replying to all of her thoughts.

With the arrival of Princess Marya life in Tambov continued even more happily than before.

The news from the army was most auspicious, both the young Rostovs were safe and well, the older brother in the regiment and the younger one in Denisov's partisan detachment.

Only old Rostov, totally ruined by the surrender of Moscow, was sad and preoccupied, he wrote letters to all his powerful acquaintances, requesting money and appointments. On one occasion Sonya discovered him in the study, sobbing over a letter he had written. "Yes, if only this had been all right too!" she thought. She locked herself in her room and cried for a long time. Late that day she wrote a letter to Nikolai in which she returned his ring, released him from his promise and requested him to ask for the hand of Princess Marya, who would bring happiness to him and the whole family. She brought this letter to the countess, laid it on the table and ran away. The letter was sent with the next courier, together with a letter along similar lines from the countess.

"Allow me to kiss your magnanimous hand," Prince Andrei said to her that evening, and they had a long, friendly conversation about Natasha.

"Has she ever really loved anyone deeply?" Andrei asked. "I know she never loved me completely. And that other one even less. But others, before?"

"There is one, it's Bezukhov," said Sonya. "But she doesn't even know it herself."

That evening in Natasha's presence Prince Andrei talked about Bezukhov and the news he had received from him. Natasha blushed. Perhaps it was because she was thinking more about Bezukhov than about the other, perhaps because with her sensitivity she sensed that they were watching her as they talked. Prince Andrei's news had come from Poncini, who had been brought to Tambov together with the other prisoners. The next day Andrei mentioned Pierre's magnanimity and kindness, recalling them from his own reminiscences and from what the prisoner had written. Sonya also spoke about Pierre, and Princess Marya did likewise.

"What are they doing to me?" thought Natasha, "They are trying to do something to me," and she looked around with puzzled concern. She considered Andrei and Sonya her best friends and that whatever they did was for her own good.

That evening Prince Andrei asked Natasha to sing in the next room and Princess Marya sat down to accompany her, and the voice which, despite two years of near neglect, had lost none of its powers of enchantment, poured forth with such strength and charm that Princess Marya began to weep and for a long time after they all seemed to be in a trance, suddenly close and dear, exchanging incoherent remarks. The following day the prisoners, whom everyone in Tambov was overjoyed to see, were invited to the house, Poncini among them. Two of them, a general and a colonel, proved to be coarse men who did not dare kiss the hands of Russian countesses and spat in the house, while one, the subtle, intelligent, melancholy Poncini, to whom everyone took a liking, pleased everyone especially by not being able to speak of Pierre without tears in his eyes and in relating Pierre's greatness of soul in captivity with the child, he rose to quite irresistible heights of Italian eloquence.

Finally a letter arrived from Pierre, saying he was alive and had left Moscow with the prisoners. And Poncini, having confessed to Andrei of Pierre's declarations and marvelling unceasingly at his chance encounter with that particular man, was sent to Natasha in order to convey to her that declaration, which now, with news of Hélène's death, could have no harmful consequences.

The old count saw all of this. It brought him no gladness. He felt depressed and sad – he felt that in all of this he was now unnecessary, that his life was over and his work was done: he had produced children, raised them and been ruined, and now they consoled and pitied him, but they had no need of him.

# XX

After the enemy's entry into Moscow and the reports denouncing Kutu-zov and the despair in St. Petersburg and the outrage and the heroic words and the renewed hopes, it all finished with our forces crossing from the Tula road to the Kaluga road beyond the Pakhra.

Why the military writers, and everyone else in the world, believe this flanking march (a term they are very fond of) to be a profound manoeuvre that saved Russia and undid Napoleon is extremely hard to understand for someone who takes nothing on trust and thinks for himself. More than a hundred different crossings could have been made to the Tula road and the Smolensk road and the Kaluga road, and the result would have been the same. In exactly the same way, the spirits of Napoleon's troops would already have fallen as they approached Mos-cow, the soldiers would have scattered and their spirits would have plunged still further as a result of the fires and pillaging in Moscow. People only make this claim because it is hard for them to see the totality of causes which bring about events, and the desire is so strong to attribute everything to the actions of one single man (just the same kind of man as I am myself), especially since this creates a hero whom we can love so much. It had to be that way, and that is the way it was.

After a month in Moscow, Napoleon and every one of his troops vaguely sensed they had gone astray and, attempting to conceal this awareness, they started back, disordered, hungry and tattered. One month earlier at Borodino they had been strong, but now, after a month in calm and comfortable quarters with good provisions in Moscow and its surroundings, they set off back at a run, frightened. It is hard to believe that all of this was the result of a flanking march beyond Krasnaya Pakhra. There were other causes, which I do not propose to list, but nor do I set forth a single, inadequate cause, claiming that as the only one.

After the despair, the Russian army and St. Petersburg came to life again. Couriers and Germans and the sovereign's generals began travel-ling frequently from St. Petersburg, for just a brief visit to the army, and Kutuzov treated these visitors with especial kindness. On the third day of the month, when Kutuzov was told that the French had withdrawn from Moscow, he began sobbing with tears of joy and, crossing himself, he said:

"Now I'll make these French eat horseflesh, like the Turk."

This dictum was frequently repeated by Kutuzov. But Kutuzov was sent a plan of action from St. Petersburg, and he had to attack very cunningly, from various directions. Kutuzov was naturally delighted at this plan but obstacles lay in his way. Bennigsen reported to the sovereign that Kutuzov had a wench dressed as a Cossack.

Bennigsen undermined Kutuzov, Kutuzov undermined Bennigsen, Ermolov undermined Konovnitsyn, Konovnitsyn undermined de Tolly and also Ermolov, Wintzengerode undermined Bennigsen and so on and so forth, in infinite combinations and variations, but they all went on living happily near Tarutino with good chefs and wines and singers and music and even women. Eventually the arrogant Lauriston arrived with a letter from Napoleon, in which Napoleon wrote that he was particularly glad of the opportunity to testify to his profound respect for the Field-Marshal. Prince Volkonsky wished to receive him alone, but Lauriston refused – Volkonsky was too lowly – and demanded a meeting with Kutuzov. There was nothing to be done. Kutuzov donned some epaulettes borrowed from Konovnitsyn and received the visitor. The generals crowded in. They all feared Kutuzov might betray them. But Kutuzov, as always, deferred everything, as did Lauriston, and Napoleon was left without an answer.

Meanwhile Murat and Miloradovich were playing the fool under a flag of truce, and one fine day the Russians attacked the French, and the French fled headlong, astonished that they had not all been taken, because they could no longer fight in the way they had before. Not all of them were taken, however, because Kutuzov had put Bennigsen in charge of matters and, in order to wrong-foot him, had granted him inadequate forces, thus greatly embittering Bennigsen, but apart from this they were also, in any case, too late – because outside the line of encirclement Shepelev was holding a drinking spree in an entire manor house and they were making merry all night and even the generals themselves were dancing. They were all good generals and good men, and I would never have mentioned their dancing and intrigues, had not all of them, annoyingly, written later in the style of Derzhavin on their love for the fatherland and the Tsar and similar such nonsense, whereas in actual fact they were mostly concerned with their dinner and a little blue ribbon, or a red one. This is a natural human aspiration, and it should not be condemned, but it must be called by its true name, otherwise it will mislead the younger generations as they gaze in aston- ishment and despair at the weaknesses which they discover in their own souls, while in Plutarch and Russian history they see nothing but heroes.

After the battle of Tarutino the French advanced within shooting distance like a bewildered hare, but Kutuzov, begrudging a shot like a professional huntsman, did not start shooting and fell back. Having reached Maly Yaroslavets on the right, however, following a small, incidental battle, the hare went running back in such a state that a mongrel cur would have caught it. And indeed, at this particular time a single sexton alone captured ninety prisoners and killed thirty men. The partisans took ten thousand prisoners. The French troops were only waiting for an excuse to lay down their arms and get out while the going was good. And indeed, the confusion in the army was quite incredible: they forgot about entire depots, commandants had no idea who was where. Every general was lugging along his string of carts full of loot, and every officer and soldier too. And like a monkey that has grabbed a fistful of nuts inside a pitcher, they would not let go and preferred to allow themselves to be taken prisoner. Where they were going and why, no one knew, least of all the great genius himself, Napoleon, since no one was giving him any information. Close around him, a certain decorum was still observed; orders, letters, reports and agendas were written, they still called each other "Sire!" "Sire! My cousin the Prince of Ekmul, the King of Naples." But they were all wretched and vile men who fully deserved all their sorrow, their pangs of conscience and desperate misfortune. The orders and reports only existed on paper, in actual fact there was chaos. As for the terror of the Cossacks – at one mere whoop, the columns simply fled without reason. Discipline was collapsing. The poverty was appalling, and to expect discipline was impossible. But afterwards, naturally, all the eventualities that could not be accommodated by the human comprehension of disaster – out of three hundred thousand, only one hundred men will comprehend – were attributed to the imaginary orders issued by an emperor of genius. Yet anyone who has been in a war knows that a fleeing bear which is wounded can be easily killed with a catapult, but not a bold and healthy one. Kutuzov was the only one who knew this. He did not know how things stood, but he knew, as old people wise in life know, that time would do everything – everything would happen of itself. And *of themselves* is the best way for historical events to happen.

## XXI

During this period, when all the French wanted was to be taken prisoner as quickly as possible, and the Russians were amusing themselves in various ways swaggering around them, Dolokhov was with the partisans. He had an entire detachment of three hundred men, and he lived with them along the Smolensk road.

Denisov was another partisan. And Denisov, now a colonel, had in his detachment young Petya Rostov, who wanted to serve with no one but Denisov, for whom he had conceived a passionate adoration from the time of his arrival in Moscow in 1806.

In addition to these two detachments, also roaming this same area, quite close by, were the detachments of a Polish count serving with the Russians, as well as those of a German, and a general.

One night, Denisov, with a beard and wearing a heavy peasant's coat and an image of St. Nicholas the Wonder-Worker on a chain, was lying on carpets spread on the floor of a ruined hut as he wrote, scratching away rapidly with his quill pen, and from time to time taking a swig from a glass filled with half rum, half tea.

Petya, with his broad, kind face and skinny adolescent limbs was sitting on a bench in the corner, glancing now and then in pious adoration at his very own Napoleon. Petya was also wearing a fantastic costume, a peasant coat adorned with cartridges like a Circassian kaftan, blue cavalry pantaloons and spurs. As soon as Denisov had finished one sheet of paper, Petya took it off to be sealed.

"May I read them?"

"Yes, take a look . . . then get them sealed . . ."

Petya read, and what he read increased his rapturous enthusiasm for his own Napoleon. What Denisov had been writing were replies to a demand by two other detachment commanders who had diplomatically invited Denisov to join forces with them, that is to say, since Denisov was junior in rank, to accept their command for an attack on Blancard's large cavalry depot, for which all the leaders of detachments were sharpening their knives, each wishing to acquire the glory of this prize. Blancard's depot, heavily encumbered with wounded, prisoners and starving men, and also, most importantly, with a train of wagons, had been forgotten by Napoleon's staff and was simply waiting for one of the Cossacks to take it. Denisov replied to one of the generals that he had already accepted the command of the other, and to the other he wrote that he had accepted the command of the first, tricking them both with formal turns of phrase, at which he was a great master, and in this manner ridding himself of both, since he himself intended to seize the depot, and with it the glory, the rank and, perhaps, the decoration.

"You've done an excellent job putting them off," said Petya in delight, not quite understanding the diplomacy and its goal.

"Take a look who's out there," said Denisov, hearing soft steps in the hall.

Off duty, in private, Petya was on familiar terms with Denisov, as was everyone, but on duty he was an adjutant. Denisov, inclined to play

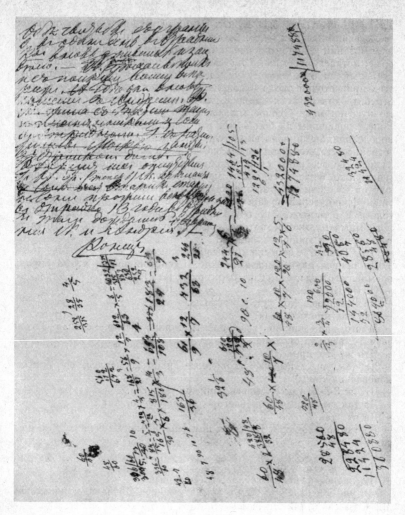

FINAL SHEET OF MANUSCRIPT 107: "THE END"
*Autograph*

at soldiering and at being Napoleon, was all the more encouraged by Petya's unswerving faith in his napoleonhood.

The steps belonged to Tikhon Shestipaly, who was led in by Petya. Tikhon Shestipaly was a peasant from Pokrovskoe. When Denisov had arrived in Pokrovskoe at the beginning of his military activity, he had received complaints about two peasant men who had taken in the French – Prokofii Ryzhy and Tikhon Shestipaly. At the time Denisov, testing his power and his ability to exercise it, had initially grown furious and ordered both of them to be shot. But Tikhon Shestipaly had thrown himself at his feet, promising to serve him faithfully, saying he had only done it out of stupidity, and Denisov had forgiven him and taken him into his detachment.

At first performing the menial work of laying campfires and fetching water, Tikhon had soon demonstrated an exceptional aptitude for partisan warfare. Once, on his way to fetch firewood, he came across some looters and killed two of them, bringing one back. Denisov jokingly took him out with his detachment, and there proved to be no man capable of bearing greater hardship, of noticing more, of approaching closer unheard and paying less attention to danger than Tikhon Shestipaly, and thus Tikhon was enlisted in the Cossacks as a sergeant and awarded a medal.

Tikhon Shestipaly was a tall, skinny peasant with arms that dangled low and looked puny but which, when they swung, struck harder than the most powerful, and with long, gangling legs which could cover seven *versts* in immense, gangling strides without tiring. He was called Shestipaly, meaning six-fingers, because he really did have small growths beside the little fingers and toes on his hands and feet, and a fortune-teller had told him that if he cut off a single one of these extra fingers and toes, then he would be done for, so Tikhon took better care of those ugly lumps of flesh than of his head. His face was long and pock-marked, with a nose that twisted down to one side and sparse, long hairs here and there on his chin. He smiled rarely, but very oddly, so oddly that when he did smile, everyone laughed. He was wounded several times, but all his wounds soon healed up, and he never visited the field hospital. He only needed to stop the blood, which he did not like to see. But he did not understand pain, just as he did not understand fear. He was dressed in a red French hussar's uniform jacket with a soft Kazan hat on his head and bast sandals. He preferred this footwear to all others. He was armed with an immense musketoon, which only he was able to load, tipping in three charges at once, and an axe and a pike.

"What is it, Tishka?" asked Denisov.

"I've brought in two," said Tikhon. (Denisov realised that meant two prisoners. He had sent Tikhon to the spot where the depot had halted, to reconnoitre.)

"Oh! From Shamshevo?"

"From Shamshevo. Out here, by the porch."

"Well, are there many folk?"

"There are, bad folk too. We could kill them all at once," said Tikhon. "I caught three straight away behind the village fence."

"Why did you bring two?"

"I just did, your honour," Tikhon said with a laugh, and Denisov and Petya also laughed automatically.

"Come on, where's the third?" Denisov asked, laughing.

"It's just, don't you be vexed, your honour, just . . ."

"Just what?"

"His clothes were so bad, like . . ." – he fell silent.

"Well, what of it?

"Well, why bother bringing him, like – a tramp."

"All right then, be off, I'll be out to them in a moment."

Tikhon left, and after him, Dolokhov came into the room, having galloped fifteen *versts* to Denisov on the same matter as Denisov was occupied with – the wish to divert him from the depot and capture it himself. Dolokhov had a word with Tikhonov's prisoners before he entered the room. He was dressed simply, in a Guard's military frock coat without epaulettes and fancy dancing boots.

"What are we doing standing still here, guarding the sea?" Dolokhov began, extending his hand to Denisov and Petya. "Why don't you take them starting from Rtishchevo, three hundred of our men are prisoners there," he said.

"But I'm waiting for help to attack the depot."

"Ah, nonsense, you won't take the depot, there are eight batallions of infantry there, you just ask, your man's brought you some of them."

Denisov laughed.

"All right, we understand you, we do," he said. "Would you like some punch?"

"No, not now, but listen here: you've collected up a lot of prisoners, give me just ten men, I need to break in some young Cossacks on someone."

Denisov shook his head.

"Why don't you kill them?" Dolokhov asked simply. "Such molly-coddling . . ."

Dolokhov fooled them all, the two generals and Denisov. Without waiting for anyone, he attacked the depot the next day, and naturally, he grabbed everything that was just waiting for a chance to be surrendered.

## XXII

Pierre was with this depot among the prisoners. On the first day's march out of Moscow his felt boots had been taken and they had been given nothing to eat except horse meat. At night they slept under the open sky. The frost was setting in. During the second day's march Pierre had felt terrible pain in his feet and noticed how chapped and cracked they were becoming. As he walked along, limping involuntarily on one leg, almost all the strength of his spirit and all his powers of observation were focused from that time onwards on those feet and that pain. He ceased to notice the passing hours, he forgot where he was, he began to forget his fears and his hopes, and he no longer wished to think about her, but thought only of that pain.

Where and when it took place he could not remember, but one thing that occurred affected him greatly. Walking along behind the carts which were loaded with paintings, and the carriages, one of which Pierre recognised as his own (it now *belonged*, so he had been told, to the Duke of Ettingen), came all the prisoners. Walking beside Pierre was an old soldier, the one who had taught him how to bind up his feet and grease them. Walking on Pierre's right was a young French soldier with a sharp nose and round, black eyes. The old Russian soldier began wheezing and kept asking for a rest.

"Forward!" shouted the corporal from behind.

Pierre began leading him by the arm, although he was limping himself. The soldier's belly was aching. He was yellow.

"Tell him, you, the one who understands," said the Frenchman. "That we're not allowed to leave those who fall behind. The orders are to shoot those who fall behind."

Pierre told the soldier this.

"It's all the same in the end," said the old soldier and then, crossing himself, he fell back. "Farewell, my Russian brothers," he said, crossing himself and bowing. And the crowd surrounding Pierre bore him, like a ship, onwards, further and further. But the grey old man sat there on the muddy road and went on bowing. Pierre looked back at the old man and heard the sergeant's shouted command to the private with the sharp nose who was walking on his right.

"Carry out the order," the sergeant shouted and pushed the young soldier by the shoulder. The soldier ran back, scowling angrily. The road turned a bend round some birch trees and Pierre, glancing round, could see only the smoke of the shot, and then the soldier, as pale and frightened as if he had seen a ghost, took up his place again without looking at anyone.

They shot that old man, just as they shot many of the crowd of two hundred men walking along with Pierre. But terrible though this was, Pierre did not blame them. They themselves were in such a bad state that some of them might even have agreed to take the old soldier's place. Feverish, their teeth chattering, they sat down at the edge of the road and stayed put. All the conversations that he overheard were about the position being hopeless, that they were done for, it only needed the Cossacks to attack and there would be nothing left. Several times everybody launched into flight at the sight of a Cossack, and sometimes simply by mistake. Pierre saw them eating raw horseflesh. But Pierre saw it all as if in a dream. All of his attention was constantly focused on his sore feet, yet he kept on walking, amazed at himself and at the level to which suffering could increase and the innate capacity of the human being for tolerating suffering. Almost every evening he said, "Today I'm finished" – but the next day he walked on again.

Pierre was aware of the general demoralisation of the troops as if he were dreaming it during those days of marching – how many days he had no idea – but his impressions were suddenly concentrated by an event that was extremely simple in essence, but had a profound effect. During one of the days of the march, three Frenchmen were walking along near him, complaining: suddenly he caught the words, "The Emperor" and everyone roused themselves, drew themselves erect and moved off the road, and a carriage preceded by an escort drove smartly past and halted a little way ahead. A general who was close to its window listened to something and removed his hat. There were loud, desperate, happy shouts: "Long live the Emperor" – and the carriage drove on.

"What did he say?"

"The Emperor, the Emperor," revitalised voices called from all sides. As though there had been no suffering at all. "Did you see what he's like! A fine fellow! Oh, our little corporal won't let anyone tread on his toes," the enthusiastic, confident voices called out. Yet everything still went on just the same: the same cold, hunger and physical effort, pointless and cruel, and the same fear, which never left the troops.

One evening during those days the officers allowed Pierre, whom they after all regarded differently from the others, to sit by the fire, and having warmed himself, he fell asleep. Pierre's salvation in these difficult times was his capacity for sound, deep sleep. Suddenly he was woken up. Afterwards, he could not tell whether what he saw was real or a dream. They woke him up and by the fire he saw a French officer with a familiar face – more than merely familiar, it was a face he knew, one with which he had had intimate dealings. Yes, it was Dolokhov, but in the uniform of a French Uhlan. He was speaking with the officers in excellent French, telling them how he had been sent to find the depot and had ridden here by chance. He complained about the disorder and a French officer echoed his words and told him things to which Dolokhov appeared to pay no attention. Catching sight of Pierre's uplifted curly head, Dolokhov betrayed no surprise, but gave a slight smile (from this smile there could be no doubt who he was) and asked casually, pointing at Pierre: "A Cossack?" They answered him. Dolokhov lit his pipe and took his leave of the officers. *"Bonne nuit, messieurs."* He mounted his horse and rode off.

Pierre went on watching him. There was a moon that night, and he could see a long way. Pierre was horrified, although comforted to know that it was only a dream, seeing him ride up to the sentries of the line and say something. "Thank God, he got through all right," Pierre thought, but just then Dolokhov suddenly turned back and came trotting up to the campfire. His smiling, handsome face was visible in the firelight.

"I almost forgot" – he was holding a note written pencil. "Can any of you tell me what these Russian words mean? 'Bezukhov, be ready with the prisoners, tomorrow I'll free you.'" And without waiting for an answer, he turned his horse and galloped off.

"Seize him!" shouted the officers, and shots rang out down the line, but Pierre saw Dolokhov gallop past it and disappear into the darkness.

The following day there was a halt at Shamshevo and in the evening the shooting began for real, Frenchmen went running past Pierre, and the first to come galloping into the village was Dolokhov. An officer with a white flag of truce ran to meet him. The French had surrendered. When Pierre approached Dolokhov, he broke into sobs for the first time in his captivity, without knowing why. Soldiers and Cossacks surrounded Bezukhov, handed him numerous handkerchiefs and took him off to spend the night in the hut in which a French general had been sleeping, but which was now Dolokhov's. The following day the prisoners filed past Dolokhov, who stood there with his hands on his hips. They were all chattering loudly.

"Anyway, one way or another, the Emperor . . ." The voices mingled together.

Dolokhov looked at them severely, putting an end to their talk with the words: "Get on, get on . . ."

Pierre was sent to Tambov, and as he passed through Kozlov, the first town untouched by war that he had seen in two months, Pierre cried for the second time, out of joy at seeing people going to church, beggars, a man selling bread loaves and a merchant's wife in a lilac headscarf and fox-fur coat, waddling in a calm, self-satisfied fashion along a church porch. Pierre never forgot this for the rest of his life. In Kozlov, Pierre found one of the letters from Andrei, who had been searching for him everywhere, and after obtaining some money, he waited there for his servants and things to arrive, and finally reached Tambov himself in late October.

Prince Andrei was no longer there, he had gone back to the army again, catching up with it outside Vilno.

# XXIII

One of the first people Andrei met in the army was Nikolai. Upon seeing him, Nikolai blushed and he rushed ardently to embrace him. Andrei realised that this was more than friendship.

"I am the very happiest of men," said Nikolai, "I've had a letter from Marya, she promises to be mine. And I have come to headquarters to request a month's leave: I've been wounded twice, but I stayed at the front. And I am also waiting for my brother Petya, who's a partisan with Denisov."

Andrei went to Nikolai's quarters, and there they sat a long time, exchanging all their news. Andrei was firmly set on applying for service again – but only with the regiment. Late in the day, Petya also arrived, full of incessant talk of the glory of Russia and of Vasilii Denisov, who had conquered an entire city, punished the Poles, been a benefactor to the Jews, received deputations and concluded peace.

"We have a whole phalanx of heroes. We have Tikhon." He did not wish to hear about any other kind of soldiering.

Unfortunately, however, that particular conquest of a city in which Petya had so greatly rejoiced had not pleased the German general who had also desired to conquer it, and since Denisov was under the German's command, the German had reprimanded Denisov and dismissed him from his heroic detachment. Petya only learned about that later, however, and for now he was utterly thrilled and talked unceasingly of the way they had driven out Napoleon, what fine people we Russians are and especially how we all are heroes . . .

Andrei and Nikolai were glad for Petya and made him tell them his whole story. In the morning, when the two men, newly related, went to the field-marshal together, each to make his own request, Kutuzov was particularly gracious and granted his permission to both of them, and evidently also wished to say a kind word to Andrei, but was unable to do so because Panna Pszezovska and her daughter, Kutuzov's god-daughter from when he was the governor in Vilno, entered the drawing room. The *pani* was a pretty little girl and Kutuzov screwed his eyes in a smile and turned to greet her, pinching her cheeks and giving her a kiss. Prince Andrei tugged Nikolai by the flap of his jacket and led him out.

"Be at the parade, both of you," Kutuzov called to them through the doorway.

"Yes, your excellency."

The following day there was an inspection; after the ceremonial march Kutuzov approached the Guards and congratulated all the troops on their victory.

"Out of five hundred thousand there is not one left and Napoleon has fled. I thank you. God has assisted me. You, Bonaparte, are a wolf – with grey fur – and I, brother, have grey hair" – and so saying, Kutuzov removed his peakless cap from his white head and inclined the hair on this head towards the assembled ranks . . .

"Hoo-rah!" roared a hundred thousand voices and Kutuzov, choking on his tears, began fumbling for his handkerchief. Nikolai stood in the entourage, between his brother and Prince Andrei. Petya was roaring furiously, "Hoorah!" and tears of joy and pride ran down his plump, boyish cheeks. Prince Andrei was smiling in barely perceptible, good-humoured mockery.

"Petrusha, enough, everyone's already stopped," said Nikolai.

"What do I care? I'm dying of ecstasy," shouted Petya, then he glanced at Prince Andrei and his smile, and he fell silent, feeling somewhat disgruntled with his future brother-in-law.

*

The two weddings were celebrated together on the same day at Otradnoe, which had now come back to life and was flourishing once again. Nikolai duly left for the regiment and entered Paris with it, where he met up yet again with Andrei.

While they were away Pierre, Natasha (now a countess in her own right), Marya and her nephew Coco, the old Count Rostov and his wife and Sonya also stayed on at Otradnoe for the whole summer and the winter of 1813 until Nikolai and Andrei could finally return.